The H.G.WELLS
COLLECTION

The H. G. WELLS COLLECTION

ARCTURUS

ARCTURUS

This edition published in 2018 by Arcturus Publishing Limited
26/27 Bickels Yard, 151–153 Bermondsey Street,
London SE1 3HA

Cover design: Peter Ridley
Cover illustration: Peter Gray

ISBN: 978-1-78428-608-8
AD005688UK

Printed in China

CONTENTS

CONTENTS

INTRODUCTION

There are few writers who have had as profound an influence on literature as Herbert George Wells. With good reason, he has been called 'the father of science fiction'. While his contemporaries were experimenting with modernism and sought to portray the modern world in intricate detail and reality, Wells instead unlocked his boundless imagination and created new worlds for readers to explore.

H. G. Wells was born in Kent in 1866. His father, Joseph Wells, was a professional cricketer but the family's income was hardly stable. It was an incident in his youth, in 1874, that set the course of his future. As an eight-year-old, he broke his leg, leaving him confined to his bed for weeks. In later years, he described it as 'one of the luckiest events of my life'. As a bored child, he turned to reading books from the local library.

Soon, reading was not enough. He wanted to write and to create his own stories. His family's challenging financial circumstances did not help him achieve his ambitions. For three years, beginning in 1880, he was forced to work as an apprentice to a draper – a career to which he was utterly unsuited. Only after this testing experience was he able to obtain a scholarship to the Normal School of Science, where he graduated in biology and began a career as a teacher.

For a decade, he wrote short stories and textbooks in his spare time while he worked in poverty. Throughout this period, he began to experiment in his writing with the idea of a 'scientific romance'. The first of these was *The Time Machine*, published in 1895. It was an astonishing success. He soon found a demand for this new type of fiction and within just six years, he had written five exceptional novels in the newly-created genre.

Today, Wells is best known for his science fiction masterpieces, but he was a prolific writer who dabbled in several genres. As the 20th century dawned, Wells wrote a number of non-science fiction novels, such as *The History of Mr Polly*, most of which contained a strong social element. By the time of his death in 1946, he had written nearly 40 books and countless short stories.

This collection brings together seven of his most powerful science fiction novels.

The Invisible Man tells the tale of a scientist who finds a way to make himself invisible, but to his dismay is unable to reverse the experiment. At once distraught and freed from the constraints of the law, Wells' disturbing and insightful novel explores the question of morality when a man is free to do as he pleases without risk of being caught.

Originally intended as a series of short stories for the *Pall Mall Gazette*, *The Time Machine* was the novel which popularized the idea of time travel.

His publisher pushed him to turn it into a full novel. In this imaginative tale, a scientist creates a time machine that he uses to travel far into the future. There he encounters an alien world and he learns of the terrifying fate that awaits humanity.

Mars, or the red planet has fascinated people for centuries. *The War of the Worlds* is the iconic tale of a Martian invasion of Earth. The most famous novel of H. G. Wells, the chilling visions of Martian killing machines and heat-rays has been adapted several times for the big screen, most successfully by Steven Spielberg in 2005.

In *The Island of Doctor Moreau*, the shipwrecked Edward Prendick finds himself rescued by the mysterious character of the title. On the island, he finds his rescuer to be a mad scientist, who is intent on creating human-animal hybrids and willing to push the boundaries of morality to its extremes.

Nearly 70 years before men first walked on the moon, H. G. Wells' was exploring what might be awaiting them in *The First Men in the Moon*. The businessman Mr Bedford and the scientist Mr Cavor make their way to the moon and discover a race of intelligent insect-like creatures called 'Selenites'.

When the Sleeper Wakes is Wells' dystopian tale of London set 203 years in the future. A man who has slept for this entire period awakes as the richest man in the world from the interest in his bank accounts, but the world he awakes to is a far more sinister place than the world in which he fell asleep.

The World Set Free was Wells' response to the sense of impending crisis of the 1910s. Predicting a violent conflagration, this novel, published just before the outbreak of the First World War in 1914, found its terrifying stories coming true far sooner than even Wells had predicted.

Wells' iconic works opened the way for the 'Golden Age' of science fiction writers of the 1930s like E. E. 'Doc' Smith, Olaf Stapledon, Isaac Asimov and Arthur C. Clarke. The lasting power of his writing comes from the strength of his social commentary as much as his from ingenious ideas. Today, all science fiction authors hold a debt to this groundbreaking late-Victorian novelist.

THE
INVISIBLE MAN

CONTENTS

CHAPTER I

The Strange Man's Arrival

The stranger came early in February, one wintry day, through a biting wind and a driving snow, the last snowfall of the year, over the down, walking from Bramblehurst railway station, and carrying a little black portmanteau in his thickly gloved hand. He was wrapped up from head to foot, and the brim of his soft felt hat hid every inch of his face but the shiny tip of his nose; the snow had piled itself against his shoulders and chest, and added a white crest to the burden he carried. He staggered into the Coach and Horses more dead than alive, and flung his portmanteau down. 'A fire,' he cried, 'in the name of human charity! A room and a fire!' He stamped and shook the snow from off himself in the bar, and followed Mrs Hall into her guest parlour to strike his bargain. And with that much introduction, that and a couple of sovereigns flung upon the table, he took up his quarters in the inn.

Mrs Hall lit the fire and left him there while she went to prepare him a meal with her own hands. A guest to stop at Iping in the winter-time was an unheard-of piece of luck, let alone a guest who was no 'haggler', and she was resolved to show herself worthy of her good fortune. As soon as the bacon was well under way, and Millie, her lymphatic maid, had been brisked up a bit by a few deftly chosen expressions of contempt, she carried the cloth, plates, and glasses into the parlour and began to lay them with the utmost *éclat*. Although the fire was burning up briskly, she was surprised to see that her visitor still wore his hat and coat, standing with his back to her and staring out of the window at the falling snow in the yard. His gloved hands were clasped behind him, and he seemed to be lost in thought. She noticed that the melting snow that still sprinkled his shoulders dripped upon her carpet. 'Can I take your hat and coat, sir?' she said, 'and give them a good dry in the kitchen?'

'No,' he said without turning.

She was not sure she had heard him, and was about to repeat her question.

He turned his head and looked at her over his shoulder. 'I prefer to keep them on,' he said with emphasis, and she noticed that he wore big blue spectacles with side-lights, and had a bushy side-whisker over his coat-collar that completely hid his cheeks and face.

'Very well, sir,' she said. 'As you like. In a bit the room will be warmer.'

He made no answer, and had turned his face away from her again, and Mrs Hall, feeling that her conversational advances were ill-timed, laid the rest of the table things in a quick staccato and whisked out of the room.

When she returned he was still standing there, like a man of stone, his back hunched, his collar turned up, his dripping hat-brim turned down, hiding his face and ears completely. She put down the eggs and bacon with considerable emphasis, and called rather than said to him, 'Your lunch is served, sir.'

'Thank you,' he said at the same time, and did not stir until she was closing the door. Then he swung round and approached the table with a certain eager quickness.

As she went behind the bar to the kitchen she heard a sound repeated at regular intervals. Chirk, chirk, chirk, it went, the sound of a spoon being rapidly whisked round a basin. 'That girl!' she said. 'There! I clean forgot it. It's her being so long!' And while she herself finished mixing the mustard, she gave Millie a few verbal stabs for her excessive slowness. She had cooked the ham and eggs, laid the table, and done everything, while Millie (help indeed!) had only succeeded in delaying the mustard. And him a new guest and wanting to stay! Then she filled the mustard pot, and, putting it with a certain stateliness upon a gold and black tea-tray, carried it into the parlour.

She rapped and entered promptly. As she did so her visitor moved quickly, so that she got but a glimpse of a white object disappearing behind the table. It would seem he was picking something from the floor. She rapped down the mustard pot on the table, and then she noticed the overcoat and hat had been taken off and put over a chair in front of the fire, and a pair of wet boots threatened rust to her steel fender. She went to these things resolutely. 'I suppose I may have them to dry now,' she said in a voice that brooked no denial.

'Leave the hat,' said her visitor, in a muffled voice, and turning she saw he had raised his head and was sitting and looking at her.

For a moment she stood gaping at him, too surprised to speak.

He held a white cloth – it was a serviette he had brought with him – over the lower part of his face, so that his mouth and jaws were completely hidden, and that was the reason of his muffled voice. But it was not that which startled Mrs Hall. It was the fact that all his forehead above his blue glasses was covered by a white bandage, and that another covered his ears, leaving not a scrap of his face exposed excepting only his pink, peaked nose. It was bright, pink, and shiny just as it had been at first. He wore a dark-brown velvet jacket with a high, black, linen-lined collar turned up about his neck. The thick black hair, escaping as it could below and between the cross bandages, projected in curious tails and horns, giving him the strangest appearance conceivable. This muffled and bandaged head was so unlike what she had anticipated, that for a moment she was rigid.

He did not remove the serviette, but remained holding it, as she saw now, with a brown gloved hand, and regarding her with his inscrutable

blue glasses. 'Leave the hat,' he said, speaking very distinctly through the white cloth.

Her nerves began to recover from the shock they had received. She placed the hat on the chair again by the fire. 'I didn't know, sir,' she began, 'that—' and she stopped embarrassed.

'Thank you,' he said drily, glancing from her to the door and then at her again.

'I'll have them nicely dried, sir, at once,' she said, and carried his clothes out of the room. She glanced at his white-swathed head and blue goggles again as she was going out of the door; but his napkin was still in front of his face. She shivered a little as she closed the door behind her, and her face was eloquent of her surprise and perplexity. 'I *never*,' she whispered. 'There!' She went quite softly to the kitchen, and was too preoccupied to ask Millie what she was messing about with *now*, when she got there.

The visitor sat and listened to her retreating feet. He glanced enquiringly at the window before he removed his serviette, and resumed his meal. He took a mouthful, glanced suspiciously at the window, took another mouthful, then rose and, taking the serviette in his hand, walked across the room and pulled the blind down to the top of the white muslin that obscured the lower panes. This left the room in a twilight. This done, he returned with an easier air to the table and his meal.

'The poor soul's had an accident or an op'ration or somethin',' said Mrs Hall. 'What a turn them bandages did give me, to be sure!'

She put on some more coal, unfolded the clothes-horse, and extended the traveller's coat upon this. 'And they goggles! Why, he looked more like a divin' helmet than a human man!' She hung his muffler on a corner of the horse. 'And holding that handkerchief over his mouth all the time. Talkin' through it! . . . Perhaps his mouth was hurt too – maybe.'

She turned round, as one who suddenly remembers. 'Bless my soul alive!' she said, going off at a tangent; 'ain't you done them taters *yet*, Millie?'

When Mrs Hall went to clear away the stranger's lunch, her idea that his mouth must also have been cut or disfigured in the accident she supposed him to have suffered, was confirmed, for he was smoking a pipe, and all the time that she was in the room he never loosened the silk muffler he had wrapped round the lower part of his face to put the mouthpiece to his lips. Yet it was not forgetfulness, for she saw he glanced at it as it smouldered out. He sat in the corner with his back to the window-blind and spoke now, having eaten and drunk and being comfortably warmed through, with less aggressive brevity than before. The reflection of the fire lent a kind of red animation to his big spectacles they had lacked hitherto.

'I have some luggage,' he said, 'at Bramblehurst station,' and he asked her how he could have it sent. He bowed his bandaged head quite politely in acknowledgment of her explanation. 'Tomorrow!' he said. 'There is no

speedier delivery?' and seemed quite disappointed when she answered, 'No.' Was she quite sure? No man with a trap who would go over?

Mrs Hall, nothing loath, answered his questions and developed a conversation. 'It's a steep road by the down, sir,' she said in answer to the question about a trap; and then, snatching at an opening, said, 'It was there a carriage was upsettled, a year ago and more. A gentleman killed, besides his coachman. Accidents, sir, happen in a moment, don't they?'

But the visitor was not to be drawn so easily. 'They do,' he said through his muffler, eyeing her quietly through his impenetrable glasses.

'But they take long enough to get well, don't they? . . . There was my sister's son, Tom, jest cut his arm with a scythe, tumbled on it in the 'ayfield, and, bless me! he was three months tied up, sir. You'd hardly believe it. It's regular given me a dread of a scythe, sir.'

'I can quite understand that,' said the visitor.

'He was afraid, one time, that he'd have to have an op'ration – he was that bad, sir.'

The visitor laughed abruptly, a bark of a laugh that he seemed to bite and kill in his mouth. '*Was* he?' he said.

'He was, sir. And no laughing matter to them as had the doing for him, as I had – my sister being took up with her little ones so much. There was bandages to do, sir, and bandages to undo. So that if I may make so bold as to say it, sir—'

'Will you get me some matches?' said the visitor, quite abruptly. 'My pipe is out.'

Mrs Hall was pulled up suddenly. It was certainly rude of him, after telling him all she had done. She gasped at him for a moment, and remembered the two sovereigns. She went for the matches.

'Thanks,' he said concisely, as she put them down, and turned his shoulder upon her and stared out of the window again. It was altogether too discouraging. Evidently he was sensitive on the topic of operations and bandages. She did not 'make so bold as to say,' however, after all. But his snubbing way had irritated her, and Millie had a hot time of it that afternoon.

The visitor remained in the parlour until four o'clock, without giving the ghost of an excuse for an intrusion. For the most part he was quite still during that time; it would seem he sat in the growing darkness smoking in the firelight, perhaps dozing.

Once or twice a curious listener might have heard him at the coals, and for the space of five minutes he was audible pacing the room. He seemed to be talking to himself. Then the armchair creaked as he sat down again.

CHAPTER II

Mr Teddy Henfrey's First Impressions

At four o'clock, when it was fairly dark and Mrs Hall was screwing up her courage to go in and ask her visitor if he would take some tea, Teddy Henfrey, the clock-jobber, came into the bar. 'My sakes! Mrs Hall,' said he, 'but this is terrible weather for thin boots!' The snow outside was falling faster.

Mrs Hall agreed, and then noticed he had his bag with him. 'Now you're here, Mr Teddy,' said she, 'I'd be glad if you'd give th' old clock in the parlour a bit of a look. 'Tis going, and it strikes well and hearty; but the hour-hand won't do nuthin' but point at six.'

And leading the way, she went across to the parlour door and rapped and entered.

Her visitor, she saw as she opened the door, was seated in the armchair before the fire, dozing it would seem, with his bandaged head drooping on one side. The only light in the room was the red glow from the fire – which lit his eyes like adverse railway signals, but left his downcast face in darkness – and the scanty vestiges of the day that came in through the open door. Everything was ruddy, shadowy, and indistinct to her, the more so since she had just been lighting the bar lamp, and her eyes were dazzled. But for a second it seemed to her that the man she looked at had an enormous mouth wide open – a vast and incredible mouth that swallowed the whole of the lower portion of his face. It was the sensation of a moment: the white-bound head, the monstrous goggle eyes, and this huge yawn below it. Then he stirred, started up in his chair, put up his hand. She opened the door wide, so that the room was lighter, and she saw him more clearly, with the muffler held up to his face just as she had seen him hold the serviette before. The shadows, she fancied, had tricked her.

'Would you mind, sir, this man a-coming to look at the clock, sir?' she said, recovering from the momentary shock.

'Look at the clock?' he said, staring round in a drowsy manner, and speaking over his hand, and then, getting more fully awake, 'Certainly.'

Mrs Hall went away to get a lamp, and he rose and stretched himself. Then came the light, and Mr Teddy Henfrey, entering, was confronted by this bandaged person. He was, he says, 'taken aback'.

'Good afternoon,' said the stranger, regarding him – as Mr Henfrey says, with a vivid sense of the dark spectacles – 'like a lobster.'

'I hope,' said Mr Henfrey, 'that it's no intrusion.'

'None whatever,' said the stranger. 'Though, I understand,' he said turning to Mrs Hall, 'that this room is really to be mine for my own private use.'

'I thought, sir,' said Mrs Hall, 'you'd prefer the clock—'

'Certainly,' said the stranger, 'certainly – but, as a rule, I like to be alone and undisturbed.

'But I'm really glad to have the clock seen to,' he said, seeing a certain hesitation in Mr Henfrey's manner. 'Very glad.' Mr Henfrey had intended to apologize and withdraw, but this anticipation reassured him. The stranger turned round with his back to the fireplace and put his hands behind his back. 'And presently,' he said, 'when the clock-mending is over, I think I should like to have some tea. But not till the clock-mending is over.'

Mrs Hall was about to leave the room – she made no conversational advances this time, because she did not want to be snubbed in front of Mr Henfrey – when her visitor asked her if she had made any arrangements about his boxes at Bramblehurst. She told him she had mentioned the matter to the postman, and that the carrier could bring them over on the morrow. 'You are certain that is the earliest?' he said.

She was certain, with a marked coldness.

'I should explain,' he added, 'what I was really too cold and fatigued to do before, that I am an experimental investigator.'

'Indeed, sir,' said Mrs Hall, much impressed.

'And my baggage contains apparatus and appliances.'

'Very useful things indeed they are, sir,' said Mrs Hall.

'And I'm very naturally anxious to get on with my enquiries.'

'Of course, sir.'

'My reason for coming to Iping,' he proceeded, with a certain deliberation of manner, 'was . . . a desire for solitude. I do not wish to be disturbed in my work. In addition to my work, an accident—'

'I thought as much,' said Mrs Hall to herself.

' – necessitates a certain retirement. My eyes – are sometimes so weak and painful that I have to shut myself up in the dark for hours together. Lock myself up. Sometimes – now and then. Not at present, certainly. At such times the slightest disturbance, the entry of a stranger into the room, is a source of excruciating annoyance to me – it is well these things should be understood.'

'Certainly, sir,' said Mrs Hall. 'And if I might make so bold as to ask—'

'That, I think, is all,' said the stranger, with that quietly irresistible air of finality he could assume at will. Mrs Hall reserved her question and sympathy for a better occasion.

After Mrs Hall had left the room, he remained standing in front of the fire, glaring, so Mr Henfrey puts it, at the clock-mending. Mr Henfrey not only took off the hands of the clock, and the face, but extracted the works; and he tried to work in as slow and quiet and unassuming a manner as possible. He worked with the lamp close to him, and the green shade threw a brilliant light upon his hands, and upon the frame and wheels, and left

the rest of the room shadowy. When he looked up, coloured patches swam in his eyes. Being constitutionally of a curious nature, he had removed the works – a quite unnecessary proceeding – with the idea of delaying his departure and perhaps falling into conversation with the stranger. But the stranger stood there, perfectly silent and still. So still, it got on Henfrey's nerves. He felt alone in the room and looked up, and there, grey and dim, was the bandaged head and huge blue lenses staring fixedly, with a mist of green spots drifting in front of them. It was so uncanny to Henfrey that for a minute they remained staring blankly at one another. Then Henfrey looked down again. Very uncomfortable position! One would like to say something. Should he remark that the weather was very cold for the time of year?

He looked up as if to take aim with that introductory shot. 'The weather—' he began.

'Why don't you finish and go?' said the rigid figure, evidently in a state of painfully suppressed rage. 'All you've got to do is to fix the hour-hand on its axle. You're simply humbugging—'

'Certainly, sir – one minute more, sir. I overlooked—' and Mr Henfrey finished and went.

But he went feeling excessively annoyed. 'Damn it!' said Mr Henfrey to himself, trudging down the village through the thawing snow; 'a man must do a clock at times, surely.'

And again, 'Can't a man look at you? – Ugly!'

And yet again, 'Seemingly not. If the police was wanting you you couldn't be more wrapped and bandaged.'

At Gleeson's corner he saw Hall, who had recently married the stranger's hostess at the Coach and Horses, and who now drove the Iping conveyance, when occasional people required it, to Sidderbridge Junction, coming towards him on his return from that place. Hall had evidently been 'stopping a bit' at Sidderbridge, to judge by his driving. ''Ow do, Teddy?' he said, passing.

'You got a rum un up home!' said Teddy.

Hall very sociably pulled up. 'What's that?' he asked.

'Rum-looking customer stopping at the Coach and Horses,' said Teddy. 'My sakes!'

And he proceeded to give Hall a vivid description of his grotesque guest. 'Looks a bit like a disguise, don't it? I'd like to see a man's face if I had him stopping in my place,' said Henfrey. 'But women are that trustful, where strangers are concerned. He's took your rooms and he ain't even given a name, Hall.'

'You don't say so!' said Hall, who was a man of sluggish apprehension.

'Yes,' said Teddy. 'By the week. Whatever he is, you can't get rid of him under the week. And he's got a lot of luggage coming tomorrow, so he says. Let's hope it won't be stones in boxes, Hall.'

He told Hall how his aunt at Hastings had been swindled by a stranger with empty portmanteaux. Altogether he left Hall vaguely suspicious. 'Get up, old girl,' said Hall. 'I s'pose I must see 'bout this.'

Teddy trudged on his way with his mind considerably relieved.

Instead of 'seeing 'bout it,' however, Hall on his return was severely rated by his wife on the length of time he had spent in Sidderbridge, and his mild enquiries were answered snappishly and in a manner not to the point. But the seed of suspicion Teddy had sown germinated in the mind of Mr Hall in spite of these discouragements. 'You wim' don't know everything,' said Mr Hall, resolved to ascertain more about the personality of his guest at the earliest possible opportunity. And after the stranger had gone to bed, which he did about half-past nine, Mr Hall went very aggressively into the parlour and looked very hard at his wife's furniture, just to show that the stranger wasn't master there, and scrutinized closely and a little contemptuously a sheet of mathematical computation the stranger had left. When retiring for the night he instructed Mrs Hall to look very closely at the stranger's luggage when it came next day.

'You mind your own business, Hall,' said Mrs Hall, 'and I'll mind mine.'

She was all the more inclined to snap at Hall because the stranger was undoubtedly an unusually strange sort of stranger, and she was by no means assured about him in her own mind. In the middle of the night she woke up dreaming of huge white heads like turnips, that came trailing after her, at the end of interminable necks, and with vast black eyes. But being a sensible woman, she subdued her terrors and turned over and went to sleep again.

CHAPTER III

The Thousand and One Bottles

So it was that on the twenty-ninth day of February, at the beginning of the thaw, this singular person fell out of infinity into Iping village. Next day his luggage arrived through the slush. And very remarkable luggage it was. There were a couple of trunks indeed, such as a rational man might need, but in addition there were a box of books – big, fat books, of which some were just in an incomprehensible handwriting – and a dozen or more crates, boxes, and cases, containing objects packed in straw, as it seemed to Hall, tugging with a casual curiosity at the straw – glass bottles. The stranger, muffled in hat, coat, gloves, and wrapper, came out impatiently to meet Fearenside's cart, while Hall was having a word or so of gossip preparatory to helping bring them in. Out he came, not noticing Fearenside's dog, who was sniffing in a *dilettante* spirit at Hall's legs. 'Come along with those boxes,' he said. 'I've been waiting long enough.'

And he came down the steps towards the tail of the cart as if to lay hands on the smaller crate.

No sooner had Fearenside's dog caught sight of him, however, than it began to bristle and growl savagely, and when he rushed down the steps it gave an undecided hop, and then sprang straight at his hand. 'Whup!' cried Hall, jumping back, for he was no hero with dogs, and Fearenside howled, 'Lie down!' and snatched his whip.

They saw the dog's teeth had slipped the hand, heard a kick, saw the dog execute a flanking jump and get home on the stranger's leg, and heard the rip of his trousering. Then the finer end of Fearenside's whip reached his property, and the dog, yelping with dismay, retreated under the wheels of the waggon. It was all the business of a swift half-minute. No one spoke, everyone shouted. The stranger glanced swiftly at his torn glove and at his leg, made as if he would stoop to the latter, then turned and rushed swiftly up the steps into the inn. They heard him go headlong across the passage and up the uncarpeted stairs to his bedroom.

'You brute, you!' said Fearenside, climbing off the waggon with his whip in his hand, while the dog watched him through the wheel. 'Come here,' said Fearenside – 'You'd better.'

Hall had stood gaping. 'He wuz bit,' said Hall. 'I'd better go and see to en,' and he trotted after the stranger. He met Mrs Hall in the passage. 'Carrier's darg,' he said 'bit en.'

He went straight upstairs, and the stranger's door being ajar, he pushed it open and was entering without any ceremony, being of a naturally sympathetic turn of mind.

The blind was down and the room dim. He caught a glimpse of a most singular thing, what seemed a handless arm waving towards him, and a face of three huge indeterminate spots on white, very like the face of a pale pansy. Then he was struck violently in the chest, hurled back, and the door slammed in his face and locked. It was so rapid that it gave him no time to observe. A waving of indecipherable shapes, a blow, and a concussion. There he stood on the dark little landing, wondering what it might be that he had seen.

A couple of minutes after, he rejoined the little group that had formed outside the Coach and Horses. There was Fearenside telling about it all over again for the second time; there was Mrs Hall saying his dog didn't have no business to bite her guests; there was Huxter, the general dealer from over the road, interrogative; and Sandy Wadgers from the forge, judicial; besides women and children, all of them saying fatuities: 'Wouldn't let en bite *me*, I knows'; ''Tasn't right *have* such dargs'; 'Whad *'e* bite 'n for, then?' and so forth.

Mr Hall, staring at them from the steps and listening, found it incredible that he had seen anything so very remarkable happen upstairs. Besides, his vocabulary was altogether too limited to express his impressions.

'He don't want no help, he says,' he said in answer to his wife's enquiry. 'We'd better be a-takin' of his luggage in.'

'He ought to have it cauterized at once,' said Mr Huxter; 'especially if it's at all inflamed.'

'I'd shoot en, that's what I'd do,' said a lady in the group.

Suddenly the dog began growling again.

'Come along,' cried an angry voice in the doorway, and there stood the muffled stranger with his collar turned up, and his hat-brim bent down. 'The sooner you get those things in the better I'll be pleased.' It is stated by an anonymous bystander that his trousers and gloves had been changed.

'Was you hurt, sir?' said Fearenside. 'I'm rare sorry the darg—'

'Not a bit,' said the stranger. 'Never broke the skin. Hurry up with those things.'

He then swore to himself, so Mr Hall asserts.

Directly the first crate was, in accordance with his directions, carried into the parlour, the stranger flung himself upon it with extraordinary eagerness, and began to unpack it, scattering the straw with an utter disregard of Mrs Hall's carpet. And from it he began to produce bottles – little fat bottles containing powders, small and slender bottles containing coloured and white fluids, fluted blue bottles labelled *Poison*, bottles with round bodies and slender necks, large green-glass bottles, large white-glass bottles, bottles with glass stoppers and frosted labels, bottles with fine corks, bottles with bungs, bottles with wooden caps, wine bottles, salad-oil bottles – putting them in rows on the chiffonnier, on the mantel, on the table under the window,

round the floor, on the bookshelf – everywhere. The chemist's shop in Bramblehurst could not boast half so many. Quite a sight it was. Crate after crate yielded bottles, until all six were empty and the table high with straw; the only things that came out of these crates besides the bottles were a number of test-tubes and a carefully packed balance.

And directly the crates were unpacked, the stranger went to the window and set to work, not troubling in the least about the litter of straw, the fire which had gone out, the box of books outside, nor for the trunks and other luggage that had gone upstairs.

When Mrs Hall took his dinner in to him, he was already so absorbed in his work, pouring little drops out of the bottles into test-tubes, that he did not hear her until she had swept away the bulk of the straw and put the tray on the table, with some little emphasis perhaps, seeing the state that the floor was in. Then he half turned his head and immediately turned it away again. But she saw he had removed his glasses; they were beside him on the table, and it seemed to her that his eye sockets were extraordinarily hollow. He put on his spectacles again, and then turned and faced her. She was about to complain of the straw on the floor when he anticipated her.

'I wish you wouldn't come in without knocking,' he said in the tone of abnormal exasperation that seemed so characteristic of him.

'I knocked, but seemingly—'

'Perhaps you did. But in my investigations – my really very urgent and necessary investigations – the slightest disturbance, the jar of a door – I must ask you—'

'Certainly, sir. You can turn the lock if you're like that, you know. Any time.'

'A very good idea,' said the stranger.

'This stror, sir, if I might make so bold as to remark—'

'Don't. If the straw makes trouble put it down in the bill.' And he mumbled at her – words suspiciously like curses.

He was so odd, standing there, so aggressive and explosive, bottle in one hand and test-tube in the other, that Mrs Hall was quite alarmed. But she was a resolute woman. 'In which case, I should like to know, sir, what you consider—'

'A shilling. Put down a shilling. Surely a shilling's enough?'

'So be it,' said Mrs Hall, taking up the table-cloth and beginning to spread it over the table. 'If you're satisfied, of course—'

He turned and sat down, with his coat-collar towards her.

All the afternoon he worked with the door locked and, as Mrs Hall testifies, for the most part in silence. But once there was a concussion and a sound of bottles ringing together as though the table had been hit, and the smash of a bottle flung violently down, and then a rapid pacing athwart

the room. Fearing 'something was the matter,' she went to the door and
listened, not caring to knock.

'I can't go on,' he was raving. 'I *can't* go on. Three hundred thousand,
four hundred thousand! The huge multitude! Cheated! All my life it may
take me! . . . Patience! Patience indeed! Fool and liar!'

There was a noise of hobnails on the bricks in the bar, and Mrs Hall had
very reluctantly to leave the rest of his soliloquy. When she returned the
room was silent again, save for the faint crepitation of his chair and the
occasional clink of a bottle. It was all over; the stranger had resumed work.

When she took in his tea she saw broken glass in the corner of the room
under the concave mirror, and a golden stain that had been carelessly wiped.
She called attention to it.

'Put it down in the bill,' snapped her visitor. 'For God's sake don't worry
me. If there's damage done, put it down in the bill,' and he went on ticking
a list in the exercise book before him.

'I'll tell you something,' said Fearenside, mysteriously. It was late in the
afternoon, and they were in the little beer-shop of Iping Hanger.

'Well?' said Teddy Henfrey.

'This chap you're speaking of, what my dog bit. Well – he's black.
Leastways, his legs are. I seed through the tear of his trousers and the tear
of his glove. You'd have expected a sort of pinky to show, wouldn't you?
Well – there wasn't none. Just blackness. I tell you, he's as black as my hat.'

'My sakes!' said Henfrey. 'It's a rummy case altogether. Why, his nose is
as pink as paint!'

'That's true,' said Fearenside. 'I knows that. And I tell 'ee what I'm
thinking. That marn's a piebald, Teddy. Black here and white there – in
patches. And he's ashamed of it. He's a kind of half-breed, and the colour's
come off patchy instead of mixing. I've heard of such things before. And it's
the common way with horses, as anyone can see.'

CHAPTER IV

Mr Cuss Interviews the Stranger

I have told the circumstances of the stranger's arrival in Iping with a certain
fullness of detail, in order that the curious impression he created may be
understood by the reader. But excepting two odd incidents, the circumstances
of his stay until the extraordinary day of the Club Festival may be passed
over very cursorily. There were a number of skirmishes with Mrs Hall on
matters of domestic discipline, but in every case until late April, when the
first signs of penury began, he over-rode her by the easy expedient of an
extra payment. Hall did not like him, and whenever he dared he talked of
the advisability of getting rid of him; but he showed his dislike chiefly by
concealing it ostentatiously, and avoiding his visitor as much as possible.
'Wait till the summer,' said Mrs Hall sagely, 'when the artisks are beginning
to come. Then we'll see. He may be a bit overbearing, but bills settled
punctual is bills settled punctual, whatever you like to say.'

The stranger did not go to church, and indeed made no difference between
Sunday and the irreligious days, even in costume. He worked, as Mrs Hall
thought, very fitfully. Some days he would come down early and be contin-
uously busy. On others he would rise late, pace his room, fretting audibly
for hours together, smoke, sleep in the armchair by the fire. Communication
with the world beyond the village he had none. His temper continued very
uncertain; for the most part his manner was that of a man suffering under
almost unendurable provocation, and once or twice things were snapped,
torn, crushed, or broken in spasmodic gusts of violence. He seemed under
a chronic irritation of the greatest intensity. His habit of talking to himself
in a low voice grew steadily upon him, but though Mrs Hall listened conscien-
tiously she could make neither head nor tail of what she heard.

He rarely went abroad by daylight, but at twilight he would go out muffled
up invisibly, whether the weather were cold or not, and he chose the lone-
liest paths and those most overshadowed by trees and banks. His goggling
spectacles and ghastly bandaged face under the penthouse of his hat, came
with a disagreeable suddenness out of the darkness upon one or two home-
going labourers, and Teddy Henfrey, tumbling out of the Scarlet Coat one
night, at half-past nine, was scared shamefully by the stranger's skull-like
head (he was walking hat in hand) lit by the sudden light of the opened
inn door. Such children as saw him at nightfall dreamt of bogies, and it
seemed doubtful whether he disliked boys more than they disliked him, or
the reverse; but there was certainly a vivid enough dislike on either side.

It was inevitable that a person of so remarkable an appearance and bearing

should form a frequent topic in such a village as Iping. Opinion was greatly divided about his occupation. Mrs Hall was sensitive on the point. When questioned, she explained very carefully that he was an 'experimental investigator,' going gingerly over the syllables as one who dreads pitfalls. When asked what an experimental investigator was, she would say with a touch of superiority that most educated people knew such things as that, and would thus explain that he 'discovered things'. Her visitor had had an accident, she said, which temporarily discoloured his face and hands, and being of a sensitive disposition, he was averse to any public notice of the fact.

Out of her hearing there was a view largely entertained that he was a criminal trying to escape from justice by wrapping himself up so as to conceal himself altogether from the eye of the police. This idea sprang from the brain of Mr Teddy Henfrey. No crime of any magnitude dating from the middle or end of February was known to have occurred. Elaborated in the imagination of Mr Gould, the probationary assistant in the National School, this theory took the form that the stranger was an Anarchist in disguise, preparing explosives, and he resolved to undertake such detective operations as his time permitted. These consisted for the most part in looking very hard at the stranger whenever they met, or in asking people who had never seen the stranger, leading questions about him. But he detected nothing.

Another school of opinion followed Mr Fearenside, and either accepted the piebald view or some modification of it; as, for instance, Silas Durgan, who was heard to assert that 'if he chooses to show enself at fairs he'd make his fortune in no time,' and being a bit of a theologian, compared the stranger to the man with the one talent. Yet another view explained the entire matter by regarding the stranger as a harmless lunatic. That had the advantage of accounting for everything straight away.

Between these main groups there were waverers and compromisers. Sussex folk have few superstitions, and it was only after the events of early April that the thought of the supernatural was first whispered in the village. Even then it was only credited among the women folk.

But whatever they thought of him, people in Iping, on the whole, agreed in disliking him. His irritability, though it might have been comprehensible to an urban brain-worker, was an amazing thing to these quiet Sussex villagers. The frantic gesticulations they surprised now and then, the headlong pace after nightfall that swept him upon them round quiet corners, the inhuman bludgeoning of all the tentative advances of curiosity, the taste for twilight that led to the closing of doors, the pulling down of blinds, the extinction of candles and lamps – who could agree with such goings on? They drew aside as he passed down the village, and when he had gone by, young humourists would up with coat-collars and down with hat-brims, and go pacing nervously after him in imitation of his occult bearing. There was a song popular at that time called the 'Bogey Man'. Miss Statchell sang it at

the schoolroom concert (in aid of the church lamps), and thereafter when-ever one or two of the villagers were gathered together and the stranger appeared, a bar or so of this tune, more or less sharp or flat, was whistled in the midst of them. Also belated little children would call 'Bogey Man!' after him, and make off tremulously elated.

Cuss, the general practitioner, was devoured by curiosity. The bandages excited his professional interest, the report of the thousand and one bottles aroused his jealous regard. All through April and May he coveted an oppor-tunity of talking to the stranger, and at last, towards Whitsuntide, he could stand it no longer, but hit upon the subscription-list for a village nurse as an excuse. He was surprised to find that Mr Hall did not know his guest's name. 'He give a name,' said Mrs Hall, an assertion which was quite unfounded, 'but I didn't rightly hear it.' She thought it seemed so silly not to know the man's name.

Cuss rapped at the parlour door and entered. There was a fairly audible imprecation from within. 'Pardon my intrusion,' said Cuss, and then the door closed and cut Mrs Hall off from the rest of the conversation.

She could hear the murmur of voices for the next ten minutes, then a cry of surprise, a stirring of feet, a chair flung aside, a bark of laughter, quick steps to the door, and Cuss appeared, his face white, his eyes staring over his shoulder. He left the door open behind him, and without looking at her strode across the hall and went down the steps, and she heard his feet hurrying along the road. He carried his hat in his hand. She stood behind the door, looking at the open door of the parlour. Then she heard the stranger laughing quietly, and then his footsteps came across the room. She could not see his face where she stood. The parlour door slammed, and the place was silent again.

Cuss went straight up the village to Bunting the vicar. 'Am I mad?' Cuss began abruptly, as he entered the shabby little study. 'Do I look like an insane person?'

'What's happened?' said the vicar, putting the ammonite on the loose sheets of his forthcoming sermon.

'That chap at the inn—'

'Well?'

'Give me something to drink,' said Cuss, and he sat down.

When his nerves had been steadied by a glass of cheap sherry, the only drink the good vicar had available, he told him of the interview he had just had. 'Went in,' he gasped, 'and began to demand a subscription for that Nurse Fund. He'd stuck his hands in his pockets as I came in, and he sat down lumpily in his chair. Sniffed. I told him I'd heard he took an interest in scientific things. He said yes. Sniffed again. Kept on sniffing all the time; evidently recently caught an infernal cold. No wonder, wrapped up like that! I developed the nurse idea, and all the while kept my eyes open. Bottles –

chemicals – everywhere. Balance, test-tubes in stands, and a smell of – evening primrose. Would he subscribe? Said he'd consider it. Asked him, point-blank, was he researching. Said he was. A long research? Got quite cross. "A damnable long research," said he, blowing the cork out, so to speak. "Oh," said I. And out came the grievance. The man was just on the boil, and my question boiled him over. He had been given a prescription, most valuable prescription – what for he wouldn't say. Was it medical? "Damn you! What are you fishing after?" I apologized. Dignified sniff and cough. He resumed. He'd read it. Five ingredients. Put it down; turned his head. Draught of air from window lifted the paper. Swish, rustle. He was working in a room with an open fireplace, he said. Saw a flicker, and there was the prescription burning and lifting chimneyward. Rushed towards it just as it whisked up chimney. So! Just at that point, to illustrate his story, out came his arm.'

'Well?'

'No hand – just an empty sleeve. Lord! I thought, *that's* a deformity! Got a cork arm, I suppose, and has taken it off. Then, I thought, there's something odd in that. What the devil keeps that sleeve up and open, if there's nothing in it? There was nothing in it, I tell you. Nothing down it, right down to the joint. I could see right down it to the elbow, and there was a glimmer of light shining through a tear of the cloth. "Good God!" I said. Then he stopped. Stared at me with those black goggles of his, and then at his sleeve.'

'Well?'

'That's all. He never said a word; just glared, and put his sleeve back in his pocket quickly. "I was saying," said he, "that there was the prescription burning, wasn't I?" Interrogative cough. "How the devil," said I, "can you move an empty sleeve like that?" "Empty sleeve?' "Yes," said I, "an empty sleeve."

"'It's an empty sleeve, is it? You saw it was an empty sleeve?" He stood up right away. I stood up too. He came towards me in three very slow steps, and stood quite close. Sniffed venomously. I didn't flinch, though I'm hanged if that bandaged knob of his, and those blinkers, aren't enough to unnerve anyone, coming quietly up to you.

"'You said it was an empty sleeve?" he said. "Certainly," I said. At staring and saying nothing a barefaced man, unspectacled, starts scratch. Then very quietly he pulled his sleeve out of his pocket again, and raised his arm towards me as though he would show it to me again. He did it very, very slowly. I looked at it. Seemed an age. "Well?"said I, clearing my throat, "there's nothing in it."

'Had to say something. I was beginning to feel frightened. I could see right down it. He extended it straight towards me, slowly, slowly, just like that, until the cuff was six inches from my face. Queer thing to see an empty sleeve come at you like that! And then—'

'Well?'

'Something – exactly like a finger and thumb it felt – nipped my nose.'

Bunting began to laugh.

'There wasn't anything there!' said Cuss, his voice running up into a shriek at the 'there'. 'It's all very well for you to laugh, but I tell you I was so startled, I hit his cuff hard, and turned around, and cut out of the room – I left him—'

Cuss stopped. There was no mistaking the sincerity of his panic. He turned round in a helpless way and took a second glass of the excellent vicar's very inferior sherry. 'When I hit his cuff,' said Cuss, 'I tell you, it felt exactly like hitting an arm. And there wasn't an arm! There wasn't the ghost of an arm!'

Mr Bunting thought it over. He looked suspiciously at Cuss. 'It's a most remarkable story,' he said. He looked very wise and grave indeed. 'It's really,' said Mr Bunting with judicial emphasis, 'a most remarkable story.'

CHAPTER V

The Burglary at the Vicarage

The facts of the burglary at the vicarage came to us chiefly through the medium of the vicar and his wife. It occurred in the small hours of Whit Monday, the day devoted in Iping to the Club festivities. Mrs Bunting, it seems, woke up suddenly in the stillness that comes before the dawn, with the strong impression that the door of their bedroom had opened and closed. She did not arouse her husband at first, but sat up in bed listening. She then distinctly heard the pad, pad, pad of bare feet coming out of the adjoining dressing-room and walking along the passage towards the staircase. As soon as she felt assured of this, she aroused the Rev. Mr Bunting as quietly as possible. He did not strike a light, but putting on his spectacles, her dressing-gown and his bath slippers, he went out on the landing to listen. He heard quite distinctly a fumbling going on at his study desk downstairs, and then a violent sneeze.

At that he returned to his bedroom, armed himself with the most obvious weapon, the poker, and descended the staircase as noiselessly as possible. Mrs Bunting came out on the landing.

The hour was about four, and the ultimate darkness of the night was past. There was a faint shimmer of light in the hall, but the study doorway yawned impenetrably black. Everything was still except the faint creaking of the stairs under Mr Bunting's tread, and the slight movements in the study. Then something snapped, the drawer was opened, and there was a rustle of papers. Then came an imprecation, and a match was struck and the study was flooded with yellow light. Mr Bunting was now in the hall, and through the crack of the door he could see the desk and the open drawer and a candle burning on the desk. But the robber he could not see. He stood there in the hall undecided what to do, and Mrs Bunting, her face white and intent, crept slowly downstairs after him. One thing kept Mr Bunting's courage; the persuasion that this burglar was a resident in the village.

They heard the chink of money, and realized that the robber had found the housekeeping reserve of gold, two pounds ten in half sovereigns altogether. At that sound Mr Bunting was nerved to abrupt action. Gripping the poker firmly, he rushed into the room, closely followed by Mrs Bunting. 'Surrender!' cried Mr Bunting, fiercely, and then stooped amazed. Apparently the room was perfectly empty.

Yet their conviction that they had, that very moment, heard somebody moving in the room had amounted to a certainty. For half a minute, perhaps,

they stood gaping, then Mrs Bunting went across the room and looked behind the screen, while Mr Bunting, by a kindred impulse, peered under the desk. Then Mrs Bunting turned back the window-curtains, and Mr Bunting looked up the chimney and probed it with the poker. Then Mrs Bunting scrutinized the wastepaper basket and Mr Bunting opened the lid of the coal-scuttle. Then they came to a stop and stood with eyes interrogating each other.

'I could have sworn—' said Mr Bunting.

'The candle!' said Mr Bunting. 'Who lit the candle?'

'The drawer!' said Mrs Bunting. 'And the money's gone!'

She went hastily to the doorway.

'Of all the extraordinary occurrences—'

There was a violent sneeze in the passage. They rushed out, and as they did so the kitchen door slammed. 'Bring the candle,' said Mr Bunting, and led the way. They both heard a sound of bolts being hastily shot back.

As he opened the kitchen door he saw through the scullery that the back door was just opening, and the faint light of early dawn displayed the dark masses of the garden beyond. He is certain that nothing went out of the door. It opened, stood open for a moment, and then closed with a slam. As it did so, the candle Mrs Bunting was carrying from the study flickered and flared. It was a minute or more before they entered the kitchen.

The place was empty. They refastened the back door, examined the kitchen, pantry, and scullery thoroughly, and at last went down into the cellar. There was not a soul to be found in the house, search as they would.

Daylight found the vicar and his wife, a quaintly costumed little couple, still marvelling about on their own ground floor by the unnecessary light of a guttering candle.

CHAPTER VI

The Furniture That Went Mad

Now it happened that in the early hours of Whit Monday, before Millie was hunted out for the day, Mr Hall and Mrs Hall both rose and went noiselessly down into the cellar. Their business there was of a private nature, and had something to do with the specific gravity of their beer. They had hardly entered the cellar when Mrs Hall found she had forgotten to bring down a bottle of sarsaparilla from their joint-room. As she was the expert and principal operator in this affair, Hall very properly went upstairs for it.

On the landing he was surprised to see that the stranger's door was ajar. He went on into his own room and found the bottle as he had been directed.

But returning with the bottle, he noticed that the bolts of the front door had been shot back, that the door was in fact simply on the latch. And with a flash of inspiration he connected this with the stranger's room upstairs and the suggestions of Mr Teddy Henfrey. He distinctly remembered holding the candle while Mrs Hall shot these bolts over night. At the sight he stopped, gaping, then with the bottle still in his hand went upstairs again. He rapped at the stranger's door. There was no answer. He rapped again; then pushed the door wide open and entered.

It was as he expected. The bed, the room also, was empty. And what was stranger, even to his heavy intelligence, on the bedroom chair and along the rail of the bed were scattered the garments, the only garments so far as he knew, and the bandages of their guest. His big slouch hat even was cocked jauntily over the bed-post.

As Hall stood there he heard his wife's voice coming out of the depth of the cellar, with that rapid telescoping of the syllables and interrogative cocking up of the final words to a high note, by which the West Sussex villager is wont to indicate a brisk impatience. 'Gearge! You gart whad a wand?'

At that he turned and hurried down to her. 'Janny,' he said, over the rail of the cellar steps, ''tas the truth what Henfrey sez. 'E's not in uz room, 'e en't. And the front door's unbolted.'

At first Mrs Hall did not understand, and as soon as she did she resolved to see the empty room for herself. Hall, still holding the bottle, went first. 'If 'e en't there,' he said, ''is close are. And what's 'e doin' 'ithout 'is close, then? 'Tas a most curious basness.'

As they came up the cellar steps they both, it was afterwards ascertained, fancied they heard the front door open and shut, but seeing it closed and nothing there, neither said a word to the other about it at the time. Mrs

Hall passed her husband in the passage and ran on first upstairs. Someone sneezed on the staircase. Hall, following six steps behind, thought that he heard her sneeze. She, going on first, was under the impression that Hall was sneezing. She flung open the door and stood regarding the room. 'Of all the curious!' she said.

She heard a sniff close behind her head as it seemed, and turning, was surprised to see Hall a dozen feet off on the topmost stair. But in another moment he was beside her. She bent forward and put her hand on the pillow and then under the clothes.

'Cold,' she said. 'He's been up this hour or more.'

As she did so, a most extraordinary thing happened. The bed-clothes gathered themselves together, leapt up suddenly into a sort of peak, and then jumped headlong over the bottom rail. It was exactly as if a hand had clutched them in the centre and flung them aside. Immediately after, the stranger's hat hopped off the bed-post, described a whirling flight in the air through the better part of a circle, and then dashed straight at Mrs Hall's face. Then as swiftly came the sponge from the washstand; and then the chair, flinging the stranger's coat and trousers carelessly aside, and laughing drily in a voice singularly like the stranger's, turned itself up with its four legs at Mrs Hall, seemed to take aim at her for a moment, and charged at her. She screamed and turned, and then the chair legs came gently but firmly against her back and impelled her and Hall out of the room. The door slammed violently and was locked. The chair and bed seemed to be executing a dance of triumph for a moment, and then abruptly everything was still.

Mrs Hall was left almost in a fainting condition in Mr Hall's arms on the landing. It was with the greatest difficulty that Mr Hall and Millie, who had been roused by her scream of alarm, succeeded in getting her downstairs, and applying the restoratives customary in such cases.

''Tas sperits,' said Mrs Hall. 'I know 'tas sperits. I've read in papers of en. Tables and chairs leaping and dancing . . .'

'Take a drop more, Janny,' said Hall. ''Twill steady ye.'

'Lock him out,' said Mrs Hall. 'Don't let him come in again. I half guessed – I might ha' known. With them goggling eyes and bandaged head, and never going to church of a Sunday. And all they bottles – more'n it's right for anyone to have. He's put the sperits into the furniture. My good old furniture! 'Twas in that very chair my poor dear mother used to sit when I was a little girl. To think it should rise up against me now!'

'Just a drop more, Janny,' said Hall. 'Your nerves is all upset.'

They sent Millie across the street through the golden five o'clock sunshine to rouse up Mr Sandy Wadgers, the blacksmith. Mr Hall's compliments and the furniture upstairs was behaving most extraordinary. Would Mr Wadgers come round? He was a knowing man, was Mr Wadgers, and very resourceful. He took quite a grave view of the case. 'Arm darmed ef thet ent witchcraft,'

was the view of Mr Sandy Wadgers. 'You want horseshoes for such gentry as he.'

He came round greatly concerned. They wanted him to lead the way upstairs to the room, but he didn't seem to be in any hurry. He preferred to talk in the passage. Over the way Huxter's apprentice came out and began taking down the shutters of the tobacco window. He was called over to join the discussion. Mr Huxter naturally followed over in the course of a few minutes. The Anglo-Saxon genius for parliamentary government asserted itself; there was a great deal of talk and no decisive action. 'Let's have the facts first,' insisted Mr Sandy Wadgers. 'Let's be sure we'd be acting perfectly right in bustin' that there door open. A door onbust is always open to bustin', but ye can't onbust a door once you've busted en.'

And suddenly and most wonderfully the door of the room upstairs opened of its own accord, and as they looked up in amazement, they saw descending the stairs the muffled figure of the stranger staring more blackly and blankly than ever with those unreasonably large blue glass eyes of his. He came down stiffly and slowly, staring all the time; he walked across the passage staring, then stopped.

'Look there!' he said, and their eyes followed the direction of his gloved finger and saw a bottle of sarsaparilla hard by the cellar door. Then he entered the parlour, and suddenly, swiftly, viciously, slammed the door in their faces.

Not a word was spoken until the last echoes of the slam had died away. They stared at one another. 'Well, if that don't lick everything!' said Mr Wadgers, and left the alternative unsaid.

'I'd go in and ask'n 'bout it,' said Wadgers, to Mr Hall. 'I'd d'mand an explanation.'

It took some time to bring the landlady's husband up to that pitch. At last he rapped, opened the door, and got as far as, 'Excuse me—'

'Go to the devil!' said the stranger in a tremendous voice, and 'Shut that door after you.' So that brief interview terminated.

CHAPTER VII

The Unveiling of the Stranger

The stranger went into the little parlour of the Coach and Horses about half-past five in the morning, and there he remained until near midday, the blinds down, the door shut, and none, after Hall's repulse, venturing near him.

All that time he must have fasted. Thrice he rang his bell, the third time furiously and continuously, but no one answered him. 'Him and his "go to the devil" indeed!' said Mrs Hall. Presently came an imperfect rumour of the burglary at the vicarage, and two and two were put together. Hall, assisted by Wadgers, went off to find Mr Shuckleforth, the magistrate, and take his advice. No one ventured upstairs. How the stranger occupied himself is unknown. Now and then he would stride violently up and down, and twice came an outburst of curses, a tearing of paper, and a violent smashing of bottles.

The little group of scared but curious people increased. Mrs Huxter came over; some gay young fellows resplendent in black ready-made jackets and *piqué* paper ties, for it was Whit Monday, joined the group with confused interrogations. Young Archie Harker distinguished himself by going up the yard and trying to peep under the window-blinds. He could see nothing, but gave reason for supposing that he did, and others of the Iping youth presently joined him.

It was the finest of all possible Whit Mondays, and down the village street stood a row of nearly a dozen booths, a shooting gallery, and on the grass by the forge were three yellow and chocolate waggons and some picturesque strangers of both sexes putting up a coconut shy. The gentlemen wore blue jerseys, the ladies white aprons and quite fashionable hats with heavy plumes. Wodger, of the Purple Fawn, and Mr Jaggers, the cobbler, who also sold old second-hand ordinary bicycles, were stretching a string of union-jacks and royal ensigns (which had originally celebrated the first Victorian Jubilee) across the road.

And inside, in the artificial darkness of the parlour, into which only one thin jet of sunlight penetrated, the stranger, hungry we must suppose, and fearful, hidden in his uncomfortable hot wrappings, pored through his dark glasses upon his paper or chinked his dirty little bottles, and occasionally swore savagely at the boys, audible if invisible, outside the windows. In the corner by the fireplace lay the fragments of half a dozen smashed bottles, and a pungent twang of chlorine tainted the air. So much we know from what was heard at the time and from what was subsequently seen in the room.

About noon he suddenly opened his parlour door and stood glaring fixedly at the three or four people in the bar. 'Mrs Hall,' he said. Somebody went sheepishly and called for Mrs Hall.

Mrs Hall appeared after an interval, a little short of breath, but all the fiercer for that. Hall was still out. She had deliberated over this scene, and she came holding a little tray with an unsettled bill upon it. 'Is it your bill you're wanting, sir?' she said.

'Why wasn't my breakfast laid? Why haven't you prepared my meals and answered my bell? Do you think I live without eating?'

'Why isn't my bill paid?' said Mrs Hall. 'That's what I want to know.'

'I told you three days ago I was awaiting a remittance—'

'I told you two days ago I wasn't going to await no remittances. You can't grumble if your breakfast waits a bit, if my bill's been waiting these five days, can you?'

The stranger swore briefly but vividly.

'Nar, nar!' from the bar.

'And I'd thank you kindly, sir, if you'd keep your swearing to yourself, sir,' said Mrs Hall.

The stranger stood looking more like an angry diving-helmet than ever. It was universally felt in the bar that Mrs Hall had the better of him. His next words showed as much.

'Look here, my good woman—' he began.

'Don't "good woman" *me*,' said Mrs Hall.

'I've told you my remittance hasn't come—'

'Remittance indeed!' said Mrs Hall.

'Still, I daresay in my pocket—'

'You told me three days ago that you hadn't anything but a sovereign's worth of silver upon you— '

'Well, I've found some more—'

''Ul-*lo*!' from the bar.

'I wonder where you found it,' said Mrs Hall.

That seemed to annoy the stranger very much. He stamped his foot. 'What do you mean?' he said.

'That I wonder where you found it,' said Mrs Hall. 'And before I take any bills or get any breakfasts, or do any such things whatsoever, you got to tell me one or two things I don't understand, and what nobody don't understand, and what everybody is very anxious to understand. I want to know what you been doing t'my chair upstairs, and I want to know how 'tis your room was empty, and how you got in again. Them as stops in this house comes in by the doors, that's the rule of the house, and that you *didn't* do, and what I want to know is how you *did* come in. And I want to know—'

Suddenly the stranger raised his gloved hands clenched, stamped his

foot, and said, 'Stop!' with such extraordinary violence that he silenced her instantly.

'You don't understand,' he said, 'who I am or what I am. I'll show you. By Heaven! I'll show you.' Then he put his open palm over his face and withdrew it. The centre of his face became a black cavity. 'Here,' he said. He stepped forward and handed Mrs Hall something which she, staring at his metamorphosed face, accepted automatically. Then, when she saw what it was, she screamed loudly, dropped it, and staggered back. The nose – it was the stranger's nose! pink and shining – rolled on the floor.

Then he removed his spectacles, and everyone in the bar gasped. He took off his hat, and with a violent gesture tore at his whiskers and bandages. For a moment they resisted him. A flash of horrible anticipation passed through the bar. 'Oh, my Gard!' said someone. Then off they came.

It was worse than anything. Mrs Hall, standing open-mouthed and horror-struck, shrieked at what she saw, and made for the door of the house. Everyone began to move. They were prepared for scars, disfigurements, tangible horrors, but *nothing*! The bandages and false hair flew across the passage into the bar, making a hobbledehoy jump to avoid them. Everyone tumbled on everyone else down the steps. For the man who stood there shouting some incoherent explanation, was a solid gesticulating figure up to the coat-collar of him, and then – nothingness, no visible thing at all!

People down the village heard shouts and shrieks, and looking up the street saw the Coach and Horses violently firing out its humanity. They saw Mrs Hall fall down and Mr Teddy Henfrey jump to avoid tumbling over her, and then they heard the frightful screams of Millie, who, emerging suddenly from the kitchen at the noise of the tumult, had come upon the headless stranger from behind. These increased suddenly.

Forthwith everyone all down the street, the sweetstuff seller, coconut shy proprietor and his assistant, the swing man, little boys and girls, rustic dandies, smart wenches, smocked elders and aproned gipsies – began running towards the inn, and in a miraculously short space of time a crowd of perhaps forty people, and rapidly increasing, swayed and hooted and enquired and exclaimed and suggested, in front of Mrs Hall's establishment. Everyone seemed eager to talk at once, and the result was babel. A small group supported Mrs Hall, who was picked up in a state of collapse. There was a conference, and the incredible evidence of a vociferous eye-witness. 'O Bogey!' 'What's he been doin', then?' 'Ain't hurt the girl, 'as 'e?' 'Run at en with a knife, I believe.' 'No 'ed, I tell ye. I don't mean no manner of speaking. I mean *marn 'ithout a 'ed*!' 'Narnsense! 'tis some conjuring trick.' 'Fetched off 'is wrapping, 'e did—'

In its struggles to see in through the open door, the crowd formed itself into a straggling wedge, with the more adventurous apex nearest the inn. 'He stood for a moment, I heerd the gal scream, and he turned. I saw her

skirts whisk, and he went after her. Didn't take ten seconds. Back he comes
with a knife in uz hand and a loaf; stood just as if he was staring. Not a
moment ago. Went in that there door. I tell 'e, 'e ain't gart no 'ed at all.
You just missed en—'

There was a disturbance behind, and the speaker stopped to step aside
for a little procession that was marching very resolutely towards the house;
first Mr Hall, very red and determined, then Mr Bobby Jaffers, the village
constable, and then the wary Mr Wadgers. They had come now armed with
a warrant.

People shouted conflicting information of the recent circumstances. "Ed
or no 'ed,' said Jaffers, 'I got to 'rest en, and 'rest en I *will*.'

Mr Hall marched up the steps, marched straight to the door of the parlour
and flung it open. 'Constable,' he said, 'do your duty.'

Jaffers marched in. Hall next, Wadgers last. They saw in the dim light
the headless figure facing them, with a gnawed crust of bread in one gloved
hand and a chunk of cheese in the other.

'That's him!' said Hall.

'What the devil's this?' came in a tone of angry expostulation from above
the collar of the figure.

'You're a damned rum customer, mister,' said Mr Jaffers. 'But 'ed or no
'ed, the warrant says "body," and duty's duty—'

'Keep off!' said the figure, starting back.

Abruptly he whipped down the bread and cheese, and Mr Hall just
grasped the knife on the table in time to save it. Off came the stranger's
left glove and was slapped in Jaffers' face. In another moment Jaffers,
cutting short some statement concerning a warrant, had gripped him by
the handless wrist and caught his invisible throat. He got a sounding
kick on the shin that made him shout, but he kept his grip. Hall sent
the knife sliding along the table to Wadgers, who acted as goalkeeper
for the offensive, so to speak, and then stepped forward as Jaffers and
the stranger swayed and staggered towards him, clutching and hitting
in. A chair stood in the way, and went aside with a crash as they came
down together.

'Get the feet,' said Jaffers between his teeth.

Mr Hall, endeavouring to act on instructions, received a sounding kick
in the ribs that disposed of him for a moment, and Mr Wadgers, seeing the
decapitated stranger had rolled over and got the upper side of Jaffers, retreated
towards the door, knife in hand, and so collided with Mr Huxter and the
Sidderbridge carter coming to the rescue of law and order. At the same
moment down came three or four bottles from the chiffonnier and shot a
web of pungency into the air of the room.

'I'll surrender,' cried the stranger, though he had Jaffers down, and in
another moment he stood up panting, a strange figure, headless and handless,

for he had pulled off his right glove now as well as his left. 'It's no good,' he said, as if sobbing for breath.

It was the strangest thing in the world to hear that voice coming as if out of empty space, but the Sussex peasants are perhaps the most matter-of-fact people under the sun. Jaffers got up also and produced a pair of handcuffs. Then he started.

'I say!' said Jaffers, brought up short by a dim realization of the incongruity of the whole business, 'Darn it! Can't use 'em as I can see.'

The stranger ran his arm down his waistcoat, and as if by a miracle the buttons to which his empty sleeve pointed became undone. Then he said something about his shin, and stooped down. He seemed to be fumbling with his shoes and socks.

'Why!' said Huxter, suddenly, 'that's not a man at all. It's just empty clothes. Look! You can see down his collar and the linings of his clothes. I could put my arm—'

He extended his hand; it seemed to meet something in mid-air, and he drew it back with a sharp exclamation. 'I wish you'd keep your fingers out of my eye,' said the aerial voice, in a tone of savage expostulation. 'The fact is, I'm all here: head, hands, legs, and all the rest of it, but it happens I'm invisible. It's a confounded nuisance, but I am. That's no reason why I should be poked to pieces by every stupid bumpkin in Iping, is it?'

The suit of clothes, now all unbuttoned and hanging loosely upon its unseen supports, stood up, arms akimbo.

Several other of the men folks had now entered the room, so that it was closely crowded. 'Invisible, eh?' said Huxter, ignoring the stranger's abuse. 'Who ever heard the likes of that?'

'It's strange, perhaps, but it's not a crime. Why am I assaulted by a policeman in this fashion?'

'Ah! that's a different matter,' said Jaffers. 'No doubt you are a bit difficult to see in this light, but I got a warrant and it's all correct. What I'm after ain't no invisibility, it's burglary. There's a house been broke into and money took.'

'Well?'

'And circumstances certainly point—'

'Stuff and nonsense!' said the Invisible Man.

'I hope so, sir; but I've got my instructions.'

'Well,' said the stranger, 'I'll come. I'll *come*. But no handcuffs.'

'It's the regular thing,' said Jaffers.

'No handcuffs,' stipulated the stranger.

'Pardon me,' said Jaffers.

Abruptly the figure sat down, and before anyone could realize what was being done, the slippers, socks, and trousers had been kicked off under the table. Then he sprang up again and flung off his coat.

'Here, stop that,' said Jaffers, suddenly realizing what was happening. He gripped at the waistcoat; it struggled, and the shirt slipped out of it and left it limp and empty in his hand. 'Hold him!' said Jaffers, loudly. 'Once he gets the things off—'

'Hold him!' cried everyone, and there was a rush at the fluttering white shirt which was now all that was visible of the stranger.

The shirt-sleeve planted a shrewd blow in Hall's face that stopped his open-armed advance, and sent him backward into old Toothsome the sexton, and in another moment the garment was lifted up and became convulsed and vacantly flapping about the arms, even as a shirt that is being thrust over a man's head. Jaffers clutched at it, and only helped to pull it off; he was struck in the mouth out of the air, and incontinently threw his truncheon and smote Teddy Henfrey savagely upon the crown of his head.

'Look out!' said everybody, fencing at random and hitting at nothing. 'Hold him! Shut the door! Don't let him loose! I got something! Here he is!' A perfect babel of noises they made. Everybody, it seemed, was being hit all at once, and Sandy Wadgers, knowing as ever and his wits sharpened by a frightful blow in the nose, reopened the door and led the rout. The others, following incontinently, were jammed for a moment in the corner by the doorway. The hitting continued. Phipps, the Unitarian, had a front tooth broken, and Henfrey was injured in the cartilage of his ear. Jaffers was struck under the jaw, and, turning, caught at something that intervened between him and Huxter in the mêlée, and prevented their coming together. He felt a muscular chest, and in another moment the whole mass of struggling, excited men shot out into the crowded hall.

'I got him!' shouted Jaffers, choking and reeling through them all, and wrestling with purple face and swelling veins against his unseen enemy.

Men staggered right and left as the extraordinary conflict swayed swiftly towards the house door, and went spinning down the half-dozen steps of the inn. Jaffers cried in a strangled voice, holding tight, nevertheless, and making play with his knee – spun around, and fell heavily undermost with his head on the gravel. Only then did his fingers relax.

There were excited cries of 'Hold him!' 'Invisible!' and so forth, and a young fellow, a stranger in the place whose name did not come to light, rushed in at once, caught something, missed his hold, and fell over the constable's prostrate body. Halfway across the road a woman screamed as something pushed by her; a dog, kicked apparently, yelped and ran howling into Huxter's yard, and with that the transit of the Invisible Man was accomplished. For a space people stood amazed and gesticulating, and then came panic, and scattered them abroad through the village as a gust scatters dead leaves.

But Jaffers lay quite still, face upward and knees bent, at the foot of the steps of the inn.

CHAPTER VIII

In Transit

The eighth chapter is exceedingly brief, and relates that Gibbons, the amateur naturalist of the district, while lying out on the spacious open downs without a soul within a couple of miles of him, as he thought, and almost dozing, heard close to him the sound as of a man coughing, sneezing, and then swearing savagely to himself; and looking, beheld nothing. Yet the voice was indisputable. It continued to swear with that breadth and variety that distinguishes the swearing of a cultivated man. It grew to a climax, diminished again, and died away in the distance, going as it seemed to him in the direction of Adderdean. It lifted to a spasmodic sneeze and ended. Gibbons had heard nothing of the morning's occurrences, but the phenomenon was so striking and disturbing that his philosophical tranquillity vanished; he got up hastily, and hurried down the steepness of the hill towards the village, as fast as he could go.

CHAPTER IX

Mr Thomas Marvel

You must picture Mr Thomas Marvel as a person of copious, flexible visage, a nose of cylindrical protrusion, a liquorish, ample, fluctuating mouth, and a beard of bristling eccentricity. His figure inclined to embonpoint; his short limbs accentuated this inclination. He wore a furry silk hat, and the frequent substitution of twine and shoelaces for buttons, apparent at critical points of his costume, marked a man essentially bachelor.

Mr Thomas Marvel was sitting with his feet in a ditch by the roadside over the down towards Adderdean, about a mile and a half out of Iping. His feet, save for socks of irregular open-work, were bare, his big toes were broad, and pricked like the ears of a watchful dog. In a leisurely manner – he did everything in a leisurely manner – he was contemplating trying on a pair of boots. They were the soundest boots he had come across for a long time, but too large for him; whereas the ones he had were, in dry weather, a very comfortable fit, but too thin-soled for damp. Mr Thomas Marvel hated roomy shoes, but then he hated damp. He had never properly thought out which he hated most, and it was a pleasant day, and there was nothing better to do. So he put the four shoes in a graceful group on the turf and looked at them. And seeing them there among the grass and springing agrimony, it suddenly occurred to him that both pairs were exceedingly ugly to see. He was not at all startled by a voice behind him.

'They're boots, anyhow,' said the voice.

'They are – charity boots,' said Mr Thomas Marvel, with his head on one side regarding them distastefully; 'and which is the ugliest pair in the whole blessed universe, I'm darned if I know!'

'H'm,' said the Voice.

'I've worn worse – in fact, I've worn none. But none so owdacious ugly, if you'll allow the expression. I've been cadging boots – in particular – for days. Because I was sick of *them*. They're sound enough, of course. But a gentleman on tramp sees such a thundering lot of his boots. And if you'll believe me, I've raised nothing in the whole blessed county, try as I would, but *them*. Look at 'em! And a good country for boots, too, in a general way. But it's just my promiscuous luck. I've got my boots in this county ten years or more. And then they treat you like this.'

'It's a beast of a county,' said the voice. 'And pigs for people.'

'Ain't it?' said Mr Thomas Marvel. 'Lord! But them boots! It beats it.'

He turned his head over his shoulder to the right, to look at the boots of his interlocutor with a view to comparisons, and lo! where the boots of his interlocutor should have been were neither legs nor boots. He was irradiated by the dawn of a great amazement. 'Where *are* yer?' said Mr Thomas Marvel over his shoulder and coming on all fours. He saw a stretch of empty downs with the wind swaying the remote green-pointed furze bushes.

'Am I drunk?' said Mr Marvel. 'Have I had visions? Was I talking to myself? What the—'

'Don't be alarmed,' said a voice.

'None of your ventriloquizing *me*,' said Mr Thomas Marvel, rising sharply to his feet. 'Where *are* yer? Alarmed, indeed!'

'Don't be alarmed,' repeated the voice.

'*You'll* be alarmed in a minute, you silly fool,' said Mr Thomas Marvel. 'Where *are* yer? Lemme get my mark on yer—

'Are yer *buried?*' said Mr Thomas Marvel, after an interval.

There was no answer. Mr Thomas Marvel stood bootless and amazed, his jacket nearly thrown off.

'Peewit,' said a peewit, very remote.

'Peewit, indeed!' said Mr Thomas Marvel. 'This ain't no time for foolery.' The down was desolate, east and west, north and south; the road with its shallow ditches and white bordering stakes, ran smooth and empty north and south, and, save for that peewit, the blue sky was empty too. 'So help me,' said Mr Thomas Marvel, shuffling his coat on to his shoulders again. 'It's the drink! I might ha' known.'

'It's not the drink,' said the voice. 'You keep your nerves steady.'

'Ow!' said Mr Marvel, and his face grew white amidst its patches. 'It's the drink!' his lips repeated noiselessly. He remained staring about him, rotating slowly backwards. 'I could have *swore* I heard a voice,' he whispered.

'Of course you did.'

'It's there again,' said Mr Marvel, closing his eyes and clasping his hand on his brow with a tragic gesture. He was suddenly taken by the collar and shaken violently, and left more dazed than ever. 'Don't be a fool,' said the voice.

'I'm – off – my – blooming – chump,' said Mr Marvel. 'It's no good. It's fretting about them blarsted boots. I'm off my blessed blooming chump. Or it's spirits.'

'Neither one thing nor the other,' said the voice. 'Listen!'

'Chump,' said Mr Marvel.

'One minute,' said the voice, penetratingly, tremulous with self-control.

'Well?' said Mr Thomas Marvel, with a strange feeling of having been dug in the chest by a finger.

'You think I'm just imagination? Just imagination?'

'What else *can* you be?' said Mr Thomas Marvel, rubbing the back of his neck.

'Very well,' said the voice, in a tone of relief. 'Then I'm going to throw flints at you till you think differently.'

'But where *are* yer?'

The voice made no answer. Whizz came a flint, apparently out of the air, and missed Mr Marvel's shoulder by a hair's breadth. Mr Marvel, turning, saw a flint jerk up into the air, trace a complicated path, hang for a moment, and then fling at his feet with almost invisible rapidity. He was too amazed to dodge. Whizz it came, and ricochetted from a bare toe into the ditch. Mr Thomas Marvel jumped a foot and howled aloud. Then he started to run, tripped over an unseen obstacle, and came head over heels into a sitting position.

'*Now*,' said the voice, as a third stone curved upward and hung in the air above the tramp. 'Am I imagination?'

Mr Marvel by way of reply struggled to his feet, and was immediately rolled over again. He lay quiet for a moment. 'If you struggle any more,' said the voice, 'I shall throw the flint at your head.'

'It's a fair do,' said Mr Thomas Marvel, sitting up, taking his wounded toe in hand and fixing his eye on the third missile. 'I don't understand it. Stones flinging themselves. Stones talking. Put yourself down. Rot away. I'm done.'

The third flint fell.

'It's very simple,' said the voice. 'I'm an invisible man.'

'Tell us something I don't know,' said Mr Marvel, gasping with pain. 'Where you've hid – how you do it – I *don't* know. I'm beat.'

'That's all,' said the voice. 'I'm invisible. That's what I want you to understand.'

'Anyone could see that. There is no need for you to be so confounded impatient, mister. *Now* then. Give us a notion. How are you hid?'

'I'm invisible. That's the great point. And what I want you to understand is this—'

'But whereabouts?' interrupted Mr Marvel.

'Here! Six yards in front of you.'

'Oh, *come*! I ain't blind. You'll be telling me next you're just thin air. I'm not one of your ignorant tramps—'

'Yes, I am – thin air. You're looking through me.'

'What! Ain't there any stuff to you. *Vox et* – what is it? – jabber. Is it that?'

'I am just a human being – solid, needing food and drink, needing covering too – But I'm invisible. You see? Invisible. Simple idea. Invisible.'

'What, real like?'

'Yes, real.'

'Let's have a hand of you,' said Marvel, 'if you *are* real. It won't be so darn out-of-the-way like, then – *Lord!*' he said, 'how you made me jump! – gripping me like that!'

He felt the hand that had closed round his wrist with his disengaged fingers, and his fingers went timorously up the arm, patted a muscular chest, and explored a bearded face. Marvel's face was astonishment.

'I'm dashed!' he said. 'If this don't beat cock-fighting! Most remarkable! – And there I can see a rabbit clean through you, 'arf a mile away! Not a bit of you visible – except—'

He scrutinized the apparently empty space keenly. 'You 'aven't been eatin' bread and cheese?' he asked, holding the invisible arm.

'You're quite right, and it's not quite assimilated into the system.'

'Ah!' said Mr Marvel. 'Sort of ghostly, though.'

'Of course, all this isn't half so wonderful as you think.'

'It's quite wonderful enough for *my* modest wants,' said Mr Thomas Marvel. 'Howjer manage it! How the dooce is it done?'

'It's too long a story. And besides—'

'I tell you, the whole business fairly beats me,' said Mr Marvel.

'What I want to say at present is this: I need help. I have come to that – I came upon you suddenly. I was wandering, mad with rage, naked, impotent. I could have murdered. And I saw you—'

'*Lord!*' said Mr Marvel.

'I came up behind you – hesitated – went on—'

Mr Marvel's expression was eloquent.

' – then stopped. "Here," I said, "is an outcast like myself. This is the man for me." So I turned back and came to you – you. And—'

'*Lord!*' said Mr Marvel. 'But I'm all in a tizzy. May I ask – How is it? And what you may be requiring in the way of help? – Invisible!'

'I want you to help me get clothes – and shelter – and then, with other things. I've left them long enough. If you won't – well! But you *will* – *must*.'

'Look here,' said Mr Marvel. 'I'm too flabbergasted. Don't knock me about any more. And leave me go. I must get steady a bit. And you've pretty near broken my toe. It's all so unreasonable. Empty downs, empty sky. Nothing visible for miles except the bosom of Nature. And then comes a voice. A voice out of heaven! And stones! And a fist – Lord!'

'Pull yourself together,' said the voice, 'for you have to do the job I've chosen for you.'

Mr Marvel blew out his cheeks, and his eyes were round.

'I've chosen you,' said the voice. 'You are the only man except some of those fools down there, who knows there is such a thing as an invisible man. You have to be my helper. Help me – and I will do great things for you. An invisible man is a man of power.' He stopped for a moment to sneeze violently.

'But if you betray me,' he said, 'if you fail to do as I direct you—' He paused and tapped Mr Marvel's shoulder smartly. Mr Marvel gave a yelp of terror at the touch. 'I don't want to betray you,' said Mr Marvel, edging away from the direction of the fingers. 'Don't you go a-thinking that, whatever you do. All I want to do is to help you – just tell me what I got to do. (Lord!) Whatever you want done, that I'm most willing to do.'

CHAPTER X

Mr Marvel's Visit to Iping

After the first gusty panic had spent itself Iping became argumentative. Scepticism suddenly reared its head, rather nervous scepticism, not at all assured of its back, but scepticism nevertheless. It is so much easier not to believe in an invisible man; and those who had actually seen him dissolve into air, or felt the strength of his arm, could be counted on the fingers of two hands. And of these witnesses Mr Wadgers was presently missing, having retired impregnably behind the bolts and bars of his own house, and Jaffers was lying stunned in the parlour of the Coach and Horses. Great and strange ideas transcending experience often have less effect upon men and women than smaller, more tangible considerations. Iping was gay with bunting, and everybody was in gala dress. Whit Monday had been looked forward to for a month or more. By the afternoon even those who believed in the Unseen were beginning to resume their little amusements in a tentative fashion, on the supposition that he had quite gone away, and with the sceptics he was already a jest. But people, sceptics and believers alike, were remarkably sociable all that day.

Haysman's meadow was gay with a tent, in which Mrs Bunting and the other ladies were preparing tea, while, without, the Sunday-school children ran races and played games under the noisy guidance of the curate and the Misses Cuss and Sackbut. No doubt there was a slight uneasiness in the air, but people for the most part had the sense to conceal whatever imaginative qualms they experienced. On the village green an inclined string, down which, clinging the while to a pulley-swung handle, one could be hurled violently against a sack at the other end, came in for considerable favour among the adolescents, as also did the swings and the coconut shies. There was also promenading, and the steam organ attached to a small roundabout filled the air with a pungent flavour of oil and with equally pungent music. Members of the Club, who had attended church in the morning, were splendid in badges of pink and green, and some of the gayer-minded had also adorned their bowler hats with brilliant-coloured favours of ribbon. Old Fletcher, whose conceptions of holiday-making were severe, was visible through the jasmine about his window or through the open door (whichever way you chose to look), poised delicately on a plank supported on two chairs, and whitewashing the ceiling of his front room.

About four o'clock a stranger entered the village from the direction of the downs. He was a short, stout person in an extraordinarily shabby top hat, and he appeared to be very much out of breath. His cheeks were alter-

nately limp and tightly puffed. His mottled face was apprehensive, and he moved with a sort of reluctant alacrity. He turned the corner of the church, and directed his way to the Coach and Horses. Among others Old Fletcher remembers seeing him, and indeed the old gentleman was so struck by his peculiar agitation that he inadvertently allowed a quantity of whitewash to run down the brush into the sleeve of his coat while regarding him.

This stranger, to the perceptions of the proprietor of the coconut shy, appeared to be talking to himself, and Mr Huxter remarked the same thing. He stopped at the foot of the Coach and Horses steps, and, according to Mr Huxter, appeared to undergo a severe internal struggle before he could induce himself to enter the house. Finally he marched up the steps, and was seen by Mr Huxter to turn to the left and open the door of the parlour. Mr Huxter heard voices from within the room and from the bar apprising the man of his error. 'That room's private!' said Hall, and the stranger shut the door clumsily and went into the bar.

In the course of a few minutes he reappeared, wiping his lips with the back of his hand with an air of quiet satisfaction that somehow impressed Mr Huxter as assumed. He stood looking about him for some moments, and then Mr Huxter saw him walk in an oddly furtive manner towards the gates of the yard, upon which the parlour window opened. The stranger, after some hesitation, leant against one of the gate-posts, produced a short clay pipe, and prepared to fill it. His fingers trembled while doing so. He lit it clumsily, and folding his arms began to smoke in a languid attitude, an attitude which his occasional glances up the yard altogether belied.

All this Mr Huxter saw over the canisters of the tobacco window, and the singularity of the man's behaviour prompted him to maintain his observation.

Presently the stranger stood up abruptly and put his pipe in his pocket. Then he vanished into the yard. Forthwith Mr Huxter, conceiving he was witness of some petty larceny, leapt round his counter and ran out into the road to intercept the thief. As he did so, Mr Marvel reappeared, his hat askew, a big bundle in a blue table-cloth in one hand, and three books tied together – as it proved afterwards with the Vicar's braces – in the other. Directly he saw Huxter he gave a sort of gasp, and turning sharply to the left, began to run. 'Stop, thief!' cried Huxter, and set off after him. Mr Huxter's sensations were vivid but brief. He saw the man just before him and spurting briskly for the church corner and the hill road. He saw the village flags and festivities beyond, and a face or so turned towards him. He bawled, 'Stop!' again. He had hardly gone ten strides before his shin was caught in some mysterious fashion, and he was no longer running, but flying with inconceivable rapidity through the air. He saw the ground suddenly close to his face. The world seemed to splash into a million whirling specks of light, and subsequent proceedings interested him no more.

CHAPTER XI

In the Coach and Horses

Now in order clearly to understand what had happened in the inn, it is necessary to go back to the moment when Mr Marvel first came into view of Mr Huxter's window.

At that precise moment Mr Cuss and Mr Bunting were in the parlour. They were seriously investigating the strange occurrences of the morning, and were, with Mr Hall's permission, making a thorough examination of the Invisible Man's belongings. Jaffers had partially recovered from his fall and had gone home in the charge of his sympathetic friends. The stranger's scattered garments had been removed by Mrs Hall and the room tidied up. And on the table under the window where the stranger had been wont to work, Cuss had hit almost at once on three big books in manuscript labelled 'Diary'.

'Diary!' said Cuss, putting the three books on the table. 'Now, at any rate, we shall learn something.' The Vicar stood with his hands on the table.

'Diary,' repeated Cuss, sitting down, putting two volumes to support the third, and opening it. 'H'm – no name on the fly-leaf. Bother! – cypher. And figures.'

The Vicar came round to look over his shoulder.

Cuss turned the pages over with a face suddenly disappointed. 'I'm – dear me! It's all cypher, Bunting.'

'There are no diagrams?' asked Mr Bunting. 'No illustrations throwing light—'

'See for yourself,' said Mr Cuss. 'Some of it's mathematical and some of it's Russian or some such language (to judge by the letters), and some of it's Greek. Now the Greek I thought *you*—'

'Of course,' said Mr Bunting, taking out and wiping his spectacles and feeling suddenly very uncomfortable, for he had no Greek left in his mind worth talking about; 'yes – the Greek, of course, may furnish a clue.'

'I'll find you a place.'

'I'd rather glance through the volumes first,' said Mr Bunting, still wiping. 'A general impression first, Cuss, and *then*, you know, we can go looking for clues.'

He coughed, put on his glasses, arranged them fastidiously, coughed again, and wished something would happen to avert the seemingly inevitable exposure. Then he took the volume Cuss handed him in a leisurely manner. And then something did happen.

The door opened suddenly.

Both gentlemen started violently, looked round, and were relieved to see a sporadically rosy face beneath a furry silk hat. 'Tap?' asked the face, and stood staring.

'No,' said both gentlemen at once.

'Over the other side, my man,' said Mr Bunting. And 'Please shut that door,' said Mr Cuss, irritably.

'All right,' said the intruder, as it seemed in a low voice curiously different from the huskiness of its first enquiry. 'Right you are,' said the intruder in the former voice. 'Stand clear!' and he vanished and closed the door.

'A sailor, I should judge,' said Mr Bunting. 'Amusing fellows, they are. Stand clear! indeed. A nautical term, referring to his getting back out of the room, I suppose.'

'I daresay so,' said Cuss. 'My nerves are all loose today. It quite made me jump – the door opening like that.'

Mr Bunting smiled as if he had not jumped. 'And now,' he said with a sigh, 'these books.'

'One minute,' said Cuss, and went and locked the door. 'Now I think we're safe from interruption.'

Someone sniffed as he did so.

'One thing is indisputable,' said Bunting, drawing up a chair next to that of Cuss. 'There certainly have been very strange things happen in Iping during the last few days – very strange. I cannot of course believe in this absurd invisibility story—'

'It's incredible,' said Cuss '– incredible. But the fact remains that I saw – I certainly saw right down his sleeve—'

'But did you – are you sure? Suppose a mirror, for instance – hallucinations are so easily produced. I don't know if you have ever seen a really good conjuror—'

'I won't argue again,' said Cuss. 'We've thrashed that out, Bunting. And just now there's these books – Ah! here's some of what I take to be Greek! Greek letters certainly.'

He pointed to the middle of the page. Mr Bunting flushed slightly and brought his face nearer, apparently finding some difficulty with his glasses. Suddenly he became aware of a strange feeling at the nape of his neck. He tried to raise his head, and encountered an immovable resistance. The feeling was a curious pressure, the grip of a heavy, firm hand, and it bore his chin irresistibly to the table. '*Don't move, little men,*' whispered a voice, '*or I'll brain you both!*' He looked into the face of Cuss, close to his own, and each saw a horrified reflection of his own sickly astonishment.

'I'm sorry to handle you so roughly,' said the Voice, 'but it's unavoidable.'

'Since when did you learn to pry into an investigator's private memoranda?' said the Voice; and two chins struck the table simultaneously, and two sets of teeth rattled.

'Since when did you learn to invade the private rooms of a man in misfortune?' and the concussion was repeated.

'Where have they put my clothes?'

'Listen,' said the Voice. 'The windows are fastened and I've taken the key out of the door. I am a fairly strong man, and I have the poker handy – besides being invisible. There's not the slightest doubt that I could kill you both and get away quite easily if I wanted to – do you understand? Very well. If I let you go will you promise not to try any nonsense and do what I tell you?'

The Vicar and the Doctor looked at one another, and the Doctor pulled a face. 'Yes,' said Mr Bunting, and the Doctor repeated it. Then the pressure on the necks relaxed, and the Doctor and the Vicar sat up, both very red in the face and wriggling their heads.

'Please keep sitting where you are,' said the Invisible Man. 'Here's the poker, you see.'

'When I came into this room,' continued the Invisible Man, after presenting the poker to the tip of the nose of each of his visitors, 'I did not expect to find it occupied, and I expected to find, in addition to my books of memoranda, an outfit of clothing. Where is it? No, don't rise. I can see it's gone. Now, just at present, though the days are quite warm enough for an invisible man to run about stark, the evenings are quite chilly. I want clothing – and other accommodation; and I must also have those three books.'

CHAPTER XII

The Invisible Man Loses His Temper

It is unavoidable that at this point the narrative should break off again, for a certain very painful reason that will presently be apparent. While these things were going on in the parlour, and while Mr Huxter was watching Mr Marvel smoking his pipe against the gate, not a dozen yards away were Mr Hall and Teddy Henfrey discussing in a state of cloudy puzzlement the one Iping topic.

Suddenly there came a violent thud against the door of the parlour, a sharp cry, and then – silence.

'*Hul*-lo!' said Teddy Henfrey.

'Hul-*lo*!' from the Tap.

Mr Hall took things in slowly but surely. 'That ain't right,' he said, and came round from behind the bar towards the parlour door.

He and Teddy approached the door together, with intent faces. Their eyes considered. 'Summat wrong,' said Hall, and Henfrey nodded agreement. Whiffs of an unpleasant chemical odour met them, and there was a muffled sound of conversation, very rapid and subdued.

'You all raight thur?' asked Hall, rapping.

The muttered conversation ceased abruptly, for a moment silence, then the conversation was resumed, in hissing whispers, then a sharp cry of 'No! no, you don't!' There came a sudden motion and the oversetting of a chair, a brief struggle. Silence again.

'What the dooce?' exclaimed Henfrey, *sotto voce*.

'You – all – raight thur?' asked Mr Hall, sharply, again.

The Vicar's voice answered with a curious jerking intonation: 'Quite ri-right. Please don't – interrupt.'

'Odd!' said Mr Henfrey.

'Odd!' said Mr Hall.

'Says, "Don't interrupt,"' said Henfrey.

'I heerd'n,' said Hall.

'And a sniff,' said Henfrey.

They remained listening. The conversation was rapid and subdued. 'I *can't*,' said Mr Bunting, his voice rising; 'I tell you, sir, I *will* not.'

'What was that?' asked Henfrey.

'Says he wi' nart,' said Hall. 'Warn't speaking to us, wuz he?'

'Disgraceful!' said Mr Bunting, within.

'Disgraceful,' said Mr Henfrey. 'I heard it – *distinct*.'

'Who's that speaking now?' asked Henfrey.

'Mr Cuss, I s'pose,' said Hall. 'Can you hear – anything?'

Silence. The sounds within indistinct and perplexing.

'Sounds like throwing the table-cloth about,' said Hall.

Mrs Hall appeared behind the bar. Hall made gestures of silence and invitation. This aroused Mrs Hall's wifely opposition. 'What yer listenin' there for, Hall?' she asked. 'Ain't you nothin' better to do – busy day like this?'

Hall tried to convey everything by grimaces and dumb show, but Mrs Hall was obdurate. She raised her voice. So Hall and Henfrey, rather crest-fallen, tiptoed back to the bar, gesticulating to explain to her.

At first she refused to see anything in what they had heard at all. Then she insisted on Hall keeping silence, while Henfrey told her his story. She was inclined to think the whole business nonsense – perhaps they were just moving the furniture about. 'I heerd'n say "disgraceful"; *that* I did,' said Hall.

'I heerd that, Mis' Hall,' said Henfrey.

'Like as not—' began Mrs Hall.

'Hsh!' said Mr Teddy Henfrey. 'Didn't I hear the window?'

'What window?' asked Mrs Hall.

'Parlour window,' said Henfrey.

Everyone stood listening intently. Mrs Hall's eyes, directed straight before her, saw without seeing the brilliant oblong of the inn door, the road white and vivid, and Huxter's shop front blistering in the June sun. Abruptly Huxter's door opened and Huxter appeared, eyes staring with excitement, arms gesticulating. '*Yap!*' cried Huxter. 'Stop thief!' and he ran obliquely across the oblong towards the yard gates, and vanished.

Simultaneously came a tumult from the parlour, and a sound of windows being closed.

Hall, Henfrey, and the human contents of the Tap rushed out at once pell-mell into the street. They saw someone whisk round the corner towards the road, and Mr Huxter executing a complicated leap in the air that ended on his face and shoulder. Down the street people were standing astonished or running towards them.

Mr Huxter was stunned. Henfrey stopped to discover this, but Hall and the two labourers from the Tap rushed at once to the corner, shouting incoherent things, and saw Mr Marvel vanishing by the corner of the church wall. They appear to have jumped to the impossible conclusion that this was the Invisible Man suddenly become visible, and set off at once along the lane in pursuit. But Hall had hardly run a dozen yards before he gave a loud shout of astonishment and went flying headlong sideways, clutching one of the labourers and bringing him to the ground. He had been charged just as one charges a man at football. The second labourer came round in a circle, stared, and conceiving that Hall had tumbled over of his own accord, turned to resume the pursuit, only to be tripped by the ankle just

as Huxter had been. Then, as the first labourer struggled to his feet, he was kicked sideways by a blow that might have felled an ox.

As he went down, the rush from the direction of the village green came round the corner. The first to appear was the proprietor of the coconut shy, a burly man in a blue jersey. He was astonished to see the lane empty save for three men sprawling absurdly on the ground. And then something happened to his rear-most foot, and he went headlong and rolled sideways just in time to graze the feet of his brother and partner, following headlong. The two were then kicked, knelt on, fallen over, and cursed by quite a number of over-hasty people.

Now when Hall and Henfrey and the labourers ran out of the house, Mrs Hall, who had been disciplined by years of experience, remained in the bar next the till. And suddenly the parlour door was opened, and Mr Cuss appeared, and without glancing at her rushed at once down the steps towards the corner. 'Hold him!' he cried. 'Don't let him drop that parcel.' He knew nothing of the existence of Marvel. For the Invisible Man had handed over the books and bundle in the yard. The face of Mr Cuss was angry and resolute, but his costume was defective, a sort of limp white kilt that could only have passed muster in Greece. 'Hold him!' he bawled. 'He's got my trousers! And every stitch of the Vicar's clothes!'

'Tend to him in a minute!' he cried to Henfrey as he passed the prostrate Huxter, and, coming round the corner to join the tumult, was promptly knocked off his feet into an indecorous sprawl. Somebody in full flight trod heavily on his finger. He yelled, struggled to regain his feet, was knocked against and thrown on all fours again, and became aware that he was involved not in a capture, but a rout. Everyone was running back to the village. He rose again and was hit severely behind the ear. He staggered and set off back to the Coach and Horses forthwith, leaping over the deserted Huxter, who was now sitting up, on his way.

Behind him as he was halfway up the inn steps he heard a sudden yell of rage, rising sharply out of the confusion of cries, and a sounding smack in someone's face. He recognized the voice as that of the Invisible Man, and the note was that of a man suddenly infuriated by a painful blow.

In another moment Mr Cuss was back in the parlour. 'He's coming back, Bunting!' he said, rushing in. 'Save yourself! He's gone mad!'

Mr Bunting was standing in the window engaged in an attempt to clothe himself in the hearth-rug and a *West Surrey Gazette*. 'Who's coming?' he said, so startled that his costume narrowly escaped disintegration.

'Invisible Man,' said Cuss, and rushed on to the window. 'We'd better clear out from here! He's fighting mad! Mad!'

In another moment he was out in the yard.

'Good Heavens!' said Mr Bunting, hesitating between two horrible alternatives. He heard a frightful struggle in the passage of the inn, and his

decision was made. He clambered out of the window, adjusted his costume hastily, and fled up the village as fast as his fat little legs would carry him.

From the moment when the Invisible Man screamed with rage and Mr Bunting made his memorable flight up the village, it became impossible to give a consecutive account of affairs in Iping. Possibly the Invisible Man's original intention was simply to cover Marvel's retreat with the clothes and books. But his temper, at no time very good, seems to have gone completely at some chance blow, and forthwith he set to smiting and overthrowing, for the mere satisfaction of hurting.

You must figure the street full of running figures, of doors slamming and fights for hiding-places. You must figure the tumult suddenly striking on the unstable equilibrium of old Fletcher's planks and two chairs, with cataclysmic results. You must figure an appalled couple caught dismally in a swing. And then the whole tumultuous rush has passed and the Iping street with its gauds and flags is deserted save for the still raging Unseen, and littered with coconuts, overthrown canvas screens, and the scattered stock in trade of a sweetstuff stall. Everywhere there is a sound of closing shutters and shoving bolts, and the only visible humanity is an occasional flitting eye under a raised eyebrow in the corner of a window pane.

The Invisible Man amused himself for a little while by breaking all the windows in the Coach and Horses, and then he thrust a street lamp through the parlour window of Mrs Gribble. He it must have been who cut the telegraph wire to Adderdean just beyond Higgins' cottage on the Adderdean road. And after that, as his peculiar qualities allowed, he passed out of human perceptions altogether, and he was neither heard, seen, nor felt in Iping any more. He vanished absolutely.

But it was the best part of two hours before any human being ventured out again into the desolation of Iping street.

CHAPTER XIII

Mr Marvel Discusses His Resignation

When the dusk was gathering and Iping was just beginning to peep timorously forth again upon the shattered wreckage of its Bank Holiday, a short, thick set man in a shabby silk hat was marching painfully through the twilight behind the beechwoods on the road to Bramblehurst. He carried three books bound together by some sort of ornamental elastic ligature, and a bundle wrapped in a blue table-cloth. His rubicund face expressed consternation and fatigue; he appeared to be in a spasmodic sort of hurry. He was accompanied by a voice other than his own, and ever and again he winced under the touch of unseen hands.

'If you give me the slip again,' said the Voice, 'if you attempt to give me the slip again—'

'Lord!' said Mr Marvel. 'That shoulder's a mass of bruises as it is.'

'On my honour,' said the Voice, 'I will kill you.'

'I didn't try to give you the slip,' said Marvel, in a voice that was not far remote from tears. 'I swear I didn't. I didn't know the blessed turning, that was all! How the devil was I to know the blessed turning? As it is, I've been knocked about—'

'You'll get knocked about a great deal more if you don't mind,' said the Voice, and Mr Marvel abruptly became silent. He blew out his cheeks, and his eyes were eloquent of despair.

'It's bad enough to let these floundering yokels explode my little secret, without *your* cutting off with my books. It's lucky for some of them they cut and ran when they did! Here am I . . . No one knew I was invisible! And now what am I to do?'

'What am *I* to do?' asked Marvel, *sotto voce*.

'It's all about. It will be in the papers! Everybody will be looking for me; everyone on their guard—' The Voice broke off into vivid curses and ceased.

The despair of Mr Marvel's face deepened, and his pace slackened.

'Go on!' said the Voice.

Mr Marvel's face assumed a greyish tint between the ruddier patches.

'Don't drop those books, stupid,' said the Voice, sharply – overtaking him.

'The fact is,' said the Voice, 'I shall have to make use of you . . . You're a poor tool, but I must.'

'I'm a *miserable* tool,' said Marvel.

'You are,' said the Voice.

'I'm the worst possible tool you could have,' said Marvel.

'I'm not strong,' he said after a discouraging silence.

'I'm not over-strong,' he repeated.

'No?'

'And my heart's weak. That little business – I pulled it through, of course – but bless you! I could have dropped.'

'Well?'

'I haven't the nerve and strength for the sort of thing you want.'

'*I'll* stimulate you.'

'I wish you wouldn't. I wouldn't like to mess up your plans, you know. But I might, out of sheer funk and misery.'

'You'd better not,' said the Voice, with quiet emphasis.

'I wish I was dead,' said Marvel.

'It ain't justice,' he said; 'you must admit . . . It seems to me I've a perfect right—'

'*Get* on!' said the Voice.

Mr Marvel mended his pace, and for a time they went in silence again.

'It's devilish hard,' said Mr Marvel.

This was quite ineffectual. He tried another tack.

'What do I make by it?' he began again in a tone of unendurable wrong.

'Oh! *shut up!*' said the Voice, with sudden amazing vigour. 'I'll see to you all right. You do what you're told. You'll do it all right. You're a fool and all that, but you'll do—'

'I tell you, sir, I'm not the man for it. Respectfully – but it *is* so—'

'If you don't shut up I shall twist your wrist again,' said the Invisible Man. 'I want to think.'

Presently two oblongs of yellow light appeared through the trees, and the square tower of a church loomed through the gloaming. 'I shall keep my hand on your shoulder,' said the Voice, 'all through the village. Go straight through and try no foolery. It will be the worse for you if you do.'

'I know that,' sighed Mr Marvel, 'I know all that.'

The unhappy-looking figure in the obsolete silk hat passed up the street of the little village with his burdens, and vanished into the gathering darkness beyond the lights of the windows.

CHAPTER XIV

At Port Stowe

Ten o'clock the next morning found Mr Marvel, unshaven, dirty, and travel-stained, sitting with the books beside him and his hands deep in his pockets, looking very weary, nervous, and uncomfortable, and inflating his cheeks at infrequent intervals, on the bench outside a little inn on the outskirts of Port Stowe. Beside him were the books, but now they were tied with string. The bundle had been abandoned in the pinewoods beyond Bramblehurst, in accordance with a change in the plans of the Invisible Man. Mr Marvel sat on the bench, and although no one took the slightest notice of him, his agitation remained at fever heat. His hands would go ever and again to his various pockets with a curious nervous fumbling.

When he had been sitting for the best part of an hour, however, an elderly mariner, carrying a newspaper, came out of the inn and sat down beside him. 'Pleasant day,' said the mariner.

Mr Marvel glanced about him with something very like terror. 'Very,' he said.

'Just seasonable weather for the time of year,' said the mariner, taking no denial.

'Quite,' said Mr Marvel.

The mariner produced a toothpick, and (saving his regard) was engrossed thereby for some minutes. His eyes meanwhile were at liberty to examine Mr Marvel's dusty figure, and the books beside him. As he had approached Mr Marvel he had heard a sound like the dropping of coins into a pocket. He was struck by the contrast of Mr Marvel's appearance with this suggestion of opulence. Thence his mind wandered back again to a topic that had taken a curiously firm hold of his imagination.

'Books?' he said suddenly, noisily finishing with the toothpick.

Mr Marvel started and looked at them. 'Oh, yes,' he said. 'Yes, they're books.'

'There's some ex-traordinary things in books,' said the mariner.

'I believe you,' said Mr Marvel.

'And some extra-ordinary things out of 'em,' said the mariner.

'True likewise,' said Mr Marvel. He eyed his interlocutor, and then glanced about him.

'There's some extraordinary things in newspapers, for example,' said the mariner.

'There are.'

'In *this* newspaper,' said the mariner.

'Ah!' said Mr Marvel.

'There's a story,' said the mariner, fixing Mr Marvel with an eye that was firm and deliberate; 'there's a story about an Invisible Man, for instance.'

Mr Marvel pulled his mouth askew and scratched his cheek and felt his ears glowing. 'What will they be writing next?' he asked faintly. 'Ostria, or America?'

'Neither,' said the mariner. 'Here.'

'Lord!' said Mr Marvel, starting.

'When I say here,' said the mariner, to Mr Marvel's intense relief, 'I don't of course mean here in this place, I mean hereabouts.'

'An Invisible Man!' said Mr Marvel. 'And what's he been up to?'

'Everything,' said the mariner, controlling Marvel with his eye, and then amplifying: 'Every Blessed Thing.'

'I ain't seen a paper these four days,' said Marvel.

'Iping's the place he started at,' said the mariner.

'In-deed!' said Mr Marvel.

'He started there. And where he came from, nobody don't seem to know. Here it is: "Peculiar Story from Iping." And it says in this paper that the evidence is extraordinary strong – extra-ordinary.'

'Lord!' said Mr Marvel.

'But then, it's an extra-ordinary story. There is a clergyman and a medical gent witnesses – saw 'im all right and proper – or leastways didn't see 'im. He was staying, it says, at the Coach an' Horses, and no one don't seem to have been aware of his misfortune, it says, aware of his misfortune, until in an Altercation in the inn, it says, his bandages on his head was torn off. It was then ob-served that his head was invisible. Attempts were At Once made to secure him, but casting off his garments, it says, he succeeded in escaping, but not until after a desperate struggle, in which he had inflicted serious injuries, it says, on our worthy and able constable, Mr J. A. Jaffers. Pretty straight story, eh? Names and everything.'

'Lord!' said Mr Marvel, looking nervously about him, trying to count the money in his pockets by his unaided sense of touch, and full of a strange and novel idea. 'It sounds most astonishing.'

'Don't it? Extra-ordinary, I call it. Never heard tell of Invisible Men before, I haven't, but nowadays one hears such a lot of extra-ordinary things – that—'

'That all he did?' asked Marvel, trying to seem at his ease.

'It's enough, ain't it?' said the mariner.

'Didn't go Back by any chance?' asked Marvel. 'Just escaped and that's all, eh?'

'All!' said the mariner. 'Why! – ain't it enough?'

'Quite enough,' said Marvel.

'I should think it was enough,' said the mariner. 'I should think it was enough.'

'He didn't have any pals – it don't say he had any pals, does it?' asked Mr Marvel, anxious.

'Ain't one of a sort enough for you?' asked the mariner. 'No, thank Heaven, as one might say, he didn't.'

He nodded his head slowly. 'It makes me regular uncomfortable, the bare thought of that chap running about the country! He is at present At Large, and from certain evidence it is supposed that he has – taken – *took*, I suppose they mean – the road to Port Stowe. You see we're right *in* it! None of your American wonders, this time. And just think of the things he might do! Where'd you be, if he took a drop over and above, and had a fancy to go for you? Suppose he wants to rob – who can prevent him? He can trespass, he can burgle, he could walk through a cordon of policemen as easy as me or you could give the slip to a blind man! Easier! For these here blind chaps hear uncommon sharp, I'm told. And wherever there was liquor he fancied—'

'He's got a tremenjous advantage, certainly,' said Mr Marvel. 'And – well. . . .'

'You're right,' said the mariner. 'He *has*.'

All this time Mr Marvel had been glancing about him intently, listening for faint footfalls, trying to detect imperceptible movements. He seemed on the point of some great resolution. He coughed behind his hand.

He looked about him again, listened, bent towards the mariner, and lowered his voice: 'The fact of it is – I happen – to know just a thing or two about this Invisible Man. From private sources.'

'Oh!' said the mariner, interested. '*You?*'

'Yes,' said Mr Marvel. 'Me.'

'Indeed!' said the mariner. 'And may I ask—'

'You'll be astonished,' said Mr Marvel behind his hand. 'It's tremenjous.'

'Indeed!' said the mariner.

'The fact is,' began Mr Marvel eagerly in a confidential undertone. Suddenly his expression changed marvellously. 'Ow!' he said. He rose stiffly in his seat. His face was eloquent of physical suffering. 'Wow!' he said.

'What's up?' said the mariner, concerned.

'Toothache,' said Mr Marvel, and put his hand to his ear. He caught hold of his books. 'I must be getting on, I think,' he said. He edged in a curious way along the seat away from his interlocutor. 'But you was just agoing to tell me about this here Invisible Man!' protested the mariner. Mr Marvel seemed to consult with himself. 'Hoax,' said a Voice. 'It's a hoax,' said Mr Marvel.

'But it's in the paper,' said the mariner.

'Hoax all the same,' said Marvel. 'I know the chap that started the lie. There ain't no Invisible Man whatsoever – Blimey.'

'But how 'bout this paper? D'you mean to say—?'

'Not a word of it,' said Marvel, stoutly.

The mariner stared, paper in hand. Mr Marvel jerkily faced about. 'Wait a bit,' said the mariner, rising and speaking slowly, 'D'you mean to say—?'

'I do,' said Mr Marvel.

'Then why did you let me go on and tell you all this blarsted stuff, then? What d'yer mean by letting a man make a fool of himself like that for? Eh?'

Mr Marvel blew out his cheeks. The mariner was suddenly very red indeed; he clenched his hands. 'I been talking here this ten minutes,' he said; 'and you, you little pot-bellied, leathery-faced son of an old boot, couldn't have the elementary manners—'

'Don't you come bandying words with *me*,' said Mr Marvel.

'Bandying words! I'm a jolly good mind—'

'Come up,' said a Voice, and Mr Marvel was suddenly whirled about and started marching off in a curious spasmodic manner. 'You'd better move on,' said the mariner. '*Who's* moving on?' said Mr Marvel. He was receding obliquely with a curious hurrying gait, with occasional violent jerks forward. Some way along the road he began a muttered monologue, protests and recriminations.

'Silly devil!' said the mariner, legs wide apart, elbows akimbo, watching the receding figure. 'I'll show you, you silly ass – hoaxing *me*! It's here – on the paper!'

Mr Marvel retorted incoherently and, receding, was hidden by a bend in the road, but the mariner still stood magnificent in the midst of the way, until the approach of a butcher's cart dislodged him. Then he turned himself towards Port Stowe. 'Full of extra-ordinary asses,' he said softly to himself. 'Just to take me down a bit – that was his silly game – It's on the paper!'

And there was another extraordinary thing he was presently to hear, that had happened quite close to him. And that was a vision of a 'fist full of money' (no less) travelling without visible agency, along by the wall at the corner of St Michael's Lane. A brother mariner had seen this wonderful sight that very morning. He had snatched at the money forthwith and had been knocked headlong, and when he had got to his feet the butterfly money had vanished. Our mariner was in the mood to believe anything, he declared, but that was a bit *too* stiff. Afterwards, however, he began to think things over.

The story of the flying money was true. And all about that neighbourhood, even from the august London and Country Banking Company, from the tills of shops and inns – doors standing that sunny weather entirely open – money had been quietly and dexterously making off that day in handfuls and rouleaux, floating quietly along by walls and shady places, dodging quickly from the approaching eyes of men. And it had, though no man had traced it, invariably ended its mysterious flight in the pocket of that agitated

gentleman in the obsolete silk hat, sitting outside the little inn on the outskirts of Port Stowe.

It was ten days after – and indeed only when the Burdock story was already old – that the mariner collated these facts and began to understand how near he had been to the wonderful Invisible Man.

CHAPTER XV

The Man Who Was Running

In the early evening time Doctor Kemp was sitting in his study in the belve-
dere on the hill overlooking Burdock. It was a pleasant little room, with three
windows – north, west, and south – and bookshelves covered with books and
scientific publications, and a broad writing-table, and, under the north window,
a microscope, glass slips, minute instruments, some cultures, and scattered
bottles of reagents. Doctor Kemp's solar lamp was lit, albeit the sky was still
bright with the sunset light, and his blinds were up because there was no
offence of peering outsiders to require them pulled down. Doctor Kemp was
a tall and slender young man, with flaxen hair and a moustache almost white,
and the work he was upon would earn him, he hoped, the fellowship of the
Royal Society, so highly did he think of it.

And his eye, presently wandering from his work, caught the sunset blazing
at the back of the hill that is over against his own. For a minute perhaps
he sat, pen in mouth, admiring the rich golden colour above the crest, and
then his attention was attracted by the little figure of a man, inky black,
running over the hill-brow towards him. He was a shortish little man, and
he wore a high hat, and he was running so fast that his legs verily twinkled.

'Another of those fools,' said Doctor Kemp. 'Like that ass who ran into
me this morning round a corner, with his "'Visible Man a-coming, sir!'' I
can't imagine what possesses people. One might think we were in the thir-
teenth century.'

He got up, went to the window, and stared at the dusky hillside, and the
dark little figure tearing down it. 'He seems in a confounded hurry,' said
Doctor Kemp, 'but he doesn't seem to be getting on. If his pockets were full
of lead, he couldn't run heavier.'

'Spurted, sir,' said Doctor Kemp.

In another moment the higher of the villas that had clambered up the
hill from Burdock had occulted the running figure. He was visible again for
a moment, and again, and then again, three times between the three detached
houses that came next, and then the terrace hid him.

'Asses!' said Doctor Kemp, swinging round on his heel and walking back
to his writing-table.

But those who saw the fugitive nearer, and perceived the abject terror
on his perspiring face, being themselves in the open roadway, did not share
in the doctor's contempt. By the man pounded, and as he ran he chinked
like a well-filled purse that is tossed to and fro. He looked neither to the
right nor the left, but his dilated eyes stared straight downhill to where the

lamps were being lit, and the people were crowded in the street. And his ill-shaped mouth fell apart, and a glairy foam lay on his lips, and his breath came hoarse and noisy. All he passed stopped and began staring up the road and down, and interrogating one another with an inkling of discomfort for the reason of his haste.

And then presently, far up the hill, a dog playing in the road yelped and ran under a gate, and as they still wondered something – a wind – a pad, pad, pad, – a sound like a panting breathing, rushed by.

People screamed. People sprang off the pavement: It passed in shouts, it passed by instinct down the hill. They were shouting in the street before Marvel was halfway there. They were bolting into houses and slamming the doors behind them, with the news. He heard it and made one last desperate spurt. Fear came striding by, rushed ahead of him, and in a moment had seized the town.

'The Invisible Man is coming! *The Invisible Man!*'

CHAPTER XVI

In the Jolly Cricketers

The Jolly Cricketers is just at the bottom of the hill, where the tram-lines begin. The barman leant his fat red arms on the counter and talked of horses with an anaemic cabman, while a black-bearded man in grey snapped up biscuit and cheese, drank Burton, and conversed in American with a policeman off duty.

'What's the shouting about!' said the anaemic cabman, going off at a tangent, trying to see up the hill over the dirty yellow blind in the low window of the inn. Somebody ran by outside. 'Fire, perhaps,' said the barman.

Footsteps approached, running heavily, the door was pushed open violently, and Marvel, weeping and dishevelled, his hat gone, the neck of his coat torn open, rushed in, made a convulsive turn, and attempted to shut the door. It was held half open by a strap.

'Coming!' he bawled, his voice shrieking with terror. 'He's coming. The 'Visible Man! After me! For Gawd's sake! 'Elp! 'Elp! 'Elp!'

'Shut the doors,' said the policeman. 'Who's coming? What's the row?' He went to the door, released the strap, and it slammed. The American closed the other door.

'Lemme go inside,' said Marvel, staggering and weeping, but still clutching the books. 'Lemme go inside. Lock me in – somewhere. I tell you he's after me. I give him the slip. He said he'd kill me and he will.'

'You're safe,' said the man with the black beard. 'The door's shut. What's it all about?'

'Lemme go inside,' said Marvel, and shrieked aloud as a blow suddenly made the fastened door shiver and was followed by a hurried rapping and a shouting outside. 'Hullo,' cried the policeman, 'who's there?' Mr Marvel began to make frantic dives at panels that looked like doors. 'He'll kill me – he's got a knife or something. For Gawd's sake—!'

'Here you are,' said the barman. 'Come in here.' And he held up the flap of the bar.

Mr Marvel rushed behind the bar as the summons outside was repeated. 'Don't open the door,' he screamed. '*Please* don't open the door. *Where* shall I hide?'

'This, this Invisible Man, then?' asked the man with the black beard, with one hand behind him. 'I guess it's about time we saw him.'

The window of the inn was suddenly smashed in, and there was a screaming and running to and fro in the street. The policeman had been standing on the settee staring out, craning to see who was at the door. He got down

with raised eyebrows. 'It's that,' he said. The barman stood in front of the bar-parlour door which was now locked on Mr Marvel, stared at the smashed window, and came round to the two other men.

Everything was suddenly quiet. 'I wish I had my truncheon,' said the policeman, going irresolutely to the door. 'Once we open, in he comes. There's no stopping him.'

'Don't you be in too much hurry about that door,' said the anaemic cabman, anxiously.

'Draw the bolts,' said the man with the black beard, 'and if he comes—' He showed a revolver in his hand.

'That won't do,' said the policeman; 'that's murder.'

'I know what country I'm in,' said the man with the beard. 'I'm going to let off at his legs. Draw the bolts.'

'Not with that blinking thing going off behind me,' said the barman, craning over the blind.

'Very well,' said the man with the black beard, and stooping down, revolver ready, drew them himself. Barman, cabman, and policeman faced about.

'Come in,' said the bearded man in an undertone, standing back and facing the unbolted doors with his pistol behind him. No one came in, the door remained closed. Five minutes afterwards when a second cabman pushed his head in cautiously, they were still waiting, and an anxious face peered out of the bar-parlour and supplied information. 'Are all the doors of the house shut?' asked Marvel. 'He's going round – prowling round. He's as artful as the devil.'

'Good Lord!' said the burly barman. 'There's the back! Just watch them doors! I say—!' He looked about him helplessly. The bar-parlour door slammed and they heard the key turn. 'There's the yard door and the private door. The yard door—'

He rushed out of the bar.

In a minute he reappeared with a carving-knife in his hand. 'The yard door was open!' he said, and his fat underlip dropped. 'He may be in the house now!' said the first cabman.

'He's not in the kitchen,' said the barman. 'There's two women there, and I've stabbed every inch of it with this little beef slicer. And they don't think he's come in. They haven't noticed—'

'Have you fastened it?' asked the first cabman.

'I'm out of frocks,' said the barman.

The man with the beard replaced his revolver. And even as he did so the flap of the bar was shut down and the bolt clicked, and then with a tremendous thud the catch of the door snapped and the bar-parlour door burst open. They heard Marvel squeal like a caught leveret, and forthwith they were clambering over the bar to his rescue. The bearded man's revolver cracked and the looking-glass at the back of the parlour started and came smashing and tinkling down.

As the barman entered the room he saw Marvel, curiously crumpled up and struggling against the door that led to the yard and kitchen. The door flew open while the barman hesitated, and Marvel was dragged into the kitchen. There was a scream and a clatter of pans. Marvel, head down, and lugging back obstinately, was forced to the kitchen door, and the bolts were drawn.

Then the policeman, who had been trying to pass the barman, rushed in, followed by one of the cabmen, gripped the wrist of the invisible hand that collared Marvel, was hit in the face and went reeling back. The door opened, and Marvel made a frantic effort to obtain a lodgment behind it. Then the cabman collared something. 'I got him,' said the cabman. The barman's red hands came clawing at the unseen. 'Here he is!' said the barman.

Mr Marvel, released, suddenly dropped to the ground and made an attempt to crawl behind the legs of the fighting men. The struggle blundered round the edge of the door. The voice of the Invisible Man was heard for the first time, yelling out sharply, as the policeman trod on his foot. Then he cried out passionately and his fists flew round like flails. The cabman suddenly whooped and doubled up, kicked under the diaphragm. The door into the bar-parlour from the kitchen slammed and covered Mr Marvel's retreat. The men in the kitchen found themselves clutching at and struggling with empty air.

'Where's he gone?' cried the man with the beard. 'Out?'

'This way,' said the policeman, stepping into the yard and stopping.

A piece of tile whizzed by his head and smashed among the crockery on the kitchen table.

'I'll show him,' shouted the man with the black beard, and suddenly a steel barrel shone over the policeman's shoulder, and five bullets had followed one another into the twilight whence the missile had come. As he fired, the man with the beard moved his hand in a horizontal curve, so that his shots radiated out into the narrow yard like spokes from a wheel.

A silence followed. 'Five cartridges,' said the man with the black beard. 'That's the best of all. Four aces and a joker. Get a lantern, someone, and come and feel about for his body.'

CHAPTER XVII

Doctor Kemp's Visitor

Doctor Kemp had continued writing in his study until the shots aroused him. Crack, crack, crack, they came one after the other.

'Hullo!' said Doctor Kemp, putting his pen into his mouth again and listening. 'Who's letting off revolvers in Burdock? What are the asses at now?'

He went to the south window, threw it up, and leaning out stared down on the network of windows, beaded gas-lamps and shops, with its black interstices of roofs that made up the town at night. 'Looks like a crowd down the hill,' he said, 'by The Cricketers,' and remained watching. Thence his eyes wandered over the town to far away where the ships' lights shone, and the pier glowed, a little illuminated, facetted pavilion like a gem of yellow light. The moon in its first quarter hung over the westward hill, and the stars were clear and almost tropically bright.

After five minutes, during which his mind had travelled into a remote speculation of social conditions of the future, and lost itself at last over the time dimension, Doctor Kemp roused himself with a sigh, pulled down the window again, and returned to his writing desk.

It must have been about an hour after this that the front door bell rang. He had been writing slackly, and with intervals of abstraction, since the shots. He sat listening. He heard the servant answer the door, and waited for her feet on the staircase, but she did not come. 'Wonder what that was,' said Doctor Kemp.

He tried to resume his work, failed, got up, went downstairs from his study to the landing, rang, and called over the balustrade to the housemaid as she appeared in the hall below. 'Was that a letter?' he asked.

'Only a runaway ring, sir,' she answered.

'I'm restless tonight,' he said to himself. He went back to his study, and this time attacked his work resolutely. In a little while he was hard at work again, and the only sounds in the room were the ticking of the clock and the subdued shrillness of his quill, hurrying in the very centre of the circle of light his lampshade threw on his table.

It was two o'clock before Doctor Kemp had finished his work for the night. He rose, yawned, and went downstairs to bed. He had already removed his coat and vest, when he noticed that he was thirsty. He took a candle and went down to the dining-room in search of a syphon and whisky.

Doctor Kemp's scientific pursuits had made him a very observant man, and as he recrossed the hall, he noticed a dark spot on the linoleum near the mat at the foot of the stairs. He went on upstairs, and then it suddenly

occurred to him to ask himself what the spot on the linoleum might be. Apparently some subconscious element was at work. At any rate, he turned with his burden, went back to the hall, put down the syphon and whisky, and bending down, touched the spot. Without any great surprise he found it had the stickiness and colour of drying blood.

He took up his burden again, and returned upstairs, looking about him and trying to account for the blood-spot. On the landing he saw something and stopped astonished. The door-handle of his own room was blood-stained.

He looked at his own hand. It was quite clean, and then he remembered that the door of his room had been open when he came down from his study, and that consequently he had not touched the handle at all. He went straight into his room, his face quite calm – perhaps a trifle more resolute than usual. His glance, wandering inquisitively, fell on the bed. On the counterpane was a mess of blood, and the sheet had been torn. He had not noticed this before because he had walked straight to the dressing-table. On the further side the bedclothes were depressed as if someone had been recently sitting there.

Then he had an odd impression that he had heard a low voice say, 'Good Heavens! *Kemp!*' But Doctor Kemp was no believer in voices.

He stood staring at the tumbled sheets. Was that really a voice? He looked about again, but noticed nothing further than the disordered and blood-stained bed. Then he distinctly heard a movement across the room, near the wash-hand stand. All men, however highly educated, retain some superstitious inklings. The feeling that is called 'eerie' came upon him. He closed the door of the room, came forward to the dressing-table, and put down his burdens. Suddenly, with a start, he perceived a coiled and blood-stained bandage of linen rag hanging in mid-air, between him and the wash-hand stand.

He stared at this in amazement. It was an empty bandage, a bandage properly tied but quite empty. He would have advanced to grasp it, but a touch arrested him, and a voice speaking quite close to him.

'Kemp!' said the Voice.

'Eh?' said Kemp, with his mouth open.

'Keep your nerve,' said the Voice. 'I'm an Invisible Man.'

Kemp made no answer for a space, simply stared at the bandage. 'Invisible Man,' he said.

'I am an Invisible Man,' repeated the Voice.

The story he had been active to ridicule only that morning rushed through Kemp's brain. He does not appear to have been either very much frightened or very greatly surprised at the moment. Realization came later.

'I thought it was all a lie,' he said. The thought uppermost in his mind was the reiterated arguments of the morning. 'Have you a bandage on?' he asked.

'Yes,' said the Invisible Man.

'Oh!' said Kemp, and then roused himself. 'I say!' he said. 'But this is nonsense. It's some trick.' He stepped forward suddenly, and his hand, extended towards the bandage, met invisible fingers.

He recoiled at the touch and his colour changed.

'Keep steady, Kemp, for God's sake! I want help badly. Stop!'

The hand gripped his arm. He struck at it.

'Kemp!' cried the Voice. 'Kemp! Keep steady!' and the grip tightened.

A frantic desire to free himself took possession of Kemp. The hand of the bandaged arm gripped his shoulder, and he was suddenly tripped and flung backwards upon the bed. He opened his mouth to shout, and the corner of the sheet was thrust between his teeth. The Invisible Man had him down grimly, but his arms were free and he struck and tried to kick savagely.

'Listen to reason, will you?' said the Invisible Man, sticking to him in spite of a pounding in the ribs. 'By Heaven! you'll madden me in a minute!'

'Lie still, you fool!' bawled the Invisible Man in Kemp's ear.

Kemp struggled for another moment and then lay still.

'If you shout, I'll smash your face,' said the Invisible Man, relieving his mouth.

'I'm an Invisible Man. It's no foolishness, and no magic. I really am an Invisible Man. And I want your help. I don't want to hurt you, but if you behave like a frantic rustic, I must. Don't you remember me, Kemp? Griffin, of University College?'

'Let me get up,' said Kemp. 'I'll stop where I am. And let me sit quiet for a minute.'

He sat up and felt his neck.

'I am Griffin, of University College, and I have made myself invisible. I am just an ordinary man – a man you have known – made invisible.'

'Griffin?' said Kemp.

'Griffin,' answered the Voice. A younger student than you were, almost an albino, six feet high, and broad, with a pink and white face and red eyes, who won the medal for chemistry.'

'I am confused,' said Kemp. 'My brain is rioting. What has this to do with Griffin?'

'I *am* Griffin.'

Kemp thought. 'It's horrible,' he said. 'But what devilry must happen to make a man invisible?'

'It's no devilry. It's a process, sane and intelligible enough—'

'It's horrible!' said Kemp. 'How on earth—?'

'It's horrible enough. But I'm wounded and in pain, and tired . . . Great God! Kemp, you are a man. Take it steady. Give me some food and drink, and let me sit down here.'

Kemp stared at the bandage as it moved across the room, then saw a basket chair dragged across the floor and come to rest near the bed. It creaked, and the seat was depressed the quarter of an inch or so. He rubbed his eyes and felt his neck again. 'This beats ghosts,' he said, and laughed stupidly.

'That's better. Thank Heaven, you're getting sensible!'

'Or silly,' said Kemp, and knuckled his eyes.

'Give me some whisky. I'm near dead.'

'It didn't feel so. Where are you? If I get up shall I run into you? *There!* all right. Whisky? Here. Where shall I give it to you?'

The chair creaked and Kemp felt the glass drawn away from him. He let go by an effort; his instinct was all against it. It came to rest poised twenty inches above the front edge of the seat of the chair. He stared at it in infinite perplexity. 'This is – this must be – hypnotism. You have suggested you are invisible.'

'Nonsense,' said the Voice.

'It's frantic.'

'Listen to me.'

'I demonstrated conclusively this morning,' began Kemp, 'that invisibility—'

'Never mind what you've demonstrated! I'm starving,' said the Voice, 'and the night is chilly – to a man without clothes.'

'Food?' said Kemp.

The tumbler of whisky tilted itself. 'Yes,' said the Invisible Man rapping it down. 'Have you got a dressing-gown?'

Kemp made some exclamation in an undertone. He walked to a wardrobe and produced a robe of dingy scarlet. 'This do?' he asked. It was taken from him. It hung limp for a moment in mid-air, fluttered weirdly, stood full and decorous buttoning itself, and sat down in his chair. 'Drawers, socks, slippers would be a comfort,' said the Unseen, curtly. 'And food.'

'Anything. But this is the insanest thing I ever was in, in my life!'

He turned out his drawers for the articles, and then went downstairs to ransack his larder. He came back with some cold cutlets and bread, pulled up a light table, and placed them before his guest. 'Never mind knives,' said his visitor, and a cutlet hung in mid-air, with a sound of gnawing.

'Invisible!' said Kemp, and sat down on a bedroom chair.

'I always like to get something about me before I eat,' said the Invisible Man, with a full mouth, eating greedily. 'Queer fancy!'

'I suppose that wrist is all right,' said Kemp.

'Trust me,' said the Invisible Man.

'Of all the strange and wonderful—'

'Exactly. But it's odd I should blunder into *your* house to get my bandaging. My first stroke of luck! Anyhow I meant to sleep in this house tonight. You

must stand that! It's a filthy nuisance, my blood showing, isn't it? Quite a
clot over there. Gets visible as it coagulates, I see. It's only the living tissue
I've changed, and only for as long as I'm alive . . . I've been in the house
three hours.'

'But how's it done?' began Kemp, in a tone of exasperation. 'Confound
it! The whole business – it's unreasonable from beginning to end.'

'Quite reasonable,' said the Invisible Man. 'Perfectly reasonable.'

He reached over and secured the whisky bottle. Kemp stared at the
devouring dressing-gown. A ray of candlelight penetrating a torn patch in
the right shoulder, made a triangle of light under the left ribs. 'What were
the shots?' he asked. 'How did the shooting begin?'

'There was a real fool of a man – a sort of confederate of mine – curse
him! who tried to steal my money. *Has* done so.'

'Is *he* invisible too?'

'No.'

'Well?'

'Can't I have some more to eat before I tell you all that? I'm hungry – in
pain. And you want me to tell stories!'

Kemp got up. '*You* didn't do any shooting?' he asked.

'Not me,' said his visitor. 'Some fool I'd never seen fired at random. A
lot of them got scared. They all got scared at me. Curse them! – I say – I
want more to eat than this, Kemp.'

'I'll see what there is to eat downstairs,' said Kemp. 'Not much, I'm afraid.'

After he had done eating, and he made a heavy meal, the Invisible Man
demanded a cigar. He bit the end savagely before Kemp could find a knife,
and cursed when the outer leaf loosened. It was strange to see him smoking;
his mouth, and throat, pharynx and nares, became visible as a sort of whirling
smoke cast.

'This blessed gift of smoking!' he said, and puffed vigorously. 'I'm lucky
to have fallen upon you, Kemp. You must help me. Fancy tumbling on you
just now! I'm in a devilish scrape. I've been mad, I think. The things I have
been through! But we will do things yet. Let me tell you—'

He helped himself to more whisky and soda. Kemp got up, looked about
him, and fetched a glass from his spare room. 'It's wild – but I suppose I
may drink.'

'You haven't changed much, Kemp, these dozen years. You fair men don't.
Cool and methodical – after the first collapse. I must tell you. We will work
together!'

'But how was it all done?' said Kemp, 'and how did you get like this?'

'For God's sake, let me smoke in peace for a little while! And then I will
begin to tell you.'

But the story was not told that night. The Invisible Man's wrist was
growing painful; he was feverish, exhausted, and his mind came round to

brood upon his chase down the hill and the struggle about the inn. He spoke in fragments of Marvel, he smoked faster, his voice grew angry. Kemp tried to gather what he could.

'He was afraid of me, I could see that he was afraid of me,' said the Invisible Man many times over. 'He meant to give me the slip – he was always casting about! What a fool I was!'

'The cur!'

'I should have killed him!'

'Where did you get the money?' asked Kemp, abruptly.

The Invisible Man was silent for a space. 'I can't tell you tonight,' he said.

He groaned suddenly and leant forward, supporting his invisible head on invisible hands. 'Kemp,' he said, 'I've had no sleep for near three days, except a couple of dozes of an hour or so. I must sleep soon.'

'Well, have my room – have this room.'

'But how can I sleep? If I sleep – he will get away. Ugh! What does it matter?'

'What's the shot wound?' asked Kemp, abruptly.

'Nothing – scratch and blood. Oh, God! How I want sleep!'

'Why not?'

The Invisible Man appeared to be regarding Kemp. 'Because I've a particular objection to being caught by my fellow men,' he said slowly.

Kemp started.

'Fool that I am!' said the Invisible Man, striking the table smartly. 'I've put the idea into your head.'

CHAPTER XVIII

The Invisible Man Sleeps

Exhausted and wounded as the Invisible Man was, he refused to accept Kemp's word that his freedom should be respected. He examined the two windows of the bedroom, drew up the blinds and opened the sashes, to confirm Kemp's statement that a retreat by them would be possible. Outside the night was very quiet and still, and the new moon was setting over the down. Then he examined the keys of the bedroom and the two dressing-room doors, to satisfy himself that these also could be made an assurance of freedom. Finally he expressed himself satisfied. He stood on the hearth rug and Kemp heard the sound of a yawn.

'I'm sorry,' said the Invisible Man, 'if I cannot tell you all that I have done tonight. But I am worn out. It's grotesque, no doubt. It's horrible! But believe me, Kemp, in spite of your arguments of this morning, it is quite a possible thing. I have made a discovery. I meant to keep it to myself. I can't. I must have a partner. And you— We can do such things— But tomorrow. Now, Kemp, I feel as though I must sleep or perish.'

Kemp stood in the middle of the room staring at the headless garment. 'I suppose I must leave you,' he said. 'It's – incredible. Three things happening like this, overturning all my preconceptions, would make me insane. But it's real! Is there anything more that I can get you?'

'Only bid me goodnight,' said Griffin.

'Good-night,' said Kemp, and shook an invisible hand. He walked sideways to the door. Suddenly the dressing-gown walked quickly towards him. 'Understand me!' said the dressing-gown. 'No attempts to hamper me, or capture me! Or—'

Kemp's face changed a little. 'I thought I gave you my word,' he said.

Kemp closed the door softly behind him, and the key was turned upon him forthwith. Then, as he stood with an expression of passive amazement on his face, the rapid feet came to the door of the dressing-room and that too was locked. Kemp slapped his brow with his hand. 'Am I dreaming? Has the world gone mad – or have I?'

He laughed, and put his hand to the locked door. 'Barred out of my own bedroom, by a flagrant absurdity!' he said.

He walked to the head of the staircase, turned, and stared at the locked doors. 'It's fact,' he said. He put his fingers to his slightly bruised neck. 'Undeniable fact!

'But—'

He shook his head hopelessly, turned, and went downstairs.

He lit the dining-room lamp, got out a cigar, and began pacing the room, ejaculating. Now and then he would argue with himself.

'Invisible!' he said.

'Is there such a thing as an invisible animal? . . . In the sea, yes. Thousands! Millions! All the larvae, all the little nauplii and tornarias, all the microscopic things, the jelly-fish. In the sea there are more things invisible than visible! I never thought of that before. And in the ponds too! All those little pond-life things, specks of colourless translucent jelly! But in air? No!

'It can't be.

'But after all – why not?

'If a man was made of glass he would still be visible.'

His meditation became profound. The bulk of three cigars had passed into the invisible or diffused as a white ash over the carpet before he spoke again. Then it was merely an exclamation. He turned aside, walked out of the room, and went into his little consulting-room and lit the gas there. It was a little room, because Doctor Kemp did not live by practice, and in it were the day's newspapers. The morning's paper lay carelessly opened and thrown aside. He caught it up, turned it over, and read the account of a 'Strange Story from Iping' that the mariner at Port Stowe had spelt over so painfully to Mr Marvel. Kemp read it swiftly.

'Wrapped up!' said Kemp. 'Disguised! Hiding it! "No one seems to have been aware of his misfortune." What the devil *is* his game?'

He dropped the paper, and his eye went seeking. 'Ah!' he said, and caught up the St James' Gazette, lying folded up as it arrived. 'Now we shall get at the truth,' said Doctor Kemp. He rent the paper open; a couple of columns confronted him. 'An Entire Village in Sussex goes Mad' was the heading.

'Good Heavens!' said Kemp, reading eagerly an incredulous account of the events in Iping, of the previous afternoon, that have already been described. Over the leaf the report in the morning paper had been reprinted.

He re-read it. 'Ran through the streets striking right and left. Jaffers insensible. Mr Huxter in great pain – still unable to describe what he saw. Painful humiliation – vicar. Woman ill with terror! Windows smashed. This extraordinary story probably a fabrication. Too good not to print – *cum grano!*'

He dropped the paper and stared blankly in front of him. 'Probably a fabrication!'

He caught up the paper again, and re-read the whole business. 'But when does the Tramp come in? Why the deuce was he chasing a tramp?'

He sat down abruptly on the surgical bench. 'He's not only invisible,' he said, 'but he's mad! Homicidal!'

When dawn came to mingle its pallor with the lamp-light and cigar smoke of the dining-room, Kemp was still pacing up and down, trying to grasp the incredible.

He was altogether too excited to sleep. His servants, descending sleepily, discovered him, and were inclined to think that over-study had worked this ill on him. He gave them extraordinary but quite explicit instructions to lay breakfast for two in the belvedere study – and then to confine themselves to the basement and ground-floor. Then he continued to pace the dining-room until the morning's paper came. That had much to say and little to tell, beyond the confirmation of the evening before, and a very badly written account of another remarkable tale from Port Burdock. This gave Kemp the essence of the happenings at the Jolly Cricketers, and the name of Marvel. 'He has made me keep with him twenty-four hours,' Marvel testified. Certain minor facts were added to the Iping story, notably the cutting of the village telegraph wire. But there was nothing to throw light on the connection between the Invisible Man and the Tramp; for Mr Marvel had supplied no information about the three books, or the money with which he was lined. The incredulous tone had vanished and a shoal of reporters and enquirers were already at work elaborating the matter.

Kemp read every scrap of the report and sent his housemaid out to get every one of the morning papers she could. These also he devoured.

'He is invisible!' he said. 'And it reads like rage growing to mania! The things he may do! The things he may do! And he's upstairs free as the air. What on earth ought I to do?'

'For instance, would it be a breach of faith if—? No.'

He went to a little untidy desk in the corner, and began a note. He tore this up half written, and wrote another. He read it over and considered it. Then he took an envelope and addressed it to 'Colonel Adye, Port Burdock'.

The Invisible Man awoke even as Kemp was doing this. He awoke in an evil temper, and Kemp, alert for every sound, heard his pattering feet rush suddenly across the bedroom overhead. Then a chair was flung over and the wash-hand stand tumbler smashed. Kemp hurried upstairs and rapped eagerly.

CHAPTER XIX

Certain First Principles

'What's the matter?' asked Kemp, when the Invisible Man admitted him.

'Nothing,' was the answer.

'But, confound it! The smash?'

'Fit of temper,' said the Invisible Man. 'Forgot this arm; and it's sore.'

'You're rather liable to that sort of thing.'

'I am.'

Kemp walked across the room and picked up the fragments of broken glass. 'All the facts are out about you,' said Kemp, standing up with the glass in his hand; 'all that happened in Iping, and down the hill. The world has become aware of its invisible citizen. But no one knows you are here.'

The Invisible Man swore.

'The secret's out. I gather it was a secret. I don't know what your plans are, but of course I'm anxious to help you.'

The Invisible Man sat down on the bed.

'There's breakfast upstairs,' said Kemp, speaking as easily as possible, and he was delighted to find his strange guest rose willingly. Kemp led the way up the narrow staircase to the belvedere.

'Before we can do anything else,' said Kemp, 'I must understand a little more about this invisibility of yours.' He had sat down, after one nervous glance out of the window, with the air of a man who has talking to do. His doubts of the sanity of the entire business flashed and vanished again as he looked across to where Griffin sat at the breakfast-table – a headless, handless dressing-gown, wiping unseen lips on a miraculously held serviette.

'It's simple enough – and credible enough,' said Griffin, putting the serviette aside and leaning the invisible head on an invisible hand.

'No doubt, to you, but—' Kemp laughed.

'Well, yes; to me it seemed wonderful at first, no doubt. But now, great God! But we will do great things yet! I came on the stuff first at Chesilstowe.'

'Chesilstowe?'

'I went there after I left London. You know I dropped medicine and took up physics? *No*; well, I did. *Light* fascinated me.'

'Ah!'

'Optical density! The whole subject is a network of riddles – a network with solutions glimmering elusively through. And being but two-and-twenty and full of enthusiasm, I said, "I will devote my life to this. This is worth while." You know what fools we are at two-and-twenty?'

'Fools then or fools now,' said Kemp.

'As though knowing could be any satisfaction to a man!

'But I went to work – like a slave. And I had hardly worked and thought about the matter six months before light came through one of the meshes suddenly – blindingly! I found a general principle of pigments and refraction – a formula, a geometrical expression involving four dimensions. Fools, common men, even common mathematicians, do not know anything of what some general expression may mean to the student of molecular physics. In the books – the books that Tramp has hidden – there are marvels, miracles! But this was not a method, it was an idea, that might lead to a method by which it would be possible, without changing any other property of matter – except, in some instances colours – to lower the refractive index of a substance, solid or liquid, to that of air – so far as all practical purposes are concerned.'

'Phew!' said Kemp. 'That's odd! But still I don't see quite – I can understand that thereby you could spoil a valuable stone, but personal invisibility is a far cry.'

'Precisely,' said Griffin. 'But consider: Visibility depends on the action of the visible bodies on light. Either a body absorbs light, or it reflects or refracts it, or does all these things. If it neither reflects nor refracts nor absorbs light, it cannot of itself be visible. You see an opaque red box, for instance, because the colour absorbs some of the light and reflects the rest, all the red part of the light, to you. If it did not absorb any particular part of the light, but reflected it all, then it would be a shining white box. Silver! A diamond box would neither absorb much of the light nor reflect much from the general surface, but just here and there where the surfaces were favourable the light would be reflected and refracted, so that you would get a brilliant appearance of flashing reflections and translucencies – a sort of skeleton of light. A glass box would not be so brilliant, nor so clearly visible, as a diamond box, because there would be less refraction and reflection. See that? From certain points of view you would see quite clearly through it. Some kinds of glass would be more visible than others, a box of flint glass would be brighter than a box of ordinary window glass. A box of very thin common glass would be hard to see in a bad light, because it would absorb hardly any light and refract and reflect very little. And if you put a sheet of common white glass in water, still more if you put it in some denser liquid than water, it would vanish almost altogether, because light passing from water to glass is only slightly refracted or reflected or indeed affected in any way. It is almost as invisible as a jet of coal gas or hydrogen is in air. And for precisely the same reason!'

'Yes,' said Kemp, 'that is pretty plain sailing.'

'And here is another fact you will know to be true. If a sheet of glass is smashed, Kemp, and beaten into a powder, it becomes much more visible while it is in the air; it becomes at last an opaque white powder. This is because the powdering multiplies the surfaces of the glass at which refraction

and reflection occur. In the sheet of glass there are only two surfaces; in the powder the light is reflected or refracted by each grain it passes through, and very little gets right through the powder. But if the white powdered glass is put into water, it forthwith vanishes. The powdered glass and water have much the same refractive index; that is, the light undergoes very little refraction or reflection in passing from one to the other.

'You make the glass invisible by putting it into a liquid of nearly the same refractive index; a transparent thing becomes invisible if it is put in any medium of almost the same refractive index. And if you will consider only a second, you will see also that the powder of glass might be made to vanish in air, if its refractive index could be made the same as that of air; for then there would be no refraction or reflection as the light passed from glass to air.'

'Yes, yes,' said Kemp. 'But a man's not powdered glass!'

'No,' said Griffin. '*He's more transparent!*'

'Nonsense!'

'That from a doctor! How one forgets! Have you already forgotten your physics, in ten years? Just think of all the things that are transparent and seem not to be so. Paper, for instance, is made up of transparent fibres, and it is white and opaque only for the same reason that a powder of glass is white and opaque. Oil white paper, fill up the interstices between the particles with oil so that there is no longer refraction or reflection except at the surfaces, and it becomes as transparent as glass. And not only paper, but cotton fibre, linen fibre, wool fibre, woody fibre, and *bone*, Kemp, *flesh*, Kemp, *hair*, Kemp, *nails* and *nerves*, Kemp, in fact the whole fabric of a man except the red of his blood and the black pigment of hair, are all made up of transparent, colourless tissue. So little suffices to make us visible one to the other. For the most part the fibres of a living creature are no more opaque than water.'

'Great Heavens!' cried Kemp. 'Of course, of course! I was thinking only last night of the sea larvae and all jelly-fish!'

'*Now* you have me! And all that I knew and had in mind a year after I left London – six years ago. But I kept it to myself. I had to do my work under frightful disadvantages. Oliver, my professor, was a scientific bounder, a journalist by instinct, a thief of ideas – he was always prying! And you know the knavish system of the scientific world. I simply would not publish, and let him share my credit. I went on working; I got nearer and nearer making my formula into an experiment, a reality. I told no living soul, because I meant to flash my work upon the world with crushing effect – and to become famous at a blow. I took up the question of pigments to fill up certain gaps. And suddenly, not by design but by accident, I made a discovery in physiology.'

'Yes?'

'You know the red colouring matter of blood; it can be made white – colourless – and remain with all the functions it has now!'

Kemp gave a cry of incredulous amazement.

The Invisible Man rose and began pacing the little study. 'You may well exclaim. I remember that night. It was late at night – in the daytime one was bothered with the gaping, silly students – and I worked then sometimes till dawn. It came suddenly, splendid and complete in my mind. I was alone; the laboratory was still, with the tall lights burning brightly and silently. In all my great moments I have been alone. "One could make an animal – a tissue – transparent! One could make it invisible! All except the pigments – I could be invisible!" I said, suddenly realizing what it meant to be an albino with such knowledge. It was overwhelming. I left the filtering I was doing, and went and stared out of the great window at the stars. "I could be invisible!" I repeated.

'To do such a thing would be to transcend magic. And I beheld, unclouded by doubt, a magnificent vision of all that invisibility might mean to a man – the mystery, the power, the freedom. Drawbacks I saw none. You have only to think! And I, a shabby, poverty-struck, hemmed-in demonstrator, teaching fools in a provincial college, might suddenly become – this. I ask you, Kemp if *you*— Anyone, I tell you, would have flung himself upon that research. And I worked three years, and every mountain of difficulty I toiled over showed another from its summit. The infinite details! And the exasperation! A professor, a provincial professor, always prying. "When are you going to publish this work of yours?" was his everlasting question. And the students, the cramped means! Three years I had of it –

'And after three years of secrecy and exasperation, I found that to complete it was impossible – impossible.'

'How?' asked Kemp.

'Money,' said the Invisible Man, and went again to stare out of the window. He turned around abruptly. 'I robbed the old man – robbed my father.

'The money was not his, and he shot himself.'

CHAPTER XX

At the House in Great Portland Street

For a moment Kemp sat in silence, staring at the back of the headless figure at the window. Then he started, struck by a thought, rose, took the Invisible Man's arm, and turned him away from the outlook.

'You are tired,' he said, 'and while I sit, you walk about. Have my chair.'

He placed himself between Griffin and the nearest window.

For a space Griffin sat silent, and then he resumed abruptly:

'I had left the Chesilstowe cottage already,' he said, 'when that happened. It was last December. I had taken a room in London, a large unfurnished room in a big ill-managed lodging-house in a slum near Great Portland Street. The room was soon full of the appliances I had bought with his money; the work was going on steadily, successfully, drawing near an end. I was like a man emerging from a thicket, and suddenly coming on some unmeaning tragedy. I went to bury him. My mind was still on this research, and I did not lift a finger to save his character. I remember the funeral, the cheap hearse, the scant ceremony, the windy frost-bitten hillside, and the old college friend of his who read the service over him – a shabby, black, bent old man with a snivelling cold.

'I remember walking back to the empty house, through the place that had once been a village and was now patched and tinkered by the jerry builders into the ugly likeness of a town. Every way the roads ran out at last into the desecrated fields and ended in rubble heaps and rank wet weeds. I remember myself as a gaunt black figure, going along the slippery, shiny pavement, and the strange sense of detachment I felt from the squalid respectability, the sordid commercialism of the place.

'I did not feel a bit sorry for my father. He seemed to me to be the victim of his own foolish sentimentality. The current cant required my attendance at his funeral, but it was really not my affair.

'But going along the High Street, my old life came back to me for a space, for I met the girl I had known ten years since. Our eyes met.

'Something moved me to turn back and talk to her. She was a very ordinary person.

'It was all like a dream, that visit to the old places. I did not feel then that I was lonely, that I had come out from the world into a desolate place. I appreciated my loss of sympathy, but I put it down to the general inanity of things. Re-entering my room seemed like the recovery of reality. There were the things I knew and loved. There stood the apparatus, the experiments

arranged and waiting. And now there was scarcely a difficulty left, beyond the planning of details.

'I will tell you, Kemp, sooner or later, all the complicated processes. We need not go into that now. For the most part, saving certain gaps I chose to remember, they are written in cypher in those books that tramp has hidden. We must hunt him down. We must get those books again. But the essential phase was to place the transparent object whose refractive index was to be lowered between two radiating centres of a sort of ethereal vibration, of which I will tell you more fully later. No, not those Röntgen vibrations – I don't know that these others of mine have been described. Yet they are obvious enough. I needed two little dynamos, and these I worked with a cheap gas engine. My first experiment was with a bit of white wool fabric. It was the strangest thing in the world to see it in the flicker of the flashes soft and white, and then to watch it fade like a wreath of smoke and vanish.

'I could scarcely believe I had done it. I put my hand into the emptiness, and there was the thing as solid as ever. I felt it awkwardly, and threw it on the floor. I had a little trouble finding it again.

'And then came a curious experience. I heard a miaow behind me, and turning, saw a lean white cat, very dirty, on the cistern cover outside the window. A thought came into my head. "Everything ready for you," I said, and went to the window, opened it, and called softly. She came in, purring – the poor beast was starving – and I gave her some milk. All my food was in a cupboard in the corner of the room. After that she went smelling round the room, evidently with the idea of making herself at home. The invisible rag upset her a bit; you should have seen her spit at it! But I made her comfortable on the pillow of my truckle-bed. And I gave her butter to get her to wash.'

'And you processed her?'

'I processed her. But giving drugs to a cat is no joke, Kemp! And the process failed.'

'Failed!'

'In two particulars. These were the claws and the pigment stuff, what is it? – at the back of the eye in a cat. You know?'

'*Tapetum*.'

'Yes, the *tapetum*. It didn't go. After I'd given the stuff to bleach the blood and done certain other things to her, I gave the beast opium, and put her and the pillow she was sleeping on, on the apparatus. And after all the rest had faded and vanished, there remained two little ghosts of her eyes.'

'Odd!'

'I can't explain it. She was bandaged and clamped, of course – so I had her safe; but she woke while she was still misty, and miaowed dismally, and someone came knocking. It was an old woman from downstairs, who

suspected me of vivisecting – a drink-sodden old creature, with only a white cat to care for in all the world. I whipped out some chloroform, applied it, and answered the door. "Did I hear a cat?" she asked. "My cat?" "Not here," said I, very politely. She was a little doubtful and tried to peer past me into the room; strange enough to her no doubt – bare walls, uncurtained windows, truckle-bed, with the gas engine vibrating, and the seethe of the radiant points, and that faint ghastly stinging of chloroform in the air. She had to be satisfied at last and went away again.'

'How long did it take?' asked Kemp.

'Three or four hours – the cat. The bones and sinews and the fat were the last to go, and the tips of the coloured hairs. And, as I say, the back part of the eye, tough, iridescent stuff it is, wouldn't go at all.

'It was night outside long before the business was over, and nothing was to be seen but the dim eyes and the claws. I stopped the gas engine, felt for and stroked the beast, which was still insensible, and then, being tired, left it sleeping on the invisible pillow and went to bed. I found it hard to sleep. I lay awake thinking weak aimless stuff, going over the experiment over and over again, or dreaming feverishly of things growing misty and vanishing about me, until everything, the ground I stood on, vanished, and so I came to that sickly falling nightmare one gets. About two, the cat began miaowing about the room. I tried to hush it by talking to it, and then I decided to turn it out. I remember the shock I had when striking a light – there were just the round eyes shining green – and nothing round them. I would have given it milk, but I hadn't any. It wouldn't be quiet, it just sat down and miaowed at the door. I tried to catch it, with an idea of putting it out of the window, but it wouldn't be caught, it vanished. Then it began miaowing in different parts of the room. At last I opened the window and made a bustle. I suppose it went out at last. I never saw any more of it.

'Then – Heaven knows why – I fell thinking of my father's funeral again, and the dismal windy hillside, until the day had come. I found sleeping was hopeless, and, locking my door after me, wandered out into the morning streets.'

'You don't mean to say there's an invisible cat at large!' said Kemp.

'If it hasn't been killed,' said the Invisible Man. 'Why not?'

'Why not?' said Kemp. 'I didn't mean to interrupt.'

'It's very probably been killed,' said the Invisible Man. 'It was alive four days after, I know, and down a grating in Great Titchfield Street; because I saw a crowd round the place, trying to see whence the miaowing came.'

He was silent for the best part of a minute. Then he resumed abruptly:

'I remember that morning before the change very vividly. I must have gone up Great Portland Street. I remember the barracks in Albany Street, and the horse soldiers coming out, and at last I found the summit of Primrose Hill. It was a sunny day in January – one of those sunny, frosty days that

came before the snow this year. My weary brain tried to formulate the position, to plot out a plan of action.

'I was surprised to find, now that my prize was within my grasp, how inconclusive its attainment seemed. As a matter of fact I was worked out; the intense stress of nearly four years' continuous work left me incapable of any strength of feeling. I was apathetic, and I tried in vain to recover the enthusiasm of my first enquiries, the passion of discovery that had enabled me to compass even the downfall of my father's grey hairs. Nothing seemed to matter. I saw pretty clearly this was a transient mood, due to overwork and want of sleep, and that either by drugs or rest it would be possible to recover my energies.

'All I could think clearly was that the thing had to be carried through; the fixed idea still ruled me. And soon, for the money I had was almost exhausted. I looked about me at the hillside, with children playing and girls watching them, and tried to think of all the fantastic advantages an invisible man would have in the world. After a time I crawled home, took some food and a strong dose of strychnine, and went to sleep in my clothes on my unmade bed. Strychnine is a grand tonic, Kemp, to take the flabbiness out of a man.'

'It's the devil,' said Kemp. 'It's the palaeolithic in a bottle.'

'I awoke vastly invigorated and rather irritable. You know?'

'I know the stuff.'

'And there was someone rapping at the door. It was my landlord with threats and enquiries, an old Polish Jew in a long grey coat and greasy slippers. I had been tormenting a cat in the night, he was sure – the old woman's tongue had been busy. He insisted on knowing all about it. The laws in this country against vivisection were very severe – he might be liable. I denied the cat. Then the vibration of the little gas engine could be felt all over the house, he said. That was true, certainly. He edged round me into the room, peering about over his German-silver spectacles, and a sudden dread came into my mind that he might carry away something of my secret. I tried to keep between him and the concentrating apparatus I had arranged, and that only made him more curious. What was I doing? Why was I always alone and secretive? Was it legal? Was it dangerous? I paid nothing but the usual rent. His had always been a most respectable house – in a disreputable neighbourhood. Suddenly my temper gave way. I told him to get out. He began to protest, to jabber of his right of entry. In a moment I had him by the collar; something ripped, and he went spinning out into his own passage. I slammed and locked the door and sat down quivering.

'He made a fuss outside, which I disregarded, and after a time he went away.

'But this brought matters to a crisis. I did not know what he would do, nor even what he had the power to do. To move to fresh apartments would

have meant delay; altogether I had barely twenty pounds left in the world, for the most part in a bank – and I could not afford that. Vanish! It was irresistible. Then there would be an enquiry, the sacking of my room.

'At the thought of the possibility of my work being exposed or interrupted at its very climax, I became very angry and active. I hurried out with my three books of notes, my cheque-book – the tramp has them now – and directed them from the nearest Post Office to a house of call for letters and parcels in Great Portland Street. I tried to go out noiselessly. Coming in, I found my landlord going quietly upstairs; he had heard the door close, I suppose. You would have laughed to see him jump aside on the landing as I came tearing after him. He glared at me as I went by him, and I made the house quiver with the slamming of my door. I heard him come shuffling up to my floor, hesitate, and go down. I set to work upon my preparations forthwith.

'It was all done that evening and night. While I was still sitting under the sickly, drowsy influence of the drugs that decolourize blood, there came a repeated knocking at the door. It ceased, footsteps went away and returned, and the knocking was resumed. There was an attempt to push something under the door – a blue paper. Then in a fit of irritation I rose and went and flung the door wide open. "Now then?" said I.

'It was my landlord, with a notice of ejectment or something. He held it out to me, saw something odd about my hands, I expect, and lifted his eyes to my face.

'For a moment he gaped. Then he gave a sort of inarticulate cry, dropped candle and writ together, and went blundering down the dark passage to the stairs. I shut the door, locked it, and went to the looking-glass. Then I understood his terror . . . My face was white – like white stone.

'But it was all horrible. I had not expected the suffering. A night of racking anguish, sickness and fainting. I set my teeth, though my skin was presently afire, all my body afire; but I lay there like grim death. I understood now how it was the cat had howled until I chloroformed it. Lucky it was I lived alone and untended in my room. There were times when I sobbed and groaned and talked. But I stuck to it . . . I became insensible and woke languid in the darkness.

'The pain had passed. I thought I was killing myself and I did not care. I shall never forget that dawn, and the strange horror of seeing that my hands had become as clouded glass, and watching them grow clearer and thinner as the day went by, until at last I could see the sickly disorder of my room through them, though I closed my transparent eyelids. My limbs became glassy, the bones and arteries faded, vanished, and the little white nerves went last. I gritted my teeth and stayed there to the end. At last only the dead tips of the fingernails remained, pallid and white, and the brown stain of some acid upon my fingers.

'I struggled up. At first I was as incapable as a swathed infant – stepping with limbs I could not see. I was weak and very hungry. I went and stared at nothing in my shaving-glass, at nothing save where an attenuated pigment still remained behind the retina of my eyes, fainter than mist. I had to hang on to the table and press my forehead against the glass.

'It was only by a frantic effort of will that I dragged myself back to the apparatus and completed the process.

'I slept during the forenoon, pulling the sheet over my eyes to shut out the light, and about midday I was awakened again by a knocking. My strength had returned. I sat up and listened and heard a whispering. I sprang to my feet and as noiselessly as possible began to detach the connections of my apparatus, and to distribute it about the room, so as to destroy the suggestions of its arrangement. Presently the knocking was renewed and voices called, first my landlord's, and then two others. To gain time I answered them. The invisible rag and pillow came to hand and I opened the window and pitched them out on to the cistern cover. As the window opened, a heavy crash came at the door. Someone had charged it with the idea of smashing the lock. But the stout bolts I had screwed up some days before stopped him. That startled me, made me angry. I began to tremble and do things hurriedly.

'I tossed together some loose paper, straw, packing paper and so forth, in the middle of the room, and turned on the gas. Heavy blows began to rain upon the door. I could not find the matches. I beat my hands on the wall with rage. I turned down the gas again, stepped out of the window on the cistern cover, very softly lowered the sash, and sat down, secure and invisible, but quivering with anger, to watch events. They split a panel, I saw, and in another moment they had broken away the staples of the bolts and stood in the open doorway. It was the landlord and his two step-sons, sturdy young men of three or four and twenty. Behind them fluttered the old hag of a woman from downstairs.

'You may imagine their astonishment to find the room empty. One of the younger men rushed to the window at once, flung it up and stared out. His staring eyes and thick-lipped bearded face came a foot from my face. I was half minded to hit his silly countenance, but I arrested my doubled fist. He stared right through me. So did the others as they joined him. The old man went and peered under the bed, and then they all made a rush for the cupboard. They had to argue about it at length in Yiddish and Cockney English. They concluded I had not answered them, that their imagination had deceived them. A feeling of extraordinary elation took the place of my anger as I sat outside the window and watched these four people – for the old lady came in, glancing suspiciously about her like a cat, trying to understand the riddle of my behaviour.

'The old man, so far as I could understand his *patois*, agreed with the old lady that I was a vivisectionist. The sons protested in garbled English that

I was an electrician, and appealed to the dynamos and radiators. They were all nervous about my arrival, although I found subsequently that they had bolted the front door. The old lady peered into the cupboard and under the bed, and one of the young men pushed up the register and stared up the chimney. One of my fellow lodgers, a costermonger who shared the opposite room with a butcher, appeared on the landing, and he was called in and told incoherent things.

'It occurred to me that the radiators, if they fell into the hands of some acute well-educated person, would give me away too much, and watching my opportunity, I came into the room and tilted one of the little dynamos off its fellow on which it was standing, and smashed both apparatus. Then, while they were trying to explain the smash, I dodged out of the room and went softly downstairs.

'I went into one of the sitting-rooms and waited until they came down, still speculating and argumentative, all a little disappointed at finding no "horrors," and all a little puzzled how they stood legally towards me. Then I slipped up again with a box of matches, fired my heap of paper and rubbish, put the chairs and bedding thereby, led the gas to the affair, by means of an india-rubber tube, and waving a farewell to the room left it for the last time.'

'You fired the house!' exclaimed Kemp.

'Fired the house. It was the only way to cover my trail – and no doubt it was insured. I slipped the bolts of the front door quietly and went out into the street. I was invisible, and I was only just beginning to realize the extraordinary advantage my invisibility gave me. My head was already teeming with plans of all the wild and wonderful things I had now impunity to do.'

CHAPTER XXI

In Oxford Street

'In going downstairs the first time I found an unexpected difficulty because I could not see my feet; indeed I stumbled twice, and there was an unaccustomed clumsiness in gripping the bolt. By not looking down, however, I managed to walk on the level passably well.

'My mood, I say, was one of exaltation. I felt as a seeing man might do, with padded feet and noiseless clothes, in a city of the blind. I experienced a wild impulse to jest, to startle people, to clap men on the back, fling people's hats astray, and generally revel in my extraordinary advantage.

'But hardly had I emerged upon Great Portland Street, however (my lodging was close to the big draper's shop there), when I heard a clashing concussion and was hit violently behind, and turning saw a man carrying a basket of soda-water syphons, and looking in amazement at his burden. Although the blow had really hurt me, I found something so irresistible in his astonishment that I laughed aloud. "The devil's in the basket," I said, and suddenly twisted it out of his hand. He let go incontinently, and I swung the whole weight into the air.

'But a fool of a cabman, standing outside a public house, made a sudden rush for this, and his extending fingers took me with excruciating violence under the ear. I let the whole down with a smash on the cabman, and then, with shouts and the clatter of feet about me, people coming out of shops, vehicles pulling up, I realized what I had done for myself, and cursing my folly, backed against a shop window and prepared to dodge out of the confusion. In a moment I should be wedged into a crowd and inevitably discovered. I pushed by a butcher boy, who luckily did not turn to see the nothingness that shoved him aside, and dodged behind the cabman's four-wheeler. I do not know how they settled the business. I hurried straight across the road, which was happily clear, and hardly heeding which way I went, in the fright of detection the incident had given me, plunged into the afternoon throng of Oxford Street.

'I tried to get into the stream of people, but they were too thick for me, and in a moment my heels were being trodden upon. I took to the gutter, the roughness of which I found painful to my feet, and forthwith the shaft of a crawling hansom dug me forcibly under the shoulder blade, reminding me that I was already bruised severely. I staggered out of the way of the cab, avoided a perambulator by a convulsive movement, and found myself behind the hansom. A happy thought saved me, and as this drove slowly along I followed in its immediate wake, trembling and astonished at the

turn of my adventure. And not only trembling, but shivering. It was a bright day in January and I was stark naked and the thin slime of mud that covered the road was freezing. Foolish as it seems to me now, I had not reckoned that, transparent or not, I was still amenable to the weather and all its consequences.

'Then suddenly a bright idea came into my head. I ran round and got into the cab. And so, shivering, scared, and sniffing with the first intimations of a cold, and with the bruises in the small of my back growing upon my attention, I drove slowly along Oxford Street and past Tottenham Court Road. My mood was as different from that in which I had sallied forth ten minutes ago as it is possible to imagine. *This* invisibility indeed! The one thought that possessed me was – how was I to get out of the scrape I was in.

'We crawled past Mudie's, and there a tall woman with five or six yellow-labelled books hailed my cab, and I sprang out just in time to escape her, shaving a railway van narrowly in my flight. I made off up the roadway to Bloomsbury Square, intending to strike north past the Museum and so get into the quiet district. I was now cruelly chilled, and the strangeness of my situation so unnerved me that I whimpered as I ran. At the northward corner of the Square a little white dog ran out of the Pharmaceutical Society's offices, and incontinently made for me, nose down.

'I had never realized it before, but the nose is to the mind of a dog what the eye is to the mind of a seeing man. Dogs perceive the scent of a man moving as men perceive his vision. This brute began barking and leaping, showing, as it seemed to me, only too plainly that he was aware of me. I crossed Great Russell Street, glancing over my shoulder as I did so, and went some way along Montague Street before I realized what I was running towards.

'Then I became aware of a blare of music, and looking along the street saw a number of people advancing out of Russell Square, red shirts, and the banner of the Salvation Army to the fore. Such a crowd, chanting in the roadway and scoffing on the pavement, I could not hope to penetrate, and dreading to go back and further from home again, and deciding on the spur of the moment, I ran up the white steps of a house facing the Museum railings, and stood there until the crowd should have passed. Happily the dog stopped at the noise of the band too, hesitated, and turned tail, running back to Bloomsbury Square again.

'On came the band, bawling with unconscious irony some hymn about "When shall we see His face?" and it seemed an interminable time to me before the tide of the crowd washed along the pavement by me. Thud, thud, thud, came the drum with a vibrating resonance, and for the moment I did not notice two urchins stopping at the railings by me. "See 'em," said one. "See what?" said the other. "Why – them footmarks – *bare*. Like what you makes in mud."

'I looked down and saw the youngsters had stopped and were gaping at the muddy footmarks I had left behind me up the newly whitened steps. The passing people elbowed and jostled them, but their confounded intelligence was arrested. "Thud, thud, thud, when, thud, shall we see, thud, his face, thud, thud." "There's a barefoot man gone up them steps, or I don't know nothing," said one. "And he ain't never come down again. And his foot was a-bleeding."

'The thick of the crowd had already passed. "Looky there, Ted," quoth the younger of the detectives, with the sharpness of surprise in his voice, and pointed straight to my feet. I looked down and saw at once the dim suggestion of their outline sketched in splashes of mud. For a moment I was paralyzed.

'"Why, that's rum," said the elder. "Dashed rum! It's just like the ghost of a foot, ain't it?" He hesitated and advanced with outstretched hand. A man pulled up short to see what he was catching, and then a girl. In another moment he would have touched me. Then I saw what to do. I made a step, the boy started back with an exclamation, and with a rapid movement I swung myself over into the portico of the next house. But the smaller boy was sharp-eyed enough to follow the movement, and before I was well down the steps and upon the pavement, he had recovered from his momentary astonishment and was shouting out that the feet had gone over the wall.

'They rushed round and saw my new footmarks flash into being on the lower step and upon the pavement. "What's up?" asked someone. "Feet! Look! Feet running!"

'Everybody in the road, except my three pursuers, was pouring along after the Salvation Army, and this blow not only impeded me but them. There was an eddy of surprise and interrogation. At the cost of bowling over one young fellow I got through, and in another moment I was rushing headlong round the circuit of Russell Square, with six or seven astonished people following my footmarks. There was no time for explanation, or else the whole host would have been after me.

'Twice I doubled round corners, thrice I crossed the road and came back upon my tracks, and then, as my feet grew hot and dry, the damp impressions began to fade. At last I had a breathing space and rubbed my feet clean with my hands, and so got away altogether. The last I saw of the chase was a little group of a dozen people perhaps, studying with infinite perplexity a slowly drying footprint that had resulted from a puddle in Tavistock Square, a footprint as isolated and incomprehensible to them as Crusoe's solitary discovery.

'This running warmed me to a certain extent, and I went on with a better courage through the maze of less frequented roads that runs hereabouts. My back had now become very stiff and sore, my tonsils were painful from the cabman's fingers, and the skin of my neck had been scratched by his nails;

my feet hurt exceedingly and I was lame from a little cut on one foot. I saw in time a blind man approaching me, and fled limping, for I feared his subtle intuitions. Once or twice accidental collisions occurred and I left people amazed, with unaccountable curses ringing in their ears. Then came something silent and quiet against my face, and across the Square fell a thin veil of slowly falling flakes of snow. I had caught a cold, and do as I would I could not avoid an occasional sneeze. And every dog that came in sight, with its pointing nose and curious sniffing, was a terror to me.

'Then came men and boys running, first one and then others, and shouting as they ran. It was a fire. They ran in the direction of my lodging, and looking back down a street I saw a mass of black smoke streaming up above the roofs and telephone wires. It was my lodging burning; my clothes, my apparatus, all my resources indeed, except my cheque-book and the three volumes of memoranda that awaited me in Great Portland Street, were there. Burning! I had burnt my boats – if ever a man did! The place was blazing.'

The Invisible Man paused and thought. Kemp glanced nervously out of the window. 'Yes?' he said. 'Go on.'

CHAPTER XXII

In the Emporium

'So last January, with the beginning of a snowstorm in the air about me –
and if it settled on me it would betray me! – weary, cold, painful,
inexpressibly wretched, and still but half convinced of my invisible quality,
I began this new life to which I am committed. I had no refuge, no appli-
ances, no human being in the world in whom I could confide. To have told
my secret would have given me away – made a mere show and rarity of me.
Nevertheless, I was half minded to accost some passer-by and throw myself
upon his mercy. But I knew too clearly the terror and brutal cruelty my
advances would evoke. I made no plans in the street. My sole object was
to get shelter from the snow, to get myself covered and warm; then I might
hope to plan. But even to me, an Invisible Man, the rows of London houses
stood latched, barred, and bolted impregnably.

'Only one thing could I see clearly before me – the cold exposure and
misery of the snowstorm and the night.

'And then I had a brilliant idea. I turned down one of the roads leading
from Gower Street to Tottenham Court Road, and found myself outside
Omniums, the big establishment where everything is to be bought – you
know the place: meat, grocery, linen, furniture, clothing, oil paintings even
– a huge meandering collection of shops rather than a shop. I had thought
I should find the doors open, but they were closed, and as I stood in the
wide entrance a carriage stopped outside, and a man in uniform – you know
the kind of personage with "*Omnium*" on his cap – flung open the door. I
contrived to enter, and walking down the shop – it was a department where
they were selling ribbons and gloves and stockings and that kind of thing
– came to a more spacious region devoted to picnic baskets and wicker
furniture.

'I did not feel safe there, however; people were going to and fro, and I
prowled restlessly about until I came upon a huge section in an upper floor
containing multitudes of bedsteads, and over these I clambered, and found
a resting-place at last among a huge pile of folded flock mattresses. The
place was already lit up and agreeably warm, and I decided to remain
where I was, keeping a cautious eye on the two or three sets of shopmen
and customers who were meandering through the place, until closing time
came. Then I should be able, I thought, to rob the place for food and
clothing, and disguised, prowl through it and examine its resources, perhaps
sleep on some of the bedding. That seemed an acceptable plan. My idea
was to procure clothing to make myself a muffled but acceptable figure,

to get money, and then to recover my books and parcels where they awaited me, take a lodging somewhere and elaborate plans for the complete realization of the advantages my invisibility gave me (as I still imagined) over my fellow men.

'Closing time arrived quickly enough. It could not have been more than an hour after I took up my position on the mattresses before I noticed the blinds of the windows being drawn, and customers being marched doorward. And then a number of brisk young men began with remarkable alacrity to tidy up the goods that remained disturbed. I left my lair as the crowds diminished, and prowled cautiously out into the less desolate parts of the shop. I was really surprised to observe how rapidly the young men and women whipped away the goods displayed for sale during the day. All the boxes of goods, the hanging fabrics, the festoons of lace, the boxes of sweets in the grocery section, the displays of this and that, were being whipped down, folded up, slapped into tidy receptacles, and everything that could not be taken down and put away had sheets of some coarse stuff like sacking flung over them. Finally all the chairs were turned up on to the counters, leaving the floor clear. Directly each of these young people had done, he or she made promptly for the door with such an expression of animation as I have rarely observed in a shop assistant before. Then came a lot of youngsters scattering sawdust and carrying pails and brooms. I had to dodge to get out of the way, and as it was, my ankle got stung with the sawdust. For some time, wandering through the swathed and darkened departments, I could hear the brooms at work. And at last a good hour or more after the shop had been closed, came a noise of locking doors. Silence came upon the place, and I found myself wandering through the vast and intricate shops, galleries, show-rooms of the place, alone. It was very still; in one place I remember passing near one of the Tottenham Court Road entrances and listening to the tapping of boot-heels of the passers-by.

'My first visit was to the place where I had seen stockings and gloves for sale. It was dark, and I had the devil of a hunt after matches, which I found at last in the drawer of the little cash desk. Then I had to get a candle. I had to tear down wrappings and ransack a number of boxes and drawers, but at last I managed to turn out what I sought; the box label called them lambswool pants, and lambswool vests. Then socks, a thick comforter, and then I went to the clothing place and got trousers, a lounge jacket, an overcoat and a slouch hat – a clerical sort of hat with the brim turned down. I began to feel a human being again, and my next thought was food.

'Upstairs was a refreshment department, and there I got cold meat. There was coffee still in the urn, and I lit the gas and warmed it up again, and altogether I did not do badly. Afterwards, prowling through the place in search of blankets – I had to put up at last with a heap of down quilts – I came upon a grocery section with a lot of chocolate and candied fruits, more

than was good for me indeed – and some white burgundy. And near that was a toy department, and I had a brilliant idea. I found some artificial noses – dummy noses, you know, and I thought of dark spectacles. But Omniums had no optical department. My nose had been a difficulty indeed – I had thought of paint. But the discovery set my mind running on wigs and masks and the like. Finally I went to sleep in a heap of down quilts, very warm and comfortable.

'My last thoughts before sleeping were the most agreeable I had had since the change. I was in a state of physical serenity, and that was reflected in my mind. I thought that I should be able to slip out unobserved in the morning with my clothes upon me, muffling my face with a white wrapper I had taken, purchase, with the money I had taken, spectacles and so forth, and so complete my disguise. I lapsed into disorderly dreams of all the fantastic things that had happened during the last few days. I saw the ugly little Jew of a landlord vociferating in his rooms; I saw his two sons marvelling, and the wrinkled old woman's gnarled face as she asked for her cat. I experienced again the strange sensation of seeing the cloth disappear, and so I came round to the windy hillside and the sniffing old clergyman mumbling "Earth to earth, ashes to ashes, dust to dust," at my father's open grave.

'You also,' said a voice, and suddenly I was being forced towards the grave. I struggled, shouted, appealed to the mourners, but they continued stonily following the service; the old clergyman, too, never faltered droning and sniffing through the ritual. I realized I was invisible and inaudible, that overwhelming forces had their grip on me. I struggled in vain, I was forced over the brink, the coffin rang hollow as I fell upon it, and the gravel came flying after me in spadefuls. Nobody heeded me, nobody was aware of me. I made convulsive struggles and awoke.

'The pale London dawn had come, the place was full of a chilly grey light that filtered round the edges of the window blinds. I sat up, and for a time I could not think where this ample apartment, with its counters, its piles of rolled stuff, its heap of quilts and cushions, its iron pillars, might be. Then, as recollection came back to me, I heard voices in conversation.

'Then far down the place, in the brighter light of some department which had already raised its blinds, I saw two men approaching. I scrambled to my feet, looking about me for some way of escape, and even as I did so the sound of my movement made them aware of me. I suppose they saw merely a figure moving quietly and quickly away. "Who's that?" cried one, and "Stop there!" shouted the other. I dashed around a corner and came full tilt – a faceless figure, mind you! – on a lanky lad of fifteen. He yelled and I bowled him over, rushed past him, turned another corner, and by a happy inspiration threw myself behind a counter. In another moment feet went running past and I heard voices shouting, "All hands to the doors!" asking what was "up," and giving one another advice how to catch me.

'Lying on the ground, I felt scared out of my wits. But – odd as it may seem – it did not occur to me at the moment to take off my clothes as I should have done. I had made up my mind, I suppose, to get away in them, and that ruled me. And then down the vista of the counters came a bawling of "Here he is!"

'I sprang to my feet, whipped a chair off the counter, and sent it whirling at the fool who had shouted, turned, came into another round a corner, sent him spinning, and rushed up the stairs. He kept his footing, gave a view hallo! and came up the staircase hot after me. Up the staircase were piled a multitude of those bright-coloured pot things – what are they?'

'Art pots,' suggested Kemp.

'That's it! Art pots. Well, I turned at the top step and swung round, plucked one out of a pile and smashed it on his silly head as he came at me. The whole pile of pots went headlong, and I heard shouting and foot-steps running from all parts. I made a mad rush for the refreshment place, and there was a man in white like a man cook, who took up the chase. I made one last desperate turn and found myself among lamps and ironmon-gery. I went behind the counter of this, and waited for my cook, and as he bolted in at the head of the chase, I doubled him up with a lamp. Down he went, and I crouched down behind the counter and began whipping off my clothes as fast as I could. Coat, jacket, trousers, shoes were all right, but a lambswool vest fits a man like a skin. I heard more men coming, my cook was lying quiet on the other side of the counter, stunned or scared speechless, and I had to make another dash for it, like a rabbit hunted out of a wood-pile.

'This way, policeman!' I heard someone shouting. I found myself in my bedstead storeroom again, and at the end of a wilderness of wardrobes. I rushed among them, went flat, got rid of my vest after infinite wriggling, and stood a free man again, panting and scared, as the policeman and three of the shopmen came round the corner. They made a rush for the vest and pants, and collared the trousers. 'He's dropping his plunder,' said one of the young men. 'He *must* be somewhere here.'

'But they did not find me all the same.

'I stood watching them hunt for me for a time, and cursing my ill-luck in losing the clothes. Then I went into the refreshment-room, drank a little milk I found there, and sat down by the fire to consider my position.

'In a little while two assistants came in and began to talk over the busi-ness very excitedly and like the fools they were. I heard a magnified account of my depredations, and other speculations as to my whereabouts. Then I fell to scheming again. The insurmountable difficulty of the place, especially now it was alarmed, was to get any plunder out of it. I went down into the warehouse to see if there was any chance of packing and addressing a parcel, but I could not understand the system of checking. About eleven o'clock,

the snow having thawed as it fell, and the day being finer and a little warmer than the previous one, I decided that the Emporium was hopeless, and went out again, exasperated at my want of success, with only the vaguest plans of action in my mind.'

CHAPTER XXIII

In Drury Lane

'But you begin now to realize,' said the Invisible Man, 'the full disadvantage of my condition. I had no shelter – no covering – to get clothing was to forego all my advantage, to make myself a strange and terrible thing. I was fasting; for to eat, to fill myself with unassimilated matter, would be to become grotesquely visible again.'

'I never thought of that,' said Kemp.

'Nor had I. And the snow had warned me of other dangers. I could not go abroad in snow – it would settle on me and expose me. Rain, too, would make me a watery outline, a glistening surface of a man – a bubble. And fog – I should be like a fainter bubble in a fog, a surface, a greasy glimmer of humanity. Moreover, as I went abroad – in the London air – I gathered dirt about my ankles, floating smuts and dust upon my skin. I did not know how long it would be before I should become visible from that cause also. But I saw clearly it could not be for long.

'Not in London at any rate.

'I went into the slums towards Great Portland Street, and found myself at the end of the street in which I had lodged. I did not go that way, because of the crowd halfway down it opposite to the still smoking ruins of the house I had fired. My most immediate problem was to get clothing. What to do with my face puzzled me. Then I saw in one of those little miscellaneous shops – news, sweets, toys, stationery, belated Christmas tomfoolery, and so forth – an array of masks and noses. I realized that problem was solved. In a flash I saw my course. I turned about, no longer aimless, and went – circuitously in order to avoid the busy ways, towards the back streets north of the Strand; for I remembered, though not very distinctly where, that some theatrical costumiers had shops in that district.

'The day was cold, with a nipping wind down the northward running streets. I walked fast to avoid being overtaken. Every crossing was a danger, every passenger a thing to watch alertly. One man as I was about to pass him at the top of Bedford Street, turned upon me abruptly and came into me, sending me into the road and almost under the wheel of a passing hansom. The verdict of the cab-rank was that he had had some sort of stroke. I was so unnerved by this encounter that I went into Covent Garden Market and sat down for some time in a quiet corner by a stall of violets, panting and trembling. I found I had caught a fresh cold, and had to turn out after a time lest my sneezes should attract attention.

'At last I reached the object of my quest, a dirty, fly-blown little shop in a byway near Drury Lane, with a window full of tinsel robes, sham jewels, wigs, slippers, dominoes and theatrical photographs. The shop was old-fashioned and low and dark, and the house rose above it for four storeys, dark and dismal. I peered through the window and, seeing no one within, entered. The opening of the door set a clanking bell ringing. I left it open, and walked round a bare costume stand, into a corner behind a cheval glass. For a minute or so no one came. Then I heard heavy feet striding across a room, and a man appeared down the shop.

'My plans were now perfectly definite. I proposed to make my way into the house, secrete myself upstairs, watch my opportunity, and when everything was quiet, rummage out a wig, mask, spectacles, and costume, and go into the world, perhaps a grotesque but still a credible figure. And incidentally of course I could rob the house of any available money.

'The man who had just entered the shop was a short, slight, hunched, beetle-browed man, with long arms and very short bandy legs. Apparently I had interrupted a meal. He stared about the shop with an expression of expectation. This gave way to surprise, and then to anger, as he saw the shop empty. "Damn the boys!" he said. He went to stare up and down the street. He came in again in a minute, kicked the door to with his foot spitefully, and went muttering back to the house door.

'I came forward to follow him, and at the noise of my movement he stopped dead. I did so too, startled by his quickness of ear. He slammed the house door in my face.

'I stood hesitating. Suddenly I heard his quick footsteps returning, and the door reopened. He stood looking about the shop like one who was still not satisfied. Then, murmuring to himself, he examined the back of the counter and peered behind some fixtures. Then he stood doubtful. He had left the house door open and I slipped into the inner room.

'It was a queer little room, poorly furnished and with a number of big masks in the corner. On the table was his belated breakfast, and it was a confoundedly exasperating thing for me, Kemp, to have to sniff his coffee and stand watching while he came in and resumed his meal. And his table manners were irritating. Three doors opened into the little room, one going upstairs and one down, but they were all shut. I could not get out of the room while he was there; I could scarcely move because of his alertness, and there was a draught down my back. Twice I strangled a sneeze just in time.

'The spectacular quality of my sensations was curious and novel, but for all that I was heartily tired and angry long before he had done his eating. But at last he made an end and putting his beggarly crockery on the black tin tray upon which he had had his teapot, and gathering all the crumbs up on the mustard stained cloth, he took the whole lot of things after him. His

burden prevented his shutting the door behind him – as he would have done; I never saw such a man for shutting doors – and I followed him into a very dirty underground kitchen and scullery. I had the pleasure of seeing him begin to wash up, and then, finding no good in keeping down there, and the brick floor being cold on my feet, I returned upstairs and sat in his chair by the fire. It was burning low, and scarcely thinking, I put on a little coal. The noise of this brought him up at once, and he stood aglare. He peered about the room and was within an ace of touching me. Even after that examination, he scarcely seemed satisfied. He stopped in the doorway and took a final inspection before he went down.

'I waited in the little parlour for an age, and at last he came up and opened the upstairs door. I just managed to get by him.

'On the staircase he stopped suddenly, so that I very nearly blundered into him. He stood looking back right into my face and listening. "I could have sworn," he said. His long hairy hand pulled at his lower lip. His eye went up and down the staircase. Then he grunted and went on up again.

'His hand was on the handle of a door, and then he stopped again with the same puzzled anger on his face. He was becoming aware of the faint sounds of my movements about him. The man must have had diabolically acute hearing. He suddenly flashed into rage. "If there's anyone in this house—" he cried with an oath, and left the threat unfinished. He put his hand in his pocket, failed to find what he wanted, and rushing past me went blundering noisily and pugnaciously downstairs. But I did not follow him. I sat on the head of the staircase until his return.

'Presently he came up again, still muttering. He opened the door of the room, and before I could enter, slammed it in my face.

'I resolved to explore the house, and spent some time in doing so as noiselessly as possible. The house was very old and tumble-down, damp so that the paper in the attics was peeling from the walls, and rat infested. Some of the door handles were stiff and I was afraid to turn them. Several rooms I did inspect were unfurnished, and others were littered with theatrical lumber, bought second-hand, I judged, from its appearance. In one room next to his I found a lot of old clothes. I began routing among these, and in my eagerness forgot again the evident sharpness of his ears. I heard a stealthy footstep and, looking up just in time, saw him peering in at the tumbled heap and holding an old-fashioned revolver in his hand. I stood perfectly still while he stared about open-mouthed and suspicious. "It must have been her," he said slowly. "Damn her!"

'He shut the door quietly, and immediately I heard the key turn in the lock. Then his footsteps retreated. I realized abruptly that I was locked in. For a minute I did not know what to do. I walked from door to window and back, and stood perplexed. A gust of anger came upon me. But I decided to inspect the clothes before I did anything further, and my first attempt

brought down a pile from an upper shelf. This brought him back, more sinister than ever. That time he actually touched me, jumped back with amazement and stood astonished in the middle of the room.

'Presently he calmed a little. "Rats," he said in an undertone, fingers on lips. He was evidently a little scared. I edged quietly out of the room, but a plank creaked. Then the infernal little brute started going all over the house, revolver in hand and locking door after door and pocketing the keys. When I realized what he was up to I had a fit of rage – I could hardly control myself sufficiently to watch my opportunity. By this time I knew he was alone in the house, and so I made no more ado, but knocked him on the head.'

'Knocked him on the head!' exclaimed Kemp.

'Yes – stunned him – as he was going downstairs. Hit him from behind with a stool that stood on the landing. He went downstairs like a bag of old boots.'

'But – I say! The common conventions of humanity—'

'Are all very well for common people. But the point was, Kemp, that I had to get out of that house in a disguise without his seeing me. I couldn't think of any other way of doing it. And then I gagged him with a Louis Quatorze vest and tied him up in a sheet.'

'Tied him up in a sheet!'

'Made a sort of bag of it. It was rather a good idea to keep the idiot scared and quiet, and a devilish hard thing to get out of – head away from the string. My dear Kemp, it's no good your sitting glaring as though I was a murderer. It had to be done. He had his revolver. If once he saw me he would be able to describe me—'

'But still,' said Kemp, 'in England – today. And the man was in his own house, and you were – well, robbing.'

'Robbing! Confound it! You'll call me a thief next! Surely, Kemp, you're not fool enough to dance on the old strings. Can't you see my position?'

'And his too,' said Kemp.

The Invisible Man stood up sharply. 'What do you mean to say?'

Kemp's face grew a trifle hard. He was about to speak and checked himself. 'I suppose, after all,' he said with a sudden change of manner, 'the thing had to be done. You were in a fix. But still—'

'Of course I was in a fix – an infernal fix. And he made me wild too – hunting me about the house, fooling about with his revolver, locking and unlocking doors. He was simply exasperating. You don't blame me, do you? You don't blame me?'

'I never blame anyone,' said Kemp. 'It's quite out of fashion. What did you do next?'

'I was hungry. Downstairs I found a loaf and some rank cheese – more than sufficient to satisfy my hunger. I took some brandy and water, and then

went up past my impromptu bag – he was lying quite still – to the room containing the old clothes. This looked out upon the street, two lace curtains brown with dirt guarding the window. I went and peered out through their interstices. Outside the day was bright – by contrast with the brown shadows of the dismal house in which I found myself, dazzlingly bright. A brisk traffic was going by, fruit carts, a hansom, a four-wheeler with a pile of boxes, a fishmonger's cart. I turned with spots of colour swimming before my eyes to the shadowy fixtures behind me. My excitement was giving place to a clear apprehension of my position again. The room was full of a faint scent of benzoline, used, I suppose, in cleaning the garments.

'I began a systematic search of the place. I should judge the hunchback had been alone in the house for some time. He was a curious person. Everything that could possibly be of service to me I collected in the clothes storeroom, and then I made a deliberate selection. I found a handbag I thought a suitable possession, and some powder, rouge, and sticking-plaster.

'I had thought of painting and powdering my face and all that there was to show of me, in order to render myself visible, but the disadvantage of this lay in the fact that I should require turpentine and other appliances and a considerable amount of time before I could vanish again. Finally I chose a mask of the better type, slightly grotesque but not more so than many human beings, dark glasses, greyish whiskers, and a wig. I could find no underclothing, but that I could buy subsequently, and for the time I swathed myself in calico dominoes and some white cashmere scarfs. I could find no socks, but the hunchback's boots were rather a loose fit and sufficed. In a desk in the shop were three sovereigns and about thirty shillings' worth of silver, and in a locked cupboard I burst in the inner room were eight pounds in gold. I could go forth into the world again, equipped.

'Then came a curious hesitation. Was my appearance really credible? I tried myself with a little bedroom looking-glass, inspecting myself from every point of view to discover any forgotten chink, but it all seemed sound. I was grotesque to the theatrical pitch, a stage miser, but I was certainly not a physical impossibility. Gathering confidence, I took my looking-glass down into the shop, pulled down the shop blinds, and surveyed myself from every point of view with the help of the cheval glass in the corner.

'I spent some minutes screwing up my courage and then unlocked the shop door and marched out into the street, leaving the little man to get out of his sheet again when he liked. In five minutes a dozen turnings intervened between me and the costumier's shop. No one appeared to notice me very pointedly. My last difficulty seemed overcome.'

He stopped again.

'And you troubled no more about the hunchback?' said Kemp.

'No,' said the Invisible Man. 'Nor have I heard what became of him. I suppose he untied himself or kicked himself out. The knots were pretty tight.'

He became silent and went to the window and stared out.

'What happened when you went out into the Strand?'

'Oh! – disillusionment again. I thought my troubles were over. Practically I thought I had impunity to do whatever I chose, everything – save to give away my secret. So I thought. Whatever I did, whatever the consequences might be, was nothing to me. I had merely to fling aside my garments and vanish. No person could hold me. I could take my money where I found it. I decided to treat myself to a sumptuous feast, and then put up at a good hotel, and accumulate a new outfit of property. I felt amazingly confident; it's not particularly pleasant recalling that I was an ass. I went into a place and was already ordering lunch, when it occurred to me that I could not eat unless I exposed my invisible face. I finished ordering the lunch, told the man I should be back in ten minutes, and went out exasperated. I don't know if you have ever been disappointed in your appetite.'

'Not quite so badly,' said Kemp, 'but I can imagine it.'

'I could have smashed the silly devils. At last, faint with the desire for tasteful food, I went into another place and demanded a private room. "I am disfigured," I said. "Badly." They looked at me curiously, but of course it was not their affair – and so at last I got my lunch. It was not particularly well served, but it sufficed; and when I had had it, I sat over a cigar, trying to plan my line of action. And outside a snowstorm was beginning.

'The more I thought it over, Kemp, the more I realized what a helpless absurdity an Invisible Man was – in a cold and dirty climate and a crowded civilized city. Before I made this mad experiment I had dreamt of a thousand advantages. That afternoon it seemed all disappointment. I went over the heads of the things a man reckons desirable. No doubt invisibility made it possible to get them, but it made it impossible to enjoy them when they are got. Ambition – what is the good of pride of place when you cannot appear there? What is the good of the love of woman when her name must needs be Delilah? I have no taste for politics, for the blackguardisms of fame, for philanthropy, for sport. What was I to do? And for this I had become a wrapped-up mystery, a swathed and bandaged caricature of a man!'

He paused, and his attitude suggested a roving glance at the window.

'But how did you get to Iping?' said Kemp, anxious to keep his guest busy talking.

'I went there to work. I had one hope. It was a half idea! I have it still. It is a full blown idea now. A way of getting back! Of restoring what I have done. When I choose. When I have done all I mean to do invisibly. And that is what I chiefly want to talk to you about now.'

'You went straight to Iping?'

'Yes. I had simply to get my three volumes of memoranda and my chequebook, my luggage and underclothing, order a quantity of chemicals to work

out this idea of mine – I will show you the calculations as soon as I get my books – and then I started. Jove! I remember the snowstorm now, and the accursed bother it was to keep the snow from damping my pasteboard nose.'

'At the end,' said Kemp, 'the day before yesterday, when they found you out, you rather – to judge by the papers—'

'I did. Rather. Did I kill that fool of a constable?'

'No,' said Kemp. 'He's expected to recover.'

'That's his luck, then. I clean lost my temper, the fools! Why couldn't they leave me alone? And that grocer lout?'

'There are no deaths expected,' said Kemp.

'I don't know about that tramp of mine,' said the Invisible Man, with an unpleasant laugh.

'By Heaven, Kemp, you don't know what rage *is*! . . . To have worked for years, to have planned and plotted, and then to get some fumbling purblind idiot messing across your course! Every conceivable sort of silly creature that has ever been created has been sent to cross me.

'If I have much more of it, I shall go wild – I shall start mowing 'em.

'As it is, they've made things a thousand times more difficult.'

'No doubt it's exasperating,' said Kemp, drily.

CHAPTER XXIV

The Plan that Failed

'But now,' said Kemp, with a side glance out of the window, 'what are we to do?'

He moved nearer his guest as he spoke in such a manner as to prevent the possibility of a sudden glimpse of the three men who were advancing up the hill road – with an intolerable slowness, as it seemed to Kemp.

'What were you planning to do when you were heading for Port Burdock? *Had* you any plan?'

'I was going to clear out of the country. But I have altered that plan rather since seeing you. I thought it would be wise, now the weather is hot and invisibility possible, to make for the South. Especially as my secret was known, and everyone would be on the lookout for a masked and muffled man. You have a line of steamers from here to France. My idea was to get aboard one and run the risks of the passage. Thence I could go by train into Spain, or else get to Algiers. It would not be difficult. There a man might always be invisible – and yet live. And do things. I was using that tramp as a money box and luggage carrier, until I decided how to get my books and things sent over to meet me.'

'That's clear.'

'And then the filthy brute must needs try and rob me! He *has* hidden my books, Kemp. Hidden my books! If I can lay my hands on him!'

'Best plan to get the books out of him first.'

'But where is he? Do you know?'

'He's in the town police station, locked up, by his own request, in the strongest cell in the place.'

'Cur!' said the Invisible Man.

'But that hangs up your plans a little.'

'We must get those books; those books are vital.'

'Certainly,' said Kemp, a little nervously, wondering if he heard footsteps outside. 'Certainly we must get those books. But that won't be difficult, if he doesn't know they're for you.'

'No,' said the Invisible Man, and thought.

Kemp tried to think of something to keep the talk going, but the Invisible Man resumed of his own accord.

'Blundering into your house, Kemp,' he said, 'changes all my plans. For you are a man that can understand. In spite of all that has happened, in spite of this publicity, of the loss of my books, of what I have suffered, there still remain great possibilities, huge possibilities—'

'You have told no one I am here?' he asked abruptly.

Kemp hesitated. 'That was implied,' he said.

'No one?' insisted Griffin.

'Not a soul.'

'Ah! Now—' The Invisible Man stood up, and sticking his arms akimbo began to pace the study.

'I made a mistake, Kemp, a huge mistake, in carrying this thing through alone. I have wasted strength, time, opportunities. Alone – it is wonderful how little a man can do alone! To rob a little, to hurt a little, and there is the end.

'What I want, Kemp, is a goal-keeper, a helper, and a hiding-place, an arrangement whereby I can sleep and eat and rest in peace, and unsuspected. I must have a confederate. With a confederate, with food and rest – a thousand things are possible.

'Hitherto I have gone on vague lines. We have to consider all that invisibility means, all that it does not mean. It means little advantage for eavesdropping and so forth – one makes sounds. It's of little help – a little help perhaps – in housebreaking and so forth. Once you've caught me you could easily imprison me. But on the other hand I am hard to catch. This invisibility, in fact, is only good in two cases: it's useful in getting away, it's useful in approaching. It's particularly useful, therefore, in killing. I can walk round a man, whatever weapon he has, choose my point, strike as I like. Dodge as I like. Escape as I like.'

Kemp's hand went to his moustache. Was that a movement downstairs?

'And it is killing we must do, Kemp.'

'It is killing we must do,' repeated Kemp. 'I'm listening to your plan, Griffin, but I'm not agreeing, mind. *Why* killing?'

'Not wanton killing, but a judicious slaying. The point is, they know there is an Invisible Man – as well as we know there is an Invisible Man. And that Invisible Man, Kemp, must now establish a Reign of Terror. Yes; no doubt it's startling. But I mean it. A Reign of Terror. He must take some town like your Burdock and terrify and dominate it. He must issue his orders. He can do that in a thousand ways – scraps of paper thrust under doors would suffice. And all who disobey his orders he must kill, and kill all who would defend them.'

'Humph!' said Kemp, no longer listening to Griffin but to the sound of his front door opening and closing.

'It seems to me, Griffin,' he said, to cover his wandering attention, 'that your confederate would be in a difficult position.'

'No one would know he was a confederate,' said the Invisible Man, eagerly. And then suddenly, '*Hush!* What's that downstairs?'

'Nothing,' said Kemp, and suddenly began to speak loud and fast. 'I don't agree to this, Griffin,' he said. 'Understand me, I don't agree to this. Why

dream of playing a game against the race? How can you hope to gain happiness? Don't be a lone wolf. Publish your results; take the world – take the nation at least – into your confidence. Think what you might do with a million helpers—'

The Invisible Man interrupted – arm extended. 'There are footsteps coming upstairs,' he said in a low voice.

'Nonsense,' said Kemp.

'Let me see,' said the Invisible Man, and advanced, arm extended, to the door.

And then things happened very swiftly. Kemp hesitated for a second and then moved to intercept him. The Invisible Man started and stood still. 'Traitor!' cried the Voice, and suddenly the dressing-gown opened, and sitting down the Unseen began to disrobe. Kemp made three swift steps to the door, and forthwith the Invisible Man – his legs had vanished – sprang to his feet with a shout. Kemp flung the door open.

As it opened, there came a sound of hurrying feet downstairs and voices.

With a quick movement Kemp thrust the Invisible Man back, sprang aside, and slammed the door. The key was outside and ready. In another moment Griffin would have been alone in the belvedere study, a prisoner. Save for one little thing. The key had been slipped in hastily that morning. As Kemp slammed the door it fell noisily upon the carpet.

Kemp's face became white. He tried to grip the door handle with both hands. For a moment he stood lugging. Then the door gave six inches. But he got it closed again. The second time it was jerked a foot wide, and the dressing-gown came wedging itself into the opening. His throat was gripped by invisible fingers, and he left his hold on the handle to defend himself. He was forced back, tripped and pitched heavily into the corner of the landing. The empty dressing-gown was flung on the top of him.

Halfway up the staircase was Colonel Adye, the recipient of Kemp's letter, the chief of the Burdock police. He was staring aghast at the sudden appearance of Kemp, followed by the extraordinary sight of clothing tossing empty in the air. He saw Kemp felled, and struggling to his feet. He saw him rush forward, and go down again, felled like an ox.

Then suddenly he was struck violently. By nothing! A vast weight, it seemed, leapt upon him, and he was hurled headlong down the staircase, with a grip on his throat and a knee in his groin. An invisible foot trod on his back, a ghostly patter passed downstairs, he heard the two police officers in the hall shout and run, and the front door of the house slammed violently.

He rolled over and sat up staring. He saw, staggering down the staircase, Kemp, dusty and disheveled, one side of his face white from a blow, his lip bleeding, and a pink dressing-gown and some underclothing held in his arms.

'My God!' cried Kemp, 'the game's up! He's gone!'

CHAPTER XXV

The Hunting of the Invisible Man

For a space Kemp was too inarticulate to make Adye understand the swift things that had just happened. They stood on the landing, Kemp speaking swiftly, the grotesque swathings of Griffin still on his arm. But presently Adye began to grasp something of the situation.

'He is mad,' said Kemp; 'inhuman. He is pure selfishness. He thinks of nothing but his own advantage, his own safety. I have listened to such a story this morning of brutal self-seeking! He has wounded men. He will kill them unless we can prevent him. He will create a panic. Nothing can stop him. He is going out now – furious!'

'He must be caught,' said Adye. 'That is certain.'

'But how?' cried Kemp, and suddenly became full of ideas. 'You must begin at once. You must set every available man to work; you must prevent his leaving this district. Once he gets away, he may go through the countryside as he wills, killing and maiming. He dreams of a reign of terror! A reign of terror, I tell you. You must set a watch on trains and roads and shipping. The garrison must help. You must wire for help. The only thing that may keep him here is the thought of recovering some books of notes he counts of value. I will tell you of that! There is a man in your police station – Marvel.'

'I know,' said Adye, 'I know. Those books – yes. But the tramp . . .'

'Says he hasn't them. But he thinks the tramp has. And you must prevent him from eating or sleeping; day and night the country must be astir for him. Food must be locked up and secured, all food, so that he will have to break his way to it. The houses everywhere must be barred against him. Heaven send us cold nights and rain! The whole countryside must begin hunting and keep hunting. I tell you, Adye, he is a danger, a disaster; unless he is pinned and secured, it is frightful to think of the things that may happen.'

'What else can we do?' said Adye. 'I must go down at once and begin organizing. But why not come? Yes – you come too! Come, and we must hold a sort of council of war – get Hopps to help – and the railway managers. By Jove! it's urgent. Come along – tell me as we go. What else is there we can do? Put that stuff down.'

In another moment Adye was leading the way downstairs. They found the front door open and the policemen standing outside staring at empty air. 'He's got away, sir,' said one.

'We must go to the central station at once,' said Adye. 'One of you go on down and get a cab to come up and meet us – quickly. And now, Kemp, what else?'

'Dogs,' said Kemp. 'Get dogs. They don't see him, but they wind him. Get dogs.'

'Good,' said Adye. 'It's not generally known, but the prison officials over at Halstead know a man with bloodhounds. Dogs. What else?'

'Bear in mind,' said Kemp, 'his food shows. After eating, his food shows until it is assimilated. So that he has to hide after eating. You must keep on beating – every thicket, every quiet corner. And put all weapons, all implements that might be weapons, away. He can't carry such things for long. And what he can snatch up and strike men with must be hidden away.'

'Good again,' said Adye. 'We shall have him yet!'

'And on the roads,' said Kemp, and hesitated.

'Yes?' said Adye.

'Powdered glass,' said Kemp. 'It's cruel, I know. But think of what he may do!'

Adye drew the air in sharply between his teeth. 'It's unsportsmanlike. I don't know. But I'll have powdered glass got ready. If he goes too far—'

'The man's become inhuman, I tell you,' said Kemp. 'I am as sure he will establish a reign of terror – so soon as he has got over the emotions of this escape – as I am sure I am talking to you. Our only chance is to be ahead. He has cut himself off from his kind. His blood be upon his own head.'

CHAPTER XXVI

The Wicksteed Murder

The Invisible Man seems to have rushed out of Kemp's house in a state of blind fury. A little child playing near Kemp's gateway was violently caught up and thrown aside, so that its ankle was broken, and thereafter for some hours the Invisible Man passed out of human perceptions. No one knows where he went nor what he did. But one can imagine him hurrying through the hot June forenoon, up the hill and on to the open downland behind Port Burdock, raging and despairing at his intolerable fate, and sheltering at last, heated and weary, amid the thickets of Hintondean, to piece together again his shattered schemes against his species. That seems the most probable refuge for him, for there it was he reasserted himself in a grimly tragical manner about two in the afternoon.

One wonders what his state of mind may have been during that time, and what plans he devised. No doubt he was almost ecstatically exasperated by Kemp's treachery, and though we may be able to understand the motives that led to that deceit, we may still imagine and even sympathize a little with the fury the attempted surprise must have occasioned. Perhaps something of the stunned astonishment of his Oxford Street experiences may have returned to him, for he had evidently counted on Kemp's co-operation in his brutal dream of a terrorized world. At any rate he vanished from human ken about midday, and no living witness can tell what he did until about half-past two. It was a fortunate thing, perhaps, for humanity, but for him it was a fatal inaction.

During that time a growing multitude of men scattered over the countryside were busy. In the morning he had still been simply a legend, a terror; in the afternoon, by virtue chiefly of Kemp's drily worded proclamation, he was presented as a tangible antagonist, to be wounded, captured, or overcome, and the countryside began organizing itself with inconceivable rapidity. By two o'clock even he might still have removed himself out of the district by getting aboard a train, but after two that became impossible. Every passenger train along the lines on a great parallelogram between Southampton, Manchester, Brighton, and Horsham, travelled with locked doors, and the goods traffic was almost entirely suspended. And in a great circle of twenty miles round Port Burdock, men armed with guns and bludgeons were presently setting out in groups of three and four, with dogs, to beat the roads and fields.

Mounted policemen rode along the country lanes, stopping at every cottage and warning the people to lock up their houses, and keep indoors

unless they were armed, and all the elementary schools had broken up by three o'clock, and the children, scared and keeping together in groups, were hurrying home. Kemp's proclamation – signed indeed by Adye – was posted over almost the whole district by four or five o'clock in the afternoon. It gave briefly but clearly all the conditions of the struggle, the necessity of keeping the Invisible Man from food and sleep, the necessity for incessant watchfulness and for a prompt attention to any evidence of his movements. And so swift and decided was the action of the authorities, so prompt and universal was the belief in this strange being, that before nightfall an area of several hundred square miles was in a stringent state of siege. And before nightfall, too, a thrill of horror went through the whole watching nervous countryside. Going from whispering mouth to mouth, swift and certain over the length and breadth of the country, passed the story of the murder of Mr Wicksteed.

If our supposition that the Invisible Man's refuge was the Hintondean thickets, then we must suppose that in the early afternoon he sallied out again bent upon some project that involved the use of a weapon. We cannot know what the project was, but the evidence that he had the iron rod in hand before he met Wicksteed is to me at least overwhelming.

Of course we can know nothing of the details of that encounter. It occurred on the edge of a gravel pit, not two hundred yards from Lord Burdock's lodge gate. Everything points to a desperate struggle – the trampled ground, the numerous wounds Mr Wicksteed received, his splintered walking-stick; but why the attack was made, save in a murderous frenzy, it is impossible to imagine. Indeed the theory of madness is almost unavoidable. Mr Wicksteed was a man of forty-five or forty-six, steward to Lord Burdock, of inoffensive habits and appearance, the very last person in the world to provoke such a terrible antagonist. Against him it would seem the Invisible Man used an iron rod dragged from a broken piece of fence. He stopped this quiet man, going quietly home to his midday meal, attacked him, beat down his feeble defences, broke his arm, felled him, and smashed his head to a jelly.

Of course, he must have dragged this rod out of the fencing before he met his victim; he must have been carrying it ready in his hand. Only two details beyond what has already been stated seem to bear on the matter. One is the circumstance that the gravel pit was not in Mr Wicksteed's direct path home, but nearly a couple of hundred yards out of his way. The other is the assertion of a little girl to the effect that, going to her afternoon school, she saw the murdered man *trotting* in a peculiar manner across a field towards the gravel pit. Her pantomime of his action suggests a man pursuing something on the ground before him and striking at it ever and again with his walking-stick. She was the last person to see him alive. He passed out of her sight to his death, the struggle being hidden

from her only by a clump of beech trees and a slight depression in the ground.

Now this, to the present writer's mind at least, lifts the murder out of the realm of the absolutely wanton. We may imagine that Griffin had taken the rod as a weapon indeed, but without any deliberate intention of using it in murder. Wicksteed may then have come by and noticed this rod inexplicably moving through the air. Without any thought of the Invisible Man – for Port Burdock is ten miles away – he may have pursued it. It is quite conceivable that he may not even have heard of the Invisible Man. One can then imagine the Invisible Man making off – quietly in order to avoid discovering his presence in the neighbourhood, and Wicksteed, excited and curious, pursuing this unaccountably locomotive object – finally striking at it.

No doubt the Invisible Man could easily have distanced his middle-aged pursuer under ordinary circumstances, but the position in which Wicksteed's body was found suggests that he had the ill luck to drive his quarry into a corner between a drift of stinging nettles and the gravel pit. To those who appreciate the extraordinary irascibility of the Invisible Man, the rest of the encounter will be easy to imagine.

But this is pure hypothesis. The only undeniable facts – for stories of children are often unreliable – are the discovery of Wicksteed's body, done to death, and of the blood-stained iron rod flung among the nettles. The abandonment of the rod by Griffin, suggests that in the emotional excitement of the affair, the purpose for which he took it – if he had a purpose – was abandoned. He was certainly an intensely egotistical and unfeeling man, but the sight of his victim, his first victim, bloody and pitiful at his feet, may have released some long pent fountain of remorse which for a time may have flooded whatever scheme of action he had contrived.

After the murder of Mr Wicksteed, he would seem to have struck across the country towards the downland. There is a story of a voice heard about sunset by a couple of men in a field near Fern Bottom. It was wailing and laughing, sobbing and groaning, and ever and again it shouted. It must have been queer hearing. It drove up across the middle of a clover field and died away towards the hills.

That afternoon the Invisible Man must have learnt something of the rapid use Kemp had made of his confidences. He must have found houses locked and secured; he may have loitered about railway stations and prowled about inns, and no doubt he read the proclamations and realized something of the nature of the campaign against him. And as the evening advanced, the fields became dotted here and there with groups of three or four men, and noisy with the yelping of dogs. These men-hunters had particular instructions in the case of an encounter as to the way they should support one another. But he avoided them all. We may understand something of his

exasperation, and it could have been none the less because he himself had
supplied the information that was being used so remorselessly against him.
For that day at least he lost heart; for nearly twenty-four hours, save when
he turned on Wicksteed, he was a hunted man. In the night, he must have
eaten and slept; for in the morning he was himself again, active, powerful,
angry, and malignant, prepared for his last great struggle against the world.

CHAPTER XXVII

The Siege of Kemp's House

Kemp read a strange missive, written in pencil on a greasy sheet of paper.

'You have been amazingly energetic and clever,' this letter ran, 'though what you stand to gain by it I cannot imagine. You are against me. For a whole day you have chased me; you have tried to rob me of a night's rest. But I have had food in spite of you, I have slept in spite of you, and the game is only beginning. The game is only beginning. There is nothing for it, but to start the Terror. This announces the first day of the Terror. Port Burdock is no longer under the Queen, tell your Colonel of Police, and the rest of them; it is under me – the Terror! This is day one of year one of the new epoch – the Epoch of the Invisible Man. I am Invisible Man the First. To begin with the rule will be easy. The first day there will be one execution for the sake of example – a man named Kemp. Death starts for him today. He may lock himself away, hide himself away, get guards about him, put on armour if he likes – Death, the unseen Death, is coming. Let him take precautions; it will impress my people. Death starts from the pillar box by midday. The letter will fall in as the postman comes along, then off! The game begins. Death starts. Help him not, my people, lest Death fall upon you also. Today Kemp is to die.'

Kemp read this letter twice, 'It's no hoax,' he said. 'That's his voice! And he means it.'

He turned the folded sheet over and saw on the addressed side of it the postmark Hintondean, and the prosaic detail '*2d. to pay*.'

He got up slowly, leaving his lunch unfinished – the letter had come by the one o'clock post – and went into his study. He rang for his housekeeper, and told her to go round the house at once, examine all the fastenings of the windows, and close all the shutters. He closed the shutters of his study himself. From a locked drawer in his bedroom he took a little revolver, examined it carefully, and put it into the pocket of his lounge jacket. He wrote a number of brief notes, one to Colonel Adye, gave them to his servant to take, with explicit instructions as to her way of leaving the house. 'There is no danger,' he said, and added a mental reservation, 'to you.' He remained meditative for a space after doing this, and then returned to his cooling lunch.

He ate with gaps of thought. Finally he struck the table sharply. 'We will have him!' he said; 'and I am the bait. He will come too far.'

He went up to the belvedere, carefully shutting every door after him. 'It's a game,' he said, 'an odd game – but the chances are all for me, Mr Griffin, in spite of your invisibility. Griffin *contra mundum* – with a vengeance.'

He stood at the window staring at the hot hillside. 'He must get food every day – and I don't envy him. Did he really sleep last night? Out in the open somewhere – secure from collisions. I wish we could get some good cold wet weather instead of the heat.'

'He may be watching me now.'

He went close to the window. Something rapped smartly against the brickwork over the frame, and made him start violently back.

'I'm getting nervous,' said Kemp. But it was five minutes before he went to the window again. 'It must have been a sparrow,' he said.

Presently he heard the front-door bell ringing, and hurried downstairs. He unbolted and unlocked the door, examined the chain, put it up, and opened cautiously without showing himself. A familiar voice hailed him. It was Adye.

'Your servant's been assaulted, Kemp,' he said round the door.

'What!' exclaimed Kemp.

'Had that note of yours taken away from her. He's close about here. Let me in.'

Kemp released the chain, and Adye entered through as narrow an opening as possible. He stood in the hall, looking with infinite relief at Kemp refastening the door. 'Note was snatched out of her hand. Scared her horribly. She's down at the station. Hysterics. He's close here. What was it about?'

Kemp swore.

'What a fool I was,' said Kemp. 'I might have known. It's not an hour's walk from Hintondean. Already?'

'What's up?' said Adye.

'Look here!' said Kemp, and led the way into his study. He handed Adye the Invisible Man's letter. Adye read it and whistled softly. 'And you—?' said Adye.

'Proposed a trap – like a fool,' said Kemp, 'and sent my proposal out by a maid servant. To him.'

Adye followed Kemp's profanity.

'He'll clear out,' said Adye.

'Not he,' said Kemp.

A resounding smash of glass came from upstairs. Adye had a silvery glimpse of a little revolver half out of Kemp's pocket. 'It's a window, upstairs!' said Kemp, and led the way up. There came a second smash while they were still on the staircase. When they reached the study they found two of the three windows smashed, half the room littered with splintered glass, and one big flint lying on the writing table. The two men stopped in the doorway, contemplating the wreckage. Kemp swore again, and as he did so the third window went with a snap like a pistol, hung starred for a moment, and collapsed in jagged, shivering triangles into the room.

'What's this for?' said Adye.

'It's a beginning,' said Kemp.

'There's no way of climbing up here?'

'Not for a cat,' said Kemp.

'No shutters?'

'Not here. All the downstairs rooms – Hullo!'

Smash, and then whack of boards hit hard came from downstairs. 'Confound him!' said Kemp. 'That must be – yes – it's one of the bedrooms. He's going to do all the house. But he's a fool. The shutters are up, and the glass will fall outside. He'll cut his feet.'

Another window proclaimed its destruction. The two men stood on the landing perplexed. 'I have it!' said Adye. 'Let me have a stick or something, and I'll go down to the station and get the bloodhounds put on. That ought to settle him! They're hard by – not ten minutes—'

Another window went the way of its fellows.

'You haven't a revolver?' asked Adye.

Kemp's hand went to his pocket. Then he hesitated. 'I haven't one – at least to spare.'

'I'll bring it back,' said Adye, 'you'll be safe here.'

Kemp, ashamed of his momentary lapse from truthfulness, handed him the weapon.

'Now for the door,' said Adye.

As they stood hesitating in the hall, they heard one of the first-floor bedroom windows crack and clash. Kemp went to the door and began to slip the bolts as silently as possible. His face was a little paler than usual. 'You must step straight out,' said Kemp. In another moment Adye was on the doorstep and the bolts were dropping back into the staples. He hesitated for a moment, feeling more comfortable with his back against the door. Then he marched, upright and square, down the steps. He crossed the lawn and approached the gate. A little breeze seemed to ripple over the grass. Something moved near him. 'Stop a bit,' said a Voice, and Adye stopped dead and his hand tightened on the revolver.

'Well?' said Adye, white and grim, and every nerve tense.

'Oblige me by going back to the house,' said the Voice, as tense and grim as Adye's.

'Sorry,' said Adye a little hoarsely, and moistened his lips with his tongue. The Voice was on his left front, he thought. Suppose he were to take his luck with a shot?

'What are you going for?' said the Voice, and there was a quick movement of the two, and a flash of sunlight from the open lip of Adye's pocket.

Adye desisted and thought. 'Where I go,' he said slowly, 'is my own business.' The words were still on his lips, when an arm came round his neck, his back felt a knee, and he was sprawling backward. He drew clumsily and fired absurdly, and in another moment he was struck in the mouth

and the revolver wrested from his grip. He made a vain clutch at a slippery limb, tried to struggle up and fell back. 'Damn!' said Adye. The Voice laughed. 'I'd kill you now if it wasn't the waste of a bullet,' it said. He saw the revolver in mid-air, six feet off, covering him.

'Well?' said Adye, sitting up.

'Get up,' said the Voice.

Adye stood up.

'Attention,' said the Voice, and then fiercely, 'Don't try any games. Remember I can see your face if you can't see mine. You've got to go back to the house.'

'He won't let me in,' said Adye.

'That's a pity,' said the Invisible Man. 'I've got no quarrel with you.'

Adye moistened his lips again. He glanced away from the barrel of the revolver and saw the sea far off very blue and dark under the midday sun, the smooth green down, the white cliff of the Head, and the multitudinous town, and suddenly he knew that life was very sweet. His eyes came back to this little metal thing hanging between heaven and earth, six yards away. 'What am I to do?' he said sullenly.

'What am I to do?' asked the Invisible Man. 'You will get help. The only thing is for you to go back.'

'I will try. If he lets me in will you promise not to rush the door?'

'I've got no quarrel with you,' said the Voice.

Kemp had hurried upstairs after letting Adye out, and now crouching among the broken glass and peering cautiously over the edge of the study window sill, he saw Adye stand parleying with the Unseen. 'Why doesn't he fire?' whispered Kemp to himself. Then the revolver moved a little and the glint of the sunlight flashed in Kemp's eyes. He shaded his eyes and tried to see the source of the blinding beam.

'Surely!' he said, 'Adye has given up the revolver.'

'Promise not to rush the door,' Adye was saying. 'Don't push a winning game too far. Give a man a chance.'

'You go back to the house. I tell you flatly I will not promise anything.'

Adye's decision seemed suddenly made. He turned towards the house, walking slowly with his hands behind him. Kemp watched him – puzzled. The revolver vanished, flashed again into sight, vanished again, and became evident on a closer scrutiny as a little dark object following Adye. Then things happened very quickly. Adye leapt backwards, swung around, clutched at this little object, missed it, threw up his hands and fell forward on his face, leaving a little puff of blue in the air. Kemp did not hear the sound of the shot. Adye writhed, raised himself on one arm, fell forward, and lay still.

For a space Kemp remained staring at the quiet carelessness of Adye's attitude. The afternoon was very hot and still, nothing seemed stirring in all the world save a couple of yellow butterflies chasing each other through

the shrubbery between the house and the road gate. Adye lay on the lawn near the gate. The blinds of all the villas down the hill road were drawn, but in one little green summer-house was a white figure, apparently an old man asleep. Kemp scrutinized the surroundings of the house for a glimpse of the revolver, but it had vanished. His eyes came back to Adye. The game was opening well.

Then came a ringing and knocking at the front door, that grew at last tumultuous, but pursuant to Kemp's instructions the servants had locked themselves into their rooms. This was followed by a silence. Kemp sat listening and then began peering cautiously out of the three windows, one after another. He went to the staircase head and stood listening uneasily. He armed himself with his bedroom poker, and went to examine the interior fastenings of the ground-floor windows again. Everything was safe and quiet. He returned to the belvedere. Adye lay motionless over the edge of the gravel just as he had fallen. Coming along the road by the villas were the housemaid and two policemen.

Everything was deadly still. The three people seemed very slow in approaching. He wondered what his antagonist was doing.

He started. There was a smash from below. He hesitated and went downstairs again. Suddenly the house resounded with heavy blows and the splintering of wood. He heard a smash and the destructive clang of the iron fastenings of the shutters. He turned the key and opened the kitchen door. As he did so, the shutters, split and splintering, came flying inward. He stood aghast. The window frame, save for one crossbar, was still intact, but only little teeth of glass remained in the frame. The shutters had been driven in with an axe, and now the axe was descending in sweeping blows upon the window frame and the iron bars defending it. Then suddenly it leapt aside and vanished. He saw the revolver lying on the path outside, and then the little weapon sprang into the air. He dodged back. The revolver cracked just too late, and a splinter from the edge of the closing door flashed over his head. He slammed and locked the door, and as he stood outside he heard Griffin shouting and laughing. Then the blows of the axe with its splitting and smashing consequences, were resumed.

Kemp stood in the passage trying to think. In a moment the Invisible Man would be in the kitchen. This door would not keep him a moment, and then –

A ringing came at the front door again. It would be the policemen. He ran into the hall, put up the chain, and drew the bolts. He made the girl speak before he dropped the chain, and the three people blundered into the house in a heap, and Kemp slammed the door again.

'The Invisible Man!' said Kemp. 'He has a revolver, with two shots – left. He's killed Adye. Shot him anyhow. Didn't you see him on the lawn? He's lying there.'

'Who?' said one of the policemen.

'Adye,' said Kemp.

'We came in the back way,' said the girl.

'What's that smashing?' asked one of the policemen.

'He's in the kitchen – or will be. He has found an axe—'

Suddenly the house was full of the Invisible Man's resounding blows on the kitchen door. The girl stared towards the kitchen, shuddered, and retreated into the dining-room. Kemp tried to explain in broken sentences. They heard the kitchen door give.

'This way,' said Kemp, starting into activity, and bundled the policemen into the dining-room doorway.

'Poker,' said Kemp, and rushed to the fender. He handed the poker he had carried to the policeman and the dining-room one to the other. He suddenly flung himself backward.

'Whup!' said one policeman, ducked, and caught the axe on his poker. The pistol snapped its penultimate shot and ripped a valuable Sidney Cooper. The second policeman brought his poker down on the little weapon, as one might knock down a wasp, and sent it rattling to the floor.

At the first clash the girl screamed, stood screaming for a moment by the fireplace, and then ran to open the shutters – possibly with an idea of escaping by the shattered window.

The axe receded into the passage, and fell to a position about two feet from the ground. They could hear the Invisible Man breathing. 'Stand away, you two,' he said. 'I want that man Kemp.'

'We want you,' said the first policeman, making a quick step forward and wiping with his poker at the Voice. The Invisible Man must have started back, and he blundered into the umbrella stand.

Then, as the policeman staggered with the swing of the blow he had aimed, the Invisible Man countered with the axe, the helmet crumpled like paper, and the blow sent the man spinning to the floor at the head of the kitchen stairs. But the second policeman, aiming behind the axe with his poker, hit something soft that snapped. There was a sharp exclamation of pain and then the axe fell to the ground. The policeman wiped again at vacancy and hit nothing; he put his foot on the axe, and struck again. Then he stood, poker clubbed, listening intent for the slightest movement.

He heard the dining-room window open, and a quick rush of feet within. His companion rolled over and sat up, with the blood running down between his eye and ear. 'Where is he?' asked the man on the floor.

'Don't know. I've hit him. He's standing somewhere in the hall. Unless he's slipped past you. Doctor Kemp – sir.'

Pause.

'Doctor Kemp,' cried the policeman again.

The second policeman began struggling to his feet. He stood up. Suddenly the faint pad of bare feet on the kitchen stairs could be heard. 'Yap!' cried the first policeman, and incontinently flung his poker. It smashed a little gas bracket.

He made as if he would pursue the Invisible Man downstairs. Then he thought better of it and stepped into the dining-room.

'Doctor Kemp—' he began, and stopped short.

'Doctor Kemp's a hero,' he said, as his companion looked over his shoulder.

The dining-room window was wide open, and neither housemaid nor Kemp was to be seen.

The second policeman's opinion of Kemp was terse and vivid.

CHAPTER XXVIII

The Hunter Hunted

Mr Heelas, Mr Kemp's nearest neighbour among the villa holders, was asleep in his summer-house when the siege of Kemp's house began. Mr Heelas was one of the sturdy minority who refused to believe 'in all this nonsense' about an Invisible Man. His wife, however, as he was subsequently to be reminded, did. He insisted upon walking about his garden just as if nothing was the matter, and he went to sleep in the afternoon in accordance with the custom of years. He slept through the smashing of the windows, and then woke up suddenly with a curious persuasion of something wrong. He looked across at Kemp's house, rubbed his eyes and looked again. Then he put his feet to the ground, and sat listening. He said he was damned, but still the strange thing was visible. The house looked as though it had been deserted for weeks – after a violent riot. Every window was broken, and every window, save those of the belvedere study, was blinded by the internal shutters.

'I could have sworn it was all right' – he looked at his watch – 'twenty minutes ago.'

He became aware of a measured concussion and the clash of glass, far away in the distance. And then, as he sat open-mouthed, came a still more wonderful thing. The shutters of the drawing-room window were flung open violently, and the housemaid in her outdoor hat and garments, appeared struggling in a frantic manner to throw up the sash. Suddenly a man appeared beside her, helping her – Doctor Kemp! In another moment the window was open, and the housemaid was struggling out; she pitched forward and vanished among the shrubs. Mr Heelas stood up, exclaiming vaguely and vehemently at all these wonderful things. He saw Kemp stand on the sill, spring from the window, and reappear almost instantaneously running along a path in the shrubbery and stooping as he ran, like a man who evades observation. He vanished behind a laburnum, and appeared again clambering over a fence that abutted on the open down. In a second he had tumbled over and was running at a tremendous pace down the slope towards Mr Heelas.

'Lord!' cried Mr Heelas, struck with an idea; 'it's that Invisible Man brute! It's right, after all!'

With Mr Heelas to think things like that was to act, and his cook watching him from the top window was amazed to see him come pelting towards the house at a good nine miles an hour. 'Thought he wasn't afraid,' said the cook. 'Mary, just come here!' There was a slamming of doors, a ringing of bells, and the voice of Mr Heelas bellowing like a bull. 'Shut the doors, shut

the windows, shut everything! – the Invisible Man is coming!' Instantly the house was full of screams and directions, and scurrying feet. He ran himself to shut the French windows that opened on the verandah; as he did so Kemp's head and shoulders and knee appeared over the edge of the garden fence. In another moment Kemp had ploughed through the asparagus, and was running across the tennis lawn to the house.

'You can't come in,' said Mr Heelas, shutting the bolts. 'I'm very sorry if he's after you, but you can't come in!'

Kemp appeared with a face of terror close to the glass, rapping and then shaking frantically at the French window. Then, seeing his efforts were useless, he ran along the verandah, vaulted the end, and went to hammer at the side door. Then he ran round by the side gate to the front of the house, and so into the hill road. And Mr Heelas staring from his window – a face of horror – had scarcely witnessed Kemp vanish, ere the asparagus was being trampled this way and that by feet unseen. At that Mr Heelas fled precipitately upstairs, and the rest of the chase is beyond his purview. But as he passed the staircase window, he heard the side gate slam.

Emerging into the hill road, Kemp naturally took the downward direction, and so it was he came to run in his own person the very race he had watched with such a critical eye from the belvedere study only four days ago. He ran it well, for a man out of training, and though his face was white and wet, his wits were cool to the last. He ran with wide strides, and wherever a patch of rough ground intervened, wherever there came a patch of raw flints, or a bit of broken glass shone dazzling, he crossed it and left the bare invisible feet that followed to take what line they would.

For the first time in his life Kemp discovered that the hill road was indescribably vast and desolate, and that the beginnings of the town far below at the hill foot were strangely remote. Never had there been a slower or more painful method of progression than running. All the gaunt villas, sleeping in the afternoon sun, looked locked and barred; no doubt they were locked and barred – by his own orders. But at any rate they might have kept a lookout for an eventuality like this! The town was rising up now, the sea had dropped out of sight behind it, and people down below were stirring. A tram was just arriving at the hill foot. Beyond that was the police station. Was that footsteps he heard behind him? Spurt.

The people below were staring at him, one or two were running, and his breath was beginning to saw in his throat. The tram was quite near now, and the Jolly Cricketers was noisily barring its doors. Beyond the tram were posts and heaps of gravel – the drainage works. He had a transitory idea of jumping into the tram and slamming the doors, and then he resolved to go for the police station. In another moment he had passed the door of the Jolly Cricketers, and was in the blistering fag end of the street, with human beings about him. The tram driver and his helper – arrested by the

sight of his furious haste – stood staring with the tram horses unhitched. Further on the astonished features of navvies appeared above the mounds of gravel.

His pace broke a little, and then he heard the swift pad of his pursuer, and leapt forward again. 'The Invisible Man!' he cried to the navvies, with a vague indicative gesture, and by an inspiration leapt the excavation and placed a burly group between him and the chase. Then abandoning the idea of the police station he turned into a little side street, rushed by a green-grocer's cart, hesitated for the tenth of a second at the door of a sweetstuff shop, and then made for the mouth of an alley that ran back into the main Hill Street again. Two or three little children were playing here, and shrieked and scattered at his apparition, and forthwith doors and windows opened and excited mothers revealed their hearts. Out he shot into Hill Street again, three hundred yards from the tram-line end, and immediately he became aware of a tumultuous vociferation and running people.

He glanced up the street towards the hill. Hardly a dozen yards off ran a huge navvy, cursing in fragments and slashing viciously with a spade, and hard behind him came the tram conductor with his fists clenched. Up the street others followed these two, striking and shouting. Down towards the town, men and women were running, and he noticed clearly one man coming out of a shop-door with a stick in his hand. 'Spread out! Spread out!' cried someone. Kemp suddenly grasped the altered condition of the chase. He stopped, and looked round, panting. 'He's close here!' he cried. 'Form a line across—'

'Aha!' shouted a voice.

He was hit hard under the ear, and went reeling, trying to face round towards his unseen antagonist. He just managed to keep his feet, and he struck a vain counter in the air. Then he was hit again under the jaw, and sprawled headlong on the ground. In another moment a knee compressed his diaphragm, and a couple of eager hands gripped his throat, but the grip of one was weaker than the other; he grasped the wrists, heard a cry of pain from his assailant, and then the spade of the navvy came whirling through the air above him, and struck something with a dull thud. He felt a drop of moisture on his face. The grip at his throat suddenly relaxed, and with a convulsive effort, Kemp loosed himself, grasped a limp shoulder, and rolled uppermost. He gripped the unseen elbows near the ground. 'I've got him!' screamed Kemp. 'Help! Help hold! He's down! Hold his feet!'

In another second there was a simultaneous rush upon the struggle, and a stranger coming into the road suddenly might have thought an exception-ally savage game of rugby football was in progress. And there was no shouting after Kemp's cry – only a sound of blows and feet and heavy breathing.

Then came a mighty effort, and the Invisible Man threw off a couple of his antagonists and rose to his knees. Kemp clung to him in front like a

hound to a stag, and a dozen hands gripped, clutched, and tore at the Unseen. The tram conductor suddenly got the neck and shoulders and lugged him back.

Down went the heap of struggling men again and rolled over. There was, I am afraid, some savage kicking. Then suddenly a wild scream of 'Mercy! Mercy!' that died down swiftly to a sound like choking.

'Get back, you fools!' cried the muffled voice of Kemp, and there was a vigorous shoving back of stalwart forms. 'He's hurt, I tell you. Stand back!'

There was a brief struggle to clear a space, and then the circle of eager faces saw the doctor kneeling, as it seemed, fifteen inches in the air, and holding invisible arms to the ground. Behind him a constable gripped invisible ankles.

'Don't you leave go of en,' cried the big navvy, holding a blood-stained spade; 'he's shamming.'

'He's not shamming,' said the doctor, cautiously raising his knee; 'and I'll hold him.' His face was bruised and already going red; he spoke thickly because of a bleeding lip. He released one hand and seemed to be feeling at the face. 'The mouth's all wet,' he said. And then, 'Good God!'

He stood up abruptly and then knelt down on the ground by the side of the thing unseen. There was a pushing and shuffling, a sound of heavy feet as fresh people turned up to increase the pressure of the crowd. People now were coming out of the houses. The doors of the Jolly Cricketers stood suddenly wide open. Very little was said.

Kemp felt about, his hand seeming to pass through empty air. 'He's not breathing,' he said, and then, 'I can't feel his heart. His side – ugh!'

Suddenly an old woman, peering under the arm of the big navvy, screamed sharply. 'Looky there!' she said, and thrust out a wrinkled finger.

And looking where she pointed, everyone saw, faint and transparent as though it was made of glass, so that veins and arteries and bones and nerves could be distinguished, the outline of a hand, a hand limp and prone. It grew clouded and opaque even as they stared.

'Hullo!' cried the constable. 'Here's his feet a-showing!'

And so, slowly, beginning at his hands and feet and creeping along his limbs to the vital centres of his body, that strange change continued. It was like the slow spreading of a poison. First came the little white nerves, a hazy grey sketch of a limb, then the glassy bones and intricate arteries, then the flesh and skin, first a faint fogginess, and then growing rapidly dense and opaque. Presently they could see his crushed chest and his shoulders, and the dim outline of his drawn and battered features.

When at last the crowd made way for Kemp to stand erect, there lay, naked and pitiful on the ground, the bruised and broken body of a young man about thirty. His hair and brow were white – not grey with age, but white with the whiteness of albinism, and his eyes were like garnets. His

hands were clenched, his eyes wide open, and his expression was one of anger and dismay.

'Cover his face!' said a man. 'For Gawd's sake, cover that face!' and three little children, pushing forward through the crowd, were suddenly twisted round and sent packing off again.

Someone brought a sheet from the Jolly Cricketers, and having covered him, they carried him into that house. And there it was, on a shabby bed in a tawdry, ill-lighted bedroom, surrounded by a crowd of ignorant and excited people, broken and wounded, betrayed and unpitied, that Griffin, the first of all men to make himself invisible, Griffin, the most gifted physicist the world has ever seen, ended in infinite disaster his strange and terrible career.

THE EPILOGUE

So ends the story of the strange and evil experiments of the Invisible Man.
And if you would learn more of him you must go to a little inn near Port
Stowe and talk to the landlord. The sign of the inn is an empty board save
for a hat and boots, and the name is the title of this story. The landlord is
a short and corpulent little man with a nose of cylindrical proportions, wiry
hair, and a sporadic rosiness of visage. Drink generously, and he will tell you
generously of all the things that happened to him after that time, and of
how the lawyers tried to do him out of the treasure found upon him.

'When they found they couldn't prove whose money was which, I'm
blessed,' he says, 'if they didn't try to make me out a blooming treasure
trove! Do I *look* like a Treasure Trove? And then a gentleman gave me a
guinea a night to tell the story at the Empire Music 'All – just to tell 'em
in my own words – barring one.'

And if you want to cut off the flow of his reminiscences abruptly, you
can always do so by asking if there weren't three manuscript books in the
story. He admits there were and proceeds to explain, with asseverations that
everybody thinks *he* has 'em! But bless you! he hasn't. 'The Invisible Man
it was took 'em off to hide 'em when I cut and ran for Port Stowe. It's that
Doctor Kemp put people on with the idea of *my* having 'em.'

And then he subsides into a pensive state, watches you furtively, bustles
nervously with glasses, and presently leaves the bar.

He is a bachelor man – his tastes were ever bachelor, and there are no
women folk in the house. Outwardly he buttons – it is expected of him
– but in his more vital privacies, in the matter of braces for example, he
still turns to string. He conducts his house without enterprise, but with
eminent decorum. His movements are slow, and he is a great thinker. But
he has a reputation for wisdom and for a respectable parsimony in the
village, and his knowledge of the roads of the South of England would
beat Cobbett.

And on Sunday mornings, every Sunday morning, all the year round,
while he is closed to the outer world, and every night after ten, he goes into
his bar parlour, bearing a glass of gin faintly tinged with water, and having
placed this down, he locks the door and examines the blinds, and even looks
under the table. And then, being satisfied of his solitude, he unlocks the
cupboard and a box in the cupboard and a drawer in that box, and produces
three volumes bound in brown leather, and places them solemnly in the
middle of the table. The covers are weather-worn and tinged with an algal
green – for once they sojourned in a ditch and some of the pages have been
washed blank by dirty water. The landlord sits down in an armchair, fills a
long clay pipe slowly – gloating over the books the while. Then he pulls one

towards him and opens it, and begins to study it – turning over the leaves backwards and forwards.

His brows are knit and his lips move painfully. 'Hex, little two up in the air, cross and a fiddle-de-dee. Lord! what a one he was for intellect!'

Presently he relaxes and leans back, and blinks through his smoke across the room at things invisible to other eyes. 'Full of secrets,' he says. 'Wonderful secrets!'

'Once I get the haul of them – *Lord!*'

'I wouldn't do what *he* did; I'd just – well!' He pulls at his pipe.

So he lapses into a dream, the undying wonderful dream of his life. And though Kemp has fished unceasingly, no human being save the landlord knows those books are there, with the subtle secret of invisibility and a dozen other strange secrets written therein. And none other will know of them until he dies.

THE
TIME MACHINE

CONTENTS

CHAPTER I

The Time Traveller (for so it will be convenient to speak of him) was expounding a recondite matter to us. His grey eyes shone and twinkled, and his usually pale face was flushed and animated. The fire burned brightly, and the soft radiance of the incandescent lights in the lilies of silver caught the bubbles that flashed and passed in our glasses. Our chairs, being his patents, embraced and caressed us rather than submitted to be sat upon, and there was that luxurious after-dinner atmosphere when thought roams gracefully free of the trammels of precision. And he put it to us in this way – marking the points with a lean forefinger – as we sat and lazily admired his earnestness over this new paradox (as we thought it) and his fecundity.

'You must follow me carefully. I shall have to controvert one or two ideas that are almost universally accepted. The geometry, for instance, they taught you at school is founded on a misconception.'

'Is not that rather a large thing to expect us to begin upon?' said Filby, an argumentative person with red hair.

'I do not mean to ask you to accept anything without reasonable ground for it. You will soon admit as much as I need from you. You know of course that a mathematical line, a line of thickness *nil*, has no real existence. They taught you that? Neither has a mathematical plane. These things are mere abstractions.'

'That is all right,' said the Psychologist.

'Nor, having only length, breadth and thickness, can a cube have a real existence.'

'There I object,' said Filby. 'Of course a solid body may exist. All real things—'

'So most people think. But wait a moment. Can an *instantaneous* cube exist?'

'Don't follow you,' said Filby.

'Can a cube that does not last for any time at all, have a real existence?'

Filby became pensive. 'Clearly,' the Time Traveller proceeded, 'any real body must have extension in *four* directions: it must have Length, Breadth, Thickness and – Duration. But through a natural infirmity of the flesh, which I will explain to you in a moment, we incline to overlook this fact. There are really four dimensions, three which we call the three planes of Space, and a fourth, Time. There is, however, a tendency to draw an unreal distinction between the former three dimensions and the latter, because it happens that our consciousness moves intermittently in one direction along the latter from the beginning to the end of our lives.'

'That,' said a very young man, making spasmodic efforts to relight his cigar over the lamp; 'that . . . very clear indeed.'

'Now, it is very remarkable that this is so extensively overlooked,' continued the Time Traveller, with a slight accession of cheerfulness. 'Really this is what is meant by the Fourth Dimension, though some people who talk about the Fourth Dimension do not know they mean it. It is only another way of looking at Time. *There is no difference between Time and any of the three dimensions of Space except that our consciousness moves along it.* But some foolish people have got hold of the wrong side of that idea. You have all heard what they have to say about this Fourth Dimension?'

'I have not,' said the Provincial Mayor.

'It is simply this. That Space, as our mathematicians have it, is spoken of as having three dimensions, which one may call Length, Breadth and Thickness, and is always definable by reference to three planes, each at right angles to the others. But some philosophical people have been asking why *three* dimensions particularly – why not another direction at right angles to the other three? – and have even tried to construct a Four-Dimension geometry. Professor Simon Newcomb was expounding this to the New York Mathematical Society only a month or so ago. You know how on a flat surface, which has only two dimensions, we can represent a figure of a Three-Dimensional solid, and similarly they think that by models of three dimensions they could represent one of four – if they could master the perspective of the thing. See?'

'I think so,' murmured the Provincial Mayor; and, knitting his brows, he lapsed into an introspective state, his lips moving as one who repeats mystic words. 'Yes, I think I see it now,' he said after some time, brightening in a quite transitory manner.

'Well, I do not mind telling you I have been at work upon this geometry of Four Dimensions for some time. Some of my results are curious. For instance, here is a portrait of a man at eight years old, another at fifteen, another at seventeen, another at twenty-three, and so on. All these are evidently sections, as it were, Three-Dimensional representations of his Four-Dimensioned being, which is a fixed and unalterable thing.

'Scientific people,' proceeded the Time Traveller, after the pause required for the proper assimilation of this, 'know very well that Time is only a kind of Space. Here is a popular scientific diagram, a weather record. This line I trace with my finger shows the movement of the barometer. Yesterday it was so high, yesterday night it fell, then this morning it rose again, and so gently upward to here. Surely the mercury did not trace this line in any of the dimensions of Space generally recognized? But certainly it traced such a line, and that line, therefore, we must conclude was along the Time-Dimension.'

'But,' said the Medical Man, staring hard at a coal in the fire, 'if Time is really only a Fourth Dimension of Space, why is it, and why has it always been, regarded as something different? And why cannot we move in Time as we move about in the other dimensions of Space?'

The Time Traveller smiled. 'Are you so sure we can move freely in Space? Right and left we can go, backward and forward freely enough, and men always have done so. I admit we move freely in two dimensions. But how about up and down? Gravitation limits us there.'

'Not exactly,' said the Medical Man. 'There are balloons.'

'But before the balloons, save for spasmodic jumping and the inequalities of the surface, man had no freedom of vertical movement.'

'Still they could move a little up and down,' said the Medical Man.

'Easier, far easier down than up.'

'And you cannot move at all in Time, you cannot get away from the present moment.'

'My dear sir, that is just where you are wrong. That is just where the whole world has gone wrong. We are always getting away from the present moment. Our mental existences, which are immaterial and have no dimensions, are passing along the Time-Dimension with a uniform velocity from the cradle to the grave. Just as we should travel *down* if we began our existence fifty miles above the earth's surface.'

'But the great difficulty is this,' interrupted the Psychologist. 'You *can* move about in all directions of Space, but you cannot move about in Time.'

'That is the germ of my great discovery. But you are wrong to say that we cannot move about in Time. For instance, if I am recalling an incident very vividly I go back to the instant of its occurrence: I become absent-minded, as you say. I jump back for a moment. Of course we have no means of staying back for any length of time, any more than a savage or an animal has of staying six feet above the ground. But a civilized man is better off than the savage in this respect. He can go up against gravitation in a balloon, and why should he not hope that ultimately he may be able to stop or accelerate his drift along the Time-Dimension, or even turn about and travel the other way?'

'Oh, *this*,' began Filby, 'is all—'

'Why not?' said the Time Traveller.

'It's against reason,' said Filby.

'What reason?' said the Time Traveller.

'You can show black is white by argument,' said Filby, 'but you will never convince me.'

'Possibly not,' said the Time Traveller. 'But now you begin to see the object of my investigations into the geometry of Four Dimensions. Long ago I had a vague inkling of a machine—'

'To travel through Time!' exclaimed the Very Young Man.

'That shall travel indifferently in any direction of Space and Time, as the driver determines.'

Filby contented himself with laughter.

'But I have experimental verification,' said the Time Traveller.

'It would be remarkably convenient for the historian,' the Psychologist suggested. 'One might travel back and verify the accepted account of the Battle of Hastings, for instance!'

'Don't you think you would attract attention?' said the Medical Man. 'Our ancestors had no great tolerance for anachronisms.'

'One might get one's Greek from the very lips of Homer and Plato,' the Very Young Man thought.

'In which case they would certainly plough you for the Little-go. The German scholars have improved Greek so much.'

'Then there is the future,' said the Very Young Man. 'Just think! One might invest all one's money, leave it to accumulate at interest, and hurry on ahead!'

'To discover a society,' said I, 'erected on a strictly communistic basis.'

'Of all the wild extravagant theories!' began the Psychologist.

'Yes, so it seemed to me, and so I never talked of it until—'

'Experimental verification!' cried I. 'You are going to verify *that?*'

'The experiment!' cried Filby, who was getting brain-weary.

'Let's see your experiment anyhow,' said the Psychologist, 'though it's all humbug, you know.'

The Time Traveller smiled round at us. Then, still smiling faintly, and with his hands deep in his trousers' pockets, he walked slowly out of the room, and we heard his slippers shuffling down the long passage to his laboratory.

The Psychologist looked at us. 'I wonder what he's got?'

'Some sleight-of-hand trick or other,' said the Medical Man, and Filby tried to tell us about a conjurer he had seen at Burslem; but before he had finished his preface the Time Traveller came back, and Filby's anecdote collapsed.

The thing the Time Traveller held in his hand was a glittering metallic framework, scarcely larger than a small clock, and very delicately made. There was ivory in it, and some transparent crystalline substance. And now I must be explicit, for this that follows – unless his explanation is to be accepted – is an absolutely unaccountable thing. He took one of the small octagonal tables that were scattered about the room, and set it in front of the fire, with two legs on the hearthrug. On this table he placed the mechanism. Then he drew up a chair, and sat down. The only other object on the table was a small shaded lamp, the bright light of which fell upon the model. There were also perhaps a dozen candles about, two in brass candlesticks upon the mantel and several in sconces, so that the room was brilliantly illuminated. I sat in a low armchair nearest the fire, and I drew this forward so as to be almost between the Time Traveller and the fireplace. Filby sat behind him, looking over his shoulder. The Medical Man and the Provincial Mayor watched him in profile from the right, the Psychologist from the left.

The Very Young Man stood behind the Psychologist. We were all on the alert. It appears incredible to me that any kind of trick, however subtly conceived and however adroitly done, could have been played upon us under these conditions.

The Time Traveller looked at us, and then at the mechanism. 'Well?' said the Psychologist.

'This little affair,' said the Time Traveller, resting his elbows upon the table and pressing his hands together above the apparatus, 'is only a model. It is my plan for a machine to travel through time. You will notice that it looks singularly askew, and that there is an odd twinkling appearance about this bar, as though it was in some way unreal.' He pointed to the part with his finger. 'Also, here is one little white lever, and here is another.'

The Medical Man got up out of his chair and peered into the thing. 'It's beautifully made,' he said.

'It took two years to make,' retorted the Time Traveller. Then, when we had all imitated the action of the Medical Man, he said: 'Now I want you clearly to understand that this lever, being pressed over, sends the machine gliding into the future, and this other reverses the motion. This saddle represents the seat of a time traveller. Presently I am going to press the lever, and off the machine will go. It will vanish, pass into future Time, and disappear. Have a good look at the thing. Look at the table too, and satisfy yourselves there is no trickery. I don't want to waste this model, and then be told I'm a quack.'

There was a minute's pause perhaps. The Psychologist seemed about to speak to me, but changed his mind. Then the Time Traveller put forth his finger towards the lever. 'No,' he said suddenly. 'Lend me your hand.' And turning to the Psychologist, he took that individual's hand in his own and told him to put out his forefinger. So that it was the Psychologist himself who sent forth the model Time Machine on its interminable voyage. We all saw the lever turn. I am absolutely certain there was no trickery. There was a breath of wind, and the lamp flame jumped. One of the candles on the mantel was blown out, and the little machine suddenly swung round, became indistinct, was seen as a ghost for a second perhaps, as an eddy of faintly glittering brass and ivory; and it was gone – vanished! Save for the lamp the table was bare.

Everyone was silent for a minute. Then Filby said he was damned.

The Psychologist recovered from his stupor, and suddenly looked under the table. At that the Time Traveller laughed cheerfully. 'Well?' he said, with a reminiscence of the Psychologist. Then, getting up, he went to the tobacco jar on the mantel, and with his back to us began to fill his pipe.

We stared at each other. 'Look here,' said the Medical Man, 'are you in earnest about this? Do you seriously believe that that machine has travelled into time?'

'Certainly,' said the Time Traveller, stooping to light a spill at the fire. Then he turned, lighting his pipe, to look at the Psychologist's face. (The Psychologist, to show that he was not unhinged, helped himself to a cigar and tried to light it uncut.) 'What is more, I have a big machine nearly finished in there' – he indicated the laboratory – 'and when that is put together I mean to have a journey on my own account.'

'You mean to say that that machine has travelled into the future?' said Filby.

'Into the future or the past – I don't, for certain, know which.'

After an interval the Psychologist had an inspiration. 'It must have gone into the past if it has gone anywhere,' he said.

'Why?' said the Time Traveller.

'Because I presume that it has not moved in space, and if it travelled into the future it would still be here all this time, since it must have travelled through this time.'

'But,' I said, 'if it travelled into the past it would have been visible when we came first into this room; and last Thursday when we were here; and the Thursday before that; and so forth!'

'Serious objections,' remarked the Provincial Mayor, with an air of impartiality, turning towards the Time Traveller.

'Not a bit,' said the Time Traveller, and, to the Psychologist: 'You think. You can explain that. It's presentation below the threshold, you know, diluted presentation.'

'Of course,' said the Psychologist, and reassured us. 'That's a simple point of psychology. I should have thought of it. It's plain enough, and helps the paradox delightfully. We cannot see it, nor can we appreciate this machine, any more than we can the spoke of a wheel spinning, or a bullet flying through the air. If it is travelling through time fifty times or a hundred times faster than we are, if it gets through a minute while we get through a second, the impression it creates will of course be only one-fiftieth or one-hundredth of what it would make if it were not travelling in time. That's plain enough.' He passed his hand through the space in which the machine had been. 'You see?' he said, laughing.

We sat and stared at the vacant table for a minute or so. Then the Time Traveller asked us what we thought of it all.

'It sounds plausible enough tonight,' said the Medical Man; 'but wait until tomorrow. Wait for the common sense of the morning.'

'Would you like to see the Time Machine itself?' asked the Time Traveller. And therewith, taking the lamp in his hand, he led the way down the long, draughty corridor to his laboratory. I remember vividly the flickering light, his queer, broad head in silhouette, the dance of the shadows, how we all followed him, puzzled but incredulous, and how there in the laboratory we beheld a larger edition of the little mechanism which we had seen vanish from before

our eyes. Parts were of nickel, parts of ivory, parts had certainly been filed or sawn out of rock crystal. The thing was generally complete, but the twisted crystalline bars lay unfinished upon the bench beside some sheets of drawings, and I took one up for a better look at it. Quartz it seemed to be.

'Look here,' said the Medical Man, 'are you perfectly serious? Or is this a trick – like that ghost you showed us last Christmas?'

'Upon that machine,' said the Time Traveller, holding the lamp aloft, 'I intend to explore time. Is that plain? I was never more serious in my life.'

None of us quite knew how to take it.

I caught Filby's eye over the shoulder of the Medical Man, and he winked at me solemnly.

CHAPTER II

I think that at that time none of us quite believed in the Time Machine. The fact is, the Time Traveller was one of those men who are too clever to be believed: you never felt that you saw all round him; you always suspected some subtle reserve, some ingenuity in ambush, behind his lucid frankness. Had Filby shown the model and explained the matter in the Time Traveller's words, we should have shown *him* far less scepticism. For we should have perceived his motives; a pork butcher could understand Filby. But the Time Traveller had more than a touch of whim among his elements, and we distrusted him. Things that would have made the fame of a less clever man seemed tricks in his hands. It is a mistake to do things too easily. The serious people who took him seriously never felt quite sure of his deportment; they were somehow aware that trusting their reputations for judgment with him was like furnishing a nursery with egg-shell china. So I don't think any of us said very much about time travelling in the interval between that Thursday and the next, though its odd potentialities ran, no doubt, in most of our minds: its plausibility, that is, its practical incredibleness, the curious possibilities of anachronism and of utter confusion it suggested. For my own part, I was particularly preoccupied with the trick of the model. That I remember discussing with the Medical Man, whom I met on Friday at the Linnaean. He said he had seen a similar thing at Tübingen, and laid considerable stress on the blowing out of the candle. But how the trick was done he could not explain.

The next Thursday I went again to Richmond – I suppose I was one of the Time Traveller's most constant guests – and, arriving late, found four or five men already assembled in his drawing-room. The Medical Man was standing before the fire with a sheet of paper in one hand and his watch in the other. I looked round for the Time Traveller, and – 'It's half-past seven now,' said the Medical Man. 'I suppose we'd better have dinner?'

'Where's—?' said I, naming our host.

'You've just come? It's rather odd. He's unavoidably detained. He asks me in this note to lead off with dinner at seven if he's not back. Says he'll explain when he comes.'

'It seems a pity to let the dinner spoil,' said the Editor of a well-known daily paper; and thereupon the Doctor rang the bell.

The Psychologist was the only person besides the Doctor and myself who had attended the previous dinner. The other men were Blank, the Editor aforementioned, a certain journalist, and another – a quiet, shy man with a beard – whom I didn't know, and who, as far as my observation went, never opened his mouth all the evening. There was some speculation at the dinner-table about the Time Traveller's absence, and I suggested time travelling, in

a half-jocular spirit. The Editor wanted that explained to him, and the Psychologist volunteered a wooden account of the 'ingenious paradox and trick' we had witnessed that day week. He was in the midst of his exposition when the door from the corridor opened slowly and without noise. I was facing the door, and saw it first. 'Hallo!' I said. 'At last!' And the door opened wider, and the Time Traveller stood before us. I gave a cry of surprise. 'Good Heavens, man, what's the matter?' cried the Medical Man, who saw him next. And the whole tableful turned towards the door.

He was in an amazing plight. His coat was dusty and dirty, and smeared with green down the sleeves; his hair disordered, and as it seemed to me greyer – either with dust and dirt or because its colour had actually faded. His face was ghastly pale; his chin had a brown cut on it – a cut half healed; his expression was haggard and drawn, as by intense suffering. For a moment he hesitated in the doorway, as if he had been dazzled by the light. Then he came into the room. He walked with just such a limp as I have seen in footsore tramps. We stared at him in silence, expecting him to speak.

He said not a word, but came painfully to the table, and made a motion towards the wine. The Editor filled a glass of champagne, and pushed it towards him. He drained it, and it seemed to do him good: for he looked round the table, and the ghost of his old smile flickered across his face. 'What on earth have you been up to, man?' said the Doctor. The Time Traveller did not seem to hear. 'Don't let me disturb you,' he said, with a certain faltering articulation. 'I'm all right.' He stopped, held out his glass for more, and took it off at a draught. 'That's good,' he said. His eyes grew brighter, and a faint colour came into his cheeks. His glance flickered over our faces with a certain dull approval, and then went round the warm and comfortable room. Then he spoke again, still as it were feeling his way among his words. 'I'm going to wash and dress, and then I'll come down and explain things. . . . Save me some of that mutton. I'm starving for a bit of meat.'

He looked across at the Editor, who was a rare visitor, and hoped he was all right. The Editor began a question. 'Tell you presently,' said the Time Traveller. 'I'm – funny! Be all right in a minute.'

He put down his glass, and walked towards the staircase door. Again I remarked his lameness and the soft padding sound of his footfall, and standing up in my place, I saw his feet as he went out. He had nothing on them but a pair of tattered, blood-stained socks. Then the door closed upon him. I had half a mind to follow, till I remembered how he detested any fuss about himself. For a minute, perhaps, my mind was wool-gathering. Then, 'Remarkable Behaviour of an Eminent Scientist,' I heard the Editor say, thinking (after his wont) in headlines. And this brought my attention back to the bright dinner-table.

'What's the game?' said the Journalist. 'Has he been doing the Amateur Cadger? I don't follow.' I met the eye of the Psychologist, and read my own

interpretation in his face. I thought of the Time Traveller limping painfully upstairs. I don't think anyone else had noticed his lameness.

The first to recover completely from this surprise was the Medical Man, who rang the bell – the Time Traveller hated to have servants waiting at dinner – for a hot plate. At that the Editor turned to his knife and fork with a grunt, and the Silent Man followed suit. The dinner was resumed. Conversation was exclamatory for a little while, with gaps of wonderment; and then the Editor got fervent in his curiosity. 'Does our friend eke out his modest income with a crossing? Or has he his Nebuchadnezzar phases?' he enquired. 'I feel assured it's this business of the Time Machine,' I said, and took up the Psychologist's account of our previous meeting. The new guests were frankly incredulous. The Editor raised objections. 'What *was* this time travelling? A man couldn't cover himself with dust by rolling in a paradox, could he?' And then, as the idea came home to him, he resorted to caricature. Hadn't they any clothes-brushes in the Future? The Journalist too, would not believe at any price, and joined the Editor in the easy work of heaping ridicule on the whole thing. They were both the new kind of journalist – very joyous, irreverent young men. 'Our Special Correspondent in the Day after Tomorrow reports,' the Journalist was saying – or rather shouting – when the Time Traveller came back. He was dressed in ordinary evening clothes, and nothing save his haggard look remained of the change that had startled me.

'I say,' said the Editor hilariously, 'these chaps here say you have been travelling into the middle of next week! Tell us all about little Rosebery, will you? What will you take for the lot?'

The Time Traveller came to the place reserved for him without a word. He smiled quietly, in his old way. 'Where's my mutton?' he said. 'What a treat it is to stick a fork into meat again!'

'Story!' cried the Editor.

'Story be damned!' said the Time Traveller. 'I want something to eat. I won't say a word until I get some peptone into my arteries. Thanks. And the salt.'

'One word,' said I. 'Have you been time travelling?'

'Yes,' said the Time Traveller, with his mouth full, nodding his head.

'I'd give a shilling a line for a verbatim note,' said the Editor. The Time Traveller pushed his glass towards the Silent Man and rang it with his fingernail; at which the Silent Man, who had been staring at his face, started convulsively, and poured him wine. The rest of the dinner was uncomfortable. For my own part, sudden questions kept on rising to my lips, and I dare say it was the same with the others. The Journalist tried to relieve the tension by telling anecdotes of Hettie Potter. The Time Traveller devoted his attention to his dinner, and displayed the appetite of a tramp. The Medical Man smoked a cigarette, and watched the Time Traveller through

his eyelashes. The Silent Man seemed even more clumsy than usual, and drank champagne with regularity and determination out of sheer nervousness. At last the Time Traveller pushed his plate away, and looked round us. 'I suppose I must apologize,' he said. 'I was simply starving. I've had a most amazing time.' He reached out his hand for a cigar, and cut the end. 'But come into the smoking-room. It's too long a story to tell over greasy plates.' And ringing the bell in passing, he led the way into the adjoining room.

'You have told Blank, and Dash, and Chose about the machine?' he said to me, leaning back in his easy-chair and naming the three new guests.

'But the thing's a mere paradox,' said the Editor.

'I can't argue tonight. I don't mind telling you the story, but I can't argue. I will,' he went on, 'tell you the story of what has happened to me, if you like, but you must refrain from interruptions. I want to tell it. Badly. Most of it will sound like lying. So be it! It's true – every word of it, all the same. I was in my laboratory at four o'clock, and since then . . . I've lived eight days . . . such days as no human being ever lived before! I'm nearly worn out, but I shan't sleep till I've told this thing over to you. Then I shall go to bed. But no interruptions! Is it agreed?'

'Agreed,' said the Editor, and the rest of us echoed 'Agreed.' And with that the Time Traveller began his story as I have set it forth. He sat back in his chair at first, and spoke like a weary man. Afterwards he got more animated. In writing it down I feel with only too much keenness the inadequacy of pen and ink – and, above all, my own inadequacy – to express its quality. You read, I will suppose, attentively enough; but you cannot see the speaker's white, sincere face in the bright circle of the little lamp, nor hear the intonation of his voice. You cannot know how his expression followed the turns of his story! Most of us hearers were in shadow, for the candles in the smoking-room had not been lighted, and only the face of the Journalist and the legs of the Silent Man from the knees downward were illuminated. At first we glanced now and again at each other. After a time we ceased to do that, and looked only at the Time Traveller's face.

CHAPTER III

'I told some of you last Thursday of the principles of the Time Machine, and showed you the actual thing itself, incomplete in the workshop. There it is now, a little travel-worn, truly; and one of the ivory bars is cracked, and a brass rail bent; but the rest of it's sound enough. I expected to finish it on Friday, but on Friday, when the putting together was nearly done, I found that one of the nickel bars was exactly one inch too short, and this I had to get remade; so that the thing was not complete until this morning. It was at ten o'clock today that the first of all Time Machines began its career. I gave it a last tap, tried all the screws again, put one more drop of oil on the quartz rod, and sat myself in the saddle. I suppose a suicide who holds a pistol to his skull feels much the same wonder at what will come next as I felt then. I took the starting lever in one hand and the stopping one in the other, pressed the first, and almost immediately the second. I seemed to reel; I felt a nightmare sensation of falling; and, looking round, I saw the laboratory exactly as before. Had anything happened? For a moment I suspected that my intellect had tricked me. Then I noted the clock. A moment before, as it seemed, it had stood at a minute or so past ten; now it was nearly half-past three!

'I drew a breath, set my teeth, gripped the starting lever with both hands, and went off with a thud. The laboratory got hazy and went dark. Mrs Watchett came in and walked, apparently without seeing me, towards the garden door. I suppose it took her a minute or so to traverse the place, but to me she seemed to shoot across the room like a rocket. I pressed the lever over to its extreme position. The night came like the turning out of a lamp, and in another moment came tomorrow. The laboratory grew faint and hazy, then fainter and ever fainter. Tomorrow night came black, then day again, night again, day again, faster and faster still. An eddying murmur filled my ears, and a strange, dumb confusedness descended on my mind.

'I am afraid I cannot convey the peculiar sensations of time travelling. They are excessively unpleasant. There is a feeling exactly like that one has upon a switchback – of a helpless headlong motion! I felt the same horrible anticipation, too, of an imminent smash. As I put on pace, night followed day like the flapping of a black wing. The dim suggestion of the laboratory seemed presently to fall away from me, and I saw the sun hopping swiftly across the sky, leaping it every minute, and every minute marking a day. I supposed the laboratory had been destroyed and I had come into the open air. I had a dim impression of scaffolding, but I was already going too fast to be conscious of any moving things. The slowest snail that ever crawled dashed by too fast for me. The twinkling succession of darkness and light was excessively painful to the eye. Then, in the intermittent

darknesses, I saw the moon spinning swiftly through her quarters from new to full, and had a faint glimpse of the circling stars. Presently, as I went on, still gaining velocity, the palpitation of night and day merged into one continuous greyness; the sky took on a wonderful deepness of blue, a splendid luminous colour like that of early twilight; the jerking sun became a streak of fire, a brilliant arch, in space; the moon a fainter fluctuating band; and I could see nothing of the stars, save now and then a brighter circle flickering in the blue.

'The landscape was misty and vague. I was still on the hillside upon which this house now stands, and the shoulder rose above me grey and dim. I saw trees growing and changing like puffs of vapour, now brown, now green; they grew, spread, shivered, and passed away. I saw huge buildings rise up faint and fair, and pass like dreams. The whole surface of the earth seemed changed – melting and flowing under my eyes. The little hands upon the dials that registered my speed raced round faster and faster. Presently I noted that the sun belt swayed up and down, from solstice to solstice, in a minute or less, and that consequently my pace was over a year a minute; and minute by minute the white snow flashed across the world, and vanished, and was followed by the bright, brief green of spring.

'The unpleasant sensations of the start were less poignant now. They merged at last into a kind of hysterical exhilaration. I remarked indeed a clumsy swaying of the machine, for which I was unable to account. But my mind was too confused to attend to it, so with a kind of madness growing upon me, I flung myself into futurity. At first I scarce thought of stopping, scarce thought of anything but these new sensations. But presently a fresh series of impressions grew up in my mind – a certain curiosity and therewith a certain dread – until at last they took complete possession of me. What strange developments of humanity, what wonderful advances upon our rudimentary civilization, I thought, might not appear when I came to look nearly into the dim elusive world that raced and fluctuated before my eyes! I saw great and splendid architecture rising about me, more massive than any buildings of our own time, and yet, as it seemed, built of glimmer and mist. I saw a richer green flow up the hillside, and remain there, without any wintry intermission. Even through the veil of my confusion the earth seemed very fair. And so my mind came round to the business of stopping.

'The peculiar risk lay in the possibility of my finding some substance in the space which I, or the machine, occupied. So long as I travelled at a high velocity through time, this scarcely mattered; I was, so to speak, attenuated – was slipping like a vapour through the interstices of intervening substances! But to come to a stop involved the jamming of myself, molecule by molecule, into whatever lay in my way; meant bringing my atoms into such intimate contact with those of the obstacle that a profound chemical reaction – possibly a far-reaching explosion – would result, and blow myself and my

apparatus out of all possible dimensions – into the Unknown. This possibility had occurred to me again and again while I was making the machine; but then I had cheerfully accepted it as an unavoidable risk – one of the risks a man has got to take! Now the risk was inevitable, I no longer saw it in the same cheerful light. The fact is that, insensibly, the absolute strangeness of everything, the sickly jarring and swaying of the machine, above all, the feeling of prolonged falling, had absolutely upset my nerve. I told myself that I could never stop, and with a gust of petulance I resolved to stop forthwith. Like an impatient fool, I lugged over the lever, and incontinently the thing went reeling over, and I was flung headlong through the air.

'There was the sound of a clap of thunder in my ears. I may have been stunned for a moment. A pitiless hail was hissing round me, and I was sitting on soft turf in front of the overset machine. Everything still seemed grey, but presently I remarked that the confusion in my ears was gone. I looked round me. I was on what seemed to be a little lawn in a garden, surrounded by rhododendron bushes, and I noticed that their mauve and purple blossoms were dropping in a shower under the beating of the hailstones. The rebounding, dancing hail hung in a cloud over the machine, and drove along the ground like smoke. In a moment I was wet to the skin. "Fine hospitality," said I, "to a man who has travelled innumerable years to see you."

'Presently I thought what a fool I was to get wet. I stood up and looked round me. A colossal figure, carved apparently in some white stone, loomed indistinctly beyond the rhododendrons through the hazy downpour. But all else of the world was invisible.

'My sensations would be hard to describe. As the columns of hail grew thinner, I saw the white figure more distinctly. It was very large, for a silver birch tree touched its shoulder. It was of white marble, in shape something like a winged sphinx, but the wings, instead of being carried vertically at the sides, were spread so that it seemed to hover. The pedestal, it appeared to me, was of bronze, and was thick with verdigris. It chanced that the face was towards me; the sightless eyes seemed to watch me; there was the faint shadow of a smile on the lips. It was greatly weather-worn, and that imparted an unpleasant suggestion of disease. I stood looking at it for a little space – half a minute, perhaps, or half an hour. It seemed to advance and to recede as the hail drove before it denser or thinner. At last I tore my eyes from it for a moment and saw that the hail curtain had worn threadbare, and that the sky was lightening with the promise of the sun.

'I looked up again at the crouching white shape, and the full temerity of my voyage came suddenly upon me. What might appear when that hazy curtain was altogether withdrawn? What might not have happened to men? What if cruelty had grown into a common passion? What if in this interval the race had lost its manliness and had developed into something inhuman, unsympathetic and overwhelmingly powerful? I might seem some old-world

savage animal, only the more dreadful and disgusting for our common like-
ness – a foul creature to be incontinently slain.

'Already I saw other vast shapes – huge buildings with intricate parapets
and tall columns, with a wooded hillside dimly creeping in upon me through
the lessening storm. I was seized with a panic fear. I turned frantically to
the Time Machine, and strove hard to readjust it. As I did so the shafts
of the sun smote through the thunderstorm. The grey downpour was swept
aside and vanished like the trailing garments of a ghost. Above me, in the
intense blue of the summer sky, some faint brown shreds of cloud whirled
into nothingness. The great buildings about me stood out clear and distinct,
shining with the wet of the thunderstorm, and picked out in white by the
unmelted hailstones piled along their courses. I felt naked in a strange
world. I felt as perhaps a bird may feel in the clear air, knowing the hawk
wings above and will swoop. My fear grew to frenzy. I took a breathing
space, set my teeth, and again grappled fiercely, wrist and knee, with the
machine. It gave under my desperate onset and turned over. It struck my
chin violently. One hand on the saddle, the other on the lever, I stood
panting heavily in attitude to mount again.

'But with this recovery of a prompt retreat my courage recovered. I looked
more curiously and less fearfully at this world of the remote future. In a
circular opening, high up in the wall of the nearer house, I saw a group of
figures clad in rich soft robes. They had seen me, and their faces were
directed towards me.

'Then I heard voices approaching me. Coming through the bushes by the
White Sphinx were the heads and shoulders of men running. One of these
emerged in a pathway leading straight to the little lawn upon which I stood
with my machine. He was a slight creature – perhaps four feet high – clad
in a purple tunic, girdled at the waist with a leather belt. Sandals or buskins
– I could not clearly distinguish which – were on his feet; his legs were bare
to the knees, and his head was bare. Noticing that, I noticed for the first
time how warm the air was.

'He struck me as being a very beautiful and graceful creature, but inde-
scribably frail. His flushed face reminded me of the more beautiful kind of
consumptive – that hectic beauty of which we used to hear so much. At the
sight of him I suddenly regained confidence. I took my hands from the machine.'

CHAPTER IV

'In another moment we were standing face to face, I and this fragile thing out of futurity. He came straight up to me and laughed into my eyes. The absence from his bearing of any sign of fear struck me at once. Then he turned to the two others who were following him and spoke to them in a strange and very sweet and liquid tongue.

'There were others coming, and presently a little group of perhaps eight or ten of these exquisite creatures were about me. One of them addressed me. It came into my head, oddly enough, that my voice was too harsh and deep for them. So I shook my head, and, pointing to my ears, shook it again. He came a step forward, hesitated, and then touched my hand. Then I felt other soft little tentacles upon my back and shoulders. They wanted to make sure I was real. There was nothing in this at all alarming. Indeed, there was something in these pretty little people that inspired confidence – a graceful gentleness, a certain childlike ease. And besides, they looked so frail that I could fancy myself flinging the whole dozen of them about like nine-pins. But I made a sudden motion to warn them when I saw their little pink hands feeling at the Time Machine. Happily then, when it was not too late, I thought of a danger I had hitherto forgotten, and reaching over the bars of the machine I unscrewed the little levers that would set it in motion, and put these in my pocket. Then I turned again to see what I could do in the way of communication.

'And then, looking more nearly into their features, I saw some further peculiarities in their Dresden-china type of prettiness. Their hair, which was uniformly curly, came to a sharp end at the neck and cheek; there was not the faintest suggestion of it on the face, and their ears were singularly minute. The mouths were small, with bright red, rather thin lips, and the little chins ran to a point. The eyes were large and mild; and – this may seem egotism on my part – I fancied even that there was a certain lack of the interest I might have expected in them.

'As they made no effort to communicate with me, but simply stood round me smiling and speaking in soft cooing notes to each other, I began the conversation. I pointed to the Time Machine and to myself. Then hesitating for a moment how to express time, I pointed to the sun. At once a quaintly pretty little figure in chequered purple and white followed my gesture, and then astonished me by imitating the sound of thunder.

'For a moment I was staggered, though the import of his gesture was plain enough. The question had come into my mind abruptly: were these creatures fools? You may hardly understand how it took me. You see I had always anticipated that the people of the year Eight Hundred and Two Thousand odd would be incredibly in front of us in knowledge, art, everything. Then

one of them suddenly asked me a question that showed him to be on the intellectual level of one of our five-year-old children – asked me, in fact, if I had come from the sun in a thunderstorm! It let loose the judgment I had suspended upon their clothes, their frail light limbs, and fragile features. A flow of disappointment rushed across my mind. For a moment I felt that I had built the Time Machine in vain.

'I nodded, pointed to the sun, and gave them such a vivid rendering of a thunderclap as startled them. They all withdrew a pace or so and bowed. Then came one laughing towards me, carrying a chain of beautiful flowers altogether new to me, and put it about my neck. The idea was received with melodious applause; and presently they were all running to and fro for flowers, and laughingly flinging them upon me until I was almost smothered with blossom. You who have never seen the like can scarcely imagine what delicate and wonderful flowers countless years of culture had created. Then someone suggested that their plaything should be exhibited in the nearest building, and so I was led past the sphinx of white marble, which had seemed to watch me all the while with a smile at my astonishment, towards a vast grey edifice of fretted stone. As I went with them the memory of my confident anticipations of a profoundly grave and intellectual posterity came, with irresistible merriment, to my mind.

'The building had a huge entry, and was altogether of colossal dimensions. I was naturally most occupied with the growing crowd of little people, and with the big open portals that yawned before me shadowy and mysterious. My general impression of the world I saw over their heads was a tangled waste of beautiful bushes and flowers, a long neglected and yet weedless garden. I saw a number of tall spikes of strange white flowers, measuring a foot perhaps across the spread of the waxen petals. They grew scattered, as if wild, among the variegated shrubs, but, as I say, I did not examine them closely at this time. The Time Machine was left deserted on the turf among the rhododendrons.

'The arch of the doorway was richly carved, but naturally I did not observe the carving very narrowly, though I fancied I saw suggestions of old Phoenician decorations as I passed through, and it struck me that they were very badly broken and weather-worn. Several more brightly clad people met me in the doorway, and so we entered, I, dressed in dingy nineteenth-century garments, looking grotesque enough, garlanded with flowers, and surrounded by an eddying mass of bright, soft-coloured robes and shining white limbs, in a melodious whirl of laughter and laughing speech.

'The big doorway opened into a proportionately great hall hung with brown. The roof was in shadow, and the windows, partially glazed with coloured glass and partially unglazed, admitted a tempered light. The floor was made up of huge blocks of some very hard white metal, not plates nor slabs – blocks, and it was so much worn, as I judged by the going to and

fro of past generations, as to be deeply channelled along the more frequented ways. Transverse to the length were innumerable tables made of slabs of polished stone, raised perhaps a foot from the floor, and upon these were heaps of fruits. Some I recognized as a kind of hypertrophied raspberry and orange, but for the most part they were strange.

'Between the tables was scattered a great number of cushions. Upon these my conductors seated themselves, signing for me to do likewise. With a pretty absence of ceremony they began to eat the fruit with their hands, flinging peel and stalks, and so forth, into the round openings in the sides of the tables. I was not loath to follow their example, for I felt thirsty and hungry. As I did so I surveyed the hall at my leisure.

'And perhaps the thing that struck me most was its dilapidated look. The stained-glass windows, which displayed only a geometrical pattern, were broken in many places, and the curtains that hung across the lower end were thick with dust. And it caught my eye that the corner of the marble table near me was fractured. Nevertheless, the general effect was extremely rich and picturesque. There were, perhaps, a couple of hundred people dining in the hall, and most of them, seated as near to me as they could come, were watching me with interest, their little eyes shining over the fruit they were eating. All were clad in the same soft and yet strong, silky material.

'Fruit, by the by, was all their diet. These people of the remote future were strict vegetarians, and while I was with them, in spite of some carnal cravings, I had to be frugivorous also. Indeed, I found afterwards that horses, cattle, sheep, dogs, had followed the Ichthyosaurus into extinction. But the fruits were very delightful; one, in particular, that seemed to be in season all the time I was there – a floury thing in a three-sided husk – was especially good, and I made it my staple. At first I was puzzled by all these strange fruits, and by the strange flowers I saw, but later I began to perceive their import.

'However, I am telling you of my fruit dinner in the distant future now. So soon as my appetite was a little checked, I determined to make a resolute attempt to learn the speech of these new men of mine. Clearly that was the next thing to do. The fruits seemed a convenient thing to begin upon, and holding one of these up I began a series of interrogative sounds and gestures. I had some considerable difficulty in conveying my meaning. At first my efforts met with a stare of surprise or inextinguishable laughter, but presently a fair-haired little creature seemed to grasp my intention and repeated a name. They had to chatter and explain the business at great length to each other, and my first attempts to make the exquisite little sounds of their language caused an immense amount of amusement. However, I felt like a schoolmaster amidst children, and persisted, and presently I had a score of noun substantives at least at my command; and then I got to demonstrative pronouns, and even the verb "to eat". But it was slow work, and the little

people soon tired and wanted to get away from my interrogations, so I determined, rather of necessity, to let them give their lessons in little doses when they felt inclined. And very little doses I found they were before long, for I never met people more indolent or more easily fatigued.

'A queer thing I soon discovered about my little hosts, and that was their lack of interest. They would come to me with eager cries of astonishment, like children, but like children they would soon stop examining me and wander away after some other toy. The dinner and my conversational beginnings ended, I noted for the first time that almost all those who had surrounded me at first were gone. It is odd, too, how speedily I came to disregard these little people. I went out through the portal into the sunlit world again as soon as my hunger was satisfied. I was continually meeting more of these men of the future, who would follow me a little distance, chatter and laugh about me, and, having smiled and gesticulated in a friendly way, leave me again to my own devices.

'The calm of evening was upon the world as I emerged from the great hall, and the scene was lit by the warm glow of the setting sun. At first things were very confusing. Everything was so entirely different from the world I had known – even the flowers. The big building I had left was situated on the slope of a broad river valley, but the Thames had shifted perhaps a mile from its present position. I resolved to mount to the summit of a crest, perhaps a mile and a half away, from which I could get a wider view of this our planet in the year Eight Hundred and Two Thousand Seven Hundred and One AD. For that, I should explain, was the date the little dials of my machine recorded.

'As I walked I was watching for every impression that could possibly help to explain the condition of ruinous splendour in which I found the world – for ruinous it was. A little way up the hill, for instance, was a great heap of granite, bound together by masses of aluminium, a vast labyrinth of precipitous walls and crumpled heaps, amidst which were thick heaps of very beautiful pagoda-like plants – nettles possibly – but wonderfully tinted with brown about the leaves, and incapable of stinging. It was evidently the derelict remains of some vast structure, to what end built I could not determine. It was here that I was destined, at a later date, to have a very strange experience – the first intimation of a still stranger discovery – but of that I will speak in its proper place.

'Looking round with a sudden thought, from a terrace on which I rested for a while, I realized that there were no small houses to be seen. Apparently the single house, and possibly even the household, had vanished. Here and there among the greenery were palace-like buildings, but the house and the cottage, which form such characteristic features of our own English landscape, had disappeared.

'"Communism," said I to myself.

'And on the heels of that came another thought. I looked at the half-dozen little figures that were following me. Then, in a flash, I perceived that all had the same form of costume, the same soft hairless visage, and the same girlish rotundity of limb. It may seem strange, perhaps, that I had not noticed this before. But everything was so strange. Now, I saw the fact plainly enough. In costume, and in all the differences of texture and bearing that now mark off the sexes from each other, these people of the future were alike. And the children seemed to my eyes to be but the miniatures of their parents. I judged, then, that the children of that time were extremely precocious, physically at least, and I found afterwards abundant verification of my opinion.

'Seeing the ease and security in which these people were living, I felt that this close resemblance of the sexes was after all what one would expect; for the strength of a man and the softness of a woman, the institution of the family, and the differentiation of occupations are mere militant necessities of an age of physical force; where population is balanced and abundant, much child-bearing becomes an evil rather than a blessing to the State; where violence comes but rarely and offspring are secure, there is less necessity – indeed there is no necessity – for an efficient family, and the specialization of the sexes with reference to their children's needs disappears. We see some beginnings of this even in our own time, and in this future age it was complete. This, I must remind you, was my speculation at the time. Later, I was to appreciate how far it fell short of the reality.

'While I was musing upon these things, my attention was attracted by a pretty little structure, like a well under a cupola. I thought in a transitory way of the oddness of wells still existing, and then resumed the thread of my speculations. There were no large buildings towards the top of the hill, and as my walking powers were evidently miraculous, I was presently left alone for the first time. With a strange sense of freedom and adventure I pushed on up to the crest.

'There I found a seat of some yellow metal that I did not recognize, corroded in places with a kind of pinkish rust and half smothered in soft moss, the armrests cast and filed into the resemblance of griffins' heads. I sat down on it, and I surveyed the broad view of our old world under the sunset of that long day. It was as sweet and fair a view as I have ever seen. The sun had already gone below the horizon and the west was flaming gold, touched with some horizontal bars of purple and crimson. Below was the valley of the Thames, in which the river lay like a band of burnished steel. I have already spoken of the great palaces dotted about among the variegated greenery, some in ruins and some still occupied. Here and there rose a white or silvery figure in the waste garden of the earth, here and there came the sharp vertical line of some cupola or obelisk. There were no hedges, no signs of proprietary rights, no evidences of agriculture; the whole earth had become a garden.

'So watching, I began to put my interpretation upon the things I had seen, and as it shaped itself to me that evening, my interpretation was something in this way. (Afterwards I found I had got only a half-truth – or only a glimpse of one facet of the truth.)

'It seemed to me that I had happened upon humanity upon the wane. The ruddy sunset set me thinking of the sunset of mankind. For the first time I began to realize an odd consequence of the social effort in which we are at present engaged. And yet, come to think, it is a logical consequence enough. Strength is the outcome of need; security sets a premium on feebleness. The work of ameliorating the conditions of life – the true civilizing process that makes life more and more secure – had gone steadily on to a climax. One triumph of a united humanity over Nature had followed another. Things that are now mere dreams had become projects deliberately put in hand and carried forward. And the harvest was what I saw!

'After all, the sanitation and the agriculture of today are still in the rudimentary stage. The science of our time has attacked but a little department of the field of human disease, but even so, it spreads its operations very steadily and persistently. Our agriculture and horticulture destroy a weed just here and there and cultivate perhaps a score or so of wholesome plants, leaving the greater number to fight out a balance as they can. We improve our favourite plants and animals – and how few they are – gradually by selective breeding; now a new and better peach, now a seedless grape, now a sweeter and larger flower, now a more convenient breed of cattle. We improve them gradually, because our ideals are vague and tentative, and our knowledge is very limited; because Nature, too, is shy and slow in our clumsy hands. Some day all this will be better organized, and still better. That is the drift of the current in spite of the eddies. The whole world will be intelligent, educated, and co-operating; things will move faster and faster towards the subjugation of Nature. In the end, wisely and carefully we shall readjust the balance of animal and vegetable life to suit our human needs.

'This adjustment, I say, must have been done, and done well; done indeed for all Time, in the space of Time across which my machine had leaped. The air was free from gnats, the earth from weeds or fungi; everywhere were fruits and sweet and delightful flowers; brilliant butterflies flew hither and thither. The ideal of preventive medicine was attained. Diseases had been stamped out. I saw no evidence of any contagious diseases during all my stay. And I shall have to tell you later that even the processes of putrefaction and decay had been profoundly affected by these changes.

'Social triumphs, too, had been effected. I saw mankind housed in splendid shelters, gloriously clothed, and as yet I had found them engaged in no toil. There were no signs of struggle, neither social nor economical struggle. The shop, the advertisement, traffic, all that commerce which constitutes the body of our world, was gone. It was natural on that golden evening that I

should jump at the idea of a social paradise. The difficulty of increasing population had been met, I guessed, and population had ceased to increase.

'But with this change in condition comes inevitably adaptations to the change. What, unless biological science is a mass of errors, is the cause of human intelligence and vigour? Hardship and freedom: conditions under which the active, strong, and subtle survive and the weaker go to the wall; conditions that put a premium upon the loyal alliance of capable men, upon self-restraint, patience, and decision. And the institution of the family, and the emotions that arise therein, the fierce jealousy, the tenderness for offspring, parental self-devotion, all found their justification and support in the imminent dangers of the young. *Now*, where are these imminent dangers? There is a sentiment arising, and it will grow, against connubial jealousy, against fierce maternity, against passion of all sorts; unnecessary things now, and things that make us uncomfortable, savage survivals, discords in a refined and pleasant life.

'I thought of the physical slightness of the people, their lack of intelligence, and those big abundant ruins, and it strengthened my belief in a perfect conquest of Nature. For after the battle comes Quiet. Humanity had been strong, energetic, and intelligent, and had used all its abundant vitality to alter the conditions under which it lived. And now came the reaction of the altered conditions.

'Under the new conditions of perfect comfort and security, that restless energy, that with us is strength, would become weakness. Even in our own time certain tendencies and desires, once necessary to survival, are a constant source of failure. Physical courage and the love of battle, for instance, are no great help – may even be hindrances – to a civilized man. And in a state of physical balance and security, power, intellectual as well as physical, would be out of place. For countless years I judged there had been no danger of war or solitary violence, no danger from wild beasts, no wasting disease to require strength of constitution, no need of toil. For such a life, what we should call the weak are as well equipped as the strong, are indeed no longer weak. Better equipped indeed they are, for the strong would be fretted by an energy for which there was no outlet. No doubt the exquisite beauty of the buildings I saw was the outcome of the last surgings of the now purposeless energy of mankind before it settled down into perfect harmony with the conditions under which it lived – the flourish of that triumph which began the last great peace. This has ever been the fate of energy in security; it takes to art and to eroticism, and then come languor and decay.

'Even this artistic impetus would at last die away – had almost died in the Time I saw. To adorn themselves with flowers, to dance, to sing in the sunlight: so much was left of the artistic spirit, and no more. Even that would fade in the end into a contented inactivity. We are kept keen on the

grindstone of pain and necessity, and, it seemed to me, that here was that hateful grindstone broken at last!

'As I stood there in the gathering dark I thought that in this simple explanation I had mastered the problem of the world – mastered the whole secret of these delicious people. Possibly the checks they had devised for the increase of population had succeeded too well, and their numbers had rather diminished than kept stationary. That would account for the abandoned ruins. Very simple was my explanation, and plausible enough – as most wrong theories are!

CHAPTER V

'As I stood there musing over this too perfect triumph of man, the full moon, yellow and gibbous, came up out of an overflow of silver light in the north-east. The bright little figures ceased to move about below, a noiseless owl flitted by, and I shivered with the chill of the night. I determined to descend and find where I could sleep.

'I looked for the building I knew. Then my eye travelled along to the figure of the White Sphinx upon the pedestal of bronze, growing distinct as the light of the rising moon grew brighter. I could see the silver birch against it. There was the tangle of rhododendron bushes, black in the pale light, and there was the little lawn. I looked at the lawn again. A queer doubt chilled my complacency. "No," said I stoutly to myself, "that was not the lawn."

'But it *was* the lawn. For the white leprous face of the sphinx was towards it. Can you imagine what I felt as this conviction came home to me? But you cannot. The Time Machine was gone!

'At once, like a lash across the face, came the possibility of losing my own age, of being left helpless in this strange new world. The bare thought of it was an actual physical sensation. I could feel it grip me at the throat and stop my breathing. In another moment I was in a passion of fear and running with great leaping strides down the slope. Once I fell headlong and cut my face; I lost no time in stanching the blood, but jumped up and ran on, with a warm trickle down my cheek and chin. All the time I ran I was saying to myself: "They have moved it a little, pushed it under the bushes out of the way." Nevertheless, I ran with all my might. All the time, with the certainty that sometimes comes with excessive dread, I knew that such assurance was folly, knew instinctively that the machine was removed out of my reach. My breath came with pain. I suppose I covered the whole distance from the hill crest to the little lawn, two miles perhaps, in ten minutes. And I am not a young man. I cursed aloud, as I ran, at my confident folly in leaving the machine, wasting good breath thereby. I cried aloud, and none answered. Not a creature seemed to be stirring in that moonlit world.

'When I reached the lawn my worst fears were realized. Not a trace of the thing was to be seen. I felt faint and cold when I faced the empty space among the black tangle of bushes. I ran round it furiously, as if the thing might be hidden in a corner, and then stopped abruptly, with my hands clutching my hair. Above me towered the sphinx, upon the bronze pedestal, white, shining, leprous, in the light of the rising moon. It seemed to smile in mockery of my dismay.

'I might have consoled myself by imagining the little people had put the mechanism in some shelter for me, had I not felt assured of their physical and intellectual inadequacy. That is what dismayed me: the sense of some

hitherto unsuspected power, through whose intervention my invention had vanished. Yet, for one thing I felt assured: unless some other age had produced its exact duplicate, the machine could not have moved in time. The attachment of the levers – I will show you the method later – prevented anyone from tampering with it in that way when they were removed. It had moved, and was hid, only in space. But then, where could it be?

'I think I must have had a kind of frenzy. I remember running violently in and out among the moonlit bushes all round the sphinx, and startling some white animal that, in the dim light, I took for a small deer. I remember, too, late that night, beating the bushes with my clenched fist until my knuckles were gashed and bleeding from the broken twigs. Then, sobbing and raving in my anguish of mind, I went down to the great building of stone. The big hall was dark, silent, and deserted. I slipped on the uneven floor, and fell over one of the malachite tables, almost breaking my shin. I lit a match and went on past the dusty curtains, of which I have told you.

'There I found a second great hall covered with cushions, upon which, perhaps, a score or so of the little people were sleeping. I have no doubt they found my second appearance strange enough, coming suddenly out of the quiet darkness with inarticulate noises and the splutter and flare of a match. For they had forgotten about matches. "Where is my Time Machine?" I began, bawling like an angry child, laying hands upon them and shaking them up together. It must have been very queer to them. Some laughed, most of them looked sorely frightened. When I saw them standing round me, it came into my head that I was doing as foolish a thing as it was possible for me to do under the circumstances, in trying to revive the sensation of fear. For, reasoning from their daylight behaviour, I thought that fear must be forgotten.

'Abruptly, I dashed down the match, and, knocking one of the people over in my course, went blundering across the big dining-hall again, out under the moonlight. I heard cries of terror and their little feet running and stumbling this way and that. I do not remember all I did as the moon crept up the sky. I suppose it was the unexpected nature of my loss that maddened me. I felt hopelessly cut off from my own kind – a strange animal in an unknown world. I must have raved to and fro, screaming and crying upon God and Fate. I have a memory of horrible fatigue, as the long night of despair wore away; of looking in this impossible place and that; of groping among moonlit ruins and touching strange creatures in the black shadows; at last, of lying on the ground near the sphinx and weeping with absolute wretchedness. I had nothing left but misery. Then I slept, and when I woke again it was full day, and a couple of sparrows were hopping round me on the turf within reach of my arm.

'I sat up in the freshness of the morning, trying to remember how I had got there, and why I had such a profound sense of desertion and despair.

Then things came clear in my mind. With the plain, reasonable daylight, I could look my circumstances fairly in the face. I saw the wild folly of my frenzy overnight, and I could reason with myself. "Suppose the worst?" I said. "Suppose the machine altogether lost – perhaps destroyed? It behoves me to be calm and patient, to learn the way of the people, to get a clear idea of the method of my loss, and the means of getting materials and tools; so that in the end, perhaps, I may make another." That would be my only hope, perhaps, but better than despair. And, after all, it was a beautiful and curious world.

'But probably, the machine had only been taken away. Still, I must be calm and patient, find its hiding-place, and recover it by force or cunning. And with that I scrambled to my feet and looked about me, wondering where I could bathe. I felt weary, stiff, and travel-soiled. The freshness of the morning made me desire an equal freshness. I had exhausted my emotion. Indeed, as I went about my business, I found myself wondering at my intense excitement overnight. I made a careful examination of the ground about the little lawn. I wasted some time in futile questionings, conveyed, as well as I was able, to such of the little people as came by. They all failed to understand my gestures; some were simply stolid, some thought it was a jest and laughed at me. I had the hardest task in the world to keep my hands off their pretty laughing faces. It was a foolish impulse, but the devil begotten of fear and blind anger was ill curbed and still eager to take advantage of my perplexity. The turf gave better counsel. I found a groove ripped in it, about midway between the pedestal of the sphinx and the marks of my feet where, on arrival, I had struggled with the overturned machine. There were other signs of removal about, with queer narrow footprints like those I could imagine made by a sloth. This directed my closer attention to the pedestal. It was, as I think I have said, of bronze. It was not a mere block, but highly decorated with deep framed panels on either side. I went and rapped at these. The pedestal was hollow. Examining the panels with care I found them discontinuous with the frames. There were no handles or keyholes, but possibly the panels, if they were doors, as I supposed, opened from within. One thing was clear enough to my mind. It took no very great mental effort to infer that my Time Machine was inside that pedestal. But how it got there was a different problem.

'I saw the heads of two orange-clad people coming through the bushes and under some blossom-covered apple trees towards me. I turned smiling to them and beckoned them to me. They came, and then, pointing to the bronze pedestal, I tried to intimate my wish to open it. But at my first gesture towards this they behaved very oddly. I don't know how to convey their expression to you. Suppose you were to use a grossly improper gesture to a delicate-minded woman – it is how she would look. They went off as if they had received the last possible insult. I tried a sweet-looking little

chap in white next, with exactly the same result. Somehow, his manner made me feel ashamed of myself. But, as you know, I wanted the Time Machine, and I tried him once more. As he turned off, like the others, my temper got the better of me. In three strides I was after him, had him by the loose part of his robe round the neck, and began dragging him towards the sphinx. Then I saw the horror and repugnance of his face, and all of a sudden I let him go.

'But I was not beaten yet. I banged with my fist at the bronze panels. I thought I heard something stir inside – to be explicit, I thought I heard a sound like a chuckle – but I must have been mistaken. Then I got a big pebble from the river, and came and hammered till I had flattened a coil in the decorations, and the verdigris came off in powdery flakes. The delicate little people must have heard me hammering in gusty outbreaks a mile away on either hand, but nothing came of it. I saw a crowd of them upon the slopes, looking furtively at me. At last, hot and tired, I sat down to watch the place. But I was too restless to watch long; I am too Occidental for a long vigil. I could work at a problem for years, but to wait inactive for twenty-four hours – that is another matter.

'I got up after a time, and began walking aimlessly through the bushes towards the hill again. "Patience," said I to myself. "If you want your machine again you must leave that sphinx alone. If they mean to take your machine away, it's little good your wrecking their bronze panels, and if they don't, you will get it back as soon as you can ask for it. To sit among all those unknown things before a puzzle like that is hopeless. That way lies monomania. Face this world. Learn its ways, watch it, be careful of too hasty guesses at its meaning. In the end you will find clues to it all." Then suddenly the humour of the situation came into my mind: the thought of the years I had spent in study and toil to get into the future age, and now my passion of anxiety to get out of it. I had made myself the most complicated and the most hopeless trap that ever a man devised. Although it was at my own expense, I could not help myself. I laughed aloud.

'Going through the big palace, it seemed to me that the little people avoided me. It may have been my fancy, or it may have had something to do with my hammering at the gates of bronze. Yet I felt tolerably sure of the avoidance. I was careful, however, to show no concern and to abstain from any pursuit of them, and in the course of a day or two things got back to the old footing. I made what progress I could in the language, and in addition I pushed my explorations here and there. Either I missed some subtle point or their language was excessively simple – almost exclusively composed of concrete substantives and verbs. There seemed to be few, if any, abstract terms, or little use of figurative language. Their sentences were usually simple and of two words, and I failed to convey or understand any but the simplest propositions. I determined to put the thought of my Time

Machine and the mystery of the bronze doors under the sphinx as much as possible in a corner of memory, until my growing knowledge would lead me back to them in a natural way. Yet a certain feeling, you may understand, tethered me in a circle of a few miles round the point of my arrival.

'So far as I could see, all the world displayed the same exuberant richness as the Thames valley. From every hill I climbed I saw the same abundance of splendid buildings, endlessly varied in material and style, the same clustering thickets of evergreens, the same blossom-laden trees and tree-ferns. Here and there water shone like silver, and beyond, the land rose into blue undulating hills, and so faded into the serenity of the sky. A peculiar feature, which presently attracted my attention, was the presence of certain circular wells, several, as it seemed to me, of a very great depth. One lay by the path up the hill, which I had followed during my first walk. Like the others, it was rimmed with bronze, curiously wrought, and protected by a little cupola from the rain. Sitting by the side of these wells, and peering down into the shafted darkness, I could see no gleam of water, nor could I start any reflection with a lighted match. But in all of them I heard a certain sound: a thud – thud – thud, like the beating of some big engine; and I discovered, from the flaring of my matches, that a steady current of air set down the shafts. Further, I threw a scrap of paper into the throat of one, and, instead of fluttering slowly down, it was at once sucked swiftly out of sight.

'After a time, too, I came to connect these wells with tall towers standing here and there upon the slopes; for above them there was often just such a flicker in the air as one sees on a hot day above a sun-scorched beach. Putting things together, I reached a strong suggestion of an extensive system of subterranean ventilation, whose true import it was difficult to imagine. I was at first inclined to associate it with the sanitary apparatus of these people. It was an obvious conclusion, but it was absolutely wrong.

'And here I must admit that I learned very little of drains and bells and modes of conveyance, and the like conveniences, during my time in this real future. In some of these visions of Utopias and coming times which I have read, there is a vast amount of detail about building, and social arrangements, and so forth. But while such details are easy enough to obtain when the whole world is contained in one's imagination, they are altogether inaccessible to a real traveller amid such realities as I found here. Conceive the tale of London which a Negro, fresh from Central Africa, would take back to his tribe! What would he know of railway companies, of social movements, of telephone and telegraph wires, of the Parcels Delivery Company, and postal orders and the like? Yet we, at least, should be willing enough to explain these things to him! And even of what he knew, how much could he make his untravelled friend either apprehend or believe? Then, think how narrow the gap between a Negro and a white man of our own times, and how wide the interval between myself and these of the Golden Age! I was sensible of

much which was unseen, and which contributed to my comfort; but save for a general impression of automatic organization, I fear I can convey very little of the difference to your mind.

'In the matter of sepulture, for instance, I could see no signs of crematoria nor anything suggestive of tombs. But it occurred to me that, possibly, there might be cemeteries (or crematoria) somewhere beyond the range of my explorings. This, again, was a question I deliberately put to myself, and my curiosity was at first entirely defeated upon the point. The thing puzzled me, and I was led to make a further remark, which puzzled me still more: that aged and infirm among this people there were none.

'I must confess that my satisfaction with my first theories of an automatic civilization and a decadent humanity did not long endure. Yet I could think of no other. Let me put my difficulties. The several big palaces I had explored were mere living places, great dining-halls and sleeping apartments. I could find no machinery, no appliances of any kind. Yet these people were clothed in pleasant fabrics that must at times need renewal, and their sandals, though undecorated, were fairly complex specimens of metalwork. Somehow such things must be made. And the little people displayed no vestige of a creative tendency. There were no shops, no workshops, no sign of importations among them. They spent all their time in playing gently, in bathing in the river, in making love in a half-playful fashion, in eating fruit and sleeping. I could not see how things were kept going.

'Then, again, about the Time Machine: something, I knew not what, had taken it into the hollow pedestal of the White Sphinx. *Why?* For the life of me I could not imagine. Those waterless wells, too, those flickering pillars. I felt I lacked a clue. I felt – how shall I put it? Suppose you found an inscription, with sentences here and there in excellent plain English, and interpolated therewith, others made up of words, of letters even, absolutely unknown to you? Well, on the third day of my visit, that was how the world of Eight Hundred and Two Thousand Seven Hundred and One presented itself to me!

'That day, too, I made a friend – of a sort. It happened that, as I was watching some of the little people bathing in a shallow, one of them was seized with cramp and began drifting downstream. The main current ran rather swiftly, but not too strongly for even a moderate swimmer. It will give you an idea, therefore, of the strange deficiency in these creatures, when I tell you that none made the slightest attempt to rescue the weakly crying little thing which was drowning before their eyes. When I realized this, I hurriedly slipped off my clothes, and, wading in at a point lower down, I caught the poor mite and drew her safe to land. A little rubbing of the limbs soon brought her round, and I had the satisfaction of seeing she was all right before I left her. I had got to such a low estimate of her kind that I did not expect any gratitude from her. In that, however, I was wrong.

'This happened in the morning. In the afternoon I met my little woman, as I believe it was, as I was returning towards my centre from an exploration, and she received me with cries of delight and presented me with a big garland of flowers – evidently made for me and me alone. The thing took my imagination. Very possibly I had been feeling desolate. At any rate I did my best to display my appreciation of the gift. We were soon seated together in a little stone arbour, engaged in conversation, chiefly of smiles. The creature's friendliness affected me exactly as a child's might have done. We passed each other flowers, and she kissed my hands. I did the same to hers. Then I tried talk, and found that her name was Weena, which, though I don't know what it meant, somehow seemed appropriate enough. That was the beginning of a queer friendship which lasted a week, and ended – as I will tell you!

'She was exactly like a child. She wanted to be with me always. She tried to follow me everywhere, and on my next journey out and about it went to my heart to tire her down, and leave her at last, exhausted and calling after me rather plaintively. But the problems of the world had to be mastered. I had not, I said to myself, come into the future to carry on a miniature flirtation. Yet her distress when I left her was very great, her expostulations at the parting were sometimes frantic, and I think, altogether, I had as much trouble as comfort from her devotion. Nevertheless she was, somehow, a very great comfort. I thought it was mere childish affection that made her cling to me. Until it was too late, I did not clearly know what I had inflicted upon her when I left her. Nor until it was too late did I clearly understand what she was to me. For, by merely seeming fond of me, and showing in her weak, futile way that she cared for me, the little doll of a creature presently gave my return to the neighbourhood of the White Sphinx almost the feeling of coming home; and I would watch for her tiny figure of white and gold so soon as I came over the hill.

'It was from her, too, that I learned that fear had not yet left the world. She was fearless enough in the daylight, and she had the oddest confidence in me; for once, in a foolish moment, I made threatening grimaces at her, and she simply laughed at them. But she dreaded the dark, dreaded shadows, dreaded black things. Darkness to her was the one thing dreadful. It was a singularly passionate emotion, and it set me thinking and observing. I discovered then, among other things, that these little people gathered into the great houses after dark, and slept in droves. To enter upon them without a light was to put them into a tumult of apprehension. I never found one out of doors, or one sleeping alone within doors, after dark. Yet I was still such a blockhead that I missed the lesson of that fear, and in spite of Weena's distress I insisted upon sleeping away from these slumbering multitudes.

'It troubled her greatly, but in the end her odd affection for me triumphed, and for five of the nights of our acquaintance, including the last night of all, she slept with her head pillowed on my arm. But my story slips away

from me as I speak of her. It must have been the night before her rescue that I was awakened about dawn. I had been restless, dreaming most disagreeably that I was drowned, and that sea anemones were feeling over my face with their soft palps. I woke with a start, and with an odd fancy that some greyish animal had just rushed out of the chamber. I tried to get to sleep again, but I felt restless and uncomfortable. It was that dim grey hour when things are just creeping out of darkness, when everything is colourless and clear cut, and yet unreal. I got up, and went down into the great hall, and so out upon the flagstones in front of the palace. I thought I would make a virtue of necessity, and see the sunrise.

'The moon was setting, and the dying moonlight and the first pallor of dawn were mingled in a ghastly half-light. The bushes were inky black, the ground a sombre grey, the sky colourless and cheerless. And up the hill I thought I could see ghosts. There several times, as I scanned the slope, I saw white figures. Twice I fancied I saw a solitary white, ape-like creature running rather quickly up the hill, and once near the ruins I saw a leash of them carrying some dark body. They moved hastily. I did not see what became of them. It seemed that they vanished among the bushes. The dawn was still indistinct, you must understand. I was feeling that chill, uncertain, early-morning feeling you may have known. I doubted my eyes.

'As the eastern sky grew brighter, and the light of the day came on and its vivid colouring returned upon the world once more, I scanned the view keenly. But I saw no vestige of my white figures. They were mere creatures of the half-light. "They must have been ghosts," I said; "I wonder whence they dated." For a queer notion of Grant Allen's came into my head, and amused me. If each generation die and leave ghosts, he argued, the world at last will get overcrowded with them. On that theory they would have grown innumerable some Eight Hundred Thousand Years hence, and it was no great wonder to see four at once. But the jest was unsatisfying, and I was thinking of these figures all the morning, until Weena's rescue drove them out of my head. I associated them in some indefinite way with the white animal I had startled in my first passionate search for the Time Machine. But Weena was a pleasant substitute. Yet all the same, they were soon destined to take far deadlier possession of my mind.

'I think I have said how much hotter than our own was the weather of this Golden Age. I cannot account for it. It may be that the sun was hotter, or the earth nearer the sun. It is usual to assume that the sun will go on cooling steadily in the future. But people, unfamiliar with such speculations as those of the younger Darwin, forget that the planets must ultimately fall back one by one into the parent body. As these catastrophes occur, the sun will blaze with renewed energy; and it may be that some inner planet had suffered this fate. Whatever the reason, the fact remains that the sun was very much hotter than we know it.

'Well, one very hot morning – my fourth, I think – as I was seeking shelter from the heat and glare in a colossal ruin near the great house where I slept and fed, there happened this strange thing: clambering among these heaps of masonry, I found a narrow gallery, whose end and side windows were blocked by fallen masses of stone. By contrast with the brilliancy outside, it seemed at first impenetrably dark to me. I entered it groping, for the change from light to blackness made spots of colour swim before me. Suddenly I halted spellbound. A pair of eyes, luminous by reflection against the daylight without, was watching me out of the darkness.

'The old instinctive dread of wild beasts came upon me. I clenched my hands and steadfastly looked into the glaring eyeballs. I was afraid to turn. Then the thought of the absolute security in which humanity appeared to be living came to my mind. And then I remembered that strange terror of the dark. Overcoming my fear to some extent, I advanced a step and spoke. I will admit that my voice was harsh and ill-controlled. I put out my hand and touched something soft. At once the eyes darted sideways, and something white ran past me. I turned with my heart in my mouth, and saw a queer little ape-like figure, its head held down in a peculiar manner, running across the sunlit space behind me. It blundered against a block of granite, staggered aside, and in a moment was hidden in a black shadow beneath another pile of ruined masonry.

'My impression of it is, of course, imperfect; but I know it was a dull white, and had strange large greyish-red eyes; also that there was flaxen hair on its head and down its back. But, as I say, it went too fast for me to see distinctly. I cannot even say whether it ran on all fours, or only with its forearms held very low. After an instant's pause I followed it into the second heap of ruins. I could not find it at first; but, after a time in the profound obscurity, I came upon one of those round well-like openings of which I have told you, half closed by a fallen pillar. A sudden thought came to me. Could this Thing have vanished down the shaft? I lit a match, and, looking down, I saw a small, white, moving creature, with large bright eyes which regarded me steadfastly as it retreated. It made me shudder. It was so like a human spider! It was clambering down the wall, and now I saw for the first time a number of metal foot and hand rests forming a kind of ladder down the shaft. Then the light burned my fingers and fell out of my hand, going out as it dropped, and when I had lit another the little monster had disappeared.

'I do not know how long I sat peering down that well. It was not for some time that I could succeed in persuading myself that the thing I had seen was human. But, gradually, the truth dawned on me: that Man had not remained one species, but had differentiated into two distinct animals: that my graceful children of the Upper-world were not the sole descendants of our generation, but that this bleached, obscene, nocturnal Thing, which had flashed before me, was also heir to all the ages.

'I thought of the flickering pillars and of my theory of an underground ventilation. I began to suspect their true import. And what, I wondered, was this Lemur doing in my scheme of a perfectly balanced organization? How was it related to the indolent serenity of the beautiful Upper-worlders? And what was hidden down there, at the foot of that shaft? I sat upon the edge of the well telling myself that, at any rate, there was nothing to fear, and that there I must descend for the solution of my difficulties. And withal I was absolutely afraid to go! As I hesitated, two of the beautiful Upper-world people came running in their amorous sport across the daylight in the shadow. The male pursued the female, flinging flowers at her as he ran.

'They seemed distressed to find me, my arm against the overturned pillar, peering down the well. Apparently it was considered bad form to remark these apertures; for when I pointed to this one, and tried to frame a question about it in their tongue, they were still more visibly distressed and turned away. But they were interested by my matches, and I struck some to amuse them. I tried them again about the well, and again I failed. So presently I left them, meaning to go back to Weena, and see what I could get from her. But my mind was already in revolution; my guesses and impressions were slipping and sliding to a new adjustment. I had now a clue to the import of these wells, to the ventilating towers, to the mystery of the ghosts; to say nothing of a hint at the meaning of the bronze gates and the fate of the Time Machine! And very vaguely there came a suggestion towards the solution of the economic problem that had puzzled me.

'Here was the new view. Plainly, this second species of Man was subterranean. There were three circumstances in particular which made me think that its rare emergence above ground was the outcome of a long-continued underground habit. In the first place, there was the bleached look common in most animals that live largely in the dark – the white fish of the Kentucky caves, for instance. Then, those large eyes, with that capacity for reflecting light, are common features of nocturnal things – witness the owl and the cat. And last of all, that evident confusion in the sunshine, that hasty yet fumbling awkward flight towards dark shadow, and that peculiar carriage of the head while in the light – all reinforced the theory of an extreme sensitiveness of the retina.

'Beneath my feet, then, the earth must be tunnelled enormously, and these tunnellings were the habitat of the new race. The presence of ventilating shafts and wells along the hill slopes – everywhere, in fact, except along the river valley – showed how universal were its ramifications. What so natural, then, as to assume that it was in this artificial Under-world that such work as was necessary to the comfort of the daylight race was done? The notion was so plausible that I at once accepted it, and went on to assume the how of this splitting of the human species. I dare say you will anticipate the shape of my theory; though, for myself, I very soon felt that it fell far short of the truth.

'At first, proceeding from the problems of our own age, it seemed clear as daylight to me that the gradual widening of the present merely temporary and social difference between the Capitalist and the Labourer, was the key to the whole position. No doubt it will seem grotesque enough to you – and wildly incredible! – and yet even now there are existing circumstances to point that way. There is a tendency to utilize underground space for the less ornamental purposes of civilization; there is the Metropolitan Railway in London, for instance, there are new electric railways, there are subways, there are underground workrooms and restaurants, and they increase and multiply. Evidently, I thought, this tendency had increased till Industry had gradually lost its birthright in the sky. I mean that it had gone deeper and deeper into larger and ever larger underground factories, spending a still-increasing amount of its time therein, till, in the end—! Even now, does not an East End worker live in such artificial conditions as practically to be cut off from the natural surface of the earth?

'Again, the exclusive tendency of richer people – due, no doubt, to the increasing refinement of their education, and the widening gulf between them and the rude violence of the poor – is already leading to the closing, in their interest, of considerable portions of the surface of the land. About London, for instance, perhaps half the prettier country is shut in against intrusion. And this same widening gulf – which is due to the length and expense of the higher educational process and the increased facilities for and temptations towards refined habits on the part of the rich – will make that exchange between class and class, that promotion by intermarriage which at present retards the splitting of our species along lines of social stratification, less and less frequent. So, in the end, above ground you must have the Haves, pursuing pleasure and comfort and beauty, and below ground the Have-nots, the Workers getting continually adapted to the conditions of their labour. Once they were there, they would no doubt have to pay rent, and not a little of it, for the ventilation of their caverns; and if they refused, they would starve or be suffocated for arrears. Such of them as were so constituted as to be miserable and rebellious would die; and, in the end, the balance being permanent, the survivors would become as well adapted to the conditions of underground life, and as happy in their way, as the Upper-world people were to theirs. As it seemed to me, the refined beauty and the etiolated pallor followed naturally enough.

'The great triumph of Humanity I had dreamed of took a different shape in my mind. It had been no such triumph of moral education and general co-operation as I had imagined. Instead, I saw a real aristocracy, armed with a perfected science and working to a logical conclusion the industrial system of today. Its triumph had not been simply a triumph over Nature, but a triumph over Nature and the fellow man. This, I must warn you, was my theory at the time. I had no convenient cicerone in the pattern of the

Utopian books. My explanation may be absolutely wrong. I still think it is the most plausible one. But even on this supposition the balanced civilization that was at last attained must have long since passed its zenith, and was now far fallen into decay. The too-perfect security of the Upper-worlders had led them to a slow movement of degeneration, to a general dwindling in size, strength, and intelligence. That I could see clearly enough already. What had happened to the Under-grounders I did not yet suspect; but from what I had seen of the Morlocks – that, by the by, was the name by which these creatures were called – I could imagine that the modification of the human type was even far more profound than among the Eloi, the beautiful race that I already knew.

'Then came troublesome doubts. Why had the Morlocks taken my Time Machine? For I felt sure it was they who had taken it. Why, too, if the Eloi were masters, could they not restore the machine to me? And why were they so terribly afraid of the dark? I proceeded, as I have said, to question Weena about this Under-world, but here again I was disappointed. At first she would not understand my questions, and presently she refused to answer them. She shivered as though the topic was unendurable. And when I pressed her, perhaps a little harshly, she burst into tears. They were the only tears, except my own, I ever saw in that Golden Age. When I saw them I ceased abruptly to trouble about the Morlocks, and was only concerned in banishing these signs of the human inheritance from Weena's eyes. And very soon she was smiling and clapping her hands, while I solemnly burned a match.

CHAPTER VI

'It may seem odd to you, but it was two days before I could follow up the new-found clue in what was manifestly the proper way. I felt a peculiar shrinking from those pallid bodies. They were just the half-bleached colour of the worms and things one sees preserved in spirit in a zoological museum. And they were filthily cold to the touch. Probably my shrinking was largely due to the sympathetic influence of the Eloi, whose disgust of the Morlocks I now began to appreciate.

'The next night I did not sleep well. Probably my health was a little disordered. I was oppressed with perplexity and doubt. Once or twice I had a feeling of intense fear for which I could perceive no definite reason. I remember creeping noiselessly into the great hall where the little people were sleeping in the moonlight – that night Weena was among them – and feeling reassured by their presence. It occurred to me even then, that in the course of a few days the moon must pass through its last quarter, and the nights grow dark, when the appearances of these unpleasant creatures from below, these whitened Lemurs, this new vermin that had replaced the old, might be more abundant. And on both these days I had the restless feeling of one who shirks an inevitable duty. I felt assured that the Time Machine was only to be recovered by boldly penetrating these underground mysteries. Yet I could not face the mystery. If only I had had a companion it would have been different. But I was so horribly alone, and even to clamber down into the darkness of the well appalled me. I don't know if you will understand my feeling, but I never felt quite safe at my back.

'It was this restlessness, this insecurity, perhaps, that drove me further and further afield in my exploring expeditions. Going to the south-westward towards the rising country that is now called Combe Wood, I observed far off, in the direction of nineteenth-century Banstead, a vast green structure, different in character from any I had hitherto seen. It was larger than the largest of the palaces or ruins I knew, and the façade had an Oriental look: the face of it having the lustre, as well as the pale-green tint, a kind of bluish-green, of a certain type of Chinese porcelain. This difference in aspect suggested a difference in use, and I was minded to push on and explore. But the day was growing late, and I had come upon the sight of the place after a long and tiring circuit; so I resolved to hold over the adventure for the following day, and I returned to the welcome and the caresses of little Weena. But next morning I perceived clearly enough that my curiosity regarding the Palace of Green Porcelain was a piece of self-deception, to enable me to shirk, by another day, an experience I dreaded. I resolved I would make the descent without further waste of time, and started out in the early morning towards a well near the ruins of granite and aluminium.

'Little Weena ran with me. She danced beside me to the well, but when she saw me lean over the mouth and look downward, she seemed strangely disconcerted. "Good-bye, little Weena," I said, kissing her; and then putting her down, I began to feel over the parapet for the climbing hooks. Rather hastily, I may as well confess, for I feared my courage might leak away! At first she watched me in amazement. Then she gave a most piteous cry, and running to me, she began to pull at me with her little hands. I think her opposition nerved me rather to proceed. I shook her off, perhaps a little roughly, and in another moment I was in the throat of the well. I saw her agonized face over the parapet, and smiled to reassure her. Then I had to look down at the unstable hooks to which I clung.

'I had to clamber down a shaft of perhaps two hundred yards. The descent was effected by means of metallic bars projecting from the sides of the well, and these being adapted to the needs of a creature much smaller and lighter than myself, I was speedily cramped and fatigued by the descent. And not simply fatigued! One of the bars bent suddenly under my weight, and almost swung me off into the blackness beneath. For a moment I hung by one hand, and after that experience I did not dare to rest again. Though my arms and back were presently acutely painful, I went on clambering down the sheer descent with as quick a motion as possible. Glancing upward, I saw the aperture, a small blue disk, in which a star was visible, while little Weena's head showed as a round black projection. The thudding sound of a machine below grew louder and more oppressive. Everything save that little disk above was profoundly dark, and when I looked up again Weena had disappeared.

'I was in an agony of discomfort. I had some thought of trying to go up the shaft again, and leave the Under-world alone. But even while I turned this over in my mind I continued to descend. At last, with intense relief, I saw dimly coming up, a foot to the right of me, a slender loophole in the wall. Swinging myself in, I found it was the aperture of a narrow horizontal tunnel in which I could lie down and rest. It was not too soon. My arms ached, my back was cramped, and I was trembling with the prolonged terror of a fall. Besides this, the unbroken darkness had had a distressing effect upon my eyes. The air was full of the throb and hum of machinery pumping air down the shaft.

'I do not know how long I lay. I was roused by a soft hand touching my face. Starting up in the darkness I snatched at my matches and, hastily striking one, I saw three stooping white creatures similar to the one I had seen above ground in the ruin, hastily retreating before the light. Living, as they did, in what appeared to me impenetrable darkness, their eyes were abnormally large and sensitive, just as are the pupils of the abysmal fishes, and they reflected the light in the same way. I have no doubt they could see me in that rayless obscurity, and they did not seem to have any fear of

me apart from the light. But, so soon as I struck a match in order to see them, they fled incontinently, vanishing into dark gutters and tunnels, from which their eyes glared at me in the strangest fashion.

'I tried to call to them, but the language they had was apparently different from that of the Upper-world people; so that I was needs left to my own unaided efforts, and the thought of flight before exploration was even then in my mind. But I said to myself, "You are in for it now," and, feeling my way along the tunnel, I found the noise of machinery grow louder. Presently the walls fell away from me, and I came to a large open space, and striking another match, saw that I had entered a vast arched cavern, which stretched into utter darkness beyond the range of my light. The view I had of it was as much as one could see in the burning of a match.

'Necessarily my memory is vague. Great shapes like big machines rose out of the dimness, and cast grotesque black shadows, in which dim spectral Morlocks sheltered from the glare. The place, by the by, was very stuffy and oppressive, and the faint halitus of freshly shed blood was in the air. Some way down the central vista was a little table of white metal, laid with what seemed a meal. The Morlocks at any rate were carnivorous! Even at the time, I remember wondering what large animal could have survived to furnish the red joint I saw. It was all very indistinct: the heavy smell, the big unmeaning shapes, the obscene figures lurking in the shadows, and only waiting for the darkness to come at me again! Then the match burned down, and stung my fingers, and fell, a wriggling red spot in the blackness.

'I have thought since how particularly ill-equipped I was for such an experience. When I had started with the Time Machine, I had started with the absurd assumption that the men of the Future would certainly be infinitely ahead of ourselves in all their appliances. I had come without arms, without medicine, without anything to smoke – at times I missed tobacco frightfully – even without enough matches. If only I had thought of a Kodak! I could have flashed that glimpse of the Underworld in a second, and examined it at leisure. But, as it was, I stood there with only the weapons and the powers that Nature had endowed me with – hands, feet and teeth; these, and four safety-matches that still remained to me.

'I was afraid to push my way in among all this machinery in the dark, and it was only with my last glimpse of light I discovered that my store of matches had run low. It had never occurred to me until that moment that there was any need to economize them, and I had wasted almost half the box in astonishing the Upper-worlders, to whom fire was a novelty. Now, as I say, I had four left, and while I stood in the dark, a hand touched mine, lank fingers came feeling over my face, and I was sensible of a peculiar unpleasant odour. I fancied I heard the breathing of a crowd of those dreadful little beings about me. I felt the box of matches in my hand being gently disengaged, and other hands behind me plucking at my clothing.

The sense of these unseen creatures examining me was indescribably unpleasant. The sudden realization of my ignorance of their ways of thinking and doing came home to me very vividly in the darkness. I shouted at them as loudly as I could. They started away, and then I could feel them approaching me again. They clutched at me more boldly, whispering odd sounds to each other. I shivered violently, and shouted again – rather discordantly. This time they were not so seriously alarmed, and they made a queer laughing noise as they came back at me. I will confess I was horribly frightened. I determined to strike another match and escape under the protection of its glare. I did so, and eking out the flicker with a scrap of paper from my pocket, I made good my retreat to the narrow tunnel. But I had scarce entered this when my light was blown out and in the blackness I could hear the Morlocks rustling like wind among leaves, and pattering like the rain, as they hurried after me.

'In a moment I was clutched by several hands, and there was no mistaking that they were trying to haul me back. I struck another light, and waved it in their dazzled faces. You can scarce imagine how nauseatingly inhuman they looked – those pale, chinless faces and great, lidless, pinkish-grey eyes! – as they stared in their blindness and bewilderment. But I did not stay to look, I promise you: I retreated again, and when my second match had ended, I struck my third. It had almost burned through when I reached the opening into the shaft. I lay down on the edge, for the throb of the great pump below made me giddy. Then I felt sideways for the projecting hooks, and, as I did so, my feet were grasped from behind, and I was violently tugged backward. I lit my last match . . . and it incontinently went out. But I had my hand on the climbing bars now, and, kicking violently, I disengaged myself from the clutches of the Morlocks and was speedily clambering up the shaft, while they stayed peering and blinking up at me: all but one little wretch who followed me for some way, and well-nigh secured my boot as a trophy.

'That climb seemed interminable to me. With the last twenty or thirty feet of it a deadly nausea came upon me. I had the greatest difficulty in keeping my hold. The last few yards was a frightful struggle against this faintness. Several times my head swam, and I felt all the sensations of falling. At last, however, I got over the well-mouth somehow, and staggered out of the ruin into the blinding sunlight. I fell upon my face. Even the soil smelt sweet and clean. Then I remember Weena kissing my hands and ears, and the voices of others among the Eloi. Then, for a time, I was insensible.

CHAPTER VII

'Now, indeed, I seemed in a worse case than before. Hitherto, except during my night's anguish at the loss of the Time Machine, I had felt a sustaining hope of ultimate escape, but that hope was staggered by these new discoveries. Hitherto I had merely thought myself impeded by the childish simplicity of the little people, and by some unknown forces which I had only to understand to overcome; but there was an altogether new element in the sickening quality of the Morlocks – a something inhuman and malign. Instinctively I loathed them. Before, I had felt as a man might feel who had fallen into a pit: my concern was with the pit and how to get out of it. Now I felt like a beast in a trap, whose enemy would come upon him soon.

'The enemy I dreaded may surprise you. It was the darkness of the new moon. Weena had put this into my head by some at first incomprehensible remarks about the Dark Nights. It was not now such a very difficult problem to guess what the coming Dark Nights might mean. The moon was on the wane: each night there was a longer interval of darkness. And I now understood to some slight degree at least the reason of the fear of the little Upper-world people for the dark. I wondered vaguely what foul villainy it might be that the Morlocks did under the new moon. I felt pretty sure now that my second hypothesis was all wrong. The Upper-world people might once have been the favoured aristocracy, and the Morlocks their mechanical servants: but that had long since passed away. The two species that had resulted from the evolution of man were sliding down towards, or had already arrived at, an altogether new relationship. The Eloi, like the Carolingian kings, had decayed to a mere beautiful futility. They still possessed the earth on sufferance: since the Morlocks, subterranean for innumerable generations, had come at last to find the daylit surface intolerable. And the Morlocks made their garments, I inferred, and maintained them in their habitual needs, perhaps through the survival of an old habit of service. They did it as a standing horse paws with his foot, or as a man enjoys killing animals in sport: because ancient and departed necessities had impressed it on the organism. But, clearly, the old order was already in part reversed. The Nemesis of the delicate ones was creeping on apace. Ages ago, thousands of generations ago, man had thrust his brother man out of the ease and the sunshine. And now that brother was coming back changed! Already the Eloi had begun to learn one old lesson anew. They were becoming reacquainted with Fear. And suddenly there came into my head the memory of the meat I had seen in the Under-world. It seemed odd how it floated into my mind: not stirred up as it were by the current of my meditations, but coming in almost like a question from outside. I tried to recall the form of it. I had a vague sense of something familiar, but I could not tell what it was at the time.

'Still, however helpless the little people in the presence of their mysterious Fear, I was differently constituted. I came out of this age of ours, this ripe prime of the human race, when Fear does not paralyse and mystery has lost its terrors. I at least would defend myself. Without further delay I determined to make myself arms and a fastness where I might sleep. With that refuge as a base, I could face this strange world with some of that confidence I had lost in realizing to what creatures night by night I lay exposed. I felt I could never sleep again until my bed was secure from them. I shuddered with horror to think how they must already have examined me.

'I wandered during the afternoon along the valley of the Thames, but found nothing that commended itself to my mind as inaccessible. All the buildings and trees seemed easily practicable to such dexterous climbers as the Morlocks, to judge by their wells, must be. Then the tall pinnacles of the Palace of Green Porcelain and the polished gleam of its walls came back to my memory; and in the evening, taking Weena like a child upon my shoulder, I went up the hills towards the south-west. The distance, I had reckoned, was seven or eight miles, but it must have been nearer eighteen. I had first seen the place on a moist afternoon when distances are deceptively diminished. In addition, the heel of one of my shoes was loose, and a nail was working through the sole – they were comfortable old shoes I wore about indoors – so that I was lame. And it was already long past sunset when I came in sight of the palace, silhouetted black against the pale yellow of the sky.

'Weena had been hugely delighted when I began to carry her, but after a while she desired me to let her down, and ran along by the side of me, occasionally darting off on either hand to pick flowers to stick in my pockets. My pockets had always puzzled Weena, but at the last she had concluded that they were an eccentric kind of vase for floral decoration. At least she utilized them for that purpose. And that reminds me! In changing my jacket I found. . . .'

The Time Traveller paused, put his hand into his pocket, and silently placed two withered flowers, not unlike very large white mallows, upon the little table. Then he resumed his narrative.

'As the hush of evening crept over the world and we proceeded over the hill crest towards Wimbledon, Weena grew tired and wanted to return to the house of grey stone. But I pointed out the distant pinnacles of the Palace of Green Porcelain to her, and contrived to make her understand that we were seeking a refuge there from her Fear. You know that great pause that comes upon things before the dusk? Even the breeze stops in the trees. To me there is always an air of expectation about that evening stillness. The sky was clear, remote, and empty save for a few horizontal bars far down in the sunset. Well, that night the expectation took the colour of my fears. In that darkling calm my senses seemed preternaturally sharpened. I fancied I could even feel the hollowness of the ground beneath my feet: could, indeed,

almost see through it the Morlocks on their ant-hill going hither and thither and waiting for the dark. In my excitement I fancied that they would receive my invasion of their burrows as a declaration of war. And why had they taken my Time Machine?

'So we went on in the quiet, and the twilight deepened into night. The clear blue of the distance faded, and one star after another came out. The ground grew dim and the trees black. Weena's fears and her fatigue grew upon her. I took her in my arms and talked to her and caressed her. Then, as the darkness grew deeper, she put her arms round my neck, and, closing her eyes, tightly pressed her face against my shoulder. So we went down a long slope into a valley, and there in the dimness I almost walked into a little river. This I waded, and went up the opposite side of the valley, past a number of sleeping houses, and by a statue – a Faun, or some such figure, minus the head. Here too were acacias. So far I had seen nothing of the Morlocks, but it was yet early in the night, and the darker hours before the old moon rose were still to come.

'From the brow of the next hill I saw a thick wood spreading wide and black before me. I hesitated at this. I could see no end to it, either to the right or the left. Feeling tired – my feet, in particular, were very sore – I carefully lowered Weena from my shoulder as I halted, and sat down upon the turf. I could no longer see the Palace of Green Porcelain, and I was in doubt of my direction. I looked into the thickness of the wood and thought of what it might hide. Under that dense tangle of branches one would be out of sight of the stars. Even were there no other lurking danger – a danger I did not care to let my imagination loose upon – there would still be all the roots to stumble over and the tree-boles to strike against.

'I was very tired, too, after the excitements of the day; so I decided that I would not face it, but would pass the night upon the open hill.

'Weena, I was glad to find, was fast asleep. I carefully wrapped her in my jacket, and sat down beside her to wait for the moonrise. The hillside was quiet and deserted, but from the black of the wood there came now and then a stir of living things. Above me shone the stars, for the night was very clear. I felt a certain sense of friendly comfort in their twinkling. All the old constellations had gone from the sky, however: that slow movement which is imperceptible in a hundred human lifetimes, had long since rearranged them in unfamiliar groupings. But the Milky Way, it seemed to me, was still the same tattered streamer of star-dust as of yore. Southward (as I judged it) was a very bright red star that was new to me; it was even more splendid than our own green Sirius. And amid all these scintillating points of light one bright planet shone kindly and steadily like the face of an old friend.

'Looking at these stars suddenly dwarfed my own troubles and all the gravities of terrestrial life. I thought of their unfathomable distance, and the slow inevitable drift of their movements out of the unknown past into

the unknown future. I thought of the great precessional cycle that the pole of the earth describes. Only forty times had that silent revolution occurred during all the years that I had traversed. And during these few revolutions all the activity, all the traditions, the complex organizations, the nations, languages, literatures, aspirations, even the mere memory of Man as I knew him, had been swept out of existence. Instead were these frail creatures who had forgotten their high ancestry, and the white Things of which I went in terror. Then I thought of the Great Fear that was between the two species, and for the first time, with a sudden shiver, came the clear knowledge of what the meat I had seen might be. Yet it was too horrible! I looked at little Weena sleeping beside me, her face white and starlike under the stars, and forthwith dismissed the thought.

'Through that long night I held my mind off the Morlocks as well as I could, and whiled away the time by trying to fancy I could find signs of the old constellations in the new confusion. The sky kept very clear, except for a hazy cloud or so. No doubt I dozed at times. Then, as my vigil wore on, came a faintness in the eastward sky, like the reflection of some colourless fire, and the old moon rose, thin and peaked and white. And close behind, and overtaking it, and overflowing it, the dawn came, pale at first, and then growing pink and warm. No Morlocks had approached us. Indeed, I had seen none upon the hill that night. And in the confidence of renewed day it almost seemed to me that my fear had been unreasonable. I stood up and found my foot with the loose heel swollen at the ankle and painful under the heel; so I sat down again, took off my shoes, and flung them away.

'I awakened Weena, and we went down into the wood, now green and pleasant instead of black and forbidding. We found some fruit wherewith to break our fast. We soon met others of the dainty ones, laughing and dancing in the sunlight as though there was no such thing in nature as the night. And then I thought once more of the meat that I had seen. I felt assured now of what it was, and from the bottom of my heart I pitied this last feeble rill from the great flood of humanity. Clearly, at some time in the Long-Ago of human decay the Morlocks' food had run short. Possibly they had lived on rats and such-like vermin. Even now man is far less discriminating and exclusive in his food than he was – far less than any monkey. His prejudice against human flesh is no deep-seated instinct. And so these inhuman sons of men—! I tried to look at the thing in a scientific spirit. After all, they were less human and more remote than our cannibal ancestors of three or four thousand years ago. And the intelligence that would have made this state of things a torment had gone. Why should I trouble myself? These Eloi were mere fatted cattle, which the ant-like Morlocks preserved and preyed upon – probably saw to the breeding of. And there was Weena dancing at my side!

'Then I tried to preserve myself from the horror that was coming upon me, by regarding it as a rigorous punishment of human selfishness. Man had been content to live in ease and delight upon the labours of his fellow man, had taken Necessity as his watchword and excuse, and in the fullness of time Necessity had come home to him. I even tried a Carlyle-like scorn of this wretched aristocracy in decay. But this attitude of mind was impossible. However great their intellectual degradation, the Eloi had kept too much of the human form not to claim my sympathy, and to make me perforce a sharer in their degradation and their Fear.

'I had at that time very vague ideas as to the course I should pursue. My first was to secure some safe place of refuge, and to make myself such arms of metal or stone as I could contrive. That necessity was immediate. In the next place, I hoped to procure some means of fire, so that I should have the weapon of a torch at hand, for nothing, I knew, would be more efficient against these Morlocks. Then I wanted to arrange some contrivance to break open the doors of bronze under the White Sphinx. I had in mind a battering ram. I had a persuasion that if I could enter those doors and carry a blaze of light before me I should discover the Time Machine and escape. I could not imagine the Morlocks were strong enough to move it far away. Weena I had resolved to bring with me to our own time. And turning such schemes over in my mind I pursued our way towards the building which my fancy had chosen as our dwelling.

CHAPTER VIII

'I found the Palace of Green Porcelain, when we approached it about noon, deserted and falling into ruin. Only ragged vestiges of glass remained in its windows, and great sheets of the green facing had fallen away from the corroded metallic framework. It lay very high upon a turfy down, and looking north-eastward before I entered it, I was surprised to see a large estuary, or even creek, where I judged Wandsworth and Battersea must once have been. I thought then – though I never followed up the thought – of what might have happened, or might be happening, to the living things in the sea.

'The material of the Palace proved on examination to be indeed porcelain, and along the face of it I saw an inscription in some unknown character. I thought, rather foolishly, that Weena might help me to interpret this, but I only learned that the bare idea of writing had never entered her head. She always seemed to me, I fancy, more human than she was, perhaps because her affection was so human.

'Within the big valves of the door – which were open and broken – we found, instead of the customary hall, a long gallery lit by many side windows. At the first glance I was reminded of a museum. The tiled floor was thick with dust, and a remarkable array of miscellaneous objects was shrouded in the same grey covering. Then I perceived, standing strange and gaunt in the centre of the hall, what was clearly the lower part of a huge skeleton. I recognized by the oblique feet that it was some extinct creature after the fashion of the Megatherium. The skull and the upper bones lay beside it in the thick dust, and in one place, where rain-water had dropped through a leak in the roof, the thing itself had been worn away. Further in the gallery was the huge skeleton barrel of a Brontosaurus. My museum hypothesis was confirmed. Going towards the side I found what appeared to be sloping shelves, and clearing away the thick dust, I found the old familiar glass cases of our own time. But they must have been air-tight to judge from the fair preservation of some of their contents.

'Clearly we stood among the ruins of some latter-day South Kensington! Here, apparently, was the Palaeontological Section, and a very splendid array of fossils it must have been, though the inevitable process of decay that had been staved off for a time, and had, through the extinction of bacteria and fungi, lost ninety-nine hundredths of its force, was nevertheless, with extreme sureness if with extreme slowness at work again upon all its treasures. Here and there I found traces of the little people in the shape of rare fossils broken to pieces or threaded in strings upon reeds. And the cases had in some instances been bodily removed – by the Morlocks as I judged. The place was very silent. The thick dust deadened our footsteps. Weena, who had been rolling a sea urchin down the sloping glass of

a case, presently came, as I stared about me, and very quietly took my hand and stood beside me.

'And at first I was so much surprised by this ancient monument of an intellectual age, that I gave no thought to the possibilities it presented. Even my preoccupation about the Time Machine receded a little from my mind.

'To judge from the size of the place, this Palace of Green Porcelain had a great deal more in it than a Gallery of Palaeontology; possibly historical galleries; it might be, even a library! To me, at least in my present circumstances, these would be vastly more interesting than this spectacle of old-time geology in decay. Exploring, I found another short gallery running transversely to the first. This appeared to be devoted to minerals, and the sight of a block of sulphur set my mind running on gunpowder. But I could find no saltpetre; indeed, no nitrates of any kind. Doubtless they had deliquesced ages ago. Yet the sulphur hung in my mind, and set up a train of thinking. As for the rest of the contents of that gallery, though on the whole they were the best preserved of all I saw, I had little interest. I am no specialist in mineralogy, and I went on down a very ruinous aisle running parallel to the first hall I had entered. Apparently this section had been devoted to natural history, but everything had long since passed out of recognition. A few shrivelled and blackened vestiges of what had once been stuffed animals, desiccated mummies in jars that had once held spirit, a brown dust of departed plants: that was all! I was sorry for that, because I should have been glad to trace the patent readjustments by which the conquest of animated nature had been attained. Then we came to a gallery of simply colossal proportions, but singularly ill-lit, the floor of it running downward at a slight angle from the end at which I entered. At intervals white globes hung from the ceiling – many of them cracked and smashed – which suggested that originally the place had been artificially lit. Here I was more in my element, for rising on either side of me were the huge bulks of big machines, all greatly corroded and many broken down, but some still fairly complete. You know I have a certain weakness for mechanism, and I was inclined to linger among these; the more so as for the most part they had the interest of puzzles, and I could make only the vaguest guesses at what they were for. I fancied that if I could solve their puzzles I should find myself in possession of powers that might be of use against the Morlocks.

'Suddenly Weena came very close to my side. So suddenly that she startled me. Had it not been for her I do not think I should have noticed that the floor of the gallery sloped at all.* The end I had come in at was quite above ground, and was lit by rare slit-like windows. As you went down the length, the ground came up against these windows, until at last there was

* It may be, of course, that the floor did not slope, but that the museum was built into the side of a hill. – Ed.

a pit like the "area" of a London house before each, and only a narrow line of daylight at the top. I went slowly along, puzzling about the machines, and had been too intent upon them to notice the gradual diminution of the light, until Weena's increasing apprehensions drew my attention. Then I saw that the gallery ran down at last into a thick darkness. I hesitated, and then, as I looked round me, I saw that the dust was less abundant and its surface less even. Further away towards the dimness, it appeared to be broken by a number of small narrow footprints. My sense of the immediate presence of the Morlocks revived at that. I felt that I was wasting my time in the academic examination of machinery. I called to mind that it was already far advanced in the afternoon, and that I had still no weapon, no refuge, and no means of making a fire. And then down in the remote blackness of the gallery I heard a peculiar pattering, and the same odd noises I had heard down the well.

'I took Weena's hand. Then, struck with a sudden idea, I left her and turned to a machine from which projected a lever not unlike those in a signal-box. Clambering upon the stand, and grasping this lever in my hands, I put all my weight upon it sideways. Suddenly Weena, deserted in the central aisle, began to whimper. I had judged the strength of the lever pretty correctly, for it snapped after a minute's strain, and I rejoined her with a mace in my hand more than sufficient, I judged, for any Morlock skull I might encounter. And I longed very much to kill a Morlock or so. Very inhuman, you may think, to want to go killing one's own descendants! But it was impossible, somehow, to feel any humanity in the things. Only my disinclination to leave Weena, and a persuasion that if I began to slake my thirst for murder my Time Machine might suffer, restrained me from going straight down the gallery and killing the brutes I heard.

'Well, mace in one hand and Weena in the other, I went out of that gallery and into another and still larger one, which at the first glance reminded me of a military chapel hung with tattered flags. The brown and charred rags that hung from the sides of it, I presently recognized as the decaying vestiges of books. They had long since dropped to pieces, and every semblance of print had left them. But here and there were warped boards and cracked metallic clasps that told the tale well enough. Had I been a literary man I might, perhaps, have moralized upon the futility of all ambition. But as it was, the thing that struck me with keenest force was the enormous waste of labour to which this sombre wilderness of rotting paper testified. At the time I will confess that I thought chiefly of the *Philosophical Transactions* and my own seventeen papers upon physical optics.

'Then, going up a broad staircase, we came to what may once have been a gallery of technical chemistry. And here I had not a little hope of useful discoveries. Except at one end where the roof had collapsed, this gallery was well preserved. I went eagerly to every unbroken case. And at last, in one

of the really airtight cases, I found a box of matches. Very eagerly I tried
them. They were perfectly good. They were not even damp. I turned to
Weena. "Dance," I cried to her in her own tongue. For now I had a weapon
indeed against the horrible creatures we feared. And so, in that derelict
museum, upon the thick soft carpeting of dust, to Weena's huge delight, I
solemnly performed a kind of composite dance, whistling *The Land of the
Leal* as cheerfully as I could. In part it was a modest can-can, in part a
step-dance, in part a skirt-dance (so far as my tail-coat permitted), and in
part original. For I am naturally inventive, as you know.

'Now, I still think that for this box of matches to have escaped the wear
of time for immemorial years was a most strange, as for me it was a most
fortunate thing. Yet, oddly enough, I found a far unlikelier substance, and
that was camphor. I found it in a sealed jar, that by chance, I suppose, had
been really hermetically sealed. I fancied at first that it was paraffin wax,
and smashed the glass accordingly. But the odour of camphor was unmis-
takable. In the universal decay this volatile substance had chanced to survive,
perhaps through many thousands of centuries. It reminded me of a sepia
painting I had once seen done from the ink of a fossil Belemnite that must
have perished and become fossilized millions of years ago. I was about to
throw it away, but I remembered that it was inflammable and burned with
a good bright flame – was, in fact, an excellent candle – and I put it in my
pocket. I found no explosives, however, nor any means of breaking down
the bronze doors. As yet my iron crowbar was the most helpful thing I had
chanced upon. Nevertheless I left that gallery greatly elated.

'I cannot tell you all the story of that long afternoon. It would require a
great effort of memory to recall my explorations in at all the proper order.
I remember a long gallery of rusting stands of arms, and how I hesitated
between my crowbar and a hatchet or a sword. I could not carry both,
however, and my bar of iron promised best against the bronze gates. There
were numbers of guns, pistols, and rifles. The most were masses of rust, but
many were of some new metal, and still fairly sound. But any cartridges or
powder there may once have been had rotted into dust. One corner I saw
was charred and shattered; perhaps, I thought, by an explosion among the
specimens. In another place was a vast array of idols – Polynesian, Mexican,
Grecian, Phoenician, every country on earth I should think. And here,
yielding to an irresistible impulse, I wrote my name upon the nose of a
steatite monster from South America that particularly took my fancy.

'As the evening drew on, my interest waned. I went through gallery after
gallery, dusty, silent, often ruinous, the exhibits sometimes mere heaps of
rust and lignite, sometimes fresher. In one place I suddenly found myself
near the model of a tin-mine, and then by the merest accident I discovered,
in an airtight case, two dynamite cartridges! I shouted "Eureka!" and smashed
the case with joy. Then came a doubt. I hesitated. Then, selecting a little

side gallery, I made my essay. I never felt such a disappointment as I did in waiting five, ten, fifteen minutes for an explosion that never came. Of course the things were dummies, as I might have guessed from their presence. I really believe that had they not been so, I should have rushed off incontinently and blown Sphinx, bronze doors, and (as it proved) my chances of finding the Time Machine, all together into non-existence.

'It was after that, I think, that we came to a little open court within the palace. It was turfed, and had three fruit trees. So we rested and refreshed ourselves. Towards sunset I began to consider our position. Night was creeping upon us, and my inaccessible hiding-place had still to be found. But that troubled me very little now. I had in my possession a thing that was, perhaps, the best of all defences against the Morlocks – I had matches! I had the camphor in my pocket, too, if a blaze were needed. It seemed to me that the best thing we could do would be to pass the night in the open, protected by a fire. In the morning there was the getting of the Time Machine. Towards that, as yet, I had only my iron mace. But now, with my growing knowledge, I felt very differently towards those bronze doors. Up to this, I had refrained from forcing them, largely because of the mystery on the other side. They had never impressed me as being very strong, and I hoped to find my bar of iron not altogether inadequate for the work.

CHAPTER IX

'We emerged from the palace while the sun was still in part above the horizon. I was determined to reach the White Sphinx early the next morning, and ere the dusk I purposed pushing through the woods that had stopped me on the previous journey. My plan was to go as far as possible that night, and then, building a fire, to sleep in the protection of its glare. Accordingly, as we went along I gathered any sticks or dried grass I saw, and presently had my arms full of such litter. Thus loaded, our progress was slower than I had anticipated, and besides Weena was tired. And I began to suffer from sleepiness too; so that it was full night before we reached the wood. Upon the shrubby hill of its edge Weena would have stopped, fearing the darkness before us; but a singular sense of impending calamity, that should indeed have served me as a warning, drove me onward. I had been without sleep for a night and two days, and I was feverish and irritable. I felt sleep coming upon me, and the Morlocks with it.

'While we hesitated, among the black bushes behind us, and dim against their blackness, I saw three crouching figures. There was scrub and long grass all about us, and I did not feel safe from their insidious approach. The forest, I calculated, was rather less than a mile across. If we could get through it to the bare hillside, there, as it seemed to me, was an altogether safer rest-ing-place; I thought that with my matches and my camphor I could contrive to keep my path illuminated through the woods. Yet it was evident that if I was to flourish matches with my hands I should have to abandon my firewood; so, rather reluctantly, I put it down. And then it came into my head that I would amaze our friends behind by lighting it. I was to discover the atrocious folly of this proceeding, but it came to my mind as an ingenious move for covering our retreat.

'I don't know if you have ever thought what a rare thing flame must be in the absence of man and in a temperate climate. The sun's heat is rarely strong enough to burn, even when it is focused by dewdrops, as is sometimes the case in more tropical districts. Lightning may blast and blacken, but it rarely gives rise to widespread fire. Decaying vegetation may occasionally smoulder with the heat of its fermentation, but this rarely results in flame. In this decadence, too, the art of fire-making had been forgotten on the earth. The red tongues that went licking up my heap of wood were an altogether new and strange thing to Weena.

'She wanted to run to it and play with it. I believe she would have cast herself into it had I not restrained her. But I caught her up, and in spite of her struggles, plunged boldly before me into the wood. For a little way the glare of my fire lit the path. Looking back presently, I could see, through the crowded stems, that from my heap of sticks the blaze had spread to some

bushes adjacent, and a curved line of fire was creeping up the grass of the hill. I laughed at that, and turned again to the dark trees before me. It was very black, and Weena clung to me convulsively, but there was still, as my eyes grew accustomed to the darkness, sufficient light for me to avoid the stems. Overhead it was simply black, except where a gap of remote blue sky shone down upon us here and there. I struck none of my matches because I had no hand free. Upon my left arm I carried my little one, in my right hand I had my iron bar.

'For some way I heard nothing but the crackling twigs under my feet, the faint rustle of the breeze above, and my own breathing and the throb of the blood-vessels in my ears. Then I seemed to know of a pattering about me. I pushed on grimly. The pattering grew more distinct, and then I caught the same queer sound and voices I had heard in the Under-world. There were evidently several of the Morlocks, and they were closing in upon me. Indeed, in another minute I felt a tug at my coat, then something at my arm. And Weena shivered violently, and became quite still.

'It was time for a match. But to get one I must put her down. I did so, and, as I fumbled with my pocket, a struggle began in the darkness about my knees, perfectly silent on her part and with the same peculiar cooing sounds from the Morlocks. Soft little hands, too, were creeping over my coat and back, touching even my neck. Then the match scratched and fizzed. I held it flaring, and saw the white backs of the Morlocks in flight amid the trees. I hastily took a lump of camphor from my pocket, and prepared to light it as soon as the match should wane. Then I looked at Weena. She was lying clutching my feet and quite motionless, with her face to the ground. With a sudden fright I stooped to her. She seemed scarcely to breathe. I lit the block of camphor and flung it to the ground, and as it split and flared up and drove back the Morlocks and the shadows, I knelt down and lifted her. The wood behind seemed full of the stir and murmur of a great company!

'She seemed to have fainted. I put her carefully upon my shoulder and rose to push on, and then there came a horrible realization. In manoeuvring with my matches and Weena, I had turned myself about several times, and now I had not the faintest idea in what direction lay my path. For all I knew, I might be facing back towards the Palace of Green Porcelain. I found myself in a cold sweat. I had to think rapidly what to do. I determined to build a fire and encamp where we were. I put Weena, still motionless, down upon a turfy bole, and very hastily, as my first lump of camphor waned, I began collecting sticks and leaves. Here and there out of the darkness round me the Morlocks' eyes shone like carbuncles.

'The camphor flickered and went out. I lit a match, and as I did so, two white forms that had been approaching Weena dashed hastily away. One was so blinded by the light that he came straight for me, and I felt his bones

grind under the blow of my fist. He gave a whoop of dismay, staggered a little way, and fell down. I lit another piece of camphor, and went on gathering my bonfire. Presently I noticed how dry was some of the foliage above me, for since my arrival on the Time Machine, a matter of a week, no rain had fallen. So, instead of casting about among the trees for fallen twigs, I began leaping up and dragging down branches. Very soon I had a choking smoky fire of green wood and dry sticks, and could economize my camphor. Then I turned to where Weena lay beside my iron mace. I tried what I could to revive her, but she lay like one dead. I could not even satisfy myself whether or not she breathed.

'Now, the smoke of the fire beat over towards me, and it must have made me heavy of a sudden. Moreover, the vapour of camphor was in the air. My fire would not need replenishing for an hour or so. I felt very weary after my exertion, and sat down. The wood, too, was full of a slumbrous murmur that I did not understand. I seemed just to nod and open my eyes. But all was dark, and the Morlocks had their hands upon me. Flinging off their clinging fingers I hastily felt in my pocket for the match-box, and – it had gone! Then they gripped and closed with me again. In a moment I knew what had happened. I had slept, and my fire had gone out, and the bitterness of death came over my soul. The forest seemed full of the smell of burning wood. I was caught by the neck, by the hair, by the arms, and pulled down. It was indescribably horrible in the darkness to feel all these soft creatures heaped upon me. I felt as if I was in a monstrous spider's web. I was overpowered, and went down. I felt little teeth nipping at my neck. I rolled over, and as I did so my hand came against my iron lever. It gave me strength. I struggled up, shaking the human rats from me, and, holding the bar short, I thrust where I judged their faces might be. I could feel the succulent giving of flesh and bone under my blows, and for a moment I was free.

'The strange exultation that so often seems to accompany hard fighting came upon me. I knew that both I and Weena were lost, but I determined to make the Morlocks pay for their meat. I stood with my back to a tree, swinging the iron bar before me. The whole wood was full of the stir and cries of them. A minute passed. Their voices seemed to rise to a higher pitch of excitement, and their movements grew faster. Yet none came within reach. I stood glaring at the blackness. Then suddenly came hope. What if the Morlocks were afraid? And close on the heels of that came a strange thing. The darkness seemed to grow luminous. Very dimly I began to see the Morlocks about me – three battered at my feet – and then I recognized, with incredulous surprise, that the others were running, in an incessant stream, as it seemed, from behind me, and away through the wood in front. And their backs seemed no longer white, but reddish. As I stood agape, I saw a little red spark go drifting across a gap of starlight between the branches,

and vanish. And at that I understood the smell of burning wood, the slumbrous murmur that was growing now into a gusty roar, the red glow, and the Morlocks' flight.

'Stepping out from behind my tree and looking back, I saw, through the black pillars of the nearer trees, the flames of the burning forest. It was my first fire coming after me. With that I looked for Weena, but she was gone. The hissing and crackling behind me, the explosive thud as each fresh tree burst into flame, left little time for reflection. My iron bar still gripped, I followed in the Morlocks' path. It was a close race. Once the flames crept forward so swiftly on my right as I ran that I was outflanked and had to strike off to the left. But at last I emerged upon a small open space, and as I did so, a Morlock came blundering towards me, and past me, and went on straight into the fire!

'And now I was to see the most weird and horrible thing, I think, of all that I beheld in that future age. This whole space was as bright as day with the reflection of the fire. In the centre was a hillock or tumulus, surmounted by a scorched hawthorn. Beyond this was another arm of the burning forest, with yellow tongues already writhing from it, completely encircling the space with a fence of fire. Upon the hillside were some thirty or forty Morlocks, dazzled by the light and heat, and blundering hither and thither against each other in their bewilderment. At first I did not realize their blindness, and struck furiously at them with my bar, in a frenzy of fear, as they approached me, killing one and crippling several more. But when I had watched the gestures of one of them groping under the hawthorn against the red sky, and heard their moans, I was assured of their absolute helplessness and misery in the glare, and I struck no more of them.

'Yet every now and then one would come straight towards me, setting loose a quivering horror that made me quick to elude him. At one time the flames died down somewhat, and I feared the foul creatures would presently be able to see me. I was thinking of beginning the fight by killing some of them before this should happen; but the fire burst out again brightly, and I stayed my hand. I walked about the hill among them and avoided them, looking for some trace of Weena. But Weena was gone.

'At last I sat down on the summit of the hillock, and watched this strange incredible company of blind things groping to and fro, and making uncanny noises to each other, as the glare of the fire beat on them. The coiling uprush of smoke streamed across the sky, and through the rare tatters of that red canopy, remote as though they belonged to another universe, shone the little stars. Two or three Morlocks came blundering into me, and I drove them off with blows of my fists, trembling as I did so.

'For the most part of that night I was persuaded it was a nightmare. I bit myself and screamed in a passionate desire to awake. I beat the ground with my hands, and got up and sat down again, and wandered here and there,

and again sat down. Then I would fall to rubbing my eyes and calling upon God to let me awake. Thrice I saw Morlocks put their heads down in a kind of agony and rush into the flames. But, at last, above the subsiding red of the fire, above the streaming masses of black smoke and the whitening and blackening tree stumps, and the diminishing numbers of these dim creatures, came the white light of the day.

'I searched again for traces of Weena, but there were none. It was plain that they had left her poor little body in the forest. I cannot describe how it relieved me to think that it had escaped the awful fate to which it seemed destined. As I thought of that, I was almost moved to begin a massacre of the helpless abominations about me, but I contained myself. The hillock, as I have said, was a kind of island in the forest. From its summit I could now make out through a haze of smoke the Palace of Green Porcelain, and from that I could get my bearings for the White Sphinx. And so, leaving the remnant of these damned souls still going hither and thither and moaning, as the day grew clearer, I tied some grass about my feet and limped on across smoking ashes and among black stems, that still pulsated internally with fire, towards the hiding-place of the Time Machine. I walked slowly, for I was almost exhausted, as well as lame, and I felt the intensest wretchedness for the horrible death of little Weena. It seemed an overwhelming calamity. Now, in this old familiar room, it is more like the sorrow of a dream than an actual loss. But that morning it left me absolutely lonely again – terribly alone. I began to think of this house of mine, of this fireside, of some of you, and with such thoughts came a longing that was pain.

'But as I walked over the smoking ashes under the bright morning sky, I made a discovery. In my trouser pocket were still some loose matches. The box must have leaked before it was lost.'

CHAPTER X

'About eight or nine in the morning I came to the same seat of yellow metal from which I had viewed the world upon the evening of my arrival. I thought of my hasty conclusions upon that evening and could not refrain from laughing bitterly at my confidence. Here was the same beautiful scene, the same abundant foliage, the same splendid palaces and magnificent ruins, the same silver river running between its fertile banks. The gay robes of the beautiful people moved hither and thither among the trees. Some were bathing in exactly the place where I had saved Weena, and that suddenly gave me a keen stab of pain. And like blots upon the landscape rose the cupolas above the ways to the Under-world. I understood now what all the beauty of the Upper-world people covered. Very pleasant was their day, as pleasant as the day of the cattle in the field. Like the cattle, they knew of no enemies and provided against no needs. And their end was the same.

'I grieved to think how brief the dream of the human intellect had been. It had committed suicide. It had set itself steadfastly towards comfort and ease, a balanced society with security and permanency as its watchword, it had attained its hopes – to come to this at last. Once, life and property must have reached almost absolute safety. The rich had been assured of his wealth and comfort, the toiler assured of his life and work. No doubt in that perfect world there had been no unemployed problem, no social question left unsolved. And a great quiet had followed.

'It is a law of nature we overlook, that intellectual versatility is the compensation for change, danger, and trouble. An animal perfectly in harmony with its environment is a perfect mechanism. Nature never appeals to intelligence until habit and instinct are useless. There is no intelligence where there is no change and no need of change. Only those animals partake of intelligence that have to meet a huge variety of needs and dangers.

'So, as I see it, the Upper-world man had drifted towards his feeble prettiness, and the Under-world to mere mechanical industry. But that perfect state had lacked one thing even for mechanical perfection – absolute permanency. Apparently as time went on, the feeding of the Under-world, however it was effected, had become disjointed. Mother Necessity, who had been staved off for a few thousand years, came back again, and she began below. The Under-world being in contact with machinery, which, however perfect, still needs some little thought outside habit, had probably retained perforce rather more initiative, if less of every other human character, than the Upper. And when other meat failed them, they turned to what old habit had hitherto forbidden. So I say I saw it in my last view of the world of Eight Hundred

and Two Thousand Seven Hundred and One. It may be as wrong an explanation as mortal wit could invent. It is how the thing shaped itself to me, and as that I give it to you.

'After the fatigues, excitements, and terrors of the past days, and in spite of my grief, this seat and the tranquil view and the warm sunlight were very pleasant. I was very tired and sleepy, and soon my theorizing passed into dozing. Catching myself at that, I took my own hint, and spreading myself out upon the turf I had a long and refreshing sleep.

'I awoke a little before sunsetting. I now felt safe against being caught napping by the Morlocks, and, stretching myself, I came on down the hill towards the White Sphinx. I had my crowbar in one hand, and the other hand played with the matches in my pocket.

'And now came a most unexpected thing. As I approached the pedestal of the sphinx I found the bronze valves were open. They had slid down into grooves.

'At that I stopped short before them, hesitating to enter.

'Within was a small apartment, and on a raised place in the corner of this was the Time Machine. I had the small levers in my pocket. So here, after all my elaborate preparations for the siege of the White Sphinx, was a meek surrender. I threw my iron bar away, almost sorry not to use it.

'A sudden thought came into my head as I stooped towards the portal. For once, at least, I grasped the mental operations of the Morlocks. Suppressing a strong inclination to laugh, I stepped through the bronze frame and up to the Time Machine. I was surprised to find it had been carefully oiled and cleaned. I have suspected since that the Morlocks had even partially taken it to pieces while trying in their dim way to grasp its purpose.

'Now as I stood and examined it, finding a pleasure in the mere touch of the contrivance, the thing I had expected happened. The bronze panels suddenly slid up and struck the frame with a clang. I was in the dark – trapped. So the Morlocks thought. At that I chuckled gleefully.

'I could already hear their murmuring laughter as they came towards me. Very calmly I tried to strike the match. I had only to fix on the levers and depart then like a ghost. But I had overlooked one little thing. The matches were of that abominable kind that light only on the box.

'You may imagine how all my calm vanished. The little brutes were close upon me. One touched me. I made a sweeping blow in the dark at them with the levers, and began to scramble into the saddle of the machine. Then came one hand upon me and then another. Then I had simply to fight against their persistent fingers for my levers, and at the same time feel for the studs over which these fitted. One, indeed, they almost got away from me. As it slipped from my hand, I had to butt in the dark with my head – I could hear

the Morlock's skull ring – to recover it. It was a nearer thing than the fight in the forest, I think, this last scramble.

'But at last the lever was fitted and pulled over. The clinging hands slipped from me. The darkness presently fell from my eyes. I found myself in the same grey light and tumult I have already described.

CHAPTER XI

'I have already told you of the sickness and confusion that comes with time travelling. And this time I was not seated properly in the saddle, but sideways and in an unstable fashion. For an indefinite time I clung to the machine as it swayed and vibrated, quite unheeding how I went, and when I brought myself to look at the dials again I was amazed to find where I had arrived. One dial records days, and another thousands of days, another millions of days, and another thousands of millions. Now, instead of reversing the levers, I had pulled them over so as to go forward with them, and when I came to look at these indicators I found that the thousands hand was sweeping round as fast as the seconds hand of a watch – into futurity.

'As I drove on, a peculiar change crept over the appearance of things. The palpitating greyness grew darker; then – though I was still travelling with prodigious velocity – the blinking succession of day and night, which was usually indicative of a slower pace, returned, and grew more and more marked. This puzzled me very much at first. The alternations of night and day grew slower and slower, and so did the passage of the sun across the sky, until they seemed to stretch through centuries. At last a steady twilight brooded over the earth, a twilight only broken now and then when a comet glared across the darkling sky. The band of light that had indicated the sun had long since disappeared; for the sun had ceased to set – it simply rose and fell in the west, and grew ever broader and more red. All trace of the moon had vanished. The circling of the stars, growing slower and slower, had given place to creeping points of light. At last, some time before I stopped, the sun, red and very large, halted motionless upon the horizon, a vast dome glowing with a dull heat, and now and then suffering a momentary extinction. At one time it had for a little while glowed more brilliantly again, but it speedily reverted to its sullen red heat. I perceived by this slowing down of its rising and setting that the work of the tidal drag was done. The earth had come to rest with one face to the sun, even as in our own time the moon faces the earth. Very cautiously, for I remembered my former headlong fall, I began to reverse my motion. Slower and slower went the circling hands until the thousands one seemed motionless and the daily one was no longer a mere mist upon its scale. Still slower, until the dim outlines of a desolate beach grew visible.

'I stopped very gently and sat upon the Time Machine, looking round. The sky was no longer blue. North-eastward it was inky black, and out of the blackness shone brightly and steadily the pale white stars. Overhead it was a deep Indian red and starless, and south-eastward it grew brighter to a glowing scarlet where, cut by the horizon, lay the huge hull of the sun, red and motionless. The rocks about me were of a harsh reddish colour, and

all the trace of life that I could see at first was the intensely green vegetation that covered every projecting point on their south-eastern face. It was the same rich green that one sees on forest moss or on the lichen in caves: plants which like these grow in a perpetual twilight.

'The machine was standing on a sloping beach. The sea stretched away to the south-west, to rise into a sharp bright horizon against the wan sky. There were no breakers and no waves, for not a breath of wind was stirring. Only a slight oily swell rose and fell like a gentle breathing, and showed that the eternal sea was still moving and living. And along the margin where the water sometimes broke was a thick incrustation of salt – pink under the lurid sky. There was a sense of oppression in my head, and I noticed that I was breathing very fast. The sensation reminded me of my only experience of mountaineering, and from that I judged the air to be more rarefied than it is now.

'Far away up the desolate slope I heard a harsh scream, and saw a thing like a huge white butterfly go slanting and fluttering up into the sky and, circling, disappear over some low hillocks beyond. The sound of its voice was so dismal that I shivered and seated myself more firmly upon the machine. Looking round me again, I saw that, quite near, what I had taken to be a reddish mass of rock was moving slowly towards me. Then I saw the thing was really a monstrous crab-like creature. Can you imagine a crab as large as yonder table, with its many legs moving slowly and uncertainly, its big claws swaying, its long antennae, like carters' whips, waving and feeling, and its stalked eyes gleaming at you on either side of its metallic front? Its back was corrugated and ornamented with ungainly bosses, and a greenish incrustation blotched it here and there. I could see the many palps of its complicated mouth flickering and feeling as it moved.

'As I stared at this sinister apparition crawling towards me, I felt a tickling on my cheek as though a fly had lighted there. I tried to brush it away with my hand, but in a moment it returned, and almost immediately came another by my ear. I struck at this, and caught something threadlike. It was drawn swiftly out of my hand. With a frightful qualm, I turned, and I saw that I had grasped the antenna of another monster crab that stood just behind me. Its evil eyes were wriggling on their stalks, its mouth was all alive with appetite, and its vast ungainly claws, smeared with an algal slime, were descending upon me. In a moment my hand was on the lever, and I had placed a month between myself and these monsters. But I was still on the same beach, and I saw them distinctly now as soon as I stopped. Dozens of them seemed to be crawling here and there, in the sombre light, among the foliated sheets of intense green.

'I cannot convey the sense of abominable desolation that hung over the world. The red eastern sky, the northward blackness, the salt Dead Sea, the stony beach crawling with these foul, slow-stirring monsters, the uniform

poisonous-looking green of the lichenous plants, the thin air that hurts one's lungs: all contributed to an appalling effect. I moved on a hundred years, and there was the same red sun – a little larger, a little duller – the same dying sea, the same chill air, and the same crowd of earthy crustacea creeping in and out among the green weed and the red rocks. And in the westward sky, I saw a curved pale line like a vast new moon.

'So I travelled, stopping ever and again, in great strides of a thousand years or more, drawn on by the mystery of the earth's fate, watching with a strange fascination the sun grow larger and duller in the westward sky, and the life of the old earth ebb away. At last, more than thirty million years hence, the huge red-hot dome of the sun had come to obscure nearly a tenth part of the darkling heavens. Then I stopped once more, for the crawling multitude of crabs had disappeared, and the red beach, save for its livid green liverworts and lichens, seemed lifeless. And now it was flecked with white. A bitter cold assailed me. Rare white flakes ever and again came eddying down. To the north-eastward, the glare of snow lay under the starlight of the sable sky and I could see an undulating crest of hillocks pinkish white. There were fringes of ice along the sea margin, with drifting masses further out; but the main expanse of that salt ocean, all bloody under the eternal sunset, was still unfrozen.

'I looked about me to see if any traces of animal life remained. A certain indefinable apprehension still kept me in the saddle of the machine. But I saw nothing moving, in earth or sky or sea. The green slime on the rocks alone testified that life was not extinct. A shallow sandbank had appeared in the sea and the water had receded from the beach. I fancied I saw some black object flopping about upon this bank, but it became motionless as I looked at it, and I judged that my eye had been deceived, and that the black object was merely a rock. The stars in the sky were intensely bright and seemed to me to twinkle very little.

'Suddenly I noticed that the circular westward outline of the sun had changed; that a concavity, a bay, had appeared in the curve. I saw this grow larger. For a minute perhaps I stared aghast at this blackness that was creeping over the day, and then I realized that an eclipse was beginning. Either the moon or the planet Mercury was passing across the sun's disk. Naturally, at first I took it to be the moon, but there is much to incline me to believe that what I really saw was the transit of an inner planet passing very near to the earth.

'The darkness grew apace; a cold wind began to blow in freshening gusts from the east, and the showering white flakes in the air increased in number. From the edge of the sea came a ripple and whisper. Beyond these lifeless sounds the world was silent. Silent? It would be hard to convey the stillness of it. All the sounds of man, the bleating of sheep, the cries of birds, the hum of insects, the stir that makes the background of our lives – all that

was over. As the darkness thickened, the eddying flakes grew more abundant, dancing before my eyes; and the cold of the air more intense. At last, one by one, swiftly, one after the other, the white peaks of the distant hills vanished into blackness. The breeze rose to a moaning wind. I saw the black central shadow of the eclipse sweeping towards me. In another moment the pale stars alone were visible. All else was rayless obscurity. The sky was absolutely black.

'A horror of this great darkness came on me. The cold, that smote to my marrow, and the pain I felt in breathing, overcame me. I shivered, and a deadly nausea seized me. Then like a red-hot bow in the sky appeared the edge of the sun. I got off the machine to recover myself. I felt giddy and incapable of facing the return journey. As I stood sick and confused I saw again the moving thing upon the shoal – there was no mistake now that it was a moving thing – against the red water of the sea. It was a round thing, the size of a football perhaps, or, it may be, bigger, and tentacles trailed down from it; it seemed black against the weltering blood-red water, and it was hopping fitfully about. Then I felt I was fainting. But a terrible dread of lying helpless in that remote and awful twilight sustained me while I clambered upon the saddle.

'So I came back. For a long time I must have been insensible upon the machine. The blinking succession of the days and nights was resumed, the sun got golden again, the sky blue. I breathed with greater freedom. The fluctuating contours of the land ebbed and flowed. The hands spun backward upon the dials. At last I saw again the dim shadows of houses, the evidences of decadent humanity. These, too, changed and passed, and others came. Presently, when the million dial was at zero, I slackened speed. I began to recognize our own pretty and familiar architecture, the thousands hand ran back to the starting-point, the night and day flapped slower and slower. Then the old walls of the laboratory came round me. Very gently, now, I slowed the mechanism down.

'I saw one little thing that seemed odd to me. I think I have told you that when I set out, before my velocity became very high, Mrs Watchett had walked across the room, travelling, as it seemed to me, like a rocket. As I returned, I passed again across that minute when she traversed the laboratory. But now her every motion appeared to be the exact inversion of her previous ones. The door at the lower end opened, and she glided quietly up the laboratory, back foremost, and disappeared behind the door by which she had previously entered. Just before that I seemed to see Hillyer for a moment; but he passed like a flash.

'Then I stopped the machine, and saw about me again the old familiar laboratory, my tools, my appliances just as I had left them. I got off the thing very shakily, and sat down upon my bench. For several minutes I trembled violently. Then I became calmer. Around me was my old workshop again, exactly as it had been. I might have slept there, and the whole thing have been a dream.

'And yet, not exactly! The thing had started from the south-east corner of the laboratory. It had come to rest again in the north-west, against the wall where you saw it. That gives you the exact distance from my little lawn to the pedestal of the White Sphinx, into which the Morlocks had carried my machine.

'For a time my brain went stagnant. Presently I got up and came through the passage here, limping, because my heel was still painful, and feeling sorely begrimed. I saw the *Pall Mall Gazette* on the table by the door. I found the date was indeed today, and looking at the timepiece, saw the hour was almost eight o'clock. I heard your voices and the clatter of plates. I hesitated – I felt so sick and weak. Then I sniffed good wholesome meat, and opened the door on you. You know the rest. I washed, and dined, and now I am telling you the story.

'I know,' he said, after a pause, 'that all this will be absolutely incredible

to you. To me the one incredible thing is that I am here tonight in this old familiar room looking into your friendly faces and telling you these strange adventures.'

He looked at the Medical Man. 'No. I cannot expect you to believe it. Take it as a lie – or a prophecy. Say I dreamed it in the workshop. Consider I have been speculating upon the destinies of our race until I have hatched this fiction. Treat my assertion of its truth as a mere stroke of art to enhance its interest. And taking it as a story, what do you think of it?'

He took up his pipe, and began, in his old accustomed manner, to tap with it nervously upon the bars of the grate. There was a momentary stillness. Then chairs began to creak and shoes to scrape upon the carpet. I took my eyes off the Time Traveller's face, and looked round at his audience. They were in the dark, and little spots of colour swam before them. The Medical Man seemed absorbed in the contemplation of our host. The Editor was looking hard at the end of his cigar – the sixth. The Journalist fumbled for his watch. The others, as far as I remember, were motionless.

The Editor stood up with a sigh. 'What a pity it is you're not a writer of stories!' he said, putting his hand on the Time Traveller's shoulder.

'You don't believe it?'

'Well—'

'I thought not.'

The Time Traveller turned to us. 'Where are the matches?' he said.

He lit one and spoke over his pipe, puffing. 'To tell you the truth . . . I hardly believe it myself . . . And yet. . . .'

His eye fell with a mute enquiry upon the withered white flowers upon the little table. Then he turned over the hand holding his pipe, and I saw he was looking at some half-healed scars on his knuckles.

The Medical Man rose, came to the lamp, and examined the flowers. 'The gynaeceum's odd,' he said. The Psychologist leant forward to see, holding out his hand for a specimen.

'I'm hanged if it isn't a quarter to one,' said the Journalist. 'How shall we get home?'

'Plenty of cabs at the station,' said the Psychologist.

'It's a curious thing,' said the Medical Man; 'but I certainly don't know the natural order of these flowers. May I have them?'

The Time Traveller hesitated. Then suddenly: 'Certainly not.'

'Where did you really get them?' said the Medical Man.

The Time Traveller put his hand to his head. He spoke like one who was trying to keep hold of an idea that eluded him. 'They were put into my pocket by Weena, when I travelled into Time.' He stared round the room. 'I'm damned if it isn't all going. This room and you and the atmosphere of every day is too much for my memory. Did I ever make a Time Machine, or a model of a Time Machine? Or is it all only a dream? They say life is a

dream, a precious poor dream at times – but I can't stand another that won't fit. It's madness. And where did the dream come from? . . . I must look at that machine. If there is one!'

He caught up the lamp swiftly, and carried it, flaring red, through the door into the corridor. We followed him. There in the flickering light of the lamp was the machine sure enough, squat, ugly, and askew; a thing of brass, ebony, ivory, and translucent glimmering quartz. Solid to the touch – for I put out my hand and felt the rail of it – and with brown spots and smears upon the ivory, and bits of grass and moss upon the lower parts, and one rail bent awry.

The Time Traveller put the lamp down on the bench, and ran his hand along the damaged rail. 'It's all right now,' he said. 'The story I told you was true. I'm sorry to have brought you out here in the cold.' He took up the lamp, and, in an absolute silence, we returned to the smoking-room.

He came into the hall with us and helped the Editor on with his coat. The Medical Man looked into his face and, with a certain hesitation, told him he was suffering from overwork, at which he laughed hugely. I remember him standing in the open doorway, bawling good night.

I shared a cab with the Editor. He thought the tale a 'gaudy lie'. For my own part I was unable to come to a conclusion. The story was so fantastic and incredible, the telling so credible and sober. I lay awake most of the night thinking about it. I determined to go next day and see the Time Traveller again.

I was told he was in the laboratory, and being on easy terms in the house, I went up to him. The laboratory, however, was empty. I stared for a minute at the Time Machine and put out my hand and touched the lever. At that the squat substantial-looking mass swayed like a bough shaken by the wind. Its instability startled me extremely, and I had a queer reminiscence of the childish days when I used to be forbidden to meddle. I came back through the corridor. The Time Traveller met me in the smoking-room. He was coming from the house. He had a small camera under one arm and a knap-sack under the other. He laughed when he saw me, and gave me an elbow to shake. 'I'm frightfully busy,' said he, 'with that thing in there.'

'But is it not some hoax?' I said. 'Do you really travel through time?'

'Really and truly I do.' And he looked frankly into my eyes. He hesitated. His eye wandered about the room. 'I only want half an hour,' he said. 'I know why you came, and it's awfully good of you. There's some magazines here. If you'll stop to lunch I'll prove you this time travelling up to the hilt, specimen and all. If you'll forgive my leaving you now?'

I consented, hardly comprehending then the full import of his words, and he nodded and went on down the corridor. I heard the door of the laboratory slam, seated myself in a chair, and took up a daily paper. What was he going to do before lunch-time? Then suddenly I was reminded by

an advertisement that I had promised to meet Richardson, the publisher, at two. I looked at my watch, and saw that I could barely save that engagement. I got up and went down the passage to tell the Time Traveller.

As I took hold of the handle of the door I heard an exclamation, oddly truncated at the end, and a click and a thud. A gust of air whirled round me as I opened the door, and from within came the sound of broken glass falling on the floor. The Time Traveller was not there. I seemed to see a ghostly, indistinct figure sitting in a whirling mass of black and brass for a moment – a figure so transparent that the bench behind with its sheets of drawings was absolutely distinct; but this phantasm vanished as I rubbed my eyes. The Time Machine had gone. Save for a subsiding stir of dust, the further end of the laboratory was empty. A pane of the skylight had, apparently, just been blown in.

I felt an unreasonable amazement. I knew that something strange had happened, and for the moment could not distinguish what the strange thing might be. As I stood staring, the door into the garden opened, and the man-servant appeared.

We looked at each other. Then ideas began to come. 'Has Mr— gone out that way?' said I.

'No, sir. No one has come out this way. I was expecting to find him here.'

At that I understood. At the risk of disappointing Richardson I stayed on, waiting for the Time Traveller; waiting for the second, perhaps still stranger story, and the specimens and photographs he would bring with him. But I am beginning now to fear that I must wait a lifetime. The Time Traveller vanished three years ago. And, as everybody knows now, he has never returned.

EPILOGUE

One cannot choose but wonder. Will he ever return? It may be that he swept back into the past, and fell among the blood-drinking, hairy savages of the Age of Unpolished Stone; into the abysses of the Cretaceous Sea; or among the grotesque saurians, the huge reptilian brutes of the Jurassic times. He may even now – if I may use the phrase – be wandering on some plesi-osaurus-haunted Oolitic coral reef, or beside the lonely saline lakes of the Triassic Age. Or did he go forward, into one of the nearer ages, in which men are still men, but with the riddles of our own time answered and its wearisome problems solved? Into the manhood of the race: for I, for my own part, cannot think that these latter days of weak experiment, fragmentary theory, and mutual discord are indeed man's culminating time! I say, for my own part. He, I know – for the question had been discussed among us long before the Time Machine was made – thought but cheerlessly of the Advancement of Mankind, and saw in the growing pile of civilization only a foolish heaping that must inevitably fall back upon and destroy its makers in the end. If that is so, it remains for us to live as though it were not so. But to me the future is still black and blank – is a vast ignorance, lit at a few casual places by the memory of his story. And I have by me, for my comfort, two strange white flowers – shrivelled now, and brown and flat and brittle – to witness that even when mind and strength had gone, gratitude and a mutual tenderness still lived on in the heart of man.

THE WAR OF THE WORLDS

But who shall dwell in these worlds if they be inhabited? . . .
Are we or they Lords of the World? . . .
And how are all things made for man?

Kepler (quoted in *The Anatomy of Melancholy*)

CONTENTS

Book One — The Coming of the Martians

Book Two — The Earth Under the Martians

BOOK ONE
THE COMING OF THE MARTIANS

CHAPTER I

The Eve of the War

No one would have believed in the last years of the nineteenth century that this world was being watched keenly and closely by intelligences greater than man's and yet as mortal as his own; that as men busied themselves about their various concerns they were scrutinized and studied, perhaps almost as narrowly as a man with a microscope might scrutinize the transient creatures that swarm and multiply in a drop of water. With infinite complacency men went to and fro over this globe about their little affairs, serene in their assurance of their empire over matter. It is possible that the infusoria under the microscope do the same. No one gave a thought to the older worlds of space as sources of human danger, or thought of them only to dismiss the idea of life upon them as impossible or improbable. It is curious to recall some of the mental habits of those departed days. At most, terrestrial men fancied there might be other men upon Mars, perhaps inferior to themselves and ready to welcome a missionary enterprise. Yet across the gulf of space, minds that are to our minds as ours are to those of the beasts that perish, intellects vast and cool and unsympathetic, regarded this earth with envious eyes, and slowly and surely drew their plans against us. And early in the twentieth century came the great disillusionment.

The planet Mars, I scarcely need remind the reader, revolves about the sun at a mean distance of 140,000,000 miles, and the light and heat it receives from the sun is barely half of that received by this world. It must be, if the nebular hypothesis has any truth, older than our world; and long before this earth ceased to be molten, life upon its surface must have begun its course. The fact that it is scarcely one-seventh of the volume of the earth must have accelerated its cooling to the temperature at which life could begin. It has air and water and all that is necessary for the support of animated existence.

Yet so vain is man, and so blinded by his vanity, that no writer, up to the very end of the nineteenth century, expressed any idea that intelligent life might have developed there far, or indeed at all, beyond its earthly level. Nor was it generally understood that since Mars is older than our earth, with scarcely a quarter of the superficial area and remoter from the sun, it necessarily follows that it is not only more distant from time's beginning but nearer its end.

The secular cooling that must someday overtake our planet has already gone far indeed with our neighbour. Its physical condition is still largely a mystery, but we know now that even in its equatorial region the midday

temperature barely approaches that of our coldest winter. Its air is much
more attenuated than ours, its oceans have shrunk until they cover but a
third of its surface, and, as its slow seasons change, huge snowcaps gather
and melt about either pole and periodically inundate its temperate zones.
That last stage of exhaustion, which to us is still incredibly remote, has
become a present-day problem for the inhabitants of Mars. The immediate
pressure of necessity has brightened their intellects, enlarged their powers,
and hardened their hearts. And looking across space with instruments,
and intelligences such as we have scarcely dreamed of, they see, at its
nearest distance only 35,000,000 of miles sunward of them, a morning star
of hope, our own warmer planet, green with vegetation and grey with
water, with a cloudy atmosphere eloquent of fertility, with glimpses through
its drifting cloud wisps of broad stretches of populous country and narrow,
navy-crowded seas.

And we men, the creatures who inhabit this earth, must be to them at
least as alien and lowly as are the monkeys and lemurs to us. The intellec-
tual side of man already admits that life is an incessant struggle for existence,
and it would seem that this too is the belief of the minds upon Mars. Their
world is far gone in its cooling and this world is still crowded with life, but
crowded only with what they regard as inferior animals. To carry warfare
sunward is, indeed, their only escape from the destruction that, generation
after generation, creeps upon them.

And before we judge of them too harshly we must remember what ruth-
less and utter destruction our own species has wrought, not only upon
animals, such as the vanished bison and the dodo, but upon its inferior
races. The Tasmanians, in spite of their human likeness, were entirely swept
out of existence in a war of extermination waged by European immigrants,
in the space of fifty years. Are we such apostles of mercy as to complain if
the Martians warred in the same spirit?

The Martians seem to have calculated their descent with amazing subtlety
– their mathematical learning is evidently far in excess of ours – and to
have carried out their preparations with a well-nigh perfect unanimity. Had
our instruments permitted it, we might have seen the gathering trouble far
back in the nineteenth century. Men like Schiaparelli watched the red
planet – it is odd, by-the-bye, that for countless centuries Mars has been
the star of war – but failed to interpret the fluctuating appearances of the
markings they mapped so well. All that time the Martians must have been
getting ready.

During the opposition of 1894 a great light was seen on the illuminated
part of the disk, first at the Lick Observatory, then by Perrotin of Nice, and
then by other observers. English readers heard of it first in the issue of *Nature*
dated August 2nd. I am inclined to think that this blaze may have been the
casting of the huge gun, in the vast pit sunk into their planet, from which

their shots were fired at us. Peculiar markings, as yet unexplained, were seen near the site of that outbreak during the next two oppositions.

The storm burst upon us six years ago now. As Mars approached opposition, Lavelle of Java set the wires of the astronomical exchange palpitating with the amazing intelligence of a huge outbreak of incandescent gas upon the planet. It had occurred towards midnight of the 12th; and the spectroscope, to which he had at once resorted, indicated a mass of flaming gas, chiefly hydrogen, moving with an enormous velocity towards this earth. This jet of fire had become invisible about a quarter past twelve. He compared it to a colossal puff of flame suddenly and violently squirted out of the planet, 'as flaming gases rushed out of a gun'.

A singularly appropriate phrase it proved. Yet the next day there was nothing of this in the papers except a little note in the *Daily Telegraph*, and the world went in ignorance of one of the gravest dangers that ever threatened the human race. I might not have heard of the eruption at all had I not met Ogilvy, the well-known astronomer, at Ottershaw. He was immensely excited at the news, and in the excess of his feelings invited me up to take a turn with him that night in a scrutiny of the red planet.

In spite of all that has happened since, I still remember that vigil very distinctly: the black and silent observatory, the shadowed lantern throwing a feeble glow upon the floor in the corner, the steady ticking of the clockwork of the telescope, the little slit in the roof – an oblong profundity with the stardust streaked across it. Ogilvy moved about, invisible but audible. Looking through the telescope, one saw a circle of deep blue and the little round planet swimming in the field. It seemed such a little thing, so bright and small and still, faintly marked with transverse stripes, and slightly flattened from the perfect round. But so little it was, so silvery warm – a pin's-head of light! It was as if it quivered, but really this was the telescope vibrating with the activity of the clockwork that kept the planet in view.

As I watched, the planet seemed to grow larger and smaller and to advance and recede, but that was simply that my eye was tired. Forty millions of miles it was from us – more than forty millions of miles of void. Few people realize the immensity of vacancy in which the dust of the material universe swims.

Near it in the field, I remember, were three faint points of light, three telescopic stars infinitely remote, and all around it was the unfathomable darkness of empty space. You know how that blackness looks on a frosty starlight night. In a telescope it seems far profounder. And invisible to me because it was so remote and small, flying swiftly and steadily towards me across that incredible distance, drawing nearer every minute by so many thousands of miles, came the Thing they were sending us, the Thing that was to bring so much struggle and calamity and death to the earth. I never dreamed of it then as I watched; no one on earth dreamed of that unerring missile.

That night, too, there was another jetting out of gas from the distant planet. I saw it. A reddish flash at the edge, the slightest projection of the outline just as the chronometer struck midnight; and at that I told Ogilvy and he took my place. The night was warm and I was thirsty, and I went stretching my legs clumsily and feeling my way in the darkness, to the little table where the siphon stood, while Ogilvy exclaimed at the streamer of gas that came out towards us.

That night another invisible missile started on its way to the earth from Mars, just a second or so under twenty-four hours after the first one. I remember how I sat on the table there in the blackness, with patches of green and crimson swimming before my eyes. I wished I had a light to smoke by, little suspecting the meaning of the minute gleam I had seen and all that it would presently bring me. Ogilvy watched till one, and then gave it up; and we lit the lantern and walked over to his house. Down below in the darkness were Ottershaw and Chertsey and all their hundreds of people, sleeping in peace.

He was full of speculation that night about the condition of Mars, and scoffed at the vulgar idea of its having inhabitants who were signalling us. His idea was that meteorites might be falling in a heavy shower upon the planet, or that a huge volcanic explosion was in progress. He pointed out to me how unlikely it was that organic evolution had taken the same direction in the two adjacent planets.

'The chances against anything man-like on Mars are a million to one,' he said.

Hundreds of observers saw the flame that night and the night after about midnight, and again the night after; and so for ten nights, a flame each night. Why the shots ceased after the tenth no one on earth has attempted to explain. It may be the gases of the firing caused the Martians inconvenience. Dense clouds of smoke or dust, visible through a powerful telescope on earth as little grey, fluctuating patches, spread through the clearness of the planet's atmosphere and obscured its more familiar features.

Even the daily papers woke up to the disturbances at last, and popular notes appeared here, there, and everywhere concerning the volcanoes upon Mars. The serio-comic periodical *Punch*, I remember, made a happy use of it in the political cartoon. And, all unsuspected, those missiles the Martians had fired at us drew earthward, rushing now at a pace of many miles a second through the empty gulf of space, hour by hour and day by day, nearer and nearer. It seems to me now almost incredibly wonderful that, with that swift fate hanging over us, men could go about their petty concerns as they did. I remember how jubilant Markham was at securing a new photograph of the planet for the illustrated paper he edited in those days. People in these latter times scarcely realize the abundance and enterprise of our nineteenth-century papers. For my own part, I was much occupied

in learning to ride the bicycle, and busy upon a series of papers discussing the probable developments of moral ideas as civilization progressed.

One night (the first missile then could scarcely have been 10,000,000 miles away) I went for a walk with my wife. It was starlight and I explained the Signs of the Zodiac to her, and pointed out Mars, a bright dot of light creeping zenithward, towards which so many telescopes were pointed. It was a warm night. Coming home, a party of excursionists from Chertsey or Isleworth passed us singing and playing music. There were lights in the upper windows of the houses as the people went to bed. From the railway station in the distance came the sound of shunting trains, ringing and rumbling, softened almost into melody by the distance. My wife pointed out to me the brightness of the red, green, and yellow signal lights hanging in a framework against the sky. It seemed so safe and tranquil.

CHAPTER II

The Falling Star

Then came the night of the first falling star. It was seen early in the morning, rushing over Winchester eastward, a line of flame high in the atmosphere. Hundreds must have seen it, and taken it for an ordinary falling star. Albin described it as leaving a greenish streak behind it that glowed for some seconds. Denning, our greatest authority on meteorites, stated that the height of its first appearance was about ninety or one hundred miles. It seemed to him that it fell to earth about one hundred miles east of him.

I was at home at that hour and writing in my study; and although my French windows face towards Ottershaw and the blind was up (for I loved in those days to look up at the night sky), I saw nothing of it. Yet this strangest of all things that ever came to earth from outer space must have fallen while I was sitting there, visible to me had I only looked up as it passed. Some of those who saw its flight say it travelled with a hissing sound. I myself heard nothing of that. Many people in Berkshire, Surrey, and Middlesex must have seen the fall of it, and, at most, have thought that another meteorite had descended. No one seems to have troubled to look for the fallen mass that night.

But very early in the morning poor Ogilvy, who had seen the shooting star and who was persuaded that a meteorite lay somewhere on the common between Horsell, Ottershaw, and Woking, rose early with the idea of finding it. Find it he did, soon after dawn, and not far from the sand pits. An enormous hole had been made by the impact of the projectile, and the sand and gravel had been flung violently in every direction over the heath, forming heaps visible a mile and a half away. The heather was on fire eastward, and a thin blue smoke rose against the dawn.

The Thing itself lay almost entirely buried in sand, amidst the scattered splinters of a fir tree it had shivered to fragments in its descent. The uncovered part had the appearance of a huge cylinder, caked over and its outline softened by a thick scaly dun-coloured incrustation. It had a diameter of about thirty yards. He approached the mass, surprised at the size and more so at the shape, since most meteorites are rounded more or less completely. It was, however, still so hot from its flight through the air as to forbid his near approach. A stirring noise within its cylinder he ascribed to the unequal cooling of its surface; for at that time it had not occurred to him that it might be hollow.

He remained standing at the edge of the pit that the Thing had made for itself, staring at its strange appearance, astonished chiefly at its unusual shape

and colour, and dimly perceiving even then some evidence of design in its arrival. The early morning was wonderfully still, and the sun, just clearing the pine trees towards Weybridge, was already warm. He did not remember hearing any birds that morning, there was certainly no breeze stirring, and the only sounds were the faint movements from within the cindery cylinder. He was all alone on the common.

Then suddenly he noticed with a start that some of the grey clinker, the ashy incrustation that covered the meteorite, was falling off the circular edge of the end. It was dropping off in flakes and raining down upon the sand. A large piece suddenly came off and fell with a sharp noise that brought his heart into his mouth.

For a minute he scarcely realized what this meant, and, although the heat was excessive, he clambered down into the pit close to the bulk to see the Thing more clearly. He fancied even then that the cooling of the body might account for this, but what disturbed that idea was the fact that the ash was falling only from the end of the cylinder.

And then he perceived that, very slowly, the circular top of the cylinder was rotating on its body. It was such a gradual movement that he discovered it only through noticing that a black mark that had been near him five minutes ago was now at the other side of the circumference. Even then he scarcely understood what this indicated, until he heard a muffled grating sound and saw the black mark jerk forward an inch or so. Then the thing came upon him in a flash. The cylinder was artificial – hollow – with an end that screwed out! Something within the cylinder was unscrewing the top!

'Good Heavens!' said Ogilvy. 'There's a man in it – men in it! Half roasted to death! Trying to escape!'

At once, with a quick mental leap, he linked the Thing with the flash upon Mars.

The thought of the confined creature was so dreadful to him that he forgot the heat and went forward to the cylinder to help turn. But luckily the dull radiation arrested him before he could burn his hands on the still-glowing metal. At that he stood irresolute for a moment, then turned, scrambled out of the pit, and set off running wildly into Woking. The time then must have been somewhere about six o'clock. He met a waggoner and tried to make him understand, but the tale he told and his appearance were so wild – his hat had fallen off in the pit – that the man simply drove on. He was equally unsuccessful with the potman who was just unlocking the doors of the public-house by Horsell Bridge. The fellow thought he was a lunatic at large and made an unsuccessful attempt to shut him into the taproom. That sobered him a little; and when he saw Henderson, the London journalist, in his garden, he called over the palings and made himself understood.

'Henderson,' he called, 'you saw that shooting star last night?'

'Well?' said Henderson.

'It's out on Horsell Common now.'

'Good Lord!' said Henderson. 'Fallen meteorite! That's good.'

'But it's something more than a meteorite. It's a cylinder – an artificial cylinder, man! And there's something inside.'

Henderson stood up with his spade in his hand.

'What's that?' he said. He was deaf in one ear.

Ogilvy told him all that he had seen. Henderson was a minute or so taking it in. Then he dropped his spade, snatched up his jacket, and came out into the road. The two men hurried back at once to the common, and found the cylinder still lying in the same position. But now the sounds inside had ceased, and a thin circle of bright metal showed between the top and the body of the cylinder. Air was either entering or escaping at the rim with a thin, sizzling sound.

They listened, rapped on the scaly burnt metal with a stick, and, meeting with no response, they both concluded the man or men inside must be insensible or dead.

Of course the two were quite unable to do anything. They shouted consolation and promises, and went off back to the town again to get help. One can imagine them, covered with sand, excited and disordered, running up the little street in the bright sunlight just as the shop folks were taking down their shutters and people were opening their bedroom windows. Henderson went into the railway station at once, in order to telegraph the news to London. The newspaper articles had prepared men's minds for the reception of the idea.

By eight o'clock a number of boys and unemployed men had already started for the common to see the 'dead men from Mars'. That was the form the story took. I heard of it first from my newspaper boy about a quarter to nine when I went out to get my *Daily Chronicle*. I was naturally startled, and lost no time in going out and across the Ottershaw bridge to the sand pits.

CHAPTER III

On Horsell Common

I found a little crowd of perhaps twenty people surrounding the huge hole in which the cylinder lay. I have already described the appearance of that colossal bulk, embedded in the ground. The turf and gravel about it seemed charred as if by a sudden explosion. No doubt its impact had caused a flash of fire. Henderson and Ogilvy were not there. I think they perceived that nothing was to be done for the present, and had gone away to breakfast at Henderson's house.

There were four or five boys sitting on the edge of the pit, with their feet dangling, and amusing themselves – until I stopped them – by throwing stones at the giant mass. After I had spoken to them about it, they began playing at 'touch' in and out of the group of bystanders.

Among these were a couple of cyclists, a jobbing gardener I employed sometimes, a girl carrying a baby, Gregg the butcher and his little boy, and two or three loafers and golf caddies who were accustomed to hang about the railway station. There was very little talking. Few of the common people in England had anything but the vaguest astronomical ideas in those days. Most of them were staring quietly at the big table-like end of the cylinder, which was still as Ogilvy and Henderson had left it. I fancy the popular expectation of a heap of charred corpses was disappointed at this inanimate bulk. Some went away while I was there, and other people came. I clambered into the pit and fancied I heard a faint movement under my feet. The top had certainly ceased to rotate.

It was only when I got thus close to it that the strangeness of this object was at all evident to me. At the first glance it was really no more exciting than an overturned carriage or a tree blown across the road. Not so much so, indeed. It looked like a rusty gas-float. It required a certain amount of scientific education to perceive that the grey scale of the Thing was no common oxide, that the yellowish-white metal that gleamed in the crack between the lid and the cylinder had an unfamiliar hue. 'Extra-terrestrial' had no meaning for most of the onlookers.

At that time it was quite clear in my own mind that the Thing had come from the planet Mars, but I judged it improbable that it contained any living creature. I thought the unscrewing might be automatic. In spite of Ogilvy, I still believed that there were men on Mars. My mind ran fancifully on the possibilities of its containing manuscript, on the difficulties in translation that might arise, whether we should find coins and models in it, and so forth. Yet it was a little too large for assurance

on this idea. I felt an impatience to see it opened. About eleven, as nothing seemed happening, I walked back, full of such thoughts, to my home in Maybury. But I found it difficult to get to work upon my abstract investigations.

In the afternoon the appearance of the common had altered very much. The early editions of the evening papers had startled London with enormous headlines:

'A MESSAGE RECEIVED FROM MARS.'

'REMARKABLE STORY FROM WOKING,'

and so forth. In addition, Ogilvy's wire to the Astronomical Exchange had roused every observatory in the three kingdoms.

There were half a dozen flies or more from the Woking station standing in the road by the sand pits, a basket-chaise from Chobham, and a rather lordly carriage. Besides that, there was quite a heap of bicycles. In addition, a large number of people must have walked, in spite of the heat of the day, from Woking and Chertsey, so that there was altogether quite a considerable crowd – one or two gaily dressed ladies among the others.

It was glaringly hot, not a cloud in the sky nor a breath of wind, and the only shadow was that of the few scattered pine trees. The burning heather had been extinguished, but the level ground towards Ottershaw was blackened as far as one could see, and still giving off vertical streamers of smoke. An enterprising sweet-stuff dealer in the Chobham Road had sent up his son with a barrow-load of green apples and ginger beer.

Going to the edge of the pit, I found it occupied by a group of about half a dozen men – Henderson, Ogilvy, and a tall, fair-haired man that I afterwards learned was Stent, the Astronomer Royal, with several workmen wielding spades and pickaxes. Stent was giving directions in a clear, high-pitched voice. He was standing on the cylinder, which was now evidently much cooler; his face was crimson and streaming with perspiration, and something seemed to have irritated him.

A large portion of the cylinder had been uncovered, though its lower end was still embedded. As soon as Ogilvy saw me among the staring crowd on the edge of the pit he called to me to come down, and asked me if I would mind going over to see Lord Hilton, the lord of the manor.

The growing crowd, he said, was becoming a serious impediment to their excavations, especially the boys. They wanted a light railing put up, and help to keep the people back. He told me that a faint stirring was occasionally still audible within the case, but that the workmen had failed to unscrew the top, as it afforded no grip to them. The case appeared to be enormously thick, and it was possible that the faint sounds we heard represented a noisy tumult in the interior.

I was very glad to do as he asked, and so become one of the privileged spectators within the contemplated enclosure. I failed to find Lord Hilton

at his house, but I was told he was expected from London by the six o'clock train from Waterloo; and as it was then about a quarter past five, I went home, had some tea, and walked up to the station to waylay him.

CHAPTER IV

The Cylinder Opens

When I returned to the common the sun was setting. Scattered groups were hurrying from the direction of Woking, and one or two persons were returning. The crowd about the pit had increased, and stood out black against the lemon yellow of the sky – a couple of hundred people, perhaps. There were raised voices, and some sort of struggle appeared to be going on about the pit. Strange imaginings passed through my mind. As I drew nearer I heard Stent's voice:

'Keep back! Keep back!'

A boy came running towards me.

'It's a-movin',' he said to me as he passed; 'a-screwin' and a-screwin' out. I don't like it. I'm a-goin' 'ome, I am.'

I went on to the crowd. There were really, I should think, two or three hundred people elbowing and jostling one another, the one or two ladies there being by no means the least active.

'He's fallen in the pit!' cried someone.

'Keep back!' said several.

The crowd swayed a little, and I elbowed my way through. Everyone seemed greatly excited. I heard a peculiar humming sound from the pit.

'I say!' said Ogilvy; 'help keep these idiots back. We don't know what's in the confounded thing, you know!'

I saw a young man, a shop assistant in Woking I believe he was, standing on the cylinder and trying to scramble out of the hole again. The crowd had pushed him in.

The end of the cylinder was being screwed out from within. Nearly two feet of shining screw projected. Somebody blundered against me, and I narrowly missed being pitched onto the top of the screw. I turned, and as I did so the screw must have come out, for the lid of the cylinder fell upon the gravel with a ringing concussion. I stuck my elbow into the person behind me, and turned my head towards the Thing again. For a moment that circular cavity seemed perfectly black. I had the sunset in my eyes.

I think everyone expected to see a man emerge – possibly something a little unlike us terrestrial men, but in all essentials a man. I know I did. But, looking, I presently saw something stirring within the shadow: greyish billowy movements, one above another, and then two luminous disks – like eyes. Then something resembling a little grey snake, about the thickness of a walking stick, coiled up out of the writhing middle, and wriggled in the air towards me – and then another.

A sudden chill came over me. There was a loud shriek from a woman behind. I half turned, keeping my eyes fixed upon the cylinder still, from which other tentacles were now projecting, and began pushing my way back from the edge of the pit. I saw astonishment giving place to horror on the faces of the people about me. I heard inarticulate exclamations on all sides. There was a general movement backwards. I saw the shopman struggling still on the edge of the pit. I found myself alone, and saw the people on the other side of the pit running off, Stent among them. I looked again at the cylinder, and ungovernable terror gripped me. I stood petrified and staring.

A big greyish rounded bulk, the size, perhaps, of a bear, was rising slowly and painfully out of the cylinder. As it bulged up and caught the light, it glistened like wet leather.

Two large dark-coloured eyes were regarding me steadfastly. The mass that framed them, the head of the thing, was rounded, and had, one might say, a face. There was a mouth under the eyes, the lipless brim of which quivered and panted, and dropped saliva. The whole creature heaved and pulsated convulsively. A lank tentacular appendage gripped the edge of the cylinder, another swayed in the air.

Those who have never seen a living Martian can scarcely imagine the strange horror of its appearance. The peculiar V-shaped mouth with its pointed upper lip, the absence of brow ridges, the absence of a chin beneath the wedge-like lower lip, the incessant quivering of this mouth, the Gorgon groups of tentacles, the tumultuous breathing of the lungs in a strange atmosphere, the evident heaviness and painfulness of movement due to the greater gravitational energy of the earth – above all, the extraordinary intensity of the immense eyes – were at once vital, intense, inhuman, crippled and monstrous. There was something fungoid in the oily brown skin, something in the clumsy deliberation of the tedious movements unspeakably nasty. Even at this first encounter, this first glimpse, I was overcome with disgust and dread.

Suddenly the monster vanished. It had toppled over the brim of the cylinder and fallen into the pit, with a thud like the fall of a great mass of leather. I heard it give a peculiar thick cry, and forthwith another of these creatures appeared darkly in the deep shadow of the aperture.

I turned and, running madly, made for the first group of trees, perhaps a hundred yards away; but I ran slantingly and stumbling, for I could not avert my face from these things.

There, among some young pine trees and furze bushes, I stopped, panting, and waited further developments. The common round the sand pits was dotted with people, standing like myself in a half-fascinated terror, staring at these creatures, or rather at the heaped gravel at the edge of the pit in which they lay. And then, with a renewed horror, I saw a round, black object bobbing up and down on the edge of the pit. It was the head of the shopman

who had fallen in, but showing as a little black object against the hot western
sun. Now he got his shoulder and knee up, and again he seemed to slip
back until only his head was visible. Suddenly he vanished, and I could have
fancied a faint shriek had reached me. I had a momentary impulse to go
back and help him that my fears overruled.

Everything was then quite invisible, hidden by the deep pit and the heap
of sand that the fall of the cylinder had made. Anyone coming along the
road from Chobham or Woking would have been amazed at the sight – a
dwindling multitude of perhaps a hundred people or more standing in a great
irregular circle, in ditches, behind bushes, behind gates and hedges, saying
little to one another and that in short, excited shouts, and staring, staring
hard at a few heaps of sand. The barrow of ginger beer stood, a queer dere-
lict, black against the burning sky, and in the sand pits was a row of deserted
vehicles with their horses feeding out of nosebags or pawing the ground.

CHAPTER V

The Heat-Ray

After the glimpse I had had of the Martians emerging from the cylinder in which they had come to the earth from their planet, a kind of fascination paralysed my actions. I remained standing knee-deep in the heather, staring at the mound that hid them. I was a battleground of fear and curiosity.

I did not dare to go back towards the pit, but I felt a passionate longing to peer into it. I began walking, therefore, in a big curve, seeking some point of vantage and continually looking at the sand heaps that hid these new-comers to our earth. Once a leash of thin black whips, like the arms of an octopus, flashed across the sunset and was immediately withdrawn, and afterwards a thin rod rose up, joint by joint, bearing at its apex a circular disk that spun with a wobbling motion. What could be going on there?

Most of the spectators had gathered in one or two groups – one a little crowd towards Woking, the other a knot of people in the direction of Chobham. Evidently they shared my mental conflict. There were few near me. One man I approached – he was, I perceived, a neighbour of mine, though I did not know his name – and accosted. But it was scarcely a time for articulate conversation.

'What ugly *brutes*!' he said. 'Good God! What ugly brutes!' He repeated this over and over again.

'Did you see a man in the pit?' I said; but he made no answer to that. We became silent, and stood watching for a time side by side, deriving, I fancy, a certain comfort in one another's company. Then I shifted my position to a little knoll that gave me the advantage of a yard or more of elevation and when I looked for him presently he was walking towards Woking.

The sunset faded to twilight before anything further happened. The crowd far away on the left, towards Woking, seemed to grow, and I heard now a faint murmur from it. The little knot of people towards Chobham dispersed. There was scarcely an intimation of movement from the pit.

It was this, as much as anything, that gave people courage, and I suppose the new arrivals from Woking also helped to restore confidence. At any rate, as the dusk came on a slow, intermittent movement upon the sand pits began, a movement that seemed to gather force as the stillness of the evening about the cylinder remained unbroken. Vertical black figures in twos and threes would advance, stop, watch, and advance again, spreading out as they did so in a thin irregular crescent that promised to enclose the pit in its attenuated horns. I, too, on my side began to move towards the pit.

Then I saw some cabmen and others had walked boldly into the sand pits, and heard the clatter of hoofs and the gride of wheels. I saw a lad trundling off the barrow of apples. And then, within thirty yards of the pit, advancing from the direction of Horsell, I noted a little black knot of men, the foremost of whom was waving a white flag.

This was the Deputation. There had been a hasty consultation, and since the Martians were evidently, in spite of their repulsive forms, intelligent creatures, it had been resolved to show them, by approaching them with signals, that we too were intelligent.

Flutter, flutter, went the flag, first to the right, then to the left. It was too far for me to recognize anyone there, but afterwards I learned that Ogilvy, Stent, and Henderson were with others in this attempt at communication. This little group had in its advance dragged inward, so to speak, the circumference of the now almost complete circle of people, and a number of dim black figures followed it at discreet distances.

Suddenly there was a flash of light, and a quantity of luminous greenish smoke came out of the pit in three distinct puffs, which drove up, one after the other, straight into the still air.

This smoke (or flame, perhaps, would be the better word for it) was so bright that the deep blue sky overhead and the hazy stretches of brown common towards Chertsey, set with black pine trees, seemed to darken abruptly as these puffs arose, and to remain the darker after their dispersal. At the same time a faint hissing sound became audible.

Beyond the pit stood the little wedge of people with the white flag at its apex, arrested by these phenomena, a little knot of small vertical black shapes upon the black ground. As the green smoke arose, their faces flashed out pallid green, and faded again as it vanished. Then slowly the hissing passed into a humming, into a long, loud, droning noise. Slowly a humped shape rose out of the pit, and the ghost of a beam of light seemed to flicker out from it.

Forthwith flashes of actual flame, a bright glare leaping from one to another, sprang from the scattered group of men. It was as if some invisible jet impinged upon them and flashed into white flame. It was as if each man were suddenly and momentarily turned to fire.

Then, by the light of their own destruction, I saw them staggering and falling, and their supporters turning to run.

I stood staring, not as yet realizing that this was death leaping from man to man in that little distant crowd. All I felt was that it was something very strange. An almost noiseless and blinding flash of light, and a man fell headlong and lay still; and as the unseen shaft of heat passed over them, pine trees burst into fire, and every dry furze bush became with one dull thud a mass of flames. And far away towards Knaphill I saw the flashes of trees and hedges and wooden buildings suddenly set alight.

It was sweeping round swiftly and steadily, this flaming death, this invisible, inevitable sword of heat. I perceived it coming towards me by the flashing bushes it touched, and was too astounded and stupefied to stir. I heard the crackle of fire in the sand pits and the sudden squeal of a horse that was as suddenly stilled. Then it was as if an invisible yet intensely heated finger were drawn through the heather between me and the Martians, and all along a curving line beyond the sand pits the dark ground smoked and crackled. Something fell with a crash far away to the left where the road from Woking station opens out on the common. Forthwith the hissing and humming ceased, and the black, dome-like object sank slowly out of sight into the pit.

All this had happened with such swiftness that I had stood motionless, dumbfounded and dazzled by the flashes of light. Had that death swept through a full circle, it must inevitably have slain me in my surprise. But it passed and spared me, and left the night about me suddenly dark and unfamiliar.

The undulating common seemed now dark almost to blackness, except where its roadways lay grey and pale under the deep blue sky of the early night. It was dark, and suddenly void of men. Overhead the stars were mustering, and in the west the sky was still a pale, bright, almost greenish blue. The tops of the pine trees and the roofs of Horsell came out sharp and black against the western afterglow. The Martians and their appliances were altogether invisible, save for that thin mast upon which their restless mirror wobbled. Patches of bush and isolated trees here and there smoked and glowed still, and the houses towards Woking station were sending up spires of flame into the stillness of the evening air.

Nothing was changed save for that and a terrible astonishment. The little group of black specks with the flag of white had been swept out of existence, and the stillness of the evening, so it seemed to me, had scarcely been broken.

It came to me that I was upon this dark common, helpless, unprotected, and alone. Suddenly, like a thing falling upon me from without, came – fear.

With an effort I turned and began a stumbling run through the heather.

The fear I felt was no rational fear, but a panic terror not only of the Martians, but of the dusk and stillness all about me. Such an extraordinary effect in unmanning me it had that I ran weeping silently as a child might do. Once I had turned, I did not dare to look back.

I remember I felt an extraordinary persuasion that I was being played with, that presently, when I was upon the very verge of safety, this mysterious death – as swift as the passage of light – would leap after me from the pit about the cylinder and strike me down.

CHAPTER VI

The Heat-Ray in the Chobham Road

It is still a matter of wonder how the Martians are able to slay men so swiftly and so silently. Many think that in some way they are able to generate an intense heat in a chamber of practically absolute non-conductivity. This intense heat they project in a parallel beam against any object they choose, by means of a polished parabolic mirror of unknown composition, much as the parabolic mirror of a lighthouse projects a beam of light. But no one has absolutely proved these details. However it is done, it is certain that a beam of heat is the essence of the matter. Heat, and invisible, instead of visible, light. Whatever is combustible flashes into flame at its touch, lead runs like water, it softens iron, cracks and melts glass, and when it falls upon water, incontinently that explodes into steam.

That night nearly forty people lay under the starlight about the pit, charred and distorted beyond recognition, and all night long the common from Horsell to Maybury was deserted and brightly ablaze.

The news of the massacre probably reached Chobham, Woking, and Ottershaw about the same time. In Woking the shops had closed when the tragedy happened, and a number of people, shop-people and so forth, attracted by the stories they had heard, were walking over the Horsell Bridge and along the road between the hedges that runs out at last upon the common. You may imagine the young people brushed up after the labours of the day, and making this novelty, as they would make any novelty, the excuse for walking together and enjoying a trivial flirtation. You may figure to yourself the hum of voices along the road in the gloaming . . .

As yet, of course, few people in Woking even knew that the cylinder had opened, though poor Henderson had sent a messenger on a bicycle to the post office with a special wire to an evening paper.

As these folks came out by twos and threes upon the open, they found little knots of people talking excitedly and peering at the spinning mirror over the sand pits, and the newcomers were, no doubt, soon infected by the excitement of the occasion.

By half-past eight, when the Deputation was destroyed, there may have been a crowd of three hundred people or more at this place, besides those who had left the road to approach the Martians nearer. There were three policemen too, one of whom was mounted, doing their best, under instructions from Stent, to keep the people back and deter them from approaching the cylinder. There was some booing from those more thoughtless and excitable souls to whom a crowd is always an occasion for noise and horse-play.

THE WAR OF THE WORLDS

Stent and Ogilvy, anticipating some possibilities of a collision, had tele-graphed from Horsell to the barracks as soon as the Martians emerged, for the help of a company of soldiers to protect these strange creatures from violence. After that they returned to lead that ill-fated advance. The descrip-tion of their death, as it was seen by the crowd, tallies very closely with my own impressions: the three puffs of green smoke, the deep humming note, and the flashes of flame.

But that crowd of people had a far narrower escape than mine. Only the fact that a hummock of heathery sand intercepted the lower part of the Heat-Ray saved them. Had the elevation of the parabolic mirror been a few yards higher, none could have lived to tell the tale. They saw the flashes and the men falling and an invisible hand, as it were, lit the bushes as it hurried towards them through the twilight. Then, with a whistling note that rose above the droning of the pit, the beam swung close over their heads, lighting the tops of the beech trees that line the road, and splitting the bricks, smashing the windows, firing the window frames, and bringing down in crumbling ruin a portion of the gable of the house nearest the corner.

In the sudden thud, hiss, and glare of the igniting trees, the panic-stricken crowd seems to have swayed hesitatingly for some moments. Sparks and burning twigs began to fall into the road, and single leaves like puffs of flame. Hats and dresses caught fire. Then came a crying from the common. There were shrieks and shouts, and suddenly a mounted policeman came galloping through the confusion with his hands clasped over his head, screaming.

'They're coming!' a woman shrieked, and incontinently everyone was turning and pushing at those behind, in order to clear their way to Woking again. They must have bolted as blindly as a flock of sheep. Where the road grows narrow and black between the high banks the crowd jammed, and a desperate struggle occurred. All that crowd did not escape; three persons at least, two women and a little boy, were crushed and trampled there, and left to die amid the terror and the darkness.

CHAPTER VII

How I Reached Home

For my own part, I remember nothing of my flight except the stress of blundering against trees and stumbling through the heather. All about me gathered the invisible terrors of the Martians; that pitiless sword of heat seemed whirling to and fro, flourishing overhead before it descended and smote me out of life. I came into the road between the crossroads and Horsell, and ran along this to the crossroads.

At last I could go no further; I was exhausted with the violence of my emotion and of my flight, and I staggered and fell by the wayside. That was near the bridge that crosses the canal by the gasworks. I fell and lay still.

I must have remained there some time.

I sat up, strangely perplexed. For a moment, perhaps, I could not clearly understand how I came there. My terror had fallen from me like a garment. My hat had gone, and my collar had burst away from its fastener. A few minutes before, there had only been three real things before me – the immensity of the night and space and nature, my own feebleness and anguish, and the near approach of death. Now it was as if something turned over, and the point of view altered abruptly. There was no sensible transition from one state of mind to the other. I was immediately the self of every day again – a decent, ordinary citizen. The silent common, the impulse of my flight, the starting flames, were as if they had been in a dream. I asked myself had these latter things indeed happened? I could not credit it.

I rose and walked unsteadily up the steep incline of the bridge. My mind was blank wonder. My muscles and nerves seemed drained of their strength. I dare say I staggered drunkenly. A head rose over the arch, and the figure of a workman carrying a basket appeared. Beside him ran a little boy. He passed me, wishing me good night. I was minded to speak to him, but did not. I answered his greeting with a meaningless mumble and went on over the bridge.

Over the Maybury arch a train, a billowing tumult of white, firelit smoke, and a long caterpillar of lighted windows, flying south – clatter, clatter, clap, rap, and it had gone. A dim group of people talked in the gate of one of the houses in the pretty little row of gables that was called Oriental Terrace. It was all so real and so familiar. And that behind me! It was frantic, fantastic! Such things, I told myself, could not be.

Perhaps I am a man of exceptional moods. I do not know how far my experience is common. At times I suffer from the strangest sense of detachment from myself and the world about me; I seem to watch it all from the

outside, from somewhere inconceivably remote, out of time, out of space, out of the stress and tragedy of it all. This feeling was very strong upon me that night. Here was another side to my dream.

But the trouble was the blank incongruity of this serenity and the swift death flying yonder, not two miles away. There was a noise of business from the gasworks, and the electric lamps were all alight. I stopped at the group of people.

'What news from the common?' said I.

There were two men and a woman at the gate.

'Eh?' said one of the men, turning.

'What news from the common?' I said.

"Ain't yer just *been* there?' asked the men.

'People seem fair silly about the common,' said the woman over the gate. 'What's it all abart?'

'Haven't you heard of the men from Mars?' said I; 'The creatures from Mars?'

'Quite enough,' said the woman over the gate. 'Thenks.' And all three of them laughed.

I felt foolish and angry. I tried and found I could not tell them what I had seen. They laughed again at my broken sentences.

'You'll hear more yet,' I said, and went on to my home.

I startled my wife at the doorway, so haggard was I. I went into the dining room, sat down, drank some wine, and so soon as I could collect myself sufficiently I told her the things I had seen. The dinner, which was a cold one, had already been served, and remained neglected on the table while I told my story.

'There is one thing,' I said, to allay the fears I had aroused; 'they are the most sluggish things I ever saw crawl. They may keep the pit and kill people who come near them, but they cannot get out of it. . . . But the horror of them!'

'Don't, dear!' said my wife, knitting her brows and putting her hand on mine.

'Poor Ogilvy!' I said. 'To think he may be lying dead there!'

My wife at least did not find my experience incredible. When I saw how deadly white her face was, I ceased abruptly.

'They may come here,' she said again and again.

I pressed her to take wine, and tried to reassure her.

'They can scarcely move,' I said.

I began to comfort her and myself by repeating all that Ogilvy had told me of the impossibility of the Martians establishing themselves on the earth. In particular I laid stress on the gravitational difficulty. On the surface of the earth the force of gravity is three times what it is on the surface of Mars. A Martian, therefore, would weigh three times more than on Mars, albeit

his muscular strength would be the same. His own body would be a cope
of lead to him. That, indeed, was the general opinion. Both *The Times* and
the *Daily Telegraph*, for instance, insisted on it the next morning, and both
overlooked, just as I did, two obvious modifying influences.

The atmosphere of the earth, we now know, contains far more oxygen
or far less argon (whichever way one likes to put it) than does Mars. The
invigorating influences of this excess of oxygen upon the Martians indisput-
ably did much to counterbalance the increased weight of their bodies. And,
in the second place, we all overlooked the fact that such mechanical intel-
ligence as the Martian possessed was quite able to dispense with muscular
exertion at a pinch.

But I did not consider these points at the time, and so my reasoning was
dead against the chances of the invaders. With wine and food, the confidence
of my own table, and the necessity of reassuring my wife, I grew by insensible
degrees courageous and secure.

'They have done a foolish thing,' said I, fingering my wineglass. 'They
are dangerous because, no doubt, they are mad with terror. Perhaps they
expected to find no living things – certainly no intelligent living things.'

'A shell in the pit' said I, 'if the worst comes to the worst will kill them all.'

The intense excitement of the events had no doubt left my perceptive
powers in a state of erethism. I remember that dinner-table with extraordi-
nary vividness even now. My dear wife's sweet anxious face peering at me
from under the pink lamp-shade, the white cloth with its silver and glass
table furniture – for in those days even philosophical writers had many little
luxuries – the crimson-purple wine in my glass, are photographically distinct.
At the end of it I sat, tempering nuts with a cigarette, regretting Ogilvy's
rashness, and denouncing the short-sighted timidity of the Martians.

So some respectable dodo in the Mauritius might have lorded it in his
nest, and discussed the arrival of that shipful of pitiless sailors in want of
animal food. 'We will peck them to death tomorrow, my dear.'

I did not know it, but that was the last civilized dinner I was to eat for
very many strange and terrible days.

CHAPTER VIII

Friday Night

The most extraordinary thing to my mind, of all the strange and wonderful things that happened upon that Friday, was the dovetailing of the commonplace habits of our social order with the first beginnings of the series of events that was to topple that social order headlong. If on Friday night you had taken a pair of compasses and drawn a circle with a radius of five miles round the Woking sand pits, I doubt if you would have had one human being outside it, unless it were some relation of Stent or of the three or four cyclists or London people lying dead on the common, whose emotions or habits were at all affected by the new-comers. Many people had heard of the cylinder, of course, and talked about it in their leisure, but it certainly did not make the sensation that an ultimatum to Germany would have done.

In London that night poor Henderson's telegram describing the gradual unscrewing of the shot was judged to be a canard, and his evening paper, after wiring for authentication from him and receiving no reply – the man was killed – decided not to print a special edition.

Even within the five-mile circle the great majority of people were inert. I have already described the behaviour of the men and women to whom I spoke. All over the district people were dining and supping; working men were gardening after the labours of the day, children were being put to bed, young people were wandering through the lanes love-making, students sat over their books.

Maybe there was a murmur in the village streets, a novel and dominant topic in the public-houses, and here and there a messenger, or even an eye-witness of the later occurrences, caused a whirl of excitement, a shouting, and a running to and fro; but for the most part the daily routine of working, eating, drinking, sleeping, went on as it had done for countless years – as though no planet Mars existed in the sky. Even at Woking station and Horsell and Chobham that was the case.

In Woking junction, until a late hour, trains were stopping and going on, others were shunting on the sidings, passengers were alighting and waiting, and everything was proceeding in the most ordinary way. A boy from the town, trenching on Smith's monopoly, was selling papers with the afternoon's news. The ringing impact of trucks, the sharp whistle of the engines from the junction, mingled with their shouts of 'Men from Mars!' Excited men came into the station about nine o'clock with incredible tidings, and caused no more disturbance than drunkards might have done. People rattling Londonwards peered into the darkness outside the carriage windows, and

saw only a rare, flickering, vanishing spark dance up from the direction of Horsell, a red glow and a thin veil of smoke driving across the stars, and thought that nothing more serious than a heath fire was happening. It was only round the edge of the common that any disturbance was perceptible. There were half a dozen villas burning on the Woking border. There were lights in all the houses on the common side of the three villages, and the people there kept awake till dawn.

A curious crowd lingered restlessly, people coming and going but the crowd remaining, both on the Chobham and Horsell bridges. One or two adventurous souls, it was afterwards found, went into the darkness and crawled quite near the Martians; but they never returned, for now and again a light-ray, like the beam of a warship's searchlight swept the common, and the Heat-Ray was ready to follow. Save for such, that big area of common was silent and desolate, and the charred bodies lay about on it all night under the stars, and all the next day. A noise of hammering from the pit was heard by many people.

So you have the state of things on Friday night. In the centre, sticking into the skin of our old planet Earth like a poisoned dart, was this cylinder. But the poison was scarcely working yet. Around it was a patch of silent common, smouldering in places, and with a few dark, dimly seen objects lying in contorted attitudes here and there. Here and there was a burning bush or tree. Beyond was a fringe of excitement, and further than that fringe the inflammation had not crept as yet. In the rest of the world the stream of life still flowed as it had flowed for immemorial years. The fever of war that would presently clog vein and artery, deaden nerve and destroy brain, had still to develop.

All night long the Martians were hammering and stirring, sleepless, inde-fatigable, at work upon the machines they were making ready, and ever and again a puff of greenish-white smoke whirled up to the starlit sky.

About eleven a company of soldiers came through Horsell, and deployed along the edge of the common to form a cordon. Later a second company marched through Chobham to deploy on the north side of the common. Several officers from the Inkerman barracks had been on the common earlier in the day, and one, Major Eden, was reported to be missing. The colonel of the regiment came to the Chobham bridge and was busy questioning the crowd at midnight. The military authorities were certainly alive to the seri-ousness of the business. About eleven, the next morning's papers were able to say, a squadron of hussars, two Maxims, and about four hundred men of the Cardigan regiment started from Aldershot.

A few seconds after midnight the crowd in the Chertsey road, Woking, saw a star fall from heaven into the pine woods to the north-west. It had a greenish colour, and caused a silent brightness like summer lightning. This was the second cylinder.

CHAPTER IX

The Fighting Begins

Saturday lives in my memory as a day of suspense. It was a day of lassitude too, hot and close, with, I am told, a rapidly fluctuating barometer. I had slept but little, though my wife had succeeded in sleeping, and I rose early. I went into my garden before breakfast and stood listening, but towards the common there was nothing stirring but a lark.

The milkman came as usual. I heard the rattle of his chariot and I went round to the side gate to ask the latest news. He told me that during the night the Martians had been surrounded by troops, and that guns were expected. Then – a familiar, reassuring note – I heard a train running towards Woking.

'They aren't to be killed,' said the milkman, 'if that can possibly be avoided.'

I saw my neighbour gardening, chatted with him for a time, and then strolled in to breakfast. It was a most unexceptional morning. My neighbour was of opinion that the troops would be able to capture or to destroy the Martians during the day.

'It's a pity they make themselves so unapproachable,' he said. 'It would be curious to know how they live on another planet; we might learn a thing or two.'

He came up to the fence and extended a handful of strawberries, for his gardening was as generous as it was enthusiastic. At the same time he told me of the burning of the pine woods about the Byfleet Golf Links.

'They say,' said he, 'that there's another of those blessed things fallen there – number two. But one's enough, surely. This lot'll cost the insurance people a pretty penny before everything's settled.' He laughed with an air of the greatest good humour as he said this. The woods, he said, were still burning, and pointed out a haze of smoke to me. 'They will be hot under foot for days, on account of the thick soil of pine needles and turf,' he said, and then grew serious over 'poor Ogilvy'.

After breakfast, instead of working, I decided to walk down towards the common. Under the railway bridge I found a group of soldiers – sappers, I think, men in small round caps, dirty red jackets unbuttoned, and showing their blue shirts, dark trousers, and boots coming to the calf. They told me no one was allowed over the canal, and, looking along the road towards the bridge, I saw one of the Cardigan men standing sentinel there. I talked with these soldiers for a time; I told them of my sight of the Martians on the previous evening. None of them had seen the Martians, and they had

but the vaguest ideas of them, so that they plied me with questions. They said that they did not know who had authorized the movements of the troops; their idea was that a dispute had arisen at the Horse Guards. The ordinary sapper is a great deal better educated than the common soldier, and they discussed the peculiar conditions of the possible fight with some acuteness. I described the Heat-Ray to them, and they began to argue among themselves.

'Crawl up under cover and rush 'em, say I,' said one.

'Get aht!' said another. 'What's cover against this 'ere 'eat? Sticks to cook yer! What we got to do is to go as near as the ground'll let us, and then drive a trench.'

'Blow yer trenches! You always want trenches; you ought to ha' been born a rabbit, Snippy.'

'Ain't they got any necks, then?' said a third, abruptly – a little, contemplative, dark man, smoking a pipe.

I repeated my description.

'Octopuses,' said he, 'that's what I calls 'em. Talk about fishers of men – fighters of fish it is this time!'

'It ain't no murder killing beasts like that,' said the first speaker.

'Why not shell the darned things strite off and finish 'em?' said the little dark man. 'You carn tell what they might do.'

'Where's your shells?' said the first speaker. 'There ain't no time. Do it in a rush, that's my tip, and do it at once.'

So they discussed it. After a while I left them, and went on to the railway station to get as many morning papers as I could.

But I will not weary the reader with a description of that long morning and of the longer afternoon. I did not succeed in getting a glimpse of the common, for even Horsell and Chobham church towers were in the hands of the military authorities. The soldiers I addressed didn't know anything; the officers were mysterious as well as busy. I found people in the town quite secure again in the presence of the military, and I heard for the first time from Marshall, the tobacconist, that his son was among the dead on the common. The soldiers had made the people on the outskirts of Horsell lock up and leave their houses.

I got back to lunch about two, very tired for, as I have said, the day was extremely hot and dull; and in order to refresh myself I took a cold bath in the afternoon. About half-past four I went up to the railway station to get an evening paper, for the morning papers had contained only a very inaccurate description of the killing of Stent, Henderson, Ogilvy, and the others. But there was little I didn't know. The Martians did not show an inch of themselves. They seemed busy in their pit, and there was a sound of hammering and an almost continuous streamer of smoke. Apparently they were busy getting ready for a struggle. 'Fresh attempts have been made

to signal, but without success,' was the stereotyped formula of the papers. A sapper told me it was done by a man in a ditch with a flag on a long pole. The Martians took as much notice of such advances as we should of the lowing of a cow.

I must confess the sight of all this armament, all this preparation, greatly excited me. My imagination became belligerent, and defeated the invaders in a dozen striking ways; something of my schoolboy dreams of battle and heroism came back. It hardly seemed a fair fight to me at that time. They seemed very helpless in that pit of theirs.

About three o'clock there began the thud of a gun at measured intervals from Chertsey or Addlestone. I learned that the smouldering pine wood into which the second cylinder had fallen was being shelled, in the hope of destroying that object before it opened. It was only about five, however, that a field gun reached Chobham for use against the first body of Martians.

About six in the evening, as I sat at tea with my wife in the summerhouse talking vigorously about the battle that was lowering upon us, I heard a muffled detonation from the common, and immediately after a gust of firing. Close on the heels of that came a violent rattling crash, quite close to us, that shook the ground; and, starting out upon the lawn, I saw the tops of the trees about the Oriental College burst into smoky red flame, and the tower of the little church beside it slide down into ruin. The pinnacle of the mosque had vanished, and the roof-line of the college itself looked as if a hundred-ton gun had been at work upon it. One of our chimneys cracked as if a shot had hit it, flew, and a piece of it came clattering down the tiles and made a heap of broken red fragments upon the flower-bed by my study window.

I and my wife stood amazed. Then I realized that the crest of Maybury Hill must be within range of the Martians' Heat-Ray now that the college was cleared out of the way.

At that I gripped my wife's arm, and without ceremony ran her out into the road. Then I fetched out the servant, telling her I would go upstairs myself for the box she was clamouring for.

'We can't possibly stay here,' I said; and as I spoke the firing reopened for a moment upon the common.

'But where are we to go?' said my wife in terror.

I thought, perplexed. Then I remembered my cousins at Leatherhead.

'Leatherhead!' I shouted above the sudden noise.

She looked away from me downhill. The people were coming out of their houses, astonished.

'How are we to get to Leatherhead?' she said.

Down the hill I saw a bevy of hussars ride under the railway bridge; three galloped through the open gates of the Oriental College; two others dismounted, and began running from house to house. The sun, shining

through the smoke that drove up from the tops of the trees, seemed blood-red, and threw an unfamiliar lurid light upon everything.

'Stop here,' said I; 'you are safe here.' And I started off at once for the Spotted Dog, for I knew the landlord had a horse and dog-cart. I ran, for I perceived that in a moment everyone upon this side of the hill would be moving. I found him in his bar, quite unaware of what was going on behind his house. A man stood with his back to me, talking to him.

'I must have a pound,' said the landlord, 'and I've no one to drive it.'

'I'll give you two,' said I, over the stranger's shoulder.

'What for?'

'And I'll bring it back by midnight,' I said.

'Lord!' said the landlord; 'What's the hurry? I'm selling my bit of a pig. Two pounds, and you bring it back? What's going on now?'

I explained hastily that I had to leave my home, and so secured the dog-cart. At the time it did not seem to me nearly so urgent that the landlord should leave his. I took care to have the cart there and then, drove it off down the road, and, leaving it in charge of my wife and servant, rushed into my house and packed a few valuables, such plate as we had, and so forth. The beech trees below the house were burning while I did this, and the palings up the road glowed red. While I was occupied in this way, one of the dismounted hussars came running up. He was going from house to house, warning people to leave. He was going on as I came out of my front door, lugging my treasures, done up in a tablecloth. I shouted after him:

'What news?'

He turned, stared, bawled something about 'crawling out in a thing like a dish cover', and ran on to the gate of the house at the crest. A sudden whirl of black smoke driving across the road hid him for a moment. I ran to my neighbour's door and rapped to satisfy myself of what I already knew, that his wife had gone to London with him and had locked up their house. I went in again, according to my promise, to get my servant's box, lugged it out, clapped it beside her on the tail of the dog-cart, and then caught the reins and jumped up into the driver's seat beside my wife. In another moment we were clear of the smoke and noise, and spanking down the opposite slope of Maybury Hill towards Old Woking.

In front was a quiet, sunny landscape, a wheat-field ahead on either side of the road, and the Maybury Inn with its swinging sign. I saw the doctor's cart ahead of me. At the bottom of the hill I turned my head to look at the hillside I was leaving. Thick streamers of black smoke shot with threads of red fire were driving up into the still air, and throwing dark shadows upon the green tree-tops eastward. The smoke already extended far away to the east and west – to the Byfleet pine woods eastward, and to Woking on the west. The road was dotted with people running towards us. And very faint now, but very distinct through the hot, quiet air, one heard the whirr of a

machine-gun that was presently stilled, and an intermittent cracking of rifles. Apparently the Martians were setting fire to everything within range of their Heat-Ray.

I am not an expert driver, and I had immediately to turn my attention to the horse. When I looked back again the second hill had hidden the black smoke. I slashed the horse with the whip, and gave him a loose rein until Woking and Send lay between us and that quivering tumult. I overtook and passed the doctor between Woking and Send.

CHAPTER X

In the Storm

Leatherhead is about twelve miles from Maybury Hill. The scent of hay was in the air through the lush meadows beyond Pyrford, and the hedges on either side were sweet and gay with multitudes of dog-roses. The heavy firing that had broken out while we were driving down Maybury Hill ceased as abruptly as it began, leaving the evening very peaceful and still. We got to Leatherhead without misadventure about nine o'clock, and the horse had an hour's rest while I took supper with my cousins and commended my wife to their care.

My wife was curiously silent throughout the drive, and seemed oppressed with forebodings of evil. I talked to her reassuringly, pointing out that the Martians were tied to the pit by sheer heaviness, and at the utmost could but crawl a little out of it; but she answered only in monosyllables. Had it not been for my promise to the innkeeper, she would, I think, have urged me to stay in Leatherhead that night. Would that I had! Her face, I remember, was very white as we parted.

For my own part, I had been feverishly excited all day. Something very like the war fever that occasionally runs through a civilized community had got into my blood, and in my heart I was not so very sorry that I had to return to Maybury that night. I was even afraid that that last fusillade I had heard might mean the extermination of our invaders from Mars. I can best express my state of mind by saying that I wanted to be in at the death.

It was nearly eleven when I started to return. The night was unexpectedly dark; to me, walking out of the lighted passage of my cousins' house, it seemed indeed black, and it was as hot and close as the day. Overhead the clouds were driving fast, albeit not a breath stirred the shrubs about us. My cousins' man lit both lamps. Happily, I knew the road intimately. My wife stood in the light of the doorway, and watched me until I jumped up into the dog-cart. Then abruptly she turned and went in, leaving my cousins side by side wishing me good hap.

I was a little depressed at first with the contagion of my wife's fears, but very soon my thoughts reverted to the Martians. At that time I was absolutely in the dark as to the course of the evening's fighting. I did not know even the circumstances that had precipitated the conflict. As I came through Ockham (for that was the way I returned, and not through Send and Old Woking) I saw along the western horizon a blood-red glow, which as I drew nearer, crept slowly up the sky. The driving clouds of the gathering thunderstorm mingled there with masses of black and red smoke.

Ripley Street was deserted, and except for a lighted window or so the village showed not a sign of life; but I narrowly escaped an accident at the corner of the road to Pyrford, where a knot of people stood with their backs to me. They said nothing to me as I passed. I do not know what they knew of the things happening beyond the hill, nor do I know if the silent houses I passed on my way were sleeping securely, or deserted and empty, or harassed and watching against the terror of the night.

From Ripley until I came through Pyrford I was in the valley of the Wey, and the red glare was hidden from me. As I ascended the little hill beyond Pyrford Church the glare came into view again, and the trees about me shivered with the first intimation of the storm that was upon me. Then I heard midnight pealing out from Pyrford Church behind me, and then came the silhouette of Maybury Hill, with its tree-tops and roofs black and sharp against the red.

Even as I beheld this a lurid green glare lit the road about me and showed the distant woods towards Addlestone. I felt a tug at the reins. I saw that the driving clouds had been pierced as it were by a thread of green fire, suddenly lighting their confusion and falling into the field to my left. It was the third falling star!

Close on its apparition, and blindingly violet by contrast, danced out the first lightning of the gathering storm, and the thunder burst like a rocket overhead. The horse took the bit between his teeth and bolted.

A moderate incline runs towards the foot of Maybury Hill, and down this we clattered. Once the lightning had begun, it went on in as rapid a succession of flashes as I have ever seen. The thunderclaps, treading one on the heels of another and with a strange crackling accompaniment, sounded more like the working of a gigantic electric machine than the usual detonating reverberations. The flickering light was blinding and confusing, and a thin hail smote gustily at my face as I drove down the slope.

At first I regarded little but the road before me, and then abruptly my attention was arrested by something that was moving rapidly down the opposite slope of Maybury Hill. At first I took it for the wet roof of a house, but one flash following another showed it to be in swift rolling movement. It was an elusive vision – a moment of bewildering darkness, and then, in a flash like daylight, the red masses of the Orphanage near the crest of the hill, the green tops of the pine trees, and this problematical object came out clear and sharp and bright.

And this Thing I saw! How can I describe it? A monstrous tripod, higher than many houses, striding over the young pine trees, and smashing them aside in its career; a walking engine of glittering metal, striding now across the heather; articulate ropes of steel dangling from it, and the clattering tumult of its passage mingling with the riot of the thunder. A flash, and it came out vividly, heeling over one way with two feet in the

air, to vanish and reappear almost instantly as it seemed, with the next flash, a hundred yards nearer. Can you imagine a milking stool tilted and bowled violently along the ground? That was the impression those instant flashes gave. But instead of a milking stool imagine it a great body of machinery on a tripod stand.

Then suddenly the trees in the pine wood ahead of me were parted, as brittle reeds are parted by a man thrusting through them; they were snapped off and driven headlong, and a second huge tripod appeared, rushing, as it seemed, headlong towards me. And I was galloping hard to meet it! At the sight of the second monster my nerve went altogether. Not stopping to look again, I wrenched the horse's head hard round to the right and in another moment the dog-cart had heeled over upon the horse; the shafts smashed noisily, and I was flung sideways and fell heavily into a shallow pool of water.

I crawled out almost immediately, and crouched, my feet still in the water, under a clump of furze. The horse lay motionless (his neck was broken, poor brute!) and by the lightning flashes I saw the black bulk of the overturned dog-cart and the silhouette of the wheel still spinning slowly. In another moment the colossal mechanism went striding by me, and passed uphill towards Pyrford.

Seen nearer, the Thing was incredibly strange, for it was no mere insensate machine driving on its way. Machine it was, with a ringing metallic pace, and long, flexible, glittering tentacles (one of which gripped a young pine tree) swinging and rattling about its strange body. It picked its road as it went striding along, and the brazen hood that surmounted it moved to and fro with the inevitable suggestion of a head looking about. Behind the main body was a huge mass of white metal like a gigantic fisherman's basket, and puffs of green smoke squirted out from the joints of the limbs as the monster swept by me. And in an instant it was gone.

So much I saw then, all vaguely for the flickering of the lightning, in blinding highlights and dense black shadows.

As it passed it set up an exultant deafening howl that drowned the thunder – 'Aloo! Aloo!' – and in another minute it was with its companion, half a mile away, stooping over something in the field. I have no doubt this Thing in the field was the third of the ten cylinders they had fired at us from Mars.

For some minutes I lay there in the rain and darkness watching, by the intermittent light, these monstrous beings of metal moving about in the distance over the hedge-tops. A thin hail was now beginning, and as it came and went their figures grew misty and then flashed into clearness again. Now and then came a gap in the lightning, and the night swallowed them up.

I was soaked with hail above and puddle-water below. It was some time before my blank astonishment would let me struggle up the bank to a drier position, or think at all of my imminent peril.

Not far from me was a little one-roomed squatter's hut of wood, surrounded by a patch of potato garden. I struggled to my feet at last, and, crouching and making use of every chance of cover, I made a run for this. I hammered at the door, but I could not make the people hear (if there were any people inside), and after a time I desisted, and, availing myself of a ditch for the greater part of the way, succeeded in crawling, unobserved by these monstrous machines, into the pine woods towards Maybury.

Under cover of this I pushed on, wet and shivering now, towards my own house. I walked among the trees trying to find the footpath. It was very dark indeed in the wood, for the lightning was now becoming infrequent, and the hail, which was pouring down in a torrent, fell in columns through the gaps in the heavy foliage.

If I had fully realized the meaning of all the things I had seen I should have immediately worked my way round through Byfleet to Street Cobham, and so gone back to rejoin my wife at Leatherhead. But that night the strangeness of things about me, and my physical wretchedness, prevented me, for I was bruised, weary, wet to the skin, deafened and blinded by the storm.

I had a vague idea of going on to my own house, and that was as much motive as I had. I staggered through the trees, fell into a ditch and bruised my knees against a plank, and finally splashed out into the lane that ran down from the College Arms. I say splashed, for the storm water was sweeping the sand down the hill in a muddy torrent. There in the darkness a man blundered into me and sent me reeling back.

He gave a cry of terror, sprang sideways, and rushed on before I could gather my wits sufficiently to speak to him. So heavy was the stress of the storm just at this place that I had the hardest task to win my way up the hill. I went close up to the fence on the left and worked my way along its palings.

Near the top I stumbled upon something soft, and, by a flash of lightning, saw between my feet a heap of black broadcloth and a pair of boots. Before I could distinguish clearly how the man lay, the flicker of light had passed. I stood over him waiting for the next flash. When it came, I saw that he was a sturdy man, cheaply but not shabbily dressed; his head was bent under his body, and he lay crumpled up close to the fence, as though he had been flung violently against it.

Overcoming the repugnance natural to one who had never before touched a dead body, I stooped and turned him over to feel for his heart. He was quite dead. Apparently his neck had been broken. The lightning flashed for a third time, and his face leaped upon me. I sprang to my feet. It was the landlord of the Spotted Dog, whose conveyance I had taken.

I stepped over him gingerly and pushed on up the hill. I made my way by the police station and the College Arms towards my own house. Nothing was burning on the hillside, though from the common there still came a red

glare and a rolling tumult of ruddy smoke beating up against the drenching hail. So far as I could see by the flashes, the houses about me were mostly uninjured. By the College Arms a dark heap lay in the road.

Down the road towards Maybury Bridge there were voices and the sound of feet, but I had not the courage to shout or to go to them. I let myself in with my latchkey, closed, locked and bolted the door, staggered to the foot of the staircase, and sat down. My imagination was full of those striding metallic monsters, and of the dead body smashed against the fence.

I crouched at the foot of the staircase with my back to the wall, shivering violently.

CHAPTER XI

At the Window

I have already said that my storms of emotion have a trick of exhausting themselves. After a time I discovered that I was cold and wet, and with little pools of water about me on the stair carpet. I got up almost mechanically, went into the dining room and drank some whisky, and then I was moved to change my clothes.

After I had done that I went upstairs to my study, but why I did so I do not know. The window of my study looks over the trees and the railway towards Horsell Common. In the hurry of our departure this window had been left open. The passage was dark, and, by contrast with the picture the window frame enclosed, the side of the room seemed impenetrably dark. I stopped short in the doorway.

The thunderstorm had passed. The towers of the Oriental College and the pine trees about it had gone, and very far away, lit by a vivid red glare, the common about the sand pits was visible. Across the light, huge black shapes, grotesque and strange, moved busily to and fro.

It seemed indeed as if the whole country in that direction was on fire – a broad hillside set with minute tongues of flame, swaying and writhing with the gusts of the dying storm, and throwing a red reflection upon the cloud-scud above. Every now and then a haze of smoke from some nearer conflagration drove across the window and hid the Martian shapes. I could not see what they were doing, nor the clear form of them, nor recognize the black objects they were busied upon. Neither could I see the nearer fire, though the reflections of it danced on the wall and ceiling of the study. A sharp, resinous tang of burning was in the air.

I closed the door noiselessly and crept towards the window. As I did so, the view opened out until, on the one hand, it reached to the houses about Woking station, and on the other to the charred and blackened pine woods of Byfleet. There was a light down below the hill, on the railway, near the arch, and several of the houses along the Maybury road and the streets near the station were glowing ruins. The light upon the railway puzzled me at first; there were a black heap and a vivid glare, and to the right of that a row of yellow oblongs. Then I perceived this was a wrecked train, the forepart smashed and on fire, the hinder carriages still upon the rails.

Between these three main centres of light – the houses, the train, and the burning county towards Chobham – stretched irregular patches of dark country, broken here and there by intervals of dimly glowing and smoking

ground. It was the strangest spectacle, that black expanse set with fire. It reminded me, more than anything else, of the Potteries at night. At first I could distinguish no people at all, though I peered intently for them. Later I saw against the light of Woking station a number of black figures hurrying one after the other across the line.

And this was the little world in which I had been living securely for years, this fiery chaos! What had happened in the last seven hours I still did not know; nor did I know, though I was beginning to guess, the relation between these mechanical colossi and the sluggish lumps I had seen disgorged from the cylinder. With a queer feeling of impersonal interest I turned my desk chair to the window, sat down, and stared at the blackened country, and particularly at the three gigantic black things that were going to and fro in the glare about the sand pits.

They seemed amazingly busy. I began to ask myself what they could be. Were they intelligent mechanisms? Such a thing I felt was impossible. Or did a Martian sit within each, ruling, directing, using, much as a man's brain sits and rules in his body? I began to compare the things to human machines, to ask myself for the first time in my life how an ironclad or a steam-engine would seem to an intelligent lower animal.

The storm had left the sky clear, and over the smoke of the burning land the little fading pin-point of Mars was dropping into the west, when a soldier came into my garden. I heard a slight scraping at the fence, and rousing myself from the lethargy that had fallen upon me, I looked down and saw him dimly, clambering over the palings. At the sight of another human being my torpor passed, and I leaned out of the window eagerly.

'Hist!' said I, in a whisper.

He stopped astride of the fence in doubt. Then he came over and across the lawn to the corner of the house. He bent down and stepped softly.

'Who's there?' he said, also whispering, standing under the window and peering up.

'Where are you going?' I asked.

'God knows.'

'Are you trying to hide?'

'That's it.'

'Come into the house,' I said.

I went down, unfastened the door, and let him in, and locked the door again. I could not see his face. He was hatless, and his coat was unbuttoned.

'My God!' he said, as I drew him in.

'What has happened?' I asked.

'What hasn't?' In the obscurity I could see he made a gesture of despair. 'They wiped us out – simply wiped us out,' he repeated again and again.

He followed me, almost mechanically, into the dining room.

'Take some whisky,' I said, pouring out a stiff dose.

He drank it. Then abruptly he sat down before the table, put his head on his arms, and began to sob and weep like a little boy, in a perfect passion of emotion, while I, with a curious forgetfulness of my own recent despair, stood beside him, wondering.

It was a long time before he could steady his nerves to answer my questions, and then he answered perplexingly and brokenly. He was a driver in the artillery, and had only come into action about seven. At that time firing was going on across the common, and it was said the first party of Martians were crawling slowly towards their second cylinder under cover of a metal shield.

Later this shield staggered up on tripod legs and became the first of the fighting-machines I had seen. The gun he drove had been unlimbered near Horsell, in order to command the sand pits, and its arrival it was that had precipitated the action. As the limber gunners went to the rear, his horse trod in a rabbit hole and came down, throwing him into a depression of the ground. At the same moment the gun exploded behind him, the ammunition blew up, there was fire all about him, and he found himself lying under a heap of charred dead men and dead horses.

'I lay still,' he said, 'scared out of my wits, with the fore quarter of a horse atop of me. We'd been wiped out. And the smell – good God! Like burnt meat! I was hurt across the back by the fall of the horse, and there I had to lie until I felt better. Just like parade it had been a minute before – then stumble, bang, swish!'

'Wiped out!' he said.

He had hid under the dead horse for a long time, peeping out furtively across the common. The Cardigan men had tried a rush, in skirmishing order, at the pit, simply to be swept out of existence. Then the monster had risen to its feet and had begun to walk leisurely to and fro across the common among the few fugitives, with its head-like hood turning about exactly like the head of a cowled human being. A kind of arm carried a complicated metallic case, about which green flashes scintillated, and out of the funnel of this there smoked the Heat-Ray.

In a few minutes there was, so far as the soldier could see, not a living thing left upon the common, and every bush and tree upon it that was not already a blackened skeleton was burning. The hussars had been on the road beyond the curvature of the ground, and he saw nothing of them. He heard the Martians rattle for a time and then become still. The giant saved Woking station and its cluster of houses until the last; then in a moment the Heat-Ray was brought to bear, and the town became a heap of fiery ruins. Then the Thing shut off the Heat-Ray, and turning its back upon the artilleryman, began to waddle away towards the smouldering pine woods that sheltered the second cylinder. As it did so a second glittering Titan built itself up out of the pit.

The second monster followed the first, and at that the artilleryman began to crawl very cautiously across the hot heather ash towards Horsell. He managed to get alive into the ditch by the side of the road, and so escaped to Woking. There his story became ejaculatory. The place was impassable. It seems there were a few people alive there, frantic for the most part and many burned and scalded. He was turned aside by the fire, and hid among some almost scorching heaps of broken wall as one of the Martian giants returned. He saw this one pursue a man, catch him up in one of its steely tentacles, and knock his head against the trunk of a pine tree. At last, after nightfall, the artilleryman made a rush for it and got over the railway embankment.

Since then he had been skulking along towards Maybury, in the hope of getting out of danger Londonward. People were hiding in trenches and cellars, and many of the survivors had made off towards Woking village and Send. He had been consumed with thirst until he found one of the water mains near the railway arch smashed, and the water bubbling out like a spring upon the road.

That was the story I got from him, bit by bit. He grew calmer telling me and trying to make me see the things he had seen. He had eaten no food since midday, he told me early in his narrative, and I found some mutton and bread in the pantry and brought it into the room. We lit no lamp for fear of attracting the Martians, and ever and again our hands would touch upon bread or meat. As he talked, things about us came darkly out of the darkness, and the trampled bushes and broken rose trees outside the window grew distinct. It would seem that a number of men or animals had rushed across the lawn. I began to see his face, blackened and haggard, as no doubt mine was also.

When we had finished eating we went softly upstairs to my study, and I looked again out of the open window. In one night the valley had become a valley of ashes. The fires had dwindled now. Where flames had been there were now streamers of smoke; but the countless ruins of shattered and gutted houses and blasted and blackened trees that the night had hidden stood out now gaunt and terrible in the pitiless light of dawn. Yet here and there some object had had the luck to escape – a white railway signal here, the end of a greenhouse there, white and fresh amid the wreckage. Never before in the history of warfare had destruction been so indiscriminate and so universal. And shining with the growing light of the east, three of the metallic giants stood about the pit, their cowls rotating as though they were surveying the desolation they had made.

It seemed to me that the pit had been enlarged, and ever and again puffs of vivid green vapour streamed up and out of it towards the brightening dawn – streamed up, whirled, broke and vanished.

Beyond were the pillars of fire about Chobham. They became pillars of bloodshot smoke at the first touch of day.

CHAPTER XII

What I Saw of the Destruction of Weybridge and Shepperton

As the dawn grew brighter we withdrew from the window from which we had watched the Martians, and went very quietly downstairs.

The artilleryman agreed with me that the house was no place to stay in. He proposed, he said, to make his way Londonward, and thence rejoin his battery – No. 12, of the Horse Artillery. My plan was to return at once to Leatherhead; and so greatly had the strength of the Martians impressed me that I had determined to take my wife to Newhaven, and go with her out of the country forthwith. For I already perceived clearly that the country about London must inevitably be the scene of a disastrous struggle before such creatures as these could be destroyed.

Between us and Leatherhead, however, lay the third cylinder, with its guarding giants. Had I been alone, I think I should have taken my chance and struck across country. But the artilleryman dissuaded me: 'It's no kindness to the right sort of wife,' he said, 'to make her a widow;' and in the end I agreed to go with him, under cover of the woods, northward as far as Street Cobham before I parted with him. Thence I would make a big detour by Epsom to reach Leatherhead.

I should have started at once, but my companion had been in active service and he knew better than that. He made me ransack the house for a flask, which he filled with whisky; and we lined every available pocket with packets of biscuits and slices of meat. Then we crept out of the house, and ran as quickly as we could down the ill-made road by which I had come overnight. The houses seemed deserted. In the road lay a group of three charred bodies close together, struck dead by the Heat-Ray; and here and there were things that people had dropped – a clock, a slipper, a silver spoon and the like poor valuables. At the corner turning up towards the post office a little cart, filled with boxes and furniture, and horseless, heeled over on a broken wheel. A cash box had been hastily smashed open and thrown under the debris.

Except the lodge at the Orphanage, which was still on fire, none of the houses had suffered very greatly here. The Heat-Ray had shaved the chimney tops and passed. Yet, save ourselves, there did not seem to be a living soul on Maybury Hill. The majority of the inhabitants had escaped, I suppose, by way of the Old Woking road – the road I had taken when I drove to Leatherhead – or they had hidden.

We went down the lane, by the body of the man in black, sodden now from the overnight hail, and broke into the woods at the foot of the hill.

We pushed through these towards the railway without meeting a soul. The woods across the line were but the scarred and blackened ruins of woods; for the most part the trees had fallen, but a certain proportion still stood, dismal grey stems, with dark brown foliage instead of green.

On our side the fire had done no more than scorch the nearer trees; it had failed to secure its footing. In one place the woodmen had been at work on Saturday; trees, felled and freshly trimmed, lay in a clearing, with heaps of sawdust by the sawing-machine and its engine. Hard by was a temporary hut, deserted. There was not a breath of wind this morning, and everything was strangely still. Even the birds were hushed, and as we hurried along I and the artilleryman talked in whispers and looked now and again over our shoulders. Once or twice we stopped to listen.

After a time we drew near the road, and as we did so we heard the clatter of hoofs and saw through the tree stems three cavalry soldiers riding slowly towards Woking. We hailed them, and they halted while we hurried towards them. It was a lieutenant and a couple of privates of the 8th Hussars, with a stand like a theodolite, which the artilleryman told me was a heliograph.

'You are the first men I've seen coming this way this morning,' said the lieutenant. 'What's brewing?'

His voice and face were eager. The men behind him stared curiously. The artilleryman jumped down the bank into the road and saluted.

'Gun destroyed last night, sir. Have been hiding. Trying to rejoin battery, sir. You'll come in sight of the Martians, I expect, about half a mile along this road.'

'What the dickens are they like?' asked the lieutenant.

'Giants in armour, sir. Hundred feet high. Three legs and a body like 'luminium, with a mighty great head in a hood, sir.'

'Get out!' said the lieutenant. 'What confounded nonsense!'

'You'll see, sir. They carry a kind of box, sir, that shoots fire and strikes you dead.'

'What d'ye mean – a gun?'

'No, sir,' and the artilleryman began a vivid account of the Heat-Ray. Halfway through, the lieutenant interrupted him and looked up at me. I was still standing on the bank by the side of the road.

'It's perfectly true,' I said.

'Well,' said the lieutenant, 'I suppose it's my business to see it too. Look here' – to the artilleryman – 'we're detailed here clearing people out of their houses. You'd better go along and report yourself to Brigadier-General Marvin, and tell him all you know. He's at Weybridge. Know the way?'

'I do,' I said; and he turned his horse southward again.

'Half a mile, you say?' said he.

'At most,' I answered, and pointed over the tree-tops southward. He thanked me and rode on, and we saw them no more.

Further along we came upon a group of three women and two children in the road, busy clearing out a labourer's cottage. They had got hold of a little hand truck, and were piling it up with unclean-looking bundles and shabby furniture. They were all too assiduously engaged to talk to us as we passed.

By Byfleet station we emerged from the pine trees, and found the country calm and peaceful under the morning sunlight. We were far beyond the range of the Heat-Ray there, and had it not been for the silent desertion of some of the houses, the stirring movement of packing in others, and the knot of soldiers standing on the bridge over the railway and staring down the line towards Woking, the day would have seemed very like any other Sunday.

Several farm waggons and carts were moving creakily along the road to Addlestone, and suddenly through the gate of a field we saw, across a stretch of flat meadow, six twelve-pounders standing neatly at equal distances pointing towards Woking. The gunners stood by the guns waiting, and the ammunition waggons were at a business-like distance. The men stood almost as if under inspection.

'That's good!' said I. 'They will get one fair shot, at any rate.'

The artilleryman hesitated at the gate.

'I shall go on,' he said.

Further on towards Weybridge, just over the bridge, there were a number of men in white fatigue jackets throwing up a long rampart, and more guns behind.

'It's bows and arrows against the lightning, anyhow,' said the artilleryman. 'They 'aven't seen that fire-beam yet.'

The officers who were not actively engaged stood and stared over the tree-tops south-westward, and the men digging would stop every now and again to stare in the same direction.

Byfleet was in a tumult; people packing, and a score of hussars, some of them dismounted, some on horseback, were hunting them about. Three or four black government waggons, with crosses in white circles, and an old omnibus, among other vehicles, were being loaded in the village street. There were scores of people, most of them sufficiently sabbatical to have assumed their best clothes. The soldiers were having the greatest difficulty in making them realize the gravity of their position. We saw one shrivelled old fellow with a huge box and a score or more of flower pots containing orchids, angrily expostulating with the corporal who would leave them behind. I stopped and gripped his arm.

'Do you know what's over there?' I said, pointing at the pine-tops that hid the Martians.

'Eh?' said he, turning. 'I was explainin' these is vallyble.'

'Death!' I shouted. 'Death is coming! Death!' And leaving him to digest

that if he could, I hurried on after the artilleryman. At the corner I looked back. The soldier had left him, and he was still standing by his box, with the pots of orchids on the lid of it, and staring vaguely over the trees.

No one in Weybridge could tell us where the headquarters were established; the whole place was in such confusion as I had never seen in any town before. Carts, carriages everywhere, the most astonishing miscellany of conveyances and horseflesh. The respectable inhabitants of the place, men in golf and boating costumes, wives prettily dressed, were packing, river-side loafers energetically helping, children excited, and, for the most part, highly delighted at this astonishing variation of their Sunday experiences. In the midst of it all the worthy vicar was very pluckily holding an early celebration, and his bell was jangling out above the excitement.

I and the artilleryman, seated on the step of the drinking fountain, made a very passable meal upon what we had brought with us. Patrols of soldiers – here no longer hussars, but grenadiers in white – were warning people to move now or to take refuge in their cellars as soon as the firing began. We saw as we crossed the railway bridge that a growing crowd of people had assembled in and about the railway station, and the swarming platform was piled with boxes and packages. The ordinary traffic had been stopped, I believe, in order to allow of the passage of troops and guns to Chertsey, and I have heard since that a savage struggle occurred for places in the special trains that were put on at a later hour.

We remained at Weybridge until midday, and at that hour we found ourselves at the place near Shepperton Lock where the Wey and Thames join. Part of the time we spent helping two old women to pack a little cart. The Wey has a treble mouth, and at this point boats are to be hired, and there was a ferry across the river. On the Shepperton side was an inn with a lawn, and beyond that the tower of Shepperton Church – it has been replaced by a spire – rose above the trees.

Here we found an excited and noisy crowd of fugitives. As yet the flight had not grown to a panic, but there were already far more people than all the boats going to and fro could enable to cross. People came panting along under heavy burdens; one husband and wife were even carrying a small outhouse door between them, with some of their household goods piled thereon. One man told us he meant to try to get away from Shepperton station.

There was a lot of shouting, and one man was even jesting. The idea people seemed to have here was that the Martians were simply formidable human beings, who might attack and sack the town, to be certainly destroyed in the end. Every now and then people would glance nervously across the Wey, at the meadows towards Chertsey, but everything over there was still.

Across the Thames, except just where the boats landed, everything was quiet, in vivid contrast with the Surrey side. The people who landed there

from the boats went tramping off down the lane. The big ferryboat had just made a journey. Three or four soldiers stood on the lawn of the inn, staring and jesting at the fugitives, without offering to help. The inn was closed, as it was now within prohibited hours.

'What's that?' cried a boatman, and 'Shut up, you fool!' said a man near me to a yelping dog. Then the sound came again, this time from the direction of Chertsey, a muffled thud – the sound of a gun.

The fighting was beginning. Almost immediately unseen batteries across the river to our right, unseen because of the trees, took up the chorus, firing heavily one after the other. A woman screamed. Everyone stood arrested by the sudden stir of battle, near us and yet invisible to us. Nothing was to be seen save flat meadows, cows feeding unconcernedly for the most part, and silvery pollard willows motionless in the warm sunlight.

'The sojers'll stop 'em,' said a woman beside me, doubtfully. A haziness rose over the tree-tops.

Then suddenly we saw a rush of smoke far away up the river, a puff of smoke that jerked up into the air and hung; and forthwith the ground heaved under foot and a heavy explosion shook the air, smashing two or three windows in the houses near, and leaving us astonished.

'Here they are!' shouted a man in a blue jersey. 'Yonder! D'yer see them? Yonder!'

Quickly, one after the other, one, two, three, four of the armoured Martians appeared, far away over the little trees, across the flat meadows that stretched towards Chertsey, and striding hurriedly towards the river. Little cowled figures they seemed at first, going with a rolling motion and as fast as flying birds.

Then, advancing obliquely towards us, came a fifth. Their armoured bodies glittered in the sun as they swept swiftly forward upon the guns, growing rapidly larger as they drew nearer. One on the extreme left, the remotest that is, flourished a huge case high in the air, and the ghostly, terrible Heat-Ray I had already seen on Friday night smote towards Chertsey, and struck the town.

At sight of these strange, swift, and terrible creatures the crowd near the water's edge seemed to me to be for a moment horror-struck. There was no screaming or shouting, but a silence. Then a hoarse murmur and a movement of feet – a splashing from the water. A man, too frightened to drop the portmanteau he carried on his shoulder, swung round and sent me staggering with a blow from the corner of his burden. A woman thrust at me with her hand and rushed past me. I turned with the rush of the people, but I was not too terrified for thought. The terrible Heat-Ray was in my mind. To get under water! That was it!

'Get under water!' I shouted, unheeded.

I faced about again, and rushed towards the approaching Martian, rushed

right down the gravelly beach and headlong into the water. Others did the same. A boatload of people putting back came leaping out as I rushed past. The stones under my feet were muddy and slippery, and the river was so low that I ran perhaps twenty feet scarcely waist-deep. Then, as the Martian towered overhead scarcely a couple of hundred yards away, I flung myself forward under the surface. The splashes of the people in the boats leaping into the river sounded like thunderclaps in my ears. People were landing hastily on both sides of the river. But the Martian machine took no more notice for the moment of the people running this way and that than a man would of the confusion of ants in a nest against which his foot has kicked. When, half suffocated, I raised my head above water, the Martian's hood pointed at the batteries that were still firing across the river, and as it advanced it swung loose what must have been the generator of the Heat-Ray.

In another moment it was on the bank, and in a stride wading halfway across. The knees of its foremost legs bent at the further bank, and in another moment it had raised itself to its full height again, close to the village of Shepperton. Forthwith the six guns which, unknown to anyone on the right bank, had been hidden behind the outskirts of that village, fired simultaneously. The sudden near concussion, the last close upon the first, made my heart jump. The monster was already raising the case generating the Heat-Ray as the first shell burst six yards above the hood.

I gave a cry of astonishment. I saw and thought nothing of the other four Martian monsters; my attention was riveted upon the nearer incident. Simultaneously two other shells burst in the air near the body as the hood twisted round in time to receive, but not in time to dodge, the fourth shell.

The shell burst clean in the face of the Thing. The hood bulged, flashed, was whirled off in a dozen tattered fragments of red flesh and glittering metal.

'Hit!' shouted I, with something between a scream and a cheer.

I heard answering shouts from the people in the water about me. I could have leaped out of the water with that momentary exultation.

The decapitated colossus reeled like a drunken giant; but it did not fall over. It recovered its balance by a miracle, and, no longer heeding its steps and with the camera that fired the Heat-Ray now rigidly upheld, it reeled swiftly upon Shepperton. The living intelligence, the Martian within the hood, was slain and splashed to the four winds of heaven, and the Thing was now but a mere intricate device of metal whirling to destruction. It drove along in a straight line, incapable of guidance. It struck the tower of Shepperton Church, smashing it down as the impact of a battering ram might have done, swerved aside, blundered on and collapsed with tremendous force into the river out of my sight.

A violent explosion shook the air, and a spout of water, steam, mud, and shattered metal shot far up into the sky. As the camera of the Heat-Ray hit

the water, the latter had immediately flashed into steam. In another moment a huge wave, like a muddy tidal bore but almost scaldingly hot, came sweeping round the bend upstream. I saw people struggling shorewards, and heard their screaming and shouting faintly above the seething and roar of the Martian's collapse.

For a moment I heeded nothing of the heat, forgot the patent need of self-preservation. I splashed through the tumultuous water, pushing aside a man in black to do so, until I could see round the bend. Half a dozen deserted boats pitched aimlessly upon the confusion of the waves. The fallen Martian came into sight downstream, lying across the river, and for the most part submerged.

Thick clouds of steam were pouring off the wreckage, and through the tumultuously whirling wisps I could see, intermittently and vaguely, the gigantic limbs churning the water and flinging a splash and spray of mud and froth into the air. The tentacles swayed and struck like living arms, and, save for the helpless purposelessness of these movements, it was as if some wounded thing were struggling for its life amid the waves. Enormous quantities of a ruddy-brown fluid were spurting up in noisy jets out of the machine.

My attention was diverted from this death flurry by a furious yelling, like that of the thing called a siren in our manufacturing towns. A man, knee-deep near the towing path, shouted inaudibly to me and pointed. Looking back, I saw the other Martians advancing with gigantic strides down the riverbank from the direction of Chertsey. The Shepperton guns spoke this time unavailingly.

At that I ducked at once under water, and, holding my breath until movement was an agony, blundered painfully ahead under the surface as long as I could. The water was in a tumult about me, and rapidly growing hotter.

When for a moment I raised my head to take breath and throw the hair and water from my eyes, the steam was rising in a whirling white fog that at first hid the Martians altogether. The noise was deafening. Then I saw them dimly, colossal figures of grey, magnified by the mist. They had passed by me, and two were stooping over the frothing, tumultuous ruins of their comrade.

The third and fourth stood beside him in the water, one perhaps two hundred yards from me, the other towards Laleham. The generators of the Heat-Rays waved high, and the hissing beams smote down this way and that.

The air was full of sound, a deafening and confusing conflict of noises – the clangorous din of the Martians, the crash of falling houses, the thud of trees, fences, sheds flashing into flame, and the crackling and roaring of fire. Dense black smoke was leaping up to mingle with the steam from the river, and as the Heat-Ray went to and fro over Weybridge its impact was

marked by flashes of incandescent white, that gave place at once to a smoky dance of lurid flames. The nearer houses still stood intact, awaiting their fate, shadowy, faint and pallid in the steam, with the fire behind them going to and fro.

For a moment perhaps I stood there, breast-high in the almost boiling water, dumbfounded at my position, hopeless of escape. Through the reek I could see the people who had been with me in the river scrambling out of the water through the reeds, like little frogs hurrying through grass from the advance of a man, or running to and fro in utter dismay on the towing-path.

Then suddenly the white flashes of the Heat-Ray came leaping towards me. The houses caved in as they dissolved at its touch, and darted out flames; the trees changed to fire with a roar. The Ray flickered up and down the towing-path, licking off the people who ran this way and that, and came down to the water's edge not fifty yards from where I stood. It swept across the river to Shepperton, and the water in its track rose in a boiling weal crested with steam. I turned shoreward.

In another moment the huge wave, well-nigh at the boiling-point had rushed upon me. I screamed aloud, and scalded, half blinded, agonized, I staggered through the leaping, hissing water towards the shore. Had my foot stumbled, it would have been the end. I fell helplessly, in full sight of the Martians, upon the broad, bare gravelly spit that runs down to mark the angle of the Wey and Thames. I expected nothing but death.

I have a dim memory of the foot of a Martian coming down within a score of yards of my head, driving straight into the loose gravel, whirling it this way and that and lifting again; of a long suspense, and then of the four carrying the debris of their comrade between them, now clear and then presently faint through a veil of smoke, receding interminably, as it seemed to me, across a vast space of river and meadow. And then, very slowly, I realized that by a miracle I had escaped.

CHAPTER XIII

How I Fell In with the Curate

After getting this sudden lesson in the power of terrestrial weapons, the Martians retreated to their original position upon Horsell Common; and in their haste, and encumbered with the debris of their smashed companion, they no doubt overlooked many such a stray and negligible victim as myself. Had they left their comrade and pushed on forthwith, there was nothing at that time between them and London but batteries of twelve-pounder guns, and they would certainly have reached the capital in advance of the tidings of their approach; as sudden, dreadful, and destructive their advent would have been as the earthquake that destroyed Lisbon a century ago.

But they were in no hurry. Cylinder followed cylinder on its interplanetary flight; every twenty-four hours brought them reinforcement. And meanwhile the military and naval authorities, now fully alive to the tremendous power of their antagonists, worked with furious energy. Every minute a fresh gun came into position until, before twilight, every copse, every row of suburban villas on the hilly slopes about Kingston and Richmond, masked an expectant black muzzle. And through the charred and desolated area – perhaps twenty square miles altogether – that encircled the Martian encampment on Horsell Common, through charred and ruined villages among the green trees, through the blackened and smoking arcades that had been but a day ago pine spinneys, crawled the devoted scouts with the heliographs that were presently to warn the gunners of the Martian approach. But the Martians now understood our command of artillery and the danger of human proximity, and not a man ventured within a mile of either cylinder, save at the price of his life.

It would seem that these giants spent the earlier part of the afternoon in going to and fro, transferring everything from the second and third cylinders – the second in Addlestone Golf Links and the third at Pyrford – to their original pit on Horsell Common. Over that, above the blackened heather and ruined buildings that stretched far and wide, stood one as sentinel, while the rest abandoned their vast fighting-machines and descended into the pit. They were hard at work there far into the night, and the towering pillar of dense green smoke that rose therefrom could be seen from the hills about Merrow, and even, it is said, from Banstead and Epsom Downs.

And while the Martians behind me were thus preparing for their next sally, and in front of me Humanity gathered for the battle, I made my way with infinite pains and labour from the fire and smoke of burning Weybridge towards London.

I saw an abandoned boat, very small and remote, drifting downstream; and throwing off the most of my sodden clothes, I went after it, gained it, and so escaped out of that destruction. There were no oars in the boat, but I contrived to paddle, as well as my parboiled hands would allow, down the river towards Halliford and Walton, going very tediously and continually looking behind me, as you may well understand. I followed the river, because I considered that the water gave me my best chance of escape should these giants return.

The hot water from the Martian's overthrow drifted downstream with me, so that for the best part of a mile I could see little of either bank. Once, however, I made out a string of black figures hurrying across the meadows from the direction of Weybridge. Halliford, it seemed, was deserted, and several of the houses facing the river were on fire. It was strange to see the place quite tranquil, quite desolate under the hot, blue sky, with the smoke and little threads of flame going straight up into the heat of the afternoon. Never before had I seen houses burning without the accompaniment of an obstructive crowd. A little further on the dry reeds up the bank were smoking and glowing, and a line of fire inland was marching steadily across a late field of hay.

For a long time I drifted, so painful and weary was I after the violence I had been through, and so intense the heat upon the water. Then my fears got the better of me again, and I resumed my paddling. The sun scorched my bare back. At last, as the bridge at Walton was coming into sight round the bend, my fever and faintness overcame my fears, and I landed on the Middlesex bank and lay down, deadly sick, amid the long grass. I suppose the time was then about four or five o'clock. I got up presently, walked perhaps half a mile without meeting a soul, and then lay down again in the shadow of a hedge. I seem to remember talking, wanderingly, to myself during that last spurt. I was also very thirsty, and bitterly regretful I had drunk no more water. It is a curious thing that I felt angry with my wife; I cannot account for it, but my impotent desire to reach Leatherhead worried me excessively.

I do not clearly remember the arrival of the curate, so that probably I dozed. I became aware of him as a seated figure in soot-smudged shirt sleeves, and with his upturned, clean-shaven face staring at a faint flickering that danced over the sky. The sky was what is called a mackerel sky – rows and rows of faint down-plumes of cloud, just tinted with the midsummer sunset.

I sat up, and at the rustle of my motion he looked at me quickly.

'Have you any water?' I asked abruptly.

He shook his head.

'You have been asking for water for the last hour,' he said.

For a moment we were silent, taking stock of each other. I dare say he found me a strange enough figure, naked, save for my water-soaked trousers

and socks, scalded, and my face and shoulders blackened by the smoke. His face was a fair weakness, his chin retreated, and his hair lay in crisp, almost flaxen curls on his low forehead; his eyes were rather large, pale blue, and blankly staring. He spoke abruptly, looking vacantly away from me.

'What does it mean?' he said. 'What do these things mean?'

I stared at him and made no answer.

He extended a thin white hand and spoke in almost a complaining tone.

'Why are these things permitted? What sins have we done? The morning service was over, I was walking through the roads to clear my brain for the afternoon, and then – fire, earthquake, death! As if it were Sodom and Gomorrah! All our work undone, all the work – What are these Martians?'

'What are we?' I answered, clearing my throat.

He gripped his knees and turned to look at me again. For half a minute, perhaps, he stared silently.

'I was walking through the roads to clear my brain,' he said. 'And suddenly – fire, earthquake, death!'

He relapsed into silence, with his chin now sunken almost to his knees. Presently he began waving his hand.

'All the work – all the Sunday-schools – What have we done – what has Weybridge done? Everything gone – everything destroyed. The church! We rebuilt it only three years ago. Gone! Swept out of existence! Why?'

Another pause, and he broke out again like one demented.

'The smoke of her burning goeth up for ever and ever!' he shouted.

His eyes flamed, and he pointed a lean finger in the direction of Weybridge.

By this time I was beginning to take his measure. The tremendous tragedy in which he had been involved – it was evident he was a fugitive from Weybridge – had driven him to the very verge of his reason.

'Are we far from Sunbury?' I said, in a matter-of-fact tone.

'What are we to do?' he asked. 'Are these creatures everywhere? Has the earth been given over to them?'

'Are we far from Sunbury?'

'Only this morning I officiated at early celebration ——'

'Things have changed,' I said, quietly. 'You must keep your head. There is still hope.'

'Hope!'

'Yes. Plentiful hope – for all this destruction!'

I began to explain my view of our position. He listened at first, but as I went on the interest dawning in his eyes gave place to their former stare, and his regard wandered from me.

'This must be the beginning of the end,' he said, interrupting me. 'The end! The great and terrible day of the Lord! When men shall call upon the mountains and the rocks to fall upon them and hide them – hide them from the face of Him that sitteth upon the throne!'

I began to understand the position. I ceased my laboured reasoning, struggled to my feet, and, standing over him, laid my hand on his shoulder.

'Be a man!' said I. 'You are scared out of your wits! What good is religion if it collapses under calamity? Think of what earthquakes and floods, wars and volcanoes, have done before to men! Did you think God had exempted Weybridge? He is not an insurance agent.'

For a time he sat in blank silence.

'But how can we escape?' he asked, suddenly. 'They are invulnerable, they are pitiless.'

'Neither the one nor, perhaps, the other,' I answered. 'And the mightier they are the more sane and wary should we be. One of them was killed yonder not three hours ago.'

'Killed!' he said, staring about him. 'How can God's ministers be killed?'

'I saw it happen.' I proceeded to tell him. 'We have chanced to come in for the thick of it,' said I, 'and that is all.'

'What is that flicker in the sky?' he asked abruptly.

I told him it was the heliograph signalling – that it was the sign of human help and effort in the sky.

'We are in the midst of it,' I said, 'quiet as it is. That flicker in the sky tells of the gathering storm. Yonder, I take it are the Martians, and Londonward, where those hills rise about Richmond and Kingston and the trees give cover, earthworks are being thrown up and guns are being placed. Presently the Martians will be coming this way again.'

And even as I spoke he sprang to his feet and stopped me by a gesture.

'Listen!' he said.

From beyond the low hills across the water came the dull resonance of distant guns and a remote weird crying. Then everything was still. A cock-chafer came droning over the hedge and past us. High in the west the crescent moon hung faint and pale above the smoke of Weybridge and Shepperton and the hot, still splendour of the sunset.

'We had better follow this path,' I said, 'northward.'

CHAPTER XIV

In London

My younger brother was in London when the Martians fell at Woking. He was a medical student working for an imminent examination, and he heard nothing of the arrival until Saturday morning. The morning papers on Saturday contained, in addition to lengthy special articles on the planet Mars, on life in the planets, and so forth, a brief and vaguely worded telegram, all the more striking for its brevity.

The Martians, alarmed by the approach of a crowd, had killed a number of people with a quick-firing gun, so the story ran. The telegram concluded with the words: 'Formidable as they seem to be, the Martians have not moved from the pit into which they have fallen, and, indeed, seem incapable of doing so. Probably this is due to the relative strength of the earth's gravitational energy.' On that last text their leader-writer expanded very comfortingly.

Of course all the students in the crammer's biology class, to which my brother went that day, were intensely interested, but there were no signs of any unusual excitement in the streets. The afternoon papers puffed scraps of news under big headlines. They had nothing to tell beyond the movements of troops about the common, and the burning of the pine woods between Woking and Weybridge, until eight. Then the *St James's Gazette*, in an extra-special edition, announced the bare fact of the interruption of telegraphic communication. This was thought to be due to the falling of burning pine trees across the line. Nothing more of the fighting was known that night, the night of my drive to Leatherhead and back.

My brother felt no anxiety about us, as he knew from the description in the papers that the cylinder was a good two miles from my house. He made up his mind to run down that night to me, in order, as he says, to see the Things before they were killed. He dispatched a telegram, which never reached me, about four o'clock, and spent the evening at a music-hall.

In London, also, on Saturday night there was a thunderstorm, and my brother reached Waterloo in a cab. On the platform from which the midnight train usually starts he learned, after some waiting, that an accident prevented trains from reaching Woking that night. The nature of the accident he could not ascertain; indeed, the railway authorities did not clearly know at that time. There was very little excitement in the station, as the officials, failing to realize that anything further than a breakdown between Byfleet and Woking junction had occurred, were running the theatre trains which usually passed through Woking round by Virginia Water or Guildford. They were

busy making the necessary arrangements to alter the route of the Southampton and Portsmouth Sunday League excursions. A nocturnal newspaper reporter, mistaking my brother for the traffic manager, to whom he bears a slight resemblance, waylaid and tried to interview him. Few people, excepting the railway officials, connected the breakdown with the Martians.

I have read, in another account of these events, that on Sunday morning 'all London was electrified by the news from Woking'. As a matter of fact, there was nothing to justify that very extravagant phrase. Plenty of Londoners did not hear of the Martians until the panic of Monday morning. Those who did took some time to realize all that the hastily worded telegrams in the Sunday papers conveyed. The majority of people in London do not read Sunday papers.

The habit of personal security, moreover, is so deeply fixed in the Londoner's mind, and startling intelligence so much a matter of course in the papers, that they could read without any personal tremors: 'About seven o'clock last night the Martians came out of the cylinder, and, moving about under an armour of metallic shields, have completely wrecked Woking station with the adjacent houses, and massacred an entire battalion of the Cardigan Regiment. No details are known. Maxims have been absolutely useless against their armour; the field guns have been disabled by them. Flying hussars have been galloping into Chertsey. The Martians appear to be moving slowly towards Chertsey or Windsor. Great anxiety prevails in West Surrey, and earthworks are being thrown up to check the advance Londonward.' That was how the Sunday *Sun* put it, and a clever and remarkably prompt 'hand-book' article in the *Referee* compared the affair to a menagerie suddenly let loose in a village.

No one in London knew positively of the nature of the armoured Martians, and there was still a fixed idea that these monsters must be sluggish: 'crawling,' 'creeping painfully' – such expressions occurred in almost all the earlier reports. None of the telegrams could have been written by an eyewitness of their advance. The Sunday papers printed separate editions as further news came to hand, some even in default of it. But there was practically nothing more to tell people until late in the afternoon, when the authorities gave the press agencies the news in their possession. It was stated that the people of Walton and Weybridge, and all the district were pouring along the roads Londonward, and that was all.

My brother went to church at the Foundling Hospital in the morning, still in ignorance of what had happened on the previous night. There he heard allusions made to the invasion, and a special prayer for peace. Coming out, he bought a *Referee*. He became alarmed at the news in this, and went again to Waterloo station to find out if communication were restored. The omnibuses, carriages, cyclists, and innumerable people walking in their best clothes seemed scarcely affected by the strange intelligence that the news

venders were disseminating. People were interested, or, if alarmed, alarmed only on account of the local residents. At the station he heard for the first time that the Windsor and Chertsey lines were now interrupted. The porters told him that several remarkable telegrams had been received in the morning from Byfleet and Chertsey stations, but that these had abruptly ceased. My brother could get very little precise detail out of them. 'There's fighting going on about Weybridge' was the extent of their information.

The train service was now very much disorganized. Quite a number of people who had been expecting friends from places on the South-Western network were standing about the station. One grey-headed old gentleman came and abused the South-Western Company bitterly to my brother. 'It wants showing up,' he said.

One or two trains came in from Richmond, Putney, and Kingston, containing people who had gone out for a day's boating and found the locks closed and a feeling of panic in the air. A man in a blue and white blazer addressed my brother, full of strange tidings.

'There's hosts of people driving into Kingston in traps and carts and things, with boxes of valuables and all that,' he said. 'They come from Molesey and Weybridge and Walton, and they say there's been guns heard at Chertsey, heavy firing, and that mounted soldiers have told them to get off at once because the Martians are coming. We heard guns firing at Hampton Court station, but we thought it was thunder. What the dickens does it all mean? The Martians can't get out of their pit, can they?'

My brother could not tell him.

Afterwards he found that the vague feeling of alarm had spread to the clients of the underground railway, and that the Sunday excursionists began to return from all over the South-Western 'lungs' – Barnes, Wimbledon, Richmond Park, Kew and so forth – at unnaturally early hours; but not a soul had anything more than vague hearsay to tell of. Everyone connected with the terminus seemed ill-tempered.

About five o'clock the gathering crowd in the station was immensely excited by the opening of the line of communication, which is almost invariably closed, between the South-Eastern and the South-Western stations, and the passage of carriage trucks bearing huge guns and carriages crammed with soldiers. These were the guns that were brought up from Woolwich and Chatham to cover Kingston. There was an exchange of pleasantries: 'You'll get eaten!' 'We're the beast-tamers!' and so forth. A little while after that a squad of police came into the station and began to clear the public off the platforms, and my brother went out into the street again.

The church bells were ringing for evensong, and a squad of Salvation Army lassies came singing down Waterloo Road. On the bridge a number of loafers were watching a curious brown scum that came drifting down the stream in patches. The sun was just setting, and the Clock Tower and

the Houses of Parliament rose against one of the most peaceful skies it is possible to imagine, a sky of gold, barred with long transverse stripes of reddish-purple cloud. There was talk of a floating body. One of the men there, a reservist he said he was, told my brother he had seen the heliograph flickering in the west.

In Wellington Street my brother met a couple of sturdy roughs who had just been rushed out of Fleet Street with still-wet newspapers and staring placards. 'Dreadful catastrophe!' they bawled one to the other down Wellington Street. 'Fighting at Weybridge! Full description! Repulse of the Martians! London in Danger!' He had to give threepence for a copy of that paper.

Then it was, and then only, that he realized something of the full power and terror of these monsters. He learned that they were not merely a handful of small sluggish creatures, but that they were minds swaying vast mechanical bodies; and that they could move swiftly and smite with such power that even the mightiest guns could not stand against them.

They were described as 'vast spider-like machines, nearly a hundred feet high, capable of the speed of an express train, and able to shoot out a beam of intense heat'. Masked batteries, chiefly of field-guns, had been planted in the country about Horsell Common, and especially between the Woking district and London. Five of the machines had been seen moving towards the Thames, and one, by a happy chance, had been destroyed. In the other cases the shells had missed, and the batteries had been at once annihilated by the Heat-Rays. Heavy losses of soldiers were mentioned, but the tone of the dispatch was optimistic.

The Martians had been repulsed; they were not invulnerable. They had retreated to their triangle of cylinders again, in the circle about Woking. Signallers with heliographs were pushing forward upon them from all sides. Guns were in rapid transit from Windsor, Portsmouth, Aldershot, Woolwich – even from the north; among others, long wire-guns of ninety-five tons from Woolwich. Altogether one hundred and sixteen were in position or being hastily placed, chiefly covering London. Never before in England had there been such a vast or rapid concentration of military material.

Any further cylinders that fell, it was hoped, could be destroyed at once by high explosives, which were being rapidly manufactured and distributed. No doubt, ran the report, the situation was of the strangest and gravest description, but the public was exhorted to avoid and discourage panic. No doubt the Martians were strange and terrible in the extreme, but at the outside there could not be more than twenty of them against our millions.

The authorities had reason to suppose, from the size of the cylinders, that at the outside there could not be more than five in each cylinder – fifteen altogether. And one at least was disposed of – perhaps more. The public would be fairly warned of the approach of danger, and elaborate measures

were being taken for the protection of the people in the threatened south-western suburbs. And so, with reiterated assurances of the safety of London and the ability of the authorities to cope with the difficulty, this quasi-proclamation closed.

This was printed in enormous type on paper so fresh that it was still wet, and there had been no time to add a word of comment. It was curious, my brother said, to see how ruthlessly the usual contents of the paper had been hacked and taken out to give this place.

All down Wellington Street people could be seen fluttering out the pink sheets and reading, and the Strand was suddenly noisy with the voices of an army of hawkers following these pioneers. Men came scrambling off buses to secure copies. Certainly this news excited people intensely, whatever their previous apathy. The shutters of a map shop in the Strand were being taken down, my brother said, and a man in his Sunday raiment, lemon-yellow gloves even, was visible inside the window hastily fastening maps of Surrey to the glass.

Going on along the Strand to Trafalgar Square, the paper in his hand, my brother saw some of the fugitives from West Surrey. There was a man with his wife and two boys and some articles of furniture in a cart such as greengrocers use. He was driving from the direction of Westminster Bridge; and close behind him came a hay waggon with five or six respectable-looking people in it, and some boxes and bundles. The faces of these people were haggard, and their entire appearance contrasted conspicuously with the Sabbath-best appearance of the people on the omnibuses. People in fashionable clothing peeped at them out of cabs. They stopped at the Square as if undecided which way to take, and finally turned eastward along the Strand. Some way behind these came a man in workday clothes, riding one of those old-fashioned tricycles with a small front wheel. He was dirty and white in the face.

My brother turned down towards Victoria, and met a number of such people. He had a vague idea that he might see something of me. He noticed an unusual number of police regulating the traffic. Some of the refugees were exchanging news with the people on the omnibuses. One was professing to have seen the Martians. 'Boilers on stilts, I tell you, striding along like men.' Most of them were excited and animated by their strange experience.

Beyond Victoria the public-houses were doing a lively trade with these arrivals. At all the street corners groups of people were reading papers, talking excitedly, or staring at these unusual Sunday visitors. They seemed to increase as night drew on, until at last the roads, my brother said, were like Epsom High Street on a Derby Day. My brother addressed several of these fugitives and got unsatisfactory answers from most.

None of them could tell him any news of Woking except one man, who assured him that Woking had been entirely destroyed on the previous night.

'I come from Byfleet,' he said; 'man on a bicycle came through the place in the early morning, and ran from door to door warning us to come away. Then came soldiers. We went out to look, and there were clouds of smoke to the south – nothing but smoke, and not a soul coming that way. Then we heard the guns at Chertsey, and folks coming from Weybridge. So I've locked up my house and come on.'

At the time there was a strong feeling in the streets that the authorities were to blame for their incapacity to dispose of the invaders without all this inconvenience.

About eight o'clock a noise of heavy firing was distinctly audible all over the south of London. My brother could not hear it for the traffic in the main thoroughfares, but by striking through the quiet back-streets to the river he was able to distinguish it quite plainly.

He walked from Westminster to his apartments near Regent's Park, about two. He was now very anxious on my account, and disturbed at the evident magnitude of the trouble. His mind was inclined to run, even as mine had run on Saturday, on military details. He thought of all those silent, expectant guns, of the suddenly nomadic countryside; he tried to imagine 'boilers on stilts' a hundred feet high.

There were one or two cartloads of refugees passing along Oxford Street, and several in the Marylebone Road, but so slowly was the news spreading that Regent Street and Portland Place were full of their usual Sunday-night promenaders, albeit they talked in groups, and along the edge of Regent's Park there were as many silent couples 'walking out' together under the scattered gas-lamps as ever there had been. The night was warm and still, and a little oppressive; the sound of guns continued intermittently, and after midnight there seemed to be sheet lightning in the south.

He read and re-read the paper, fearing the worst had happened to me. He was restless, and after supper prowled out again aimlessly. He returned and tried in vain to divert his attention to his examination notes. He went to bed a little after midnight, and was awakened from lurid dreams in the small hours of Monday by the sound of door knockers, feet running in the street, distant drumming, and a clamour of bells. Red reflections danced on the ceiling. For a moment he lay astonished, wondering whether day had come or the world gone mad. Then he jumped out of bed and ran to the window.

His room was an attic and as he thrust his head out, up and down the street there were a dozen echoes to the noise of his window-sash, and heads in every kind of night disarray appeared. Enquiries were being shouted. 'They are coming!' bawled a policeman, hammering at the door; 'the Martians are coming!' and hurried to the next door.

The sound of drumming and trumpeting came from the Albany Street Barracks, and every church within earshot was hard at work killing sleep

with a vehement disorderly tocsin. There was a noise of doors opening, and window after window in the houses opposite flashed from darkness into yellow illumination.

Up the street came galloping a closed carriage, bursting abruptly into noise at the corner, rising to a clattering climax under the window, and dying away slowly in the distance. Close on the rear of this came a couple of cabs, the forerunners of a long procession of flying vehicles, going for the most part to Chalk Farm station, where the North-Western special trains were loading up, instead of coming down the gradient into Euston.

For a long time my brother stared out of the window in blank astonishment, watching the policemen hammering at door after door, and delivering their incomprehensible message. Then the door behind him opened, and the man who lodged across the landing came in, dressed only in shirt, trousers, and slippers, his braces loose about his waist, his hair disordered from his pillow.

'What the devil is it?' he asked. 'A fire? What a devil of a row!'

They both craned their heads out of the window, straining to hear what the policemen were shouting. People were coming out of the side-streets, and standing in groups at the corners talking.

'What the devil is it all about?' said my brother's fellow lodger.

My brother answered him vaguely and began to dress, running with each garment to the window in order to miss nothing of the growing excitement. And presently men selling unnaturally early newspapers came bawling into the street:

'London in danger of suffocation! The Kingston and Richmond defences forced! Fearful massacres in the Thames Valley!'

And all about him – in the rooms below, in the houses on each side and across the road, and behind in the Park Terraces and in the hundred other streets of that part of Marylebone, and the Westbourne Park district and St. Pancras, and westward and northward in Kilburn and St John's Wood and Hampstead, and eastward in Shoreditch and Highbury and Haggerston and Hoxton, and, indeed, through all the vastness of London from Ealing to East Ham – people were rubbing their eyes, and opening windows to stare out and ask aimless questions, dressing hastily as the first breath of the coming storm of Fear blew through the streets. It was the dawn of the great panic. London, which had gone to bed on Sunday night oblivious and inert, was awakened, in the small hours of Monday morning, to a vivid sense of danger.

Unable from his window to learn what was happening, my brother went down and out into the street, just as the sky between the parapets of the houses grew pink with the early dawn. The flying people on foot and in vehicles grew more numerous every moment. 'Black Smoke!' he heard people crying, and again, 'Black Smoke!' The contagion of such a unanimous fear

was inevitable. As my brother hesitated on the door-step, he saw another news-vender approaching, and got a paper forthwith. The man was running away with the rest, and selling his papers for a shilling each as he ran – a grotesque mingling of profit and panic.

And from this paper my brother read that catastrophic dispatch of the Commander-in-Chief:

'The Martians are able to discharge enormous clouds of a black and poisonous vapour by means of rockets. They have smothered our batteries, destroyed Richmond, Kingston, and Wimbledon, and are advancing slowly towards London, destroying everything on the way. It is impossible to stop them. There is no safety from the Black Smoke but in instant flight.'

That was all, but it was enough. The whole population of the great six-million city was stirring, slipping, running; presently it would be pouring *en masse* northward.

'Black Smoke!' the voices cried. 'Fire!'

The bells of the neighbouring church made a jangling tumult, a cart carelessly driven smashed, amid shrieks and curses, against the water trough up the street. Sickly yellow lights went to and fro in the houses, and some of the passing cabs flaunted unextinguished lamps. And overhead the dawn was growing brighter, clear and steady and calm.

He heard footsteps running to and fro in the rooms, and up and down stairs behind him. His landlady came to the door, loosely wrapped in dressing-gown and shawl; her husband followed ejaculating.

As my brother began to realize the import of all these things, he turned hastily to his own room, put all his available money – some ten pounds altogether – into his pockets, and went out again into the streets.

CHAPTER XV

What Had Happened in Surrey

It was while the curate had sat and talked so wildly to me under the hedge in the flat meadows near Halliford, and while my brother was watching the fugitives stream over Westminster Bridge, that the Martians had resumed the offensive. So far as one can ascertain from the conflicting accounts that have been put forth, the majority of them remained busied with preparations in the Horsell pit until nine that night, hurrying on some operation that disengaged huge volumes of green smoke.

But three certainly came out about eight o'clock and, advancing slowly and cautiously, made their way through Byfleet and Pyrford towards Ripley and Weybridge, and so came in sight of the expectant batteries against the setting sun. These Martians did not advance in a body, but in a line, each perhaps a mile and a half from his nearest fellow. They communicated with one another by means of siren-like howls, running up and down the scale from one note to another.

It was this howling and firing of the guns at Ripley and St George's Hill that we had heard at Upper Halliford. The Ripley gunners, unseasoned artillery volunteers who ought never to have been placed in such a position, fired one wild, premature, ineffectual volley, and bolted on horse and foot through the deserted village, while the Martian, without using his Heat-Ray, walked serenely over their guns, stepped gingerly among them, passed in front of them, and so came unexpectedly upon the guns in Painshill Park, which he destroyed.

The St George's Hill men, however, were better led or of a better mettle. Hidden by a pine wood as they were, they seem to have been quite unsuspected by the Martian nearest to them. They laid their guns as deliberately as if they had been on parade, and fired at about a thousand yards' range.

The shells flashed all round him, and he was seen to advance a few paces, stagger, and go down. Everybody yelled together, and the guns were reloaded in frantic haste. The overthrown Martian set up a prolonged ululation, and immediately a second glittering giant, answering him, appeared over the trees to the south. It would seem that a leg of the tripod had been smashed by one of the shells. The whole of the second volley flew wide of the Martian on the ground, and, simultaneously, both his companions brought their Heat-Rays to bear on the battery. The ammunition blew up, the pine trees all about the guns flashed into fire, and only one or two of the men who were already running over the crest of the hill escaped.

After this it would seem that the three took counsel together and halted, and the scouts who were watching them report that they remained absolutely stationary for the next half hour. The Martian who had been overthrown crawled tediously out of his hood, a small brown figure, oddly suggestive from that distance of a speck of blight, and apparently engaged in the repair of his support. About nine he had finished, for his cowl was then seen above the trees again.

It was a few minutes past nine that night when these three sentinels were joined by four other Martians, each carrying a thick black tube. A similar tube was handed to each of the three, and the seven proceeded to distribute themselves at equal distances along a curved line between St George's Hill, Weybridge, and the village of Send, south-west of Ripley.

A dozen rockets sprang out of the hills before them so soon as they began to move, and warned the waiting batteries about Ditton and Esher. At the same time four of their fighting machines, similarly armed with tubes, crossed the river, and two of them, black against the western sky, came into sight of myself and the curate as we hurried wearily and painfully along the road that runs northward out of Halliford. They moved, as it seemed to us, upon a cloud, for a milky mist covered the fields and rose to a third of their height.

At this sight the curate cried faintly in his throat, and began running; but I knew it was no good running from a Martian, and I turned aside and crawled through dewy nettles and brambles into the broad ditch by the side of the road. He looked back, saw what I was doing, and turned to join me.

The two halted, the nearer to us standing and facing Sunbury, the remoter being a grey indistinctness towards the evening star, away towards Staines.

The occasional howling of the Martians had ceased; they took up their positions in the huge crescent about their cylinders in absolute silence. It was a crescent with twelve miles between its horns. Never since the devising of gunpowder was the beginning of a battle so still. To us and to an observer about Ripley it would have had precisely the same effect – the Martians seemed in solitary possession of the darkling night, lit only as it was by the slender moon, the stars, the afterglow of the daylight, and the ruddy glare from St George's Hill and the woods of Painshill.

But facing that crescent everywhere – at Staines, Hounslow, Ditton, Esher, Ockham, behind hills and woods south of the river, and across the flat grass meadows to the north of it, wherever a cluster of trees or village houses gave sufficient cover – the guns were waiting. The signal rockets burst and rained their sparks through the night and vanished, and the spirit of all those watching batteries rose to a tense expectation. The Martians had but to advance into the line of fire, and instantly those motionless black forms of men, those guns glittering so darkly in the early night, would explode into a thunderous fury of battle.

No doubt the thought that was uppermost in a thousand of those vigilant minds, even as it was uppermost in mine, was the riddle – how much they understood of us. Did they grasp that we in our millions were organized, disciplined, working together? Or did they interpret our spurts of fire, the sudden stinging of our shells, our steady investment of their encampment, as we should the furious unanimity of onslaught in a disturbed hive of bees? Did they dream they might exterminate us? (At that time no one knew what food they needed.) A hundred such questions struggled together in my mind as I watched that vast sentinel shape. And in the back of my mind was the sense of all the huge unknown and hidden forces Londonward. Had they prepared pitfalls? Were the powder mills at Hounslow ready as a snare? Would the Londoners have the heart and courage to make a greater Moscow of their mighty province of houses?

Then, after an interminable time, as it seemed to us, crouching and peering through the hedge, came a sound like the distant concussion of a gun. Another nearer, and then another. And then the Martian beside us raised his tube on high and discharged it, gunwise, with a heavy report that made the ground heave. The one towards Staines answered him. There was no flash, no smoke, simply that loaded detonation.

I was so excited by these heavy minute-guns following one another that I so far forgot my personal safety and my scalded hands as to clamber up into the hedge and stare towards Sunbury. As I did so a second report followed, and a big projectile hurtled overhead towards Hounslow. I expected at least to see smoke or fire, or some such evidence of its work. But all I saw was the deep-blue sky above, with one solitary star, and the white mist spreading wide and low beneath. And there had been no crash, no answering explosion. The silence was restored; the minute lengthened to three.

'What has happened?' said the curate, standing up beside me.

'Heaven knows!' said I.

A bat flickered by and vanished. A distant tumult of shouting began and ceased. I looked again at the Martian, and saw he was now moving eastward along the riverbank, with a swift, rolling motion.

Every moment I expected the fire of some hidden battery to spring upon him; but the evening calm was unbroken. The figure of the Martian grew smaller as he receded, and presently the mist and the gathering night had swallowed him up. By a common impulse we clambered higher. Towards Sunbury was a dark appearance, as though a conical hill had suddenly come into being there, hiding our view of the further country; and then, remoter across the river, over Walton, we saw another such summit. These hill-like forms grew lower and broader even as we stared.

Moved by a sudden thought, I looked northward, and there I perceived a third of these cloudy black kopjes had risen.

Everything had suddenly become very still. Far away to the south-east, marking the quiet, we heard the Martians hooting to one another, and then the air quivered again with the distant thud of their guns. But the earthly artillery made no reply.

Now at the time we could not understand these things, but later I was to learn the meaning of these ominous kopjes that gathered in the twilight. Each of the Martians, standing in the great crescent I have described, had discharged, by means of the gunlike tube he carried, a huge canister over whatever hill, copse, cluster of houses, or other possible cover for guns, chanced to be in front of him. Some fired only one of these, some two – as in the case of the one we had seen; the one at Ripley is said to have discharged no fewer than five at that time. These canisters smashed on striking the ground – they did not explode – and incontinently disengaged an enormous volume of heavy, inky vapour, coiling and pouring upward in a huge and ebony cumulus cloud, a gaseous hill that sank and spread itself slowly over the surrounding country. And the touch of that vapour, the inhaling of its pungent wisps, was death to all that breathes.

It was heavy, this vapour, heavier than the densest smoke, so that, after the first tumultuous uprush and outflow of its impact, it sank down through the air and poured over the ground in a manner rather liquid than gaseous, abandoning the hills, and streaming into the valleys and ditches and water-courses even as I have heard the carbonic-acid gas that pours from volcanic clefts is wont to do. And where it came upon water some chemical action occurred, and the surface would be instantly covered with a powdery scum that sank slowly and made way for more. The scum was absolutely insoluble, and it is a strange thing, seeing the instant effect of the gas, that one could drink without hurt the water from which it had been strained. The vapour did not diffuse as a true gas would do. It hung together in banks, flowing sluggishly down the slope of the land and driving reluctantly before the wind, and very slowly it combined with the mist and moisture of the air, and sank to the earth in the form of dust. Save that an unknown element giving a group of four lines in the blue of the spectrum is concerned, we are still entirely ignorant of the nature of this substance.

Once the tumultuous upheaval of its dispersion was over, the black smoke clung so closely to the ground, even before its precipitation, that fifty feet up in the air, on the roofs and upper stories of high houses and on great trees, there was a chance of escaping its poison altogether, as was proved even that night at Street Cobham and Ditton.

The man who escaped at the former place tells a wonderful story of the strangeness of its coiling flow, and how he looked down from the church spire and saw the houses of the village rising like ghosts out of its inky nothingness. For a day and a half he remained there, weary, starving and

sun-scorched, the earth under the blue sky and against the prospect of the distant hills a velvet-black expanse, with red roofs, green trees, and, later, black-veiled shrubs and gates, barns, out-houses, and walls, rising here and there into the sunlight.

But that was at Street Cobham, where the black vapour was allowed to remain until it sank of its own accord into the ground. As a rule the Martians, when it had served its purpose, cleared the air of it again by wading into it and directing a jet of steam upon it.

This they did with the vapour-banks near us, as we saw in the starlight from the window of a deserted house at Upper Halliford, whither we had returned. From there we could see the searchlights on Richmond Hill and Kingston Hill going to and fro, and about eleven the windows rattled, and we heard the sound of the huge siege guns that had been put in position there. These continued intermittently for the space of a quarter of an hour, sending chance shots at the invisible Martians at Hampton and Ditton, and then the pale beams of the electric light vanished, and were replaced by a bright red glow.

Then the fourth cylinder fell – a brilliant green meteor – as I learned afterwards, in Bushey Park. Before the guns on the Richmond and Kingston line of hills began, there was a fitful cannonade far away in the south-west, due, I believe, to guns being fired haphazard before the black vapour could overwhelm the gunners.

So, setting about it as methodically as men might smoke out a wasps' nest, the Martians spread this strange stifling vapour over the Londonward country. The horns of the crescent slowly moved apart, until at last they formed a line from Hanwell to Coombe and Malden. All night through their destructive tubes advanced. Never once, after the Martian at St George's Hill was brought down, did they give the artillery the ghost of a chance against them. Wherever there was a possibility of guns being laid for them unseen, a fresh canister of the black vapour was discharged, and where the guns were openly displayed the Heat-Ray was brought to bear.

By midnight the blazing trees along the slopes of Richmond Park and the glare of Kingston Hill threw their light upon a network of black smoke, blotting out the whole valley of the Thames and extending as far as the eye could reach. And through this two Martians slowly waded, and turned their hissing steam jets this way and that.

They were sparing of the Heat-Ray that night, either because they had but a limited supply of material for its production or because they did not wish to destroy the country but only to crush and overawe the opposition they had aroused. In the latter aim they certainly succeeded. Sunday night was the end of the organised opposition to their movements. After that no body of men would stand against them, so hopeless was the enterprise. Even the crews of the torpedo-boats and destroyers that had brought their

quick-firers up the Thames refused to stop, mutinied, and went down again. The only offensive operation men ventured upon after that night was the preparation of mines and pitfalls, and even in that their energies were frantic and spasmodic.

One has to imagine, as well as one may, the fate of those batteries towards Esher, waiting so tensely in the twilight. Survivors there were none. One may picture the orderly expectation, the officers alert and watchful, the gunners ready, the ammunition piled to hand, the limber gunners with their horses and waggons, the groups of civilian spectators standing as near as they were permitted, the evening stillness, the ambulances and hospital tents with the burned and wounded from Weybridge; then the dull resonance of the shots the Martians fired, and the clumsy projectile whirling over the trees and houses and smashing amid the neighbouring fields.

One may picture, too, the sudden shifting of the attention, the swiftly spreading coils and bellyings of that blackness advancing headlong, towering heavenward, turning the twilight to a palpable darkness, a strange and horrible antagonist of vapour striding upon its victims, men and horses near it seen dimly, running, shrieking, falling headlong, shouts of dismay, the guns suddenly abandoned, men choking and writhing on the ground, and the swift broadening-out of the opaque cone of smoke. And then night and extinction – nothing but a silent mass of impenetrable vapour hiding its dead.

Before dawn the black vapour was pouring through the streets of Richmond, and the disintegrating organism of government was, with a last expiring effort, rousing the population of London to the necessity of flight.

CHAPTER XVI

The Exodus from London

So you understand the roaring wave of fear that swept through the greatest city in the world just as Monday was dawning – the stream of flight rising swiftly to a torrent, lashing in a foaming tumult round the railway stations, banked up into a horrible struggle about the shipping in the Thames, and hurrying by every available channel northward and eastward. By ten o'clock the police organization, and by midday even the railway organizations, were losing coherency, losing shape and efficiency, guttering, softening, running at last in that swift liquefaction of the social body.

All the railway lines north of the Thames and the South-Eastern people at Cannon Street had been warned by midnight on Sunday, and trains were being filled. People were fighting savagely for standing-room in the carriages even at two o'clock. By three, people were being trampled and crushed even in Bishopsgate Street, a couple of hundred yards or more from Liverpool Street station; revolvers were fired, people stabbed, and the policemen who had been sent to direct the traffic, exhausted and infuriated, were breaking the heads of the people they were called out to protect.

And as the day advanced and the engine-drivers and stokers refused to return to London, the pressure of the flight drove the people in an ever-thickening multitude away from the stations and along the northward-running roads. By midday a Martian had been seen at Barnes, and a cloud of slowly sinking black vapour drove along the Thames and across the flats of Lambeth, cutting off all escape over the bridges in its sluggish advance. Another bank drove over Ealing, and surrounded a little island of survivors on Castle Hill, alive, but unable to escape.

After a fruitless struggle to get aboard a North-Western train at Chalk Farm – the engines of the trains that had loaded in the goods yard there *ploughed* through shrieking people, and a dozen stalwart men fought to keep the crowd from crushing the driver against his furnace – my brother emerged upon the Chalk Farm road, dodged across through a hurrying swarm of vehicles, and had the luck to be foremost in the sack of a cycle shop. The front tyre of the machine he got was punctured in dragging it through the window, but he got up and off, notwithstanding, with no further injury than a cut wrist. The steep foot of Haverstock Hill was impassable owing to several overturned horses, and my brother struck into Belsize Road.

So he got out of the fury of the panic, and, skirting the Edgware Road, reached Edgware about seven, fasting and wearied, but well ahead of the crowd. Along the road people were standing in the roadway, curious,

wondering. He was passed by a number of cyclists, some horsemen, and two motor-cars. A mile from Edgware the rim of the wheel broke, and the machine became unrideable. He left it by the roadside and trudged through the village. There were shops half opened in the main street of the place, and people crowded on the pavement and in the doorways and windows, staring astonished at this extraordinary procession of fugitives that was beginning. He succeeded in getting some food at an inn.

For a time he remained in Edgware not knowing what next to do. The flying people increased in number. Many of them, like my brother, seemed inclined to loiter in the place. There was no fresh news of the invaders from Mars.

At that time the road was crowded, but as yet far from congested. Most of the fugitives at that hour were mounted on cycles, but there were soon motor-cars, hansom cabs, and carriages hurrying along, and the dust hung in heavy clouds along the road to St Albans.

It was perhaps a vague idea of making his way to Chelmsford, where some friends of his lived, that at last induced my brother to strike into a quiet lane running eastward. Presently he came upon a stile, and, crossing it, followed a footpath north-eastward. He passed near several farmhouses and some little places whose names he did not learn. He saw few fugitives until, in a grass lane towards High Barnet, he happened upon two ladies who became his fellow travellers. He came upon them just in time to save them.

He heard their screams, and, hurrying round the corner, saw a couple of men struggling to drag them out of the little pony-chaise in which they had been driving, while a third with difficulty held the frightened pony's head. One of the ladies, a short woman dressed in white, was simply screaming; the other, a dark, slender figure, slashed at the man who gripped her arm with a whip she held in her disengaged hand.

My brother immediately grasped the situation, shouted, and hurried towards the struggle. One of the men desisted and turned towards him, and my brother, realizing from his antagonist's face that a fight was unavoidable, and being an expert boxer, went into him forthwith and sent him down against the wheel of the chaise.

It was no time for pugilistic chivalry and my brother laid him quiet with a kick, and gripped the collar of the man who pulled at the slender lady's arm. He heard the clatter of hoofs, the whip stung across his face, a third antagonist struck him between the eyes, and the man he held wrenched himself free and made off down the lane in the direction from which he had come.

Partly stunned, he found himself facing the man who had held the horse's head, and became aware of the chaise receding from him down the lane, swaying from side to side, and with the women in it looking back. The man before him, a burly rough, tried to close, and he stopped him with a blow

in the face. Then, realizing that he was deserted, he dodged round and made off down the lane after the chaise, with the sturdy man close behind him, and the fugitive, who had turned now, following remotely.

Suddenly he stumbled and fell; his immediate pursuer went headlong, and he rose to his feet to find himself with a couple of antagonists again. He would have had little chance against them had not the slender lady very pluckily pulled up and returned to his help. It seems she had had a revolver all this time, but it had been under the seat when she and her companion were attacked. She fired at six yards' distance, narrowly missing my brother. The less courageous of the robbers made off, and his companion followed him, cursing his cowardice. They both stopped in sight down the lane, where the third man lay insensible.

'Take this!' said the slender lady, and she gave my brother her revolver.

'Go back to the chaise,' said my brother, wiping the blood from his split lip.

She turned without a word – they were both panting – and they went back to where the lady in white struggled to hold back the frightened pony.

The robbers had evidently had enough of it. When my brother looked again they were retreating.

'I'll sit here,' said my brother, 'if I may'; and he got upon the empty front seat. The lady looked over her shoulder.

'Give me the reins,' she said, and laid the whip along the pony's side. In another moment a bend in the road hid the three men from my brother's eyes.

So, quite unexpectedly, my brother found himself, panting, with a cut mouth, a bruised jaw, and bloodstained knuckles, driving along an unknown lane with these two women.

He learned they were the wife and the younger sister of a surgeon living at Stanmore, who had come in the small hours from a dangerous case at Pinner, and heard at some railway station on his way of the Martian advance. He had hurried home, roused the women – their servant had left them two days before – packed some provisions, put his revolver under the seat – luckily for my brother – and told them to drive on to Edgware, with the idea of getting a train there. He stopped behind to tell the neighbours. He would overtake them, he said, at about half-past four in the morning, and now it was nearly nine and they had seen nothing of him. They could not stop in Edgware because of the growing traffic through the place, and so they had come into this side lane.

That was the story they told my brother in fragments when presently they stopped again, nearer to New Barnet. He promised to stay with them, at least until they could determine what to do, or until the missing man arrived, and professed to be an expert shot with the revolver – a weapon strange to him – in order to give them confidence.

They made a sort of encampment by the wayside, and the pony became happy in the hedge. He told them of his own escape out of London, and all that he knew of these Martians and their ways. The sun crept higher in the sky, and after a time their talk died out and gave place to an uneasy state of anticipation. Several wayfarers came along the lane, and of these my brother gathered such news as he could. Every broken answer he had deepened his impression of the great disaster that had come on humanity, deepened his persuasion of the immediate necessity for prosecuting this flight. He urged the matter upon them.

'We have money,' said the slender woman, and hesitated.

Her eyes met my brother's, and her hesitation ended.

'So have I,' said my brother.

She explained that they had as much as thirty pounds in gold, besides a five-pound note, and suggested that with that they might get upon a train at St Albans or New Barnet. My brother thought that was hopeless, seeing the fury of the Londoners to crowd upon the trains, and broached his own idea of striking across Essex towards Harwich and thence escaping from the country altogether.

Mrs Elphinstone – that was the name of the woman in white – would listen to no reasoning, and kept calling upon 'George'; but her sister-in-law was astonishingly quiet and deliberate, and at last agreed to my brother's suggestion. So, designing to cross the Great North Road, they went on towards Barnet, my brother leading the pony to save it as much as possible.

As the sun crept up the sky the day became excessively hot, and under foot a thick, whitish sand grew burning and blinding, so that they travelled only very slowly. The hedges were grey with dust. And as they advanced towards Barnet a tumultuous murmuring grew stronger.

They began to meet more people. For the most part these were staring before them, murmuring indistinct questions, jaded, haggard, unclean. One man in evening dress passed them on foot, his eyes on the ground. They heard his voice, and, looking back at him, saw one hand clutched in his hair and the other beating invisible things. His paroxysm of rage over, he went on his way without once looking back.

As my brother's party went on towards the crossroads to the south of Barnet they saw a woman approaching the road across some fields on their left, carrying a child and with two other children; and then passed a man in dirty black, with a thick stick in one hand and a small portmanteau in the other. Then round the corner of the lane, from between the villas that guarded it at its confluence with the high road, came a little cart drawn by a sweating black pony and driven by a sallow youth in a bowler hat, grey with dust. There were three girls, East End factory girls, and a couple of little children crowded in the cart.

'This'll tike us rahnd Edgware?' asked the driver, wild-eyed, white-faced; and when my brother told him it would if he turned to the left, he whipped up at once without the formality of thanks.

My brother noticed a pale grey smoke or haze rising among the houses in front of them, and veiling the white facade of a terrace beyond the road that appeared between the backs of the villas. Mrs Elphinstone suddenly cried out at a number of tongues of smoky red flame leaping up above the houses in front of them against the hot, blue sky. The tumultuous noise resolved itself now into the disorderly mingling of many voices, the gride of many wheels, the creaking of waggons, and the staccato of hoofs. The lane came round sharply not fifty yards from the crossroads.

'Good Heavens!' cried Mrs Elphinstone. 'What is this you are driving us into?'

My brother stopped.

For the main road was a boiling stream of people, a torrent of human beings rushing northward, one pressing on another. A great bank of dust, white and luminous in the blaze of the sun, made everything within twenty feet of the ground grey and indistinct and was perpetually renewed by the hurrying feet of a dense crowd of horses and of men and women on foot, and by the wheels of vehicles of every description.

'Way!' my brother heard voices crying. 'Make way!'

It was like riding into the smoke of a fire to approach the meeting point of the lane and road; the crowd roared like a fire, and the dust was hot and pungent. And, indeed, a little way up the road a villa was burning and sending rolling masses of black smoke across the road to add to the confusion.

Two men came past them. Then a dirty woman, carrying a heavy bundle and weeping. A lost retriever dog, with hanging tongue, circled dubiously round them, scared and wretched, and fled at my brother's threat.

So much as they could see of the road Londonward between the houses to the right was a tumultuous stream of dirty, hurrying people, pent in between the villas on either side; the black heads, the crowded forms, grew into distinctness as they rushed towards the corner, hurried past, and merged their individuality again in a receding multitude that was swallowed up at last in a cloud of dust.

'Go on! Go on!' cried the voices. 'Way! Way!'

One man's hands pressed on the back of another. My brother stood at the pony's head. Irresistibly attracted, he advanced slowly, pace by pace, down the lane.

Edgware had been a scene of confusion, Chalk Farm a riotous tumult, but this was a whole population in movement. It is hard to imagine that host. It had no character of its own. The figures poured out past the corner, and receded with their backs to the group in the lane. Along the margin

came those who were on foot threatened by the wheels, stumbling in the ditches, blundering into one another.

The carts and carriages crowded close upon one another, making little way for those swifter and more impatient vehicles that darted forward every now and then when an opportunity showed itself of doing so, sending the people scattering against the fences and gates of the villas.

'Push on!' was the cry. 'Push on! They are coming!'

In one cart stood a blind man in the uniform of the Salvation Army, gesticulating with his crooked fingers and bawling, 'Eternity! Eternity!' His voice was hoarse and very loud so that my brother could hear him long after he was lost to sight in the dust. Some of the people who crowded in the carts whipped stupidly at their horses and quarrelled with other drivers; some sat motionless, staring at nothing with miserable eyes; some gnawed their hands with thirst, or lay prostrate in the bottoms of their conveyances. The horses' bits were covered with foam, their eyes bloodshot.

There were cabs, carriages, shop-carts, waggons, beyond counting; a mail cart, a road-cleaner's cart marked 'Vestry of St Pancras,' a huge timber waggon crowded with roughs. A brewer's dray rumbled by with its two near wheels splashed with fresh blood.

'Clear the way!' cried the voices. 'Clear the way!'

'Eter-nity! Eter-nity!' came echoing down the road.

There were sad, haggard women tramping by, well dressed, with children that cried and stumbled, their dainty clothes smothered in dust, their weary faces smeared with tears. With many of these came men, sometimes helpful, sometimes lowering and savage. Fighting side by side with them pushed some weary street outcast in faded black rags, wide-eyed, loud-voiced, and foul-mouthed. There were sturdy workmen thrusting their way along, wretched, unkempt men, clothed like clerks or shop-men, struggling spasmodically; a wounded soldier my brother noticed, men dressed in the clothes of railway porters, one wretched creature in a nightshirt with a coat thrown over it.

But varied as its composition was, certain things all that host had in common. There were fear and pain on their faces, and fear behind them. A tumult up the road, a quarrel for a place in a waggon, sent the whole host of them quickening their pace; even a man so scared and broken that his knees bent under him was galvanized for a moment into renewed activity. The heat and dust had already been at work upon this multitude. Their skins were dry, their lips black and cracked. They were all thirsty, weary, and footsore. And amid the various cries one heard disputes, reproaches, groans of weariness and fatigue; the voices of most of them were hoarse and weak. Through it all ran a refrain:

'Way! Way! The Martians are coming!'

Few stopped and came aside from that flood. The lane opened slantingly into the main road with a narrow opening, and had a delusive appearance of coming from the direction of London. Yet a kind of eddy of people drove into its mouth; weaklings elbowed out of the stream, who for the most part rested but a moment before plunging into it again. A little way down the lane, with two friends bending over him, lay a man with a bare leg, wrapped about with bloody rags. He was a lucky man to have friends.

A little old man, with a grey military moustache and a filthy black frock coat, limped out and sat down beside the trap, removed his boot – his sock was blood-stained – shook out a pebble, and hobbled on again; and then a little girl of eight or nine, all alone, threw herself under the hedge close by my brother, weeping.

'I can't go on! I can't go on!'

My brother woke from his torpor of astonishment and lifted her up, speaking gently to her, and carried her to Miss Elphinstone. So soon as my brother touched her she became quite still, as if frightened.

'Ellen!' shrieked a woman in the crowd, with tears in her voice – 'Ellen!' And the child suddenly darted away from my brother, crying 'Mother!'

'They are coming,' said a man on horseback, riding past along the lane.

'Out of the way, there!' bawled a coachman, towering high; and my brother saw a closed carriage turning into the lane.

The people crushed back on one another to avoid the horse. My brother pushed the pony and chaise back into the hedge, and the man drove by and stopped at the turn of the way. It was a carriage, with a pole for a pair of horses, but only one was in the traces. My brother saw dimly through the dust that two men lifted out something on a white stretcher and put it gently on the grass beneath the privet hedge.

One of the men came running to my brother.

'Where is there any water?' he said. 'He is dying fast, and very thirsty. It is Lord Garrick.'

'Lord Garrick!' said my brother; 'The Chief Justice?'

'The water?' he said.

'There may be a tap,' said my brother, 'in some of the houses. We have no water. I dare not leave my people.'

The man pushed against the crowd towards the gate of the corner house.

'Go on!' said the people, thrusting at him. 'They are coming! Go on!'

Then my brother's attention was distracted by a bearded, eagle-faced man lugging a small handbag, which split even as my brother's eyes rested on it and disgorged a mass of sovereigns that seemed to break up into separate coins as it struck the ground. They rolled hither and thither among the struggling feet of men and horses. The man stopped and looked stupidly at the heap, and the shaft of a cab struck his shoulder and sent him reeling. He gave a shriek and dodged back, and a cartwheel shaved him narrowly.

'Way!' cried the men all about him. 'Make way!'

So soon as the cab had passed, he flung himself, with both hands open, upon the heap of coins, and began thrusting handfuls in his pocket. A horse rose close upon him, and in another moment, half rising, he had been borne down under the horse's hoofs.

'Stop!' screamed my brother, and pushing a woman out of his way, tried to clutch the bit of the horse.

Before he could get to it, he heard a scream under the wheels, and saw through the dust the rim passing over the poor wretch's back. The driver of the cart slashed his whip at my brother, who ran round behind the cart. The multitudinous shouting confused his ears. The man was writhing in the dust among his scattered money, unable to rise, for the wheel had broken his back, and his lower limbs lay limp and dead. My brother stood up and yelled at the next driver, and a man on a black horse came to his assistance.

'Get him out of the road,' said he; and, clutching the man's collar with his free hand, my brother lugged him sideways. But he still clutched after his money, and regarded my brother fiercely, hammering at his arm with a handful of gold. 'Go on! Go on!' shouted angry voices behind.

'Way! Way!'

There was a smash as the pole of a carriage crashed into the cart that the man on horseback stopped. My brother looked up, and the man with the gold twisted his head round and bit the wrist that held his collar. There was a concussion, and the black horse came staggering sideways, and the carthorse pushed beside it. A hoof missed my brother's foot by a hair's breadth. He released his grip on the fallen man and jumped back. He saw anger change to terror on the face of the poor wretch on the ground, and in a moment he was hidden and my brother was borne backward and carried past the entrance of the lane, and had to fight hard in the torrent to recover it.

He saw Miss Elphinstone covering her eyes, and a little child, with all a child's want of sympathetic imagination, staring with dilated eyes at a dusty something that lay black and still, ground and crushed under the rolling wheels. 'Let us go back!' he shouted, and began turning the pony round. 'We cannot cross this – hell,' he said and they went back a hundred yards the way they had come, until the fighting crowd was hidden. As they passed the bend in the lane my brother saw the face of the dying man in the ditch under the privet, deadly white and drawn, and shining with perspiration. The two women sat silent, crouching in their seat and shivering.

Then beyond the bend my brother stopped again. Miss Elphinstone was white and pale, and her sister-in-law sat weeping, too wretched even to call upon 'George'. My brother was horrified and perplexed. So soon as they had retreated he realized how urgent and unavoidable it was to attempt this crossing. He turned to Miss Elphinstone, suddenly resolute.

'We must go that way,' he said, and led the pony round again.

For the second time that day this girl proved her quality. To force their way into the torrent of people, my brother plunged into the traffic and held back a cab horse, while she drove the pony across its head. A waggon locked wheels for a moment and ripped a long splinter from the chaise. In another moment they were caught and swept forward by the stream. My brother, with the cabman's whip marks red across his face and hands, scrambled into the chaise and took the reins from her.

'Point the revolver at the man behind,' he said, giving it to her, 'if he presses us too hard. No! – point it at his horse.'

Then he began to look out for a chance of edging to the right across the road. But once in the stream he seemed to lose volition, to become a part of that dusty rout. They swept through Chipping Barnet with the torrent; they were nearly a mile beyond the centre of the town before they had fought across to the opposite side of the way. It was din and confusion indescribable; but in and beyond the town the road forks repeatedly, and this to some extent relieved the stress.

They struck eastward through Hadley, and there on either side of the road, and at another place further on they came upon a great multitude of people drinking at the stream, some fighting to come at the water. And further on, from a lull near East Barnet, they saw two trains running slowly one after the other without signal or order – trains swarming with people, with men even among the coals behind the engines – going northward along the Great Northern Railway. My brother supposes they must have filled outside London, for at that time the furious terror of the people had rendered the central termini impossible.

Near this place they halted for the rest of the afternoon, for the violence of the day had already utterly exhausted all three of them. They began to suffer the beginnings of hunger; the night was cold, and none of them dared to sleep. And in the evening many people came hurrying along the road nearby their stopping place, fleeing from unknown dangers before them, and going in the direction from which my brother had come.

CHAPTER XVII

The 'Thunder Child'

Had the Martians aimed only at destruction, they might on Monday have annihilated the entire population of London, as it spread itself slowly through the home counties. Not only along the road through Barnet, but also through Edgware and Waltham Abbey, and along the roads eastward to Southend and Shoeburyness, and south of the Thames to Deal and Broadstairs, poured the same frantic rout. If one could have hung that June morning in a balloon in the blazing blue above London every northward and eastward road running out of the tangled maze of streets would have seemed stippled black with the streaming fugitives, each dot a human agony of terror and physical distress. I have set forth at length in the last chapter my brother's account of the road through Chipping Barnet, in order that my readers may realize how that swarming of black dots appeared to one of those concerned. Never before in the history of the world had such a mass of human beings moved and suffered together. The legendary hosts of Goths and Huns, the hugest armies Asia has ever seen, would have been but a drop in that current. And this was no disciplined march; it was a stampede – a stampede gigantic and terrible – without order and without a goal, six million people unarmed and unprovisioned, driving headlong. It was the beginning of the rout of civilization, of the massacre of mankind.

Directly below him the balloonist would have seen the network of streets far and wide, houses, churches, squares, crescents, gardens – already derelict – spread out like a huge map, and in the southward *blotted*. Over Ealing, Richmond, Wimbledon, it would have seemed as if some monstrous pen had flung ink upon the chart. Steadily, incessantly, each black splash grew and spread, shooting out ramifications this way and that, now banking itself against rising ground, now pouring swiftly over a crest into a new-found valley, exactly as a gout of ink would spread itself upon blotting paper.

And beyond, over the blue hills that rise southward of the river, the glittering Martians went to and fro, calmly and methodically spreading their poison cloud over this patch of country and then over that, laying it again with their steam jets when it had served its purpose, and taking possession of the conquered country. They do not seem to have aimed at extermination so much as at complete demoralization and the destruction of any opposition. They exploded any stores of powder they came upon, cut every telegraph, and wrecked the railways here and there. They were hamstringing mankind. They seemed in no hurry to extend the field of their operations, and did not come beyond the central part of London all that day. It is possible that

a very considerable number of people in London stuck to their houses through Monday morning. Certain it is that many died at home suffocated by the Black Smoke.

Until about midday the Pool of London was an astonishing scene. Steamboats and shipping of all sorts lay there, tempted by the enormous sums of money offered by fugitives, and it is said that many who swam out to these vessels were thrust off with boat-hooks and drowned. About one o'clock in the afternoon the thinning remnant of a cloud of the black vapour appeared between the arches of Blackfriars Bridge. At that the Pool became a scene of mad confusion, fighting, and collision, and for some time a multitude of boats and barges jammed in the northern arch of the Tower Bridge, and the sailors and lightermen had to fight savagely against the people who swarmed upon them from the riverfront. People were actually clambering down the piers of the bridge from above.

When, an hour later, a Martian appeared beyond the Clock Tower and waded down the river, nothing but wreckage floated above Limehouse.

Of the falling of the fifth cylinder I have presently to tell. The sixth star fell at Wimbledon. My brother, keeping watch beside the women in the chaise in a meadow, saw the green flash of it far beyond the hills. On Tuesday the little party, still set upon getting across the sea, made its way through the swarming country towards Colchester. The news that the Martians were now in possession of the whole of London was confirmed. They had been seen at Highgate, and even, it was said, at Neasden. But they did not come into my brother's view until the morrow.

That day the scattered multitudes began to realize the urgent need of provisions. As they grew hungry the rights of property ceased to be regarded. Farmers were out to defend their cattle-sheds, granaries, and ripening root crops with arms in their hands. A number of people now, like my brother, had their faces eastward, and there were some desperate souls even going back towards London to get food. These were chiefly people from the northern suburbs, whose knowledge of the Black Smoke came by hearsay. He heard that about half the members of the government had gathered at Birmingham, and that enormous quantities of high explosives were being prepared to be used in automatic mines across the Midland counties.

He was also told that the Midland Railway Company had replaced the desertions of the first day's panic, had resumed traffic, and was running northward trains from St Albans to relieve the congestion of the home counties. There was also a placard in Chipping Ongar announcing that large stores of flour were available in the northern towns and that within twenty -four hours bread would be distributed among the starving people in the neighbourhood. But this intelligence did not deter him from the plan of escape he had formed, and the three pressed eastward all day, and heard no more of the bread distribution than this promise. Nor, as a matter of fact,

did anyone else hear more of it. That night fell the seventh star, falling upon Primrose Hill. It fell while Miss Elphinstone was watching, for she took that duty alternately with my brother. She saw it.

On Wednesday the three fugitives – they had passed the night in a field of unripe wheat – reached Chelmsford, and there a body of the inhabitants, calling itself the Committee of Public Supply, seized the pony as provisions, and would give nothing in exchange for it but the promise of a share in it the next day. Here there were rumours of Martians at Epping, and news of the destruction of Waltham Abbey Powder Mills in a vain attempt to blow up one of the invaders.

People were watching for Martians here from the church towers. My brother, very luckily for him as it chanced, preferred to push on at once to the coast rather than wait for food, although all three of them were very hungry. By midday they passed through Tillingham, which, strangely enough, seemed to be quite silent and deserted, save for a few furtive plunderers hunting for food. Near Tillingham they suddenly came in sight of the sea, and the most amazing crowd of shipping of all sorts that it is possible to imagine.

For after the sailors could no longer come up the Thames, they came on to the Essex coast, to Harwich and Walton and Clacton, and afterwards to Foulness and Shoebury, to bring off the people. They lay in a huge sickle-shaped curve that vanished into mist at last towards the Naze. Close inshore was a multitude of fishing smacks – English, Scotch, French, Dutch, and Swedish; steam launches from the Thames, yachts, electric boats; and beyond were ships of large burden, a multitude of filthy colliers, trim merchantmen, cattle ships, passenger boats, petroleum tanks, ocean tramps, an old white transport even, neat white and grey liners from Southampton and Hamburg; and along the blue coast across the Blackwater my brother could make out dimly a dense swarm of boats chaffering with the people on the beach, a swarm which also extended up the Blackwater almost to Maldon.

About a couple of miles out lay an ironclad, very low in the water, almost, to my brother's perception, like a water-logged ship. This was the ram *Thunder Child*. It was the only warship in sight, but far away to the right over the smooth surface of the sea – for that day there was a dead calm – lay a serpent of black smoke to mark the next ironclads of the Channel Fleet, which hovered in an extended line, steam up and ready for action, across the Thames estuary during the course of the Martian conquest, vigilant and yet powerless to prevent it.

At the sight of the sea, Mrs Elphinstone, in spite of the assurances of her sister-in-law, gave way to panic. She had never been out of England before, she would rather die than trust herself friendless in a foreign country, and so forth. She seemed, poor woman, to imagine that the French and the Martians might prove very similar. She had been growing increasingly hyster-

ical, fearful and depressed during the two days' journeyings. Her great idea was to return to Stanmore. Things had been always well and safe at Stanmore. They would find George at Stanmore.

It was with the greatest difficulty they could get her down to the beach, where presently my brother succeeded in attracting the attention of some men on a paddle steamer from the Thames. They sent a boat and drove a bargain for thirty-six pounds for the three. The steamer was going, these men said, to Ostend.

It was about two o'clock when my brother, having paid their fares at the gangway, found himself safely aboard the steamboat with his charges. There was food aboard, albeit at exorbitant prices, and the three of them contrived to eat a meal on one of the seats forward.

There were already a couple of score of passengers aboard, some of whom had expended their last money in securing a passage, but the captain lay off the Blackwater until five in the afternoon, picking up passengers until the seated decks were even dangerously crowded. He would probably have remained longer had it not been for the sound of guns that began about that hour in the south. As if in answer, the ironclad seaward fired a small gun and hoisted a string of flags. A jet of smoke sprang out of her funnels.

Some of the passengers were of opinion that this firing came from Shoeburyness, until it was noticed that it was growing louder. At the same time, far away in the south-east the masts and upperworks of three ironclads rose one after the other out of the sea, beneath clouds of black smoke. But my brother's attention speedily reverted to the distant firing in the south. He fancied he saw a column of smoke rising out of the distant grey haze.

The little steamer was already flapping her way eastward of the big crescent of shipping, and the low Essex coast was growing blue and hazy, when a Martian appeared, small and faint in the remote distance, advancing along the muddy coast from the direction of Foulness. At that the captain on the bridge swore at the top of his voice with fear and anger at his own delay, and the paddles seemed infected with his terror. Every soul aboard stood at the bulwarks or on the seats of the steamer and stared at that distant shape, higher than the trees or church towers inland, and advancing with a leisurely parody of a human stride.

It was the first Martian my brother had seen, and he stood, more amazed than terrified, watching this Titan advancing deliberately towards the shipping, wading further and further into the water as the coast fell away. Then, far away beyond the Crouch, came another, striding over some stunted trees, and then yet another, still further off, wading deeply through a shiny mudflat that seemed to hang halfway up between sea and sky. They were all stalking seaward, as if to intercept the escape of the multitudinous vessels that were crowded between Foulness and the Naze. In spite of the throbbing

exertions of the engines of the little paddle-boat, and the pouring foam that her wheels flung behind her, she receded with terrifying slowness from this ominous advance.

Glancing north-westward, my brother saw the large crescent of shipping already writhing with the approaching terror; one ship passing behind another, another coming round from broadside to end on, steamships whistling and giving off volumes of steam, sails being let out, launches rushing hither and thither. He was so fascinated by this and by the creeping danger away to the left that he had no eyes for anything seaward. And then a swift movement of the steamboat (she had suddenly come round to avoid being run down) flung him headlong from the seat upon which he was standing. There was a shouting all about him, a trampling of feet, and a cheer that seemed to be answered faintly. The steamboat lurched and rolled him over upon his hands.

He sprang to his feet and saw to starboard, and not a hundred yards from their heeling, pitching boat, a vast iron bulk like the blade of a plough tearing through the water, tossing it on either side in huge waves of foam that leaped towards the steamer, flinging her paddles helplessly in the air, and then sucking her deck down almost to the waterline.

A douche of spray blinded my brother for a moment. When his eyes were clear again he saw the monster had passed and was rushing landward. Big iron upperworks rose out of this headlong structure, and from that twin funnels projected and spat a smoking blast shot with fire. It was the torpedo ram *Thunder Child*, steaming headlong, coming to the rescue of the threatened shipping.

Keeping his footing on the heaving deck by clutching the bulwarks, my brother looked past this charging leviathan at the Martians again, and he saw the three of them now close together, and standing so far out to sea that their tripod supports were almost entirely submerged. Thus sunken, and seen in remote perspective, they appeared far less formidable than the huge iron bulk in whose wake the steamer was pitching so helplessly. It would seem they were regarding this new antagonist with astonishment. To their intelligence, it may be, the giant was even such another as themselves. The *Thunder Child* fired no gun, but simply drove full speed towards them. It was probably her not firing that enabled her to get so near the enemy as she did. They did not know what to make of her. One shell, and they would have sent her to the bottom forthwith with the Heat-Ray.

She was steaming at such a pace that in a minute she seemed halfway between the steamboat and the Martians – a diminishing black bulk against the receding horizontal expanse of the Essex coast.

Suddenly the foremost Martian lowered his tube and discharged a canister of the black gas at the ironclad. It hit her larboard side and glanced off in an inky jet that rolled away to seaward, an unfolding torrent of Black Smoke,

from which the ironclad drove clear. To the watchers from the steamer, low in the water and with the sun in their eyes, it seemed as though she were already among the Martians.

They saw the gaunt figures separating and rising out of the water as they retreated shoreward, and one of them raised the camera-like generator of the Heat-Ray. He held it pointing obliquely downward, and a bank of steam sprang from the water at its touch. It must have driven through the iron of the ship's side like a white-hot iron rod through paper.

A flicker of flame went up through the rising steam, and then the Martian reeled and staggered. In another moment he was cut down, and a great body of water and steam shot high in the air. The guns of the *Thunder Child* sounded through the reek, going off one after the other, and one shot splashed the water high close by the steamer, ricocheted towards the other flying ships to the north, and smashed a smack to matchwood.

But no one heeded that very much. At the sight of the Martian's collapse the captain on the bridge yelled inarticulately, and all the crowding passengers on the steamer's stern shouted together. And then they yelled again. For, surging out beyond the white tumult, drove something long and black, the flames streaming from its middle parts, its ventilators and funnels spouting fire.

She was alive still; the steering gear, it seems, was intact and her engines working. She headed straight for a second Martian, and was within a hundred yards of him when the Heat-Ray came to bear. Then with a violent thud, a blinding flash, her decks, her funnels, leaped upward. The Martian staggered with the violence of her explosion, and in another moment the flaming wreckage, still driving forward with the impetus of its pace, had struck him and crumpled him up like a thing of cardboard. My brother shouted involuntarily. A boiling tumult of steam hid everything again.

'Two!' yelled the captain.

Everyone was shouting. The whole steamer from end to end rang with frantic cheering that was taken up first by one and then by all in the crowding multitude of ships and boats that was driving out to sea.

The steam hung upon the water for many minutes, hiding the third Martian and the coast altogether. And all this time the boat was paddling steadily out to sea and away from the fight; and when at last the confusion cleared, the drifting bank of black vapour intervened, and nothing of the *Thunder Child* could be made out, nor could the third Martian be seen. But the ironclads to seaward were now quite close and standing in towards shore past the steamboat.

The little vessel continued to beat its way seaward, and the ironclads receded slowly towards the coast, which was hidden still by a marbled bank of vapour, part steam, part black gas, eddying and combining in the strangest way. The fleet of refugees was scattering to the north-east; several smacks

284 H. G. WELLS

were sailing between the ironclads and the steamboat. After a time, and before they reached the sinking cloud-bank, the warships turned northward, and then abruptly went about and passed into the thickening haze of evening southward. The coast grew faint, and at last indistinguishable amid the low banks of clouds that were gathering about the sinking sun.

Then suddenly out of the golden haze of the sunset came the vibration of guns, and a form of black shadows moving. Everyone struggled to the rail of the steamer and peered into the blinding furnace of the west, but nothing was to be distinguished clearly. A mass of smoke rose slanting and barred the face of the sun. The steamboat throbbed on its way through an interminable suspense.

The sun sank into grey clouds, the sky flushed and darkened, the evening star trembled into sight. It was deep twilight when the captain cried out and pointed. My brother strained his eyes. Something rushed up into the sky out of the greyness – rushed slantingly upward and very swiftly into the luminous clearness above the clouds in the western sky; something flat and broad, and very large, that swept round in a vast curve, grew smaller, sank slowly, and vanished again into the grey mystery of the night. And as it flew it rained down darkness upon the land.

BOOK TWO
THE EARTH UNDER
THE MARTIANS

CHAPTER I

Under Foot

In the first book I have wandered so much from my own adventures to tell of the experiences of my brother that all through the last two chapters I and the curate have been lurking in the empty house at Halliford whither we fled to escape the Black Smoke. There I will resume. We stopped there all Sunday night and all the next day – the day of the panic – in a little island of daylight, cut off by the Black Smoke from the rest of the world. We could do nothing but wait in aching inactivity during those two weary days.

My mind was occupied by anxiety for my wife. I figured her at Leatherhead, terrified, in danger, mourning me already as a dead man. I paced the rooms and cried aloud when I thought of how I was cut off from her, of all that might happen to her in my absence. My cousin I knew was brave enough for any emergency, but he was not the sort of man to realize danger quickly, to rise promptly. What was needed now was not bravery, but circumspection. My only consolation was to believe that the Martians were moving London-ward and away from her. Such vague anxieties keep the mind sensitive and painful. I grew very weary and irritable with the curate's perpetual ejaculations; I tired of the sight of his selfish despair. After some ineffectual remonstrance I kept away from him, staying in a room – evidently a children's schoolroom – containing globes, forms, and copybooks. When he followed me thither, I went to a box room at the top of the house and, in order to be alone with my aching miseries, locked myself in.

We were hopelessly hemmed in by the Black Smoke all that day and the morning of the next. There were signs of people in the next house on Sunday evening – a face at a window and moving lights, and later the slamming of a door. But I do not know who these people were, nor what became of them. We saw nothing of them next day. The Black Smoke drifted slowly riverward all through Monday morning, creeping nearer and nearer to us, driving at last along the roadway outside the house that hid us.

A Martian came across the fields about midday, laying the stuff with a jet of superheated steam that hissed against the walls, smashed all the windows it touched, and scalded the curate's hand as he fled out of the front room. When at last we crept across the sodden rooms and looked out again, the country northward was as though a black snowstorm had passed over it. Looking towards the river, we were astonished to see an unaccountable redness mingling with the black of the scorched meadows.

For a time we did not see how this change affected our position, save that we were relieved of our fear of the Black Smoke. But later I perceived that we were no longer hemmed in, that now we might get away. So soon as I realized that the way of escape was open, my dream of action returned. But the curate was lethargic, unreasonable.

'We are safe here,' he repeated; 'safe here.'

I resolved to leave him – would that I had! Wiser now for the artillery-man's teaching, I sought out food and drink. I had found oil and rags for my burns, and I also took a hat and a flannel shirt that I found in one of the bedrooms. When it was clear to him that I meant to go alone – had reconciled myself to going alone – he suddenly roused himself to come. And all being quiet throughout the afternoon, we started about five o'clock, as I should judge, along the blackened road to Sunbury.

In Sunbury, and at intervals along the road, were dead bodies lying in contorted attitudes, horses as well as men, overturned carts and luggage, all covered thickly with black dust. That pall of cindery powder made me think of what I had read of the destruction of Pompeii. We got to Hampton Court without misadventure, our minds full of strange and unfamiliar appearances, and at Hampton Court our eyes were relieved to find a patch of green that had escaped the suffocating drift. We went through Bushey Park, with its deer going to and fro under the chestnuts, and some men and women hurrying in the distance towards Hampton, and so we came to Twickenham. These were the first people we saw.

Away across the road the woods beyond Ham and Petersham were still afire. Twickenham was uninjured by either Heat-Ray or Black Smoke, and there were more people about here, though none could give us news. For the most part they were like ourselves, taking advantage of a lull to shift their quarters. I have an impression that many of the houses here were still occupied by scared inhabitants, too frightened even for flight. Here, too, the evidence of a hasty rout was abundant along the road. I remember most vividly three smashed bicycles in a heap, pounded into the road by the wheels of subsequent carts. We crossed Richmond Bridge about half-past eight. We hurried across the exposed bridge, of course, but I noticed floating down the stream a number of red masses, some many feet across. I did not know what these were – there was no time for scrutiny – and I put a more horrible interpretation on them than they deserved. Here again on the Surrey side were black dust that had once been smoke, and dead bodies – a heap near the approach to the station; but we had no glimpse of the Martians until we were some way towards Barnes.

We saw in the blackened distance a group of three people running down a side street towards the river, but otherwise it seemed deserted. Up the hill Richmond town was burning briskly; outside the town of Richmond there was no trace of the Black Smoke.

Then, suddenly, as we approached Kew, came a number of people running, and the upperworks of a Martian fighting-machine loomed in sight over the housetops, not a hundred yards away from us. We stood aghast at our danger, and had the Martian looked down we must immediately have perished. We were so terrified that we dared not go on, but turned aside and hid in a shed in a garden. There the curate crouched, weeping silently, and refusing to stir again.

But my fixed idea of reaching Leatherhead would not let me rest, and in the twilight I ventured out again. I went through a shrubbery, and along a passage beside a big house standing in its own grounds, and so emerged upon the road towards Kew. The curate I left in the shed, but he came hurrying after me.

That second start was the most foolhardy thing I ever did. For it was manifest the Martians were about us. No sooner had the curate overtaken me than we saw either the fighting-machine we had seen before or another, far away across the meadows in the direction of Kew Lodge. Four or five little black figures hurried before it across the green-grey of the field, and in a moment it was evident this Martian pursued them. In three strides he was among them, and they ran radiating from his feet in all directions. He used no Heat-Ray to destroy them, but picked them up one by one. Apparently he tossed them into the great metallic carrier which projected behind him, much as a workman's basket hangs over his shoulder.

It was the first time I realized that the Martians might have any other purpose than destruction with defeated humanity. We stood for a moment petrified, then turned and fled through a gate behind us into a walled garden, fell into, rather than found, a fortunate ditch, and lay there, scarce daring to whisper to each other until the stars were out.

I suppose it was nearly eleven o'clock before we gathered courage to start again, no longer venturing into the road, but sneaking along hedgerows and through plantations, and watching keenly through the darkness, he on the right and I on the left, for the Martians, who seemed to be all about us. In one place we blundered upon a scorched and blackened area, now cooling and ashen, and a number of scattered dead bodies of men, burned horribly about the heads and trunks but with their legs and boots mostly intact; and of dead horses, fifty feet, perhaps, behind a line of four ripped guns and smashed gun carriages.

Sheen, it seemed, had escaped destruction, but the place was silent and deserted. Here we happened on no dead, though the night was too dark for us to see into the side roads of the place. In Sheen my companion suddenly complained of faintness and thirst, and we decided to try one of the houses.

The first house we entered, after a little difficulty with the window, was a small semi-detached villa, and I found nothing eatable left in the place

but some mouldy cheese. There was, however, water to drink; and I took a
hatchet, which promised to be useful in our next house-breaking.

We then crossed to a place where the road turns towards Mortlake. Here
there stood a white house within a walled garden, and in the pantry of this
domicile we found a store of food – two loaves of bread in a pan, an uncooked
steak, and the half of a ham. I give this catalogue so precisely because, as
it happened, we were destined to subsist upon this store for the next fort-
night. Bottled beer stood under a shelf, and there were two bags of haricot
beans and some limp lettuces. This pantry opened into a kind of wash-up
kitchen, and in this was firewood; there was also a cupboard, in which we
found nearly a dozen of burgundy, tinned soups and salmon, and two tins
of biscuits.

We sat in the adjacent kitchen in the dark – for we dared not strike a
light – and ate bread and ham, and drank beer out of the same bottle. The
curate, who was still timorous and restless, was now, oddly enough, for
pushing on, and I was urging him to keep up his strength by eating when
the thing happened that was to imprison us.

'It can't be midnight yet,' I said, and then came a blinding glare of
vivid green light. Everything in the kitchen leaped out, clearly visible in
green and black, and vanished again. And then followed such a concus-
sion as I have never heard before or since. So close on the heels of this
as to seem instantaneous came a thud behind me, a clash of glass, a
crash and rattle of falling masonry all about us, and the plaster of the
ceiling came down upon us, smashing into a multitude of fragments upon
our heads. I was knocked headlong across the floor against the oven
handle and stunned. I was insensible for a long time, the curate told me,
and when I came to we were in darkness again, and he, with a face wet,
as I found afterwards, with blood from a cut forehead, was dabbing water
over me.

For some time I could not recollect what had happened. Then things
came to me slowly. A bruise on my temple asserted itself.

'Are you better?' asked the curate in a whisper.

At last I answered him. I sat up.

'Don't move,' he said. 'The floor is covered with smashed crockery from
the dresser. You can't possibly move without making a noise, and I fancy
they are outside.'

We both sat quite silent, so that we could scarcely hear each other
breathing. Everything seemed deadly still, but once something near us, some
plaster or broken brickwork, slid down with a rumbling sound. Outside and
very near was an intermittent, metallic rattle.

'That!' said the curate, when presently it happened again.

'Yes,' I said. 'But what is it?'

'A Martian!' said the curate.

I listened again.

'It was not like the Heat-Ray,' I said, and for a time I was inclined to think one of the great fighting-machines had stumbled against the house, as I had seen one stumble against the tower of Shepperton Church.

Our situation was so strange and incomprehensible that for three or four hours, until the dawn came, we scarcely moved. And then the light filtered in, not through the window, which remained black, but through a triangular aperture between a beam and a heap of broken bricks in the wall behind us. The interior of the kitchen we now saw greyly for the first time.

The window had been burst in by a mass of garden mould, which flowed over the table upon which we had been sitting and lay about our feet. Outside, the soil was banked high against the house. At the top of the window frame we could see an uprooted drainpipe. The floor was littered with smashed hardware; the end of the kitchen towards the house was broken into, and since the daylight shone in there, it was evident the greater part of the house had collapsed. Contrasting vividly with this ruin was the neat dresser, stained in the fashion, pale green, and with a number of copper and tin vessels below it, the wallpaper imitating blue and white tiles, and a couple of coloured supplements fluttering from the walls above the kitchen range.

As the dawn grew clearer, we saw through the gap in the wall the body of a Martian, standing sentinel, I suppose, over the still glowing cylinder. At the sight of that we crawled as circumspectly as possible out of the twilight of the kitchen into the darkness of the scullery.

Abruptly the right interpretation dawned upon my mind.

'The fifth cylinder,' I whispered, 'the fifth shot from Mars, has struck this house and buried us under the ruins!'

For a time the curate was silent, and then he whispered:

'God have mercy upon us!'

I heard him presently whimpering to himself.

Save for that sound we lay quite still in the scullery; I for my part scarce dared breathe, and sat with my eyes fixed on the faint light of the kitchen door. I could just see the curate's face, a dim, oval shape, and his collar and cuffs. Outside there began a metallic hammering, then a violent hooting, and then again, after a quiet interval, a hissing like the hissing of an engine. These noises, for the most part problematical, continued intermittently, and seemed if anything to increase in number as time wore on. Presently a measured thudding and a vibration that made everything about us quiver and the vessels in the pantry ring and shift, began and continued. Once the light was eclipsed, and the ghostly kitchen doorway became absolutely dark. For many hours we must have crouched there, silent and shivering, until our tired attention failed . . .

At last I found myself awake and very hungry. I am inclined to believe we must have spent the greater portion of a day before that awakening. My hunger was at a stride so insistent that it moved me to action. I told the curate I was going to seek food, and felt my way towards the pantry. He made me no answer, but so soon as I began eating the faint noise I made stirred him up and I heard him crawling after me.

CHAPTER II

What We Saw from the Ruined House

After eating we crept back to the scullery, and there I must have dozed again, for when presently I looked round I was alone. The thudding vibration continued with wearisome persistence. I whispered for the curate several times, and at last felt my way to the door of the kitchen. It was still daylight, and I perceived him across the room, lying against the triangular hole that looked out upon the Martians. His shoulders were hunched, so that his head was hidden from me.

I could hear a number of noises almost like those in an engine shed; and the place rocked with that beating thud. Through the aperture in the wall I could see the top of a tree touched with gold and the warm blue of a tranquil evening sky. For a minute or so I remained watching the curate, and then I advanced, crouching and stepping with extreme care amid the broken crockery that littered the floor.

I touched the curate's leg, and he started so violently that a mass of plaster went sliding down outside and fell with a loud impact. I gripped his arm, fearing he might cry out, and for a long time we crouched motionless. Then I turned to see how much of our rampart remained. The detachment of the plaster had left a vertical slit open in the debris, and by raising myself cautiously across a beam I was able to see out of this gap into what had been overnight a quiet suburban roadway. Vast, indeed, was the change that we beheld.

The fifth cylinder must have fallen right into the midst of the house we had first visited. The building had vanished, completely smashed, pulverized, and dispersed by the blow. The cylinder lay now far beneath the original foundations – deep in a hole, already vastly larger than the pit I had looked into at Woking. The earth all round it had splashed under that tremendous impact – 'splashed' is the only word – and lay in heaped piles that hid the masses of the adjacent houses. It had behaved exactly like mud under the violent blow of a hammer. Our house had collapsed backward; the front portion, even on the ground floor, had been destroyed completely; by a chance the kitchen and scullery had escaped, and stood buried now under soil and ruins, closed in by tons of earth on every side save towards the cylinder. Over that aspect we hung now on the very edge of the great circular pit the Martians were engaged in making. The heavy beating sound was evidently just behind us, and ever and again a bright green vapour drove up like a veil across our peephole.

The cylinder was already opened in the centre of the pit, and on the further edge of the pit, amid the smashed and gravel-heaped shrubbery, one of the great fighting-machines, deserted by its occupant, stood stiff and tall against the evening sky. At first I scarcely noticed the pit and the cylinder, although it has been convenient to describe them first, on account of the extraordinary glittering mechanism I saw busy in the excavation, and on account of the strange creatures that were crawling slowly and painfully across the heaped mould near it.

The mechanism it certainly was that held my attention first. It was one of those complicated fabrics that have since been called handling-machines, and the study of which has already given such an enormous impetus to terrestrial invention. As it dawned upon me first, it presented a sort of metallic spider with five jointed, agile legs, and with an extraordinary number of jointed levers, bars, and reaching and clutching tentacles about its body. Most of its arms were retracted, but with three long tentacles it was fishing out a number of rods, plates, and bars which lined the covering and apparently strengthened the walls of the cylinder. These, as it extracted them, were lifted out and deposited upon a level surface of earth behind it.

Its motion was so swift, complex, and perfect that at first I did not see it as a machine, in spite of its metallic glitter. The fighting-machines were co-ordinated and animated to an extraordinary pitch, but nothing to compare with this. People who have never seen these structures, and have only the ill-imagined efforts of artists or the imperfect descriptions of such eye-witnesses as myself to go upon, scarcely realize that living quality.

I recall particularly the illustration of one of the first pamphlets to give a consecutive account of the war. The artist had evidently made a hasty study of one of the fighting-machines, and there his knowledge ended. He presented them as tilted, stiff tripods, without either flexibility or subtlety, and with an altogether misleading monotony of effect. The pamphlet containing these renderings had a considerable vogue, and I mention them here simply to warn the reader against the impression they may have created. They were no more like the Martians I saw in action than a Dutch doll is like a human being. To my mind, the pamphlet would have been much better without them.

At first, I say, the handling-machine did not impress me as a machine, but as a crab-like creature with a glittering integument, the controlling Martian whose delicate tentacles actuated its movements seeming to be simply the equivalent of the crab's cerebral portion. But then I perceived the resemblance of its grey-brown, shiny, leathery integument to that of the other sprawling bodies beyond, and the true nature of this dexterous workman dawned upon me. With that realization my interest shifted to those other creatures, the real Martians. Already I had had a transient impression of these, and the first nausea no longer obscured my observation. Moreover, I was concealed and motionless, and under no urgency of action.

They were, I now saw, the most unearthly creatures it is possible to conceive. They were huge round bodies – or, rather, heads – about four feet in diameter, each body having in front of it a face. This face had no nostrils – indeed, the Martians do not seem to have had any sense of smell, but it had a pair of very large dark-coloured eyes, and just beneath this a kind of fleshy beak. In the back of this head or body – I scarcely know how to speak of it – was the single tight tympanic surface, since known to be anatomically an ear, though it must have been almost useless in our dense air. In a group round the mouth were sixteen slender, almost whiplike tentacles, arranged in two bunches of eight each. These bunches have since been named rather aptly, by that distinguished anatomist, Professor Howes, the *hands*. Even as I saw these Martians for the first time they seemed to be endeavouring to raise themselves on these hands, but of course, with the increased weight of terrestrial conditions, this was impossible. There is reason to suppose that on Mars they may have progressed upon them with some facility.

The internal anatomy, I may remark here, as dissection has since shown, was almost equally simple. The greater part of the structure was the brain, sending enormous nerves to the eyes, ear, and tactile tentacles. Besides this were the bulky lungs, into which the mouth opened, and the heart and its vessels. The pulmonary distress caused by the denser atmosphere and greater gravitational attraction was only too evident in the convulsive movements of the outer skin.

And this was the sum of the Martian organs. Strange as it may seem to a human being, all the complex apparatus of digestion, which makes up the bulk of our bodies, did not exist in the Martians. They were heads – merely heads. Entrails they had none. They did not eat, much less digest. Instead, they took the fresh, living blood of other creatures, and *injected* it into their own veins. I have myself seen this being done, as I shall mention in its place. But, squeamish as I may seem, I cannot bring myself to describe what I could not endure even to continue watching. Let it suffice to say, blood obtained from a still living animal, in most cases from a human being, was run directly by means of a little pipette into the recipient canal . . .

The bare idea of this is no doubt horribly repulsive to us, but at the same time I think that we should remember how repulsive our carnivorous habits would seem to an intelligent rabbit.

The physiological advantages of the practice of injection are undeniable, if one thinks of the tremendous waste of human time and energy occasioned by eating and the digestive process. Our bodies are half made up of glands and tubes and organs, occupied in turning heterogeneous food into blood. The digestive processes and their reaction upon the nervous system sap our strength and colour our minds. Men go happy or miserable as they have healthy or unhealthy livers, or sound gastric glands. But the Martians were lifted above all these organic fluctuations of mood and emotion.

Their undeniable preference for men as their source of nourishment is partly explained by the nature of the remains of the victims they had brought with them as provisions from Mars. These creatures, to judge from the shrivelled remains that have fallen into human hands, were bipeds with flimsy, silicious skeletons (almost like those of the silicious sponges) and feeble musculature, standing about six feet high and having round, erect heads, and large eyes in flinty sockets. Two or three of these seem to have been brought in each cylinder, and all were killed before earth was reached. It was just as well for them, for the mere attempt to stand upright upon our planet would have broken every bone in their bodies.

And while I am engaged in this description, I may add in this place certain further details which, although they were not all evident to us at the time, will enable the reader who is unacquainted with them to form a clearer picture of these offensive creatures.

In three other points their physiology differed strangely from ours. Their organisms did not sleep, any more than the heart of man sleeps. Since they had no extensive muscular mechanism to recuperate, that periodical extinction was unknown to them. They had little or no sense of fatigue, it would seem. On earth they could never have moved without effort, yet even to the last they kept in action. In twenty-four hours they did twenty-four hours of work, as even on earth is perhaps the case with the ants.

In the next place, wonderful as it seems in a sexual world, the Martians were absolutely without sex, and therefore without any of the tumultuous emotions that arise from that difference among men. A young Martian, there can now be no dispute, was really born upon earth during the war, and it was found attached to its parent, partially *budded* off, just as young lily-bulbs bud off, or like the young animals in the fresh-water polyp.

In man, in all the higher terrestrial animals, such a method of increase has disappeared; but even on this earth it was certainly the primitive method. Among the lower animals, up even to those first cousins of the vertebrated animals, the Tunicates, the two processes occur side by side, but finally the sexual method superseded its competitor altogether. On Mars, however, just the reverse has apparently been the case.

It is worthy of remark that a certain speculative writer of quasi-scientific repute, writing long before the Martian invasion, did forecast for man a final structure not unlike the actual Martian condition. His prophecy, I remember, appeared in November or December, 1893, in a long-defunct publication, the *Pall Mall Budget*, and I recall a caricature of it in a pre-Martian periodical called *Punch*. He pointed out – writing in a foolish, facetious tone – that the perfection of mechanical appliances must ultimately supersede limbs; the perfection of chemical devices, digestion; that such organs as hair, external nose, teeth, ears, and chin were no longer essential parts of the human being, and that the tendency of natural selection would lie in the direction

of their steady diminution through the coming ages. The brain alone remained a cardinal necessity. Only one other part of the body had a strong case for survival, and that was the hand, 'teacher and agent of the brain'. While the rest of the body dwindled, the hands would grow larger.

There is many a true word written in jest, and here in the Martians we have beyond dispute the actual accomplishment of such a suppression of the animal side of the organism by the intelligence. To me it is quite credible that the Martians may be descended from beings not unlike ourselves, by a gradual development of brain and hands (the latter giving rise to the two bunches of delicate tentacles at last) at the expense of the rest of the body. Without the body the brain would, of course, become a mere selfish intelligence, without any of the emotional substratum of the human being.

The last salient point in which the systems of these creatures differed from ours was in what one might have thought a very trivial particular. Micro-organisms, which cause so much disease and pain on earth, have either never appeared upon Mars or Martian sanitary science eliminated them ages ago. A hundred diseases, all the fevers and contagions of human life, consumption, cancers, tumours and such morbidities, never enter the scheme of their life. And speaking of the differences between the life on Mars and terrestrial life, I may allude here to the curious suggestions of the red weed.

Apparently the vegetable kingdom in Mars, instead of having green for a dominant colour, is of a vivid blood-red tint. At any rate, the seeds which the Martians (intentionally or accidentally) brought with them gave rise in all cases to red-coloured growths. Only that known popularly as the red weed, however, gained any footing in competition with terrestrial forms. The red creeper was quite a transitory growth, and few people have seen it growing. For a time, however, the red weed grew with astonishing vigour and luxuriance. It spread up the sides of the pit by the third or fourth day of our imprisonment, and its cactus-like branches formed a carmine fringe to the edges of our triangular window. And afterwards I found it broadcast throughout the country, and especially wherever there was a stream of water.

The Martians had what appears to have been an auditory organ, a single round drum at the back of the head-body, and eyes with a visual range not very different from ours except that, according to Philips, blue and violet were as black to them. It is commonly supposed that they communicated by sounds and tentacular gesticulations; this is asserted, for instance, in the able but hastily compiled pamphlet (written evidently by someone not an eye-witness of Martian actions) to which I have already alluded, and which, so far, has been the chief source of information concerning them. Now no surviving human being saw so much of the Martians in action as I did. I take no credit to myself for an accident, but the fact is so. And I assert that I watched them closely time after time, and that I have seen four, five and

(once) six of them sluggishly performing the most elaborately complicated operations together without either sound or gesture. Their peculiar hooting invariably preceded feeding; it had no modulation, and was, I believe, in no sense a signal, but merely the expiration of air preparatory to the suctional operation. I have a certain claim to at least an elementary knowledge of psychology, and in this matter I am convinced – as firmly as I am convinced of anything – that the Martians interchanged thoughts without any physical intermediation. And I have been convinced of this in spite of strong preconceptions. Before the Martian invasion, as an occasional reader here or there may remember, I had written with some little vehemence against the telepathic theory.

The Martians wore no clothing. Their conceptions of ornament and decorum were necessarily different from ours; and not only were they evidently much less sensible of changes of temperature than we are, but changes of pressure do not seem to have affected their health at all seriously. Yet though they wore no clothing, it was in the other artificial additions to their bodily resources that their great superiority over man lay. We men, with our bicycles and road-skates, our Lilienthal soaring-machines, our guns and sticks and so forth, are just in the beginning of the evolution that the Martians have worked out. They have become practically mere brains, wearing different bodies according to their needs just as men wear suits of clothes and take a bicycle in a hurry or an umbrella in the wet. And of their appliances, perhaps nothing is more wonderful to a man than the curious fact that what is the dominant feature of almost all human devices in mechanism is absent – the *wheel* is absent; among all the things they brought to earth there is no trace or suggestion of their use of wheels. One would have at least expected it in locomotion. And in this connection it is curious to remark that even on this earth Nature has never hit upon the wheel, or has preferred other expedients to its development. And not only did the Martians either not know of (which is incredible), or abstain from, the wheel, but in their apparatus singularly little use is made of the fixed pivot or relatively fixed pivot, with circular motions thereabout confined to one plane. Almost all the joints of the machinery present a complicated system of sliding parts moving over small but beautifully curved friction bearings. And while upon this matter of detail, it is remarkable that the long leverages of their machines are in most cases actuated by a sort of sham musculature of the disks in an elastic sheath; these disks become polarized and drawn closely and powerfully together when traversed by a current of electricity. In this way the curious parallelism to animal motions, which was so striking and disturbing to the human beholder, was attained. Such quasi-muscles abounded in the crab-like handling-machine which, on my first peeping out of the slit, I watched unpacking the cylinder. It seemed infinitely more alive than the actual Martians lying beyond it in the sunset

light, panting, stirring ineffectual tentacles, and moving feebly after their vast journey across space.

While I was still watching their sluggish motions in the sunlight, and noting each strange detail of their form, the curate reminded me of his presence by pulling violently at my arm. I turned to a scowling face, and silent, eloquent lips. He wanted the slit, which permitted only one of us to peep through; and so I had to forego watching them for a time while he enjoyed that privilege.

When I looked again, the busy handling-machine had already put together several of the pieces of apparatus it had taken out of the cylinder into a shape having an unmistakable likeness to its own; and down on the left a busy little digging mechanism had come into view, emitting jets of green vapour and working its way round the pit, excavating and embanking in a methodical and discriminating manner. This it was which had caused the regular beating noise, and the rhythmic shocks that had kept our ruinous refuge quivering. It piped and whistled as it worked. So far as I could see, the thing was without a directing Martian at all.

CHAPTER III

The Days of Imprisonment

The arrival of a second fighting-machine drove us from our peephole into the scullery, for we feared that from his elevation the Martian might see down upon us behind our barrier. At a later date we began to feel less in danger of their eyes, for to an eye in the dazzle of the sunlight outside our refuge must have been blank blackness, but at first the slightest suggestion of approach drove us into the scullery in heart-throbbing retreat. Yet terrible as was the danger we incurred, the attraction of peeping was for both of us irresistible. And I recall now with a sort of wonder that, in spite of the infinite danger in which we were between starvation and a still more terrible death, we could yet struggle bitterly for that horrible privilege of sight. We would race across the kitchen in a grotesque way between eagerness and the dread of making a noise, and strike each other, and thrust and kick, within a few inches of exposure.

The fact is that we had absolutely incompatible dispositions and habits of thought and action, and our danger and isolation only accentuated the incompatibility. At Halliford I had already come to hate the curate's trick of helpless exclamation, his stupid rigidity of mind. His endless muttering monologue vitiated every effort I made to think out a line of action, and drove me at times, thus pent up and intensified, almost to the verge of craziness. He was as lacking in restraint as a silly woman. He would weep for hours together, and I verily believe that to the very end this spoiled child of life thought his weak tears in some way efficacious. And I would sit in the darkness unable to keep my mind off him by reason of his importunities. He ate more than I did, and it was in vain I pointed out that our only chance of life was to stop in the house until the Martians had done with their pit, that in that long patience a time might presently come when we should need food. He ate and drank impulsively in heavy meals at long intervals. He slept little.

As the days wore on, his utter carelessness of any consideration so intensified our distress and danger that I had, much as I loathed doing it, to resort to threats, and at last to blows. That brought him to reason for a time. But he was one of those weak creatures, void of pride, timorous, anaemic, hateful souls, full of shifty cunning, who face neither God nor man, who face not even themselves.

It is disagreeable for me to recall and write these things, but I set them down that my story may lack nothing. Those who have escaped the dark and terrible aspects of life will find my brutality, my flash of rage in our final

tragedy, easy enough to blame; for they know what is wrong as well as any, but not what is possible to tortured men. But those who have been under the shadow, who have gone down at last to elemental things, will have a wider charity.

And while within we fought out our dark, dim contest of whispers, snatched food and drink, and gripping hands and blows, without, in the pitiless sunlight of that terrible June, was the strange wonder, the unfamiliar routine of the Martians in the pit. Let me return to those first new experiences of mine. After a long time I ventured back to the peephole, to find that the new-comers had been reinforced by the occupants of no fewer than three of the fighting-machines. These last had brought with them certain fresh appliances that stood in an orderly manner about the cylinder. The second handling-machine was now completed, and was busied in serving one of the novel contrivances the big machine had brought. This was a body resembling a milk can in its general form, above which oscillated a pear-shaped receptacle, and from which a stream of white powder flowed into a circular basin below.

The oscillatory motion was imparted to this by one tentacle of the handling-machine. With two spatulate hands the handling-machine was digging out and flinging masses of clay into the pear-shaped receptacle above, while with another arm it periodically opened a door and removed rusty and blackened clinkers from the middle part of the machine.

Another steely tentacle directed the powder from the basin along a ribbed channel towards some receiver that was hidden from me by the mound of bluish dust. From this unseen receiver a little thread of green smoke rose vertically into the quiet air. As I looked, the handling-machine, with a faint and musical clinking, extended, telescopic fashion, a tentacle that had been a moment before a mere blunt projection, until its end was hidden behind the mound of clay. In another second it had lifted a bar of white aluminium into sight, untarnished as yet, and shining dazzlingly, and deposited it in a growing stack of bars that stood at the side of the pit. Between sunset and starlight this dexterous machine must have made more than a hundred such bars out of the crude clay, and the mound of bluish dust rose steadily until it topped the side of the pit.

The contrast between the swift and complex movements of these contrivances and the inert panting clumsiness of their masters was acute, and for days I had to tell myself repeatedly that these latter were indeed the living of the two things.

The curate had possession of the slit when the first men were brought to the pit. I was sitting below, huddled up, listening with all my ears. He made a sudden movement backward, and I, fearful that we were observed, crouched in a spasm of terror. He came sliding down the rubbish and crept beside me in the darkness, inarticulate, gesticulating, and for a moment I

shared his panic. His gesture suggested a resignation of the slit, and after a
little while my curiosity gave me courage, and I rose up, stepped across him,
and clambered up to it. At first I could see no reason for his frantic behav-
iour. The twilight had now come, the stars were little and faint, but the pit
was illuminated by the flickering green fire that came from the aluminium-
making. The whole picture was a flickering scheme of green gleams and
shifting rusty black shadows, strangely trying to the eyes. Over and through
it all went the bats, heeding it not at all. The sprawling Martians were no
longer to be seen, the mound of blue-green powder had risen to cover them
from sight, and a fighting-machine, with its legs contracted, crumpled, and
abbreviated, stood across the corner of the pit. And then, amid the clangour
of the machinery, came a drifting suspicion of human voices, that I enter-
tained at first only to dismiss.

I crouched, watching this fighting-machine closely, satisfying myself now
for the first time that the hood did indeed contain a Martian. As the green
flames lifted I could see the oily gleam of his integument and the brightness
of his eyes. And suddenly I heard a yell, and saw a long tentacle reaching
over the shoulder of the machine to the little cage that hunched upon its
back. Then something – something struggling violently – was lifted high
against the sky, a black, vague enigma against the starlight; and as this black
object came down again, I saw by the green brightness that it was a man.
For an instant he was clearly visible. He was a stout, ruddy, middle-aged
man, well dressed; three days before, he must have been walking the world,
a man of considerable consequence. I could see his staring eyes and gleams
of light on his studs and watch chain. He vanished behind the mound, and
for a moment there was silence. And then began a shrieking and a sustained
and cheerful hooting from the Martians.

I slid down the rubbish, struggled to my feet, clapped my hands over my
ears, and bolted into the scullery. The curate, who had been crouching
silently with his arms over his head, looked up as I passed, cried out quite
loudly at my desertion of him, and came running after me.

That night, as we lurked in the scullery, balanced between our horror
and the terrible fascination this peeping had, although I felt an urgent need
of action I tried in vain to conceive some plan of escape; but afterwards,
during the second day, I was able to consider our position with great clear-
ness. The curate, I found, was quite incapable of discussion; this new and
culminating atrocity had robbed him of all vestiges of reason or forethought.
Practically he had already sunk to the level of an animal. But as the saying
goes, I gripped myself with both hands. It grew upon my mind, once I could
face the facts, that terrible as our position was, there was as yet no justifi-
cation for absolute despair. Our chief chance lay in the possibility of the
Martians making the pit nothing more than a temporary encampment. Or
even if they kept it permanently, they might not consider it necessary to

guard it, and a chance of escape might be afforded us. I also weighed very carefully the possibility of our digging a way out in a direction away from the pit, but the chances of our emerging within sight of some sentinel fighting-machine seemed at first too great. And I should have had to do all the digging myself. The curate would certainly have failed me.

It was on the third day, if my memory serves me right, that I saw the lad killed. It was the only occasion on which I actually saw the Martians feed. After that experience I avoided the hole in the wall for the better part of a day. I went into the scullery, removed the door, and spent some hours digging with my hatchet as silently as possible; but when I had made a hole about a couple of feet deep the loose earth collapsed noisily, and I did not dare continue. I lost heart, and lay down on the scullery floor for a long time, having no spirit even to move. And after that I abandoned altogether the idea of escaping by excavation.

It says much for the impression the Martians had made upon me that at first I entertained little or no hope of our escape being brought about by their overthrow through any human effort. But on the fourth or fifth night I heard a sound like heavy guns.

It was very late in the night, and the moon was shining brightly. The Martians had taken away the excavating-machine, and, save for a fighting-machine that stood in the remoter bank of the pit and a handling-machine that was buried out of my sight in a corner of the pit immediately beneath my peephole, the place was deserted by them. Except for the pale glow from the handling-machine and the bars and patches of white moonlight the pit was in darkness, and, except for the clinking of the handling-machine, quite still. That night was a beautiful serenity; save for one planet, the moon seemed to have the sky to herself. I heard a dog howling, and that familiar sound it was that made me listen. Then I heard quite distinctly a booming exactly like the sound of great guns. Six distinct reports I counted, and after a long interval six again. And that was all.

CHAPTER IV

The Death of the Curate

It was on the sixth day of our imprisonment that I peeped for the last time, and presently found myself alone. Instead of keeping close to me and trying to oust me from the slit, the curate had gone back into the scullery. I was struck by a sudden thought. I went back quickly and quietly into the scullery. In the darkness I heard the curate drinking. I snatched in the darkness, and my fingers caught a bottle of burgundy.

For a few minutes there was a tussle. The bottle struck the floor and broke, and I desisted and rose. We stood panting and threatening each other. In the end I planted myself between him and the food, and told him of my determination to begin a discipline. I divided the food in the pantry, into rations to last us ten days. I would not let him eat any more that day. In the afternoon he made a feeble effort to get at the food. I had been dozing, but in an instant I was awake. All day and all night we sat face to face, I weary but resolute, and he weeping and complaining of his immediate hunger. It was, I know, a night and a day, but to me it seemed – it seems now – an interminable length of time.

And so our widened incompatibility ended at last in open conflict. For two vast days we struggled in undertones and wrestling contests. There were times when I beat and kicked him madly, times when I cajoled and persuaded him, and once I tried to bribe him with the last bottle of burgundy, for there was a rain-water pump from which I could get water. But neither force nor kindness availed; he was indeed beyond reason. He would neither desist from his attacks on the food nor from his noisy babbling to himself. The rudimentary precautions to keep our imprisonment endurable he would not observe. Slowly I began to realize the complete overthrow of his intelligence, to perceive that my sole companion in this close and sickly darkness was a man insane.

From certain vague memories I am inclined to think my own mind wandered at times. I had strange and hideous dreams whenever I slept. It sounds paradoxical, but I am inclined to think that the weakness and insanity of the curate warned me, braced me, and kept me a sane man.

On the eighth day he began to talk aloud instead of whispering, and nothing I could do would moderate his speech.

'It is just, O God!' he would say, over and over again. 'It is just. On me and mine be the punishment laid. We have sinned, we have fallen short. There was poverty, sorrow; the poor were trodden in the dust, and I held my peace. I preached acceptable folly – my God, what folly! – when I should

have stood up, though I died for it, and called upon them to repent – repent! . . . Oppressors of the poor and needy . . . ! The wine press of God!'

Then he would suddenly revert to the matter of the food I withheld from him, praying, begging, weeping, at last threatening. He began to raise his voice – I prayed him not to. He perceived a hold on me – he threatened he would shout and bring the Martians upon us. For a time that scared me; but any concession would have shortened our chance of escape beyond estimating. I defied him, although I felt no assurance that he might not do this thing. But that day, at any rate, he did not. He talked with his voice rising slowly, through the greater part of the eighth and ninth days – threats, entreaties, mingled with a torrent of half-sane and always frothy repentance for his vacant sham of God's service, such as made me pity him. Then he slept awhile, and began again with renewed strength, so loudly that I must needs make him desist.

'Be still!' I implored.

He rose to his knees, for he had been sitting in the darkness near the copper.

'I have been still too long,' he said, in a tone that must have reached the pit, 'and now I must bear my witness. Woe unto this unfaithful city! Woe! Woe! Woe! Woe! Woe! To the inhabitants of the earth by reason of the other voices of the trumpet ——'

'Shut up!' I said, rising to my feet, and in a terror lest the Martians should hear us. 'For God's sake ——'

'Nay,' shouted the curate, at the top of his voice, standing likewise and extending his arms. 'Speak! The word of the Lord is upon me!'

In three strides he was at the door leading into the kitchen.

'I must bear my witness! I go! It has already been too long delayed.'

I put out my hand and felt the meat chopper hanging to the wall. In a flash I was after him. I was fierce with fear. Before he was halfway across the kitchen I had overtaken him. With one last touch of humanity I turned the blade back and struck him with the butt. He went headlong forward and lay stretched on the ground. I stumbled over him and stood panting. He lay still.

Suddenly I heard a noise without, the run and smash of slipping plaster, and the triangular aperture in the wall was darkened. I looked up and saw the lower surface of a handling-machine coming slowly across the hole. One of its gripping limbs curled amid the debris; another limb appeared, feeling its way over the fallen beams. I stood petrified, staring. Then I saw through a sort of glass plate near the edge of the body the face, as we may call it, and the large dark eyes of a Martian, peering, and then a long metallic snake of tentacle came feeling slowly through the hole.

I turned by an effort, stumbled over the curate, and stopped at the scullery door. The tentacle was now some way, two yards or more, in the

room, and twisting and turning, with queer sudden movements, this way and that. For a while I stood fascinated by that slow, fitful advance. Then, with a faint, hoarse cry, I forced myself across the scullery. I trembled violently; I could scarcely stand upright. I opened the door of the coal cellar, and stood there in the darkness staring at the faintly lit doorway into the kitchen, and listening. Had the Martian seen me? What was it doing now?

Something was moving to and fro there, very quietly; every now and then it tapped against the wall, or started on its movements with a faint metallic ringing, like the movements of keys on a split-ring. Then a heavy body – I knew too well what – was dragged across the floor of the kitchen towards the opening. Irresistibly attracted, I crept to the door and peeped into the kitchen. In the triangle of bright outer sunlight I saw the Martian, in its Briareus of a handling-machine, scrutinizing the curate's head. I thought at once that it would infer my presence from the mark of the blow I had given him.

I crept back to the coal-cellar, shut the door, and began to cover myself up as much as I could, and as noiselessly as possible in the darkness, among the firewood and coal therein. Every now and then I paused, rigid, to hear if the Martian had thrust its tentacles through the opening again.

Then the faint metallic jingle returned. I traced it slowly feeling over the kitchen. Presently I heard it nearer – in the scullery, as I judged. I thought that its length might be insufficient to reach me. I prayed copiously. It passed, scraping faintly across the cellar door. An age of almost intolerable suspense intervened; then I heard it fumbling at the latch! It had found the door! The Martians understood doors!

It worried at the catch for a minute, perhaps, and then the door opened.

In the darkness I could just see the thing – like an elephant's trunk more than anything else – waving towards me and touching and examining the wall, coals, wood and ceiling. It was like a black worm swaying its blind head to and fro.

Once, even, it touched the heel of my boot. I was on the verge of screaming; I bit my hand. For a time the tentacle was silent. I could have fancied it had been withdrawn. Presently, with an abrupt click, it gripped something – I thought it had me! – and seemed to go out of the cellar again. For a minute I was not sure. Apparently it had taken a lump of coal to examine.

I seized the opportunity of slightly shifting my position, which had become cramped, and then listened. I whispered passionate prayers for safety.

Then I heard the slow, deliberate sound creeping towards me again. Slowly, slowly it drew near, scratching against the walls and tapping the furniture.

While I was still doubtful, it rapped smartly against the cellar door and closed it. I heard it go into the pantry, and the biscuit-tins rattled and a

bottle smashed, and then came a heavy bump against the cellar door. Then silence that passed into an infinity of suspense.

Had it gone?

At last I decided that it had.

It came into the scullery no more; but I lay all the tenth day in the close darkness, buried among coals and firewood, not daring even to crawl out for the drink for which I craved. It was the eleventh day before I ventured so far from my security.

CHAPTER V

The Stillness

My first act before I went into the pantry was to fasten the door between the kitchen and the scullery. But the pantry was empty; every scrap of food had gone. Apparently, the Martian had taken it all on the previous day. At that discovery I despaired for the first time. I took no food, or no drink either, on the eleventh or the twelfth day.

At first my mouth and throat were parched, and my strength ebbed sensibly. I sat about in the darkness of the scullery, in a state of despondent wretchedness. My mind ran on eating. I thought I had become deaf, for the noises of movement I had been accustomed to hear from the pit had ceased absolutely. I did not feel strong enough to crawl noiselessly to the peephole, or I would have gone there.

On the twelfth day my throat was so painful that, taking the chance of alarming the Martians, I attacked the creaking rain-water pump that stood by the sink, and got a couple of glassfuls of blackened and tainted rain-water. I was greatly refreshed by this, and emboldened by the fact that no enquiring tentacle followed the noise of my pumping.

During these days, in a rambling, inconclusive way, I thought much of the curate and of the manner of his death.

On the thirteenth day I drank some more water, and dozed and thought disjointedly of eating and of vague impossible plans of escape. Whenever I dozed I dreamt of horrible phantasms, of the death of the curate, or of sumptuous dinners; but, asleep or awake, I felt a keen pain that urged me to drink again and again. The light that came into the scullery was no longer grey, but red. To my disordered imagination it seemed the colour of blood.

On the fourteenth day I went into the kitchen, and I was surprised to find that the fronds of the red weed had grown right across the hole in the wall, turning the half-light of the place into a crimson-coloured obscurity.

It was early on the fifteenth day that I heard a curious, familiar sequence of sounds in the kitchen, and, listening, identified it as the snuffing and scratching of a dog. Going into the kitchen, I saw a dog's nose peering in through a break among the ruddy fronds. This greatly surprised me. At the scent of me he barked shortly.

I thought if I could induce him to come into the place quietly I should be able, perhaps, to kill and eat him; and in any case, it would be advisable to kill him, lest his actions attracted the attention of the Martians.

I crept forward, saying 'Good dog!' very softly; but he suddenly withdrew his head and disappeared.

I listened – I was not deaf – but certainly the pit was still. I heard a sound like the flutter of a bird's wings, and a hoarse croaking, but that was all.

For a long while I lay close to the peephole, but not daring to move aside the red plants that obscured it. Once or twice I heard a faint pitter-patter like the feet of the dog going hither and thither on the sand far below me, and there were more birdlike sounds, but that was all. At length, encouraged by the silence, I looked out.

Except in the corner, where a multitude of crows hopped and fought over the skeletons of the dead the Martians had consumed, there was not a living thing in the pit.

I stared about me, scarcely believing my eyes. All the machinery had gone. Save for the big mound of greyish-blue powder in one corner, certain bars of aluminium in another, the black birds, and the skeletons of the killed, the place was merely an empty circular pit in the sand.

Slowly I thrust myself out through the red weed, and stood upon the mound of rubble. I could see in any direction save behind me, to the north, and neither Martians nor sign of Martians were to be seen. The pit dropped sheerly from my feet, but a little way along the rubbish afforded a practicable slope to the summit of the ruins. My chance of escape had come. I began to tremble.

I hesitated for some time, and then, in a gust of desperate resolution, and with a heart that throbbed violently, I scrambled to the top of the mound in which I had been buried so long.

I looked about again. To the northward, too, no Martian was visible.

When I had last seen this part of Sheen in the daylight it had been a straggling street of comfortable white and red houses, interspersed with abundant shady trees. Now I stood on a mound of smashed brickwork, clay, and gravel, over which spread a multitude of red cactus-shaped plants, knee-high, without a solitary terrestrial growth to dispute their footing. The trees near me were dead and brown, but further a network of red threads scaled the still living stems.

The neighbouring houses had all been wrecked, but none had been burned; their walls stood, sometimes to the second story, with smashed windows and shattered doors. The red weed grew tumultuously in their roofless rooms. Below me was the great pit, with the crows struggling for its refuse. A number of other birds hopped about among the ruins. Far away I saw a gaunt cat slink crouchingly along a wall, but traces of men there were none.

The day seemed, by contrast with my recent confinement, dazzlingly bright, the sky a glowing blue. A gentle breeze kept the red weed that covered every scrap of unoccupied ground gently swaying. And oh, the sweetness of the air!

CHAPTER VI

The Work of Fifteen Days

For some time I stood tottering on the mound regardless of my safety. Within that noisome den from which I had emerged I had thought with a narrow intensity only of our immediate security. I had not realized what had been happening to the world, had not anticipated this startling vision of unfamiliar things. I had expected to see Sheen in ruins – I found about me the landscape, weird and lurid, of another planet.

For that moment I touched an emotion beyond the common range of men, yet one that the poor brutes we dominate know only too well. I felt as a rabbit might feel returning to his burrow and suddenly confronted by the work of a dozen busy navvies digging the foundations of a house. I felt the first inkling of a thing that presently grew quite clear in my mind, that oppressed me for many days, a sense of dethronement, a persuasion that I was no longer a master, but an animal among the animals, under the Martian heel. With us it would be as with them, to lurk and watch, to run and hide; the fear and empire of man had passed away.

But so soon as this strangeness had been realized it passed, and my dominant motive became the hunger of my long and dismal fast. In the direction away from the pit I saw, beyond a red-covered wall, a patch of garden ground unburied. This gave me a hint, and I went knee-deep, and sometimes neck-deep, in the red weed. The density of the weed gave me a reassuring sense of hiding. The wall was some six feet high, and when I attempted to clamber it I found I could not lift my feet to the crest. So I went along by the side of it, and came to a corner and a rockwork that enabled me to get to the top, and tumble into the garden I coveted. Here I found some young onions, a couple of gladiolus bulbs, and a quantity of immature carrots, all of which I secured, and, scrambling over a ruined wall, went on my way through scarlet and crimson trees towards Kew – it was like walking through an avenue of gigantic blood drops – possessed with two ideas: to get more food, and to limp, as soon and as far as my strength permitted, out of this accursed unearthly region of the pit.

Some way further, in a grassy place, was a group of mushrooms which also I devoured, and then I came upon a brown sheet of flowing shallow water, where meadows used to be. These fragments of nourishment served only to whet my hunger. At first I was surprised at this flood in a hot, dry summer, but afterwards I discovered that it was caused by the tropical exuberance of the red weed. Directly this extraordinary growth encountered water it straightway became gigantic and of unparalleled

fecundity. Its seeds were simply poured down into the water of the Wey and Thames, and its swiftly growing and titanic water fronds speedily choked both those rivers.

At Putney, as I afterwards saw, the bridge was almost lost in a tangle of this weed, and at Richmond, too, the Thames water poured in a broad and shallow stream across the meadows of Hampton and Twickenham. As the waters spread the weed followed them, until the ruined villas of the Thames valley were for a time lost in this red swamp, whose margin I explored, and much of the desolation the Martians had caused was concealed.

In the end the red weed succumbed almost as quickly as it had spread. A cankering disease, due, it is believed, to the action of certain bacteria, presently seized upon it. Now by the action of natural selection, all terrestrial plants have acquired a resisting power against bacterial diseases – they never succumb without a severe struggle, but the red weed rotted like a thing already dead. The fronds became bleached, and then shrivelled and brittle. They broke off at the least touch, and the waters that had stimulated their early growth carried their last vestiges out to sea.

My first act on coming to this water was, of course, to slake my thirst. I drank a great deal of it and, moved by an impulse, gnawed some fronds of red weed; but they were watery, and had a sickly, metallic taste. I found the water was sufficiently shallow for me to wade securely, although the red weed impeded my feet a little; but the flood evidently got deeper towards the river, and I turned back to Mortlake. I managed to make out the road by means of occasional ruins of its villas and fences and lamps, and so presently I got out of this spate and made my way to the hill going up towards Roehampton and came out on Putney Common.

Here the scenery changed from the strange and unfamiliar to the wreckage of the familiar: patches of ground exhibited the devastation of a cyclone, and in a few score yards I would come upon perfectly undisturbed spaces, houses with their blinds trimly drawn and doors closed, as if they had been left for a day by the owners, or as if their inhabitants slept within. The red weed was less abundant; the tall trees along the lane were free from the red creeper. I hunted for food among the trees, finding nothing, and I also raided a couple of silent houses, but they had already been broken into and ransacked. I rested for the remainder of the daylight in a shrubbery, being, in my enfeebled condition, too fatigued to push on.

All this time I saw no human beings, and no signs of the Martians. I encountered a couple of hungry-looking dogs, but both hurried circuitously away from the advances I made them. Near Roehampton I had seen two human skeletons – not bodies, but skeletons, picked clean – and in the wood by me I found the crushed and scattered bones of several cats and rabbits and the skull of a sheep. But though I gnawed parts of these in my mouth, there was nothing to be got from them.

After sunset I struggled on along the road towards Putney, where I think the Heat-Ray must have been used for some reason. And in the garden beyond Roehampton I got a quantity of immature potatoes, sufficient to stay my hunger. From this garden one looked down upon Putney and the river. The aspect of the place in the dusk was singularly desolate: blackened trees, blackened, desolate ruins, and down the hill the sheets of the flooded river, red-tinged with the weed. And over all – silence. It filled me with indescribable terror to think how swiftly that desolating change had come.

For a time I believed that mankind had been swept out of existence, and that I stood there alone, the last man left alive. Hard by the top of Putney Hill I came upon another skeleton, with the arms dislocated and removed several yards from the rest of the body. As I proceeded I became more and more convinced that the extermination of mankind was, save for such stragglers as myself, already accomplished in this part of the world. The Martians, I thought, had gone on and left the country desolated, seeking food elsewhere. Perhaps even now they were destroying Berlin or Paris, or it might be they had gone northward.

CHAPTER VII

The Man on Putney Hill

I spent that night in the inn that stands at the top of Putney Hill, sleeping in a made bed for the first time since my flight to Leatherhead. I will not tell the needless trouble I had breaking into that house – afterwards I found the front door was on the latch – nor how I ransacked every room for food, until just on the verge of despair, in what seemed to me to be a servant's bedroom, I found a rat-gnawed crust and two tins of pineapple. The place had been already searched and emptied. In the bar I afterwards found some biscuits and sandwiches that had been overlooked. The latter I could not eat, they were too rotten, but the former not only stayed my hunger, but filled my pockets. I lit no lamps, fearing some Martian might come beating that part of London for food in the night. Before I went to bed I had an interval of restlessness, and prowled from window to window, peering out for some sign of these monsters. I slept little. As I lay in bed I found myself thinking consecutively – a thing I do not remember to have done since my last argument with the curate. During all the intervening time my mental condition had been a hurrying succession of vague emotional states or a sort of stupid receptivity. But in the night my brain, reinforced, I suppose, by the food I had eaten, grew clear again, and I thought.

Three things struggled for possession of my mind: the killing of the curate, the whereabouts of the Martians, and the possible fate of my wife. The former gave me no sensation of horror or remorse to recall; I saw it simply as a thing done, a memory infinitely disagreeable but quite without the quality of remorse. I saw myself then as I see myself now, driven step by step towards that hasty blow, the creature of a sequence of accidents leading inevitably to that. I felt no condemnation; yet the memory, static, unprogressive, haunted me. In the silence of the night, with that sense of the nearness of God that sometimes comes into the stillness and the darkness, I stood my trial, my only trial, for that moment of wrath and fear. I retraced every step of our conversation from the moment when I had found him crouching beside me, heedless of my thirst, and pointing to the fire and smoke that streamed up from the ruins of Weybridge. We had been incapable of co-operation – grim chance had taken no heed of that. Had I foreseen, I should have left him at Halliford. But I did not foresee; and crime is to foresee and do. And I set this down as I have set all this story down, as it was. There were no witnesses – all these things I might have concealed. But I set it down, and the reader must form his judgment as he will.

And when, by an effort, I had set aside that picture of a prostrate body, I faced the problem of the Martians and the fate of my wife. For the former I had no data; I could imagine a hundred things, and so, unhappily, I could for the latter. And suddenly that night became terrible. I found myself sitting up in bed, staring at the dark. I found myself praying that the Heat-Ray might have suddenly and painlessly struck her out of being. Since the night of my return from Leatherhead I had not prayed. I had uttered prayers, fetish prayers, had prayed as heathens mutter charms when I was in extremity; but now I prayed indeed, pleading steadfastly and sanely, face to face with the darkness of God. Strange night! Strangest in this, that so soon as dawn had come, I, who had talked with God, crept out of the house like a rat leaving its hiding place – a creature scarcely larger, an inferior animal, a thing that for any passing whim of our masters might be hunted and killed. Perhaps they also prayed confidently to God. Surely, if we have learned nothing else, this war has taught us pity – pity for those witless souls that suffer our dominion.

The morning was bright and fine, and the eastern sky glowed pink, and was fretted with little golden clouds. In the road that runs from the top of Putney Hill to Wimbledon was a number of poor vestiges of the panic torrent that must have poured Londonward on the Sunday night after the fighting began. There was a little two-wheeled cart inscribed with the name of Thomas Lobb, Greengrocer, New Malden, with a smashed wheel and an abandoned tin trunk; there was a straw hat trampled into the now hardened mud, and at the top of West Hill a lot of blood-stained glass about the overturned water trough. My movements were languid, my plans of the vaguest. I had an idea of going to Leatherhead, though I knew that there I had the poorest chance of finding my wife. Certainly, unless death had overtaken them suddenly, my cousins and she would have fled thence; but it seemed to me I might find or learn there whither the Surrey people had fled. I knew I wanted to find my wife, that my heart ached for her and the world of men, but I had no clear idea how the finding might be done. I was also sharply aware now of my intense loneliness. From the corner I went, under cover of a thicket of trees and bushes, to the edge of Wimbledon Common, stretching wide and far.

That dark expanse was lit in patches by yellow gorse and broom; there was no red weed to be seen, and as I prowled, hesitating, on the verge of the open, the sun rose, flooding it all with light and vitality. I came upon a busy swarm of little frogs in a swampy place among the trees. I stopped to look at them, drawing a lesson from their stout resolve to live. And presently, turning suddenly, with an odd feeling of being watched, I beheld something crouching amid a clump of bushes. I stood regarding this. I made a step towards it, and it rose up and became a man armed with a cutlass. I approached him slowly. He stood silent and motionless, regarding me.

As I drew nearer I perceived he was dressed in clothes as dusty and filthy as my own; he looked, indeed, as though he had been dragged through a culvert. Nearer, I distinguished the green slime of ditches mixing with the pale drab of dried clay and shiny, coaly patches. His black hair fell over his eyes, and his face was dark and dirty and sunken, so that at first I did not recognize him. There was a red cut across the lower part of his face.

'Stop!' he cried, when I was within ten yards of him, and I stopped. His voice was hoarse. 'Where do you come from?' he said.

I thought, surveying him.

'I come from Mortlake,' I said. 'I was buried near the pit the Martians made about their cylinder. I have worked my way out and escaped.'

'There is no food about here,' he said. 'This is my country. All this hill down to the river, and back to Clapham, and up to the edge of the common. There is only food for one. Which way are you going?'

I answered slowly.

'I don't know,' I said. 'I have been buried in the ruins of a house thirteen or fourteen days. I don't know what has happened.'

He looked at me doubtfully, then started, and looked with a changed expression.

'I've no wish to stop about here,' said I. 'I think I shall go to Leatherhead, for my wife was there.'

He shot out a pointing finger.

'It is you,' said he; 'the man from Woking. And you weren't killed at Weybridge?'

I recognized him at the same moment.

'You are the artilleryman who came into my garden.'

'Good luck!' he said. 'We are lucky ones! Fancy *you*!' He put out a hand, and I took it. 'I crawled up a drain,' he said. 'But they didn't kill everyone. And after they went away I got off towards Walton across the fields. But – it's not sixteen days altogether – and your hair is grey.' He looked over his shoulder suddenly. 'Only a rook,' he said. 'One gets to know that birds have shadows these days. This is a bit open. Let us crawl under those bushes and talk.'

'Have you seen any Martians?' I said. 'Since I crawled out—'

'They've gone away across London,' he said. 'I guess they've got a bigger camp there. Of a night, all over there, Hampstead way, the sky is alive with their lights. It's like a great city, and in the glare you can just see them moving. By daylight you can't. But nearer – I haven't seen them—' (he counted on his fingers) 'five days. Then I saw a couple across Hammersmith way carrying something big. And the night before last' – he stopped and spoke impressively – 'it was just a matter of lights, but it was something up in the air. I believe they've built a flying-machine, and are learning to fly.'

I stopped, on hands and knees, for we had come to the bushes.

'Fly!'

'Yes,' he said, 'fly.'

I went on into a little bower, and sat down.

'It is all over with humanity,' I said. 'If they can do that they will simply go round the world.'

He nodded.

'They will. But – it will relieve things over here a bit. And besides—' He looked at me. 'Aren't you satisfied it *is* up with humanity? I am. We're down; we're beat.'

I stared. Strange as it may seem, I had not arrived at this fact – a fact perfectly obvious so soon as he spoke. I had still held a vague hope; rather, I had kept a lifelong habit of mind. He repeated his words, 'We're beat.' They carried absolute conviction.

'It's all over,' he said. 'They've lost *one* – just *one*. And they've made their footing good and crippled the greatest power in the world. They've walked over us. The death of that one at Weybridge was an accident. And these are only pioneers. They kept on coming. These green stars – I've seen none these five or six days, but I've no doubt they're falling somewhere every night. Nothing's to be done. We're under! We're beat!'

I made him no answer. I sat staring before me, trying in vain to devise some countervailing thought.

'This isn't a war,' said the artilleryman. 'It never was a war, any more than there's war between man and ants.'

Suddenly I recalled the night in the observatory.

'After the tenth shot they fired no more – at least, until the first cylinder came.'

'How do you know?' said the artilleryman. I explained. He thought. 'Something wrong with the gun,' he said. 'But what if there is? They'll get it right again. And even if there's a delay, how can it alter the end? It's just men and ants. There's the ants builds their cities, live their lives, have wars, revolutions, until the men want them out of the way, and then they go out of the way. That's what we are now – just ants. Only ——'

'Yes,' I said.

'We're eatable ants.'

We sat looking at each other.

'And what will they do with us?' I said.

'That's what I've been thinking,' he said; 'that's what I've been thinking. After Weybridge I went south – thinking. I saw what was up. Most of the people were hard at it squealing and exciting themselves. But I'm not so fond of squealing. I've been in sight of death once or twice; I'm not an ornamental soldier, and at the best and worst, death – it's just death. And it's the man that keeps on thinking comes through. I saw everyone tracking

away south. Says I, "Food won't last this way," and I turned right back. I went for the Martians like a sparrow goes for man. All round' – he waved a hand to the horizon – 'they're starving in heaps, bolting, treading on each other . . .'

He saw my face, and halted awkwardly.

'No doubt lots who had money have gone away to France,' he said. He seemed to hesitate whether to apologize, met my eyes, and went on: 'There's food all about here. Canned things in shops; wines, spirits, mineral waters; and the water mains and drains are empty. Well, I was telling you what I was thinking. "Here's intelligent things," I said, "and it seems they want us for food. First, they'll smash us up – ships, machines, guns, cities, all the order and organization. All that will go. If we were the size of ants we might pull through. But we're not. It's all too bulky to stop. That's the first certainty." Eh?'

I assented.

'It is; I've thought it out. Very well, then – next; at present we're caught as we're wanted. A Martian has only to go a few miles to get a crowd on the run. And I saw one, one day, out by Wandsworth, picking houses to pieces and routing among the wreckage. But they won't keep on doing that. So soon as they've settled all our guns and ships, and smashed our railways, and done all the things they are doing over there, they will begin catching us systematic, picking the best and storing us in cages and things. That's what they will start doing in a bit. Lord! They haven't begun on us yet. Don't you see that?'

'Not begun!' I exclaimed.

'Not begun. All that's happened so far is through our not having the sense to keep quiet – worrying them with guns and such foolery. And losing our heads, and rushing off in crowds to where there wasn't any more safety than where we were. They don't want to bother us yet. They're making their things – making all the things they couldn't bring with them, getting things ready for the rest of their people. Very likely that's why the cylinders have stopped for a bit, for fear of hitting those who are here. And instead of our rushing about blind, on the howl, or getting dynamite on the chance of busting them up, we've got to fix ourselves up according to the new state of affairs. That's how I figure it out. It isn't quite according to what a man wants for his species, but it's about what the facts point to. And that's the principle I acted upon. Cities, nations, civilization, progress – it's all over. That game's up. We're beat.'

'But if that is so, what is there to live for?'

The artilleryman looked at me for a moment.

'There won't be any more blessed concerts for a million years or so; there won't be any Royal Academy of Arts, and no nice little feeds at restaurants. If it's amusement you're after, I reckon the game is up. If you've got any

drawing-room manners or a dislike to eating peas with a knife or dropping aitches, you'd better chuck 'em away. They ain't no further use.'

'You mean ——'

'I mean that men like me are going on living – for the sake of the breed. I tell you, I'm grim set on living. And if I'm not mistaken, you'll show what insides *you've* got, too, before long. We aren't going to be exterminated. And I don't mean to be caught either, and tamed and fattened and bred like a thundering ox. Ugh! Fancy those brown creepers!'

'You don't mean to say ——'

'I do. I'm going on, under their feet. I've got it planned; I've thought it out. We men are beat. We don't know enough. We've got to learn before we've got a chance. And we've got to live and keep independent while we learn. See! That's what has to be done.'

I stared, astonished, and stirred profoundly by the man's resolution.

'Great God!' cried I. 'But you are a man indeed!' And suddenly I gripped his hand.

'Eh!' he said, with his eyes shining. 'I've thought it out, eh?'

'Go on,' I said.

'Well, those who mean to escape their catching must get ready. I'm getting ready. Mind you, it isn't all of us that are made for wild beasts; and that's what it's got to be. That's why I watched you. I had my doubts. You're slender. I didn't know that it was you, you see, or just how you'd been buried. All these – the sort of people that lived in these houses, and all those damn little clerks that used to live down that way – they'd be no good. They haven't any spirit in them – no proud dreams and no proud lusts; and a man who hasn't one or the other – Lord! What is he but funk and precautions? They just used to skedaddle off to work – I've seen hundreds of 'em, bit of breakfast in hand, running wild and shining to catch their little season-ticket train, for fear they'd get dismissed if they didn't; working at businesses they were afraid to take the trouble to understand; skedaddling back for fear they wouldn't be in time for dinner; keeping indoors after dinner for fear of the back streets, and sleeping with the wives they married, not because they wanted them, but because they had a bit of money that would make for safety in their one little miserable skedaddle through the world. Lives insured and a bit invested for fear of accidents. And on Sundays – fear of the hereafter. As if hell was built for rabbits! Well, the Martians will just be a godsend to these. Nice roomy cages, fattening food, careful breeding, no worry. After a week or so chasing about the fields and lands on empty stomachs, they'll come and be caught cheerful. They'll be quite glad after a bit. They'll wonder what people did before there were Martians to take care of them. And the bar loafers, and mashers, and singers – I can imagine them. I can imagine them,' he said, with a sort of sombre gratification. 'There'll be any amount of sentiment and religion loose among them.

THE WAR OF THE WORLDS

There's hundreds of things I saw with my eyes that I've only begun to see clearly these last few days. There's lots will take things as they are – fat and stupid; and lots will be worried by a sort of feeling that it's all wrong, and that they ought to be doing something. Now whenever things are so that a lot of people feel they ought to be doing something, the weak, and those who go weak with a lot of complicated thinking, always make for a sort of do-nothing religion, very pious and superior, and submit to persecution and the will of the Lord. Very likely you've seen the same thing. It's energy in a gale of funk, and turned clean inside out. These cages will be full of psalms and hymns and piety. And those of a less simple sort will work in a bit of – what is it? – eroticism.'

He paused.

'Very likely these Martians will make pets of some of them; train them to do tricks – who knows? – get sentimental over the pet boy who grew up and had to be killed. And some, maybe, they will train to hunt us.'

'No,' I cried, 'that's impossible! No human being ——'

'What's the good of going on with such lies?' said the artilleryman. 'There's men who'd do it cheerful. What nonsense to pretend there isn't!'

And I succumbed to his conviction.

'If they come after me,' he said; 'Lord, if they come after me!' and subsided into a grim meditation.

I sat contemplating these things. I could find nothing to bring against this man's reasoning. In the days before the invasion no one would have questioned my intellectual superiority to his – I, a professed and recognized writer on philosophical themes, and he, a common soldier; and yet he had already formulated a situation that I had scarcely realized.

'What are you doing?' I said presently. 'What plans have you made?'

He hesitated.

'Well, it's like this,' he said. 'What have we to do? We have to invent a sort of life where men can live and breed, and be sufficiently secure to bring the children up. Yes – wait a bit, and I'll make it clearer what I think ought to be done. The tame ones will go like all tame beasts; in a few generations they'll be big, beautiful, rich-blooded, stupid – rubbish! The risk is that we who keep wild will go savage – degenerate into a sort of big, savage rat . . . You see, how I mean to live is underground. I've been thinking about the drains. Of course those who don't know drains think horrible things; but under this London are miles and miles – hundreds of miles – and a few days rain and London empty will leave them sweet and clean. The main drains are big enough and airy enough for anyone. Then there's cellars, vaults, stores, from which bolting passages may be made to the drains. And the railway tunnels and subways. Eh? You begin to see? And we form a band – able-bodied, clean-minded men. We're not going to pick up any rubbish that drifts in. Weaklings go out again.'

'As you meant me to go?'

'Well – I parleyed, didn't I?'

'We won't quarrel about that. Go on.'

'Those who stop obey orders. Able-bodied, clean-minded women we want also – mothers and teachers. No lackadaisical ladies – no blasted rolling eyes. We can't have any weak or silly. Life is real again, and the useless and cumbersome and mischievous have to die. They ought to die. They ought to be willing to die. It's a sort of disloyalty, after all, to live and taint the race. And they can't be happy. Moreover, dying's none so dreadful; it's the funking makes it bad. And in all those places we shall gather. Our district will be London. And we may even be able to keep a watch, and run about in the open when the Martians keep away. Play cricket, perhaps. That's how we shall save the race. Eh? It's a possible thing? But saving the race is nothing in itself. As I say, that's only being rats. It's saving our knowledge and adding to it is the thing. There men like you come in. There's books, there's models. We must make great safe places down deep, and get all the books we can; not novels and poetry swipes, but ideas, science books. That's where men like you come in. We must go to the British Museum and pick all those books through. Especially we must keep up our science – learn more. We must watch these Martians. Some of us must go as spies. When it's all working, perhaps I will. Get caught, I mean. And the great thing is, we must leave the Martians alone. We mustn't even steal. If we get in their way, we clear out. We must show them we mean no harm. Yes, I know. But they're intelligent things, and they won't hunt us down if they have all they want, and think we're just harmless vermin.'

The artilleryman paused and laid a brown hand upon my arm.

'After all, it may not be so much we may have to learn before – Just imagine this: four or five of their fighting machines suddenly starting off – Heat-Rays right and left, and not a Martian in 'em. Not a Martian in 'em, but men – men who have learned the way how. It may be in my time, even – those men. Fancy having one of them lovely things, with its Heat-Ray wide and free! Fancy having it in control! What would it matter if you smashed to smithereens at the end of the run, after a bust like that? I reckon the Martians'll open their beautiful eyes! Can't you see them, man? Can't you see them hurrying, hurrying – puffing and blowing and hooting to their other mechanical affairs? Something out of gear in every case. And swish, bang, rattle, swish! Just as they are fumbling over it, *swish* comes the Heat-Ray, and, behold! Man has come back to his own.'

For a while the imaginative daring of the artilleryman, and the tone of assurance and courage he assumed, completely dominated my mind. I believed unhesitatingly both in his forecast of human destiny and in the practicability of his astonishing scheme, and the reader who thinks me susceptible and foolish must contrast his position, reading steadily with all

his thoughts about his subject, and mine, crouching fearfully in the bushes and listening, distracted by apprehension. We talked in this manner through the early morning time, and later crept out of the bushes, and, after scanning the sky for Martians, hurried precipitately to the house on Putney Hill where he had made his lair. It was the coal cellar of the place, and when I saw the work he had spent a week upon – it was a burrow scarcely ten yards long, which he designed to reach to the main drain on Putney Hill – I had my first inkling of the gulf between his dreams and his powers. Such a hole I could have dug in a day. But I believed in him sufficiently to work with him all that morning until past midday at his digging. We had a garden-barrow and shot the earth we removed against the kitchen range. We refreshed ourselves with a tin of mock-turtle soup and wine from the neighbouring pantry. I found a curious relief from the aching strangeness of the world in this steady labour. As we worked, I turned his project over in my mind, and presently objections and doubts began to arise; but I worked there all the morning, so glad was I to find myself with a purpose again. After working an hour I began to speculate on the distance one had to go before the cloaca was reached, the chances we had of missing it altogether. My immediate trouble was why we should dig this long tunnel, when it was possible to get into the drain at once down one of the manholes, and work back to the house. It seemed to me, too, that the house was inconveniently chosen, and required a needless length of tunnel. And just as I was beginning to face these things, the artilleryman stopped digging, and looked at me.

'We're working well,' he said. He put down his spade. 'Let us knock off a bit' he said. 'I think it's time we reconnoitred from the roof of the house.'

I was for going on, and after a little hesitation he resumed his spade; and then suddenly I was struck by a thought. I stopped, and so did he at once.

'Why were you walking about the common,' I said, 'instead of being here?'

'Taking the air,' he said. 'I was coming back. It's safer by night.'

'But the work?'

'Oh, one can't always work,' he said, and in a flash I saw the man plain. He hesitated, holding his spade. 'We ought to reconnoitre now,' he said, 'because if any come near they may hear the spades and drop upon us unawares.'

I was no longer disposed to object. We went together to the roof and stood on a ladder peeping out of the roof door. No Martians were to be seen, and we ventured out on the tiles, and slipped down under shelter of the parapet.

From this position a shrubbery hid the greater portion of Putney, but we could see the river below, a bubbly mass of red weed, and the low parts of Lambeth flooded and red. The red creeper swarmed up the trees about the old palace, and their branches stretched gaunt and dead, and set with shrivelled leaves, from amid its clusters. It was strange how entirely dependent

both these things were upon flowing water for their propagation. About us neither had gained a footing; laburnums, pink mays, snowballs, and trees of arbor-vitae, rose out of laurels and hydrangeas, green and brilliant into the sunlight. Beyond Kensington dense smoke was rising, and that and a blue haze hid the northward hills.

The artilleryman began to tell me of the sort of people who still remained in London.

'One night last week,' he said, 'some fools got the electric light in order, and there was all Regent Street and the Circus ablaze, crowded with painted and ragged drunkards, men and women, dancing and shouting till dawn. A man who was there told me. And as the day came they became aware of a fighting-machine standing near by the Langham and looking down at them. Heaven knows how long he had been there. It must have given some of them a nasty turn. He came down the road towards them, and picked up nearly a hundred too drunk or frightened to run away.'

Grotesque gleam of a time no history will ever fully describe!

From that, in answer to my questions, he came round to his grandiose plans again. He grew enthusiastic. He talked so eloquently of the possibility of capturing a fighting-machine that I more than half believed in him again. But now that I was beginning to understand something of his quality, I could divine the stress he laid on doing nothing precipitately. And I noted that now there was no question that he personally was to capture and fight the great machine.

After a time we went down to the cellar. Neither of us seemed disposed to resume digging, and when he suggested a meal, I was nothing loath. He became suddenly very generous, and when we had eaten he went away and returned with some excellent cigars. We lit these, and his optimism glowed. He was inclined to regard my coming as a great occasion.

'There's some champagne in the cellar,' he said.

'We can dig better on this Thames-side burgundy,' said I.

'No,' said he; 'I am host today. Champagne! Great God! We've a heavy enough task before us! Let us take a rest and gather strength while we may. Look at these blistered hands!'

And pursuant to this idea of a holiday, he insisted upon playing cards after we had eaten. He taught me euchre, and after dividing London between us, I taking the northern side and he the southern, we played for parish points. Grotesque and foolish as this will seem to the sober reader, it is absolutely true, and what is more remarkable, I found the card game and several others we played extremely interesting.

Strange mind of man that, with our species upon the edge of extermination or appalling degradation, with no clear prospect before us but the chance of a horrible death, we could sit following the chance of this painted pasteboard, and playing the 'joker' with vivid delight. Afterwards he taught me

poker, and I beat him at three tough chess games. When dark came we decided to take the risk, and lit a lamp.

After an interminable string of games, we supped, and the artilleryman finished the champagne. We went on smoking the cigars. He was no longer the energetic regenerator of his species I had encountered in the morning. He was still optimistic, but it was a less kinetic, a more thoughtful optimism. I remember he wound up with my health, proposed in a speech of small variety and considerable intermittence. I took a cigar, and went upstairs to look at the lights of which he had spoken that blazed so greenly along the Highgate hills.

At first I stared unintelligently across the London valley. The northern hills were shrouded in darkness; the fires near Kensington glowed redly, and now and then an orange-red tongue of flame flashed up and vanished in the deep blue night. All the rest of London was black. Then, nearer, I perceived a strange light, a pale, violet-purple fluorescent glow, quivering under the night breeze. For a space I could not understand it, and then I knew that it must be the red weed from which this faint irradiation proceeded. With that realization my dormant sense of wonder, my sense of the proportion of things, awoke again. I glanced from that to Mars, red and clear, glowing high in the west, and then gazed long and earnestly at the darkness of Hampstead and Highgate.

I remained a very long time upon the roof, wondering at the grotesque changes of the day. I recalled my mental states from the midnight prayer to the foolish card-playing. I had a violent revulsion of feeling. I remember I flung away the cigar with a certain wasteful symbolism. My folly came to me with glaring exaggeration. I seemed a traitor to my wife and to my kind; I was filled with remorse. I resolved to leave this strange undisciplined dreamer of great things to his drink and gluttony, and to go on into London. There, it seemed to me, I had the best chance of learning what the Martians and my fellowmen were doing. I was still upon the roof when the late moon rose.

CHAPTER VIII

Dead London

After I had parted from the artilleryman, I went down the hill, and by the High Street across the bridge to Fulham. The red weed was tumultuous at that time, and nearly choked the bridge roadway; but its fronds were already whitened in patches by the spreading disease that presently removed it so swiftly.

At the corner of the lane that runs to Putney Bridge station I found a man lying. He was as black as a sweep with the black dust, alive, but help-lessly and speechlessly drunk. I could get nothing from him but curses and furious lunges at my head. I think I should have stayed by him but for the brutal expression of his face.

There was black dust along the roadway from the bridge onwards, and it grew thicker in Fulham. The streets were horribly quiet. I got food – sour, hard, and mouldy, but quite eatable – in a baker's shop here. Some way towards Walham Green the streets became clear of powder, and I passed a white terrace of houses on fire; the noise of the burning was an absolute relief. Going on towards Brompton, the streets were quiet again.

Here I came once more upon the black powder in the streets and upon dead bodies. I saw altogether about a dozen in the length of the Fulham Road. They had been dead many days, so that I hurried quickly past them. The black powder covered them over, and softened their outlines. One or two had been disturbed by dogs.

Where there was no black powder, it was curiously like a Sunday in the City, with the closed shops, the houses locked up and the blinds drawn, the desertion, and the stillness. In some places plunderers had been at work, but rarely at other than the provision and wine shops. A jeweller's window had been broken open in one place, but apparently the thief had been disturbed, and a number of gold chains and a watch lay scattered on the pavement. I did not trouble to touch them. Further on was a tattered woman in a heap on a doorstep; the hand that hung over her knee was gashed and bled down her rusty brown dress, and a smashed magnum of champagne formed a pool across the pavement. She seemed asleep, but she was dead.

The further I penetrated into London, the profounder grew the stillness. But it was not so much the stillness of death – it was the stillness of suspense, of expectation. At any time the destruction that had already singed the north-western borders of the metropolis, and had annihilated Ealing and Kilburn, might strike among these houses and leave them smoking ruins. It was a city condemned and derelict . . .

In South Kensington the streets were clear of dead and of black powder. It was near South Kensington that I first heard the howling. It crept almost imperceptibly upon my senses. It was a sobbing alternation of two notes, 'Ulla, ulla, ulla, ulla,' keeping on perpetually. When I passed streets that ran northward it grew in volume, and houses and buildings seemed to deaden and cut it off again. It came in a full tide down Exhibition Road. I stopped, staring towards Kensington Gardens, wondering at this strange, remote wailing. It was as if that mighty desert of houses had found a voice for its fear and solitude.

'Ulla, ulla, ulla, ulla,' wailed that superhuman note – great waves of sound sweeping down the broad, sunlit roadway, between the tall buildings on each side. I turned northwards, marvelling, towards the iron gates of Hyde Park. I had half a mind to break into the Natural History Museum and find my way up to the summits of the towers, in order to see across the park. But I decided to keep to the ground, where quick hiding was possible, and so went on up the Exhibition Road. All the large mansions on each side of the road were empty and still, and my footsteps echoed against the sides of the houses. At the top, near the park gate, I came upon a strange sight – a bus over-turned, and the skeleton of a horse picked clean. I puzzled over this for a time, and then went on to the bridge over the Serpentine. The voice grew stronger and stronger, though I could see nothing above the housetops on the north side of the park, save a haze of smoke to the north-west.

'Ulla, ulla, ulla, ulla,' cried the voice, coming, as it seemed to me, from the district about Regent's Park. The desolating cry worked upon my mind. The mood that had sustained me passed. The wailing took possession of me. I found I was intensely weary, footsore, and now again hungry and thirsty.

It was already past noon. Why was I wandering alone in this city of the dead? Why was I alone when all London was lying in state, and in its black shroud? I felt intolerably lonely. My mind ran on old friends that I had forgotten for years. I thought of the poisons in the chemists' shops, of the liquors the wine merchants stored; I recalled the two sodden creatures of despair, who so far as I knew, shared the city with myself . . .

I came into Oxford Street by the Marble Arch, and here again were black powder and several bodies, and an evil, ominous smell from the gratings of the cellars of some of the houses. I grew very thirsty after the heat of my long walk. With infinite trouble I managed to break into a public-house and get food and drink. I was weary after eating, and went into the parlour behind the bar, and slept on a black horsehair sofa I found there.

I awoke to find that dismal howling still in my ears, 'Ulla, ulla, ulla, ulla.' It was now dusk, and after I had routed out some biscuits and a cheese in the bar – there was a meat safe, but it contained nothing but maggots – I wandered on through the silent residential squares to Baker Street – Portman

Square is the only one I can name – and so came out at last upon Regent's Park. And as I emerged from the top of Baker Street, I saw far away over the trees in the clearness of the sunset the hood of the Martian giant from which this howling proceeded. I was not terrified. I came upon him as if it were a matter of course. I watched him for some time, but he did not move. He appeared to be standing and yelling, for no reason that I could discover.

I tried to formulate a plan of action. That perpetual sound of 'Ulla, ulla, ulla, ulla,' confused my mind. Perhaps I was too tired to be very fearful. Certainly I was more curious to know the reason of this monotonous crying than afraid. I turned back away from the park and struck into Park Road, intending to skirt the park, went along under the shelter of the terraces, and got a view of this stationary, howling Martian from the direction of St John's Wood. A couple of hundred yards out of Baker Street I heard a yelping chorus, and saw, first a dog with a piece of putrescent red meat in his jaws coming headlong towards me, and then a pack of starving mongrels in pursuit of him. He made a wide curve to avoid me, as though he feared I might prove a fresh competitor. As the yelping died away down the silent road, the wailing sound of 'Ulla, ulla, ulla, ulla,' reasserted itself.

I came upon the wrecked handling-machine halfway to St. John's Wood station. At first I thought a house had fallen across the road. It was only as I clambered among the ruins that I saw, with a start, this mechanical Samson lying, with its tentacles bent and smashed and twisted, among the ruins it had made. The forepart was shattered. It seemed as if it had driven blindly straight at the house, and had been overwhelmed in its overthrow. It seemed to me then that this might have happened by a handling-machine escaping from the guidance of its Martian. I could not clamber among the ruins to see it, and the twilight was now so far advanced that the blood with which its seat was smeared, and the gnawed gristle of the Martian that the dogs had left, were invisible to me.

Wondering still more at all that I had seen, I pushed on towards Primrose Hill. Far away, through a gap in the trees, I saw a second Martian, as motionless as the first, standing in the park towards the Zoological Gardens, and silent. A little beyond the ruins about the smashed handling-machine I came upon the red weed again, and found the Regent's Canal, a spongy mass of dark-red vegetation.

As I crossed the bridge, the sound of 'Ulla, ulla, ulla, ulla,' ceased. It was, as it were, cut off. The silence came like a thunderclap.

The dusky houses about me stood faint and tall and dim; the trees towards the park were growing black. All about me the red weed clambered among the ruins, writhing to get above me in the dimness. Night, the mother of fear and mystery, was coming upon me. But while that voice sounded the solitude, the desolation, had been endurable; by virtue of it London had still seemed alive, and the sense of life about me had upheld me. Then

suddenly a change, the passing of something – I knew not what – and then a stillness that could be felt. Nothing but this gaunt quiet.

London about me gazed at me spectrally. The windows in the white houses were like the eye sockets of skulls. About me my imagination found a thousand noiseless enemies moving. Terror seized me, a horror of my temerity. In front of me the road became pitchy black as though it was tarred, and I saw a contorted shape lying across the pathway. I could not bring myself to go on. I turned down St John's Wood Road, and ran headlong from this unendurable stillness towards Kilburn. I hid from the night and the silence, until long after midnight, in a cabmen's shelter in Harrow Road. But before the dawn my courage returned, and while the stars were still in the sky I turned once more towards Regent's Park. I missed my way among the streets, and presently saw down a long avenue, in the half-light of the early dawn, the curve of Primrose Hill. On the summit, towering up to the fading stars, was a third Martian, erect and motionless like the others.

An insane resolve possessed me. I would die and end it. And I would save myself even the trouble of killing myself. I marched on recklessly towards this Titan, and then, as I drew nearer and the light grew, I saw that a multitude of black birds was circling and clustering about the hood. At that my heart gave a bound, and I began running along the road.

I hurried through the red weed that choked St Edmund's Terrace (I waded breast-high across a torrent of water that was rushing down from the waterworks towards the Albert Road), and emerged upon the grass before the rising of the sun. Great mounds had been heaped about the crest of the hill, making a huge redoubt of it – it was the final and largest place the Martians had made – and from behind these heaps there rose a thin smoke against the sky. Against the sky line an eager dog ran and disappeared. The thought that had flashed into my mind grew real, grew credible. I felt no fear, only a wild, trembling exultation, as I ran up the hill towards the motionless monster. Out of the hood hung lank shreds of brown, at which the hungry birds pecked and tore.

In another moment I had scrambled up the earthen rampart and stood upon its crest, and the interior of the redoubt was below me. A mighty space it was, with gigantic machines here and there within it, huge mounds of material and strange shelter places. And scattered about it, some in their overturned war-machines, some in the now rigid handling-machines, and a dozen of them stark and silent and laid in a row, were the Martians – *dead!* – slain by the putrefactive and disease bacteria against which their systems were unprepared; slain as the red weed was being slain; slain, after all man's devices had failed, by the humblest things that God, in his wisdom, has put upon this earth.

For so it had come about, as indeed I and many men might have foreseen had not terror and disaster blinded our minds. These germs of disease have

taken toll of humanity since the beginning of things – taken toll of our prehuman ancestors since life began here. But by virtue of this natural selection of our kind we have developed resisting power; to no germs do we succumb without a struggle, and to many – those that cause putrefaction in dead matter, for instance – our living frames are altogether immune. But there are no bacteria in Mars, and directly these invaders arrived, directly they drank and fed, our microscopic allies began to work their overthrow. Already when I watched them they were irrevocably doomed, dying and rotting even as they went to and fro. It was inevitable. By the toll of a billion deaths man has bought his birthright of the earth, and it is his against all comers; it would still be his were the Martians ten times as mighty as they are. For neither do men live nor die in vain.

Here and there they were scattered, nearly fifty altogether, in that great gulf they had made, overtaken by a death that must have seemed to them as incomprehensible as any death could be. To me also at that time this death was incomprehensible. All I knew was that these things that had been alive and so terrible to men were dead. For a moment I believed that the destruction of Sennacherib had been repeated, that God had repented, that the Angel of Death had slain them in the night.

I stood staring into the pit, and my heart lightened gloriously, even as the rising sun struck the world to fire about me with his rays. The pit was still in darkness; the mighty engines, so great and wonderful in their power and complexity, so unearthly in their tortuous forms, rose weird and vague and strange out of the shadows towards the light. A multitude of dogs, I could hear, fought over the bodies that lay darkly in the depth of the pit, far below me. Across the pit on its further lip, flat and vast and strange, lay the great flying-machine with which they had been experimenting upon our denser atmosphere when decay and death arrested them. Death had come not a day too soon. At the sound of a cawing overhead I looked up at the huge fighting-machine that would fight no more for ever, at the tattered red shreds of flesh that dripped down upon the overturned seats on the summit of Primrose Hill.

I turned and looked down the slope of the hill to where, enhaloed now in birds, stood those other two Martians that I had seen overnight, just as death had overtaken them. The one had died, even as it had been crying to its companions; perhaps it was the last to die, and its voice had gone on perpetually until the force of its machinery was exhausted. They glittered now, harmless tripod towers of shining metal, in the brightness of the rising sun.

All about the pit, and saved as by a miracle from everlasting destruction, stretched the great Mother of Cities. Those who have only seen London veiled in her sombre robes of smoke can scarcely imagine the naked clearness and beauty of the silent wilderness of houses.

Eastward, over the blackened ruins of the Albert Terrace and the splintered spire of the church, the sun blazed dazzling in a clear sky, and here and there some facet in the great wilderness of roofs caught the light and glared with a white intensity.

Northward were Kilburn and Hampsted, blue and crowded with houses; westward the great city was dimmed; and southward, beyond the Martians, the green waves of Regent's Park, the Langham Hotel, the dome of the Albert Hall, the Imperial Institute and the giant mansions of the Brompton Road came out clear and little in the sunrise, the jagged ruins of Westminster rising hazily beyond. Far away and blue were the Surrey hills, and the towers of the Crystal Palace glittered like two silver rods. The dome of St Paul's was dark against the sunrise, and injured, I saw for the first time, by a huge gaping cavity on its western side.

And as I looked at this wide expanse of houses and factories and churches, silent and abandoned; as I thought of the multitudinous hopes and efforts, the innumerable hosts of lives that had gone to build this human reef, and of the swift and ruthless destruction that had hung over it all; when I realized that the shadow had been rolled back, and that men might still live in the streets, and this dear vast dead city of mine be once more alive and powerful, I felt a wave of emotion that was near akin to tears.

The torment was over. Even that day the healing would begin. The survivors of the people scattered over the country – leaderless, lawless, foodless, like sheep without a shepherd – the thousands who had fled by sea, would begin to return; the pulse of life, growing stronger and stronger, would beat again in the empty streets and pour across the vacant squares. Whatever destruction was done, the hand of the destroyer was stayed. All the gaunt wrecks, the blackened skeletons of houses that stared so dismally at the sunlit grass of the hill, would presently be echoing with the hammers of the restorers and ringing with the tapping of their trowels. At the thought I extended my hands towards the sky and began thanking God. In a year, thought I – in a year . . .

With overwhelming force came the thought of myself, of my wife, and the old life of hope and tender helpfulness that had ceased for ever.

CHAPTER IX

Wreckage

And now comes the strangest thing in my story. Yet, perhaps, it is not alto-gether strange. I remember, clearly and coldly and vividly, all that I did that day until the time that I stood weeping and praising God upon the summit of Primrose Hill. And then I forget.

Of the next three days I know nothing. I have learned since that, so far from my being the first discoverer of the Martian overthrow, several such wanderers as myself had already discovered this on the previous night. One man – the first – had gone to St Martin's-le-Grand, and, while I sheltered in the cabmen's hut, had contrived to telegraph to Paris. Thence the joyful news had flashed all over the world; a thousand cities, chilled by ghastly apprehensions, suddenly flashed into frantic illumina-tions; they knew of it in Dublin, Edinburgh, Manchester, Birmingham, at the time when I stood upon the verge of the pit. Already men, weeping with joy, as I have heard, shouting and staying their work to shake hands and shout, were making up trains, even as near as Crewe, to descend upon London. The church bells that had ceased a fortnight since suddenly caught the news, until all England was bell-ringing. Men on cycles, lean-faced, unkempt, scorched along every country lane shouting of unhoped deliverance, shouting to gaunt, staring figures of despair. And for the food! Across the Channel, across the Irish Sea, across the Atlantic, corn, bread, and meat were tearing to our relief. All the shipping in the world seemed going Londonward in those days. But of all this I have no memory. I drifted – a demented man. I found myself in a house of kindly people, who had found me on the third day wandering, weeping, and raving through the streets of St John's Wood. They have told me since that I was singing some insane doggerel about 'The Last Man Left Alive! Hurrah! The Last Man Left Alive!' Troubled as they were with their own affairs, these people, whose name, much as I would like to express my gratitude to them, I may not even give here, nevertheless cumbered themselves with me, sheltered me, and protected me from myself. Apparently they had learned something of my story from me during the days of my lapse.

Very gently, when my mind was assured again, did they break to me what they had learned of the fate of Leatherhead. Two days after I was imprisoned it had been destroyed, with every soul in it, by a Martian. He had swept it out of existence, as it seemed, without any provocation, as a boy might crush an ant hill, in the mere wantonness of power.

I was a lonely man, and they were very kind to me. I was a lonely man and a sad one, and they bore with me. I remained with them four days after my recovery. All that time I felt a vague, a growing craving to look once more on whatever remained of the little life that seemed so happy and bright in my past. It was a mere hopeless desire to feast upon my misery. They dissuaded me. They did all they could to divert me from this morbidity. But at last I could resist the impulse no longer, and, promising faithfully to return to them, and parting, as I will confess, from these four-day friends with tears, I went out again into the streets that had lately been so dark and strange and empty.

Already they were busy with returning people; in places even there were shops open, and I saw a drinking fountain running water.

I remember how mockingly bright the day seemed as I went back on my melancholy pilgrimage to the little house at Woking, how busy the streets and vivid the moving life about me. So many people were abroad everywhere, busied in a thousand activities, that it seemed incredible that any great proportion of the population could have been slain. But then I noticed how yellow were the skins of the people I met, how shaggy the hair of the men, how large and bright their eyes, and that every other man still wore his dirty rags. Their faces seemed all with one of two expressions – a leaping exultation and energy or a grim resolution. Save for the expression of the faces, London seemed a city of tramps. The vestries were indiscriminately distributing bread sent us by the French government. The ribs of the few horses showed dismally. Haggard special constables with white badges stood at the corners of every street. I saw little of the mischief wrought by the Martians until I reached Wellington Street, and there I saw the red weed clambering over the buttresses of Waterloo Bridge.

At the corner of the bridge, too, I saw one of the common contrasts of that grotesque time – a sheet of paper flaunting against a thicket of the red weed, transfixed by a stick that kept it in place. It was the placard of the first newspaper to resume publication – the *Daily Mail*. I bought a copy for a blackened shilling I found in my pocket. Most of it was in blank, but the solitary compositor who did the thing had amused himself by making a grotesque scheme of advertisement stereo on the back page. The matter he printed was emotional; the news organization had not as yet found its way back. I learned nothing fresh except that already in one week the examination of the Martian mechanisms had yielded astonishing results. Among other things, the article assured me what I did not believe at the time, that the 'Secret of Flying,' was discovered. At Waterloo I found the free trains that were taking people to their homes. The first rush was already over. There were few people in the train, and I was in no mood for casual conversation. I got a compartment to myself, and sat with folded arms, looking greyly at the sunlit devastation that flowed past the windows. And just

outside the terminus the train jolted over temporary rails, and on either side of the railway the houses were blackened ruins. To Clapham Junction the face of London was grimy with powder of the Black Smoke, in spite of two days of thunderstorms and rain, and at Clapham Junction the line had been wrecked again; there were hundreds of out-of-work clerks and shopmen working side by side with the customary navvies, and we were jolted over a hasty relaying.

All down the line from there the aspect of the country was gaunt and unfamiliar; Wimbledon particularly had suffered. Walton, by virtue of its unburned pine woods, seemed the least hurt of any place along the line. The Wandle, the Mole, every little stream, was a heaped mass of red weed, in appearance between butcher's meat and pickled cabbage. The Surrey pine woods were too dry, however, for the festoons of the red climber. Beyond Wimbledon, within sight of the line, in certain nursery grounds, were the heaped masses of earth about the sixth cylinder. A number of people were standing about it, and some sappers were busy in the midst of it. Over it flaunted a Union Jack, flapping cheerfully in the morning breeze. The nursery grounds were everywhere crimson with the weed, a wide expanse of livid colour cut with purple shadows, and very painful to the eye. One's gaze went with infinite relief from the scorched greys and sullen reds of the foreground to the blue-green softness of the eastward hills.

The line on the London side of Woking station was still undergoing repair, so I descended at Byfleet station and took the road to Maybury, past the place where I and the artilleryman had talked to the hussars, and on by the spot where the Martian had appeared to me in the thunderstorm. Here, moved by curiosity, I turned aside to find, among a tangle of red fronds, the warped and broken dog-cart with the whitened bones of the horse scattered and gnawed. For a time I stood regarding these vestiges . . .

Then I returned through the pine wood, neck-high with red weed here and there, to find the landlord of the Spotted Dog had already found burial, and so came home past the College Arms. A man standing at an open cottage door greeted me by name as I passed.

I looked at my house with a quick flash of hope that faded immediately. The door had been forced; it was unfast and was opening slowly as I approached.

It slammed again. The curtains of my study fluttered out of the open window from which I and the artilleryman had watched the dawn. No one had closed it since. The smashed bushes were just as I had left them nearly four weeks ago. I stumbled into the hall, and the house felt empty. The stair carpet was ruffled and discoloured where I had crouched, soaked to the skin from the thunderstorm the night of the catastrophe. Our muddy footsteps I saw still went up the stairs.

I followed them to my study, and found lying on my writing-table still, with the selenite paper weight upon it, the sheet of work I had left on the afternoon of the opening of the cylinder. For a space I stood reading over my abandoned arguments. It was a paper on the probable development of Moral Ideas with the development of the civilizing process; and the last sentence was the opening of a prophecy: 'In about two hundred years,' I had written, 'we may expect—' The sentence ended abruptly. I remembered my inability to fix my mind that morning, scarcely a month gone by, and how I had broken off to get my *Daily Chronicle* from the newsboy. I remembered how I went down to the garden gate as he came along, and how I had listened to his odd story of 'Men from Mars'.

I came down and went into the dining room. There were the mutton and the bread, both far gone now in decay, and a beer bottle overturned, just as I and the artilleryman had left them. My home was desolate. I perceived the folly of the faint hope I had cherished so long. And then a strange thing occurred. 'It is no use,' said a voice. 'The house is deserted. No one has been here these ten days. Do not stay here to torment yourself. No one escaped but you.'

I was startled. Had I spoken my thought aloud? I turned, and the French window was open behind me. I made a step to it, and stood looking out.

And there, amazed and afraid, even as I stood amazed and afraid, were my cousin and my wife – my wife white and tearless. She gave a faint cry.

'I came,' she said. 'I knew – knew ——'

She put her hand to her throat – swayed. I made a step forward, and caught her in my arms.

CHAPTER X

The Epilogue

I cannot but regret, now that I am concluding my story, how little I am able to contribute to the discussion of the many debatable questions which are still unsettled. In one respect I shall certainly provoke criticism. My particular province is speculative philosophy. My knowledge of comparative physiology is confined to a book or two, but it seems to me that Carver's suggestions as to the reason of the rapid death of the Martians is so probable as to be regarded almost as a proven conclusion. I have assumed that in the body of my narrative.

At any rate, in all the bodies of the Martians that were examined after the war, no bacteria except those already known as terrestrial species were found. That they did not bury any of their dead, and the reckless slaughter they perpetrated, point also to an entire ignorance of the putrefactive process. But probable as this seems, it is by no means a proven conclusion.

Neither is the composition of the Black Smoke known, which the Martians used with such deadly effect, and the generator of the Heat-Rays remains a puzzle. The terrible disasters at the Ealing and South Kensington laboratories have disinclined analysts for further investigations upon the latter. Spectrum analysis of the black powder points unmistakably to the presence of an unknown element with a brilliant group of three lines in the green, and it is possible that it combines with argon to form a compound which acts at once with deadly effect upon some constituent in the blood. But such unproven speculations will scarcely be of interest to the general reader, to whom this story is addressed. None of the brown scum that drifted down the Thames after the destruction of Shepperton was examined at the time, and now none is forthcoming.

The results of an anatomical examination of the Martians, so far as the prowling dogs had left such an examination possible, I have already given. But everyone is familiar with the magnificent and almost complete specimen in spirits at the Natural History Museum, and the countless drawings that have been made from it; and beyond that the interest of their physiology and structure is purely scientific.

A question of graver and universal interest is the possibility of another attack from the Martians. I do not think that nearly enough attention is being given to this aspect of the matter. At present the planet Mars is in conjunction, but with every return to opposition I, for one, anticipate a renewal of their adventure. In any case, we should be prepared. It seems to me that it should be possible to define the position of the gun from which

the shots are discharged, to keep a sustained watch upon this part of the planet, and to anticipate the arrival of the next attack.

In that case the cylinder might be destroyed with dynamite or artillery before it was sufficiently cool for the Martians to emerge, or they might be butchered by means of guns so soon as the screw opened. It seems to me that they have lost a vast advantage in the failure of their first surprise. Possibly they see it in the same light.

Lessing has advanced excellent reasons for supposing that the Martians have actually succeeded in effecting a landing on the planet Venus. Seven months ago now, Venus and Mars were in alignment with the sun; that is to say, Mars was in opposition from the point of view of an observer on Venus. Subsequently a peculiar luminous and sinuous marking appeared on the unillumined half of the inner planet, and almost simultaneously a faint dark mark of a similar sinuous character was detected upon a photograph of the Martian disk. One needs to see the drawings of these appearances in order to appreciate fully their remarkable resemblance in character.

At any rate, whether we expect another invasion or not, our views of the human future must be greatly modified by these events. We have learned now that we cannot regard this planet as being fenced in and a secure abiding-place for Man; we can never anticipate the unseen good or evil that may come upon us suddenly out of space. It may be that in the larger design of the universe this invasion from Mars is not without its ultimate benefit for men; it has robbed us of that serene confidence in the future which is the most fruitful source of decadence, the gifts to human science it has brought are enormous, and it has done much to promote the conception of the commonweal of mankind. It may be that across the immensity of space the Martians have watched the fate of these pioneers of theirs and learned their lesson, and that on the planet Venus they have found a securer settlement. Be that as it may, for many years yet there will certainly be no relaxation of the eager scrutiny of the Martian disk, and those fiery darts of the sky, the shooting stars, will bring with them as they fall an unavoidable apprehension to all the sons of men.

The broadening of men's views that has resulted can scarcely be exaggerated. Before the cylinder fell there was a general persuasion that through all the deep of space no life existed beyond the petty surface of our minute sphere. Now we see further. If the Martians can reach Venus, there is no reason to suppose that the thing is impossible for men, and when the slow cooling of the sun makes this earth uninhabitable, as at last it must do, it may be that the thread of life that has begun here will have streamed out and caught our sister planet within its toils.

Dim and wonderful is the vision I have conjured up in my mind of life spreading slowly from this little seed-bed of the solar system throughout the inanimate vastness of sidereal space. But that is a remote dream. It may be,

on the other hand, that the destruction of the Martians is only a reprieve. To them, and not to us, perhaps, is the future ordained.

I must confess the stress and danger of the time have left an abiding sense of doubt and insecurity in my mind. I sit in my study writing by lamp-light, and suddenly I see again the healing valley below set with writhing flames, and feel the house behind and about me empty and desolate. I go out into the Byfleet Road, and vehicles pass me, a butcher-boy in a cart, a cabful of visitors, a workman on a bicycle, children going to school, and suddenly they become vague and unreal, and I hurry again with the artilleryman through the hot, brooding silence. Of a night I see the black powder darkening the silent streets, and the contorted bodies shrouded in that layer; they rise upon me tattered and dog-bitten. They gibber and grow fiercer, paler, uglier, mad distortions of humanity at last, and I wake, cold and wretched, in the darkness of the night.

I go to London and see the busy multitudes in Fleet Street and the Strand, and it comes across my mind that they are but the ghosts of the past, haunting the streets that I have seen silent and wretched, going to and fro, phantasms in a dead city, the mockery of life in a galvanized body. And strange, too, it is to stand on Primrose Hill, as I did but a day before writing this last chapter, to see the great province of houses, dim and blue through the haze of the smoke and mist, vanishing at last into the vague lower sky, to see the people walking to and fro among the flower-beds on the hill, to see the sightseers about the Martian machine that stands there still, to hear the tumult of playing children, and to recall the time when I saw it all bright and clear-cut, hard and silent, under the dawn of that last great day . . .

And strangest of all is it to hold my wife's hand again, and to think that I have counted her, and that she has counted me, among the dead.

THE ISLAND OF DOCTOR MOREAU

CONTENTS

CONTENTS

INTRODUCTION

On February the 1st 1887, the *Lady Vain* was lost by collision with a derelict when about the latitude 1° S and longitude 107° W.

On January the 5th, 1888 – that is eleven months and four days after – my uncle, Edward Prendick, a private gentleman, who certainly went aboard the *Lady Vain* at Callao, and who had been considered drowned, was picked up in latitude 5° 3' S and longitude 101° W in a small open boat of which the name was illegible, but which is supposed to have belonged to the missing schooner *Ipecacuanha*. He gave such a strange account of himself that he was supposed demented. Subsequently he alleged that his mind was a blank from the moment of his escape from the *Lady Vain*. His case was discussed among psychologists at the time as a curious instance of the lapse of memory consequent upon physical and mental stress. The following narrative was found among his papers by the undersigned, his nephew and heir, but unaccompanied by any definite request for publication.

The only island known to exist in the region in which my uncle was picked up is Noble's Isle, a small volcanic islet and uninhabited. It was visited in 1891 by *H. M. S. Scorpion*. A party of sailors then landed, but found nothing living thereon except certain curious white moths, some hogs and rabbits, and some rather peculiar rats. So that this narrative is without confirmation in its most essential particular. With that understood, there seems no harm in putting this strange story before the public in accordance, as I believe, with my uncle's intentions. There is at least this much in its behalf: my uncle passed out of human knowledge about latitude 5° S and longitude 105° W, and reappeared in the same part of the ocean after a space of eleven months. In some way he must have lived during the interval. And it seems that a schooner called the *Ipecacuanha* with a drunken captain, John Davies, did start from Africa with a puma and certain other animals aboard in January, 1887, that the vessel was well known at several ports in the South Pacific, and that it finally disappeared from those seas (with a considerable amount of copra aboard), sailing to its unknown fate from Bayna in December 1887, a date that tallies entirely with my uncle's story.

CHARLES EDWARD PRENDICK

CHAPTER I

In the Dinghy of the Lady Vain

I do not propose to add anything to what has already been written concerning the loss of the *Lady Vain*. As everyone knows, she collided with a derelict when ten days out from Callao. The longboat, with seven of the crew, was picked up eighteen days after by H. M. gunboat *Myrtle*, and the story of their terrible privations has become quite as well known as the far more horrible *Medusa* case. But I have to add to the published story of the *Lady Vain* another, possibly as horrible and far stranger. It has hitherto been supposed that the four men who were in the dinghy perished, but this is incorrect. I have the best of evidence for this assertion: I was one of the four men.

But in the first place I must state that there never were four men in the dinghy – the number was three. Constans, who was 'seen by the captain to jump into the gig,'* luckily for us and unluckily for himself did not reach us. He came down out of the tangle of ropes under the stays of the smashed bowsprit, some small rope caught his heel as he let go, and he hung for a moment head downward, and then fell and struck a block or spar floating in the water. We pulled towards him, but he never came up.

I say luckily for us he did not reach us, and I might almost say luckily for himself; for we had only a small beaker of water and some soddened ship's biscuits with us, so sudden had been the alarm, so unprepared the ship for any disaster. We thought the people on the launch would be better provisioned (though it seems they were not), and we tried to hail them. They could not have heard us, and the next morning when the drizzle cleared – which was not until past midday – we could see nothing of them. We could not stand up to look about us, because of the pitching of the boat. The two other men who had escaped so far with me were a man named Helmar, a passenger like myself, and a seaman whose name I don't know – a short sturdy man, with a stammer.

We drifted famishing, and, after our water had come to an end, tormented by an intolerable thirst, for eight days altogether. After the second day the sea subsided slowly to a glassy calm. It is quite impossible for the ordinary reader to imagine those eight days. He has not, luckily for himself, anything in his memory to imagine with. After the first day we said little to one another, and lay in our places in the boat and stared at the horizon, or watched, with eyes that grew larger and more haggard every day, the misery

* *Daily News*, 17 March 1887

and weakness gaining upon our companions. The sun became pitiless. The water ended on the fourth day, and we were already thinking strange things and saying them with our eyes; but it was, I think, the sixth before Helmar gave voice to the thing we had all been thinking. I remember our voices were dry and thin, so that we bent towards one another and spared our words. I stood out against it with all my might, was rather for scuttling the boat and perishing together among the sharks that followed us; but when Helmar said that if his proposal was accepted we should have drink, the sailor came round to him.

I would not draw lots however, and in the night the sailor whispered to Helmar again and again, and I sat in the bows with my clasp-knife in my hand, though I doubt if I had the stuff in me to fight; and in the morning I agreed to Helmar's proposal, and we handed halfpence to find the odd man.

The lot fell upon the sailor; but he was the strongest of us and would not abide by it, and attacked Helmar with his hands. They grappled together and almost stood up. I crawled along the boat to them, intending to help Helmar by grasping the sailor's leg; but the sailor stumbled with the swaying of the boat, and the two fell upon the gunwale and rolled overboard together. They sank like stones. I remember laughing at that, and wondering why I laughed. The laugh caught me suddenly like a thing from without.

I lay across one of the thwarts for I know not how long, thinking that if I had the strength I would drink sea-water and madden myself to die quickly. And even as I lay there I saw, with no more interest than if it had been a picture, a sail come up towards me over the skyline. My mind must have been wandering, and yet I remember all that happened, quite distinctly. I remember how my head swayed with the seas, and the horizon with the sail above it danced up and down; but I also remember as distinctly that I had a persuasion that I was dead, and that I thought what a jest it was that they should come too late by such a little to catch me in my body.

For an endless period, as it seemed to me, I lay with my head on the thwart watching the schooner (she was a little ship, schooner-rigged fore and aft) come up out of the sea. She kept tacking to and fro in a widening compass, for she was sailing dead into the wind. It never entered my head to attempt to attract attention, and I do not remember anything distinctly after the sight of her side until I found myself in a little cabin aft. There's a dim half-memory of being lifted up to the gangway, and of a big round countenance covered with freckles and surrounded with red hair staring at me over the bulwarks. I also had a disconnected impression of a dark face, with extraordinary eyes, close to mine; but that I thought was a nightmare, until I met it again. I fancy I recollect some stuff being poured in between my teeth; and that is all.

CHAPTER II

The Man Who Was Going Nowhere.

The cabin in which I found myself was small and rather untidy. A youngish man with flaxen hair, a bristly straw-coloured moustache, and a dropping nether lip, was sitting and holding my wrist. For a minute we stared at each other without speaking. He had watery grey eyes, oddly void of expression. Then just overhead came a sound like an iron bedstead being knocked about, and the low angry growling of some large animal. At the same time the man spoke. He repeated his question, 'How do you feel now?'

I think I said I felt all right. I could not recollect how I had got there. He must have seen the question in my face, for my voice was inaccessible to me.

'You were picked up in a boat, starving. The name on the boat was the *Lady Vain*, and there were spots of blood on the gunwale.'

At the same time my eye caught my hand, so thin that it looked like a dirty skin-purse full of loose bones, and all the business of the boat came back to me.

'Have some of this,' said he, and gave me a dose of some scarlet stuff, iced.

It tasted like blood, and made me feel stronger.

'You were in luck,' said he, 'to get picked up by a ship with a medical man aboard.' He spoke with a slobbering articulation, with the ghost of a lisp.

'What ship is this?' I said slowly, hoarse from my long silence.

'It's a little trader from Arica and Callao. I never asked where she came from in the beginning, – out of the land of born fools, I guess. I'm a passenger myself, from Arica. The silly ass who owns her – he's captain too, named Davis – he's lost his certificate, or something. You know the kind of man – calls the thing the *Ipecacuanha*, of all silly, infernal names; though when there's much of a sea without any wind, she certainly acts according.'

(Then the noise overhead began again, a snarling growl and the voice of a human being together. Then another voice, telling some 'Heaven-forsaken idiot' to desist.)

'You were nearly dead,' said my interlocutor. 'It was a very near thing, indeed. But I've put some stuff into you now. Notice your arm's sore? Injections. You've been insensible for nearly thirty hours.'

I thought slowly. (I was distracted now by the yelping of a number of dogs.) 'Am I eligible for solid food?' I asked.

'Thanks to me,' he said. 'Even now the mutton is boiling.'

'Yes,' I said with assurance; 'I could eat some mutton.'

H. G. WELLS

'But,' said he with a momentary hesitation, 'you know I'm dying to hear of how you came to be alone in that boat.' I thought I detected a certain suspicion in his eyes.

'*Damn that howling!*' He suddenly left the cabin, and I heard him in violent controversy with someone, who seemed to me to talk gibberish in response to him. The matter sounded as though it ended in blows, but in that I thought my ears were mistaken. Then he shouted at the dogs, and returned to the cabin.

'Well?' said he in the doorway. 'You were just beginning to tell me.'

I told him my name, Edward Prendick, and how I had taken to Natural History as a relief from the dullness of my comfortable independence.

He seemed interested in this. 'I've done some science myself. I did my Biology at University College – getting out the ovary of the earthworm and the radula of the snail, and all that. Lord! It's ten years ago. But go on, go on, tell me about the boat!'

He was evidently satisfied with the frankness of my story, which I told in concise sentences enough, for I felt horribly weak; and when it was finished he reverted at once to the topic of Natural History and his own biological studies. He began to question me closely about Tottenham Court Road and Gower Street. 'Is Caplatzi still flourishing? What a shop that was!' He had evidently been a very ordinary medical student, and drifted incontinently to the topic of the music halls. He told me some anecdotes.

'Left it all,' he said, 'ten years ago. How jolly it all used to be! But I made a young ass of myself – played myself out before I was twenty-one. I daresay it's all different now. But I must look up that ass of a cook, and see what he's done to your mutton.'

The growling overhead was renewed, so suddenly and with so much savage anger that it startled me. 'What's that?' I called after him, but the door had closed. He came back again with the boiled mutton, and I was so excited by the appetizing smell of it that I forgot the noise of the beast that had troubled me.

After a day of alternate sleep and feeding I was so far recovered as to be able to get from my bunk to the scuttle, and see the green seas trying to keep pace with us. I judged the schooner was running before the wind. Montgomery – that was the name of the flaxen-haired man – came in again as I stood there, and I asked him for some clothes. He lent me some duck things of his own, for those I had worn in the boat had been thrown overboard. They were rather loose for me, for he was large and long in his limbs. He told me casually that the captain was three-parts drunk in his own cabin. As I assumed the clothes, I began asking him some questions about the destination of the ship. He said the ship was bound to Hawaii, but that it had to land him first.

'Where?' said I.

'It's an island, where I live. So far as I know, it hasn't got a name.'

He stared at me with his nether lip dropping, and looked so wilfully stupid all of a sudden that it came into my head that he desired to avoid my questions. I had the discretion to ask no more.

CHAPTER III

The Strange Face

We left the cabin and found a man at the companion obstructing our way. He was standing on the ladder with his back to us, peering over the combing of the hatchway. He was, I could see, a misshapen man, short, broad, and clumsy, with a crooked back, a hairy neck, and a head sunk between his shoulders. He was dressed in dark-blue serge, and had peculiarly thick, coarse, black hair. I heard the unseen dogs growl furiously, and forthwith he ducked back – coming into contact with the hand I put out to fend him off from myself. He turned with animal swiftness.

In some indefinable way the black face thus flashed upon me shocked me profoundly. It was a singularly deformed one. The facial part projected, forming something dimly suggestive of a muzzle, and the huge half-open mouth showed as big white teeth as I had ever seen in a human mouth. His eyes were bloodshot at the edges, with scarcely a rim of white round the hazel pupils. There was a curious glow of excitement in his face.

'Confound you!' said Montgomery. 'Why the devil don't you get out of the way?'

The black-faced man started aside without a word. I went on up the companion, staring at him instinctively as I did so. Montgomery stayed at the foot for a moment. 'You have no business here, you know,' he said in a deliberate tone. 'Your place is forward.'

The black-faced man cowered. 'They – won't have me forward.' He spoke slowly, with a queer hoarse quality in his voice.

'Won't have you forward!' said Montgomery, in a menacing voice. 'But I tell you to go!' He was on the brink of saying something further, then looked up at me suddenly and followed me up the ladder.

I had paused half way through the hatchway, looking back, still astonished beyond measure at the grotesque ugliness of this black-faced creature. I had never beheld such a repulsive and extraordinary face before, and yet – if the contradiction is credible – I experienced at the same time an odd feeling that in some way I *had* already encountered exactly the features and gestures that now amazed me. Afterwards it occurred to me that probably I had seen him as I was lifted aboard; and yet that scarcely satisfied my suspicion of a previous acquaintance. Yet how one could have set eyes on so singular a face and yet have forgotten the precise occasion, passed my imagination.

Montgomery's movement to follow me released my attention, and I turned and looked about me at the flush deck of the little schooner. I was already half prepared by the sounds I had heard for what I saw. Certainly I never

beheld a deck so dirty. It was littered with scraps of carrot, shreds of green stuff, and indescribable filth. Fastened by chains to the mainmast were a number of grisly staghounds, who now began leaping and barking at me, and by the mizzen a huge puma was cramped in a little iron cage far too small even to give it turning room. Further under the starboard bulwark were some big hutches containing a number of rabbits, and a solitary llama was squeezed in a mere box of a cage forward. The dogs were muzzled by leather straps. The only human being on deck was a gaunt and silent sailor at the wheel.

The patched and dirty spankers were tense before the wind, and up aloft the little ship seemed carrying every sail she had. The sky was clear, the sun midway down the western sky; long waves, capped by the breeze with froth, were running with us. We went past the steersman to the taffrail, and saw the water come foaming under the stern and the bubbles go dancing and vanishing in her wake. I turned and surveyed the unsavoury length of the ship.

'Is this an ocean menagerie?' said I.

'Looks like it,' said Montgomery.

'What are these beasts for? Merchandise, curios? Does the captain think he is going to sell them somewhere in the South Seas?'

'It looks like it, doesn't it?' said Montgomery, and turned towards the wake again.

Suddenly we heard a yelp and a volley of furious blasphemy from the companion hatchway, and the deformed man with the black face came up hurriedly. He was immediately followed by a heavy red-haired man in a white cap. At the sight of the former the staghounds, who had all tired of barking at me by this time, became furiously excited, howling and leaping against their chains. The black hesitated before them, and this gave the red-haired man time to come up with him and deliver a tremendous blow between the shoulder-blades. The poor devil went down like a felled ox, and rolled in the dirt among the furiously excited dogs. It was lucky for him that they were muzzled. The red-haired man gave a yawp of exultation and stood staggering, and as it seemed to me in serious danger of either going backwards down the companion hatchway or forwards upon his victim.

So soon as the second man had appeared, Montgomery had started forward. 'Steady on there!' he cried, in a tone of remonstrance. A couple of sailors appeared on the forecastle. The black-faced man, howling in a singular voice, rolled about under the feet of the dogs. No one attempted to help him. The brutes did their best to worry him, butting their muzzles at him. There was a quick dance of their lithe grey-figured bodies over the clumsy, prostrate figure. The sailors forward shouted, as though it was admirable sport. Montgomery gave an angry exclamation, and went striding down the deck, and I followed him. The black-faced man scrambled up and

staggered forward, going and leaning over the bulwark by the main shrouds, where he remained, panting and glaring over his shoulder at the dogs. The red-haired man laughed a satisfied laugh.

'Look here, Captain,' said Montgomery, with his lisp a little accentuated, gripping the elbows of the red-haired man, 'this won't do!'

I stood behind Montgomery. The captain came half round, and regarded him with the dull and solemn eyes of a drunken man. 'Wha' won't do?' he said, and added, after looking sleepily into Montgomery's face for a minute, 'Blasted Sawbones!'

With a sudden movement he shook his arms free, and after two ineffectual attempts stuck his freckled fists into his side pockets.

'That man's a passenger,' said Montgomery. 'I'd advise you to keep your hands off him.'

'Go to hell!' said the captain, loudly. He suddenly turned and staggered towards the side. 'Do what I like on my own ship,' he said.

I think Montgomery might have left him then, seeing the brute was drunk; but he only turned a shade paler, and followed the captain to the bulwarks.

'Look you here, Captain,' he said; 'that man of mine is not to be ill-treated. He has been hazed ever since he came aboard.'

For a minute, alcoholic fumes kept the captain speechless. 'Blasted Sawbones!' was all he considered necessary.

I could see that Montgomery had one of those slow, pertinacious tempers that will warm day after day to a white heat, and never again cool to forgiveness; and I saw too that this quarrel had been some time growing. 'The man's drunk,' said I, perhaps officiously; 'you'll do no good.'

Montgomery gave an ugly twist to his dropping lip. 'He's always drunk. Do you think that excuses his assaulting his passengers?'

'My ship,' began the captain, waving his hand unsteadily towards the cages, 'was a clean ship. Look at it now!' It was certainly anything but clean. 'Crew,' continued the captain, 'clean, respectable crew.'

'You agreed to take the beasts.'

'I wish I'd never set eyes on your infernal island. What the devil – want beasts for on an island like that? Then, that man of yours – understood he was a man. He's a lunatic; and he hadn't no business aft. Do you think the whole damned ship belongs to you?'

'Your sailors began to haze the poor devil as soon as he came aboard.'

'That's just what he is – he's a devil, an ugly devil! My men can't stand him. I can't stand him. None of us can't stand him. Nor you either!'

Montgomery turned away. 'You leave that man alone, anyhow,' he said, nodding his head as he spoke.

But the captain meant to quarrel now. He raised his voice. 'If he comes this end of the ship again I'll cut his insides out, I tell you. Cut out his blasted insides! Who are you, to tell me what I'm to do? I tell you I'm

captain of this ship – captain and owner. I'm the law here, I tell you – the law and the prophets. I bargained to take a man and his attendant to and from Arica, and bring back some animals. I never bargained to carry a mad devil and a silly Sawbones, a—'

Well, never mind what he called Montgomery. I saw the latter take a step forward, and interposed. 'He's drunk,' said I. The captain began some abuse even fouler than the last. 'Shut up!' I said, turning on him sharply, for I had seen danger in Montgomery's white face. With that I brought the downpour on myself.

However, I was glad to avert what was uncommonly near a scuffle, even at the price of the captain's drunken ill-will. I do not think I have ever heard quite so much vile language come in a continuous stream from any man's lips before, though I have frequented eccentric company enough. I found some of it hard to endure, though I am a mild-tempered man; but, certainly, when I told the captain to 'shut up' I had forgotten that I was merely a bit of human flotsam, cut off from my resources and with my fare unpaid; a mere casual dependant on the bounty, or speculative enterprise, of the ship. He reminded me of it with considerable vigour; but at any rate I prevented a fight.

CHAPTER IV

At the Schooner's Rail

That night land was sighted after sundown, and the schooner hove to. Montgomery intimated that was his destination. It was too far to see any details; it seemed to me then simply a low-lying patch of dim blue in the uncertain blue-grey sea. An almost vertical streak of smoke went up from it into the sky.

The captain was not on deck when it was sighted. After he had vented his wrath on me he had staggered below, and I understand he went to sleep on the floor of his own cabin. The mate practically assumed the command. He was the gaunt, taciturn individual we had seen at the wheel. Apparently he was in an evil temper with Montgomery. He took not the slightest notice of either of us. We dined with him in a sulky silence, after a few ineffectual efforts on my part to talk. It struck me too that the men regarded my companion and his animals in a singularly unfriendly manner. I found Montgomery very reticent about his purpose with these creatures, and about his destination; and though I was sensible of a growing curiosity as to both, I did not press him.

We remained talking on the quarter deck until the sky was thick with stars. Except for an occasional sound in the yellow-lit forecastle and a movement of the animals now and then, the night was very still. The puma lay crouched together, watching us with shining eyes, a black heap in the corner of its cage. The dogs seemed to be asleep. Montgomery produced some cigars.

He talked to me of London in a tone of half-painful reminiscence, asking all kinds of questions about changes that had taken place. He spoke like a man who had loved his life there, and had been suddenly and irrevocably cut off from it. I gossiped as well as I could of this and that. All the time the strangeness of him was shaping itself in my mind; and as I talked I peered at his odd, pallid face in the dim light of the binnacle lantern behind me. Then I looked out at the darkling sea, where in the dimness his little island was hidden.

This man, it seemed to me, had come out of Immensity merely to save my life. Tomorrow he would drop over the side, and vanish again out of my existence. Even had it been under commonplace circumstances, it would have made me a trifle thoughtful; but in the first place was the singularity of an educated man living on this unknown little island, and coupled with that the extraordinary nature of his luggage. I found myself repeating the captain's question. What did he want with the beasts? Why, too, had he

pretended they were not his when I had remarked about them at first? Then, again, in his personal attendant there was a bizarre quality which had impressed me profoundly. These circumstances threw a haze of mystery round the man. They laid hold of my imagination, and hampered my tongue.

Towards midnight our talk of London died away, and we stood side by side leaning over the bulwarks and staring dreamily over the silent, starlit sea, each pursuing his own thoughts. It was the atmosphere for sentiment, and I began upon my gratitude.

'If I may say it,' said I, after a time, 'you have saved my life.'

'Chance,' he answered. 'Just chance.'

'I prefer to make my thanks to the accessible agent.'

'Thank no one. You had the need, and I had the knowledge; and I injected and fed you much as I might have collected a specimen. I was bored and wanted something to do. If I'd been jaded that day, or hadn't liked your face, well – it's a curious question where you would have been now!'

This damped my mood a little. 'At any rate—' I began.

'It's a chance, I tell you,' he interrupted, 'as everything is in a man's life. Only the asses won't see it! Why am I here now, an outcast from civilization, instead of being a happy man enjoying all the pleasures of London? Simply because eleven years ago – I lost my head for ten minutes on a foggy night.'

He stopped. 'Yes?' said I.

'That's all.'

We relapsed into silence. Presently he laughed. 'There's something in this starlight that loosens one's tongue. I'm an ass, and yet somehow I would like to tell you.'

'Whatever you tell me, you may rely upon my keeping to myself – if that's it.'

He was on the point of beginning, and then shook his head, doubtfully.

'Don't,' said I. 'It is all the same to me. After all, it is better to keep your secret. There's nothing gained but a little relief if I respect your confidence. If I don't – well?'

He grunted undecidedly. I felt I had him at a disadvantage, had caught him in the mood of indiscretion; and to tell the truth I was not curious to learn what might have driven a young medical student out of London. I have an imagination. I shrugged my shoulders and turned away. Over the taffrail leant a silent black figure, watching the stars. It was Montgomery's strange attendant. It looked over its shoulder quickly with my movement, then looked away again.

It may seem a little thing to you, perhaps, but it came like a sudden blow to me. The only light near us was a lantern at the wheel. The creature's face was turned for one brief instant out of the dimness of the stern towards this illumination, and I saw that the eyes that glanced at me shone with a pale-green light.

I did not know then that a reddish luminosity, at least, is not uncommon in human eyes. The thing came to me as stark inhumanity. That black figure with its eyes of fire struck down through all my adult thoughts and feelings, and for a moment the forgotten horrors of childhood came back to my mind. Then the effect passed as it had come. An uncouth black figure of a man, a figure of no particular import, hung over the taffrail against the starlight, and I found Montgomery was speaking to me.

'I'm thinking of turning in, then,' said he, 'if you've had enough of this.'

I answered him incongruously. We went below, and he wished me good-night at the door of my cabin.

That night I had some very unpleasant dreams. The waning moon rose late. Its light struck a ghostly white beam across my cabin, and made an ominous shape on the planking by my bunk. Then the staghounds woke, and began howling and baying; so that I dreamt fitfully, and scarcely slept until the approach of dawn.

CHAPTER V

The Man Who Had Nowhere to Go

In the early morning (it was the second morning after my recovery, and I believe the fourth after I was picked up), I awoke through an avenue of tumultuous dreams – dreams of guns and howling mobs – and became sensible of a hoarse shouting above me. I rubbed my eyes and lay listening to the noise, doubtful for a little while of my whereabouts. Then came a sudden pattering of bare feet, the sound of heavy objects being thrown about, a violent creaking and the rattling of chains. I heard the swish of the water as the ship was suddenly brought round, and a foamy yellow-green wave flew across the little round window and left it streaming. I jumped into my clothes and went on deck.

As I came up the ladder I saw against the flushed sky – for the sun was just rising – the broad back and red hair of the captain, and over his shoulder the puma spinning from a tackle rigged on to the mizzen spanker-boom. The poor brute seemed horribly scared, and crouched in the bottom of its little cage.

'Overboard with 'em!' bawled the captain. 'Overboard with 'em! We'll have a clean ship soon of the whole bilin' of 'em.'

He stood in my way, so that I had perforce to tap his shoulder to come on deck. He came round with a start, and staggered back a few paces to stare at me. It needed no expert eye to tell that the man was still drunk.

'Hullo!' said he, stupidly; and then with a light coming into his eyes, 'Why, it's Mister – Mister?'

'Prendick,' said I.

'Prendick be damned!' said he. 'Shut-up – that's your name. Mister Shut-up.'

It was no good answering the brute; but I certainly did not expect his next move. He held out his hand to the gangway by which Montgomery stood talking to a massive grey-haired man in dirty blue flannels, who had apparently just come aboard.

'That way, Mister Blasted Shut-up! That way!' roared the captain.

Montgomery and his companion turned as he spoke.

'What do you mean?' I said.

'That way, Mister Blasted Shut-up – that's what I mean! Overboard, Mister Shut-up – and sharp! We're cleaning the ship out – cleaning the whole blessed ship out; and overboard you go!'

I stared at him dumbfounded. Then it occurred to me that it was exactly the thing I wanted. The lost prospect of a journey as sole passenger with this quarrelsome sot was not one to mourn over. I turned towards Montgomery.

'Can't have you,' said Montgomery's companion, concisely.

'You can't have me!' said I, aghast. He had the squarest and most resolute face I ever set eyes upon.

'Look here,' I began, turning to the captain.

'Overboard!' said the captain. 'This ship ain't for beasts and cannibals and worse than beasts, any more. Overboard you go, Mister Shut-up. If they can't have you, you goes adrift. But, anyhow, you go – with your friends. I've done with this blessed island for evermore, amen! I've had enough of it.'

'But, Montgomery,' I appealed.

He distorted his lower lip, and nodded his head hopelessly at the grey-haired man beside him, to indicate his powerlessness to help me.

'I'll see to *you*, presently,' said the captain.

Then began a curious three-cornered altercation. Alternately I appealed to one and another of the three men, – first to the grey-haired man to let me land, and then to the drunken captain to keep me aboard. I even bawled entreaties to the sailors. Montgomery said never a word, only shook his head. 'You're going overboard, I tell you,' was the captain's refrain. 'Law be damned! I'm king here.'

At last I must confess my voice suddenly broke in the middle of a vigorous threat. I felt a gust of hysterical petulance, and went aft and stared dismally at nothing.

Meanwhile the sailors progressed rapidly with the task of unshipping the packages and caged animals. A large launch, with two standing lugs, lay under the lee of the schooner; and into this the strange assortment of goods were swung. I did not then see the hands from the island that were receiving the packages, for the hull of the launch was hidden from me by the side of the schooner. Neither Montgomery nor his companion took the slightest notice of me, but busied themselves in assisting and directing the four or five sailors who were unloading the goods. The captain went forward interfering rather than assisting. I was alternately despairful and desperate. Once or twice as I stood waiting there for things to accomplish themselves, I could not resist an impulse to laugh at my miserable quandary. I felt all the wretcheder for the lack of a breakfast. Hunger and a lack of blood-corpuscles take all the manhood from a man. I perceived pretty clearly that I had not the stamina either to resist what the captain chose to do to expel me, or to force myself upon Montgomery and his companion. So I waited passively upon fate; and the work of transferring Montgomery's possessions to the launch went on as if I did not exist.

Presently that work was finished, and then came a struggle. I was hauled, resisting weakly enough, to the gangway. Even then I noticed the oddness of the brown faces of the men who were with Montgomery in the launch; but the launch was now fully laden, and was shoved off hastily. A broadening gap of green water appeared under me, and I pushed back with all my strength

to avoid falling headlong. The hands in the launch shouted derisively, and I heard Montgomery curse at them; and then the captain, the mate and one of the seamen helping him ran me aft towards the stern.

The dinghy of the *Lady Vain* had been towing behind; it was half full of water, had no oars, and was quite unvictualled. I refused to go aboard her, and flung myself full length on the deck. In the end, they swung me into her by a rope (for they had no stern ladder), and then they cut me adrift.

I drifted slowly from the schooner. In a kind of stupor I watched all hands take to the rigging, and slowly but surely she came round to the wind; the sails fluttered, and then bellied out as the wind came into them. I stared at her weather-beaten side heeling steeply towards me; and then she passed out of my range of view.

I did not turn my head to follow her. At first I could scarcely believe what had happened. I crouched in the bottom of the dinghy, stunned and staring blankly at the vacant, oily sea. Then I realized that I was in that little hell of mine again, now half swamped; and looking back over the gunwale, I saw the schooner standing away from me, with the red-haired captain mocking at me over the taffrail, and turning towards the island saw the launch growing smaller as she approached the beach.

Abruptly the cruelty of this desertion became clear to me. I had no means of reaching the land unless I should chance to drift there. I was still weak, you must remember, from my exposure in the boat; I was empty and very faint, or I should have had more heart. But as it was I suddenly began to sob and weep, as I had never done since I was a little child. The tears ran down my face. In a passion of despair I struck with my fists at the water in the bottom of the boat, and kicked savagely at the gunwale. I prayed aloud for God to let me die.

CHAPTER VI

The Evil-Looking Boatmen

But the islanders, seeing that I was really adrift, took pity on me. I drifted very slowly to the eastward, approaching the island slantingly; and presently I saw, with hysterical relief, the launch come round and return towards me. She was heavily laden, and I could make out as she drew nearer Montgomery's white-haired, broad-shouldered companion sitting cramped up with the dogs and several packing-cases in the stern sheets. This individual stared fixedly at me without moving or speaking. The black-faced cripple was glaring at me as fixedly in the bows near the puma. There were three other men besides, three strange brutish-looking fellows, at whom the staghounds were snarling savagely. Montgomery, who was steering, brought the boat by me, and rising, caught and fastened my painter to the tiller to tow me, for there was no room aboard.

I had recovered from my hysterical phase by this time and answered his hail, as he approached, bravely enough. I told him the dinghy was nearly swamped, and he reached me a piggin. I was jerked back as the rope tightened between the boats. For some time I was busy baling.

It was not until I had got the water under (for the water in the dinghy had been shipped; the boat was perfectly sound) that I had leisure to look at the people in the launch again.

The white-haired man I found was still regarding me steadfastly, but with an expression, as I now fancied, of some perplexity. When my eyes met his, he looked down at the staghound that sat between his knees. He was a powerfully built man, as I have said, with a fine forehead and rather heavy features; but his eyes had that odd drooping of the skin above the lids which often comes with advancing years, and the fall of his heavy mouth at the corners gave him an expression of pugnacious resolution. He talked to Montgomery in a tone too low for me to hear.

From him my eyes travelled to his three men; and a strange crew they were. I saw only their faces, yet there was something in their faces – I knew not what – that gave me a queer spasm of disgust. I looked steadily at them, and the impression did not pass, though I failed to see what had occasioned it. They seemed to me then to be brown men; but their limbs were oddly swathed in some thin, dirty, white stuff down even to the fingers and feet: I have never seen men so wrapped up before, and women so only in the East. They wore turbans too, and thereunder peered out their elfin faces at me – faces with protruding lower jaws and bright eyes. They had lank black hair, almost like horsehair, and seemed as they sat to exceed in stature any

race of men I have seen. The white-haired man, who I knew was a good six feet in height, sat a head below any one of the three. I found afterwards that really none were taller than myself; but their bodies were abnormally long, and the thigh-part of the leg short and curiously twisted. At any rate, they were an amazingly ugly gang, and over the heads of them under the forward lug peered the black face of the man whose eyes were luminous in the dark. As I stared at them, they met my gaze; and then first one and then another turned away from my direct stare, and looked at me in an odd, furtive manner. It occurred to me that I was perhaps annoying them, and I turned my attention to the island we were approaching.

It was low, and covered with thick vegetation – chiefly a kind of palm that was new to me. From one point a thin white thread of vapour rose slantingly to an immense height, and then frayed out like a down feather. We were now within the embrace of a broad bay flanked on either hand by a low promontory. The beach was of dull grey sand, and sloped steeply up to a ridge, perhaps sixty or seventy feet above the sea-level, and irregularly set with trees and undergrowth. Half way up was a square enclosure of some greyish stone, which I found subsequently was built partly of coral and partly of pumiceous lava. Two thatched roofs peeped from within this enclosure.

A man stood awaiting us at the water's edge. I fancied while we were still far off that I saw some other and very grotesque-looking creatures scuttle into the bushes upon the slope; but I saw nothing of these as we drew nearer. This man was of a moderate size, and with a black Negroid face. He had a large, almost lipless, mouth, extraordinary lank arms, long thin feet and bow legs, and stood with his heavy face thrust forward staring at us. He was dressed like Montgomery and his white-haired companion, in jacket and trousers of blue serge. As we came still nearer, this individual began to run to and fro on the beach, making the most grotesque movements.

At a word of command from Montgomery, the four men in the launch sprang up, and with singularly awkward gestures struck the lugs. Montgomery steered us round and into a narrow little dock excavated in the beach. Then the man on the beach hastened towards us. This dock, as I call it, was really a mere ditch just long enough at this phase of the tide to take the longboat.

I heard the bows ground in the sand, staved the dinghy off the rudder of the big boat with my piggin, and freeing the painter, landed. The three muffled men, with the clumsiest movements, scrambled out upon the sand, and forthwith set to landing the cargo, assisted by the man on the beach. I was struck especially by the curious movements of the legs of the three swathed and bandaged boatmen – not stiff they were, but distorted in some odd way, almost as if they were jointed in the wrong place. The dogs were still snarling, and strained at their chains after these men, as the white-haired man landed with them.

The three big fellows spoke to one another in odd guttural tones, and the man who had waited for us on the beach began chattering to them excitedly – a foreign language, as I fancied – as they laid hands on some bales piled near the stern. Somewhere I had heard such a voice before, and I could not think where. The white-haired man stood, holding in a tumult of six dogs, and bawling orders over their din. Montgomery, having unshipped the rudder, landed likewise, and all set to work at unloading. I was too faint, what with my long fast and the sun beating down on my bare head, to offer any assistance.

Presently the white-haired man seemed to recollect my presence, and came up to me. 'You look,' said he, 'as though you had scarcely breakfasted.' His little eyes were a brilliant black under his heavy brows. 'I must apologize for that. Now you are our guest, we must make you comfortable – though you are uninvited, you know.' He looked keenly into my face. 'Montgomery says you are an educated man, Mr Prendick; says you know something of science. May I ask what that signifies?'

I told him I had spent some years at the Royal College of Science, and had done some researches in biology under Huxley. He raised his eyebrows slightly at that.

'That alters the case a little, Mr Prendick,' he said, with a trifle more respect in his manner. 'As it happens, we are biologists here. This is a biological station – of a sort.' His eye rested on the men in white who were busily hauling the puma, on rollers, towards the walled yard. 'I and Montgomery, at least,' he added. Then, 'When you will be able to get away, I can't say. We're off the track to anywhere. We see a ship once in a twelvemonth or so.'

He left me abruptly, and went up the beach past this group, and I think entered the enclosure. The other two men were with Montgomery, erecting a pile of smaller packages on a low-wheeled truck. The llama was still on the launch with the rabbit hutches; the staghounds were still lashed to the thwarts. The pile of things completed, all three men laid hold of the truck and began shoving the ton-weight or so upon it after the puma. Presently Montgomery left them, and coming back to me held out his hand.

'I'm glad,' said he, 'for my own part. That captain was a silly ass. He'd have made things lively for you.'

'It was you,' said I, 'that saved me again.'

'That depends. You'll find this island an infernally rum place, I promise you. I'd watch my goings carefully, if I were you. He—' He hesitated, and seemed to alter his mind about what was on his lips. 'I wish you'd help me with these rabbits,' he said.

His procedure with the rabbits was singular. I waded in with him, and helped him lug one of the hutches ashore. No sooner was that done than he opened the door of it, and tilting the thing on one end turned its living contents out on the ground. They fell in a struggling heap one on the top

of the other. He clapped his hands, and forthwith they went off with that hopping run of theirs, fifteen or twenty of them I should think, up the beach.

'Increase and multiply, my friends,' said Montgomery. 'Replenish the island. Hitherto we've had a certain lack of meat here.'

As I watched them disappearing, the white-haired man returned with a brandy-flask and some biscuits. 'Something to go on with, Prendick,' said he, in a far more familiar tone than before. I made no ado, but set to work on the biscuits at once, while the white-haired man helped Montgomery to release about a score more of the rabbits. Three big hutches, however, went up to the house with the puma. The brandy I did not touch, for I have been an abstainer from my birth.

CHAPTER VII

The Locked Door

The reader will perhaps understand that at first everything was so strange about me, and my position was the outcome of such unexpected adventures, that I had no discernment of the relative strangeness of this or that thing. I followed the llama up the beach, and was overtaken by Montgomery, who asked me not to enter the stone enclosure. I noticed then that the puma in its cage and the pile of packages had been placed outside the entrance to this quadrangle.

I turned and saw that the launch had now been unloaded, run out again, and was being beached, and the white-haired man was walking towards us. He addressed Montgomery.

'And now comes the problem of this uninvited guest. What are we to do with him?'

'He knows something of science,' said Montgomery.

'I'm itching to get to work again – with this new stuff,' said the white-haired man, nodding towards the enclosure. His eyes grew brighter.

'I daresay you are,' said Montgomery, in anything but a cordial tone.

'We can't send him over there, and we can't spare the time to build him a new shanty; and we certainly can't take him into our confidence just yet.'

'I'm in your hands,' said I. I had no idea of what he meant by 'over there'.

'I've been thinking of the same things,' Montgomery answered. 'There's my room with the outer door—'

'That's it,' said the elder man, promptly, looking at Montgomery, and all three of us went towards the enclosure. 'I'm sorry to make a mystery, Mr Prendick; but you'll remember you're uninvited. Our little establishment here contains a secret or so, is a kind of Bluebeard's Chamber, in fact. Nothing very dreadful, really, to a sane man; but just now, as we don't know you—'

'Decidedly,' said I, 'I should be a fool to take offence at any want of confidence.'

He twisted his heavy mouth into a faint smile – he was one of those saturnine people who smile with the corners of the mouth down – and bowed his acknowledgment of my complaisance. The main entrance to the enclosure was passed; it was a heavy wooden gate, framed in iron and locked, with the cargo of the launch piled outside it, and at the corner we came to a small doorway I had not previously observed. The white-haired man produced a bundle of keys from the pocket of his greasy blue jacket, opened this door, and entered. His keys, and the elaborate locking-up of the place

even while it was still under his eye, struck me as peculiar. I followed him, and found myself in a small apartment, plainly but not uncomfortably furnished and with its inner door, which was slightly ajar, opening into a paved courtyard. This inner door Montgomery at once closed. A hammock was slung across the darker corner of the room, and a small unglazed window defended by an iron bar looked out towards the sea.

This the white-haired man told me was to be my apartment; and the inner door, which 'for fear of accidents,' he said, he would lock on the other side, was my limit inward. He called my attention to a convenient deck chair before the window, and to an array of old books, chiefly, I found, surgical works and editions of the Latin and Greek classics (languages I cannot read with any comfort), on a shelf near the hammock. He left the room by the outer door, as if to avoid opening the inner one again.

'We usually have our meals in here,' said Montgomery, and then, as if in doubt, went out after the other. 'Moreau!' I heard him call, and for the moment I do not think I noticed. Then as I handled the books on the shelf it came up in consciousness: Where had I heard the name of Moreau before? I sat down before the window, took out the biscuits that still remained to me, and ate them with an excellent appetite. Moreau!

Through the window I saw one of those unaccountable men in white, lugging a packing-case along the beach. Presently the window frame hid him. Then I heard a key inserted and turned in the lock behind me. After a little while I heard through the locked door the noise of the staghounds, that had now been brought up from the beach. They were not barking, but sniffing and growling in a curious fashion. I could hear the rapid patter of their feet, and Montgomery's voice soothing them.

I was very much impressed by the elaborate secrecy of these two men regarding the contents of the place, and for some time I was thinking of that and of the unaccountable familiarity of the name of Moreau; but so odd is the human memory that I could not then recall that well-known name in its proper connection. From that my thoughts went to the indefinable queerness of the deformed man on the beach. I never saw such a gait, such odd motions as he pulled at the box. I recalled that none of these men had spoken to me, though most of them I had found looking at me at one time or another in a peculiarly furtive manner, quite unlike the frank stare of your unsophisticated savage. Indeed, they had all seemed remarkably taciturn, and when they did speak, endowed with very uncanny voices. What was wrong with them? Then I recalled the eyes of Montgomery's ungainly attendant.

Just as I was thinking of him he came in. He was now dressed in white, and carried a little tray with some coffee and boiled vegetables thereon. I could hardly repress a shuddering recoil as he came, bending amiably, and placed the tray before me on the table. Then astonishment paralysed me.

Under his stringy black locks I saw his ear; it jumped upon me suddenly close to my face. The man had pointed ears, covered with a fine brown fur!

'Your breakfast, sair,' he said.

I stared at his face without attempting to answer him. He turned and went towards the door, regarding me oddly over his shoulder. I followed him out with my eyes; and as I did so, by some odd trick of unconscious cerebration, there came surging into my head the phrase 'The Moreau – Hollows' was it? 'The Moreau—' Ah! It sent my memory back ten years. 'The Moreau Horrors!' The phrase drifted loose in my mind for a moment, and then I saw it in red lettering on a little buff-coloured pamphlet, to read which made one shiver and creep. Then I remembered distinctly all about it. That long-forgotten pamphlet came back with startling vividness to my mind. I had been a mere lad then, and Moreau was, I suppose, about fifty – a prominent and masterful physiologist, well known in scientific circles for his extraordinary imagination and his brutal directness in discussion.

Was this the same Moreau? He had published some very astonishing facts in connection with the transfusion of blood, and in addition was known to be doing valuable work on morbid growths. Then suddenly his career was closed. He had to leave England. A journalist obtained access to his laboratory in the capacity of laboratory-assistant, with the deliberate intention of making sensational exposures; and by the help of a shocking accident (if it was an accident), his gruesome pamphlet became notorious. On the day of its publication a wretched dog, flayed and otherwise mutilated, escaped from Moreau's house.

It was in the silly season, and a prominent editor, a cousin of the temporary laboratory-assistant, appealed to the conscience of the nation. It was not the first time that conscience has turned against the methods of research. The doctor was simply howled out of the country. It may be that he deserved to be; but I still think that the tepid support of his fellow-investigators and his desertion by the great body of scientific workers was a shameful thing. Yet some of his experiments, by the journalist's account, were wantonly cruel. He might perhaps have purchased his social peace by abandoning his investigations; but he apparently preferred the latter, as most men would who have once fallen under the overmastering spell of research. He was unmarried, and had indeed nothing but his own interests to consider.

I felt convinced that this must be the same man. Everything pointed to it. It dawned upon me to what end the puma and the other animals – which had now been brought with other luggage into the enclosure behind the house – were destined; and a curious faint odour, the halitus of something familiar, an odour that had been in the background of my consciousness hitherto, suddenly came forward into the forefront of my thoughts. It was the antiseptic odour of the operating-room. I heard the puma growling through the wall, and one of the dogs yelped as though it had been struck.

Yet surely, and especially to another scientific man, there was nothing so horrible in vivisection as to account for this secrecy; and by some odd leap in my thoughts the pointed ears and luminous eyes of Montgomery's attendant came back again before me with the sharpest definition. I stared before me out at the green sea, frothing under a freshening breeze, and let these and other strange memories of the last few days chase one another through my mind.

What could it all mean? A locked enclosure on a lonely island, a notorious vivisector, and these crippled and distorted men?

CHAPTER VIII

The Crying of the Puma

Montgomery interrupted my tangle of mystification and suspicion about one o'clock, and his grotesque attendant followed him with a tray bearing bread, some herbs and other eatables, a flask of whisky, a jug of water, and three glasses and knives. I glanced askance at this strange creature, and found him watching me with his queer, restless eyes. Montgomery said he would lunch with me, but that Moreau was too preoccupied with some work to come.

'Moreau!' said I. 'I know that name.'

'The devil you do!' said he. 'What an ass I was to mention it to you! I might have thought. Anyhow, it will give you an inkling of our – mysteries. Whisky?'

'No, thanks; I'm an abstainer.'

'I wish I'd been. But it's no use locking the door after the steed is stolen. It was that infernal stuff which led to my coming here – that, and a foggy night. I thought myself in luck at the time, when Moreau offered to get me off. It's queer—'

'Montgomery,' said I, suddenly, as the outer door closed, 'why has your man pointed ears?'

'Damn!' he said, over his first mouthful of food. He stared at me for a moment, and then repeated, 'Pointed ears?'

'Little points to them,' said I, as calmly as possible, with a catch in my breath; 'and a fine brown fur at the edges?'

He helped himself to whisky and water with great deliberation. 'I was under the impression – that his hair covered his ears.'

'I saw them as he stooped by me to put that coffee you sent to me on the table. And his eyes shine in the dark.'

By this time Montgomery had recovered from the surprise of my question. 'I always thought,' he said deliberately, with a certain accentuation of his flavouring of lisp, 'that there *was* something the matter with his ears, from the way he covered them. What were they like?'

I was persuaded from his manner that this ignorance was a pretence. Still, I could hardly tell the man that I thought him a liar. 'Pointed,' I said; 'rather small and furry – distinctly furry. But the whole man is one of the strangest beings I ever set eyes on.'

A sharp, hoarse cry of animal pain came from the enclosure behind us. Its depth and volume testified to the puma. I saw Montgomery wince.

'Yes?' he said.

'Where did you pick up the creature?'

'San Francisco. He's an ugly brute, I admit. Half-witted, you know. Can't remember where he came from. But I'm used to him, you know. We both are. How does he strike you?'

'He's unnatural,' I said. 'There's something about him – don't think me fanciful, but it gives me a nasty little sensation, a tightening of my muscles, when he comes near me. It's a touch – of the diabolical, in fact.'

Montgomery had stopped eating while I told him this. 'Rum!' he said. 'I can't see it.' He resumed his meal. 'I had no idea of it,' he said, and masticated. 'The crew of the schooner must have felt it the same. Made a dead set at the poor devil. You saw the captain?'

Suddenly the puma howled again, this time more painfully. Montgomery swore under his breath. I had half a mind to attack him about the men on the beach. Then the poor brute within gave vent to a series of short, sharp cries.

'Your men on the beach,' said I; 'what race are they?'

'Excellent fellows, aren't they?' said he, absentmindedly, knitting his brows as the animal yelled out sharply.

I said no more. There was another outcry worse than the former. He looked at me with his dull grey eyes, and then took some more whisky. He tried to draw me into a discussion about alcohol, professing to have saved my life with it. He seemed anxious to lay stress on the fact that I owed my life to him. I answered him distractedly.

Presently our meal came to an end; the misshapen monster with the pointed ears cleared the remains away, and Montgomery left me alone in the room again. All the time he had been in a state of ill-concealed irritation at the noise of the vivisected puma. He had spoken of his odd want of nerve, and left me to the obvious application.

I found myself that the cries were singularly irritating, and they grew in depth and intensity as the afternoon wore on. They were painful at first, but their constant resurgence at last altogether upset my balance. I flung aside a crib of Horace I had been reading, and began to clench my fists, to bite my lips, and to pace the room. Presently I got to stopping my ears with my fingers.

The emotional appeal of those yells grew upon me steadily, grew at last to such an exquisite expression of suffering that I could stand it in that confined room no longer. I stepped out of the door into the slumberous heat of the late afternoon, and walking past the main entrance – locked again, I noticed – turned the corner of the wall.

The crying sounded even louder out of doors. It was as if all the pain in the world had found a voice. Yet had I known such pain was in the next room, and had it been dumb, I believe – I have thought since – I could have stood it well enough. It is when suffering finds a voice and sets our

nerves quivering that this pity comes troubling us. But in spite of the brilliant sunlight and the green fans of the trees waving in the soothing sea-breeze, the world was a confusion, blurred with drifting black and red phantasms, until I was out of earshot of the house in the stone wall.

CHAPTER IX

The Thing in the Forest

I strode through the undergrowth that clothed the ridge behind the house, scarcely heeding whither I went; passed on through the shadow of a thick cluster of straight-stemmed trees beyond it, and so presently found myself some way on the other side of the ridge, and descending towards a streamlet that ran through a narrow valley. I paused and listened. The distance I had come, or the intervening masses of thicket, deadened any sound that might be coming from the enclosure. The air was still. Then with a rustle a rabbit emerged, and went scampering up the slope before me. I hesitated, and sat down in the edge of the shade.

The place was a pleasant one. The rivulet was hidden by the luxuriant vegetation of the banks save at one point, where I caught a triangular patch of its glittering water. On the further side I saw through a bluish haze a tangle of trees and creepers, and above these again the luminous blue of the sky. Here and there a splash of white or crimson marked the blooming of some trailing epiphyte. I let my eyes wander over this scene for a while, and then began to turn over in my mind again the strange peculiarities of Montgomery's man. But it was too hot to think elaborately, and presently I fell into a tranquil state midway between dozing and waking.

From this I was aroused, after I know not how long, by a rustling amidst the greenery on the other side of the stream. For a moment I could see nothing but the waving summits of the ferns and reeds. Then suddenly upon the bank of the stream appeared something – at first I could not distinguish what it was. It bowed its round head to the water, and began to drink. Then I saw it was a man, going on all-fours like a beast. He was clothed in bluish cloth, and was of a copper-coloured hue, with black hair. It seemed that grotesque ugliness was an invariable character of these islanders. I could hear the suck of the water at his lips as he drank.

I leant forward to see him better, and a piece of lava, detached by my hand, went pattering down the slope. He looked up guiltily, and his eyes met mine. Forthwith he scrambled to his feet, and stood wiping his clumsy hand across his mouth and regarding me. His legs were scarcely half the length of his body. So, staring one another out of countenance, we remained for perhaps the space of a minute. Then, stopping to look back once or twice, he slunk off among the bushes to the right of me, and I heard the swish of the fronds grow faint in the distance and die away. Long after he had disappeared, I remained sitting up staring in the direction of his retreat. My drowsy tranquillity had gone.

I was startled by a noise behind me, and turning suddenly saw the flapping white tail of a rabbit vanishing up the slope. I jumped to my feet. The apparition of this grotesque, half-bestial creature had suddenly populated the stillness of the afternoon for me. I looked around me rather nervously, and regretted that I was unarmed. Then I thought that the man I had just seen had been clothed in bluish cloth, had not been naked as a savage would have been; and I tried to persuade myself from that fact that he was after all probably a peaceful character, that the dull ferocity of his countenance belied him.

Yet I was greatly disturbed at the apparition. I walked to the left along the slope, turning my head about and peering this way and that among the straight stems of the trees. Why should a man go on all-fours and drink with his lips? Presently I heard an animal wailing again, and taking it to be the puma, I turned about and walked in a direction diametrically opposite to the sound. This led me down to the stream, across which I stepped and pushed my way up through the undergrowth beyond.

I was startled by a great patch of vivid scarlet on the ground, and going up to it found it to be a peculiar fungus, branched and corrugated like a foliaceous lichen, but deliquescing into slime at the touch; and then in the shadow of some luxuriant ferns I came upon an unpleasant thing – the dead body of a rabbit covered with shining flies, but still warm and with the head torn off. I stopped aghast at the sight of the scattered blood. Here at least was one visitor to the island disposed of!

There were no traces of other violence about it. It looked as though it had been suddenly snatched up and killed; and as I stared at the little furry body came the difficulty of how the thing had been done. The vague dread that had been in my mind since I had seen the inhuman face of the man at the stream grew distincter as I stood there. I began to realize the hardihood of my expedition among these unknown people. The thicket about me became altered to my imagination. Every shadow became something more than a shadow – became an ambush; every rustle became a threat. Invisible things seemed watching me. I resolved to go back to the enclosure on the beach. I suddenly turned away and thrust myself violently, possibly even frantically, through the bushes, anxious to get a clear space about me again.

I stopped just in time to prevent myself emerging upon an open space. It was a kind of glade in the forest, made by a fall; seedlings were already starting up to struggle for the vacant space; and beyond, the dense growth of stems and twining vines and splashes of fungus and flowers closed in again. Before me, squatting together upon the fungoid ruins of a huge fallen tree and still unaware of my approach, were three grotesque human figures.

One was evidently a female; the other two were men. They were naked, save for swathings of scarlet cloth about the middle; and their skins were of a dull pinkish drab colour, such as I had seen in no savages before. They

had fat, heavy, chinless faces, retreating foreheads, and a scant bristly hair upon their heads. I never saw such bestial-looking creatures.

They were talking, or at least one of the men was talking to the other two, and all three had been too closely interested to heed the rustling of my approach. They swayed their heads and shoulders from side to side. The speaker's words came thick and sloppy, and though I could hear them distinctly I could not distinguish what he said. He seemed to me to be reciting some complicated gibberish. Presently his articulation became shriller, and spreading his hands he rose to his feet.

At that the others began to gibber in unison, also rising to their feet, spreading their hands and swaying their bodies in rhythm with their chant. I noticed then the abnormal shortness of their legs, and their lank, clumsy feet. All three began slowly to circle round, raising and stamping their feet and waving their arms; a kind of tune crept into their rhythmic recitation, and a refrain – 'Aloola,' or 'Balloola,' it sounded like. Their eyes began to sparkle, and their ugly faces to brighten, with an expression of strange pleasure. Saliva dripped from their lipless mouths.

Suddenly, as I watched their grotesque and unaccountable gestures, I perceived clearly for the first time what it was that had offended me, what had given me the two inconsistent and conflicting impressions of utter strangeness and yet of the strangest familiarity. The three creatures engaged in this mysterious rite were human in shape, and yet human beings with the strangest air about them of some familiar animal. Each of these creatures, despite its human form, its rag of clothing, and the rough humanity of its bodily form, had woven into it – into its movements, into the expression of its countenance, into its whole presence – some now irresistible suggestion of a hog, a swinish taint, the unmistakable mark of the beast.

I stood overcome by this amazing realization and then the most horrible questionings came rushing into my mind. They began leaping in the air, first one and then the other, whooping and grunting. Then one slipped, and for a moment was on all fours – to recover, indeed, forthwith. But that transitory gleam of the true animalism of these monsters was enough.

I turned as noiselessly as possible, and becoming every now and then rigid with the fear of being discovered, as a branch cracked or a leaf rustled, I pushed back into the bushes. It was long before I grew bolder, and dared to move freely. My only idea for the moment was to get away from these foul beings, and I scarcely noticed that I had emerged upon a faint pathway amidst the trees. Then suddenly traversing a little glade, I saw with an unpleasant start two clumsy legs among the trees, walking with noiseless footsteps parallel with my course, and perhaps thirty yards away from me. The head and upper part of the body were hidden by a tangle of creeper. I stopped abruptly, hoping the creature did not see me. The feet stopped as I did. So nervous was I that I controlled an impulse to headlong flight with the utmost difficulty.

Then looking hard, I distinguished through the interlacing network the head and body of the brute I had seen drinking. He moved his head. There was an emerald flash in his eyes as he glanced at me from the shadow of the trees, a half-luminous colour that vanished as he turned his head again. He was motionless for a moment, and then with a noiseless tread began running through the green confusion. In another moment he had vanished behind some bushes. I could not see him, but I felt that he had stopped and was watching me again.

What on earth was he – man or beast? What did he want with me? I had no weapon, not even a stick. Flight would be madness. At any rate the Thing, whatever it was, lacked the courage to attack me. Setting my teeth hard, I walked straight towards him. I was anxious not to show the fear that seemed chilling my backbone. I pushed through a tangle of tall white-flowered bushes, and saw him twenty paces beyond, looking over his shoulder at me and hesitating. I advanced a step or two, looking steadfastly into his eyes.

'Who are you?' said I.

He tried to meet my gaze. 'No!' he said suddenly, and turning went bounding away from me through the undergrowth. Then he turned and stared at me again. His eyes shone brightly out of the dusk under the trees.

My heart was in my mouth; but I felt my only chance was to bluff, and walked steadily towards him. He turned again, and vanished into the dusk. Once more I thought I caught the glint of his eyes, and that was all.

For the first time I realized how the lateness of the hour might affect me. The sun had set some minutes since, the swift dusk of the tropics was already fading out of the eastern sky, and a pioneer moth fluttered silently by my head. Unless I would spend the night among the unknown dangers of the mysterious forest, I must hasten back to the enclosure. The thought of a return to that pain-haunted refuge was extremely disagreeable, but still more so was the idea of being overtaken in the open by darkness and all that darkness might conceal. I gave one more look into the blue shadows that had swallowed up this odd creature, and then retraced my way down the slope towards the stream, going as I judged in the direction from which I had come.

I walked eagerly, perplexed by all these things, and presently found myself in a level place among scattered trees. The colourless clearness that comes after the sunset flush was darkling; the blue sky above grew momentarily deeper, and the little stars one by one pierced the attenuated light; the interspaces of the trees, the gaps in the further vegetation, that had been hazy blue in the daylight, grew black and mysterious. I pushed on. The colour vanished from the world. The tree-tops rose against the luminous blue sky in inky silhouette, and all below that outline melted into one formless blackness. Presently the trees grew thinner, and the shrubby under-

growth more abundant. Then there was a desolate space covered with a white sand, and then another expanse of tangled bushes. I did not remember crossing the sand-opening before. I began to be tormented by a faint rustling upon my right hand. I thought at first it was fancy, for whenever I stopped there was silence, save for the evening breeze in the tree-tops. Then when I turned to hurry on again there was an echo to my footsteps.

I turned away from the thickets, keeping to the more open ground, and endeavouring by sudden turns now and then to surprise something in the act of creeping upon me. I saw nothing, and nevertheless my sense of another presence grew steadily. I increased my pace, and after some time came to a slight ridge, crossed it, and turned sharply, regarding it steadfastly from the further side. It came out black and clear-cut against the darkling sky; and presently a shapeless lump heaved up momentarily against the skyline and vanished again. I felt assured now that my tawny-faced antagonist was stalking me once more; and coupled with that was another unpleasant realization, that I had lost my way.

For a time I hurried on hopelessly perplexed, and pursued by that stealthy approach. Whatever it was, the Thing either lacked the courage to attack me, or it was waiting to take me at some disadvantage. I kept studiously to the open. At times I would turn and listen; and presently I had half persuaded myself that my pursuer had abandoned the chase, or was a mere creation of my disordered imagination. Then I heard the sound of the sea. I quickened my footsteps almost into a run, and immediately there was a stumble in my rear.

I turned suddenly, and stared at the uncertain trees behind me. One black shadow seemed to leap into another. I listened, rigid, and heard nothing but the creep of the blood in my ears. I thought that my nerves were unstrung, and that my imagination was tricking me, and turned resolutely towards the sound of the sea again.

In a minute or so the trees grew thinner, and I emerged upon a bare, low headland running out into the sombre water. The night was calm and clear, and the reflection of the growing multitude of the stars shivered in the tranquil heaving of the sea. Some way out, the wash upon an irregular band of reef shone with a pallid light of its own. Westward I saw the zodiacal light mingling with the yellow brilliance of the evening star. The coast fell away from me to the east, and westward it was hidden by the shoulder of the cape. Then I recalled the fact that Moreau's beach lay to the west.

A twig snapped behind me, and there was a rustle. I turned, and stood facing the dark trees. I could see nothing – or else I could see too much. Every dark form in the dimness had its ominous quality, its peculiar sugges-tion of alert watchfulness. So I stood for perhaps a minute, and then, with an eye to the trees still, turned westward to cross the headland; and as I moved, one among the lurking shadows moved to follow me.

My heart beat quickly. Presently the broad sweep of a bay to the westward became visible, and I halted again. The noiseless shadow halted a dozen yards from me. A little point of light shone on the further bend of the curve, and the grey sweep of the sandy beach lay faint under the starlight. Perhaps two miles away was that little point of light. To get to the beach I should have to go through the trees where the shadows lurked, and down a bushy slope.

I could see the Thing rather more distinctly now. It was no animal, for it stood erect. At that I opened my mouth to speak, and found a hoarse phlegm choked my voice. I tried again, and shouted, 'Who is there?' There was no answer. I advanced a step. The Thing did not move, only gathered itself together. My foot struck a stone. That gave me an idea. Without taking my eyes off the black form before me, I stooped and picked up this lump of rock; but at my motion the Thing turned abruptly as a dog might have done, and slunk obliquely into the further darkness. Then I recalled a schoolboy expedient against big dogs, and twisted the rock into my handkerchief, and gave this a turn round my wrist. I heard a movement further off among the shadows, as if the Thing was in retreat. Then suddenly my tense excitement gave way; I broke into a profuse perspiration and fell a-trembling, with my adversary routed and this weapon in my hand.

It was some time before I could summon resolution to go down through the trees and bushes upon the flank of the headland to the beach. At last I did it at a run; and as I emerged from the thicket upon the sand, I heard some other body come crashing after me. At that I completely lost my head with fear, and began running along the sand. Forthwith there came the swift patter of soft feet in pursuit. I gave a wild cry, and redoubled my pace. Some dim, black things about three or four times the size of rabbits went running or hopping up from the beach towards the bushes as I passed.

So long as I live, I shall remember the terror of that chase. I ran near the water's edge, and heard every now and then the splash of the feet that gained upon me. Far away, hopelessly far, was the yellow light. All the night about us was black and still. Splash, splash, came the pursuing feet, nearer and nearer. I felt my breath going, for I was quite out of training; it whooped as I drew it, and I felt a pain like a knife at my side. I perceived the Thing would come up with me long before I reached the enclosure, and, desperate and sobbing for my breath, I wheeled round upon it and struck at it as it came up to me – struck with all my strength. The stone came out of the sling of the handkerchief as I did so.

As I turned, the Thing, which had been running on all fours, rose to its feet, and the missile fell fair on its left temple. The skull rang loud, and the animal-man blundered into me, thrust me back with its hands, and went staggering past me to fall headlong upon the sand with its face in the water; and there it lay still.

I could not bring myself to approach that black heap. I left it there, with the water rippling round it, under the still stars, and giving it a wide berth pursued my way towards the yellow glow of the house; and presently, with a positive effect of relief, came the pitiful moaning of the puma, the sound that had originally driven me out to explore this mysterious island. At that, though I was faint and horribly fatigued, I gathered together all my strength, and began running again towards the light. I thought I heard a voice calling me.

CHAPTER X

The Crying of the Man

AS I drew near the house I saw that the light shone from the open door of my room; and then I heard coming from out of the darkness at the side of that orange oblong of light, the voice of Montgomery shouting, 'Prendick!'

I continued running. Presently I heard him again. I replied by a feeble 'Hullo!' and in another moment had staggered up to him.

'Where have you been?' said he, holding me at arm's length, so that the light from the door fell on my face. 'We have both been so busy that we forgot you until about half an hour ago.' He led me into the room and sat me down in the deck chair. For awhile I was blinded by the light. 'We did not think you would start to explore this island of ours without telling us,' he said; and then, 'I was afraid— ! But – what – hullo!'

My last remaining strength slipped from me, and my head fell forward on my chest. I think he found a certain satisfaction in giving me brandy.

'For God's sake,' said I, 'fasten that door.'

'You've been meeting some of our curiosities, eh?' said he.

He locked the door and turned to me again. He asked me no questions, but gave me some more brandy and water and pressed me to eat. I was in a state of collapse. He said something vague about his forgetting to warn me, and asked me briefly when I left the house and what I had seen.

I answered him as briefly, in fragmentary sentences. 'Tell me what it all means,' said I, in a state bordering on hysterics.

'It's nothing so very dreadful,' said he. 'But I think you have had about enough for one day.' The puma suddenly gave a sharp yell of pain. At that he swore under his breath. 'I'm damned,' said he, 'if this place is not as bad as Gower Street, with its cats.'

'Montgomery,' said I, 'what was that thing that came after me? Was it a beast or was it a man?'

'If you don't sleep tonight,' he said, 'you'll be off your head tomorrow.'

I stood up in front of him. 'What was that thing that came after me?' I asked.

He looked me squarely in the eyes, and twisted his mouth askew. His eyes, which had seemed animated a minute before, went dull. 'From your account,' said he, 'I'm thinking it was a bogle.'

I felt a gust of intense irritation, which passed as quickly as it came. I flung myself into the chair again, and pressed my hands on my forehead. The puma began once more.

Montgomery came round behind me and put his hand on my shoulder.

'Look here, Prendick,' he said, 'I had no business to let you drift out into this silly island of ours. But it's not so bad as you feel, man. Your nerves are worked to rags. Let me give you something that will make you sleep. *That* – will keep on for hours yet. You must simply get to sleep, or I won't answer for it.'

I did not reply. I bowed forward, and covered my face with my hands. Presently he returned with a small measure containing a dark liquid. This he gave me. I took it unresistingly, and he helped me into the hammock.

When I awoke, it was broad day. For a little while I lay flat, staring at the roof above me. The rafters, I observed, were made out of the timbers of a ship. Then I turned my head, and saw a meal prepared for me on the table. I perceived that I was hungry, and prepared to clamber out of the hammock, which, very politely anticipating my intention, twisted round and deposited me upon all fours on the floor.

I got up and sat down before the food. I had a heavy feeling in my head, and only the vaguest memory at first of the things that had happened overnight. The morning breeze blew very pleasantly through the unglazed window, and that and the food contributed to the sense of animal comfort which I experienced. Presently the door behind me – the door inward towards the yard of the enclosure – opened. I turned and saw Montgomery's face.

'All right?' said he. 'I'm frightfully busy.' And he shut the door. Afterwards I discovered that he forgot to re-lock it.

Then I recalled the expression of his face the previous night, and with that the memory of all I had experienced reconstructed itself before me. Even as that fear came back to me came a cry from within; but this time it was not the cry of a puma. I put down the mouthful that hesitated upon my lips, and listened. Silence, save for the whisper of the morning breeze. I began to think my ears had deceived me.

After a long pause I resumed my meal, but with my ears still vigilant. Presently I heard something else, very faint and low. I sat as if frozen in my attitude. Though it was faint and low, it moved me more profoundly than all that I had hitherto heard of the abominations behind the wall. There was no mistake this time in the quality of the dim, broken sounds; no doubt at all of their source. For it was groaning, broken by sobs and gasps of anguish. It was no brute this time; it was a human being in torment!

As I realized this I rose, and in three steps had crossed the room, seized the handle of the door into the yard, and flung it open before me.

'Prendick, man! Stop!' cried Montgomery, intervening.

A startled deerhound yelped and snarled. There was blood, I saw, in the sink – brown, and some scarlet – and I smelt the peculiar smell of carbolic acid. Then through an open doorway beyond, in the dim light of the shadow, I saw something bound painfully upon a framework, scarred, red, and bandaged; and then blotting this out appeared the face of old Moreau, white and

terrible. In a moment he had gripped me by the shoulder with a hand that was smeared red, had twisted me off my feet, and flung me headlong back into my own room. He lifted me as though I was a little child. I fell at full length upon the floor, and the door slammed and shut out the passionate intensity of his face. Then I heard the key turn in the lock, and Montgomery's voice in expostulation.

'Ruin the work of a lifetime,' I heard Moreau say.

'He does not understand,' said Montgomery. and other things that were inaudible.

'I can't spare the time yet,' said Moreau.

The rest I did not hear. I picked myself up and stood trembling, my mind a chaos of the most horrible misgivings. Could it be possible, I thought, that such a thing as the vivisection of men was carried on here? The question shot like lightning across a tumultuous sky; and suddenly the clouded horror of my mind condensed into a vivid realization of my own danger.

CHAPTER XI

The Hunting of the Man

It came before my mind with an unreasonable hope of escape that the outer door of my room was still open to me. I was convinced now, absolutely assured, that Moreau had been vivisecting a human being. All the time since I had heard his name, I had been trying to link in my mind in some way the grotesque animalism of the islanders with his abominations; and now I thought I saw it all. The memory of his work on the transfusion of blood recurred to me. These creatures I had seen were the victims of some hideous experiment. These sickening scoundrels had merely intended to keep me back, to fool me with their display of confidence, and presently to fall upon me with a fate more horrible than death – with torture; and after torture the most hideous degradation it is possible to conceive – to send me off a lost soul, a beast, to the rest of their Comus rout.

I looked round for some weapon. Nothing. Then with an inspiration I turned over the deck chair, put my foot on the side of it, and tore away the side rail. It happened that a nail came away with the wood, and projecting, gave a touch of danger to an otherwise petty weapon. I heard a step outside, and incontinently flung open the door and found Montgomery within a yard of it. He meant to lock the outer door! I raised this nailed stick of mine and cut at his face; but he sprang back. I hesitated a moment, then turned and fled, round the corner of the house. 'Prendick, man!' I heard his astonished cry, 'don't be a silly ass, man!'

Another minute, thought I, and he would have had me locked in, and as ready as a hospital rabbit for my fate. He emerged behind the corner, for I heard him shout, 'Prendick!' Then he began to run after me, shouting things as he ran. This time running blindly, I went north-eastward in a direction at right angles to my previous expedition. Once, as I went running headlong up the beach, I glanced over my shoulder and saw his attendant with him. I ran furiously up the slope, over it, then turning eastward along a rocky valley fringed on either side with jungle I ran for perhaps a mile altogether, my chest straining, my heart beating in my ears; and then hearing nothing of Montgomery or his man, and feeling upon the verge of exhaustion, I doubled sharply back towards the beach as I judged, and lay down in the shelter of a canebrake. There I remained for a long time, too fearful to move, and indeed too fearful even to plan a course of action. The wild scene about me lay sleeping silently under the sun, and the only sound near me was the thin hum of some small gnats that had discovered me. Presently I became aware of a drowsy breathing sound, the soughing of the sea upon the beach.

After about an hour I heard Montgomery shouting my name, far away to the north. That set me thinking of my plan of action. As I interpreted it then, this island was inhabited only by these two vivisectors and their animalized victims. Some of these no doubt they could press into their service against me if need arose. I knew both Moreau and Montgomery carried revolvers; and, save for a feeble bar of deal spiked with a small nail, the merest mockery of a mace, I was unarmed.

So I lay still there, until I began to think of food and drink; and at that thought the real hopelessness of my position came home to me. I knew no way of getting anything to eat. I was too ignorant of botany to discover any resort of root or fruit that might lie about me; I had no means of trapping the few rabbits upon the island. It grew blanker the more I turned the prospect over. At last in the desperation of my position, my mind turned to the animal men I had encountered. I tried to find some hope in what I remembered of them. In turn I recalled each one I had seen, and tried to draw some augury of assistance from my memory.

Then suddenly I heard a staghound bay, and at that realized a new danger. I took little time to think, or they would have caught me then, but snatching up my nailed stick, rushed headlong from my hiding place towards the sound of the sea. I remember a growth of thorny plants, with spines that stabbed like penknives. I emerged bleeding and with torn clothes upon the lip of a long creek opening northward. I went straight into the water without a minute's hesitation, wading up the creek, and presently finding myself knee-deep in a little stream. I scrambled out at last on the westward bank, and with my heart beating loudly in my ears, crept into a tangle of ferns to await the issue. I heard the dog (there was only one) draw nearer, and yelp when it came to the thorns. Then I heard no more, and presently began to think I had escaped.

The minutes passed; the silence lengthened out, and at last after an hour of security my courage began to return to me. By this time I was no longer very much terrified or very miserable. I had, as it were, passed the limit of terror and despair. I felt now that my life was practically lost, and that persuasion made me capable of daring anything. I had even a certain wish to encounter Moreau face to face; and as I had waded into the water, I remembered that if I were too hard pressed at least one path of escape from torment still lay open to me – they could not very well prevent my drowning myself. I had half a mind to drown myself then; but an odd wish to see the whole adventure out, a queer, impersonal, spectacular interest in myself, restrained me. I stretched my limbs, sore and painful from the pricks of the spiny plants, and stared around me at the trees; and, so suddenly that it seemed to jump out of the green tracery about it, my eyes lit upon a black face watching me. I saw that it was the simian creature who had met the launch upon the beach. He was clinging to the oblique

stem of a palm tree. I gripped my stick, and stood up facing him. He began chattering. 'You, you, you,' was all I could distinguish at first. Suddenly he dropped from the tree, and in another moment was holding the fronds apart and staring curiously at me.

I did not feel the same repugnance towards this creature which I had experienced in my encounters with the other Beast Men. 'You,' he said, 'in the boat.' He was a man, then – at least as much of a man as Montgomery's attendant – for he could talk.

'Yes,' I said, 'I came in the boat. From the ship.'

'Oh!' he said, and his bright, restless eyes travelled over me, to my hands, to the stick I carried, to my feet, to the tattered places in my coat, and the cuts and scratches I had received from the thorns. He seemed puzzled at something. His eyes came back to my hands. He held his own hand out and counted his digits slowly, 'One, two, three, four, five – eh?'

I did not grasp his meaning then; afterwards I was to find that a great proportion of these Beast People had malformed hands, lacking sometimes even three digits. But guessing this was in some way a greeting, I did the same thing by way of reply. He grinned with immense satisfaction. Then his swift roving glance went round again; he made a swift movement – and vanished. The fern fronds he had stood between came swishing together.

I pushed out of the brake after him, and was astonished to find him swinging cheerfully by one lank arm from a rope of creepers that looped down from the foliage overhead. His back was to me.

'Hullo!' said I.

He came down with a twisting jump, and stood facing me.

'I say,' said I, 'where can I get something to eat?'

'Eat!' he said. 'Eat man's food, now.' And his eye went back to the swing of ropes. 'At the huts.'

'But where are the huts?'

'Oh!'

'I'm new, you know.'

At that he swung round, and set off at a quick walk. All his motions were curiously rapid. 'Come along,' said he.

I went with him to see the adventure out. I guessed the huts were some rough shelter where he and some more of these Beast People lived. I might perhaps find them friendly, find some handle in their minds to take hold of. I did not know how far they had forgotten their human heritage.

My ape-like companion trotted along by my side, with his hands hanging down and his jaw thrust forward. I wondered what memory he might have in him. 'How long have you been on this island?' said I.

'How long?' he asked; and after having the question repeated, he held up three fingers.

The creature was little better than an idiot. I tried to make out what he

meant by that, and it seems I bored him. After another question or two he suddenly left my side and went leaping at some fruit that hung from a tree. He pulled down a handful of prickly husks and went on eating the contents. I noted this with satisfaction, for here at least was a hint for feeding. I tried him with some other questions, but his chattering, prompt responses were as often as not quite at cross purposes with my question. Some few were appropriate, others quite parrot-like.

I was so intent upon these peculiarities that I scarcely noticed the path we followed. Presently we came to trees, all charred and brown, and so to a bare place covered with a yellow-white incrustation, across which a drifting smoke, pungent in whiffs to nose and eyes, went drifting. On our right, over a shoulder of bare rock, I saw the level blue of the sea. The path coiled down abruptly into a narrow ravine between two tumbled and knotty masses of blackish scoriae. Into this we plunged.

It was extremely dark, this passage, after the blinding sunlight reflected from the sulphurous ground. Its walls grew steep, and approached each other. Blotches of green and crimson drifted across my eyes. My conductor stopped suddenly. 'Home!' said he, and I stood in a floor of a chasm that was at first absolutely dark to me. I heard some strange noises, and thrust the knuckles of my left hand into my eyes. I became aware of a disagreeable odour, like that of a monkey's cage ill-cleaned. Beyond, the rock opened again upon a gradual slope of sunlit greenery, and on either hand the light smote down through narrow ways into the central gloom.

CHAPTER XII

The Sayers of the Law

Then something cold touched my hand. I started violently, and saw close to me a dim pinkish thing, looking more like a flayed child than anything else in the world. The creature had exactly the mild but repulsive features of a sloth, the same low forehead and slow gestures.

As the first shock of the change of light passed, I saw about me more distinctly. The little sloth-like creature was standing and staring at me. My conductor had vanished. The place was a narrow passage between high walls of lava, a crack in the knotted rock, and on either side interwoven heaps of sea-mat, palm fans and reeds leaning against the rock formed rough and impenetrably dark dens. The winding way up the ravine between these was scarcely three yards wide, and was disfigured by lumps of decaying fruit pulp and other refuse, which accounted for the disagreeable stench of the place.

The little pink sloth creature was still blinking at me when my Ape-man reappeared at the aperture of the nearest of these dens, and beckoned me in. As he did so a slouching monster wriggled out of one of the places, further up this strange street, and stood up in featureless silhouette against the bright green beyond, staring at me. I hesitated, having half a mind to bolt the way I had come; and then, determined to go through with the adventure, I gripped my nailed stick about the middle and crawled into the little evil-smelling lean-to after my conductor.

It was a semi-circular space, shaped like the half of a beehive; and against the rocky wall that formed the inner side of it was a pile of variegated fruits, coconuts among others. Some rough vessels of lava and wood stood about the floor, and one on a rough stool. There was no fire. In the darkest corner of the hut sat a shapeless mass of darkness that grunted 'Hey!' as I came in, and my Ape-man stood in the dim light of the doorway and held out a split coconut to me as I crawled into the other corner and squatted down. I took it, and began gnawing it as serenely as possible in spite of a certain trepidation and the nearly intolerable closeness of the den. The little pink sloth creature stood in the aperture of the hut, and something else with a drab face and bright eyes came staring over its shoulder.

'Hey!' came out of the lump of mystery opposite. 'It is a man.'

'It is a man,' gabbled my conductor, 'a man, a man, a five-man, like me.'

'Shut up!' said the voice from the dark, and grunted. I gnawed my coconut amid an impressive stillness.

I peered hard into the blackness, but could distinguish nothing.

'It is a man,' the voice repeated. 'He comes to live with us?'

It was a thick voice, with something in it – a kind of whistling overtone
– that struck me as peculiar; but the English accent was strangely good.

The Ape-man looked at me as though he expected something. I perceived
the pause was interrogative. 'He comes to live with you,' I said.

'It is a man. He must learn the Law.'

I began to distinguish now a deeper blackness in the black, a vague outline
of a hunched-up figure. Then I noticed the opening of the place was dark-
ened by two more black heads. My hand tightened on my stick.

The thing in the dark repeated in a louder tone, 'Say the words.' I had
missed its last remark. 'Not to go on all-fours; that is the Law,' it repeated
in a kind of sing-song.

I was puzzled.

'Say the words,' said the Ape-man, repeating, and the figures in the
doorway echoed this, with a threat in the tone of their voices.

I realized that I had to repeat this idiotic formula; and then began the
insanest ceremony. The voice in the dark began intoning a mad litany, line
by line, and I and the rest to repeat it. As they did so, they swayed from
side to side in the oddest way, and beat their hands upon their knees; and
I followed their example. I could have imagined I was already dead and in
another world. That dark hut, these grotesque dim figures, just flecked here
and there by a glimmer of light, and all of them swaying in unison and
chanting,

'Not to go on all-fours; that is the Law. Are we not Men?
'Not to suck up Drink; that is the Law. Are we not Men?
'Not to eat Fish or Flesh; that is the Law. Are we not Men?
'Not to claw the Bark of Trees; that is the Law. Are we not Men?
'Not to chase other Men; that is the Law. Are we not Men?'

And so from the prohibition of these acts of folly, on to the prohibition
of what I thought then were the maddest, most impossible and most indecent
things one could well imagine. A kind of rhythmic fervour fell on all of us;
we gabbled and swayed faster and faster, repeating this amazing Law.
Superficially the contagion of these brutes was upon me, but deep down
within me the laughter and disgust struggled together. We ran through a
long list of prohibitions, and then the chant swung round to a new formula.

'His is the House of Pain.
'His is the Hand that makes.
'His is the Hand that wounds.
'His is the Hand that heals.'

And so on for another long series, mostly quite incomprehensible gibberish
to me about Him, whoever he might be. I could have fancied it was a dream,
but never before have I heard chanting in a dream.

'His is the lightning flash,' we sang. 'His is the deep, salt sea.'

A horrible fancy came into my head that Moreau, after animalizing these

men, had infected their dwarfed brains with a kind of deification of himself.
However, I was too keenly aware of white teeth and strong claws about me
to stop my chanting on that account.

'*His* are the stars in the sky.'

At last that song ended. I saw the Ape-man's face shining with perspi-
ration; and my eyes being now accustomed to the darkness, I saw more
distinctly the figure in the corner from which the voice came. It was the
size of a man, but it seemed covered with a dull grey hair almost like a Skye
terrier. What was it? What were they all? Imagine yourself surrounded by
all the most horrible cripples and maniacs it is possible to conceive, and you
may understand a little of my feelings with these grotesque caricatures of
humanity about me.

'He is a five-man, a five-man, a five-man – like me,' said the Ape-man.

I held out my hands. The grey creature in the corner leant forward.

'Not to run on all-fours; that is the Law. Are we not Men?' he said.

He put out a strangely distorted talon and gripped my fingers. The thing
was almost like the hoof of a deer produced into claws. I could have yelled
with surprise and pain. His face came forward and peered at my nails,
came forward into the light of the opening of the hut and I saw with a
quivering disgust that it was like the face of neither man nor beast, but a
mere shock of grey hair, with three shadowy over-archings to mark the
eyes and mouth.

'He has little nails,' said this grisly creature in his hairy beard. 'It is well.'

He threw my hand down, and instinctively I gripped my stick.

'Eat roots and herbs; it is His will,' said the Ape-man.

'I am the Sayer of the Law,' said the grey figure. 'Here come all that be
new to learn the Law. I sit in the darkness and say the Law.'

'It is even so,' said one of the beasts in the doorway.

'Evil are the punishments of those who break the Law. None escape.'

'None escape,' said the Beast Folk, glancing furtively at one another.

'None, none,' said the Ape-man – 'none escape. See! I did a little thing,
a wrong thing, once. I jabbered, jabbered, stopped talking. None could
understand. I am burnt, branded in the hand. He is great. He is good!'

'None escape,' said the grey creature in the corner.

'None escape,' said the Beast People, looking askance at one another.

'For everyone the want that is bad,' said the grey Sayer of the Law. 'What
you will want we do not know; we shall know. Some want to follow things
that move, to watch and slink and wait and spring; to kill and bite, bite
deep and rich, sucking the blood. It is bad. "Not to chase other Men; that
is the Law. *Are we not Men?* Not to eat Flesh or Fish; that is the Law. *Are
we not Men?*"'

'None escape,' said a dappled brute standing in the doorway.

'For everyone the want is bad,' said the grey Sayer of the Law. 'Some

want to go tearing with teeth and hands into the roots of things, snuffing into the earth. It is bad.'

'None escape,' said the men in the door.

'Some go clawing trees; some go scratching at the graves of the dead; some go fighting with foreheads or feet or claws; some bite suddenly, none giving occasion; some love uncleanness.'

'None escape,' said the Ape-man, scratching his calf.

'None escape,' said the little pink sloth creature.

'Punishment is sharp and sure. Therefore learn the Law. Say the words.'

And incontinently he began again the strange litany of the Law, and again I and all these creatures began singing and swaying. My head reeled with this jabbering and the close stench of the place; but I kept on, trusting to find presently some chance of a new development.

'Not to go on all-fours; that is the Law. *Are we not Men?*'

We were making such a noise that I noticed nothing of a tumult outside, until someone, who I think was one of the two Swine Men I had seen, thrust his head over the little pink sloth creature and shouted something excitedly, something that I did not catch. Incontinently those at the opening of the hut vanished; my Ape-man rushed out; the thing that had sat in the dark followed him (I only observed that it was big and clumsy, and covered with silvery hair), and I was left alone. Then before I reached the aperture I heard the yelp of a staghound.

In another moment I was standing outside the hovel, my chair-rail in my hand, every muscle of me quivering. Before me were the clumsy backs of perhaps a score of these Beast People, their misshapen heads half hidden by their shoulder-blades. They were gesticulating excitedly. Other half-animal faces glared interrogation out of the hovels. Looking in the direction in which they faced, I saw coming through the haze under the trees beyond the end of the passage of dens the dark figure and awful white face of Moreau. He was holding the leaping staghound back, and close behind him came Montgomery revolver in hand.

For a moment I stood horror-struck. I turned and saw the passage behind me blocked by another heavy brute, with a huge grey face and twinkling little eyes, advancing towards me. I looked round and saw to the right of me and a half-dozen yards in front of me a narrow gap in the wall of rock through which a ray of light slanted into the shadows.

'Stop!' cried Moreau as I strode towards this, and then, 'Hold him!'

At that, first one face turned towards me and then others. Their bestial minds were happily slow. I dashed my shoulder into a clumsy monster who was turning to see what Moreau meant, and flung him forward into another. I felt his hands fly round, clutching at me and missing me. The little pink sloth creature dashed at me, and I gashed down its ugly face with the nail in my stick and in another minute was scrambling up a steep side pathway,

a kind of sloping chimney, out of the ravine. I heard a howl behind me, and cries of 'Catch him!' 'Hold him!' and the grey-faced creature appeared behind me and jammed his huge bulk into the cleft. 'Go on! Go on!' they howled. I clambered up the narrow cleft in the rock and came out upon the sulphur on the westward side of the village of the Beast Men.

That gap was altogether fortunate for me, for the narrow chimney, slanting obliquely upward, must have impeded the nearer pursuers. I ran over the white space and down a steep slope, through a scattered growth of trees, and came to a low-lying stretch of tall reeds, through which I pushed into a dark, thick undergrowth that was black and succulent under foot. As I plunged into the reeds, my foremost pursuers emerged from the gap. I broke my way through this undergrowth for some minutes. The air behind me and about me was soon full of threatening cries. I heard the tumult of my pursuers in the gap up the slope, then the crashing of the reeds, and every now and then the crackling crash of a branch. Some of the creatures roared like excited beasts of prey. The staghound yelped to the left. I heard Moreau and Montgomery shouting in the same direction. I turned sharply to the right. It seemed to me even then that I heard Montgomery shouting for me to run for my life.

Presently the ground gave, rich and oozy, under my feet; but I was desperate and went headlong into it, struggled through knee-deep, and so came to a winding path among tall canes. The noise of my pursuers passed away to my left. In one place three strange, pink, hopping animals, about the size of cats, bolted before my footsteps. This pathway ran up hill, across another open space covered with white incrustation, and plunged into a cane-brake again. Then suddenly it turned parallel with the edge of a steep-walled gap, which came without warning, like the ha-ha of an English park – turned with an unexpected abruptness. I was still running with all my might, and I never saw this drop until I was flying headlong through the air.

I fell on my forearms and head, among thorns, and rose with a torn ear and bleeding face. I had fallen into a precipitous ravine, rocky and thorny, full of a hazy mist which drifted about me in wisps, and with a narrow streamlet from which this mist came meandering down the centre. I was astonished at this thin fog in the full blaze of daylight; but I had no time to stand wondering then. I turned to my right, downstream, hoping to come to the sea in that direction, and so have my way open to drown myself. It was only later I found that I had dropped my nailed stick in my fall.

Presently the ravine grew narrower for a space, and carelessly I stepped into the stream. I jumped out again pretty quickly, for the water was almost boiling. I noticed too there was a thin sulphurous scum drifting upon its coiling water. Almost immediately came a turn in the ravine, and the indistinct blue horizon. The nearer sea was flashing the sun from a myriad facets. I saw my death before me; but I was hot and panting, with the warm blood oozing out

on my face and running pleasantly through my veins. I felt more than a touch of exultation too, at having distanced my pursuers. It was not in me then to go out and drown myself yet. I stared back the way I had come.

I listened. Save for the hum of the gnats and the chirp of some small insects that hopped among the thorns, the air was absolutely still. Then came the yelp of a dog, very faint, and a chattering and gibbering, the snap of a whip, and voices. They grew louder, then fainter again. The noise receded up the stream and faded away. For a while the chase was over; but I knew now how much hope of help for me lay in the Beast People.

CHAPTER XIII

A Parley

I turned again and went on down towards the sea. I found the hot stream broadened out to a shallow, weedy sand, in which an abundance of crabs and long-bodied, many-legged creatures started from my footfall. I walked to the very edge of the salt water, and then I felt I was safe. I turned and stared, arms akimbo, at the thick green behind me, into which the steamy ravine cut like a smoking gash. But, as I say, I was too full of excitement and (a true saying, though those who have never known danger may doubt it) too desperate to die.

Then it came into my head that there was one chance before me yet. While Moreau and Montgomery and their bestial rabble chased me through the island, might I not go round the beach until I came to their enclosure – make a flank march upon them, in fact, and then with a rock lugged out of their loosely built wall, perhaps, smash in the lock of the smaller door and see what I could find (knife, pistol or whatnot) to fight them with when they returned? It was at any rate something to try.

So I turned to the westward and walked along by the water's edge. The setting sun flashed his blinding heat into my eyes. The slight Pacific tide was running in with a gentle ripple. Presently the shore fell away southward, and the sun came round upon my right hand. Then suddenly, far in front of me, I saw first one and then several figures emerging from the bushes – Moreau, with his grey staghound, then Montgomery, and two others. At that I stopped.

They saw me, and began gesticulating and advancing. I stood watching them approach. The two Beast Men came running forward to cut me off from the undergrowth, inland. Montgomery came, running also, but straight towards me. Moreau followed slower with the dog.

At last I roused myself from my inaction, and turning seaward walked straight into the water. The water was very shallow at first. I was thirty yards out before the waves reached to my waist. Dimly I could see the intertidal creatures darting away from my feet.

'What are you doing, man?' cried Montgomery.

I turned, standing waist deep, and stared at them. Montgomery stood panting at the margin of the water. His face was bright red with exertion, his long flaxen hair blown about his head, and his dropping nether lip showed his irregular teeth. Moreau was just coming up, his face pale and firm, and the dog at his hand barked at me. Both men had heavy whips. Further up the beach stared the Beast Men.

'What am I doing? I am going to drown myself,' said I.

Montgomery and Moreau looked at each other. 'Why?' asked Moreau.

'Because that is better than being tortured by you.'

'I told you so,' said Montgomery, and Moreau said something in a low tone.

'What makes you think I shall torture you?' asked Moreau.

'What I saw,' I said. 'And those – yonder.'

'Hush!' said Moreau, and held up his hand.

'I will not,' said I. 'They were men: what are they now? I at least will not be like them.'

I looked past my interlocutors. Up the beach were M'ling, Montgomery's attendant, and one of the white-swathed brutes from the boat. Further up, in the shadow of the trees, I saw my little Ape-man, and behind him some other dim figures.

'Who are these creatures?' said I, pointing to them and raising my voice more and more that it might reach them. 'They were men, men like your-selves, whom you have infected with some bestial taint – men whom you have enslaved, and whom you still fear.

'You who listen,' I cried, pointing now to Moreau and shouting past him to the Beast Men – 'You who listen! Do you not see these men still fear you, go in dread of you? Why, then, do you fear them? You are many—'

'For God's sake,' cried Montgomery, 'stop that, Prendick!'

'Prendick!' cried Moreau.

They both shouted together, as if to drown my voice; and behind them lowered the staring faces of the Beast Men, wondering, their deformed hands hanging down, their shoulders hunched up. They seemed, as I fancied, to be trying to understand me, to remember, I thought, something of their human past.

I went on shouting, I scarcely remember what – that Moreau and Montgomery could be killed, that they were not to be feared: that was the burden of what I put into the heads of the Beast People. I saw the green-eyed man in the dark rags, who had met me on the evening of my arrival, come out from among the trees, and others followed him, to hear me better. At last for want of breath I paused.

'Listen to me for a moment,' said the steady voice of Moreau; 'and then say what you will.'

'Well?' said I.

He coughed, thought, then shouted: 'Latin, Prendick! Bad Latin, schoolboy Latin; but try and understand. *Hi non sunt homines; sunt animalia qui nos habemus* – vivisected. A humanizing process. I will explain. Come ashore.'

I laughed. 'A pretty story,' said I. 'They talk, build houses. They were men. It's likely I'll come ashore.'

'The water just beyond where you stand is deep – and full of sharks.'

'That's my way,' said I. 'Short and sharp. Presently.'

'Wait a minute.' He took something out of his pocket that flashed back the sun, and dropped the object at his feet. 'That's a loaded revolver,' said he. 'Montgomery here will do the same. Now we are going up the beach until you are satisfied the distance is safe. Then come and take the revolvers.'

'Not I! You have a third between you.'

'I want you to think over things, Prendick. In the first place, I never asked you to come upon this island. If we vivisected men, we should import men, not beasts. In the next, we had you drugged last night, had we wanted to work you any mischief; and in the next, now your first panic is over and you can think a little, is Montgomery here quite up to the character you give him? We have chased you for your good. Because this island is full of inimical phenomena. Besides, why should we want to shoot you when you have just offered to drown yourself?'

'Why did you set – your people onto me when I was in the hut?'

'We felt sure of catching you, and bringing you out of danger. Afterwards we drew away from the scent, for your good.'

I mused. It seemed just possible. Then I remembered something again. 'But I saw,' said I, 'in the enclosure—'

'That was the puma.'

'Look here, Prendick,' said Montgomery, 'you're a silly ass! Come out of the water and take these revolvers, and talk. We can't do anything more than we could do now.'

I will confess that then, and indeed always, I distrusted and dreaded Moreau; but Montgomery was a man I felt I understood.

'Go up the beach,' said I, after thinking, and added, 'holding your hands up.'

'Can't do that,' said Montgomery, with an explanatory nod over his shoulder. 'Undignified.'

'Go up to the trees, then,' said I, 'as you please.'

'It's a damned silly ceremony,' said Montgomery.

Both turned and faced the six or seven grotesque creatures, who stood there in the sunlight, solid, casting shadows, moving, and yet so incredibly unreal. Montgomery cracked his whip at them, and forthwith they all turned and fled helter-skelter into the trees; and when Montgomery and Moreau were at a distance I judged sufficient, I waded ashore, and picked up and examined the revolvers. To satisfy myself against the subtlest trickery, I discharged one at a round lump of lava, and had the satisfaction of seeing the stone pulverized and the beach splashed with lead. Still I hesitated for a moment.

'I'll take the risk,' said I, at last; and with a revolver in each hand I walked up the beach towards them.

'That's better,' said Moreau, without affectation. 'As it is, you have wasted the best part of my day with your confounded imagination.' And with a touch of contempt which humiliated me, he and Montgomery turned and went on in silence before me.

The knot of Beast Men, still wondering, stood back among the trees. I passed them as serenely as possible. One started to follow me, but retreated again when Montgomery cracked his whip. The rest stood silent – watching. They may once have been animals; but I never before saw an animal trying to think.

CHAPTER XIV

Doctor Moreau Explains*

'And now, Prendick, I will explain,' said Doctor Moreau, so soon as we had eaten and drunk. 'I must confess that you are the most dictatorial guest I ever entertained. I warn you that this is the last I shall do to oblige you. The next thing you threaten to commit suicide about, I shan't do – even at some personal inconvenience.'

He sat in my deck chair, a cigar half consumed in his white, dexterous-looking fingers. The light of the swinging lamp fell on his white hair; he stared through the little window out at the starlight. I sat as far away from him as possible, the table between us and the revolvers to hand. Montgomery was not present. I did not care to be with the two of them in such a little room.

'You admit that the vivisected human being, as you called it, is, after all, only the puma?' said Moreau. He had made me visit that horror in the inner room, to assure myself of its inhumanity.

'It is the puma,' I said, 'still alive, but so cut and mutilated as I pray I may never see living flesh again. Of all vile—'

'Never mind that,' said Moreau; 'at least, spare me those youthful horrors. Montgomery used to be just the same. You admit that it is the puma. Now be quiet, while I reel off my physiological lecture to you.'

And forthwith, beginning in the tone of a man supremely bored, but presently warming a little, he explained his work to me. He was very simple and convincing. Now and then there was a touch of sarcasm in his voice. Presently I found myself hot with shame at our mutual positions.

The creatures I had seen were not men, had never been men. They were animals, humanized animals – triumphs of vivisection.

'You forget all that a skilled vivisector can do with living things,' said Moreau. 'For my own part, I'm puzzled why the things I have done here have not been done before. Small efforts, of course, have been made – amputation, tongue-cutting, excisions. Of course you know a squint may be induced or cured by surgery? Then in the case of excisions you have all kinds of secondary changes, pigmentary disturbances, modifications of the passions, alterations in the secretion of fatty tissue. I have no doubt you have heard of these things?'

* NOTE. The substance of the chapter entitled 'Doctor Moreau Explains', which contains the essential idea of the story, appeared as a middle article in the Saturday Review in January 1895. This is the only portion of this story that has been previously published, and it has been entirely recast to adapt it to the narrative form.

'Of course,' said I. 'But these foul creatures of yours—'

'All in good time,' said he, waving his hand at me; 'I am only beginning. Those are trivial cases of alteration. Surgery can do better things than that. There is building up as well as breaking down and changing. You have heard, perhaps, of a common surgical operation resorted to in cases where the nose has been destroyed: a flap of skin is cut from the forehead, turned down on the nose, and heals in the new position. This is a kind of grafting in a new position of part of an animal upon itself. Grafting of freshly obtained material from another animal is also possible – the case of teeth, for example. The grafting of skin and bone is done to facilitate healing: the surgeon places in the middle of the wound pieces of skin snipped from another animal, or fragments of bone from a victim freshly killed. Hunter's cockspur – possibly you have heard of that – flourished on the bull's neck; and the rhinoceros rats of the Algerian Zouaves are also to be thought of – monsters manufactured by transferring a slip from the tail of an ordinary rat to its snout, and allowing it to heal in that position.'

'Monsters manufactured!' said I. 'Then you mean to tell me—'

'Yes. These creatures you have seen are animals carven and wrought into new shapes. To that, to the study of the plasticity of living forms, my life has been devoted. I have studied for years, gaining in knowledge as I go. I see you look horrified, and yet I am telling you nothing new. It all lay in the surface of practical anatomy years ago, but no one had the temerity to touch it. It is not simply the outward form of an animal which I can change. The physiology, the chemical rhythm of the creature, may also be made to undergo an enduring modification – of which vaccination and other methods of inoculation with living or dead matter are examples that will, no doubt, be familiar to you. A similar operation is the transfusion of blood – with which subject, indeed, I began. These are all familiar cases. Less so, and probably far more extensive, were the operations of those mediaeval practitioners who made dwarfs and beggar-cripples, show-monsters – some vestiges of whose art still remain in the preliminary manipulation of the young mountebank or contortionist. Victor Hugo gives an account of them in *L'Homme qui Rit*. – But perhaps my meaning grows plain now. You begin to see that it is a possible thing to transplant tissue from one part of an animal to another, or from one animal to another; to alter its chemical reactions and methods of growth; to modify the articulations of its limbs; and, indeed, to change it in its most intimate structure?

'And yet this extraordinary branch of knowledge has never been sought as an end, and systematically, by modern investigators until I took it up! Some such things have been hit upon in the last resort of surgery; most of the kindred evidence that will recur to your mind has been demonstrated as it were by accident – by tyrants, by criminals, by the breeders of horses and dogs, by all kinds of untrained clumsy-handed men working for their

own immediate ends. I was the first man to take up this question armed
with antiseptic surgery, and with a really scientific knowledge of the laws of
growth. Yet one would imagine it must have been practised in secret before.
Such creatures as the Siamese Twins.... And in the vaults of the Inquisition.
No doubt their chief aim was artistic torture, but some at least of the inquis-
itors must have had a touch of scientific curiosity.'

'But,' said I, 'these things – these animals *talk*!'

He said that was so, and proceeded to point out that the possibility of
vivisection does not stop at a mere physical metamorphosis. A pig may be
educated. The mental structure is even less determinate than the bodily. In
our growing science of hypnotism we find the promise of a possibility of
superseding old inherent instincts by new suggestions, grafted upon or
replacing the inherited fixed ideas. Very much indeed of what we call moral
education, he said, is such an artificial modification and perversion of instinct;
pugnacity is trained into courageous self-sacrifice, and suppressed sexuality
into religious emotion. And the great difference between man and monkey
is in the larynx, he continued – in the incapacity to frame delicately different
sound-symbols by which thought could be sustained. In this I failed to agree
with him, but with a certain incivility he declined to notice my objection.
He repeated that the thing was so, and continued his account of his work.

I asked him why he had taken the human form as a model. There
seemed to me then, and there still seems to me now, a strange wickedness
in that choice.

He confessed that he had chosen that form by chance. 'I might just as
well have worked to form sheep into llamas and llamas into sheep. I suppose
there is something in the human form that appeals to the artistic turn of
mind more powerfully than any animal shape can. But I've not confined
myself to man-making. Once or twice—' He was silent, for a minute perhaps.
'These years! How they have slipped by! And here I have wasted a day
saving your life, and am now wasting an hour explaining myself!'

'But,' said I, 'I still do not understand. Where is your justification for
inflicting all this pain? The only thing that could excuse vivisection to me
would be some application—'

'Precisely,' said he. 'But, you see, I am differently constituted. We are on
different platforms. You are a materialist.'

'I am *not* a materialist,' I began hotly.

'In my view – in my view. For it is just this question of pain that parts
us. So long as visible or audible pain turns you sick; so long as your own
pains drive you; so long as pain underlies your propositions about sin, – so
long, I tell you, you are an animal, thinking a little less obscurely what an
animal feels. This pain—'

I gave an impatient shrug at such sophistry.

'Oh, but it is such a little thing! A mind truly opened to what science

has to teach must see that it is a little thing. It may be that, save in this little planet, this speck of cosmic dust, invisible long before the nearest star could be attained – it may be, I say, that nowhere else does this thing called pain occur. But the laws we feel our way towards.... Why, even on this earth, even among living things, what pain is there?'

As he spoke he drew a little penknife from his pocket, opened the smaller blade, and moved his chair so that I could see his thigh. Then, choosing the place deliberately, he drove the blade into his leg and withdrew it.

'No doubt,' he said, 'you have seen that before. It does not hurt a pin-prick. But what does it show? The capacity for pain is not needed in the muscle, and it is not placed there – is but little needed in the skin, and only here and there over the thigh is a spot capable of feeling pain. Pain is simply our intrinsic medical adviser to warn us and stimulate us. Not all living flesh is painful; nor is all nerve, not even all sensory nerve. There's no taint of pain, real pain, in the sensations of the optic nerve. If you wound the optic nerve, you merely see flashes of light – just as disease of the auditory nerve merely means a humming in our ears. Plants do not feel pain, nor the lower animals; it's possible that such animals as the starfish and crayfish do not feel pain at all. Then with men, the more intelligent they become, the more intelligently they will see after their own welfare, and the less they will need the goad to keep them out of danger. I never yet heard of a useless thing that was not ground out of existence by evolution sooner or later. Did you? And pain gets needless.

'Then I am a religious man, Prendick, as every sane man must be. It may be, I fancy, that I have seen more of the ways of this world's Maker than you – for I have sought his laws, in my way, all my life, while you, I understand, have been collecting butterflies. And I tell you, pleasure and pain have nothing to do with heaven or hell. Pleasure and pain – bah! What is your theologian's ecstasy but Mahomet's houri in the dark? This store which men and women set on pleasure and pain, Prendick, is the mark of the beast upon them – the mark of the beast from which they came! Pain! Pain and pleasure, they are for us only so long as we wriggle in the dust.

'You see, I went on with this research just the way it led me. That is the only way I ever heard of true research going. I asked a question, devised some method of obtaining an answer, and got a fresh question. Was this possible or that possible? You cannot imagine what this means to an investigator, what an intellectual passion grows upon him! You cannot imagine the strange, colourless delight of these intellectual desires! The thing before you is no longer an animal, a fellow creature, but a problem! Sympathetic pain – all I know of it I remember as a thing I used to suffer from years ago. I wanted – it was the one thing I wanted – to find out the extreme limit of plasticity in a living shape.'

'But,' said I, 'the thing is an abomination—'

'To this day I have never troubled about the ethics of the matter,' he continued. 'The study of Nature makes a man at last as remorseless as Nature. I have gone on, not heeding anything but the question I was pursuing; and the material has – dripped into the huts yonder. It is nearly eleven years since we came here, I and Montgomery and six Kanakas. I remember the green stillness of the island and the empty ocean about us, as though it was yesterday. The place seemed waiting for me.

'The stores were landed and the house was built. The Kanakas founded some huts near the ravine. I went to work here upon what I had brought with me. There were some disagreeable things happened at first. I began with a sheep, and killed it after a day and a half by a slip of the scalpel. I took another sheep, and made a thing of pain and fear and left it bound up to heal. It looked quite human to me when I had finished it; but when I went to it I was discontented with it. It remembered me, and was terrified beyond imagination; and it had no more than the wits of a sheep. The more I looked at it the clumsier it seemed, until at last I put the monster out of its misery. These animals without courage, these fear-haunted, pain-driven things, without a spark of pugnacious energy to face torment – they are no good for man-making.

'Then I took a gorilla I had; and upon that, working with infinite care and mastering difficulty after difficulty, I made my first man. All the week, night and day, I moulded him. With him it was chiefly the brain that needed moulding; much had to be added, much changed. I thought him a fair specimen of the Negroid type when I had finished him, and he lay bandaged, bound, and motionless before me. It was only when his life was assured that I left him and came into this room again, and found Montgomery much as you are. He had heard some of the cries as the thing grew human – cries like those that disturbed you so. I didn't take him completely into my confidence at first. And the Kanakas too, had realized something of it. They were scared out of their wits by the sight of me. I got Montgomery over to me – in a way; but I and he had the hardest job to prevent the Kanakas deserting. Finally they did; and so we lost the yacht. I spent many days educating the brute – altogether I had him for three or four months. I taught him the rudiments of English; gave him ideas of counting; even made the thing read the alphabet. But at that he was slow, though I've met with idiots slower. He began with a clean sheet, mentally; had no memories left in his mind of what he had been. When his scars were quite healed, and he was no longer anything but painful and stiff, and able to converse a little, I took him yonder and introduced him to the Kanakas as an interesting stowaway.

'They were horribly afraid of him at first, somehow – which offended me rather, for I was conceited about him; but his ways seemed so mild, and he was so abject, that after a time they received him and took his education in hand. He was quick to learn, very imitative and adaptive, and built himself

a hovel rather better, it seemed to me, than their own shanties. There was one among the boys a bit of a missionary, and he taught the thing to read, or at least to pick out letters, and gave him some rudimentary ideas of morality; but it seems the beast's habits were not all that is desirable.

'I rested from work for some days after this, and was in a mind to write an account of the whole affair to wake up English physiology. Then I came upon the creature squatting up in a tree and gibbering at two of the Kanakas who had been teasing him. I threatened him, told him the inhumanity of such a proceeding, aroused his sense of shame, and came home resolved to do better before I took my work back to England. I have been doing better. But somehow the things drift back again: the stubborn beast-flesh grows day by day back again. But I mean to do better things still. I mean to conquer that. This puma—

'But that's the story. All the Kanaka boys are dead now; one fell overboard off the launch, and one died of a wounded heel that he poisoned in some way with plant-juice. Three went away in the yacht, and I suppose and hope were drowned. The other one – was killed. Well, I have replaced them. Montgomery went on much as you are disposed to do at first, and then—

'What became of the other one?' said I, sharply, – 'the other Kanaka who was killed?'

'The fact is, after I had made a number of human creatures I made a Thing—' He hesitated.

'Yes?' said I.

'It was killed.'

'I don't understand,' said I; 'Do you mean to say—'

'It killed the Kanaka – yes. It killed several other things that it caught. We chased it for a couple of days. It only got loose by accident – I never meant it to get away. It wasn't finished. It was purely an experiment. It was a limbless thing, with a horrible face, that writhed along the ground in a serpentine fashion. It was immensely strong, and in infuriating pain. It lurked in the woods for some days, until we hunted it; and then it wriggled into the northern part of the island, and we divided the party to close in upon it. Montgomery insisted upon coming with me. The man had a rifle; and when his body was found, one of the barrels was curved into the shape of an S and very nearly bitten through. Montgomery shot the thing. After that I stuck to the ideal of humanity – except for little things.'

He became silent. I sat in silence watching his face.

'So for twenty years altogether – counting nine years in England – I have been going on; and there is still something in everything I do that defeats me, makes me dissatisfied, challenges me to further effort. Sometimes I rise above my level, sometimes I fall below it; but always I fall short of the things I dream. The human shape I can get now, almost with ease, so that it is lithe and graceful, or thick and strong; but often there is trouble

with the hands and the claws – painful things, that I dare not shape too freely. But it is in the subtle grafting and reshaping one must needs do to the brain that my trouble lies. The intelligence is often oddly low, with unaccountable blank ends, unexpected gaps. And least satisfactory of all is something that I cannot touch, somewhere – I cannot determine where – in the seat of the emotions. Cravings, instincts, desires that harm humanity, a strange hidden reservoir to burst forth suddenly and inundate the whole being of the creature with anger, hate, or fear.

'These creatures of mine seemed strange and uncanny to you so soon as you began to observe them; but to me, just after I make them, they seem to be indisputably human beings. It's afterwards, as I observe them, that the persuasion fades. First one animal trait, then another, creeps to the surface and stares out at me. But I will conquer yet! Each time I dip a living creature into the bath of burning pain, I say, "This time I will burn out all the animal; this time I will make a rational creature of my own!" After all, what is ten years? Men have been a hundred thousand in the making.'

He thought darkly. 'But I am drawing near the fastness. This puma of mine—'

After a silence, 'And they revert. As soon as my hand is taken from them the beast begins to creep back, begins to assert itself again.' Another long silence.

'Then you take the things you make into those dens?' said I.

'They go. I turn them out when I begin to feel the beast in them, and presently they wander there. They all dread this house and me. There is a kind of travesty of humanity over there. Montgomery knows about it, for he interferes in their affairs. He has trained one or two of them to our service. He's ashamed of it, but I believe he half likes some of those beasts. It's his business, not mine. They only sicken me with a sense of failure. I take no interest in them. I fancy they follow in the lines the Kanaka missionary marked out, and have a kind of mockery of a rational life, poor beasts! There's something they call the Law. Sing hymns about "all thine". They build themselves their dens, gather fruit and pull herbs – marry even. But I can see through it all, see into their very souls, and see there nothing but the souls of beasts, beasts that perish, anger and the lusts to live and gratify themselves.... Yet they're odd; complex, like everything else alive. There is a kind of upward striving in them, part vanity, part waste sexual emotion, part waste curiosity. It only mocks me. I have some hope of this puma. I have worked hard at her head and brain....

'And now,' said he, standing up after a long gap of silence, during which we had each pursued our own thoughts, 'what do you think? Are you in fear of me still?'

I looked at him, and saw but a white-faced, white-haired man, with calm eyes. Save for his serenity, the touch almost of beauty that resulted from his set tranquillity and his magnificent build, he might have passed muster among a hundred other comfortable old gentlemen. Then I shivered. By way of answer to his second question, I handed him a revolver with either hand.

'Keep them,' he said, and snatched at a yawn. He stood up, stared at me for a moment, and smiled. 'You have had two eventful days,' said he. 'I should advise some sleep. I'm glad it's all clear. Good night.' He thought me over for a moment, then went out by the inner door. I immediately turned the key in the outer one.

I sat down again; sat for a time in a kind of stagnant mood, so weary, emotionally, mentally and physically, that I could not think beyond the point at which he had left me. The black window stared at me like an eye. At last with an effort I put out the light and got into the hammock. Very soon I was asleep.

CHAPTER XV

Concerning the Beast Folk

I woke early. Moreau's explanation stood before my mind, clear and definite, from the moment of my awakening. I got out of the hammock and went to the door to assure myself that the key was turned. Then I tried the window bar, and found it firmly fixed. That these man-like creatures were in truth only bestial monsters, mere grotesque travesties of men, filled me with a vague uncertainty of their possibilities which was far worse than any definite fear.

A tapping came at the door, and I heard the glutinous accents of M'ling speaking. I pocketed one of the revolvers (keeping one hand upon it), and opened to him.

'Good morning, sair,' he said, bringing in, in addition to the customary herb breakfast, an ill-cooked rabbit. Montgomery followed him. His roving eye caught the position of my arm and he smiled askew.

The puma was resting to heal that day; but Moreau, who was singularly solitary in his habits, did not join us. I talked with Montgomery to clear my ideas of the way in which the Beast Folk lived. In particular, I was urgent to know how these inhuman monsters were kept from falling upon Moreau and Montgomery and from rending one another.

He explained to me that the comparative safety of Moreau and himself was due to the limited mental scope of these monsters. In spite of their increased intelligence and the tendency of their animal instincts to reawaken, they had certain fixed ideas implanted by Moreau in their minds, which absolutely bounded their imaginations. They were really hypnotized; had been told that certain things were impossible, and that certain things were not to be done, and these prohibitions were woven into the texture of their minds beyond any possibility of disobedience or dispute.

Certain matters, however, in which old instinct was at war with Moreau's convenience, were in a less stable condition. A series of propositions called the Law (I had already heard them recited) battled in their minds with the deep-seated, ever-rebellious cravings of their animal natures. This Law they were ever repeating, I found, and ever breaking. Both Montgomery and Moreau displayed particular solicitude to keep them ignorant of the taste of blood; they feared the inevitable suggestions of that flavour.

Montgomery told me that the Law, especially among the feline Beast People, became oddly weakened about nightfall; that then the animal was at its strongest; that a spirit of adventure sprang up in them at the dusk, when they would dare things they never seemed to dream about by day. To that I owed my stalking by the Leopard-man, on the night of my arrival.

But during these earlier days of my stay they broke the Law only furtively and after dark; in the daylight there was a general atmosphere of respect for its multifarious prohibitions.

And here perhaps I may give a few general facts about the island and the Beast People. The island, which was of irregular outline and lay low upon the wide sea, had a total area, I suppose, of seven or eight square miles.* It was volcanic in origin, and was now fringed on three sides by coral reefs; some fumaroles to the northward, and a hot spring, were the only vestiges of the forces that had long since originated it. Now and then a faint quiver of earthquake would be sensible, and sometimes the ascent of the spire of smoke would be rendered tumultuous by gusts of steam; but that was all. The population of the island, Montgomery informed me, now numbered rather more than sixty of these strange creations of Moreau's art, not counting the smaller monstrosities which lived in the undergrowth and were without human form. Altogether he had made nearly a hundred and twenty; but many had died, and others – like the writhing Footless Thing of which he had told me – had come by violent ends. In answer to my question, Montgomery said that they actually bore offspring, but that these generally died. When they lived, Moreau took them and stamped the human form upon them. There was no evidence of the inheritance of their acquired human characteristics. The females were less numerous than the males, and liable to much furtive persecution in spite of the monogamy the Law enjoined.

It would be impossible for me to describe these Beast People in detail; my eye has had no training in details, and unhappily I cannot sketch. Most striking, perhaps, in their general appearance was the disproportion between the legs of these creatures and the length of their bodies; and yet – so relative is our idea of grace – my eye became habituated to their forms, and at last I even fell in with their persuasion that my own long thighs were ungainly. Another point was the forward carriage of the head and the clumsy and inhuman curvature of the spine. Even the Ape-man lacked that inward sinuous curve of the back which makes the human figure so graceful. Most had their shoulders hunched clumsily, and their short forearms hung weakly at their sides. Few of them were conspicuously hairy, at least until the end of my time upon the island.

The next most obvious deformity was in their faces, almost all of which were prognathous, malformed about the ears, with large and protuberant noses, very furry or very bristly hair, and often strangely coloured or strangely placed eyes. None could laugh, though the Ape-man had a mirthless grin. Beyond these general characters their heads had little in common; each preserved the quality of its particular species: the human mark distorted but did not hide the leopard, the ox, or the sow, or other animal or animals,

* This description corresponds in every respect to Noble's Isle – C E P

from which the creature had been moulded. The voices, too, varied exceedingly. The hands were always malformed; and though some surprised me by their unexpected human appearance, almost all were deficient in the number of the digits, clumsy about the fingernails, and lacking any tactile sensibility.

The two most formidable Animal Men were the Leopard-man and a creature made of hyena and swine. Larger than these were the three bull creatures who pulled in the boat. Then came the silvery-hairy man, who was also the Sayer of the Law, M'ling, and a satyr-like creature of ape and goat. There were three Swine-men and a Swine-woman, a horse-rhinoceros creature, and several other females whose sources I did not ascertain. There were several wolf creatures, a bear-bull, and a Saint-Bernard-man. I have already described the Ape-man, and there was a particularly hateful (and evil-smelling) old woman made of vixen and bear, whom I hated from the beginning. She was said to be a passionate votary of the Law. Smaller creatures were certain dappled youths and my little sloth creature. But enough of this catalogue.

At first I had a shivering horror of the brutes, felt all too keenly that they were still brutes; but insensibly I became a little habituated to the idea of them, and moreover I was affected by Montgomery's attitude towards them. He had been with them so long that he had come to regard them as almost normal human beings. His London days seemed a glorious, impossible past to him. Only once in a year or so did he go to Arica to deal with Moreau's agent, a trader in animals there. He hardly met the finest type of mankind in that seafaring village of Spanish mongrels. The men aboard ship, he told me, seemed at first just as strange to him as the Beast Men seemed to me – unnaturally long in the leg, flat in the face, prominent in the forehead, suspicious, dangerous, and cold-hearted. In fact, he did not like men: his heart had warmed to me, he thought, because he had saved my life. I fancied even then that he had a sneaking kindness for some of these metamorphosed brutes, a vicious sympathy with some of their ways, but that he attempted to veil it from me at first.

M'ling, the black-faced man, Montgomery's attendant, the first of the Beast Folk I had encountered, did not live with the others across the island, but in a small kennel at the back of the enclosure. The creature was scarcely so intelligent as the Ape-man, but far more docile, and the most human-looking of all the Beast Folk; and Montgomery had trained it to prepare food, and indeed to discharge all the trivial domestic offices that were required. It was a complex trophy of Moreau's horrible skill – a bear, tainted with dog and ox, and one of the most elaborately made of all his creatures. It treated Montgomery with a strange tenderness and devotion. Sometimes he would notice it, pat it, call it half-mocking, half-jocular names, and so make it caper with extraordinary delight; sometimes he would ill-treat it, especially after he had been at the whisky, kicking it, beating it, pelting it

with stones or lighted fusees. But whether he treated it well or ill, it loved
nothing so much as to be near him.

I say I became habituated to the Beast People, so that a thousand things
which had seemed unnatural and repulsive speedily became natural and
ordinary to me. I suppose everything in existence takes its colour from the
average hue of our surroundings. Montgomery and Moreau were too pecu-
liar and individual to keep my general impressions of humanity well defined.
I would see one of the clumsy bovine creatures who worked the launch
treading heavily through the undergrowth, and find myself asking, trying
hard to recall, how he differed from some really human yokel trudging home
from his mechanical labours; or I would meet the Fox-bear woman's vulpine,
shifty face, strangely human in its speculative cunning, and even imagine I
had met it before in some city byway.

Yet every now and then the beast would flash out upon me beyond doubt
or denial. An ugly-looking man, a hunchbacked human savage to all appear-
ance, squatting in the aperture of one of the dens, would stretch his arms
and yawn, showing with startling suddenness scissor-edged incisors and
sabre-like canines, keen and brilliant as knives. Or in some narrow pathway,
glancing with a transitory daring into the eyes of some lithe, white-swathed
female figure, I would suddenly see (with a spasmodic revulsion) that she
had slit-like pupils, or glancing down note the curving nail with which she
held her shapeless wrap about her. It is a curious thing, by the by, for which
I am quite unable to account, that these weird creatures – the females, I
mean – had in the earlier days of my stay an instinctive sense of their own
repulsive clumsiness, and displayed in consequence a more than human
regard for the decency and decorum of extensive costume.

CHAPTER XVI

How the Beast Folk Tasted Blood

My inexperience as a writer betrays me, and I wander from the thread of my story.

After I had breakfasted with Montgomery, he took me across the island to see the fumarole and the source of the hot spring into whose scalding waters I had blundered on the previous day. Both of us carried whips and loaded revolvers. While going through a leafy jungle on our road thither, we heard a rabbit squealing. We stopped and listened, but we heard no more; and presently we went on our way, and the incident dropped out of our minds. Montgomery called my attention to certain little pink animals with long hind legs that went leaping through the undergrowth. He told me they were creatures made of the offspring of the Beast People, that Moreau had invented. He had fancied they might serve for meat, but a rabbit-like habit of devouring their young had defeated this intention. I had already encountered some of these creatures – once during my moonlight flight from the Leopard-man, and once during my pursuit by Moreau on the previous day. By chance, one hopping to avoid us leapt into the hole caused by the uprooting of a wind-blown tree; before it could extricate itself we managed to catch it. It spat like a cat, scratched and kicked vigorously with its hind-legs, and made an attempt to bite; but its teeth were too feeble to inflict more than a painless pinch. It seemed to me rather a pretty little creature; and as Montgomery stated that it never destroyed the turf by burrowing, and was very clean in its habits, I should imagine it might prove a convenient substitute for the common rabbit in gentlemen's parks.

We also saw on our way the trunk of a tree barked in long strips and splintered deeply. Montgomery called my attention to this. 'Not to claw bark of trees, *that* is the Law,' he said. 'Much some of them care for it!' It was after this, I think, that we met the Satyr and the Ape-man. The Satyr was a gleam of classical memory on the part of Moreau – his face ovine in expression, like the coarser Hebrew type; his voice a harsh bleat, his nether extremities Satanic. He was gnawing the husk of a pod-like fruit as he passed us. Both of them saluted Montgomery.

'Hail,' said they, 'to the Other with the Whip!'

'There's a Third with a Whip now,' said Montgomery. 'So you'd better mind!'

'Was he not made?' said the Ape-man. 'He said – he said he was made.'

The Satyr-man looked curiously at me. 'The Third with the Whip, he that walks weeping into the sea, has a thin white face.'

'He has a thin long whip,' said Montgomery.

'Yesterday he bled and wept,' said the Satyr. 'You never bleed nor weep. The Master does not bleed nor weep.'

'Ollendorffian beggar!' said Montgomery. 'You'll bleed and weep if you don't look out!'

'He has five fingers, he is a five-man like me,' said the Ape-man.

'Come along, Prendick,' said Montgomery, taking my arm; and I went on with him.

The Satyr and the Ape-man stood watching us and making other remarks to each other.

'He says nothing,' said the Satyr. 'Men have voices.'

'Yesterday he asked me of things to eat,' said the Ape-man. 'He did not know.'

Then they spoke inaudible things, and I heard the Satyr laughing.

It was on our way back that we came upon the dead rabbit. The red body of the wretched little beast was rent to pieces, many of the ribs stripped white, and the backbone indisputably gnawed.

At that Montgomery stopped. 'Good God!' said he, stooping down, and picking up some of the crushed vertebrae to examine them more closely. 'Good God!' he repeated. 'What can this mean?'

'Some carnivore of yours has remembered its old habits,' I said after a pause. 'This backbone has been bitten through.'

He stood staring, with his face white and his lip pulled askew. 'I don't like this,' he said slowly.

'I saw something of the same kind,' said I, 'the first day I came here.'

'The devil you did! What was it?'

'A rabbit with its head twisted off.'

'The day you came here?'

'The day I came here. In the undergrowth at the back of the enclosure, when I went out in the evening. The head was completely wrung off.'

He gave a long, low whistle.

'And what is more, I have an idea which of your brutes did the thing. It's only a suspicion, you know. Before I came on the rabbit I saw one of your monsters drinking in the stream.'

'Sucking his drink?'

'Yes.'

'"Not to suck your drink; that is the Law." Much the brutes care for the Law, eh, when Moreau's not about!'

'It was the brute who chased me.'

'Of course,' said Montgomery; 'it's just the way with carnivores. After a kill, they drink. It's the taste of blood, you know. What was the brute like?' he continued. 'Would you know him again?' He glanced about us, standing astride over the mess of dead rabbit, his eyes roving among the shadows and

screens of greenery, the lurking-places and ambuscades of the forest that bounded us in. 'The taste of blood,' he said again.

He took out his revolver, examined the cartridges in it and replaced it. Then he began to pull at his dropping lip.

'I think I should know the brute again,' I said. 'I stunned him. He ought to have a handsome bruise on the forehead of him.'

'But then we have to *prove* that he killed the rabbit,' said Montgomery. 'I wish I'd never brought the things here.'

I should have gone on, but he stayed there thinking over the mangled rabbit in a puzzle-headed way. As it was, I went to such a distance that the rabbit's remains were hidden.

'Come on!' I said.

Presently he woke up and came towards me. 'You see,' he said, almost in a whisper, 'they are all supposed to have a fixed idea against eating anything that runs on land. If some brute has by any accident tasted blood—'

We went on some way in silence. 'I wonder what can have happened,' he said to himself. Then, after a pause again: 'I did a foolish thing the other day. That servant of mine – I showed him how to skin and cook a rabbit. It's odd – I saw him licking his hands – It never occurred to me.'

Then: 'We must put a stop to this. I must tell Moreau.'

He could think of nothing else on our homeward journey.

Moreau took the matter even more seriously than Montgomery, and I need scarcely say that I was affected by their evident consternation.

'We must make an example,' said Moreau. 'I've no doubt in my own mind that the Leopard-man was the sinner. But how can we prove it? I wish, Montgomery, you had kept your taste for meat in hand, and gone without these exciting novelties. We may find ourselves in a mess yet, through it.'

'I was a silly ass,' said Montgomery. 'But the thing's done now; and you said I might have them, you know.'

'We must see to the thing at once,' said Moreau. 'I suppose if anything should turn up, M'ling can take care of himself?'

'I'm not so sure of M'ling,' said Montgomery. 'I think I ought to know him.'

In the afternoon, Moreau, Montgomery, myself and M'ling went across the island to the huts in the ravine. We three were armed; M'ling carried the little hatchet he used in chopping firewood, and some coils of wire. Moreau had a huge cowherd's horn slung over his shoulder.

'You will see a gathering of the Beast People,' said Montgomery. 'It is a pretty sight!'

Moreau said not a word on the way, but the expression of his heavy, white-fringed face was grimly set.

We crossed the ravine down which smoked the stream of hot water, and followed the winding pathway through the canebrakes until we reached a

wide area covered over with a thick, powdery yellow substance which I believe was sulphur. Above the shoulder of a weedy bank the sea glittered. We came to a kind of shallow natural amphitheatre, and here the four of us halted. Then Moreau sounded the horn, and broke the sleeping stillness of the tropical afternoon. He must have had strong lungs. The hooting note rose and rose amidst its echoes, to at last an ear-penetrating intensity.

'Ah!' said Moreau, letting the curved instrument fall to his side again.

Immediately there was a crashing through the yellow canes, and a sound of voices from the dense green jungle that marked the morass through which I had run on the previous day. Then at three or four points on the edge of the sulphurous area appeared the grotesque forms of the Beast People hurrying towards us. I could not help a creeping horror, as I perceived first one and then another trot out from the trees or reeds and come shambling along over the hot dust. But Moreau and Montgomery stood calmly enough; and, perforce, I stuck beside them.

First to arrive was the Satyr, strangely unreal for all that he cast a shadow and tossed the dust with his hoofs. After him from the brake came a monstrous lout, a thing of horse and rhinoceros, chewing a straw as it came; then appeared the Swine-woman and two Wolf-women; then the Fox-bear witch, with her red eyes in her peaked red face, and then others – all hurrying eagerly. As they came forward they began to cringe towards Moreau and chant, quite regardless of one another, fragments of the latter half of the litany of the Law – 'His is the Hand that wounds; His is the Hand that heals,' and so forth. As soon as they had approached within a distance of perhaps thirty yards they halted, and bowing on knees and elbows began flinging the white dust upon their heads.

Imagine the scene if you can! We three blue-clad men, with our misshapen black-faced attendant, standing in a wide expanse of sunlit yellow dust under the blazing blue sky, and surrounded by this circle of crouching and gesticulating monstrosities – some almost human save in their subtle expression and gestures, some like cripples, some so strangely distorted as to resemble nothing but the denizens of our wildest dreams; and, beyond, the reedy lines of a canebrake in one direction, a dense tangle of palm trees on the other, separating us from the ravine with the huts, and to the north the hazy horizon of the Pacific Ocean.

'Sixty-two, sixty-three,' counted Moreau. 'There are four more.'

'I do not see the Leopard-man,' said I.

Presently Moreau sounded the great horn again, and at the sound of it all the Beast People writhed and grovelled in the dust. Then, slinking out of the canebrake, stooping near the ground and trying to join the dust-throwing circle behind Moreau's back, came the Leopard-man. The last of the Beast People to arrive was the little Ape-man. The earlier animals, hot and weary with their grovelling, shot vicious glances at him.

'Cease!' said Moreau, in his firm, loud voice; and the Beast People sat back upon their hams and rested from their worshipping.

'Where is the Sayer of the Law?' said Moreau, and the hairy-grey monster bowed his face in the dust.

'Say the words!' said Moreau.

Forthwith all in the kneeling assembly, swaying from side to side and dashing up the sulphur with their hands – first the right hand and a puff of dust, and then the left – began once more to chant their strange litany. When they reached, 'Not to eat Flesh or Fish, that is the Law,' Moreau held up his lank white hand.

'*Stop!*' he cried, and there fell absolute silence upon them all.

I think they all knew and dreaded what was coming. I looked round at their strange faces. When I saw their wincing attitudes and the furtive dread in their bright eyes, I wondered that I had ever believed them to be men.

'That Law has been broken!' said Moreau.

'None escape,' from the faceless creature with the silvery hair. 'None escape,' repeated the kneeling circle of Beast People.

'Who is he?' cried Moreau, and looked round at their faces, cracking his whip. I fancied the Hyena-swine looked dejected, so too did the Leopard-man. Moreau stopped, facing this creature, who cringed towards him with the memory and dread of infinite torment.

'Who is he?' repeated Moreau, in a voice of thunder.

'Evil is he who breaks the Law,' chanted the Sayer of the Law.

Moreau looked into the eyes of the Leopard-man, and seemed to be dragging the very soul out of the creature.

'Who breaks the Law—' said Moreau, taking his eyes off his victim, and turning towards us (it seemed to me there was a touch of exultation in his voice).

'Goes back to the House of Pain,' they all clamoured – 'goes back to the House of Pain, O Master!'

'Back to the House of Pain – back to the House of Pain,' gabbled the Ape-man, as though the idea was sweet to him.

'Do you hear?' said Moreau, turning back to the criminal. 'My friend – hullo!'

For the Leopard-man, released from Moreau's eye, had risen straight from his knees, and now, with eyes aflame and his huge feline tusks flashing out from under his curling lips, leapt towards his tormentor. I am convinced that only the madness of unendurable fear could have prompted this attack. The whole circle of threescore monsters seemed to rise about us. I drew my revolver. The two figures collided. I saw Moreau reeling back from the Leopard-man's blow. There was a furious yelling and howling all about us. Everyone was moving rapidly. For a moment I thought it was a general revolt. The furious face of the Leopard-man flashed by mine, with M'ling close in pursuit. I saw

the yellow eyes of the Hyena-swine blazing with excitement, his attitude as if he were half resolved to attack me. The Satyr, too, glared at me over the Hyena-swine's hunched shoulders. I heard the crack of Moreau's pistol, and saw the pink flash dart across the tumult. The whole crowd seemed to swing round in the direction of the glint of fire, and I too was swung round by the magnetism of the movement. In another second I was running, one of a tumultuous shouting crowd, in pursuit of the escaping Leopard-man.

That is all I can tell definitely. I saw the Leopard-man strike Moreau, and then everything spun about me until I was running headlong. M'ling was ahead, close in pursuit of the fugitive. Behind, their tongues already lolling out, ran the Wolf-women in great leaping strides. The Swine folk followed, squealing with excitement, and the two Bull-men in their swathings of white. Then came Moreau in a cluster of the Beast People, his wide-brimmed straw hat blown off, his revolver in hand, and his lank white hair streaming out. The Hyena-swine ran beside me, keeping pace with me and glancing furtively at me out of his feline eyes, and the others came pattering and shouting behind us.

The Leopard-man went bursting his way through the long canes, which sprang back as he passed, and rattled in M'ling's face. We others in the rear found a trampled path for us when we reached the brake. The chase lay through the brake for perhaps a quarter of a mile, and then plunged into a dense thicket, which retarded our movements exceedingly, though we went through it in a crowd together – fronds flicking into our faces, ropy creepers catching us under the chin or gripping our ankles, thorny plants hooking into and tearing cloth and flesh together.

'He has gone on all-fours through this,' panted Moreau, now just ahead of me.

'None escape,' said the Wolf-bear, laughing into my face with the exultation of hunting.

We burst out again among rocks, and saw the quarry ahead running lightly on all-fours and snarling at us over his shoulder. At that the Wolf Folk howled with delight. The Thing was still clothed, and at a distance its face still seemed human; but the carriage of its four limbs was feline, and the furtive droop of its shoulder was distinctly that of a hunted animal. It leapt over some thorny yellow-flowering bushes, and was hidden. M'ling was halfway across the space.

Most of us now had lost the first speed of the chase, and had fallen into a longer and steadier stride. I saw as we traversed the open that the pursuit was now spreading from a column into a line. The Hyena-swine still ran close to me, watching me as it ran, every now and then puckering its muzzle with a snarling laugh. At the edge of the rocks the Leopard-man, realizing that he was making for the projecting cape upon which he had stalked me on the night of my arrival, had doubled in the undergrowth; but Montgomery

had seen the manoeuvre, and turned him again. So, panting, tumbling against rocks, torn by brambles, impeded by ferns and reeds, I helped to pursue the Leopard-man who had broken the Law, and the Hyena-swine ran, laughing savagely, by my side. I staggered on, my head reeling and my heart beating against my ribs, tired almost to death, and yet not daring to lose sight of the chase lest I should be left alone with this horrible companion. I staggered on in spite of infinite fatigue and the dense heat of the tropical afternoon.

At last the fury of the hunt slackened. We had pinned the wretched brute into a corner of the island. Moreau, whip in hand, marshalled us all into an irregular line, and we advanced now slowly, shouting to one another as we advanced and tightening the cordon about our victim. He lurked noiseless and invisible in the bushes through which I had run from him during that midnight pursuit.

'Steady!' cried Moreau, 'steady!' as the ends of the line crept round the tangle of undergrowth and hemmed the brute in.

''Ware a rush!' came the voice of Montgomery from beyond the thicket.

I was on the slope above the bushes; Montgomery and Moreau beat along the beach beneath. Slowly we pushed in among the fretted network of branches and leaves. The quarry was silent.

'Back to the House of Pain, the House of Pain, the House of Pain!' yelped the voice of the Ape-man, some twenty yards to the right.

When I heard that, I forgave the poor wretch all the fear he had inspired in me. I heard the twigs snap and the boughs swish aside before the heavy tread of the Horse-rhinoceros upon my right. Then suddenly through a polygon of green, in the half darkness under the luxuriant growth, I saw the creature we were hunting. I halted. He was crouched together into the smallest possible compass, his luminous green eyes turned over his shoulder regarding me.

It may seem a strange contradiction in me – I cannot explain the fact, – but now, seeing the creature there in a perfectly animal attitude, with the light gleaming in its eyes and its imperfectly human face distorted with terror, I realized again the fact of its humanity. In another moment other of its pursuers would see it, and it would be overpowered and captured, to experience once more the horrible tortures of the enclosure. Abruptly I slipped out my revolver, aimed between its terror-struck eyes, and fired. As I did so, the Hyena-swine saw the Thing, and flung itself upon it with an eager cry, thrusting thirsty teeth into its neck. All about me the green masses of the thicket were swaying and cracking as the Beast People came rushing together. One face and then another appeared.

'Don't kill it, Prendick!' cried Moreau. 'Don't kill it!' and I saw him stooping as he pushed through under the fronds of the big ferns.

In another moment he had beaten off the Hyena-swine with the handle of his whip, and he and Montgomery were keeping away the excited

carnivorous Beast People, and particularly M'ling, from the still quivering body. The hairy-grey Thing came sniffing at the corpse under my arm. The other animals, in their animal ardour, jostled me to get a nearer view.

'Confound you, Prendick!' said Moreau. 'I wanted him.'

'I'm sorry,' said I, though I was not. 'It was the impulse of the moment.' I felt sick with exertion and excitement. Turning, I pushed my way out of the crowding Beast People and went on alone up the slope towards the higher part of the headland. Under the shouted directions of Moreau I heard the three white-swathed Bull-men begin dragging the victim down towards the water.

It was easy now for me to be alone. The Beast People manifested a quite human curiosity about the dead body, and followed it in a thick knot, sniffing and growling at it as the Bull-men dragged it down the beach. I went to the headland and watched the Bull-men, black against the evening sky as they carried the weighted dead body out to sea; and like a wave across my mind came the realization of the unspeakable aimlessness of things upon the island. Upon the beach among the rocks beneath me were the Ape-man, the Hyena-swine, and several other of the Beast People, standing about Montgomery and Moreau. They were all still intensely excited, and all overflowing with noisy expressions of their loyalty to the Law; yet I felt an absolute assurance in my own mind that the Hyena-swine was implicated in the rabbit-killing. A strange persuasion came upon me, that, save for the grossness of the line, the grotesqueness of the forms, I had here before me the whole balance of human life in miniature, the whole interplay of instinct, reason, and fate in its simplest form. The Leopard-man had happened to go under: that was all the difference. Poor brute!

Poor brutes! I began to see the viler aspect of Moreau's cruelty. I had not thought before of the pain and trouble that came to these poor victims after they had passed from Moreau's hands. I had shivered only at the days of actual torment in the enclosure. But now that seemed to me the lesser part. Before, they had been beasts, their instincts fitly adapted to their surround-ings, and happy as living things may be. Now they stumbled in the shackles of humanity, lived in a fear that never died, fretted by a law they could not understand; their mock-human existence, begun in an agony, was one long internal struggle, one long dread of Moreau – and for what? It was the wantonness of it that stirred me.

Had Moreau had any intelligible object, I could have sympathized at least a little with him. I am not so squeamish about pain as that. I could have forgiven him a little even, had his motive been only hate. But he was so irresponsible, so utterly careless! His curiosity, his mad, aimless investigations, drove him on; and the Things were thrown out to live a year or so, to struggle and blunder and suffer, and at last to die painfully. They were wretched in themselves; the old animal hate moved them to trouble one

another; the Law held them back from a brief hot struggle and a decisive end to their natural animosities.

In those days my fear of the Beast People went the way of my personal fear for Moreau. I fell indeed into a morbid state, deep and enduring, and alien to fear, which has left permanent scars upon my mind. I must confess that I lost faith in the sanity of the world when I saw it suffering the painful disorder of this island. A blind Fate, a vast pitiless mechanism, seemed to cut and shape the fabric of existence and I, Moreau (by his passion for research), Montgomery (by his passion for drink), the Beast People with their instincts and mental restrictions, were torn and crushed, ruthlessly, inevitably, amid the infinite complexity of its incessant wheels. But this condition did not come all at once: I think indeed that I anticipate a little in speaking of it now.

CHAPTER XVII

A Catastrophe

Scarcely six weeks passed before I had lost every feeling but dislike and abhorrence for this infamous experiment of Moreau's. My one idea was to get away from these horrible caricatures of my Maker's image, back to the sweet and wholesome intercourse of men. My fellow creatures, from whom I was thus separated, began to assume idyllic virtue and beauty in my memory. My first friendship with Montgomery did not increase. His long separation from humanity, his secret vice of drunkenness, his evident sympathy with the Beast People, tainted him to me. Several times I let him go alone among them. I avoided intercourse with them in every possible way. I spent an increasing proportion of my time upon the beach, looking for some liberating sail that never appeared – until one day there fell upon us an appalling disaster, which put an altogether different aspect upon my strange surroundings.

It was about seven or eight weeks after my landing – rather more, I think, though I had not troubled to keep account of the time – when this catastrophe occurred. It happened in the early morning – I should think about six. I had risen and breakfasted early, having been aroused by the noise of three Beast Men carrying wood into the enclosure.

After breakfast I went to the open gateway of the enclosure, and stood there smoking a cigarette and enjoying the freshness of the early morning. Moreau presently came round the corner of the enclosure and greeted me. He passed by me, and I heard him behind me unlock and enter his laboratory. So indurated was I at that time to the abomination of the place that I heard without a touch of emotion the puma victim begin another day of torture. It met its persecutor with a shriek, almost exactly like that of an angry virago.

Then suddenly something happened – I do not know what, to this day. I heard a short, sharp cry behind me, a fall, and turning saw an awful face rushing upon me – not human, not animal, but hellish, brown, seamed with red branching scars, red drops starting out upon it, and the lidless eyes ablaze. I threw up my arm to defend myself from the blow that flung me headlong with a broken forearm; and the great monster, swathed in lint and with red-stained bandages fluttering about it, leapt over me and passed. I rolled over and over down the beach, tried to sit up, and collapsed upon my broken arm. Then Moreau appeared, his massive white face all the more terrible for the blood that trickled from his forehead. He carried a revolver in one hand. He scarcely glanced at me, but rushed off at once in pursuit of the puma.

I tried the other arm and sat up. The muffled figure in front ran in great striding leaps along the beach, and Moreau followed her. She turned her head and saw him, then doubling abruptly made for the bushes. She gained upon him at every stride. I saw her plunge into them, and Moreau, running slantingly to intercept her, fired and missed as she disappeared. Then he too vanished in the green confusion. I stared after them, and then the pain in my arm flamed up, and with a groan I staggered to my feet. Montgomery appeared in the doorway, dressed, and with his revolver in his hand.

'Great God, Prendick!' he said, not noticing that I was hurt, 'That brute's loose! Tore the fetter out of the wall! Have you seen them?' Then sharply, seeing I gripped my arm, 'What's the matter?'

'I was standing in the doorway,' said I.

He came forward and took my arm. 'Blood on the sleeve,' said he, and rolled back the flannel. He pocketed his weapon, felt my arm about painfully, and led me inside. 'Your arm is broken,' he said, and then, 'Tell me exactly how it happened – what happened?'

I told him what I had seen; told him in broken sentences, with gasps of pain between them, and very dexterously and swiftly he bound my arm meanwhile. He slung it from my shoulder, stood back and looked at me.

'You'll do,' he said. 'And now?' He thought. Then he went out and locked the gates of the enclosure. He was absent some time.

I was chiefly concerned about my arm. The incident seemed merely one more of many horrible things. I sat down in the deck chair, and I must admit swore heartily at the island. The first dull feeling of injury in my arm had already given way to a burning pain when Montgomery reappeared. His face was rather pale, and he showed more of his lower gums than ever.

'I can neither see nor hear anything of him,' he said. 'I've been thinking he may want my help.' He stared at me with his expressionless eyes. 'That was a strong brute,' he said. 'It simply wrenched its fetter out of the wall.' He went to the window, then to the door, and there turned to me. 'I shall go after him,' he said. 'There's another revolver I can leave with you. To tell you the truth, I feel anxious somehow.'

He obtained the weapon, and put it ready to my hand on the table; then went out, leaving a restless contagion in the air. I did not sit long after he left, but took the revolver in hand and went to the doorway.

The morning was as still as death. Not a whisper of wind was stirring; the sea was like polished glass, the sky empty, the beach desolate. In my half-excited, half-feverish state, this stillness of things oppressed me. I tried to whistle, and the tune died away. I swore again – the second time that morning. Then I went to the corner of the enclosure and stared inland at the green bush that had swallowed up Moreau and Montgomery. When would they return, and how? Then far away up the beach a little grey Beast Man appeared, ran down to the water's edge and began splashing about. I

strolled back to the doorway, then to the corner again, and so began pacing to and fro like a sentinel upon duty. Once I was arrested by the distant voice of Montgomery bawling, 'Coo-ee – Moreau!' My arm became less painful, but very hot. I got feverish and thirsty. My shadow grew shorter. I watched the distant figure until it went away again. Would Moreau and Montgomery never return? Three sea birds began fighting for some stranded treasure.

Then from far away behind the enclosure I heard a pistol-shot. A long silence, and then came another. Then a yelling cry nearer, and another dismal gap of silence. My unfortunate imagination set to work to torment me. Then suddenly a shot close by. I went to the corner, startled, and saw Montgomery – his face scarlet, his hair disordered, and the knee of his trousers torn. His face expressed profound consternation. Behind him slouched the Beast Man, M'ling, and round M'ling's jaws were some queer dark stains.

'Has he come?' said Montgomery.

'Moreau?' said I. 'No.'

'My God!' The man was panting, almost sobbing. 'Go back in,' he said, taking my arm. 'They're mad. They're all rushing about mad. What can have happened? I don't know. I'll tell you, when my breath comes. Where's some brandy?'

Montgomery limped before me into the room and sat down in the deck chair. M'ling flung himself down just outside the doorway and began panting like a dog. I got Montgomery some brandy and water. He sat staring in front of him at nothing, recovering his breath. After some minutes he began to tell me what had happened.

He had followed their track for some way. It was plain enough at first on account of the crushed and broken bushes, white rags torn from the puma's bandages, and occasional smears of blood on the leaves of the shrubs and undergrowth. He lost the track, however, on the stony ground beyond the stream where I had seen the Beast Man drinking, and went wandering aimlessly westward shouting Moreau's name. Then M'ling had come to him carrying a light hatchet. M'ling had seen nothing of the puma affair; had been felling wood, and heard him calling. They went on shouting together. Two Beast Men came crouching and peering at them through the under-growth, with gestures and a furtive carriage that alarmed Montgomery by their strangeness. He hailed them, and they fled guiltily. He stopped shouting after that, and after wandering some time further in an undecided way, determined to visit the huts.

He found the ravine deserted.

Growing more alarmed every minute, he began to retrace his steps. Then it was he encountered the two Swine-men I had seen dancing on the night of my arrival; bloodstained they were about the mouth, and intensely excited. They came crashing through the ferns, and stopped with

fierce faces when they saw him. He cracked his whip in some trepidation, and forthwith they rushed at him. Never before had a Beast Man dared to do that. One he shot through the head; M'ling flung himself upon the other, and the two rolled grappling. M'ling got his brute under and with his teeth in its throat, and Montgomery shot that too as it struggled in M'ling's grip. He had some difficulty in inducing M'ling to come on with him. Thence they had hurried back to me. On the way, M'ling had suddenly rushed into a thicket and driven out an under-sized Ocelot-man, also blood-stained, and lame through a wound in the foot. This brute had run a little way and then turned savagely at bay, and Montgomery – with a certain wantonness, I thought – had shot him.

'What does it all mean?' said I.

He shook his head, and turned once more to the brandy.

CHAPTER XVIII

The Finding of Moreau

When I saw Montgomery swallow a third dose of brandy, I took it upon myself to interfere. He was already more than half fuddled. I told him that some serious thing must have happened to Moreau by this time, or he would have returned before this, and that it behoved us to ascertain what that catastrophe was. Montgomery raised some feeble objections, and at last agreed. We had some food, and then all three of us started.

It is possibly due to the tension of my mind, at the time, but even now that start into the hot stillness of the tropical afternoon is a singularly vivid impression. M'ling went first, his shoulder hunched, his strange black head moving with quick starts as he peered first on this side of the way and then on that. He was unarmed; his axe he had dropped when he encountered the Swine-man. Teeth were *his* weapons when it came to fighting. Montgomery followed with stumbling footsteps, his hands in his pockets, his face downcast; he was in a state of muddled sullenness with me on account of the brandy. My left arm was in a sling (it was lucky it was my left), and I carried my revolver in my right. Soon we traced a narrow path through the wild luxuriance of the island, going north-westward; and presently M'ling stopped, and became rigid with watchfulness. Montgomery almost staggered into him, and then stopped too. Then, listening intently, we heard coming through the trees the sound of voices and footsteps approaching us.

'He is dead,' said a deep, vibrating voice.

'He is not dead; he is not dead,' jabbered another.

'We saw, we saw,' said several voices.

'Hullo!' suddenly shouted Montgomery, 'Hullo, there!'

'Confound you!' said I, and gripped my pistol.

There was a silence, then a crashing among the interlacing vegetation, first here, then there, and then half-a-dozen faces appeared – strange faces, lit by a strange light. M'ling made a growling noise in his throat. I recognized the Ape-man: I had indeed already identified his voice, and two of the white-swathed brown-featured creatures I had seen in Montgomery's boat. With these were the two dappled brutes and that grey, horribly crooked creature who said the Law, with grey hair streaming down its cheeks, heavy grey eyebrows, and grey locks pouring off from a central parting upon its sloping forehead – a heavy, faceless thing, with strange red eyes, looking at us curiously from amidst the green.

For a space no one spoke. Then Montgomery hiccoughed, 'Who – said he was dead?'

The Monkey-man looked guiltily at the hairy-grey Thing. 'He is dead,' said this monster. 'They saw.'

There was nothing threatening about this detachment, at any rate. They seemed awestricken and puzzled.

'Where is he?' said Montgomery.

'Beyond,' and the grey creature pointed.

'Is there a Law now?' asked the Ape-man. 'Is it still to be this and that? Is he dead indeed?'

'Is there a Law?' repeated the man in white. 'Is there a Law, thou Other with the Whip?'

'He is dead,' said the hairy-grey Thing. And they all stood watching us.

'Prendick,' said Montgomery, turning his dull eyes to me. 'He's dead, evidently.'

I had been standing behind him during this colloquy. I began to see how things lay with them. I suddenly stepped in front of Montgomery and lifted up my voice: 'Children of the Law,' I said, 'he is *not* dead!' M'ling turned his sharp eyes on me. 'He has changed his shape; he has changed his body,' I went on. 'For a time you will not see him. He is – there,' I pointed upward, 'where he can watch you. You cannot see him, but he can see you. Fear the Law!'

I looked at them squarely. They flinched.

'He is great, he is good,' said the Ape-man, peering fearfully upward among the dense trees.

'And the other Thing?' I demanded.

'The Thing that bled, and ran screaming and sobbing – that is dead too,' said the grey Thing, still regarding me.

'That's well,' grunted Montgomery.

'The Other with the Whip—' began the grey Thing.

'Well?' said I.

'Said he was dead.'

But Montgomery was still sober enough to understand my motive in denying Moreau's death. 'He is not dead,' he said slowly, 'not dead at all. No more dead than I am.'

'Some,' said I, 'have broken the Law: they will die. Some have died. Show us now where his old body lies – the body he cast away because he had no more need of it.'

'It is this way, Man who walked in the Sea,' said the grey Thing.

And with these six creatures guiding us, we went through the tumult of ferns and creepers and tree stems towards the north-west. Then came a yelling, a crashing among the branches, and a little pink homunculus rushed by us shrieking. Immediately after appeared a feral monster in headlong pursuit, blood-bedabbled, who was amongst us almost before he could stop his career. The grey Thing leapt aside. M'ling, with a snarl, flew at it, and

was struck aside. Montgomery fired and missed, bowed his head, threw up his arm, and turned to run. I fired, and the Thing still came on; fired again, point-blank, into its ugly face. I saw its features vanish in a flash: its face was driven in. Yet it passed me, gripped Montgomery, and holding him, fell headlong beside him and pulled him sprawling upon itself in its death-agony.

I found myself alone with M'ling, the dead brute and the prostrate man. Montgomery raised himself slowly and stared in a muddled way at the shattered Beast Man beside him. It more than half sobered him. He scrambled to his feet. Then I saw the grey Thing returning cautiously through the trees.

'See,' said I, pointing to the dead brute, 'is the Law not alive? This came of breaking the Law.'

He peered at the body. 'He sends the Fire that kills,' said he, in his deep voice, repeating part of the Ritual. The others gathered round and stared for a space.

At last we drew near the westward extremity of the island. We came upon the gnawed and mutilated body of the puma, its shoulder-bone smashed by a bullet, and perhaps twenty yards further found at last what we sought. Moreau lay face downward in a trampled space in a canebrake. One hand was almost severed at the wrist and his silvery hair was dabbled in blood. His head had been battered in by the fetters of the puma. The broken canes beneath him were smeared with blood. His revolver we could not find. Montgomery turned him over. Resting at intervals, and with the help of the seven Beast People (for he was a heavy man), we carried Moreau back to the enclosure. The night was darkling. Twice we heard unseen creatures howling and shrieking past our little band, and once the little pink sloth creature appeared and stared at us, and vanished again. But we were not attacked again. At the gates of the enclosure our company of Beast People left us, M'ling going with the rest. We locked ourselves in, and then took Moreau's mangled body into the yard and laid it upon a pile of brushwood. Then we went into the laboratory and put an end to all we found living there.

CHAPTER XIX

Montgomery's 'Bank Holiday'

When this was accomplished, and we had washed and eaten, Montgomery and I went into my little room and seriously discussed our position for the first time. It was then near midnight. He was almost sober, but greatly disturbed in his mind. He had been strangely under the influence of Moreau's personality: I do not think it had ever occurred to him that Moreau could die. This disaster was the sudden collapse of the habits that had become part of his nature in the ten or more monotonous years he had spent on the island. He talked vaguely, answered my questions crookedly, wandered into general questions.

'This silly ass of a world,' he said; 'what a muddle it all is! I haven't had any life. I wonder when it's going to begin. Sixteen years being bullied by nurses and schoolmasters at their own sweet will; five in London grinding hard at medicine, bad food, shabby lodgings, shabby clothes, shabby vice, a blunder – I didn't know any better – and hustled off to this beastly island. Ten years here! What's it all for, Prendick? Are we bubbles blown by a baby?'

It was hard to deal with such ravings. 'The thing we have to think of now,' said I, 'is how to get away from this island.'

'What's the good of getting away? I'm an outcast. Where am I to join on? It's all very well for *you*, Prendick. Poor old Moreau! We can't leave him here to have his bones picked. As it is.... And besides, what will become of the decent part of the Beast Folk?'

'Well,' said I, 'that will do tomorrow. I've been thinking we might make the brushwood into a pyre and burn his body – and those other things. Then what will happen with the Beast Folk?'

'I don't know. I suppose those that were made of beasts of prey will make silly asses of themselves sooner or later. We can't massacre the lot – can we? I suppose that's what *your* humanity would suggest? But they'll change. They are sure to change.'

He talked thus inconclusively until at last I felt my temper going.

'Damnation!' he exclaimed at some petulance of mine; 'Can't you see I'm in a worse hole than you are?' And he got up, and went for the brandy. 'Drink!' he said returning, 'You logic-chopping, chalky-faced saint of an atheist, drink!'

'Not I,' said I, and sat grimly watching his face under the yellow paraffin flare, as he drank himself into a garrulous misery.

I have a memory of infinite tedium. He wandered into a maudlin defence of the Beast People and of M'ling. M'ling, he said, was the only thing that

had ever really cared for him. And suddenly an idea came to him.

'I'm damned!' said he, staggering to his feet and clutching the brandy bottle.

By some flash of intuition I knew what it was he intended. 'You don't give drink to that beast!' I said, rising and facing him.

'Beast!' said he. 'You're the beast. He takes his liquor like a Christian. Come out of the way, Prendick!'

'For God's sake,' said I.

'Get – out of the way!' he roared, and suddenly whipped out his revolver.

'Very well,' said I, and stood aside, half-minded to fall upon him as he put his hand upon the latch, but deterred by the thought of my useless arm. 'You've made a beast of yourself – to the beasts you may go.'

He flung the doorway open, and stood half facing me between the yellow lamp-light and the pallid glare of the moon; his eye-sockets were blotches of black under his stubbly eyebrows.

'You're a solemn prig, Prendick, a silly ass! You're always fearing and fancying. We're on the edge of things. I'm bound to cut my throat tomorrow. I'm going to have a damned Bank Holiday tonight.' He turned and went out into the moonlight. 'M'ling!' he cried; 'M'ling, old friend!'

Three dim creatures in the silvery light came along the edge of the wan beach – one a white-wrapped creature, the other two blotches of blackness following it. They halted, staring. Then I saw M'ling's hunched shoulders as he came round the corner of the house.

'Drink!' cried Montgomery, 'Drink, you brutes! Drink and be men! Damme, I'm the cleverest. Moreau forgot this; this is the last touch. Drink, I tell you!' And waving the bottle in his hand he started off at a kind of quick trot to the westward, M'ling ranging himself between him and the three dim creatures who followed.

I went to the doorway. They were already indistinct in the mist of the moon-light before Montgomery halted. I saw him administer a dose of the raw brandy to M'ling, and saw the five figures melt into one vague patch.

'Sing!' I heard Montgomery shout – 'Sing all together, "Confound old Prendick!" That's right; now again, "Confound old Prendick!"'

The black group broke up into five separate figures, and wound slowly away from me along the band of shining beach. Each went howling at his own sweet will, yelping insults at me, or giving whatever other vent this new inspiration of brandy demanded. Presently I heard Montgomery's voice shouting, 'Right turn!' and they passed with their shouts and howls into the blackness of the landward trees. Slowly, very slowly, they receded into silence.

The peaceful splendour of the night healed again. The moon was now past the meridian and travelling down the west. It was at its full, and very bright, riding through the empty blue sky. The shadow of the wall lay, a yard wide and of inky blackness, at my feet. The eastward sea was a featureless

grey, dark and mysterious; and between the sea and the shadow the grey sands (of volcanic glass and crystals) flashed and shone like a beach of diamonds. Behind me the paraffin lamp flared hot and ruddy.

Then I shut the door, locked it, and went into the enclosure where Moreau lay beside his latest victims – the staghounds and the llama and some other wretched brutes – with his massive face calm even after his terrible death, and with the hard eyes open, staring at the dead white moon above. I sat down upon the edge of the sink, and with my eyes upon that ghastly pile of silvery light and ominous shadows began to turn over my plans. In the morning I would gather some provisions in the dinghy, and after setting fire to the pyre before me, push out into the desolation of the high sea once more. I felt that for Montgomery there was no help; that he was, in truth, half akin to these Beast Folk, unfitted for human kindred.

I do not know how long I sat there scheming. It must have been an hour or so. Then my planning was interrupted by the return of Montgomery to my neighbourhood. I heard a yelling from many throats, a tumult of exultant cries passing down towards the beach, whooping and howling, and excited shrieks that seemed to come to a stop near the water's edge. The riot rose and fell; I heard heavy blows and the splintering smash of wood, but it did not trouble me then. A discordant chanting began.

My thoughts went back to my means of escape. I got up, brought the lamp, and went into a shed to look at some kegs I had seen there. Then I became interested in the contents of some biscuit tins, and opened one. I saw something out of the tail of my eye – a red flicker – and turned sharply.

Behind me lay the yard, vividly black-and-white in the moonlight, and the pile of wood and faggots on which Moreau and his mutilated victims lay, one over another. They seemed to be gripping one another in one last revengeful grapple. His wounds gaped, black as night, and the blood that had dripped lay in black patches upon the sand. Then I saw, without under-standing, the cause of my phantom – a ruddy glow that came and danced and went upon the wall opposite. I misinterpreted this, fancied it was a reflection of my flickering lamp, and turned again to the stores in the shed. I went on rummaging among them, as well as a one-armed man could, finding this convenient thing and that, and putting them aside for tomorrow's launch. My movements were slow, and the time passed quickly. Presently the daylight crept upon me.

The chanting died down, giving place to a clamour; then it began again, and suddenly broke into a tumult. I heard cries of, 'More! More!' a sound like quarrelling, and a sudden wild shriek. The quality of the sounds changed so greatly that it arrested my attention. I went out into the yard and listened. Then cutting like a knife across the confusion came the crack of a revolver.

I rushed at once through my room to the little doorway. As I did so I heard some of the packing-cases behind me go sliding down and smash

together with a clatter of glass on the floor of the shed. But I did not heed
these. I flung the door open and looked out.

Up the beach by the boathouse a bonfire was burning, raining up sparks
into the indistinctness of the dawn. Around this struggled a mass of black
figures. I heard Montgomery call my name. I began to run at once towards
this fire, revolver in hand. I saw the pink tongue of Montgomery's pistol
lick out once, close to the ground. He was down. I shouted with all my
strength and fired into the air. I heard someone cry, 'The Master!' The
knotted black struggle broke into scattering units, the fire leapt and sank
down. The crowd of Beast People fled in sudden panic before me, up the
beach. In my excitement I fired at their retreating backs as they disappeared
among the bushes. Then I turned to the black heaps upon the ground.

Montgomery lay on his back, with the hairy grey Beast-man sprawling
across his body. The brute was dead, but still gripping Montgomery's throat
with its curving claws. Near by lay M'ling on his face and quite still, his
neck bitten open and the upper part of the smashed brandy bottle in his
hand. Two other figures lay near the fire – the one motionless, the other
groaning fitfully, every now and then raising its head slowly, then dropping
it again.

I caught hold of the grey man and pulled him off Montgomery's body;
his claws drew down the torn coat reluctantly as I dragged him away.
Montgomery was dark in the face and scarcely breathing. I splashed sea-water
on his face and pillowed his head on my rolled-up coat. M'ling was dead.
The wounded creature by the fire – it was a Wolf-brute with a bearded grey
face – lay, I found, with the fore part of its body upon the still glowing
timber. The wretched thing was injured so dreadfully that in mercy I blew
its brains out at once. The other brute was one of the Bull-men swathed in
white. He too was dead. The rest of the Beast People had vanished from
the beach.

I went to Montgomery again and knelt beside him, cursing my ignorance
of medicine. The fire beside me had sunk down, and only charred beams of
timber glowing at the central ends and mixed with a grey ash of brushwood
remained. I wondered casually where Montgomery had got his wood. Then
I saw that the dawn was upon us. The sky had grown brighter, the setting
moon was becoming pale and opaque in the luminous blue of the day. The
sky to the eastward was rimmed with red.

Suddenly I heard a thud and a hissing behind me, and, looking round,
sprang to my feet with a cry of horror. Against the warm dawn great
tumultuous masses of black smoke were boiling up out of the enclosure,
and through their stormy darkness shot flickering threads of blood-red
flame. Then the thatched roof caught. I saw the curving charge of the
flames across the sloping straw. A spurt of fire jetted from the window of
my room.

I knew at once what had happened. I remembered the crash I had heard. When I had rushed out to Montgomery's assistance, I had overturned the lamp.

The hopelessness of saving any of the contents of the enclosure stared me in the face. My mind came back to my plan of flight, and turning swiftly I looked to see where the two boats lay upon the beach. They were gone! Two axes lay upon the sands beside me; chips and splinters were scattered broadcast, and the ashes of the bonfire were blackening and smoking under the dawn. Montgomery had burnt the boats to revenge himself upon me and prevent our return to mankind!

A sudden convulsion of rage shook me. I was almost moved to batter his foolish head in, as he lay there helpless at my feet. Then suddenly his hand moved, so feebly, so pitifully, that my wrath vanished. He groaned, and opened his eyes for a minute. I knelt down beside him and raised his head. He opened his eyes again, staring silently at the dawn, and then they met mine. The lids fell.

'Sorry,' he said presently, with an effort. He seemed trying to think. 'The last,' he murmured, 'the last of this silly universe. What a mess—'

I listened. His head fell helplessly to one side. I thought some drink might revive him; but there was neither drink nor vessel in which to bring drink at hand. He seemed suddenly heavier. My heart went cold. I bent down to his face, put my hand through the rent in his blouse. He was dead; and even as he died a line of white heat, the limb of the sun, rose eastward beyond the projection of the bay, splashing its radiance across the sky and turning the dark sea into a weltering tumult of dazzling light. It fell like a glory upon his death-shrunken face.

I let his head fall gently upon the rough pillow I had made for him, and stood up. Before me was the glittering desolation of the sea, the awful solitude upon which I had already suffered so much; behind me the island, hushed under the dawn, its Beast People silent and unseen. The enclosure, with all its provisions and ammunition, burnt noisily, with sudden gusts of flame, a fitful crackling, and now and then a crash. The heavy smoke drove up the beach away from me, rolling low over the distant tree-tops towards the huts in the ravine. Beside me were the charred vestiges of the boats and these five dead bodies.

Then out of the bushes came three Beast People, with hunched shoulders, protruding heads, misshapen hands awkwardly held, and inquisitive, unfriendly eyes and advanced towards me with hesitating gestures.

CHAPTER XX

Alone with the Beast Folk

I faced these people, facing my fate in them, single-handed now – literally single-handed, for I had a broken arm. In my pocket was a revolver with two empty chambers. Among the chips scattered about the beach lay the two axes that had been used to chop up the boats. The tide was creeping in behind me. There was nothing for it but courage. I looked squarely into the faces of the advancing monsters. They avoided my eyes, and their quivering nostrils investigated the bodies that lay beyond me on the beach. I took half-a-dozen steps, picked up the blood-stained whip that lay beneath the body of the Wolf-man, and cracked it. They stopped and stared at me.

'Salute!' said I. 'Bow down!'

They hesitated. One bent his knees. I repeated my command, with my heart in my mouth, and advanced upon them. One knelt, then the other two.

I turned and walked towards the dead bodies, keeping my face towards the three kneeling Beast Men, very much as an actor passing up the stage faces the audience.

'They broke the Law,' said I, putting my foot on the Sayer of the Law. 'They have been slain – even the Sayer of the Law; even the Other with the Whip. Great is the Law! Come and see.'

'None escape,' said one of them, advancing and peering.

'None escape,' said I. 'Therefore hear and do as I command.' They stood up, looking questioningly at one another.

'Stand there,' said I.

I picked up the hatchets and swung them by their heads from the sling of my arm; turned Montgomery over; picked up his revolver still loaded in two chambers, and bending down to rummage, found half-a-dozen cartridges in his pocket.

'Take him,' said I, standing up again and pointing with the whip; 'take him, and carry him out and cast him into the sea.'

They came forward, evidently still afraid of Montgomery, but still more afraid of my cracking red whiplash; and after some fumbling and hesitation, some whip-cracking and shouting, they lifted him gingerly, carried him down to the beach, and went splashing into the dazzling welter of the sea.

'On!' said I, 'On! Carry him far.'

They went in up to their armpits and stood regarding me.

'Let go,' said I; and the body of Montgomery vanished with a splash. Something seemed to tighten across my chest.

'Good!' said I, with a break in my voice; and they came back, hurrying and fearful, to the margin of the water, leaving long wakes of black in the silver. At the water's edge they stopped, turning and glaring into the sea as though they presently expected Montgomery to arise therefrom and exact vengeance.

'Now these,' said I, pointing to the other bodies.

They took care not to approach the place where they had thrown Montgomery into the water, but instead carried the four dead Beast People slantingly along the beach for perhaps a hundred yards before they waded out and cast them away.

As I watched them disposing of the mangled remains of M'ling, I heard a light footfall behind me, and turning quickly saw the big Hyena-swine perhaps a dozen yards away. His head was bent down, his bright eyes were fixed upon me, his stumpy hands clenched and held close by his side. He stopped in this crouching attitude when I turned, his eyes a little averted.

For a moment we stood eye to eye. I dropped the whip and snatched at the pistol in my pocket; for I meant to kill this brute, the most formidable of any left now upon the island, at the first excuse. It may seem treacherous, but so I was resolved. I was far more afraid of him than of any other two of the Beast Folk. His continued life was I knew a threat against mine.

I was perhaps a dozen seconds collecting myself. Then cried I, 'Salute! Bow down!'

His teeth flashed upon me in a snarl. 'Who are *you* that I should—'

Perhaps a little too spasmodically I drew my revolver, aimed quickly and fired. I heard him yelp, saw him run sideways and turn, knew I had missed, and clicked back the cock with my thumb for the next shot. But he was already running headlong, jumping from side to side, and I dared not risk another miss. Every now and then he looked back at me over his shoulder. He went slanting along the beach, and vanished beneath the driving masses of dense smoke that were still pouring out from the burning enclosure. For some time I stood staring after him. I turned to my three obedient Beast Folk again and signalled them to drop the body they still carried. Then I went back to the place by the fire where the bodies had fallen and kicked the sand until all the brown bloodstains were absorbed and hidden.

I dismissed my three serfs with a wave of the hand, and went up the beach into the thickets. I carried my pistol in my hand, my whip thrust with the hatchets in the sling of my arm. I was anxious to be alone, to think out the position in which I was now placed. A dreadful thing that I was only beginning to realize was that over all this island there was now no safe place where I could be alone and secure to rest or sleep. I had recovered strength amazingly since my landing, but I was still inclined to be nervous and to break down under any great stress. I felt that I ought to cross the island and establish myself with the Beast People, and make myself secure in their

confidence. But my heart failed me. I went back to the beach, and turning eastward past the burning enclosure, made for a point where a shallow spit of coral sand ran out towards the reef. Here I could sit down and think, my back to the sea and my face against any surprise. And there I sat, chin on knees, the sun beating down upon my head and unspeakable dread in my mind, plotting how I could live on against the hour of my rescue (if ever rescue came). I tried to review the whole situation as calmly as I could, but it was difficult to clear the thing of emotion.

I began turning over in my mind the reason of Montgomery's despair. 'They will change,' he said; 'they are sure to change.' And Moreau, what was it that Moreau had said? 'The stubborn beast-flesh grows day by day back again.' Then I came round to the Hyena-swine. I felt sure that if I did not kill that brute, he would kill me. The Sayer of the Law was dead: worse luck. They knew now that we of the Whips could be killed even as they themselves were killed. Were they peering at me already out of the green masses of ferns and palms over yonder, watching until I came within their spring? Were they plotting against me? What was the Hyena-swine telling them? My imagination was running away with me into a morass of unsubstantial fears.

My thoughts were disturbed by a crying of sea birds hurrying towards some black object that had been stranded by the waves on the beach near the enclosure. I knew what that object was, but I had not the heart to go back and drive them off. I began walking along the beach in the opposite direction, designing to come round the eastward corner of the island and so approach the ravine of the huts, without traversing the possible ambuscades of the thickets.

Perhaps half a mile along the beach I became aware of one of my three Beast Folk advancing out of the landward bushes towards me. I was now so nervous with my own imaginings that I immediately drew my revolver. Even the propitiatory gestures of the creature failed to disarm me. He hesitated as he approached.

'Go away!' cried I.

There was something very suggestive of a dog in the cringing attitude of the creature. It retreated a little way, very like a dog being sent home, and stopped, looking at me imploringly with canine brown eyes.

'Go away,' said I. 'Do not come near me.'

'May I not come near you?' it said.

'No; go away,' I insisted, and snapped my whip. Then putting my whip in my teeth, I stooped for a stone, and with that threat drove the creature away.

So in solitude I came round by the ravine of the Beast People, and hiding among the weeds and reeds that separated this crevice from the sea I watched such of them as appeared, trying to judge from their gestures and appearance

how the death of Moreau and Montgomery and the destruction of the House of Pain had affected them. I know now the folly of my cowardice. Had I kept my courage up to the level of the dawn, had I not allowed it to ebb away in solitary thought, I might have grasped the vacant sceptre of Moreau and ruled over the Beast People. As it was I lost the opportunity, and sank to the position of a mere leader among my fellows.

Towards noon certain of them came and squatted basking in the hot sand. The imperious voices of hunger and thirst prevailed over my dread. I came out of the bushes, and, revolver in hand, walked down towards these seated figures. One, a Wolf-woman, turned her head and stared at me, and then the others. None attempted to rise or salute me. I felt too faint and weary to insist, and I let the moment pass.

'I want food,' said I, almost apologetically, and drawing near.

'There is food in the huts,' said an Ox-boar-man, drowsily, and looking away from me.

I passed them, and went down into the shadow and odours of the almost deserted ravine. In an empty hut I feasted on some specked and half-decayed fruit; and then after I had propped some branches and sticks about the opening, and placed myself with my face towards it and my hand upon my revolver, the exhaustion of the last thirty hours claimed its own, and I fell into a light slumber, hoping that the flimsy barricade I had erected would cause sufficient noise in its removal to save me from surprise.

CHAPTER XXI

The Reversion of the Beast Folk

In this way I became one among the Beast People in the Island of Doctor Moreau. When I awoke, it was dark about me. My arm ached in its bandages. I sat up, wondering at first where I might be. I heard coarse voices talking outside. Then I saw that my barricade had gone, and that the opening of the hut stood clear. My revolver was still in my hand.

I heard something breathing, saw something crouched together close beside me. I held my breath, trying to see what it was. It began to move slowly, interminably. Then something soft and warm and moist passed across my hand. All my muscles contracted. I snatched my hand away. A cry of alarm began and was stifled in my throat. Then I just realized what had happened sufficiently to stay my fingers on the revolver.

'Who is that?' I said in a hoarse whisper, the revolver still pointed.

'I – Master.'

'Who are you?'

'They say there is no Master now. But I know, I know. I carried the bodies into the sea, O Walker in the Sea! The bodies of those you slew. I am your slave, Master.'

'Are you the one I met on the beach?' I asked.

'The same, Master.'

The Thing was evidently faithful enough, for it might have fallen upon me as I slept. 'It is well,' I said, extending my hand for another licking kiss. I began to realize what its presence meant, and the tide of my courage flowed. 'Where are the others?' I asked.

'They are mad; they are fools,' said the Dog-man. 'Even now they talk together beyond there. They say, "The Master is dead. The Other with the Whip is dead. That Other who walked in the Sea is as we are. We have no Master, no Whips, no House of Pain, any more. There is an end. We love the Law, and will keep it; but there is no Pain, no Master, no Whips for ever again." So they say. But I know, Master, I know.'

I felt in the darkness, and patted the Dog-man's head. 'It is well,' I said again.

'Presently you will slay them all,' said the Dog-man.

'Presently,' I answered, 'I will slay them all – after certain days and certain things have come to pass. Every one of them save those you spare, every one of them shall be slain.'

'What the Master wishes to kill, the Master kills,' said the Dog-man with a certain satisfaction in his voice.

'And that their sins may grow,' I said, 'let them live in their folly until their time is ripe. Let them not know that I am the Master.'

'The Master's will is sweet,' said the Dog-man, with the ready tact of his canine blood.

'But one has sinned,' said I. 'Him I will kill, whenever I may meet him. When I say to you, "*That is he*," see that you fall upon him. And now I will go to the men and women who are assembled together.'

For a moment the opening of the hut was blackened by the exit of the Dog-man. Then I followed and stood up, almost in the exact spot where I had been when I had heard Moreau and his staghound pursuing me. But now it was night, and all the miasmatic ravine about me was black; and beyond, instead of a green, sunlit slope, I saw a red fire, before which hunched, grotesque figures moved to and fro. Further were the thick trees, a bank of darkness, fringed above with the black lace of the upper branches. The moon was just riding up on the edge of the ravine, and like a bar across its face drove the spire of vapour that was for ever streaming from the fumaroles of the island.

'Walk by me,' said I, nerving myself; and side by side we walked down the narrow way, taking little heed of the dim Things that peered at us out of the huts.

None about the fire attempted to salute me. Most of them disregarded me, ostentatiously. I looked round for the Hyena-swine, but he was not there. Altogether, perhaps twenty of the Beast Folk squatted, staring into the fire or talking to one another.

'He is dead, he is dead! the Master is dead!' said the voice of the Ape-man to the right of me. 'The House of Pain – there is no House of Pain!'

'He is not dead,' said I, in a loud voice. 'Even now he watches us!'

This startled them. Twenty pairs of eyes regarded me.

'The House of Pain is gone,' said I. 'It will come again. The Master you cannot see; yet even now he listens among you.'

'True, true!' said the Dog-man.

They were staggered at my assurance. An animal may be ferocious and cunning enough, but it takes a real man to tell a lie.

'The Man with the Bandaged Arm speaks a strange thing,' said one of the Beast Folk.

'I tell you it is so,' I said. 'The Master and the House of Pain will come again. Woe be to him who breaks the Law!'

They looked curiously at one another. With an affectation of indifference I began to chop idly at the ground in front of me with my hatchet. They looked, I noticed, at the deep cuts I made in the turf.

Then the Satyr raised a doubt. I answered him. Then one of the dappled things objected, and an animated discussion sprang up round the fire. Every moment I began to feel more convinced of my present security. I talked now

without the catching in my breath, due to the intensity of my excitement, that had troubled me at first. In the course of about an hour I had really convinced several of the Beast Folk of the truth of my assertions, and talked most of the others into a dubious state. I kept a sharp eye for my enemy the Hyena-swine, but he never appeared. Every now and then a suspicious movement would startle me, but my confidence grew rapidly. Then as the moon crept down from the zenith, one by one the listeners began to yawn (showing the oddest teeth in the light of the sinking fire), and first one and then another retired towards the dens in the ravine; and I, dreading the silence and darkness, went with them, knowing I was safer with several of them than with one alone.

In this manner began the longer part of my sojourn upon this Island of Doctor Moreau. But from that night until the end came, there was but one thing happened to tell save a series of innumerable small unpleasant details and the fretting of an incessant uneasiness. So that I prefer to make no chronicle for that gap of time, to tell only one cardinal incident of the ten months I spent as an intimate of these half-humanized brutes. There is much that sticks in my memory that I could write – things that I would cheerfully give my right hand to forget; but they do not help the telling of the story.

In the retrospect it is strange to remember how soon I fell in with these monsters' ways, and gained my confidence again. I had my quarrels with them of course, and could show some of their teeth-marks still; but they soon gained a wholesome respect for my trick of throwing stones and for the bite of my hatchet. And my Saint-Bernard-dog-man's loyalty was of infinite service to me. I found their simple scale of honour was based mainly on the capacity for inflicting trenchant wounds. Indeed, I may say – without vanity, I hope – that I held something like pre-eminence among them. One or two, whom in a rare access of high spirits I had scarred rather badly, bore me a grudge; but it vented itself chiefly behind my back, and at a safe distance from my missiles, in grimaces.

The Hyena-swine avoided me, and I was always on the alert for him. My inseparable Dog-man hated and dreaded him intensely. I really believe that was at the root of the brute's attachment to me. It was soon evident to me that the former monster had tasted blood, and gone the way of the Leopard-man. He formed a lair somewhere in the forest, and became solitary. Once I tried to induce the Beast Folk to hunt him, but I lacked the authority to make them co-operate for one end. Again and again I tried to approach his den and come upon him unaware; but always he was too acute for me, and saw or winded me and got away. He too made every forest pathway dangerous to me and my ally with his lurking ambuscades. The Dog-man scarcely dared to leave my side.

In the first month or so the Beast Folk, compared with their latter condition, were human enough, and for one or two besides my canine

friend I even conceived a friendly tolerance. The little pink sloth creature displayed an odd affection for me, and took to following me about. The Monkey-man bored me, however; he assumed, on the strength of his five digits, that he was my equal, and was for ever jabbering at me – jabbering the most arrant nonsense. One thing about him entertained me a little: he had a fantastic trick of coining new words. He had an idea, I believe, that to gabble about names that meant nothing was the proper use of speech. He called it 'Big Thinks' to distinguish it from 'Little Thinks', the sane everyday interests of life. If ever I made a remark he did not understand, he would praise it very much, ask me to say it again, learn it by heart, and go off repeating it, with a word wrong here or there, to all the milder of the Beast People. He thought nothing of what was plain and comprehensible. I invented some very curious 'Big Thinks' for his especial use. I think now that he was the silliest creature I ever met; he had developed in the most wonderful way the distinctive silliness of man without losing one jot of the natural folly of a monkey.

This, I say, was in the earlier weeks of my solitude among these brutes. During that time they respected the usage established by the Law, and behaved with general decorum. Once I found another rabbit torn to pieces – by the Hyena-swine, I am assured – but that was all. It was about May when I first distinctly perceived a growing difference in their speech and carriage, a growing coarseness of articulation, a growing disinclination to talk. My Monkey-man's jabber multiplied in volume but grew less and less comprehensible, more and more simian. Some of the others seemed altogether slipping their hold upon speech, though they still understood what I said to them at that time. (Can you imagine language, once clear-cut and exact, softening and guttering, losing shape and import, becoming mere lumps of sound again?) And they walked erect with an increasing difficulty. Though they evidently felt ashamed of themselves, every now and then I would come upon one or another running on toes and finger-tips, and quite unable to recover the vertical attitude. They held things more clumsily; drinking by suction, feeding by gnawing, grew commoner every day. I realized more keenly than ever what Moreau had told me about the 'stubborn beast-flesh'. They were reverting, and reverting very rapidly.

Some of them – the pioneers in this, I noticed with some surprise, were all females – began to disregard the injunction of decency, deliberately for the most part. Others even attempted public outrages upon the institution of monogamy. The tradition of the Law was clearly losing its force. I cannot pursue this disagreeable subject.

My Dog-man imperceptibly slipped back to the dog again; day by day he became dumb, quadrupedal, hairy. I scarcely noticed the transition from the companion on my right hand to the lurching dog at my side.

As the carelessness and disorganization increased from day to day, the

lane of dwelling places, at no time very sweet, became so loathsome that I left it, and going across the island made myself a hovel of boughs amid the black ruins of Moreau's enclosure. Some memory of pain, I found, still made that place the safest from the Beast Folk.

It would be impossible to detail every step of the lapsing of these monsters, – to tell how, day by day, the human semblance left them; how they gave up bandagings and wrappings, abandoned at last every stitch of clothing; how the hair began to spread over the exposed limbs; how their foreheads fell away and their faces projected; how the quasi-human intimacy I had permitted myself with some of them in the first month of my loneliness became a shuddering horror to recall.

The change was slow and inevitable. For them and for me it came without any definite shock. I still went among them in safety, because no jolt in the downward glide had released the increasing charge of explosive animalism that ousted the human day by day. But I began to fear that soon now that shock must come. My Saint-Bernard-brute followed me to the enclosure every night, and his vigilance enabled me to sleep at times in something like peace. The little pink sloth-thing became shy and left me, to crawl back to its natural life once more among the tree branches. We were in just the state of equilibrium that would remain in one of those 'Happy Family' cages which animal-tamers exhibit, if the tamer were to leave it for ever.

Of course these creatures did not decline into such beasts as the reader has seen in zoological gardens – into ordinary bears, wolves, tigers, oxen, swine, and apes. There was still something strange about each; in each Moreau had blended this animal with that. One perhaps was ursine chiefly, another feline chiefly, another bovine chiefly; but each was tainted with other creatures – a kind of generalized animalism appearing through the specific dispositions. And the dwindling shreds of the humanity still startled me every now and then – a momentary recrudescence of speech perhaps, an unexpected dexterity of the forefeet, a pitiful attempt to walk erect.

I too must have undergone strange changes. My clothes hung about me as yellow rags, through whose rents showed the tanned skin. My hair grew long, and became matted together. I am told that even now my eyes have a strange brightness, a swift alertness of movement.

At first I spent the daylight hours on the southward beach watching for a ship, hoping and praying for a ship. I counted on the *Ipecacuanha* returning as the year wore on; but she never came. Five times I saw sails, and thrice smoke; but nothing ever touched the island. I always had a bonfire ready, but no doubt the volcanic reputation of the island was taken to account for that.

It was only about September or October that I began to think of making a raft. By that time my arm had healed, and both my hands were at my service again. At first, I found my helplessness appalling. I had never done

any carpentry or suchlike work in my life, and I spent day after day in experimental chopping and binding among the trees. I had no ropes, and could hit on nothing wherewith to make ropes; none of the abundant creepers seemed limber or strong enough, and with all my litter of scientific education I could not devise any way of making them so. I spent more than a fortnight grubbing among the black ruins of the enclosure and on the beach where the boats had been burnt, looking for nails and other stray pieces of metal that might prove of service. Now and then some Beast-creature would watch me, and go leaping off when I called to it. There came a season of thunder storms and heavy rain, which greatly retarded my work; but at last the raft was completed.

I was delighted with it. But with a certain lack of practical sense which has always been my bane, I had made it a mile or more from the sea; and before I had dragged it down to the beach the thing had fallen to pieces. Perhaps it is as well that I was saved from launching it; but at the time my misery at my failure was so acute that for some days I simply moped on the beach, and stared at the water and thought of death.

I did not, however, mean to die, and an incident occurred that warned me unmistakably of the folly of letting the days pass so – for each fresh day was fraught with increasing danger from the Beast People.

I was lying in the shade of the enclosure wall, staring out to sea, when I was startled by something cold touching the skin of my heel, and starting round found the little pink sloth creature blinking into my face. He had long since lost speech and active movement, and the lank hair of the little brute grew thicker every day and his stumpy claws more askew. He made a moaning noise when he saw he had attracted my attention, went a little way towards the bushes and looked back at me.

At first I did not understand, but presently it occurred to me that he wished me to follow him; and this I did at last – slowly, for the day was hot. When we reached the trees he clambered into them, for he could travel better among their swinging creepers than on the ground. And suddenly in a trampled space I came upon a ghastly group. My Saint-Bernard-creature lay on the ground, dead; and near his body crouched the Hyena-swine, gripping the quivering flesh with its misshapen claws, gnawing at it, and snarling with delight. As I approached, the monster lifted its glaring eyes to mine, its lips went trembling back from its red-stained teeth, and it growled menacingly. It was not afraid and not ashamed; the last vestige of the human taint had vanished. I advanced a step further, stopped, and pulled out my revolver. At last I had him face to face.

The brute made no sign of retreat; but its ears went back, its hair bristled, and its body crouched together. I aimed between the eyes and fired. As I did so, the Thing rose straight at me in a leap, and I was knocked over like a ninepin. It clutched at me with its crippled hand, and struck me in the

face. Its spring carried it over me. I fell under the hind part of its body; but luckily I had hit as I meant, and it had died even as it leapt. I crawled out from under its unclean weight and stood up trembling, staring at its quivering body. That danger at least was over; but this, I knew was only the first of the series of relapses that must come.

I burnt both of the bodies on a pyre of brushwood; but after that I saw that unless I left the island my death was only a question of time. The Beast People by that time had, with one or two exceptions, left the ravine and made themselves lairs according to their taste among the thickets of the island. Few prowled by day, most of them slept, and the island might have seemed deserted to a newcomer; but at night the air was hideous with their calls and howling. I had half a mind to make a massacre of them; to build traps, or fight them with my knife. Had I possessed sufficient cartridges, I should not have hesitated to begin the killing. There could now be scarcely a score left of the dangerous carnivores; the braver of these were already dead. After the death of this poor dog of mine, my last friend, I too adopted to some extent the practice of slumbering in the daytime in order to be on my guard at night. I rebuilt my den in the walls of the enclosure, with such a narrow opening that anything attempting to enter must necessarily make a considerable noise. The creatures had lost the art of fire too, and recovered their fear of it. I turned once more, almost passionately now, to hammering together stakes and branches to form a raft for my escape.

I found a thousand difficulties. I am an extremely unhandy man (my schooling was over before the days of Slöjd); but most of the requirements of a raft I met at last in some clumsy, circuitous way or other, and this time I took care of the strength. The only insurmountable obstacle was that I had no vessel to contain the water I should need if I floated forth upon these untravelled seas. I would have even tried pottery, but the island contained no clay. I used to go moping about the island trying with all my might to solve this one last difficulty. Sometimes I would give way to wild outbursts of rage, and hack and splinter some unlucky tree in my intolerable vexation. But I could think of nothing.

And then came a day, a wonderful day, which I spent in ecstasy. I saw a sail to the south-west, a small sail like that of a little schooner; and forthwith I lit a great pile of brushwood, and stood by it in the heat of it, and the heat of the midday sun, watching. All day I watched that sail, eating or drinking nothing, so that my head reeled; and the Beasts came and glared at me, and seemed to wonder, and went away. It was still distant when night came and swallowed it up; and all night I toiled to keep my blaze bright and high, and the eyes of the Beasts shone out of the darkness, marvelling. In the dawn the sail was nearer, and I saw it was the dirty lug-sail of a small boat. But it sailed strangely. My eyes were weary with watching, and I peered and could not believe them. Two men were in the

boat, sitting low down – one by the bows, the other at the rudder. The head was not kept to the wind; it yawed and fell away.

As the day grew brighter, I began waving the last rag of my jacket to them; but they did not notice me, and sat still, facing each other. I went to the lowest point of the low headland, and gesticulated and shouted. There was no response, and the boat kept on her aimless course, making slowly, very slowly, for the bay. Suddenly a great white bird flew up out of the boat, and neither of the men stirred nor noticed it; it circled round, and then came sweeping overhead with its strong wings outspread.

Then I stopped shouting, and sat down on the headland and rested my chin on my hands and stared. Slowly, slowly, the boat drove past towards the west. I would have swum out to it, but something – a cold, vague fear – kept me back. In the afternoon the tide stranded the boat, and left it a hundred yards or so to the westward of the ruins of the enclosure. The men in it were dead, had been dead so long that they fell to pieces when I tilted the boat on its side and dragged them out. One had a shock of red hair, like the captain of the *Ipecacuanha*, and a dirty white cap lay in the bottom of the boat.

As I stood beside the boat, three of the Beasts came slinking out of the bushes and sniffing towards me. One of my spasms of disgust came upon me. I thrust the little boat down the beach and clambered on board her. Two of the brutes were Wolf-beasts, and came forward with quivering nostrils and glittering eyes; the third was the horrible nondescript of bear and bull. When I saw them approaching those wretched remains, heard them snarling at one another and caught the gleam of their teeth, a frantic horror succeeded my repulsion. I turned my back upon them, struck the lug and began paddling out to sea. I could not bring myself to look behind me.

I lay, however, between the reef and the island that night, and the next morning went round to the stream and filled the empty keg aboard with water. Then, with such patience as I could command, I collected a quantity of fruit, and waylaid and killed two rabbits with my last three cartridges. While I was doing this I left the boat moored to an inward projection of the reef, for fear of the Beast People.

CHAPTER XXII

The Man Alone

In the evening I started, and drove out to sea before a gentle wind from the south-west, slowly, steadily; and the island grew smaller and smaller, and the lank spire of smoke dwindled to a finer and finer line against the hot sunset. The ocean rose up around me, hiding that low, dark patch from my eyes. The daylight, the trailing glory of the sun, went streaming out of the sky, was drawn aside like some luminous curtain, and at last I looked into the blue gulf of immensity which the sunshine hides, and saw the floating hosts of the stars. The sea was silent, the sky was silent. I was alone with the night and silence.

So I drifted for three days, eating and drinking sparingly, and meditating upon all that had happened to me – not desiring very greatly then to see men again. One unclean rag was about me, my hair a black tangle: no doubt my discoverers thought me a madman.

It is strange, but I felt no desire to return to mankind. I was only glad to be quit of the foulness of the Beast People. And on the third day I was picked up by a brig from Apia to San Francisco. Neither the captain nor the mate would believe my story, judging that solitude and danger had made me mad; and fearing their opinion might be that of others, I refrained from telling my adventure further, and professed to recall nothing that had happened to me between the loss of the *Lady Vain* and the time when I was picked up again – the space of a year.

I had to act with the utmost circumspection to save myself from the suspicion of insanity. My memory of the Law, of the two dead sailors, of the ambuscades of the darkness, of the body in the canebrake, haunted me; and, unnatural as it seems, with my return to mankind came, instead of that confidence and sympathy I had expected, a strange enhancement of the uncertainty and dread I had experienced during my stay upon the island. No one would believe me; I was almost as queer to men as I had been to the Beast People. I may have caught something of the natural wildness of my companions. They say that terror is a disease, and anyhow I can witness that for several years now a restless fear has dwelt in my mind – such a restless fear as a half-tamed lion cub may feel.

My trouble took the strangest form. I could not persuade myself that the men and women I met were not also another, still passably human, Beast People, animals half wrought into the outward image of human souls, and that they would presently begin to revert – to show first this bestial mark and then that. But I have confided my case to a strangely able man

– a man who had known Moreau, and seemed half to credit my story; a mental specialist – and he has helped me mightily, though I do not expect that the terror of that island will ever altogether leave me. At most times it lies far in the back of my mind, a mere distant cloud, a memory and a faint distrust; but there are times when the little cloud spreads until it obscures the whole sky. Then I look about me at my fellow men; and I go in fear. I see faces, keen and bright; others dull or dangerous; others, unsteady, insincere – none that have the calm authority of a reasonable soul. I feel as though the animal was surging up through them; that presently the degradation of the Islanders will be played over again on a larger scale. I know this is an illusion; that these seeming men and women about me are indeed men and women – men and women for ever, perfectly reasonable creatures, full of human desires and tender solicitude, emancipated from instinct and the slaves of no fantastic Law – beings altogether different from the Beast Folk. Yet I shrink from them, from their curious glances, their enquiries and assistance, and long to be away from them and alone. For that reason I live near the broad free downland, and can escape thither when this shadow is over my soul; and very sweet is the empty downland then, under the wind-swept sky.

When I lived in London the horror was well-nigh insupportable. I could not get away from men: their voices came through windows; locked doors were flimsy safeguards. I would go out into the streets to fight with my delusion, and prowling women would mew after me; furtive, craving men glance jealously at me; weary, pale workers go coughing by me with tired eyes and eager paces, like wounded deer dripping blood; old people, bent and dull, pass murmuring to themselves; and, all unheeding, a ragged tail of gibing children. Then I would turn aside into some chapel – and even there, such was my disturbance, it seemed that the preacher gibbered 'Big Thinks,' even as the Ape-man had done; or into some library, and there the intent faces over the books seemed but patient creatures waiting for prey. Particularly nauseous were the blank, expressionless faces of people in trains and omnibuses; they seemed no more my fellow creatures than dead bodies would be, so that I did not dare to travel unless I was assured of being alone. And even it seemed that I too was not a reasonable creature, but only an animal tormented with some strange disorder in its brain which sent it to wander alone, like a sheep stricken with gid.

This is a mood, however, that comes to me now, I thank God, more rarely. I have withdrawn myself from the confusion of cities and multitudes, and spend my days surrounded by wise books – bright windows in this life of ours, lit by the shining souls of men. I see few strangers, and have but a small household. My days I devote to reading and to experiments in chemistry, and I spend many of the clear nights in the study of astronomy. There is – though I do not know how there is or why there is – a sense of infinite

peace and protection in the glittering hosts of heaven. There it must be, I think, in the vast and eternal laws of matter, and not in the daily cares and sins and troubles of men, that whatever is more than animal within us must find its solace and its hope. I hope, or I could not live.

And so, in hope and solitude, my story ends.

<div align="right">EDWARD PRENDICK.</div>

THE FIRST MEN IN THE MOON

'Three thousand stadia from the earth to the moon . . .
Marvel not, my comrade, if I appear talking to you on
super-terrestrial and aerial topics. The long and the short
of the matter is that I am running over the order of a
Journey I have lately made.'

– Lucian's *Icaromenippus*

CONTENTS

CHAPTER I

Mr Bedford Meets Mr Cavor at Lympne

As I sit down to write here amidst the shadows of vine-leaves under the blue sky of southern Italy, it comes to me with a certain quality of astonishment that my participation in these amazing adventures of Mr Cavor was, after all, the outcome of the purest accident. It might have been anyone. I fell into these things at a time when I thought myself removed from the slightest possibility of disturbing experiences. I had gone to Lympne because I had imagined it the most uneventful place in the world. 'Here, at any rate,' said I, 'I shall find peace and a chance to work!'

And this book is the sequel. So utterly at variance is Destiny with all the little plans of men.

I may perhaps mention here that very recently I had come an ugly cropper in certain business enterprises. Sitting now surrounded by all the circumstances of wealth, there is a luxury in admitting my extremity. I can admit, even, that to a certain extent my disasters were conceivably of my own making. It may be there are directions in which I have some capacity, but the conduct of business operations is not among these. But in those days I was young, and my youth among other objectionable forms took that of a pride in my capacity for affairs. I am young still in years, but the things that have happened to me have rubbed something of the youth from my mind. Whether they have brought any wisdom to light below it is a more doubtful matter.

It is scarcely necessary to go into the details of the speculations that landed me at Lympne, in Kent. Nowadays even about business transactions there is a strong spice of adventure. I took risks. In these things there is invariably a certain amount of give and take, and it fell to me finally to do the giving. Reluctantly enough. Even when I had got out of everything, one cantankerous creditor saw fit to be malignant. Perhaps you have met that flaming sense of outraged virtue, or perhaps you have only felt it. He ran me hard. It seemed to me, at last, that there was nothing for it but to write a play, unless I wanted to drudge for my living as a clerk. I have a certain imagination, and luxurious tastes, and I meant to make a vigorous fight for it before that fate overtook me. In addition to my belief in my powers as a business man, I had always in those days had an idea that I was equal to writing a very good play. It is not, I believe, a very uncommon persuasion. I knew there is nothing a man can do outside legitimate business transactions that has such opulent possibilities, and very probably that biased my opinion. I had, indeed, got into the habit of regarding this unwritten drama as a

convenient little reserve put by for a rainy day. That rainy day had come
and I set to work.

I soon discovered that writing a play was a longer business than I had
supposed; at first I had reckoned ten days for it, and it was to have a *pied-
à-terre* while it was in hand that I came to Lympne. I reckoned myself lucky
in getting that little bungalow. I got it on a three years' agreement. I put in
a few sticks of furniture, and while the play was in hand I did my own
cooking. My cooking would have shocked Mrs Bond. And yet, you know,
it had flavour. I had a coffee-pot, a sauce-pan for eggs, and one for potatoes,
and a frying-pan for sausages and bacon – such was the simple apparatus of
my comfort. One cannot always be magnificent, but simplicity is always a
possible alternative. For the rest I laid in an eighteen-gallon cask of beer on
credit, and a trustful baker came each day. It was not, perhaps, in the style
of Sybaris, but I have had worse times. I was a little sorry for the baker, who
was a very decent man indeed, but even for him I hoped.

Certainly if anyone wants solitude, the place is Lympne. It is in the clay
part of Kent, and my bungalow stood on the edge of an old sea cliff and
stared across the flats of Romney Marsh at the sea. In very wet weather the
place is almost inaccessible, and I have heard that at times the postman
used to traverse the more succulent portions of his route with boards upon
his feet. I never saw him doing so, but I can quite imagine it. Outside the
doors of the few cottages and houses that make up the present village big
birch besoms are stuck, to wipe off the worst of the clay, which will give
some idea of the texture of the district. I doubt if the place would be there
at all, if it were not a fading memory of things gone for ever. It was the big
port of England in Roman times, Portus Lemanis, and now the sea is four
miles away. All down the steep hill are boulders and masses of Roman
brickwork, and from it old Watling Street, still paved in places, starts like
an arrow to the north. I used to stand on the hill and think of it all, the
galleys and legions, the captives and officials, the women and traders, the
speculators like myself, all the swarm and tumult that came clanking in and
out of the harbour. And now just a few lumps of rubble on a grassy slope,
and a sheep or two – and me! And where the port had been were the levels
of the marsh, sweeping round in a broad curve to distant Dungeness, and
dotted here and there with tree clumps and the church towers of old mediæval
towns that are following Lemanis now towards extinction.

That outlook on the marsh was, indeed, one of the finest views I have
ever seen. I suppose Dungeness was fifteen miles away; it lay like a raft
on the sea, and further westward were the hills by Hastings under the
setting sun. Sometimes they hung close and clear, sometimes they were
faded and low, and often the drift of the weather took them clean out of
sight. And all the nearer parts of the marsh were laced and lit by ditches
and canals.

The window at which I worked looked over the skyline of this crest, and it was from this window that I first set eyes on Cavor. It was just as I was struggling with my scenario, holding down my mind to the sheer hard work of it, and naturally enough he arrested my attention.

The sun had set, the sky was a vivid tranquillity of green and yellow, and against that he came out black – the oddest little figure.

He was a short, round-bodied, thin-legged little man, with a jerky quality in his motions; he had seen fit to clothe his extraordinary mind in a cricket cap, an overcoat, and cycling knickerbockers and stockings. Why he did so I do not know, for he never cycled and he never played cricket. It was a fortuitous concurrence of garments, arising I know not how. He gesticulated with his hands and arms, and jerked his head about and *buzzed*. He buzzed like something electric. You never heard such buzzing. And ever and again he cleared his throat with a most extraordinary noise.

There had been rain, and that spasmodic walk of his was enhanced by the extreme slipperiness of the footpath. Exactly as he came against the sun he stopped, pulled out a watch, hesitated. Then with a sort of convulsive gesture he turned and retreated with every manifestation of haste, no longer gesticulating, but going with ample strides that showed the relatively large size of his feet – they were, I remember, grotesquely exaggerated in size by adhesive clay – to the best possible advantage.

This occurred on the first day of my sojourn, when my play-writing energy was at its height, and I regarded the incident simply as an annoying distraction – the waste of five minutes. I returned to my scenario. But when next evening the apparition was repeated with remarkable precision, and again the next evening, and indeed every evening when rain was not falling, concentration upon the scenario became a considerable effort. 'Confound the man,' said I, 'one would think he was learning to be a marionette!' and for several evenings I cursed him pretty heartily.

Then my annoyance gave way to amazement and curiosity. Why on earth should a man do this thing? On the fourteenth evening I could stand it no longer, and so soon as he appeared I opened the French window, crossed the verandah, and directed myself to the point where he invariably stopped.

He had his watch out as I came up to him. He had a chubby, rubicund face with reddish brown eyes – previously I had seen him only against the light. 'One moment, sir,' said I as he turned.

He stared. 'One moment,' he said, 'certainly. Or if you wish to speak to me for longer, and it is not asking too much – your moment is up – would it trouble you to accompany me?'

'Not in the least,' said I, placing myself beside him.

'My habits are regular. My time for intercourse – limited.'

'This, I presume, is your time for exercise?'

'It is. I come here to enjoy the sunset.'

'You don't.'

'Sir?'

'You never look at it.'

'Never look at it?'

'No. I've watched you thirteen nights, and not once have you looked at the sunset – not once.'

He knitted his brows like one who encounters a problem.

'Well, I enjoy the sunlight – the atmosphere – I go along this path, through that gate' – he jerked his head over his shoulder – 'and round—'

'You don't. You never have been. It's all nonsense. There isn't a way. Tonight, for instance—'

'Oh! Tonight! Let me see. Ah! I just glanced at my watch, saw that I had already been out just three minutes over the precise half-hour, decided there was not time to go round, turned—'

'You always do.'

He looked at me – reflected. 'Perhaps I do, now I come to think of it. But what was it you wanted to speak to me about?'

'Why, this!'

'This?'

'Yes. Why do you do it? Every night you come making a noise—'

'Making a noise?'

'Like this' – I imitated his buzzing noise.

He looked at me, and it was evident the buzzing awakened distaste. 'Do I do *that*?' he asked.

'Every blessed evening.'

'I had no idea.'

He stopped dead. He regarded me gravely. 'Can it be,' he said, 'that I have formed a Habit?'

'Well, it looks like it. Doesn't it?'

He pulled down his lower lip between finger and thumb. He regarded a puddle at his feet.

'My mind is much occupied,' he said. 'And you want to know *why*! Well, sir, I can assure you that not only do I not know why I do these things, but I did not even know I did them. Come to think, it is just as you say; I never *have* been beyond that field. . . . And these things annoy you?'

For some reason I was beginning to relent towards him. 'Not *annoy*,' I said. 'But – imagine yourself writing a play!'

'I couldn't.'

'Well, anything that needs concentration.'

'Ah!' he said, 'Of course,' and meditated. His expression became so eloquent of distress, that I relented still more. After all, there *is* a touch of aggression in demanding of a man you don't know why he hums on a public footpath.

'You see,' he said weakly, 'it's a habit.'

'Oh, I recognize that.'

'I must stop it.'

'But not if it puts you out. After all, I had no business – it's something of a liberty.'

'Not at all, sir,' he said, 'not at all. I am greatly indebted to you. I should guard myself against these things. In future I will. Could I trouble you – once again? That noise?'

'Something like this,' I said. 'Zuzzoo, zuzzoo. But really, you know—'

'I am greatly obliged to you. In fact, I know I am getting absurdly absent-minded. You are quite justified, sir – perfectly justified. Indeed, I am indebted to you. The thing shall end. And now, sir, I have already brought you further than I should have done.'

'I do hope my impertinence—'

'Not at all, sir, not at all.'

We regarded each other for a moment. I raised my hat and wished him a good evening. He responded convulsively, and so we went our ways.

At the stile I looked back at his receding figure. His bearing had changed remarkably, he seemed limp, shrunken. The contrast with his former gesticulating, zuzzoing self took me in some absurd way as pathetic. I watched him out of sight. Then wishing very heartily I had kept to my own business, I returned to my bungalow and my play.

The next evening I saw nothing of him, nor the next. But he was very much in my mind, and it had occurred to me that as a sentimental comic character he might serve a useful purpose in the development of my plot. The third day he called upon me.

For a time I was puzzled to think what had brought him. He made indifferent conversation in the most formal way, then abruptly he came to business. He wanted to buy me out of my bungalow.

'You see,' he said, 'I don't blame you in the least, but you've destroyed a habit, and it disorganizes my day. I've walked past here for years – years. No doubt I've hummed. . . . You've made all that impossible!'

I suggested he might try some other direction.

'No. There is no other direction. This is the only one. I've enquired. And now – every afternoon at four – I come to a dead wall.'

'But, my dear sir, if the thing is so important to you—'

'It's vital. You see, I'm – I'm an investigator – I am engaged in a scientific research. I live—' he paused and seemed to think. 'Just over there,' he said, and pointed suddenly dangerously near my eye. 'The house with white chimneys you see just over the trees. And my circumstances are abnormal – abnormal. I am on the point of completing one of the most important demonstrations – I can assure you one of *the most important* demonstrations that have ever been made. It requires constant thought, constant mental

ease and activity. And the afternoon was my brightest time! – Effervescing with new ideas – new points of view.'

'But why not come by still?'

'It would be all different. I should be self-conscious. I should think of you at your play – watching me irritated – instead of thinking of my work. No! I must have the bungalow.'

I meditated. Naturally, I wanted to think the matter over thoroughly before anything decisive was said. I was generally ready enough for business in those days, and selling always attracted me; but in the first place it was not my bungalow, and even if I sold it to him at a good price I might get inconvenienced in the delivery of goods if the current owner got wind of the transaction, and in the second I was, well – undischarged. It was clearly a business that required delicate handling. Moreover, the possibility of his being in pursuit of some valuable invention also interested me. It occurred to me that I would like to know more of this research, not with any dishonest intention, but simply with an idea that to know what it was would be a relief from play-writing. I threw out feelers.

He was quite willing to supply information. Indeed, once he was fairly under way the conversation became a monologue. He talked like a man long pent up, who has had it over with himself again and again. He talked for nearly an hour, and I must confess I found it a pretty stiff bit of listening. But through it all there was the undertone of satisfaction one feels when one is neglecting work one has set oneself. During that first interview I gathered very little of the drift of his work. Half his words were technicalities entirely strange to me, and he illustrated one or two points with what he was pleased to call elementary mathematics, computing on an envelope with a copying-ink pencil, in a manner that made it hard even to seem to understand. 'Yes,' I said; 'yes. Go on!' Nevertheless I made out enough to convince me that he was no mere crank playing at discoveries. In spite of his crank-like appearance there was a force about him that made that impossible. Whatever it was, it was a thing with mechanical possibilities. He told me of a work-shed he had, and of three assistants – originally jobbing carpenters – whom he had trained. Now, from the work-shed to the patent office is clearly only one step. He invited me to see those things. I accepted readily, and took care, by a remark or so, to underline that. The proposed transfer of the bungalow remained very conveniently in suspense.

At last he rose to depart, with an apology for the length of his call. Talking over his work was, he said, a pleasure enjoyed only too rarely. It was not often he found such an intelligent listener as myself, he mingled very little with professional scientific men.

'So much pettiness,' he explained; 'so much intrigue! And really, when one has an idea – a novel, fertilizing idea – I don't want to be uncharitable, but—'

I am a man who believes in impulses. I made what was perhaps a rash proposition. But you must remember that I had been alone, play-writing in Lympne, for fourteen days, and my compunction for his ruined walk still hung about me. 'Why not,' said I, 'make this your new habit? In the place of the one I spoilt? At least, until we can settle about the bungalow. What you want is to turn over your work in your mind. That you have always done during your afternoon walk. Unfortunately that's over – you can't get things back as they were. But why not come and talk about your work to me; use me as a sort of wall against which you may throw your thoughts and catch them again? It's certain I don't know enough to steal your ideas myself – and I know no scientific men—'

I stopped. He was considering. Evidently the thing attracted him. 'But I'm afraid I should bore you,' he said.

'You think I'm too dull?'

'Oh no; but technicalities—'

'Anyhow, you've interested me immensely this afternoon.'

'Of course it *would* be a great help to me. Nothing clears up one's ideas so much as explaining them. Hitherto—'

'My dear sir, say no more.'

'But really can you spare the time?'

'There is no rest like change of occupation,' I said, with profound conviction.

The affair was over. On my verandah steps he turned. 'I am already greatly indebted to you,' he said.

I made an interrogative noise.

'You have completely cured me of that ridiculous habit of humming,' he explained.

I think I said I was glad to be of any service to him, and he turned away.

Immediately the train of thought that our conversation had suggested must have resumed its sway. His arms began to wave in their former fashion. The faint echo of 'zuzzoo' came back to me on the breeze. . . .

Well, after all, that was not my affair. . . .

He came the next day, and again the next day after that, and delivered two lectures on physics to our mutual satisfaction. He talked with an air of being extremely lucid about the 'ether' and 'tubes of force' and 'gravitational potential' and things like that, and I sat in my other folding-chair and said, 'Yes,' 'Go on,' 'I follow you,' to keep him going. It was tremendously difficult stuff, but I do not think he ever suspected how much I did not understand him. There were moments when I doubted whether I was well employed, but at any rate I was resting from that confounded play. Now and then things gleamed on me clearly for a space, only to vanish just when I thought I had hold of them. Sometimes my attention failed altogether, and I would give it up and sit and stare at him, wondering whether, after

all, it would not be better to use him as a central figure in a good farce and let all this other stuff slide. And then, perhaps, I would catch on again for a bit.

At the earliest opportunity I went to see his house. It was large and carelessly furnished; there were no servants other than his three assistants, and his dietary and private life were characterized by a philosophical simplicity. He was a water-drinker, a vegetarian, and all those logical disciplinary things. But the sight of his equipment settled many doubts. It looked like business from cellar to attic – an amazing little place to find in an out-of-the-way village. The ground-floor rooms contained benches and apparatus, the bakehouse and scullery boiler had developed into respectable furnaces, dynamos occupied the cellar, and there was a gasometer in the garden. He showed it to me with all the confiding zest of a man who has been living too much alone. His seclusion was overflowing now in an excess of confidence, and I had the good luck to be the recipient.

The three assistants were creditable specimens of the class of 'handy-men' from which they came. Conscientious if unintelligent, strong, civil and willing. One, Spargus, who did the cooking and all the metal work, had been a sailor; a second, Gibbs, was a joiner; and the third was an ex-jobbing gardener, and now general assistant. They were the merest labourers. All the intelligent work was done by Cavor. Theirs was the darkest ignorance compared even with my muddled impression.

And now, as to the nature of these enquiries. Here, unhappily, comes a grave difficulty. I am no scientific expert, and if I were to attempt to set forth in the highly scientific language of Mr Cavor the aim to which his experiments tended, I am afraid I should confuse not only the reader but myself, and almost certainly I should make some blunder that would bring upon me the mockery of every up-to-date student of mathematical physics in the country. The best thing I can do therefore is, I think, to give my impressions in my own inexact language, without any attempt to wear a garment of knowledge to which I have no claim.

The object of Mr Cavor's search was a substance that should be 'opaque' – he used some other word I have forgotten, but 'opaque' conveys the idea – to 'all forms of radiant energy'. 'Radiant energy', he made me understand, was anything like light or heat, or those Röntgen Rays there was so much talk about a year or so ago, or the electric waves of Marconi, or gravitation. All these things, he said, *radiate* out from centres, and act on bodies at a distance, whence comes the term 'radiant energy'. Now almost all substances are opaque to some form or other of radiant energy. Glass, for example, is transparent to light, but much less so to heat, so that it is useful as a fire-screen; and alum is transparent to light, but blocks heat completely. A solution of iodine in carbon bisulphide, on the other hand, completely blocks light, but is quite transparent to heat. It will hide a fire from you, but permit all its

warmth to reach you. Metals are not only opaque to light and heat, but also to electrical energy, which passes through both iodine solution and glass almost as though they were not interposed. And so on.

Now all known substances are 'transparent' to gravitation. You can use screens of various sorts to cut off the light or heat, or electrical influence of the sun, or the warmth of the earth from anything; you can screen things by sheets of metal from Marconi's rays, but nothing will cut off the gravitational attraction of the sun or the gravitational attraction of the earth. Yet why there should be nothing is hard to say. Cavor did not see why such a substance should not exist, and certainly I could not tell him. I had never thought of such a possibility before. He showed me by calculations on paper, which Lord Kelvin, no doubt, or Professor Lodge, or Professor Karl Pearson, or any of those great scientific people might have understood, but which simply reduced me to a hopeless muddle, that not only was such a substance possible, but that it must satisfy certain conditions. It was an amazing piece of reasoning. Much as it amazed and exercised me at the time, it would be impossible to reproduce it here. 'Yes,' I said to it all, 'yes; go on!' Suffice it for this story that he believed he might be able to manufacture this possible substance opaque to gravitation out of a complicated alloy of metals and something new – a new element, I fancy – called, I believe, *helium*, which was sent to him from London in sealed stone jars. Doubt has been thrown upon this detail, but I am almost certain it was *helium* he had sent him in sealed stone jars. It was certainly something very gaseous and thin. If only I had taken notes. . . .

But then, how was I to foresee the necessity of taking notes?

Anyone with the merest germ of an imagination will understand the extraordinary possibilities of such a substance, and will sympathize a little with the emotion I felt as this understanding emerged from the haze of abstruse phrases in which Cavor expressed himself. Comic relief in a play indeed! It was some time before I would believe that I had interpreted him aright, and I was very careful not to ask questions that would have enabled him to gauge the profundity of misunderstanding into which he dropped his daily exposition. But no one reading the story of it here will sympathize fully, because from my barren narrative it will be impossible to gather the strength of my conviction that this astonishing substance was positively going to be made.

I do not recall that I gave my play an hour's consecutive work at any time after my visit to his house. My imagination had other things to do. There seemed no limit to the possibilities of the stuff; whichever way I tried I came on miracles and revolutions. For example, if one wanted to lift a weight, however enormous, one had only to get a sheet of this substance beneath it, and one might lift it with a straw. My first natural impulse was to apply this principle to guns and ironclads, and all the material and methods

of war, and from that to shipping, locomotion, building, every conceivable form of human industry. The chance that had brought me into the very birth-chamber of this new time – it was an epoch, no less – was one of those chances that come once in a thousand years. The thing unrolled, it expanded and expanded. Among other things I saw in it my redemption as a business man. I saw a parent company, and daughter companies, applications to right of us, applications to left, rings and trusts, privileges and concessions spreading and spreading, until one vast, stupendous Cavorite company ran and ruled the world.

And I was in it!

I took my line straight away. I knew I was staking everything, but I jumped there and then.

'We're on absolutely the biggest thing that has ever been invented,' I said, and put the accent on 'we'. 'If you want to keep me out of this, you'll have to do it with a gun. I'm coming down to be your fourth labourer tomorrow.'

He seemed surprised at my enthusiasm, but not a bit suspicious or hostile. Rather, he was self-depreciatory.

He looked at me doubtfully. 'But do you really think—?' he said. 'And your play! How about that play?'

'It's vanished!' I cried. 'My dear sir, don't you see what you've got? Don't you see what you're going to do?'

That was merely a rhetorical turn, but positively, he didn't. At first I could not believe it. He had not had the beginning of the inkling of an idea. This astonishing little man had been working on purely theoretical grounds the whole time! When he said it was 'the most important' research the world had ever seen, he simply meant it squared up so many theories, settled so much that was in doubt; he had troubled no more about the application of the stuff he was going to turn out than if he had been a machine that makes guns. This was a possible substance, and he was going to make it! *V'la tout*, as the Frenchman says.

Beyond that, he was childish! If he made it, it would go down to posterity as Cavorite or Cavorine, and he would be made an FRS, and his portrait given away as a scientific worthy with *Nature*, and things like that. And that was all he saw! He would have dropped this bombshell into the world as though he had discovered a new species of gnat, if it had not happened that I had come along. And there it would have lain and fizzled, like one or two other little things these scientific people have lit and dropped about us.

When I realized this, it was I did the talking, and Cavor who said 'Go on!'. I jumped up. I paced the room, gesticulating like a boy of twenty. I tried to make him understand his duties and responsibilities in the matter – *our* duties and responsibilities in the matter. I assured him we might make wealth enough to work any sort of social revolution we fancied, we might

own and order the whole world. I told him of companies and patents, and the case for secret processes. All these things seemed to take him much as his mathematics had taken me. A look of perplexity came into his ruddy little face. He stammered something about indifference to wealth, but I brushed all that aside. He had got to be rich, and it was no good his stammering. I gave him to understand the sort of man I was, and that I had had very considerable business experience. I did not tell him I was an undischarged bankrupt at the time, because that was temporary, but I think I reconciled my evident poverty with my financial claims. And quite insensibly, in the way such projects grow, the understanding of a Cavorite monopoly grew up between us. He was to make the stuff, and I was to make the boom.

I stuck like a leech to the 'we' – 'you' and 'I' didn't exist for me.

His idea was that the profits I spoke of might go to endow research, but that, of course, was a matter we had to settle later. 'That's all right,' I shouted, 'that's all right.' The great point, as I insisted, was to get the thing done.

'Here is a substance,' I cried, 'no home, no factory, no fortress, no ship can dare to be without – more universally applicable even than a patent medicine! There isn't a solitary aspect of it, not one of its ten thousand possible uses that will not make us rich, Cavor, beyond the dreams of avarice!'

'No!' he said. 'I begin to see. It's extraordinary how one gets new points of view by talking over things!'

'And as it happens you have just talked to the right man!'

'I suppose no one,' he said, 'is absolutely *averse* to enormous wealth. Of course there is one thing—'

He paused. I stood still.

'It is just possible, you know, that we may not be able to make it after all! It may be one of those things that are a theoretical possibility, but a practical absurdity. Or when we make it, there may be some little hitch—!'

'We'll tackle the hitch when it comes,' said I.

CHAPTER II

The First Making of Cavorite

But Cavor's fears were groundless, so far as the actual making was concerned. On the 14th of October 1899 this incredible substance was made!

Oddly enough, it was made at last by accident, when Mr Cavor least expected it. He had fused together a number of metals and certain other things – I wish I knew the particulars now! – and he intended to leave the mixture a week and then allow it to cool slowly. Unless he had miscalculated, the last stage in the combination would occur when the stuff sank to a temperature of 60° Fahrenheitenheit. But it chanced that, unknown to Cavor, dissension had arisen about the furnace tending. Gibbs, who had previously seen to this, had suddenly attempted to shift it to the man who had been a gardener, on the score that coal was soil, being dug, and therefore could not possibly fall within the province of a joiner; the man who had been a jobbing gardener alleged, however, that coal was a metallic or ore-like substance, let alone that he was a cook. But Spargus insisted on Gibbs doing the coaling, seeing that he was a joiner and that coal is notoriously fossil wood. Consequently Gibbs ceased to replenish the furnace, and no one else did so, and Cavor was too much immersed in certain interesting problems concerning a Cavorite flying machine (neglecting the resistance of the air and one or two other points) to perceive that anything was wrong. And the premature birth of his invention took place just as he was coming across the field to my bungalow for our afternoon talk and tea.

I remember the occasion with extreme vividness. The water was boiling, and everything was prepared, and the sound of his 'zuzzoo' had brought me out upon the verandah. His active little figure was black against the autumnal sunset, and to the right the chimneys of his house just rose above a gloriously tinted group of trees. Remoter rose the Wealden Hills, faint and blue, while to the left the hazy marsh spread out spacious and serene. And then—!

The chimneys jerked heavenward, smashing into a string of bricks as they rose, and the roof and a miscellany of furniture followed. Then overtaking them came a huge white flame. The trees about the building swayed and whirled and tore themselves to pieces, that sprang towards the flare. My ears were smitten with a clap of thunder that left me deaf on one side for life, and all about me windows smashed, unheeded.

I took three steps from the verandah towards Cavor's house, and even as I did so came the wind.

Instantly my coat tails were over my head, and I was progressing in great

leaps and bounds, and quite against my will, towards him. In the same moment the discoverer was seized, whirled about, and flew through the screaming air. I saw one of my chimney pots hit the ground within six yards of me, leap a score of feet, and so hurry in great strides towards the focus of the disturbance. Cavor, kicking and flapping, came down again, rolled over and over on the ground for a space, struggled up and was lifted and borne forward at an enormous velocity, vanishing at last among the labouring, lashing trees that writhed about his house.

A mass of smoke and ashes, and a square of bluish shining substance rushed up towards the zenith. A large fragment of fencing came sailing past me, dropped edgeways, hit the ground and fell flat, and then the worst was over. The aerial commotion fell swiftly until it was a mere strong gale, and I became once more aware that I had breath and feet. By leaning back against the wind I managed to stop, and could collect such wits as still remained to me.

In that instant the whole face of the world had changed. The tranquil sunset had vanished, the sky was dark with scurrying clouds, everything was flattened and swaying with the gale. I glanced back to see if my bungalow was still in a general way standing, then staggered forward towards the trees amongst which Cavor had vanished, and through whose tall and leaf-denuded branches shone the flames of his burning house.

I entered the copse, dashing from one tree to another and clinging to them, and for a space I sought him in vain. Then amidst a heap of smashed branches and fencing that had banked itself against a portion of his garden wall I perceived something stir. I made a run for this, but before I reached it a brown object separated itself, rose on two muddy legs and protruded two drooping, bleeding hands. Some tattered ends of garment fluttered out from its middle portion and streamed before the wind.

For a moment I did not recognize this earthy lump, and then I saw that it was Cavor, caked in the mud in which he had rolled. He leant forward against the wind, rubbing the dirt from his eyes and mouth.

He extended a muddy lump of hand, and staggered a pace towards me. His face worked with emotion, little lumps of mud kept falling from it. He looked as damaged and pitiful as any living creature I have ever seen, and his remark therefore amazed me exceedingly. ''Gratulate me,' he gasped; ''gratulate me!'

'Congratulate you!' said I. 'Good Heavens! What for?'

'I've done it.'

'You *have*. What on earth caused that explosion?'

A gust of wind blew his words away. I understood him to say that it wasn't an explosion at all. The wind hurled me into collision with him, and we stood clinging to one another.

'Try and get back to my bungalow,' I bawled in his ear. He did not hear

me, and shouted something about 'three martyrs – science', and also some-
thing about 'not much good'. At the time he laboured under the impression
that his three attendants had perished in the whirlwind. Happily this was
incorrect. Directly he had left for my bungalow they had gone off to the
public-house in Lympne to discuss the question of the furnaces over some
trivial refreshment.

I repeated my suggestion of getting back to my bungalow, and this time
he understood. We clung arm in arm and started, and managed at last to
reach the shelter of as much roof as was left to me. For a space we sat in
armchairs and panted. All the windows were broken, and the lighter articles
of furniture were in great disorder, but no irrevocable damage was done.
Happily the kitchen door had stood the pressure upon it, so that all my
crockery and cooking materials had survived. The oil stove was still burning,
and I put on the water to boil again for tea. And that prepared, I could
turn on Cavor for his explanation.

'Quite correct,' he insisted; 'quite correct. I've done it, and it's all right.'

'But,' I protested, 'all right? Why, there can't be a rick standing, or a
fence or a thatched roof undamaged for twenty miles around. . . .'

'It's all right – *really*. I didn't, of course, foresee this little upset. My mind
was preoccupied with another problem, and I'm apt to disregard these prac-
tical side issues. But it's all right—'

'My dear sir,' I cried, 'don't you see you've done thousands of pounds'
worth of damage?'

'There, I throw myself on your discretion. I'm not a practical man, of
course, but don't you think they will regard it as a cyclone?'

'But the explosion—'

'It was *not* an explosion. It's perfectly simple. Only, as I say, I'm apt to
overlook these little things. It's that zuzzoo business on a larger scale.
Inadvertently I made this substance of mine, this Cavorite, in a thin, wide
sheet. . . .'

He paused. 'You are quite clear that the stuff is opaque to gravitation,
that it cuts off things from gravitating towards each other?'

'Yes,' said I. 'Yes.'

'Well, so soon as it reached a temperature of 60° Fahrenheit. and the
process of its manufacture was complete, the air above it, the portions of roof
and ceiling and floor above it ceased to have weight. I suppose you know
– everybody knows nowadays – that, as a usual thing, the air *has* weight, that
it presses on everything at the surface of the earth, presses in all directions,
with a pressure of fourteen and a half pounds to the square inch?'

'I know that,' said I. 'Go on.'

'I know that too,' he remarked. 'Only this shows you how useless know-
ledge is unless you apply it. You see, over our Cavorite this ceased to be the
case, the air there ceased to exert any pressure, and the air round it and

not over the Cavorite was exerting a pressure of fourteen pounds and a half to the square inch upon this suddenly weightless air. Ah! You begin to see! The air all about the Cavorite crushed in upon the air above it with irresistible force. The air above the Cavorite was forced upward violently, the air that rushed in to replace it immediately lost weight, ceased to exert any pressure, followed suit, blew the ceiling through and the roof off. . . .

'You perceive,' he said, 'it formed a sort of atmospheric fountain, a kind of chimney in the atmosphere. And if the Cavorite itself hadn't been loose and so got sucked up the chimney, does it occur to you what would have happened?'

I thought. 'I suppose,' I said, 'the air would be rushing up and up over that infernal piece of stuff now.'

'Precisely,' he said. 'A huge fountain—'

'Spouting into space! Good Heavens! Why, it would have squirted all the atmosphere of the earth away! It would have robbed the world of air! It would have been the death of all mankind! That little lump of stuff!'

'Not exactly into space,' said Cavor, 'but as bad – practically. It would have whipped the air off the world as one peels a banana, and flung it thousands of miles. It would have dropped back again, of course – but on an asphyxiated world! From our point of view very little better than if it never came back!'

I stared. As yet I was too amazed to realize how all my expectations had been upset. 'What do you mean to do now?' I asked.

'In the first place, if I may borrow a garden trowel I will remove some of this earth with which I am encased, and then if I may avail myself of your domestic conveniences I will have a bath. This done, we will converse more at leisure. It will be wise, I think' – he laid a muddy hand on my arm – 'if nothing were said of this affair beyond ourselves. I know I have caused great damage – probably even dwelling-houses may be ruined here and there upon the countryside. But on the other hand, I cannot possibly pay for the damage I have done, and if the real cause of this is published, it will lead only to heart-burning and the obstruction of my work. One cannot foresee *everything*, you know, and I cannot consent for one moment to add the burthen of practical considerations to my theorizing. Later on, when you have come in with your practical mind, and Cavorite is floated – floated *is* the word, isn't it? – and it has realized all you anticipate for it, we may set matters right with these persons. But not now – not now. If no other explanation is offered, people, in the present unsatisfactory state of meteorological science, will ascribe all this to a cyclone; there might be a public subscription, and as my house has collapsed and been burnt, I should in that case receive a considerable share in the compensation, which would be extremely helpful to the prosecution of our researches. But if it is known that *I* caused this, there will be no public

subscription, and everybody will be put out. Practically I should never get a chance of working in peace again. My three assistants may or may not have perished. That is a detail. If they have, it is no great loss; they were more zealous than able, and this premature event must be largely due to their joint neglect of the furnace. If they have not perished, I doubt if they have the intelligence to explain the affair. They will accept the cyclone story. And if, during the temporary unfitness of my house for occupation, I may lodge in one of the untenanted rooms of this bungalow of yours—'

He paused and regarded me.

A man of such possibilities, I reflected, is no ordinary guest to entertain.

'Perhaps,' said I, rising to my feet, 'we had better begin by looking for a trowel,' and I led the way to the scattered vestiges of the greenhouse.

And while he was having his bath I considered the entire question alone. It was clear there were drawbacks to Mr Cavor's society I had not foreseen. The absent-mindedness that had just escaped depopulating the terrestrial globe, might at any moment result in some other grave inconvenience. On the other hand I was young, my affairs were in a mess, and I was in just the mood for reckless adventure – with a chance of something good at the end of it. I had quite settled in my mind that I was to have half at least in that aspect of the affair. Fortunately I held my bungalow, as I have already explained, on a three-year agreement, without being responsible for repairs; and my furniture, such as there was of it, had been hastily purchased, was unpaid for, insured, and altogether devoid of associations. In the end I decided to keep on with him, and see the business through.

Certainly the aspect of things had changed very greatly. I no longer doubted at all the enormous possibilities of the substance, but I began to have doubts about the gun-carriage and the patent boots.

We set to work at once to reconstruct his laboratory and proceed with our experiments. Cavor talked more on my level than he had ever done before, when it came to the question of how we should make the stuff next.

'Of course we must make it again,' he said, with a sort of glee I had not expected in him, 'of course we must make it again. We have caught a Tartar, perhaps, but we have left the theoretical behind us for good and all. If we can possibly avoid wrecking this little planet of ours, we will. But – there *must* be risks! There must be. In experimental work there always are. And here, as a practical man, *you* must come in. For my own part it seems to me we might make it edgeways, perhaps, and very thin. Yet I don't know. I have a certain dim perception of another method. I can hardly explain it yet. But curiously enough it came into my mind, while I was rolling over and over in the mud before the wind, and very doubtful how the whole adventure was to end, as being absolutely the thing I ought to have done.'

Even with my aid we found some little difficulty, and meanwhile we kept at work restoring the laboratory. There was plenty to do before it was absolutely necessary to decide upon the precise form and method of our second attempt. Our only hitch was the strike of the three labourers, who objected to my activity as a foreman. But that matter we compromised after two days' delay.

CHAPTER III

The Building of the Sphere

I remember the occasion very distinctly when Cavor told me of his idea of the sphere. He had had intimations of it before, but at the time it seemed to come to him in a rush. We were returning to the bungalow for tea, and on the way he fell humming. Suddenly he shouted, 'That's it! That finishes it! A sort of roller blind!'

'Finishes what?' I asked.

'Space – anywhere! The moon!'

'What do you mean?'

'Mean? Why – it must be a sphere! That's what I mean!'

I saw I was out of it, and for a time I let him talk in his own fashion. I hadn't the ghost of an idea then of his drift. But after he had taken tea he made it clear to me.

'It's like this,' he said. 'Last time I ran this stuff that cuts things off from gravitation into a flat tank with an overlap that held it down. And directly it had cooled and the manufacture was completed all that uproar happened, nothing above it weighed anything, the air went squirting up, the house squirted up, and if the stuff itself hadn't squirted up too, I don't know what would have happened! But suppose the substance is loose, and quite free to go up?'

'It will go up at once!'

'Exactly. With no more disturbance than firing a big gun.'

'But what good will that do?'

'I'm going up with it!'

I put down my teacup and stared at him.

'Imagine a sphere,' he explained, 'large enough to hold two people and their luggage. It will be made of steel lined with thick glass; it will contain a proper store of solidified air, concentrated food, water-distilling apparatus, and so forth. And enamelled, as it were, on the outer steel—'

'Cavorite?'

'Yes.'

'But how will you get inside?'

'There was a similar problem about a dumpling.'

'Yes, I know. But how?'

'That's perfectly easy. An air-tight manhole is all that is needed. That, of course, will have to be a little complicated; there will have to be a valve, so that things may be thrown out, if necessary, without much loss of air.'

'Like Jules Verne's thing in "A Trip to the Moon"?'

But Cavor was not a reader of fiction.

'I begin to see,' I said slowly. 'And you could get in and screw yourself up while the Cavorite was warm, and as soon as it cooled it would become impervious to gravitation, and off you would fly—'

'At a tangent.'

'You would go off in a straight line—' I stopped abruptly. 'What is to prevent the thing travelling in a straight line into space for ever?' I asked. 'You're not safe to get anywhere, and if you do – how will you get back?'

'I've just thought of that,' said Cavor. 'That's what I meant when I said the thing is finished. The inner glass sphere can be air-tight and, except for the manhole, continuous, and the steel sphere can be made in sections, each section capable of rolling up after the fashion of a roller blind. These can easily be worked by springs, and released and checked by electricity conveyed by platinum wires fused through the glass. All that is merely a question of detail. So you see, that except for the thickness of the blind rollers, the Cavorite exterior of the sphere will consist of windows or blinds, whichever you like to call them. Well, when all these windows or blinds are shut, no light, no heat, no gravitation, no radiant energy of any sort will get at the inside of the sphere, it will fly on through space in a straight line, as you say. But open a window, imagine one of the windows open! Then at once any heavy body that chances to be in that direction will attract us—'

I sat taking it in.

'You see?' he said.

'Oh, I *see*.'

'Practically we shall be able to tack about in space just as we wish. Get attracted by this and that.'

'Oh yes. *That's* clear enough. Only—'

'Well?'

'I don't quite see what we shall do it for! It's really only jumping off the world and back again.'

'Surely! For example, one might go to the moon.'

'And when one got there! What would you find?'

'We should see— Oh! Consider the new knowledge.'

'Is there air there?'

'There may be.'

'It's a fine idea,' I said, 'but it strikes me as a large order all the same. The moon! I'd much rather try some smaller things first.'

'They're out of the question, because of the air difficulty.'

'Why not apply that idea of spring blinds – Cavorite blinds in strong steel cases – to lifting weights?'

'It wouldn't work,' he insisted. 'After all, to go into outer space is not so much worse, if at all, than a polar expedition. Men go on polar expeditions.'

'Not business men. And besides, they get paid for polar expeditions. And

if anything goes wrong there are relief parties. But this – it's just firing ourselves off the world for nothing.'

'Call it prospecting.'

'You'll have to call it that. . . . One might make a book of it perhaps,' I said.

'I have no doubt there will be minerals,' said Cavor.

'For example?'

'Oh! Sulphur, ores, gold perhaps, possibly new elements.'

'Cost of carriage,' I said. 'You know you're *not* a practical man. The moon's a quarter of a million miles away.'

'It seems to me it wouldn't cost much to cart any weight anywhere if you packed it in a Cavorite case.'

I had not thought of that. 'Delivered free on head of purchaser, eh?'

'It isn't as though we were confined to the moon.'

'You mean—'

'There's Mars – clear atmosphere, novel surroundings, exhilarating sense of lightness. It might be pleasant to go there.'

'Is there air on Mars?'

'Oh yes!'

'Seems as though you might run it as a sanatorium. By the way, how far is Mars?'

'Two hundred million miles at present,' said Cavor airily; 'and you go close by the sun.'

My imagination was picking itself up again. 'After all,' I said, 'there's something in these things. There's travel—'

An extraordinary possibility came rushing into my mind. Suddenly I saw, as in a vision, the whole solar system threaded with Cavorite liners and spheres *de luxe*. 'Rights of pre-emption,' came floating into my head – planetary rights of pre-emption. I recalled the old Spanish monopoly in American gold. It wasn't as though it was just this planet or that – it was all of them. I stared at Cavor's rubicund face, and suddenly my imagination was leaping and dancing. I stood up, I walked up and down; my tongue was unloosened.

'I'm beginning to take it in,' I said; 'I'm beginning to take it in.' The transition from doubt to enthusiasm seemed to take scarcely any time at all. 'But this is tremendous!' I cried. 'This is Imperial! I haven't been dreaming of this sort of thing.'

Once the chill of my opposition was removed, his own pent-up excitement had play. He too got up and paced. He too gesticulated and shouted. We behaved like men inspired. We *were* men inspired.

'We'll settle all that!' he said in answer to some incidental difficulty that had pulled me up. 'We'll soon settle all that! We'll start the drawings for mouldings this very night.'

'We'll start them now,' I responded, and we hurried off to the laboratory to begin upon this work forthwith.

I was like a child in Wonderland all that night. The dawn found us both still at work – we kept our electric light going heedless of the day. I remember now exactly how those drawings looked. I shaded and tinted, while Cavor drew – smudged and haste-marked they were in every line, but wonderfully correct. We got out the orders for the steel blinds and frames we needed from that night's work, and the glass sphere was designed within a week. We gave up our afternoon conversations and our old routine altogether. We worked, and we slept and ate when we could work no longer for hunger and fatigue. Our enthusiasm infected even our three men, though they had no idea what the sphere was for. Through those days the man Gibbs gave up walking, and went everywhere, even across the room, at a sort of fussy run.

And it grew – the sphere. December passed, January – I spent a day with a broom sweeping a path through the snow from bungalow to laboratory – February, March. By the end of March the completion was in sight. In January had come a team of horses, a huge packing-case; we had our thick glass sphere now ready, and in position under the crane we had rigged to sling it into the steel shell. All the bars and blinds of the steel shell – it was not really a spherical shell, but polyhedral, with a roller blind to each facet – had arrived by February, and the lower half was bolted together. The Cavorite was half made by March, the metallic paste had gone through two of the stages in its manufacture, and we had plastered quite half of it on to the steel bars and blinds. It was astonishing how closely we kept to the lines of Cavor's first inspiration in working out the scheme. When the bolting together of the sphere was finished, he proposed to remove the rough roof of the temporary laboratory in which the work was done, and build a furnace about it. So the last stage of Cavorite making, in which the paste is heated to a dull red glow in a stream of helium, would be accomplished when it was already on the sphere.

And then we had to discuss and decide what provisions we were to take – compressed foods, concentrated essences, steel cylinders containing reserve oxygen, an arrangement for removing carbonic acid and waste from the air and restoring oxygen by means of sodium peroxide, water condensers, and so forth. I remember the little heap they made in the corner – tins, and rolls, and boxes – convincingly matter-of-fact.

It was a strenuous time, with little chance of thinking. But one day, when we were drawing near the end, an odd mood came over me. I had been bricking up the furnace all the morning, and I sat down by these possessions dead beat. Everything seemed dull and incredible.

'But look here, Cavor,' I said. 'After all! What's it all for?'

He smiled. 'The thing now is to go.'

'The moon,' I reflected. 'But what do you expect? I thought the moon was a dead world.'

He shrugged his shoulders.

'What do you expect?'

'We're going to see.'

'*Are* we?' I said, and stared before me.

'You are tired,' he remarked. 'You'd better take a walk this afternoon.'

'No,' I said obstinately; 'I'm going to finish this brickwork.'

And I did, and insured myself a night of insomnia.

I don't think I have ever had such a night.

I had some bad times before my business collapse, but the very worst of those was sweet slumber compared to this infinity of aching wakefulness. I was suddenly in the most enormous funk at the thing we were going to do.

I do not remember before that night thinking at all of the risks we were running. Now they came like that array of spectres that once beleaguered Prague, and camped around me. The strangeness of what we were about to do, the unearthliness of it, overwhelmed me. I was like a man awakened out of pleasant dreams to the most horrible surroundings. I lay, eyes wide open, and the sphere seemed to get more flimsy and feeble, and Cavor more unreal and fantastic, and the whole enterprise madder and madder every moment.

I got out of bed and wandered about. I sat at the window and stared at the immensity of space. Between the stars was the void, the unfathomable darkness! I tried to recall the fragmentary knowledge of astronomy I had gained in my irregular reading, but it was all too vague to furnish any idea of the things we might expect. At last I got back to bed and snatched some moments of sleep – moments of nightmare rather – in which I fell and fell and fell for evermore into the abyss of the sky.

I astonished Cavor at breakfast. I told him shortly, 'I'm not coming with you in the sphere.'

I met all his protests with a sullen persistence. 'The thing's too mad,' I said, 'and I won't come. The thing's too mad.'

I would not go with him to the laboratory. I fretted about my bungalow for a time, and then took hat and stick and set off alone, I knew not whither. It chanced to be a glorious morning: a warm wind and deep blue sky, the first green of spring abroad, and multitudes of birds singing. I lunched on beef and beer in a little public-house near Elham, and startled the landlord by remarking *apropos* of the weather, 'A man who leaves the world when days of this sort are about is a fool!'

'That's what I says when I heerd on it!' said the landlord, and I found that for one poor soul at least this world had proved excessive, and there had been a throat-cutting. I went on with a new twist to my thoughts.

In the afternoon I had a pleasant sleep in a sunny place, and went my way refreshed.

I came to a comfortable-looking inn near Canterbury. It was bright with creepers, and the landlady was a clean old woman and took my eye. I found I had just enough money to pay for my lodging with her. I decided to stop the night there. She was a talkative body, and among many other particulars I learnt she had never been to London. 'Canterbury's as far as ever I been,' she said. 'I'm not one of your gad-about sort.'

'How would you like a trip to the moon?' I cried.

'I never did hold with them ballooneys,' she said, evidently under the impression that this was a common excursion enough. 'I wouldn't go up in one – not for ever so.'

This struck me as being funny. After I had supped I sat on a bench by the door of the inn and gossiped with two labourers about brick-making, and motor-cars, and the cricket of last year. And in the sky a faint new crescent, blue and vague as a distant Alp, sank westward over the sun.

The next day I returned to Cavor. 'I am coming,' I said. 'I've been a little out of order, that's all.'

That was the only time I felt any serious doubt of our enterprise. Nerves purely! After that I worked a little more carefully, and took a trudge for an hour every day. And at last, save for the heating in the furnace, our labours were at an end.

CHAPTER IV

Inside the Sphere

'Go on,' said Cavor, as I sat across the edge of the manhole and looked down into the black interior of the sphere. We two were alone. It was evening, the sun had set, and the stillness of the twilight was upon everything.

I drew my other leg inside and slid down the smooth glass to the bottom of the sphere, then turned to take the cans of food and other impedimenta from Cavor. The interior was warm, the thermometer stood at eighty, and as we should lose little or none of this by radiation, we were dressed in shoes and thin flannels. We had, however, a bundle of thick woollen clothing and several thick blankets to guard against mischance. By Cavor's direction I placed the packages, the cylinders of oxygen, and so forth, loosely about my feet, and soon we had everything in. He walked about the roofless shed for a time seeking anything we had overlooked, and then crawled in after me. I noted something in his hand.

'What have you got there?' I asked.

'Haven't you brought anything to read?'

'Good Lord! No.'

'I forgot to tell you. There are uncertainties – the voyage may last – we may be weeks!'

'But—'

'We shall be floating in this sphere with absolutely no occupation.'

'I wish I'd known—'

He peered out of the manhole. 'Look!' he said. 'There's something there!'

'Is there time?'

'We shall be an hour.'

I looked out. It was an old number of *Tit-Bits* that one of the men must have brought. Further away in the corner I saw a torn *Lloyds' News*. I scrambled back into the sphere with these things. 'What have you got?' I said.

I took the book from his hand and read, 'The Works of William Shakespeare.'

He coloured slightly. 'My education has been so purely scientific—' he said apologetically.

'Never read him?'

'Never.'

'He knew a little you know – in an irregular sort of way.'

'Precisely what I am told,' said Cavor.

I assisted him to screw in the glass cover of the manhole, and then he pressed a stud to close the corresponding blind in the outer case. The little oblong of twilight vanished. We were in darkness.

For a time neither of us spoke. Although our case would not be impervious to sound, everything was very still. I perceived there was nothing to grip when the shock of our start should come, and I realized that I should be uncomfortable for want of a chair.

'Why have we no chairs?' I asked.

'I've settled all that,' said Cavor. 'We shan't need them.'

'Why not?'

'You will see,' he said, in the tone of a man who refuses to talk.

I became silent. Suddenly it had come to me clear and vivid that I was a fool to be inside that sphere. Even now, I asked myself, is it too late to withdraw? The world outside the sphere, I knew, would be cold and inhospitable enough to me – for weeks I had been living on subsidies from Cavor – but after all, would it be as cold as the infinite zero, as inhospitable as empty space? If it had not been for the appearance of cowardice, I believe that even then I should have made him let me out. But I hesitated on that score, and hesitated, and grew fretful and angry, and the time passed.

There came a little jerk, a noise like champagne being uncorked in another room, and a faint whistling sound. For just one instant I had a sense of enormous tension, a transient conviction that my feet were pressing downward with a force of countless tons. It lasted for an infinitesimal time.

But it stirred me to action. 'Cavor!' I said into the darkness, 'my nerve's in rags. . . . I don't think—'

I stopped. He made no answer.

'Confound it!' I cried; 'I'm a fool! What business have I here? I'm not coming, Cavor. The thing's too risky. I'm getting out.'

'You can't,' he said.

'Can't! We'll soon see about that!'

He made no answer for ten seconds. 'It's too late for us to quarrel now, Bedford,' he said. 'That little jerk was the start. Already we are flying as swiftly as a bullet up into the gulf of space.'

'I—' I said, and then it didn't seem to matter what happened. For a time I was, as it were, stunned; I had nothing to say. It was just as if I had never heard of this idea of leaving the world before. Then I perceived an unaccountable change in my bodily sensations. It was a feeling of lightness, of unreality. Coupled with that was a queer sensation in the head, an apoplectic effect almost, and a thumping of blood-vessels at the ears. Neither of these feelings diminished as time went on, but at last I got so used to them that I experienced no inconvenience.

I heard a click, and a little glow lamp came into being.

I saw Cavor's face, as white as I felt my own to be. We regarded one another in silence. The transparent blackness of the glass behind him made him seem as though he floated in a void.

'Well, we're committed,' I said at last.

'Yes,' he said, 'we're committed.'

'Don't move,' he exclaimed, at some suggestion of a gesture. 'Let your muscles keep quite lax – as if you were in bed. We are in a little universe of our own. Look at those things!'

He pointed to the loose cases and bundles that had been lying on the blankets in the bottom of the sphere. I was astonished to see that they were floating now nearly a foot from the spherical wall. Then I saw from his shadow that Cavor was no longer leaning against the glass. I thrust out my hand behind me, and found that I too was suspended in space, clear of the glass.

I did not cry out nor gesticulate, but fear came upon me. It was like being held and lifted by something – you know not what. The mere touch of my hand against the glass moved me rapidly. I understood what had happened, but that did not prevent my being afraid. We were cut off from all exterior gravitation, only the attraction of objects within our sphere had effect. Consequently everything that was not fixed to the glass was falling – slowly because of the slightness of our masses – towards the centre of gravity of our little world, which seemed to be somewhere about the middle of the sphere, but rather nearer to myself than Cavor, on account of my greater weight.

'We must turn round,' said Cavor, 'and float back to back, with the things between us.'

It was the strangest sensation conceivable, floating thus loosely in space, at first indeed horribly strange, and when the horror passed, not disagreeable at all, exceeding restful; indeed, the nearest thing in earthly experience to it that I know is lying on a very thick, soft feather bed. But the quality of utter detachment and independence! I had not reckoned on things like this. I had expected a violent jerk at starting, a giddy sense of speed. Instead I felt – as if I were disembodied. It was not like the beginning of a journey; it was like the beginning of a dream.

CHAPTER V

The Journey to the Moon

Presently Cavor extinguished the light. He said we had not overmuch energy stored, and that what we had we must economize for reading. For a time, whether it was long or short I do not know, there was nothing but blank darkness.

A question floated up out of the void. 'How are we pointing?' I said. 'What is our direction?'

'We are flying away from the earth at a tangent, and as the moon is near her third quarter we are going somewhere towards her. I will open a blind—'

Came a click, and then a window in the outer case yawned open. The sky outside was as black as the darkness within the sphere, but the shape of the open window was marked by an infinite number of stars.

Those who have only seen the starry sky from the earth cannot imagine its appearance when the vague half-luminous veil of our air has been withdrawn. The stars we see on earth are the mere scattered survivors that penetrate our misty atmosphere. But now at last I could realize the meaning of the hosts of heaven!

Stranger things we were presently to see, but that airless, star-dusted sky! Of all things, I think that will be one of the last I shall forget.

The little window vanished with a click, another beside it snapped open and instantly closed, and then a third, and for a moment I had to close my eyes because of the blinding splendour of the waning moon.

For a space I had to stare at Cavor and the white-lit things about me to season my eyes to light again, before I could turn them towards that pallid glare.

Four windows were open in order that the gravitation of the moon might act upon all the substances in our sphere. I found I was no longer floating freely in space, but that my feet were resting on the glass in the direction of the moon. The blankets and cases of provisions were also creeping slowly down the glass, and presently came to rest so as to block out a portion of the view. It seemed to me, of course, that I looked 'down' when I looked at the moon. On earth 'down' means earthward, the way things fall, and 'up' the reverse direction. Now the pull of gravitation was towards the moon, and for all I knew to the contrary our earth was overhead. And, of course, when all the Cavorite blinds were closed, 'down' was towards the centre of our sphere, and 'up' towards its outer wall.

It was curiously unlike earthly experience, too, to have the light coming *up* to one. On earth light falls from above, or comes slanting down sideways,

but here it came from beneath our feet, and to see our shadows we had to look up.

At first it gave me a sort of vertigo to stand only on thick glass and look down upon the moon through hundreds of thousands of miles of vacant space; but this sickness passed very speedily. And then – the splendour of the sight!

The reader may imagine it best if he will lie on the ground some warm summer's night and look between his upraised feet at the moon, but for some reason, probably because the absence of air made it so much more luminous, the moon seemed already considerably larger than it does from earth. The minutest details of its surface were acutely clear. And since we did not see it through air, its outline was bright and sharp, there was no glow or halo about it, and the star-dust that covered the sky came right to its very margin, and marked the outline of its unilluminated part. And as I stood and stared at the moon between my feet, that perception of the impossible that had been with me off and on ever since our start, returned again with tenfold conviction.

'Cavor,' I said, 'this takes me queerly. Those companies we were going to run, and all that about minerals?'

'Well?'

'I don't see 'em here.'

'No,' said Cavor; 'but you'll get over all that.'

'I suppose I'm made to turn right side up again. Still, *this*— For a moment I could half believe there never was a world.'

'That copy of *Lloyds' News* might help you.'

I stared at the paper for a moment, then held it above the level of my face, and found I could read it quite easily. I struck a column of mean little advertisements. 'A gentleman of private means is willing to lend money,' I read. I knew that gentleman. Then somebody eccentric wanted to sell a Cutaway bicycle, 'quite new and cost £15', for five pounds; and a lady in distress wished to dispose of some fish knives and forks, 'a wedding present', at a great sacrifice. No doubt some simple soul was sagely examining these knives and forks, and another triumphantly riding off on that bicycle, and a third trustfully consulting that benevolent gentleman of means even as I read. I laughed, and let the paper drift from my hand.

'Are we visible from the earth?' I asked.

'Why?'

'I knew someone who was rather interested in astronomy. It occurred to me that it would be rather odd if – my friend – chanced to be looking through some telescope.'

'It would need the most powerful telescope on earth even now to see us as the minutest speck.'

For a time I stared in silence at the moon.

'It's a world,' I said; 'one feels that infinitely more than one ever did on earth. People perhaps—'

'People!' he exclaimed. 'No! Banish all that! Think yourself a sort of ultra-arctic voyager exploring the desolate places of space. Look at it!'

He waved his hand at the shining whiteness below. 'It's dead – dead! Vast extinct volcanoes, lava wildernesses, tumbled wastes of snow, or frozen carbonic acid, or frozen air, and everywhere landslip seams and cracks and gulfs. Nothing happens. Men have watched this planet systematically with telescopes for over two hundred years. How much change do you think they have seen?'

'None.'

'They have traced two indisputable landslips, a doubtful crack and one slight periodic change of colour, and that's all.'

'I didn't know they'd traced even that.'

'Oh yes. But as for people!'

'By the way,' I asked, 'how small a thing will the biggest telescopes show upon the moon?'

'One could see a fair-sized church. One could certainly see any towns or buildings, or anything like the handiwork of men. There might perhaps be insects, something in the way of ants, for example, so that they could hide in deep burrows from the lunar night, or some new sort of creatures having no earthly parallel. That is the most probable thing, if we are to find life there at all. Think of the difference in conditions! Life must fit itself to a day as long as fourteen earthly days, a cloudless sun-blaze of fourteen days, and then a night of equal length, growing ever colder and colder under these cold, sharp stars. In that night there must be cold, the ultimate cold, absolute zero, 273° Centigrade below the earthly freezing point. Whatever life there is must hibernate through *that*, and rise again each day.'

He mused. 'One can imagine something worm-like,' he said, 'taking its air solid as an earth-worm swallows earth, or thick-skinned monsters—'

'By-the-by,' I said, 'why didn't we bring a gun?'

He did not answer that question. 'No,' he concluded, 'we just have to go. We shall see when we get there.'

I remembered something. 'Of course, there's my minerals, anyhow,' I said; 'whatever the conditions may be.'

Presently he told me he wished to alter our course a little by letting the earth tug at us for a moment. He was going to open one earthward blind for thirty seconds. He warned me that it would make my head swim, and advised me to extend my hands against the glass to break my fall. I did as he directed, and thrust my feet against the bales of food cases and air cylinders to prevent their falling upon me. Then with a click the window flew open. I fell clumsily upon hands and face, and saw for a moment between my black extended fingers our mother earth – a planet in a downward sky.

We were still very near – Cavor told me the distance was perhaps eight hundred miles – and the huge terrestrial disk filled all heaven. But already it was plain to see that the world was a globe. The land below us was in twilight and vague, but westward the vast grey stretches of the Atlantic shone like molten silver under the receding day. I think I recognized the cloud-dimmed coastlines of France and Spain and the south of England, and then, with a click, the shutter closed again, and I found myself in a state of extraordinary confusion sliding slowly over the smooth glass.

When at last things settled themselves in my mind again, it seemed quite beyond question that the moon was 'down' and under my feet, and that the earth was somewhere away on the level of the horizon – the earth that had been 'down' to me and my kindred since the beginning of things.

So slight were the exertions required of us, so easy did the practical annihilation of our weight make all we had to do, that the necessity for taking refreshment did not occur to us for nearly six hours (by Cavor's chronometer) after our start. I was amazed at that lapse of time. Even then I was satisfied with very little. Cavor examined the apparatus for absorbing carbonic acid and water, and pronounced it to be in satisfactory order, our consumption of oxygen having been extraordinarily slight. And our talk being exhausted for the time, and there being nothing further for us to do, we gave way to a curious drowsiness that had come upon us, and spreading our blankets on the bottom of the sphere in such a manner as to shut out most of the moonlight, wished each other good-night, and almost immediately fell asleep.

And so, sleeping, and sometimes talking and reading a little, and at times eating, although without any keenness of appetite,* but for the most part in a sort of quiescence that was neither waking nor slumber, we fell through a space of time that had neither night nor day in it, silently, softly, and swiftly down towards the moon.

* It is a curious thing that while we were in the sphere we felt not the slightest desire for food, nor did we feel the want of it when we abstained. At first we forced our appetites, but afterwards we fasted completely. Altogether we did not consume one-hundredth part of the compressed provisions we had brought with us. The amount of carbonic acid we breathed was also unnaturally low, but why this was, I am quite unable to explain.

CHAPTER VI

The Landing on the Moon

I remember how one day Cavor suddenly opened six of our shutters and blinded me so that I cried aloud at him. The whole area was moon, a stupendous scimitar of white dawn with its edge hacked out by notches of darkness, the crescent shore of an ebbing tide of darkness, out of which peaks and pinnacles came climbing into the blaze of the sun. I take it the reader has seen pictures or photographs of the moon, so that I need not describe the broader features of that landscape, those spacious ringlike ranges vaster than any terrestrial mountains, their summits shining in the day, their shadows harsh and deep, the grey disordered plains, the ridges, hills, and craterlets, all passing at last from a blazing illumination into a common mystery of black. Athwart this world we were flying scarcely a hundred miles above its crests and pinnacles. And now we could see, what no eye on earth will ever see, that under the blaze of the day the harsh outlines of the rocks and ravines of the plains and crater floor grew grey and indistinct under a thickening haze, that the white of their lit surfaces broke into lumps and patches, and broke again and shrank and vanished, and that here and there strange tints of brown and olive grew and spread.

But little time we had for watching then. For now we had come to the real danger of our journey. We had to drop ever closer to the moon as we spun about it, to slacken our pace and watch our chance, until at last we could dare to drop upon its surface.

For Cavor that was a time of intense exertion; for me it was an anxious inactivity. I seemed perpetually to be getting out of his way. He leapt about the sphere from point to point with an agility that would have been impossible on earth. He was perpetually opening and closing the Cavorite windows, making calculations, consulting his chronometer by means of the glow lamp during those last eventful hours. For a long time we had all our windows closed and hung silently in darkness, hurling through space.

Then he was feeling for the shutter studs, and suddenly four windows were open. I staggered and covered my eyes, drenched and scorched and blinded by the unaccustomed splendour of the sun beneath my feet. Then again the shutters snapped, leaving my brain spinning in a darkness that pressed against the eyes. And after that I floated in another vast, black silence.

Then Cavor switched on the electric light, and told me he proposed to bind all our luggage together with the blankets about it, against the concussion of our descent. We did this with our windows closed, because in that way our goods arranged themselves naturally at the centre of the sphere.

That too was a strange business; we two men floating loose in that spherical space, and packing and pulling ropes. Imagine it if you can! No up nor down, and every effort resulting in unexpected movements. Now I would be pressed against the glass with the full force of Cavor's thrust, now I would be kicking helplessly in a void. Now the star of the electric light would be overhead, now under foot. Now Cavor's feet would float up before my eyes, and now we would be crossways to each other. But at last our goods were safely bound together in a big soft bale, all except two blankets with head holes that we were to wrap about ourselves.

Then for a flash Cavor opened a window moonward, and we saw that we were dropping towards a huge central crater with a number of minor craters grouped in a sort of cross about it. And then again Cavor flung our little sphere open to the scorching, blinding sun. I think he was using the sun's attraction as a brake. 'Cover yourself with a blanket,' he cried, thrusting himself from me, and for a moment I did not understand.

Then I hauled the blanket from beneath my feet and got it about me and over my head and eyes. Abruptly he closed the shutters again, snapped one open again and closed it, then suddenly began snapping them all open, each safely into its steel roller. There came a jar, and then we were rolling over and over, bumping against the glass and against the big bale of our luggage, and clutching at each other, and outside some white substance splashed as if we were rolling down a slope of snow. . . .

Over, clutch, bump, clutch, bump, over. . . .

Came a thud, and I was half buried under the bale of our possessions, and for a space everything was still. Then I could hear Cavor puffing and grunting, and the snapping of a shutter in its sash. I made an effort, thrust back our blanket-wrapped luggage, and emerged from beneath it. Our open windows were just visible as a deeper black set with stars.

We were still alive, and we were lying in the darkness of the shadow of the wall of the great crater into which we had fallen.

We sat getting our breath again, and feeling the bruises on our limbs. I don't think either of us had had a very clear expectation of such rough handling as we had received. I struggled painfully to my feet. 'And now,' said I, 'to look at the landscape of the moon! But—! It's tremendously dark, Cavor!'

The glass was dewy, and as I spoke I wiped at it with my blanket. 'We're half-an-hour or so beyond the day,' he said. 'We must wait.'

It was impossible to distinguish anything. We might have been in a sphere of steel for all that we could see. My rubbing with the blanket simply smeared the glass, and as fast as I wiped it, it became opaque again with freshly condensed moisture mixed with an increasing quantity of blanket hairs. Of course I ought not to have used the blanket. In my efforts to clear the glass I slipped upon the damp surface, and hurt my shin against one of the oxygen cylinders that protruded from our bale.

The thing was exasperating – it was absurd.

Here we were just arrived upon the moon, amidst we knew not what wonders, and all we could see was the grey and streaming wall of the bubble in which we had come.

'Confound it!' I said. 'But at this rate we might have stopped at home;' and I squatted on the bale and shivered, and drew my blanket closer about me.

Abruptly the moisture turned to spangles and fronds of frost. 'Can you reach the electric heater?' said Cavor. 'Yes – that black knob. Or we shall freeze.'

I did not wait to be told twice. 'And now,' said I, 'what are we to do?'

'Wait,' he said.

'Wait?'

'Of course. We shall have to wait until our air gets warm again, and then this glass will clear. We can't do anything till then. It's night here yet; we must wait for the day to overtake us. Meanwhile, don't you feel hungry?'

For a space I did not answer him, but sat fretting. I turned reluctantly from the smeared puzzle of the glass and stared at his face. 'Yes,' I said, 'I am hungry. I feel somehow enormously disappointed. I had expected – I don't know what I had expected, but not this.'

I summoned my philosophy, and rearranging my blanket about me sat down on the bale again and began my first meal on the moon. I don't think I finished it – I forget. Presently, first in patches, then running rapidly together into wider spaces, came the clearing of the glass, came the drawing of the misty veil that hid the moon world from our eyes.

We peered out upon the landscape of the moon.

CHAPTER VII

Sunrise on the Moon

As we saw it first it was the wildest and most desolate of scenes. We were in an enormous amphitheatre, a vast circular plain, the floor of the giant crater. Its cliff-like walls closed us in on every side. From the westward the light of the unseen sun fell upon them, reaching to the very foot of the cliff, and showed a disordered escarpment of drab and greyish rock, lined here and there with banks and crevices of snow. This was perhaps a dozen miles away, but at first no intervening atmosphere diminished in the slightest the minutely detailed brilliancy with which these things glared at us. They stood out clear and dazzling against a background of starry blackness that seemed to our earthly eyes rather a gloriously spangled velvet curtain than the spaciousness of the sky.

The eastward cliff was at first merely a starless selvedge to the starry dome. No rosy flush, no creeping pallor, announced the commencing day. Only the Corona, the Zodiacal light, a huge cone-shaped, luminous haze, pointing up towards the splendour of the morning star, warned us of the imminent nearness of the sun.

Whatever light was about us was reflected by the westward cliffs. It showed a huge undulating plain, cold and grey, a grey that deepened eastward into the absolute raven darkness of the cliff shadow. Innumerable rounded grey summits, ghostly hummocks, billows of snowy substance, stretching crest beyond crest into the remote obscurity, gave us our first inkling of the distance of the crater wall. These hummocks looked like snow. At the time I thought they were snow. But they were not – they were mounds and masses of frozen air!

So it was at first, and then, sudden, swift, and amazing, came the lunar day.

The sunlight had crept down the cliff, it touched the drifted masses at its base and incontinently came striding with seven-leagued boots towards us. The distant cliff seemed to shift and quiver, and at the touch of the dawn a reek of grey vapour poured upward from the crater floor, whirls and puffs and drifting wraiths of grey, thicker and broader and denser, until at last the whole westward plain was steaming like a wet handkerchief held before the fire, and the westward cliffs were no more than a refracted glare beyond.

'It is air,' said Cavor. 'It must be air – or it would not rise like this – at the mere touch of a sunbeam. And at this pace . . .'

He peered upwards. 'Look!' he said.

'What?' I asked.

'In the sky. Already. On the blackness – a little touch of blue. See! The

stars seem larger. And the little ones and all those dim nebulosities we saw in empty space – they are hidden!'

Swiftly, steadily the day approached us. Grey summit after grey summit was overtaken by the blaze, and turned to a smoking white intensity. At last there was nothing to the west of us but a bank of surging fog, the tumultuous advance and ascent of cloudy haze. The distant cliff had receded further and further, had loomed and changed through the whirl, and foundered and vanished at last in its confusion.

Nearer came that steaming advance, nearer and nearer, coming as fast as the shadow of a cloud before the south-west wind. About us rose a thin anticipatory haze.

Cavor gripped my arm.

'What?' I said.

'Look! The sunrise! The sun!'

He turned me about and pointed to the brow of the eastward cliff, looming above the haze about us, scarce lighter than the darkness of the sky. But now its line was marked by strange reddish shapes, tongues of vermilion flame that writhed and danced. I fancied it must be spirals of vapour that had caught the light and made this crest of fiery tongues against the sky, but indeed it was the solar prominences I saw, a crown of fire about the sun that is forever hidden from earthly eyes by our atmospheric veil.

And then – the sun!

Steadily, inevitably came a brilliant line, came a thin edge of intolerable effulgence that took a circular shape, became a bow, became a blazing sceptre, and hurled a shaft of heat at us as though it was a spear.

It seemed verily to stab my eyes! I cried aloud and turned about blinded, groping for my blanket beneath the bale.

And with that incandescence came a sound, the first sound that had reached us from without since we left the earth, a hissing and rustling, the stormy trailing of the aerial garment of the advancing day. And with the coming of the sound and the light the sphere lurched, and blinded and dazzled we staggered helplessly against each other. It lurched again, and the hissing grew louder. I had shut my eyes perforce, I was making clumsy efforts to cover my head with my blanket, and this second lurch sent me helplessly off my feet. I fell against the bale, and opening my eyes had a momentary glimpse of the air just outside our glass. It was running – it was boiling – like snow into which a white-hot rod is thrust. What had been solid air had suddenly at the touch of the sun become a paste, a mud, a slushy liquefaction, that hissed and bubbled into gas.

There came a still more violent whirl of the sphere, and we had clutched one another. In another moment we were spun about again. Round we went and over, and then I was on all fours. The lunar dawn had hold of us. It meant to show us little men what the moon could do with us.

I caught a second glimpse of things without, puffs of vapour, half-liquid slush, excavated, sliding, falling, sliding. We dropped into darkness. I went down with Cavor's knees in my chest. Then he seemed to fly away from me, and for a moment I lay with all the breath out of my body staring upward. A toppling crag of the melting stuff had splashed over us, buried us, and now it thinned and boiled off us. I saw the bubbles dancing on the glass above. I heard Cavor exclaiming feebly.

Then some huge landslip in the thawing air had caught us, and spluttering expostulation, we began to roll down a slope, rolling faster and faster, leaping crevasses and rebounding from banks, faster and faster, westward into the white-hot boiling tumult of the lunar day.

Clutching at one another we spun about, pitched this way and that, our bale of packages leaping at us, pounding at us. We collided, we gripped, we were torn asunder – our heads met, and the whole universe burst into fiery darts and stars! On the earth we should have smashed one another a dozen times, but on the moon, luckily for us, our weight was only one-sixth of what it is terrestrially, and we fell very mercifully. I recall a sensation of utter sickness, a feeling as if my brain were upside down within my skull, and then—

Something was at work upon my face, some thin feelers worried my ears. Then I discovered the brilliance of the landscape around was mitigated by blue spectacles. Cavor bent over me, and I saw his face upside down, his eyes also protected by tinted goggles. His breath came irregularly, and his lip was bleeding from a bruise. 'Better?' he said, wiping the blood with the back of his hand.

Everything seemed swaying for a space, but that was simply my giddiness. I perceived that he had closed some of the shutters in the outer sphere to save me from the direct blaze of the sun. I was aware that everything about us was very brilliant.

'Lord!' I gasped. 'But this—!'

I craned my neck to see. I perceived there was a blinding glare outside, an utter change from the gloomy darkness of our first impressions. 'Have I been insensible long?' I asked.

'I don't know – the chronometer is broken. Some little time . . . My dear chap! I have been afraid . . .'

I lay for a space taking this in. I saw his face still bore evidences of emotion. For a while I said nothing. I passed an inquisitive hand over my contusions, and surveyed his face for similar damages. The back of my right hand had suffered most, and was skinless and raw. My forehead was bruised and had bled. He handed me a little measure with some of the restorative – I forget the name of it – he had brought with us. After a time I felt a little better. I began to stretch my limbs carefully. Soon I could talk.

'It wouldn't have done,' I said, as though there had been no interval. 'No! It *wouldn't*.'

He thought, his hands hanging over his knees. He peered through the glass and then stared at me. 'Good Lord!' he said. '*No!*'

'What has happened?' I asked after a pause. 'Have we jumped to the tropics?'

'It was as I expected. This air has evaporated – if it is air. At any rate, it has evaporated and the surface of the moon is showing. We are lying on a bank of earthy rock. Here and there bare soil is exposed. A queer sort of soil!'

It occurred to him that it was unnecessary to explain. He assisted me into a sitting position, and I could see with my own eyes.

CHAPTER VIII

A Lunar Morning

The harsh emphasis, the pitiless black and white of the scenery had altogether disappeared. The glare of the sun had taken upon itself a faint tinge of amber; the shadows upon the cliff of the crater wall were deeply purple. To the eastward a dark bank of fog still crouched and sheltered from the sunrise, but to the westward the sky was blue and clear. I began to realize the length of my insensibility.

We were no longer in a void. An atmosphere had arisen about us. The outline of things had gained in character, had grown acute and varied; save for a shadowed space of white substance here and there, white substance that was no longer air but snow, the arctic appearance had gone altogether. Everywhere broad rusty brown spaces of bare and tumbled earth spread to the blaze of the sun. Here and there at the edge of the snowdrifts were transient little pools and eddies of water, the only things stirring in that expanse of barrenness. The sunlight inundated the upper two blinds of our sphere and turned our climate to high summer, but our feet were still in shadow, and the sphere was lying upon a drift of snow.

And scattered here and there upon the slope, and emphasized by little white threads of unthawed snow upon their shady sides, were shapes like sticks, dry twisted sticks of the same rusty hue as the rock upon which they lay. That caught one's thoughts sharply. Sticks! On a lifeless world? Then as my eye grew more accustomed to the texture of their substance, I perceived that almost all this surface had a fibrous texture, like the carpet of brown needles one finds beneath the shade of pine trees.

'Cavor!' I said.

'Yes.'

'It may be a dead world now – but once—'

Something arrested my attention. I had discovered among these needles a number of little round objects. And it seemed to me that one of these had moved.

'Cavor,' I whispered.

'What?'

But I did not answer at once. I stared incredulous. For an instant I could not believe my eyes. I gave an inarticulate cry. I gripped his arm. I pointed. 'Look!' I cried, finding my tongue. 'There! Yes! And there!'

His eyes followed my pointing finger. 'Eh?' he said.

How can I describe the thing I saw? It is so petty a thing to state, and yet it seemed so wonderful, so pregnant with emotion. I have said that

amidst the stick-like litter were these rounded bodies, these little oval bodies that might have passed as very small pebbles. And now first one and then another had stirred, had rolled over and cracked, and down the crack of each of them showed a minute line of yellowish green, thrusting outward to meet the hot encouragement of the newly risen sun. For a moment that was all, and then there stirred and burst a third!

'It is a seed,' said Cavor. And then I heard him whisper very softly, '*Life!*'

'Life!' And immediately it poured upon us that our vast journey had not been made in vain, that we had come to no arid waste of minerals, but to a world that lived and moved! We watched intensely. I remember I kept rubbing the glass before me with my sleeve, jealous of the faintest suspicion of mist.

The picture was clear and vivid only in the middle of the field. All about that centre the dead fibres and seeds were magnified and distorted by the curvature of the glass. But we could see enough! One after another all down the sunlit slope these miraculous little brown bodies burst and gaped apart, like seed-pods, like the husks of fruits; opened eager mouths that drank in the heat and light pouring in a cascade from the newly risen sun.

Every moment more of these seed coats ruptured, and even as they did so the swelling pioneers overflowed their rent-distended seed-cases, and passed into the second stage of growth. With a steady assurance, a swift deliberation, these amazing seeds thrust a rootlet downward to the earth and a queer little bundle-like bud into the air. In a little while the whole slope was dotted with minute plantlets standing at attention in the blaze of the sun.

They did not stand for long. The bundle-like buds swelled and strained and opened with a jerk, thrusting out a coronet of little sharp tips, spreading a whorl of tiny, spiky, brownish leaves, that lengthened rapidly, lengthened visibly even as we watched. The movement was slower than any animal's, swifter than any plant's I have ever seen before. How can I suggest it to you – the way that growth went on? The leaf tips grew so that they moved onward even while we looked at them. The brown seed-case shrivelled and was absorbed with an equal rapidity. Have you ever on a cold day taken a thermometer into your warm hand and watched the little thread of mercury creep up the tube? These moon plants grew like that.

In a few minutes, as it seemed, the buds of the more forward of these plants had lengthened into a stem and were even putting forth a second whorl of leaves, and all the slope that had seemed so recently a lifeless stretch of litter was now dark with the stunted olive-green herbage of bristling spikes that swayed with the vigour of their growing.

I turned about, and behold! Along the upper edge of a rock to the eastward a similar fringe in a scarcely less forward condition swayed and bent, dark against the blinding glare of the sun. And beyond this fringe was the

silhouette of a plant mass, branching clumsily like a cactus, and swelling visibly, swelling like a bladder that fills with air.

Then to the westward also I discovered that another such distended form was rising over the scrub. But here the light fell upon its sleek sides, and I could see that its colour was a vivid orange hue. It rose as one watched it; if one looked away from it for a minute and then back, its outline had changed; it thrust out blunt congested branches until in a little time it rose a coralline shape of many feet in height. Compared with such a growth the terrestrial puff-ball, which will sometimes swell a foot in diameter in a single night, would be a hopeless laggard. But then the puff-ball grows against a gravitational pull six times that of the moon. Beyond, out of gullies and flats that had been hidden from us, but not from the quickening sun, over reefs and banks of shining rock, a bristling beard of spiky and fleshy vegetation was straining into view, hurrying tumultuously to take advantage of the brief day in which it must flower and fruit and seed again and die. It was like a miracle, that growth. So, one must imagine, the trees and plants arose at the Creation and covered the desolation of the new-made earth.

Imagine it! Imagine that dawn! The resurrection of the frozen air, the stirring and quickening of the soil, and then this silent uprising of vegetation, this unearthly ascent of fleshiness and spikes. Conceive it all lit by a blaze that would make the intensest sunlight of earth seem watery and weak. And still around this stirring jungle, wherever there was shadow, lingered banks of bluish snow. And to have the picture of our impression complete, you must bear in mind that we saw it all through a thick bent glass, distorting it as things are distorted by a lens, acute only in the centre of the picture, and very bright there, and towards the edges magnified and unreal.

CHAPTER IX

Prospecting Begins

We ceased to gaze. We turned to each other, the same thought, the same question in our eyes. For these plants to grow, there must be some air, however attenuated, air that we also should be able to breathe.

'The manhole?' I said.

'Yes!' said Cavor, 'If it is air we see!'

'In a little while,' I said, 'these plants will be as high as we are. Suppose – suppose after all— Is it certain? How do you know that stuff is air? It may be nitrogen – it may be carbonic acid even!'

'That is easy,' he said, and set about proving it. He produced a big piece of crumpled paper from the bale, lit it, and thrust it hastily through the manhole valve. I bent forward and peered down through the thick glass for its appearance outside, that little flame on whose evidence depended so much!

I saw the paper drop out and lie lightly upon the snow. The pink flame of its burning vanished. For an instant it seemed to be extinguished. And then I saw a little blue tongue upon the edge of it that trembled, and crept, and spread!

Quietly the whole sheet, save where it lay in immediate contact with the snow, charred and shrivelled and sent up a quivering thread of smoke. There was no doubt left to me; the atmosphere of the moon was either pure oxygen or air, and capable therefore – unless its tenuity was excessive – of supporting our alien life. We might emerge – and live!

I sat down with my legs on either side of the manhole and prepared to unscrew it, but Cavor stopped me. 'There is first a little precaution,' he said. He pointed out that although it was certainly an oxygenated atmosphere outside, it might still be so rarified as to cause us grave injury. He reminded me of mountain sickness, and of the bleeding that often afflicts aeronauts who have ascended too swiftly, and he spent some time in the preparation of a sickly-tasting drink which he insisted on my sharing. It made me feel a little numb, but otherwise had no effect on me. Then he permitted me to begin unscrewing.

Presently the glass stopper of the manhole was so far undone that the denser air within our sphere began to escape along the thread of the screw, singing as a kettle sings before it boils. Thereupon he made me desist. It speedily became evident that the pressure outside was very much less than it was within. How much less it was we had no means of telling.

I sat grasping the stopper with both hands, ready to close it again if, in spite of our intense hope, the lunar atmosphere should after all prove too rarified for us, and Cavor sat with a cylinder of compressed oxygen at hand to restore our pressure. We looked at one another in silence, and then at the fantastic vegetation that swayed and grew visibly and noiselessly without. And ever that shrill piping continued.

My blood-vessels began to throb in my ears, and the sound of Cavor's movements diminished. I noted how still everything had become, because of the thinning of the air.

As our air sizzled out from the screw the moisture of it condensed in little puffs.

Presently I experienced a peculiar shortness of breath, that lasted indeed during the whole of the time of our exposure to the moon's exterior atmosphere, and a rather unpleasant sensation about the ears and fingernails and the back of the throat grew upon my attention, and presently passed off again.

But then came vertigo and nausea that abruptly changed the quality of my courage. I gave the lid of the manhole half a turn and made a hasty explanation to Cavor; but now he was the more sanguine. He answered me in a voice that seemed extraordinarily small and remote, because of the thinness of the air that carried the sound. He recommended a nip of brandy, and set me the example, and presently I felt better. I turned the manhole stopper back again. The throbbing in my ears grew louder, and then I remarked that the piping note of the outrush had ceased. For a time I could not be sure that it had ceased.

'Well?' said Cavor in the ghost of a voice.

'Well?' said I.

'Shall we go on?'

I thought. 'Is this all?'

'If you can stand it.'

By way of answer I went on unscrewing. I lifted the circular operculum from its place and laid it carefully on the bale. A flake or so of snow whirled and vanished as that thin and unfamiliar air took possession of our sphere. I knelt, and then seated myself at the edge of the manhole, peering over it. Beneath, within a yard of my face, lay the untrodden snow of the moon.

There came a little pause. Our eyes met.

'It doesn't distress your lungs too much?' said Cavor.

'No,' I said. 'I can stand this.'

He stretched out his hand for his blanket, thrust his head through its central hole and wrapped it about him. He sat down on the edge of the manhole, he let his feet drop until they were within six inches of the lunar ground. He hesitated for a moment, then thrust himself forward, dropped these intervening inches, and stood upon the untrodden soil of the moon.

As he stepped forward he was refracted grotesquely by the edge of the glass. He stood for a moment looking this way and that. Then he drew himself together and leapt.

The glass distorted everything, but it seemed to me even then to be an extremely big leap. He had at one bound become remote. He seemed twenty or thirty feet off. He was standing high upon a rocky mass and gesticulating back to me. Perhaps he was shouting – but the sound did not reach me. But how the deuce had he done this? I felt like a man who has just seen a new conjuring trick.

In a puzzled state of mind I too dropped through the manhole. I stood up. Just in front of me the snowdrift had fallen away and made a sort of ditch. I made a step and jumped.

I found myself flying through the air, saw the rock on which he stood coming to meet me, clutched it and clung in a state of infinite amazement.

I gasped a painful laugh. I was tremendously confused. Cavor bent down and shouted in piping tones for me to be careful.

I had forgotten that on the moon, with only an eighth part of the earth's mass and a quarter of its diameter, my weight was barely a sixth what it was on earth. But now that fact insisted on being remembered.

'We are out of Mother Earth's leading-strings now,' he said.

With a guarded effort I raised myself to the top, and moving as cautiously as a rheumatic patient, stood up beside him under the blaze of the sun. The sphere lay behind us on its dwindling snowdrift thirty feet away.

As far as the eye could see over the enormous disorder of rocks that formed the crater floor, the same bristling scrub that surrounded us was starting into life, diversified here and there by bulging masses of a cactus form, and scarlet and purple lichens that grew so fast they seemed to crawl over the rocks. The whole area of the crater seemed to me then to be one similar wilderness up to the very foot of the surrounding cliff.

This cliff was apparently bare of vegetation save at its base, and with buttresses and terraces and platforms that did not very greatly attract our attention at the time. It was many miles away from us in every direction, we seemed to be almost at the centre of the crater, and we saw it through a certain haziness that drove before the wind. For there was even a wind now in the thin air, a swift yet weak wind that chilled exceedingly but exerted little pressure. It was blowing round the crater, as it seemed, to the hot illuminated side from the foggy darkness under the sunward wall. It was difficult to look into this eastward fog; we had to peer with half-closed eyes beneath the shade of our hands, because of the fierce intensity of the motionless sun.

'It seems to be deserted,' said Cavor, 'absolutely desolate.'

I looked about me again. I retained even then a clinging hope of some quasi-human evidence, some pinnacle of building, some house or engine,

but everywhere one looked spread the tumbled rocks in peaks and crests, and the darting scrub and those bulging cacti that swelled and swelled, a flat negation as it seemed of all such hope.

'It looks as though these plants had it to themselves,' I said. 'I see no trace of any other creature.'

'No insects – no birds – no! Not a trace, not a scrap nor particle of animal life. If there was – what would they do in the night? . . . No; there's just these plants alone.'

I shaded my eyes with my hand. 'It's like the landscape of a dream. These things are less like earthly land plants than the things one imagines among the rocks at the bottom of the sea. Look at that yonder! One might imagine it a lizard changed into a plant. And the glare!'

'This is only the fresh morning,' said Cavor.

He sighed and looked about him. 'This is no world for men,' he said. 'And yet in a way – it appeals.'

He became silent for a time, then commenced his meditative humming.

I started at a gentle touch, and found a thin sheet of livid lichen lapping over my shoe. I kicked at it and it fell to powder, and each speck began to grow.

I heard Cavor exclaim sharply, and perceived that one of the fixed bayonets of the scrub had pricked him.

He hesitated, his eyes sought among the rocks about us. A sudden blaze of pink had crept up a ragged pillar of crag. It was a most extraordinary pink, a livid magenta.

'Look!' said I, turning, and behold Cavor had vanished!

For an instant I stood transfixed. Then I made a hasty step to look over the verge of the rock. But in my surprise at his disappearance I forgot once more that we were on the moon. The thrust of my foot that I made in striding would have carried me a yard on earth; on the moon it carried me six – a good five yards over the edge. For the moment the thing had something of the effect of those nightmares when one falls and falls. For while one falls sixteen feet in the first second of a fall on earth, on the moon one falls two, and with only a sixth of one's weight. I fell, or rather I jumped down, about ten yards I suppose. It seemed to take quite a long time, five or six seconds, I should think. I floated through the air and fell like a feather, knee-deep in a snowdrift in the bottom of a gully of blue-grey, white-veined rock.

I looked about me. 'Cavor!' I cried; but no Cavor was visible.

'Cavor!' I cried louder, and the rocks echoed me.

I turned fiercely to the rocks and clambered to the summit of them. 'Cavor!' I cried. My voice sounded like the voice of a lost lamb.

The sphere, too, was not in sight, and for a moment a horrible feeling of desolation pinched my heart.

Then I saw him. He was laughing and gesticulating to attract my attention. He was on a bare patch of rock twenty or thirty yards away. I could not hear his voice, but 'jump' said his gestures. I hesitated, the distance seemed enormous. Yet I reflected that surely I must be able to clear a greater distance than Cavor.

I made a step back, gathered myself together, and leapt with all my might. I seemed to shoot right up in the air as though I should never come down. . . .

It was horrible and delightful, and as wild as a nightmare, to go flying off in this fashion. I realized my leap had been altogether too violent. I flew clean over Cavor's head and beheld a spiky confusion in a gully spreading to meet my fall. I gave a yelp of alarm. I put out my hands and straightened my legs.

I hit a huge fungoid bulk that burst all about me, scattering a mass of orange spores in every direction, and covering me with orange powder. I rolled over spluttering, and came to rest convulsed with breathless laughter.

I became aware of Cavor's little round face peering over a bristling hedge. He shouted some faded enquiry. 'Eh?' I tried to shout, but could not do so for want of breath. He made his way towards me, coming gingerly among the bushes.

'We've got to be careful,' he said. 'This moon has no discipline. She'll let us smash ourselves.'

He helped me to my feet. 'You exerted yourself too much,' he said, dabbing at the yellow stuff with his hand to remove it from my garments.

I stood passive and panting, allowing him to beat off the jelly from my knees and elbows and lecture me upon my misfortunes. 'We don't quite allow for the gravitation. Our muscles are scarcely educated yet. We must practise a little, when you have got your breath.'

I pulled two or three little thorns out of my hand, and sat for a time on a boulder of rock. My muscles were quivering, and I had that feeling of personal disillusionment that comes at the first fall to the learner of cycling on earth.

It suddenly occurred to Cavor that the cold air in the gully, after the brightness of the sun, might give me a fever. So we clambered back into the sunlight. We found that beyond a few abrasions I had received no serious injuries from my tumble, and at Cavor's suggestion we were presently looking round for some safe and easy landing-place for my next leap. We chose a rocky slab some ten yards off, separated from us by a little thicket of olive-green spikes.

'Imagine it there!' said Cavor, who was assuming the airs of a trainer, and he pointed to a spot about four feet from my toes. This leap I managed without difficulty, and I must confess I found a certain satisfaction in Cavor's falling short by a foot or so and tasting the spikes of the scrub. 'One has

to be careful, you see,' he said, pulling out his thorns, and with that he ceased to be my mentor, and became my fellow learner in the art of lunar locomotion.

We chose a still easier jump and did it without difficulty, and then leapt back again, and to and fro several times, accustoming our muscles to the new standard. I could never have believed had I not experienced it, how rapid that adaptation would be. In a very little time indeed, certainly after fewer than thirty leaps, we could judge the effort necessary for a distance with almost terrestrial assurance.

And all this time the lunar plants were growing around us, higher and denser and more entangled, every moment thicker and taller, spiked plants, green cactus masses, fungi, fleshy and lichenous things, strangest radiate and sinuous shapes. But we were so intent upon our leaping, that for a time we gave no heed to their unfaltering expansion.

An extraordinary elation had taken possession of us. Partly, I think, it was our sense of release from the confinement of the sphere. Mainly, however, the thin sweetness of the air, which I am certain contained a much larger proportion of oxygen than our terrestrial atmosphere. In spite of the strange quality of all about us, I felt as adventurous and experimental as a cockney would do placed for the first time among mountains; and I do not think it occurred to either of us, face to face though we were with the Unknown, to be very greatly afraid.

We were bitten by a spirit of enterprise. We selected a lichenous kopje perhaps fifteen yards away, and landed neatly on its summit one after the other. 'Good!' we cried to each other; 'Good!' and Cavor made three steps and went off to a tempting slope of snow a good twenty yards and more beyond. I stood for a moment struck by the grotesque effect of his soaring figure – his dirty cricket cap, and spiky hair, his little round body, his arms and his knickerbockered legs tucked up tightly – against the weird spacious-ness of the lunar scene. A gust of laughter seized me, and then I stepped off to follow. Plump! I dropped beside him.

We made a few gargantuan strides, leapt three or four times more, and sat down at last in a lichenous hollow. Our lungs were painful. We sat holding our sides and recovering our breath, looking appreciation at one another. Cavor panted something about 'amazing sensations'. And then came a thought into my head. For the moment it did not seem a particularly appalling thought, simply a natural question arising out of the situation.

'By the way,' I said, 'where exactly is the sphere?'

Cavor looked at me. 'Eh?'

The full meaning of what we were saying struck me sharply.

'Cavor!' I cried, laying a hand on his arm, 'Where is the sphere?'

CHAPTER X

Lost Men in the Moon

His face caught something of my dismay. He stood up and stared about him at the scrub that fenced us in and rose about us, straining upward in a passion of growth. He put a dubious hand to his lips. He spoke with a sudden lack of assurance. 'I think,' he said slowly, 'we left it . . . somewhere . . . about *there*.'

He pointed a hesitating finger that wavered in an arc.

'I'm not sure.' His look of consternation deepened. 'Anyhow,' he said, with his eyes on me, 'it can't be far.'

We had both stood up. We made unmeaning ejaculations, our eyes sought in the twining, thickening jungle round about us.

All about us on the sunlit slopes frothed and swayed the darting shrubs, the swelling cactus, the creeping lichens, and wherever the shade remained the snowdrifts lingered. North, south, east, and west spread an identical monotony of unfamiliar forms. And somewhere, buried already among this tangled confusion, was our sphere, our home, our only provision, our only hope of escape from this fantastic wilderness of ephemeral growths into which we had come.

'I think, after all,' he said, pointing suddenly, 'it might be over there.'

'No,' I said. 'We have turned in a curve. See! Here is the mark of my heels. It's clear the thing must be more to the eastward, much more. No! – The sphere must be over there.'

'I *think*,' said Cavor, 'I kept the sun upon my right all the time.'

'Every leap, it seems to *me*,' I said, 'my shadow flew before me.'

We stared into one another's eyes. The area of the crater had become enormously vast to our imaginations, the growing thickets already impenetrably dense.

'Good Heavens! What fools we have been!'

'It's evident that we must find it again,' said Cavor, 'and that soon. The sun grows stronger. We should be fainting with the heat already if it wasn't so dry. And . . . I'm hungry.'

I stared at him. I had not suspected this aspect of the matter before. But it came to me at once – a positive craving. 'Yes,' I said with emphasis. 'I am hungry too.'

He stood up with a look of active resolution. 'Certainly we must find the sphere.'

As calmly as possible we surveyed the interminable reefs and thickets that formed the floor of the crater, each of us weighing in silence the chances of our finding the sphere before we were overtaken by heat and hunger.

'It can't be fifty yards from here,' said Cavor, with indecisive gestures. 'The only thing is to beat round about until we come upon it.'

'That is all we can do,' I said, without any alacrity to begin our hunt. 'I wish this confounded spike bush did not grow so fast!'

'That's just it,' said Cavor. 'But it *was* lying on a bank of snow.'

I stared about me in the vain hope of recognizing some knoll or shrub that had been near the sphere. But everywhere was a confusing sameness, everywhere the aspiring bushes, the distending fungi, the dwindling snow banks, steadily and inevitably changed. The sun scorched and stung, the faintness of an unaccountable hunger mingled with our infinite perplexity. And even as we stood there, confused and lost amidst unprecedented things, we became aware for the first time of a sound upon the moon other than the stir of the growing plants, the faint sighing of the wind, or those that we ourselves had made.

Boom . . . Boom . . . Boom . . .

It came from beneath our feet, a sound in the earth. We seemed to hear it with our feet as much as with our ears. Its dull resonance was muffled by distance, thick with the quality of intervening substance. No sound that I can imagine could have astonished us more, or have changed more completely the quality of things about us. For this sound, rich, slow, and deliberate, seemed to us as though it could be nothing but the striking of some gigantic buried clock.

Boom . . . Boom . . . Boom . . .

Sound suggestive of still cloisters, of sleepless nights in crowded cities, of vigils and the awaited hour, of all that is orderly and methodical in life, booming out pregnant and mysterious in this fantastic desert! To the eye everything was unchanged: the desolation of bushes and cacti waving silently in the wind, stretched unbroken to the distant cliffs, the still dark sky was empty overhead, and the hot sun hung and burned. And through it all, a warning, a threat, throbbed this enigma of sound.

Boom . . . Boom . . . Boom . . .

We questioned one another in faint and faded voices. 'A clock?'

'Like a clock!'

'What is it?'

'What can it be?'

'Count,' was Cavor's belated suggestion, and at that word the striking ceased.

The silence, the rhythmic disappointment of the silence, came as a fresh shock. For a moment one could doubt whether one had ever heard a sound. Or whether it might not still be going on. Had I indeed heard a sound?

I felt the pressure of Cavor's hand upon my arm. He spoke in an undertone, as though he feared to wake some sleeping thing. 'Let us keep together,' he whispered, 'and look for the sphere. We must get back to the sphere. This is beyond our understanding.'

'Which way shall we go?'

He hesitated. An intense persuasion of presences, of unseen things about us and near us, dominated our minds. What could they be? Where could they be? Was this arid desolation, alternately frozen and scorched, only the outer rind and mask of some subterranean world? And if so, what sort of world? What sort of inhabitants might it not presently disgorge upon us?

And then, stabbing the aching stillness as vivid and sudden as an unexpected thunderclap, came a clang and rattle as though great gates of metal had suddenly been flung apart.

It arrested our steps. We stood gaping helplessly. Then Cavor stole towards me.

'I do not understand!' he whispered close to my face. He waved his hand vaguely skyward, the vague suggestion of still vaguer thoughts.

'A hiding-place! If anything came . . .'

I looked about us. I nodded my head in assent to him.

We started off, moving stealthily with the most exaggerated precautions against noise. We went towards a thicket of scrub. A clangour like hammers flung about a boiler hastened our steps. 'We must crawl,' whispered Cavor.

The lower leaves of the bayonet plants, already overshadowed by the newer ones above, were beginning to wilt and shrivel so that we could thrust our way in among the thickening stems without serious injury. A stab in the face or arm we did not heed. At the heart of the thicket I stopped, and stared panting into Cavor's face.

'Subterranean,' he whispered. 'Below.'

'They may come out.'

'We must find the sphere!'

'Yes,' I said; 'but how?'

'Crawl till we come to it.'

'But if we don't?'

'Keep hidden. See what they are like.'

'We will keep together,' said I.

He thought. 'Which way shall we go?'

'We must take our chance.'

We peered this way and that. Then very circumspectly, we began to crawl through the lower jungle, making, so far as we could judge, a circuit, halting now at every waving fungus, at every sound, intent only on the sphere from which we had so foolishly emerged. Ever and again from out of the earth beneath us came concussions, beatings, strange, inexplicable, mechanical sounds; and once, and then again, we thought we heard something, a faint rattle and tumult, borne to us through the air. But fearful as we were we dared essay no vantage-point to survey the crater. For long we saw nothing of the beings whose sounds were so abundant and insistent. But for the faintness of our hunger and the drying of our throats that crawling would

have had the quality of a very vivid dream. It was so absolutely unreal. The only element with any touch of reality was these sounds.

Figure it to yourself! About us the dreamlike jungle, with the silent bayonet leaves darting overhead, and the silent, vivid, sun-splashed lichens under our hands and knees, waving with the vigour of their growth as a carpet waves when the wind gets beneath it. Ever and again one of the bladder fungi, bulging and distending under the sun, loomed upon us. Ever and again some novel shape in vivid colour obtruded. The very cells that built up these plants were as large as my thumb, like beads of coloured glass. And all these things were saturated in the unmitigated glare of the sun, were seen against a sky that was bluish black and spangled still, in spite of the sunlight, with a few surviving stars. Strange! The very forms and texture of the stones were strange. It was all strange, the feeling of one's body was unprecedented, every other movement ended in a surprise. The breath sucked thin in one's throat, the blood flowed through one's ears in a throbbing tide – thud, thud, thud, thud. . . .

And ever and again came gusts of turmoil, hammering, the clanging and throb of machinery, and presently – the bellowing of great beasts!

CHAPTER XI

The Mooncalf Pastures

So we two poor terrestrial castaways, lost in that wild-growing moon jungle, crawled in terror before the sounds that had come upon us. We crawled, as it seemed, a long time before we saw either Selenite or mooncalf, though we heard the bellowing and gruntulous noises of these latter continually drawing nearer to us. We crawled through stony ravines, over snow slopes, amidst fungi that ripped like thin bladders at our thrust, emitting a watery humour, over a perfect pavement of things like puff-balls, and beneath interminable thickets of scrub. And ever more hopelessly our eyes sought for our abandoned sphere. The noise of the mooncalves would at times be a vast flat calf-like sound, at times it rose to an amazed and wrathy bellowing, and again it would become a clogged bestial sound, as though these unseen creatures had sought to eat and bellow at the same time.

Our first view was but an inadequate transitory glimpse, yet none the less disturbing because it was incomplete. Cavor was crawling in front at the time, and he first was aware of their proximity. He stopped dead, arresting me with a single gesture.

A crackling and smashing of the scrub appeared to be advancing directly upon us, and then, as we squatted close and endeavoured to judge of the nearness and direction of this noise, there came a terrific bellow behind us, so close and vehement that the tops of the bayonet scrub bent before it, and one felt the breath of it hot and moist. And, turning about, we saw indistinctly through a crowd of swaying stems the mooncalf's shining sides, and the long line of its back loomed out against the sky.

Of course it is hard for me now to say how much I saw at that time, because my impressions were corrected by subsequent observation. First of all impressions was its enormous size; the girth of its body was some fourscore feet, its length perhaps two hundred. Its sides rose and fell with its laboured breathing. I perceived that its gigantic, flabby body lay along the ground, and that its skin was of a corrugated white, dappling into blackness along the backbone. But of its feet we saw nothing. I think also that we saw then the profile at least of the almost brainless head, with its fat-encumbered neck, its slobbering omnivorous mouth, its little nostrils, and tight shut eyes. (For the mooncalf invariably shuts its eyes in the presence of the sun.) We had a glimpse of a vast red pit as it opened its mouth to bleat and bellow again; we had a breath from the pit, and then the monster heeled over like a ship, dragged forward along the ground, creasing all its leathery skin, rolled again, and so wallowed past us, smashing a path amidst the scrub, and was

speedily hidden from our eyes by the dense interlacings beyond. Another appeared more distantly, and then another, and then, as though he was guiding these animated lumps of provender to their pasture, a Selenite came momentarily into ken. My grip upon Cavor's foot became convulsive at the sight of him, and we remained motionless and peering long after he had passed out of our range.

By contrast with the mooncalves he seemed a trivial being, a mere ant, scarcely five feet high. He was wearing garments of some leathery substance, so that no portion of his actual body appeared, but of this, of course, we were entirely ignorant. He presented himself, therefore, as a compact, bris-tling creature, having much of the quality of a complicated insect, with whip-like tentacles and a clanging arm projecting from his shining cylindrical body case. The form of his head was hidden by his enormous many-spiked helmet – we discovered afterwards that he used the spikes for prodding refractory mooncalves – and a pair of goggles of darkened glass, set very much at the side, gave a bird-like quality to the metallic apparatus that covered his face. His arms did not project beyond his body case, and he carried himself upon short legs that, wrapped though they were in warm coverings, seemed to our terrestrial eyes inordinately flimsy. They had very short thighs, very long shanks, and little feet.

In spite of his heavy-looking clothing, he was progressing with what would be, from the terrestrial point of view, very considerable strides, and his clanging arm was busy. The quality of his motion during the instant of his passing suggested haste and a certain anger, and soon after we had lost sight of him we heard the bellow of a mooncalf change abruptly into a short, sharp squeal, followed by the scuffle of its acceleration. And gradually that bellowing receded, and then came to an end, as if the pastures sought had been attained.

We listened. For a space the moon world was still. But it was some time before we resumed our crawling search for the vanished sphere.

When next we saw mooncalves they were some little distance away from us in a place of tumbled rocks. The less vertical surfaces of the rocks were thick with a speckled green plant growing in dense mossy clumps, upon which these creatures were browsing. We stopped at the edge of the reeds amidst which we were crawling at the sight of them, peering out at them and looking round for a second glimpse of a Selenite. They lay against their food like stupendous slugs, huge, greasy hulls, eating greedily and noisily, with a sort of sobbing avidity. They seemed monsters of mere fatness, clumsy and overwhelmed to a degree that would make a Smithfield ox seem a model of agility. Their busy, writhing, chewing mouths, and eyes closed, together with the appetizing sound of their munching, made up an effect of animal enjoyment that was singularly stimulating to our empty frames.

'Hogs!' said Cavor with unusual passion. 'Disgusting hogs!' and after one

glare of angry envy crawled off through the bushes to our right. I stayed long enough to see that the speckled plant was quite hopeless for human nourishment, then crawled after him, nibbling a quill of it between my teeth.

Presently we were arrested again by the proximity of a Selenite, and this time we were able to observe him more exactly. Now we could see that the Selenite covering was indeed clothing, and not a sort of crustacean integument. He was quite similar in his costume to the former one we had glimpsed, except that ends of something like wadding were protruding from his neck, and he stood on a promontory of rock and moved his head this way and that, as though he was surveying the crater. We lay quite still, fearing to attract his attention if we moved, and after a time he turned about and disappeared.

We came upon another drove of mooncalves bellowing up a ravine, and then we passed over a place of sounds, sounds of beating machinery, as if some huge hall of industry came near the surface there. And while these sounds were still about us we came to the edge of a great open space, perhaps two hundred yards in diameter, and perfectly level. Save for a few lichens that advanced from its margin this space was bare, and presented a powdery surface of a dusty yellow colour. We were afraid to strike out across this space, but as it presented less obstruction to our crawling than the scrub, we went down upon it and began very circumspectly to skirt its edge.

For a little while the noises from below ceased, and everything, save for the faint stir of the growing vegetation, was very still. Then abruptly there began an uproar, louder, more vehement, and nearer than any we had so far heard. Of a certainty it came from below. Instinctively we crouched as flat as we could, ready for a prompt plunge into the thicket beside us. Each knock and throb seemed to vibrate through our bodies. Louder grew this throbbing and beating, and that irregular vibration increased until the whole moon world seemed to be jerking and pulsing.

'Cover,' whispered Cavor, and I turned towards the bushes.

At that instant came a thud like the thud of a gun, and then a thing happened – it still haunts me in my dreams. I had turned my head to look at Cavor's face, and thrust out my hand in front of me as I did so. And my hand met nothing! Plunged suddenly into a bottomless hole!

My chest hit something hard, and I found myself with my chin on the edge of an unfathomable abyss that had suddenly opened beneath me, my hand extended stiffly into the void. The whole of that flat circular area was no more than a gigantic lid, that was now sliding sideways from off the pit it had covered into a slot prepared for it.

Had it not been for Cavor I think I should have remained rigid, hanging over this margin and staring into the enormous gulf below, until at last the edges of the slot scraped me off and hurled me into its depths. But Cavor had not received the shock that had paralysed me. He had been a little

distance from the edge when the lid had first opened, and perceiving the peril that held me helpless, gripped my legs and pulled me backward. I came into a sitting position, crawled away from the edge for a space on all fours, then staggered up and ran after him across the thundering, quivering sheet of metal. It seemed to be swinging open with a steadily accelerated velocity, and the bushes in front of me shifted sideways as I ran.

I was none too soon. Cavor's back vanished amidst the bristling thicket, and as I scrambled up after him, the monstrous valve came into its position with a clang. For a long time we lay panting, not daring to approach the pit.

But at last very cautiously and bit by bit we crept into a position from which we could peer down. The bushes about us creaked and waved with the force of a breeze that was blowing down the shaft. We could see nothing at first except smooth vertical walls descending at last into an impenetrable black. And then very gradually we became aware of a number of very faint and little lights going to and fro.

For a time that stupendous gulf of mystery held us so that we forgot even our sphere. In time, as we grew more accustomed to the darkness, we could make out very small, dim, elusive shapes moving about among those needle-point illuminations. We peered amazed and incredulous, understanding so little that we could find no words to say. We could distinguish nothing that would give us a clue to the meaning of the faint shapes we saw.

'What can it be?' I asked; 'What can it be?'

'The engineering! . . . They must live in these caverns during the night, and come out during the day.'

'Cavor!' I said. 'Can they be – *that* – it was something like – men?'

'*That* was not a man.'

'We dare risk nothing!'

'We dare do nothing until we find the sphere!'

'We can do nothing until we find the sphere.'

He assented with a groan and stirred himself to move. He stared about him for a space, sighed, and indicated a direction. We struck out through the jungle. For a time we crawled resolutely, then with diminishing vigour. Presently among great shapes of flabby purple there came a noise of trampling and cries about us. We lay close, and for a long time the sounds went to and fro and very near. But this time we saw nothing. I tried to whisper to Cavor that I could hardly go without food much longer, but my mouth had become too dry for whispering.

'Cavor,' I said, 'I must have food.'

He turned a face full of dismay towards me. 'It's a case for holding out,' he said.

'But I *must*,' I said, 'and look at my lips!'

'I've been thirsty some time.'

'If only some of that snow had remained!'

'It's clean gone! We're driving from arctic to tropical at the rate of a degree a minute. . . .'

I gnawed my hand.

'The sphere!' he said. 'There is nothing for it but the sphere.'

We roused ourselves to another spurt of crawling. My mind ran entirely on edible things, on the hissing profundity of summer drinks, more particularly I craved for beer. I was haunted by the memory of a sixteen gallon cask that had swaggered in my Lympne cellar. I thought of the adjacent larder, and especially of steak and kidney pie – tender steak and plenty of kidney, and rich, thick gravy between. Ever and again I was seized with fits of hungry yawning. We came to flat places overgrown with fleshy red things, monstrous coralline growths; as we pushed against them they snapped and broke. I noted the quality of the broken surfaces. The confounded stuff certainly looked of a biteable texture. Then it seemed to me that it smelt rather well.

I picked up a fragment and sniffed at it.

'Cavor,' I said in a hoarse undertone.

He glanced at me with his face screwed up. 'Don't,' he said. I put down the fragment, and we crawled on through this tempting fleshiness for a space.

'Cavor,' I asked, 'why *not*?'

'Poison,' I heard him say, but he did not look round.

We crawled some way before I decided.

'I'll chance it,' said I.

He made a belated gesture to prevent me. I stuffed my mouth full. He crouched watching my face, his own twisted into the oddest expression. 'It's good,' I said.

'O Lord!' he cried.

He watched me munch, his face wrinkled between desire and disapproval, then suddenly succumbed to appetite, and began to tear off huge mouthfuls. For a time we did nothing but eat.

The stuff was not unlike a terrestrial mushroom, only it was much laxer in texture, and, as one swallowed it, it warmed the throat. At first we experienced a mere mechanical satisfaction in eating; then our blood began to run warmer, and we tingled at the lips and fingers, and then new and slightly irrelevant ideas came bubbling up in our minds.

'It's good,' said I. 'Infernally good! What a home for our surplus population! Our poor surplus population,' and I broke off another large portion.

It filled me with a curiously benevolent satisfaction that there was such good food in the moon. The depression of my hunger gave way to an irrational exhilaration. The dread and discomfort in which I had been living vanished entirely. I perceived the moon no longer as a planet from which I most earnestly desired the means of escape, but as a possible refuge for human destitution. I think I forgot the Selenites, the mooncalves, the lid and the noises completely so soon as I had eaten that fungus.

Cavor replied to my third repetition of my 'surplus population' remark
with similar words of approval. I felt that my head swam, but I put this down
to the stimulating effect of food after a long fast. 'Ess'lent discov'ry yours,
Cavor,' said I. 'Se'nd on'y to the 'tato.'

'Whajer mean?' asked Cavor. ''Scovery of the moon – se'nd on'y to the 'tato?'

I looked at him, shocked at his suddenly hoarse voice, and by the badness
of his articulation. It occurred to me in a flash that he was intoxicated,
possibly by the fungus. It also occurred to me that he erred in imagining
that he had discovered the moon; he had not discovered it, he had only
reached it. I tried to lay my hand on his arm and explain this to him, but
the issue was too subtle for his brain. It was also unexpectedly difficult to
express. After a momentary attempt to understand me – I remember
wondering if the fungus had made my eyes as fishy as his – he set off upon
some observations on his own account.

'We are,' he announced with a solemn hiccup, 'the creashurs o' what we
eat and drink.'

He repeated this, and as I was now in one of my subtle moods, I deter-
mined to dispute it. Possibly I wandered a little from the point. But Cavor
certainly did not attend at all properly. He stood up as well as he could,
putting a hand on my head to steady himself, which was disrespectful, and
stood staring about him, quite devoid now of any fear of the moon beings.

I tried to point out that this was dangerous for some reason that was
not perfectly clear to me, but the word 'dangerous' had somehow got
mixed with 'indiscreet', and came out rather more like 'injurious' than
either; and after an attempt to disentangle them, I resumed my argument,
addressing myself principally to the unfamiliar but attentive coralline
growths on either side. I felt that it was necessary to clear up this confu-
sion between the moon and a potato at once – I wandered into a long
parenthesis on the importance of precision of definition in argument. I
did my best to ignore the fact that my bodily sensations were no longer
agreeable.

In some way that I have now forgotten, my mind was led back to projects
of colonization. 'We must annex this moon,' I said. 'There must be no shilly-
shally. This is part of the White Man's Burden. Cavor – we are – *hic* – Satap
– mean Satraps! Nempire Cæsar never dreamt. B'in all the newspapers.
Cavorecia. Bedfordecia. Bedfordecia – *hic* – Limited. Mean – unlimited!
Practically.'

Certainly I was intoxicated.

I embarked upon an argument to show the infinite benefits our arrival
would confer on the moon. I involved myself in a rather difficult proof that
the arrival of Columbus was, on the whole, beneficial to America. I found
I had forgotten the line of argument I had intended to pursue, and continued
to repeat 'Sim'lar to C'lumbus,' to fill up time.

From that point my memory of the action of that abominable fungus becomes confused. I remember vaguely that we declared our intention of standing no nonsense from any confounded insects, that we decided it ill became men to hide shamefully upon a mere satellite, that we equipped ourselves with huge armfuls of the fungus – whether for missile purposes or not I do not know – and, heedless of the stabs of the bayonet scrub, we started forth into the sunshine.

Almost immediately we must have come upon the Selenites. There were six of them, and they were marching in single file over a rocky place, making the most remarkable piping and whining sounds. They all seemed to become aware of us at once, all instantly became silent and motionless, like animals, with their faces turned towards us.

For a moment I was sobered.

'Insects,' murmured Cavor, 'insects! And they think I'm going to crawl about on my stomach – on my vertebrated stomach!

'Stomach,' he repeated slowly, as though he chewed the indignity.

Then suddenly, with a shout of fury, he made three vast strides and leapt towards them. He leapt badly; he made a series of somersaults in the air, whirled right over them, and vanished with an enormous splash amidst the cactus bladders. What the Selenites made of this amazing, and to my mind undignified irruption from another planet, I have no means of guessing. I seem to remember the sight of their backs as they ran in all directions, but I am not sure. All these last incidents before oblivion came are vague and faint in my mind. I know I made a step to follow Cavor, and tripped and fell headlong among the rocks. I was, I am certain, suddenly and vehemently ill. I seem to remember a violent struggle, and being gripped by metallic clasps. . . .

My next clear recollection is that we were prisoners at we knew not what depth beneath the moon's surface; we were in darkness amidst strange distracting noises; our bodies were covered with scratches and bruises, and our heads racked with pain.

CHAPTER XII

The Selenite's Face

I found myself sitting crouched together in a tumultuous darkness. For a long time I could not understand where I was, nor how I had come to this perplexity. I thought of the cupboard into which I had been thrust at times when I was a child, and then of a very dark and noisy bedroom in which I had slept during an illness. But these sounds about me were not the noises I had known, and there was a thin flavour in the air like the wind of a stable. Then I supposed we must still be at work upon the sphere, and that somehow I had got into the cellar of Cavor's house. I remembered we had finished the sphere, and fancied I must still be in it and travelling through space.

'Cavor,' I said, 'cannot we have some light?'

There came no answer.

'Cavor!' I insisted.

I was answered by a groan. 'My head!' I heard him say; 'my head!'

I attempted to press my hands to my brow, which ached, and discovered they were tied together. This startled me very much. I brought them up to my mouth and felt the cold smoothness of metal. They were chained together. I tried to separate my legs, and made out they were similarly fastened, and also that I was fastened to the ground by a much thicker chain about the middle of my body.

I was more frightened than I had yet been by anything in all our strange experiences. For a time I tugged silently at my bonds. 'Cavor!' I cried out sharply. 'Why am I tied? Why have you tied me hand and foot?'

'I haven't tied you,' he answered. 'It's the Selenites.'

The Selenites! My mind hung on that for a space. Then my memories came back to me: the snowy desolation, the thawing of the air, the growth of the plants, our strange hopping and crawling among the rocks and vegetation of the crater. All the distress of our frantic search for the sphere returned to me. . . . Finally the opening of the great lid that covered the pit!

Then as I strained to trace our later movements down to our present plight, the pain in my head became intolerable. I came to an insurmountable barrier, an obstinate blank.

'Cavor!'

'Yes?'

'Where are we?'

'How should I know?'

'Are we dead?'

'What nonsense!'

'They've got us, then!'

He made no answer but a grunt. The lingering traces of the poison seemed to make him oddly irritable.

'What do you mean to do?'

'How should I know what to do?'

'Oh, very well!' said I, and became silent. Presently I was roused from a stupor. 'O Lord!' I cried; 'I wish you'd stop that buzzing!'

We lapsed into silence again, listening to the dull confusion of noises like the muffled sounds of a street or factory that filled our ears. I could make nothing of it, my mind pursued first one rhythm and then another, and questioned it in vain. But after a long time I became aware of a new and sharper element, not mingling with the rest but standing out, as it were, against that cloudy background of sound. It was a series of relatively very little definite sounds, tappings and rubbings, like a loose spray of ivy against a window or a bird moving about upon a box. We listened and peered about us, but the darkness was a velvet pall. There followed a noise like the subtle movement of the wards of a well-oiled lock. And then there appeared before me, hanging as it seemed in an immensity of black, a thin bright line.

'Look!' whispered Cavor very softly.

'What is it?'

'I don't know.'

We stared.

The thin bright line became a band, and broader and paler. It took upon itself the quality of a bluish light falling upon a whitewashed wall. It ceased to be parallel-sided; it developed a deep indentation on one side. I turned to remark this to Cavor, and was amazed to see his ear in a brilliant illumination – all the rest of him in shadow. I twisted my head round as well as my bonds would permit. 'Cavor,' I said, 'it's behind!'

His ear vanished – gave place to an eye!

Suddenly the crack that had been admitting the light broadened out, and revealed itself as the space of an opening door. Beyond was a sapphire vista, and in the doorway stood a grotesque outline silhouetted against the glare.

We both made convulsive efforts to turn, and failing, sat staring over our shoulders at this. My first impression was of some clumsy quadruped with lowered head. Then I perceived it was the slender pinched body and short and extremely attenuated bandy legs of a Selenite, with his head depressed between his shoulders. He was without the helmet and body covering they wear upon the exterior.

He was a blank, black figure to us, but instinctively our imaginations supplied features to his very human outline. I, at least, took it instantly

that he was somewhat hunchbacked, with a high forehead and long features.

He came forward three steps and paused for a time. His movements seemed absolutely noiseless. Then he came forward again. He walked like a bird, his feet fell one in front of the other. He stepped out of the ray of light that came through the doorway, and it seemed as though he vanished altogether in the shadow.

For a moment my eyes sought him in the wrong place, and then I perceived him standing facing us both in the full light. Only the human features I had attributed to him were not there at all!

Of course I ought to have expected that, only I didn't. It came to me as an absolute, for a moment an overwhelming, shock. It seemed as though it wasn't a face, as though it must needs be a mask, a horror, a deformity, that would presently be disavowed or explained. There was no nose, and the thing had dull bulging eyes at the side – in the silhouette I had supposed they were ears. There were no ears . . . I have tried to draw one of these heads, but I cannot. There was a mouth, downwardly curved, like a human mouth in a face that stares ferociously. . . .

The neck on which the head was poised was jointed in three places, almost like the short joints in the leg of a crab. The joints of the limbs I could not see, because of the puttee-like straps in which they were swathed, and which formed the only clothing the being wore.

There the thing was, looking at us!

At the time my mind was taken up by the mad impossibility of the creature. I suppose he also was amazed, and with more reason, perhaps, for amazement than we. Only – confound him! – he did not show it. We did at least know what had brought about this meeting of incompatible creatures. But conceive how it would seem to decent Londoners, for example, to come upon a couple of living things, as big as men and absolutely unlike any other earthly animals, careering about among the sheep in Hyde Park! It must have taken him like that.

Figure us! We were bound hand and foot, fagged and filthy; our beards two inches long, our faces scratched and bloody. Cavor you must imagine in his knickerbockers (torn in several places by the bayonet scrub), his Jaeger shirt and old cricket cap, his wiry hair wildly disordered, a tail to every quarter of the heavens. In that blue light his face did not look red but very dark, his lips and the drying blood upon my hands seemed black. If possible I was in a worse plight than he, on account of the yellow fungus into which I had jumped. Our jackets were unbuttoned, and our shoes had been taken off and lay at our feet. And we were sitting with our backs to this queer bluish light, peering at such a monster as Dürer might have invented.

Cavor broke the silence; started to speak, went hoarse, and cleared his

throat. Outside began a terrific bellowing, as if a mooncalf were in trouble. It ended in a shriek, and everything was still again.

Presently the Selenite turned about, flickered into the shadow, stood for a moment retrospective at the door, and then closed it on us; and once more we were in that murmurous mystery of darkness into which we had awakened.

CHAPTER XIII

Mr Cavor Makes Some Suggestions

For a time neither of us spoke. To focus together all the things we had brought upon ourselves, seemed beyond my mental powers.

'They've got us,' I said at last.

'It was that fungus.'

'Well – if I hadn't taken it we should have fainted and starved.'

'We might have found the sphere.'

I lost my temper at his persistence, and swore to myself. For a time we hated one another in silence. I drummed with my fingers on the floor between my knees, and gritted the links of my fetters together. Presently I was forced to talk again.

'What do you make of it, anyhow?' I asked humbly.

'They are reasonable creatures – they can make things and do things – Those lights we saw . . .'

He stopped. It was clear he could make nothing of it.

When he spoke again it was to confess, 'After all, they are more human than we had a right to expect. I suppose—'

He stopped irritatingly.

'Yes?'

'I suppose, anyhow – on any planet where there is an intelligent animal – it will carry its brain case upward, and have hands, and walk erect. . . .'

Presently he broke away in another direction.

'We are some way in,' he said. 'I mean – perhaps a couple of thousand feet or more.'

'Why?'

'It's cooler. And our voices are so much louder. That faded quality – it has altogether gone. And the feeling in one's ears and throat.'

I had not noted that, but I did now.

'The air is denser. We must be some depth – a mile even, we may be – inside the moon.'

'We never thought of a world inside the moon.'

'No.'

'How could we?'

'We might have done. Only – one gets into habits of mind.'

He thought for a time.

'*Now*,' he said, 'it seems such an obvious thing.

'Of course! The moon must be enormously cavernous, with an atmosphere within, and at the centre of its caverns a sea.

'One knew that the moon had a lower specific gravity than the earth, one knew that it had little air or water outside, one knew, too, that it was sister planet to the earth, and that it was unaccountable that it should be different in composition. The inference that it was hollowed out was as clear as day. And yet one never saw it as a fact. Kepler, of course—'

His voice had the interest now of a man who has discovered a pretty sequence of reasoning.

'Yes,' he said, 'Kepler with his *sub-volvani* was right after all.'

'I wish you had taken the trouble to find that out before we came,' I said.

He answered nothing, buzzing to himself softly as he pursued his thoughts. My temper was going. 'What do you think has become of the sphere, anyhow?' I asked.

'Lost,' he said, like a man who answers an uninteresting question.

'Among those plants?'

'Unless they find it.'

'And then?'

'How can I tell?'

'Cavor,' I said, with a sort of hysterical bitterness, 'things look bright for my Company. . . .'

He made no answer.

'Good Lord!' I exclaimed. 'Just think of all the trouble we took to get into this pickle! What did we come for? What are we after? What was the moon to us or we to the moon? We wanted too much, we tried too much. We ought to have started the little things first. It was you proposed the moon! Those Cavorite spring blinds! I am certain we could have worked them for terrestrial purposes. Certain! Did you really understand what I proposed? A steel cylinder—'

'Rubbish!' said Cavor.

We ceased to converse.

For a time Cavor kept up a broken monologue without much help from me.

'If they find it,' he began, 'if they find it . . . what will they do with it? Well, that's a question. It may be that's *the* question. They won't understand it, anyhow. If they understood that sort of thing they would have come long since to the earth. Would they? Why shouldn't they? But they would have sent something – They couldn't keep their hands off such a possibility. No! But they will examine it. Clearly they are intelligent and inquisitive. They will examine it – get inside it – trifle with the studs. Off! . . . That would mean the moon for us for all the rest of our lives. Strange creatures, strange knowledge . . .'

'As for strange knowledge—' said I, and language failed me.

'Look here, Bedford,' said Cavor, 'you came on this expedition of your own free will.'

'You said to me, "Call it prospecting."'

'There's always risks in prospecting.'

'Especially when you do it unarmed and without thinking out every possibility.'

'I was so taken up with the sphere. The thing rushed on us, and carried us away.'

'Rushed on *me*, you mean.'

'Rushed on me just as much. How was *I* to know when I set to work on molecular physics that the business would bring me here – of all places?'

'It's this accursed science,' I cried. 'It's the very Devil. The mediæval priests and persecutors were right and the Moderns are all wrong. You tamper with it – and it offers you gifts. And directly you take them it knocks you to pieces in some unexpected way. Old passions and new weapons – now it upsets your religion, now it upsets your social ideas, now it whirls you off to desolation and misery!'

'Anyhow, it's no use your quarrelling with me *now*. These creatures – these Selenites, or whatever we choose to call them – have got us tied hand and foot. Whatever temper you choose to go through with it in, you will have to go through with it. . . . We have experiences before us that will need all our coolness.'

He paused as if he required my assent. But I sat sulking. 'Confound your science!' I said.

'The problem is communication. Gestures, I fear, will be different. Pointing, for example. No creatures but men and monkeys point.'

That was too obviously wrong for me. 'Pretty nearly every animal,' I cried, 'points with its eyes or nose.'

Cavor meditated over that. 'Yes,' he said at last, 'and we don't. There's such differences – such differences!

'One might . . . But how can I tell? There is speech. The sounds they make, a sort of fluting and piping. I don't see how we are to imitate that. Is it their speech, that sort of thing? They may have different senses, different means of communication. Of course they are minds and we are minds; there must be something in common. Who knows how far we may not get to an understanding?'

'The things are outside us,' I said. 'They're more different from us than the strangest animals on earth. They are a different clay. What is the good of talking like this?'

Cavor thought. 'I don't see that. Where there are minds they will have something *similar* – even though they have been evolved on different planets. Of course if it was a question of instincts, if we or they are no more than animals—'

'Well, *are* they? They're much more like ants on their hind legs than human beings, and who ever got to any sort of understanding with ants?'

'But these machines and clothing! No, I don't hold with you, Bedford. The difference is wide—'

'It's insurmountable.'

'The resemblance must bridge it. I remember reading once a paper by the late Professor Galton on the possibility of communication between the planets. Unhappily, at that time it did not seem probable that that would be of any material benefit to me, and I fear I did not give it the attention I should have done – in view of this state of affairs. Yet . . . Now, let me see!

'His idea was to begin with those broad truths that must underlie all conceivable mental existences and establish a basis on those. The great principles of geometry, to begin with. He proposed to take some leading proposition of Euclid's, and show by construction that its truth was known to us, to demonstrate, for example, that the angles at the base of an isosceles triangle are equal, and that if the equal sides be produced the angles on the other side of the base are equal also, or that the square on the hypotenuse of a right-angled triangle is equal to the sum of the squares on the two other sides. By demonstrating our knowledge of these things we should demonstrate our possession of a reasonable intelligence . . . Now, suppose I . . . I might draw the geometrical figure with a wet finger, or even trace it in the air . . .'

He fell silent. I sat meditating his words. For a time his wild hope of communication, of interpretation, with these weird beings held me. Then that angry despair that was a part of my exhaustion and physical misery resumed its sway. I perceived with a sudden novel vividness the extraordinary folly of everything I had ever done. 'Ass!' I said; 'Oh, ass, unutterable ass . . . I seem to exist only to go about doing preposterous things . . . Why did we ever leave the thing? . . . Hopping about looking for patents and concessions in the craters of the moon! . . . If only we had had the sense to fasten a handkerchief to a stick to show where we had left the sphere!'

I subsided, fuming.

'It is clear,' meditated Cavor, 'they are intelligent. One can hypotheticate certain things. As they have not killed us at once, they must have ideas of mercy. Mercy! At any rate of restraint. Possibly of intercourse. They may meet us. And this apartment and the glimpses we had of its guardian. These fetters! A high degree of intelligence . . .'

'I wish to Heaven,' cried I, 'I'd thought even twice! Plunge after plunge. First one fluky start and then another. It was my confidence in you! Why didn't I stick to my play? That was what I was equal to. That was my world and the life I was made for. I could have finished that play. I'm certain . . . it was a good play. I had the scenario as good as done. Then . . . Conceive it! leaping to the moon! Practically – I've thrown my life away! That old woman in the inn near Canterbury had better sense.'

I looked up, and stopped in mid-sentence. The darkness had given place to that bluish light again. The door was opening, and several noiseless

Selenites were coming into the chamber. I became quite still, staring at their grotesque faces.

Then suddenly my sense of disagreeable strangeness changed to interest. I perceived that the foremost and second carried bowls. One elemental need at least our minds could understand in common. They were bowls of some metal that, like our fetters, looked dark in that bluish light; and each contained a number of whitish fragments. All the cloudy pain and misery that oppressed me rushed together and took the shape of hunger. I eyed these bowls wolfishly, and, though it returned to me in dreams, at that time it seemed a small matter that at the end of the arms that lowered one towards me were not hands, but a sort of flap and thumb, like the end of an elephant's trunk.

The stuff in the bowl was loose in texture, and whitish brown in colour – rather like lumps of some cold soufflé, and it smelt faintly like mushrooms. From a partially divided carcass of a mooncalf that we presently saw, I am inclined to believe it must have been mooncalf flesh.

My hands were so tightly chained that I could barely contrive to reach the bowl; but when they saw the effort I made, two of them dexterously released one of the turns about my wrist. Their tentacle hands were soft and cold to my skin. I immediately seized a mouthful of the food. It had the same laxness in texture that all organic structures seem to have upon the moon; it tasted rather like a *gauffre* or a damp meringue, but in no way was it disagreeable. I took two other mouthfuls. 'I *wanted* – foo'!' said I, tearing off a still larger piece. . . .

For a time we ate with an utter absence of self-consciousness. We ate and presently drank like tramps in a soup kitchen. Never before nor since have I been hungry to the ravenous pitch, and save that I have had this very experience I could never have believed that, a quarter of a million of miles out of our proper world, in utter perplexity of soul, surrounded, watched, touched by beings more grotesque and inhuman than the worst creations of a nightmare, it would be possible for me to eat in utter forgetfulness of all these things. They stood about us watching us, and ever and again making a slight elusive twittering that stood them, I suppose, in the stead of speech. I did not even shiver at their touch. And when the first zeal of my feeding was over, I could note that Cavor, too, had been eating with the same shameless abandon.

CHAPTER XIV

Experiments in Intercourse

When at last we had made an end of eating, the Selenites linked our hands closely together again, and then untwisted the chains about our feet and rebound them, so as to give us a limited freedom of movement. Then they unfastened the chains about our waists. To do all this they had to handle us freely, and ever and again one of their queer heads came down close to my face, or a soft tentacle-hand touched my head or neck. I don't remember that I was afraid then or repelled by their proximity. I think that our incurable anthropomorphism made us imagine there were human heads inside their masks. The skin, like everything else, looked bluish, but that was on account of the light; and it was hard and shiny, quite in the beetle-wing fashion, not soft, or moist, or hairy, as a vertebrated animal's would be. Along the crest of the head was a low ridge of whitish spines running from back to front, and a much larger ridge curved on either side over the eyes. The Selenite who untied me used his mouth to help his hands.

'They seem to be releasing us,' said Cavor. 'Remember we are on the moon! Make no sudden movements!'

'Are you going to try that geometry?'

'If I get a chance. But, of course, they may make an advance first.'

We remained passive, and the Selenites, having finished their arrangements, stood back from us, and seemed to be looking at us. I say seemed to be, because as their eyes were at the side and not in front, one had the same difficulty in determining the direction in which they were looking as one has in the case of a hen or a fish. They conversed with one another in their reedy tones, that seemed to me impossible to imitate or define. The door behind us opened wider, and, glancing over my shoulder, I saw a vague large space beyond, in which quite a little crowd of Selenites were standing. They seemed a curiously miscellaneous rabble.

'Do they want us to imitate those sounds?' I asked Cavor.

'I don't think so,' he said.

'It seems to me that they are trying to make us understand something.'

'I can't make anything of their gestures. Do you notice this one, who is worrying with his head like a man with an uncomfortable collar?'

'Let us shake our heads at him.'

We did that, and finding it ineffectual, attempted an imitation of the Selenites' movements. That seemed to interest them. At any rate they all set up the same movement. But as that seemed to lead to nothing, we desisted at last and so did they, and fell into a piping argument among

themselves. Then one of them, shorter and very much thicker than the others, and with a particularly wide mouth, squatted down suddenly beside Cavor, and put his hands and feet in the same posture as Cavor's were bound, and then by a dexterous movement stood up.

'Cavor,' I shouted, 'they want us to get up!'

He stared open-mouthed. 'That's it!' he said.

And with much heaving and grunting, because our hands were tied together, we contrived to struggle to our feet. The Selenites made way for our elephantine heavings, and seemed to twitter more volubly. As soon as we were on our feet the thick-set Selenite came and patted each of our faces with his tentacles, and walked towards the open doorway. That also was plain enough, and we followed him. We saw that four of the Selenites standing in the doorway were much taller than the others, and clothed in the same manner as those we had seen in the crater, namely, with spiked round helmets and cylindrical body cases, and that each of the four carried a goad with spike and guard made of that same dull-looking metal as the bowls. These four closed about us, one on either side of each of us, as we emerged from our chamber into the cavern from which the light had come.

We did not get our impression of that cavern all at once. Our attention was taken up by the movements and attitudes of the Selenites immediately about us, and by the necessity of controlling our motion, lest we should startle and alarm them and ourselves by some excessive stride. In front of us was the short, thick-set being who had solved the problem of asking us to get up, moving with gestures that seemed, almost all of them, intelligible to us, inviting us to follow him. His spout-like face turned from one of us to the other with a quickness that was clearly interrogative. For a time, I say, we were taken up with these things.

But at last the great place that formed a background to our movements asserted itself. It became apparent that the source of much, at least, of the tumult of sounds which had filled our ears ever since we had recovered from the stupefaction of the fungus was a vast mass of machinery in active movement, whose flying and whirling parts were visible indistinctly over the heads and between the bodies of the Selenites who walked about us. And not only did the web of sounds that filled the air proceed from this mechanism, but also the peculiar blue light that irradiated the whole place. We had taken it as a natural thing that a subterranean cavern should be artificially lit, and even now, though the fact was patent to my eyes, I did not really grasp its import until presently the darkness came. The meaning and structure of this huge apparatus we saw I cannot explain, because we neither of us learnt what it was for or how it worked. One after another, big shafts of metal flung out and up from its centre, their heads travelling in what seemed to me to be a parabolic path; each dropped a sort of dangling arm as it rose towards the apex of its flight and plunged down

into a vertical cylinder, forcing this down before it. About it moved the shapes of tenders, little figures that seemed vaguely different from the beings about us. As each of the three dangling arms of the machine plunged down, there was a clank and then a roaring, and out of the top of the vertical cylinder came pouring this incandescent substance that lit the place, and ran over as milk runs over a boiling pot, and dripped luminously into a tank of light below. It was a cold blue light, a sort of phosphorescent glow but infinitely brighter, and from the tanks into which it fell it ran in conduits athwart the cavern.

Thud, thud, thud, thud, came the sweeping arms of this unintelligible apparatus, and the light substance hissed and poured. At first the thing seemed only reasonably large and near to us, and then I saw how exceedingly little the Selenites upon it seemed, and I realized the full immensity of cavern and machine. I looked from this tremendous affair to the faces of the Selenites with a new respect. I stopped, and Cavor stopped, and stared at this thunderous engine.

'But this is stupendous!' I said. 'What can it be for?'

Cavor's blue-lit face was full of an intelligent respect. 'I can't dream! Surely these beings— Men could not make a thing like that! Look at those arms, are they on connecting rods?'

The thick-set Selenite had gone some paces unheeded. He came back and stood between us and the great machine. I avoided seeing him, because I guessed somehow that his idea was to beckon us onward. He walked away in the direction he wished us to go, and turned and came back, and flicked our faces to attract our attention.

Cavor and I looked at one another.

'Cannot we show him we are interested in the machine?' I said.

'Yes,' said Cavor. 'We'll try that.' He turned to our guide and smiled, and pointed to the machine, and pointed again, and then to his head, and then to the machine. By some defect of reasoning he seemed to imagine that broken English might help these gestures. 'Me look 'im,' he said, 'me think 'im very much. Yes.'

His behaviour seemed to check the Selenites in their desire for our progress for a moment. They faced one another, their queer heads moved, the twittering voices came quick and liquid. Then one of them, a lean, tall creature, with a sort of mantle added to the puttee in which the others were dressed, twisted his elephant trunk of a hand about Cavor's waist, and pulled him gently to follow our guide, who again went on ahead.

Cavor resisted. 'We may just as well begin explaining ourselves now. They may think we are new animals, a new sort of mooncalf perhaps! It is most important that we should show an intelligent interest from the outset.'

He began to shake his head violently. 'No, no,' he said, 'me not come on one minute. Me look at 'im.'

'Isn't there some geometrical point you might bring in *apropos* of that affair?' I suggested, as the Selenites conferred again.

'Possibly a parabolic—' he began.

He yelled loudly, and leaped six feet or more!

One of the four armed moon-men had pricked him with a goad!

I turned on the goad-bearer behind me with a swift threatening gesture, and he started back. This and Cavor's sudden shout and leap clearly astonished all the Selenites. They receded hastily, facing us. For one of those moments that seem to last for ever, we stood in angry protest, with a scattered semicircle of these inhuman beings about us.

'He pricked me!' said Cavor, with a catching of the voice.

'I saw him,' I answered.

'Confound it!' I said to the Selenites; 'We're not going to stand that! What on earth do you take us for?'

I glanced quickly right and left. Far away across the blue wilderness of cavern I saw a number of other Selenites running towards us; broad and slender they were, and one with a larger head than the others. The cavern spread wide and low, and receded in every direction into darkness. Its roof, I remember, seemed to bulge down as if with the weight of the vast thickness of rocks that prisoned us. There was no way out of it – no way out of it. Above, below, in every direction, was the unknown, and these inhuman creatures, with goads and gestures, confronting us, and we two unsupported men!

CHAPTER XV

The Giddy Bridge

Just for a moment that hostile pause endured. I suppose that both we and the Selenites did some very rapid thinking. My clearest impression was that there was nothing to put my back against, and that we were bound to be surrounded and killed. The overwhelming folly of our presence there loomed over me in black, enormous reproach. Why had I ever launched myself on this mad, inhuman expedition?

Cavor came to my side and laid his hand on my arm. His pale and terrified face was ghastly in the blue light.

'We can't do anything,' he said. 'It's a mistake. They don't understand. We must go. As they want us to go.'

I looked down at him, and then at the fresh Selenites who were coming to help their fellows. 'If I had my hands free—'

'It's no use,' he panted.

'No.'

'We'll go.'

And he turned about and led the way in the direction that had been indicated for us.

I followed, trying to look as subdued as possible, and feeling at the chains about my wrists. My blood was boiling. I noted nothing more of that cavern, though it seemed to take a long time before we had marched across it, or if I noted anything I forgot it as I saw it. My thoughts were concentrated, I think, upon my chains and the Selenites, and particularly upon the helmeted ones with the goads. At first they marched parallel with us, and at a respectful distance, but presently they were overtaken by three others, and then they drew nearer, until they were within arm's length again. I winced like a beaten horse as they came near to us. The shorter, thicker Selenite marched at first on our right flank, but presently came in front of us again.

How well the picture of that grouping has bitten into my brain: the back of Cavor's downcast head just in front of me, and the dejected droop of his shoulders, and our guide's gaping visage, perpetually jerking about him, and the goad-bearers on either side, watchful, yet open-mouthed – a blue monochrome. And, after all, I *do* remember one other thing besides the purely personal affair, which is, that a sort of gutter came presently across the floor of the cavern, and then ran along by the side of the path of rock we followed. And it was full of that same bright blue luminous stuff that flowed out of the great machine. I walked close beside it, and I can testify it radiated not

a particle of heat. It was brightly shining, and yet it was neither warmer nor colder than anything else in the cavern.

Clang, clang, clang, we passed right under the thumping levers of another vast machine, and so came at last to a wide tunnel, in which we could even hear the pad, pad of our shoeless feet, and which, save for the trickling thread of blue to the right of us, was quite unlit. The shadows made gigantic travesties of our shapes and those of the Selenites on the irregular wall and roof of the tunnel. Ever and again crystals in the walls of the tunnel scintillated like gems, ever and again the tunnel expanded into a stalactitic cavern, or gave off branches that vanished into darkness.

We seemed to be marching down that tunnel for a long time. 'Trickle, trickle,' went the flowing light very softly, and our footfalls and their echoes made an irregular paddle, paddle.

My mind settled down to the question of my chains. If I were to slip off one turn *so*, and then to twist it *so* . . .

If I tried to do it very gradually, would they see I was slipping my wrist out of the looser turn? If they did, what would they do?

'Bedford,' said Cavor, 'it goes down. It keeps on going down.'

His remark roused me from my sullen preoccupation.

'If they wanted to kill us,' he said, dropping back to come level with me, 'there is no reason why they should not have done it.'

'No,' I admitted, 'that's true.'

'They don't understand us,' he said, 'they think we are merely strange animals, some wild sort of mooncalf birth, perhaps. It will be only when they have observed us better that they will begin to think we have minds—'

'When you trace those geometrical problems,' said I.

'It may be that.'

We tramped on for a space.

'You see,' said Cavor, 'these may be Selenites of a lower class.'

'The infernal fools!' said I viciously, glancing at their exasperating faces.

'If we endure what they do to us—'

'We've got to endure it,' said I.

'There may be others less stupid. This is the mere outer fringe of their world. It must go down and down, cavern, passage, tunnel, down at last to the sea – hundreds of miles below.'

His words made me think of the mile or so of rock and tunnel that might be over our heads already. It was like a weight dropping on my shoulders. 'Away from the sun and air,' I said. 'Even a mine half a mile deep is stuffy.'

'This is not, anyhow. It's probable— Ventilation! The air would blow from the dark side of the moon to the sunlit, and all the carbonic acid would well out there and feed those plants. Up this tunnel, for example, there is quite a breeze. And what a world it must be. The earnest we have in that shaft, and those machines—'

'And the goad,' I said. 'Don't forget the goad!'

He walked a little in front of me for a time.

'Even that goad—' he said.

'Well?'

'I was angry at the time. But – it was perhaps necessary we should get on. They have different skins, and probably different nerves. They may not understand our objection – just as a being from Mars might not like our earthly habit of nudging—'

'They'd better be careful how they nudge *me*.'

'And about that geometry. After all, their way is a way of understanding, too. They begin with the elements of life and not of thought. Food. Compulsion. Pain. They strike at fundamentals.'

'There's no doubt about *that*,' I said.

He went on to talk of the enormous and wonderful world into which we were being taken. I realized slowly from his tone, that even now he was not absolutely in despair at the prospect of going ever deeper into this inhuman planet-burrow. His mind ran on machines and invention, to the exclusion of a thousand dark things that beset me. It wasn't that he intended to make any use of these things, he simply wanted to know them.

'After all,' he said, 'this is a tremendous occasion. It is the meeting of two worlds! What are we going to see? Think of what is below us here.'

'We shan't see much if the light isn't better,' I remarked.

'This is only the outer crust. Down below – on this scale – there will be everything. Do you notice how different they seem one from another? The story we shall take back!'

'Some rare sort of animal,' I said, 'might comfort himself in that way while they were bringing him to the Zoo. . . . It doesn't follow that we are going to be shown all these things.'

'When they find we have reasonable minds,' said Cavor, 'they will want to learn about the earth. Even if they have no generous emotions, they will teach in order to learn. . . . And the things they must know! The unanticipated things!'

He went on to speculate on the possibility of their knowing things he had never hoped to learn on earth, speculating in that way, with a raw wound from that goad already in his skin! Much that he said I forget, for my attention was drawn to the fact that the tunnel along which we had been marching was opening out wider and wider. We seemed, from the feeling of the air, to be going out into a huge space. But how big the space might really be we could not tell, because it was unlit. Our little stream of light ran in a dwindling thread and vanished far ahead. Presently the rocky walls had vanished altogether on either hand. There was nothing to be seen but the path in front of us and the trickling, hurrying rivulet of blue phosphorescence. The figures of Cavor and the guiding Selenite marched before

me, the sides of their legs and heads that were towards the rivulet were clear and bright blue, their darkened sides, now that the reflection of the tunnel wall no longer lit them, merged indistinguishably in the darkness beyond.

And soon I perceived that we were approaching a declivity of some sort, because the little blue stream dipped suddenly out of sight.

In another moment, as it seemed, we had reached the edge. The shining stream gave one meander of hesitation and then rushed over. It fell to a depth at which the sound of its descent was absolutely lost to us. Far below was a bluish glow, a sort of blue mist – at an infinite distance below. And the darkness the stream dropped out of became utterly void and black, save that a thing like a plank projected from the edge of the cliff and stretched out and faded and vanished altogether. There was a warm air blowing up out of the gulf.

For a moment I and Cavor stood as near the edge as we dared, peering into a blue-tinged profundity. And then our guide was pulling at my arm.

Then he left me, and walked to the end of that plank and stepped upon it, looking back. Then when he perceived we watched him, he turned about and went on along it, walking as surely as though he was on firm earth. For a moment his form was distinct, then he became a blue blur, and then vanished into the obscurity. I became aware of some vague shape looming darkly out of the black.

There was a pause. 'Surely—!' said Cavor.

One of the other Selenites walked a few paces out upon the plank, and turned and looked back at us unconcernedly. The others stood ready to follow after us. Our guide's expectant figure reappeared. He was returning to see why we had not advanced.

'What is that beyond there?' I asked.

'I can't see.'

'We can't cross this at any price,' said I.

'I could not go three steps on it,' said Cavor, 'even with my hands free.'

We looked at each other's drawn faces in blank consternation.

'They can't know what it is to be giddy!' said Cavor.

'It's quite impossible for us to walk that plank.'

'I don't believe they see as we do. I've been watching them. I wonder if they know this is simply blackness for us. How can we make them understand?'

'Anyhow, we must make them understand.'

I think we said these things with a vague half hope the Selenites might somehow understand. I knew quite clearly that all that was needed was an explanation. Then as I saw their faces, I realized that an explanation was impossible. Just here it was that our resemblances were not going to bridge our differences. Well, I wasn't going to walk the plank, anyhow. I slipped

my wrist very quickly out of the coil of chain that was loose, and then began to twist my wrists in opposite directions. I was standing nearest to the bridge, and as I did this two of the Selenites laid hold of me, and pulled me gently towards it.

I shook my head violently. 'No go,' I said, 'no use. You don't understand.'

Another Selenite added his compulsion. I was forced to step forward.

'I've got an idea,' said Cavor; but I knew his ideas.

'Look here!' I exclaimed to the Selenites. 'Steady on! It's all very well for you—'

I sprang round upon my heel. I burst out into curses. For one of the armed Selenites had stabbed me behind with his goad.

I wrenched my wrists free from the little tentacles that held them. I turned on the goad-bearer. 'Confound you!' I cried. 'I've warned you of that. What on earth do you think I'm made of, to stick that into me? If you touch me again—!'

By way of answer he pricked me forthwith.

I heard Cavor's voice in alarm and entreaty. Even then I think he wanted to compromise with these creatures. 'I say, Bedford,' he cried, 'I know a way!' But the sting of that second stab seemed to set free some pent-up reserve of energy in my being. Instantly the link of the wrist-chain snapped, and with it snapped all considerations that had held us unresisting in the hands of these moon creatures. For that second, at least, I was mad with fear and anger. I took no thought of consequences. I hit straight out at the face of the thing with the goad. The chain was twisted round my fist. . . .

There came another of these beastly surprises of which the moon world is full.

My mailed hand seemed to go clean through him. He smashed like – like some softish sort of sweet with liquid in it! He broke right in! He squelched and splashed. It was like hitting a damp toadstool. The flimsy body went spinning a dozen yards, and fell with a flabby impact. I was astonished. I was incredulous that any living thing could be so flimsy. For an instant I could have believed the whole thing a dream.

Then it had become real and imminent again. Neither Cavor nor the other Selenites seemed to have done anything from the time when I had turned about to the time when the dead Selenite hit the ground. Everyone stood back from us two, everyone alert. That arrest seemed to last at least a second after the Selenite was down. Everyone must have been taking the thing in. I seem to remember myself standing with my arm half retracted, trying also to take it in. 'What next?' clamoured my brain; 'What next?' Then in a moment everyone was moving!

I perceived we must get our chains loose, and that before we could do this these Selenites had to be beaten off. I faced towards the group of the

three goad-bearers. Instantly one threw his goad at me. It swished over my head, and I suppose went flying into the abyss behind.

I leaped right at him with all my might as the goad flew over me. He turned to run as I jumped, and I bore him to the ground, came down right upon him, and slipped upon his smashed body and fell. He seemed to wriggle under my foot.

I came into a sitting position, and on every hand the blue backs of the Selenites were receding into the darkness. I bent a link by main force and untwisted the chain that had hampered me about the ankles, and sprang to my feet, with the chain in my hand. Another goad, flung javelin-wise, whistled by me, and I made a rush towards the darkness out of which it had come. Then I turned back towards Cavor, who was still standing in the light of the rivulet near the gulf convulsively busy with his wrists, and at the same time jabbering nonsense about his idea.

'Come on!' I cried.

'My hands!' he answered.

Then, realizing that I dared not run back to him, because my ill-calculated steps might carry me over the edge, he came shuffling towards me, with his hands held out before him.

I gripped his chains at once to unfasten them.

'Where are they?' he panted.

'Run away. They'll come back. They're throwing things! Which way shall we go?'

'By the light. To that tunnel. Eh?'

'Yes,' said I, and his hands were free.

I dropped on my knees and fell to work on his ankle bonds. Whack came something – I know not what – and splashed the livid streamlet into drops about us. Far away on our right a piping and whistling began.

I whipped the chain off his feet, and put it in his hand. 'Hit with that!' I said, and without waiting for an answer, set off in big bounds along the path by which we had come. I had a nasty sort of feeling that these things could jump out of the darkness on to my back. I heard the impact of his leaps come following after me.

We ran in vast strides. But that running, you must understand, was an altogether different thing from any running on earth. On earth one leaps and almost instantly hits the ground again, but on the moon, because of its weaker pull, one shot through the air for several seconds before one came to earth. In spite of our violent hurry this gave an effect of long pauses, pauses in which one might have counted seven or eight. 'Step,' and one soared off! All sorts of questions ran through my mind: 'Where are the Selenites? What will they do? Shall we ever get to that tunnel? Is Cavor far behind? Are they likely to cut him off?' Then whack, stride, and off again for another step.

I saw a Selenite running in front of me, his legs going exactly as a man's would go on earth, saw him glance over his shoulder, and heard him shriek as he ran aside out of my way into the darkness. He was, I think, our guide, but I am not sure. Then in another vast stride the walls of rock had come into view on either hand, and in two more strides I was in the tunnel, and tempering my pace to its low roof. I went on to a bend, then stopped and turned back, and plug, plug, plug, Cavor came into view, splashing into the stream of blue light at every stride, and grew larger and blundered into me. We stood clutching each other. For a moment, at least, we had shaken off our captors and were alone.

We were both very much out of breath. We spoke in panting, broken sentences.

'You've spoilt it all!' panted Cavor.

'Nonsense,' I cried. 'It was that or death!'

'What are we to do?'

'Hide.'

'How can we?'

'It's dark enough.'

'But where?'

'Up one of these side caverns.'

'And then?'

'Think.'

'Right – come on.'

We strode on, and presently came to a radiating dark cavern. Cavor was in front. He hesitated, and chose a black mouth that seemed to promise good hiding. He went towards it and turned.

'It's dark,' he said.

'Your legs and feet will light us. You're wet with that luminous stuff.'

'But—'

A tumult of sounds, and in particular a sound like a clanging gong, advancing up the main tunnel, became audible. It was horribly suggestive of a tumultuous pursuit. We made a bolt for the unlit side cavern forthwith. As we ran along it our way was lit by the irradiation of Cavor's legs. 'It's lucky,' I panted, 'they took off our boots, or we should fill this place with clatter.' On we rushed, taking as small steps as we could to avoid striking the roof of the cavern. After a time we seemed to be gaining on the uproar. It became muffled, it dwindled, it died away.

I stopped and looked back, and I heard the pad, pad of Cavor's feet receding. Then he stopped also. 'Bedford,' he whispered; 'there's a sort of light in front of us.'

I looked, and at first could see nothing. Then I perceived his head and shoulders dimly outlined against a fainter darkness. I saw, also, that this mitigation of the darkness was not blue, as all the other light within the

moon had been, but a pallid grey, a very vague, faint white, the daylight colour. Cavor noted this difference as soon or sooner than I did, and I think, too, that it filled him with much the same wild hope.

'Bedford,' he whispered, and his voice trembled. 'That light – it is possible—'

He did not dare to say the thing he hoped. Then came a pause. Suddenly I knew by the sound of his feet that he was striding towards that pallor. I followed him with a beating heart.

CHAPTER XVI

Points of View

The light grew stronger as we advanced. In a little time it was nearly as strong as the phosphorescence on Cavor's legs. Our tunnel was expanding into a cavern, and this new light was at the further end of it. I perceived something that set my hopes leaping and bounding.

'Cavor,' I said, 'it comes from above! I am certain it comes from above!'

He made no answer, but hurried on.

Indisputably it was a grey light; a silvery light.

In another moment we were beneath it. It filtered down through a chink in the walls of the cavern, and as I stared up, drip, came a drop of water upon my face. I started and stood aside – drip, fell another drop quite audibly on the rocky floor.

'Cavor,' I said, 'if one of us lifts the other, he can reach that crack!'

'I'll lift you,' he said, and incontinently hoisted me as though I was a baby.

I thrust an arm into the crack, and just at my fingertips found a little ledge by which I could hold. I could see the white light was very much brighter now. I pulled myself up by two fingers with scarcely an effort, though on earth I weigh twelve stone, reached to a still higher corner of rock, and so got my feet on the narrow ledge. I stood up and searched up the rocks with my fingers; the cleft broadened out upwardly. 'It's climbable,' I said to Cavor. 'Can you jump up to my hand if I hold it down to you?'

I wedged myself between the sides of the cleft, rested knee and foot on the ledge, and extended a hand. I could not see Cavor, but I could hear the rustle of his movements as he crouched to spring. Then whack and he was hanging to my arm – and no heavier than a kitten! I lugged him up until he had a hand on my ledge, and could release me.

'Confound it!' I said, 'Anyone could be a mountaineer on the moon;' and so set myself in earnest to the climbing. For a few minutes I clambered steadily, and then I looked up again. The cleft opened out steadily, and the light was brighter. Only—

It was not daylight after all!

In another moment I could see what it was, and at the sight I could have beaten my head against the rocks with disappointment. For I beheld simply an irregularly sloping open space, and all over its slanting floor stood a forest of little club-shaped fungi, each shining gloriously with that pinkish silvery light. For a moment I stared at their soft radiance, then sprang

forward and upward among them. I plucked up half a dozen and flung them against the rocks, and then sat down, laughing bitterly, as Cavor's ruddy face came into view.

'It's phosphorescence again!' I said. 'No need to hurry. Sit down and make yourself at home.' And as he spluttered over our disappointment, I began to lob more of these growths into the cleft.

'I thought it was daylight,' he said.

'Daylight!' cried I. 'Daybreak, sunset, clouds, and windy skies! Shall we ever see such things again?'

As I spoke, a little picture of our world seemed to rise before me, bright and little and clear, like the background of some old Italian picture. 'The sky that changes, and the sea that changes, and the hills and the green trees and the towns and cities shining in the sun. Think of a wet roof at sunset, Cavor! Think of the windows of a westward house!'

He made no answer.

'Here we are burrowing in this beastly world that isn't a world, with its inky ocean hidden in some abominable blackness below, and outside that torrid day and that death stillness of night. And all those things that are chasing us now, beastly men of leather – insect men, that come out of a nightmare! After all, they're right! What business have we here smashing them and disturbing their world? For all we know the whole planet is up and after us already. In a minute we may hear them whimpering, and their gongs going. What are we to do? Where are we to go? Here we are as comfortable as snakes from Jamrach's loose in a Surbiton villa!'

'It was your fault,' said Cavor.

'My fault!' I shouted. 'Good Lord!'

'I had an idea!'

'Curse your ideas!'

'If we had refused to budge—'

'Under these goads?'

'Yes. They would have carried us!'

'Over that bridge?'

'Yes. They must have carried us from outside.'

'I'd rather be carried by a fly across a ceiling. Good Heavens!'

I resumed my destruction of the fungi. Then suddenly I saw something that struck me even then.

'Cavor,' I said, 'these chains are of gold!'

He was thinking intently, with his hands gripping his cheeks. He turned his head slowly and stared at me, and when I had repeated my words, at the twisted chain about his right hand. 'So they are,' he said, 'so they are.' His face lost its transitory interest even as he looked. He hesitated for a moment, then went on with his interrupted meditation. I sat for a space puzzling over the fact that I had only just observed this, until I considered

the blue light in which we had been, and which had taken all the colour out of the metal. And from that discovery I also started upon a train of thought that carried me wide and far. I forgot that I had just been asking what business we had in the moon. Gold—

It was Cavor who spoke first. 'It seems to me that there are two courses open to us.'

'Well?'

'Either we can attempt to make our way – fight our way if necessary – out to the exterior again, and then hunt for our sphere until we find it, or the cold of the night comes to kill us, or else—'

He paused. 'Yes?' I said, though I knew what was coming.

'We might attempt once more to establish some sort of understanding with the minds of the people in the moon.'

'So far as I'm concerned – it's the first.'

'I doubt.'

'I don't.'

'You see,' said Cavor, 'I do not think we can judge the Selenites by what we have seen of them. Their central world, their civilized world will be far below in the profounder caverns about their sea. This region of the crust in which we are is an outlying district, a pastoral region. At any rate, that is my interpretation. These Selenites we have seen may be only the equivalent of cowboys and engine tenders. Their use of goads – in all probability mooncalf goads – the lack of imagination they show in expecting us to be able to do just what they can do, their indisputable brutality, all seem to point to something of that sort. But if we endured—'

'Neither of us could endure a six-inch plank across the bottomless pit for very long.'

'No,' said Cavor; 'but then—'

'I *won't*,' I said.

He discovered a new line of possibilities. 'Well, suppose we got ourselves into some corner, where we could defend ourselves against these hinds and labourers. If, for example, we could hold out for a week or so, it is probable that the news of our appearance would filter down to the more intelligent and populous parts—'

'If they exist.'

'They must exist, or whence came those tremendous machines?'

'That's possible, but it's the worst of the two chances.'

'We might write up inscriptions on walls—'

'How do we know their eyes would see the sort of marks we made?'

'If we cut them—'

'That's possible, of course.'

I took up a new thread of thought. 'After all,' I said, 'I suppose you don't think these Selenites so infinitely wiser than men.'

'They must know a lot more – or at least a lot of different things.'

'Yes, but—' I hesitated.

'I think you'll quite admit, Cavor, that you're rather an exceptional man.'

'How?'

'Well, you – you're a rather lonely man – have been, that is. You haven't married.'

'Never wanted to. But why—?'

'And you never grew richer than you happened to be?'

'Never wanted that either.'

'You've just rooted after knowledge?'

'Well, a certain curiosity is natural—'

'You think so. That's just it. You think every other mind wants to *know*. I remember once, when I asked you why you conducted all these researches, you said you wanted your FRS, and to have the stuff called Cavorite, and things like that. You know perfectly well you didn't do it for that; but at the time my question took you by surprise, and you felt you ought to have something to look like a motive. Really you conducted researches because you *had* to. It's your twist.'

'Perhaps it is—'

'It isn't one man in a million has that twist. Most men want – well, various things, but very few want knowledge for its own sake. *I* don't, I know perfectly well. Now, these Selenites seem to be a driving, busy sort of being, but how do you know that even the most intelligent will take an interest in us or our world? I don't believe they'll even know we have a world. They never come out at night – they'd freeze if they did. They've probably never seen any heavenly body at all except the blazing sun. How are they to know there *is* another world? What does it matter to them if they do? Well, even if they *have* had a glimpse of a few stars, or even of the earth crescent, what of that? Why should people living *inside* a planet trouble to observe that sort of thing? Men wouldn't have done it except for the seasons and sailing; why should the moon people? . . .

'Well, suppose there are a few philosophers like yourself. They are just the very Selenites who'll never hear of our existence. Suppose a Selenite had dropped on the earth when you were at Lympne, you'd have been the last man in the world to hear he had come. You never read a newspaper! You see the chances against you. Well, it's for these chances we're sitting here doing nothing while precious time is flying. I tell you we've got into a fix. We've come unarmed, we've lost our sphere, we've got no food, we've shown ourselves to the Selenites, and made them think we're strange, strong, dangerous animals; and unless these Selenites are perfect fools, they'll set about now and hunt us till they find us, and when they find us they'll try and take us if they can, and kill us if they can't, and that's the end of the matter. If they take us, they'll probably kill us, through some misunder-

standing. After we're done for, they may discuss us perhaps, but we shan't get much fun out of that.'

'Go on.'

'On the other hand, here's gold knocking about like cast iron at home. If only we can get some of it back, if only we can find our sphere again before they do, and get back, then—'

'Yes?'

'We might put the thing on a sounder footing. Come back in a bigger sphere with guns.'

'Good Lord!' cried Cavor, as though that was horrible.

I shied another luminous fungus down the cleft.

'Look here, Cavor,' I said, 'I've half the voting power anyhow in this affair, and this is a case for a practical man. I'm a practical man, and you are not. I'm not going to trust to Selenites and geometrical diagrams again, if I can help it . . . That's all. Get back. Drop all this secrecy – or most of it. And come again.'

He reflected. 'When I came to the moon,' he said, 'I ought to have come alone.'

'The question before the meeting,' I said, 'is how to get back to the sphere.'

For a time we nursed our knees in silence. Then he seemed to decide for my reasons.

'I think,' he said, 'one can get data. It is clear that while the sun is on this side of the moon the air will be blowing through this planet sponge from the dark side hither. On this side, at any rate, the air will be expanding and flowing out of the moon caverns into the craters . . . Very well, there's a draught here.'

'So there is.'

'And that means that this is not a dead end; somewhere behind us this cleft goes on and up. The draught is blowing up, and that is the way we have to go. If we try and get up any sort of chimney or gully there is, we shall not only get out of these passages where they are hunting for us—'

'But suppose the gully is too narrow?'

'We'll come down again.'

'Ssh!' I said suddenly; 'what's that?'

We listened. At first it was an indistinct murmur, and then one picked out the clang of a gong. 'They must think we are mooncalves,' said I, 'to be frightened at that.'

'They're coming along that passage,' said Cavor.

'They must be.'

'They'll not think of the cleft. They'll go past.'

I listened again for a space. 'This time,' I whispered, 'they're likely to have some sort of weapon.'

Then suddenly I sprang to my feet. 'Good Heavens, Cavor!' I cried. 'But
they *will*! They'll see the fungi I have been pitching down. They'll—!'

I didn't finish my sentence. I turned about and made a leap over the
fungus tops towards the upper end of the cavity. I saw that the space turned
upward and became a draughty cleft again, ascending to impenetrable dark-
ness. I was about to clamber up into this, and then with a happy inspiration
turned back.

'What are you doing?' asked Cavor.

'Go on!' said I, and went back and got two of the shining fungi, and
putting one into the breast pocket of my flannel jacket, so that it stuck out
to light our climbing, went back with the other for Cavor. The noise of the
Selenites was now so loud that it seemed they must be already beneath the
cleft. But it might be they would have difficulty in clambering into it, or
might hesitate to ascend it against our possible resistance. At any rate, we
had now the comforting knowledge of the enormous muscular superiority
our birth in another planet gave us. In another minute I was clambering
with gigantic vigour after Cavor's blue-lit heels.

CHAPTER XVII

The Fight in the Cave of the Moon Butchers

I do not know how far we clambered before we came to the grating. It may be we ascended only a few hundred feet, but at the time it seemed to me we might have hauled and jammed and hopped and wedged ourselves through a mile or more of vertical ascent. Whenever I recall that time, there comes into my head the heavy clank of our golden chains that followed every movement. Very soon my knuckles and knees were raw, and I had a bruise on one cheek. After a time the first violence of our efforts diminished, and our movements became more deliberate and less painful. The noise of the pursuing Selenites had died away altogether. It seemed almost as though they had not traced us up the crack after all, in spite of the tell-tale heap of broken fungi that must have lain beneath it. At times the cleft narrowed so much that we could scarce squeeze up it; at others it expanded into great drusy cavities, studded with prickly crystals, or thickly beset with dull, shining fungoid pimples. Sometimes it twisted spirally, and at other times slanted down nearly to the horizontal direction. Ever and again there was the intermittent drip and trickle of water by us. Once or twice it seemed to us that small living things had rustled out of our reach, but what they were we never saw. They may have been venomous beasts for all I know, but they did us no harm, and we were now tuned to a pitch when a weird creeping thing more or less mattered little. And at last, far above, came the familiar bluish light again, and then we saw that it filtered through a grating that barred our way.

We whispered as we pointed this out to one another, and became more and more cautious in our ascent. Presently we were close under the grating, and by pressing my face against its bars I could see a limited portion of the cavern beyond. It was clearly a large space, and lit no doubt by some rivulet of the same blue light that we had seen flow from the beating machinery. An intermittent trickle of water dropped ever and again between the bars near my face.

My first endeavour was naturally to see what might be upon the floor of the cavern, but our grating lay in a depression whose rim hid all this from our eyes. Our foiled attention then fell back upon the suggestion of the various sounds we heard, and presently my eye caught a number of faint shadows that played across the dim roof far overhead.

Indisputably there were several Selenites, perhaps a considerable number, in this space, for we could hear the noises of their intercourse, and faint sounds that I identified as their footfalls. There was also a succession of

regularly repeated sounds – chid, chid, chid – which began and ceased, suggestive of a knife or spade hacking at some soft substance. Then came a clank as if of chains, a whistle and a rumble as of a truck running over a hollowed place, and then again that chid, chid, chid resumed. The shadows told of shapes that moved quickly and rhythmically, in agreement with that regular sound, and rested when it ceased.

We put our heads close together, and began to discuss these things in noiseless whispers.

'They are occupied,' I said, 'they are occupied in some way.'

'Yes.'

'They're not seeking us, or thinking of us.'

'Perhaps they have not heard of us.'

'Those others are hunting about below. If suddenly we appeared here—'

We looked at one another.

'There might be a chance to parley,' said Cavor.

'No,' I said. 'Not as we are.'

For a space we remained, each occupied by his own thoughts.

Chid, chid, chid went the chopping, and the shadows moved to and fro.

I looked at the grating. 'It's flimsy,' I said. 'We might bend two of the bars and crawl through.'

We wasted a little time in vague discussion. Then I took one of the bars in both hands, and got my feet up against the rock until they were almost on a level with my head, and so thrust against the bar. It bent so suddenly that I almost slipped. I clambered about and bent the adjacent bar in the opposite direction, and then took the luminous fungus from my pocket and dropped it down the fissure.

'Don't do anything hastily,' whispered Cavor, as I twisted myself up through the opening I had enlarged. I had a glimpse of busy figures as I came through the grating, and immediately bent down, so that the rim of the depression in which the grating lay hid me from their eyes, and so lay flat, signalling advice to Cavor as he also prepared to come through. Presently we were side by side in the depression, peering over the edge at the cavern and its occupants.

It was a much larger cavern than we had supposed from our first glimpse of it, and we looked up from the lowest portion of its sloping floor. It widened out as it receded from us, and its roof came down and hid the remoter portion altogether. And lying in a line along its length, vanishing at last far away in that tremendous perspective, were a number of huge shapes, huge pallid hulls, upon which the Selenites were busy. At first they seemed big white cylinders of vague import. Then I noted the heads upon them lying towards us, eyeless and skinless like the heads of sheep at a butcher's, and perceived they were the carcasses of mooncalves being cut up, much as the crew of a whaler might cut up a moored whale. They were cutting off the

flesh in strips, and on some of the further trunks the white ribs were showing. It was the sound of their hatchets that made that chid, chid. Some way away a thing like a trolley cable, drawn and loaded with chunks of lax meat, was running up the slope of the cavern floor. This enormous long avenue of hulls that were destined to be food, gave us a sense of the vast populousness of the moon world second only to the effect of our first glimpse down the shaft.

It seemed to me at first that the Selenites must be standing on trestle-supported planks,* and then I saw that the planks and supports and their hatchets were really of the same leaden hue as my fetters had seemed before white light came to bear on them. A number of very thick-looking crowbars lay about the floor, and had apparently assisted to turn the dead mooncalf over on its side. They were perhaps six feet long, with shaped handles, very tempting-looking weapons. The whole place was lit by three transverse streams of the blue fluid.

We lay for a long time noting all these things in silence. 'Well?' said Cavor at last.

I crouched lower and turned to him. I had come upon a brilliant idea. 'Unless they lowered those bodies by a crane,' I said, 'we must be nearer the surface than I thought.'

'Why?'

'The mooncalf doesn't hop, and it hasn't got wings.'

He peered over the edge of the hollow again. 'I wonder now . . .' he began. 'After all, we have never gone far from the surface—'

I stopped him by a grip on his arm. I had heard a noise from the cleft below us!

We twisted ourselves about, and lay as still as death, with every sense alert. In a little while I did not doubt that something was quietly ascending the cleft. Very slowly and quite noiselessly I assured myself of a good grip on my chain, and waited for that something to appear.

'Just look at those chaps with the hatchets again,' I said.

'They're all right,' said Cavor.

I took a sort of provisional aim at the gap in the grating. I could hear now quite distinctly the soft twittering of the ascending Selenites, the dab of their hands against the rock, and the falling of dust from their grips as they clambered.

Then I could see that there was something moving dimly in the blackness below the grating, but what it might be I could not distinguish. The

* I do not remember seeing any wooden things on the moon; doors, tables, everything corresponding to our terrestrial joinery was made of metal, and I believe for the most part of gold, which as a metal would, of course, naturally recommend itself – other things being equal – on account of the ease in working it, and its toughness and durability.

whole thing seemed to hang fire just for a moment – then smash! I had sprung to my feet, struck savagely at something that had flashed out at me. It was the keen point of a spear. I have thought since that its length in the narrowness of the cleft must have prevented its being sloped to reach me. Anyhow, it shot out from the grating like the tongue of a snake, and missed and flew back and flashed again. But the second time I snatched and caught it, and wrenched it away, but not before another had darted ineffectually at me.

I shouted with triumph as I felt the hold of the Selenite resist my pull for a moment and give, and then I was jabbing down through the bars, amidst squeals from the darkness, and Cavor had snapped off the other spear, and was leaping and flourishing it beside me, and making inefficient jabs. Clang, clang, came up through the grating, and then an axe hurtled through the air and whacked against the rocks beyond, to remind me of the fleshers at the carcasses up the cavern.

I turned, and they were all coming towards us in open order waving their axes. They were short, thick, little beggars, with long arms, strikingly different from the ones we had seen before. If they had not heard of us before, they must have realized the situation with incredible swiftness. I stared at them for a moment, spear in hand. 'Guard that grating, Cavor,' I cried, howled to intimidate them, and rushed to meet them. Two of them missed with their hatchets, and the rest fled incontinently. Then the two also were sprinting away up the cavern, with hands clenched and heads down. I never saw men run like them!

I knew the spear I had was no good for me. It was thin and flimsy, only effectual for a thrust, and too long for a quick recover. So I only chased the Selenites as far as the first carcass, and stopped there and picked up one of the crowbars that were lying about. It felt comfortingly heavy, and equal to smashing any number of Selenites. I threw away my spear, and picked up a second crowbar for the other hand. I felt five times better than I had with the spear. I shook the two threateningly at the Selenites, who had come to a halt in a little crowd far away up the cavern, and then turned about to look at Cavor.

He was leaping from side to side of the grating, making threatening jabs with his broken spear. That was all right. It would keep the Selenites down – for a time at any rate. I looked up the cavern again. What on earth were we going to do now?

We were cornered in a sort of way already. But these butchers up the cavern had been surprised, they were probably scared, and they had no special weapons, only those little hatchets of theirs. And that way lay escape. Their sturdy little forms – ever so much shorter and thicker than the mooncalf herds – were scattered up the slope in a way that was eloquent of indecision. I had the moral advantage of a mad bull in a street. But for

all that, there seemed a tremendous crowd of them. Very probably there was. Those Selenites down the cleft had certainly some infernally long spears. It might be they had other surprises for us. . . . But – confound it! – if we charged up the cave we should let them up behind us, and if we didn't, those little brutes up the cave would probably get reinforced. Heaven alone knew what tremendous engines of warfare – guns, bombs, terrestrial torpedoes – this unknown world below our feet, this vaster world of which we had only pricked the outer cuticle, might not presently send up to our destruction. It became clear the only thing to do was to charge! It became clearer as the legs of a number of fresh Selenites appeared running down the cavern towards us.

'Bedford!' cried Cavor, and behold, he was halfway between me and the grating!

'Go back!' I cried. 'What are you doing—'

'They've got – it's like a gun!'

And struggling in the grating between those defensive spears appeared the head and shoulders of a singularly lean and angular Selenite, bearing some complicated apparatus.

I realized Cavor's utter incapacity for the fight we had in hand. For a moment I hesitated. Then I rushed past him whirling my crowbars, and shouting to confound the aim of the Selenite. He was aiming in the queerest way with the thing against his stomach. '*Chuzz!*' The thing wasn't a gun; it went off like a cross-bow more, and dropped me in the middle of a leap.

I didn't fall down, I simply came down a little shorter than I should have done if I hadn't been hit, and from the feel of my shoulder the thing might have tapped me and glanced off. Then my left hand hit against the shaft, and I perceived there was a sort of spear sticking half through my shoulder. The moment after I got home with the crowbar in my right hand, and hit the Selenite fair and square. He collapsed – he crushed and crumpled – his head smashed like an egg.

I dropped a crowbar, pulled the spear out of my shoulder, and began to jab it down the grating into the darkness. At each jab came a shriek and twitter. Finally I hurled the spear down upon them with all my strength, leapt up, picked up the crowbar again, and started for the multitude up the cavern.

'Bedford!' cried Cavor. 'Bedford!' as I flew past him.

I seem to remember his footsteps coming on behind me.

Step, leap . . . whack, step, leap . . . Each leap seemed to last ages. With each, the cave opened out and the number of Selenites visible increased. At first they seemed all running about like ants in a disturbed ant-hill, one or two waving hatchets and coming to meet me, more running away, some bolting sideways into the avenue of carcasses, then presently others came in sight carrying spears, and then others. I saw a most extraordinary thing,

all hands and feet, bolting for cover. The cavern grew darker further up. Flick! Something flew over my head. Flick! As I soared in mid-stride I saw a spear hit and quiver in one of the carcasses to my left. Then, as I came down, one hit the ground before me, and I heard the remote 'chuzz!' with which their things were fired. Flick, flick! For a moment it was a shower. They were volleying!

I stopped dead.

I don't think I thought clearly then. I seem to remember a kind of stereo-typed phrase running through my mind: 'Zone of fire, seek cover!' I know I made a dash for the space between two of the carcasses, and stood there panting and feeling very wicked.

I looked round for Cavor, and for a moment it seemed as if he had vanished from the world. Then he came out of the darkness between the row of the carcasses and the rocky wall of the cavern. I saw his little face, dark and blue, and shining with perspiration and emotion.

He was saying something, but what it was I did not heed. I had realized that we might work from mooncalf to mooncalf up the cave until we were near enough to charge home. It was charge or nothing. 'Come on!' I said, and led the way.

'Bedford!' he cried unavailingly.

My mind was busy as we went up that narrow alley between the dead bodies and the wall of the cavern. The rocks curved about – they could not enfilade us. Though in that narrow space we could not leap, yet with our earth-born strength we were still able to go very much faster than the Selenites. I reckoned we should presently come right among them. Once we were on them, they would be nearly as formidable as black beetles. Only – there would first of all be a volley. I thought of a stratagem. I whipped off my flannel jacket as I ran.

'Bedford!' panted Cavor behind me.

I glanced back. 'What?' said I.

He was pointing upward over the carcasses. 'White light!' he said. 'White light again!'

I looked, and it was even so, a faint white ghost of twilight in the remoter cavern roof. That seemed to give me double strength.

'Keep close,' I said. A flat, long Selenite dashed out of the darkness, and squealed and fled. I halted, and stopped Cavor with my hand. I hung my jacket over my crowbar, ducked round the next carcass, dropped jacket and crowbar, showed myself, and darted back.

'Chuzz – flick,' just one arrow came. We were close on the Selenites, and they were standing in a crowd, broad, short and tall together, with a little battery of their shooting implements pointing down the cave. Three or four other arrows followed the first, and then their fire ceased.

I stuck out my head, and escaped by a hair's-breadth. This time I drew

a dozen shots or more, and heard the Selenites shouting and twittering as if with excitement as they shot. I picked up jacket and crowbar again.

'*Now!*' said I, and thrust out the jacket.

'Chuzz-zz-zz-zz! Chuzz!' In an instant my jacket had grown a thick beard of arrows, and they were quivering all over the carcass behind us. Instantly I slipped the crowbar out of the jacket, dropped the jacket – for all I know to the contrary it is lying up there in the moon now – and rushed out upon them.

For a minute perhaps it was massacre. I was too fierce to discriminate, and the Selenites were probably too scared to fight. At any rate they made no sort of fight against me. I saw scarlet, as the saying is. I remember I seemed to be wading among those leathery, thin things as a man wades through tall grass, mowing and hitting, first right, then left; smash, smash. Little drops of moisture flew about. I trod on things that crushed and piped and went slippery. The crowd seemed to open and close and flow like water. They seemed to have no combined plan whatever. There were spears flew about me, I was grazed over the ear by one. I was stabbed once in the arm and once in the cheek, but I only found that out afterwards, when the blood had had time to run and cool and feel wet.

What Cavor did I do not know. For a space it seemed that this fighting had lasted for an age, and must needs go on for ever. Then suddenly it was all over, and there was nothing to be seen but the backs of heads bobbing up and down as their owners ran in all directions. . . . I seemed altogether unhurt. I ran forward some paces, shouting, then turned about. I was amazed.

I had come right through them in vast flying strides, they were all behind me, and running hither and thither to hide.

I felt an enormous astonishment at the evaporation of the great fight into which I had hurled myself, and not a little of exultation. It did not seem to me that I had discovered the Selenites were unexpectedly flimsy, but that I was unexpectedly strong. I laughed stupidly. This fantastic moon!

I glanced for a moment at the smashed and writhing bodies that were scattered over the cavern floor, with a vague idea of further violence, then hurried on after Cavor.

CHAPTER XVIII

In the Sunlight

Presently we saw that the cavern before us opened on a hazy void. In another moment we had emerged upon a sort of slanting gallery that projected into a vast circular space, a huge cylindrical pit running vertically up and down. Round this pit the slanting gallery ran without any parapet or protection for a turn and a half, and then plunged high above into the rock again. Somehow it reminded me then of one of those spiral turns of the railway through the Saint Gothard. It was all tremendously huge. I can scarcely hope to convey to you the titanic proportion of all that place, the titanic effect of it. Our eyes followed up the vast declivity of the pit wall, and overhead and far above we beheld a round opening set with faint stars, and half of the lip about it well-nigh blinding with the white light of the sun. At that we cried aloud simultaneously.

'Come on!' I said, leading the way.

'But there?' said Cavor, and very carefully stepped nearer the edge of the gallery. I followed his example, and craned forward and looked down, but I was dazzled by that gleam of light above, and I could see only a bottomless darkness with spectral patches of crimson and purple floating therein. Yet if I could not see, I could hear. Out of this darkness came a sound, a sound like the angry hum one can hear if one puts one's ear outside a hive of bees, a sound out of that enormous hollow, it may be, four miles beneath our feet. . . .

For a moment I listened, then tightened my grip on my crowbar, and led the way up the gallery.

'This must be the shaft we looked down upon,' said Cavor. 'Under that lid.'

'And below there, is where we saw the lights.'

'The lights!' said he. 'Yes – the lights of the world that now we shall never see.'

'We'll come back,' I said, for now we had escaped so much I was rashly sanguine that we should recover the sphere.

His answer I did not catch.

'Eh?' I asked.

'It doesn't matter,' he answered, and we hurried on in silence.

I suppose that slanting lateral way was four or five miles long, allowing for its curvature, and it ascended at a slope that would have made it almost impossibly steep on earth, but which one strode up easily under lunar conditions. We saw only two Selenites during all that portion of our flight,

and directly they became aware of us they ran headlong. It was clear that the knowledge of our strength and violence had reached them. Our way to the exterior was unexpectedly plain. The spiral gallery straightened into a steeply ascendent tunnel, its floor bearing abundant traces of the mooncalves, and so straight and short in proportion to its vast arch, that no part of it was absolutely dark. Almost immediately it began to lighten, and then far off and high up, and quite blindingly brilliant, appeared its opening on the exterior, a slope of Alpine steepness surmounted by a crest of bayonet shrub, tall and broken down now, and dry and dead, in spiky silhouette against the sun.

And it is strange that we men, to whom this very vegetation had seemed so weird and horrible a little time ago, should now behold it with the emotion a home-coming exile might feel at sight of his native land. We welcomed even the rareness of the air that made us pant as we ran, and which rendered speaking no longer the easy thing that it had been, but an effort to make oneself heard. Larger grew the sunlit circle above us, and larger, and all the nearer tunnel sank into a rim of indistinguishable black. We saw the dead bayonet shrub no longer with any touch of green in it, but brown and dry and thick, and the shadow of its upper branches high out of sight made a densely interlaced pattern upon the tumbled rocks. And at the immediate mouth of the tunnel was a wide trampled space where the mooncalves had come and gone.

We came out upon this space at last into a light and heat that hit and pressed upon us. We traversed the exposed area painfully, and clambered up a slope among the scrub stems, and sat down at last panting in a high place beneath the shadow of a mass of twisted lava. Even in the shade the rock felt hot.

The air was intensely hot, and we were in great physical discomfort, but for all that we were no longer in a nightmare. We seemed to have come to our own province again, beneath the stars. All the fear and stress of our flight through the dim passages and fissures below had fallen from us. That last fight had filled us with an enormous confidence in ourselves so far as the Selenites were concerned. We looked back almost incredulously at the black opening from which we had just emerged. Down there it was, in a blue glow that now in our memories seemed the next thing to absolute darkness, we had met with things like mad mockeries of men, helmet-headed creatures, and had walked in fear before them, and had submitted to them until we could submit no longer. And, behold, they had smashed like wax and scattered like chaff, and fled and vanished like the creatures of a dream!

I rubbed my eyes, doubting whether we had not slept and dreamt these things by reason of the fungus we had eaten, and suddenly discovered the blood upon my face, and then that my shirt was sticking painfully to my shoulder and arm.

'Confound it!' I said, gauging my injuries with an investigatory hand, and suddenly that distant tunnel mouth became, as it were, a watching eye.

'Cavor!' I said; 'what are they going to do now? And what are we going to do?'

He shook his head, with his eyes fixed upon the tunnel. 'How can one tell what they will do?'

'It depends on what they think of us, and I don't see how we can begin to guess that. And it depends upon what they have in reserve. It's as you say, Cavor, we have touched the merest outside of this world. They may have all sorts of things inside here. Even with those shooting things they might make it bad for us. . . .

'Yet after all,' I said, 'even if we *don't* find the sphere at once, there is a chance for us. We might hold out. Even through the night. We might go down there again and make a fight for it.'

I stared about me with speculative eyes. The character of the scenery had altered altogether by reason of the enormous growth and subsequent drying of the scrub. The crest on which we sat was high, and commanded a wide prospect of the crater landscape, and we saw it now all sere and dry in the late autumn of the lunar afternoon. Rising one behind the other were long slopes and fields of trampled brown where the mooncalves had pastured, and far away in the full blaze of the sun a drove of them basked slumberously, scattered shapes, each with a blot of shadow against it like sheep on the side of a down. But never a sign of a Selenite was to be seen. Whether they had fled on our emergence from the interior passages, or whether they were accustomed to retire after driving out the mooncalves, I cannot guess. At the time I believed the former was the case.

'If we were to set fire to all this stuff,' I said, 'we might find the sphere among the ashes.'

Cavor did not seem to hear me. He was peering under his hand at the stars, that still, in spite of the intense sunlight, were abundantly visible in the sky. 'How long do you think we have been here?' he asked at last.

'Been where?'

'On the moon.'

'Two earthly days, perhaps.'

'More nearly ten. Do you know, the sun is past its zenith, and sinking in the west. In four days' time or less, it will be night.'

'But – we've only eaten once!'

'I know that. And— But there are the stars!'

'But why should time seem different because we are on a smaller planet?'

'I don't know. There it is!'

'How does one tell time?'

'Hunger – fatigue – all those things are different. Everything is different – everything. To me it seems that since first we came out of the sphere has

been only a question of hours – long hours – at most.'

'Ten days,' I said; 'that leaves—' I looked up at the sun for a moment, and then saw that it was halfway from the zenith to the western edge of things. 'Four days! . . . Cavor, we mustn't sit here and dream. How do you think we may begin?'

I stood up. 'We must get a fixed point we can recognize – we might hoist a flag, or a handkerchief, or something – and quarter the ground, and work round that.'

He stood up beside me.

'Yes,' he said, 'there is nothing for it but to hunt the sphere. Nothing. We may find it – certainly we may find it. And if not—'

'We must keep on looking.'

He looked this way and that, glanced up at the sky and down at the tunnel, and astonished me by a sudden gesture of impatience. 'Oh! But we have done foolishly! To have come to this pass! Think how it might have been, and the things we might have done!'

'We may do something yet.'

'Never the thing we might have done. Here below our feet is a world. Think of what that world must be! Think of that machine we saw, and the lid and the shaft! They were just remote outlying things, and those creatures we have seen and fought with no more than ignorant peasants, dwellers in the outskirts, yokels and labourers half akin to brutes. Down below! Caverns beneath caverns, tunnels, structures, ways . . . It must open out, and be greater and wider and more populous as one descends. Assuredly. Right down at last to the central sea that washes round the core of the moon. Think of its inky waters under the spare lights – if, indeed, their eyes *need* lights! Think of the cascading tributaries pouring down their channels to feed it! Think of the tides upon its surface, and the rush and swirl of its ebb and flow! Perhaps they have ships that go upon it, perhaps down there are mighty cities and swarming ways, and wisdom and order passing the wit of man. And we may die here upon it, and never see the masters who *must* be – ruling over these things! We may freeze and die here, and the air will freeze and thaw upon us, and then—! Then they will come upon us, come on our stiff and silent bodies, and find the sphere we cannot find, and they will understand at last too late all the thought and effort that ended here in vain!'

His voice for all that speech sounded like the voice of someone heard in a telephone, weak and far away.

'But the darkness,' I said.

'One might get over that.'

'How?'

'I don't know. How am I to know? One might carry a torch, one might have a lamp; the others – might understand.'

He stood for a moment with his hands held down and a rueful face,

staring out over the waste that defied him. Then with a gesture of renun-
ciation he turned towards me with proposals for the systematic hunting of
the sphere.

'We can return,' I said.

He looked about him. 'First of all we shall have to get to earth.'

'We could bring back lamps to carry and climbing irons, and a hundred
necessary things.'

'Yes,' he said.

'We can take back an earnest of success in this gold.'

He looked at my golden crowbars, and said nothing for a space. He stood
with his hands clasped behind his back, staring across the crater. At last
he sighed and spoke. 'It was I found the way here, but to find a way isn't
always to be master of a way. If I take my secret back to earth, what will
happen? I do not see how I can keep my secret for a year, for even a part
of a year. Sooner or later it must come out, even if other men rediscover
it. And then . . . Governments and powers will struggle to get hither, they
will fight against one another, and against these moon people; it will only
spread warfare and multiply the occasions of war. In a little while, in a very
little while, if I tell my secret, this planet to its deepest galleries will be
strewn with human dead. Other things are doubtful, but that is certain . . .
It is not as though man had any use for the moon. What good would the
moon be to men? Even of their own planet what have they made but a
battleground and theatre of infinite folly? Small as his world is, and short
as his time, he has still in his little life down there far more than he can
do. No! Science has toiled too long forging weapons for fools to use. It is
time she held her hand. Let him find it out for himself again – in a thou-
sand years' time.'

'There are methods of secrecy,' I said.

He looked up at me and smiled. 'After all,' he said, 'why should one
worry? There is little chance of our finding the sphere, and down below
things are brewing. It's simply the human habit of hoping till we die that
makes us think of return. Our troubles are only beginning. We have shown
these moon folk violence, we have given them a taste of our quality, and
our chances are about as good as a tiger's that has got loose and killed a
man in Hyde Park. The news of us must be running down from gallery to
gallery, down towards the central parts. . . . No sane beings will ever let us
take that sphere back to earth after so much as they have seen of us.'

'We aren't improving our chances,' said I, 'by sitting here.'

We stood up side by side.

'After all,' he said, 'we must separate. We must stick up a handkerchief
on these tall spikes here and fasten it firmly, and from this as a centre we
must work over the crater. You must go westward, moving out in semicircles
to and fro towards the setting sun. You must move first with your shadow

on your right until it is at right angles with the direction of your handkerchief, and then with your shadow on your left. And I will do the same to the east. We will look into every gully, examine every skerry of rocks; we will do all we can to find my sphere. If we see Selenites we will hide from them as well as we can. For drink we must take snow, and if we feel the need of food, we must kill a mooncalf if we can, and eat such flesh as it has – raw – and so each will go his own way.'

'And if one of us comes upon the sphere?'

'He must come back to the white handkerchief, and stand by it and signal to the other.'

'And if neither—?'

Cavor glanced up at the sun. 'We go on seeking until the night and cold overtake us.'

'Suppose the Selenites have found the sphere and hidden it?'

He shrugged his shoulders.

'Or if presently they come hunting us?'

He made no answer.

'You had better take a club,' I said.

He shook his head, and stared away from me across the waste.

But for a moment he did not start. He looked round at me shyly, hesitated. '*Au revoir*,' he said.

I felt an odd stab of emotion. A sense of how we had galled each other, and particularly how I must have galled him, came to me. 'Confound it,' thought I, 'we might have done better!' I was on the point of asking him to shake hands – for that, somehow, was how I felt just then – when he put his feet together and leapt away from me towards the north. He seemed to drift through the air as a dead leaf would do, fell lightly, and leapt again. I stood for a moment watching him, then faced westward reluctantly, pulled myself together, and with something of the feeling of a man who leaps into icy water, selected a leaping point, and plunged forward to explore my solitary half of the moon world. I dropped rather clumsily among rocks, stood up and looked about me, clambered on to a rocky slab, and leapt again. . . .

When presently I looked for Cavor he was hidden from my eyes, but the handkerchief showed out bravely on its headland, white in the blaze of the sun.

I determined not to lose sight of that handkerchief whatever might betide.

CHAPTER XIX

Mr Bedford Alone

In a little while it seemed to me as though I had always been alone on the moon. I hunted for a time with a certain intentness, but the heat was still very great, and the thinness of the air felt like a hoop about one's chest. I came presently into a hollow basin bristling with tall, brown, dry fronds about its edge, and I sat down under these to rest and cool. I intended to rest for only a little while. I put down my clubs beside me, and sat resting my chin on my hands. I saw with a sort of colourless interest that the rocks of the basin, where here and there the crackling dry lichens had shrunk away to show them, were all veined and splattered with gold, that here and there bosses of rounded and wrinkled gold projected from among the litter. What did that matter now? A sort of languor had possession of my limbs and mind, I did not believe for a moment that we should ever find the sphere in that vast desiccated wilderness. I seemed to lack a motive for effort until the Selenites should come. Then I supposed I should exert myself, obeying that unreasonable imperative that urges a man before all things to preserve and defend his life, albeit he may preserve it only to die more painfully in a little while.

Why had we come to the moon?

The thing presented itself to me as a perplexing problem. What is this spirit in man that urges him for ever to depart from happiness and security, to toil, to place himself in danger, to risk even a reasonable certainty of death? It dawned upon me up there in the moon as a thing I ought always to have known, that man is not made simply to go about being safe and comfortable and well fed and amused. Almost any man, if you put the thing to him, not in words, but in the shape of opportunities, will show that he knows as much. Against his interest, against his happiness, he is constantly being driven to do unreasonable things. Some force not himself impels him, and go he must. But why? Why? Sitting there in the midst of that useless moon gold, amidst the things of another world, I took count of all my life. Assuming I was to die a castaway upon the moon, I failed altogether to see what purpose I had served. I got no light on that point, but at any rate it was clearer to me than it had ever been in my life before that I was not serving my own purpose, that all my life I had in truth never served the purposes of my private life. Whose purposes, what purposes, was I serving? ... I ceased to speculate on why we had come to the moon, and took a wider sweep. Why had I come to the earth? Why had I a private life at all? ... I lost myself at last in bottomless speculations. ...

My thoughts became vague and cloudy, no longer leading in definite directions. I had not felt heavy or weary – I cannot imagine one doing so upon the moon – but I suppose I was greatly fatigued. At any rate I slept.

Slumbering there rested me greatly, I think, and the sun was setting and the violence of the heat abating, through all the time I slumbered. When at last I was roused from my slumbers by a remote clamour, I felt active and capable again. I rubbed my eyes and stretched my arms. I rose to my feet – I was a little stiff – and at once prepared to resume my search. I shouldered my golden clubs, one on each shoulder, and went on out of the ravine of the gold-veined rocks.

The sun was certainly lower, much lower than it had been; the air was very much cooler. I perceived I must have slept some time. It seemed to me that a faint touch of misty blueness hung about the western cliff. I leapt to a little boss of rock and surveyed the crater. I could see no signs of mooncalves or Selenites, nor could I see Cavor, but I could see my handkerchief afar off, spread out on its thicket of thorns. I looked about me, and then leapt forward to the next convenient view-point.

I beat my way round in a semicircle, and back again in a still remoter crescent. It was very fatiguing and hopeless. The air was really very much cooler, and it seemed to me that the shadow under the westward cliff was growing broad. Ever and again I stopped and reconnoitred, but there was no sign of Cavor, no sign of Selenites; and it seemed to me the mooncalves must have been driven into the interior again – I could see none of them. I became more and more desirous of seeing Cavor. The winged outline of the sun had sunk now, until it was scarcely the distance of its diameter from the rim of the sky. I was oppressed by the idea that the Selenites would presently close their lids and valves, and shut us out under the inexorable onrush of the lunar night. It seemed to me high time that he abandoned his search, and that we took counsel together. I felt how urgent it was that we should decide soon upon our course. We had failed to find the sphere, we no longer had time to seek it, and once these valves were closed with us outside, we were lost men. The great night of space would descend upon us – that blackness of the void which is the only absolute death. All my being shrank from that approach. We must get into the moon again, though we were slain in doing it. I was haunted by a vision of our freezing to death, of our hammering with our last strength on the valve of the great pit.

I took no thought any more of the sphere. I thought only of finding Cavor again. I was half inclined to go back into the moon without him, rather than seek him until it was too late. I was already halfway back towards our handkerchief, when suddenly—

I saw the sphere!

I did not find it so much as it found me. It was lying much further to the westward than I had gone, and the sloping rays of the sinking sun

reflected from its glass had suddenly proclaimed its presence in a dazzling beam. For an instant I thought this was some new device of the Selenites against us, and then I understood.

I threw up my arms, shouted a ghostly shout, and set off in vast leaps towards it. I missed one of my leaps and dropped into a deep ravine and twisted my ankle, and after that I stumbled at almost every leap. I was in a state of hysterical agitation, trembling violently, and quite breathless long before I got to it. Three times at least I had to stop with my hands resting on my side, and spite of the thin dryness of the air, the perspiration was wet upon my face.

I thought of nothing but the sphere until I reached it, I forgot even my trouble of Cavor's whereabouts. My last leap flung me with my hands hard against its glass; then I lay against it panting, and trying vainly to shout, 'Cavor! Here is the sphere!' When I had recovered a little I peered through the thick glass, and the things inside seemed tumbled. I stooped to peer closer. Then I attempted to get in. I had to hoist it over a little to get my head through the manhole. The screw stopper was inside, and I could see now that nothing had been touched, nothing had suffered. It lay there as we had left it when we had dropped out amidst the snow.

For a time I was wholly occupied in making and remaking this inventory. I found I was trembling violently. It was good to see that familiar dark interior again! I cannot tell you how good. Presently I crept inside and sat down among the things. I looked through the glass at the moon world and shivered. I placed my gold clubs upon the bale, and sought out and took a little food; not so much because I wanted it, but because it was there. Then it occurred to me that it was time to go out and signal for Cavor. But I did not go out and signal for Cavor forthwith. Something held me to the sphere.

After all, everything was coming right. There would be still time for us to get more of the magic stone that gives one mastery over men. Away there, close handy, was gold for the picking up; and the sphere would travel as well half full of gold as though it were empty. We could go back now, masters of ourselves and our world, and then—

I roused myself at last, and with an effort got myself out of the sphere. I shivered as I emerged, for the evening air was growing very cold. I stood in the hollow staring about me. I scrutinized the bushes round me very carefully before I leapt to the rocky shelf hard by, and took once more what had been my first leap in the moon. But now I made it with no effort whatever.

The growth and decay of the vegetation had gone on apace, and the whole aspect of the rocks had changed, but still it was possible to make out the slope on which the seeds had germinated, and the rocky mass from which we had taken our first view of the crater. But the spiky shrub on the slope stood brown and sere now, and thirty feet high, and cast long shadows that stretched out of sight, and the little seeds that clustered in its upper

branches were brown and ripe. Its work was done, and it was brittle and ready to fall and crumple under the freezing air, so soon as the nightfall came. And the huge cacti, that had swollen as we watched them, had long since burst and scattered their spores to the four quarters of the moon. Amazing little corner in the universe – the landing-place of men!

Some day, thought I, I will have an inscription standing there right in the midst of the hollow. It came to me, if only this teeming world within knew of the full import of the moment, how furious its tumult would become!

But as yet it could scarcely be dreaming of the significance of our coming. For if it did, the crater would surely be an uproar of pursuit, instead of as still as death! I looked about for some place from which I might signal to Cavor, and saw that same patch of rock to which he had leapt from my present standpoint, still bare and barren in the sun. For a moment I hesitated at going so far from the sphere. Then with a pang of shame at that hesitation, I leapt. . . .

From this vantage point I surveyed the crater again. Far away at the top of the enormous shadow I cast was the little white handkerchief fluttering on the bushes. It was very little and very far, and Cavor was not in sight. It seemed to me that by this time he ought to be looking for me. That was the agreement. But he was nowhere to be seen.

I stood waiting and watching, hands shading my eyes, expecting every moment to distinguish him. Very probably I stood there for quite a long time. I tried to shout, and was reminded of the thinness of the air. I made an undecided step back towards the sphere. But a lurking dread of the Selenites made me hesitate to signal my whereabouts by hoisting one of our sleeping-blankets on to the adjacent scrub. I searched the crater again.

It had an effect of emptiness that chilled me. And it was still! Any sound from the Selenites in the world beneath, even had died away. It was as still as death. Save for the faint stir of the shrub about me in the little breeze that was rising, there was no sound nor shadow of a sound. And the breeze blew chill.

Confound Cavor!

I took a deep breath. I put my hands to the sides of my mouth. 'Cavor!' I bawled, and the sound was like some manikin shouting far away.

I looked at the handkerchief, I looked behind me at the broadening shadow of the westward cliff, I looked under my hand at the sun. It seemed to me that almost visibly it was creeping down the sky.

I felt I must act instantly if I was to save Cavor. I whipped off my vest and flung it as a mark on the sere bayonets of the shrubs behind me, and then set off in a straight line towards the handkerchief. Perhaps it was a couple of miles away – a matter of a few hundred leaps and strides. I have already told how one seemed to hang through those lunar leaps. In each suspense I sought Cavor, and marvelled why he should be hidden. In

each leap I could feel the sun setting behind me. Each time I touched the ground I was tempted to go back.

A last leap and I was in the depression below our handkerchief, a stride, and I stood on our former vantage point within arm's reach of it. I stood up straight and scanned the world about me, between its lengthening bars of shadow. Far away, down a long declivity, was the opening of the tunnel up which we had fled, and my shadow reached towards it, stretched towards it, and touched it, like a finger of the night.

Not a sign of Cavor, not a sound in all the stillness, only that the stir and waving of the scrub and of the shadows increased. And suddenly and violently I shivered. 'Cav—' I began, and realized once more the uselessness of the human voice in that thin air.

Silence. The silence of death.

Then it was my eye caught something – a little thing, lying perhaps fifty yards away down the slope, amidst a litter of bent and broken branches. What was it? I knew, and yet for some reason I would not know.

I went nearer to it. It was the little cricket cap Cavor had worn. I did not touch it, I stood looking at it.

I saw then that the scattered branches about it had been forcibly smashed and trampled. I hesitated, stepped forward and picked it up.

I stood with Cavor's cap in my hand, staring at the trampled reeds and thorns about me. On some of them were little smears of something dark, something that I dared not touch. A dozen yards away, perhaps, the rising breeze dragged something into view, something small and vividly white.

It was a little piece of paper crumpled tightly, as though it had been clutched tightly. I picked it up, and on it were smears of red. My eye caught faint pencil marks. I smoothed it out, and saw uneven and broken writing ending at last in a crooked streak upon the paper.

I set myself to decipher this.

'I have been injured about the knee, I think my kneecap is hurt, and I cannot run or crawl,' it began – pretty distinctly written.

Then less legibly: 'They have been chasing me for some time, and it is only a question of' – the word 'time' seemed to have been written here and erased in favour of something illegible – 'before they get me. They are beating all about me.'

Then the writing became convulsive. 'I can hear them,' I guessed the tracing meant, and then it was quite unreadable for a space. Then came a little string of words that were quite distinct: 'a different sort of Selenite altogether, who appears to be directing the—' The writing became a mere hasty confusion again.

'They have larger brain cases – much larger, and slenderer bodies, and very short legs. They make gentle noises, and move with organized deliberation. . . .

'And though I am wounded and helpless here, their appearance still gives me hope—' That was like Cavor. 'They have not shot at me or attempted . . . injury. I intend—'

Then came the sudden streak of the pencil across the paper, and on the back and edges – blood!

And as I stood there stupid and perplexed, with this dumbfounding relic in my hand, something very soft and light and chill touched my hand for a moment and ceased to be, and then a thing, a little white speck, drifted athwart a shadow. It was a tiny snowflake, the first snowflake, the herald of the night.

I looked up with a start, and the sky had darkened now almost to blackness, and was thick with a gathering multitude of coldly watchful stars. I looked eastward, and the light of that shrivelled world was touched with a sombre bronze; westward, and the sun, robbed now by a thickening white mist of half its heat and splendour, was touching the crater rim, was sinking out of sight, and all the shrubs and jagged and tumbled rocks stood out against it in a bristling disorder of black shapes. Into the great lake of darkness westward, a vast wreath of mist was sinking. A cold wind set all the crater shivering. Suddenly, for a moment, I was in a puff of falling snow, and all the world about me grey and dim.

And then it was I heard, not loud and penetrating as at first, but faint and dim like a dying voice, that tolling, that same tolling that had welcomed the coming of the day: Boom! . . . Boom! . . . Boom! . . .

It echoed about the crater, it seemed to throb with the throbbing of the greater stars, the blood-red crescent of the sun's disk sank as it tolled out: Boom! . . . Boom! . . . Boom!

What had happened to Cavor? All through that tolling I stood there stupidly, and at last the tolling ceased.

And suddenly the open mouth of the tunnel down below there shut like an eye and vanished out of sight.

Then indeed was I alone.

Over me, around me, closing in on me, embracing me ever nearer, was the Eternal; that which was before the beginning, and that which triumphs over the end; that enormous void in which all light and life and being is but the thin and vanishing splendour of a falling star, the cold, the stillness, the silence – the infinite and final Night of space.

The sense of solitude and desolation became the sense of an overwhelming presence that stooped towards me, that almost touched me.

'No,' I cried. 'No! Not yet! not yet! Wait! Wait! Oh wait!' My voice went up to a shriek. I flung the crumpled paper from me, scrambled back to the crest to take my bearings, and then, with all the will that was in me, leapt out towards the mark I had left, dim and distant now in the very margin of the shadow.

Leap, leap, leap, and each leap was seven ages.

Before me the pale serpent-girdled section of the sun sank and sank, and the advancing shadow swept to seize the sphere before I could reach it. I was two miles away, a hundred leaps or more, and the air about me was thinning out as it thins under an air-pump, and the cold was gripping at my joints. But had I died, I should have died leaping. Once, and then again my foot slipped on the gathering snow as I leapt and shortened my leap; once I fell short into bushes that crashed and smashed into dusty chips and nothingness, and once I stumbled as I dropped, and rolled head over heels into a gully, and rose bruised and bleeding and confused as to my direction.

But such incidents were as nothing to the intervals, those awful pauses when one drifted through the air towards that pouring tide of night. My breathing made a piping noise, and it was as though knives were whirling in my lungs. My heart seemed to beat against the top of my brain. 'Shall I reach it? O Heaven! Shall I reach it?'

My whole being became anguish.

'Lie down!' screamed my pain and despair; 'Lie down!'

The nearer I struggled, the more awfully remote it seemed. I was numb, I stumbled, I bruised and cut myself and did not bleed.

It was in sight.

I fell on all fours, and my lungs whooped.

I crawled. The frost gathered on my lips, icicles hung from my moustache, I was white with the freezing atmosphere.

I was a dozen yards from it. My eyes had become dim. 'Lie down!' screamed despair; 'Lie down!'

I touched it, and halted. 'Too late!' screamed despair; 'Lie down!'

I fought stiffly with it. I was on the manhole lip, a stupefied, half-dead being. The snow was all about me. I pulled myself in. There lurked within a little warmer air.

The snowflakes – the airflakes – danced in about me, as I tried with chilling hands to thrust the valve in and spun it tight and hard. I sobbed. 'I will,' I chattered in my teeth. And then, with fingers that quivered and felt brittle, I turned to the shutter studs.

As I fumbled with the switches – for I had never controlled them before – I could see dimly through the steaming glass the blazing red streamers of the sinking sun, dancing and flickering through the snowstorm, and the black forms of the scrub thickening and bending and breaking beneath the accumulating snow. Thicker whirled the snow and thicker, black against the light. What if even now the switches overcame me?

Then something clicked under my hands, and in an instant that last vision of the moon world was hidden from my eyes. I was in the silence and darkness of the inter-planetary sphere.

CHAPTER XX

Mr Bedford in Infinite Space

It was almost as though I had been killed. Indeed, I could imagine a man suddenly and violently killed would feel very much as I did. One moment, a passion of agonizing existence and fear; the next, darkness and stillness, neither light nor life nor sun, moon nor stars, the blank infinite. Although the thing was done by my own act, although I had already tasted this very effect in Cavor's company, I felt astonished, dumbfounded, and overwhelmed. I seemed to be borne upward into an enormous darkness. My fingers floated off the studs, I hung as if I were annihilated, and at last very softly and gently I came against the bale and the golden chain, and the crowbars that had drifted to the middle of the sphere.

I do not know how long that drifting took. In the sphere of course, even more than on the moon, one's earthly time sense was ineffectual. At the touch of the bale it was as if I had awakened from a dreamless sleep. I immediately perceived that if I wanted to keep awake and alive I must get a light or open a window, so as to get a grip of something with my eyes. And besides I was cold. I kicked off from the bale, therefore, clawed on to the thin cords within the glass, crawled along until I got to the manhole rim, and so got my bearings for the light and blind studs, took a shove off, and flying once round the bale, and getting a scare from something big and flimsy that was drifting loose, I got my hand on the cord quite close to the studs, and reached them. I lit the little lamp first of all to see what it was I had collided with, and discovered that old copy of *Lloyd's News* had slipped its moorings, and was adrift in the void. That brought me out of the infinite to my own proper dimensions again. It made me laugh and pant for a time, and suggested the idea of a little oxygen from one of the cylinders. After that I lit the heater until I felt warm, and then I took food. Then I set to work in a very gingerly fashion on the Cavorite blinds, to see if I could guess by any means how the sphere was travelling.

The first blind I opened I shut at once, and hung for a time flattened and blinded by the sunlight that had hit me. After thinking a little I started upon the windows at right angles to this one, and got the huge crescent moon and the little crescent earth behind it, the second time. I was amazed to find how far I was from the moon. I had reckoned that not only should I have little or none of the 'kick-off' that the earth's atmosphere had given us at our start, but that the tangential 'fly off' of the moon's spin would be at least twenty-eight times less than the earth's. I had expected to discover myself hanging over our crater, and on the edge of the night, but

all that was now only a part of the outline of the white crescent that filled the sky. And Cavor—?

He was already infinitesimal.

I tried to imagine what could have happened to him. But at that time I could think of nothing but death. I seemed to see him, bent and smashed at the foot of some interminably high cascade of blue. And all about him the stupid insects stared. . . .

Under the inspiring touch of the drifting newspaper I became practical again for a while. It was quite clear to me that what I had to do was to get back to earth, but as far as I could see I was drifting away from it. Whatever had happened to Cavor, even if he was still alive, which seemed to me incredible after that blood-stained scrap, I was powerless to help him. There he was, living or dead behind the mantle of that rayless night, and there he must remain at least until I could summon our fellow men to his assistance. Should I do that? Something of the sort I had in my mind; to come back to earth if it were possible, and then as maturer consideration might determine, either to show and explain the sphere to a few discreet persons, and act with them, or else to keep my secret, sell my gold, obtain weapons, provisions, and an assistant, and return with these advantages to deal on equal terms with the flimsy people of the moon, to rescue Cavor, if that were still possible, and at any rate to procure a sufficient supply of gold to place my subsequent proceedings on a firmer basis. But that was hoping far; I had first to get back.

I set myself to decide just exactly how the return to earth could be contrived. As I struggled with that problem I ceased to worry about what I should do when I got there. At last my only care was to get back.

I puzzled out at last that my best chance would be to drop back towards the moon as near as I dared in order to gather velocity, then to shut my windows and fly behind it, and when I was past to open my earthward windows, and so get off at a good pace homeward. But whether I should ever reach the earth by that device, or whether I might not simply find myself spinning about it in some hyperbolic or parabolic curve or other, I could not tell. Later I had a happy inspiration, and by opening certain windows to the moon, which had appeared in the sky in front of the earth, I turned my course aside so as to head off the earth, which it had become evident to me I must pass behind without some such expedient. I did a very great deal of complicated thinking over these problems – for I am no mathematician – and in the end I am certain it was much more my good luck than my reasoning that enabled me to hit the earth. Had I known then, as I know now, the mathematical chances there were against me, I doubt if I should have troubled even to touch the studs to make any attempt. And having puzzled out what I considered to be the thing to do, I opened all my moonward windows, and squatted down – the effort lifted me for a

time some feet or so into the air, and I hung there in the oddest way – and waited for the crescent to get bigger and bigger until I felt I was near enough for safety. Then I would shut the windows, fly past the moon with the velocity I had got from it – if I did not smash upon it – and so go on towards the earth.

And that is what I did.

At last I felt my moonward start was sufficient. I shut out the sight of the moon from my eyes, and in a state of mind that was, I now recall, incredibly free from anxiety or any distressful quality, I sat down to begin a vigil in that little speck of matter in infinite space that would last until I should strike the earth. The heater had made the sphere tolerably warm, the air had been refreshed by the oxygen, and except for that faint congestion of the head that was always with me while I was away from earth, I felt entire physical comfort. I had extinguished the light again, lest it should fail me in the end; I was in darkness, save for the earthshine and the glitter of the stars below me. Everything was so absolutely silent and still that I might indeed have been the only being in the universe, and yet, strangely enough, I had no more feeling of loneliness or fear than if I had been lying in bed on earth. Now, this seems all the stranger to me, since during my last hours in that crater of the moon, the sense of my utter loneliness had been an agony. . . .

Incredible as it will seem, this interval of time that I spent in space has no sort of proportion to any other interval of time in my life. Sometimes it seemed as though I sat through immeasurable eternities like some god upon a lotus leaf, and again as though there was a momentary pause as I leapt from moon to earth. In truth, it was altogether some weeks of earthly time. But I had done with care and anxiety, hunger or fear, for that space. I floated, thinking with a strange breadth and freedom of all that we had undergone, and of all my life and motives, and the secret issues of my being. I seemed to myself to have grown greater and greater, to have lost all sense of movement; to be floating amidst the stars, and always the sense of earth's littleness and the infinite littleness of my life upon it, was implicit in my thoughts.

I can't profess to explain the things that happened in my mind. No doubt they could all be traced directly or indirectly to the curious physical conditions under which I was living. I set them down here just for what they are worth, and without any comment. The most prominent quality of it was a pervading doubt of my own identity. I became, if I may so express it, dissociate from Bedford; I looked down on Bedford as a trivial, incidental thing with which I chanced to be connected. I saw Bedford in many relations – as an ass or as a poor beast, where I had hitherto been inclined to regard him with a quiet pride as a very spirited or rather forcible person. I saw him not only as an ass, but as the son of many generations of asses. I reviewed his

schooldays and his early manhood, and his first encounter with love, very much as one might review the proceedings of an ant in the sand. . . . Something of that period of lucidity I regret still hangs about me, and I doubt if I shall ever recover the full-bodied self-satisfaction of my early days. But at the time the thing was not in the least painful, because I had that extraordinary persuasion that, as a matter of fact, I was no more Bedford than I was anyone else, but only a mind floating in the still serenity of space. Why should I be disturbed about this Bedford's shortcomings? I was not responsible for him or them.

For a time I struggled against this really very grotesque delusion. I tried to summon the memory of vivid moments, of tender or intense emotions to my assistance; I felt that if I could recall one genuine twinge of feeling the growing severance would be stopped. But I could not do it. I saw Bedford rushing down Chancery Lane, hat on the back of his head, coat tails flying out, *en route* for his public examination. I saw him dodging and bumping against, and even saluting, other similar little creatures in that swarming gutter of people. Me? I saw Bedford that same evening in the sitting-room of a certain lady, and his hat was on the table beside him, and it wanted brushing badly, and he was in tears. Me? I saw him with that lady in various attitudes and emotions – I never felt so detached before. . . . I saw him hurrying off to Lympne to write a play, and accosting Cavor, and in his shirt sleeves working at the sphere, and walking out to Canterbury because he was afraid to come! Me? I did not believe it.

I still reasoned that all this was hallucination due to my solitude, and the fact that I had lost all weight and sense of resistance. I endeavoured to recover that sense by banging myself about the sphere, by pinching my hands and clasping them together. Among other things I lit the light, captured that torn copy of *Lloyd's*, and read those convincingly realistic advertisements again about the Cutaway bicycle, and the gentleman of private means, and the lady in distress who was selling those 'forks and spoons'. There was no doubt they existed surely enough, and, said I, 'This is your world, and you are Bedford, and you are going back to live among things like that for all the rest of your life.' But the doubts within me could still argue: 'It is not you that is reading, it is Bedford, but you are not Bedford, you know. That's just where the mistake comes in.'

'Confound it!' I cried; 'And if I am not Bedford, what am I?'

But in that direction no light was forthcoming, though the strangest fancies came drifting into my brain, queer remote suspicions, like shadows seen from far away . . . Do you know, I had a sort of idea that really I was something quite outside not only the world, but all worlds, and out of space and time, and that this poor Bedford was just a peephole through which I looked at life? . . .

Bedford! However I disavowed him, there I was most certainly bound up with him, and I knew that wherever or whatever I might be, I must needs feel the stress of his desires, and sympathize with all his joys and sorrows until his life should end. And with the dying of Bedford – what then? . . .

Enough of this remarkable phase of my experiences! I tell it here simply to show how one's isolation and departure from this planet touched not only the functions and feeling of every organ of the body, but indeed also the very fabric of the mind, with strange and unanticipated disturbances. All through the major portion of that vast space journey I hung thinking of such immaterial things as these, hung dissociated and apathetic, a cloudy megalomaniac, as it were, amidst the stars and planets in the void of space; and not only the world to which I was returning, but the blue-lit caverns of the Selenites, their helmet faces, their gigantic and wonderful machines, and the fate of Cavor, dragged helpless into that world, seemed infinitely minute and altogether trivial things to me.

Until at last I began to feel the pull of the earth upon my being, drawing me back again to the life that is real for men. And then, indeed, it grew clearer and clearer to me that I was quite certainly Bedford after all, and returning after amazing adventures to this world of ours, and with a life that I was very likely to lose in this return. I set myself to puzzle out the conditions under which I must fall to earth.

CHAPTER XXI

Mr Bedford at Littlestone

My line of flight was about parallel with the surface as I came into the upper air. The temperature of the sphere began to rise forthwith. I knew it behoved me to drop at once. Far below me, in a darkling twilight, stretched a great expanse of sea. I opened every window I could, and fell – out of sunshine into evening, and out of evening into night. Vaster grew the earth and vaster, swallowing up the stars, and the silvery translucent starlit veil of cloud it wore spread out to catch me. At last the world seemed no longer a sphere but flat, and then concave. It was no longer a planet in the sky, but the world of Man. I shut all but an inch or so of earthward window, and dropped with a slackening velocity. The broadening water, now so near that I could see the dark glitter of the waves, rushed up to meet me. The sphere became very hot. I snapped the last strip of window, and sat scowling and biting my knuckles, waiting for the impact. . . .

The sphere hit the water with a huge splash: it must have sent it fathoms high. At the splash I flung the Cavorite shutters open. Down I went, but slower and slower, and then I felt the sphere pressing against my feet, and so drove up again as a bubble drives. And at the last I was floating and rocking upon the surface of the sea, and my journey in space was at an end.

The night was dark and overcast. Two yellow pin-points far away showed the passing of a ship, and nearer was a red glare that came and went. Had not the electricity of my glow-lamp exhausted itself, I could have got picked up that night. In spite of the inordinate fatigue I was beginning to feel, I was excited now, and for a time hopeful, in a feverish, impatient way, that so my travelling might end.

But at last I ceased to move about, and sat, wrists on knees, staring at a distant red light. It swayed up and down, rocking, rocking. My excitement passed. I realized I had yet to spend another night at least in the sphere. I perceived myself infinitely heavy and fatigued. And so I fell asleep.

A change in my rhythmic motion awakened me. I peered through the refracting glass, and saw that I had come aground upon a huge shallow of sand. Far away I seemed to see houses and trees, and seaward a curved, vague distortion of a ship hung between sea and sky.

I stood up and staggered. My one desire was to emerge. The manhole was upward, and I wrestled with the screw. Slowly I opened the manhole. At last the air was singing in again as once it had sung out. But this time I did not wait until the pressure was adjusted. In another moment I had the weight of

the window on my hands, and I was open, wide open, to the old familiar sky of earth.

The air hit me on the chest so that I gasped. I dropped the glass screw. I cried out, put my hands to my chest, and sat down. For a time I was in pain. Then I took deep breaths. At last I could rise and move about again.

I tried to thrust my head through the manhole, and the sphere rolled over. It was as though something had lugged my head down directly it emerged. I ducked back sharply, or I should have been pinned face under water. After some wriggling and shoving I managed to crawl out upon sand, over which the retreating waves still came and went.

I did not attempt to stand up. It seemed to me that my body must be suddenly changed to lead. Mother Earth had her grip on me now – no Cavorite intervening. I sat down heedless of the water that came over my feet.

It was dawn, a grey dawn, rather overcast, but showing here and there a long patch of greenish grey. Some way out a ship was lying at anchor, a pale silhouette of a ship with one yellow light. The water came rippling in in long shallow waves. Away to the right curved the land, a shingle bank with little hovels, and at last a lighthouse, a sailing mark and a point. Inland stretched a space of level sand, broken here and there by pools of water, and ending a mile away perhaps in a low shore of scrub. To the north-east some isolated watering-place was visible, a row of gaunt lodging-houses, the tallest things that I could see on earth, dull dabs against the brightening sky. What strange men can have reared these vertical piles in such an amplitude of space I do not know. There they are, like pieces of Brighton lost in the waste.

For a long time I sat there, yawning and rubbing my face. At last I struggled to rise. It made me feel that I was lifting a weight. I stood up.

I stared at the distant houses. For the first time since our starvation in the crater I thought of earthly food. 'Bacon,' I whispered, 'eggs. Good toast and good coffee . . . And how the devil am I going to get all this stuff to Lympne?' I wondered where I was. It was an east shore anyhow, and I had seen Europe before I dropped.

I heard footsteps scrunching in the sand, and a little round-faced, friendly-looking man in flannels, with a bathing towel wrapped about his shoulders, and his bathing dress over his arm, appeared up the beach. I knew instantly that I must be in England. He was staring almost intently at the sphere and me. He advanced staring. I daresay I looked a ferocious savage enough – dirty, unkempt, to an indescribable degree; but it did not occur to me at the time. He stopped at a distance of twenty yards. 'Hul-lo, my man!' he said doubtfully.

'Hullo yourself!' said I.

He advanced, reassured by that. 'What on earth is that thing?' he asked.

'Can you tell me where I am?' I asked.

'That's Littlestone,' he said, pointing to the houses; 'and that's Dungeness! Have you just landed? What's that thing you've got? Some sort of machine?'

'Yes.'

'Have you floated ashore? Have you been wrecked or something? What is it?'

I meditated swiftly. I made an estimate of the little man's appearance as he drew nearer. 'By Jove!' he said, 'You've had a time of it! I thought you— Well – where were you cast away? Is that thing a sort of floating thing for saving life?'

I decided to take that line for the present. I made a few vague affirmatives. 'I want help,' I said hoarsely. 'I want to get some stuff up the beach – stuff I can't very well leave about.' I became aware of three other pleasant-looking young men with towels, blazers, and straw hats, coming down the sands towards me. Evidently the early bathing section of this Littlestone!

'Help!' said the young man; 'Rather!' He became vaguely active. 'What particularly do you want done?' He turned round and gesticulated. The three young men accelerated their pace. In a minute they were about me, plying me with questions I was indisposed to answer. 'I'll tell all that later,' I said. 'I'm dead beat. I'm a rag.'

'Come up to the hotel,' said the foremost little man. 'We'll look after that thing there.'

I hesitated. 'I can't,' I said. 'In that sphere there's two big bars of gold.'

They looked incredulously at one another, then at me with a new enquiry. I went to the sphere, stooped, crept in, and presently they had the Selenites' crowbars and the broken chain before them. If I had not been so horribly fagged I could have laughed at them. It was like kittens round a beetle. They didn't know what to do with the stuff. The fat little man stooped and lifted the end of one of the bars, and then dropped it with a grunt. Then they all did.

'It's lead, or gold!' said one.

'Oh, it's *gold!*' said another.

'Gold, right enough,' said the third.

Then they all stared at me, and then they all stared at the ship lying at anchor.

'I say!' cried the little man. 'But where did you get that?'

I was too tired to keep up a lie. 'I got it in the moon.'

I saw them stare at one another.

'Look here!' said I. 'I'm not going to argue now. Help me carry these lumps of gold up to the hotel – I guess, with rests, two of you can manage one, and I'll trail this chain thing – and I'll tell you more when I've had some food.'

'And how about that thing?'

'It won't hurt there,' I said. 'Anyhow – confound it! – it must stop there now. If the tide comes up, it will float all right.'

And in a state of enormous wonderment, these young men most obediently hoisted my treasures on their shoulders, and with limbs that felt like lead I headed a sort of procession towards that distant fragment of 'sea-front'. Halfway there we were reinforced by two awe-stricken little girls with spades, and later a lean little boy, with a penetrating sniff, appeared. He was, I remember, wheeling a bicycle, and he accompanied us at a distance of about a hundred yards on our right flank, and then, I suppose, gave us up as uninteresting, mounted his bicycle, and rode off over the level sands in the direction of the sphere.

I glanced back after him.

'*He* won't touch it,' said the stout young man reassuringly, and I was only too willing to be reassured.

At first something of the grey of the morning was in my mind, but presently the sun disengaged itself from the level clouds of the horizon and lit the world, and turned the leaden sea to glittering waters. My spirits rose. A sense of the vast importance of the things I had done and had yet to do came with the sunlight into my mind. I laughed aloud as the foremost man staggered under my gold. When indeed I took my place in the world, how amazed the world would be!

If it had not been for my inordinate fatigue, the landlord of the Littlestone hotel would have been amusing, as he hesitated between my gold and my respectable company on the one hand, and my filthy appearance on the other. But at last I found myself in a terrestrial bathroom once more with warm water to wash myself with, and a change of raiment, preposterously small indeed, but anyhow clean, that the genial little man had lent me. He lent me a razor too, but I could not screw up my resolution to attack even the outposts of the bristling beard that covered my face.

I sat down to an English breakfast and ate with a sort of languid appetite – an appetite many weeks old, and very decrepit – and stirred myself to answer the questions of the four young men. And I told them the truth.

'Well,' said I, 'as you press me – I got it in the moon.'

'The moon?'

'Yes, the moon in the sky.'

'But how do you mean?'

'What I say, confound it!'

'That you have just come from the moon?'

'Exactly! Through space – in that ball.' And I took a delicious mouthful of egg. I made a private note that when I went back to the moon I would take a box of eggs.

I could see clearly that they did not believe one word of what I told them, but evidently they considered me the most respectable liar they had ever

met. They glanced at one another, and then concentrated the fire of their eyes on me. I fancy they expected a clue to me in the way I helped myself to salt. They seemed to find something significant in my peppering my egg. These strangely shaped masses of gold they had staggered under held their minds. There the lumps lay in front of me, each worth thousands of pounds, and as impossible for anyone to steal as a house or a piece of land. As I looked at their curious faces over my coffee-cup, I realized something of the enormous wilderness of explanations into which I should have to wander to render myself comprehensible again.

'You don't *really* mean—' began the youngest young man, in the tone of one who speaks to an obstinate child.

'Just pass me that toast-rack,' I said, and shut him up completely.

'But look here, I say,' began one of the others. 'We're not going to believe that, you know.'

'Ah, well,' said I, and shrugged my shoulders.

'He doesn't want to tell us,' said the youngest young man in a stage aside; and then, with an appearance of great *sang-froid*, 'You don't mind if I take a cigarette?'

I waved him a cordial assent, and proceeded with my breakfast. Two of the others went and looked out of the further window and talked inaudibly. I was struck by a thought. 'The tide,' I said, 'is running out?'

There was a pause, a doubt who should answer me. 'It's near the ebb,' said the fat little man.

'Well, anyhow,' I said, 'it won't float far.'

I decapitated my third egg, and began a little speech. 'Look here,' I said. 'Please don't imagine I'm surly or telling you uncivil lies, or anything of that sort. I'm forced almost to be a little short and mysterious. I can quite understand this is as queer as it can be, and that your imaginations must be going it. I can assure you, you're in at a memorable time. But I can't make it clear to you now – it's impossible. I give you my word of honour I've come from the moon, and that's all I can tell you. . . . All the same I'm tremendously obliged to you, you know, tremendously. I hope that my manner hasn't in any way given you offence.'

'Oh, not in the least!' said the youngest young man affably. 'We can quite understand,' and staring hard at me all the time, he heeled his chair back until it very nearly upset, and recovered with some exertion. 'Not a bit of it,' said the fat young man. 'Don't you imagine *that*!' and they all got up and dispersed, and walked about and lit cigarettes, and generally tried to show they were perfectly amiable and disengaged, and entirely free from the slightest curiosity about me and the sphere. 'I'm going to keep an eye on that ship out there all the same,' I heard one of them remarking in an undertone. If only they could have forced themselves to it, they would, I believe, even have gone out and left me. I went on with my third egg.

'The weather,' the fat little man remarked presently, 'has been immense, has it not? I don't know *when* we have had such a summer. . . .'

Phoo – whizz! Like a tremendous rocket!

And somewhere a window was broken. . . .

'What's that?' said I.

'It isn't—?' cried the little man, and rushed to the corner window.

All the others rushed to the window likewise. I sat staring at them.

Suddenly I leapt up, knocked over my third egg, and rushed for the window also. I had just thought of something. 'Nothing to be seen there,' cried the little man, rushing for the door.

'It's that boy!' I cried, bawling in hoarse fury; 'It's that accursed boy!' and turning about I pushed the waiter aside – he was just bringing me some more toast – and rushed violently out of the room and down and out upon the queer little esplanade in front of the hotel.

The sea, which had been smooth, was rough now with hurrying cat's-paws, and all about where the sphere had been was tumbled water like the wake of a ship. Above, a little puff of cloud whirled like dispersing smoke, and the three or four people on the beach were staring up with interrogative faces towards the point of that unexpected report. And that was all! Boots and waiter and the four young men in blazers came rushing out behind me. Shouts came from windows and doors, and all sorts of worrying people came into sight – agape.

For a time I stood there, too overwhelmed by this new development to think of the people.

At first I was too stunned to see the thing as any definite disaster – I was just stunned, as a man is by some accidental violent blow. It is only afterwards he begins to appreciate his specific injury.

'Good Lord!'

I felt as though somebody was pouring funk out of a can down the back of my neck. My legs became feeble. I had got the first intimation of what the disaster meant for me. There was that confounded boy – sky high! I was utterly 'left'. There was the gold in the coffee-room – my only possession on earth. How would it all work out? The general effect was of a gigantic unmanageable confusion.

'I say,' said the voice of the little man behind. 'I *say*, you know.'

I wheeled about, and there were twenty or thirty people, a sort of irreg- ular investment of people, all bombarding me with dumb interrogation, with infinite doubt and suspicion. I felt the compulsion of their eyes intolerably. I groaned aloud.

'I *can't*!' I shouted. 'I tell you I can't! I'm not equal to it! You must puzzle and – and be damned to you!'

I gesticulated convulsively. He receded a step as though I had threatened him. I made a bolt through them into the hotel. I charged back into the

coffee-room, rang the bell furiously. I gripped the waiter as he entered. 'D'ye hear?' I shouted. 'Get help and carry these bars up to my room right away.'

He failed to understand me, and I shouted and raved at him. A scared-looking little old man in a green apron appeared, and further two of the young men in flannels. I made a dash at them and commandeered their services. As soon as the gold was in my room I felt free to quarrel. 'Now get out,' I shouted; 'all of you get out if you don't want to see a man go mad before your eyes!' And I helped the waiter by the shoulder as he hesitated in the doorway. And then, as soon as I had the door locked on them all, I tore off the little man's clothes again, shied them right and left, and got into bed forthwith. And there I lay swearing and panting and cooling for a very long time.

At last I was calm enough to get out of bed and ring up the round-eyed waiter for a flannel nightshirt, a soda and whisky, and some good cigars. And these things being procured me, after an exasperating delay that drove me several times to the bell, I locked the door again and proceeded very deliberately to look the entire situation in the face.

The net result of the great experiment presented itself as an absolute failure. It was a rout, and I was the sole survivor. It was an absolute collapse, and this was the final disaster. There was nothing for it but to save myself, and as much as I could in the way of prospects from our *débâcle*. At one fatal crowning blow all my vague resolutions of return and recovery had vanished. My intention of going back to the moon, of getting a sphereful of gold, and afterwards of having a fragment of Cavorite analysed and so recovering the great secret – perhaps, finally, even of recovering Cavor's body – all these ideas vanished altogether.

I was the sole survivor, and that was all.

I think that going to bed was one of the luckiest ideas I have ever had in an emergency. I really believe I should either have got loose-headed or done some fatal, indiscreet thing. But there, locked in and secure from all interruption, I could think out the position in all its bearings and make my arrangements at leisure.

Of course it was quite clear to me what had happened to the boy. He had crawled into the sphere, meddled with the studs, shut the Cavorite windows, and gone up. It was highly improbable he had screwed in the manhole stopper, and, even if he had, the chances were a thousand to one against his getting back. It was fairly evident that he would gravitate with my bales to somewhere near the middle of the sphere and remain there, and so cease to be a legitimate terrestrial interest, however remarkable he might seem to the inhabitants of some remote quarter of space. I very speedily convinced myself on that point. And as for any responsibility I might have in the matter, the more I reflected upon that, the clearer it

became that if only I kept quiet about things, I need not trouble myself about that. If I was faced by sorrowing parents demanding their lost boy, I had merely to demand my lost sphere – or ask them what they meant. At first I had had a vision of weeping parents and guardians, and all sorts of complications; but now I saw that I simply had to keep my mouth shut, and nothing in that way could arise.

And, indeed, the more I lay and smoked and thought, the more evident became the wisdom of impenetrability.

It is within the right of every British citizen, provided he does not commit damage nor indecorum, to appear suddenly wherever he pleases, and as ragged and filthy as he pleases, and with whatever amount of virgin gold he sees fit to encumber himself, and no one has any right at all to hinder and detain him in this procedure. I formulated that at last to myself, and repeated it over as a sort of private Magna Charta of my liberty.

Once I had put that issue on one side, I could take up and consider in an equable manner certain considerations I had scarcely dared to think of before, namely, those arising out of the circumstances of my bankruptcy. But now, looking at this matter calmly and at leisure, I could see that if only I suppressed my identity by a temporary assumption of some less well-known name, and if I retained the two months' beard that had grown upon me, the risks of any annoyance from the spiteful creditor to whom I have already alluded became very small indeed. From that to a definite course of rational worldly action was plain sailing. It was all amazingly petty, no doubt, but what was there remaining for me to do?

Whatever I did I was resolved that I would keep myself level and right side up.

I ordered up writing materials, and addressed a letter to the New Romney Bank – the nearest, the waiter informed me – telling the manager I wished to open an account with him, and requesting him to send two trustworthy persons properly authenticated in a cab with a good horse to fetch some hundredweight of gold with which I happened to be encumbered. I signed the letter 'Blake,' which seemed to me to be a thoroughly respectable sort of name. This done, I got a Folkestone Blue Book, picked out an outfitter, and asked him to send a cutter to measure me for a drab tweed suit, ordering at the same time a valise, dressing bag, brown boots, shirts, hats (to fit) and so forth; and from a watchmaker I also ordered a watch. And these letters being despatched, I had up as good a lunch as the hotel could give, and then lay smoking a cigar, as calm and ordinary as possible, until in accordance with my instructions two duly authenticated clerks came from the bank and weighed and took away my gold. After which I pulled the clothes over my ears in order to drown any knocking, and went very comfortably to sleep.

I went to sleep. No doubt it was a prosaic thing for the first man back from the moon to do, and I can imagine that the young and imaginative

reader will find my behaviour disappointing. But I was horribly fatigued and bothered, and – confound it! – what else was there to do? There certainly was not the remotest chance of my being believed, if I had told my story then, and it would certainly have subjected me to intolerable annoyances. I went to sleep. When at last I woke up again I was ready to face the world, as I have always been accustomed to face it since I came to years of discretion. And so I got away to Italy, and there it is I am writing this story. If the world will not have it as fact, then the world may take it as fiction. It is no concern of mine.

And now that the account is finished, I am amazed to think how completely this adventure is gone and done with. Everybody believes that Cavor was a not very brilliant scientific experimenter who blew up his house and himself at Lympne, and they explain the bang that followed my arrival at Littlestone by a reference to the experiments with explosives that are going on continually at the government establishment of Lydd, two miles away. I must confess that hitherto I have not acknowledged my share in the disappearance of Master Tommy Simmons, which was that little boy's name. That, perhaps, may prove a difficult item of corroboration to explain away. They account for my appearance in rags with two bars of indisputable gold upon the Littlestone beach in various ingenious ways – it doesn't worry me what they think of me. They say I have strung all these things together to avoid being questioned too closely as to the source of my wealth. I would like to see the man who could invent a story that would hold together like this one. Well, they must take it as fiction – there it is.

I have told my story – and now I suppose I have to take up the worries of this terrestrial life again. Even if one has been to the moon, one has still to earn a living. So I am working here at Amalfi, on the scenario of that play I sketched before Cavor came walking into my world, and I am trying to piece my life together as it was before ever I saw him. I must confess that I find it hard to keep my mind on the play when the moonshine comes into my room. It is full moon here, and last night I was out on the pergola for hours, staring away at that shining blankness that hides so much. Imagine it! Tables and chairs, and trestles and bars of gold! Confound it! – If only one could hit on that Cavorite again! But a thing like that doesn't come twice in a life. Here I am, a little better off than I was at Lympne, and that is all. And Cavor has committed suicide in a more elaborate way than any human being ever did before. So the story closes as finally and completely as a dream. It fits in so little with all the other things of life, so much of it is so utterly remote from all human experience, the leaping, the eating, the breathing, and these weightless times, that indeed there are moments when, in spite of my moon gold, I do more than half believe myself that the whole thing was a dream. . . .

CHAPTER XXII

The Astonishing Communication of Mr Julius Wendigee

When I had finished my account of my return to the earth at Littlestone I wrote 'The End', made a flourish, and threw my pen aside, fully believing that the whole story of the First Men in the Moon was done. Not only had I done this, but I had placed my manuscript in the hands of a literary agent, had permitted it to be sold, had seen the greater portion of it appear in the *Strand Magazine*, and was setting to work again upon the scenario of the play I had commenced at Lympne before I realized that the end was not yet. And then, following me from Amalfi to Algiers, there reached me (it is now about six months ago) one of the most astounding communications I have ever been fated to receive. Briefly, it informed me that Mr Julius Wendigee, a Dutch electrician, who has been experimenting with certain apparatus akin to the apparatus used by Mr Tesla in America, in the hope of discovering some method of communication with Mars, was receiving day by day a curiously fragmentary message in English, which was indisputably emanating from Mr Cavor in the moon.

At first I thought the thing was an elaborate practical joke by someone who had seen the manuscript of my narrative. I answered Mr Wendigee jestingly, but he replied in a manner that put such suspicion altogether aside, and in a state of inconceivable excitement I hurried from Algiers to the little observatory upon the Monte Rosa in which he was working. In the presence of his record and his appliances – and above all of the messages from Cavor that were coming to hand – my lingering doubts vanished. I decided at once to accept a proposal he made me to remain with him, assisting him to take down the record from day to day, and endeavouring with him to send a message back to the moon. Cavor, we learnt, was not only alive but free, in the midst of an almost inconceivable community of these ant-like beings, these ant-men, in the blue darkness of the lunar caves. He was lamed, it seemed, but otherwise in quite good health – in better health, he distinctly said, than he usually enjoyed on earth. He had had a fever, but it had left no bad effects. But curiously enough he seemed to be labouring under a conviction that I was either dead in the moon crater or lost in the deep of space.

His message began to be received by Mr Wendigee when that gentleman was engaged in quite a different investigation. The reader will no doubt recall the little excitement that began the century, arising out of an announcement by Mr Nikola Tesla, the American electrical celebrity, that he had received a message from Mars. His announcement renewed attention to a

fact that had long been familiar to scientific people, namely: that from some unknown source in space, waves of electro-magnetic disturbance, entirely similar to those used by Signor Marconi for his wireless telegraphy, are constantly reaching the earth. Besides Mr Tesla quite a number of other observers have been engaged in perfecting apparatus for receiving and recording these vibrations, though few would go so far as to consider them actual messages from some extra-terrestrial sender. Among that few, however, we must certainly count Mr Wendigee. Ever since 1898 he had devoted himself almost entirely to this subject, and being a man of ample means he had erected an observatory on the flanks of Monte Rosa, in a position singularly adapted in every way for such observations.

My scientific attainments, I must admit, are not great, but so far as they enable me to judge, Mr Wendigee's contrivances for detecting and recording any disturbances in the electro-magnetic conditions of space are singularly original and ingenious. And by a happy combination of circumstances they were set up and in operation about two months before Cavor made his first attempt to call up the earth. Consequently we have fragments of his communication even from the beginning. Unhappily, they are only fragments, and the most momentous of all the things that he had to tell humanity – the instructions, that is, for the making of Cavorite, if, indeed, he ever transmitted them – have throbbed themselves away unrecorded into space. We never succeeded in getting a response back to Cavor. He was unable to tell, therefore, what we had received or what we had missed; nor, indeed, did he certainly know that anyone on earth was really aware of his efforts to reach us. And the persistence he displayed in sending eighteen long descriptions of lunar affairs – as they would be if we had them complete – shows how much his mind must have turned back towards his native planet since he left it two years ago.

You can imagine how amazed Mr Wendigee must have been when he discovered his record of electro-magnetic disturbances interlaced by Cavor's straightforward English. Mr Wendigee knew nothing of our wild journey moonward, and suddenly – this English out of the void!

It is well the reader should understand the conditions under which it would seem these messages were sent. Somewhere within the moon Cavor certainly had access for a time to a considerable amount of electrical apparatus, and it would seem he rigged up – perhaps furtively – a transmitting arrangement of the Marconi type. This he was able to operate at irregular intervals: sometimes for only half an hour or so, sometimes for three or four hours at a stretch. At these times he transmitted his earthward message, regardless of the fact that the relative position of the moon and points upon the earth's surface is constantly altering. As a consequence of this and of the necessary imperfections of our recording instruments his communication comes and goes in our records in an extremely fitful manner; it becomes

blurred; it 'fades out' in a mysterious and altogether exasperating way. And added to this is the fact that he was not an expert operator; he had partly forgotten, or never completely mastered, the code in general use, and as he became fatigued he dropped words and misspelt in a curious manner.

Altogether we have probably lost quite half of the communications he made, and much we have is damaged, broken, and partly effaced. In the abstract that follows the reader must be prepared therefore for a considerable amount of break, hiatus, and change of topic. Mr Wendigee and I are collaborating in a complete and annotated edition of the Cavor record, which we hope to publish, together with a detailed account of the instruments employed, beginning with the first volume in January next. That will be the full and scientific report, of which this is only the popular first transcript. But here we give at least sufficient to complete the story I have told, and to give the broad outlines of the state of that other world so near, so akin, and yet so dissimilar to our own.

CHAPTER XXIII

An Abstract of the Six Messages First Received from Mr Cavor

The two earlier messages of Mr Cavor may very well be reserved for that larger volume. They simply tell, with greater brevity and with a difference in several details that is interesting, but not of any vital importance, the bare facts of the making of the sphere and our departure from the world. Throughout, Cavor speaks of me as a man who is dead, but with a curious change of temper as he approaches our landing on the moon. 'Poor Bedford', he says of me, and 'this poor young man'; and he blames himself for inducing a young man 'by no means well equipped for such adventures' to leave a planet 'on which he was indisputably fitted to succeed' on so precarious a mission. I think he underrates the part my energy and practical capacity played in bringing about the realization of his theoretical sphere. 'We arrived,' he says, with no more account of our passage through space than if we had made a journey of common occurrence in a railway train.

And then he becomes increasingly unfair to me. Unfair, indeed, to an extent I should not have expected in a man trained in the search for truth. Looking back over my previously written account of these things, I must insist that I have been altogether juster to Cavor than he has been to me. I have extenuated little and suppressed nothing. But his account is: –

'It speedily became apparent that the entire strangeness of our circumstances and surroundings – great loss of weight, attenuated but highly oxygenated air, consequent exaggeration of the results of muscular effort, rapid development of weird plants from obscure spores, lurid sky – was exciting my companion unduly. On the moon his character seemed to deteriorate. He became impulsive, rash and quarrelsome. In a little while his folly in devouring some gigantic vesicles and his consequent intoxication led to our capture by the Selenites – before we had had the slightest opportunity of properly observing their ways. . . .'

(He says, you observe, nothing of his own concession to these same 'vesicles'.)

And he goes on from that point to say that: 'We came to a difficult passage with them, and Bedford mistaking certain gestures of theirs' – pretty gestures they were! – 'gave way to a panic violence. He ran amuck, killed three, and perforce I had to flee with him after the outrage. Subsequently we fought with a number who endeavoured to bar our way, and slew seven or eight more. It says much for the tolerance of these beings that on my recapture I was not instantly slain. We made our way to the exterior and separated in the crater of our arrival, to increase our chances of recovering

our sphere. But presently I came upon a body of Selenites, led by two who were curiously different, even in form, from any of those we had seen hitherto, with larger heads and smaller bodies, and much more elaborately wrapped about. And after evading them for some time I fell into a crevasse, cut my head rather badly and displaced my patella, and, finding crawling very painful, decided to surrender – if they would still permit me to do so. This they did, and, perceiving my helpless condition, carried me with them again into the moon. And of Bedford I have heard or seen nothing more, nor, so far as I can gather, has any Selenite. Either the night overtook him in the crater, or else, which is more probable, he found the sphere, and, desiring to steal a march upon me, made off with it – only, I fear, to find it uncontrollable, and to meet a more lingering fate in outer space.'

And with that Cavor dismisses me and goes on to more interesting topics. I dislike the idea of seeming to use my position as his editor to deflect his story in my own interest, but I am obliged to protest here against the turn he gives these occurrences. He says nothing about that gasping message on the blood-stained paper in which he told, or attempted to tell, a very different story. The dignified self-surrender is an altogether new view of the affair that has come to him, I must insist, since he began to feel secure among the lunar people; and as for the 'stealing a march' conception, I am quite willing to let the reader decide between us on what he has before him. I know I am not a model man – I have made no pretence to be. But am I *that?*

However, that is the sum of my wrongs. From this point I can edit Cavor with an untroubled mind, for he mentions me no more.

It would seem the Selenites who had come upon him carried him to some point in the interior down 'a great shaft' by means of what he describes as 'a sort of balloon'. We gather from the rather confused passage in which he describes this, and from a number of chance allusions and hints in other and subsequent messages, that this 'great shaft' is one of an enormous system of artificial shafts that run, each from what is called a lunar 'crater', downwards for very nearly a hundred miles towards the central portion of our satellite. These shafts communicate by transverse tunnels, they throw out abysmal caverns and expand into great globular places; the whole of the moon's substance for a hundred miles inward, indeed, is a mere sponge of rock. 'Partly,' says Cavor, 'this sponginess is natural, but very largely it is due to the enormous industry of the Selenites in the past. The enormous circular mounds of the excavated rock and earth it is that form these great circles about the tunnels known to earthly astronomers (misled by a false analogy) as volcanoes.'

It was down this shaft they took him, in this 'sort of balloon' he speaks of, at first into an inky blackness and then into a region of continually increasing phosphorescence. Cavor's despatches show him to be curiously

regardless of detail for a scientific man, but we gather that this light was due to the streams and cascades of water – 'no doubt containing some phosphorescent organism' – that flowed ever more abundantly downward towards the Central Sea. And as he descended, he says, 'The Selenites also became luminous.' And at last far below him he saw, as it were, a lake of heatless fire, the waters of the Central Sea, glowing and eddying in strange perturbation, 'like luminous blue milk that is just on the boil'.

'This Lunar Sea,' says Cavor, in a later passage, 'is not a stagnant ocean; a solar tide sends it in a perpetual flow around the lunar axis, and strange storms and boilings and rushings of its waters occur, and at times cold winds and thunderings that ascend out of it into the busy ways of the great ant-hill above. It is only when the water is in motion that it gives out light; in its rare seasons of calm it is black. Commonly, when one sees it, its waters rise and fall in an oily swell, and flakes and big rafts of shining, bubbly foam drift with the sluggish, faintly glowing current. The Selenites navigate its cavernous straits and lagoons in little shallow boats of a canoe-like shape; and even before my journey to the galleries about the Grand Lunar, who is Master of the Moon, I was permitted to make a brief excursion on its waters.

'The caverns and passages are naturally very tortuous. A large proportion of these ways are known only to expert pilots among the fishermen, and not infrequently Selenites are lost for ever in their labyrinths. In their remoter recesses, I am told, strange creatures lurk, some of them terrible and dangerous creatures that all the science of the moon has been unable to exterminate. There is particularly the Rapha, an inextricable mass of clutching tentacles that one hacks to pieces only to multiply; and the Tzee, a darting creature that is never seen, so subtly and suddenly does it slay. . . .'

He gives us a gleam of description.

'I was reminded on this excursion of what I have read of the Mammoth Caves; if only I had had a yellow flambeau instead of the pervading blue light, and a solid-looking boatman with an oar instead of a scuttle-faced Selenite working an engine at the back of the canoe, I could have imagined I had suddenly got back to earth. The rocks about us were very various, sometimes black, sometimes pale blue and veined, and once they flashed and glittered as though we had come into a mine of sapphires. And below one saw the ghostly phosphorescent fishes flash and vanish in the hardly less phosphorescent deep. Then, presently, a long ultramarine vista down the turgid stream of one of the channels of traffic, and a landing-stage, and then, perhaps, a glimpse up the enormous crowded shaft of one of the vertical ways.

'In one great place heavy with glistening stalactites a number of boats were fishing. We went alongside one of these and watched the long-armed fishing Selenites winding in a net. They were little, hunchbacked insects, with very strong arms, short, bandy legs, and crinkled face-masks. As they

pulled at it that net seemed the heaviest thing I had come upon in the moon; it was loaded with weights – no doubt of gold – and it took a long time to draw, for in those waters the larger and more edible fish lurk deep. The fish in the net came up like a blue moonrise – a blaze of darting, tossing blue.

'Among their catch was a many-tentaculate, evil-eyed black thing, ferociously active, whose appearance they greeted with shrieks and twitters, and which with quick, nervous movements they hacked to pieces by means of little hatchets. All its dissevered limbs continued to lash and writhe in a vicious manner. Afterwards, when fever had hold of me, I dreamt again and again of that bitter, furious creature rising so vigorous and active out of the unknown sea. It was the most active and malignant thing of all the living creatures I have yet seen in this world inside the moon. . . .

'The surface of this sea must be very nearly two hundred miles (if not more) below the level of the moon's exterior; all the cities of the moon lie, I learnt, immediately above this Central Sea, in such cavernous spaces and artificial galleries as I have described, and they communicate with the exterior by enormous vertical shafts which open invariably in what are called by earthly astronomers the "craters" of the moon. The lid covering one such aperture I had already seen during the wanderings that had preceded my capture.

'Upon the condition of the less central portion of the moon I have not yet arrived at very precise knowledge. There is an enormous system of caverns in which the mooncalves shelter during the night; and there are abattoirs and the like – in one of these it was that I and Bedford fought with the Selenite butchers – and I have since seen balloons laden with meat descending out of the upper dark. I have as yet scarcely learnt as much of these things as a Zulu in London would learn about the British corn supplies in the same time. It is clear, however, that these vertical shafts and the vegetation of the surface must play an essential role in ventilating and keeping fresh the atmosphere of the moon. At one time, and particularly on my first emergence from my prison, there was certainly a cold wind blowing *down* the shaft, and later there was a kind of sirocco upward that corresponded with my fever. For at the end of about three weeks I fell ill of an indefinable sort of fever, and in spite of sleep and the quinine tabloids that very fortunately I had brought in my pocket, I remained ill and fretting miserably, almost to the time when I was taken into the presence of the Grand Lunar, who is Master of the Moon.

'I will not dilate on the wretchedness of my condition,' he remarks, 'during those days of ill-health.' And he goes on with great amplitude with details I omit here. 'My temperature,' he concludes, 'kept abnormally high for a long time, and I lost all desire for food. I had stagnant waking intervals, and sleep tormented by dreams, and at one phase I was, I remember, so weak as

to be earth-sick and almost hysterical. I longed almost intolerably for colour to break the everlasting blue. . . .'

He reverts again presently to the topic of this sponge caught lunar atmosphere. I am told by astronomers and physicists that all he tells is in absolute accordance with what was already known of the moon's condition. Had earthly astronomers had the courage and imagination to push home a bold induction, says Mr Wendigee, they might have foretold almost everything that Cavor has to say of the general structure of the moon. They know now pretty certainly that moon and earth are not so much satellite and primary as smaller and greater sisters, made out of one mass, and consequently made of the same material. And since the density of the moon is only three-fifths that of the earth, there can be nothing for it but that she is hollowed out by a great system of caverns. There was no necessity, said Sir Jabez Flap, FRS, that most entertaining exponent of the facetious side of the stars, that we should ever have gone to the moon to find out such easy inferences, and points the pun with an allusion to Gruyère, but he certainly might have announced his knowledge of the hollowness of the moon before. And if the moon is hollow, then the apparent absence of air and water is, of course, quite easily explained. The sea lies within at the bottom of the caverns, and the air travels through the great sponge of galleries, in accordance with simple physical laws. The caverns of the moon, on the whole, are very windy places. As the sunlight comes round the moon the air in the outer galleries on that side is heated, its pressure increases, some flows out on the exterior and mingles with the evaporating air of the craters (where the plants remove its carbonic acid), while the greater portion flows round through the galleries to replace the shrinking air of the cooling side that the sunlight has left. There is, therefore, a constant eastward breeze in the air of the outer galleries, and an up-flow during the lunar day up the shafts, complicated, of course, very greatly by the varying shape of the galleries, and the ingenious contrivances of the Selenite mind. . . .

CHAPTER XXIV

The Natural History of the Selenites

The messages of Cavor from the sixth up to the sixteenth are for the most part so much broken, and they abound so in repetitions, that they scarcely form a consecutive narrative. They will be given in full, of course, in the scientific report, but here it will be far more convenient to continue simply to abstract and quote as in the former chapter. We have subjected every word to a keen critical scrutiny, and my own brief memories and impressions of lunar things have been of inestimable help in interpreting what would otherwise have been impenetrably dark. And, naturally, as living beings our interest centres far more upon the strange community of lunar insects in which he was living, it would seem, as an honoured guest than upon the mere physical condition of their world.

I have already made it clear, I think, that the Selenites I saw resembled man in maintaining the erect attitude, and in having four limbs, and I have compared the general appearance of their heads and the jointing of their limbs to that of insects. I have mentioned, too, the peculiar consequence of the smaller gravitation of the moon on their fragile slightness. Cavor confirms me upon all these points. He calls them 'animals', though of course they fall under no division of the classification of earthly creatures, and he points out 'the insect type of anatomy had, fortunately for men, never exceeded a relatively very small size on earth'. The largest terrestrial insects, living or extinct, do not, as a matter of fact, measure 6 inches in length; 'but here, against the lesser gravitation of the moon, a creature certainly as much an insect as vertebrate seems to have been able to attain to human and ultrahuman dimensions.'

He does not mention the ant, but throughout his allusions the ant is continually being brought before my mind, in its sleepless activity, in its intelligence and social organization, in its structure, and more particularly in the fact that it displays, in addition to the two forms, the male and the female form, that almost all other animals possess, a number of other sexless creatures, workers, soldiers, and the like, differing from one another in structure, character, power and use, and yet all members of the same species. For these Selenites, also, have a great variety of forms. Of course they are not only colossally greater in size than ants, but also, in Cavor's opinion at least, in intelligence, morality, and social wisdom are they colossally greater than men. And instead of the four or five different forms of ant that are found, there are almost innumerably different forms of Selenite. I have endeavoured to indicate the very considerable difference observable

in such Selenites of the outer crust as I happened to encounter; the differ-
ences in size and proportions were certainly as wide as the differences
between the most widely separated races of men. But such differences as
I saw fade absolutely to nothing in comparison with the huge distinctions
of which Cavor tells. It would seem the exterior Selenites I saw were,
indeed, mostly engaged in kindred occupations – mooncalf herds, butchers,
fleshers and the like. But within the moon, practically unsuspected by me,
there are, it seems, a number of other sorts of Selenite, differing in size,
differing in the relative size of part to part, differing in power and appear-
ance, and yet not different species of creatures, but only different forms of
one species, and retaining through all their variations a certain common
likeness that marks their specific unity. The moon is, indeed, a sort of vast
ant-hill, only, instead of there being only four or five sorts of ant, there are
many hundred different sorts of Selenite, and almost every gradation
between one sort and another.

It would seem the discovery came upon Cavor very speedily. I infer rather
than learn from his narrative that he was captured by the mooncalf herds
under the direction of those other Selenites who 'have larger brain cases
(heads?) and very much shorter legs'. Finding he would not walk even under
the goad, they carried him into darkness, crossed a narrow, plank-like bridge
that may have been the identical bridge I had refused, and put him down
in something that must have seemed at first to be some sort of lift. This was
the balloon – it had certainly been absolutely invisible to us in the darkness
– and what had seemed to me a mere plank-walking into the void was really,
no doubt, the passage of the gangway. In this he descended towards constantly
more luminous caverns of the moon. At first they descended in silence –
save for the twitterings of the Selenites – and then into a stir of windy
movement. In a little while the profound blackness had made his eyes so
sensitive that he began to see more and more of the things about him, and
at last the vague took shape.

'Conceive an enormous cylindrical space,' says Cavor in his seventh
message, 'a quarter of a mile across, perhaps; very dimly lit at first and then
brighter, with big platforms twisting down its sides in a spiral that vanishes
at last below in a blue profundity; and lit even more brightly – one could
not tell how or why. Think of the well of the very largest spiral staircase or
lift-shaft that you have ever looked down, and magnify that by a hundred.
Imagine it at twilight seen through blue glass. Imagine yourself looking down
that; only imagine also that you feel extraordinarily light, and have got rid
of any giddy feeling you might have on earth, and you will have the first
conditions of my impression. Round this enormous shaft imagine a broad
gallery running in a much steeper spiral than would be credible on earth,
and forming a steep road protected from the gulf only by a little parapet
that vanishes at last in perspective a couple of miles below.

'Looking up, I saw the very fellow of the downward vision; it had, of course, the effect of looking into a very steep cone. A wind was blowing down the shaft, and far above I fancy I heard, growing fainter and fainter, the bellowing of the mooncalves that were being driven down again from their evening pasturage on the exterior. And up and down the spiral galleries were scattered numerous moon people, pallid, faintly self-luminous beings, regarding our appearance or busied on unknown errands.

'Either I fancied it or a flake of snow came drifting down on the icy breeze. And then, falling like a snowflake, a little figure, a little man-insect clinging to a parachute, drove down very swiftly towards the central places of the moon.

'The big-headed Selenite sitting beside me, seeing me move my head with the gesture of one who saw, pointed with his trunk-like "hand" and indicated a sort of jetty coming into sight very far below: a little landing-stage, as it were, hanging into the void. As it swept up towards us our pace diminished very rapidly, and in a few moments, as it seemed, we were abreast of it and at rest. A mooring-rope was flung and grasped, and I found myself pulled down to a level with a great crowd of Selenites, who jostled to see me.

'It was an incredible crowd. Suddenly and violently there was forced upon my attention the vast amount of difference there is amongst these beings of the moon.

'Indeed, there seemed not two alike in all that jostling multitude. They differed in shape, they differed in size, they rang all the horrible changes on the theme of Selenite form! Some bulged and overhung, some ran about among the feet of their fellows. All of them had a grotesque and disquieting suggestion of an insect that has somehow contrived to mock humanity; but all seemed to present an incredible exaggeration of some particular feature: one had a vast right fore-limb, an enormous antennal arm, as it were; one seemed all leg, poised, as it were, on stilts; another protruded the edge of his face mask into a nose-like organ that made him startlingly human until one saw his expressionless gaping mouth. The strange and (except for the want of mandibles and palps) most insect-like head of the mooncalf-minders underwent, indeed, the most incredible transformations: here it was broad and low, here high and narrow; here its leathery brow was drawn out into horns and strange features; here it was whiskered and divided, and there with a grotesquely human profile. One distortion was particularly conspicuous. There were several brain cases distended like bladders to a huge size, with the face mask reduced to quite small proportions. There were several amazing forms, with heads reduced to microscopic proportions and blobby bodies; and fantastic, flimsy things that existed, it would seem, only as a basis for vast, trumpet-like protrusions of the lower part of the mask. And oddest of all, as it seemed to me for the moment, two or three of these weird inhabitants of a subterranean world, a world sheltered by innumerable miles

of rock from sun or rain, *carried umbrellas* in their tentaculate hands! – Real terrestrial-looking umbrellas! And then I thought of the parachutist I had watched descend.

'These moon people behaved exactly as a human crowd might have done in similar circumstances: they jostled and thrust one another, they shoved one another aside, they even clambered upon one another to get a glimpse of me. Every moment they increased in numbers, and pressed more urgently upon the discs of my ushers' – Cavor does not explain what he means by this – 'every moment fresh shapes emerged from the shadows and forced themselves upon my astounded attention. And presently I was signed and helped into a sort of litter, and lifted up on the shoulders of strong-armed bearers, and so borne through the twilight over this seething multitude towards the apartments that were provided for me in the moon. All about me were eyes, faces, masks, a leathery noise like the rustling of beetle wings, and a great bleating and cricket-like twittering of Selenite voices. . . .'

We gather he was taken to a 'hexagonal apartment', and there for a space he was confined. Afterwards he was given a much more considerable liberty; indeed, almost as much freedom as one has in a civilized town on earth. And it would appear that the mysterious being who is the ruler and master of the moon appointed two Selenites 'with large heads' to guard and study him, and to establish whatever mental communications were possible with him. And, amazing and incredible as it may seem, these two creatures, these fantastic men-insects, these beings of another world, were presently communicating with Cavor by means of terrestrial speech.

Cavor speaks of them as Phi-oo and Tsi-puff. Phi-oo, he says, was about 5 feet high; he had small, slender legs about 18 inches long, and slight feet of the common lunar pattern. On these balanced a little body, throbbing with the pulsations of his heart. He had long, soft, many-jointed arms ending in a tentacled grip, and his neck was many-jointed in the usual way, but exceptionally short and thick. His head, says Cavor – apparently alluding to some previous description that has gone astray in space – 'is of the common lunar type, but strangely modified. The mouth has the usual expressionless gape, but it is unusually small and pointing downward, and the mask is reduced to the size of a large flat nose-flap. On either side are the little eyes.

'The rest of the head is distended into a huge globe, and the chitinous leathery cuticle of the mooncalf herds thins out to a mere membrane, through which the pulsating brain movements are distinctly visible. He is a creature, indeed, with a tremendously hypertrophied brain, and with the rest of his organism both relatively and absolutely dwarfed.'

In another passage Cavor compares the back view of him to Atlas supporting the world. Tsi-puff, it seems, was a very similar insect, but his

My thoughts became vague and cloudy, no longer leading in definite directions. I had not felt heavy or weary – I cannot imagine one doing so upon the moon – but I suppose I was greatly fatigued. At any rate I slept.

Slumbering there rested me greatly, I think, and the sun was setting and the violence of the heat abating, through all the time I slumbered. When at last I was roused from my slumbers by a remote clamour, I felt active and capable again. I rubbed my eyes and stretched my arms. I rose to my feet – I was a little stiff – and at once prepared to resume my search. I shouldered my golden clubs, one on each shoulder, and went on out of the ravine of the gold-veined rocks.

The sun was certainly lower, much lower than it had been; the air was very much cooler. I perceived I must have slept some time. It seemed to me that a faint touch of misty blueness hung about the western cliff. I leapt to a little boss of rock and surveyed the crater. I could see no signs of moon-calves or Selenites, nor could I see Cavor, but I could see my handkerchief afar off, spread out on its thicket of thorns. I looked about me, and then leapt forward to the next convenient view-point.

I beat my way round in a semicircle, and back again in a still remoter crescent. It was very fatiguing and hopeless. The air was really very much cooler, and it seemed to me that the shadow under the westward cliff was growing broad. Ever and again I stopped and reconnoitred, but there was no sign of Cavor, no sign of Selenites; and it seemed to me the mooncalves must have been driven into the interior again – I could see none of them. I became more and more desirous of seeing Cavor. The winged outline of the sun had sunk now, until it was scarcely the distance of its diameter from the rim of the sky. I was oppressed by the idea that the Selenites would presently close their lids and valves, and shut us out under the inexorable onrush of the lunar night. It seemed to me high time that he abandoned his search, and that we took counsel together. I felt how urgent it was that we should decide soon upon our course. We had failed to find the sphere, we no longer had time to seek it, and once these valves were closed with us outside, we were lost men. The great night of space would descend upon us – that blackness of the void which is the only absolute death. All my being shrank from that approach. We must get into the moon again, though we were slain in doing it. I was haunted by a vision of our freezing to death, of our hammering with our last strength on the valve of the great pit.

I took no thought any more of the sphere. I thought only of finding Cavor again. I was half inclined to go back into the moon without him, rather than seek him until it was too late. I was already halfway back towards our handkerchief, when suddenly—

I saw the sphere!

I did not find it so much as it found me. It was lying much further to the westward than I had gone, and the sloping rays of the sinking sun

reflected from its glass had suddenly proclaimed its presence in a dazzling beam. For an instant I thought this was some new device of the Selenites against us, and then I understood.

I threw up my arms, shouted a ghostly shout, and set off in vast leaps towards it. I missed one of my leaps and dropped into a deep ravine and twisted my ankle, and after that I stumbled at almost every leap. I was in a state of hysterical agitation, trembling violently, and quite breathless long before I got to it. Three times at least I had to stop with my hands resting on my side, and spite of the thin dryness of the air, the perspiration was wet upon my face.

I thought of nothing but the sphere until I reached it, I forgot even my trouble of Cavor's whereabouts. My last leap flung me with my hands hard against its glass; then I lay against it panting, and trying vainly to shout, 'Cavor! Here is the sphere!' When I had recovered a little I peered through the thick glass, and the things inside seemed tumbled. I stooped to peer closer. Then I attempted to get in. I had to hoist it over a little to get my head through the manhole. The screw stopper was inside, and I could see now that nothing had been touched, nothing had suffered. It lay there as we had left it when we had dropped out amidst the snow.

For a time I was wholly occupied in making and remaking this inventory. I found I was trembling violently. It was good to see that familiar dark interior again! I cannot tell you how good. Presently I crept inside and sat down among the things. I looked through the glass at the moon world and shivered. I placed my gold clubs upon the bale, and sought out and took a little food; not so much because I wanted it, but because it was there. Then it occurred to me that it was time to go out and signal for Cavor. But I did not go out and signal for Cavor forthwith. Something held me to the sphere.

After all, everything was coming right. There would be still time for us to get more of the magic stone that gives one mastery over men. Away there, close handy, was gold for the picking up; and the sphere would travel as well half full of gold as though it were empty. We could go back now, masters of ourselves and our world, and then—

I roused myself at last, and with an effort got myself out of the sphere. I shivered as I emerged, for the evening air was growing very cold. I stood in the hollow staring about me. I scrutinized the bushes round me very carefully before I leapt to the rocky shelf hard by, and took once more what had been my first leap in the moon. But now I made it with no effort whatever.

The growth and decay of the vegetation had gone on apace, and the whole aspect of the rocks had changed, but still it was possible to make out the slope on which the seeds had germinated, and the rocky mass from which we had taken our first view of the crater. But the spiky shrub on the slope stood brown and sere now, and thirty feet high, and cast long shadows that stretched out of sight, and the little seeds that clustered in its upper

branches were brown and ripe. Its work was done, and it was brittle and ready to fall and crumple under the freezing air, so soon as the nightfall came. And the huge cacti, that had swollen as we watched them, had long since burst and scattered their spores to the four quarters of the moon. Amazing little corner in the universe – the landing-place of men!

Some day, thought I, I will have an inscription standing there right in the midst of the hollow. It came to me, if only this teeming world within knew of the full import of the moment, how furious its tumult would become!

But as yet it could scarcely be dreaming of the significance of our coming. For if it did, the crater would surely be an uproar of pursuit, instead of as still as death! I looked about for some place from which I might signal to Cavor, and saw that same patch of rock to which he had leapt from my present standpoint, still bare and barren in the sun. For a moment I hesitated at going so far from the sphere. Then with a pang of shame at that hesitation, I leapt. . . .

From this vantage point I surveyed the crater again. Far away at the top of the enormous shadow I cast was the little white handkerchief fluttering on the bushes. It was very little and very far, and Cavor was not in sight. It seemed to me that by this time he ought to be looking for me. That was the agreement. But he was nowhere to be seen.

I stood waiting and watching, hands shading my eyes, expecting every moment to distinguish him. Very probably I stood there for quite a long time. I tried to shout, and was reminded of the thinness of the air. I made an undecided step back towards the sphere. But a lurking dread of the Selenites made me hesitate to signal my whereabouts by hoisting one of our sleeping-blankets on to the adjacent scrub. I searched the crater again.

It had an effect of emptiness that chilled me. And it was still! Any sound from the Selenites in the world beneath, even had died away. It was as still as death. Save for the faint stir of the shrub about me in the little breeze that was rising, there was no sound nor shadow of a sound. And the breeze blew chill.

Confound Cavor!

I took a deep breath. I put my hands to the sides of my mouth. 'Cavor!' I bawled, and the sound was like some manikin shouting far away.

I looked at the handkerchief, I looked behind me at the broadening shadow of the westward cliff, I looked under my hand at the sun. It seemed to me that almost visibly it was creeping down the sky.

I felt I must act instantly if I was to save Cavor. I whipped off my vest and flung it as a mark on the sere bayonets of the shrubs behind me, and then set off in a straight line towards the handkerchief. Perhaps it was a couple of miles away – a matter of a few hundred leaps and strides. I have already told how one seemed to hang through those lunar leaps. In each suspense I sought Cavor, and marvelled why he should be hidden. In

each leap I could feel the sun setting behind me. Each time I touched the ground I was tempted to go back.

A last leap and I was in the depression below our handkerchief, a stride, and I stood on our former vantage point within arm's reach of it. I stood up straight and scanned the world about me, between its lengthening bars of shadow. Far away, down a long declivity, was the opening of the tunnel up which we had fled, and my shadow reached towards it, stretched towards it, and touched it, like a finger of the night.

Not a sign of Cavor, not a sound in all the stillness, only that the stir and waving of the scrub and of the shadows increased. And suddenly and violently I shivered. 'Cav—' I began, and realized once more the uselessness of the human voice in that thin air.

Silence. The silence of death.

Then it was my eye caught something – a little thing, lying perhaps fifty yards away down the slope, amidst a litter of bent and broken branches. What was it? I knew, and yet for some reason I would not know.

I went nearer to it. It was the little cricket cap Cavor had worn. I did not touch it, I stood looking at it.

I saw then that the scattered branches about it had been forcibly smashed and trampled. I hesitated, stepped forward and picked it up.

I stood with Cavor's cap in my hand, staring at the trampled reeds and thorns about me. On some of them were little smears of something dark, something that I dared not touch. A dozen yards away, perhaps, the rising breeze dragged something into view, something small and vividly white.

It was a little piece of paper crumpled tightly, as though it had been clutched tightly. I picked it up, and on it were smears of red. My eye caught faint pencil marks. I smoothed it out, and saw uneven and broken writing ending at last in a crooked streak upon the paper.

I set myself to decipher this.

'I have been injured about the knee, I think my kneecap is hurt, and I cannot run or crawl,' it began – pretty distinctly written.

Then less legibly: 'They have been chasing me for some time, and it is only a question of' – the word 'time' seemed to have been written here and erased in favour of something illegible – 'before they get me. They are beating all about me.'

Then the writing became convulsive. 'I can hear them,' I guessed the tracing meant, and then it was quite unreadable for a space. Then came a little string of words that were quite distinct: 'a different sort of Selenite altogether, who appears to be directing the—' The writing became a mere hasty confusion again.

'They have larger brain cases – much larger, and slenderer bodies, and very short legs. They make gentle noises, and move with organized deliberation. . . .

'And though I am wounded and helpless here, their appearance still gives me hope—' That was like Cavor. 'They have not shot at me or attempted . . . injury. I intend—'

Then came the sudden streak of the pencil across the paper, and on the back and edges – blood!

And as I stood there stupid and perplexed, with this dumbfounding relic in my hand, something very soft and light and chill touched my hand for a moment and ceased to be, and then a thing, a little white speck, drifted athwart a shadow. It was a tiny snowflake, the first snowflake, the herald of the night.

I looked up with a start, and the sky had darkened now almost to blackness, and was thick with a gathering multitude of coldly watchful stars. I looked eastward, and the light of that shrivelled world was touched with a sombre bronze; westward, and the sun, robbed now by a thickening white mist of half its heat and splendour, was touching the crater rim, was sinking out of sight, and all the shrubs and jagged and tumbled rocks stood out against it in a bristling disorder of black shapes. Into the great lake of darkness westward, a vast wreath of mist was sinking. A cold wind set all the crater shivering. Suddenly, for a moment, I was in a puff of falling snow, and all the world about me grey and dim.

And then it was I heard, not loud and penetrating as at first, but faint and dim like a dying voice, that tolling, that same tolling that had welcomed the coming of the day: Boom! . . . Boom! . . . Boom! . . .

It echoed about the crater, it seemed to throb with the throbbing of the greater stars, the blood-red crescent of the sun's disk sank as it tolled out: Boom! . . . Boom! . . . Boom!

What had happened to Cavor? All through that tolling I stood there stupidly, and at last the tolling ceased.

And suddenly the open mouth of the tunnel down below there shut like an eye and vanished out of sight.

Then indeed was I alone.

Over me, around me, closing in on me, embracing me ever nearer, was the Eternal; that which was before the beginning, and that which triumphs over the end; that enormous void in which all light and life and being is but the thin and vanishing splendour of a falling star, the cold, the stillness, the silence – the infinite and final Night of space.

The sense of solitude and desolation became the sense of an overwhelming presence that stooped towards me, that almost touched me.

'No,' I cried. 'No! Not yet! not yet! Wait! Wait! Oh wait!' My voice went up to a shriek. I flung the crumpled paper from me, scrambled back to the crest to take my bearings, and then, with all the will that was in me, leapt out towards the mark I had left, dim and distant now in the very margin of the shadow.

Leap, leap, leap, and each leap was seven ages.

Before me the pale serpent-girdled section of the sun sank and sank, and the advancing shadow swept to seize the sphere before I could reach it. I was two miles away, a hundred leaps or more, and the air about me was thinning out as it thins under an air-pump, and the cold was gripping at my joints. But had I died, I should have died leaping. Once, and then again my foot slipped on the gathering snow as I leapt and shortened my leap; once I fell short into bushes that crashed and smashed into dusty chips and nothingness, and once I stumbled as I dropped, and rolled head over heels into a gully, and rose bruised and bleeding and confused as to my direction.

But such incidents were as nothing to the intervals, those awful pauses when one drifted through the air towards that pouring tide of night. My breathing made a piping noise, and it was as though knives were whirling in my lungs. My heart seemed to beat against the top of my brain. 'Shall I reach it? O Heaven! Shall I reach it?'

My whole being became anguish.

'Lie down!' screamed my pain and despair; 'Lie down!'

The nearer I struggled, the more awfully remote it seemed. I was numb, I stumbled, I bruised and cut myself and did not bleed.

It was in sight.

I fell on all fours, and my lungs whooped.

I crawled. The frost gathered on my lips, icicles hung from my moustache, I was white with the freezing atmosphere.

I was a dozen yards from it. My eyes had become dim. 'Lie down!' screamed despair; 'Lie down!'

I touched it, and halted. 'Too late!' screamed despair; 'Lie down!'

I fought stiffly with it. I was on the manhole lip, a stupefied, half-dead being. The snow was all about me. I pulled myself in. There lurked within a little warmer air.

The snowflakes – the airflakes – danced in about me, as I tried with chilling hands to thrust the valve in and spun it tight and hard. I sobbed. 'I will,' I chattered in my teeth. And then, with fingers that quivered and felt brittle, I turned to the shutter studs.

As I fumbled with the switches – for I had never controlled them before – I could see dimly through the steaming glass the blazing red streamers of the sinking sun, dancing and flickering through the snowstorm, and the black forms of the scrub thickening and bending and breaking beneath the accumulating snow. Thicker whirled the snow and thicker, black against the light. What if even now the switches overcame me?

Then something clicked under my hands, and in an instant that last vision of the moon world was hidden from my eyes. I was in the silence and darkness of the inter-planetary sphere.

CHAPTER XX

Mr Bedford in Infinite Space

It was almost as though I had been killed. Indeed, I could imagine a man suddenly and violently killed would feel very much as I did. One moment, a passion of agonizing existence and fear; the next, darkness and stillness, neither light nor life nor sun, moon nor stars, the blank infinite. Although the thing was done by my own act, although I had already tasted this very effect in Cavor's company, I felt astonished, dumbfounded, and overwhelmed. I seemed to be borne upward into an enormous darkness. My fingers floated off the studs, I hung as if I were annihilated, and at last very softly and gently I came against the bale and the golden chain, and the crowbars that had drifted to the middle of the sphere.

I do not know how long that drifting took. In the sphere of course, even more than on the moon, one's earthly time sense was ineffectual. At the touch of the bale it was as if I had awakened from a dreamless sleep. I immediately perceived that if I wanted to keep awake and alive I must get a light or open a window, so as to get a grip of something with my eyes. And besides I was cold. I kicked off from the bale, therefore, clawed on to the thin cords within the glass, crawled along until I got to the manhole rim, and so got my bearings for the light and blind studs, took a shove off, and flying once round the bale, and getting a scare from something big and flimsy that was drifting loose, I got my hand on the cord quite close to the studs, and reached them. I lit the little lamp first of all to see what it was I had collided with, and discovered that old copy of *Lloyd's News* had slipped its moorings, and was adrift in the void. That brought me out of the infinite to my own proper dimensions again. It made me laugh and pant for a time, and suggested the idea of a little oxygen from one of the cylinders. After that I lit the heater until I felt warm, and then I took food. Then I set to work in a very gingerly fashion on the Cavorite blinds, to see if I could guess by any means how the sphere was travelling.

The first blind I opened I shut at once, and hung for a time flattened and blinded by the sunlight that had hit me. After thinking a little I started upon the windows at right angles to this one, and got the huge crescent moon and the little crescent earth behind it, the second time. I was amazed to find how far I was from the moon. I had reckoned that not only should I have little or none of the 'kick-off' that the earth's atmosphere had given us at our start, but that the tangential 'fly off' of the moon's spin would be at least twenty-eight times less than the earth's. I had expected to discover myself hanging over our crater, and on the edge of the night, but

all that was now only a part of the outline of the white crescent that filled the sky. And Cavor—?

He was already infinitesimal.

I tried to imagine what could have happened to him. But at that time I could think of nothing but death. I seemed to see him, bent and smashed at the foot of some interminably high cascade of blue. And all about him the stupid insects stared. . . .

Under the inspiring touch of the drifting newspaper I became practical again for a while. It was quite clear to me that what I had to do was to get back to earth, but as far as I could see I was drifting away from it. Whatever had happened to Cavor, even if he was still alive, which seemed to me incredible after that blood-stained scrap, I was powerless to help him. There he was, living or dead behind the mantle of that rayless night, and there he must remain at least until I could summon our fellow men to his assistance. Should I do that? Something of the sort I had in my mind; to come back to earth if it were possible, and then as maturer consideration might determine, either to show and explain the sphere to a few discreet persons, and act with them, or else to keep my secret, sell my gold, obtain weapons, provisions, and an assistant, and return with these advantages to deal on equal terms with the flimsy people of the moon, to rescue Cavor, if that were still possible, and at any rate to procure a sufficient supply of gold to place my subsequent proceedings on a firmer basis. But that was hoping far; I had first to get back.

I set myself to decide just exactly how the return to earth could be contrived. As I struggled with that problem I ceased to worry about what I should do when I got there. At last my only care was to get back.

I puzzled out at last that my best chance would be to drop back towards the moon as near as I dared in order to gather velocity, then to shut my windows and fly behind it, and when I was past to open my earthward windows, and so get off at a good pace homeward. But whether I should ever reach the earth by that device, or whether I might not simply find myself spinning about it in some hyperbolic or parabolic curve or other, I could not tell. Later I had a happy inspiration, and by opening certain windows to the moon, which had appeared in the sky in front of the earth, I turned my course aside so as to head off the earth, which it had become evident to me I must pass behind without some such expedient. I did a very great deal of complicated thinking over these problems – for I am no mathematician – and in the end I am certain it was much more my good luck than my reasoning that enabled me to hit the earth. Had I known then, as I know now, the mathematical chances there were against me, I doubt if I should have troubled even to touch the studs to make any attempt. And having puzzled out what I considered to be the thing to do, I opened all my moonward windows, and squatted down – the effort lifted me for a

time some feet or so into the air, and I hung there in the oddest way – and waited for the crescent to get bigger and bigger until I felt I was near enough for safety. Then I would shut the windows, fly past the moon with the velocity I had got from it – if I did not smash upon it – and so go on towards the earth.

And that is what I did.

At last I felt my moonward start was sufficient. I shut out the sight of the moon from my eyes, and in a state of mind that was, I now recall, incredibly free from anxiety or any distressful quality, I sat down to begin a vigil in that little speck of matter in infinite space that would last until I should strike the earth. The heater had made the sphere tolerably warm, the air had been refreshed by the oxygen, and except for that faint conges-tion of the head that was always with me while I was away from earth, I felt entire physical comfort. I had extinguished the light again, lest it should fail me in the end; I was in darkness, save for the earthshine and the glitter of the stars below me. Everything was so absolutely silent and still that I might indeed have been the only being in the universe, and yet, strangely enough, I had no more feeling of loneliness or fear than if I had been lying in bed on earth. Now, this seems all the stranger to me, since during my last hours in that crater of the moon, the sense of my utter loneliness had been an agony. . . .

Incredible as it will seem, this interval of time that I spent in space has no sort of proportion to any other interval of time in my life. Sometimes it seemed as though I sat through immeasurable eternities like some god upon a lotus leaf, and again as though there was a momentary pause as I leapt from moon to earth. In truth, it was altogether some weeks of earthly time. But I had done with care and anxiety, hunger or fear, for that space. I floated, thinking with a strange breadth and freedom of all that we had undergone, and of all my life and motives, and the secret issues of my being. I seemed to myself to have grown greater and greater, to have lost all sense of movement; to be floating amidst the stars, and always the sense of earth's littleness and the infinite littleness of my life upon it, was implicit in my thoughts.

I can't profess to explain the things that happened in my mind. No doubt they could all be traced directly or indirectly to the curious physical condi-tions under which I was living. I set them down here just for what they are worth, and without any comment. The most prominent quality of it was a pervading doubt of my own identity. I became, if I may so express it, disso-ciate from Bedford; I looked down on Bedford as a trivial, incidental thing with which I chanced to be connected. I saw Bedford in many relations – as an ass or as a poor beast, where I had hitherto been inclined to regard him with a quiet pride as a very spirited or rather forcible person. I saw him not only as an ass, but as the son of many generations of asses. I reviewed his

schooldays and his early manhood, and his first encounter with love, very much as one might review the proceedings of an ant in the sand. . . . Something of that period of lucidity I regret still hangs about me, and I doubt if I shall ever recover the full-bodied self-satisfaction of my early days. But at the time the thing was not in the least painful, because I had that extraordinary persuasion that, as a matter of fact, I was no more Bedford than I was anyone else, but only a mind floating in the still serenity of space. Why should I be disturbed about this Bedford's shortcomings? I was not responsible for him or them.

For a time I struggled against this really very grotesque delusion. I tried to summon the memory of vivid moments, of tender or intense emotions to my assistance; I felt that if I could recall one genuine twinge of feeling the growing severance would be stopped. But I could not do it. I saw Bedford rushing down Chancery Lane, hat on the back of his head, coat tails flying out, *en route* for his public examination. I saw him dodging and bumping against, and even saluting, other similar little creatures in that swarming gutter of people. Me? I saw Bedford that same evening in the sitting-room of a certain lady, and his hat was on the table beside him, and it wanted brushing badly, and he was in tears. Me? I saw him with that lady in various attitudes and emotions – I never felt so detached before. . . . I saw him hurrying off to Lympne to write a play, and accosting Cavor, and in his shirt sleeves working at the sphere, and walking out to Canterbury because he was afraid to come! Me? I did not believe it.

I still reasoned that all this was hallucination due to my solitude, and the fact that I had lost all weight and sense of resistance. I endeavoured to recover that sense by banging myself about the sphere, by pinching my hands and clasping them together. Among other things I lit the light, captured that torn copy of *Lloyd's*, and read those convincingly realistic advertisements again about the Cutaway bicycle, and the gentleman of private means, and the lady in distress who was selling those 'forks and spoons'. There was no doubt they existed surely enough, and, said I, 'This is your world, and you are Bedford, and you are going back to live among things like that for all the rest of your life.' But the doubts within me could still argue: 'It is not you that is reading, it is Bedford, but you are not Bedford, you know. That's just where the mistake comes in.'

'Confound it!' I cried; 'And if I am not Bedford, what am I?'

But in that direction no light was forthcoming, though the strangest fancies came drifting into my brain, queer remote suspicions, like shadows seen from far away . . . Do you know, I had a sort of idea that really I was something quite outside not only the world, but all worlds, and out of space and time, and that this poor Bedford was just a peephole through which I looked at life? . . .

Bedford! However I disavowed him, there I was most certainly bound up with him, and I knew that wherever or whatever I might be, I must needs feel the stress of his desires, and sympathize with all his joys and sorrows until his life should end. And with the dying of Bedford – what then? . . .

Enough of this remarkable phase of my experiences! I tell it here simply to show how one's isolation and departure from this planet touched not only the functions and feeling of every organ of the body, but indeed also the very fabric of the mind, with strange and unanticipated disturbances. All through the major portion of that vast space journey I hung thinking of such immaterial things as these, hung dissociated and apathetic, a cloudy megalomaniac, as it were, amidst the stars and planets in the void of space; and not only the world to which I was returning, but the blue-lit caverns of the Selenites, their helmet faces, their gigantic and wonderful machines, and the fate of Cavor, dragged helpless into that world, seemed infinitely minute and altogether trivial things to me.

Until at last I began to feel the pull of the earth upon my being, drawing me back again to the life that is real for men. And then, indeed, it grew clearer and clearer to me that I was quite certainly Bedford after all, and returning after amazing adventures to this world of ours, and with a life that I was very likely to lose in this return. I set myself to puzzle out the conditions under which I must fall to earth.

CHAPTER XXI

Mr Bedford at Littlestone

My line of flight was about parallel with the surface as I came into the upper air. The temperature of the sphere began to rise forthwith. I knew it behoved me to drop at once. Far below me, in a darkling twilight, stretched a great expanse of sea. I opened every window I could, and fell – out of sunshine into evening, and out of evening into night. Vaster grew the earth and vaster, swallowing up the stars, and the silvery translucent starlit veil of cloud it wore spread out to catch me. At last the world seemed no longer a sphere but flat, and then concave. It was no longer a planet in the sky, but the world of Man. I shut all but an inch or so of earthward window, and dropped with a slackening velocity. The broadening water, now so near that I could see the dark glitter of the waves, rushed up to meet me. The sphere became very hot. I snapped the last strip of window, and sat scowling and biting my knuckles, waiting for the impact. . . .

The sphere hit the water with a huge splash: it must have sent it fathoms high. At the splash I flung the Cavorite shutters open. Down I went, but slower and slower, and then I felt the sphere pressing against my feet, and so drove up again as a bubble drives. And at the last I was floating and rocking upon the surface of the sea, and my journey in space was at an end.

The night was dark and overcast. Two yellow pin-points far away showed the passing of a ship, and nearer was a red glare that came and went. Had not the electricity of my glow-lamp exhausted itself, I could have got picked up that night. In spite of the inordinate fatigue I was beginning to feel, I was excited now, and for a time hopeful, in a feverish, impatient way, that so my travelling might end.

But at last I ceased to move about, and sat, wrists on knees, staring at a distant red light. It swayed up and down, rocking, rocking. My excitement passed. I realized I had yet to spend another night at least in the sphere. I perceived myself infinitely heavy and fatigued. And so I fell asleep.

A change in my rhythmic motion awakened me. I peered through the refracting glass, and saw that I had come aground upon a huge shallow of sand. Far away I seemed to see houses and trees, and seaward a curved, vague distortion of a ship hung between sea and sky.

I stood up and staggered. My one desire was to emerge. The manhole was upward, and I wrestled with the screw. Slowly I opened the manhole. At last the air was singing in again as once it had sung out. But this time I did not wait until the pressure was adjusted. In another moment I had the weight of

the window on my hands, and I was open, wide open, to the old familiar sky of earth.

The air hit me on the chest so that I gasped. I dropped the glass screw. I cried out, put my hands to my chest, and sat down. For a time I was in pain. Then I took deep breaths. At last I could rise and move about again.

I tried to thrust my head through the manhole, and the sphere rolled over. It was as though something had lugged my head down directly it emerged. I ducked back sharply, or I should have been pinned face under water. After some wriggling and shoving I managed to crawl out upon sand, over which the retreating waves still came and went.

I did not attempt to stand up. It seemed to me that my body must be suddenly changed to lead. Mother Earth had her grip on me now – no Cavorite intervening. I sat down heedless of the water that came over my feet.

It was dawn, a grey dawn, rather overcast, but showing here and there a long patch of greenish grey. Some way out a ship was lying at anchor, a pale silhouette of a ship with one yellow light. The water came rippling in in long shallow waves. Away to the right curved the land, a shingle bank with little hovels, and at last a lighthouse, a sailing mark and a point. Inland stretched a space of level sand, broken here and there by pools of water, and ending a mile away perhaps in a low shore of scrub. To the north-east some isolated watering-place was visible, a row of gaunt lodging-houses, the tallest things that I could see on earth, dull dabs against the brightening sky. What strange men can have reared these vertical piles in such an amplitude of space I do not know. There they are, like pieces of Brighton lost in the waste.

For a long time I sat there, yawning and rubbing my face. At last I struggled to rise. It made me feel that I was lifting a weight. I stood up.

I stared at the distant houses. For the first time since our starvation in the crater I thought of earthly food. 'Bacon,' I whispered, 'eggs. Good toast and good coffee . . . And how the devil am I going to get all this stuff to Lympne?' I wondered where I was. It was an east shore anyhow, and I had seen Europe before I dropped.

I heard footsteps scrunching in the sand, and a little round-faced, friendly-looking man in flannels, with a bathing towel wrapped about his shoulders, and his bathing dress over his arm, appeared up the beach. I knew instantly that I must be in England. He was staring almost intently at the sphere and me. He advanced staring. I daresay I looked a ferocious savage enough – dirty, unkempt, to an indescribable degree; but it did not occur to me at the time. He stopped at a distance of twenty yards. 'Hul-lo, my man!' he said doubtfully.

'Hullo yourself!' said I.

He advanced, reassured by that. 'What on earth is that thing?' he asked.

'Can you tell me where I am?' I asked.

'That's Littlestone,' he said, pointing to the houses; 'and that's Dungeness! Have you just landed? What's that thing you've got? Some sort of machine?'

'Yes.'

'Have you floated ashore? Have you been wrecked or something? What is it?'

I meditated swiftly. I made an estimate of the little man's appearance as he drew nearer. 'By Jove!' he said, 'You've had a time of it! I thought you— Well – where were you cast away? Is that thing a sort of floating thing for saving life?'

I decided to take that line for the present. I made a few vague affirmatives. 'I want help,' I said hoarsely. 'I want to get some stuff up the beach – stuff I can't very well leave about.' I became aware of three other pleasant-looking young men with towels, blazers, and straw hats, coming down the sands towards me. Evidently the early bathing section of this Littlestone!

'Help!' said the young man; 'Rather!' He became vaguely active. 'What particularly do you want done?' He turned round and gesticulated. The three young men accelerated their pace. In a minute they were about me, plying me with questions I was indisposed to answer. 'I'll tell all that later,' I said. 'I'm dead beat. I'm a rag.'

'Come up to the hotel,' said the foremost little man. 'We'll look after that thing there.'

I hesitated. 'I can't,' I said. 'In that sphere there's two big bars of gold.'

They looked incredulously at one another, then at me with a new enquiry. I went to the sphere, stooped, crept in, and presently they had the Selenites' crowbars and the broken chain before them. If I had not been so horribly fagged I could have laughed at them. It was like kittens round a beetle. They didn't know what to do with the stuff. The fat little man stooped and lifted the end of one of the bars, and then dropped it with a grunt. Then they all did.

'It's lead, or gold!' said one.

'Oh, it's *gold*!' said another.

'Gold, right enough,' said the third.

Then they all stared at me, and then they all stared at the ship lying at anchor.

'I say!' cried the little man. 'But where did you get that?'

I was too tired to keep up a lie. 'I got it in the moon.'

I saw them stare at one another.

'Look here!' said I. 'I'm not going to argue now. Help me carry these lumps of gold up to the hotel – I guess, with rests, two of you can manage one, and I'll trail this chain thing – and I'll tell you more when I've had some food.'

'And how about that thing?'

'It won't hurt there,' I said. 'Anyhow – confound it! – it must stop there now. If the tide comes up, it will float all right.'

And in a state of enormous wonderment, these young men most obediently hoisted my treasures on their shoulders, and with limbs that felt like lead I headed a sort of procession towards that distant fragment of 'sea-front'. Halfway there we were reinforced by two awe-stricken little girls with spades, and later a lean little boy, with a penetrating sniff, appeared. He was, I remember, wheeling a bicycle, and he accompanied us at a distance of about a hundred yards on our right flank, and then, I suppose, gave us up as uninteresting, mounted his bicycle, and rode off over the level sands in the direction of the sphere.

I glanced back after him.

'*He* won't touch it,' said the stout young man reassuringly, and I was only too willing to be reassured.

At first something of the grey of the morning was in my mind, but presently the sun disengaged itself from the level clouds of the horizon and lit the world, and turned the leaden sea to glittering waters. My spirits rose. A sense of the vast importance of the things I had done and had yet to do came with the sunlight into my mind. I laughed aloud as the foremost man staggered under my gold. When indeed I took my place in the world, how amazed the world would be!

If it had not been for my inordinate fatigue, the landlord of the Littlestone hotel would have been amusing, as he hesitated between my gold and my respectable company on the one hand, and my filthy appearance on the other. But at last I found myself in a terrestrial bathroom once more with warm water to wash myself with, and a change of raiment, preposterously small indeed, but anyhow clean, that the genial little man had lent me. He lent me a razor too, but I could not screw up my resolution to attack even the outposts of the bristling beard that covered my face.

I sat down to an English breakfast and ate with a sort of languid appetite – an appetite many weeks old, and very decrepit – and stirred myself to answer the questions of the four young men. And I told them the truth.

'Well,' said I, 'as you press me – I got it in the moon.'

'The moon?'

'Yes, the moon in the sky.'

'But how do you mean?'

'What I say, confound it!'

'That you have just come from the moon?'

'Exactly! Through space – in that ball.' And I took a delicious mouthful of egg. I made a private note that when I went back to the moon I would take a box of eggs.

I could see clearly that they did not believe one word of what I told them, but evidently they considered me the most respectable liar they had ever

met. They glanced at one another, and then concentrated the fire of their eyes on me. I fancy they expected a clue to me in the way I helped myself to salt. They seemed to find something significant in my peppering my egg. These strangely shaped masses of gold they had staggered under held their minds. There the lumps lay in front of me, each worth thousands of pounds, and as impossible for anyone to steal as a house or a piece of land. As I looked at their curious faces over my coffee-cup, I realized something of the enormous wilderness of explanations into which I should have to wander to render myself comprehensible again.

'You don't *really* mean—' began the youngest young man, in the tone of one who speaks to an obstinate child.

'Just pass me that toast-rack,' I said, and shut him up completely.

'But look here, I say,' began one of the others. 'We're not going to believe that, you know.'

'Ah, well,' said I, and shrugged my shoulders.

'He doesn't want to tell us,' said the youngest young man in a stage aside; and then, with an appearance of great *sang-froid*, 'You don't mind if I take a cigarette?'

I waved him a cordial assent, and proceeded with my breakfast. Two of the others went and looked out of the further window and talked inaudibly. I was struck by a thought. 'The tide,' I said, 'is running out?'

There was a pause, a doubt who should answer me. 'It's near the ebb,' said the fat little man.

'Well, anyhow,' I said, 'it won't float far.'

I decapitated my third egg, and began a little speech. 'Look here,' I said. 'Please don't imagine I'm surly or telling you uncivil lies, or anything of that sort. I'm forced almost to be a little short and mysterious. I can quite understand this is as queer as it can be, and that your imaginations must be going it. I can assure you, you're in at a memorable time. But I can't make it clear to you now – it's impossible. I give you my word of honour I've come from the moon, and that's all I can tell you. . . . All the same I'm tremendously obliged to you, you know, tremendously. I hope that my manner hasn't in any way given you offence.'

'Oh, not in the least!' said the youngest young man affably. 'We can quite understand,' and staring hard at me all the time, he heeled his chair back until it very nearly upset, and recovered with some exertion. 'Not a bit of it,' said the fat young man. 'Don't you imagine *that*!' and they all got up and dispersed, and walked about and lit cigarettes, and generally tried to show they were perfectly amiable and disengaged, and entirely free from the slightest curiosity about me and the sphere. 'I'm going to keep an eye on that ship out there all the same,' I heard one of them remarking in an undertone. If only they could have forced themselves to it, they would, I believe, even have gone out and left me. I went on with my third egg.

'The weather,' the fat little man remarked presently, 'has been immense, has it not? I don't know *when* we have had such a summer. . . .'

Phoo – whizz! Like a tremendous rocket!

And somewhere a window was broken. . . .

'What's that?' said I.

'It isn't—?' cried the little man, and rushed to the corner window.

All the others rushed to the window likewise. I sat staring at them.

Suddenly I leapt up, knocked over my third egg, and rushed for the window also. I had just thought of something. 'Nothing to be seen there,' cried the little man, rushing for the door.

'It's that boy!' I cried, bawling in hoarse fury; 'It's that accursed boy!' and turning about I pushed the waiter aside – he was just bringing me some more toast – and rushed violently out of the room and down and out upon the queer little esplanade in front of the hotel.

The sea, which had been smooth, was rough now with hurrying cat's-paws, and all about where the sphere had been was tumbled water like the wake of a ship. Above, a little puff of cloud whirled like dispersing smoke, and the three or four people on the beach were staring up with interrogative faces towards the point of that unexpected report. And that was all! Boots and waiter and the four young men in blazers came rushing out behind me. Shouts came from windows and doors, and all sorts of worrying people came into sight – agape.

For a time I stood there, too overwhelmed by this new development to think of the people.

At first I was too stunned to see the thing as any definite disaster – I was just stunned, as a man is by some accidental violent blow. It is only afterwards he begins to appreciate his specific injury.

'Good Lord!'

I felt as though somebody was pouring funk out of a can down the back of my neck. My legs became feeble. I had got the first intimation of what the disaster meant for me. There was that confounded boy – sky high! I was utterly 'left'. There was the gold in the coffee-room – my only possession on earth. How would it all work out? The general effect was of a gigantic unmanageable confusion.

'I say,' said the voice of the little man behind. 'I *say*, you know.'

I wheeled about, and there were twenty or thirty people, a sort of irregular investment of people, all bombarding me with dumb interrogation, with infinite doubt and suspicion. I felt the compulsion of their eyes intolerably. I groaned aloud.

'I *can't*!' I shouted. 'I tell you I can't! I'm not equal to it! You must puzzle and – and be damned to you!'

I gesticulated convulsively. He receded a step as though I had threatened him. I made a bolt through them into the hotel. I charged back into the

coffee-room, rang the bell furiously. I gripped the waiter as he entered. 'D'ye hear?' I shouted. 'Get help and carry these bars up to my room right away.'

He failed to understand me, and I shouted and raved at him. A scared-looking little old man in a green apron appeared, and further two of the young men in flannels. I made a dash at them and commandeered their services. As soon as the gold was in my room I felt free to quarrel. 'Now get out,' I shouted; 'all of you get out if you don't want to see a man go mad before your eyes!' And I helped the waiter by the shoulder as he hesitated in the doorway. And then, as soon as I had the door locked on them all, I tore off the little man's clothes again, shied them right and left, and got into bed forthwith. And there I lay swearing and panting and cooling for a very long time.

At last I was calm enough to get out of bed and ring up the round-eyed waiter for a flannel nightshirt, a soda and whisky, and some good cigars. And these things being procured me, after an exasperating delay that drove me several times to the bell, I locked the door again and proceeded very deliberately to look the entire situation in the face.

The net result of the great experiment presented itself as an absolute failure. It was a rout, and I was the sole survivor. It was an absolute collapse, and this was the final disaster. There was nothing for it but to save myself, and as much as I could in the way of prospects from our *débâcle*. At one fatal crowning blow all my vague resolutions of return and recovery had vanished. My intention of going back to the moon, of getting a sphereful of gold, and afterwards of having a fragment of Cavorite analysed and so recovering the great secret – perhaps, finally, even of recovering Cavor's body – all these ideas vanished altogether.

I was the sole survivor, and that was all.

I think that going to bed was one of the luckiest ideas I have ever had in an emergency. I really believe I should either have got loose-headed or done some fatal, indiscreet thing. But there, locked in and secure from all interruption, I could think out the position in all its bearings and make my arrangements at leisure.

Of course it was quite clear to me what had happened to the boy. He had crawled into the sphere, meddled with the studs, shut the Cavorite windows, and gone up. It was highly improbable he had screwed in the manhole stopper, and, even if he had, the chances were a thousand to one against his getting back. It was fairly evident that he would gravitate with my bales to somewhere near the middle of the sphere and remain there, and so cease to be a legitimate terrestrial interest, however remarkable he might seem to the inhabitants of some remote quarter of space. I very speedily convinced myself on that point. And as for any responsibility I might have in the matter, the more I reflected upon that, the clearer it

became that if only I kept quiet about things, I need not trouble myself about that. If I was faced by sorrowing parents demanding their lost boy, I had merely to demand my lost sphere – or ask them what they meant. At first I had had a vision of weeping parents and guardians, and all sorts of complications; but now I saw that I simply had to keep my mouth shut, and nothing in that way could arise.

And, indeed, the more I lay and smoked and thought, the more evident became the wisdom of impenetrability.

It is within the right of every British citizen, provided he does not commit damage nor indecorum, to appear suddenly wherever he pleases, and as ragged and filthy as he pleases, and with whatever amount of virgin gold he sees fit to encumber himself, and no one has any right at all to hinder and detain him in this procedure. I formulated that at last to myself, and repeated it over as a sort of private Magna Charta of my liberty.

Once I had put that issue on one side, I could take up and consider in an equable manner certain considerations I had scarcely dared to think of before, namely, those arising out of the circumstances of my bankruptcy. But now, looking at this matter calmly and at leisure, I could see that if only I suppressed my identity by a temporary assumption of some less well-known name, and if I retained the two months' beard that had grown upon me, the risks of any annoyance from the spiteful creditor to whom I have already alluded became very small indeed. From that to a definite course of rational worldly action was plain sailing. It was all amazingly petty, no doubt, but what was there remaining for me to do?

Whatever I did I was resolved that I would keep myself level and right side up.

I ordered up writing materials, and addressed a letter to the New Romney Bank – the nearest, the waiter informed me – telling the manager I wished to open an account with him, and requesting him to send two trustworthy persons properly authenticated in a cab with a good horse to fetch some hundredweight of gold with which I happened to be encumbered. I signed the letter 'Blake,' which seemed to me to be a thoroughly respectable sort of name. This done, I got a Folkestone Blue Book, picked out an outfitter, and asked him to send a cutter to measure me for a drab tweed suit, ordering at the same time a valise, dressing bag, brown boots, shirts, hats (to fit) and so forth; and from a watchmaker I also ordered a watch. And these letters being despatched, I had up as good a lunch as the hotel could give, and then lay smoking a cigar, as calm and ordinary as possible, until in accordance with my instructions two duly authenticated clerks came from the bank and weighed and took away my gold. After which I pulled the clothes over my ears in order to drown any knocking, and went very comfortably to sleep.

I went to sleep. No doubt it was a prosaic thing for the first man back from the moon to do, and I can imagine that the young and imaginative

reader will find my behaviour disappointing. But I was horribly fatigued and bothered, and – confound it! – what else was there to do? There certainly was not the remotest chance of my being believed, if I had told my story then, and it would certainly have subjected me to intolerable annoyances. I went to sleep. When at last I woke up again I was ready to face the world, as I have always been accustomed to face it since I came to years of discretion. And so I got away to Italy, and there it is I am writing this story. If the world will not have it as fact, then the world may take it as fiction. It is no concern of mine.

And now that the account is finished, I am amazed to think how completely this adventure is gone and done with. Everybody believes that Cavor was a not very brilliant scientific experimenter who blew up his house and himself at Lympne, and they explain the bang that followed my arrival at Littlestone by a reference to the experiments with explosives that are going on continually at the government establishment of Lydd, two miles away. I must confess that hitherto I have not acknowledged my share in the disappearance of Master Tommy Simmons, which was that little boy's name. That, perhaps, may prove a difficult item of corroboration to explain away. They account for my appearance in rags with two bars of indisputable gold upon the Littlestone beach in various ingenious ways – it doesn't worry me what they think of me. They say I have strung all these things together to avoid being questioned too closely as to the source of my wealth. I would like to see the man who could invent a story that would hold together like this one. Well, they must take it as fiction – there it is.

I have told my story – and now I suppose I have to take up the worries of this terrestrial life again. Even if one has been to the moon, one has still to earn a living. So I am working here at Amalfi, on the scenario of that play I sketched before Cavor came walking into my world, and I am trying to piece my life together as it was before ever I saw him. I must confess that I find it hard to keep my mind on the play when the moonshine comes into my room. It is full moon here, and last night I was out on the pergola for hours, staring away at that shining blankness that hides so much. Imagine it! Tables and chairs, and trestles and bars of gold! Confound it! – If only one could hit on that Cavorite again! But a thing like that doesn't come twice in a life. Here I am, a little better off than I was at Lympne, and that is all. And Cavor has committed suicide in a more elaborate way than any human being ever did before. So the story closes as finally and completely as a dream. It fits in so little with all the other things of life, so much of it is so utterly remote from all human experience, the leaping, the eating, the breathing, and these weightless times, that indeed there are moments when, in spite of my moon gold, I do more than half believe myself that the whole thing was a dream. . . .

CHAPTER XXII

The Astonishing Communication of Mr Julius Wendigee

When I had finished my account of my return to the earth at Littlestone I wrote 'The End', made a flourish, and threw my pen aside, fully believing that the whole story of the First Men in the Moon was done. Not only had I done this, but I had placed my manuscript in the hands of a literary agent, had permitted it to be sold, had seen the greater portion of it appear in the *Strand Magazine*, and was setting to work again upon the scenario of the play I had commenced at Lympne before I realized that the end was not yet. And then, following me from Amalfi to Algiers, there reached me (it is now about six months ago) one of the most astounding communications I have ever been fated to receive. Briefly, it informed me that Mr Julius Wendigee, a Dutch electrician, who has been experimenting with certain apparatus akin to the apparatus used by Mr Tesla in America, in the hope of discovering some method of communication with Mars, was receiving day by day a curiously fragmentary message in English, which was indisputably emanating from Mr Cavor in the moon.

At first I thought the thing was an elaborate practical joke by someone who had seen the manuscript of my narrative. I answered Mr Wendigee jestingly, but he replied in a manner that put such suspicion altogether aside, and in a state of inconceivable excitement I hurried from Algiers to the little observatory upon the Monte Rosa in which he was working. In the presence of his record and his appliances – and above all of the messages from Cavor that were coming to hand – my lingering doubts vanished. I decided at once to accept a proposal he made me to remain with him, assisting him to take down the record from day to day, and endeavouring with him to send a message back to the moon. Cavor, we learnt, was not only alive but free, in the midst of an almost inconceivable community of these ant-like beings, these ant-men, in the blue darkness of the lunar caves. He was lamed, it seemed, but otherwise in quite good health – in better health, he distinctly said, than he usually enjoyed on earth. He had had a fever, but it had left no bad effects. But curiously enough he seemed to be labouring under a conviction that I was either dead in the moon crater or lost in the deep of space.

His message began to be received by Mr Wendigee when that gentleman was engaged in quite a different investigation. The reader will no doubt recall the little excitement that began the century, arising out of an announce-ment by Mr Nikola Tesla, the American electrical celebrity, that he had received a message from Mars. His announcement renewed attention to a

fact that had long been familiar to scientific people, namely: that from some unknown source in space, waves of electro-magnetic disturbance, entirely similar to those used by Signor Marconi for his wireless telegraphy, are constantly reaching the earth. Besides Mr Tesla quite a number of other observers have been engaged in perfecting apparatus for receiving and recording these vibrations, though few would go so far as to consider them actual messages from some extra-terrestrial sender. Among that few, however, we must certainly count Mr Wendigee. Ever since 1898 he had devoted himself almost entirely to this subject, and being a man of ample means he had erected an observatory on the flanks of Monte Rosa, in a position singularly adapted in every way for such observations.

My scientific attainments, I must admit, are not great, but so far as they enable me to judge, Mr Wendigee's contrivances for detecting and recording any disturbances in the electro-magnetic conditions of space are singularly original and ingenious. And by a happy combination of circumstances they were set up and in operation about two months before Cavor made his first attempt to call up the earth. Consequently we have fragments of his communication even from the beginning. Unhappily, they are only fragments, and the most momentous of all the things that he had to tell humanity – the instructions, that is, for the making of Cavorite, if, indeed, he ever transmitted them – have throbbed themselves away unrecorded into space. We never succeeded in getting a response back to Cavor. He was unable to tell, therefore, what we had received or what we had missed; nor, indeed, did he certainly know that anyone on earth was really aware of his efforts to reach us. And the persistence he displayed in sending eighteen long descriptions of lunar affairs – as they would be if we had them complete – shows how much his mind must have turned back towards his native planet since he left it two years ago.

You can imagine how amazed Mr Wendigee must have been when he discovered his record of electro-magnetic disturbances interlaced by Cavor's straightforward English. Mr Wendigee knew nothing of our wild journey moonward, and suddenly – this English out of the void!

It is well the reader should understand the conditions under which it would seem these messages were sent. Somewhere within the moon Cavor certainly had access for a time to a considerable amount of electrical apparatus, and it would seem he rigged up – perhaps furtively – a transmitting arrangement of the Marconi type. This he was able to operate at irregular intervals: sometimes for only half an hour or so, sometimes for three or four hours at a stretch. At these times he transmitted his earthward message, regardless of the fact that the relative position of the moon and points upon the earth's surface is constantly altering. As a consequence of this and of the necessary imperfections of our recording instruments his communication comes and goes in our records in an extremely fitful manner; it becomes

blurred; it 'fades out' in a mysterious and altogether exasperating way. And added to this is the fact that he was not an expert operator; he had partly forgotten, or never completely mastered, the code in general use, and as he became fatigued he dropped words and misspelt in a curious manner.

Altogether we have probably lost quite half of the communications he made, and much we have is damaged, broken, and partly effaced. In the abstract that follows the reader must be prepared therefore for a considerable amount of break, hiatus, and change of topic. Mr Wendigee and I are collaborating in a complete and annotated edition of the Cavor record, which we hope to publish, together with a detailed account of the instruments employed, beginning with the first volume in January next. That will be the full and scientific report, of which this is only the popular first transcript. But here we give at least sufficient to complete the story I have told, and to give the broad outlines of the state of that other world so near, so akin, and yet so dissimilar to our own.

CHAPTER XXIII

An Abstract of the Six Messages First Received from Mr Cavor

The two earlier messages of Mr Cavor may very well be reserved for that larger volume. They simply tell, with greater brevity and with a difference in several details that is interesting, but not of any vital importance, the bare facts of the making of the sphere and our departure from the world. Throughout, Cavor speaks of me as a man who is dead, but with a curious change of temper as he approaches our landing on the moon. 'Poor Bedford', he says of me, and 'this poor young man'; and he blames himself for inducing a young man 'by no means well equipped for such adventures' to leave a planet 'on which he was indisputably fitted to succeed' on so precarious a mission. I think he underrates the part my energy and practical capacity played in bringing about the realization of his theoretical sphere. 'We arrived,' he says, with no more account of our passage through space than if we had made a journey of common occurrence in a railway train.

And then he becomes increasingly unfair to me. Unfair, indeed, to an extent I should not have expected in a man trained in the search for truth. Looking back over my previously written account of these things, I must insist that I have been altogether juster to Cavor than he has been to me. I have extenuated little and suppressed nothing. But his account is: –

'It speedily became apparent that the entire strangeness of our circumstances and surroundings – great loss of weight, attenuated but highly oxygenated air, consequent exaggeration of the results of muscular effort, rapid development of weird plants from obscure spores, lurid sky – was exciting my companion unduly. On the moon his character seemed to deteriorate. He became impulsive, rash and quarrelsome. In a little while his folly in devouring some gigantic vesicles and his consequent intoxication led to our capture by the Selenites – before we had had the slightest opportunity of properly observing their ways. . . .'

(He says, you observe, nothing of his own concession to these same 'vesicles'.)

And he goes on from that point to say that: 'We came to a difficult passage with them, and Bedford mistaking certain gestures of theirs' – pretty gestures they were! – 'gave way to a panic violence. He ran amuck, killed three, and perforce I had to flee with him after the outrage. Subsequently we fought with a number who endeavoured to bar our way, and slew seven or eight more. It says much for the tolerance of these beings that on my recapture I was not instantly slain. We made our way to the exterior and separated in the crater of our arrival, to increase our chances of recovering

our sphere. But presently I came upon a body of Selenites, led by two who were curiously different, even in form, from any of those we had seen hitherto, with larger heads and smaller bodies, and much more elaborately wrapped about. And after evading them for some time I fell into a crevasse, cut my head rather badly and displaced my patella, and, finding crawling very painful, decided to surrender – if they would still permit me to do so. This they did, and, perceiving my helpless condition, carried me with them again into the moon. And of Bedford I have heard or seen nothing more, nor, so far as I can gather, has any Selenite. Either the night overtook him in the crater, or else, which is more probable, he found the sphere, and, desiring to steal a march upon me, made off with it – only, I fear, to find it uncontrollable, and to meet a more lingering fate in outer space.'

And with that Cavor dismisses me and goes on to more interesting topics. I dislike the idea of seeming to use my position as his editor to deflect his story in my own interest, but I am obliged to protest here against the turn he gives these occurrences. He says nothing about that gasping message on the blood-stained paper in which he told, or attempted to tell, a very different story. The dignified self-surrender is an altogether new view of the affair that has come to him, I must insist, since he began to feel secure among the lunar people; and as for the 'stealing a march' conception, I am quite willing to let the reader decide between us on what he has before him. I know I am not a model man – I have made no pretence to be. But am I *that*?

However, that is the sum of my wrongs. From this point I can edit Cavor with an untroubled mind, for he mentions me no more.

It would seem the Selenites who had come upon him carried him to some point in the interior down 'a great shaft' by means of what he describes as 'a sort of balloon'. We gather from the rather confused passage in which he describes this, and from a number of chance allusions and hints in other and subsequent messages, that this 'great shaft' is one of an enormous system of artificial shafts that run, each from what is called a lunar 'crater', downwards for very nearly a hundred miles towards the central portion of our satellite. These shafts communicate by transverse tunnels, they throw out abysmal caverns and expand into great globular places; the whole of the moon's substance for a hundred miles inward, indeed, is a mere sponge of rock. 'Partly,' says Cavor, 'this sponginess is natural, but very largely it is due to the enormous industry of the Selenites in the past. The enormous circular mounds of the excavated rock and earth it is that form these great circles about the tunnels known to earthly astronomers (misled by a false analogy) as volcanoes.'

It was down this shaft they took him, in this 'sort of balloon' he speaks of, at first into an inky blackness and then into a region of continually increasing phosphorescence. Cavor's despatches show him to be curiously

regardless of detail for a scientific man, but we gather that this light was due to the streams and cascades of water – 'no doubt containing some phosphorescent organism' – that flowed ever more abundantly downward towards the Central Sea. And as he descended, he says, 'The Selenites also became luminous.' And at last far below him he saw, as it were, a lake of heatless fire, the waters of the Central Sea, glowing and eddying in strange perturbation, 'like luminous blue milk that is just on the boil'.

'This Lunar Sea,' says Cavor, in a later passage, 'is not a stagnant ocean; a solar tide sends it in a perpetual flow around the lunar axis, and strange storms and boilings and rushings of its waters occur, and at times cold winds and thunderings that ascend out of it into the busy ways of the great ant-hill above. It is only when the water is in motion that it gives out light; in its rare seasons of calm it is black. Commonly, when one sees it, its waters rise and fall in an oily swell, and flakes and big rafts of shining, bubbly foam drift with the sluggish, faintly glowing current. The Selenites navigate its cavernous straits and lagoons in little shallow boats of a canoe-like shape; and even before my journey to the galleries about the Grand Lunar, who is Master of the Moon, I was permitted to make a brief excursion on its waters.

'The caverns and passages are naturally very tortuous. A large proportion of these ways are known only to expert pilots among the fishermen, and not infrequently Selenites are lost for ever in their labyrinths. In their remoter recesses, I am told, strange creatures lurk, some of them terrible and dangerous creatures that all the science of the moon has been unable to exterminate. There is particularly the Rapha, an inextricable mass of clutching tentacles that one hacks to pieces only to multiply; and the Tzee, a darting creature that is never seen, so subtly and suddenly does it slay. . . .'

He gives us a gleam of description.

'I was reminded on this excursion of what I have read of the Mammoth Caves; if only I had had a yellow flambeau instead of the pervading blue light, and a solid-looking boatman with an oar instead of a scuttle-faced Selenite working an engine at the back of the canoe, I could have imagined I had suddenly got back to earth. The rocks about us were very various, sometimes black, sometimes pale blue and veined, and once they flashed and glittered as though we had come into a mine of sapphires. And below one saw the ghostly phosphorescent fishes flash and vanish in the hardly less phosphorescent deep. Then, presently, a long ultramarine vista down the turgid stream of one of the channels of traffic, and a landing-stage, and then, perhaps, a glimpse up the enormous crowded shaft of one of the vertical ways.

'In one great place heavy with glistening stalactites a number of boats were fishing. We went alongside one of these and watched the long-armed fishing Selenites winding in a net. They were little, hunchbacked insects, with very strong arms, short, bandy legs, and crinkled face-masks. As they

pulled at it that net seemed the heaviest thing I had come upon in the moon; it was loaded with weights – no doubt of gold – and it took a long time to draw, for in those waters the larger and more edible fish lurk deep. The fish in the net came up like a blue moonrise – a blaze of darting, tossing blue.

'Among their catch was a many-tentaculate, evil-eyed black thing, ferociously active, whose appearance they greeted with shrieks and twitters, and which with quick, nervous movements they hacked to pieces by means of little hatchets. All its dissevered limbs continued to lash and writhe in a vicious manner. Afterwards, when fever had hold of me, I dreamt again and again of that bitter, furious creature rising so vigorous and active out of the unknown sea. It was the most active and malignant thing of all the living creatures I have yet seen in this world inside the moon. . . .

'The surface of this sea must be very nearly two hundred miles (if not more) below the level of the moon's exterior; all the cities of the moon lie, I learnt, immediately above this Central Sea, in such cavernous spaces and artificial galleries as I have described, and they communicate with the exterior by enormous vertical shafts which open invariably in what are called by earthly astronomers the "craters" of the moon. The lid covering one such aperture I had already seen during the wanderings that had preceded my capture.

'Upon the condition of the less central portion of the moon I have not yet arrived at very precise knowledge. There is an enormous system of caverns in which the mooncalves shelter during the night; and there are abattoirs and the like – in one of these it was that I and Bedford fought with the Selenite butchers – and I have since seen balloons laden with meat descending out of the upper dark. I have as yet scarcely learnt as much of these things as a Zulu in London would learn about the British corn supplies in the same time. It is clear, however, that these vertical shafts and the vegetation of the surface must play an essential role in ventilating and keeping fresh the atmosphere of the moon. At one time, and particularly on my first emergence from my prison, there was certainly a cold wind blowing *down* the shaft, and later there was a kind of sirocco upward that corresponded with my fever. For at the end of about three weeks I fell ill of an indefinable sort of fever, and in spite of sleep and the quinine tabloids that very fortunately I had brought in my pocket, I remained ill and fretting miserably, almost to the time when I was taken into the presence of the Grand Lunar, who is Master of the Moon.

'I will not dilate on the wretchedness of my condition,' he remarks, 'during those days of ill-health.' And he goes on with great amplitude with details I omit here. 'My temperature,' he concludes, 'kept abnormally high for a long time, and I lost all desire for food. I had stagnant waking intervals, and sleep tormented by dreams, and at one phase I was, I remember, so weak as

to be earth-sick and almost hysterical. I longed almost intolerably for colour
to break the everlasting blue. . . .'

He reverts again presently to the topic of this sponge caught lunar atmos-
phere. I am told by astronomers and physicists that all he tells is in absolute
accordance with what was already known of the moon's condition. Had
earthly astronomers had the courage and imagination to push home a bold
induction, says Mr Wendigee, they might have foretold almost everything
that Cavor has to say of the general structure of the moon. They know now
pretty certainly that moon and earth are not so much satellite and primary
as smaller and greater sisters, made out of one mass, and consequently made
of the same material. And since the density of the moon is only three-fifths
that of the earth, there can be nothing for it but that she is hollowed out
by a great system of caverns. There was no necessity, said Sir Jabez Flap,
FRS, that most entertaining exponent of the facetious side of the stars, that
we should ever have gone to the moon to find out such easy inferences,
and points the pun with an allusion to Gruyère, but he certainly might have
announced his knowledge of the hollowness of the moon before. And if the
moon is hollow, then the apparent absence of air and water is, of course,
quite easily explained. The sea lies within at the bottom of the caverns, and
the air travels through the great sponge of galleries, in accordance with
simple physical laws. The caverns of the moon, on the whole, are very windy
places. As the sunlight comes round the moon the air in the outer galleries
on that side is heated, its pressure increases, some flows out on the exterior
and mingles with the evaporating air of the craters (where the plants remove
its carbonic acid), while the greater portion flows round through the galleries
to replace the shrinking air of the cooling side that the sunlight has left.
There is, therefore, a constant eastward breeze in the air of the outer galleries,
and an up-flow during the lunar day up the shafts, complicated, of course,
very greatly by the varying shape of the galleries, and the ingenious contriv-
ances of the Selenite mind. . . .

CHAPTER XXIV

The Natural History of the Selenites

The messages of Cavor from the sixth up to the sixteenth are for the most part so much broken, and they abound so in repetitions, that they scarcely form a consecutive narrative. They will be given in full, of course, in the scientific report, but here it will be far more convenient to continue simply to abstract and quote as in the former chapter. We have subjected every word to a keen critical scrutiny, and my own brief memories and impressions of lunar things have been of inestimable help in interpreting what would otherwise have been impenetrably dark. And, naturally, as living beings our interest centres far more upon the strange community of lunar insects in which he was living, it would seem, as an honoured guest than upon the mere physical condition of their world.

I have already made it clear, I think, that the Selenites I saw resembled man in maintaining the erect attitude, and in having four limbs, and I have compared the general appearance of their heads and the jointing of their limbs to that of insects. I have mentioned, too, the peculiar consequence of the smaller gravitation of the moon on their fragile slightness. Cavor confirms me upon all these points. He calls them 'animals', though of course they fall under no division of the classification of earthly creatures, and he points out 'the insect type of anatomy had, fortunately for men, never exceeded a relatively very small size on earth'. The largest terrestrial insects, living or extinct, do not, as a matter of fact, measure 6 inches in length; 'but here, against the lesser gravitation of the moon, a creature certainly as much an insect as vertebrate seems to have been able to attain to human and ultrahuman dimensions.'

He does not mention the ant, but throughout his allusions the ant is continually being brought before my mind, in its sleepless activity, in its intelligence and social organization, in its structure, and more particularly in the fact that it displays, in addition to the two forms, the male and the female form, that almost all other animals possess, a number of other sexless creatures, workers, soldiers, and the like, differing from one another in structure, character, power and use, and yet all members of the same species. For these Selenites, also, have a great variety of forms. Of course they are not only colossally greater in size than ants, but also, in Cavor's opinion at least, in intelligence, morality, and social wisdom are they colossally greater than men. And instead of the four or five different forms of ant that are found, there are almost innumerably different forms of Selenite. I have endeavoured to indicate the very considerable difference observable

in such Selenites of the outer crust as I happened to encounter; the differ-
ences in size and proportions were certainly as wide as the differences
between the most widely separated races of men. But such differences as
I saw fade absolutely to nothing in comparison with the huge distinctions
of which Cavor tells. It would seem the exterior Selenites I saw were,
indeed, mostly engaged in kindred occupations – mooncalf herds, butchers,
fleshers and the like. But within the moon, practically unsuspected by me,
there are, it seems, a number of other sorts of Selenite, differing in size,
differing in the relative size of part to part, differing in power and appear-
ance, and yet not different species of creatures, but only different forms of
one species, and retaining through all their variations a certain common
likeness that marks their specific unity. The moon is, indeed, a sort of vast
ant-hill, only, instead of there being only four or five sorts of ant, there are
many hundred different sorts of Selenite, and almost every gradation
between one sort and another.

It would seem the discovery came upon Cavor very speedily. I infer rather
than learn from his narrative that he was captured by the mooncalf herds
under the direction of those other Selenites who 'have larger brain cases
(heads?) and very much shorter legs'. Finding he would not walk even under
the goad, they carried him into darkness, crossed a narrow, plank-like bridge
that may have been the identical bridge I had refused, and put him down
in something that must have seemed at first to be some sort of lift. This was
the balloon – it had certainly been absolutely invisible to us in the darkness
– and what had seemed to me a mere plank-walking into the void was really,
no doubt, the passage of the gangway. In this he descended towards constantly
more luminous caverns of the moon. At first they descended in silence –
save for the twitterings of the Selenites – and then into a stir of windy
movement. In a little while the profound blackness had made his eyes so
sensitive that he began to see more and more of the things about him, and
at last the vague took shape.

'Conceive an enormous cylindrical space,' says Cavor in his seventh
message, 'a quarter of a mile across, perhaps; very dimly lit at first and then
brighter, with big platforms twisting down its sides in a spiral that vanishes
at last below in a blue profundity; and lit even more brightly – one could
not tell how or why. Think of the well of the very largest spiral staircase or
lift-shaft that you have ever looked down, and magnify that by a hundred.
Imagine it at twilight seen through blue glass. Imagine yourself looking down
that; only imagine also that you feel extraordinarily light, and have got rid
of any giddy feeling you might have on earth, and you will have the first
conditions of my impression. Round this enormous shaft imagine a broad
gallery running in a much steeper spiral than would be credible on earth,
and forming a steep road protected from the gulf only by a little parapet
that vanishes at last in perspective a couple of miles below.

'Looking up, I saw the very fellow of the downward vision; it had, of course, the effect of looking into a very steep cone. A wind was blowing down the shaft, and far above I fancy I heard, growing fainter and fainter, the bellowing of the mooncalves that were being driven down again from their evening pasturage on the exterior. And up and down the spiral galleries were scattered numerous moon people, pallid, faintly self-luminous beings, regarding our appearance or busied on unknown errands.

'Either I fancied it or a flake of snow came drifting down on the icy breeze. And then, falling like a snowflake, a little figure, a little man-insect clinging to a parachute, drove down very swiftly towards the central places of the moon.

'The big-headed Selenite sitting beside me, seeing me move my head with the gesture of one who saw, pointed with his trunk-like "hand" and indicated a sort of jetty coming into sight very far below: a little landing-stage, as it were, hanging into the void. As it swept up towards us our pace diminished very rapidly, and in a few moments, as it seemed, we were abreast of it and at rest. A mooring-rope was flung and grasped, and I found myself pulled down to a level with a great crowd of Selenites, who jostled to see me.

'It was an incredible crowd. Suddenly and violently there was forced upon my attention the vast amount of difference there is amongst these beings of the moon.

'Indeed, there seemed not two alike in all that jostling multitude. They differed in shape, they differed in size, they rang all the horrible changes on the theme of Selenite form! Some bulged and overhung, some ran about among the feet of their fellows. All of them had a grotesque and disquieting suggestion of an insect that has somehow contrived to mock humanity; but all seemed to present an incredible exaggeration of some particular feature: one had a vast right fore-limb, an enormous antennal arm, as it were; one seemed all leg, poised, as it were, on stilts; another protruded the edge of his face mask into a nose-like organ that made him startlingly human until one saw his expressionless gaping mouth. The strange and (except for the want of mandibles and palps) most insect-like head of the mooncalf-minders underwent, indeed, the most incredible transformations: here it was broad and low, here high and narrow; here its leathery brow was drawn out into horns and strange features; here it was whiskered and divided, and there with a grotesquely human profile. One distortion was particularly conspic-uous. There were several brain cases distended like bladders to a huge size, with the face mask reduced to quite small proportions. There were several amazing forms, with heads reduced to microscopic proportions and blobby bodies; and fantastic, flimsy things that existed, it would seem, only as a basis for vast, trumpet-like protrusions of the lower part of the mask. And oddest of all, as it seemed to me for the moment, two or three of these weird inhabitants of a subterranean world, a world sheltered by innumerable miles

of rock from sun or rain, *carried umbrellas* in their tentaculate hands! – Real terrestrial-looking umbrellas! And then I thought of the parachutist I had watched descend.

'These moon people behaved exactly as a human crowd might have done in similar circumstances: they jostled and thrust one another, they shoved one another aside, they even clambered upon one another to get a glimpse of me. Every moment they increased in numbers, and pressed more urgently upon the discs of my ushers' – Cavor does not explain what he means by this – 'every moment fresh shapes emerged from the shadows and forced themselves upon my astounded attention. And presently I was signed and helped into a sort of litter, and lifted up on the shoulders of strong-armed bearers, and so borne through the twilight over this seething multitude towards the apartments that were provided for me in the moon. All about me were eyes, faces, masks, a leathery noise like the rustling of beetle wings, and a great bleating and cricket-like twittering of Selenite voices. . . .'

We gather he was taken to a 'hexagonal apartment', and there for a space he was confined. Afterwards he was given a much more considerable liberty; indeed, almost as much freedom as one has in a civilized town on earth. And it would appear that the mysterious being who is the ruler and master of the moon appointed two Selenites 'with large heads' to guard and study him, and to establish whatever mental communications were possible with him. And, amazing and incredible as it may seem, these two creatures, these fantastic men-insects, these beings of another world, were presently communicating with Cavor by means of terrestrial speech.

Cavor speaks of them as Phi-oo and Tsi-puff. Phi-oo, he says, was about 5 feet high; he had small, slender legs about 18 inches long, and slight feet of the common lunar pattern. On these balanced a little body, throbbing with the pulsations of his heart. He had long, soft, many-jointed arms ending in a tentacled grip, and his neck was many-jointed in the usual way, but exceptionally short and thick. His head, says Cavor – apparently alluding to some previous description that has gone astray in space – 'is of the common lunar type, but strangely modified. The mouth has the usual expressionless gape, but it is unusually small and pointing downward, and the mask is reduced to the size of a large flat nose-flap. On either side are the little eyes.

'The rest of the head is distended into a huge globe, and the chitinous leathery cuticle of the mooncalf herds thins out to a mere membrane, through which the pulsating brain movements are distinctly visible. He is a creature, indeed, with a tremendously hypertrophied brain, and with the rest of his organism both relatively and absolutely dwarfed.'

In another passage Cavor compares the back view of him to Atlas supporting the world. Tsi-puff, it seems, was a very similar insect, but his

heart – not a flutter. *That* doesn't make me feel as if there was a man present. In a sense it's more dead than death, for these doctors tell me that even the hair has stopped growing. Now with the proper dead, the hair will go on growing—'

'I know,' said Warming, with a flash of pain in his expression.

They peered through the glass again. Graham was indeed in a strange state, in the flaccid phase of a trance, but a trance unprecedented in medical history. Trances had lasted for as much as a year before – but at the end of that time it had ever been a waking or a death; sometimes first one and then the other. Isbister noted the marks the physicians had made in injecting nourishment, for that device had been resorted to to postpone collapse; he pointed them out to Warming, who had been trying not to see them.

'And while he has been lying here,' said Isbister, with the zest of a life freely spent, 'I have changed my plans in life; married, raised a family, my eldest lad – I hadn't begun to think of sons then – is an American citizen, and looking forward to leaving Harvard. There's a touch of grey in my hair. And this man, not a day older nor wiser (practically) than I was in my downy days. It's curious to think of.'

Warming turned. 'And I have grown old too. I played cricket with him when I was still only a lad. And he looks a young man still. Yellow perhaps. But that *is* a young man nevertheless.'

'And there's been the War,' said Isbister.

'From beginning to end.'

'I've understood,' said Isbister after a pause, 'that he had some moderate property of his own?'

'That is so,' said Warming. He coughed primly. 'As it happens – I have charge of it.'

'Ah!' Isbister thought, hesitated and spoke: 'No doubt – his keep here is not expensive – no doubt it will have improved – accumulated?'

'It has. He will wake up very much better off – if he wakes – than when he slept.'

'As a business man,' said Isbister, 'that thought has naturally been in my mind. I have, indeed, sometimes thought that, speaking commercially, of course, this sleep may be a very good thing for him. That he knows what he is about, so to speak, in being insensible so long. If he had lived straight on—'

'I doubt if he would have premeditated as much,' said Warming. 'He was not a far-sighted man. In fact—'

'Yes?'

'We differed on that point. I stood to him somewhat in the relation of a guardian. You have probably seen enough of affairs to recognize that occasionally a certain friction—. But even if that was the case, there is a doubt

whether he will ever wake. This sleep exhausts slowly, but it exhausts. Apparently he is sliding slowly, very slowly and tediously, down a long slope, if you can understand me?'

'It will be a pity to lose his surprise. There's been a lot of change these twenty years. It's Rip Van Winkle come real.'

'There has been a lot of change certainly,' said Warming. And, among other changes, I have changed. I am an old man.'

Isbister hesitated, and then feigned a belated surprise. 'I shouldn't have thought it.'

'I was forty-three when his bankers – you remember you wired to his bankers – sent on to me.'

'I got their address from the cheque book in his pocket,' said Isbister.

'Well, the addition is not difficult,' said Warming.

There was another pause, and then Isbister gave way to an unavoidable curiosity. 'He may go on for years yet,' he said, and had a moment of hesitation. 'We have to consider that. His affairs, you know, may fall some day into the hands of – someone else, you know.'

'That, if you will believe me, Mr Isbister, is one of the problems most constantly before my mind. We happen to be – as a matter of fact, there are no very trustworthy connections of ours. It is a grotesque and unprecedented position.'

'It is,' said Isbister. 'As a matter of fact, it's a case for a public trustee, if only we had such a functionary.'

'It seems to me it's a case for some public body, some practically undying guardian. If he really is going on living – as the doctors, some of them, think. As a matter of fact, I have gone to one or two public men about it. But, so far, nothing has been done.'

'It wouldn't be a bad idea to hand him over to some public body – the British Museum Trustees, or the Royal College of Physicians. Sounds a bit odd, of course, but the whole situation is odd.'

'The difficulty is to induce them to take him.'

'Red tape, I suppose?'

'Partly.'

Pause. 'It's a curious business, certainly,' said Isbister. 'And compound interest has a way of mounting up.'

'It has,' said Warming. 'And now the gold supplies are running short there is a tendency towards . . . appreciation.'

'I've felt that,' said Isbister with a grimace. 'But it makes it better for *him*.'

'If he wakes.'

'If he wakes,' echoed Isbister. 'Do you notice the pinched-ill look of his nose, and the way in which his eyelids sink?'

Warming looked and thought for a space. 'I doubt if he will wake,' he said at last.

WHEN THE SLEEPER WAKES

'I never properly understood,' said Isbister, 'what it was brought this on. He told me something about overstudy. I've often been curious.'

'He was a man of considerable gifts, but spasmodic, emotional. He had grave domestic troubles, divorced his wife, in fact, and it was as a relief from that, I think, that he took up politics of the rabid sort. He was a fanatical Radical – a Socialist – or typical Liberal, as they used to call themselves, of the advanced school. Energetic – flighty – undisciplined. Overwork upon a controversy did this for him. I remember the pamphlet he wrote – a curious production. Wild, whirling stuff. There were one or two prophecies. Some of them are already exploded, some of them are established facts. But for the most part to read such a thesis is to realize how full the world is of unanticipated things. He will have much to learn, much to unlearn, when he wakes. If ever a waking comes.'

'I'd give anything to be there,' said Isbister, 'just to hear what he would say to it all.'

'So would I,' said Warming. 'Aye! So would I,' with an old man's sudden turn to self pity. 'But I shall never see him wake.'

He stood looking thoughtfully at the waxen figure. 'He will never wake,' he said at last. He sighed 'He will never wake again.'

CHAPTER III

The Awakening

But Warming was wrong in that. An awakening came.

What a wonderfully complex thing, this simple-seeming unity – the self! Who can trace its reintegration as morning after morning we awaken, the flux and confluence of its countless factors interweaving, rebuilding, the dim first stirrings of the soul, the growth and synthesis of the unconscious to the subconscious, the subconscious to dawning consciousness, until at last we recognize ourselves again. And as it happens to most of us after the night's sleep, so it was with Graham at the end of his vast slumber. A dim cloud of sensation taking shape, a cloudy dreariness, and he found himself vaguely somewhere, recumbent, faint, but alive.

The pilgrimage towards a personal being seemed to traverse vast gulfs, to occupy epochs. Gigantic dreams that were terrible realities at the time, left vague perplexing memories, strange creatures, strange scenery, as if from another planet. There was a distinct impression, too, of a momentous conversation, of a name – he could not tell what name – that was subsequently to recur, of some queer long-forgotten sensation of vein and muscle, of a feeling of vast hopeless effort, the effort of a man near drowning in darkness. Then came a panorama of dazzling unstable confluent scenes. . . .

Graham became aware his eyes were open and regarding some unfamiliar thing.

It was something white, the edge of something, a frame of wood. He moved his head slightly, following the contour of this shape. It went up beyond the top of his eyes. He tried to think where he might be. Did it matter, seeing he was so wretched? The colour of his thoughts was a dark depression. He felt the featureless misery of one who wakes towards the hour of dawn. He had an uncertain sense of whispers and footsteps hastily receding.

The movement of his head involved a perception of extreme physical weakness. He supposed he was in bed in the hotel at the place in the valley – but he could not recall that white edge. He must have slept. He remembered now that he had wanted to sleep. He recalled the cliff and waterfall again, and then recollected something about talking to a passer-by. . . .

How long had he slept? What was that sound of pattering feet? And that rise and fall, like the murmur of breakers on pebbles? He put out a languid hand to reach his watch from the chair whereon it was his habit to place it, and touched some smooth hard surface like glass. This was so unexpected that it startled him extremely. Quite suddenly he rolled over, stared for a

moment, and struggled into a sitting position. The effort was unexpectedly difficult, and it left him giddy and weak – and amazed.

He rubbed his eyes. The riddle of his surroundings was confusing but his mind was quite clear – evidently his sleep had benefited him. He was not in a bed at all as he understood the word, but lying naked on a very soft and yielding mattress, in a trough of dark glass. The mattress was partly transparent, a fact he observed with a strange sense of insecurity, and below it was a mirror reflecting him greyly. About his arm – and he saw with a shock that his skin was strangely dry and yellow – was bound a curious apparatus of rubber, bound so cunningly that it seemed to pass into his skin above and below. And this strange bed was placed in a case of green-ish-coloured glass (as it seemed to him), a bar in the white framework of which had first arrested his attention. In the corner of the case was a stand of glittering and delicately made apparatus, for the most part quite strange appliances, though a maximum and minimum thermometer was recognizable.

The slightly greenish tint of the glass-like substance which surrounded him on every hand obscured what lay behind, but he perceived it was a vast apartment of splendid appearance, and with a very large and simple white archway facing him. Close to the walls of the cage were articles of furniture, a table covered with a silvery cloth, silvery like the side of a fish, a couple of graceful chairs, and on the table a number of dishes with substances piled on them, a bottle and two glasses. He realized that he was intensely hungry.

He could see no human being, and after a period of hesitation scrambled off the translucent mattress and tried to stand on the clean white floor of his little apartment. He had miscalculated his strength, however, and stag-gered and put his hand against the glass-like pane before him to steady himself. For a moment it resisted his hand, bending outward like a distended bladder, then it broke with a slight report and vanished – a pricked bubble. He reeled out into the general space of the hall, greatly astonished. He caught at the table to save himself, knocking one of the glasses to the floor – it rang but did not break – and sat down in one of the armchairs.

When he had a little recovered he filled the remaining glass from the bottle and drank – a colourless liquid it was, but not water, with a pleasing faint aroma and taste and a quality of immediate support and stimulus. He put down the vessel and looked about him.

The apartment lost none of its size and magnificence now that the greenish transparency that had intervened was removed. The archway he saw led to a flight of steps, going downward without the intermediation of a door, to a spacious transverse passage. This passage ran between polished pillars of some white-veined substance of deep ultramarine, and along it came the sound of human movements, and voices and a deep undeviating droning note. He sat, now fully awake, listening alertly, forgetting the viands in his attention.

Then with a shock he remembered that he was naked, and casting about him for covering, saw a long black robe thrown on one of the chairs beside him. This he wrapped about him and sat down again, trembling.

His mind was still a surging perplexity. Clearly he had slept, and had been removed in his sleep. But where? And who were those people, the distant crowd beyond the deep blue pillars? Boscastle? He poured out and partially drank another glass of the colourless fluid.

What was this place? – This place that to his senses seemed subtly quivering like a thing alive? He looked about him at the clean and beautiful form of the apartment, unstained by ornament, and saw that the roof was broken in one place by a circular shaft full of light, and, as he looked, a steady, sweeping shadow blotted it out and passed, and came again and passed. 'Beat, beat,' that sweeping shadow had a note of its own in the subdued tumult that filled the air.

He would have called out, but only a little sound came into his throat. Then he stood up, and, with the uncertain steps of a drunkard, made his way towards the archway. He staggered down the steps, tripped on the corner of the black cloak he had wrapped about himself, and saved himself by catching at one of the blue pillars.

The passage ran down a cool vista of blue and purple, and ended remotely in a railed space like a balcony, brightly lit and projecting into a space of haze, a space like the interior of some gigantic building. Beyond and remote were vast and vague architectural forms. The tumult of voices rose now loud and clear, and on the balcony and with their backs to him, gesticulating and apparently in animated conversation, were three figures, richly dressed in loose and easy garments of bright soft colourings. The noise of a great multitude of people poured up over the balcony, and once it seemed the top of a banner passed, and once some brightly coloured object, a pale blue cap or garment thrown up into the air perhaps, flashed athwart the space and fell. The shouts sounded like English, there was a reiteration of 'Wake!' He heard some indistinct shrill cry, and abruptly the three men began laughing.

'Ha, ha, ha!' laughed one – a red-haired man in a short purple robe. 'When the Sleeper wakes – *when!*'

He turned his eyes full of merriment along the passage. His face changed, the whole man changed, became rigid. The other two turned swiftly at his exclamation and stood motionless. Their faces assumed an expression of consternation, an expression that deepened into awe.

Suddenly Graham's knees bent beneath him, his arm against the pillar collapsed limply, he staggered forward and fell upon his face.

CHAPTER IV

The Sound of a Tumult

Graham's last impression before he fainted was of a clamorous ringing of bells. He learnt afterwards that he was insensible, hanging between life and death, for the better part of an hour. When he recovered his senses, he was back on his translucent couch, and there was a stirring warmth at heart and throat. The dark apparatus, he perceived, had been removed from his arm, which was bandaged. The white framework was still about him, but the greenish transparent substance that had filled it was altogether gone. A man in a deep violet robe, one of those who had been on the balcony, was looking keenly into his face.

Remote but insistent was a clamour of bells and confused sounds, that suggested to his mind the picture of a great number of people shouting together. Something seemed to fall across this tumult, a door suddenly closed.

Graham moved his head. 'What does this all mean?' he said slowly. 'Where am I?'

He saw the red-haired man who had been first to discover him. A voice seemed to be asking what he had said, and was abruptly stilled.

The man in violet answered in a soft voice, speaking English with a slightly foreign accent, or so at least it seemed to the Sleeper's ears, 'You are quite safe. You were brought hither from where you fell asleep. It is quite safe. You have been here some time – sleeping. In a trance.'

He said something further that Graham could not hear, and a little phial was handed across to him. Graham felt a cooling spray, a fragrant mist played over his forehead for a moment, and his sense of refreshment increased. He closed his eyes in satisfaction.

'Better?' asked the man in violet, as Graham's eyes reopened. He was a pleasant-faced man of thirty, perhaps, with a pointed flaxen beard, and a clasp of gold at the neck of his violet robe.

'Yes,' said Graham.

'You have been asleep some time. In a cataleptic trance. You have heard? Catalepsy? It may seem strange to you at first, but I can assure you everything is well.'

Graham did not answer, but these words served their reassuring purpose. His eyes went from face to face of the three people about him. They were regarding him strangely. He knew he ought to be somewhere in Cornwall, but he could not square these things with that impression.

A matter that had been in his mind during his last waking moments at

Boscastle recurred, a thing resolved upon and somehow neglected. He cleared his throat.

'Have you wired my cousin?' he asked. 'E. Warming, 27 Chancery Lane?'

They were all assiduous to hear. But he had to repeat it. 'What an odd *blurr* in his accent!' whispered the red-haired man. 'Wire, sir?' said the young man with the flaxen beard, evidently puzzled.

'He means send an electric telegram,' volunteered the third, a pleasant-faced youth of nineteen or twenty. The flaxen-bearded man gave a cry of comprehension. 'How stupid of me! You may be sure everything shall be done, sir,' he said to Graham. 'I am afraid it would be difficult to – *wire* to your cousin. He is not in London now. But don't trouble about arrangements yet; you have been asleep a very long time and the important thing is to get over that, sir.' (Graham concluded the word was sir, but this man pronounced it 'sire'.)

'Oh!' said Graham, and became quiet.

It was all very puzzling, but apparently these people in unfamiliar dress knew what they were about. Yet they were odd and the room was odd. It seemed he was in some newly established place. He had a sudden flash of suspicion. Surely this wasn't some hall of public exhibition! If it was he would give Warming a piece of his mind. But it scarcely had that character. And in a place of public exhibition he would not have discovered himself naked.

Then suddenly, quite abruptly, he realized what had happened. There was no perceptible interval of suspicion, no dawn to his knowledge. Abruptly he knew that his trance had lasted for a vast interval; as if by some process of thought-reading he interpreted the awe in the faces that peered into his. He looked at them strangely, full of intense emotion. It seemed they read his eyes. He framed his lips to speak and could not. A queer impulse to hide his knowledge came into his mind almost at the moment of his discovery. He looked at his bare feet, regarding then silently. His impulse to speak passed. He was trembling exceedingly.

They gave him some pink fluid with a greenish fluorescence and a meaty taste, and the assurance of returning strength grew.

'That – that makes me feel better,' he said hoarsely, and there were murmurs of respectful approval. He knew now quite clearly. He made to speak again, and again he could not.

He pressed his throat and tried a third time. 'How long?' he asked in a level voice. 'How long have I been asleep?'

'Some considerable time,' said the flaxen-bearded man, glancing quickly at the others.

'How long?'

'A very long time.'

'Yes – yes,' said Graham, suddenly testy. 'But I want— Is it – it is – some years? Many years? There was something – I forget what. I feel – confused.

But you—' He sobbed. 'You need not fence with me. How long—?'

He stopped, breathing irregularly. He squeezed his eyes with his knuckles and sat waiting for an answer.

They spoke in undertones.

'Five or six?' he asked faintly. 'More?'

'Very much more than that.'

'More!'

'More.'

He looked at them and it seemed as though imps were twitching the muscles of his face. He looked his question.

'Many years,' said the man with the red beard.

Graham struggled into a sitting position. He wiped a rheumy tear from his face with a lean hand. 'Many years!' he repeated. He shut his eyes tight, opened them, and sat looking about him, from one unfamiliar thing to another.

'How many years?' he asked.

'You must be prepared to be surprised.'

'Well?'

'More than a gross of years.'

He was irritated at the strange word. 'More than a *what*?'

Two of them spoke together. Some quick remarks that were made about 'decimal' he did not catch.

'How long did you say?' asked Graham. 'How long? Don't look like that. Tell me.'

Among the remarks in an undertone, his ear caught six words: 'More than a couple of centuries.'

'*What?*' he cried, turning on the youth who he thought had spoken. 'Who says—? What was that? A couple of *centuries*!'

'Yes,' said the man with the red beard. 'Two hundred years.'

Graham repeated the words. He had been prepared to hear of a vast repose, and yet these concrete centuries defeated him.

'Two hundred years,' he said again, with the figure of a great gulf opening very slowly in his mind; and then, 'Oh, but—!'

They said nothing.

'You – did you say—?'

'Two hundred years. Two centuries of years,' said the man with the red beard.

There was a pause. Graham looked at their faces and saw that what he had heard was indeed true.

'But it can't be,' he said querulously. 'I am dreaming. Trances. Trances don't last. That is not right – this is a joke you have played upon me! Tell me – some days ago, perhaps, I was walking along the coast of Cornwall—?'

His voice failed him.

The man with the flaxen beard hesitated. 'I'm not very strong in history, sir,' he said weakly, and glanced at the others.

'That was it, sir,' said the youngster. 'Boscastle, in the old Duchy of Cornwall – it's in the south-west country beyond the dairy meadows. There is a house there still. I have been there.'

'Boscastle!' Graham turned his eyes to the youngster. 'That was it – Boscastle. Little Boscastle. I fell asleep – somewhere there. I don't exactly remember. I don't exactly remember.'

He pressed his brows and whispered, 'More than *two hundred years!*'

He began to speak quickly with a twitching face, but his heart was cold within him. 'But if it *is* two hundred years, every soul I know, every human being that ever I saw or spoke to before I went to sleep, must be dead.'

They did not answer him.

'The Queen and the Royal Family, her Ministers, of Church and State. High and low, rich and poor, one with another.. . . Is there England still?

'That's a comfort! Is there London?

'This *is* London, eh? And you are my assistant-custodian; assistant-custodian. And these—? Eh? Assistant-custodians too?'

He sat with a gaunt stare on his face. 'But why am I here? No! Don't talk. Be quiet. Let me—'

He sat silent, rubbed his eyes, and, uncovering them, found another little glass of pinkish fluid held towards him. He took the dose. It was almost immediately sustaining. Directly he had taken it he began to weep naturally and refreshingly.

Presently he looked at their faces, suddenly laughed through his tears, a little foolishly. 'But – two – hun – dred – years!' he said. He grimaced hysterically and covered up his face again.

After a space he grew calm. He sat up, his hands hanging over his knees in almost precisely the same attitude in which Isbister had found him on the cliff at Pentargen. His attention was attracted by a thick domineering voice, the footsteps of an advancing personage. 'What are you doing? Why was I not warned? Surely you could tell? Someone will suffer for this. The man must be kept quiet. Are the doorways closed? All the doorways? He must be kept perfectly quiet. He must not be told. Has he been told anything?'

The man with the fair beard made some inaudible remark, and Graham looking over his shoulder saw approaching a very short, fat and thickset beardless man, with aquiline nose and heavy neck and chin. Very thick black and slightly sloping eyebrows that almost met over his nose and overhung deep grey eyes gave his face an oddly formidable expression. He scowled momentarily at Graham and then his regard returned to the man with the flaxen beard. 'These others,' he said in a voice of extreme irritation. 'You had better go.'

'Go?' said the red-bearded man.

'Certainly – go now. But see the doorways are closed as you go.'

The two men addressed turned obediently, after one reluctant glance at Graham, and instead of going through the archway as he expected, walked straight to the dead wall of the apartment opposite the archway. And then came a strange thing: a long strip of this apparently solid wall rolled up with a snap, hung over the two retreating men and fell again, and immediately Graham was alone with the new comer and the purple-robed man with the flaxen beard.

For a space the thickset man took not the slightest notice of Graham, but proceeded to interrogate the other – obviously his subordinate – upon the treatment of their charge. He spoke clearly, but in phrases only partially intelligible to Graham. The awakening seemed not only a matter of surprise but of consternation and annoyance to him. He was evidently profoundly excited.

'You must not confuse his mind by telling him things,' he repeated again and again. 'You must not confuse his mind.'

His questions answered, he turned quickly and eyed the awakened sleeper with an ambiguous expression.

'Feel queer?' he asked.

'Very.'

'The world, what you see of it, seems strange to you?'

'I suppose I have to live in it, strange as it seems.'

'I suppose so, now.'

'In the first place, hadn't I better have some clothes?'

'They—' said the thickset man and stopped, and the flaxen-bearded man met his eye and went away. 'You will very speedily have clothes,' said the thickset man.

'Is it true indeed, that I have been asleep two hundred—?' asked Graham.

'They have told you that, have they? Two hundred and three, as a matter of fact.'

Graham accepted the indisputable now with raised eyebrows and depressed mouth. He sat silent for a moment, and then asked a question, 'Is there a mill or dynamo near here?' He did not wait for an answer. 'Things have changed tremendously, I suppose?' he said.

'What is that shouting?' he asked abruptly.

'Nothing,' said the thickset man impatiently. 'It's people. You'll understand better later – perhaps. As you say, things have changed.' He spoke shortly, his brows were knit, and he glanced about him like a man trying to decide in an emergency. 'We must get you clothes and so forth, at any rate. Better wait here until some can be procured. No one will come near you. You want shaving.'

Graham rubbed his chin.

The man with the flaxen beard came back towards them, turned suddenly, listened for a moment, lifted his eyebrows at the older man, and hurried off through the archway towards the balcony. The tumult of shouting grew louder, and the thickset man turned and listened also. He cursed suddenly under his breath, and turned his eyes upon Graham with an unfriendly expression. It was a surge of many voices, rising and falling, shouting and screaming, and once came a sound like blows and sharp cries, and then a snapping like the crackling of dry sticks. Graham strained his ears to draw some single thread of sound from the woven tumult.

Then he perceived, repeated again and again, a certain formula. For a time he doubted his ears. But surely these were the words: 'Show us the Sleeper! Show us the Sleeper!'

The thickset man rushed suddenly to the archway.

'Wild!' he cried. 'How do they know? Do they know? Or is it guessing?'

There was perhaps an answer.

'I can't come,' said the thickset man; 'I have *him* to see to. But shout from the balcony.'

There was an inaudible reply.

'Say he is not awake. Anything! I leave it to you.'

He came hurrying back to Graham. 'You must have clothes at once,' he said. 'You cannot stop here – and it will be impossible to—'

He rushed away, Graham shouting unanswered questions after him. In a moment he was back.

'I can't tell you what is happening. It is too complex to explain. In a moment you shall have your clothes made. Yes – in a moment. And then I can take you away from here. You will find out our troubles soon enough.'

'But those voices. They were shouting—?'

'Something about the Sleeper – that's you. They have some twisted idea. I don't know what it is. I know nothing.'

A shrill bell jetted acutely across the indistinct mingling of remote noises, and this brusque person sprang to a little group of appliances in the corner of the room. He listened for a moment, regarding a ball of crystal, nodded, and said a few indistinct words; then he walked to the wall through which the two men had vanished. It rolled up again like a curtain, and he stood waiting.

Graham lifted his arm and was astonished to find what strength the restoratives had given him. He thrust one leg over the side of the couch and then the other. His head no longer swam. He could scarcely credit his rapid recovery. He sat feeling his limbs.

The man with the flaxen beard re-entered from the archway, and as he did so the cage of a lift came sliding down in front of the thickset man, and a lean, grey-bearded man, carrying a roll, and wearing a tightly-fitting costume of dark green, appeared therein.

'This is the tailor,' said the thickset man with an introductory gesture. 'It will never do for you to wear that black. I cannot understand how it got here. But I shall. I shall. You will be as rapid as possible?' he said to the tailor.

The man in green bowed, and, advancing, seated himself by Graham on the bed. His manner was calm, but his eyes were full of curiosity. 'You will find the fashions altered, Sire,' he said. He glanced from under his brows at the thickset man.

He opened the roller with a quick movement, and a confusion of brilliant fabrics poured out over his knees. 'You lived, Sire, in a period essentially cylindrical – the Victorian. With a tendency to the hemisphere in hats. Circular curves always. Now—' He flicked out a little appliance the size and appearance of a keyless watch, whirled the knob, and behold – a little figure in white appeared kinetoscope fashion on the dial, walking and turning. The tailor caught up a pattern of bluish white satin. 'That is my conception of your immediate treatment,' he said.

The thickset man came and stood by the shoulder of Graham.

'We have very little time,' he said.

'Trust me,' said the tailor. 'My machine follows. What do you think of this?'

'What is that?' asked the man from the nineteenth century.

'In your days they showed you a fashion-plate,' said the tailor, 'but this is our modern development. See here.' The little figure repeated its evolutions, but in a different costume. 'Or this,' and with a click another small figure in a more voluminous type of robe marched on to the dial. The tailor was very quick in his movements, and glanced twice towards the lift as he did these things.

It rumbled again, and a crop-haired anaemic lad with features of the Chinese type, clad in coarse pale blue canvas, appeared together with a complicated machine, which he pushed noiselessly on little castors into the room. Incontinently the little kinetoscope was dropped, Graham was invited to stand in front of the machine and the tailor muttered some instructions to the crop-haired lad, who answered in guttural tones and with words Graham did not recognize. The boy then went to conduct an incomprehensible monologue in the corner, and the tailor pulled out a number of slotted arms terminating in little discs, pulling them out until the discs were flat against the body of Graham, one at each shoulder blade, one at the elbows, one at the neck and so forth, so that at last there were, perhaps, two score of them upon his body and limbs. At the same time, some other person entered the room by the lift, behind Graham. The tailor set moving a mechanism that initiated a faint-sounding rhythmic movement of parts in the machine, and in another moment he was knocking up the levers and Graham was released. The tailor replaced his cloak of black, and the man

with the flaxen beard proffered him a little glass of some refreshing fluid. Graham saw over the rim of the glass a pale-faced young man regarding him with a singular fixity.

The thickset man had been pacing the room fretfully, and now turned and went through the archway towards the balcony, from which the noise of a distant crowd still came in gusts and cadences. The crop-headed lad handed the tailor a roll of the bluish satin and the two began fixing this in the mechanism in a manner reminiscent of a roll of paper in a nineteenth-century printing machine. Then they ran the entire thing on its easy, noise-less bearings across the room to a remote corner where a twisted cable looped rather gracefully from the wall. They made some connection and the machine became energetic and swift.

'What is that doing?' asked Graham, pointing with the empty glass to the busy figures and trying to ignore the scrutiny of the newcomer. 'Is that – some sort of force – laid on?'

'Yes,' said the man with the flaxen beard.

'Who is *that*?' He indicated the archway behind him.

The man in purple stroked his little beard, hesitated, and answered in an undertone, 'He is Howard, your chief guardian. You see, Sire – it's a little difficult to explain. The Council appoints a guardian and assistants. This hall has under certain restrictions been public. In order that people might satisfy themselves. We have barred the doorways for the first time. But I think – if you don't mind, I will leave him to explain.'

'Odd' said Graham. 'Guardian? Council?' Then turning his back on the new comer, he asked in an undertone, 'Why is this man glaring at me? Is he a mesmerist?'

'Mesmerist! He is a capillotomist.'

'Capillotomist!'

'Yes – one of the chief. His yearly fee is sixdoz lions.'

It sounded sheer nonsense. Graham snatched at the last phrase with an unsteady mind. 'Sixdoz lions?' he said.

'Didn't you have lions? I suppose not. You had the old pounds? They are our monetary units.'

'But what was that you said – sixdoz?'

'Yes. Six dozen, Sire. Of course things, even these little things, have altered. You lived in the days of the decimal system, the Arab system – tens, and little hundreds and thousands. We have eleven numerals now. We have single figures for both ten and eleven, two figures for a dozen, and a dozen dozen makes a gross, a great hundred, you know, a dozen gross a dozand, and a dozand dozand a myriad. Very simple?'

'I suppose so,' said Graham. 'But about this cap – what was it?'

The man with the flaxen beard glanced over his shoulder.

'Here are your clothes!' he said. Graham turned round sharply and saw

the tailor standing at his elbow smiling, and holding some palpably new garments over his arm. The crop-headed boy, by means of one finger, was impelling the complicated machine towards the lift by which he had arrived. Graham stared at the completed suit. 'You don't mean to say—!'

'Just made,' said the tailor. He dropped the garments at the feet of Graham, walked to the bed on which Graham had so recently been lying, flung out the translucent mattress, and turned up the looking-glass. As he did so a furious bell summoned the thickset man to the corner. The man with the flaxen beard rushed across to him and then hurried out by the archway.

The tailor was assisting Graham into a dark purple combination garment, stockings, vest, and pants in one, as the thickset man came back from the corner to meet the man with the flaxen beard returning from the balcony. They began speaking quickly in an undertone, their bearing had an unmistakable quality of anxiety. Over the purple under-garment came a complex but graceful garment of bluish white, and Graham was clothed in the fashion once more and saw himself, sallow-faced, unshaven and shaggy still, but at least naked no longer, and in some indefinable unprecedented way graceful.

'I must shave,' he said regarding himself in the glass.

'In a moment,' said Howard.

The persistent stare ceased. The young man closed his eyes, reopened them, and with a lean hand extended, advanced on Graham. Then he stopped, with his hand slowly gesticulating, and looked about him.

'A seat,' said Howard impatiently, and in a moment the flaxen-bearded man had a chair behind Graham. 'Sit down, please,' said Howard.

Graham hesitated, and in the other hand of the wild-eyed man he saw the glint of steel.

'Don't you understand, Sire?' cried the flaxen-bearded man with hurried politeness. 'He is going to cut your hair.'

'Oh!' cried Graham enlightened. 'But you called him –

'A capillotomist – precisely! He is one of the finest artists in the world.'

Graham sat down abruptly. The flaxen-bearded man disappeared. The capillotomist came forward with graceful gestures, examined Graham's ears and surveyed him, felt the back of his head, and would have sat down again to regard him but for Howard's audible impatience. Forthwith with rapid movements and a succession of deftly handled implements he shaved Graham's chin, clipped his moustache, and cut and arranged his hair. All this he did without a word, with something of the rapt air of a poet inspired. And as soon as he had finished Graham was handed a pair of shoes.

Suddenly a loud voice shouted – it seemed from a piece of machinery in the corner – 'At once – at once. The people know all over the city. Work is being stopped. Work is being stopped. Wait for nothing, but come.'

This shout appeared to perturb Howard exceedingly. By his gestures it seemed to Graham that he hesitated between two directions. Abruptly he went towards the corner where the apparatus stood about the little crystal ball. As he did so the undertone of tumultuous shouting from the archway that had continued during all these occurrences rose to a mighty sound, roared as if it were sweeping past, and fell again as if receding swiftly. It drew Graham after it with an irresistible attraction. He glanced at the thickset man, and then obeyed his impulse. In two strides he was down the steps and in the passage, and, in a score he was out upon the balcony upon which the three men had been standing.

CHAPTER V

The Moving Ways

He went to the railings of the balcony and stared upward. An exclamation of surprise at his appearance, and the movements of a number of people came from the spacious area below.

His first impression was of overwhelming architecture. The place into which he looked was an aisle of Titanic buildings, curving spaciously in either direction. Overhead mighty cantilevers sprang together across the huge width of the place, and a tracery of translucent material shut out the sky. Gigantic globes of cool white light shamed the pale sunbeams that filtered down through the girders and wires. Here and there a gossamer suspension bridge dotted with foot passengers flung across the chasm and the air was webbed with slender cables. A cliff of edifice hung above him, he perceived as he glanced upward, and the opposite façade was grey and dim and broken by great archings, circular perforations, balconies, buttresses, turret projections, myriads of vast windows, and an intricate scheme of architectural relief. Athwart these ran inscriptions horizontally and obliquely in an unfamiliar lettering. Here and there close to the roof cables of a peculiar stoutness were fastened, and drooped in a steep curve to circular openings on the opposite side of the space, and even as Graham noted these a remote and tiny figure of a man clad in pale blue arrested his attention. This little figure was far overhead across the space beside the higher fastening of one of these festoons, hanging forward from a little ledge of masonry and handling some well-nigh invisible strings dependent from the line. Then suddenly, with a swoop that sent Graham's heart into his mouth, this man had rushed down the curve and vanished through a round opening on the hither side of the way. Graham had been looking up as he came out upon the balcony, and the things he saw above and opposed to him had at first seized his attention to the exclusion of anything else. Then suddenly he discovered the roadway! It was not a roadway at all, as Graham understood such things, for in the nineteenth century the only roads and streets were beaten tracks of motionless earth, jostling rivulets of vehicles between narrow footways. But this roadway was three hundred feet across, and it moved; it moved, all save the middle, the lowest part. For a moment, the motion dazzled his mind. Then he understood.

Under the balcony this extraordinary roadway ran swiftly to Graham's right, an endless flow rushing along as fast as a nineteenth-century express train, an endless platform of narrow transverse overlapping slats with little

interspaces that permitted it to follow the curvatures of the street. Upon it were seats, and here and there little kiosks, but they swept by too swiftly for him to see what might be therein. From this nearest and swiftest platform a series of others descended to the centre of the space. Each moved to the right, each perceptibly slower than the one above it, but the difference in pace was small enough to permit anyone to step from any platform to the one adjacent, and so walk uninterruptedly from the swiftest to the motionless middle way. Beyond this middle way was another series of endless platforms rushing with varying pace to Graham's left. And seated in crowds upon the two widest and swiftest platforms, or stepping from one to another down the steps, or swarming over the central space, was an innumerable and wonderfully diversified multitude of people.

'You must not stop here,' shouted Howard suddenly at his side. 'You must come away at once.'

Graham made no answer. He heard without hearing. The platforms ran with a roar and the people were shouting. He perceived women and girls with flowing hair, beautifully robed, with bands crossing between the breasts. These first came out of the confusion. Then he perceived that the dominant note in that kaleidoscope of costume was the pale blue that the tailor's boy had worn. He became aware of cries of 'The Sleeper. What has happened to the Sleeper?' and it seemed as though the rushing platforms before him were suddenly spattered with the pale buff of human faces, and then still more thickly. He saw pointing fingers. He perceived that the motionless central area of this huge arcade just opposite to the balcony was densely crowded with blue-clad people. Some sort of struggle had sprung into life. People seemed to be pushed up the running platforms on either side, and carried away against their will. They would spring off so soon as they were beyond the thick of the confusion, and run back towards the conflict.

'It is the Sleeper. Verily it is the Sleeper,' shouted voices. 'That is never the Sleeper,' shouted others. More and more faces were turned to him. At the intervals along this central area Graham noted openings, pits, apparently the heads of staircases going down with people ascending out of them and descending into them. The struggle it seemed centred about the one of these nearest to him. People were running down the moving platforms to this, leaping dexterously from platform to platform. The clustering people on the higher platforms seemed to divide their interest between this point and the balcony. A number of sturdy little figures clad in a uniform of bright red, and working methodically together, were employed it seemed in preventing access to this descending staircase. About them a crowd was rapidly accumulating. Their brilliant colour contrasted vividly with the whitish-blue of their antagonists, for the struggle was indisputable.

He saw these things with Howard shouting in his ear and shaking his arm. And then suddenly Howard was gone and he stood alone.

The cries of 'The Sleeper' grew in volume, and the people on the nearer platform were standing up. The nearer swifter platform he perceived was empty to the right of him, and far across the space the platform running in the opposite direction was coming crowded and passing away bare. With incredible swiftness a vast crowd had gathered in the central space before his eyes; a dense swaying mass of people, and the shouts grew from a fitful crying to a voluminous incessant clamour: 'The Sleeper! The Sleeper!' and yells and cheers, a waving of garments and cries of 'Stop the ways!' They were also crying another name strange to Graham. It sounded like 'Ostrog'. The slower platforms were soon thick with active people, running against the movement so as to keep themselves opposite to him.

'Stop the ways,' they cried. Agile figures ran up swiftly from the centre to the swift road nearest to him, were borne rapidly past him, shouting strange, unintelligible things, and ran back obliquely to the central way. One thing he distinguished: 'It is indeed the Sleeper. It is indeed the Sleeper,' they testified.

For a space Graham stood motionless. Then he became vividly aware that all this concerned him. He was pleased at his wonderful popularity, he bowed, and, seeking a gesture of longer range, waved his arm. He was astonished at the violence of uproar that this provoked. The tumult about the descending stairway rose to furious violence. He became aware of crowded balconies, of men sliding along ropes, of men in trapeze-like seats hurling athwart the space. He heard voices behind him, a number of people descending the steps through the archway; he suddenly perceived that his guardian Howard was back again and gripping his arm painfully, and shouting inaudibly in his ear.

He turned, and Howard's face was white. 'Come back,' he heard. 'They will stop the ways. The whole city will be in confusion.'

There appeared a number of men hurrying along the passage of blue pillars behind Howard, the red-haired man, the man with the flaxen beard, a tall man in vivid vermilion, a crowd of others in red carrying staves, and all these people had anxious eager faces.

'Get him away,' cried Howard.

'But why?' said Graham. 'I don't see—'

'You must come away!' said the man in red in a resolute voice. His face and eyes were resolute, too. Graham's glances went from face to face, and he was suddenly aware of that most disagreeable flavour in life, compulsion. Someone gripped his arm. . . .

He was being dragged away. It seemed as though the tumult suddenly became two, as if half the shouts that had come in from this wonderful

roadway had sprung into the passages of the great building behind him. Marvelling and confused, feeling an impotent desire to resist, Graham was half led, half thrust, along the passage of blue pillars, and suddenly he found himself alone with Howard in a lift and moving swiftly upward.

CHAPTER VI

The Hall of the Atlas

From the moment when the tailor had bowed his farewell to the moment when Graham found himself in the lift, was altogether barely five minutes. And as yet the haze of his vast interval of sleep hung about him, as yet the initial strangeness of his being alive at all in this remote age touched everything with wonder, with a sense of the irrational, with something of the quality of a realistic dream. He was still detached, an astonished spectator, still but half involved in life. What he had seen, and especially the last crowded tumult, framed in the setting of the balcony, had a spectacular turn, like a thing witnessed from the box of a theatre. 'I don't understand,' he said. 'What was the trouble? My mind is in a whirl. Why were they shouting? What is the danger?'

'We have our troubles,' said Howard. His eyes avoided Graham's enquiry. 'This is a time of unrest. And, in fact, your appearance, your waking just now, has a sort of connection—'

He spoke jerkily, like a man not quite sure of his breathing. He stopped abruptly.

'I don't understand,' said Graham.

'It will be clearer later,' said Howard.

He glanced uneasily upward, as though he found the progress of the lift slow.

'I shall understand better, no doubt, when I have seen my way about a little,' said Graham puzzled. 'It will be – it is bound to be perplexing. At present it is all so strange. Anything seems possible. Anything. In the details even. Your counting, I understand, is different.'

The lift stopped, and they stepped out into a narrow but very long passage between high walls, along which ran an extraordinary number of tubes and big cables.

'What a huge place this is!' said Graham. 'Is it all one building? What place is it?'

'This is one of the city ways for various public services. Light and so forth.'

'Was it a social trouble – that – in the great roadway place? How are you governed? Have you still a police?'

'Several,' said Howard.

'Several?'

'About fourteen.'

'I don't understand.'

'Very probably not. Our social order will probably seem very complex to

you. To tell you the truth, I don't understand it myself very clearly. Nobody does. You will, perhaps – bye and bye. We have to go to the Council.'

Graham's attention was divided between the urgent necessity of his enquiries and the people in the passages and halls they were traversing. For a moment his mind would be concentrated upon Howard and the halting answers he made, and then he would lose the thread in response to some vivid unexpected impression. Along the passages, in the halls, half the people seemed to be men in the red uniform. The pale blue canvas that had been so abundant in the aisle of moving ways did not appear. Invariably these men looked at him, and saluted him and Howard as they passed.

He had a clear vision of entering a long corridor, and there were a number of girls sitting on low seats and as though in a class. He saw no teacher, but only a novel apparatus from which he fancied a voice proceeded. The girls regarded him and his conductor, he thought, with curiosity and astonishment. But he was hurried on before he could form a clear idea of the gathering. He judged they knew Howard and not himself, and that they wondered who he was. This Howard, it seemed, was a person of importance. But then he was also merely Graham's guardian. That was odd.

There came a passage in twilight, and into this passage a footway hung so that he could see the feet and ankles of people going to and fro thereon, but no more of them. Then vague impressions of galleries and of casual astonished passers-by turning round to stare after the two of them with their red-clad guard.

The stimulus of the restoratives he had taken was only temporary. He was speedily fatigued by this excessive haste. He asked Howard to slacken his speed. Presently he was in a lift that had a window upon the great street space, but this was glazed and did not open, and they were too high for him to see the moving platforms below. But he saw people going to and fro along cables and along strange, frail-looking bridges.

Thence they passed across the street and at a vast height above it. They crossed by means of a narrow bridge closed in with glass, so clear that it made him giddy even to remember it. The floor of it also was of glass. From his memory of the cliffs between Newquay and Boscastle, so remote in time, and so recent in his experience, it seemed to him that they must be near four hundred feet above the moving ways. He stopped, looked down between his legs upon the swarming blue and red multitudes, minute and foreshortened, struggling and gesticulating still towards the little balcony far below, a little toy balcony, it seemed, where he had so recently been standing. A thin haze and the glare of the mighty globes of light obscured everything. A man seated in a little open-work cradle shot by from some point still higher than the little narrow bridge, rushing down a cable as swiftly almost as if he were falling. Graham stopped involuntarily to watch this strange

passenger vanish in a great circular opening below, and then his eyes went back to the tumultuous struggle.

Along one of the swifter ways rushed a thick crowd of red spots. This broke up into individuals as it approached the balcony, and went pouring down the slower ways towards the dense struggling crowd on the central area. These men in red appeared to be armed with sticks or truncheons; they seemed to be striking and thrusting. A great shouting, cries of wrath, screaming, burst out and came up to Graham, faint and thin. 'Go on,' cried Howard, laying hands on him.

Another man rushed down a cable. Graham suddenly glanced up to see whence he came, and beheld through the glassy roof and the network of cables and girders, dim rhythmically passing forms like the vans of windmills, and between them glimpses of a remote and pallid sky. Then Howard had thrust him forward across the bridge, and he was in a little narrow passage decorated with geometrical patterns.

'I want to see more of that,' cried Graham, resisting.

'No, no,' cried Howard, still gripping his arm. 'This way. You must go this way.' And the men in red following them seemed ready to enforce his orders.

Some Negroes in a curious wasp-like uniform of black and yellow appeared down the passage, and one hastened to throw up a sliding shutter that had seemed a door to Graham, and led the way through it. Graham found himself in a gallery overhanging the end of a great chamber. The attendant in black and yellow crossed this, thrust up a second shutter and stood waiting.

This place had the appearance of an ante-room. He saw a number of people in the central space, and at the opposite end a large and imposing doorway at the top of a flight of steps, heavily curtained but giving a glimpse of some still larger hall beyond. He perceived white men in red and other Negroes in black and yellow standing stiffly about those portals.

As they crossed the gallery he heard a whisper from below, 'The Sleeper,' and was aware of a turning of heads, a hum of observation. They entered another little passage in the wall of this ante-chamber, and then he found himself on an iron-railed gallery of metal that passed round the side of the great hall he had already seen through the curtains. He entered the place at the corner, so that he received the fullest impression of its huge proportions. The black man in the wasp uniform stood aside like a well-trained servant, and closed the valve behind him.

Compared with any of the places Graham had see thus far, this second hall appeared to be decorated with extreme richness. On a pedestal at the remote end, and more brilliantly lit than any other object, was a gigantic white figure of Atlas, strong and strenuous, the globe upon his bowed shoulders. It was the first thing to strike his attention, it was so vast, so patiently and painfully real, so white and simple. Save for this figure and for a dais in the centre, the wide floor of the place was a shining vacancy.

The dais was remote in the greatness of the area; it would have looked a mere slab of metal had it not been for the group of seven men who stood about a table on it, and gave an inkling of its proportions. They were all dressed in white robes, they seemed to have arisen that moment from their seats, and they were regarding Graham steadfastly. At the end of the table he perceived the glitter of some mechanical appliances.

Howard led him along the end gallery until they were opposite this mighty labouring figure. Then he stopped. The two men in red who had followed them into the gallery came and stood on either hand of Graham.

'You must remain here,' murmured Howard, 'for a few moments,' and, without waiting for a reply, hurried away along the gallery.

'But *why?*' began Graham.

He moved as if to follow Howard, and found his path obstructed by one of the men in red. 'You have to wait here, Sire,' said the man in red.

'*Why?*'

'Orders, Sire.'

'Whose orders?'

'Our orders, Sire.'

Graham looked his exasperation.

'What place is this?' he said presently. 'Who are those men?'

'They are the lords of the Council, Sire.'

'What Council?'

'*The* Council.'

'Oh!' said Graham, and after an equally ineffectual attempt at the other man, went to the railing and stared at the distant men in white, who stood watching him and whispering together.

The Council? He perceived there were now eight, though how the new-comer had arrived he had not observed. They made no gestures of greeting; they stood regarding him as in the nineteenth century a group of men might have stood in the street regarding a distant balloon that had suddenly floated into view. What council could it be that gathered there, that little body of men beneath the significant white Atlas, secluded from every eavesdropper in this impressive spaciousness? And why should he be brought to them, and be looked at strangely and spoken of inaudibly? Howard appeared beneath, walking quickly across the polished floor towards them. As he drew near he bowed and performed certain peculiar movements, apparently of a ceremonious nature. Then he ascended the steps of the dais, and stood by the apparatus at the end of the table.

Graham watched that visible inaudible conversation. Occasionally, one of the white-robed men would glance towards him. He strained his ears in vain. The gesticulation of two of the speakers became animated. He glanced from them to the passive faces of his attendants. . . . When he looked again Howard was extending his hands and moving his head like a man who

protests. He was interrupted, it seemed, by one of the white-robed men rapping the table.

The conversation lasted an interminable time to Graham's sense. His eyes rose to the still giant at whose feet the Council sat. Thence they wandered at last to the walls of the hall. It was decorated in long painted panels of a quasi-Japanese type, many of them very beautiful. These panels were grouped in a great and elaborate framing of dark metal, which passed into the metallic caryatidae of the galleries, and the great structural lines of the interior. The facile grace of these panels enhanced the mighty white effort that laboured in the centre of the scheme. Graham's eyes came back to the Council, and Howard was descending the steps. As he drew nearer his features could be distinguished, and Graham saw that he was flushed and blowing out his cheeks. His countenance was still disturbed when presently he reappeared along the gallery.

'This way,' he said concisely, and they went on in silence to a little door that opened at their approach. The two men in red stopped on either side of this door. Howard and Graham passed in, and Graham, glancing back, saw the white-robed Council still standing in a close group and looking at him. Then the door closed behind him with a heavy thud, and for the first time since his awakening he was in silence. The floor, even, was noiseless to his feet.

Howard opened another door, and they were in the first of two contiguous chambers furnished in white and green. 'What Council was that?' began Graham. 'What were they discussing? What have they to do with me?' Howard closed the door carefully, heaved a huge sigh, and said something in an undertone. He walked slanting ways across the room and turned, blowing out his cheeks again. 'Ugh!' he grunted, a man relieved.

Graham stood regarding him.

'You must understand,' began Howard abruptly, avoiding Graham's eyes, 'that our social order is very complex. A half explanation, a bare unqualified statement would give you false impressions. As a matter of fact – it is a case of compound interest partly – your small fortune, and the fortune of your cousin Warming which was left to you – and certain other beginnings – have become very considerable. And in other ways that will be hard for you to understand, you have become a person of significance – of very considerable significance – involved in the world's affairs.'

He stopped.

'Yes?' said Graham.

'We have grave social troubles.'

'Yes?'

'Things have come to such a pass that, in fact, it is advisable to seclude you here.'

'Keep me prisoner!' exclaimed Graham.

'Well – to ask you to keep in seclusion.'

Graham turned on him. 'This is strange!' he said.

'No harm will be done you.'

'No harm!'

'But you must be kept here—'

'While I learn my position, I presume.'

'Precisely.'

'Very well then. Begin. Why *harm?*'

'Not now.'

'Why not?'

'It is too long a story, Sire.'

'All the more reason I should begin at once. You say I am a person of importance. What was that shouting I heard? Why is a great multitude shouting and excited because my trance is over, and who are the men in white in that huge council chamber?'

'All in good time, Sire,' said Howard. 'But not crudely, not crudely. This is one of those flimsy times when no man has a settled mind. Your awakening – no one expected your awakening. The Council is consulting.'

'What council?'

'The Council you saw.'

Graham made a petulant movement. 'This is not right,' he said. 'I should be told what is happening.'

'You must wait. Really you must wait.'

Graham sat down abruptly. 'I suppose since I have waited so long to resume life,' he said, 'that I must wait a little longer.'

'That is better,' said Howard. 'Yes, that is much better. And I must leave you alone. For a space. While I attend the discussion in the Council. I am sorry.'

He went towards the noiseless door, hesitated and vanished.

Graham walked to the door, tried it, found it securely fastened in some way he never came to understand, turned about, paced the room restlessly, made the circuit of the room, and sat down. He remained sitting for some time with folded arms and knitted brow, biting his fingernails and trying to piece together the kaleidoscopic impressions of this first hour of awakened life; the vast mechanical spaces, the endless series of chambers and passages, the great struggle that roared and splashed through these strange ways, the little group of remote unsympathetic men beneath the colossal Atlas, Howard's mysterious behaviour. There was an inkling of some vast inheritance already in his mind – a vast inheritance perhaps misapplied – of some unprecedented importance and opportunity. What had he to do? And this room's secluded silence was eloquent of imprisonment!

It came into Graham's mind with irresistible conviction that this series of magnificent impressions was a dream. He tried to shut his eyes and succeeded, but that time-honoured device led to no awakening.

Presently he began to touch and examine all the unfamiliar appointments of the two small rooms in which he found himself.

In a long oval panel of mirror he saw himself and stopped astonished. He was clad in a graceful costume of purple and bluish white, with a little greyshot beard trimmed to a point, and his hair, its blackness streaked now with bands of grey, arranged over his forehead in an unfamiliar but graceful manner. He seemed a man of five-and-forty perhaps. For a moment he did not perceive this was himself.

A flash of laughter came with the recognition. 'To call on old Warming like this!' he exclaimed. 'And make him take me out to lunch!'

Then he thought of meeting first one and then another of the few familiar acquaintances of his early manhood, and in the midst of his amusement realized that every soul with whom he might jest had died many score of years ago. The thought smote him abruptly and keenly; he stopped short, the expression of his face changed to a white consternation.

The tumultuous memory of the moving platforms and the huge façade of that wonderful street reasserted itself. The shouting multitudes came back clear and vivid, and those remote, inaudible, unfriendly councilors in white. He felt himself a little figure, very small and ineffectual, pitifully conspicuous. And all about him, the world was – *strange*.

CHAPTER VII

In the Silent Rooms

Presently Graham resumed his examination of his apartments. Curiosity kept him moving in spite of his fatigue. The inner room, he perceived, was high, and its ceiling dome-shaped, with an oblong aperture in the centre, opening into a funnel in which a wheel of broad fans seemed to be rotating, apparently driving the air up the shaft. The faint humming note of its easy motion was the only clear sound in that quiet place. As these vanes sprang up one after the other, Graham could get transient glimpses of the sky. He was surprised to see a star.

This drew his attention to the fact that the bright lighting of these rooms was due to a multitude of very faint glow lamps set about the cornices. There were no windows. And he began to recall that along all the vast chambers and passages he had traversed with Howard he had observed no windows at all. Had there been windows? There were windows on the street indeed, but were they for light? Or was the whole city lit day and night for evermore, so that there was no night there?

And another thing dawned upon him. There was no fireplace in either room. Was the season summer, and were these merely summer apartments, or was the whole City uniformly heated or cooled? He became interested in these questions, began examining the smooth texture of the walls, the simply constructed bed, the ingenious arrangements by which the labour of bedroom service was practically abolished. And over everything was a curious absence of deliberate ornament, a bare grace of form and colour, that he found very pleasing to the eye. There were several very comfortable chairs, a light table on silent runners carrying several bottles of fluids and glasses, and two plates bearing a clear substance like jelly. Then he noticed there were no books, no newspapers, no writing materials. 'The world has changed indeed,' he thought.

He observed one entire side of the outer room was set with rows of peculiar double cylinders inscribed with green lettering on white that harmonized with the decorative scheme of the room, and in the centre of this side projected a little apparatus about a yard square and having a white smooth face to the room. A chair faced this. He had a transitory idea that these cylinders might be books, or a modern substitute for books, but at first it did not seem so.

The lettering on the cylinders puzzled him. At first sight it seemed like Russian. Then he noticed a suggestion of mutilated English about certain of the words.

'Ɵi Man huwdbi Kiŋ'

forced itself on him as 'The Man who would be King'. 'Phonetic spelling,' he said. He remembered reading a story with that title, then he recalled the story vividly, one of the best stories in the world. But this thing before him was not a book as he understood it. He puzzled out the titles of two adjacent cylinders. *The Heart of Darkness* he had never heard of before, nor *The Madonna of the Future* – no doubt if they were indeed stories, they were by post-Victorian authors.

He puzzled over this peculiar cylinder for some time and replaced it. Then he turned to the square apparatus and examined that. He opened a sort of lid and found one of the double cylinders within, and on the upper edge a little stud like the stud of an electric bell. He pressed this and a rapid clicking began and ceased. He became aware of voices and music, and noticed a play of colour on the smooth front face. He suddenly realized what this might be, and stepped back to regard it.

On the flat surface was now a little picture, very vividly coloured, and in this picture were figures that moved. Not only did they move, but they were conversing in clear small voices. It was exactly like reality viewed through an inverted opera glass and heard through a long tube. His interest was seized at once by the situation, which presented a man pacing up and down and vociferating angry things to a pretty but petulant woman. Both were in the picturesque costume that seemed so strange to Graham. 'I have worked,' said the man, 'but what have you been doing?'

'Ah!' said Graham. He forgot everything else, and sat down in the chair. Within five minutes he heard himself named, heard 'when the Sleeper wakes' used jestingly as a proverb for remote postponement, and passed himself by, a thing remote and incredible. But in a little while he knew those two people like intimate friends.

At last the miniature drama came to an end, and the square face of the apparatus was blank again.

It was a strange world into which he had been permitted to see, unscrupulous, pleasure-seeking, energetic, subtle, a world too of dire economic struggle; there were allusions he did not understand, incidents that conveyed strange suggestions of altered moral ideals, flashes of dubious enlightenment. The blue canvas that bulked so largely in his first impression of the city ways appeared again and again as the costume of the common people. He had no doubt the story was contemporary, and its intense realism was undeniable. And the end had been a tragedy that oppressed him. He sat staring at the blankness.

He started and rubbed his eyes. He had been so absorbed in the latter-day substitute for a novel that he awoke to the little green and white room with more than a touch of the surprise of his first awakening.

He stood up, and abruptly he was back in his own wonderland. The clearness of the kinetoscope drama passed, and the struggle in the vast place of streets, the ambiguous Council, the swift phases of his waking hour, came back. These people had spoken of the Council with suggestions of a vague universality of power. And they had spoken of the Sleeper; it had not really struck him vividly at the time that he was the Sleeper. He had to recall precisely what they had said.

He walked into the bedroom and peered up through the quick intervals of the revolving fan. As the fan swept round, a dim turmoil like the noise of machinery came in rhythmic eddies. All else was silence. Though the perpetual day still irradiated his apartments, he perceived the little intermittent strip of sky was now deep blue – black almost, with a dust of little stars.

He resumed his examination of the rooms. He could find no way of opening the padded door, no bell nor other means of calling for attendance. His feeling of wonder was in abeyance; but he was curious, anxious for information. He wanted to know exactly how he stood to these new things. He tried to compose himself to wait until someone came to him. Presently he became restless and eager for information, for distraction, for fresh sensations.

He went back to the apparatus in the other room, and had soon puzzled out the method of replacing the cylinders by others. As he did so, it came into his mind that it must be these little appliances had fixed the language so that it was still clear and understandable after two hundred years. The haphazard cylinders he substituted displayed a musical fantasia. At first it was beautiful, and then it was sensuous. He presently recognized what appeared to him to be an altered version of the story of Tannhauser. The music was unfamiliar. But the rendering was realistic, and with a contemporary unfamiliarity. Tannhauser did not go to a Venusberg, but to a Pleasure City. What was a Pleasure City? A dream, surely, the fancy of a fantastic, voluptuous writer.

He became interested, curious. The story developed with a flavour of strangely twisted sentimentality. Suddenly he did not like it. He liked it less as it proceeded.

He had a revulsion of feeling. These were no pictures, no idealizations, but photographed realities. He wanted no more of the twenty-second-century Venusberg. He forgot the part played by the model in nineteenth-century art, and gave way to an archaic indignation. He rose, angry and half ashamed at himself for witnessing this thing even in solitude. He pulled forward the apparatus, and with some violence sought for a means of stopping its action. Something snapped. A violet spark stung and convulsed his arm and the thing was still. When he attempted next day to replace these Tannhauser cylinders by another pair, he found the apparatus broken. . . .

He struck out a path oblique to the room and paced to and fro, struggling with intolerable vast impressions. The things he had derived from the cylinders

and the things he had seen, conflicted, confused him. It seemed to him the most amazing thing of all that in his thirty years of life he had never tried to shape a picture of these coming times. 'We were making the future,' he said, 'and hardly any of us troubled to think what future we were making. And here it is!'

'What have they got to, what has been done? How do I come into the midst of it all?' The vastness of street and house he was prepared for, the multitudes of people. But conflicts in the city ways! And the systematized sensuality of a class of rich men!

He thought of Bellamy, the hero of whose Socialistic Utopia had so oddly anticipated this actual experience. But here was no Utopia, no Socialistic state. He had already seen enough to realize that the ancient antithesis of luxury, waste and sensuality on the one hand and abject poverty on the other, still prevailed. He knew enough of the essential factors of life to understand that correlation. And not only were the buildings of the city gigantic and the crowds in the street gigantic, but the voices he had heard in the ways, the uneasiness of Howard, the very atmosphere spoke of gigantic discontent. What country was he in? Still England it seemed, and yet strangely 'un-English'. His mind glanced at the rest of the world, and saw only an enigmatical veil.

He prowled about his apartment, examining everything as a caged animal might do. He felt very tired, felt that feverish exhaustion that does not admit of rest. He listened for long spaces under the ventilator to catch some distant echo of the tumults he felt must be proceeding in the city.

He began to talk to himself. 'Two hundred and three years!' he said to himself over and over again, laughing stupidly. 'Then I am two hundred and thirty-three years old! The oldest inhabitant. Surely they haven't reversed the tendency of our time and gone back to the rule of the oldest. My claims are indisputable. Mumble, mumble. I remember the Bulgarian atrocities as though it was yesterday. 'Tis a great age! Ha ha!' He was surprised at first to hear himself laughing, and then laughed again deliberately and louder. Then he realized that he was behaving foolishly. 'Steady,' he said. 'Steady!'

His pacing became more regular. 'This new world,' he said. 'I don't understand it. Why? . . . But it is all *why!*'

'I suppose they can fly and do all sorts of things Let me try and remember just how it began.'

He was surprised at first to find how vague the memories of his first thirty years had become. He remembered fragments, for the most part trivial moments, things of no great importance that he had observed. His boyhood seemed the most accessible at first, he recalled school books and certain lessons in mensuration. Then he revived the more salient features of his life, memories of the wife long since dead, her magic influence now gone beyond corruption, of his rivals and friends and betrayers, of the swift decision of

this issue and that, and then of his, last years of misery, of fluctuating resolves, and at last of his strenuous studies. In a little while he perceived he had it all again; dim perhaps, like metal long laid aside, but in no way defective or injured, capable of re-polishing. And the hue of it was a deepening misery. Was it worth re-polishing? By a miracle he had been lifted out of a life that had become intolerable.

He reverted to his present condition. He wrestled with the facts in vain. It became an inextricable tangle. He saw the sky through the ventilator pink with dawn. An old persuasion came out of the dark recesses of his memory. 'I must sleep,' he said. It appeared as a delightful relief from this mental distress and from the growing pain and heaviness of his limbs. He went to the strange little bed, lay down and was presently asleep.

He was destined to become very familiar indeed with these apartments before he left them, for he remained imprisoned for three days. During that time no one, except Howard, entered his prison. The marvel of his fate mingled with and in some way minimized the marvel of his survival. He had awakened to mankind it seemed only to be snatched away into this unac-countable solitude. Howard came regularly with subtly sustaining and nutritive fluids, and light and pleasant foods, quite strange to Graham. He always closed the door carefully as he entered. On matters of detail he was increasingly obliging, but the bearing of Graham on the great issues that were evidently being contested so closely beyond the sound-proof walls that enclosed him, he would not elucidate. He evaded, as politely as possible, every question on the position of affairs in the outer world.

And in those three days Graham's incessant thoughts went far and wide. All that he had seen, all this elaborate contrivance to prevent him seeing, worked together in his mind. Almost every possible interpretation of his position he debated – even as it chanced, the right interpretation. Things that presently happened to him became at least credible, by virtue of this seclusion. When at length the moment of his release arrived, it found him prepared.

Howard's bearing went far to deepen Graham's impression of his own strange importance; the door between its opening and closing seemed to admit with him a breath of momentous happening. His enquiries became more definite and searching. Howard retreated through protests and diffi-culties. The awakening was unforeseen, he repeated; it happened to have fallen in with the trend of a social convulsion.

'To explain it I must tell you the history of a gross and a half of years,' protested Howard.

'The thing is this,' said Graham. 'You are afraid of something I shall do. In some way I am arbitrator – I might be arbitrator.'

'It is not that. But you have – I may tell you this much – the automatic increase of your property puts great possibilities of interference in your

hands. And in certain other ways you have influence, with your eighteenth-century notions.'

'Nineteenth-century,' corrected Graham.

'With your old-world notions, anyhow, ignorant as you are of every feature of our State.'

'Am I a fool?'

'Certainly not.'

'Do I seem to be the sort of man who would act rashly?'

'You were never expected to act at all. No one counted on your awakening. No one dreamt you would ever awake. The Council had surrounded you with antiseptic conditions. As a matter of fact, we thought that you were dead – a mere arrest of decay. And – but it is too complex. We dare not suddenly – while you are still half awake.'

'It won't do,' said Graham. 'Suppose it is as you say – why am I not being crammed night and day with facts and warnings and all the wisdom of the time to fit me for my responsibilities? Am I any wiser now than two days ago, if it is two days, when I awoke?'

Howard pulled his lip.

'I am beginning to feel – every hour I feel more clearly – a sense of complex concealment of which you are the face. Is this Council, or committee, or whatever they are, cooking the accounts of my estate? Is that it?'

'That note of suspicion—' said Howard.

'Ugh!' said Graham. 'Now, mark my words, it will be ill for those who have put me here. It will be ill. I am alive. Make no doubt of it, I am alive. Every day my pulse is stronger and my mind clearer and more vigorous. No more quiescence. I am a man come back to life. And I want to *live*—'

'*Live!*'

Howard's face lit with an idea. He came towards Graham and spoke in an easy confidential tone.

'The Council secludes you here for your good. You are restless. Naturally – an energetic man! You find it dull here. But we are anxious that everything you may desire – every desire – every sort of desire . . . There may be something. Is there any sort of company?'

He paused meaningly.

'Yes,' said Graham thoughtfully. 'There is.'

'Ah! *Now!* We have treated you neglectfully.'

'The crowds in yonder streets of yours.'

'That,' said Howard, 'I am afraid—. But—'

Graham began pacing the room. Howard stood near the door watching him. The implication of Howard's suggestion was only half evident to Graham Company? Suppose he were to accept the proposal, demand some sort of *company*? Would there be any possibilities of gathering from the conversation

of this additional person some vague inkling of the struggle that had broken out so vividly at his waking moment? He meditated again, and the suggestion took colour. He turned on Howard abruptly.

'What do you mean by company?'

Howard raised his eyes and shrugged his shoulders. 'Human beings,' he said, with a curious smile on his heavy face.

'Our social ideas,' he said, 'have a certain increased liberality, perhaps, in comparison with your times. If a man wishes to relieve such a tedium as this – by feminine society, for instance. We think it no scandal. We have cleared our minds of formulae. There is in our city a class, a necessary class, no longer despised – discreet—'

Graham stopped dead.

'It would pass the time,' said Howard. 'It is a thing I should perhaps have thought of before, but, as a matter of fact, so much is happening—'

He indicated the exterior world.

Graham hesitated. For a moment the figure of a possible woman that his imagination suddenly created dominated his mind with an intense attraction. Then he flashed into anger.

'No!' he shouted.

He began striding rapidly up and down the room. 'Everything you say, everything you do, convinces me – of some great issue in which I am concerned. I do not want to pass the time, as you call it. Yes, I know. Desire and indulgence are life in a sense – and Death! Extinction! In my life before I slept I had worked out that pitiful question. I will not begin again. There is a city, a multitude—. And meanwhile I am here like a rabbit in a bag.'

His rage surged high. He choked for a moment and began to wave his clenched fists. He gave way to an anger fit, he swore archaic curses. His gestures had the quality of physical threats.

'I do not know who your party may be. I am in the dark, and you keep me in the dark. But I know this, that I am secluded here for no good purpose. For no good purpose. I warn you, I warn you of the consequences. Once I come at my power—'

He realized that to threaten thus might be a danger to himself. He stopped. Howard stood regarding him with a curious expression.

'I take it this is a message to the Council,' said Howard.

Graham had a momentary impulse to leap upon the man, fell or stun him. It must have shown upon his face; at any rate Howard's movement was quick. In a second the noiseless door had closed again, and the man from the nineteenth century was alone.

For a moment he stood rigid, with clenched hands half raised. Then he flung them down. 'What a fool I have been!' he said, and gave way to his anger again, stamping about the room and shouting curses. For a long time he kept himself in a sort of frenzy, raging at his position, at his own folly,

at the knaves who had imprisoned him. He did this because he did not want to look calmly at his position. He clung to his anger – because he was afraid of fear.

Presently he was reasoning with himself This imprisonment was unaccountable, but no doubt the legal forms – new legal forms – of the time permitted it. It must, of course, be legal. These people were two hundred years further on in the march of civilization than the Victorian generation. It was not likely they would be less – humane. Yet they had cleared their minds of formulae! Was humanity a formula as well as chastity?

His imagination set to work to suggest things that might be done to him. The attempts of his reason to dispose of these suggestions, though for the most part logically valid, were quite unavailing. 'Why should anything be done to me?'

'If the worst comes to the worst,' he found himself saying at last, 'I can give up what they want. But what do they want? And why don't they ask me for it instead of cooping me up?'

He returned to his former preoccupation with the Council's possible intentions. He began to reconsider the details of Howard's behaviour, sinister glances, inexplicable hesitations. Then, for a time, his mind circled about the idea of escaping from these rooms; but whither could he escape into this vast, crowded world? He would be worse off than a Saxon yeoman suddenly dropped into nineteenth-century London. And besides, how could anyone escape from these rooms?

'How can it benefit anyone if harm should happen to me?'

He thought of the tumult, the great social trouble of which he was so unaccountably the axis. A text, irrelevant enough and yet curiously insistent, came floating up out of the darkness of his memory. This also a Council had said:

'It is expedient for us that one man should die for the people.'

CHAPTER VIII

The Roof Spaces

As the fans in the circular aperture of the inner room rotated and permitted glimpses of the night, dim sounds drifted in thereby. And Graham, standing underneath, wrestling darkly with the unknown powers that imprisoned him, and which he had now deliberately challenged, was startled by the sound of a voice.

He peered up and saw in the intervals of the rotation, dark and dim, the face and shoulders of a man regarding him. Then a dark hand was extended, the swift vane struck it, swung round and beat on with a little brownish patch on the edge of its thin blade, and something began to fall therefrom upon the floor, dripping silently.

Graham looked down, and there were spots of blood at his feet. He looked up again in a strange excitement. The figure had gone.

He remained motionless – his every sense intent upon the flickering patch of darkness, for outside it was high night. He became aware of some faint, remote, dark specks floating lightly through the outer air. They came down towards him, fitfully, eddyingly, and passed aside out of the uprush from the fan. A gleam of light flickered, the specks flashed white, and then the darkness came again. Warmed and lit as he was, he perceived that it was snowing within a few feet of him.

Graham walked across the room and came back to the ventilator again. He saw the head of a man pass near. There was a sound of whispering. Then a smart blow on some metallic substance, effort, voices, and the vanes stopped. A gust of snowflakes whirled into the room, and vanished before they touched the floor. 'Don't be afraid,' said a voice.

Graham stood under the fan. 'Who are you?' he whispered.

For a moment there was nothing but a swaying of the fan, and then the head of a man was thrust cautiously into the opening. His face appeared nearly inverted to Graham; his dark hair was wet with dissolving flakes of snow upon it. His arm went up into the darkness holding something unseen. He had a youthful face and bright eyes, and the veins of his forehead were swollen. He seemed to be exerting himself to maintain his position.

For several seconds neither he nor Graham spoke.

'You were the Sleeper?' said the stranger at last.

'Yes,' said Graham. 'What do you want with me?'

'I come from Ostrog, Sire.'

'Ostrog?'

The man in the ventilator twisted his head round so that his profile was towards Graham. He appeared to be listening. Suddenly there was a hasty exclamation, and the intruder sprang back just in time to escape the sweep of the released fan. And when Graham peered up there was nothing visible but the slowly falling snow.

It was perhaps a quarter of an hour before anything returned to the ventilator. But at last came the same metallic interference again; the fans stopped and the face reappeared. Graham had remained all this time in the same place, alert and tremulously excited.

'Who are you? What do you want?' he said.

'We want to speak to you, Sire,' said the intruder. 'We want – I can't hold the thing. We have been trying to find a way to you these three days.'

'Is it rescue?' whispered Graham. 'Escape?'

'Yes, Sire. If you will.'

'You are my party – the party of the Sleeper?'

'Yes, Sire.'

'What am I to do?' said Graham.

There was a struggle. The stranger's arm appeared, and his hand was bleeding. His knees came into view over the edge of the funnel. 'Stand away from me,' he said, and he dropped rather heavily on his hands and one shoulder at Graham's feet. The released ventilator whirled noisily. The stranger rolled over, sprang up nimbly and stood panting, hand to a bruised shoulder, and with his bright eyes on Graham.

'You are indeed the Sleeper,' he said. 'I saw you asleep. When it was the law that anyone might see you.'

'I am the man who was in the trance,' said Graham. 'They have imprisoned me here. I have been here since I awoke – at least three days.'

The intruder seemed about to speak, heard something, glanced swiftly at the door, and suddenly left Graham and ran towards it, shouting quick incoherent words. A bright wedge of steel flashed in his hand, and he began tap, tap, a quick succession of blows upon the hinges. 'Mind!' cried a voice. 'Oh!' The voice came from above.

Graham glanced up, saw the soles of two feet, ducked, was struck on the shoulder by one of them, and a heavy weight bore him to the earth. He fell on his knees and forward, and the weight went over his head. He knelt up and saw a second man from above seated before him.

'I did not see you, Sire,' panted the man. He rose and assisted Graham to arise. 'Are you hurt, Sire?' he panted. A succession of heavy blows on the ventilator began, something fell close to Graham's face, and a shivering edge of white metal danced, fell over, and lay flat upon the floor.

'What is this?' cried Graham, confused and looking at the ventilator. 'Who are you? What are you going to do? Remember, I understand nothing.'

'Stand back,' said the stranger, and drew him from under the ventilator

as another fragment of metal fell heavily.

'We want you to come, Sire,' panted the newcomer, and Graham, glancing at his face again, saw a new cut had changed from white to red on his forehead, and a couple of little trickles of blood were starting therefrom. 'Your people call for you.'

'Come where? My people?'

'To the hall above the markets. Your life is in danger here. We have spies. We learned but just in time. The Council has decided – this very day – either to drug or kill you. And everything is ready. The people are drilled, the wind-vane police, the engineers, and half the way-gearers are with us. We have the halls crowded – shouting. The whole city shouts against the Council. We have arms.' He wiped the blood with his hand. 'Your life here is not worth—'

'But why arms?'

'The people have risen to protect you, Sire. What?'

He turned quickly as the man who had first come down made a hissing with his teeth. Graham saw the latter start back, gesticulate to them to conceal themselves, and move as if to hide behind the opening door.

As he did so Howard appeared, a little tray in one hand and his heavy face downcast. He started, looked up, the door slammed behind him, the tray tilted sideways, and the steel wedge struck him behind the ear. He went down like a felled tree, and lay as he fell athwart the floor of the outer room. The man who had struck him bent hastily, studied his face for a moment, rose, and returned to his work at the door.

'Your poison!' said a voice in Graham's ear.

Then abruptly they were in darkness. The innumerable cornice lights had been extinguished. Graham saw the aperture of the ventilator with ghostly snow whirling above it and dark figures moving hastily. Three knelt on the fan. Some dim thing – a ladder – was being lowered through the opening, and a hand appeared holding a fitful yellow light.

He had a moment of hesitation. But the manner of these men, their swift alacrity, their words, marched so completely with his own fears of the Council, with his idea and hope of a rescue, that it lasted not a moment. And his people awaited him!

'I do not understand,' he said, 'I trust. Tell me what to do.'

The man with the cut brow gripped Graham's arm. 'Clamber up the ladder,' he whispered. 'Quick. They will have heard—'

Graham felt for the ladder with extended hands, put his foot on the lower rung, and, turning his head, saw over the shoulder of the nearest man, in the yellow flicker of the light, the first-comer astride over Howard and still working at the door. Graham turned to the ladder again, and was thrust by his conductor and helped up by those above, and then he was standing on something hard and cold and slippery outside the ventilating funnel.

He shivered. He was aware of a great difference in the temperature. Half a dozen men stood about him, and light flakes of snow touched hands and face and melted. For a moment it was dark, then for a flash a ghastly violet white, and then everything was dark again.

He saw he had come out upon the roof of the vast City structure which had replaced the miscellaneous houses, streets and open spaces of Victorian London. The place upon which he stood was level, with huge serpentine cables lying athwart it in every direction. The circular wheels of a number of windmills loomed indistinct and gigantic through the darkness and snow-fall, and roared with a varying loudness as the fitful white light smote up from below, touched the snow eddies with a transient glitter, and made an evanescent spectre in the night; and here and there, low down, some vaguely outlined wind-driven mechanism flickered with livid sparks.

All this he appreciated in a fragmentary manner as his rescuers stood about him. Someone threw a thick soft cloak of fur-like texture about him, and fastened it by buckled straps at waist and shoulders. Things were said briefly, decisively. Someone thrust him forward.

Before his mind was yet clear a dark shape gripped his arm. 'This way,' said this shape, urging him along, and pointed Graham across the flat roof in the direction of a dim semicircular haze of light. Graham obeyed.

'Mind!' said a voice, as Graham stumbled against a cable. 'Between them and not across them,' said the voice. And, 'We must hurry.'

'Where are the people?' said Graham. 'The people you said awaited me?'

The stranger did not answer. He left Graham's arm as the path grew narrower, and led the way with rapid strides. Graham followed blindly. In a minute he found himself running. 'Are the others coming?' he panted, but received no reply. His companion glanced back and ran on. They came to a sort of pathway of open metal-work, transverse to the direction they had come, and they turned aside to follow this. Graham looked back, but the snowstorm had hidden the others.

'Come on!' said his guide. Running now, they drew near a little windmill spinning high in the air. 'Stoop,' said Graham's guide, and they avoided an endless band running roaring up to the shaft of the vane. 'This way!' and they were ankle deep in a gutter full of drifted thawing snow, between two low walls of metal that presently rose waist high. 'I will go first,' said the guide. Graham drew his cloak about him and followed. Then suddenly came a narrow abyss across which the gutter leapt to the snowy darkness of the further side. Graham peeped over the side once and the gulf was black. For a moment he regretted his flight. He dared not look again, and his brain spun as he waded through the half liquid snow.

Then out of the gutter they clambered and hurried across a wide flat space damp with thawing snow, and for half its extent dimly translucent to lights that went to and fro underneath. He hesitated at this unstable-looking

substance, but his guide ran on unheeding, and so they came to and clambered up slippery steps to the rim of a great dome of glass. Round this they went. Far below a number of people seemed to be dancing, and music filtered through the dome. . . . Graham fancied he heard a shouting through the snowstorm, and his guide hurried him on with a new spurt of haste. They clambered panting to a space of huge windmills, one so vast that only the lower edge of its vanes came rushing into sight and rushed up again and was lost in the night and the snow. They hurried for a time through the colossal metallic tracery of its supports, and came at last above a place of moving platforms like the place into which Graham had looked from the balcony. They crawled across the sloping transparency that covered this street of platforms, crawling on hands and knees because of the slipperiness of the snowfall.

For the most part the glass was bedewed, and Graham saw only hazy suggestions of the forms below, but near the pitch of the transparent roof the glass was clear, and he found himself looking sheerly down upon it all. For awhile, in spite of the urgency of his guide, he gave way to vertigo and lay spread-eagled on the glass, sick and paralysed. Far below, mere stirring specks and dots, went the people of the unsleeping city in their perpetual daylight, and the moving platforms ran on their incessant journey. Messengers and men on unknown businesses shot along the drooping cables and the frail bridges were crowded with men. It was like peering into a gigantic glass hive, and it lay vertically below him with only a tough glass of unknown thickness to save him from a fall. The street showed warm and lit, and Graham was wet now to the skin with thawing snow, and his feet were numbed with cold. For a space he could not move.

'Come on!' cried his guide, with terror in his voice. 'Come on!'

Graham reached the pitch of the roof by an effort.

Over the ridge, following his guide's example, he turned about and slid backward down the opposite slope very swiftly, amid a little avalanche of snow. While he was sliding he thought of what would happen if some broken gap should come in his way. At the edge he stumbled to his feet, ankle-deep in slush, thanking heaven for an opaque footing again. His guide was already clambering up a metal screen to a level expanse.

Through the spare snowflakes above this loomed another line of vast windmills, and then suddenly the amorphous tumult of the rotating wheels was pierced with a deafening sound. It was a mechanical shrilling of extraordinary intensity that seemed to come simultaneously from every point of the compass.

'They have missed us already!' cried Graham's guide in an accent of terror, and suddenly, with a blinding flash, the night became day.

Above the driving snow, from the summits of the wind-wheels, appeared vast masts carrying globes of livid light. They receded in illimitable vistas in

every direction. As far as his eye could penetrate the snowfall they glared.

'Get on this,' cried Graham's conductor, and thrust him forward to a long grating of snowless metal that ran like a band between two slightly sloping expanses of snow. It felt warm to Graham's benumbed feet, and a faint eddy of steam rose from it.

'Come on!' shouted his guide ten yards off, and, without waiting, ran swiftly through the incandescent glare towards the iron supports of the next range of wind-wheels. Graham, recovering from his astonishment, followed as fast, convinced of his imminent capture.

In a score of seconds they were within a tracery of glare and black shadows shot with moving bars beneath the monstrous wheels. Graham's conductor ran on for some time, and suddenly darted sideways and vanished into a black shadow in the corner of the foot of a huge support. In another moment Graham was beside him.

They cowered panting and stared out.

The scene upon which Graham looked was very wild and strange. The snow had now almost ceased; only a belated flake passed now and again across the picture. But the broad stretch of level before them was a ghastly white, broken only by gigantic masses and moving shapes and lengthy strips of impenetrable darkness, vast ungainly Titans of shadow. All about them, huge metallic structures, iron girders, inhumanly vast as it seemed to him, interlaced, and the edges of wind-wheels, scarcely moving in the lull, passed in great shining curves more and more steeply up into a luminous haze. Wherever the snow-spangled light struck down, beams and girders, and incessant bands running with a halting, indomitable resolution passed upward and downward into the black. And with all that mighty activity, with an omnipresent sense of motive and design, this snow-clad desolation of mechanism seemed void of all human presence save themselves, seemed as trackless and deserted and unfrequented by men as some inaccessible Alpine snowfield.

'They will be chasing us,' cried the leader. 'We are scarcely halfway there yet. Cold as it is we must hide here for a space – at least until it snows more thickly again.'

His teeth chattered in his head.

'Where are the markets?' asked Graham staring out. 'Where are all the people?'

The other made no answer.

'*Look!*' whispered Graham, crouched close, and became very still.

The snow had suddenly become thick again, and sliding with the whirling eddies out of the black pit of the sky came something, vague and large and very swift. It came down in a steep curve and swept round, wide wings extended and a trail of white condensing steam behind it, rose with an easy swiftness and went gliding up the air, swept horizontally forward in a wide

curve, and vanished again in the steaming specks of snow. And, through the ribs of its body, Graham saw two little men, very minute and active, searching the snowy areas about him, as it seemed to him, with field-glasses. For a second they were clear, then hazy through a thick whirl of snow, then small and distant, and in a minute they were gone.

'*Now!*' cried his companion. 'Come!'

He pulled Graham's sleeve, and incontinently the two were running headlong down the arcade of ironwork beneath the wind-wheels. Graham, running blindly, collided with his leader, who had turned back on him suddenly. He found himself within a dozen yards of a black chasm. It extended as far as he could see right and left. It seemed to cut off their progress in either direction.

'Do as I do,' whispered his guide. He lay down and crawled to the edge, thrust his head over and twisted until one leg hung. He seemed to feel for something with his foot, found it, and went sliding over the edge into the gulf. His head reappeared. 'It is a ledge,' he whispered. 'In the dark all the way along. Do as I did.'

Graham hesitated, went down upon all fours, crawled to the edge, and peered into a velvety blackness. For a sickly moment he had courage neither to go on nor retreat, then he sat and hung his leg down, felt his guide's hands pulling at him, had a horrible sensation of sliding over the edge into the unfathomable, splashed, and felt himself in a slushy gutter, impenetrably dark.

'This way,' whispered the voice, and he began crawling along the gutter through the trickling thaw, pressing himself against the wall. They continued along it for some minutes. He seemed to pass through a hundred stages of misery, to pass minute after minute through a hundred degrees of cold, damp, and exhaustion. In a little while he ceased to feel his hands and feet.

The gutter sloped downwards. He observed that they were now many feet below the edge of the buildings. Rows of spectral white shapes like the ghosts of blind-drawn windows rose above them. They came to the end of a cable fastened above one of these white windows, dimly visible and dropping into impenetrable shadows. Suddenly his hand came against his guide's.

'Still!' whispered the latter very softly.

He looked up with a start and saw the huge wings of the flying machine gliding slowly and noiselessly overhead athwart the broad band of snow-flecked grey-blue sky. In a moment it was hidden again.

'Keep still; they were just turning.'

For a while both were motionless, then Graham's companion stood up, and reaching towards the fastenings of the cable fumbled with some indistinct tackle.

'What is that?' asked Graham.

The only answer was a faint cry. The man crouched motionless. Graham

peered and saw his face dimly. He was staring down the long ribbon of sky, and Graham, following his eyes, saw the flying machine small and faint and remote. Then he saw that the wings spread on either side, that it headed towards them, that every moment it grew larger. It was following the edge of the chasm towards them.

The man's movements became convulsive. He thrust two crossbars into Graham's hand. Graham could not see them, he ascertained their form by feeling. They were slung by thin cords to the cable. On the cord were hand grips of some soft elastic substance. 'Put the cross between your legs,' whispered the guide hysterically, 'and grip the holdfasts. Grip tightly, grip!'

Graham did as he was told.

'Jump,' said the voice. 'In Heaven's name, jump!'

For one momentous second Graham could not speak. He was glad afterwards that darkness hid his face. He said nothing. He began to tremble violently. He looked sideways at the swift shadow that swallowed up the sky as it rushed upon him.

'Jump! Jump – in God's name! Or they will have us,' cried Graham's guide, and in the violence of his passion thrust him forward.

Graham tottered convulsively, gave a sobbing cry, a cry in spite of himself, and then, as the flying machine swept over them, fell forward into the pit of that darkness, seated on the cross wood and holding the ropes with the clutch of death. Something cracked, something rapped smartly against a wall. He heard the pulley of the cradle hum on its rope. He heard the aeronauts shout. He felt a pair of knees digging into his back. . . . He was sweeping headlong through the air, falling through the air. All his strength was in his hands. He would have screamed but he had no breath.

He shot into a blinding light that made him grip the tighter. He recognized the great passage with the running ways, the hanging lights and interlacing girders. They rushed upward and by him. He had a momentary impression of a great circular aperture yawning to swallow him up.

He was in the dark again, falling, falling, gripping with aching hands, and behold! a clap of sound, a burst of light, and he was in a brightly lit hall with a roaring multitude of people beneath his feet. The people! His people! A proscenium, a stage rushed up towards him, and his cable swept down to a circular aperture to the right of this. He felt he was travelling slower, and suddenly very much slower. He distinguished shouts of 'Saved! The Master. He is safe!' The stage rushed up towards him with rapidly diminishing swiftness. Then—

He heard the man clinging behind him shout as if suddenly terrified, and this shout was echoed by a shout from below. He felt that he was no longer gliding along the cable but falling with it. There was a tumult of yells, screams and cries. He felt something soft against his extended hand, and the impact of a broken fall quivering through his arm. . . .

He wanted to be still and the people were lifting him. He believed afterwards he was carried to the platform and given some drink, but he was never sure. He did not notice what became of his guide. When his mind was clear again he was on his feet; eager hands were assisting him to stand. He was in a big alcove, occupying the position that in his previous experience had been devoted to the lower boxes. If this was indeed a theatre.

A mighty tumult was in his ears, a thunderous roar, the shouting of a countless multitude. 'It is the Sleeper! The Sleeper is with us!'

'The Sleeper is with us! The Master – the Owner! The Master is with us. He is safe.'

Graham had a surging vision of a great hall crowded with people. He saw no individuals, he was conscious of a froth of pink faces, of waving arms and garments, he felt the occult influence of a vast crowd pouring over him, buoying him up. There were balconies, galleries, great archways giving remoter perspectives, and everywhere people, a vast arena of people, densely packed and cheering. Across the nearer space lay the collapsed cable like a huge snake. It had been cut by the men of the flying machine at its upper end, and had crumpled down into the hall. Men seemed to be hauling this out of the way. But the whole effect was vague, the very buildings throbbed and leapt with the roar of the voices.

He stood unsteadily and looked at those about him. Someone supported him by one arm. 'Let me go into a little room,' he said, weeping; 'a little room,' and could say no more. A man in black stepped forward, took his disengaged arm. He was aware of officious men opening a door before him. Someone guided him to a seat. He staggered. He sat down heavily and covered his face with his hands; he was trembling violently, his nervous control was at an end. He was relieved of his cloak, he could not remember how; his purple hose he saw were black with wet. People were running about him, things were happening, but for some time he gave no heed to them.

He had escaped. A myriad of cries told him that. He was safe. These were the people who were on his side. For a space he sobbed for breath, and then he sat still with his face covered. The air was full of the shouting of innumerable men.

CHAPTER IX

The People March

He became aware of someone urging a glass of clear fluid upon his attention, looked up and discovered this was a dark young man in a yellow garment. He took the dose forthwith, and in a moment he was glowing. A tall man in a black robe stood by his shoulder, and pointed to the half-open door into the hall. This man was shouting close to his ear and yet what was said was indistinct because of the tremendous uproar from the great theatre. Behind the man was a girl in a silvery grey robe, whom Graham, even in this confusion, perceived to be beautiful. Her dark eyes, full of wonder and curiosity, were fixed on him, her lips trembled apart. A partially opened door gave a glimpse of the crowded hall, and admitted a vast uneven tumult, a hammering, clapping and shouting that died away and began again, and rose to a thunderous pitch, and so continued intermittently all the time that Graham remained in the little room. He watched the lips of the man in black and gathered that he was making some clumsy explanation.

He stared stupidly for some moments at these things and then stood up abruptly; he grasped the arm of this shouting person.

'Tell me!' he cried. 'Who am I? Who am I?'

The others came nearer to hear his words. 'Who am I?' His eyes searched their faces.

'They have told him nothing!' cried the girl.

'Tell me, tell me!' cried Graham.

'You are the Master of the Earth. You are owner of half the world.'

He did not believe he heard aright. He resisted the persuasion. He pretended not to understand, not to hear. He lifted his voice again. 'I have been awake three days – a prisoner three days. I judge there is some struggle between a number of people in this city – it is London?'

'Yes,' said the younger man.

'And those who meet in the great hall with the white Atlas? How does it concern me? In some way it has to do with me. Why, I don't know. Drugs? It seems to me that while I have slept the world has gone mad. I have gone mad. Who are those Councillors under the Atlas? Why should they try to drug me?'

'To keep you insensible,' said the man in yellow. 'To prevent your interference.'

'But *why*?'

'Because *you* are the Atlas, Sire,' said the man in yellow. 'The world is on your shoulders. They rule it in your name.'

The sounds from the hall had died into a silence threaded by one mono-
tonous voice. Now suddenly, trampling on these last words, came a deafening
tumult, a roaring and thundering, cheer crowded on cheer, voices hoarse
and shrill, beating, overlapping, and while it lasted the people in the little
room could not hear each other shout.

Graham stood, his intelligence clinging helplessly to the thing he had just
heard. 'The Council,' he repeated blankly, and then snatched at a name
that had struck him. 'But who is Ostrog?' he said.

'He is the organizer – the organizer of the revolt. Our Leader – in your name.'

'In my name? – And you? Why is he not here?'

'He – has deputed us. I am his brother – his half-brother, Lincoln. He wants
you to show yourself to these people and then come on to him. That is why
he was sent. He is at the wind-vane offices directing. The people are marching.'

'In your name,' shouted the younger man. 'They have ruled, crushed,
tyrannized. At last even—'

'In my name! My name! Master?'

The younger man suddenly became audible in a pause of the outer thunder,
indignant and vociferous, a high penetrating voice under his red aquiline
nose and bushy moustache. 'No one expected you to wake. No one expected
you to wake. They were cunning. Damned tyrants! But they were taken by
surprise. They did not know whether to drug you, hypnotize you, kill you.'

Again the hall dominated everything.

'Ostrog is at the wind-vane offices ready—. Even now there is a rumour
of fighting beginning.'

The man who had called himself Lincoln came close to him. 'Ostrog has
it planned. Trust him. We have our organizations ready. We shall seize the
flying stages—. Even now he may be doing that. Then—'

'This public theatre,' bawled the man in yellow, 'is only a contingent. We
have five myriads of drilled men—'

'We have arms,' cried Lincoln. 'We have plans. A leader. Their police have
gone from the streets and are massed in the—' (inaudible). 'It is now or
never. The Council is rocking – They cannot trust even their drilled men—'

'Hear the people calling to you!'

Graham's mind was like a night of moon and swift clouds, now dark and
hopeless, now clear and ghastly. He was Master of the Earth, he was a man
sodden with thawing snow. Of all his fluctuating impressions the dominant
ones presented an antagonism; on the one hand was the White Council,
powerful, disciplined, few, the White Council from which he had just
escaped; and on the other, monstrous crowds, packed masses of indistin-
guishable people clamouring his name, hailing him Master. The other side
had imprisoned him, debated his death. These shouting thousands beyond
the little doorway had rescued him. But why these things should be so he
could not understand.

The door opened, Lincoln's voice was swept away and drowned, and a rush of people followed on the heels of the tumult. These intruders came towards him and Lincoln gesticulating. The voices without explained their soundless lips. 'Show us the Sleeper, show us the Sleeper!' was the burden of the uproar. Men were bawling for 'Order! Silence!'

Graham glanced towards the open doorway, and saw a tall, oblong picture of the hall beyond, a waving, incessant confusion of crowded, shouting faces, men and women together, waving pale blue garments, extended hands. Many were standing, one man in rags of dark brown, a gaunt figure, stood on the seat and waved a black cloth. He met the wonder and expectation of the girl's eyes. What did these people expect from him. He was dimly aware that the tumult outside had changed its character, was in some way beating, marching. His own mind, too, changed for a space he did not recognize the influence that was transforming him. But a moment that was near to panic passed. He tried to make audible enquiries of what was required of him.

Lincoln was shouting in his ear, but Graham was deafened to that. All the others save the woman gesticulated towards the hall. He perceived what had happened to the uproar. The whole mass of people was chanting together. It was not simply a song, the voices were gathered together and upborne by a torrent of instrumental music, music like the music of an organ, a woven texture of sounds, full of trumpets, full of flaunting banners, full of the march and pageantry of opening war. And the feet of the people were beating time – tramp, tramp.

He was urged towards the door. He obeyed mechanically. The strength of that chant took hold of him, stirred him, emboldened him. The hall opened to him, a vast welter of fluttering colour swaying to the music.

'Wave your arm to them,' said Lincoln. 'Wave your arm to them.'

'This,' said a voice on the other side, 'he must have this.' Arms were about his neck detaining him in the doorway, and a black mantle hung from his shoulders. He threw his arm free of this and followed Lincoln. He perceived the girl in grey close to him, her face lit, her gesture onward. For the instant she became to him, flushed and eager as she was, an embodiment of the song. He emerged in the alcove again. Incontinently the mounting waves of the song broke upon his appearing, and flashed up into a foam of shouting. Guided by Lincoln's hand he marched obliquely across the centre of the stage facing the people.

The hall was a vast and intricate space – galleries, balconies, broad spaces of amphitheatral steps, and great archways. Far away, high up, seemed the mouth of a huge passage full of struggling humanity. The whole multitude was swaying in congested masses. Individual figures sprang out of the tumult, impressed him momentarily, and lost definition again. Close to the platform swayed a beautiful fair woman, carried by three men, her

hair across her face and brandishing a green staff. Next this group an old
careworn man in blue canvas maintained his place in the crush with
difficulty, and behind shouted a hairless face, a great cavity of toothless
mouth. A voice called that enigmatical word 'Ostrog'. All his impressions
were vague save the massive emotion of that trampling song. The multitude
were beating time with their feet – marking time, tramp, tramp, tramp,
tramp. The green weapons waved, flashed and slanted. Then he saw those
nearest to him on a level space before the stage were marching in front
of him, passing towards a great archway, shouting 'To the Council!' Tramp,
tramp, tramp, tramp. He raised his arm, and the roaring was redoubled.
He remembered he had to shout 'March!' His mouth shaped inaudible
heroic words. He waved his arm again and pointed to the archway, shouting
'Onward!'. They were no longer marking time, they were marching; tramp,
tramp, tramp, tramp. In that host were bearded men, old men, youths,
fluttering robed bare-armed women, girls. Men and women of the new
age! Rich robes, grey rags fluttered together in the whirl of their movement
amidst the dominant blue. A monstrous black banner jerked its way to
the right. He perceived a blue-clad Negro, a shrivelled woman in yellow,
then a group of tall fair-haired, white-faced, blue-clad men pushed theat-
rically past him. He noted two Chinamen. A tall, sallow, dark-haired,
shining-eyed youth, white clad from top to toe, clambered up towards the
platform shouting loyally, and sprang down again and receded, looking
backward. Heads, shoulders, hands clutching weapons, all were swinging
with those marching cadences.

Faces came out of the confusion to him as he stood there, eyes met his
and passed and vanished. Men gesticulated to him, shouted inaudible
personal things. Most of the faces were flushed, but many were ghastly
white. And disease was there, and many a hand that waved to him was
gaunt and lean. Men and women of the new age! Strange and incredible
meeting! As the broad stream passed before him to the right, tributary
gangways from the remote uplands of the hall thrust downward in an
incessant replacement of people; tramp, tramp, tramp, tramp. The unison
of the song was enriched and complicated by the massive echoes of arches
and passages. Men and women mingled in the ranks; tramp, tramp, tramp,
tramp. The whole world seemed marching. Tramp, tramp, tramp, tramp;
his brain was tramping. The garments waved onward, the faces poured by
more abundantly.

Tramp, tramp, tramp, tramp; at Lincoln's pressure he turned towards the
archway, walking unconsciously in that rhythm, scarcely noticing his move-
ment for the melody and stir of it. The multitude, the gesture and song, all
moved in that direction, the flow of people smote downward until the
upturned faces were below the level of his feet. He was aware of a path
before him, of a suite about him, of guards and dignities, and Lincoln on

his right hand. Attendants intervened, and ever and again blotted out the sight of the multitude to the left. Before him went the backs of the guards in black – three and three and three. He was marched along a little railed way, and crossed above the archway, with the torrent dipping to flow beneath, and shouting up to him. He did not know whither he went; he did not want to know. He glanced back across a flaming spaciousness of hall. Tramp, tramp, tramp, tramp.

CHAPTER X

The Battle of the Darkness

He was no longer in the hall. He was marching along a gallery overhanging one of the great streets of the moving platforms that traversed the city. Before him and behind him tramped his guards. The whole concave of the moving ways below was a congested mass of people marching, tramping to the left, shouting, waving hands and arms, pouring along a huge vista, shouting as they came into view, shouting as they passed, shouting as they receded, until the globes of electric light receding in perspective dropped down it seemed and hid the swarming bare heads. Tramp, tramp, tramp, tramp.

The song roared up to Graham now, no longer upborne by music, but coarse and noisy, and the beating of the marching feet, tramp, tramp, tramp, tramp, interwove with a thunderous irregularity of footsteps from the undisciplined rabble that poured along the higher ways.

Abruptly he noted a contrast. The buildings on the opposite side of the way seemed deserted, the cables and bridges that laced across the aisle were empty and shadowy. It came into Graham's mind that these also should have swarmed with people.

He felt a curious emotion – throbbing – very fast! He stopped again. The guards before him marched on; those about him stopped as he did. He saw the direction of their faces. The throbbing had something to do with the lights. He too looked up.

At first it seemed to him a thing that affected the lights simply, an isolated phenomenon, having no bearing on the things below. Each huge globe of blinding whiteness was as it were clutched, compressed in a systole that was followed by a transitory diastole, and again a systole like a tightening grip, darkness, light, darkness, in rapid alternation.

Graham became aware that this strange behaviour of the lights had to do with the people below. The appearance of the houses and ways, the appearance of the packed masses changed, became a confusion of vivid lights and leaping shadows. He saw a multitude of shadows had sprung into aggressive existence, seemed rushing up, broadening, widening, growing with steady swiftness – to leap suddenly back and return reinforced. The song and the tramping had ceased. The unanimous march, he discovered, was arrested, there were eddies, a flow sideways, shouts of 'The lights!' Voices were crying together one thing. 'The lights!' cried these voices. 'The lights!' He looked down. In this dancing death of the lights the area of the street had suddenly become a monstrous struggle. The huge white globes became purple-white, purple with a reddish glow, flickered, flickered faster and faster,

fluttered between light and extinction, ceased to flicker and became mere fading specks of glowing red in a vast obscurity. In ten seconds the extinction was accomplished, and there was only this roaring darkness, a black monstrosity that had suddenly swallowed up those glittering myriads of men.

He felt invisible forms about him; his arms were gripped. Something rapped sharply against his shin. A voice bawled in his ear, 'It is all right – all right.'

Graham shook off the paralysis of his first astonishment. He struck his forehead against Lincoln's and bawled, 'What is this darkness?'

'The Council has cut the currents that light the city. We must wait – stop. The people will go on. They will—'

His voice was drowned. Voices were shouting, 'Save the Sleeper. Take care of the Sleeper.' A guard stumbled against Graham and hurt his hand by an inadvertent blow of his weapon. A wild tumult tossed and whirled about him, growing, as it seemed, louder, denser, more furious each moment. Fragments of recognizable sounds drove towards him, were whirled away from him as his mind reached out to grasp them. Voices seemed to be shouting conflicting orders, other voices answered. There were suddenly a succession of piercing screams close beneath them.

A voice bawled in his ear, 'The red police,' and receded forthwith beyond his questions.

A crackling sound grew to distinctness, and therewith a leaping of faint flashes along the edge of the further ways. By their light Graham saw the heads and bodies of a number of men, armed with weapons like those of his guards, leap into an instant's dim visibility. The whole area began to crackle, to flash with little instantaneous streaks of light, and abruptly the darkness rolled back like a curtain.

A glare of light dazzled his eyes, a vast seething expanse of struggling men confused his mind. A shout, a burst of cheering, came across the ways. He looked up to see the source of the light. A man hung far overhead from the upper part of a cable, holding by a rope the blinding star that had driven the darkness back. He wore a red uniform.

Graham's eyes fell to the ways again. A wedge of red a little way along the vista caught his eye. He saw it was a dense mass of red-clad men jammed on the higher further way, their backs against the pitiless cliff of building, and surrounded by a dense crowd of antagonists. They were fighting. Weapons flashed and rose and fell, heads vanished at the edge of the contest, and other heads replaced them, the little flashes from the green weapons became little jets of smoky grey while the light lasted.

Abruptly the flare was extinguished and the ways were an inky darkness once more, a tumultuous mystery.

He felt something thrusting against him. He was being pushed along the gallery. Someone was shouting – it might be at him. He was too confused to hear. He was thrust against the wall, and a number of people blundered

past him. It seemed to him that his guards were struggling with one another.

Suddenly the cable-hung star-holder appeared again, and the whole scene was white and dazzling. The band of red-coats seemed broader and nearer; its apex was halfway down the ways towards the central aisle. And raising his eyes Graham saw that a number of these men had also appeared now in the darkened lower galleries of the opposite building, and were firing over the heads of their fellows below at the boiling confusion of people on the lower ways. The meaning of these things dawned upon him. The march of the people had come upon an ambush at the very outset. Thrown into confusion by the extinction of the lights they were now being attacked by the red police. Then he became aware that he was standing alone, that his guards and Lincoln were along the gallery in the direction along which he had come before the darkness fell. He saw they were gesticulating to him wildly, running back towards him. A great shouting came from across the ways. Then it seemed as though the whole face of the darkened building opposite was lined and speckled with red-clad men. And they were pointing over to him and shouting. 'The Sleeper! Save the Sleeper!' shouted a multitude of throats.

Something struck the wall above his head. He looked up at the impact and saw a star-shaped splash of silvery metal. He saw Lincoln near him. Felt his arm gripped. Then, pat, pat; he had been missed twice.

For a moment he did not understand this. The street was hidden, everything was hidden, as he looked. The second flare had burned out.

Lincoln had gripped Graham by the arm, was lugging him along the gallery. 'Before the next light!' he cried. His haste was contagious. Graham's instinct of self-preservation overcame the paralysis of his incredulous astonishment. He became for a time the blind creature of the fear of death. He ran, stumbling because of the uncertainty of the darkness, blundered into his guards as they turned to run with him. Haste was his one desire, to escape this perilous gallery upon which he was exposed. A third glare came close on its predecessors. With it came a great shouting across the ways, an answering tumult from the ways. The red-coats below, he saw, had now almost gained the central passage. Their countless faces turned towards him, and they shouted. The white façade opposite was densely stippled with red. All these wonderful things concerned him, turned upon him as a pivot. These were the guards of the Council attempting to recapture him.

Lucky it was for him that these shots were the first fired in anger for a hundred and fifty years. He heard bullets whacking over his head, felt a splash of molten metal sting his ear, and perceived without looking that the whole opposite façade, an unmasked ambuscade of red police, was crowded and bawling and firing at him.

Down went one of his guards before him, and Graham, unable to stop, leapt the writhing body.

In another second he had plunged, unhurt, into a black passage, and incontinently someone, coming, it may be, in a transverse direction, blundered violently into him. He was hurling down a staircase in absolute darkness. He reeled, and was struck again, and came against a wall with his hands. He was crushed by a weight of struggling bodies, whirled round, and thrust to the right. A vast pressure pinned him. He could not breathe, his ribs seemed cracking. He felt a momentary relaxation, and then the whole mass of people moving together, bore him back towards the great theatre from which he had so recently come.

There were moments when his feet did not touch the ground. Then he was staggering and shoving. He heard shouts of 'They are coming!' and a muffled cry close to him. His foot blundered against something soft, he heard a hoarse scream under foot. He heard shouts of 'The Sleeper!' but he was too confused to speak. He heard the green weapons crackling. For a space he lost his individual will, became an atom in a panic, blind, unthinking, mechanical. He thrust and pressed back and writhed in the pressure, kicked presently against a step, and found himself ascending a slope. And abruptly the faces all about him leapt out of the black, visible, ghastly white and astonished, terrified, perspiring, in a livid glare. One face, a young man's, was very near to him, not twenty inches away. At the time it was but a passing incident of no emotional value, but afterwards it came back to him in his dreams. For this young man, wedged upright in the crowd for a time, had been shot and was already dead.

A fourth white star must have been lit by the man on the cable. Its light came glaring in through vast windows and arches and showed Graham that he was now one of a dense mass of flying black figures pressed back across the lower area of the great theatre. This time the picture was livid and fragmentary, slashed and barred with black shadows. He saw that quite near to him the red guards were fighting their way through the people. He could not tell whether they saw him. He looked for Lincoln and his guards. He saw Lincoln near the stage of the theatre surrounded in a crowd of black-badged revolutionaries, lifted up and staring to and fro as if seeking him. Graham perceived that he himself was near the opposite edge of the crowd, that behind him, separated by a barrier, sloped the now vacant seats of the theatre. A sudden idea came to him, and he began fighting his way towards the barrier. As he reached it the glare came to an end.

In a moment he had thrown off the great cloak that not only impeded his movements but made him conspicuous, and had slipped it from his shoulders. He heard someone trip in its folds. In another he was scaling the barrier and had dropped into the blackness on the further side. Then feeling his way he came to the lower end of an ascending gangway. In the darkness the sound of firing ceased and the roar of feet and voices lulled. Then suddenly he came to an unexpected step and tripped and fell. As he did so

pools and islands amidst the darkness about him leapt to vivid light again, the uproar surged louder and the glare of the fifth white star shone through the vast fenestrations of the theatre walls.

He rolled over among some seats, heard a shouting and the whirring rattle of weapons, struggled up and was knocked back again, perceived that a number of black-badged men were all about him firing at the rebels below, leaping from seat to seat, crouching among the seats to reload. Instinctively he crouched amidst the seats, as stray shots ripped the pneumatic cushions and cut bright slashes on their soft metal frames. Instinctively he marked the direction of the gangways, the most plausible way of escape for him so soon as the veil of darkness fell again.

A young man in faded blue garments came vaulting over the seats. 'Hullo!' he said, with his flying feet within six inches of the crouching Sleeper's face.

He stared without any sign of recognition, turned to fire, fired, and, shouting, 'To hell with the Council!' was about to fire again. Then it seemed to Graham that the half of this man's neck had vanished. A drop of moisture fell on Graham's cheek. The green weapon stopped half raised. For a moment the man stood still with his face suddenly expressionless, then he began to slant forward. His knees bent. Man and darkness fell together. At the sound of his fall Graham rose up and ran for his life until a step down to the gangway tripped him. He scrambled to his feet, turned up the gangway and ran on.

When the sixth star glared he was already close to the yawning throat of a passage. He ran on the swifter for the light, entered the passage and turned a corner into absolute night again. He was knocked sideways, rolled over, and recovered his feet. He found himself one of a crowd of invisible fugitives pressing in one direction. His one thought now was their thought also; to escape out of this fighting. He thrust and struck, staggered, ran, was wedged tightly, lost ground and then was clear again.

For some minutes he was running through the darkness along a winding passage, and then he crossed some wide and open space, passed down a long incline, and came at last down a flight of steps to a level place. Many people were shouting, 'They are coming! The guards are coming. They are firing. Get out of the fighting. The guards are firing. It will be safe in Seventh Way. Along here to Seventh Way!' There were women and children in the crowd as well as men.

The crowd converged on an archway, passed through a short throat and emerged on a wider space again, lit dimly. The black figures about him spread out and ran up what seemed in the twilight to be a gigantic series of steps. He followed. The people dispersed to the right and left . . . He perceived that he was no longer in a crowd. He stopped near the highest step. Before him, on that level, were groups of seats and a little kiosk. He went up to this and, stopping in the shadow of its eaves, looked about him panting.

Everything was vague and grey, but he recognized that these great steps were a series of platforms of the 'ways,' now motionless again. The platform slanted up on either side, and the tall buildings rose beyond, vast dim ghosts, their inscriptions and advertisements indistinctly seen, and up through the girders and cables was a faint interrupted ribbon of pallid sky. A number of people hurried by. From their shouts and voices, it seemed they were hurrying to join the fighting. Other less noisy figures flitted timidly among the shadows.

From very far away down the street he could hear the sound of a struggle. But it was evident to him that this was not the street into which the theatre opened. That former fight, it seemed, had suddenly dropped out of sound and hearing. And – grotesque thought! – they were fighting for him!

For a space he was like a man who pauses in the reading of a vivid book, and suddenly doubts what he has been taking unquestioningly. At that time he had little mind for details; the whole effect was a huge astonishment. Oddly enough, while the flight from the Council prison, the great crowd in the hall, and the attack of the red police upon the swarming people were clearly present in his mind, it cost him an effort to piece in his awakening and to revive the meditative interval of the Silent Rooms. At first his memory leapt these things and took him back to the cascade at Pentargen quivering in the wind, and all the sombre splendours of the sunlit Cornish coast. The contrast touched everything with unreality. And then the gap filled, and he began to comprehend his position.

It was no longer absolutely a riddle, as it had been in the Silent Rooms. At least he had the strange, bare outline now. He was in some way the owner of half the world, and great political parties were fighting to possess him. On the one hand was the White Council, with its red police, set resolutely, it seemed, on the usurpation of his property and perhaps his murder; on the other, the revolution that had liberated him, with this unseen 'Ostrog' as its leader. And the whole of this gigantic city was convulsed by their struggle. Frantic development of his world! 'I do not understand,' he cried. 'I do not understand!'

He had slipped out between the contending parties into this liberty of the twilight. What would happen next? What was happening? He figured the red-clad men as busily hunting him, driving the black-badged revolutionists before them.

At any rate chance had given him a breathing space. He could lurk unchallenged by the passers-by, and watch the course of things. His eye followed up the intricate dim immensity of the twilight buildings, and it came to him as a thing infinitely wonderful, that above there the sun was rising, and the world was lit and glowing with the old familiar light of day. In a little while he had recovered his breath. His clothing had already dried upon him from the snow.

He wandered for miles along these twilight ways, speaking to no one, accosted by no one – a dark figure among dark figures – the coveted man out of the past, the inestimable unintentional owner of half the world. Wherever there were lights or dense crowds, or exceptional excitement he was afraid of recognition, and watched and turned back or went up and down by the middle stairways, into some transverse system of ways at a lower or higher level. And though he came on no more fighting, the whole city stirred with battle. Once he had to run to avoid a marching multitude of men that swept the street. Everyone abroad seemed involved. For the most part they were men, and they carried what he judged were weapons. It seemed as though the struggle was concentrated mainly in the quarter of the city from which he came. Ever and again a distant roaring, the remote suggestion of that conflict, reached his ears. Then his caution and his curiosity struggled together. But his caution prevailed, and he continued wandering away from the fighting – so far as he could judge. He went unmolested, unsuspected through the dark. After a time he ceased to hear even a remote echo of the battle, fewer and fewer people passed him, until at last the Titanic streets became deserted. The frontages of the buildings grew plain and harsh; he seemed to have come to a district of vacant warehouses. Solitude crept upon him – his pace slackened.

He became aware of a growing fatigue. At times he would turn aside and seat himself on one of the numerous seats of the upper ways. But a feverish restlessness, the knowledge of his vital implication in his struggle, would not let him rest in any place for long. Was the struggle on his behalf alone?

And then in a desolate place came the shock of an earthquake – a roaring and thundering – a mighty wind of cold air pouring through the city, the smash of glass, the slip and thud of falling masonry – a series of gigantic concussions. A mass of glass and ironwork fell from the remote roofs into the middle gallery, not a hundred yards away from him, and in the distance were shouts and running. He, too, was startled to an aimless activity, and ran first one way and then as aimlessly back.

A man came running towards him. His self-control returned. 'What have they blown up?' asked the man breathlessly. 'That was an explosion,' and before Graham could speak he had hurried on.

The great buildings rose dimly, veiled by a perplexing twilight, albeit the rivulet of sky above was now bright with day. He noted many strange features, understanding none at the time; he even spelt out many of the inscriptions in Phonetic lettering. But what profits it to decipher a confusion of odd-looking letters resolving itself, after painful strain of eye and mind, into 'Here is Eadhamite,' or, 'Labour Bureau – Little Side?' Grotesque thought, that in all probability some or all of these cliff-like houses were his!

The perversity of his experience came to him vividly. In actual fact he had made such a leap in time as romancers have imagined again and again.

And that fact realized, he had been prepared. His mind had, as it were, seated itself for a spectacle. And no spectacle, but a great vague danger, unsympathetic shadows and veils of darkness. Somewhere through the labyrinthine obscurity his death sought him. Would he, after all, be killed before he saw? It might be that even at the next shadowy corner his destruction ambushed. A great desire to see, a great longing to know, arose in him.

He became fearful of corners. It seemed to him that there was safety in concealment. Where could he hide to be inconspicuous when the lights returned? At last he sat down upon a seat in a recess on one of the higher ways, conceiving he was alone there.

He squeezed his knuckles into his weary eyes. Suppose when he looked again he found the dark through of parallel ways and that intolerable altitude of edifice, gone? Suppose he were to discover the whole story of these last few days, the awakening, the shouting multitudes, the darkness and the fighting, a phantasmagoria, a new and more vivid sort of dream. It must be a dream; it was so inconsecutive, so reasonless. Why were the people fighting for him? Why should this saner world regard him as Owner and Master?

So he thought, sitting blinded, and then he looked again, half hoping in spite of his ears to see some familiar aspect of the life of the nineteenth century, to see, perhaps, the little harbour of Boscastle about him, the cliffs of Pentargen, or the bedroom of his home. But fact takes no heed of human hopes. A squad of men with a black banner tramped athwart the nearer shadows, intent on conflict, and beyond rose that giddy wall of frontage, vast and dark, with the dim incomprehensible lettering showing faintly on its face.

'It is no dream,' he said, 'no dream.' And he bowed his face upon his hands.

CHAPTER XI

The Old Man Who Knew Everything

He was startled by a cough close at hand.

He turned sharply, and peering, saw a small, hunched-up figure sitting a couple of yards off in the shadow of the enclosure.

'Have ye any news?' asked the high-pitched wheezy voice of a very old man.

Graham hesitated. 'None,' he said.

'I stay here till the lights come again,' said the old man. 'These blue scoundrels are everywhere – everywhere.'

Graham's answer was inarticulate assent. He tried to see the old man but the darkness hid his face. He wanted very much to respond, to talk, but he did not know how to begin.

'Dark and damnable,' said the old man suddenly. 'Dark and damnable. Turned out of my room among all these dangers.'

'That's hard,' ventured Graham. 'That's hard on you.'

'Darkness. An old man lost in the darkness. And all the world gone mad. War and fighting. The police beaten and rogues abroad. Why don't they bring some Negroes to protect us? . . . No more dark passages for me. I fell over a dead man.'

'You're safer with company,' said the old man, 'if it's company of the right sort,' and peered frankly. He rose suddenly and came towards Graham.

Apparently the scrutiny was satisfactory. The old man sat down as if relieved to be no longer alone. 'Eh!' he said, 'But this is a terrible time! War and fighting, and the dead lying there – men, strong men, dying in the dark. Sons! I have three sons. God knows where they are tonight.'

The voice ceased. Then repeated quavering: 'God knows where they are tonight.'

Graham stood revolving a question that should not betray his ignorance. Again the old man's voice ended the pause.

'This Ostrog will win,' he said. 'He will win. And what the world will be like under him no one can tell. My sons are under the wind-vanes, all three. One of my daughters-in-law was his mistress for a while. His mistress! We're not common people. Though they've sent me to wander tonight and take my chance. . . . I knew what was going on. Before most people. But this darkness! And to fall over a dead body suddenly in the dark!'

His wheezy breathing could be heard.

'Ostrog!' said Graham.

'The greatest Boss the world has ever seen,' said the voice.

Graham ransacked his mind. 'The Council has few friends among the people,' he hazarded.

'Few friends. And poor ones at that. They've had their time. Eh! They should have kept to the clever ones. But twice they held election. And Ostrog. And now it has burst out and nothing can stay it, nothing can stay it. Twice they rejected Ostrog – Ostrog the Boss. I heard of his rages at the time – he was terrible. Heaven save them! For nothing on earth can now, he has raised the Labour Companies upon them. No one else would have dared. All the blue canvas armed and marching! He will go through with it. He will go through.'

He was silent for a little while. 'This Sleeper,' he said, and stopped.

'Yes,' said Graham. 'Well?'

The senile voice sank to a confidential whisper, the dim, pale face came close. 'The real Sleeper—'

'Yes,' said Graham.

'Died years ago.'

'What?' said Graham, sharply.

'Years ago. Died. Years ago.'

'You don't say so!' said Graham.

'I do. I do say so. He died. This Sleeper who's woke up – they changed in the night. A poor, drugged insensible creature. But I mustn't tell all I know. I mustn't tell all I know.'

For a little while he muttered inaudibly. His secret was too much for him. 'I don't know the ones that put him to sleep – that was before my time – but I know the man who injected the stimulants and woke him again. It was ten to one – wake or kill. Wake or kill. Ostrog's way.'

Graham was so astonished at these things that he had to interrupt, to make the old man repeat his words, to re-question vaguely, before he was sure of the meaning and folly of what he heard. And his awakening had not been natural! Was that an old man's senile superstition, too, or had it any truth in it? Feeling in the dark corners of his memory, he presently came on something that might conceivably be an impression of some such stimulating effect. It dawned upon him that he had happened upon a lucky encounter, that at last he might learn something of the new age. The old man wheezed a while and spat, and then the piping, reminiscent voice resumed:

'The first time they rejected him. I've followed it all.'

'Rejected whom?' said Graham. 'The Sleeper?'

'Sleeper? No. Ostrog. He was terrible – terrible! And he was promised then, promised certainly the next time. Fools they were – not to be more afraid of him. Now all the city's his millstone, and such as we, dust ground upon it. Dust ground upon it. Until he set to work – the workers cut each other's throats, and murdered a Chinaman or a Labour policeman now and then, and left the rest of us in peace. Dead bodies! Robbing! Darkness! Such

a thing hasn't been this gross of years. Eh! – But 'tis ill on small folks when the great fall out! It's ill.'

'Did you say – there had not been – what? – for a gross of years?'

'Eh?' said the old man.

The old man said something about clipping his words, and made him repeat this a third time. 'Fighting and slaying, and weapons in hand, and fools bawling freedom and the like,' said the old man. 'Not in all my life has there been that. These are like the old days – for sure – when the Paris people broke out – three gross of years ago. That's what I mean hasn't been. But it's the world's way. It had to come back. I know. I know. This five years Ostrog has been working, and there has been trouble and trouble, and hunger and threats and high talk and arms. Blue canvas and murmurs. No one safe. Everything sliding and slipping. And now here we are! Revolt and fighting, and the Council come to its end.'

'You are rather well-informed on these things,' said Graham.

'I know what I hear. It isn't all Babble Machine with me.'

'No,' said Graham, wondering what Babble Machine might be. 'And you are certain this Ostrog – you are certain Ostrog organized this rebellion and arranged for the waking of the Sleeper? Just to assert himself – because he was not elected to the Council?

'Everyone knows that, I should think,' said the old man. 'Except – just fools. He meant to be master somehow. In the Council or not. Everyone who knows anything knows that. And here we are with dead bodies lying in the dark! Why, where have you been if you haven't heard all about the trouble between Ostrog and the Verneys? And what do you think the troubles are about? The Sleeper? Eh? You think the Sleeper's real and woke of his own accord – eh?'

'I'm a dull man, older than I look, and forgetful,' said Graham. 'Lots of things that have happened – especially of late years—. If I was the Sleeper, to tell you the truth, I couldn't know less about them.'

'Eh!' said the voice. 'Old, are you? You don't sound so very old! But its not everyone keeps his memory to my time of life – truly. But these notorious things! But you're not so old as me – not nearly so old as me. Well! I ought not to judge other men by myself, perhaps. I'm young – for so old a man. Maybe you're old for so young.'

'That's it,' said Graham. 'And I've a queer history. I know very little. And history! Practically I know no history. The Sleeper and Julius Caesar are all the same to me. It's interesting to hear you talk of these things.'

'I know a few things,' said the old man. 'I know a thing or two. But—. Hark!'

The two men became silent, listening. There was heavy thud, a concussion that made their seat shiver. The passers-by stopped, shouted to one another. The old man was full of questions; he shouted to a man who passed

near. Graham, emboldened by his example, got up and accosted others. None knew what had happened.

He returned to the seat and found the old man muttering vague inter-rogations in an undertone. For a while they said nothing to one another.

The sense of this gigantic struggle, so near and yet so remote, oppressed Graham's imagination. Was this old man right, was the report of the people right, and were the revolutionaries winning? Or were they all in error, and were the red guards driving all before them? At any time the flood of warfare might pour into this silent quarter of the city and seize upon him again. It behoved him to learn all he could while there was time. He turned suddenly to the old man with a question and left it unsaid. But his motion moved the old man to speech again.

'Eh! But how things work together!' said the old man. 'This Sleeper that all the fools put their trust in! I've the whole history of it – I was always a good one for histories. When I was a boy – I'm that old – I used to read printed books. You'd hardly think it. Likely you've seen none – they rot and dust so – and the Sanitary Company burns them to make ashlarite. But they were convenient in their dirty way. Oh I learnt a lot. These new-fangled Babble Machines – they don't seem new-fangled to you, eh? – they're easy to hear, easy to forget. But I've traced all the Sleeper business from the first.'

'You will scarcely believe it,' said Graham slowly, 'I'm so ignorant – I've been so preoccupied in my own little affairs, my circumstances have been so odd – I know nothing of this Sleeper's history. Who was he?'

'Eh!' said the old man. 'I know. I know. He was a poor nobody, and set on a playful woman, poor soul! And he fell into a trance. There's the old things they had, those brown things – silver photographs – still showing him as he lay, a gross and a half years ago – a gross and a half of years.'

'Set on a playful woman, poor soul,' said Graham softly to himself, and then aloud, 'Yes – well! Go on.'

'You must know he had a cousin named Warming a solitary man without children, who made a big fortune speculating in roads – the first Eadhamite roads. But surely you've heard? No? Why? He bought all the patent rights and made a big company. In those days there were grosses of grosses of separate businesses and business companies. Grosses of grosses! His roads killed the railroads – the old things – in two dozen years; he bought up and Eadhamited the tracks. And because he didn't want to break up his great property or let in shareholders, he left it all to the Sleeper, and put it under a Board of Trustees that he had picked and trained. He knew then the Sleeper wouldn't wake, that he would go on sleeping, sleeping till he died. He knew that quite well! And plump! A man in the United States, who had lost two sons in a boat accident, followed that up with another great bequest. His trustees found themselves with a dozen myriads of lions'-worth

or more of property at the very beginning.'

'What was his name?'

'Graham.'

'No, I mean – that American's.'

'Isbister.'

'Isbister!' cried Graham. 'Why, I don't even know the name.'

'Of course not,' said the old man. 'Of course not. People don't learn much in the schools nowadays. But I know all about him. He was a rich American who went from England, and he left the Sleeper even more than Warming. How he made it? That I don't know. Something about pictures by machinery. But he made it and left it, and so the Council had its start. It was just a council of trustees at first.'

'And how did it grow?'

'Eh! – But you're not up to things. Money attracts money – and twelve brains are better than one. They played it cleverly. They worked politics with money, and kept on adding to the money by working currency and tariffs. They grew – they grew. And for years the twelve trustees hid the growing of the Sleeper's estate, under double names and company titles and all that. The Council spread by title deed, mortgage, share, every political party, every newspaper they bought. If you listen to the old stories you will see the Council growing and growing. Billions and billions of lions at last – the Sleeper's estate. And all growing out of a whim – out of this Warming's will, and an accident to Isbister's sons.

'Men are strange,' said the old man. 'The strange thing to me is how the Council worked together so long. As many as twelve. But they worked in cliques from the first. And they've slipped back. In my young days speaking of the Council was like an ignorant man speaking of God. We didn't think they could do wrong. We didn't know of their women and all that! Or else I've got wiser.

'Men are strange,' said the old man. 'Here are you, young and ignorant, and me – sevendy years old, and I might reasonably be forgetting – explaining it all to you short and clear.

'Sevendy,' he said, 'sevendy, and I hear and see – hear better than I see. And reason clearly, and keep myself up to all the happenings of things. Sevendy!

'Life is strange. I was twaindy before Ostrog was a baby. I remember him long before he'd pushed his way to the head of the Wind-vane Control. I've seen many changes. Eh! I've worn the blue. And at last I've come to see this crush and darkness and tumult and dead men carried by in heaps on the ways. And all his doing! All his doing!'

His voice died away in scarcely articulate praises of Ostrog.

Graham thought. 'Let me see,' he said, 'if I have it right.'

He extended a hand and ticked off points upon his fingers. 'The Sleeper

has been asleep—'

'Changed,' said the old man.

'Perhaps. And meanwhile the Sleeper's property grew in the hands of Twelve Trustees, until it swallowed up nearly all the great ownership of the world. The Twelve Trustees – by virtue of this property have become virtually masters of the world. Because they are the paying power – just as the old English Parliament used to be—'

'Eh!' said the old man. 'That's so – that's a good comparison. You're not so—'

'And now this Ostrog – has suddenly revolutionized the world by waking the Sleeper – whom no one but the superstitious, common people had ever dreamt would wake again – raising the Sleeper to claim his property from the Council, after all these years.'

The old man endorsed this statement with a cough.

'It's strange,' he said, 'to meet a man who learns these things for the first time tonight.'

'Aye,' said Graham, 'it's strange.'

'Have you been in a Pleasure City?' said the old man. 'All my life I've longed—' He laughed. 'Even now,' he said, 'I could enjoy a little fun. Enjoy seeing things, anyhow.' He mumbled a sentence Graham did not understand.

'The Sleeper – when did he awake?' said Graham suddenly.

'Three days ago.'

'Where is he?'

'Ostrog has him. He escaped from the Council not four hours ago. My dear sir, where were you at the time? He was in the hall of the markets – where the fighting has been. All the city was screaming about it. All the Babble Machines! Everywhere it was shouted. Even the fools who speak for the Council were admitting it. Everyone was rushing off to see him – everyone was getting arms. Were you drunk or asleep? And even then! But you're joking! Surely you're pretending. It was to stop the shouting of the Babble Machines and prevent the people gathering that they turned off the electricity – and put this damned darkness upon us. Do you mean to say—?'

'I had heard the Sleeper was rescued,' said Graham. 'But – to come back a minute. Are you sure Ostrog has him?'

'He won't let him go,' said the old man.

'And the Sleeper. Are you sure he is not genuine? I have never heard—'

'So all the fools think. So they think. As if there wasn't a thousand things that were never heard. I know Ostrog too well for that. Did I tell you? In a way I'm a sort of relation of Ostrog's. A sort of relation. Through my daughter-in-law.'

'I suppose—'

'Well?'

'I suppose there's no chance of this Sleeper asserting himself. I suppose he's certain to be a puppet – in Ostrog's hands or the Council's, as soon as the struggle is over.'

'In Ostrog's hands – certainly. Why shouldn't he be a puppet? Look at his position. Everything done for him, every pleasure possible. Why should he want to assert himself?'

'What are these Pleasure Cities?' said Graham, abruptly.

The old man made him repeat the question. When at last he was assured of Graham's words, he nudged him violently. 'That's *too* much,' said he. 'You're poking fun at an old man. I've been suspecting you know more than you pretend.'

'Perhaps I do,' said Graham. 'But no! Why should I go on acting? No, I do not know what a Pleasure City is.'

The old man laughed in an intimate way.

'What is more, I do not know how to read your letters, I do not know what money you use, I do not know what foreign countries there are. I do not know where I am. I cannot count. I do not know where to get food, nor drink, nor shelter.'

'Come, come,' said the old man, 'if you had a glass of drink, now, would you put it in your ear or your eye?'

'I want you to tell me all these things.'

'He, he! Well, gentlemen who dress in silk must have their fun.' A withered hand caressed Graham's arm for a moment. 'Silk. Well, well! But, all the same, I wish I was the man who was put up as the Sleeper. He'll have a fine time of it. All the pomp and pleasure. He's a queer-looking face. When they used to let anyone go to see him, I've got tickets and been. The image of the real one, as the photographs show him, this substitute used to be. Yellow. But he'll get fed up. It's a queer world. Think of the luck of it. The luck of it. I expect he'll be sent to Capri. It's the best fun for a greener.'

His cough overtook him again. Then he began mumbling enviously of pleasures and strange delights. 'The luck of it, the luck of it! All my life I've been in London, hoping to get my chance.'

'But you don't know that the Sleeper died,' said Graham, suddenly.

The old man made him repeat his words.

'Men don't live beyond ten dozen. It's not in the order of things,' said the old man. 'I'm not a fool. Fools may believe it, but not me.'

Graham became angry with the old man's assurance. 'Whether you are a fool or not,' he said, 'it happens you are wrong about the Sleeper.'

'Eh?'

'You are wrong about the Sleeper. I haven't told you before, but I will tell you now. You are wrong about the Sleeper.'

'How do you know? I thought you didn't know anything – not even about Pleasure Cities.'

Graham paused.

'You don't know,' said the old man. 'How are you to know? It's very few men—'

'I *am* the Sleeper.'

He had to repeat it.

There was a brief pause. 'There's a silly thing to say, sir, if you'll excuse me. It might get you into trouble in a time like this,' said the old man. Graham, slightly dashed, repeated his assertion.

'I was saying I was the Sleeper. That years and years ago I did, indeed, fall asleep, in a little stone-built village, in the days when there were hedge-rows, and villages, and inns, and all the countryside cut up into little pieces, little fields. Have you never heard of those days? And it is I – I who speak to you – who awakened again these four days since.'

'Four days since! – The Sleeper! But they've got the Sleeper. They have him and they won't let him go. Nonsense! You've been talking sensibly enough up to now. I can see it as though I was there. There will be Lincoln like a keeper just behind him; they won't let him go about alone. Trust them. You're a queer fellow. One of these fun pokers. I see now why you have been clipping your words so oddly, but—'

He stopped abruptly, and Graham could see his gesture.

'As if Ostrog would let the Sleeper run about alone! No, you're telling that to the wrong man altogether. Eh! As if I should believe. What's your game? And besides, we've been talking of the Sleeper.'

Graham stood up. 'Listen,' he said. 'I am the Sleeper.'

'You're an odd man,' said the old man, 'to sit here in the dark, talking clipped, and telling a lie of that sort. But—'

Graham's exasperation fell to laughter. 'It is preposterous,' he cried. 'Preposterous. The dream must end. It gets wilder and wilder. Here am I – in this damned twilight – I never knew a dream in twilight before – an anachronism by two hundred years and trying to persuade an old fool that I am myself, and meanwhile— Ugh!'

He moved in gusty irritation and went striding. In a moment the old man was pursuing him. 'Eh! But don't go!' cried the old man. 'I'm an old fool, I know. Don't go. Don't leave me in all this darkness.'

Graham hesitated, stopped. Suddenly the folly of telling his secret flashed into his mind.

'I didn't mean to offend you – disbelieving you,' said the old man coming near. 'It's no manner of harm. Call yourself the Sleeper if it pleases you. 'Tis a foolish trick.'

Graham hesitated, turned abruptly and went on his way.

For a time he heard the old man's hobbling pursuit and his wheezy cries receding. But at last the darkness swallowed him, and Graham saw him no more.

CHAPTER XII

Ostrog

Graham could now take a clearer view of his position. For a long time yet he wandered, but after the talk of the old man his discovery of this Ostrog was clear in his mind as the final inevitable decision. One thing was evident, those who were at the headquarters of the revolt had succeeded very admirably in suppressing the fact of his disappearance. But every moment he expected to hear the report of his death or of his recapture by the Council.

Presently a man stopped before him. 'Have you heard?' he said.

'No!' said Graham starting.

'Near a dozand,' said the man, 'a dozand men!' and hurried on.

A number of men and a girl passed in the darkness, gesticulating and shouting: 'Capitulated! Given up!' 'A dozand of men.' 'Two dozand of men.' 'Ostrog, Hurrah! Ostrog, Hurrah!' These cries receded, became indistinct.

Other shouting men followed. For a time his attention was absorbed in the fragments of speech he heard. He had a doubt whether all were speaking English. Scraps floated to him, scraps like pidgin English, blurred and mangled distortions. He dared accost no one with questions. The impression the people gave him jarred altogether with his preconceptions of the struggle and confirmed the old man's faith in Ostrog. It was only slowly he could bring himself to believe that all these people were rejoicing at the defeat of the Council, that the Council which had pursued him with such power and vigour was after all the weaker of the two sides in conflict. And if that was so, how did it affect him? Several times he hesitated on the verge of fundamental questions. Once he turned and walked for a long way after a little man of rotund inviting outline, but he was unable to master confidence to address him.

It was only slowly that it came to him that he might ask for the 'wind-vane offices', whatever the 'wind-vane offices' might be. His first enquiry simply resulted in a direction to go on towards Westminster. His second led to the discovery of a short cut in which he was speedily lost. He was told to leave the ways to which he had hitherto confined himself – knowing no other means of transit – and to plunge down one of the middle staircases into the blackness of a crossway. Thereupon came some trivial adventures; chief of these an ambiguous encounter with a gruff-voiced invisible creature speaking in a strange dialect that seemed at first a strange tongue, a thick flow of speech with the drifting corpses of English words therein, the dialect of the latter-day vile. Then another voice drew near, a girl's voice singing, 'tralala tralala'. She spoke to Graham, her English touched with something

of the same quality. She professed to have lost her sister, she blundered needlessly into him he thought, caught hold of him and laughed. But a word of vague remonstrance sent her into the unseen again.

The sounds about him increased. Stumbling people passed him, speaking excitedly. 'They have surrendered!' 'The Council! Surely not the Council!' 'They are saying so in the Ways.' The passage seemed wider. Suddenly the wall fell away. He was in a great space and people were stirring remotely. He enquired his way of an indistinct figure. 'Strike straight across,' said a woman's voice. He left his guiding wall, and in a moment had stumbled against a little table on which were utensils of glass. Graham's eyes, now attuned to darkness, made out a long vista with tables on either side. He went down this. At one or two of the tables he heard a clang of glass and a sound of eating. There were people then cool enough to dine, or daring enough to steal a meal in spite of social convulsion and darkness. Far off and high up he presently saw a pallid light of a semi-circular shape. As he approached this, a black edge came up and hid it. He stumbled at steps and found himself in a gallery. He heard a sobbing, and found two scared little girls crouched by a railing. These children became silent at the near sound of feet. He tried to console them, but they were very still until he left them. Then as he receded he could hear them sobbing again.

Presently he found himself at the foot of a staircase and near a wide opening. He saw a dim twilight above this and ascended out of the blackness into a street of moving Ways again. Along this a disorderly swarm of people marched shouting. They were singing snatches of the song of the revolt, most of them out of tune. Here and there torches flared creating brief hysterical shadows. He asked his way and was twice puzzled by that same thick dialect. His third attempt won an answer he could understand. He was two miles from the wind-vane offices in Westminster, but the way was easy to follow.

When at last he did approach the district of the wind-vane offices it seemed to him, from the cheering processions that came marching along the Ways, from the tumult of rejoicing, and finally from the restoration of the lighting of the city, that the overthrow of the Council must already be accomplished. And still no news of his absence came to his ears.

The re-illumination of the city came with startling abruptness. Suddenly he stood blinking, all about him men halted dazzled, and the world was incandescent. The light found him already upon the outskirts of the excited crowds that choked the Ways near the wind-vane offices, and the sense of visibility and exposure that came with it turned his colourless intention of joining Ostrog to a keen anxiety.

For a time he was jostled, obstructed, and endangered by men hoarse and weary with cheering his name, some of them bandaged and bloody in his cause. The frontage of the wind-vane offices was illuminated by some moving

picture, but what it was he could not see, because in spite of his strenuous attempts the density of the crowd prevented his approaching it. From the fragments of speech he caught, he judged it conveyed news of the fighting about the Council House. Ignorance and indecision made him slow and ineffective in his movements. For a time he could not conceive how he was to get within the unbroken façade of this place. He made his way slowly into the midst of this mass of people, until he realized that the descending staircase of the central Way led to the interior of the buildings. This gave him a goal, but the crowding in the central path was so dense that it was long before he could reach it. And even then he encountered intricate obstruction, and had an hour of vivid argument first in this guard-room and then in that before he could get a note taken to the one man of all men who was most eager to see him. His story was laughed to scorn at one place, and wiser for that, when at last he reached a second stairway he professed simply to have news of extraordinary importance for Ostrog. What it was he would not say. They sent his note reluctantly. For a long time he waited in a little room at the foot of the lift shaft, and thither at last came Lincoln, eager, apologetic, astonished. He stopped in the doorway scrutinizing Graham, then rushed forward effusively.

'Yes,' he cried. 'It is you. And you are not dead!'

Graham made a brief explanation.

'My brother is waiting,' explained Lincoln. 'He is alone in the wind-vane offices. We feared you had been killed in the theatre. He doubted – and things are very urgent still in spite of what we are telling them *there* – or he would have come to you.'

They ascended a lift, passed along a narrow passage, crossed a great hall, empty save for two hurrying messengers, and entered a comparatively little room, whose only furniture was a long settee and a large oval disc of cloudy, shifting grey, hung by cables from the wall. There Lincoln left Graham for a space, and he remained alone without understanding the shifting smoky shapes that drove slowly across this disc.

His attention was arrested by a sound that began abruptly. It was cheering, the frantic cheering of a vast but very remote crowd, a roaring exultation. This ended as sharply as it had begun, like a sound heard between the opening and shutting of a door. In the outer room was a noise of hurrying steps and a melodious clinking as if a loose chain was running over the teeth of a wheel.

Then he heard the voice of a woman, the rustle of unseen garments. 'It is Ostrog!' he heard her say. A little bell rang fitfully, and then everything was still again.

Presently came voices, footsteps and movement without. The footsteps of some one person detached itself from the other sounds and drew near, firm, evenly measured steps. The curtain lifted slowly. A tall, white-haired

man, clad in garments of cream-coloured silk, appeared, regarding Graham
from under his raised arm.

For a moment the white form remained holding the curtain, then dropped
it and stood before it. Graham's first impression was of a very broad forehead,
very pale blue eyes deep sunken under white brows, an aquiline nose, and
a heavily lined resolute mouth. The folds of flesh over the eyes, the drooping
of the corners of the mouth contradicted the upright bearing, and said the
man was old. Graham rose to his feet instinctively, and for a moment the
two men stood in silence, regarding each other.

'You are Ostrog?' said Graham.

'I am Ostrog.'

'The Boss?'

'So I am called.'

Graham felt the inconvenience of the silence. 'I have to thank you chiefly,
I understand, for my safety,' he said presently.

'We were afraid you were killed,' said Ostrog. 'Or sent to sleep again – for
ever. We have been doing everything to keep our secret – the secret of your
disappearance. Where have you been? How did you get here?'

Graham told him briefly.

Ostrog listened in silence.

He smiled faintly. 'Do you know what I was doing when they came to
tell me you had come?'

'How can I guess?'

'Preparing your double.'

'My double?'

'A man as like you as we could find. We were going to hypnotize him, to
save him the difficulty of acting. It was imperative. The whole of this revolt
depends on the idea that you are awake, alive, and with us. Even now a
great multitude of people has gathered in the theatre clamouring to see you.
They do not trust . . . You know, of course – something of your position?'

'Very little,' said Graham.

'It is like this.' Ostrog walked a pace or two into the room and turned.
'You are absolute owner,' he said, 'of more than half the world. As a result
of that you are practically King. Your powers are limited in many intricate
ways, but you are the figurehead, the popular symbol of government. This
White Council, the Council of Trustees as it is called.'

'I have heard the vague outline of these things.'

'I wondered.'

'I came upon a garrulous old man.'

'I see . . . Our masses – the word comes from your days – you know, of
course, that we still have masses – regard you as our actual ruler. Just as a
great number of people in your days regarded the Crown as the ruler. They
are discontented – the masses all over the earth – with the rule of your

Trustees. For the most part it is the old discontent, the old quarrel of the common man with his commonness – the misery of work and discipline and unfitness. But your Trustees have ruled ill. In certain matters, in the administration of the Labour Companies, for example, they have been unwise. They have given endless opportunities. Already we of the popular party were agitating for reforms – when your waking came. Came! If it had been contrived it could not have come more opportunely.' He smiled. 'The public mind, making no allowance for your years of quiescence, had already hit on the thought of waking you and appealing to you, and – Flash!'

He indicated the outbreak by a gesture, and Graham moved his head to show that he understood.

'The Council muddled – quarrelled. They always do. They could not decide what to do with you. You know how they imprisoned you?'

'I see. I see. And now – we win?'

'We win. Indeed we win. Tonight, in five swift hours. Suddenly we struck everywhere. The wind-vane people, the Labour Company and its millions, burst the bonds. We got the pull of the aeropiles.'

He paused. 'Yes,' said Graham, guessing that aeropile meant flying machine.

'That was, of course, essential. Or they could have got away. All the city rose, every third man almost was in it! All the blue, all the public services, save only just a few aeronauts and about half the red police. You were rescued, and their own police of the Ways – not half of them could be massed at the Council House – have been broken up, disarmed or killed. All London is ours – now. Only the Council House remains.

'Half of those who remain to them of the red police were lost in that foolish attempt to recapture you. They lost their heads when they lost you. They flung all they had at the theatre. We cut them off from the Council House there. Truly tonight has been a night of victory. Everywhere your star has blazed. A day ago – the White Council ruled as it has ruled for a gross of years, for a century and a half of years, and then, with only a little whispering, a covert arming here and there, suddenly – so!'

'I am very ignorant,' said Graham. 'I suppose—. I do not clearly understand the conditions of this fighting. If you could explain. Where is the Council? Where is the fight?'

Ostrog stepped across the room, something clicked, and suddenly, save for an oval glow, they were in darkness. For a moment Graham was puzzled.

Then he saw that the cloudy grey disc had taken depth and colour, had assumed the appearance of an oval window looking out upon a strange unfamiliar scene.

At the first glance he was unable to guess what this scene might be. It was a daylight scene, the daylight of a wintry day, grey and clear. Across the picture, and halfway as it seemed between him and the remoter view, a stout cable of twisted white wire stretched vertically. Then he perceived that the

rows of great wind-wheels he saw, the wide intervals, the occasional gulfs of darkness, were akin to those through which he had fled from the Council House. He distinguished an orderly file of red figures marching across an open space between files of men in black, and realized before Ostrog spoke that he was looking down on the upper surface of latter-day London. The overnight snows had gone. He judged that this mirror was some modern replacement of the camera obscura, but that matter was not explained to him. He saw that though the file of red figures was trotting from left to right, yet they were passing out of the picture to the left. He wondered momentarily, and then saw that the picture was passing slowly, panorama fashion, across the oval.

'In a moment you will see the fighting,' said Ostrog at his elbow. 'Those fellows in red you notice are prisoners. This is the roof space of London – all the houses are practically continuous now. The streets and public squares are covered in. The gaps and chasms of your time have disappeared.'

Something out of focus obliterated half the picture. Its form suggested a man. There was a gleam of metal, a flash, something that swept across the oval, as the eyelid of a bird sweeps across its eye, and the picture was clear again. And now Graham beheld men running down among the wind-wheels, pointing weapons from which jetted out little smoky flashes. They swarmed thicker and thicker to the right, gesticulating – it might be they were shouting, but of that the picture told nothing. They and the wind-wheels passed slowly and steadily across the field of the mirror.

'Now,' said Ostrog, 'comes the Council House,' and slowly a black edge crept into view and gathered Graham's attention. Soon it was no longer an edge but a cavity, a huge blackened space amidst the clustering edifices, and from it thin spires of smoke rose into the pallid winter sky. Gaunt ruinous masses of the building, mighty truncated piers and girders, rose dismally out of this cavernous darkness. And over these vestiges of some splendid place, countless minute men were clambering, leaping, swarming.

'This is the Council House,' said Ostrog. 'Their last stronghold. And the fools wasted enough ammunition to hold out for a month in blowing up the buildings all about them – to stop our attack. You heard the smash? It shattered half the brittle glass in the city.'

And while he spoke, Graham saw that beyond this sea of ruins, over-hanging it and rising to a great height, was a ragged mass of white building. This mass had been isolated by the ruthless destruction of its surroundings. Black gaps marked the passages the disaster had torn apart; big halls had been slashed open and the decoration of their interiors showed dismally in the wintry dawn, and down the jagged wall hung festoons of divided cables and twisted ends of lines and metallic rods. And amidst all the vast details moved little red specks, the red-clothed defenders of the Council. Every now and then faint flashes illuminated the bleak shadows. At the first sight

it seemed to Graham that an attack upon this isolated white building was in progress, but then he perceived that the party of the revolt was not advancing but, sheltered amidst the colossal wreckage that encircled this last ragged stronghold of the red-garbed men, was keeping up a fitful firing.

And not ten hours ago he had stood beneath the ventilating fans in a little chamber within that remote building wondering what was happening in the world!

Looking more attentively as this warlike episode moved silently across the centre of the mirror, Graham saw that the white building was surrounded on every side by ruins, and Ostrog proceeded to describe in concise phrases how its defenders had sought by such destruction to isolate themselves from a storm. He spoke of the loss of men that huge downfall had entailed in an indifferent tone. He indicated an improvised mortuary among the wreckage showed ambulances swarming like cheese-mites along a ruinous groove that had once been a street of moving ways. He was more interested in pointing out the parts of the Council House, the distribution of the besiegers. In a little while the civil contest that had convulsed London was no longer a mystery to Graham. It was no tumultuous revolt had occurred that night, no equal warfare, but a splendidly organized *coup d'état*. Ostrog's grasp of details was astonishing; he seemed to know the business of even the smallest knot of black and red specks that crawled amidst these places.

He stretched a huge black arm across the luminous picture, and showed the room whence Graham had escaped, and across the chasm of ruins the course of his flight. Graham recognized the gulf across which the gutter ran, and the wind-wheels where he had crouched from the flying machine. The rest of his path had succumbed to the explosion. He looked again at the Council House, and it was already half hidden, and on the right a hillside with a cluster of domes and pinnacles, hazy, dim and distant, was gliding into view.

'And the Council is really overthrown?' he said.

'Overthrown,' said Ostrog.

'And I—. Is it indeed true that I?'

'You are Master of the World.'

'But that white flag—'

'That is the flag of the Council – the flag of the Rule of the World. It will fall. The fight is over. Their attack on the theatre was their last frantic struggle. They have only a thousand men or so, and some of these men will be disloyal. They have little ammunition. And we are reviving the ancient arts. We are casting guns.'

'But – help. Is this city the world?'

'Practically this is all they have left to them of their empire. Abroad the cities have either revolted with us or wait the issue. Your awakening has perplexed them, paralysed them.'

'But haven't the Council flying machines? Why is there no fighting with them?'

'They had. But the greater part of the aeronauts were in the revolt with us. They wouldn't take the risk of fighting on our side, but they would not stir against us. We *had* to get a pull with the aeronauts. Quite half were with us, and the others knew it. Directly they knew you had got away, those looking for you dropped. We killed the man who shot at you – an hour ago. And we occupied the flying stages at the outset in every city we could, and so stopped and captured the greater aeroplanes, and as for the little flying machines that turned out – for some did – we kept up too straight and steady a fire for them to get near the Council House. If they dropped they couldn't rise again, because there's no clear space about there for them to get up. Several we have smashed, several others have dropped and surrendered, the rest have gone off to the Continent to find a friendly city if they can before their fuel runs out. Most of these men were only too glad to be taken prisoner and kept out of harm's way. Upsetting in a flying machine isn't a very attractive prospect. There's no chance for the Council that way. Its days are done.'

He laughed and turned to the oval reflection again to show Graham what he meant by flying stages. Even the four nearer ones were remote and obscured by a thin morning haze. But Graham could perceive they were very vast structures, judged even by the standard of the things about them.

And then as these dim shapes passed to the left there came again the sight of the expanse across which the disarmed men in red had been marching. And then the black ruins, and then again the beleaguered white fastness of the Council. It appeared no longer a ghostly pile, but glowing amber in the sunlight, for a cloud shadow had passed. About it the pigmy struggle still hung in suspense, but now the red defenders were no longer firing.

So, in a dusky stillness, the man from the nineteenth century saw the closing scene of the great revolt, the forcible establishment of his rule. With a quality of startling discovery it came to him that this was his world, and not that other he had left behind; that this was no spectacle to culminate and cease; that in this world lay whatever life was still before him, lay all his duties and dangers and responsibilities. He turned with fresh questions. Ostrog began to answer them, and then broke off abruptly. 'But these things I must explain more fully later. At present there are – duties. The people are coming by the moving ways towards this ward from every part of the city – the markets and theatres are densely crowded. You are just in time for them. They are clamouring to see you. And abroad they want to see you. Paris, New York, Chicago, Denver, Capri – thousands of cities are up and in a tumult, undecided, and clamouring to see you. They have clamoured that you should be awakened for years, and now it is done they will scarcely believe—'

'But surely – I can't go . . .'

Ostrog answered from the other side of the room, and the picture on the oval disc paled and vanished as the light jerked back again. 'There are kinetotele-photographs,' he said. 'As you bow to the people here – all over the world myriads of myriads of people, packed and still in darkened halls, will see you also. In black and white, of course – not like this. And you will hear their shouts reinforcing the shouting in the hall.

'And there is an optical contrivance we shall use,' said Ostrog, 'used by some of the posturers and women dancers. It may be novel to you. You stand in a very bright light, and they see not you but a magnified image of you thrown on a screen – so that even the furthest man in the remotest gallery can, if he chooses, count your eyelashes.'

Graham clutched desperately at one of the questions in his mind. 'What is the population of London?'

'Eight and twaindy myriads.'

'Eight and what?'

'More than thirty-three millions.'

These figures went beyond Graham's imagination 'You will be expected to say something,' said Ostrog. 'Not what you used to call a Speech, but what our people call a Word – just one sentence, six or seven words. Something formal. If I might suggest – "I have awakened and my heart is with you." That is the sort of thing they want.'

'What was that?' asked Graham.

'"I am awakened and my heart is with you." And bow – bow royally. But first we must get you black robes – for black is your colour. Do you mind? And then they will disperse to their homes.'

Graham hesitated. 'I am in your hands,' he said.

Ostrog was clearly of that opinion. He thought for a moment, turned to the curtain and called brief directions to some unseen attendants. Almost immediately a black robe, the very fellow of the black robe Graham had worn in the theatre, was brought. And as he threw it about his shoulders there came from the room without the shrilling of a high-pitched bell. Ostrog turned in interrogation to the attendant, then suddenly seemed to change his mind, pulled the curtain aside and disappeared.

For a moment Graham stood with the deferential attendant listening to Ostrog's retreating steps. There was a sound of quick question and answer and of men running. The curtain was snatched back and Ostrog reappeared, his massive face glowing with excitement. He crossed the room in a stride, clicked the room into darkness, gripped Graham's arm and pointed to the mirror.

'Even as we turned away,' he said.

Graham saw his index finger, black and colossal, above the mirrored Council House. For a moment he did not understand. And then he perceived

that the flagstaff that had carried the white banner was bare.

'Do you mean—?' he began.

'The Council has surrendered. Its rule is at an end for evermore.'

'Look!' and Ostrog pointed to a coil of black that crept in little jerks up the vacant flagstaff, unfolding as it rose.

The oval picture paled as Lincoln pulled the curtain aside and entered. 'They are clamourous,' he said.

Ostrog kept his grip of Graham's arm.

'We have raised the people,' he said. 'We have given them arms. For today at least their wishes must be law.'

Lincoln held the Curtain open for Graham and Ostrog to pass through.

On his way to the markets Graham had a transitory glance of a long narrow white-walled room in which men in the universal blue canvas were carrying covered things like biers, and about which men in medical purple hurried to and fro. From this room came groans and wailing. He had an impression of an empty blood-stained couch, of men on other couches, bandaged and blood-stained. It was just a glimpse from a railed footway and then a buttress hid the place and they were going on towards the markets.

The roar of the multitude was near now: it leapt to thunder. And, arresting his attention, a fluttering of black banners, the waving of blue canvas and brown rags, and the swarming vastness of the theatre near the public markets came into view down a long passage. The picture opened out. He perceived they were entering the great theatre of his first appearance, the great theatre he had last seen as a chequer-work of glare and blackness in his flight from the red police. This time he entered it along a gallery at a level high above the stage. The place was now brilliantly lit again. He sought the gangway up which he had fled, but he could not tell it from among its dozens of fellows; nor could he see anything of the smashed seats, deflated cushions, and such like traces of the fight because of the density of the people. Except the stage the whole place was closely packed. Looking down the effect was a vast area of stippled pink, each dot a still upturned face regarding him. At his appearance with Ostrog the cheering died away, the singing died away, a common interest stilled and unified the disorder. It seemed as though every individual of those myriads was watching him.

CHAPTER XIII

The End of the Old Order

So far as Graham was able to judge, it was near midday when the white banner of the Council fell. But some hours had to elapse before it was possible to effect the formal capitulation, and so after he had spoken his 'Word' he retired to his new apartments in the wind-vane offices. The continuous excitement of the last twelve hours had left him inordinately fatigued, even his curiosity was exhausted; for a space he sat inert and passive with open eyes, and for a space he slept. He was roused by two medical attendants, come prepared with stimulants to sustain him through the next occasion. After he had taken their drugs and bathed by their advice in cold water, he felt a rapid return of interest and energy, and was presently able and willing to accompany Ostrog through several miles (as it seemed) of passages, lifts, and slides to the closing scene of the White Council's rule.

The way ran deviously through a maze of buildings. They came at last to a passage that curved about, and showed broadening before him an oblong opening, clouds hot with sunset, and the ragged skyline of the ruinous Council House. A tumult of shouts came drifting up to him. In another moment they had come out high up on the brow of the cliff of torn buildings that overhung the wreckage. The vast area opened to Graham's eyes, none the less strange and wonderful for the remote view he had had of it in the oval mirror.

This rudely amphitheatral space seemed now the better part of a mile to its outer edge. It was gold-lit on the left hand, catching the sunlight, and below and to the right clear and cold in the shadow. Above the shadowy grey Council House that stood in the midst of it, the great black banner of the surrender still hung in sluggish folds against the blazing sunset. Severed rooms, halls and passages gaped strangely, broken masses of metal projected dismally from the complex wreckage, vast masses of twisted cable dropped like tangled seaweed, and from its base came a tumult of innumerable voices, violent concussions, and the sound of trumpets. All about this great white pile was a ring of desolation; the smashed and blackened masses, the gaunt foundations and ruinous lumber of the fabric that had been destroyed by the Council's orders, skeletons of girders, Titanic masses of wall, forests of stout pillars. Amongst the sombre wreckage beneath, running water flashed and glistened, and far away across the space, out of the midst of a vague vast mass of buildings, there thrust the twisted end of a water-main, two hundred feet in the air, thunderously spouting a shining cascade. And everywhere great multitudes of people.

Wherever there was space and foothold, people swarmed, little people, small and minutely clear, except where the sunset touched them to indistinguishable gold. They clambered up the tottering walls, they clung in wreaths and groups about the high-standing pillars. They swarmed along the edges of the circle of ruins. The air was full of their shouting, and they were pressing and swaying towards the central space.

The upper storeys of the Council House seemed deserted, not a human being was visible. Only the drooping banner of the surrender hung heavily against the light. The dead were within the Council House, or hidden by the swarming people, or carried away. Graham could see only a few neglected bodies in gaps and corners of the ruins, and amidst the flowing water.

'Will you let them see you, Sire?' said Ostrog. 'They are very anxious to see you.'

Graham hesitated, and then walked forward to where the broken verge of wall dropped sheer. He stood looking down, a lonely, tall, black figure against the sky.

Very slowly the swarming ruins became aware of him. And as they did so little bands of black-uniformed men appeared remotely, thrusting through the crowds towards the Council House. He saw little black heads become pink, looking at him, saw by that means a wave of recognition sweep across the space. It occurred to him that he should accord them some recognition. He held up his arm, then pointed to the Council House and dropped his hand. The voices below became unanimous, gathered volume, came up to him as multitudinous wavelets of cheering.

The western sky was a pallid bluish green, and Jupiter shone high in the south, before the capitulation was accomplished. Above was a slow insensible change, the advance of night serene and beautiful; below was hurry, excitement, conflicting orders, pauses, spasmodic developments of organization, a vast ascending clamour and confusion. Before the Council came out, toiling perspiring men, directed by a conflict of shouts, carried forth hundreds of those who had perished in the hand-to-hand conflict within those long passages and chambers. . . .

Guards in black lined the way that the Council would come, and as far as the eye could reach into the hazy blue twilight of the ruins, and swarming now at every possible point in the captured Council House and along the shattered cliff of its circumadjacent buildings, were innumerable people, and their voices even when they were not cheering, were as the soughing of the sea upon a pebble beach. Ostrog had chosen a huge commanding pile of crushed and overthrown masonry, and on this a stage of timbers and metal girders was being hastily constructed. Its essential parts were complete, but humming and clangorous machinery still glared fitfully in the shadows beneath this temporary edifice.

The stage had a small higher portion on which Graham stood with Ostrog and Lincoln close beside him, a little in advance of a group of minor officers. A broader lower stage surrounded this quarter-deck, and on this were the black-uniformed guards of the revolt armed with the little green weapons whose very names Graham still did not know. Those standing about him perceived that his eyes wandered perpetually from the swarming people in the twilight ruins about him to the darkling mass of the White Council House, whence the Trustees would presently come, and to the gaunt cliffs of ruin that encircled him, and so back to the people. The voices of the crowd swelled to a deafening tumult.

He saw the Councillors first afar off in the glare of one of the temporary lights that marked their path, a little group of white figures blinking in a black archway. In the Council House they had been in darkness. He watched them approaching, drawing nearer past first this blazing electric star and then that; the minatory roar of the crowd over whom their power had lasted for a hundred and fifty years marched along beside them. As they drew still nearer their faces came out weary, white and anxious. He saw them blinking up through the glare about him and Ostrog. He contrasted their strange cold looks in the Hall of Atlas. . . . Presently he could recognize several of them; the man who had rapped the table at Howard, a burly man with a red beard, and one delicate-featured, short, dark man with a peculiarly long skull. He noted that two were whispering together and looking behind him at Ostrog. Next there came a tall, dark and handsome man, walking down-cast. Abruptly he glanced up, his eyes touched Graham for a moment, and passed beyond him to Ostrog. The way that had been made for them was so contrived that they had to march past and curve about before they came to the sloping path of planks that ascended to the stage where their surrender was to be made.

'The Master, the Master! God and the Master,' shouted the people. 'To hell with the Council!' Graham looked at their multitudes, receding beyond counting into a shouting haze, and then at Ostrog beside him, white and steadfast and still. His eye went again to the little group of White Councillors. And then he looked up at the familiar quiet stars overhead. The marvellous element in his fate was suddenly vivid. Could that be his indeed, that little life in his memory two hundred years gone by – and this as well?

CHAPTER XIV

From the Crow's Nest

And so after strange delays and through an avenue of doubt and battle, this man from the nineteenth century came at last to his position at the head of that complex world.

At first when he rose from the long deep sleep that followed his rescue and the surrender of the Council, he did not recognize his surroundings. By an effort he gained a clue in his mind, and all that had happened came back to him, at first with a quality of insincerity like a story heard, like something read out of a book. And even before his memories were clear, the exultation of his escape, the wonder of his prominence were back in his mind. He was owner of half the world; Master of the Earth. This new great age was in the completest sense his. He no longer hoped to discover his experiences a dream; he became anxious now to convince himself that they were real.

An obsequious valet assisted him to dress under the direction of a dignified chief attendant, a little man whose face proclaimed him Japanese, albeit he spoke English like an Englishman. From the latter he learnt something of the state of affairs. Already the revolution was an accepted fact; already business was being resumed throughout the city. Abroad the downfall of the Council had been received for the most part with delight. Nowhere was the Council popular, and the thousand cities of Western America, after two hundred years still jealous of New York, London, and the East, had risen almost unanimously two days before at the news of Graham's imprisonment. Paris was fighting within itself. The rest of the world hung in suspense.

While he was breaking his fast, the sound of a telephone bell jetted from a corner, and his chief attendant called his attention to the voice of Ostrog making polite enquiries. Graham interrupted his refreshment to reply. Very shortly Lincoln arrived, and Graham at once expressed a strong desire to talk to people and to be shown more of the new life that was opening before him. Lincoln informed him that in three hours' time a representative gathering of officials and their wives would be held in the state apartments of the wind-vane Chief. Graham's desire to traverse the ways of the city was, however, at present impossible, because of the enormous excitement of the people. It was, however, quite possible for him to take a bird's-eye view of the city from the crow's nest of the wind-vane keeper. To this accordingly Graham was conducted by his attendant. Lincoln, with a graceful compliment to the attendant, apologized for not accompanying them, on account of the present pressure of administrative work.

Higher even than the most gigantic wind-wheels hung this crow's nest, a clear thousand feet above the roofs, a little disc-shaped speck on a spear of metallic filigree, cable stayed. To its summit Graham was drawn in a little wire-hung cradle. Halfway down the frail-seeming stem was a light gallery about which hung a cluster of tubes – minute they looked from above – rotating slowly on the ring of its outer rail. These were the specula, *en rapport* with the wind-vane keeper's mirrors, in one of which Ostrog had shown him the coming of his rule. His Japanese attendant ascended before him and they spent nearly an hour asking and answering questions.

It was a day full of the promise and quality of spring. The touch of the wind warmed. The sky was an intense blue and the vast expanse of London shone dazzling under the morning sun. The air was clear of smoke and haze, sweet as the air of a mountain glen.

Save for the irregular oval of ruins about the House of the Council and the black flag of the surrender that fluttered there, the mighty city seen from above showed few signs of the swift revolution that had, to his imagination, in one night and one day, changed the destinies of the world. A multitude of people still swarmed over these ruins, and the huge openwork stagings in the distance from which started in times of peace the service of aeroplanes to the various great cities of Europe and America, were also black with the victors. Across a narrow way of planking raised on trestles that crossed the ruins a crowd of workmen were busy restoring the connection between the cables and wires of the Council House and the rest of the city, preparatory to the transfer thither of Ostrog's headquarters from the wind-vane buildings.

For the rest the luminous expanse was undisturbed. So vast was its serenity in comparison with the areas of disturbance, that presently Graham, looking beyond them, could almost forget the thousands of men lying out of sight in the artificial glare within the quasi-subterranean labyrinth, dead or dying of the overnight wounds, forget the improvised wards with the hosts of surgeons, nurses, and bearers feverishly busy, forget, indeed, all the wonder, consternation and novelty under the electric lights. Down there in the hidden ways of the anthill he knew that the revolution triumphed, that black everywhere carried the day, black favours, black banners, black festoons across the streets. And out here, under the fresh sunlight, beyond the crater of the fight, as if nothing had happened to the earth, the forest of wind-vanes that had grown from one or two while the Council had ruled, roared peacefully upon their incessant duty.

Far away, spiked, jagged and indented by the wind-vanes, the Surrey Hills rose blue and faint; to the north and nearer, the sharp contours of Highgate and Muswell Hill were similarly jagged. And all over the countryside, he knew, on every crest and hill, where once the hedges had interlaced, and cottages, churches, inns, and farmhouses had nestled among their trees,

wind-wheels similar to those he saw and bearing like them vast advertise-
ments, gaunt and distinctive symbols of the new age, cast their whirling
shadows and stored incessantly the energy that flowed away incessantly
through all the arteries of the city. And underneath these wandered the
countless flocks and herds of the British Food Trust, his property, with their
lonely guards and keepers.

Not a familiar outline anywhere broke the cluster of gigantic shapes below.
St Paul's he knew survived, and many of the old buildings in Westminster,
embedded out of sight, arched over and covered in among the giant growths
of this great age. The Thames, too, made no fall and gleam of silver to break
the wilderness of the city; the thirsty water-mains drank up every drop of
its waters before they reached the walls. Its bed and estuary scoured and
sunken, was now a canal of sea water, and a race of grimy bargemen brought
the heavy materials of trade from the Pool thereby beneath the very feet of
the workers. Faint and dim in the eastward between earth and sky hung the
clustering masts of the colossal shipping in the Pool. For all the heavy traffic,
for which there was no need of haste, came in gigantic sailing ships from
the ends of the earth, and the heavy goods for which there was urgency in
mechanical ships of a smaller swifter sort.

And to the south over the hills, came vast aqueducts with sea water for
the sewers and in three separate directions, ran pallid lines – the roads,
stippled with moving grey specks. On the first occasion that offered he was
determined to go out and see these roads. That would come after the flying
ship he was presently to try. His attendant officer described them as a pair
of gently curving surfaces a hundred yards wide, each one for the traffic
going in one direction, and made of a substance called Eadhamite – an
artificial substance, so far as he could gather, resembling toughened glass.
Along this shot a strange traffic of narrow rubber-shod vehicles, great single
wheels, two- and four-wheeled vehicles, sweeping along at velocities of from
one to six miles a minute. Railroads had vanished; a few embankments
remained as rust-crowned trenches here and there. Some few formed the
cores of Eadhamite ways.

Among the first things to strike his attention had been the great fleets
of advertisement balloons and kites that receded in irregular vistas northward
and southward along the lines of the aeroplane journeys. No great aeroplanes
were to be seen. Their passages had ceased, and only one little-seeming
aeropile circled high in the blue distance above the Surrey Hills, an unim-
pressive soaring speck.

A thing Graham had already learnt, and which he found very hard to
imagine, was that nearly all the towns in the country, and almost all the
villages, had disappeared. Here and there only, he understood, some gigantic
hotel-like edifice stood amid square miles of some single cultivation and
preserved the name of a town – as Bournemouth, Wareham, or Swanage.

Yet the officer had speedily convinced him how inevitable such a change
had been. The old order had dotted the country with farmhouses, and every
two or three miles was the ruling landlord's estate, and the place of the inn
and cobbler, the grocer's shop and church – the village. Every eight miles
or so was the country town, where lawyer, corn merchant, wool-stapler,
saddler, veterinary surgeon, doctor, draper, milliner and so forth lived. Every
eight miles – simply because that eight-mile marketing journey, four there
and back, was as much as was comfortable for the farmer. But directly the
railways came into play, and after them the light railways, and all the swift
new motor-cars that had replaced waggons and horses, and so soon as the
high roads began to be made of wood, and rubber, and Eadhamite, and all
sorts of elastic durable substances – the necessity of having such frequent
market towns disappeared. And the big towns grew. They drew the worker
with the gravitational force of seemingly endless work, the employer with
their suggestions of an infinite ocean of labour.

And as the standard of comfort rose, as the complexity of the mechanism
of living increased, life in the country had become more and more costly,
or narrow and impossible. The disappearance of vicar and squire, the extinc-
tion of the general practitioner by the city specialist, had robbed the village
of its last touch of culture. After telephone, kinematograph and phonograph
had replaced newspaper, book, schoolmaster, and letter, to live outside the
range of the electric cables was to live an isolated savage. In the country
were neither means of being clothed nor fed (according to the refined
conceptions of the time), no efficient doctors for an emergency, no company
and no pursuits.

Moreover, mechanical appliances in agriculture made one engineer the
equivalent of thirty labourers. So, inverting the condition of the city clerk in
the days when London was scarce inhabitable because of the coaly foulness
of its air, the labourers now came hurrying by road or air to the city and its
life and delights at night to leave it again in the morning. The city had swal-
lowed up humanity; man had entered upon a new stage in his development.
First had come the nomad, the hunter, then had followed the agriculturist of
the agricultural state, whose towns and cities and ports were but the head-
quarters and markets of the countryside. And now, logical consequence of an
epoch of invention, was this huge new aggregation of men.

Save London, there were only four other cities in Britain – Edinburgh,
Portsmouth, Manchester and Shrewsbury. Such things as these, simple state-
ments of fact though they were to contemporary men, strained Graham's
imagination to picture. And when he glanced 'over beyond there' at the
strange things that existed on the Continent, it failed him altogether.

He had a vision of city beyond city, cities on great plains, cities beside
great rivers, vast cities along the sea margin, cities girdled by snowy moun-
tains. Over a great part of the earth the English tongue was spoken; taken

together with its Spanish-American and Hindoo and Negro and 'pidgin' dialects, it was the everyday language of two-thirds of the people of the earth. On the Continent, save as remote and curious survivals, three other languages alone held sway – German, which reached to Antioch and Genoa and jostled Spanish English at Cadiz, a Gallicized Russian which met the Indian English in Persia and Kurdistan and the pidgin English in Peking, and French still clear and brilliant, the language of lucidity, which shared the Mediterranean with the Indian English and German and reached through an Negro dialect to the Congo.

And everywhere now, through the city-set earth, save in the administered 'black-belt' territories of the tropics, the same cosmopolitan social organiza- tion prevailed, and everywhere from Pole to Equator his property and his responsibilities extended. The whole world was civilized; the whole world dwelt in cities; the whole world was property.

Over the British Empire and throughout America his ownership was scarcely disguised, Congress and Parliament were usually regarded as antique, curious gatherings. And even in the two Empires of Russia and Germany, the influence of his wealth was conceivably of enormous weight. There, of course, came problems – possibilities, but, uplifted as he was, even Russia and Germany seemed sufficiently remote. And of the quality of the black- belt administration, and of what that might mean for him he thought, after the fashion of his former days, not at all. That it should hang like a threat over the spacious vision before him could not enter his nineteenth-century mind. But his mind turned at once from the scenery to the thought of a vanished dread. 'What of the yellow peril?' he asked, and Asano made him explain. The Chinese spectre had vanished. Chinaman and European were at peace. The twentieth century had discovered with reluctant certainty that the average Chinaman was as civilized, more moral and far more intel- ligent than the average European serf, and had repeated on a gigantic scale the fraternization of Scot and Englishman that happened in the seventeenth century. As Asano put it, 'They thought it over. They found we were white men after all.' Graham turned again to the view and his thoughts took a new direction.

Out of the dim south-west, glittering and strange, voluptuous, and in some way terrible, shone those Pleasure Cities, of which the kine- matograph-phonograph and the old man in the street had spoken. Strange places reminiscent of the legendary Sybaris, cities of art and beauty, merce- nary art and mercenary beauty, sterile wonderful cities of motion and music, whither repaired all who profited by the fierce, inglorious, economic struggle that went on in the glaring labyrinth below.

Fierce he knew it was. How fierce he could judge from the fact that these latter-day people referred back to the England of the nineteenth century as the figure of an idyllic easy-going life. He turned his eyes to the scene

immediately before him again, trying to conceive the big factories of that intricate maze.

Northward he knew were the potters, makers not only of earthenware and china, but of the kindred pastes and compounds a subtler mineralogical chemistry had devised; there were the makers of statuettes and wall ornaments and much intricate furniture; there too were the factories where feverishly competitive authors devised their phonograph discourses and advertisements and arranged the groupings and developments for their perpetually startling and novel kinematographic dramatic works. Thence, too, flashed the world-wide messages, the world-wide falsehoods of the newstellers, the chargers of the telephonic machines that had replaced the newspapers of the past.

To the westward beyond the smashed Council House were the voluminous offices of municipal control and government; and to the eastward, towards the port, the trading quarters, the huge public markets, the theatres, houses of resort, betting palaces, miles of billiard saloons, baseball and football circuses, wild beast rings and the innumerable temples of the Christian and quasi-Christian sects, the Mahomedans, Buddhists, Gnostics, Spook Worshippers, the Incubus Worshippers, the Furniture Worshippers, and so forth; and to the south again a vast manufacture of textiles, pickles, wines and condiments. And from point to point tore the countless multitudes along the roaring mechanical ways. A gigantic hive, of which the winds were tireless servants, and the ceaseless wind-vanes an appropriate crown and symbol.

He thought of the unprecedented population that had been sucked up by this sponge of halls and galleries – the thirty-three million lives that were playing out each its own brief ineffectual drama below him, and the complacency that the brightness of the day and the space and splendour of the view, and above all the sense of his own importance had begotten, dwindled and perished. Looking down from this height over the city it became at last possible to conceive this overwhelming multitude of thirty-three millions, the reality of the responsibility he would take upon himself, the vastness of the human maelstrom over which his slender kingship hung.

He tried to figure the individual life. It astonished him to realize how little the common man had changed in spite of the visible change in his conditions. Life and property, indeed, were secure from violence almost all over the world, zymotic diseases, bacterial diseases of all sorts had practically vanished, everyone had a sufficiency of food and clothing, was warmed in the city ways and sheltered from the weather – so much the almost mechanical progress of science and the physical organization of society had accomplished. But the crowd, he was already beginning to discover, was a crowd still, helpless in the hands of demagogue and organizer, individually cowardly, individually swayed by appetite, collectively incalculable. The memory of countless figures in pale blue canvas came before his mind.

Millions of such men and women below him, he knew, had never been out of the city, had never seen beyond the little round of unintelligent grudging participation in the world's business, and unintelligent dissatisfied sharing in its tawdrier pleasures. He thought of the hopes of his vanished contemporaries, and for a moment the dream of London in Morris's quaint old *News from Nowhere*, and the perfect land of Hudson's beautiful *Crystal Age* – appeared before him in an atmosphere of infinite loss. He thought of his own hopes.

For in the latter days of that passionate life that lay now so far behind him, the conception of a free and equal manhood had become a very real thing to him. He had hoped, as indeed his age had hoped, rashly taking it for granted, that the sacrifice of the many to the few would some day cease, that a day was near when every child born of woman should have a fair and assured chance of happiness. And here, after two hundred years, the same hope, still unfulfilled, cried passionately through the city. After two hundred years, he knew, greater than ever, grown with the city to gigantic proportions, were poverty and helpless labour and all the sorrows of his time.

Already he knew something of the history of the intervening years. He had heard now of the moral decay that had followed the collapse of supernatural religion in the minds of ignoble man, the decline of public honour, the ascendency of wealth. For men who had lost their belief in God had still kept their faith in property, and wealth ruled a venial world.

His Japanese attendant, Asano, in expounding the political history of the intervening two centuries, drew an apt image from a seed eaten by insect parasites. First there is the original seed, ripening vigorously enough. And then comes some insect and lays an egg under the skin, and behold! in a little while the seed is a hollow shape with an active grub inside that has eaten out its substance. And then comes some secondary parasite, some ichneumon fly, and lays an egg within this grub, and behold! that, too, is a hollow shape, and the new living thing is inside its predecessor's skin which itself is snug within the seed coat. And the seed coat still keeps its shape, most people think it a seed still, and for all one knows it may still think itself a seed, vigorous and alive.

'Your Victorian kingdom,' said Asano, 'was like that – kingship with the heart eaten out. The landowners – the barons and gentry – began ages ago with King John; there were lapses, but they beheaded King Charles, and ended practically with King George mere husk of a king . . . the real power in the hands of their parliament. But the Parliament – the organ of the land-holding tenant-ruling gentry – did not keep its power long. The change had already come in the nineteenth century. The franchises had been broadened until it included masses of ignorant men, "urban myriads", who went in their featureless thousands to vote together. And the natural consequence of a swarming constituency is the rule of the party organization. Power was

passing even in the Victorian time to the party machinery, secret, complex, and corrupt. Very speedily power was in the hands of great men of business who financed the machines. A time came when the real power and interest of the Empire rested visibly between the two party councils, ruling by newspapers and electoral organizations – two small groups of rich and able men, working at first in opposition, then presently together.'

There was a reaction of a genteel ineffectual sort. There were numberless books in existence, Asano said, to prove that – the publication of some of them was as early as Graham's sleep – a whole literature of reaction in fact. The party of the reaction seems to have locked itself into its study and rebelled with unflinching determination – on paper. The urgent necessity of either capturing or depriving the party councils of power is a common suggestion underlying all the thoughtful work of the early twentieth century, both in America and England. In most of these things America was a little earlier than England, though both countries drove the same way.

That counter-revolution never came. It could never organize and keep pure. There was not enough of the old sentimentality, the old faith in right-eousness, left among men. Any organization that became big enough to influence the polls became complex enough to be undermined, broken up, or bought outright by capable rich men. Socialistic and Popular, Reactionary and Purity Parties were all at last mere Stock Exchange counters, selling their principles to pay for their electioneering. And the great concern of the rich was naturally to keep property intact, the board clear for the game of trade. Just as the feudal concern had been to keep the board clear for hunting and war. The whole world was exploited, a battlefield of businesses; and financial convulsions, the scourge of currency manipulation, tariff wars, made more human misery during the twentieth century – because the wretched-ness was dreary life instead of speedy death – than had war, pestilence and famine, in the darkest hours of earlier history.

His own part in the development of this time he now knew clearly enough. Through the successive phases in the development of this mechan-ical civilization, aiding and presently directing its development, there had grown a new power, the Council, the board of his trustees. At first it had been a mere chance union of the millions of Isbister and Warming, a mere property holding company, the creation of two childless testators' whims, but the collective talent of its first constitution had speedily guided it to a vast influence, until by title deed, loan and share, under a hundred disguises and pseudonyms it had ramified through the fabric of the American and English States.

Wielding an enormous influence and patronage, the Council had early assumed a political aspect; and in its development it had continually used its wealth to tip the beam of political decisions and its political advantages to grasp yet more and more wealth. At last the party organizations of two

hemispheres were in its hands; it became an inner council of political control. Its last struggle was with the tacit alliance of the great Jewish families. But these families were linked only by a feeble sentiment, at any time inheritance might fling a huge fragment of their resources to a minor, a woman or a fool, marriages and legacies alienated hundreds of thousands at one blow. The Council had no such breach in its continuity. Steadily, steadfastly it grew.

The original Council was not simply twelve men of exceptional ability; they fused, it was a council of genius. It struck boldly for riches, for political influence, and the two subserved each other. With amazing foresight it spent great sums of money on the art of flying, holding that invention back against an hour foreseen. It used the patent laws, and a thousand half-legal expedients, to hamper all investigators who refused to work with it. In the old days it never missed a capable man. It paid his price. Its policy in those days was vigorous – unerring, and against it as it grew steadily and incessantly was only the chaotic selfish rule of the casually rich. In a hundred years Graham had become almost exclusive owner of Africa, of South America, of France, of London, of England and all its influence – for all practical purposes, that is – a power in North America – then the dominant power in America. The Council bought and organized China, drilled Asia, crippled the Old World empires, undermined them financially, fought and defeated them.

And this spreading usurpation of the world was so dexterously performed – a proteus – hundreds of banks, companies, syndicates, masked the Council's operations – that it was already far advanced before common men suspected the tyranny that had come. The Council never hesitated, never faltered. Means of communication, land, buildings, governments, municipalities, the territorial companies of the tropics, every human enterprise, it gathered greedily. And it drilled and marshalled its men, its railway police, its roadway police, its house guards, and drain and cable guards, its hosts of land-workers. Their unions it did not fight, but it undermined and betrayed and bought them. It bought the world at last. And, finally, its culminating stroke was the introduction of flying.

When the Council, in conflict with the workers in some of its huge monopolies, did something flagrantly illegal and that without even the ordinary civility of bribery, the old Law, alarmed for the profits of its complaisance, looked about it for weapons. But there were no more armies, no fighting navies; the age of Peace had come. The only possible warships were the great steam vessels of the Council's Navigation Trust. The police forces they controlled; the police of the railways, of the ships, of their agricultural estates, their time-keepers and order-keepers, outnumbered the neglected little forces of the old country and municipal organizations ten to one. And they produced flying machines. There were men alive still who could

remember the last great debate in the London House of Commons – the
legal party, the party against the Council was in a minority, but it made a
desperate fight – and how the members came crowding out upon the terrace
to see these great unfamiliar winged shapes circling quietly overhead. The
Council had soared to its power. The last sham of a democracy that had
permitted unlimited irresponsible property was at an end.

Within one hundred and fifty years of Graham's falling asleep, his Council
had thrown off its disguises and ruled openly, supreme in his name. Elections
had become a cheerful formality, a septennial folly, an ancient unmeaning
custom; a social Parliament as ineffectual as the convocation of the
Established Church in Victorian times assembled now and then; and a
legitimate King of England, disinherited, drunken and witless, played fool-
ishly in a second-rate music-hall.

So the magnificent dream of the nineteenth century, the noble project
of universal individual liberty and universal happiness, touched by a disease
of honour, crippled by a superstition of absolute property, crippled by the
religious feuds that had robbed the common citizens of education, robbed
men of standards of conduct, and brought the sanctions of morality to
utter contempt, had worked itself out in the face of invention and ignoble
enterprise, first to a warring plutocracy, and finally to the rule of a supreme
plutocrat. His Council at last had ceased even to trouble to have its decrees
endorsed by the constitutional authorities, and he a motionless, sunken,
yellow-skinned figure had lain, neither dead nor living, recognizably and
immediately Master of the Earth. And awoke at last to find himself – Master
of that inheritance! Awoke to stand under the cloudless empty sky and
gaze down upon the greatness of his dominion.

To what end had he awakened? Was this city, this hive of hopeless toilers,
the final refutation of his ancient hopes? Or was the fire of liberty, the fire
that had blazed and waned in the years of his past life, still smouldering
below there? He thought of the stir and impulse of the song of the revolu-
tion. Was that song merely the trick of a demagogue, to be forgotten when
its purpose was served? Was the hope that still stirred within him only the
memory of abandoned things, the vestige of a creed outworn? Or had it a
wider meaning, an import interwoven with the destiny of man?

To what end had he awakened, what was there for him to do? Humanity
was spread below him like a map. He thought of the millions and millions
of humanity following each other unceasingly for ever out of the darkness
of non-existence into the darkness of death. To what end? Aim there must
be, but it transcended his power of thought. He saw for the first time clearly
his own infinite littleness, saw stark and terrible the tragic contrast of human
strength and the craving of the human heart. For that little while he knew
himself for the petty accident he was, and knew therewith the greatness of
his desire. And suddenly his littleness was intolerable, his aspiration was

intolerable, and there came to him an irresistible impulse to pray. And he prayed. He prayed vague, incoherent, contradictory things, his soul strained up through time and space and all the fleeting multitudinous confusion of being, towards something – he scarcely knew what – towards something that could comprehend his striving and endure.

A man and a woman were far below on a roof space to the southward enjoying the freshness of the morning air. The man had brought out a perspective glass to spy upon the Council House and he was showing her how to use it. Presently their curiosity was satisfied, they could see no traces of bloodshed from their position, and after a survey of the empty sky she came round to the crow's nest. And there she saw two little black figures, so small it was hard to believe they were men, one who watched and one who gesticulated with hands outstretched to the silent emptiness of Heaven.

She handed the glass to the man. He looked and exclaimed:

'I believe it is the Master. Yes. I am sure. It is the Master!'

He lowered the glass and looked at her. 'Waving his hands about almost as if he was praying. I wonder what he is up to. Worshipping the sun? There weren't Parsees in this country in his time, were there?'

He looked again. 'He's stopped it now. It was a chance attitude, I suppose.' He put down the glass and became meditative. 'He won't have anything to do but enjoy himself – just enjoy himself. Ostrog will boss the show, of course. Ostrog will have to, because of keeping all these Labourer fools in bounds. Them and their song! And got it all by sleeping, dear eyes – just sleeping. It's a wonderful world.'

CHAPTER XV

Prominent People

The state apartments of the wind-vane keeper would have seemed astonishingly intricate to Graham had he entered them fresh from his nineteenth-century life, but already he was growing accustomed to the scale of the new time. They can scarcely be described as halls and rooms, seeing that a complicated system of arches, bridges, passages and galleries divided and united every part of the great space. He came out through one of the now familiar sliding panels upon a plateau of landing at the head of a flight of very broad and gentle steps, with men and women far more brilliantly dressed than any he had hitherto seen ascending and descending. From this position he looked down a vista of intricate ornament in lustreless white and mauve and purple, spanned by bridges that seemed wrought of porcelain and filigree, and terminating far off in a cloudy mystery of perforated screens.

Glancing upward, he saw tier above tier of ascending galleries with faces looking down upon him. The air was full of the babble of innumerable voices and of a music that descended from above, a gay and exhilarating music whose source he never discovered.

The central aisle was thick with people, but by no means uncomfortably crowded; altogether that assembly must have numbered many thousands. They were brilliantly, even fantastically dressed, the men as fancifully as the women, for the sobering influence of the Puritan conception of dignity upon masculine dress had long since passed away. The hair of the men, too, though it was rarely worn long, was commonly curled in a manner that suggested the barber, and baldness had vanished from the earth. Frizzy straight-cut masses that would have charmed Rossetti abounded, and one gentleman, who was pointed out to Graham under the mysterious title of an 'amorist', wore his hair in two becoming plaits *à la* Marguerite. The pigtail was in evidence; it would seem that citizens of Chinese extraction were no longer ashamed of their race. There was little uniformity of fashion apparent in the forms of clothing worn. The more shapely men displayed their symmetry in trunk hose, and here were puffs and slashes, and there a cloak and there a robe. The fashions of the days of Leo the Tenth were perhaps the prevailing influence, but the aesthetic conceptions of the Far East were also patent. Masculine *embonpoint*, which in Victorian times would have been subjected to the tightly buttoned perils, the ruthless exaggeration of tight-legged tight-armed evening dress, now formed but the basis of a wealth of dignity and drooping folds. Graceful slenderness abounded also. To Graham, a typically stiff man from a typically stiff period, not only did these men seem altogether

too graceful in person, but altogether too expressive in their vividly expres-
sive faces. They gesticulated, they expressed surprise, interest, amusement,
above all, they expressed the emotions excited in their minds by the ladies
about them with astonishing frankness. Even at the first glance it was evident
that women were in a great majority.

The ladies in the company of these gentlemen displayed in dress, bearing
and manner alike, less emphasis and more intricacy. Some affected a classical
simplicity of robing and subtlety of fold, after the fashion of the First French
Empire, and flashed conquering arms and shoulders as Graham passed.
Others had closely fitting dresses without seam or belt at the waist, sometimes
with long folds falling from the shoulders. The delightful confidences of
evening dress had not been diminished by the passage of two centuries.

Everyone's movements seemed graceful. Graham remarked to Lincoln
that he saw men as Raphael's cartoons walking, and Lincoln told him that
the attainment of an appropriate set of gestures was part of every rich person's
education. The Master's entry was greeted with a sort of tittering applause,
but these people showed their distinguished manners by not crowding upon
him nor annoying him by any persistent scrutiny, as he descended the steps
towards the floor of the aisle.

He had already learnt from Lincoln that these were the leaders of existing
London society; almost every person there that night was either a powerful
official or the immediate connection of a powerful official. Many had returned
from the European Pleasure Cities expressly to welcome him. The aeronautic
authorities, whose defection had played a part in the overthrow of the
Council only second to Graham's, were very prominent, and so, too, was
the Wind-vane Control. Amongst others there were several of the more
prominent officers of the Food Trust; the controller of the European Piggeries
had a particularly melancholy and interesting countenance and a daintily
cynical manner. A bishop in full canonicals passed athwart Graham's vision,
conversing with a gentleman dressed exactly like the traditional Chaucer,
including even the laurel wreath.

'Who is that?' he asked almost involuntarily

'The Bishop of London,' said Lincoln.

'No – the other, I mean.'

'Poet Laureate.'

'You still—?'

'He doesn't make poetry, of course. He's a cousin of Wotton – one of the
Councillors. But he's one of the Red Rose Royalists – a delightful club – and
they keep up the tradition of these things.'

'Asano told me there was a King.'

'The King doesn't belong. They had to expel him. It's the Stuart blood,
I suppose; but really—'

'Too much?'

'Far too much.'

Graham did not quite follow all this, but it seemed part of the general inversion of the new age. He bowed condescendingly to his first introduction. It was evident that subtle distinctions of class prevailed even in this assembly, that only to a small proportion of the guests, to an inner group, did Lincoln consider it appropriate to introduce him. This first introduction was the Master Aeronaut, a man whose sun-tanned face contrasted oddly with the delicate complexions about him. Just at present his critical defection from the Council made him a very important person indeed.

His manner contrasted very favourably, according to Graham's ideas, with the general bearing. He made a few commonplace remarks, assurances of loyalty and frank enquiries about the Master's health. His manner was breezy, his accent lacked the easy staccato of latter-day English. He made it admirably clear to Graham that he was a bluff 'aerial dog' – he used that phrase – that there was no nonsense about him, that he was a thoroughly manly fellow and old-fashioned at that, that he didn't profess to know much, and that what he did not know was not worth knowing He made a manly bow, ostentatiously free from obsequiousness, and passed.

'I am glad to see that type endures,' said Graham

'Phonographs and kinematographs,' said Lincoln, a little spitefully. 'He has studied from the life.' Graham glanced at the burly form again. It was oddly reminiscent.

'As a matter of fact we bought him,' said Lincoln. 'Partly. And partly he was afraid of Ostrog. Everything rested with him.'

He turned sharply to introduce the Surveyor-General of the Public School Trust. This person was a willowy figure in a blue-grey academic gown; he beamed down upon Graham through pince-nez of a Victorian pattern, and illustrated his remarks by gestures of a beautifully manicured hand. Graham was immediately interested in this gentleman's functions, and asked him a number of singularly direct questions. The Surveyor-General seemed quietly amused at the Master's fundamental bluntness. He was a little vague as to the monopoly of education his Company possessed; it was done by contract with the syndicate that ran the numerous London Municipalities, but he waxed enthusiastic over educational progress since the Victorian times. 'We have conquered Cram,' he said, 'completely conquered Cram – there is not an examination left in the world. Aren't you glad?'

'How do you get the work done?' asked Graham.

'We make it attractive – as attractive as possible. And if it does not attract then – we let it go. We cover an immense field.'

He proceeded to details, and they had a lengthy conversation. The Surveyor-General mentioned the names of Pestalozzi and Froebel with profound respect, although he displayed no intimacy with their epoch-making works. Graham learnt that University Extension still existed in a

modified form. 'There is a certain type of girl, for example,' said the Surveyor-General, dilating with a sense of his usefulness, 'with a perfect passion for severe studies – when they are not too difficult you know. We cater for them by the thousand. At this moment,' he said with a Napoleonic touch, 'nearly five hundred phonographs are lecturing in different parts of London on the influence exercised by Plato and Swift on the love affairs of Shelley, Hazlitt and Burns. And afterwards they write essays on the lectures, and their names in order of merit are put in conspicuous places. You see how your little germ has grown? The illiterate middle class of your days has quite passed away.'

'About the public elementary schools,' said Graham. 'Do you control them?'

The Surveyor-General did, 'entirely'. Now, Graham, in his later democratic days, had taken a keen interest in these and his questioning quickened. Certain casual phrases that had fallen from the old man with whom he had talked in the darkness recurred to him. The Surveyor-General, in effect, endorsed the old man's words. 'We have abolished Cram,' he said, a phrase Graham was beginning to interpret as the abolition of all sustained work. The Surveyor-General became sentimental. 'We try and make the elementary schools very pleasant for the little children. They will have to work so soon. Just a few simple principles – obedience – industry.'

'You teach them very little?'

'Why should we? It only leads to trouble and discontent. We amuse them. Even as it is – there are troubles – agitations. Where the labourers get the ideas, one cannot tell. They tell one another. There are socialistic dreams – anarchy even! Agitators *will* get to work among them. I take it – I have always taken it – that my foremost duty is to fight against popular discontent. Why should people be made unhappy?'

'I wonder,' said Graham thoughtfully. 'But there are a great many things I want to know.'

Lincoln, who had stood watching Graham's face throughout the conversation, intervened. 'There are others,' he said in an undertone.

The Surveyor-General of Schools gesticulated himself away. 'Perhaps,' said Lincoln, intercepting a casual glance, 'you would like to know some of these ladies?'

The daughter of the Manager of the Piggeries of the European Food Trust was a particularly charming little person with red hair and animated blue eyes. Lincoln left him awhile to converse with her, and she displayed herself as quite an enthusiast for the 'dear old times', as she called them, that had seen the beginning of his trance. As she talked she smiled, and her eyes smiled in a manner that demanded reciprocity.

'I have tried,' she said, 'countless times – to imagine those old romantic days. And to you – they are memories. How strange and crowded the world must seem to you! I have seen photographs and pictures of the old times,

the little isolated houses built of bricks made out of burnt mud and all black with soot from your fires, the railway bridges, the simple advertisements, the solemn savage Puritanical men in strange black coats and those tall hats of theirs, iron railway trains on iron bridges overhead, horses and cattle, and even dogs running half wild about the streets. And suddenly, you have come into this!'

'Into this,' said Graham.

'Out of your life – out of all that was familiar.'

'The old life was not a happy one,' said Graham. 'I do not regret that.'

She looked at him quickly. There was a brief pause. She sighed encouragingly. 'No?'

'No,' said Graham. 'It was a little life – and unmeaning. But this—. We thought the world complex and crowded and civilized enough. Yet I see – although in this world I am barely four days old – looking back on my own time, that it was a queer, barbaric time – the mere beginning of this new order. The mere beginning of this new order. You will find it hard to understand how little I know.'

'You may ask me what you like,' she said, smiling at him.

'Then tell me who these people are. I'm still very much in the dark about them. It's puzzling. Are there any Generals?'

'Men in hats and feathers?'

'Of course not. No. I suppose they are the men who control the great public businesses. Who is that distinguished-looking man?'

'That? He's a most important officer. That is Morden. He is managing director of the Antibilious Pill Company. I have heard that his workers sometimes turn out a myriad myriad pills a day in the twenty-four hours. Fancy a myriad myriad!'

'A myriad myriad. No wonder he looks proud,' said Graham. 'Pills! What a wonderful time it is! That man in purple?'

'He is not quite one of the inner circle, you know. But we like him. He is really clever and very amusing. He is one of the heads of the Medical Faculty of our London University. All medical men, you know, are shareholders in the Medical Faculty Company, and wear that purple. You have to be – to be qualified. But of course, people who are paid by fees for *doing* something—' She smiled away the social pretensions of all such people.

'Are any of your great artists or authors here?'

'No authors. They are mostly such queer people – and so preoccupied about themselves. And they quarrel so dreadfully! They will fight, some of them, for precedence on staircases! Dreadful, isn't it? But I think Wraysbury, the fashionable capillotomist, is here. From Capri.'

'Capillotomist,' said Graham. 'Ah! I remember. An artist! Why not?'

'We have to cultivate him,' she said apologetically. 'Our heads are in his hands.' She smiled.

Graham hesitated at the invited compliment, but his glance was expres-
sive. 'Have the arts grown with the rest of civilized things?' he said. 'Who
are your great painters?'

She looked at him doubtfully. Then laughed. 'For a moment,' she said, 'I
thought you meant—' She laughed again. 'You mean, of course, those good
men you used to think so much of because they could cover great spaces
of canvas with oil-colours? Great oblongs. And people used to put the things
in gilt frames and hang them up in rows in their square rooms. We haven't
any. People grew tired of that sort of thing.'

'But what did you think I meant?'

She put a finger significantly on a cheek whose glow was above suspicion,
and smiled and looked very arch and pretty and inviting. 'And here,' and
she indicated her eyelid.

Graham had an adventurous moment. Then a grotesque memory of a
picture he had somewhere seen of Uncle Toby and the Widow flashed across
his mind. An archaic shame came upon him. He became acutely aware that
he was visible to a great number of interested people. 'I see,' he remarked
inadequately. He turned awkwardly away from her fascinating facility. He
looked about him to meet a number of eyes that immediately occupied
themselves with other things. Possibly he coloured a little. 'Who is that
talking with the lady in saffron?' he asked, avoiding her eyes.

The person in question, he learnt, was one of the great organizers of the
American theatres just fresh from a gigantic production in Mexico. His face
reminded Graham of a bust of Caligula. Another striking-looking man was
the Black Labour Master. The phrase at the time made no deep impression,
but afterwards it recurred: – the Black Labour Master? The little lady, in no
degree embarrassed, pointed out to him a charming little woman as one of
the subsidiary wives of the Anglican Bishop of London. She added encomiums
on the episcopal courage – hitherto there had been a rule of clerical
monogamy – 'neither a natural nor an expedient condition of things. Why
should the natural development of the affections be dwarfed and restricted
because a man is a priest?'

'And, by the by,' she added, 'are you an Anglican?' Graham was on the
verge of hesitating enquiries about the status of a 'subsidiary wife', apparently
a euphemistic phrase, when Lincoln's return broke off this very suggestive and
interesting conversation. They crossed the aisle to where a tall man in crimson,
and two charming persons in Burmese costume (as it seemed to him) awaited
him diffidently. From their civilities he passed to other presentations.

In a little while his multitudinous impressions began to organize themselves
into a general effect. At first the glitter of the gathering had raised all the
democrat in Graham; he had felt hostile and satirical. But it is not in human
nature to resist an atmosphere of courteous regard. Soon the music, the
light, the play of colours, the shining arms and shoulders about him, the

touch of hands, the transient interest of smiling faces, the frothing sound of skillfully modulated voices, the atmosphere of compliment, interest and respect, had woven together into a fabric of indisputable pleasure. Graham for a time forgot his spacious resolutions. He gave way insensibly to the intoxication of the position that was conceded him, his manner became less conscious, more convincingly regal, his feet walked assuredly, the black robe fell with a bolder fold and pride ennobled his voice. After all this was a brilliant, interesting world.

His glance went approvingly over the shifting colours of the people, it rested here and there in kindly criticism upon a face. Presently it occurred to him that he owed some apology to the charming little person with the red hair and blue eyes. He felt guilty of a clumsy snub. It was not princely to ignore her advances, even if his policy necessitated their rejection. He wondered if he should see her again. And suddenly a little thing touched all the glamour of this brilliant gathering and changed its quality.

He looked up and saw passing across a bridge of porcelain and looking down upon him, a face that was almost immediately hidden, the face of the girl he had seen overnight in the little room beyond the theatre after his escape from the Council. And she was looking with much the same expression of curious expectation, of uncertain intentness, upon his proceedings.

For the moment he did not remember when he had seen her, and then with recognition came a vague memory of the stirring emotions of their first encounter. But the dancing web of melody about him kept the air of that great marching song from his memory.

The lady to whom he was talking repeated her remark, and Graham recalled himself to the quasi-regal flirtation upon which he was engaged.

But from that moment a vague restlessness, a feeling that grew to dissatisfaction, came into his mind. He was troubled as if by some half-forgotten duty, by the sense of things important slipping from him amidst this light and brilliance. The attraction that these bright ladies who crowded about him were beginning to exercise ceased. He no longer made vague and clumsy responses to the subtly amorous advances that he was now assured were being made to him, and his eyes wandered for another sight of that face that had appealed so strongly to his sense of beauty. But he did not see her again until he was awaiting Lincoln's return to leave this assembly. In answer to his request Lincoln had promised that an attempt should be made to fly that afternoon, if the weather permitted. He had gone to make certain necessary arrangements.

Graham was in one of the upper galleries in conversation with a bright-eyed lady on the subject of Eadhamite – the subject was his choice and not hers. He had interrupted her warm assurances of personal devotion with a matter-of-fact enquiry. He found her, as he had already found several other latter-day women that night, less well informed than charming. Suddenly,

struggling against the eddying drift of nearer melody, the song of the Revolt, the great song he had heard in the Hall, hoarse and massive, came beating down to him.

He glanced up startled, and perceived above him an *oeil de boeuf* through which this song had come, and beyond, the upper courses of cable, the blue haze, and the pendant fabric of the lights of the public ways. He heard the song break into a tumult of voices and cease. But now he perceived quite clearly the drone and tumult of the moving platforms and a murmur of many people. He had a vague persuasion that he could not account for, a sort of instinctive feeling that outside in the ways a huge crowd must be watching this place in which their Master amused himself. He wondered what they might be thinking.

Though the song had stopped so abruptly, though the special music of this gathering reasserted itself, the motif of the marching song, once it had begun, lingered in his mind.

The bright-eyed lady was still struggling with the mysteries of Eadhamite when he perceived the girl he had seen in the theatre again. She was coming now along the gallery towards him; he saw her first before she saw him. She was dressed in a faintly luminous grey, her dark hair about her brows was like a cloud, and as he saw her the cold light from the circular opening into the ways fell upon her downcast face.

The lady in trouble about the Eadhamite saw the change in his expression, and grasped her opportunity to escape. 'Would you care to know that girl, Sire?' she asked boldly. 'She is Helen Wotton – a niece of Ostrog's. She knows a great many serious things. She is one of the most serious persons alive. I am sure you will like her.'

In another moment Graham was talking to the girl, and the bright-eyed lady had fluttered away.

'I remember you quite well,' said Graham. 'You were in that little room. When all the people were singing and beating time with their feet. Before I walked across the Hall.'

Her momentary embarrassment passed. She looked up at him, and her face was steady. 'It was wonderful,' she said, hesitated, and spoke with a sudden effort. 'All those people would have died for you, Sire. Countless people did die for you that night.'

Her face glowed. She glanced swiftly aside to see that no other heard her words.

Lincoln appeared some way off along the gallery, making his way through the press towards them. She saw him and turned to Graham strangely eager, with a swift change to confidence and intimacy. 'Sire,' she said quickly, 'I cannot tell you now and here. But the common people are very unhappy; they are oppressed – they are misgoverned. Do not forget the people, who faced death – death that you might live.'

'I know nothing—' began Graham.

'I cannot tell you now.'

Lincoln's face appeared close to them. He bowed an apology to the girl.

'You find the new world pleasant, Sire?' asked Lincoln, with smiling deference, and indicating the space and splendour of the gathering by one comprehensive gesture. 'At any rate, you find it changed.'

'Yes,' said Graham, 'changed. And yet, after all, not so greatly changed.'

'Wait till you are in the air,' said Lincoln. 'The wind has fallen; even now an aeropile awaits you.'

The girl's attitude awaited dismissal.

Graham glanced at her face, was on the verge of a question, found a warning in her expression, bowed to her and turned to accompany Lincoln.

CHAPTER XVI

The Aeropile

For a while, as Graham went through the passages of the wind-vane offices with Lincoln, he was preoccupied. But, by an effort, he attended to the things which Lincoln was saying. Soon his preoccupation vanished. Lincoln was talking of flying. Graham had a strong desire to know more of this new human attainment. He began to ply Lincoln with questions. He had followed the crude beginnings of aerial navigation very keenly in his previous life; he was delighted to find the familiar names of Maxim and Pilcher, Langley and Chanute, and, above all, of the aerial proto-martyr Lillienthal, still honoured by men.

Even during his previous life two lines of investigation had pointed clearly to two distinct types of contrivance as possible, and both of these had been realized. On the one hand was the great engine-driven aeroplane, a double row of horizontal floats with a big aerial screw behind, and on the other the nimbler aeropile. The aeroplanes flew safely only in a calm or moderate wind, and sudden storms, occurrences that were now accurately predictable, rendered them for all practical purposes useless. They were built of enormous size – the usual stretch of wing being six hundred feet or more, and the length of the fabric a thousand feet. They were for passenger traffic alone. The lightly swung car they carried was from a hundred to a hundred and fifty feet in length. It was hung in a peculiar manner in order to minimize the complex vibration that even a moderate wind produced, and for the same reason the little seats within the car – each passenger remained seated during the voyage – were slung with great freedom of movement. The starting of the mechanism was only possible from a gigantic car on the rail of a specially constructed stage. Graham had seen these vast stages, the flying stages, from the crow's nest very well. Six huge blank areas they were, with a giant 'carrier' stage on each.

The choice of descent was equally circumscribed, an accurately plane surface being needed for safe grounding. Apart from the destruction that would have been caused by the descent of this great expanse of sail and metal, and the impossibility of its rising again, the concussion of an irregular surface, a tree-set hillside, for instance, or an embankment, would be sufficient to pierce or damage the framework, to smash the ribs of the body, and perhaps kill those aboard.

At first Graham felt disappointed with these cumbersome contrivances, but he speedily grasped the fact that smaller machines would have been unremunerative, for the simple reason that their carrying power would be

disproportionately diminished with diminished size. Moreover, the huge size of these things enabled them – and it was a consideration of primary importance – to traverse the air at enormous speeds, and so run no risks of unanticipated weather. The briefest journey performed, that from London to Paris, took about three-quarters of an hour, but the velocity attained was not high; the leap to New York occupied about two hours, and by timing oneself carefully at the intermediate stations it was possible in quiet weather to go around the world in a day.

The little aeropiles (as for no particular reason they were distinctively called) were of an altogether different type. Several of these were going to and fro in the air. They were designed to carry only one or two persons, and their manufacture and maintenance was so costly as to render them the monopoly of the richer sort of people. Their sails, which were brilliantly coloured, consisted only of two pairs of lateral air floats in the same plane, and of a screw behind. Their small size rendered a descent in any open space neither difficult nor disagreeable, and it was possible to attach pneumatic wheels or even the ordinary motors for terrestrial traffic to them, and so carry them to a convenient starting place. They required a special sort of swift car to throw them into the air, but such a car was efficient in any open place clear of high buildings or trees. Human aeronautics, Graham perceived, were evidently still a long way behind the instinctive gift of the albatross or the fly-catcher. One great influence that might have brought the aeropile to a more rapid perfection had been withheld; these inventions had never been used in warfare. The last great international struggle had occurred before the usurpation of the Council.

The Flying Stages of London were collected together in an irregular crescent on the southern side of the river. They formed three groups of two each and retained the names of ancient suburban hills or villages. They were named in order, Roehampton, Wimbledon Park, Streatham, Norwood, Blackheath, and Shooter's Hill. They were uniform structures rising high above the general roof surfaces. Each was about four thousand yards long and a thousand broad, and constructed of the compound of aluminium and iron that had replaced iron in architecture. Their higher tiers formed an openwork of girders through which lifts and staircases ascended. The upper surface was a uniform expanse, with portions – the starting carriers – that could be raised and were then able to run on very slightly inclined rails to the end of the fabric. Save for any aeropiles or aeroplanes that were in port these open surfaces were kept clear for arrivals.

During the adjustment of the aeroplanes it was the custom for passengers to wait in the system of theatres, restaurants, news-rooms, and places of pleasure and indulgence of various sorts that interwove with the prosperous shops below. This portion of London was in consequence commonly the gayest of all its districts, with something of the meretricious gaiety of a

seaport or city of hotels. And for those who took a more serious view of aeronautics, the religious quarters had flung out an attractive colony of devotional chapels, while a host of brilliant medical establishments competed to supply physical preparatives for the journey. At various levels through the mass of chambers and passages beneath these, ran, in addition to the main moving ways of the city which laced and gathered here, a complex system of special passages and lifts and slides, for the convenient interchange of people and luggage between stage and stage. And a distinctive feature of the architecture of this section was the ostentatious massiveness of the metal piers and girders that everywhere broke the vistas and spanned the halls and passages, crowding and twining up to meet the weight of the stages and the weighty impact of the aeroplanes overhead.

Graham went to the flying stages by the public ways. He was accompanied by Asano, his Japanese attendant. Lincoln was called away by Ostrog, who was busy with his administrative concerns. A strong guard of the wind-vane police awaited the Master outside the wind-vane offices, and they cleared a space for him on the upper moving platform. His passage to the flying stages was unexpected, nevertheless a considerable crowd gathered and followed him to his destination. As he went along, he could hear the people shouting his name, and saw numberless men and women and children in blue come swarming up the staircases in the central path, gesticulating and shouting. He could not hear what they shouted. He was struck again by the evident existence of a vulgar dialect among the poor of the city. When at last he descended, his guards were immediately surrounded by a dense excited crowd. Afterwards it occurred to him that some had attempted to reach him with petitions. His guards cleared a passage for him with difficulty.

He found an aeropile in charge of an aeronaut awaiting him on the westward stage. Seen close this mechanism was no longer small. As it lay on its launching carrier upon the wide expanse of the flying stage, its aluminium body skeleton was as big as the hull of a twenty-ton yacht. Its lateral supporting sails braced and stayed with metal nerves almost like the nerves of a bee's wing, and made of some sort of glassy artificial membrane, cast their shadow over many hundreds of square yards. The chairs for the engineer and his passenger hung free to swing by a complex tackle, within the protecting ribs of the frame and well abaft the middle. The passenger's chair was protected by a wind-guard and guarded about with metallic rods carrying air cushions. It could, if desired, be completely closed in, but Graham was anxious for novel experiences, and desired that it should be left open. The aeronaut sat behind a glass that sheltered his face. The passenger could secure himself firmly in his seat, and this was almost unavoidable on landing, or he could move along by means of a little rail and rod to a locker at the stem of the machine, where his personal luggage, his wraps and restoratives were placed, and which also with the seats, served

as a makeweight to the parts of the central engine that projected to the propeller at the stern.

The engine was very simple in appearance. Asano, pointing out the parts of this apparatus to him, told him that, like the gas-engine of Victorian days, it was of the explosive type, burning a small drop of a substance called 'fomile' at each stroke. It consisted simply of reservoir and piston about the long fluted crank of the propeller shaft. So much Graham saw of the machine.

The flying stage about him was empty save for Asano and their suite of attendants. Directed by the aeronaut he placed himself in his seat. He then drank a mixture containing ergot – a dose, he learnt, invariably administered to those about to fly, and designed to counteract the possible effect of diminished air pressure upon the system. Having done so, he declared himself ready for the journey. Asano took the empty glass from him, stepped through the bars of the hull, and stood below on the stage waving his hand. Suddenly he seemed to slide along the stage to the right and vanish.

The engine was beating, the propeller spinning, and for a second the stage and the buildings beyond were gliding swiftly and horizontally past Graham's eye; then these things seemed to tilt up abruptly. He gripped the little rods on either side of him instinctively. He felt himself moving upward, heard the air whistle over the top of the windscreen. The propeller screw moved round with powerful rhythmic impulses – one, two, three, pause; one, two, three – which the engineer controlled very delicately. The machine began a quivering vibration that continued throughout the flight, and the roof areas seemed running away to starboard very quickly and growing rapidly smaller. He looked from the face of the engineer through the ribs of the machine. Looking sideways, there was nothing very startling in what he saw – a rapid funicular railway might have given the same sensations. He recognized the Council House and the Highgate Ridge. And then he looked straight down between his feet.

For a moment physical terror possessed him, a passionate sense of insecurity. He held tight. For a second or so he could not lift his eyes. Some hundred feet or more sheer below him was one of the big wind-vanes of south-west London, and beyond it the southernmost flying stage crowded with little black dots. These things seemed to be falling away from him. For a second he had an impulse to pursue the earth. He set his teeth, he lifted his eyes by a muscular effort, and the moment of panic passed.

He remained for a space with his teeth set hard, his eyes staring into the sky. Throb, throb, throb – beat, went the engine; throb, throb, throb – beat. He gripped his bars tightly, glanced at the aeronaut, and saw a smile upon his sun-tanned face. He smiled in return – perhaps a little artificially. 'A little strange at first,' he shouted before he recalled his dignity. But he dared not look down again for some time. He stared over the aeronaut's head to where a rim of vague blue horizon crept up the sky. For a little while he

could not banish the thought of possible accidents from his mind. Throb, throb, throb – beat; suppose some trivial screw went wrong in that supporting engine! Suppose—! He made a grim effort to dismiss all such suppositions. After a while they did at least abandon the foreground of his thoughts. And up he went steadily, higher and higher into the clear air.

Once the mental shock of moving unsupported through the air was over, his sensations ceased to be unpleasant, became very speedily pleasurable. He had been warned of air sickness. But he found the pulsating movement of the aeropile as it drove up the faint south-west breeze was very little in excess of the pitching of a boat head on to broad rollers in a moderate gale, and he was constitutionally a good sailor. And the keenness of the more rarefied air into which they ascended produced a sense of lightness and exhilaration. He looked up and saw the blue sky above fretted with cirrus clouds. His eye came cautiously down through the ribs and bars to a shining flight of white birds that hung in the lower sky. For a space he watched these. Then going lower and less apprehensively, he saw the slender figure of the wind-vane keeper's crow's nest shining golden in the sunlight and growing smaller every moment. As his eye fell with more confidence now, there came a blue line of hills, and then London, already to leeward, an intricate space of roofing. Its near edge came sharp and clear, and banished his last apprehensions in a shock of surprise. For the boundary of London was like a wall, like a cliff, a steep fall of three or four hundred feet, a frontage broken only by terraces here and there, a complex decorative façade.

That gradual passage of town into country through an extensive sponge of suburbs, which was so characteristic a feature of the great cities of the nineteenth century, existed no longer. Nothing remained of it but a waste of ruins here, variegated and dense with thickets of the heterogeneous growths that had once adorned the gardens of the belt, interspersed among levelled brown patches of sown ground, and verdant stretches of winter greens. The latter even spread among the vestiges of houses. But for the most part the reefs and skerries of ruins, the wreckage of suburban villas, stood among their streets and roads, queer islands amidst the levelled expanses of green and brown, abandoned indeed by the inhabitants years since, but too substantial, it seemed', to be cleared out of the way of the wholesale horticultural mechanisms of the time.

The vegetation of this waste undulated and frothed amidst the countless cells of crumbling house walls, and broke along the foot of the city wall in a surf of bramble and holly and ivy and teazle and tall grasses. Here and there gaudy pleasure palaces towered amidst the puny remains of Victorian times, and cable ways slanted to them from the city. That winter day they seemed deserted. Deserted, too, were the artificial gardens among the ruins. The city limits were indeed as sharply defined as in the ancient days when the gates were shut at nightfall and the robber foeman prowled to the very

walls. A huge semi-circular throat poured out a vigorous traffic upon the Eadhamite Bath Road. So the first prospect of the world beyond the city flashed on Graham, and dwindled. And when at last he could look vertically downward again, he saw below him the vegetable fields of the Thames valley – innumerable minute oblongs of ruddy brown, intersected by shining threads, the sewage ditches.

His exhilaration increased rapidly, became a sort of intoxication. He found himself drawing deep breaths of air, laughing aloud, desiring to shout. After a time that desire became too strong for him, and he shouted.

The machine had now risen as high as was customary with aeropiles, and they began to curve about towards the south. Steering, Graham perceived, was effected by the opening or closing of one or two thin strips of membrane in one or other of the otherwise rigid wings, and by the movement of the whole engine backward or forward along its supports. The aeronaut set the engine gliding slowly forward along its rail and opened the valve of the leeward wing until the stem of the aeropile was horizontal and pointing southward. And in that direction they drove with a slight list to leeward, and with a slow alternation of movement, first a short, sharp ascent and then a long downward glide that was very swift and pleasing. During these downward glides the propellor was inactive altogether. These ascents gave Graham a glorious sense of successful effort; the descents through the rarefied air were beyond all experience. He wanted never to leave the upper air again.

For a time he was intent upon the minute details of the landscape that ran swiftly northward beneath him. Its minute, clear detail pleased him exceedingly. He was impressed by the ruin of the houses that had once dotted the country, by the vast treeless expanse of country from which all farms and villages had gone, save for crumbling ruins. He had known the thing was so, but seeing it so was an altogether different matter. He tried to make out places he had known within the hollow basin of the world below, but at first he could distinguish no data now that the Thames valley was left behind. Soon, however, they were driving over a sharp chalk hill that he recognized as the Guildford Hog's Back, because of the familiar outline of the gorge at its eastward end, and because of the ruins of the town that rose steeply on either lip of this gorge. And from that he made out other points, Leith Hill, the sandy wastes of Aldershot, and so forth. The Downs escarpment was set with gigantic slow-moving wind-wheels. Save where the broad Eadhamite Portsmouth Road, thickly dotted with rushing shapes, followed the course of the old railway, the gorge of the Wey was choked with thickets.

The whole expanse of the Downs escarpment, so far as the grey haze permitted him to see, was set with wind-wheels to which the largest of the city was but a younger brother. They stirred with a stately motion before

the south-west wind. And here and there were patches dotted with the sheep of the British Food Trust, and here and there a mounted shepherd made a spot of black. Then rushing under the stern of the aeropile came the Wealden Heights, the line of Hindhead, Pitch Hill, and Leith Hill, with a second row of wind-wheels that seemed striving to rob the downland whirlers of their share of breeze. The purple heather was speckled with yellow gorse, and on the further side a drove of black oxen stampeded before a couple of mounted men. Swiftly these swept behind, and dwindled and lost colour, and became scarce moving specks that were swallowed up in haze.

And when these had vanished in the distance Graham heard a peewit wailing close at hand. He perceived he was now above the South Downs, and staring over his shoulder saw the battlements of Portsmouth Landing Stage towering over the ridge of Portsdown Hill. In another moment there came into sight a spread of shipping like floating cities, the little white cliffs of the Needles dwarfed and sunlit, and the grey and glittering waters of the narrow sea. They seemed to leap the Solent in a moment, and in a few seconds the Isle of Wight was running past, and then beneath him spread a wider and wider extent of sea, here purple with the shadow of a cloud, here grey, here a burnished mirror, and here a spread of cloudy greenish blue. The Isle of Wight grew smaller and smaller. In a few more minutes a strip of grey haze detached itself from other strips that were clouds, descended out of the sky and became a coastline – sunlit and pleasant – the coast of northern France. It rose, it took colour, became definite and detailed, and the counterpart of the Downland of England was speeding by below.

In a little time, as it seemed, Paris came above the horizon, and hung there for a space, and sank out of sight again as the aeropile circled about to the north again. But he perceived the Eiffel Tower still standing, and beside it a huge dome surmounted by a pinpoint Colossus. And he perceived, too, though he did not understand it at the time, a slanting drift of smoke. The aeronaut said something about 'trouble in the underways,' that Graham did not heed at the time. But he marked the minarets and towers and slender masses that streamed skyward above the city wind-vanes, and knew that in the matter of grace at least Paris still kept in front of her larger rival. And even as he looked a pale blue shape ascended very swiftly from the city like a dead leaf driving up before a gale. It curved round and soared towards them growing rapidly larger and larger. The aeronaut was saying something. 'What?' said Graham, loath to take his eyes from this. 'Aeroplane, Sire,' bawled the aeronaut pointing.

They rose and curved about northward as it drew nearer. Nearer it came and nearer, larger and larger. The throb, throb, throb – beat, of the aeropile's flight, that had seemed so potent and so swift, suddenly appeared slow by comparison with this tremendous rush. How great the monster seemed, how

swift and steady! It passed quite closely beneath them, driving along silently, a vast spread of wire-netted translucent wings, a thing alive. Graham had a momentary glimpse of the rows and rows of wrapped-up passengers, slung in their little cradles behind windscreens, of a white-clothed engineer crawling against the gale along a ladder way, of spouting engines beating together, of the whirling wind-screw, and of a wide waste of wing. He exulted in the sight. And in an instant the thing had passed.

It rose slightly and their own little wings swayed in the rush of its flight. It fell and grew smaller. Scarcely had they moved, as it seemed, before it was again only a flat blue thing that dwindled in the sky. This was the aeroplane that went to and fro between London and Paris. In fair weather and in peaceful times it came and went four times a day.

They beat across the Channel, slowly as it seemed now, to Graham's enlarged ideas, and Beachy Head rose greyly to the left of them.

'Land,' called the aeronaut, his voice small against the whistling of the air over the windscreen.

'Not yet,' bawled Graham, laughing. 'Not land yet. I want to learn more of this machine.'

'I meant—' said the aeronaut.

'I want to learn more of this machine,' repeated Graham.

'I'm coming to you,' he said, and had flung himself free of his chair and taken a step along the guarded rail between them. He stopped for a moment, and his colour changed and his hands tightened. Another step and he was clinging close to the aeronaut. He felt a weight on his shoulder, the pressure of the air. His hat was a whirling speck behind. The wind came in gusts over his windscreen and blew his hair in streamers past his cheek. The aeronaut made some hasty adjustments for the shifting of the centres of gravity and pressure.

'I want to have these things explained,' said Graham. 'What do you do when you move that engine forward?'

The aeronaut hesitated. Then he answered, 'They are complex, Sire.'

'I don't mind,' shouted Graham. 'I don't mind.'

There was a moment's pause. 'Aeronautics is the secret – the privilege—'

'I know. But I'm the Master, and I mean to know.' He laughed, full of this novel realization of power that was his gift from the upper air.

The aeropile curved about, and the keen fresh wind cut across Graham's face and his garment lugged at his body as the stem pointed round to the west. The two men looked into each other's eyes.

'Sire, there are rules—'

'Not where I am concerned,' said Graham. 'You seem to forget.'

The aeronaut scrutinized his face. 'No,' he said. 'I do not forget, Sire. But in all the earth – no man who is not a sworn aeronaut – has ever a chance. They come as passengers—'

'I have heard something of the sort. But I'm not going to argue these points. Do you know why I have slept two hundred years? To fly!'

'Sire,' said the aeronaut, 'the rules – if I break the rules—'

Graham waved the penalties aside.

'Then if you will watch me—'

'No,' said Graham, swaying and gripping tight as the machine lifted its nose again for an ascent. 'That's not my game. I want to do it myself. Do it myself if I smash for it! No! I will. See, I am going to clamber by this to come and share your seat. Steady! I mean to fly of my own accord if I smash at the end of it. I will have something to pay for my sleep. Of all other things—. In my past it was my dream to fly. Now – keep your balance.'

'A dozen spies are watching me, Sire!'

Graham's temper was at end. Perhaps he chose it should be. He swore. He swung himself round the intervening mass of levers and the aeropile swayed.

'Am I Master of the Earth?' he said. 'Or is your Society? Now. Take your hands off those levers, and hold my wrists. Yes – so. And now, how do we turn her nose down to the glide?'

'Sire,' said the aeronaut.

'What is it?'

'You will protect me?'

'Lord! Yes! If I have to burn London. Now!'

And with that promise Graham bought his first lesson in aerial navigation. 'It's clearly to your advantage, this journey,' he said with a loud laugh – for the air was like strong wine – 'to teach me quickly and well. Do I pull this? Ah! So! Hullo!'

'Back, Sire! Back!'

'Back – right. One – two – three – good God! Ah! Up she goes! But this is living!'

And now the machine began to dance the strangest figures in the air. Now it would sweep round a spiral of scarcely a hundred yards diameter, now it would rush up into the air and swoop down again, steeply, swiftly, falling like a hawk, to recover in a rushing loop that swept it high again. In one of these descents it seemed driving straight at the drifting park of balloons in the south-east, and only curved about and cleared them by a sudden recovery of dexterity. The extraordinary swiftness and smoothness of the motion, the extraordinary effect of the rarefied air upon his constitution, threw Graham into a careless fury.

But at last a queer incident came to sober him, to send him flying down once more to the crowded life below with all its dark insoluble riddles. As he swooped, came a tap and something flying past, and a drop like a drop of rain. Then as he went on down he saw something like a white rag whirling down in his wake. 'What was that?' he asked. 'I did not see.'

The aeronaut glanced, and then clutched at the lever to recover, for they were sweeping down. When the aeropile was rising again he drew a deep breath and replied. 'That,' and he indicated the white thing still fluttering down, 'was a swan.'

'I never saw it,' said Graham.

The aeronaut made no answer, and Graham saw little drops upon his forehead.

They drove horizontally while Graham clambered back to the passenger's place out of the lash of the wind. And then came a swift rush down, with the wind-screw whirling to check their fall, and the flying stage growing broad and dark before them. The sun, sinking over the chalk hills in the west, fell with them, and left the sky a blaze of gold.

Soon men could be seen as little specks. He heard a noise coming up to meet him, a noise like the sound of waves upon a pebbly beach, and saw that the roofs about the flying stage were dark with his people rejoicing over his safe return. A dark mass was crushed together under the stage, a dark-ness stippled with innumerable faces, and quivering with the minute oscillation of waved white handkerchiefs and waving hands.

CHAPTER XVII

Three Days

Lincoln awaited Graham in an apartment beneath the flying stages. He seemed curious to learn all that had happened, pleased to hear of the extraordinary delight and interest which Graham took in flying. Graham was in a mood of enthusiasm. 'I must learn to fly,' he cried. 'I must master that. I pity all poor souls who have died without this opportunity. The sweet swift air! It is the most wonderful experience in the world.'

'You will find our new times full of wonderful experiences,' said Lincoln. 'I do not know what you will care to do now. We have music that may seem novel.'

'For the present,' said Graham, 'flying holds me. Let me learn more of that. Your aeronaut was saying there is some trades union objection to one's learning.'

'There is, I believe,' said Lincoln. 'But for you—! If you would like to occupy yourself with that, we can make you a sworn aeronaut tomorrow.'

Graham expressed his wishes vividly and talked of his sensations for a while. 'And as for affairs,' he asked abruptly, 'how are things going on?'

Lincoln waved affairs aside. 'Ostrog will tell you that tomorrow,' he said. 'Everything is settling down. The Revolution accomplishes itself all over the world. Friction is inevitable here and there, of course; but your rule is assured. You may rest secure with things in Ostrog's hands.'

'Would it be possible for me to be made a sworn aeronaut, as you call it, forthwith – before I sleep?' said Graham, pacing. 'Then I could be at it the very first thing tomorrow again.'

'It would be possible,' said Lincoln thoughtfully. 'Quite possible. Indeed, it shall be done.' He laughed. 'I came prepared to suggest amusements, but you have found one for yourself. I will telephone to the aeronautical offices from here and we will return to your apartments in the Wind-Vane Control. By the time you have dined the aeronauts will be able to come. You don't think that after you have dined, you might prefer—?' He paused.

'Yes,' said Graham.

'We had prepared a show of dancers – they have been brought from the Capri theatre.'

'I hate ballets,' said Graham, shortly. 'Always did. That other—. That's not what I want to see. We had dancers in the old days. For the matter of that, they had them in ancient Egypt. But flying—'

'True,' said Lincoln. 'Though our dancers—'

'They can afford to wait,' said Graham; 'they can afford to wait. I know.

I'm not a Latin. There's questions I want to ask some expert – about your machinery. I'm keen. I want no distractions.'

'You have the world to choose from,' said Lincoln; 'whatever you want is yours.'

Asano appeared, and under the escort of a strong guard they returned through the city streets to Graham's apartments. Far larger crowds had assembled to witness his return than his departure had gathered, and the shouts and cheering of these masses of people sometimes drowned Lincoln's answers to the endless questions Graham's aerial journey had suggested. At first Graham had acknowledged the cheering and cries of the crowd by bows and gestures, but Lincoln warned him that such a recognition would be considered incorrect behaviour. Graham, already a little wearied by rhythmic civilities, ignored his subjects for the remainder of his public progress.

Directly they arrived at his apartments Asano departed in search of kinematographic renderings of machinery in motion, and Lincoln despatched Graham's commands for models of machines and small machines to illustrate the various mechanical advances of the last two centuries. The little group of appliances for telegraphic communication attracted the Master so strongly that his delightfully prepared dinner, served by a number of charmingly dexterous girls, waited for a space. The habit of smoking had almost ceased from the face of the earth, but when he expressed a wish for that indulgence, enquiries were made and some excellent cigars were discovered in Florida, and sent to him by pneumatic dispatch while the dinner was still in progress. Afterwards came the aeronauts, and a feast of ingenious wonders in the hands of a latter-day engineer. For the time, at any rate, the neat dexterity of counting and numbering machines, building machines, spinning engines, patent doorways, explosive motors, grain and water elevators, slaughter-house machines and harvesting appliances, was more fascinating to Graham than any bayadere. 'We were savages,' was his refrain, 'we were savages. We were in the stone age – compared with this. . . . And what else have you?'

There came also practical psychologists with some very interesting developments in the art of hypnotism. The names of Milne Bramwell, Fechner, Liebault, William James, Myers and Gurney, he found, bore a value now that would have astonished their contemporaries. Several practical applications of psychology were now in general use; it had largely superseded drugs, antiseptics and anaesthetics in medicine; was employed by almost all who had any need of mental concentration. A real enlargement of human faculty seemed to have been effected in this direction. The feats of 'calculating boys', the wonders, as Graham had been wont to regard them, of mesmerizers, were now within the range of anyone who could afford the services of a skilled hypnotist. Long ago the old examination methods in education had been destroyed by these expedients. Instead of years of study, candidates had substituted a few weeks of trances, and during the trances expert coaches

had simply to repeat all the points necessary for adequate answering, adding a suggestion of the post-hypnotic recollection of these points. In process mathematics particularly, this aid had been of singular service, and it was now invariably invoked by such players of chess and games of manual dexterity as were still to be found. In fact, all operations conducted under finite rules, of a quasi-mechanical sort that is, were now systematically relieved from the wanderings of imagination and emotion, and brought to an unexampled pitch of accuracy. Little children of the labouring classes, so soon as they were of sufficient age to be hypnotized, were thus converted into beautifully punctual and trustworthy machine minders, and released forthwith from the long, long thoughts of youth. Aeronautical pupils, who gave way to giddiness, could be relieved from their imaginary terrors. In every street were hypnotists ready to print permanent memories upon the mind. If anyone desired to remember a name, a series of numbers, a song or a speech, it could be done by this method, and conversely memories could be effaced, habits removed, and desires eradicated – a sort of psychic surgery was, in fact, in general use. Indignities, humbling experiences, were thus forgotten, amorous widows would obliterate their previous husbands, angry lovers release themselves from their slavery. To graft desires, however, was still impossible, and the facts of thought transference were yet unsystematized. The psychologists illustrated their expositions with some astounding experiments in mnemonics made through the agency of a troupe of pale-faced children in blue.

Graham, like most of the people of his former time, distrusted the hypnotist, or he might then and there have eased his mind of many painful preoccupations. But in spite of Lincoln's assurances he held to the old theory that to be hypnotized was in some way the surrender of his personality, the abdication of his will. At the banquet of wonderful experiences that was beginning, he wanted very keenly to remain absolutely himself.

The next day, and another day, and yet another day passed in such interests as these. Each day Graham spent many hours in the glorious entertainment of flying. On the third day he soared across middle France, and within sight of the snow-clad Alps. These vigorous exercises gave him restful sleep, and each day saw a great stride in his health from the spiritless anaemia of his first awakening. And whenever he was not in the air, and awake, Lincoln was assiduous in the cause of his amusement; all that was novel and curious in contemporary invention was brought to him, until at last his appetite for novelty was well-nigh glutted. One might fill a dozen inconsecutive volumes with the strange things they exhibited. Each afternoon he held his court for an hour or so. He speedily found his interest in his contemporaries becoming personal and intimate. At first he had been alert chiefly for unfamiliarity and peculiarity; any foppishness in their dress, any discordance with his preconceptions of nobility in their status and manners had jarred upon him, and it was remarkable to him how soon that strangeness

and the faint hostility that arose from it, disappeared; how soon he came to appreciate the true perspective of his position, and see the old Victorian days remote and quaint. He found himself particularly amused by the red-haired daughter of the Manager of the European Piggeries. On the second day after dinner he made the acquaintance of a latter-day dancing girl, and found her an astonishing artist. And after that, more hypnotic wonders. On the third day Lincoln was moved to suggest that the Master should repair to a Pleasure City, but this Graham declined, nor would he accept the services of the hypnotists in his aeronautical experiments. The link of locality held him to London; he found a perpetual wonder in topographical identifications that he would have missed abroad. 'Here – or a hundred feet below here,' he could say, 'I used to eat my midday cutlets during my London University days. Underneath here was Waterloo and the perpetual hunt for confusing trains. Often have I stood waiting down there, bag in hand, and stared up into the sky above the forest of signals, little thinking I should walk some day a hundred yards in the air. And now in that very sky that was once a grey smoke canopy, I circle in an aeropile.'

During those three days Graham was so occupied with such distractions that the vast political movements in progress outside his quarters had but a small share of his attention. Those about him told him little. Daily came Ostrog, the Boss, his Grand Vizier, his mayor of the palace, to report in vague terms the steady establishment of his rule; 'a little trouble' soon to be settled in this city, 'a slight disturbance' in that. The song of the social revolt came to him no more; he never learned that it had been forbidden in the municipal limits; and all the great emotions of the crow's nest slumbered in his mind.

But on the second and third of the three days he found himself, in spite of his interest in the daughter of the Pig Manager, or it may be by reason of the thoughts her conversation suggested, remembering the girl Helen Wotton, who had spoken to him so oddly at the wind-vane keeper's gathering. The impression she had made was a deep one, albeit the incessant surprise of novel circumstances had kept him from brooding upon it for a space. But now her memory was coming to its own. He wondered what she had meant by those broken half-forgotten sentences; the picture of her eyes and the earnest passion of her face became more vivid as his mechanical interests faded. Her beauty came compellingly between him and certain immediate temptations of ignoble passion. But he did not see her again until three full days were past.

CHAPTER XVIII

Graham Remembers

She came upon him at last in a little gallery that ran from the wind-vane offices towards his state apartments. The gallery was long and narrow, with a series of recesses, each with an arched fenestration that looked upon a court of palms. He came upon her suddenly in one of these recesses. She was seated. She turned her head at the sound of his footsteps and started at the sight of him. Every touch of colour vanished from her face. She rose instantly, made a step towards him as if to address him, and hesitated. He stopped and stood still, expectant. Then he perceived that a nervous tumult silenced her, perceived too, that she must have sought speech with him to be waiting for him in this place.

He felt a regal impulse to assist her. 'I have wanted to see you,' he said. 'A few days ago you wanted to tell me something – you wanted to tell me of the people. What was it you had to tell me?'

She looked at him with troubled eyes.

'You said the people were unhappy?'

For a moment she was silent still.

'It must have seemed strange to you,' she said abruptly.

'It did. And yet—'

'It was an impulse.'

'Well?'

'That is all.'

She looked at him with a face of hesitation. She spoke with an effort. 'You forget,' she said, drawing a deep breath.

'What?'

'The people—'

'Do you mean—?'

'You forget the people.'

He looked interrogative.

'Yes. I know you are surprised. For you do not understand what you are. You do not know the things that are happening.'

'Well?'

'You do not understand.'

'Not clearly, perhaps. But – tell me.'

She turned to him with sudden resolution. 'It is so hard to explain. I have meant to, I have wanted to. And now – I cannot. I am not ready with words. But about you – there is something. It is Wonder. Your sleep – your awakening. These things are miracles. To me at least – and to all the common

people. You who lived and suffered and died, you who were a common citizen, wake again, live again, to find yourself Master almost of the earth.'

'Master of the Earth,' he said. 'So they tell me. But try and imagine how little I know of it.'

'Cities – Trusts – the Labour Company—'

'Principalities, powers, dominions – the power and the glory. Yes, I have heard them shout. I know. I am Master. King, if you wish. With Ostrog, the Boss—'

He paused.

She turned upon him and surveyed his face with a curious scrutiny. 'Well?'

He smiled. 'To take the responsibility.'

'That is what we have begun to fear.' For a moment she said no more. 'No,' she said slowly. 'You will take the responsibility. You will take the responsibility. The people look to you.'

She spoke softly. 'Listen! For at least half the years of your sleep – in every generation – multitudes of people, in every generation greater multitudes of people, have prayed that you might awake – *prayed*.'

Graham moved to speak and did not.

She hesitated, and a faint colour crept back to her cheek. 'Do you know that you have been to myriads – King Arthur, Barbarossa – the King who would come in his own good time and put the world right for them?'

'I suppose the imagination of the people—'

'Have you not heard our proverb "When the Sleeper wakes"? While you lay insensible and motionless there – thousands came. Thousands. Every first of the month you lay in state with a white robe upon you and the people filed by you. When I was a little girl I saw you like that, with your face white and calm.'

She turned her face from him and looked steadfastly at the painted wall before her. Her voice fell. 'When I was a little girl I used to look at your face . . . it seemed to me fixed and waiting, like the patience of God.'

'That is what we thought of you,' she said. 'That is how you seemed to us.'

She turned shining eyes to him, her voice was clear and strong. 'In the city, in the earth, a myriad myriad men and women are waiting to see what you will do, full of strange incredible expectations.'

'Yes?'

'Ostrog – no one – can take that responsibility.'

Graham looked at her in surprise, at her face lit with emotion. She seemed at first to have spoken with an effort, and to have fired herself by speaking.

'Do you think,' she said, 'that you who have lived that little life so far away in the past, you who have fallen into and risen out of this miracle of sleep – do you think that the wonder and reverence and hope of half the world has gathered about you only that you may live another little life? . . . That you may shift the responsibility to any other man?'

'I know how great this kingship of mine is,' he said haltingly. 'I know how great it seems. But is it real? It is incredible – dreamlike. Is it real, or is it only a great delusion?'

'It is real,' she said; 'if you dare.'

'After all, like all kingship, my kingship is Belief. It is an illusion in the minds of men.'

'If you dare!' she said.

'But—'

'Countless men,' she said, 'and while it is in their minds – they will obey.'

'But I know nothing. That is what I had in mind. I know nothing. And these others – the Councillors, Ostrog. They are wiser, cooler, they know so much, every detail. And, indeed, what are these miseries of which you speak? What am I to know? Do you mean—'

He stopped blankly.

'I am still hardly more than a girl,' she said. 'But to me the world seems full of wretchedness. The world has altered since your day, altered very strangely. I have prayed that I might see you and tell you these things. The world has changed. As if a canker had seized it – and robbed life of – everything worth having.'

She turned a flushed face upon him, moving suddenly. 'Your days were the days of freedom. Yes – I have thought. I have been made to think, for my life – has not been happy. Men are no longer free – no greater, no better than the men of your time. That is not all. This city – is a prison. Every city now is a prison. Mammon grips the key in his hand. Myriads, countless myriads, toil from the cradle to the grave. Is that right? Is that to be – for ever? Yes, far worse than in your time. All about us, beneath us, sorrow and pain. All the shallow delight of such life as you find about you, is separated by just a little from a life of wretchedness beyond any telling Yes, the poor know it – they know they suffer. These countless multitudes who faced death for you two nights since! You owe your life to them.'

'Yes,' said Graham, slowly. 'Yes. I owe my life to them.'

'You come,' she said, 'from the days when this new tyranny of the cities was scarcely beginning. It is a tyranny – a tyranny. In your days the feudal warlords had gone, and the new lordship of wealth had still to come. Half the men in the world still lived out upon the free countryside. The cities had still to devour them. I have heard the stories out of the old books – there was nobility! Common men led lives of love and faithfulness then – they did a thousand things. And you – you come from that time.'

'It was not—. But never mind. How is it now—?'

'Gain and the Pleasure Cities! Or slavery – unthanked, unhonoured slavery.'

'Slavery!' he said.

'Slavery.'

'You don't mean to say that human beings are chattels.'

'Worse. That is what I want you to know, what I want you to see. I know you do not know. They will keep things from you, they will take you presently to a Pleasure City. But you have noticed men and women and children in pale blue canvas, with thin yellow faces and dull eyes?'

'Everywhere.'

'Speaking a horrible dialect, coarse and weak.'

'I have heard it.'

'They are the slaves – your slaves. They are the slaves of the Labour Company you own.'

'The Labour Company! In some way – that is familiar. Ah! now I remember. I saw it when I was wandering about the city, after the lights returned, great fronts of buildings coloured pale blue. Do you really mean—?'

'Yes. How can I explain it to you? Of course the blue uniform struck you. Nearly a third of our people wear it – more assume it now every day. This Labour Company has grown imperceptibly.'

'What *is* this Labour Company?' asked Graham.

'In the old times, how did you manage with starving people?'

'There was the workhouse – which the parishes maintained.'

'Workhouse! Yes – there was something. In our history lessons. I remember now. The Labour Company ousted the workhouse. It grew – partly – out of something – you, perhaps, may remember it – an emotional religious organ-ization called the Salvation Army – that became a business company. In the first place it was almost a charity. To save people from workhouse rigours. Now I come to think of it, it was one of the earliest properties your Trustees acquired. They bought the Salvation Army and reconstructed it as this. The idea in the first place was to give work to starving homeless people.'

'Yes.'

'Nowadays there are no workhouses, no refuges and charities, nothing but that Company. Its offices are everywhere. That blue is its colour. And any man, woman or child who comes to be hungry and weary and with neither home nor friend nor resort, must go to the Company in the end – or seek some way of death. The Euthanasy is beyond their means – for the poor there is no easy death. And at any hour in the day or night there is food, shelter and a blue uniform for all comers – that is the first condition of the Company's incorporation – and in return for a day's shelter the Company extracts a day's work, and then returns the visitor's proper clothing and sends him or her out again.'

'Yes?'

'Perhaps that does not seem so terrible to you. In your days men starved in your streets. That was bad. But they died – men. These people in blue—. The proverb runs: "Blue canvas once and ever". The Company trades in their labour, and it has taken care to assure itself of the supply. People come

to it starving and helpless – they eat and sleep for a night and day, they – work for a day, and at the end of the day they go out again. If they have worked well they have a penny or so – enough for a theatre or a cheap dancing place, or a kinematograph story, or a dinner or a bet. They wander about after that is spent. Begging is prevented by the police of the ways. Besides, no one gives. They come back again the next day or the day after – brought back by the same incapacity that brought them first. At last their proper clothing wears out, or their rags get so shabby that they are ashamed. Then they must work for months to get fresh. If they want fresh. A great number of children are born under the Company's care. The mother owes them a month thereafter – the children they cherish and educate until they are fourteen, and they pay two years' service. You may be sure these children are educated for the blue canvas. And so it is the Company works.'

'And none are destitute in the city?'

'None. They are either in blue canvas or in prison.'

'If they will not work?'

'Most people will work at that pitch, and the Company has powers. There are stages of unpleasantness in the work – stoppage of food – and a man or woman who has refused to work once is known by a thumb-marking system in the Company's offices all over the world. Besides, who can leave the city poor? To go to Paris costs two Lions. And for insubordination there are the prisons – dark and miserable – out of sight below. There are prisons now for many things.'

'And a third of the people wear this blue canvas?'

'More than a third. Toilers, living without pride or delight or hope, with the stories of Pleasure Cities ringing in their ears, mocking their shameful lives, their privations and hardships. Too poor even for the Euthanasy, the rich man's refuge from life. Dumb, crippled millions, countless millions, all the world about, ignorant of anything but limitations and unsatisfied desires. They are born, they are thwarted and they die. That is the state to which we have come.'

For a space Graham sat downcast.

'But there has been a revolution,' he said. 'All these things will be changed.' Ostrog—'

'That is our hope. That is the hope of the world. But Ostrog will not do it. He is a politician. To him it seems things must be like this. He does not mind. He takes it for granted. All the rich, all the influential, all who are happy, come at last to take these miseries for granted. They use the people in their politics, they live in ease by their degradation. But you – you who come from a happier age – it is to you the people look. To you.'

He looked at her face. Her eyes were bright with unshed tears. He felt a rush of emotion. For a moment he forgot this city, he forgot the race, and all those vague remote voices, in the immediate humanity of her beauty.

'But what am I to do?' he said with his eyes upon her.

'Rule,' she answered, bending towards him and speaking in a low tone. 'Rule the world as it has never been ruled, for the good and happiness of men. For you might rule it – you could rule it.

'The people are stirring. All over the world the people are stirring. It wants but a word – but a word from you – to bring them all together. Even the middle sort of people are restless unhappy.

'They are not telling you the things that are happening. The people will not go back to their drudgery – they refuse to be disarmed. Ostrog has awakened something greater than he dreamt of – he has awakened hopes.'

His heart was beating fast. He tried to seem judicial, to weigh considerations.

'They only want their leader,' she said.

'And then?'

'You could do what you would; – the world is yours.'

He sat, no longer regarding her. Presently he spoke. 'The old dreams, and the thing I have dreamt, liberty, happiness. Are they dreams? Could one man – *one man*—?' His voice sank and ceased.

'Not one man, but all men – give them only a leader to speak the desire of their hearts.'

He shook his head, and for a time there was silence.

He looked up suddenly, and their eyes met. 'I have not your faith,' he said. 'I have not your youth. I am here with power that mocks me. No – let me speak. I want to do – not right – I have not the strength for that – but something rather right than wrong. It will bring no millennium, but I am resolved now that I will rule. What you have said has awakened me. . . . You are right. Ostrog must know his place. And I will learn—. . . One thing I promise you. This Labour slavery shall end.'

'And you will rule?'

'Yes. Provided—. There is one thing.'

'Yes?'

'That you will help me.'

'I! – a girl!'

'Yes. Does it not occur to you I am absolutely alone?'

She started and for an instant her eyes had pity. 'Need you ask whether I will help you?' she said.

She stood before him, beautiful, worshipful, and her enthusiasm and the greatness of their theme was like a great gulf fixed between them. To touch her, to clasp her hand, was a thing beyond hope. 'Then I will rule indeed,' he said slowly. 'I will rule—.' He paused. 'With you.'

There came a tense silence, and then the beating of a clock striking the hour. She made him no answer. Graham rose.

'Even now,' he said, 'Ostrog will be waiting.' He hesitated, facing her.

'When I have asked him certain questions—. There is much I do not know. It may be, that I will go to see with my own eyes the things of which you have spoken. And when I return—?'

'I shall know of your going and coming. I will wait for you here again.'

He stood for a moment regarding her.

'I knew,' she said, and stopped.

He waited, but she said no more. They regarded one another steadfastly, questioningly, and then he turned from her towards the wind-vane office.

CHAPTER XIX

Ostrog's Point of View

Graham found Ostrog waiting to give a formal account of his day's stewardship. On previous occasions he had passed over this ceremony as speedily as possible, in order to resume his aerial experiences, but now he began to ask quick short questions. He was very anxious to take up his empire forthwith. Ostrog brought flattering reports of the development of affairs abroad. In Paris and Berlin, Graham perceived that he was saying, there had been trouble, not organized resistance indeed, but insubordinate proceedings. 'After all these years,' said Ostrog, when Graham pressed enquiries, 'the Commune has lifted its head again. That is the real nature of the struggle, to be explicit.' But order had been restored in these cities. Graham, the more deliberately judicial for the stirring emotions he felt, asked if there had been any fighting. 'A little,' said Ostrog. 'In one quarter only. But the Senegalese division of our African agricultural police – the Consolidated African Companies have a very well-drilled police – was ready, and so were the aeroplanes. We expected a little trouble in the continental cities, and in America. But things are very quiet in America. They are satisfied with the overthrow of the Council. For the time.'

'Why should you expect trouble?' asked Graham abruptly.

'There is a lot of discontent – social discontent.'

'The Labour Company?'

'You are learning,' said Ostrog with a touch of surprise. 'Yes. It is chiefly the discontent with the Labour Company. It was that discontent supplied the motive force of this overthrow – that and your awakening.'

'Yes?'

Ostrog smiled. He became explicit. 'We had to stir up their discontent, we had to revive the old ideals of universal happiness – all men equal – all men happy – no luxury that everyone may not share – ideas that have slumbered for two hundred years. You know that? We had to revive these ideals, impossible as they are – in order to overthrow the Council. And now—'

'Well?'

'Our revolution is accomplished, and the Council is overthrown, and people whom we have stirred up remain surging. There was scarcely enough fighting. . . . We made promises, of course. It is extraordinary how violently and rapidly this vague out-of-date humanitarianism has revived and spread. We who sowed the seed even, have been astonished. In Paris, as I say – we have had to call in a little external help.'

'And here?'

'There is trouble. Multitudes will not go back to work. There is a general strike. Half the factories are empty and the people are swarming in the Ways. They are talking of a Commune. Men in silk and satin have been insulted in the streets. The blue canvas is expecting all sorts of things from you. . . . Of course there is no need for you to trouble. We are setting the Babble Machines to work with counter suggestions in the cause of law and order. We must keep the grip tight; that is all.'

Graham thought. He perceived a way of asserting himself. But he spoke with restraint.

'Even to the pitch of bringing a Negro police,' he said.

'They are useful,' said Ostrog. 'They are fine loyal brutes, with no wash of ideas in their heads – such as our rabble has. The Council should have had them as police of the Ways, and things might have been different. Of course, there is nothing to fear except rioting and wreckage. You can manage your own wings now, and you can soar away to Capri if there is any smoke or fuss. We have the pull of all the great things; the aeronauts are privileged and rich, the closest trades union in the world, and so are the engineers of the wind-vanes. We have the air, and the mastery of the air is the mastery of the earth. No one of any ability is organizing against us. They have no leaders – only the sectional leaders of the secret society we organized before your very opportune awakening. Mere busy bodies and sentimentalists they are and bitterly jealous of each other. None of them is man enough for a central figure. The only trouble will be a disorganized upheaval. To be frank – that may happen. But it won't interrupt your aeronautics. The days when the People could make revolutions are past.'

'I suppose they are,' said Graham. 'I suppose they are.' He mused. 'This world of yours has been full of surprises to me. In the old days we dreamt of a wonderful democratic life, of a time when all men would be equal and happy.'

Ostrog looked at him steadfastly. 'The day of democracy is past,' he said. 'Past for ever. That day began with the bowmen of Crecy, it ended when marching infantry, when common men in masses ceased to win the battles of the world, when costly cannon, great ironclads, and strategic railways became the means of power. Today is the day of wealth. Wealth now is power as it never was power before – it commands earth and sea and sky. All power is for those who can handle wealth. . . . You must accept facts, and these are facts. The world for the Crowd! The Crowd as Ruler! Even in your days that creed had been tried and condemned. Today it has only one believer – a multiplex, silly one – the mall in the Crowd.'

Graham did not answer immediately. He stood lost in sombre preoccupations.

'No,' said Ostrog. 'The day of the common man is past. On the open countryside one man is as good as another, or nearly as good. The earlier

aristocracy had a precarious tenure of strength and audacity. They were tempered – tempered. There were insurrections, duels, riots. The first real aristocracy, the first permanent aristocracy, came in with castles and armour, and vanished before the musket and bow. But this is the second aristocracy. The real one. Those days of gunpowder and democracy were only an eddy in the stream. The common man now is a helpless unit. In these days we have this great machine of the city, and an organization complex beyond his understanding.'

'Yet,' said Graham, 'there is something resists, something you are holding down – something that stirs and presses.'

'You will see,' said Ostrog, with a forced smile that would brush these diffi-cult questions aside. 'I have not roused the force to destroy myself – trust me.'

'I wonder,' said Graham.

Ostrog stared.

'*Must* the world go this way?' said Graham, with his emotions at the speaking point. 'Must it indeed go in this way? Have all our hopes been vain?'

'What do you mean?' said Ostrog. 'Hopes?'

'I came from a democratic age. And I find an aristocratic tyranny!'

'Well – but you are the chief tyrant.'

Graham shook his head.

'Well,' said Ostrog, 'take the general question. It is the way that change has always travelled. Aristocracy, the prevalence of the best – the suffering and extinction of the unfit, and so to better things.'

'But aristocracy! Those people I met—'

'Oh! Not *those*!' said Ostrog. 'But for the most part they go to their death. Vice and pleasure! They have no children. That sort of stuff will die out. If the world keeps to one road, that is, if there is no turning back. An easy road to excess, convenient Euthanasia for the pleasure seekers singed in the flame, that is the way to improve the race!'

'Pleasant extinction,' said Graham. 'Yet—.' He thought for an instant. 'There is that other thing – the Crowd, the great mass of poor men. Will that die out? That will not die out. And it suffers, its suffering is a force that even you—'

Ostrog moved impatiently, and when he spoke, he spoke rather less evenly than before.

'Don't you trouble about these things,' he said. 'Everything will be settled in a few days now. The Crowd is a huge foolish beast. What if it does not die out? Even if it does not die, it can still be tamed and driven. I have no sympathy with servile men. You heard those people shouting and singing two nights ago. They were *taught* that song. If you had taken any man there in cold blood and asked why he shouted, he could not have told you. They think they are shouting for you, that they are loyal and devoted to you. Just

then they were ready to slaughter the Council. Today – they are already murmuring against those who have overthrown the Council.'

'No, no,' said Graham. 'They shouted because their lives were dreary, without joy or pride, and because in me – in me – they hoped.'

'And what was their hope? What is their hope? What right have they to hope? They work ill and they want the reward of those who work well. The hope of mankind – what is it? That some day the Over-man may come, that some day the inferior, the weak and the bestial may be subdued or eliminated. Subdued if not eliminated. The world is no place for the bad, the stupid, the enervated. Their duty – it's a fine duty too! – is to die. The death of the failure! That is the path by which the beast rose to manhood, by which man goes on to higher things.'

Ostrog took a pace, seemed to think, and turned on Graham. 'I can imagine how this great world state of ours seems to a Victorian Englishman. You regret all the old forms of representative government – their spectres still haunt the world, the voting councils and parliaments and all that eighteenth-century tomfoolery. You feel moved against our Pleasure Cities. I might have thought of that – had I not been busy. But you will learn better. The people are mad with envy – they would be in sympathy with you. Even in the streets now, they clamour to destroy the Pleasure Cities. But the Pleasure Cities are the excretory organs of the State, attractive places that year after year draw together all that is weak and vicious, all that is lascivious and lazy, all the easy roguery of the world, to a graceful destruction. They go there, they have their time, they die childless, all the pretty silly lascivious women die childless, and mankind is the better. If the people were sane they would not envy the rich their way of death. And you would emancipate the silly brainless workers that we have enslaved, and try to make their lives easy and pleasant again. Just as they have sunk to what they are fit for.' He smiled a smile that irritated Graham oddly. 'You will learn better. I know those ideas; in my boyhood I read your Shelley and dreamt of Liberty. There is no liberty, save wisdom and self-control. Liberty is within – not without. It is each man's own affair. Suppose – which is impossible – that these swarming yelping fools in blue get the upper hand of us, what then? They will only fall to other masters. So long as there are sheep Nature will insist on beasts of prey. It would mean but a few hundred years' delay. The coming of the aristocrat is fatal and assured. The end will be the Over-man – for all the mad protests of humanity. Let them revolt, let them win and kill me and my like. Others will arise – other masters. The end will be the same.'

'I wonder,' said Graham doggedly.

For a moment he stood downcast.

'But I must see these things for myself,' he said, suddenly assuming a tone of confident mastery. 'Only by seeing can I understand. I must learn. That

is what I want to tell you, Ostrog. I do not want to be King in a Pleasure
City; that is not my, pleasure. I have spent enough time with aeronautics
– and those other things. I must learn how people live now, how the common
life has developed. Then I shall understand these things better. I must learn
how common people live – the labour people more especially – how they
work, marry, bear children, die—.'

'You get that from our realistic novelists,' suggested Ostrog, suddenly
preoccupied.

'I want reality,' said Graham, 'not realism.'

'There are difficulties,' said Ostrog, and thought. 'On the whole perhaps—.
'I did not expect—.

'I had thought—. And yet, perhaps—. You say you want to go through
the Ways of the city and see the common people.'

Suddenly he came to some conclusion. 'You would need to go disguised,'
he said. 'The city is intensely excited, and the discovery of your presence
among them might create a fearful tumult. Still this wish of yours to go into
this city – this idea of yours—. Yes, now I think the thing over it seems to
me not altogether—. It can be contrived. If you would really find an interest
in that! You are, of course, Master. You can go soon if you like. A disguise
for this excursion Asano will be able to manage. He would go with you.
After all it is not a bad idea of yours.'

'You will not want to consult me in any matter?' asked Graham suddenly,
struck by an odd suspicion.

'Oh, dear no! No! I think you may trust affairs to me for a time, at any
rate,' said Ostrog, smiling. 'Even if we differ—.'

Graham glanced at him sharply.

'There is no fighting likely to happen soon?' he asked abruptly.

'Certainly not.'

'I have been thinking about these Negroes. I don't believe the people
intend any hostility to me, and, after all, I am the Master. I do not want any
Negroes brought to London. It is an archaic prejudice perhaps, but I have
peculiar feelings about Europeans and the subject races. Even about Paris—.'

Ostrog stood watching him from under his drooping brows. 'I am not
bringing Negroes to London,' he said slowly. 'But if—.'

'You are not to bring armed Negroes to London, whatever happens,' said
Graham. 'In that matter I am quite decided.'

Ostrog, after a pause, decided not to speak, and bowed deferentially.

CHAPTER XX

In the City Ways

And that night, unknown and unsuspected, Graham, dressed in the costume of an inferior wind-vane official keeping holiday, and accompanied by Asano in Labour Company canvas, surveyed the city through which he had wandered when it was veiled in darkness. But now he saw it lit and waking, a whirlpool of life. In spite of the surging and swaying of the forces of revolution, in spite of the unusual discontent, the mutterings of the greater struggle of which the first revolt was but the prelude, the myriad streams of commerce still flowed wide and strong. He knew now something of the dimensions and quality of the new age, but he was not prepared for the infinite surprise of the detailed view, for the torrent of colour and vivid impressions that poured past him.

This was his first real contact with the people of these latter days. He realized that all that had gone before, saving his glimpses of the public theatres and markets, had had its element of seclusion, had been a movement within the comparatively narrow political quarter, that all his previous experiences had revolved immediately about the question of his own position. But here was the city at the busiest hours of night, the people to a large extent returned to their own immediate interests, the resumption of the real informal life, the common habits of the new time.

They emerged at first into a street whose opposite ways were crowded with the blue canvas liveries. This swarm Graham saw was a portion of a procession – it was odd to see a procession parading the city *seated*. They carried banners of coarse black stuff with red letters. 'No disarmament', said the banners, for the most part in crudely daubed letters and with variant spelling, and 'Why should we disarm?' 'No disarming.' 'No disarming.' Banner after banner went by, a stream of banners flowing past, and at last at the end, the song of the revolt and a noisy band of strange instruments. 'They all ought to be at work,' said Asano. 'They have had no food these two days, or they have stolen it.'

Presently Asano made a detour to avoid the congested crowd that gaped upon the occasional passage of dead bodies from hospital to a mortuary, the gleanings after death's harvest of the first revolt.

That night few people were sleeping, everyone was abroad. A vast excitement, perpetual crowds perpetually changing, surrounded Graham; his mind was confused and darkened by an incessant tumult, by the cries and enigmatical fragments of the social struggle that was as yet only beginning. Everywhere festoons and banners of black and strange decorations, intensified

the quality of his popularity. Everywhere he caught snatches of that crude thick dialect that served the illiterate class, the class, that is, beyond the reach of phonograph culture, in their common-place intercourse. Everywhere this trouble of disarmament was in the air, with a quality of immediate stress of which he had no inkling during his seclusion in the wind-vane quarter. He perceived that as soon as he returned he must discuss this with Ostrog, this and the greater issues of which it was the expression, in a far more conclusive way than he had so far done. Perpetually that night, even in the earlier hours of their wanderings about the city, the spirit of unrest and revolt swamped his attention, to the exclusion of countless strange things he might otherwise have observed.

This preoccupation made his impressions fragmentary. Yet amidst so much that was strange and vivid, no subject, however personal and insistent, could exert undivided sway. There were spaces when the revolutionary movement passed clean out of his mind, was drawn aside like a curtain from before some startling new aspect of the time. Helen had swayed his mind to this intense earnestness of enquiry, but there came times when she, even, receded beyond his conscious thoughts. At one moment, for example, he found they were traversing the religious quarter, for the easy transit about the city afforded by the moving ways rendered sporadic churches and chapels no longer necessary – and his attention was vividly arrested by the façade of one of the Christian sects.

They were travelling seated on one of the swift upper ways, the place leapt upon them at a bend and advanced rapidly towards them. It was covered with inscriptions from top to base, in vivid white and blue, save where a vast and glaring kinematograph transparency presented a realistic New Testament scene, and where a vast festoon of black to show that the popular religion followed the popular politics, hung across the lettering Graham had already become familiar with the phonotype writing and these inscriptions arrested him, being to his sense for the most part almost incredible blasphemy. Among the less offensive were: 'Salvation on the First Floor and turn to the Right.' 'Put your Money on your Maker.' 'The Sharpest Conversion in London, Expert Operators! Look Slippy!' 'What Christ would say to the Sleeper – Join the Up-to-date Saints!' 'Be a Christian – without hindrance to your present Occupation.' 'All the Brightest Bishops on the Bench tonight and Prices as Usual.' 'Brisk Blessings for Busy Businessmen.'

'But this is appalling!' said Graham, as that deafening scream of mercantile piety towered above them.

'What is appalling?' asked his little officer, apparently seeking vainly for anything unusual in this shrieking enamel.

'This! Surely the essence of religion is reverence.'

'Oh that!' Asano looked at Graham. 'Does it shock you?' he said in the

tone of one who makes a discovery. 'I suppose it would, of course. I had forgotten. Nowadays the competition for attention is so keen, and people simply haven't the leisure to attend to their souls, you know, as they used to do.' He smiled. 'In the old days you had quiet Sabbaths and the countryside. Though somewhere I've read of Sunday afternoons that—'

'But, *that*,' said Graham, glancing back at the receding blue and white. 'That is surely not the only—'

'There are hundreds of different ways. But, of course, if a sect doesn't *tell* it doesn't pay. Worship has moved with the times. There are high-class sects with quieter ways – costly incense and personal attentions and all that. These people are extremely popular and prosperous. They pay several dozen lions for those apartments to the Council – to you, I should say.'

Graham still felt a difficulty with the coinage, and this mention of a dozen lions brought him abruptly to that matter. In a moment the screaming temples and their swarming touts were forgotten in this new interest. A turn of a phrase suggested, and an answer confirmed the idea that gold and silver were both demonetized, that stamped gold which had begun its reign amidst the merchants of Phoenicia was at last dethroned. The change had been graduated but swift, brought about by an extension of the system of cheques that had even in his previous life already practically superseded gold in all the larger business transactions. The common traffic of the city, the common currency indeed of all the world, was conducted by means of the little brown, green and pink council cheques for small amounts, printed with a blank payee. Asano had several with him, and at the first opportunity he supplied the gaps in his set. They were printed not on tearable paper, but on a semi-transparent fabric of silken, flexibility, interwoven with silk. Across them all sprawled a facsimile of Graham's signature, his first encounter with the curves and turns of that familiar autograph for two hundred and three years.

Some intermediary experiences made no impression sufficiently vivid to prevent the matter of the disarmament claiming his thoughts again; a blurred picture of a Theosophist temple that promised MIRACLES in enormous letters of unsteady fire was least submerged perhaps, but then came the view of the dining hall in Northumberland Avenue. That interested him very greatly.

By the energy and thought of Asano he was able to view this place from a little screened gallery reserved for the attendants of the tables. The building was pervaded by a distant muffled hooting, piping and bawling, of which he did not at first understand the import, but which recalled a certain mysterious leathery voice he had heard after the resumption of the lights on the night of his solitary wandering.

He had grown accustomed now to vastness and great numbers of people, nevertheless this spectacle held him for a long time. It was as he watched

the table service more immediately beneath, and interspersed with many questions and answers concerning details, that the realization of the full significance of the feast of several thousand people came to him.

It was his constant surprise to find that points that one might have expected to strike vividly at the very outset never occurred to him until some trivial detail suddenly shaped as a riddle and pointed to the obvious thing he had overlooked. In this matter, for instance, it had not occurred to him that this continuity of the city, this exclusion of weather, these vast halls and ways, involved the disappearance of the household; that the typical Victorian 'home', the little brick cell containing kitchen and scullery, living rooms and bedrooms, had, save for the ruins that diversified the countryside, vanished as surely as the wattle hut. But now he saw what had indeed been manifest from the first, that London, regarded as a living place, was no longer an aggregation of houses but a prodigious hotel, an hotel with a thousand classes of accommodation, thousands of dining halls, chapels, theatres, markets and places of assembly, a synthesis of enterprises, of which he chiefly was the owner. People had their sleeping rooms, with, it might be, antechambers, rooms that were always sanitary at least whatever the degree of comfort and privacy, and for the rest they lived much as many people had lived in the new-made giant hotels of the Victorian days, eating, reading, thinking, playing, conversing, all in places of public resort, going to their work in the industrial quarters of the city or doing business in their offices in the trading section.

He perceived at once how necessarily this state of affairs had developed from the Victorian city. The fundamental reason for the modern city had ever been the economy of co-operation. The chief thing to prevent the merging of the separate households in his own generation was simply the still imperfect civilization of the people, the strong barbaric pride, passions and prejudices, the jealousies, rivalries and violence of the middle and lower classes, which had necessitated the entire separation of contiguous households. But the change, the taming of the people, had been in rapid progress even then. In his brief thirty years of previous life he had seen an enormous extension of the habit of consuming meals from home, the casually patronized horse-box coffee-house had given place to the open and crowded Aerated Bread Shop for instance, women's clubs had had their beginning, and an immense development of reading rooms, lounges and libraries had witnessed to the growth of social confidence. Those promises had by this time attained to their complete fulfilment. The locked and barred household had passed away.

These people below him belonged, he learnt, to the lower middle class, the class just above the blue labourers, a class so accustomed in the Victorian period to feed with every precaution of privacy that its members, when occasion confronted them with a public meal, would usually hide their

embarrassment under horseplay or a markedly militant demeanour. But these gaily, if lightly dressed people below, albeit vivacious, hurried and uncommunicative, were dexterously mannered and certainly quite at their ease with regard to one another.

He noted a slight significant thing; the table, as far as he could see, was and remained delightfully neat, there was nothing to parallel the confusion, the broadcast crumbs, the splashes of viand and condiment, the overturned drink and displaced ornaments, which would have marked the stormy progress of the Victorian meal. The table furniture was very different. There were no ornaments, no flowers, and the table was without a cloth, being made, he learnt, of a solid substance having the texture and appearance of damask. He discerned that this damask substance was patterned with gracefully designed trade advertisements.

In a sort of recess before each diner was a complete apparatus of porcelain and metal. There was one plate of white porcelain, and by means of taps for hot and cold volatile fluids the diner washed this himself between the courses; he also washed his elegant white metal knife and fork and spoon as occasion required.

Soup and the chemical wine that was the common drink were delivered by similar taps, and the remaining covers travelled automatically in tastefully arranged dishes down the table along silver rails. The diner stopped these and helped himself at his discretion. They appeared at a little door at one end of the table, and vanished at the other. That turn of democratic sentiment in decay, that ugly pride of menial souls, which renders equals loth to wait on one another, was very strong he found among these people. He was so preoccupied with these details that it was only just as he was leaving the place that he remarked the huge advertisement dioramas that marched majestically along the upper walls and proclaimed the most remarkable commodities.

Beyond this place they came into a crowded hall, and he discovered the cause of the noise that had perplexed him. They paused at a turnstile at which a payment was made.

Graham's attention was immediately arrested by a violent, loud hoot, followed by a vast leathery voice. 'The Master is sleeping peacefully,' it said vociferately. 'He is in excellent health. He is going to devote the rest of his life to aeronautics. He says women are more beautiful than ever. Galloop! Wow! Our wonderful civilization astonishes him beyond measure. Beyond all measure. Galloop. He puts great trust in Boss Ostrog, absolute confidence in Boss Ostrog. Ostrog is to be his chief minister; is authorized to remove or reinstate public officers – all patronage will be in his hands. All patronage in the hands of Boss Ostrog! The Councillors have been sent back to their own prison above the Council House.'

Graham stopped at the first sentence, and, looking up, beheld a foolish

trumpet face from which this was brayed. This was the General Intelligence Machine. For a space it seemed to be gathering breath, and a regular throbbing from its cylindrical body was audible. Then it trumpeted 'Galloop, Galloop,' and broke out again.

'Paris is now pacified. All resistance is over. Galloop! The black police hold every position of importance in the city. They fought with great bravery, singing songs written in praise of their ancestors by the poet Kipling. Once or twice they got out of hand, and tortured and mutilated wounded and captured insurgents, men and women. Moral – don't go rebelling. Haha! Galloop, Galloop! They are lively fellows. Lively brave fellows. Let this be a lesson to the disorderly banderlog of this city. Yah! Banderlog! Filth of the earth! Galloop, Galloop!'

The voice ceased. There was a confused murmur of disapproval among the crowd. 'Damned niggers.' A man began to harangue near them. 'Is this the Master's doing, brothers? Is this the Master's doing?'

'Black police!' said Graham. 'What is that? You don't mean—'

Asano touched his arm and gave him a warning look, and forthwith another of these mechanisms screamed deafeningly and gave tongue in a shrill voice. 'Yahaha, Yahah, Yap! Hear a live paper yelp! Live paper. Yaha! Shocking outrage in Paris. Yahahah! The Parisians exasperated by the black police to the pitch of assassination. Dreadful reprisals. Savage times come again. Blood! Blood! Yaha!' The nearer Babble Machine hooted stupendously, 'Galloop, Galloop,' drowned the end of the sentence, and proceeded in a rather flatter note than before with novel comments on the horrors of disorder. 'Law and order must be maintained,' said the nearer Babble Machine.

'But,' began Graham.

'Don't ask questions here,' said Asano, 'or you will be involved in an argument.'

'Then let us go on,' said Graham, 'for I want to know more of this.'

As he and his companion pushed their way through the excited crowd that swarmed beneath these voices, towards the exit, Graham conceived more clearly the proportion and features of this room. Altogether, great and small, there must have been nearly a thousand of these erections, piping, hooting, bawling and gabbling in that great space, each with its crowd of excited listeners, the majority of them men dressed in blue canvas. There were all sizes of machines, from the little gossiping mechanisms that chuckled out mechanical sarcasm in odd corners, through a number of grades to such fifty-foot giants as that which had first hooted over Graham.

This place was unusually crowded, because of the intense public interest in the course of affairs in Paris. Evidently the struggle had been much more savage than Ostrog had represented it. All the mechanisms were discoursing

upon that topic, and the repetition of the people made the huge hive buzz with such phrases as 'Lynched policemen,' 'Women burnt alive,' 'Fuzzy Wuzzy.' 'But does the Master allow such things?' asked a man near him. 'Is this the beginning of the Master's rule?'

Is *this* the beginning of the Master's rule? For a long time after he had left the place, the hooting, whistling and braying of the machines pursued him; 'Galloop, Galloop,' 'Yahahah, Yaha, Yap! Yaha!' Is *this* the beginning of the Master's rule?

Directly they were out upon the ways he began to question Asano closely on the nature of the Parisian struggle. 'This disarmament! What was their trouble? What does it all mean?' Asano seemed chiefly anxious to reassure him that it was 'all right'. 'But these outrages!' 'You cannot have an omelette,' said Asano, 'without breaking eggs. It is only the rough people. Only in one part of the city. All the rest is all right. The Parisian labourers are the wildest in the world, except ours.'

'What! The Londoners?'

'No, the Japanese. They have to be kept in order.'

'But burning women alive!'

'A Commune!' said Asano. 'They would rob you of your property. They would do away with property and give the world over to mob rule. You are Master, the world is yours. But there will be no Commune here. There is no need for black police here.

'And every consideration has been shown. It is their own Negroes – French-speaking Negroes. Senegal regiments, and Niger and Timbuctoo.'

'Regiments?' said Graham, 'I thought there was only one—.'

'No,' said Asano, and glanced at him. 'There is more than one.'

Graham felt unpleasantly helpless.

'I did not think,' he began and stopped abruptly He went off at a tangent to ask for information about these Babble Machines. For the most part, the crowd present had been shabbily or even raggedly dressed, and Graham learnt that so far as the more prosperous classes were concerned, in all the more comfortable private apartments of the city were fixed Babble Machines that would speak directly a lever was pulled. The tenant of the apartment could connect this with the cables of any of the great News Syndicates that he preferred. When he learnt this presently, he demanded the reason for their absence from his own suite of apartments. Asano stared. 'I never thought,' he said. 'Ostrog must have had them removed.'

Graham stared. 'How was I to know?' he exclaimed.

'Perhaps he thought they would annoy you,' said Asano.

'They must be replaced directly I return,' said Graham after an interval.

He found a difficulty in understanding that this news room and the dining hall were not great central places, that such establishments were repeated almost beyond counting all over the city. But ever and again during the

night's expedition his ears, in some new quarter would pick out from the tumult of the ways the peculiar hooting of the organ of Boss Ostrog, 'Galloop, Galloop!' or the shrill 'Yahaha, Yaha, Yap! – Hear a live paper yelp!' of its chief rival.

Repeated, too, everywhere, were such *crèches* as the one he now entered. It was reached by a lift, and by a glass bridge that flung across the dining hall and traversed the ways at a slight upward angle. To enter the first section of the place necessitated the use of his solvent signature under Asano's direction. They were immediately attended to by a man in a violet robe and gold clasp, the insignia of practising medical men. He perceived from this man's manner that his identity was known, and proceeded to ask questions on the strange arrangements of the place without reserve.

On either side of the passage, which was silent and padded, as if to deaden the footfall, were narrow little doors, their size and arrangement suggestive of the cells of a Victorian prison. But the upper portion of each door was of the same greenish transparent stuff that had enclosed him at his awakening, and within, dimly seen, lay, in every case, a very young baby in a little nest of wadding. Elaborate apparatus watched the atmosphere and rang a bell far away in the central office at the slightest departure from the optimum of temperature and moisture. A system of such *crèches* had almost entirely replaced the hazardous adventures of the old-world nursing. The attendant presently called Graham's attention to the wet nurses, a vista of mechanical figures, with arms, shoulders and breasts of astonishingly realistic modelling, articulation, and texture, but mere brass tripods below, and having in the place of features a flat disc bearing advertisements likely to be of interest to mothers.

Of all the strange things that Graham came upon that night, none jarred more upon his habits of thought than this place. The spectacle of the little pink creatures, their feeble limbs swaying uncertainly in vague first movements, left alone, without embrace or endearment, was wholly repugnant to him. The attendant doctor was of a different opinion. His statistical evidence showed beyond dispute that in the Victorian times the most dangerous passage of life was the arms of the mother, that there human mortality had ever been most terrible. On the other hand this *crèche* company, the International Crèche Syndicate, lost not one half per cent of the million babies or so that formed its peculiar care. But Graham's prejudice was too strong even for those figures.

Along one of the many passages of the place they presently came upon a young couple in the usual blue canvas peering through the transparency and laughing hysterically at the bald head of their first-born. Graham's face must have showed his estimate of them, for their merriment ceased and they looked abashed. But this little incident accentuated his sudden realization of the gulf between his habits of thought and the ways of the new age. He

passed on to the crawling rooms and the Kindergarten, perplexed and distressed. He found the endless long playrooms were empty! The latter-day children at least still spent their nights in sleep. As they went through these, the little officer pointed out the nature of the toys, developments of those devised by that inspired sentimentalist Froebel. There were nurses here, but much was done by machines that sang and danced and dandled.

Graham was still not clear upon many points. 'But so many orphans,' he said perplexed, reverting to a first misconception, and learnt again that they were not orphans.

So soon as they had left the *crèche* he began to speak of the horror the babies in their incubating cases had caused him. 'Is motherhood gone?' he said. 'Was it a cant? Surely it was an instinct. This seems so unnatural – abominable almost.'

'Along here we shall come to the dancing place,' said Asano by way of reply. 'It is sure to be crowded. In spite of all the political unrest it will be crowded. The women take no great interest in politics – except a few here and there. You will see the mothers – most young women in London are mothers. In that class it is considered a creditable thing to have one child – a proof of animation. Few middle-class people have more than one. With the Labour Company it is different. As for motherhood! They still take an immense pride in the children. They come here to look at them quite often.'

'Then do you mean that the population of the world—?'

'Is falling? Yes. Except among the people under the Labour Company. They are reckless—.'

The air was suddenly dancing with music, and down a way they approached obliquely, set with gorgeous pillars as it seemed of clear amethyst, flowed a concourse of gay people and a tumult of merry cries and laughter. He saw curled heads, wreathed brows, and a happy intricate flutter of gamboge pass triumphant across the picture.

'You will see,' said Asano with a faint smile 'The world has changed. In a moment you will see the mothers of the new age. Come this way. We shall see those yonder again very soon.'

They ascended a certain height in a swift lift, and changed to a slower one. As they went on the music grew upon them, until it was near and full and splendid, and, moving with its glorious intricacies they could distinguish the beat of innumerable dancing feet. They made a payment at a turnstile, and emerged upon the wide gallery that overlooked the dancing place, and upon the full enchantment of sound and sight.

'Here,' said Asano, 'are the fathers and mothers of the little ones you saw.'

The hall was not so richly decorated as that of the Atlas, but saving that, it was, for its size, the most splendid Graham had seen. The beautiful white-limbed figures that supported the galleries reminded him once more of the restored magnificence of sculpture; they seemed to writhe in engaging

attitudes, their faces laughed. The source of the music that filled the place was hidden, and the whole vast shining floor was thick with dancing couples. 'Look at them,' said the little officer, 'see how much they show of motherhood.'

The gallery they stood upon ran along the upper edge of a huge screen that cut the dancing hall on one side from a sort of outer hall that showed through broad arches the incessant onward rush of the city ways. In this outer hall was a great crowd of less brilliantly dressed people, as numerous almost as those who danced within, the great majority wearing the blue uniform of the Labour Company that was now so familiar to Graham. Too poor to pass the turnstiles to the festival, they were yet unable to keep away from the sound of its seductions. Some of them even had cleared spaces, and were dancing also, fluttering their rags in the air. Some shouted as they danced, jests and odd allusions Graham did not understand. Once someone began whistling the refrain of the revolutionary song, but it seemed as though that beginning was promptly suppressed. The corner was dark and Graham could not see. He turned to the hall again. Above the caryatidae were marble busts of men whom that age esteemed great moral emancipators and pioneers; for the most part their names were strange to Graham, though he recognized Grant Allen, Le Gallienne, Nietzsche, Shelley and Goodwin. Great black festoons and eloquent sentiments reinforced the huge inscription that partially defaced the upper end of the dancing place, and asserted that 'The Festival of the Awakening' was in progress.

'Myriads are taking holiday or staying from work because of that, quite apart from the labourers who refuse to go back,' said Asano. 'These people are always ready for holidays.'

Graham walked to the parapet and stood leaning over, looking down at the dancers. Save for two or three remote whispering couples, who had stolen apart, he and his guide had the gallery to themselves. A warm breath of scent and vitality came up to him. Both men and women below were lightly clad, bare-armed, open-necked, as the universal warmth of the city permitted. The hair of the men was often a mass of effeminate curls, their chins were always shaven, and many of them had flushed or coloured cheeks. Many of the women were very pretty, and all were dressed with elaborate coquetry. As they swept by beneath, he saw ecstatic faces with eyes half closed in pleasure.

'What sort of people are these?' he asked abruptly.

'Workers – prosperous workers. What you would have called the middle class. Independent tradesmen with little separate businesses have vanished long ago, but there are store servers, managers, engineers of a hundred sorts. Tonight is a holiday of course, and every dancing place in the city will be crowded, and every place of worship.'

'But – the women?'

'The same. There's a thousand forms of work for women now. But you had the beginning of the independent working-woman in your days. Most women are independent now. Most of these are married more or less – there are a number of methods of contract – and that gives them more money, and enables them to enjoy themselves.'

'I see,' said Graham looking at the flushed faces, the flash and swirl of movement, and still thinking of that nightmare of pink helpless limbs. 'And these are – mothers.'

'Most of them.'

'The more I see of these things the more complex I find your problems. This, for instance, is a surprise. That news from Paris was a surprise.'

In a little while he spoke again:

'These are mothers. Presently, I suppose, I shall get into the modern way of seeing things. I have old habits of mind clinging about me – habits based, I suppose, on needs that are over and done with. Of course, in our time, a woman was supposed not only to bear children, but to cherish them, to devote herself to them, to educate them – all the essentials of moral and mental education a child owed its mother. Or went without. Quite a number, I admit, went without. Nowadays, clearly, there is no more need for such care than if they were butterflies. I see that! Only there was an ideal – that figure of a grave, patient woman, silently and serenely mistress of a home, mother and maker of men – to love her was a sort of worship—'

He stopped and repeated, 'A sort of worship.'

'Ideals change,' said the little man, 'as needs change.'

Graham awoke from an instant reverie and Asano repeated his words. Graham's mind returned to the thing at hand.

'Of course I see the perfect reasonableness of this Restraint, soberness, the matured thought, the unselfish a act, they are necessities of the barbarous state, the life of dangers. Dourness is man's tribute to unconquered nature. But man has conquered nature now for all practical purposes – his political affairs are managed by Bosses with a black police – and life is joyous.'

He looked at the dancers again. 'Joyous,' he said.

'There are weary moments,' said the little officer, reflectively.

'They all look young. Down there I should be visibly the oldest man. And in my own time I should have passed as middle-aged.'

'They are young. There are few old people in this class in the work cities.'

'How is that?'

'Old people's lives are not so pleasant as they used to be, unless they are rich to hire lovers and helpers. And we have an institution called Euthanasy.'

'Ah! That Euthanasy!' said Graham. 'The easy death?'

'The easy death. It is the last pleasure. The Euthanasy Company does it

well. People will pay the sum – it is a costly thing – long beforehand, go off to some pleasure city and return impoverished and weary, very weary.'

'There is a lot left for me to understand,' said Graham after a pause. 'Yet I see the logic of it all. Our array of angry virtues and sour restraints was the consequence of danger and insecurity. The Stoic, the Puritan, even in my time, were vanishing types. In the old days man was armed against Pain, now he is eager for Pleasure. There lies the difference. Civilization has driven pain and danger so far off – for well-to-do people. And only well-to-do people matter now. I have been asleep two hundred years.'

For a minute they leant on the balustrading, following the intricate evolution of the dance. Indeed the scene was very beautiful.

'Before God,' said Graham, suddenly, 'I would rather be a wounded sentinel freezing in the snow than one of these painted fools!'

'In the snow,' said Asano, 'one might think differently.'

'I am uncivilized,' said Graham, not heeding him. 'That is the trouble. I am primitive – Palaeolithic. *Their* fountain of rage and fear and anger is sealed and closed, the habits of a lifetime make them cheerful and easy and delightful. You must bear with my nineteenth-century shocks and disgusts. These people, you say, are skilled workers and so forth. And while these dance, men are fighting – men are dying in Paris to keep the world – that they may dance.'

Asano smiled faintly. 'For that matter, men are dying in London,' he said.

There was a moment's silence.

'Where do these sleep?' asked Graham.

'Above and below – an intricate warren.'

'And where do they work? This is – the domestic life.'

'You will see little work tonight. Half the workers are out or under arms. Half these people are keeping holiday. But we will go to the work places if you wish it.'

For a time Graham watched the dancers, then suddenly turned away. 'I want to see the workers. I have seen enough of these,' he said.

Asano led the way along the gallery across the dancing hall. Presently they came to a transverse passage that brought a breath of fresher, colder air.

Asano glanced at this passage as they went past, stopped, went back to it, and turned to Graham with a smile. 'Here, Sire,' he said, 'is something – will be familiar to you at least – and yet––. But I will not tell you. Come!'

He led the way along a closed passage that presently became cold. The reverberation of their feet told that this passage was a bridge. They came into a circular gallery that was glazed in from the outer weather, and so reached a circular chamber which seemed familiar, though Graham could not recall distinctly when he had entered it before. In this was a ladder – the first ladder he had seen since his awakening – up which they went, and

came into a high, dark, cold place in which was another almost vertical ladder. This they ascended, Graham still perplexed.

But at the top he understood, and recognized the metallic bars to which he clung. He was in the cage under the ball of St Paul's. The dome rose but a little way above the general contour of the city, into the still twilight, and sloped away, shining greasily under a few distant lights, into a circum-ambient ditch of darkness.

Out between the bars he looked upon the wind-clear northern sky and saw the starry constellations all unchanged. Capella hung in the west, Vega was rising, and the seven glittering points of the Great Bear swept overhead in their stately circle about the Pole.

He saw these stars in a clear gap of sky. To the east and south the great circular shapes of complaining wind-wheels blotted out the heavens, so that the glare about the Council House was hidden. To the south-west hung Orion, showing like a pallid ghost through a tracery of iron-work and interlacing shapes above a dazzling coruscation of lights. A bellowing and siren screaming that came from the flying stages warned the world that one of the aeroplanes was ready to start. He remained for a space gazing towards the glaring stage. Then his eyes went back to the northward constellations.

For a long time he was silent. 'This,' he said at last, smiling in the shadow, 'seems the strangest thing of all. To stand in the dome of St Paul's and look once more upon these familiar, silent stars!'

Thence Graham was taken by Asano along devious ways to the great gambling and business quarters where the bulk of the fortunes in the city were lost and made. It impressed him as a well-nigh interminable series of very high halls, surrounded by tiers upon tiers of galleries into which opened thousands of offices, and traversed by a complicated multitude of bridges, footways, aerial motor rails, and trapeze and cable leaps. And here more than anywhere the note of vehement vitality, of uncontrollable, hasty activity, rose high. Everywhere was violent advertisement, until his brain swam at the tumult of light and colour. And Babble Machines of a peculiarly rancid tone were abundant and filled the air with strenuous squealing and an idiotic slang. 'Skin your eyes and slide,' 'Gewhoop, Bonanza,' 'Gollipers come and hark!'

The place seemed to him to be dense with people either profoundly agitated or swelling with obscure cunning, yet he learnt that the place was comparatively empty, that the great political convulsion of the last few days had reduced transactions to an unprecedented minimum. In one huge place were long avenues of roulette tables, each with an excited, undignified crowd about it; in another a yelping Babel of white-faced women and red-necked leathery-lunged men bought and sold the shares of an absolutely fictitious business undertaking which, every five minutes, paid a dividend

of ten per cent and cancelled a certain proportion of its shares by means
of a lottery wheel.

These business activities were prosecuted with an energy that readily
passed into violence, and Graham approaching a dense crowd found at its
centre a couple of prominent merchants in violent controversy with teeth
and nails on some delicate point of business etiquette. Something still
remained in life to be fought for. Further he had a shock at a vehement
announcement in phonetic letters of scarlet flame, each twice the height
of a man, that 'WE ASSURE THE PROPRAIET'R. WE ASSURE THE
PROPRAIET'R.'

'Who's the proprietor?' he asked.

'You.'

'But what do they assure me?' he asked. 'What do they assure me?'

'Didn't you have assurance?'

Graham thought. 'Insurance?'

'Yes – insurance. I remember that was the older word. They are insuring
your life. Dozands of people are taking out policies, myriads of lions are
being put on you. And further on other people are buying annuities. They
do that on everybody who is at all prominent. Look there!'

A crowd of people surged and roared, and Graham saw a vast black screen
suddenly illuminated in still larger letters of burning purple. 'Anuetes on the
Propraiet'r – x 5 pr. G.' The people began to boo and shout at this, a number
of hard breathing, wild-eyed men came running past, clawing with hooked
fingers at the air. There was a furious crush about a little doorway.

Asano did a brief calculation. 'Seventeen per cent per annum is their
annuity on you. They would not pay so much per cent if they could see you
now, Sire. But they do not know. Your own annuities used to be a very safe
investment, but now you are sheer gambling, of course. This is probably a
desperate bid. I doubt if people will get their money.'

The crowd of would-be annuitants grew so thick about them that for
some time they could move neither forward nor backward. Graham noticed
what appeared to him to be a high proportion of women among the spec-
ulators, and was reminded again of the economical independence of their
sex. They seemed remarkably well able to take care of themselves in the
crowd, using their elbows with particular skill, as he learnt to his cost. One
curly-headed person caught in the pressure for a space, looked steadfastly
at him several times, almost as if she recognized him, and then, edging
deliberately towards him, touched his hand with her arm in a scarcely
accidental manner, and made it plain by a look as ancient as Chaldea that
he had found favour in her eyes. And then a lank, grey-bearded man,
perspiring copiously in a noble passion of self-help, blind to all earthly things
save that glaring bait, thrust between them in a cataclysmal rush towards
that alluring 'x 5 pr. G.'

'I want to get out of this,' said Graham to Asano. 'This is not what I came to see. Show me the workers. I want to see the people in blue. These parasitic lunatics—'

He found himself wedged in a struggling mass of people, and this hopeful sentence went unfinished.

CHAPTER XXI

The Underside

From the Business Quarter they presently passed by the running ways into a remote quarter of the city, where the bulk of the manufactures was done. On their way the platforms crossed the Thames twice, and passed in a broad viaduct across one of the great roads that entered the city from the north. In both cases his impression was swift and in both very vivid. The river was a broad wrinkled glitter of black sea water, overarched by buildings, and vanishing either way into a blackness starred with receding lights. A string of black barges passed seaward, manned by blue-clad men. The road was a long and very broad and high tunnel, along which big-wheeled machines drove noiselessly and swiftly. Here, too, the distinctive blue of the Labour Company was in abundance. The smoothness of the double tracks, the largeness and the lightness of the big pneumatic wheels in proportion to the vehicular body, struck Graham most vividly. One lank and very high carriage with longitudinal metallic rods hung with the dripping carcasses of many hundred sheep arrested his attention unduly. Abruptly the edge of the archway cut and blotted out the picture.

Presently they left the way and descended by a lift and traversed a passage that sloped downward, and so came to a descending lift again. The appearance of things changed. Even the pretence of architectural ornament disappeared, the lights diminished in number and size, the architecture became more and more massive in proportion to the spaces as the factory quarters were reached. And in the dusty biscuit-making place of the potters, among the felspar mills in the furnace rooms of the metal workers, among the incandescent lakes of crude Eadhamite, the blue canvas clothing was on man, woman and child.

Many of these great and dusty galleries were silent avenues of machinery, endless raked out ashen furnaces testified to the revolutionary dislocation, but wherever there was work it was being done by slow-moving workers in blue canvas. The only people not in blue canvas were the overlookers of the work-places and the orange-clad Labour Police. And fresh from the flushed faces of the dancing halls, the voluntary vigours of the business quarter, Graham could note the pinched faces, the feeble muscles, and weary eyes of many of the latter-day workers. Such as he saw at work were noticeably inferior in physique to the few gaily dressed managers and forewomen who were directing their labours. The burly labourers of the Victorian times had followed the dray horse and all such living force producers, to extinction; the place of his costly muscles was taken by some dexterous machine. The

latter-day labourer, male as well as female, was essentially a machine-minder and feeder, a servant and attendant, or an artist under direction.

The women, in comparison with those Graham remembered, were as a class distinctly plain and flat-chested. Two hundred years of emancipation from the moral restraints of Puritanical religion, two hundred years of city life, had done their work in eliminating the strain of feminine beauty and vigour from the blue canvas myriads. To be brilliant physically or mentally, to be in any way attractive or exceptional, had been and was still a certain way of emancipation to the drudge, a line of escape to the Pleasure City and its splendours and delights, and at last to the Euthanasy and peace. To be steadfast against such inducements was scarcely to be expected of meanly nourished souls. In the young cities of Graham's former life, the newly aggregated labouring mass had been a diverse multitude, still stirred by the tradition of personal honour and a high morality; now it was differentiating into a distinct class, with a moral and physical difference of its own – even with a dialect of its own.

They penetrated downward, ever downward, towards the working places. Presently they passed underneath one of the streets of the moving ways, and saw its platforms running on their rails far overhead, and chinks of white lights between the transverse slits. The factories that were not working were sparsely lighted; to Graham they and their shrouded aisles of giant machines seemed plunged in gloom, and even where work was going on the illumination was far less brilliant than upon the public ways.

Beyond the blazing lakes of Eadhamite he came to the warren of the jewellers, and, with some difficulty and by using his signature, obtained admission to these galleries. They were high and dark, and rather cold. In the first a few men were making ornaments of gold filigree, each man at a little bench by himself, and with a little shaded light. The long vista of light patches, with the nimble fingers brightly lit and moving among the gleaming yellow coils, and the intent face like the face of a ghost, in each shadow had the oddest effect.

The work was beautifully executed, but without any strength of modelling or drawing, for the most part intricate grotesques or the ringing of the changes on a geometrical motif. These workers wore a peculiar white uniform without pockets or sleeves. They assumed this on coming to work, but at night they were stripped and examined before they left the premises of the Company. In spite of every precaution, the Labour policeman told them in a depressed tone, the Company was not infrequently robbed.

Beyond was a gallery of women busied in cutting and setting slabs of artificial ruby, and next to these were men and women busied together upon the slabs of copper net that formed the basis of *cloisonné* tiles. Many of these workers had lips and nostrils a livid white, due to a disease caused by a peculiar purple enamel that chanced to be much in fashion. Asano apologized

to Graham for the offence of their faces, but excused himself on the score
of the convenience of this route. 'This is what I wanted to see,' said Graham;
'this is what I wanted to see,' trying to avoid a start at a particularly striking
disfigurement that suddenly stared him in the face.

'She might have done better with herself than that,' said Asano.

Graham made some indignant comments.

'But, Sire, we simply could not stand that stuff without the purple,' said
Asano. 'In your days people could stand such crudities, they were nearer
the barbaric by two hundred years.'

They continued along one of the lower galleries of this *cloisonné* factory,
and came to a little bridge that spanned a vault. Looking over the parapet,
Graham saw that beneath was a wharf under yet more tremendous archings
than any he had seen. Three barges, smothered in floury dust, were being
unloaded of their cargoes of powdered felspar by a multitude of coughing
men, each guiding a little truck; the dust filled the place with a choking
mist, and turned the electric glare yellow. The vague shadows of these
workers gesticulated about their feet, and rushed to and fro against a long
stretch of whitewashed wall. Every now and then one would stop to cough.

A shadowy, huge mass of masonry rising out of the inky water, brought
to Graham's mind the thought of the multitude of ways and galleries and
lifts that rose floor above floor overhead between him and the sky. The men
worked in silence under the supervision of two of the Labour Police; their
feet made a hollow thunder on the planks along which they went to and
fro. And as he looked at this scene, some hidden voice in the darkness
began to sing.

'Stop that!' shouted one of the policemen, but the order was disobeyed,
and first one and then all the white-stained men who were working there
had taken up the beating refrain, singing it defiantly – the Song of the
Revolt. The feet upon the planks thundered now to the rhythm of the song,
tramp, tramp, tramp. The policeman who had shouted glanced at his fellow,
and Graham saw him shrug his shoulders. He made no further effort to
stop the singing.

And so they went through these factories and places of toil, seeing many
painful and grim things. But why should the gentle reader be depressed?
Surely to a refined nature our present world is distressing enough without
bothering ourselves about these miseries to come. We shall not suffer anyhow.
Our children may, but what is that to us? That walk left on Graham's mind
a maze of memories, fluctuating pictures of swathed halls, and crowded
vaults seen through clouds of dust, of intricate machines, the racing threads
of looms, the heavy beat of stamping machinery, the roar and rattle of belt
and armature, of ill-lit subterranean aisles of sleeping places, illimitable vistas
of pin-point lights. And here the smell of tanning, and here the reek of a
brewery and here, unprecedented reeks. And everywhere were pillars and

cross archings of such a massiveness as Graham had never before seen, thick Titans of greasy, shining brickwork crushed beneath the vast weight of that complex city world, even as these anaemic millions were crushed by its complexity. And everywhere were pale features, lean limbs, disfigurement and degradation.

Once and again, and again a third time, Graham heard the Song of the Revolt during his long, unpleasant research in these places, and once he saw a confused struggle down a passage, and learnt that a number of these serfs had seized their bread before their work was done. Graham was ascending towards the ways again when he saw a number of blue-clad children running down a transverse passage, and presently perceived the reason of their panic in a company of the Labour Police armed with clubs, trotting towards some unknown disturbance. And then came a remote disorder. But for the most part this remnant that worked, worked hopelessly. All the spirit that was left in fallen humanity was above in the streets that night, calling for the Master, and valiantly and noisily keeping its arms.

They emerged from these wanderings and stood blinking in the bright light of the middle passage of the platforms again. They became aware of the remote hooting and yelping of the machines of one of the General Intelligence Offices, and suddenly came men running, and along the platforms and about the ways everywhere was a shouting and crying. Then a woman with a face of mute white terror, and another who gasped and shrieked as she ran.

'What has happened now?' said Graham, puzzled, for he could not understand their thick speech. Then he heard it in English and perceived that the thing that everyone was shouting, that men yelled to one another, that women took up screaming, that was passing like the first breeze of a thunderstorm, chill and sudden through the city, was this: 'Ostrog has ordered the Black Police to London. The Black Police are coming from South Africa. . . . The Black Police. The Black Police.'

Asano's face was white and astonished; he hesitated, looked at Graham's face, and told him the thing he already knew. 'But how can they know?' asked Asano.

Graham heard someone shouting. 'Stop all work. Stop all work,' and a swarthy hunchback, ridiculously gay in green and gold, came leaping down the platforms toward him, bawling again and again in good English, 'This is Ostrog's doing, Ostrog the Knave! The Master is betrayed.' His voice was hoarse and a thin foam dropped from his ugly shouting mouth. He yelled an unspeakable horror that the Black Police had done in Paris, and so passed shrieking, 'Ostrog the Knave!'

For a moment Graham stood still, for it had come upon him again that these things were a dream. He looked up at the great cliff of buildings on either side, vanishing into blue haze at last above the lights, and down to

the roaring tiers of platforms, and the shouting, running people who were gesticulating past. 'The Master is betrayed!' they cried. 'The Master is betrayed!'

Suddenly the situation shaped itself in his mind real and urgent. His heart began to beat fast and strong.

'It has come,' he said. 'I might have known. The hour has come.'

He thought swiftly. 'What am I to do?'

'Go back to the Council House,' said Asano.

'Why should I not appeal—? The people are here.'

'You will lose time. They will doubt if it is you. But they will mass about the Council House. There you will find their leaders. Your strength is there – with them.'

'Suppose this is only a rumour?'

'It sounds true,' said Asano.

'Let us have the facts,' said Graham.

Asano shrugged his shoulders. 'We had better get towards the Council House,' he cried. 'That is where they will swarm. Even now the ruins may be impassable.'

Graham regarded him doubtfully and followed him.

They went up the stepped platforms to the swiftest one, and there Asano accosted a labourer. The answers to his questions were in the thick, vulgar speech.

'What did he say?' asked Graham.

'He knows little, but he told me that the Black Police would have arrived here before the people knew – had not someone in the wind-vane offices learnt. He said a girl.'

'A girl? Not?'

'He said a girl – he did not know who she was. Who came out from the Council House crying aloud, and told the men at work among the ruins.'

And then another thing was shouted, something that turned an aimless tumult into determinate movements, it came like a wind along the street. 'To your Wards, to your Wards. Every man get arms. Every man to his Ward!'

CHAPTER XXII

The Struggle in the Council House

As Asano and Graham hurried along to the ruins about the Council House, they saw everywhere the excitement of the people rising. 'To your Wards! To your Wards!' Everywhere men and women in blue were hurrying from unknown subterranean employments, up the staircases of the middle path – at one place Graham saw an arsenal of the revolutionary committee besieged by a crowd of shouting men, at another a couple of men in the hated yellow uniform of the Labour Police, pursued by a gathering crowd, fled precipitately along the swift way that went in the opposite direction.

The cries of 'To your Wards!' became at last a continuous shouting as they drew near the Government quarter. Many of the shouts were unintelligible. 'Ostrog has betrayed us,' one man bawled in a hoarse voice, again and again, dinning that refrain into Graham's ear until it haunted him. This person stayed close beside Graham and Asano on the swift way, shouting to the people who swarmed on the lower platforms as he rushed past them. His cry about Ostrog alternated with some incomprehensible orders. Presently he went leaping down and disappeared.

Graham's mind was filled with the din. His plans were vague and unformed. He had one picture of some commanding position from which he could address the multitudes, another of meeting Ostrog face to face. He was full of rage, of tense muscular excitement, his hands gripped, his lips were pressed together.

The way to the Council House across the ruins was impassable, but Asano met that difficulty and took Graham into the premises of the central post-office. The post-office was nominally at work, but the blue-clothed porters moved sluggishly or had stopped to stare through the arches of their galleries at the shouting men who were going by outside. 'Every man to his Ward! Every man to his Ward!' Here, by Asano's advice, Graham revealed his identity.

They crossed to the Council House by a cable cradle. Already in the brief interval since the capitulation of the Councillors a great change had been wrought in the appearance of the ruins. The spurting cascades of the ruptured sea-water mains had been captured and tamed, and huge temporary pipes ran overhead along a flimsy-looking fabric of girders. The sky was laced with restored cables and wires that served the Council House, and a mass of new fabric with cranes and other building machines going to and fro upon it, projected to the left of the white pile.

The moving ways that ran across this area had been restored, albeit for

once running under the open sky. These were the ways that Graham had seen from the little balcony in the hour of his awakening, not nine days since, and the hall of his trance had been on the further side, where now shapeless piles of smashed and shattered masonry were heaped together.

It was already high day and the sun was shining brightly. Out of their tall caverns of blue electric light came the swift ways crowded with multitudes of people, who poured off them and gathered ever denser over the wreckage and confusion of the ruins. The air was full of their shouting, and they were pressing and swaying towards the central building. For the most part that shouting mass consisted of shapeless swarms, but here and there Graham could see that a rude discipline struggled to establish itself. And every voice clamoured for order in the chaos. 'To your Wards! Every man to his Ward!'

The cable carried them into a hall which Graham recognized as the ante-chamber to the Hall of the Atlas, about the gallery of which he had walked days ago with Howard to show himself to the vanished Council, an hour from his awakening. Now the place was empty except for two cable attendants. These men seemed hugely astonished to recognize the Sleeper in the man who swung down from the cross seat.

'Where is Helen Wotton?' he demanded. 'Where is Helen Wotton?'

They did not know.

'Then where is Ostrog? I must see Ostrog forthwith. He has disobeyed me. I have come back to take things out of his hands.' Without waiting for Asano, he went straight across the place, ascended the steps at the further end, and, pulling the curtain aside, found himself facing the perpetually labouring Titan.

The Hall was empty. Its appearance had changed very greatly since his first sight of it. It had suffered serious injury in the violent struggle of the first outbreak. On the right-hand side of the great figure the upper half of the wall had been torn away for nearly two hundred feet of its length, and a sheet of the same glassy film that had enclosed Graham at his awakening had been drawn across the gap. This deadened, but did not altogether exclude the roar of the people outside. 'Wards! Wards! Wards!' they seemed to be saying. Through it there were visible the beams and supports of metal scaffoldings that rose and fell according to the requirements of a great crowd of workmen. An idle building machine, with lank arms of red-painted metal that caught the still plastic blocks of mineral paste and swung them neatly into position, stretched gauntly across this green tinted picture. On it were still a number of workmen staring at the crowd below. For a moment he stood regarding these things, and Asano overtook him.

'Ostrog,' said Asano, 'will be in the small offices beyond there.' The little man looked livid now and his eyes searched Graham's face.

They had scarcely advanced ten paces from the curtain before a little panel to the left of the Atlas rolled up, and Ostrog, accompanied by Lincoln

and followed by two black-and-yellow-clad Negroes, appeared crossing the remote corner of the hall, towards a second panel that was raised and open. 'Ostrog,' shouted Graham, and at the sound of his voice the little party turned astonished.

Ostrog said something to Lincoln and advanced alone.

Graham was the first to speak. His voice was loud and dictatorial. 'What is this I hear?' he asked. 'Are you bringing Negroes here – to keep the people down?'

'It is none too soon,' said Ostrog. 'They have been getting out of hand more and more, since the revolt. I under-estimated—'

'Do you mean that these infernal Negroes are on the way?'

'On the way. As it is, you have seen the people – outside?'

'No wonder! But – after what was said. You have taken too much on yourself, Ostrog.'

Ostrog said nothing, but drew nearer.

'These Negroes must not come to London,' said Graham. 'I am Master and they shall not come.'

Ostrog glanced at Lincoln, who at once came towards them with his two attendants close behind him. 'Why not?' asked Ostrog.

'White men must be mastered by white men. Besides—'

'The Negroes are only an instrument.'

'But that is not the question. I am the Master. I mean to be the Master. And I tell you these Negroes shall not come.'

'The people—'

'I believe in the people.'

'Because you are an anachronism. You are a man out of the Past – an accident. You are Owner perhaps of half the property in the world. But you are not Master. You do not know enough to be Master.'

He glanced at Lincoln again. 'I know now what you think – I can guess something of what you mean to do. Even now it is not too late to warn you. You dream of human equality – of a socialistic order – you have all those worn-out dreams of the nineteenth century fresh and vivid in your mind, and you would rule this age that you do not understand.'

'Listen!' said Graham. 'You can hear it – a sound like the sea. Not voices – but a voice. Do you altogether understand?'

'We taught them that,' said Ostrog.

'Perhaps. Can you teach them to forget it? But enough of this! These Negroes must not come.'

There was a pause and Ostrog looked him in the eyes.

'They will,' he said.

'I forbid it,' said Graham.

'They have started.'

'I will not have it.'

'No,' said Ostrog. 'Sorry as I am to follow the method of the Council—. For your own good – you must not side with disorder. And now that you are here—. It was kind of you to come here.'

Lincoln laid his hand on Graham's shoulder. Abruptly Graham realized the enormity of his blunder in coming to the Council House. He turned towards the curtains that separated the hall from the antechamber. The clutching hand of Asano intervened. In another moment Lincoln had grasped Graham's cloak.

He turned and struck at Lincoln's face, and incontinently a Negro had him by collar and arm. He wrenched himself away, his sleeve tore noisily, and he stumbled back, to be tripped by the other attendant. Then he struck the ground heavily and he was staring at the distant ceiling of the hall.

He shouted, rolled over, struggling fiercely, clutched an attendant's leg and threw him headlong, and struggled to his feet.

Lincoln appeared before him, went down heavily again with a blow under the point of the jaw and lay still. Graham made two strides, stumbled. And then Ostrog's arm was round his neck, he was pulled over backward, fell heavily, and his arms were pinned to the ground. After a few violent efforts he ceased to struggle and lay staring at Ostrog's heaving throat.

'You – are – a prisoner,' panted Ostrog, exulting. 'You – were rather a fool – to come back.'

Graham turned his head about and perceived through the irregular green window in the walls of the hall the men who had been working the building cranes gesticulating excitedly to the people below them. They had seen!

Ostrog followed his eyes and started. He shouted something to Lincoln, but Lincoln did not move. A bullet smashed among the mouldings above the Atlas. The two sheets of transparent matter that had been stretched across this gap were rent, the edges of the torn aperture darkened, curved, ran rapidly towards the framework, and in a moment the Council Chamber stood open to the air. A chilly gust blew in by the gap, bringing with it a war of voices from the ruinous spaces without, an elvish babblement, 'Save the Master!' 'What are they doing to the Master?' 'The Master is betrayed!'

And then he realized that Ostrog's attention was distracted, that Ostrog's grip had relaxed, and, wrenching his arms free, he struggled to his knees. In another moment he had thrust Ostrog back, and he was on one foot, his hand gripping Ostrog's throat, and Ostrog's hands clutching the silk about his neck. But now men were coming towards them from the dais – men whose intentions he misunderstood. He had a glimpse of someone running in the distance towards the curtains of the antechamber, and then Ostrog had slipped from him and these newcomers were upon him. To his infinite astonishment, they seized him. They obeyed the shouts of Ostrog.

He was lugged a dozen yards before he realized that they were not friends – that they were dragging him towards the open panel. When he saw this

he pulled back, he tried to fling himself down, he shouted for help with all his strength. And this time there were answering cries.

The grip upon his neck relaxed, and behold! In the lower corner of the rent upon the wall, first one and then a number of little black figures appeared shouting and waving arms. They came leaping down from the gap into the light gallery that had led to the Silent Rooms. They ran along it, so near were they that Graham could see the weapons in their hands, Then Ostrog was shouting in his ear to the men who held him, and once more he was struggling with all his strength against their endeavours to thrust him towards the opening that yawned to receive him. 'They can't come down,' panted Ostrog. 'They daren't fire. It's all right. We'll save him from them yet.'

For long minutes as it seemed to Graham that inglorious struggle continued. His clothes were rent in a dozen places, he was covered in dust, one hand had been trodden upon. He could hear the shouts of his supporters, and once he heard shots. He could feel his strength giving way, feel his efforts wild and aimless. But no help came, and surely, irresistibly, that black, yawning opening came nearer.

The pressure upon him relaxed and he struggled up. He saw Ostrog's grey head receding and perceived that he was no longer held. He turned about and came full into a man in black. One of the green weapons cracked close to him, a drift of pungent smoke came into his face, and a steel blade flashed. The huge chamber span about him.

He saw a man in pale blue stabbing one of the black and yellow attendants not three yards from his face. Then hands were upon him again.

He was being pulled in two, directions now. It seemed as though people were shouting to him. He wanted to understand and could not. Someone was clutching about his thighs, he was being hoisted in spite of his vigorous efforts. He understood suddenly, he ceased to struggle. He was lifted up on men's shoulders and carried away from that devouring panel. Ten thousand throats were cheering.

He saw men in blue and black hurrying after the retreating Ostrogites and firing. Lifted up, he saw now across the whole expanse of the hall beneath the Atlas image, saw that he was being carried towards the raised platform in the centre of the place. The far end of the hall was already full of people running towards him. They were looking at him and cheering.

He became aware that a sort of bodyguard surrounded him. Active men about him shouted vague orders. He saw close at hand the black moustached man in yellow who had been among those who had greeted him in the public theatre, shouting directions. The hall was already densely packed with swaying people, the little metal gallery sagged with a shouting load, the curtains at the end had been torn away, and the ante-chamber was revealed densely crowded. He could scarcely make the man near him hear for the tumult about them. 'Where has Ostrog gone?' he asked.

The man he questioned pointed over the heads towards the lower panels about the hall on the side opposite the gap. They stood open, and armed men, blue clad with black sashes, were running through them and vanishing into the chambers and passages beyond. It seemed to Graham that a sound of firing drifted through the riot. He was carried in a staggering curve across the great hall towards an opening beneath the gap.

He perceived men working with a sort of rude discipline to keep the crowd off him, to make a space clear about him. He passed out of the hall, and saw a crude, new wall rising blankly before him topped by blue sky. He was swung down to his feet; someone gripped his arm and guided him. He found the man in yellow close at hand. They were taking him up a narrow stairway of brick, and close at hand rose the great red-painted masses, the cranes and levers and the still engines of the big building machine.

He was at the top of the steps. He was hurried across a narrow railed footway, and suddenly with a vast shouting the amphitheatre of ruins opened again before him. 'The Master is with us! The Master! The Master!' The shout swept athwart the lake of faces like a wave, broke against the distant cliff of ruins, and came back in a welter of cries. 'The Master is on our side!'

Graham perceived that he was no longer encompassed by people, that he was standing upon a little temporary platform of white metal, part of a flimsy-seeming scaffolding that laced about the great mass of the Council House. Over all the huge expanse of the ruins, swayed and eddied the shouting people; and here and there the black banners of the revolutionary societies ducked and swayed and formed rare nuclei of organization in the chaos. Up the steep stairs of wall and scaffolding by which his rescuers had reached the opening in the Atlas Chamber, clung a solid crowd, and little energetic black figures clinging to pillars and projections were strenuous to induce these congested masses to stir. Behind him, at a higher point on the scaffolding, a number of men struggled upwards with the flapping folds of a huge black standard. Through the yawning gap in the walls below him he could look down upon the packed attentive multitudes in the Hall of the Atlas. The distant flying stages to the south came out bright and vivid, brought nearer as it seemed by an unusual translucency of the air. A solitary aeropile beat up from the central stage as if to meet the coming aeroplanes.

'What has become of Ostrog?' asked Graham, and even as he spoke he saw that all eyes were turned from him towards the crest of the Council House building. He looked also in this direction of universal attention. For a moment he saw nothing but the jagged corner of a wall, hard and clear against the sky. Then in the shadow he perceived the interior of a room and recognized with a start the green and white decorations of his former prison. And coming quickly across this opened room and up to the very verge of the cliff of the ruins came a little white clad figure followed by two other smaller seeming figures in black and yellow. He heard the man beside him

exclaim 'Ostrog,' and turned to ask a question. But he never did, because of the startled exclamation of another of those who were with him and a lank finger suddenly pointing. He looked, and behold the aeropile that had been rising from the flying stage when last he had looked in that direction, was driving towards them. The swift steady flight was still novel enough to hold his attention.

Nearer it came, growing rapidly larger and larger, until it had swept over the further edge of the ruins and into view of the dense multitudes below. It drooped across the space and rose and passed overhead, rising to clear the mass of the Council House, a filmy translucent shape with the solitary aeronaut peering down through its ribs. It vanished beyond the skyline of the ruins.

Graham transferred his attention to Ostrog. He was signalling with his hands, and his attendants were busy breaking down the wall beside him. In another moment the aeropile came into view again, a little thing far away, coming round in a wide curve and going slower.

Then suddenly the man in yellow shouted: 'What are they doing? What are the people doing? Why is Ostrog left there? Why is he not captured? They will lift him – the aeropile will lift him! Ah!'

The exclamation was echoed by a shout from the ruins. The rattling sound of the green weapons drifted across the intervening gulf to Graham, and, looking down, he saw a number of black and yellow uniforms running along one of the galleries that lay open to the air below the promontory upon which Ostrog stood. They fired as they ran at men unseen, and then emerged a number of pale blue figures in pursuit. These minute fighting figures had the oddest effect; they seemed as they ran like little model soldiers in a toy. This queer appearance of a house cut open gave that struggle amidst furniture and passages a quality of unreality. It was perhaps two hundred yards away from him, and very nearly fifty above the heads in the ruins below. The black and yellow men ran into an open archway, and turned and fired a volley. One of the blue pursuers striding forward close to the edge, flung up his arms, staggered sideways, seemed to Graham's sense to hang over the edge for several seconds, and fell headlong down. Graham saw him strike a projecting corner, fly out, head over heels, head over heels, and vanish behind the red arm of the building machine.

And then a shadow came between Graham and the sun. He looked up and the sky was clear, but he knew the aeropile had passed. Ostrog had vanished. The man in yellow thrust before him, zealous and perspiring, pointing and blatant.

'They are grounding!' cried the man in yellow. 'They are grounding. Tell the people to fire at him. Tell them to fire at him!'

Graham could not understand. He heard loud voices repeating these enigmatical orders.

Suddenly over the edge of the ruins he saw the prow of the aeropile come gliding and stop with a jerk. In a moment Graham understood that the thing had grounded in order that Ostrog might escape by it. He saw a blue haze climbing out of the gulf, perceived that the people below him were now firing up at the projecting stem.

A man beside him cheered hoarsely, and he saw that the blue rebels had gained the archway that had been contested by the men in black and yellow a moment before, and were running in a continual stream along the open passage.

And suddenly the aeropile slipped over the edge of the Council House and fell. It dropped, tilting at an angle of forty-five degrees, and dropping so steeply that it seemed to Graham, it seemed perhaps to most of those below, that it could not possibly rise again.

It fell so closely past him that he could see Ostrog clutching the guides of the seat, with his grey hair streaming; see the white-faced aeronaut wrenching over the lever that drove the engine along its guides. He heard the apprehensive vague cry of innumerable men below.

Graham clutched the railing before him and gasped. The second seemed an age. The lower fan of the aeropile passed within an ace of touching the people, who yelled and screamed and trampled one another below.

And then it rose.

For a moment it looked as if it could not possibly clear the opposite cliff, and then that it could not possibly clear the wind-wheel that rotated beyond.

And behold! It was clear and soaring, still heeling sideways, upward, upward into the wind-swept sky.

The suspense of the moment gave place to a fury of exasperation as the swarming people realized that Ostrog had escaped them. With belated activity they renewed their fire, until the rattling wove into a roar, until the whole area became dim and blue and the air pungent with the thin smoke of their weapons.

Too late! The aeropile dwindled smaller and smaller, and curved about and swept gracefully downward to the flying stage from which it had so lately risen. Ostrog had escaped.

For a while a confused babblement arose from the ruins, and then the universal attention came back to Graham, perched high among the scaffolding. He saw the faces of the people turned towards him, heard their shouts at his rescue. From the throat of the ways came the song of the revolt spreading like a breeze across that swaying sea of men.

The little group of men about him shouted congratulations on his escape. The man in yellow was close to him, with a set face and shining eyes. And the song was rising, louder and louder; tramp, tramp, tramp, tramp.

Slowly the realization came of the full meaning of these things to him, the perception of the swift change in his position. Ostrog, who had stood

beside him whenever he had faced that shouting multitude before, was beyond there – the antagonist. There was no one to rule for him any longer. Even the people about him, the leaders and organizers of the multitude, looked to see what he would do, looked to him to act, awaited his orders. He was king indeed. His puppet reign was at an end.

He was very intent to do the thing that was expected of him. His nerves and muscles were quivering, his mind was perhaps a little confused, but he felt neither fear nor anger. His hand that had been trodden upon throbbed and was hot. He was a little nervous about his bearing. He knew he was not afraid, but he was anxious not to seem afraid. In his former life he had often been more excited in playing games of skill. He was desirous of imme-diate action, he knew he must not think too much in detail of the huge complexity of the struggle about him lest he should be paralysed by the sense of its intricacy.

Over there those square blue shapes, the flying stages, meant Ostrog; against Ostrog he was fighting for the world.

CHAPTER XXIII

While the Aeroplanes Were Coming

For a time the Master of the Earth was not even master of his own mind. Even his will seemed a will not his own, his own acts surprised him and were but a part of the confusion of strange experiences that poured across his being. These things were definite, the aeroplanes were coming, Helen Wotton had warned the people of their coming, and he was Master of the Earth. Each of these facts seemed struggling for complete possession of his thoughts. They protruded from a background of swarming halls, elevated passages, rooms jammed with ward leaders in council, kinematograph and telephone rooms, and windows looking out on a seething sea of marching men. The man in yellow, and men whom he fancied were called Ward Leaders, were either propelling him forward or following him obediently; it was hard to tell. Perhaps they were doing a little of both. Perhaps some power unseen and unsuspected, propelled them all. He was aware that he was going to make a proclamation to the People of the Earth, aware of certain grandiose phrases floating in his mind as the thing he meant to say. Many little things happened, and then he found himself with the man in yellow entering a little room where this proclamation of his was to be made.

This room was grotesquely latter-day in its appointments. In the centre was a bright oval lit by shaded electric lights from above. The rest was in shadow, and the double finely fitting doors through which he came from the swarming Hall of the Atlas made the place very still. The dead thud of these as they closed behind him, the sudden cessation of the tumult in which he had been living for hours, the quivering circle of light, the whispers and quick noiseless movements of vaguely visible attendants in the shadows, had a strange effect upon Graham. The huge ears of a phonographic mechanism gaped in a battery for his words, the black eyes of great photographic cameras awaited his beginning, beyond metal rods and coils glittered dimly, and something whirled about with a droning hum. He walked into the centre of the light, and his shadow drew together black and sharp to a little blot at his feet.

The vague shape of the thing he meant to say was already in his mind. But this silence, this isolation, the sudden withdrawal from that contagious crowd, this silent audience of gaping, glaring machines had not been in his anticipation. All his supports seemed withdrawn together; he seemed to have dropped into this suddenly, suddenly to have discovered himself. In a moment he was changed. He found that he now feared to be inadequate,

he feared to be theatrical, he feared the quality of his voice, the quality of his wit, astonished, he turned to the man in yellow with a propitiatory gesture. 'For a moment,' he said, 'I must wait. I did not think it would be like this. I must think of the thing I have to say.'

While he was still hesitating there came an agitated messenger with news that the foremost aeroplanes were passing over Arawan.

'Arawan?' he said. 'Where is that? But anyhow, they are coming. They will be here. When?'

'By twilight.'

'Great God! In only a few hours. What news of the flying stages?' he asked.

'The people of the south-west wards are ready.'

'Ready!'

He turned impatiently to the blank circles of the lenses again.

'I suppose it must be a sort of speech. Would to God I knew certainly the thing that should be said! Aeroplanes at Arawan! They must have started before the main fleet. And the people only ready! Surely . . .'

'Oh! what does it matter whether I speak well or ill?' he said, and felt the light grow brighter.

He had framed some vague sentence of democratic sentiment when suddenly doubts overwhelmed him. His belief in his heroic quality and calling he found had altogether lost its assured conviction. The picture of a little strutting futility in a windy waste of incomprehensible destinies replaced it. Abruptly it was perfectly clear to him that this revolt against Ostrog was premature, foredoomed to failure, the impulse of passionate inadequacy against inevitable things. He thought of that swift flight of aeroplanes like the swoop of Fate towards him. He was astonished that he could have seen things in any other light. In that final emergency he debated, thrust debate resolutely aside, determined at all costs to go through with the thing he had undertaken. And he could find no word to begin. Even as he stood, awkward, hesitating, with an indiscrete apology for his inability trembling on his lips, came the noise of many people crying out, the running to and fro of feet. 'Wait,' cried someone, and a door opened. 'She is coming,' said the voices. Graham turned, and the watching lights waned.

Through the open doorway he saw a slight grey figure advancing across a spacious hall. His heart leapt. It was Helen Wotton. Behind and about her marched a riot of applause. The man in yellow came out of the nearer shadows into the circle of light.

'This is the girl who told us what Ostrog had done,' he said.

Her face was aflame, and the heavy coils of her black hair fell about her shoulders. The folds of the soft silk robe she wore streamed from her and floated in the rhythm of her advance. She drew nearer and nearer, and his heart was beating fast. All his doubts were gone. The shadow of the doorway

fell athwart her face and she was near him. 'You have not betrayed us?' she
cried. 'You are with us?'

'Where have you been?' said Graham.

'At the office of the south-west wards. Until ten minutes since I did not
know you had returned. I went to the office of the south-west wards to find
the Ward Leaders in order that they might tell the people.'

'I came back so soon as I heard—.'

'I knew,' she cried, 'knew you would be with us. And it was I – it was I
that told them. They have risen. All the world is rising. The people have
awakened. Thank God that I did not act in vain! You are Master still.'

'You told them' he said slowly, and he saw that in spite of her steady eyes
her lips trembled and her throat rose and fell.

'I told them. I knew of the order. I was here. I heard that the Negroes
were to come to London to guard you and to keep the people down – to
keep you a prisoner. And I stopped it. I came out and told the people. And
you are Master still.'

Graham glanced at the black lenses of the cameras, the vast listening
ears, and back to her face. 'I am Master still,' he said slowly, and the swift
rush of a fleet of aeroplanes passed across his thoughts.

'And you did this? You, who are the niece of Ostrog.'

'For you,' she cried. 'For you! That you for whom the world has waited
should not be cheated of your power.'

Graham stood for a space, wordless, regarding her. His doubts and ques-
tionings had fled before her presence. He remembered the things that he
had meant to say. He faced the cameras again and the light about him grew
brighter. He turned again towards her.

'You have saved me,' he said; 'you have saved my power. And the battle
is beginning. God knows what this night will see – but not dishonour.'

He paused. He addressed himself to the unseen multitudes who stared
upon him through those grotesque black eyes. At first he spoke slowly. 'Men
and women of the new age,' he said; 'you have arisen to do battle for the
race. . . . There is no easy victory before us.'

He stopped to gather words. The thoughts that had been in his mind
before she came returned, but transfigured, no longer touched with the
shadow of a possible irrelevance. 'This night is a beginning,' he cried. 'This
battle that is coming, this battle that rushes upon us tonight, is only a
beginning. All your lives, it may be, you must fight. Take no thought though
I am beaten, though I am utterly overthrown.'

He found the thing in his mind too vague for words. He paused momen-
tarily, and broke into vague exhortations, and then a rush of speech came
upon him. Much that he said was but the humanitarian commonplace of a
vanished age, but the conviction of his voice touched it to vitality. He stated
the case of the old days to the people of the new age, to the girl at his side.

'I come out of the past to you,' he said, 'with the memory of an age that hoped. My age was an age of dreams – of beginnings, an age of noble hopes; throughout the world we had made an end of slavery; throughout the world we had spread the desire and anticipation that wars might cease, that all men and women might live nobly, in freedom and peace. . . . So we hoped in the days that are past. And what of those hopes? How is it with man after two hundred years?

'Great cities, vast powers, a collective greatness beyond our dreams. For that we did not work, and that has come. But how is it with the little lives that make up this greater life? How is it with the common lives? As it has ever been – sorrow and labour, lives cramped and unfulfilled, lives tempted by power, tempted by wealth, and gone to waste and folly. The old faiths have faded and changed, the new faith—. Is there a new faith?'

Things that he had long wished to believe, he found that he believed. He plunged at belief and seized it, and clung for a time at her level. He spoke gustily, in broken incomplete sentences, but with all his heart and strength, of this new faith within him. He spoke of the greatness of self-abnegation, of his belief in an immortal life of Humanity in which we live and move and have our being. His voice rose and fell, and the recording appliances hummed their hurried applause, dim attendants watched him out of the shadow. Through all those doubtful places his sense of that silent spectator beside him sustained his sincerity. For a few glorious moments he was carried away; he felt no doubt of his heroic quality, no doubt of his heroic words, he had it all straight and plain. His eloquence limped no longer. And at last he made an end to speaking. 'Here and now,' he cried, 'I make my will. All that is mine in the world I give to the people of the world. All that is mine in the world I give to the people of the world. I give it to you, and myself I give to you. And as God wills, I will live for you, or I will die.'

He ended with a florid gesture and turned about. He found the light of his present exaltation reflected in the face of the girl. Their eyes met; her eyes were swimming with tears of enthusiasm. They seemed to be urged towards each other. They clasped hands and stood gripped, facing one another, in an eloquent silence. She whispered. 'I knew,' she whispered. 'I knew.' He could not speak, he crushed her hand in his. His mind was the theatre of gigantic passions.

The man in yellow was beside them. Neither had noted his coming. He was saying that the south-west Wards were marching. 'I never expected it so soon,' he cried. 'They have done wonders. You must send them a word to help them on their way.'

Graham dropped Helen's hand and stared at him absent-mindedly. Then with a start he returned to his previous preoccupation about the flying stages.

'Yes,' he said. 'That is good, that is good.' He weighed a message. 'Tell them – well done South-West.'

He turned his eyes to Helen Wotton again. His face expressed his struggle between conflicting ideas. 'We must capture the flying stages,' he explained. 'Unless we can do that they will land Negroes. At all costs we must prevent that.'

He felt even as he spoke that this was not what had been in his mind before the interruption. He saw a touch of surprise in her eyes. She seemed about to speak and a shrill bell drowned her voice.

It occurred to Graham that she expected him to lead these marching people, that that was the thing he had to do. He made the offer abruptly. He addressed the man in yellow, but he spoke to her. He saw her face respond. 'Here I am doing nothing,' he said.

'It is impossible,' protested the man in yellow. 'It is a fight in a warren. Your place is here.'

He explained elaborately. He motioned towards the room where Graham must wait, he insisted no other course was possible. 'We must know where you are,' he said. 'At any moment a crisis may arise needing your presence and decision.' The room was a luxurious little apartment with news machines and a broken mirror that had once been *en rapport* with the crow's nest specula. It seemed a matter of course to Graham that Helen should stop with him.

A picture had drifted through his mind of such a vast dramatic struggle as the masses in the ruins had suggested. But here was no spectacular battlefield such as he imagined. Instead was seclusion – and suspense. It was only as the afternoon wore on that he pieced together a truer picture of the fight that was raging, inaudibly and invisibly, within four miles of him, beneath the Roehampton stage. A strange and unprecedented contest it was, a battle that was a hundred thousand little battles, a battle in a sponge of ways and channels, fought out of sight of sky or sun under the electric glare, fought out in a vast confusion by multitudes untrained in arms, led chiefly by acclamation, multitudes dulled by mindless labour and enervated by the tradition of two hundred years of servile security against multitudes demoralized by lives of venial privilege and sensual indulgence. They had no artillery, no differentiation into this force or that; the only weapon on either side was the little green metal carbine, whose secret manufacture and sudden distribution in enormous quantities had been one of Ostrog's culminating moves against the Council. Few had had any experience with this weapon, many had never discharged one, many who carried it came unprovided with ammunition; never was wilder firing in the history of warfare. It was a battle of amateurs, a hideous experimental warfare, armed rioters fighting armed rioters, armed rioters swept forward by the words and fury of a song, by the tramping sympathy of their numbers, pouring in countless myriads towards the smaller ways, the disabled lifts, the galleries slippery with blood, the halls and passages choked with smoke,

beneath the flying stages, to learn there when retreat was hopeless the ancient mysteries of warfare. And overhead save for a few sharpshooters upon the roof spaces and for a few bands and threads of vapour that multiplied and darkened towards the evening, the day was a clear serenity. Ostrog it seems had no bombs at command and in all the earlier phases of the battle the aeropiles played no part. Not the smallest cloud was there to break the empty brilliance of the sky. It seemed as though it held itself vacant until the aeroplanes should come.

Ever and again there was news of these, drawing nearer, from this Mediterranean port and then that, and presently from the south of France. But of the new guns that Ostrog had made and which were known to be in the city came no news in spite of Graham's urgency, nor any report of successes from the dense felt of fighting strands about the flying stages. Section after section of the Labour Societies reported itself assembled, reported itself marching, and vanished from knowledge into the labyrinth of that warfare What was happening there? Even the busy Ward leaders did not know. In spite of the opening and closing of doors, the hasty messengers, the ringing of bells and the perpetual clitter-clack of recording implements, Graham felt isolated, strangely inactive, inoperative.

Their isolation seemed at times the strangest, the most unexpected of all the things that had happened since his awakening. It had something of the quality of that inactivity that comes in dreams. A tumult, the stupendous realization of a world struggle between Ostrog and himself, and then this confined quiet little room with its mouthpieces and bells and broken mirror!

Now the door would be closed and they were alone together; they seemed sharply marked off then from all the unprecedented world storm that rushed together without, vividly aware of one another, only concerned with one another. Then the door would open again, messengers would enter, or a sharp bell would stab their quiet privacy, and it was like a window in a well built brightly lit house flung open suddenly to a hurricane. The dark hurry and tumult, the stress and vehemence of the battle rushed in and overwhelmed them. They were no longer persons but mere spectators, mere impressions of a tremendous convulsion. They became unreal even to themselves, miniatures of personality, indescribably small, and the two antagonistic realities, the only realities in being were first the city, that throbbed and roared yonder in a belated frenzy of defence and secondly the aeroplanes hurling inexorably towards them over the round shoulder of the world.

At first their mood had been one of exalted confidence, a great pride had possessed them, a pride in one another for the greatness of the issues they had challenged. At first he had walked the room eloquent with a transitory persuasion of his tremendous destiny. But slowly uneasy intimations of their coming defeat touched his spirit. There came a long period in which they were alone. He changed his theme, became egotistical, spoke

of the wonder of his sleep, of the little life of his memories, remote yet minute and clear, like something seen through an inverted opera-glass, and all the brief play of desires and errors that had made his former life. She said little, but the emotion in her face followed the tones in his voice, and it seemed to him he had at last a perfect understanding. He reverted from pure reminiscence to that sense of greatness she imposed upon him. 'And through it all, this destiny was before me,' he said; 'this vast inheritance of which I did not dream.'

Insensibly their heroic preoccupation with the revolutionary struggle passed to the question of their relationship. He began to question her. She told him of the days before his awakening, spoke with a brief vividness of the girlish dreams that had given a bias to her life, of the incredulous emotions his awakening had aroused. She told him too of a tragic circumstance of her girlhood that had darkened her life, quickened her sense of injustice and opened her heart prematurely to the wider sorrows of the world. For a little time, so far as he was concerned, the great war about them was but the vast ennobling background to these personal things.

In an instant these personal relations were submerged. There came messengers to tell that a great fleet of aeroplanes was rushing between the sky and Avignon. He went to the crystal dial in the corner and assured himself that the thing was so. He went to the chart room and consulted a map to measure the distances of Avignon, New Arawan, and London. He made swift calculations. He went to the room of the Ward Leaders to ask for news of the fight for the stages – and there was no one there. After a time he came back to her.

His face had changed. It had dawned upon him that the struggle was perhaps more than half over, that Ostrog was holding his own, that the arrival of the aeroplanes would mean a panic that might leave him helpless. A chance phrase in the message had given him a glimpse of the reality that came. Each of these soaring giants bore its thousand half savage Negroes to the death grapple of the city. Suddenly his humanitarian enthusiasm showed flimsy. Only two of the Ward Leaders were in their room, when presently he repaired thither, the Hall of the Atlas seemed empty. He fancied a change in the bearing of the attendants in the outer rooms. A sombre disillusionment darkened his mind. She looked at him anxiously when he returned to her.

'No news,' he said with an assumed carelessness in answer to her eyes.

Then he was moved to frankness. 'Or rather – bad news. We are losing. We are gaining no ground and the aeroplanes draw nearer and nearer.'

He walked the length of the room and turned.

'Unless we can capture those flying stages in the next hour – there will be horrible things. We shall be beaten.

'No!' she said. 'We have justice – we have the people. We have God on our side.'

'Ostrog has discipline – he has plans. Do you know, out there just now I felt—. When I heard that these aeroplanes were a stage nearer, I felt as if I were fighting the machinery of fate.'

She made no answer for a while. 'We have done right,' she said at last.

He looked at her doubtfully. 'We have done what we could. But does this depend upon us? Is it not an older sin, a wider sin?'

'What do you mean?' she asked.

'These blacks are savages, ruled by force, used as force. And they have been under the rule of the whites two hundred years. Is it not a race quarrel? The race sinned – the race pays.'

'But these labourers, these poor people of London—!'

'Vicarious atonement. To stand wrong is to share the guilt.'

She looked keenly at him, astonished at the new aspect he presented.

Without came the shrill ringing of a bell, the sound of feet and the gabble of a phonographic message. The man in yellow appeared. 'Yes?' said Graham.

'They are at Vichy.'

'Where are the attendants who were in the great Hall of the Atlas?' asked Graham abruptly.

Presently the Babble Machine rang again. 'We may win yet,' said the man in yellow, going out to it. 'If only we can find where Ostrog has hidden his guns. Everything hangs on that now. Perhaps this—'

Graham followed him. But the only news was of the aeroplanes. They had reached Orleans.

Graham returned to Helen. 'No news,' he said 'No news.'

'And we can do nothing?'

'Nothing.'

He paced impatiently. Suddenly the swift anger that was his nature swept upon him. 'Curse this complex world!' he cried. 'And all the inventions of men! That a man must die like a rat in a snare and never see his foe! Oh, for one blow! . . .'

He turned with an abrupt change in his manner. 'That's nonsense,' he said. 'I am a savage.'

He paced and stopped. 'After all London and Paris are only two cities. All the temperate zone has risen. What if London is doomed and Paris destroyed? These are but accidents.' Again came the mockery of news to call him to fresh enquiries. He returned with a graver face and sat down beside her.

'The end must be near,' he said. 'The people it seems have fought and died in tens of thousands, the ways about Roehampton must be like a smoked beehive. And they have died in vain. They are still only at the sub stage. The aeroplanes are near Paris. Even were a gleam of success to come now, there would be nothing to do, there would be no time to do anything before they were upon us. The guns that might have saved us are mislaid. Mislaid!

Think of the disorder of things! Think of this foolish tumult, that cannot even find its weapons! Oh, for one aeropile – just one! For the want of that I am beaten. Humanity is beaten and our cause is lost! My kingship, my headlong foolish kingship will not last a night. And I have egged on the people to fight—.'

'They would have fought anyhow.'

'I doubt it. I have come among them—'

'No,' she cried, 'not that. If defeat comes – if you die—. But even that cannot be, it cannot be, after all these years.'

'Ah! We have meant well. But – do you indeed believe—?'

'If they defeat you,' she cried, 'you have spoken. Your word has gone like a great wind through the world, fanning liberty into a flame. What if the flame sputters a little! Nothing can change the spoken word. Your message will have gone forth . . .'

'To what end? It may be. It may be. You know I said, when you told me of these things dear God! but that was scarcely a score of hours ago! – I said that I had not your faith. Well – at any rate there is nothing to do now. . . .'

'You have not my faith! Do you mean—? You are sorry?'

'No,' he said hurriedly, 'no! Before God – no!' His voice changed. 'But—. I think – I have been indiscreet. I knew little – I grasped too hastily. . . .'

He paused. He was ashamed of this avowal. 'There is one thing that makes up for all. I have known you. Across this gulf of time I have come to you. The rest is done. It is done. With you, too, it has been something more – or something less—'

He paused with his face searching hers, and without clamoured the unheeded message that the aeroplanes were rising into the sky of Amiens.

She put her hand to her throat, and her lips were white. She stared before her as if she saw some horrible possibility. Suddenly her features changed. 'Oh, but I have been honest!' she cried, and then, 'Have I been honest? I loved the world and freedom, I hated cruelty and oppression. Surely it was that.'

'Yes,' he said, 'yes. And we have done what it lay in us to do. We have given our message, our message! We have started Armageddon! But now—. Now that we have, it may be our last hour, together, now that all these greater things are done. . . .'

He stopped. She sat in silence. Her face was a white riddle.

For a moment they heeded nothing of a sudden stir outside, a running to and fro, and cries. Then Helen started to an attitude of tense attention. 'It is—,' she cried and stood up, speechless, incredulous, triumphant. And Graham, too, heard. Metallic voices were shouting 'Victory!' Yes it was 'Victory!' He stood up also with the light of a desperate hope in his eyes.

Bursting through the curtains appeared the man in yellow, startled and

dishevelled with excitement. 'Victory,' he cried, 'victory! The people are winning. Ostrog's people have collapsed.'

She rose. 'Victory?' And her voice was hoarse and faint.

'What do you mean?' asked Graham. 'Tell me! What?'

'We have driven them out of the under galleries at Norwood, Streatham is afire and burning wildly, and Roehampton is ours. *Ours!* – And we have taken the aeropile that lay thereon.'

For an instant Graham and Helen stood in silence, their hearts were beating fast, they looked at one another. For one last moment there gleamed in Graham his dream of empire, of kingship, with Helen by his side. It gleamed, and passed.

A shrill bell rang. An agitated grey-headed man appeared from the room of the Ward Leaders. 'It is all over,' he cried.

'What matters it now that we have Roehampton? The aeroplanes have been sighted at Boulogne!'

'The Channel!' said the man in yellow. He calculated swiftly. 'Half an hour.'

'They still have three of the flying stages,' said the old man.

'Those guns?' cried Graham.

'We cannot mount them – in half an hour.'

'Do you mean they are found?'

'Too late,' said the old man.

'If we could stop them another hour!' cried the man in yellow.

'Nothing can stop them now,' said the old man, 'they have near a hundred aeroplanes in the first fleet.'

'Another hour?' asked Graham.

'To be so near!' said the Ward Leader. 'Now that we have found those guns. To be so near—. If once we could get them out upon the roof spaces.'

'How long would that take?' asked Graham suddenly.

'An hour – certainly.'

'Too late,' cried the Ward Leader, 'too late.'

'*Is* it too late?' said Graham. 'Even now—. An hour!'

He had suddenly perceived a possibility. He tried to speak calmly, but his face was white. 'There is one chance. You said there was an aeropile—?'

'On the Roehampton stage, Sire.'

'Smashed?'

'No. It is lying crossways to the carrier. It might be got upon the guides – easily. But there is no aeronaut—.'

Graham glanced at the two men and then at Helen. He spoke after a long pause. 'We have no aeronauts?'

'None.'

'The aeroplanes are clumsy,' he said thoughtfully, 'compared with the aeropiles.'

He turned suddenly to Helen. His decision was made. 'I must do it.'

'Do what?'

'Go to this flying stage – to this aeropile.'

'What do you mean?'

'I am an aeronaut. After all—. Those days for which you reproached me were not wasted.'

He turned to the old man in yellow. 'Put the aeropile upon the guides.'

The man in yellow hesitated.

'What do you mean to do?' cried Helen.

'This aeropile – it is a chance—.'

'You don't mean—?'

'To fight – yes. To fight in the air. I have thought before—. An aeroplane is a clumsy thing. A resolute man—!'

'But – never since flying began—' cried the man in yellow.

'There has been no need. But now the time has come. Tell them now – send them my message – to put it upon the guides.'

The old man dumbly interrogated the man in yellow, nodded, and hurried out.

Helen made a step towards Graham. Her face was white. 'But – How can one fight? You will be killed.'

'Perhaps. Yet, not to do it – or to let someone else attempt it—.'

He stopped, he could speak no more, he swept the alternative aside by a gesture, and they stood looking at one another.

'You are right,' she said at last in a low tone. 'You are right. If it can be done . . . must go.'

He moved a step towards her, and she stepped back, her white face struggled against him and resisted him. 'No,' she gasped. 'I cannot bear—. Go now.'

He extended his hands stupidly. She clenched her fists. 'Go now,' she cried. 'Go now.'

He hesitated and understood. He threw his hands up in a queer half-theatrical gesture. He had no word to say. He turned from her.

The man in yellow moved towards the door with clumsy belated tact. But Graham stepped past him. He went striding through the room where the Ward Leader bawled at a telephone directing that the aeropile should be put upon the guides.

The man in yellow glanced at Helen's still figure, hesitated and hurried after him. Graham did not once look back, he did not speak until the curtain of the ante-chamber of the great hall fell behind him. Then he turned his head with curt swift directions upon his bloodless lips.

CHAPTER XXIV

The Coming of the Aeroplanes

Two men in pale blue were lying in the irregular line that stretched along the edge of the captured Roehampton stage from end to end, grasping their carbines and peering into the shadows of the stage called Wimbledon Park. Now and then they spoke to one another. They spoke the mutilated English of their class and period. The fire of the Ostrogites had dwindled and ceased, and few of the enemy had been seen for some time. But the echoes of the fight that was going on now far below in the lower galleries of that stage, came every now and then between the staccato of shots from the popular side. One of these men was describing to the other how he had seen a man down below there dodge behind a girder, and had aimed at a guess and hit him cleanly as he dodged too far. 'He's down there still,' said the marksman. 'See that little patch. Yes. Between those bars.'

A few yards behind them lay a dead stranger, face upward to the sky, with the blue canvas of his jacket smoldering in a circle about the neat bullet hole on his chest. Close beside him a wounded man, with a leg swathed about, sat with an expressionless face and watched the progress of that burning. Gigantic behind them, athwart the carrier lay the captured aeropile.

'I can't see him *now*,' said the second man in a tone of provocation.

The marksman became foul-mouthed and high-voiced in his earnest endeavour to make things plain. And suddenly, interrupting him, came a noisy shouting from the substage.

'What's going on now,' he said, and raised himself on one arm to stare at the stairheads in the central groove of the stage. A number of blue figures were coming up these, and swarming across the stage to the aeropile.

'We don't want all these fools,' said his friend. 'They only crowd up and spoil shots. What are they after?'

'Ssh! – they're shouting something.'

The two men listened. The swarming new-comers had crowded densely about the aeropile. Three Ward Leaders, conspicuous by their black mantles and badges, clambered into the body and appeared above it. The rank and file flung themselves upon the vanes, gripping hold of the edges, until the entire outline of the thing was manned, in some places three deep. One of the marksmen knelt up. 'They're putting it on the carrier – that's what they're after.'

He rose to his feet, his friend rose also. 'What's the good?' said his friend. 'We've got no aeronauts.'

'That's what they're doing anyhow.' He looked at his rifle, looked at the struggling crowd, and suddenly turning to the wounded man. 'Mind these,

mate,' he said, handing his carbine and cartridge belt; and in a moment he
was running towards the aeropile. For a quarter of an hour he was a perspiring
Titan, lugging, thrusting, shouting and heeding shouts, and then the thing
was done, and he stood with a multitude of others cheering their own
achievement. By this time he knew, what indeed everyone in the city knew,
that the Master, raw learner though he was, intended to fly this machine
himself, was coming even now to take control of it, would let no other man
attempt it.

'He who takes the greatest danger, he who bears the heaviest burden,
that man is King,' so the Master was reported to have spoken. And even as
this man cheered, and while the beads of sweat still chased one another
from the disorder of his hair, he heard the thunder of a greater tumult, and
in fitful snatches the beat and impulse of the revolutionary song. He saw
through a gap in the people that a thick stream of heads still poured up the
stairway. 'The Master is coming,' shouted voices, 'the Master is coming,' and
the crowd about him grew denser and denser. He began to thrust himself
towards the central groove. 'The Master is coming!' 'The Sleeper, the Master!'
'God and the Master!' roared the voices.

And suddenly quite close to him were the black uniforms of the revolu-
tionary guard, and for the first and last time in his life he saw Graham, saw
him quite nearly. A tall, dark man in a flowing black robe, with a white,
resolute face and eyes fixed steadfastly before him; a man who for all the
little things about him held neither ears nor eyes nor thoughts. . . .

For all his days that man remembered the passing of Graham's bloodless
face. In a moment it had gone and he was fighting in the swaying crowd.
A lad weeping with terror thrust against him, pressing towards the stairways,
yelling 'Clear for the aeropile!' The bell that clears the flying stage became
a loud unmelodious clanging.

With that clanging in his ears Graham drew near the aeropile, marched
into the shadow of its tilting wing. He became aware that a number of
people about him were offering to accompany him, and waved their offers
aside. He wanted to think how one started the engine. The bell clanged
faster and faster, and the feet of the retreating people roared faster and
louder. The man in yellow was assisting him to mount through the ribs of
the body. He clambered into the aeronaut's place, fixing himself very care-
fully and deliberately. What was it? The man in yellow was pointing to two
aeropiles driving upward in the southern sky. No doubt they were looking
for the coming aeroplanes. That – presently – the thing to do now was to
start. Things were being shouted at him, questions, warnings. They bothered
him. He wanted to think about the aeropile, to recall every item of his
previous experience. He waved the people from him, saw the man in yellow
dropping off through the ribs, saw the crowd cleft down the line of the
girders by his gesture.

For a moment he was motionless, staring at the levers, the wheel by which the engine shifted, and all the delicate appliances of which he knew so little. His eye caught a spirit level with the bubble towards him, and he remembered something, spent a dozen seconds in swinging the engine forward until the bubble floated in the centre of the tube. He noted that the people were not shouting, knew they watched his deliberation. A bullet smashed on the bar above his head. Who fired? Was the line clear of people? He stood up to see and sat down again.

In another second the propeller was spinning, and he was rushing down the guides. He gripped the wheel and swung the engine back to lift the stem. Then it was the people shouted. In a moment he was throbbing with the quiver of the engine, and the shouts dwindled swiftly behind, rushed down to silence. The wind whistled over the edges of the screen, and the world sank away from him very swiftly.

Throb, throb, throb – throb, throb, throb; up he drove. He fancied himself free of all excitement, felt cool and deliberate. He lifted the stem still more, opened one valve on his left wing and swept round and up. He looked down with a steady head, and up. One of the Ostrogite aeropiles was driving across his course, so that he drove obliquely towards it and would pass below it at a steep angle. Its little aeronauts were peering down at him. What did they mean to do? His mind became active. One, he saw, held a weapon pointing, seemed prepared to fire. What did they think he meant to do? In a moment he understood their tactics, and his resolution was taken. His momentary lethargy was past. He opened two more valves to his left, swung round, end on to this hostile machine, closed his valves, and shot straight at it, stem and windscreen shielding him from the shot. They tilted a little as if to clear him. He flung up his stem.

Throb, throb, throb – pause – throb, throb – he set his teeth, his face into an involuntary grimace, and crash! He struck it! He struck upward beneath the nearer wing.

Very slowly the wing of his antagonist seemed to broaden as the impetus of his blow turned it up. He saw the full breadth of it and then it slid downward out of his sight.

He felt his stem going down, his hands tightened on the levers, whirled and rammed the engine back. He felt the jerk of a clearance, the nose of the machine jerked upward steeply, and for a moment he seemed to be lying on his back. The machine was reeling and staggering, it seemed to be dancing on its screw. He made a huge effort, hung for a moment on the levers, and slowly the engine came forward again. He was driving upward but no longer so steeply. He gasped for a moment and flung himself at the levers again. The wind whistled about him. One further effort and he was almost level. He could breathe. He turned his head for the first time to see what had become of his antagonists. Turned back to the levers for a moment and

looked again. For a moment he could have believed they were annihilated. And then he saw between the two stages to the east was a chasm, and down this something, a slender edge, fell swiftly and vanished, as a sixpence falls down a crack.

At first he did not understand, and then a wild joy possessed him. He shouted at the top of his voice, an inarticulate shout, and drove higher and higher up the sky. Throb, throb, throb, pause, throb, throb, throb. 'Where was the other aeropile?' he thought. 'They too—.' As he looked round the empty heavens he had a momentary fear that this machine had risen above him, and then he saw it alighting on the Norwood stage. They had meant shooting. To risk being rammed headlong two thousand feet in the air was beyond their latter-day courage. The combat was declined.

For a little while he circled, then swooped in a steep descent towards the westward stage. Throb throb throb, throb throb throb. The twilight was creeping on apace, the smoke from the Streatham stage that had been so dense and dark, was now a pillar of fire, and all the laced curves of the moving ways and the translucent roofs and domes and the chasms between the buildings were glowing softly now, lit by the tempered radiance of the electric light that the glare of the way overpowered. The three efficient stages that the Ostrogites held – for Wimbledon Park was useless because of the fire from Roehampton, and Streatham was a furnace – were glowing with guide lights for the coming aeroplanes. As he swept over the Roehampton stage he saw the dark masses of the people thereon. He heard a clap of frantic cheering, heard a bullet from the Wimbledon Park stage tweet through the air, and went beating up above the Surrey wastes. He felt a breath of wind from the south-west, and lifted his westward wing as he had learnt to do, and so drove upward heeling into the rare swift upper air. Throb throb throb – throb throb throb.

Up he drove and up, to that pulsating rhythm, until the country beneath was blue and indistinct, and London spread like a little map traced in light, like the mere model of a city near the brim of the horizon. The south-west was a sky of sapphire over the shadowy rim of the world, and ever as he drove upward the multitude of stars increased.

And behold! In the southward, low down and glittering swiftly nearer, were two little patches of nebulous light. And then two more, and then a nebulous glow of swiftly driving shapes. Presently he could count them. There were four and twenty. The first fleet of aeroplanes had come! Beyond appeared a yet greater glow.

He swept round in a half circle, staring at this advancing fleet. It flew in a wedge-like shape, a triangular flight of gigantic phosphorescent shapes sweeping nearer through the lower air. He made a swift calculation of their pace, and spun the little wheel that brought the engine forward. He touched a lever and the throbbing effort of the engine ceased. He began to fall, fell

swifter and swifter. He aimed at the apex of the wedge. He dropped like a stone through the whistling air. It seemed scarce a second from that soaring moment before he struck the foremost aeroplane.

No man of all that black multitude saw the coming of his fate, no man among them dreamt of the hawk that struck downward upon him out of the sky. Those who were not limp in the agonies of air-sickness, were craning their black necks and staring to see the filmy city that was rising out of the haze, the rich and splendid city to which 'Massa Boss' had brought their obedient muscles. Bright teeth gleamed and the glossy faces shone. They had heard of Paris. They knew they were to have lordly times among the 'poor white' trash.

And suddenly Graham struck them.

He had aimed at the body of the aeroplane, but at the very last instant a better idea had flashed into his mind. He twisted about and struck near the edge of the starboard wing with all his accumulated weight. He was jerked back as he struck. His prow went gliding across its smooth expanse towards the rim. He felt the forward rush of the huge fabric sweeping him and his aeropile along with it, and for a moment that seemed an age he could not tell what was happening. He heard a thousand throats yelling, and perceived that his machine was balanced on the edge of the gigantic float, and driving down, down; glanced over his shoulder and saw the back-bone of the aeroplane and the opposite float swaying up. He had a vision through the ribs of sliding chairs, staring faces, and hands clutching at the tilting guide bars. The fenestrations in the further float flashed open as the aeronaut tried to right her. Beyond, he saw a second aeroplane leaping steeply to escape the whirl of its heeling fellow. The broad area of swaying wings seemed to jerk upward. He felt his aeropile had dropped clear, that the monstrous fabric, clean overturned, hung like a sloping wall above him.

He did not clearly understand that he had struck the side float of the aeroplane and slipped off, but he perceived that he was flying free on the down glide and rapidly nearing earth. What had he done? His heart throbbed like a noisy engine in his throat and for a perilous instant he could not move his levers because of the paralysis of his hands. He wrenched the levers to throw his engine back, fought for two seconds against the weight of it, felt himself righting, driving horizontally, set the engine beating again.

He looked upward and saw two aeroplanes glide shouting far overhead, looked back, and saw the main body of the fleet opening out and rushing upward and outward; saw the one he had struck fall edgewise on and strike like a gigantic knife-blade along the wind-wheels below it.

He put down his stern and looked again. He drove up heedless of his direction as he watched. He saw the wind-vanes give, saw the huge fabric strike the earth, saw its downward vanes crumple with the weight of its descent, and then the whole mass turned over and smashed, upside down, upon the sloping wheels. Throb, throb, throb, pause. Suddenly from the

heaving wreckage a thin tongue of white fire licked up towards the zenith. And then he was aware of a huge mass flying through the air towards him, and turned upwards just in time to escape the charge – if it was a charge – of a second aeroplane. It whirled by below, sucked him down a fathom, and nearly turned him over in the gust of its close passage.

He became aware of three others rushing towards him, aware of the urgent necessity of beating above them. Aeroplanes were all about him, circling wildly to avoid him, as it seemed. They drove past him, above, below, eastward and westward. Far away to the westward was the sound of a collision, and two falling flares. Far away to the southward a second squadron was coming. Steadily he beat upward. Presently all the aeroplanes were below him, but for a moment he doubted the height he had of them, and did not swoop again. And then he came down upon a second victim and all its load of soldiers saw him coming. The big machine heeled and swayed as the fear-maddened men scrambled to the stern for their weapons. A score of bullets sung through the air, and there flashed a star in the thick glass windscreen that protected him. The aeroplane slowed and dropped to foil his stroke, and dropped too low. Just in time he saw the wind-wheels of Bromley hill rushing up towards him, and spun about and up as the aeroplane he had chased crashed among them. All its voices wove into a felt of yelling. The great fabric seemed to be standing on end for a second among the heeling and splintering vanes, and then it flew to pieces. Huge splinters came flying through the air, its engines burst like shells. A hot rush of flame shot overhead into the darkling sky.

'Two!' he cried, with a bomb from overhead bursting as it fell, and forthwith he was beating up again. A glorious exhilaration possessed him now, a giant activity. His troubles about humanity, about his inadequacy, were gone for ever. He was a man in battle rejoicing in his power. Aeroplanes seemed radiating from him in every direction, intent only upon avoiding him, the yelling of their packed passengers came in short gusts as they swept by. He chose his third quarry, struck hastily and did but turn it on edge. It escaped him, to smash against the tall cliff of London wall. Flying from that impact he skimmed the darkling ground so nearly he could see a frightened rabbit bolting up a slope. He jerked up steeply, and found himself driving over south London with the air about him vacant. To the right of him a wild riot of signal rockets from the Ostrogites banged tumultuously in the sky. To the south the wreckage of half a dozen air-ships flamed, and east and west and north the air-ships fled before him. They drove away to the east and north, and went about in the south, for they could not pause in the air. In their present confusion any attempt at evolution would have meant disastrous collisions. He could scarcely realize the thing he had done. In every quarter aeroplanes were receding. They were receding. They dwindled smaller and smaller. They were in flight!

He passed two hundred feet or so above the Roehampton stage. It was black with people and noisy with their frantic shouting. But why was the Wimbledon Park stage black and cheering, too? The smoke and flame of Streatham now hid the three further stages. He curved about and rose to see them and the northern quarters. First came the square masses of Shooter's Hill into sight from behind the smoke, lit and orderly with the aeroplane that had landed and its disembarking Negroes. Then came Blackheath, and then under the corner of the reek the Norwood stage. On Blackheath no aeroplane had landed but an aeropile lay upon the guides. Norwood was covered by a swarm of little figures running to and fro in a passionate confusion. Why? Abruptly he understood. The stubborn defence of the flying stages was over, the people were pouring into the under-ways of these last strongholds of Ostrog's usurpation. And then, from far away on the northern border of the city, full of glorious import to him, came a sound, a signal, a note of triumph, the leaden thud of a gun. His lips fell apart, his face was disturbed with emotion.

He drew an immense breath. 'They win,' he shouted to the empty air; 'The people win!' The sound of a second gun came like an answer. And then he saw the aeropile on Blackheath was running down its guides to launch. It lifted clean and rose. It shot up into the air, driving straight southward and away from him.

In an instant it came to him what this meant. It must needs be Ostrog in flight. He shouted and dropped towards it. He had the momentum of his elevation and fell slanting down the air and very swiftly. It rose steeply at his approach. He allowed for its velocity and drove straight upon it.

It suddenly became a mere flat edge, and behold! He was past it, and driving headlong down with all the force of his futile blow.

He was furiously angry. He reeled the engine back along its shaft and went circling up. He saw Ostrog's machine beating up a spiral before him. He rose straight towards it, won above it by virtue of the impetus of his swoop and by the advantage and weight of a man. He dropped headlong – dropped and missed again! As he rushed past he saw the face of Ostrog's aeronaut confident and cool and in Ostrog's attitude a wincing resolution. Ostrog was looking steadfastly away from him – to the south. He realized with a gleam of wrath how bungling his flight must be. Below he saw the Croydon hills. He jerked upwards and once more he gained on his enemy.

He glanced over his shoulder and his attention was arrested by a strange thing. The eastward stage, the one on Shooter's Hill, appeared to lift; a flash changing to a tall grey shape, a cowled figure of smoke and dust, jerked into the air. For a moment this cowled figure stood motionless, dropping huge masses of metal from its shoulders, and then it began to uncoil a dense head of smoke. The people had blown it up, aeroplane and all! As suddenly a second flash and grey shape sprang up from the Norwood stage. And even

as he stared at this came a dead report, and the air wave of the first explo-
sion struck him. He was flung up and sideways.

For a moment the aeropile fell nearly edgewise with her nose down, and
seemed to hesitate whether to overset altogether. He stood on his wind-
shield wrenching the wheel that swayed up over his head. And then the
shock of the second explosion took his machine sideways.

He found himself clinging to one of the ribs of his machine, and the air
was blowing past him and *upwards*. He seemed to be hanging quite still in
the air, with the wind blowing up past him. It occurred to him that he was
falling. Then he was sure that he was falling. He could not look down.

He found himself recapitulating with incredible swiftness all that had
happened since his awakening, the days of doubt, the days of Empire, and
at last the tumultuous discovery of Ostrog's calculated treachery, he was
beaten but London was saved. London was saved!

The thought had a quality of utter unreality. Who was he? Why was he
holding so tightly with his hands? Why could he not leave go? In such a fall
as this countless dreams have ended. But in a moment he would wake. . . .

His thoughts ran swifter and swifter. He wondered if he should see Helen
again. It seemed so unreasonable that he should not see her again. It *must*
be a dream! Yet surely he would meet her. She at least was real. She was
real. He would wake and meet her.

Although he could not look at it, he was suddenly aware that the earth
was very near.

THE WORLD
SET FREE

We Are All Things That Make And Pass,
Striving Upon A Hidden Mission,
Out To The Open Sea.

To Frederick Soddy's 'Interpretation Of Radium'
This Story, Which Owes Long Passages
To The Eleventh Chapter Of That Book,
Acknowledges And Inscribes Itself

CONTENTS

PREFACE

The World Set Free was written in 1913 and published early in 1914, and it is the latest of a series of three fantasias of possibility, stories which all turn on the possible developments in the future of some contemporary force or group of forces. *The World Set Free* was written under the immediate shadow of the Great War. Every intelligent person in the world felt that disaster was impending and knew no way of averting it, but few of us realized in the earlier half of 1914 how near the crash was to us. The reader will be amused to find that here it is put off until the year 1956. He may naturally want to know the reason for what will seem now a quite extraordinary delay. As a prophet, the author must confess he has always been inclined to be rather a slow prophet. The war aeroplane in the world of reality, for example, beat the forecast in Anticipations by about twenty years or so. I suppose a desire not to shock the sceptical reader's sense of use and wont and perhaps a less creditable disposition to hedge, have something to do with this dating forward of one's main events, but in the particular case of *The World Set Free* there was, I think, another motive in holding the Great War back, and that was to allow the chemist to get well forward with his discovery of the release of atomic energy. 1956 – or for that matter 2056 – may be none too late for that crowning revolution in human potentialities. And apart from this procrastination of over forty years, the guess at the opening phase of the war was fairly lucky; the forecast of an alliance of the Central Empires, the opening campaign through the Netherlands, and the despatch of the British Expeditionary Force were all justified before the book had been published six months. And the opening section of Chapter II remains now, after the reality has happened, a fairly adequate diagnosis of the essentials of the matter. One happy hit (in Chapter II, Section 2), on which the writer may congratulate himself, is the forecast that under modern conditions it would be quite impossible for any great general to emerge to supremacy and concentrate the enthusiasm of the armies of either side. There could be no Alexanders or Napoleons. And we soon heard the scientific corps muttering, 'These old fools,' exactly as it is here foretold.

These, however, are small details, and the misses in the story far outnumber the hits. It is the main thesis which is still of interest now; the thesis that because of the development of scientific knowledge, separate sovereign states and separate sovereign empires are no longer possible in the world, that to attempt to keep on with the old system is to heap disaster upon disaster for mankind and perhaps to destroy our race altogether. The remaining interest of this book now is the sustained validity of this thesis and the discussion of the possible ending of war on the earth. I have supposed a sort of epidemic of sanity to break out among the rulers of states

and the leaders of mankind. I have represented the native common sense of the French mind and of the English mind – for manifestly King Egbert is meant to be 'God's Englishman' – leading mankind towards a bold and resolute effort of salvage and reconstruction. Instead of which, as the school book footnotes say, compare today's newspaper. Instead of a frank and honourable gathering of leading men, Englishman meeting German and Frenchman Russian, brothers in their offences and in their disaster, upon the hills of Brissago, beheld in Geneva at the other end of Switzerland a poor little League of (Allied) Nations (excluding the United States, Russia and most of the 'subject peoples' of the world), meeting obscurely amidst a worldwide disregard to make impotent gestures at the leading problems of the debacle. Either the disaster has not been vast enough yet or it has not been swift enough to inflict the necessary moral shock and achieve the necessary moral revulsion. Just as the world of 1913 was used to an increasing prosperity and thought that increase would go on for ever, so now it would seem the world is growing accustomed to a steady glide towards social disintegration, and thinks that that too can go on continually and never come to a final bump. So soon do use and wont establish themselves, and the most flaming and thunderous of lessons pale into disregard.

The question whether a Leblanc is still possible, the question whether it is still possible to bring about an outbreak of creative sanity in mankind, to avert this steady glide to destruction, is now one of the most urgent in the world. It is clear that the writer is temperamentally disposed to hope that there is such a possibility. But he has to confess that he sees few signs of any such breadth of understanding and steadfastness of will as an effectual effort to turn the rush of human affairs demands. The inertia of dead ideas and old institutions carries us on towards the rapids. Only in one direction is there any plain recognition of the idea of a human commonweal as some-thing overriding any national and patriotic consideration, and that is in the working class movement throughout the world. And labour internationalism is closely bound up with conceptions of a profound social revolution. If world peace is to be attained through labour internationalism, it will have to be attained at the price of the completest social and economic reconstruction and by passing through a phase of revolution that will certainly be violent, that may be very bloody, which may be prolonged through a long period, and may in the end fail to achieve anything but social destruction. Nevertheless, the fact remains that it is in the labour class, and the labour class alone, that any conception of a world rule and a world peace has so far appeared. The dream of *The World Set Free*, a dream of highly educated and highly favoured leading and ruling men, voluntarily setting themselves to the task of reshaping the world, has thus far remained a dream.

H. G. Wells. Easton Glebe, Dunmow, 1921.

PRELUDE

The Sun Snarers

SECTION I

THE history of mankind is the history of the attainment of external power. Man is the tool-using, fire-making animal. From the outset of his terrestrial career we find him supplementing the natural strength and bodily weapons of a beast by the heat of burning and the rough implement of stone. So he passed beyond the ape. From that he expands. Presently he added to himself the power of the horse and the ox, he borrowed the carrying strength of water and the driving force of the wind, he quickened his fire by blowing, and his simple tools, pointed first with copper and then with iron, increased and varied and became more elaborate and efficient. He sheltered his heat in houses and made his way easier by paths and roads. He complicated his social relationships and increased his efficiency by the division of labour. He began to store up knowledge. Contrivance followed contrivance, each making it possible for a man to do more. Always down the lengthening record, save for a set-back ever and again, he is doing more. . . . A quarter of a million years ago the utmost man was a savage, a being scarcely articulate, sheltering in holes in the rocks, armed with a rough-hewn flint or a fire-pointed stick, naked, living in small family groups, killed by some younger man so soon as his first virile activity declined. Over most of the great wildernesses of earth you would have sought him in vain; only in a few temperate and sub-tropical river valleys would you have found the squatting lairs of his little herds, a male, a few females, a child or so.

He knew no future then, no kind of life except the life he led. He fled the cave-bear over the rocks full of iron ore and the promise of sword and spear; he froze to death upon a ledge of coal; he drank water muddy with the clay that would one day make cups of porcelain; he chewed the ear of wild wheat he had plucked and gazed with a dim speculation in his eyes at the birds that soared beyond his reach. Or suddenly he became aware of the scent of another male and rose up roaring, his roars the formless precursors of moral admonitions. For he was a great individualist, that original, he suffered none other than himself.

So through the long generations, this heavy precursor, this ancestor of all of us, fought and bred and perished, changing almost imperceptibly.

Yet he changed. That keen chisel of necessity which sharpened the tiger's claw age by age and fined down the clumsy Orchippus to the swift grace of the horse, was at work upon him – is at work upon him still. The clumsier

and more stupidly fierce among him were killed soonest and oftenest; the finer hand, the quicker eye, the bigger brain, the better balanced body prevailed; age by age, the implements were a little better made, the man a little more delicately adjusted to his possibilities. He became more social; his herd grew larger; no longer did each man kill or drive out his growing sons; a system of taboos made them tolerable to him, and they revered him alive and soon even after he was dead, and were his allies against the beasts and the rest of mankind. (But they were forbidden to touch the women of the tribe, they had to go out and capture women for themselves, and each son fled from his stepmother and hid from her lest the anger of the Old Man should be roused. All the world over, even to this day, these ancient inevitable taboos can be traced.) And now instead of caves came huts and hovels, and the fire was better tended and there were wrappings and garments; and so aided, the creature spread into colder climates, carrying food with him, storing food – until sometimes the neglected grass-seed sprouted again and gave a first hint of agriculture.

And already there were the beginnings of leisure and thought.

Man began to think. There were times when he was fed, when his lusts and his fears were all appeased, when the sun shone upon the squatting-place and dim stirrings of speculation lit his eyes. He scratched upon a bone and found resemblance and pursued it and began pictorial art, moulded the soft, warm clay of the river brink between his fingers, and found a pleasure in its patternings and repetitions, shaped it into the form of vessels, and found that it would hold water. He watched the streaming river, and wondered from what bountiful breast this incessant water came; he blinked at the sun and dreamt that perhaps he might snare it and spear it as it went down to its resting-place amidst the distant hills. Then he was roused to convey to his brother that once indeed he had done so – at least that someone had done so – he mixed that perhaps with another dream almost as daring, that one day a mammoth had been beset; and therewith began fiction – pointing a way to achievement – and the august prophetic procession of tales.

For scores and hundreds of centuries, for myriads of generations that life of our fathers went on. From the beginning to the ripening of that phase of human life, from the first clumsy eolith of rudely chipped flint to the first implements of polished stone, was two or three thousand centuries, ten or fifteen thousand generations. So slowly, by human standards, did humanity gather itself together out of the dim intimations of the beast. And that first glimmering of speculation, that first story of achievement, that story-teller bright-eyed and flushed under his matted hair, gesticulating to his gaping, incredulous listener, gripping his wrist to keep him attentive, was the most marvellous beginning this world has ever seen. It doomed the mammoths, and it began the setting of that snare that shall catch the sun.

SECTION 2

That dream was but a moment in a man's life, whose proper business it seemed was to get food and kill his fellows and beget after the manner of all that belongs to the fellowship of the beasts. About him, hidden from him by the thinnest of veils, were the untouched sources of Power, whose magnitude we scarcely do more than suspect even today, Power that could make his every conceivable dream come real. But the feet of the race were in the way of it, though he died blindly unknowing.

At last, in the generous levels of warm river valleys, where food is abundant and life very easy, the emerging human overcoming his earlier jealousies, becoming, as necessity persecuted him less urgently, more social and tolerant and amenable, achieved a larger community. There began a division of labour, certain of the older men specialized in knowledge and direction, a strong man took the fatherly leadership in war, and priest and king began to develop their roles in the opening drama of man's history. The priest's solicitude was seed-time and harvest and fertility, and the king ruled peace and war. In a hundred river valleys about the warm, temperate zone of the earth there were already towns and temples, a score of thousand years ago. They flourished unrecorded, ignoring the past and unsuspicious of the future, for as yet writing had still to begin.

Very slowly did man increase his demand upon the illimitable wealth of Power that offered itself on every hand to him. He tamed certain animals, he developed his primordially haphazard agriculture into a ritual, he added first one metal to his resources and then another, until he had copper and tin and iron and lead and gold and silver to supplement his stone, he hewed and carved wood, made pottery, paddled down his river until he came to the sea, discovered the wheel and made the first roads. But his chief activity for a hundred centuries and more was the subjugation of himself and others to larger and larger societies. The history of man is not simply the conquest of external power; it is first the conquest of those distrusts and fiercenesses, that self-concentration and intensity of animalism, that tie his hands from taking his inheritance. The ape in us still resents association. From the dawn of the age of polished stone to the achievement of the Peace of the World, man's dealings were chiefly with himself and his fellow man, trading, bargaining, law-making, propitiating, enslaving, conquering, exterminating, and every little increment in Power, he turned at once and always turns to the purposes of this confused elaborate struggle to socialize. To incorporate and comprehend his fellow men into a community of purpose became the last and greatest of his instincts. Already before the last polished phase of the stone age was over he had become a political animal. He made astonishingly far-reaching discoveries within himself, first of counting and then of writing and making records, and with that his town communities began to stretch out to dominion; in the valleys of the Nile, the Euphrates, and

the great Chinese rivers, the first empires and the first written laws had their beginnings. Men specialized for fighting and rule as soldiers and knights. Later, as ships grew seaworthy, the Mediterranean which had been a barrier became a highway, and at last out of a tangle of pirate polities came the great struggle of Carthage and Rome. The history of Europe is the history of the victory and breaking up of the Roman Empire. Every ascendant monarch in Europe up to the last, aped Caesar and called himself Kaiser or Tsar or Imperator or Kasir-i-Hind. Measured by the duration of human life it is a vast space of time between that first dynasty in Egypt and the coming of the aeroplane, but by the scale that looks back to the makers of the eoliths, it is all of it a story of yesterday.

Now during this period of two hundred centuries or more, this period of the warring states, while men's minds were chiefly preoccupied by politics and mutual aggression, their progress in the acquirement of external Power was slow – rapid in comparison with the progress of the old stone age, but slow in comparison with this new age of systematic discovery in which we live. They did not very greatly alter the weapons and tactics of warfare, the methods of agriculture, seamanship, their knowledge of the habitable globe, or the devices and utensils of domestic life between the days of the early Egyptians and the days when Christopher Columbus was a child. Of course, there were inventions and changes, but there were also retrogressions; things were found out and then forgotten again; it was, on the whole, a progress, but it contained no steps; the peasant life was the same, there were already priests and lawyers and town craftsmen and territorial lords and rulers, doctors, wise women, soldiers and sailors in Egypt and China and Assyria and south-eastern Europe at the beginning of that period, and they were doing much the same things and living much the same life as they were in Europe in A.D. 1500. The English excavators of the year A.D. 1900 could delve into the remains of Babylon and Egypt and disinter legal documents, domestic accounts, and family correspondence that they could read with the completest sympathy. There were great religious and moral changes throughout the period, empires and republics replaced one another, Italy tried a vast experiment in slavery, and indeed slavery was tried again and again and failed and failed and was still to be tested again and rejected again in the New World; Christianity and Mohammedanism swept away a thousand more specialized cults, but essentially these were progressive adaptations of mankind to material conditions that must have seemed fixed for ever. The idea of revolutionary changes in the material conditions of life would have been entirely strange to human thought through all that time.

Yet the dreamer, the story-teller, was there still, waiting for his opportunity amidst the busy preoccupations, the comings and goings, the wars and processions, the castle building and cathedral building, the arts and loves, the small diplomacies and incurable feuds, the crusades and trading journeys

of the middle ages. He no longer speculated with the untrammelled free-
dom of the stone-age savage; authoritative explanations of everything barred
his path; but he speculated with a better brain, sat idle and gazed at circling
stars in the sky and mused upon the coin and crystal in his hand. Whenever
there was a certain leisure for thought throughout these times, then men
were to be found dissatisfied with the appearances of things, dissatisfied with
the assurances of orthodox belief, uneasy with a sense of unread symbols in
the world about them, questioning the finality of scholastic wisdom. Through
all the ages of history there were men to whom this whisper had come of
hidden things about them. They could no longer lead ordinary lives nor
content themselves with the common things of this world once they had
heard this voice. And mostly they believed not only that all this world was
as it were a painted curtain before things unguessed at, but that these secrets
were Power. Hitherto Power had come to men by chance, but now there
were these seekers seeking, seeking among rare and curious and perplexing
objects, sometimes finding some odd utilizable thing, sometimes deceiving
themselves with fancied discovery, sometimes pretending to find. The world
of every day laughed at these eccentric beings, or found them annoying and
ill-treated them, or was seized with fear and made saints and sorcerers and
warlocks of them, or with covetousness and entertained them hopefully; but
for the greater part heeded them not at all. Yet they were of the blood of
him who had first dreamt of attacking the mammoth; every one of them
was of his blood and descent; and the thing they sought, all unwittingly, was
the snare that will some day catch the sun.

SECTION 3

Such a man was that Leonardo da Vinci, who went about the court of Sforza
in Milan in a state of dignified abstraction. His common-place books are
full of prophetic subtlety and ingenious anticipations of the methods of the
early aviators. Durer was his parallel and Roger Bacon – whom the Franciscans
silenced – of his kindred. Such a man again in an earlier city was Hero of
Alexandria, who knew of the power of steam nineteen hundred years before
it was first brought into use. And earlier still was Archimedes of Syracuse,
and still earlier the legendary Daedalus of Cnossos. All up and down the
record of history whenever there was a little leisure from war and brutality
the seekers appeared. And half the alchemists were of their tribe.

When Roger Bacon blew up his first batch of gunpowder one might have
supposed that men would have gone at once to the explosive engine. But
they could see nothing of the sort. They were not yet beginning to think of
seeing things; their metallurgy was all too poor to make such engines even
had they thought of them. For a time they could not make instruments
sound enough to stand this new force even for so rough a purpose as hurling

a missile. Their first guns had barrels of coopered timber, and the world waited for more than five hundred years before the explosive engine came.

Even when the seekers found, it was at first a long journey before the world could use their findings for any but the roughest, most obvious purposes. If man in general was not still as absolutely blind to the unconquered energies about him as his paleolithic precursor, he was at best purblind.

SECTION 4

The latent energy of coal and the power of steam waited long on the verge of discovery, before they began to influence human lives.

There were no doubt many such devices as Hero's toys devised and forgotten, time after time, in courts and palaces, but it needed that coal should be mined and burning with plenty of iron at hand before it dawned upon men that here was something more than a curiosity. And it is to be remarked that the first recorded suggestion for the use of steam was in war; there is an Elizabethan pamphlet in which it is proposed to fire shot out of corked iron bottles full of heated water. The mining of coal for fuel, the smelting of iron upon a larger scale than men had ever done before, the steam pumping engine, the steam-engine and the steam-boat, followed one another in an order that had a kind of logical necessity. It is the most interesting and instructive chapter in the history of the human intelligence, the history of steam from its beginning as a fact in human consciousness to the perfection of the great turbine engines that preceded the utilization of intra-molecular power. Nearly every human being must have seen steam, seen it incuriously for many thousands of years; the women in particular were always heating water, boiling it, seeing it boil away, seeing the lids of vessels dance with its fury; millions of people at different times must have watched steam pitching rocks out of volcanoes like cricket balls and blowing pumice into foam, and yet you may search the whole human record through, letters, books, inscriptions, pictures, for any glimmer of a realization that here was force, here was strength to borrow and use. . . . Then suddenly man woke up to it, the railways spread like a network over the globe, the ever enlarging iron steamships began their staggering fight against wind and wave.

Steam was the first-comer in the new powers, it was the beginning of the Age of Energy that was to close the long history of the Warring States.

But for a long time men did not realize the importance of this novelty. They would not recognize, they were not able to recognize that anything fundamental had happened to their immemorial necessities. They called the steam-engine the 'iron horse' and pretended that they had made the most partial of substitutions. Steam machinery and factory production were visibly revolutionizing the conditions of industrial production, population was

streaming steadily in from the countryside and concentrating in hitherto unthought-of masses about a few city centres, food was coming to them over enormous distances upon a scale that made the one sole precedent, the corn ships of imperial Rome, a petty incident; and a huge migration of peoples between Europe and Western Asia and America was in Progress, and – nobody seems to have realized that something new had come into human life, a strange swirl different altogether from any previous circling and mutation, a swirl like the swirl when at last the lock gates begin to open after a long phase of accumulating water and eddying inactivity. . . .

The sober Englishman at the close of the nineteenth century could sit at his breakfast-table, decide between tea from Ceylon or coffee from Brazil, devour an egg from France with some Danish ham, or eat a New Zealand chop, wind up his breakfast with a West Indian banana, glance at the latest telegrams from all the world, scrutinize the prices current of his geographically distributed investments in South Africa, Japan, and Egypt, and tell the two children he had begotten (in the place of his father's eight) that he thought the world changed very little. They must play cricket, keep their hair cut, go to the old school he had gone to, shirk the lessons he had shirked, learn a few scraps of Horace and Virgil and Homer for the confusion of cads, and all would be well with them. . . .

SECTION 5

Electricity, though it was perhaps the earlier of the two to be studied, invaded the common life of men a few decades after the exploitation of steam. To electricity also, in spite of its provocative nearness all about him, mankind had been utterly blind for incalculable ages. Could anything be more emphatic than the appeal of electricity for attention? It thundered at man's ears, it signalled to him in blinding flashes, occasionally it killed him, and he could not see it as a thing that concerned him enough to merit study. It came into the house with the cat on any dry day and crackled insinuatingly whenever he stroked her fur. It rotted his metals when he put them together. . . . There is no single record that anyone questioned why the cat's fur crackles or why hair is so unruly to brush on a frosty day, before the sixteenth century. For endless years man seems to have done his very successful best not to think about it at all; until this new spirit of the Seeker turned itself to these things.

How often things must have been seen and dismissed as unimportant, before the speculative eye and the moment of vision came! It was Gilbert, Queen Elizabeth's court physician, who first puzzled his brains with rubbed amber and bits of glass and silk and shellac, and so began the quickening of the human mind to the existence of this universal presence. And even then the science of electricity remained a mere little group of curious facts

for nearly two hundred years, connected perhaps with magnetism – a mere guess that – perhaps with the lightning. Frogs' legs must have hung by copper hooks from iron railings and twitched upon countless occasions before Galvani saw them. Except for the lightning conductor, it was 250 years after Gilbert before electricity stepped out of the cabinet of scientific curiosities into the life of the common man. . . . Then suddenly, in the half-century between 1880 and 1930, it ousted the steam-engine and took over traction, it ousted every other form of household heating, abolished distance with the perfected wireless telephone and the telephotograph. . . .

SECTION 6

And there was an extraordinary mental resistance to discovery and invention for at least a hundred years after the scientific revolution had begun. Each new thing made its way into practice against a scepticism that amounted at times to hostility. One writer upon these subjects gives a funny little domestic conversation that happened, he says, in the year 1898, within ten years, that is to say, of the time when the first aviators were fairly on the wing. He tells us how he sat at his desk in his study and conversed with his little boy.

His little boy was in profound trouble. He felt he had to speak very seriously to his father, and as he was a kindly little boy he did not want to do it too harshly.

This is what happened.

'I wish, Daddy,' he said, coming to his point, 'that you wouldn't write all this stuff about flying. The chaps rot me.'

'Yes!' said his father.

'And old Broomie, the Head I mean, he rots me. Everybody rots me.'

'But there is going to be flying – quite soon.'

The little boy was too well bred to say what he thought of that. 'Anyhow,' he said, 'I wish you wouldn't write about it.'

'You'll fly – lots of times – before you die,' the father assured him.

The little boy looked unhappy.

The father hesitated. Then he opened a drawer and took out a blurred and under-developed photograph. 'Come and look at this,' he said.

The little boy came round to him. The photograph showed a stream and a meadow beyond, and some trees, and in the air a black, pencil-like object with flat wings on either side of it. It was the first record of the first apparatus heavier than air that ever maintained itself in the air by mechanical force. Across the margin was written: 'Here we go up, up, up – from S. P. Langley, Smithsonian Institution, Washington.'

The father watched the effect of this reassuring document upon his son. 'Well?' he said.

'That,' said the schoolboy, after reflection, 'is only a model.'

'Model today, man tomorrow.'

The boy seemed divided in his allegiance. Then he decided for what he believed quite firmly to be omniscience. 'But old Broomie,' he said, 'he told all the boys in his class only yesterday, "no man will ever fly." No one, he says, who has ever shot grouse or pheasants on the wing would ever believe anything of the sort. . . .'

Yet that boy lived to fly across the Atlantic and edit his father's reminiscences.

SECTION 7

At the close of the nineteenth century as a multitude of passages in the literature of that time witness, it was thought that the fact that man had at last had successful and profitable dealings with the steam that scalded him and the electricity that flashed and banged about the sky at him, was an amazing and perhaps a culminating exercise of his intelligence and his intellectual courage. The air of 'Nunc Dimittis' sounds in same of these writings. 'The great things are discovered,' wrote Gerald Brown in his summary of the nineteenth century. 'For us there remains little but the working out of detail.' The spirit of the seeker was still rare in the world; education was unskilled, unstimulating, scholarly, and but little valued, and few people even then could have realized that Science was still but the flimsiest of trial sketches and discovery scarcely beginning. No one seems to have been afraid of science and its possibilities. Yet now where there had been but a score or so of seekers, there were many thousands, and for one needle of speculation that had been probing the curtain of appearances in 1800, there were now hundreds. And already Chemistry, which had been content with her atoms and molecules for the better part of a century, was preparing herself for that vast next stride that was to revolutionize the whole life of man from top to bottom.

One realizes how crude was the science of that time when one considers the case of the composition of air. This was determined by that strange genius and recluse, that man of mystery, that disembowelled intelligence, Henry Cavendish, towards the end of the eighteenth century. So far as he was concerned the work was admirably done. He separated all the known ingredients of the air with a precision altogether remarkable; he even put it upon record that he had some doubt about the purity of the nitrogen. For more than a hundred years his determination was repeated by chemists all the world over, his apparatus was treasured in London, he became, as they used to say, 'classic,' and always, at every one of the innumerable repetitions of his experiment, that sly element argon was hiding among the nitrogen (and with a little helium and traces of other substances, and indeed all the hints that might have led to the new departures of the twentieth-century

chemistry), and every time it slipped unobserved through the professorial fingers that repeated his procedure.

Is it any wonder then with this margin of inaccuracy, that up to the very dawn of the twentieth century, scientific discovery was still rather a procession of happy accidents than an orderly conquest of nature?

Yet the spirit of seeking was spreading steadily through the world. Even the schoolmaster could not check it. For the mere handful who grew up to feel wonder and curiosity about the secrets of nature in the nineteenth century, there were now, at the beginning of the twentieth, myriads escaping from the limitations of intellectual routine and the habitual life, in Europe, in America, North and South, in Japan, in China, and all about the world.

It was in 1910 that the parents of young Holsten, who was to be called by a whole generation of scientific men 'the greatest of European chemists', were staying in a villa near Santo Domenico, between Fiesole and Florence. He was then only fifteen, but he was already distinguished as a mathematician and possessed by a savage appetite to understand. He had been particularly attracted by the mystery of phosphorescence and its apparent unrelatedness to every other source of light. He was to tell afterwards in his reminiscences how he watched the fireflies drifting and glowing among the dark trees in the garden of the villa under the warm blue night sky of Italy; how he caught and kept them in cages, dissected them, first studying the general anatomy of insects very elaborately, and how he began to experiment with the effect of various gases and varying temperature upon their light. Then the chance present of a little scientific toy invented by Sir William Crookes, a toy called the spinthariscope, on which radium particles impinge upon sulphide of zinc and make it luminous, induced him to associate the two sets of phenomena. It was a happy association for his enquiries. It was a rare and fortunate thing, too, that anyone with the mathematical gift should have been taken by these curiosities.

SECTION 8

And while the boy Holsten was mooning over his fireflies at Fiesole, a certain professor of physics named Rufus was giving a course of afternoon lectures upon Radium and Radio-Activity in Edinburgh. They were lectures that had attracted a very considerable amount of attention. He gave them in a small lecture-theatre that had become more and more congested as his course proceeded. At his concluding discussion it was crowded right up to the ceiling at the back, and there people were standing, standing without any sense of fatigue, so fascinating did they find his suggestions. One youngster in particular, a chuckle-headed, scrub-haired lad from the Highlands, sat hugging his knee with great sand-red hands and drinking in every word, eyes aglow, cheeks flushed, and ears burning.

'And so,' said the professor, 'we see that this Radium, which seemed at first a fantastic exception, a mad inversion of all that was most established and fundamental in the constitution of matter, is really at one with the rest of the elements. It does noticeably and forcibly what probably all the other elements are doing with an imperceptible slowness. It is like the single voice crying aloud that betrays the silent breathing multitude in the darkness. Radium is an element that is breaking up and flying to pieces. But perhaps all elements are doing that at less perceptible rates. Uranium certainly is; thorium – the stuff of this incandescent gas mantle – certainly is; actinium. I feel that we are but beginning the list. And we know now that the atom, that once we thought hard and impenetrable, and indivisible and final and – lifeless – lifeless, is really a reservoir of immense energy. That is the most wonderful thing about all this work. A little while ago we thought of the atoms as we thought of bricks, as solid building material, as substantial matter, as unit masses of lifeless stuff, and behold! these bricks are boxes, treasure boxes, boxes full of the intensest force. This little bottle contains about a pint of uranium oxide; that is to say, about fourteen ounces of the element uranium. It is worth about a pound. And in this bottle, ladies and gentlemen, in the atoms in this bottle there slumbers at least as much energy as we could get by burning a hundred and sixty tons of coal. If at a word, in one instant I could suddenly release that energy here and now it would blow us and everything about us to fragments; if I could turn it into the machinery that lights this city, it could keep Edinburgh brightly lit for a week. But at present no man knows, no man has an inkling of how this little lump of stuff can be made to hasten the release of its store. It does release it, as a burn trickles. Slowly the uranium changes into radium, the radium changes into a gas called the radium emanation, and that again to what we call radium A, and so the process goes on, giving out energy at every stage, until at last we reach the last stage of all, which is, so far as we can tell at present, lead. But we cannot hasten it.'

'I take ye, man,' whispered the chuckle-headed lad, with his red hands tightening like a vice upon his knee. 'I take ye, man. Go on! Oh, go on!'

The professor went on after a little pause. 'Why is the change gradual?' he asked. 'Why does only a minute fraction of the radium disintegrate in any particular second? Why does it dole itself out so slowly and so exactly? Why does not all the uranium change to radium and all the radium change to the next lowest thing at once? Why this decay by driblets; why not a decay en masse? . . . Suppose presently we find it is possible to quicken that decay?'

The chuckle-headed lad nodded rapidly. The wonderful inevitable idea was coming. He drew his knee up towards his chin and swayed in his seat with excitement. 'Why not?' he echoed. 'Why not?'

The professor lifted his forefinger.

'Given that knowledge,' he said, 'mark what we should be able to do! We should not only be able to use this uranium and thorium; not only should we have a source of power so potent that a man might carry in his hand the energy to light a city for a year, fight a fleet of battleships, or drive one of our giant liners across the Atlantic; but we should also have a clue that would enable us at last to quicken the process of disintegration in all the other elements, where decay is still so slow as to escape our finest measurements. Every scrap of solid matter in the world would become an available reservoir of concentrated force. Do you realize, ladies and gentlemen, what these things would mean for us?'

The scrub head nodded. 'Oh! Go on. Go on.'

'It would mean a change in human conditions that I can only compare to the discovery of fire, that first discovery that lifted man above the brute. We stand today towards radio-activity as our ancestor stood towards fire before he had learnt to make it. He knew it then only as a strange thing utterly beyond his control, a flare on the crest of the volcano, a red destruction that poured through the forest. So it is that we know radio-activity today. This – this is the dawn of a new day in human living. At the climax of that civilization which had its beginning in the hammered flint and the fire-stick of the savage, just when it is becoming apparent that our ever-increasing needs cannot be borne indefinitely by our present sources of energy, we discover suddenly the possibility of an entirely new civilization. The energy we need for our very existence, and with which Nature supplies us still so grudgingly, is in reality locked up in inconceivable quantities all about us. We cannot pick that lock at present, but—'

He paused. His voice sank so that everybody strained a little to hear him. '—we will.'

He put up that lean finger again, his solitary gesture.

'And then,' he said. . . .

'Then that perpetual struggle for existence, that perpetual struggle to live on the bare surplus of Nature's energies will cease to be the lot of Man. Man will step from the pinnacle of this civilization to the beginning of the next. I have no eloquence, ladies and gentlemen, to express the vision of man's material destiny that opens out before me. I see the desert continents transformed, the poles no longer wildernesses of ice, the whole world once more Eden. I see the power of man reach out among the stars. . . .'

He stopped abruptly with a catching of the breath that many an actor or orator might have envied.

The lecture was over, the audience hung silent for a few seconds, sighed, became audible, stirred, fluttered, prepared for dispersal. More light was turned on and what had been a dim mass of figures became a bright confusion of movement. Some of the people signalled to friends, some crowded down towards the platform to examine the lecturer's apparatus and make

notes of his diagrams. But the chuckle-headed lad with the scrub hair wanted no such detailed frittering away of the thoughts that had inspired him. He wanted to be alone with them; he elbowed his way out almost fiercely, he made himself as angular and bony as a cow, fearing lest someone should speak to him, lest someone should invade his glowing sphere of enthusiasm.

He went through the streets with a rapt face, like a saint who sees visions. He had arms disproportionately long, and ridiculous big feet.

He must get alone, get somewhere high out of all this crowding of commonness, of everyday life.

He made his way to the top of Arthur's Seat, and there he sat for a long time in the golden evening sunshine, still, except that ever and again he whispered to himself some precious phrase that had stuck in his mind.

'If,' he whispered, 'if only we could pick that lock. . . .'

The sun was sinking over the distant hills. Already it was shorn of its beams, a globe of ruddy gold, hanging over the great banks of cloud that would presently engulf it.

'Eh!' said the youngster. 'Eh!'

He seemed to wake up at last out of his entrancement, and the red sun was there before his eyes. He stared at it, at first without intelligence, and then with a gathering recognition. Into his mind came a strange echo of that ancestral fancy, that fancy of a Stone Age savage, dead and scattered bones among the drift two hundred thousand years ago.

'Ye auld thing,' he said – and his eyes were shining, and he made a kind of grabbing gesture with his hand; 'ye auld red thing. . . . We'll have ye yet.'

CHAPTER I

The New Source of Energy

SECTION I

The problem which was already being mooted by such scientific men as Ramsay, Rutherford, and Soddy, in the very beginning of the twentieth century, the problem of inducing radio-activity in the heavier elements and so tapping the internal energy of atoms, was solved by a wonderful combination of induction, intuition, and luck by Holsten so soon as the year 1933. From the first detection of radio-activity to its first subjugation to human purpose measured little more than a quarter of a century. For twenty years after that, indeed, minor difficulties prevented any striking practical application of his success, but the essential thing was done, this new boundary in the march of human progress was crossed, in that year. He set up atomic disintegration in a minute particle of bismuth; it exploded with great violence into a heavy gas of extreme radio-activity, which disintegrated in its turn in the course of seven days, and it was only after another year's work that he was able to show practically that the last result of this rapid release of energy was gold. But the thing was done – at the cost of a blistered chest and an injured finger, and from the moment when the invisible speck of bismuth flashed into riving and rending energy, Holsten knew that he had opened a way for mankind, however narrow and dark it might still be, to worlds of limitless power. He recorded as much in the strange diary biography he left the world, a diary that was up to that particular moment a mass of speculations and calculations, and which suddenly became for a space an amazingly minute and human record of sensations and emotions that all humanity might understand.

He gives, in broken phrases and often single words, it is true, but none the less vividly for that, a record of the twenty-four hours following the demonstration of the correctness of his intricate tracery of computations and guesses. 'I thought I should not sleep,' he writes – the words he omitted are supplied in brackets – [on account of] 'pain in [the] hand and chest and [the] wonder of what I had done. . . . Slept like a child.'

He felt strange and disconcerted the next morning; he had nothing to do, he was living alone in apartments in Bloomsbury, and he decided to go up to Hampstead Heath, which he had known when he was a little boy as a breezy playground. He went up by the underground tube that was then the recognized means of travel from one part of London to another, and walked up Heath Street from the tube station to the open heath. He found it a gully of planks and scaffoldings between the hoardings of house-wreckers.

The spirit of the times had seized upon that narrow, steep, and winding thoroughfare, and was in the act of making it commodious and interesting, according to the remarkable ideals of Neo-Georgian aestheticism. Such is the illogical quality of humanity that Holsten, fresh from work that was like a petard under the seat of current civilization, saw these changes with regret. He had come up Heath Street perhaps a thousand times, had known the windows of all the little shops, spent hours in the vanished cinematograph theatre, and marvelled at the high-flung early Georgian houses upon the westward bank of that old gully of a thoroughfare; he felt strange with all these familiar things gone. He escaped at last with a feeling of relief from this choked alley of trenches and holes and cranes, and emerged upon the old familiar scene about the White Stone Pond. That, at least, was very much as it used to be.

There were still the fine old red-brick houses to left and right of him; the reservoir had been improved by a portico of marble, the white-fronted inn with the clustering flowers above its portico still stood out at the angle of the ways, and the blue view to Harrow Hill and Harrow spire, a view of hills and trees and shining waters and wind-driven cloud shadows, was like the opening of a great window to the ascending Londoner. All that was very reassuring. There was the same strolling crowd, the same perpetual miracle of motors dodging through it harmlessly, escaping headlong into the country from the Sabbatical stuffiness behind and below them. There was a band still, a women's suffrage meeting – for the suffrage women had won their way back to the tolerance, a trifle derisive, of the populace again – socialist orators, politicians, a band, and the same wild uproar of dogs, frantic with the gladness of their one blessed weekly release from the back yard and the chain. And away along the road to the Spaniards strolled a vast multitude, saying, as ever, that the view of London was exceptionally clear that day.

Young Holsten's face was white. He walked with that uneasy affectation of ease that marks an overstrained nervous system and an under-exercised body. He hesitated at the White Stone Pond whether to go to the left of it or the right, and again at the fork of the roads. He kept shifting his stick in his hand, and every now and then he would get in the way of people on the footpath or be jostled by them because of the uncertainty of his movements. He felt, he confesses, 'inadequate to ordinary existence'. He seemed to himself to be something inhuman and mischievous. All the people about him looked fairly prosperous, fairly happy, fairly well adapted to the lives they had to lead – a week of work and a Sunday of best clothes and mild promenading – and he had launched something that would disorganize the entire fabric that held their contentments and ambitions and satisfactions together. 'Felt like an imbecile who has presented a box full of loaded revolvers to a Creche,' he notes.

He met a man named Lawson, an old school-fellow, of whom history now

knows only that he was red-faced and had a terrier. He and Holsten walked together and Holsten was sufficiently pale and jumpy for Lawson to tell him he overworked and needed a holiday. They sat down at a little table outside the County Council house of Golders Hill Park and sent one of the waiters to the Bull and Bush for a couple of bottles of beer, no doubt at Lawson's suggestion. The beer warmed Holsten's rather dehumanised system. He began to tell Lawson as clearly as he could to what his great discovery amounted. Lawson feigned attention, but indeed he had neither the knowledge nor the imagination to understand. 'In the end, before many years are out, this must eventually change war, transit, lighting, building, and every sort of manufacture, even agriculture, every material human concern—'

Then Holsten stopped short. Lawson had leapt to his feet. 'Damn that dog!' cried Lawson. 'Look at it now. Hi! Here! Phewoo – phewoo phewoo! Come *here*, Bobs! Come *here*!'

The young scientific man, with his bandaged hand, sat at the green table, too tired to convey the wonder of the thing he had sought so long, his friend whistled and bawled for his dog, and the Sunday people drifted about them through the spring sunshine. For a moment or so Holsten stared at Lawson in astonishment, for he had been too intent upon what he had been saying to realize how little Lawson had attended.

Then he remarked, '*Well!*' and smiled faintly, and – finished the tankard of beer before him.

Lawson sat down again. 'One must look after one's dog,' he said, with a note of apology. 'What was it you were telling me?'

SECTION 2

In the evening Holsten went out again. He walked to Saint Paul's Cathedral, and stood for a time near the door listening to the evening service. The candles upon the altar reminded him in some odd way of the fireflies at Fiesole. Then he walked back through the evening lights to Westminster. He was oppressed, he was indeed scared, by his sense of the immense consequences of his discovery. He had a vague idea that night that he ought not to publish his results, that they were premature, that some secret association of wise men should take care of his work and hand it on from generation to generation until the world was riper for its practical application. He felt that nobody in all the thousands of people he passed had really awakened to the fact of change, they trusted the world for what it was, not to alter too rapidly, to respect their trusts, their assurances, their habits, their little accustomed traffics and hard-won positions.

He went into those little gardens beneath the over-hanging, brightly-lit masses of the Savoy Hotel and the Hotel Cecil. He sat down on a seat and became aware of the talk of the two people next to him. It was the talk of

a young couple evidently on the eve of marriage. The man was congratulating himself on having regular employment at last; 'they like me,' he said, 'and I like the job. If I work up – in'r dozen years or so I ought to be gettin' somethin' pretty comfortable. That's the plain sense of it, Hetty. There ain't no reason whatsoever why we shouldn't get along very decently – very decently indeed.'

The desire for little successes amidst conditions securely fixed! So it struck upon Holsten's mind. He added in his diary, 'I had a sense of all this globe as that. . . .'

By that phrase he meant a kind of clairvoyant vision of this populated world as a whole, of all its cities and towns and villages, its high roads and the inns beside them, its gardens and farms and upland pastures, its boatmen and sailors, its ships coming along the great circles of the ocean, its time-tables and appointments and payments and dues as it were one unified and progressive spectacle. Sometimes such visions came to him; his mind, accustomed to great generalizations and yet acutely sensitive to detail, saw things far more comprehensively than the minds of most of his contemporaries. Usually the teeming sphere moved on to its predestined ends and circled with a stately swiftness on its path about the sun. Usually it was all a living progress that altered under his regard. But now fatigue a little deadened him to that incessancy of life, it seemed now just an eternal circling. He lapsed to the commoner persuasion of the great fixities and recurrencies of the human routine. The remoter past of wandering savagery, the inevitable changes of tomorrow were veiled, and he saw only day and night, seed-time and harvest, loving and begetting, births and deaths, walks in the summer sunlight and tales by the winter fireside, the ancient sequence of hope and acts and age perennially renewed, eddying on for ever and ever, save that now the impious hand of research was raised to overthrow this drowsy, gently humming, habitual, sunlit spinning-top of man's existence. . . .

For a time he forgot wars and crimes and hates and persecutions, famine and pestilence, the cruelties of beasts, weariness and the bitter wind, failure and insufficiency and retrocession. He saw all mankind in terms of the humble Sunday couple upon the seat beside him, who schemed their inglorious outlook and improbable contentments. 'I had a sense of all this globe as that.'

His intelligence struggled against this mood and struggled for a time in vain. He reassured himself against the invasion of this disconcerting idea that he was something strange and inhuman, a loose wanderer from the flock returning with evil gifts from his sustained unnatural excursions amidst the darknesses and phosphorescences beneath the fair surfaces of life. Man had not been always thus; the instincts and desires of the little home, the little plot, was not all his nature; also he was an adventurer, an experimenter, an unresting curiosity, an insatiable desire. For a few thousand generations

indeed he had tilled the earth and followed the seasons, saying his prayers, grinding his corn and trampling the October winepress, yet not for so long but that he was still full of restless stirrings.

'If there have been home and routine and the field,' thought Holsten, 'there have also been wonder and the sea.'

He turned his head and looked up over the back of the seat at the great hotels above him, full of softly shaded lights and the glow and colour and stir of feasting. Might his gift to mankind mean simply more of that? . . .

He got up and walked out of the garden, surveyed a passing tram-car, laden with warm light, against the deep blues of evening, dripping and trailing long skirts of shining reflection; he crossed the Embankment and stood for a time watching the dark river and turning ever and again to the lit buildings and bridges. His mind began to scheme conceivable replacements of all those clustering arrangements. . . .

'It has begun,' he writes in the diary in which these things are recorded. 'It is not for me to reach out to consequences I cannot foresee. I am a part, not a whole; I am a little instrument in the armoury of Change. If I were to burn all these papers, before a score of years had passed, some other man would be doing this. . . .

SECTION 3

Holsten, before he died, was destined to see atomic energy dominating every other source of power, but for some years yet a vast network of difficulties in detail and application kept the new discovery from any effective invasion of ordinary life. The path from the laboratory to the workshop is sometimes a tortuous one; electro-magnetic radiations were known and demonstrated for twenty years before Marconi made them practically available, and in the same way it was twenty years before induced radio-activity could be brought to practical utilization. The thing, of course, was discussed very much, more perhaps at the time of its discovery than during the interval of technical adaptation, but with very little realization of the huge economic revolution that impended. What chiefly impressed the journalists of 1933 was the production of gold from bismuth and the realization albeit upon unprofitable lines of the alchemist's dreams; there was a considerable amount of discussion and expectation in that more intelligent section of the educated publics of the various civilized countries which followed scientific development; but for the most part the world went about its business – as the inhabitants of those Swiss villages which live under the perpetual threat of overhanging rocks and mountains go about their business – just as though the possible was impossible, as though the inevitable was postponed for ever because it was delayed.

It was in 1953 that the first Holsten-Roberts engine brought induced

radio-activity into the sphere of industrial production, and its first general use was to replace the steam-engine in electrical generating stations. Hard upon the appearance of this came the Dass-Tata engine – the invention of two among the brilliant galaxy of Bengali inventors the modernization of Indian thought was producing at this time – which was used chiefly for automobiles, aeroplanes, waterplanes, and such-like, mobile purposes. The American Kemp engine, differing widely in principle but equally practicable, and the Krupp-Erlanger came hard upon the heels of this, and by the autumn of 1954 a gigantic replacement of industrial methods and machinery was in progress all about the habitable globe. Small wonder was this when the cost, even of these earliest and clumsiest of atomic engines, is compared with that of the power they superseded. Allowing for lubrication the Dass-Tata engine, once it was started cost a penny to run thirty-seven miles, and added only nine and quarter pounds to the weight of the carriage it drove. It made the heavy alcohol-driven automobile of the time ridiculous in appearance as well as preposterously costly. For many years the price of coal and every form of liquid fuel had been clambering to levels that made even the revival of the draft horse seem a practicable possibility, and now with the abrupt relaxation of this stringency, the change in appearance of the traffic upon the world's roads was instantaneous. In three years the frightful armoured monsters that had hooted and smoked and thundered about the world for four awful decades were swept away to the dealers in old metal, and the highways thronged with light and clean and shimmering shapes of silvered steel. At the same time a new impetus was given to aviation by the relatively enormous power for weight of the atomic engine, it was at last possible to add Redmayne's ingenious helicopter ascent and descent engine to the vertical propeller that had hitherto been the sole driving force of the aeroplane without overweighting the machine, and men found themselves possessed of an instrument of flight that could hover or ascend or descend vertically and gently as well as rush wildly through the air. The last dread of flying vanished. As the journalists of the time phrased it, this was the epoch of the Leap into the Air. The new atomic aeroplane became indeed a mania; everyone of means was frantic to possess a thing so controllable, so secure and so free from the dust and danger of the road, and in France alone in the year 1943 thirty thousand of these new aeroplanes were manufactured and licensed, and soared humming softly into the sky.

And with an equal speed atomic engines of various types invaded industrialism. The railways paid enormous premiums for priority in the delivery of atomic traction engines, atomic smelting was embarked upon so eagerly as to lead to a number of disastrous explosions due to inexperienced handling of the new power, and the revolutionary cheapening of both materials and electricity made the entire reconstruction of domestic buildings a matter merely dependent upon a reorganization of the methods of the builder and

the house-furnisher. Viewed from the side of the new power and from the point of view of those who financed and manufactured the new engines and material it required the age of the Leap into the Air was one of astonishing prosperity. Patent-holding companies were presently paying dividends of five or six hundred per cent. and enormous fortunes were made and fantastic wages earned by all who were concerned in the new developments. This prosperity was not a little enhanced by the fact that in both the Dass-Tata and Holsten-Roberts engines one of the recoverable waste products was gold – the former disintegrated dust of bismuth and the latter dust of lead – and that this new supply of gold led quite naturally to a rise in prices throughout the world.

This spectacle of feverish enterprise was productivity, this crowding flight of happy and fortunate rich people – every great city was as if a crawling ant-hill had suddenly taken wing – was the bright side of the opening phase of the new epoch in human history. Beneath that brightness was a gathering darkness, a deepening dismay. If there was a vast development of production there was also a huge destruction of values. These glaring factories working night and day, these glittering new vehicles swinging noiselessly along the roads, these flights of dragonflies that swooped and soared and circled in the air, were indeed no more than the brightnesses of lamps and fires that gleam out when the world sinks towards twilight and the night. Between these high lights accumulated disaster, social catastrophe. The coal mines were manifestly doomed to closure at no very distant date, the vast amount of capital invested in oil was becoming unsaleable, millions of coal miners, steel workers upon the old lines, vast swarms of unskilled or under-skilled labourers in innumerable occupations, were being flung out of employment by the superior efficiency of the new machinery, the rapid fall in the cost of transit was destroying high land values at every centre of population, the value of existing house property had become problematical, gold was undergoing headlong depreciation, all the securities upon which the credit of the world rested were slipping and sliding, banks were tottering, the stock exchanges were scenes of feverish panic; – this was the reverse of the spectacle, these were the black and monstrous under-consequences of the Leap into the Air.

There is a story of a demented London stockbroker running out into Threadneedle Street and tearing off his clothes as he ran. 'The Steel Trust is scrapping the whole of its plant,' he shouted. 'The State Railways are going to scrap all their engines. Everything's going to be scrapped – everything. Come and scrap the mint, you fellows, come and scrap the mint!'

In the year 1955 the suicide rate for the United States of America quadrupled any previous record. There was an enormous increase also in violent crime throughout the world. The thing had come upon an unprepared humanity; it seemed as though human society was to be smashed by its own magnificent gains.

For there had been no foresight of these things. There had been no attempt anywhere even to compute the probable dislocations this flood of inexpensive energy would produce in human affairs. The world in these days was not really governed at all, in the sense in which government came to be understood in subsequent years. Government was a treaty, not a design; it was forensic, conservative, disputatious, unseeing, unthinking, uncreative; throughout the world, except where the vestiges of absolutism still sheltered the court favourite and the trusted servant, it was in the hands of the predominant caste of lawyers, who had an enormous advantage in being the only trained caste. Their professional education and every circumstance in the manipulation of the fantastically naive electoral methods by which they clambered to power, conspired to keep them contemptuous of facts, conscientiously unimaginative, alert to claim and seize advantages, and suspicious of every generosity. Government was an obstructive business of energetic fractions, progress went on outside of and in spite of public activities, and legislation was the last crippling recognition of needs so clamorous and imperative and facts so aggressively established as to invade even the dingy seclusions of the judges and threaten the very existence of the otherwise inattentive political machine.

The world was so little governed that with the very coming of plenty, in the full tide of an incalculable abundance, when everything necessary to satisfy human needs and everything necessary to realize such will and purpose as existed then in human hearts was already at hand, one has still to tell of hardship, famine, anger, confusion, conflict, and incoherent suffering. There was no scheme for the distribution of this vast new wealth that had come at last within the reach of men; there was no clear conception that any such distribution was possible. As one attempts a comprehensive view of those opening years of the new age, as one measures it against the latent achievement that later years have demonstrated, one begins to measure the blindness, the narrowness, the insensate unimaginative individualism of the pre-atomic time. Under this tremendous dawn of power and freedom, under a sky ablaze with promise, in the very presence of science standing like some bountiful goddess over all the squat darknesses of human life, holding patiently in her strong arms, until men chose to take them, security, plenty, the solution of riddles, the key of the bravest adventures, in her very presence, and with the earnest of her gifts in court, the world was to witness such things as the squalid spectacle of the Dass-Tata patent litigation.

There in a stuffy court in London, a grimy oblong box of a room, during the exceptional heat of the May of 1956, the leading counsel of the day argued and shouted over a miserable little matter of more royalties or less and whether the Dass-Tata company might not bar the Holsten-Roberts methods of utilizing the new power. The Dass-Tata people were indeed making a strenuous attempt to secure a world monopoly in atomic engineering.

The judge, after the manner of those times, sat raised above the court, wearing a preposterous gown and a foolish huge wig, the counsel also wore dirty-looking little wigs and queer black gowns over their usual costume, wigs and gowns that were held to be necessary to their pleading, and upon unclean wooden benches stirred and whispered artful-looking solicitors, busily scribbling reporters, the parties to the case, expert witnesses, interested people, and a jostling confusion of subpoenaed persons, briefless young barristers (forming a style on the most esteemed and truculent examples) and casual eccentric spectators who preferred this pit of iniquity to the free sunlight outside. Everyone was damply hot, the examining King's Counsel wiped the perspiration from his huge, clean-shaven upper lip; and into this atmosphere of grasping contention and human exhalations the daylight filtered through a window that was manifestly dirty. The jury sat in a double pew to the left of the judge, looking as uncomfortable as frogs that have fallen into an ash-pit, and in the witness-box lied the would-be omnivorous Dass, under cross-examination. . . .

Holsten had always been accustomed to publish his results so soon as they appeared to him to be sufficiently advanced to furnish a basis for further work, and to that confiding disposition and one happy flash of adaptive invention the alert Dass owed his claim. . . .

But indeed a vast multitude of such sharp people were clutching, patenting, pre-empting, monopolizing this or that feature of the new development, seeking to subdue this gigantic winged power to the purposes of their little lusts and avarice. That trial is just one of innumerable disputes of the same kind. For a time the face of the world festered with patent legislation. It chanced, however, to have one oddly dramatic feature in the fact that Holsten, after being kept waiting about the court for two days as a beggar might have waited at a rich man's door, after being bullied by ushers and watched by policemen, was called as a witness, rather severely handled by counsel, and told not to 'quibble' by the judge when he was trying to be absolutely explicit.

The judge scratched his nose with a quill pen, and sneered at Holsten's astonishment round the corner of his monstrous wig. Holsten was a great man, was he? Well, in a law-court great men were put in their places.

'We want to know has the plaintiff added anything to this or hasn't he?' said the judge, 'we don't want to have your views whether Sir Philip Dass's improvements were merely superficial adaptations or whether they were implicit in your paper. No doubt – after the manner of inventors – you think most things that were ever likely to be discovered are implicit in your papers. No doubt also you think too that most subsequent additions and modifications are merely superficial. Inventors have a way of thinking that. The law isn't concerned with that sort of thing. The law has nothing to do with the vanity of inventors. The law is concerned with the question whether these

patent rights have the novelty the plantiff claims for them. What that admission may or may not stop, and all these other things you are saying in your overflowing zeal to answer more than the questions addressed to you – none of these things have anything whatever to do with the case in hand. It is a matter of constant astonishment to me in this court to see how you scientific men, with all your extraordinary claims to precision and veracity, wander and wander so soon as you get into the witness-box. I know no more unsatisfactory class of witness. The plain and simple question is, has Sir Philip Dass made any real addition to existing knowledge and methods in this matter or has he not? We don't want to know whether they were large or small additions nor what the consequences of your admission may be. That you will leave to us.'

Holsten was silent.

'Surely?' said the judge, almost pityingly.

'No, he hasn't,' said Holsten, perceiving that for once in his life he must disregard infinitesimals.

'Ah!' said the judge, 'Now why couldn't you say that when counsel put the question? . . .'

An entry in Holsten's diary-autobiography, dated five days later, runs: 'Still amazed. The law is the most dangerous thing in this country. It is hundreds of years old. It hasn't an idea. The oldest of old bottles and this new wine, the most explosive wine. Something will overtake them.'

SECTION 4

There was a certain truth in Holsten's assertion that the law was 'hundreds of years old'. It was, in relation to current thought and widely accepted ideas, an archaic thing. While almost all the material and methods of life had been changing rapidly and were now changing still more rapidly, the law-courts and the legislatures of the world were struggling desperately to meet modern demands with devices and procedures, conceptions of rights and property and authority and obligation that dated from the rude compromises of relatively barbaric times. The horse-hair wigs and antic dresses of the British judges, their musty courts and overbearing manners, were indeed only the outward and visible intimations of profounder anachronisms. The legal and political organization of the earth in the middle twentieth century was indeed everywhere like a complicated garment, outworn yet strong, that now fettered the governing body that once it had protected.

Yet that same spirit of free-thinking and outspoken publication that in the field of natural science had been the beginning of the conquest of nature, was at work throughout all the eighteenth and nineteenth centuries preparing the spirit of the new world within the degenerating body of the old. The idea of a greater subordination of individual interests and established institutions

to the collective future, is traceable more and more clearly in the literature of those times, and movement after movement fretted itself away in criticism of and opposition to first this aspect and then that of the legal, social, and political order. Already in the early nineteenth century Shelley, with no scrap of alternative, is denouncing the established rulers of the world as Anarchs, and the entire system of ideas and suggestions that was known as Socialism, and more particularly its international side, feeble as it was in creative proposals or any method of transition, still witnesses to the growth of a conception of a modernized system of inter-relationships that should supplant the existing tangle of proprietary legal ideas.

The word 'Sociology' was invented by Herbert Spencer, a popular writer upon philosophical subjects, who flourished about the middle of the nineteenth century, but the idea of a state, planned as an electric-traction system is planned, without reference to pre-existing apparatus, upon scientific lines, did not take a very strong hold upon the popular imagination of the world until the twentieth century. Then, the growing impatience of the American people with the monstrous and socially paralysing party systems that had sprung out of their absurd electoral arrangements, led to the appearance of what came to be called the 'Modern State' movement, and a galaxy of brilliant writers, in America, Europe, and the East, stirred up the world to the thought of bolder rearrangements of social interaction, property, employment, education, and government, than had ever been contemplated before. No doubt these Modern State ideas were very largely the reflection upon social and political thought of the vast revolution in material things that had been in progress for two hundred years, but for a long time they seemed to be having no more influence upon existing institutions than the writings of Rousseau and Voltaire seemed to have had at the time of the death of the latter. They were fermenting in men's minds, and it needed only just such social and political stresses as the coming of the atomic mechanisms brought about, to thrust them forward abruptly into crude and startling realization.

SECTION 5

Frederick Barnet's *Wander Jahre* is one of those autobiographical novels that were popular throughout the third and fourth decades of the twentieth century. It was published in 1970, and one must understand *Wander Jahre* rather in a spiritual and intellectual than in a literal sense. It is indeed an allusive title, carrying the world back to the Wilhelm Meister of Goethe, a century and a half earlier.

Its author, Frederick Barnet, gives a minute and curious history of his life and ideas between his nineteenth and his twenty-third birthdays. He was neither a very original nor a very brilliant man, but he had a trick of

circumstantial writing; and though no authentic portrait was to survive for
the information of posterity, he betrays by a score of casual phrases that he
was short, sturdy, inclined to be plump, with a 'rather blobby' face, and
full, rather projecting blue eyes. He belonged until the financial debacle of
1956 to the class of fairly prosperous people, he was a student in London,
he aeroplaned to Italy and then had a pedestrian tour from Genoa to Rome,
crossed in the air to Greece and Egypt, and came back over the Balkans
and Germany. His family fortunes, which were largely invested in bank
shares, coal mines, and house property, were destroyed. Reduced to penury,
he sought to earn a living. He suffered great hardship, and was then caught
up by the war and had a year of soldiering, first as an officer in the English
infantry and then in the army of pacification. His book tells all these things
so simply and at the same time so explicitly, that it remains, as it were, an
eye by which future generations may have at least one man's vision of the
years of the Great Change.

And he was, he tells us, a 'Modern State' man 'by instinct' from the
beginning. He breathed in these ideas in the class rooms and laboratories
of the Carnegie Foundation school that rose, a long and delicately beautiful
facade, along the South Bank of the Thames opposite the ancient dignity
of Somerset House. Such thought was interwoven with the very fabric of
that pioneer school in the educational renascence in England. After the
customary exchange years in Heidelberg and Paris, he went into the classical
school of London University. The older so-called 'classical' education of
the British pedagogues, probably the most paralysing, ineffective and foolish
routine that ever wasted human life, had already been swept out of this
great institution in favour of modern methods; and he learnt Greek and
Latin as well as he had learnt German, Spanish and French, so that he
wrote and spoke them freely, and used them with an unconscious ease in
his study of the foundation civilizations of the European system to which
they were the key. (This change was still so recent that he mentions an
encounter in Rome with an 'Oxford don' who 'spoke Latin with a Wiltshire
accent and manifest discomfort, wrote Greek letters with his tongue out,
and seemed to think a Greek sentence a charm when it was a quotation
and an impropriety when it wasn't'.)

Barnet saw the last days of the coal-steam engines upon the English
railways and the gradual cleansing of the London atmosphere as the
smoke-creating sea-coal fires gave place to electric heating. The building of
laboratories at Kensington was still in progress, and he took part in the
students' riots that delayed the removal of the Albert Memorial. He carried
a banner with 'We like Funny Statuary' on one side, and on the other 'Seats
and Canopies for Statues, Why should our Great Departed Stand in the
Rain?'. He learnt the rather athletic aviation of those days at the University
grounds at Sydenham, and he was fined for flying over the new prison for

political libellers at Wormwood Scrubs, 'in a manner calculated to exhilarate the prisoners while at exercise'. That was the time of the attempted suppression of any criticism of the public judicature and the place was crowded with journalists who had ventured to call attention to the dementia of Chief Justice Abrahams. Barnet was not a very good aviator, he confesses he was always a little afraid of his machine – there was excellent reason for everyone to be afraid of those clumsy early types – and he never attempted steep descents or very high flying. He also, he records, owned one of those oil-driven motor-bicycles whose clumsy complexity and extravagant filthiness still astonish the visitors to the museum of machinery at South Kensington. He mentions running over a dog and complains of the ruinous price of 'spatchcocks' in Surrey. 'Spatchcocks,' it seems, was a slang term for crushed hens.

He passed the examinations necessary to reduce his military service to a minimum, and his want of any special scientific or technical qualification and a certain precocious corpulence that handicapped his aviation indicated the infantry of the line as his sphere of training. That was the most generalized form of soldiering. The development of the theory of war had been for some decades but little assisted by any practical experience. What fighting had occurred in recent years had been fighting in minor or uncivilized states, with peasant or barbaric soldiers and with but a small equipment of modern contrivances, and the great powers of the world were content for the most part to maintain armies that sustained in their broader organization the traditions of the European wars of thirty and forty years before. There was the infantry arm to which Barnet belonged and which was supposed to fight on foot with a rifle and be the main portion of the army. There were cavalry forces (horse soldiers), having a ratio to the infantry that had been determined by the experiences of the Franco-German war in 1871. There was also artillery, and for some unexplained reason much of this was still drawn by horses; though there were also in all the European armies a small number of motor-guns with wheels so constructed that they could go over broken ground. In addition there were large developments of the engineering arm, concerned with motor transport, motor-bicycle scouting, aviation, and the like.

No first-class intelligence had been sought to specialize in and work out the problem of warfare with the new appliances and under modern conditions, but a succession of able jurists, Lord Haldane, Chief Justice Briggs and that very able King's Counsel, Philbrick, had reconstructed the army frequently and thoroughly and placed it at last, with the adoption of national service, upon a footing that would have seemed very imposing to the public of 1900. At any moment the British Empire could now put a million and a quarter of arguable soldiers upon the board of *Welt-Politik*. The traditions of Japan and the Central European armies were more princely and less forensic; the Chinese still refused resolutely to become a military power,

and maintained a small standing army upon the American model that was said, so far as it went, to be highly efficient, and Russia, secured by a stringent administration against internal criticism, had scarcely altered the design of a uniform or the organization of a battery since the opening decades of the century. Barnet's opinion of his military training was manifestly a poor one, his Modern State ideas disposed him to regard it as a bore, and his common sense condemned it as useless. Moreover, his habit of body made him peculiarly sensitive to the fatigues and hardships of service.

'For three days in succession we turned out before dawn and – for no earthly reason – without breakfast,' he relates. 'I suppose that is to show us that when the Day comes the first thing will be to get us thoroughly uncomfortable and rotten. We then proceeded to Kriegspiel, according to the mysterious ideas of those in authority over us. On the last day we spent three hours under a hot if early sun getting over eight miles of country to a point we could have reached in a motor omnibus in nine minutes and a half – I did it the next day in that – and then we made a massed attack upon entrenchments that could have shot us all about three times over if only the umpires had let them. Then came a little bayonet exercise, but I doubt if I am sufficiently a barbarian to stick this long knife into anything living. Anyhow in this battle I shouldn't have had a chance. Assuming that by some miracle I hadn't been shot three times over, I was far too hot and blown when I got up to the entrenchments even to lift my beastly rifle. It was those others would have begun the sticking. . . .

'For a time we were watched by two hostile aeroplanes; then our own came up and asked them not to, and – the practice of aerial warfare still being unknown – they very politely desisted and went away and did dives and circles of the most charming description over the Fox Hills.'

All Barnet's accounts of his military training were written in the same half-contemptuous, half-protesting tone. He was of opinion that his chances of participating in any real warfare were very slight, and that, if after all he should participate, it was bound to be so entirely different from these peace manoeuvres that his only course as a rational man would be to keep as observantly out of danger as he could until he had learnt the tricks and possibilities of the new conditions. He states this quite frankly. Never was a man more free from sham heroics.

SECTION 6

Barnet welcomed the appearance of the atomic engine with the zest of masculine youth in all fresh machinery, and it is evident that for some time he failed to connect the rush of wonderful new possibilities with the financial troubles of his family. 'I knew my father was worried,' he admits. That cast the smallest of shadows upon his delighted departure for Italy and

Greece and Egypt with three congenial companions in one of the new atomic models. They flew over the Channel Isles and Touraine, he mentions, and circled about Mont Blanc – 'These new helicopters, we found,' he notes, 'had abolished all the danger and strain of sudden drops to which the old-time aeroplanes were liable' – and then he went on by way of Pisa, Paestum, Ghirgenti and Athens, to visit the pyramids by moonlight, flying thither from Cairo, and to follow the Nile up to Khartum. Even by later standards, it must have been a very gleeful holiday for a young man, and it made the tragedy of his next experiences all the darker. A week after his return his father, who was a widower, announced himself ruined, and committed suicide by means of an unscheduled opiate.

At one blow Barnet found himself flung out of the possessing, spending, enjoying class to which he belonged, penniless and with no calling by which he could earn a living. He tried teaching and some journalism, but in a little while he found himself on the underside of a world in which he had always reckoned to live in the sunshine. For innumerable men such an experience has meant mental and spiritual destruction, but Barnet, in spite of his bodily gravitation towards comfort, showed himself when put to the test, of the more valiant modern quality. He was saturated with the creative stoicism of the heroic times that were already dawning, and he took his difficulties and discomforts stoutly as his appointed material, and turned them to expression.

Indeed, in his book, he thanks fortune for them. 'I might have lived and died,' he says, 'in that neat fool's paradise of secure lavishness above there. I might never have realized the gathering wrath and sorrow of the ousted and exasperated masses. In the days of my own prosperity things had seemed to me to be very well arranged.' Now from his new point of view he was to find they were not arranged at all; that government was a compromise of aggressions and powers and lassitudes, and law a convention between interests, and that the poor and the weak, though they had many negligent masters, had few friends.

'I had thought things were looked after,' he wrote. 'It was with a kind of amazement that I tramped the roads and starved – and found that no one in particular cared.'

He was turned out of his lodging in a backward part of London.

'It was with difficulty I persuaded my landlady – she was a needy widow, poor soul, and I was already in her debt – to keep an old box for me in which I had locked a few letters, keepsakes and the like. She lived in great fear of the Public Health and Morality Inspectors, because she was sometimes too poor to pay the customary tip to them, but at last she consented to put it in a dark tiled place under the stairs, and then I went forth into the world – to seek first the luck of a meal and then shelter.'

He wandered down into the thronging gayer parts of London, in which a year or so ago he had been numbered among the spenders.

London, under the Visible Smoke Law, by which any production of visible
smoke with or without excuse was punishable by a fine, had already ceased
to be the sombre smoke-darkened city of the Victorian time; it had been,
and indeed was, constantly being rebuilt, and its main streets were already
beginning to take on those characteristics that distinguished them throughout
the latter half of the twentieth century. The insanitary horse and the
plebeian bicycle had been banished from the roadway, which was now of a
resilient, glass-like surface, spotlessly clean; and the foot passenger was
restricted to a narrow vestige of the ancient footpath on either side of the
track and forbidden at the risk of a fine, if he survived, to cross the roadway.
People descended from their automobiles upon this pavement and went
through the lower shops to the lifts and stairs to the new ways for pedes-
trians, the Rows, that ran along the front of the houses at the level of the
first story, and, being joined by frequent bridges, gave the newer parts of
London a curiously Venetian appearance. In some streets there were upper
and even third-story Rows. For most of the day and all night the shop
windows were lit by electric light, and many establishments had made, as
it were, canals of public footpaths through their premises in order to increase
their window space.

Barnet made his way along this night-scene rather apprehensively since
the police had power to challenge and demand the Labour Card of any
indigent-looking person, and if the record failed to show he was in employ-
ment, dismiss him to the traffic pavement below.

But there was still enough of his former gentility about Barnet's appear-
ance and bearing to protect him from this; the police, too, had other things
to think of that night, and he was permitted to reach the galleries about
Leicester Square – that great focus of London life and pleasure.

He gives a vivid description of the scene that evening. In the centre
was a garden raised on arches lit by festoons of lights and connected with
the Rows by eight graceful bridges, beneath which hummed the interlacing
streams of motor traffic, pulsating as the current alternated between east
and west and north and south. Above rose great frontages of intricate
rather than beautiful reinforced porcelain, studded with lights, barred by
bold illuminated advertisements, and glowing with reflections. There were
the two historical music halls of this place, the Shakespeare Memorial
Theatre, in which the municipal players revolved perpetually through the
cycle of Shakespeare's plays, and four other great houses of refreshment
and entertainment whose pinnacles streamed up into the blue obscurity
of the night. The south side of the square was in dark contrast to the
others; it was still being rebuilt, and a lattice of steel bars surmounted by
the frozen gestures of monstrous cranes rose over the excavated sites of
vanished Victorian buildings.

This framework attracted Barnet's attention for a time to the exclusion

of other interests. It was absolutely still, it had a dead rigidity, a stricken inaction, no one was at work upon it and all its machinery was quiet; but the constructor's globes of vacuum light filled its every interstice with a quivering green moonshine and showed alert but motionless – soldier sentinels!

He asked a passing stroller, and was told that the men had struck that day against the use of an atomic riveter that would have doubled the individual efficiency and halved the number of steel workers.

'Shouldn't wonder if they didn't get chucking bombs,' said Barnet's informant, hovered for a moment, and then went on his way to the Alhambra music hall.

Barnet became aware of an excitement in the newspaper kiosks at the corners of the square. Something very sensational had been flashed upon the transparencies. Forgetting for a moment his penniless condition, he made his way over a bridge to buy a paper, for in those days the papers, which were printed upon thin sheets of metallic foil, were sold at determinate points by specially licensed purveyors. Half over, he stopped short at a change in the traffic below; and was astonished to see that the police signals were restricting vehicles to the half roadway. When presently he got within sight of the transparencies that had replaced the placards of Victorian times, he read of the Great March of the Unemployed that was already in progress through the West End, and so without expenditure he was able to understand what was coming.

He watched, and his book describes this procession which the police had considered it unwise to prevent and which had been spontaneously organized in imitation of the Unemployed Processions of earlier times. He had expected a mob but there was a kind of sullen discipline about the procession when at last it arrived. What seemed for a time an unending column of men marched wearily, marched with a kind of implacable futility, along the roadway underneath him. He was, he says, moved to join them, but instead he remained watching. They were a dingy, shabby, ineffective-looking multitude, for the most part incapable of any but obsolete and superseded types of labour. They bore a few banners with the time-honoured inscription: 'Work, not Charity,' but otherwise their ranks were unadorned.

They were not singing, they were not even talking, there was nothing truculent nor aggressive in their bearing, they had no definite objective they were just marching and showing themselves in the more prosperous parts of London. They were a sample of that great mass of unskilled cheap labour which the now still cheaper mechanical powers had superseded for evermore. They were being 'scrapped' – as horses had been 'scrapped'.

Barnet leant over the parapet watching them, his mind quickened by his own precarious condition. For a time, he says, he felt nothing but despair at

the sight; what should be done, what could be done for this gathering surplus of humanity? They were so manifestly useless – and incapable – and pitiful.

What were they asking for?

They had been overtaken by unexpected things. Nobody had foreseen—

It flashed suddenly into his mind just what the multitudinous shambling enigma below meant. It was an appeal against the unexpected, an appeal to those others who, more fortunate, seemed wiser and more powerful, for something – for *intelligence*. This mute mass, weary footed, rank following rank, protested its persuasion that some of these others must have foreseen these dislocations – that anyhow they ought to have foreseen – and arranged.

That was what this crowd of wreckage was feeling and seeking so dumbly to assert.

'Things came to me like the turning on of a light in a darkened room,' he says. 'These men were praying to their fellow creatures as once they prayed to God! The last thing that men will realize about anything is that it is inanimate. They had transferred their animation to mankind. They still believed there was intelligence somewhere, even if it was careless or malignant. . . . It had only to be aroused to be conscience-stricken, to be moved to exertion. . . . And I saw, too, that as yet *there was no such intelligence*. The world waits for intelligence. That intelligence has still to be made, that will for good and order has still to be gathered together, out of scraps of impulse and wandering seeds of benevolence and whatever is fine and creative in our souls, into a common purpose. It's something still to come. . . .'

It is characteristic of the widening thought of the time that this not very heroical young man who, in any previous age, might well have been altogether occupied with the problem of his own individual necessities, should be able to stand there and generalize about the needs of the race.

But upon all the stresses and conflicts of that chaotic time there was already dawning the light of a new era. The spirit of humanity was escaping, even then it was escaping, from its extreme imprisonment in individuals. Salvation from the bitter intensities of self, which had been a conscious religious end for thousands of years, which men had sought in mortifications, in the wilderness, in meditation, and by innumerable strange paths, was coming at last with the effect of naturalness into the talk of men, into the books they read, into their unconscious gestures, into their newspapers and daily purposes and everyday acts. The broad horizons, the magic possibilities that the spirit of the seeker had revealed to them, were charming them out of those ancient and instinctive preoccupations from which the very threat of hell and torment had failed to drive them. And this young man, homeless and without provision even for the immediate hours, in the presence of social disorganization, distress, and perplexity, in a blazing wilderness of thoughtless pleasure that blotted out the stars, could think as he tells us he thought.

'I saw life plain,' he wrote. 'I saw the gigantic task before us, and the very splendour of its intricate and immeasurable difficulty filled me with exaltation. I saw that we have still to discover government, that we have still to discover education, which is the necessary reciprocal of government, and that all this – in which my own little speck of a life was so manifestly overwhelmed – this and its yesterday in Greece and Rome and Egypt were nothing, the mere first dust swirls of the beginning, the movements and dim murmurings of a sleeper who will presently be awake. . . .'

SECTION 7

And then the story tells, with an engaging simplicity, of his descent from this ecstatic vision of reality.

'Presently I found myself again, and I was beginning to feel cold and a little hungry.'

He bethought himself of the John Burns Relief Offices which stood upon the Thames Embankment. He made his way through the galleries of the booksellers and the National Gallery, which had been open continuously day and night to all decently dressed people now for more than twelve years, and across the rose-gardens of Trafalgar Square, and so by the hotel colonnade to the Embankment. He had long known of these admirable offices, which had swept the last beggars and matchsellers and all the casual indigent from the London streets, and he believed that he would, as a matter of course, be able to procure a ticket for food and a night's lodgings and some indication of possible employment.

But he had not reckoned upon the new labour troubles, and when he got to the Embankment he found the offices hopelessly congested and besieged by a large and rather unruly crowd. He hovered for a time on the outskirts of the waiting multitude, perplexed and dismayed, and then he became aware of a movement, a purposive trickling away of people, up through the arches of the great buildings that had arisen when all the railway stations were removed to the south side of the river, and so to the covered ways of the Strand. And here, in the open glare of midnight, he found unemployed men begging, and not only begging, but begging with astonishing assurance, from the people who were emerging from the small theatres and other such places of entertainment which abounded in that thoroughfare.

This was an altogether unexampled thing. There had been no begging in London streets for a quarter of a century. But that night the police were evidently unwilling or unable to cope with the destitute who were invading those well-kept quarters of the town. They had become stonily blind to anything but manifest disorder.

Barnet walked through the crowd, unable to bring himself to ask; indeed his bearing must have been more valiant than his circumstances, for twice

he says that he was begged from. Near the Trafalgar Square gardens, a girl with reddened cheeks and blackened eyebrows, who was walking alone, spoke to him with a peculiar friendliness.

'I'm starving,' he said to her abruptly.

'Oh! Poor dear!' she said; and with the impulsive generosity of her kind, glanced round and slipped a silver piece into his hand. . . .

It was a gift that, in spite of the precedent of De Quincey, might under the repressive social legislation of those times have brought Barnet within reach of the prison lash. But he took it, he confesses, and thanked her as well as he was able, and went off very gladly to get food.

SECTION 8

A day or so later – and again his freedom to go as he pleased upon the roads may be taken as a mark of increasing social disorganization and police embarrassment – he wandered out into the open country. He speaks of the roads of that plutocratic age as being 'fenced with barbed wire against unpropertied people', of the high-walled gardens and trespass warnings that kept him to the dusty narrowness of the public ways. In the air, happy rich people were flying, heedless of the misfortunes about them, as he himself had been flying two years ago, and along the road swept the new traffic, light and swift and wonderful. One was rarely out of earshot of its whistles and gongs and siren cries even in the field paths or over the open downs. The officials of the labour exchanges were everywhere overworked and infuriated, the casual wards were so crowded that the surplus wanderers slept in ranks under sheds or in the open air, and since giving to wayfarers had been made a punishable offence there was no longer friendship or help for a man from the rare foot passenger or the wayside cottage. . . .

'I wasn't angry,' said Barnet. 'I saw an immense selfishness, a monstrous disregard for anything but pleasure and possession in all those people above us, but I saw how inevitable that was, how certainly if the richest had changed places with the poorest, that things would have been the same. What else can happen when men use science and every new thing that science gives, and all their available intelligence and energy to manufacture wealth and appliances, and leave government and education to the rustling traditions of hundreds of years ago? Those traditions come from the dark ages when there was really not enough for everyone, when life was a fierce struggle that might be masked but could not be escaped. Of course this famine grabbing, this fierce dispossession of others, must follow from such a disharmony between material and training. Of course the rich were vulgar and the poor grew savage and every added power that came to men made the rich richer and the poor less necessary and less free. The men I met in the casual wards and the relief offices were all smouldering for revolt, talking

of justice and injustice and revenge. I saw no hope in that talk, nor in anything but patience. . . .'

But he did not mean a passive patience. He meant that the method of social reconstruction was still a riddle, that no effectual rearrangement was possible until this riddle in all its tangled aspects was solved. 'I tried to talk to those discontented men,' he wrote, 'but it was hard for them to see things as I saw them. When I talked of patience and the larger scheme, they answered, "But then we shall all be dead" – and I could not make them see, what is so simple to my own mind, that that did not affect the question. Men who think in lifetimes are of no use to statesmanship.'

He does not seem to have seen a newspaper during those wanderings, and a chance sight of the transparency of a kiosk in the market-place at Bishop's Stortford announcing a 'Grave International Situation' did not excite him very much. There had been so many grave international situations in recent years.

This time it was talk of the Central European powers suddenly attacking the Slav Confederacy, with France and England going to the help of the Slavs.

But the next night he found a tolerable meal awaiting the vagrants in the casual ward, and learnt from the workhouse master that all serviceable trained men were to be sent back on the morrow to their mobilization centres. The country was on the eve of war. He was to go back through London to Surrey. His first feeling, he records, was one of extreme relief that his days of 'hopeless battering at the underside of civilization' were at an end. Here was something definite to do, something definitely provided for. But his relief was greatly modified when he found that the mobilization arrangements had been made so hastily and carelessly that for nearly thirty-six hours at the improvised depot at Epsom he got nothing either to eat or to drink but a cup of cold water. The depot was absolutely unprovisioned, and no one was free to leave it.

CHAPTER II

The Last War

SECTION I

Viewed from the standpoint of a sane and ambitious social order, it is diffi-
cult to understand, and it would be tedious to follow, the motives that
plunged mankind into the war that fills the histories of the middle decades
of the twentieth century.

It must always be remembered that the political structure of the world
at that time was everywhere extraordinarily behind the collective intelli-
gence. That is the central fact of that history. For two hundred years there
had been no great changes in political or legal methods and pretensions,
the utmost change had been a certain shifting of boundaries and slight
readjustment of procedure, while in nearly every other aspect of life there
had been fundamental revolutions, gigantic releases, and an enormous
enlargement of scope and outlook. The absurdities of courts and the
indignities of representative parliamentary government, coupled with the
opening of vast fields of opportunity in other directions, had withdrawn
the best intelligences more and more from public affairs. The ostensible
governments of the world in the twentieth century were following in the
wake of the ostensible religions. They were ceasing to command the services
of any but second-rate men. After the middle of the eighteenth century
there are no more great ecclesiastics upon the world's memory, after the
opening of the twentieth no more statesmen. Everywhere one finds an
energetic, ambitious, short-sighted, common-place type in the seats of
authority, blind to the new possibilities and litigiously reliant upon the
traditions of the past.

Perhaps the most dangerous of those outworn traditions were the bound-
aries of the various 'sovereign states', and the conception of a general
predominance in human affairs on the part of some one particular state.
The memory of the empires of Rome and Alexander squatted, an unlaid
carnivorous ghost, in the human imagination – it bored into the human
brain like some grisly parasite and filled it with disordered thoughts and
violent impulses. For more than a century the French system exhausted its
vitality in belligerent convulsions, and then the infection passed to the
German-speaking peoples who were the heart and centre of Europe, and
from them onward to the Slavs. Later ages were to store and neglect the
vast insane literature of this obsession, the intricate treaties, the secret
agreements, the infinite knowingness of the political writer, the cunning
refusals to accept plain facts, the strategic devices, the tactical manoeuvres,

the records of mobilizations and counter-mobilizations. It ceased to be credible almost as soon as it ceased to happen, but in the very dawn of the new age their state craftsmen sat with their historical candles burning, and, in spite of strange, new reflections and unfamiliar lights and shadows, still wrangling and planning to rearrange the maps of Europe and the world.

It was to become a matter for subtle enquiry how far the millions of men and women outside the world of these specialists sympathized and agreed with their portentous activities. One school of psychologists inclined to minimize this participation, but the balance of evidence goes to show that there were massive responses to these suggestions of the belligerent schemer. Primitive man had been a fiercely combative animal; innumerable generations had passed their lives in tribal warfare, and the weight of tradition, the example of history, the ideals of loyalty and devotion fell in easily enough with the incitements of the international mischief-maker. The political ideas of the common man were picked up haphazard, there was practically nothing in such education as he was given that was ever intended to fit him for citizenship as such (that conception only appeared, indeed, with the development of Modern State ideas), and it was therefore a comparatively easy matter to fill his vacant mind with the sounds and fury of exasperated suspicion and national aggression.

For example, Barnet describes the London crowd as noisily patriotic when presently his battalion came up from the depot to London, to entrain for the French frontier. He tells of children and women and lads and old men cheering and shouting, of the streets and rows hung with the flags of the Allied Powers, of a real enthusiasm even among the destitute and unemployed. The Labour Bureaux were now partially transformed into enrolment offices, and were centres of hotly patriotic excitement. At every convenient place upon the line on either side of the Channel Tunnel there were enthusiastic spectators, and the feeling in the regiment, if a little stiffened and darkened by grim anticipations, was none the less warlike.

But all this emotion was the fickle emotion of minds without established ideas; it was with most of them, Barnet says, as it was with himself, a natural response to collective movement, and to martial sounds and colours, and the exhilarating challenge of vague dangers. And people had been so long oppressed by the threat of and preparation for war that its arrival came with an effect of positive relief.

SECTION 2

The plan of campaign of the Allies assigned the defence of the lower Meuse to the English, and the troop-trains were run direct from the various British depots to the points in the Ardennes where they were intended to entrench themselves.

Most of the documents bearing upon the campaign were destroyed during the war, from the first the scheme of the Allies seems to have been confused, but it is highly probable that the formation of an aerial park in this region, from which attacks could be made upon the vast industrial plant of the lower Rhine, and a flanking raid through Holland upon the German naval establishments at the mouth of the Elbe, were integral parts of the original project. Nothing of this was known to such pawns in the game as Barnet and his company, whose business it was to do what they were told by the mysterious intelligences at the direction of things in Paris, to which city the Whitehall staff had also been transferred. From first to last these directing intelligences remained mysterious to the body of the army, veiled under the name of 'Orders'. There was no Napoleon, no Caesar to embody enthusiasm. Barnet says, 'We talked of Them. *They* are sending us up into Luxembourg. *They* are going to turn the Central European right.'

Behind the veil of this vagueness the little group of more or less worthy men which constituted Headquarters was beginning to realize the enormity of the thing it was supposed to control. . . .

In the great hall of the War Control, whose windows looked out across the Seine to the Trocadero and the palaces of the western quarter, a series of big-scale relief maps were laid out upon tables to display the whole seat of war, and the staff-officers of the control were continually busy shifting the little blocks which represented the contending troops, as the reports and intelligence came drifting in to the various telegraphic bureaux in the adjacent rooms. In other smaller apartments there were maps of a less detailed sort, upon which, for example, the reports of the British Admiralty and of the Slav commanders were recorded as they kept coming to hand. Upon these maps, as upon chessboards, Marshal Dubois, in consultation with General Viard and the Earl of Delhi, was to play the great game for world supremacy against the Central European powers. Very probably he had a definite idea of his game; very probably he had a coherent and admirable plan.

But he had reckoned without a proper estimate either of the new strategy of aviation or of the possibilities of atomic energy that Holsten had opened for mankind. While he planned entrenchments and invasions and a frontier war, the Central European generalship was striking at the eyes and the brain. And while, with a certain diffident hesitation, he developed his gambit that night upon the lines laid down by Napoleon and Moltke, his own scientific corps in a state of mutinous activity was preparing a blow for Berlin. 'These old fools!' was the key in which the scientific corps was thinking.

The War Control in Paris, on the night of July the second, was an impressive display of the paraphernalia of scientific military organization, as the first half of the twentieth century understood it. To one human

being at least the consulting commanders had the likeness of world-wielding gods.

She was a skilled typist, capable of nearly sixty words a minute, and she had been engaged in relay with other similar women to take down orders in duplicate and hand them over to the junior officers in attendance, to be forwarded and filed. There had come a lull, and she had been sent out from the dictating room to take the air upon the terrace before the great hall and to eat such scanty refreshment as she had brought with her until her services were required again.

From her position upon the terrace this young woman had a view not only of the wide sweep of the river below her, and all the eastward side of Paris from the Arc de Triomphe to Saint Cloud, great blocks and masses of black or pale darkness with pink and golden flashes of illumination and endless interlacing bands of dotted lights under a still and starless sky, but also the whole spacious interior of the great hall with its slender pillars and gracious arching and clustering lamps was visible to her. There, over a wilderness of tables, lay the huge maps, done on so large a scale that one might fancy them small countries; the messengers and attendants went and came perpetually, altering, moving the little pieces that signified hundreds and thousands of men, and the great commander and his two consultants stood amidst all these things and near where the fighting was nearest, scheming, directing. They had but to breathe a word and presently away there, in the world of reality, the punctual myriads moved. Men rose up and went forward and died. The fate of nations lay behind the eyes of these three men. Indeed they were like gods.

Most godlike of the three was Dubois. It was for him to decide; the others at most might suggest. Her woman's soul went out to this grave, handsome, still, old man, in a passion of instinctive worship.

Once she had taken words of instruction from him direct. She had awaited them in an ecstasy of happiness – and fear. For her exaltation was made terrible by the dread that some error might dishonour her. . . .

She watched him now through the glass with all the unpenetrating minuteness of an impassioned woman's observation.

He said little, she remarked. He looked but little at the maps. The tall Englishman beside him was manifestly troubled by a swarm of ideas, conflicting ideas; he craned his neck at every shifting of the little red, blue, black, and yellow pieces on the board, and wanted to draw the commander's attention to this and that. Dubois listened, nodded, emitted a word and became still again, brooding like the national eagle.

His eyes were so deeply sunken under his white eyebrows that she could not see his eyes; his moustache overhung the mouth from which those words of decision came. Viard, too, said little; he was a dark man with a drooping head and melancholy, watchful eyes. He was more intent upon the French

right, which was feeling its way now through Alsace to the Rhine. He was, she knew, an old colleague of Dubois; he knew him better, she decided, he trusted him more than this unfamiliar Englishman. . . .

Not to talk, to remain impassive and as far as possible in profile; these were the lessons that old Dubois had mastered years ago. To seem to know all, to betray no surprise, to refuse to hurry – itself a confession of miscalculation; by attention to these simple rules, Dubois had built up a steady reputation from the days when he had been a promising junior officer, a still, almost abstracted young man, deliberate but ready. Even then men had looked at him and said: 'He will go far.' Through fifty years of peace he had never once been found wanting, and at manoeuvres his impassive persistence had perplexed and hypnotized and defeated many a more actively intelligent man. Deep in his soul Dubois had hidden his one profound discovery about the modern art of warfare, the key to his career. And this discovery was that *nobody knew*, that to act therefore was to blunder, that to talk was to confess; and that the man who acted slowly and steadfastly and above all silently, had the best chance of winning through. Meanwhile one fed the men. Now by this same strategy he hoped to shatter those mysterious unknowns of the Central European command. Delhi might talk of a great flank march through Holland, with all the British submarines and hydroplanes and torpedo craft pouring up the Rhine in support of it; Viard might crave for brilliance with the motor bicycles, aeroplanes, and ski-men among the Swiss mountains, and a sudden swoop upon Vienna; the thing was to listen – and wait for the other side to begin experimenting. It was all experimenting. And meanwhile he remained in profile, with an air of assurance – like a man who sits in an automobile after the chauffeur has had his directions.

And everyone about him was the stronger and surer for that quiet face, that air of knowledge and unruffled confidence. The clustering lights threw a score of shadows of him upon the maps, great bunches of him, versions of a commanding presence, lighter or darker, dominated the field, and pointed in every direction. Those shadows symbolized his control. When a messenger came from the wireless room to shift this or that piece in the game, to replace under amended reports one Central European regiment by a score, to draw back or thrust out or distribute this or that force of the Allies, the Marshal would turn his head and seem not to see, or look and nod slightly, as a master nods who approves a pupil's self-correction. 'Yes, that's better.'

How wonderful he was, thought the woman at the window, how wonderful it all was. This was the brain of the western world, this was Olympus with the warring earth at its feet. And he was guiding France, France so long a resentful exile from imperialism, back to her old predominance.

It seemed to her beyond the desert of a woman that she should be privileged to participate. . . .

It is hard to be a woman, full of the stormy impulse to personal devotion, and to have to be impersonal, abstract, exact, punctual. She must control herself. . . .

She gave herself up to fantastic dreams, dreams of the days when the war would be over and victory enthroned. Then perhaps this harshness, this armour would be put aside and the gods might unbend. Her eyelids drooped. . . .

She roused herself with a start. She became aware that the night outside was no longer still. That there was an excitement down below on the bridge and a running in the street and a flickering of searchlights among the clouds from some high place away beyond the Trocadero. And then the excitement came surging up past her and invaded the hall within.

One of the sentinels from the terrace stood at the upper end of the room, gesticulating and shouting something.

And all the world had changed. A kind of throbbing. She couldn't understand. It was as if all the water-pipes and concealed machinery and cables of the ways beneath, were beating – as pulses beat. And about her blew something like a wind – a wind that was dismay.

Her eyes went to the face of the Marshal as a frightened child might look towards its mother.

He was still serene. He was frowning slightly, she thought, but that was natural enough, for the Earl of Delhi, with one hand gauntly gesticulating, had taken him by the arm and was all too manifestly disposed to drag him towards the great door that opened on the terrace. And Viard was hurrying towards the huge windows and doing so in the strangest of attitudes, bent forward and with eyes upturned.

Something up there?

And then it was as if thunder broke overhead.

The sound struck her like a blow. She crouched together against the masonry and looked up. She saw three black shapes swooping down through the torn clouds, and from a point a little below two of them, there had already started curling trails of red. . . .

Everything else in her being was paralysed, she hung through moments that seemed infinities, watching those red missiles whirl down towards her.

She felt torn out of the world. There was nothing else in the world but a crimson-purple glare and sound, deafening, all-embracing, continuing sound. Every other light had gone out about her and against this glare hung slanting walls, pirouetting pillars, projecting fragments of cornices, and a disorderly flight of huge angular sheets of glass. She had an impression of a great ball of crimson-purple fire like a maddened living thing that seemed to be whirling about very rapidly amidst a chaos of falling masonry, that seemed to be attacking the earth furiously, that seemed to be burrowing into it like a blazing rabbit. . . .

She had all the sensations of waking up out of a dream.

She found she was lying face downward on a bank of mould and that a little rivulet of hot water was running over one foot. She tried to raise herself and found her leg was very painful. She was not clear whether it was night or day nor where she was; she made a second effort, wincing and groaning, and turned over and got into a sitting position and looked about her.

Everything seemed very silent. She was, in fact, in the midst of a vast uproar, but she did not realize this because her hearing had been destroyed.

At first she could not join on what she saw to any previous experience.

She seemed to be in a strange world, a soundless, ruinous world, a world of heaped broken things. And it was lit – and somehow this was more familiar to her mind than any other fact about her – by a flickering, purplish-crimson light. Then close to her, rising above a confusion of debris, she recognized the Trocadero; it was changed, something had gone from it, but its outline was unmistakable. It stood out against a streaming, whirling uprush of red-lit steam. And with that she recalled Paris and the Seine and the warm, overcast evening and the beautiful, luminous organization of the War Control. . . .

She drew herself a little way up the slope of earth on which she lay, and examined her surroundings with an increasing understanding . . .

The earth on which she was lying projected like a cape into the river. Quite close to her was a brimming lake of dammed-up water, from which these warm rivulets and torrents were trickling. Wisps of vapour came into circling existence a foot or so from its mirror-surface. Near at hand and reflected exactly in the water was the upper part of a familiar-looking stone pillar. On the side of her away from the water the heaped ruins rose steeply in a confused slope up to a glaring crest. Above and reflecting this glare towered pillowed masses of steam rolling swiftly upward to the zenith. It was from this crest that the livid glow that lit the world about her proceeded, and slowly her mind connected this mound with the vanished buildings of the War Control.

'*Mais!*' she whispered, and remained with staring eyes quite motionless for a time, crouching close to the warm earth.

Then presently this dim, broken human thing began to look about it again. She began to feel the need of fellowship. She wanted to question, wanted to speak, wanted to relate her experience. And her foot hurt her atrociously. There ought to be an ambulance. A little gust of querulous criticisms blew across her mind. This surely was a disaster! Always after a disaster there should be ambulances and helpers moving about . . .

She craned her head. There was something there. But everything was so still!

'*Monsieur!*' she cried. Her ears, she noted, felt queer, and she began to suspect that all was not well with them.

It was terribly lonely in this chaotic strangeness, and perhaps this man

– if it was a man, for it was difficult to see – might for all his stillness be merely insensible. He might have been stunned. . . .

The leaping glare beyond sent a ray into his corner and for a moment every little detail was distinct. It was Marshal Dubois. He was lying against a huge slab of the war map. To it there stuck and from it there dangled little wooden objects, the symbols of infantry and cavalry and guns, as they were disposed upon the frontier. He did not seem to be aware of this at his back, he had an effect of inattention, not indifferent attention, but as if he were thinking. . . .

She could not see the eyes beneath his shaggy brows, but it was evident he frowned. He frowned slightly, he had an air of not wanting to be disturbed. His face still bore that expression of assured confidence, that conviction that if things were left to him France might obey in security. . . .

She did not cry out to him again, but she crept a little nearer. A strange surmise made her eyes dilate. With a painful wrench she pulled herself up so that she could see completely over the intervening lumps of smashed-up masonry. Her hand touched something wet, and after one convulsive movement she became rigid.

It was not a whole man there; it was a piece of a man, the head and shoulders of a man that trailed down into a ragged darkness and a pool of shining black. . . .

And even as she stared the mound above her swayed and crumbled, and a rush of hot water came pouring over her. Then it seemed to her that she was dragged downward. . . .

SECTION 3

When the rather brutish young aviator with the bullet head and the black hair close-cropped *en brosse*, who was in charge of the French special scientific corps, heard presently of this disaster to the War Control, he was so wanting in imagination in any sphere but his own, that he laughed. Small matter to him that Paris was burning. His mother and father and sister lived at Caudebec; and the only sweetheart he had ever had, and it was poor love-making then, was a girl in Rouen. He slapped his second-in-command on the shoulder. 'Now,' he said, 'there's nothing on earth to stop us going to Berlin and giving them tit-for-tat. . . . Strategy and reasons of state – they're over. . . . Come along, my boy, and we'll just show these old women what we can do when they let us have our heads.'

He spent five minutes telephoning and then he went out into the courtyard of the chateau in which he had been installed and shouted for his automobile. Things would have to move quickly because there was scarcely an hour and a half before dawn. He looked at the sky and noted with satisfaction a heavy bank of clouds athwart the pallid east.

He was a young man of infinite shrewdness, and his material and aero-planes were scattered all over the countryside, stuck away in barns, covered with hay, hidden in woods. A hawk could not have discovered any of them without coming within reach of a gun. But that night he only wanted one of the machines, and it was handy and quite prepared under a tarpaulin between two ricks not a couple of miles away; he was going to Berlin with that and just one other man. Two men would be enough for what he meant to do. . . .

He had in his hands the black complement to all those other gifts science was urging upon unregenerate mankind, the gift of destruction, and he was an adventurous rather than a sympathetic type. . . .

He was a dark young man with something Negroid about his gleaming face. He smiled like one who is favoured and anticipates great pleasures. There was an exotic richness, a chuckling flavour, about the voice in which he gave his orders, and he pointed his remarks with the long finger of a hand that was hairy and exceptionally big.

'We'll give them tit-for-tat,' he said. 'We'll give them tit-for-tat. No time to lose, boys. . . .'

And presently over the cloud-banks that lay above Westphalia and Saxony the swift aeroplane, with its atomic engine as noiseless as a dancing sunbeam and its phosphorescent gyroscopic compass, flew like an arrow to the heart of the Central European hosts.

It did not soar very high; it skimmed a few hundred feet above the banked darknesses of cumulus that hid the world, ready to plunge at once into their wet obscurities should some hostile flier range into vision. The tense young steersman divided his attention between the guiding stars above and the level, tumbled surfaces of the vapour strata that hid the world below. Over great spaces those banks lay as even as a frozen lava-flow and almost as still, and then they were rent by ragged areas of translucency, pierced by clear chasms, so that dim patches of the land below gleamed remotely through abysses. Once he saw quite distinctly the plan of a big railway station outlined in lamps and signals, and once the flames of a burning rick showing livid through a boiling drift of smoke on the side of some great hill. But if the world was masked it was alive with sounds. Up through that vapour floor came the deep roar of trains, the whistles of horns of motor-cars, a sound of rifle fire away to the south, and as he drew near his destination the crowing of cocks. . . .

The sky above the indistinct horizons of this cloud sea was at first starry and then paler with a light that crept from north to east as the dawn came on. The Milky Way was invisible in the blue, and the lesser stars vanished. The face of the adventurer at the steering-wheel, darkly visible ever and again by the oval greenish glow of the compass face, had something of that firm beauty which all concentrated purpose gives, and something of the

happiness of an idiot child that has at last got hold of the matches. His companion, a less imaginative type, sat with his legs spread wide over the long, coffin-shaped box which contained in its compartments the three atomic bombs, the new bombs that would continue to explode indefinitely and which no one so far had ever seen in action. Hitherto Carolinum, their essential substance, had been tested only in almost infinitesimal quantities within steel chambers embedded in lead. Beyond the thought of great destruction slumbering in the black spheres between his legs, and a keen resolve to follow out very exactly the instructions that had been given him, the man's mind was a blank. His aquiline profile against the starlight expressed nothing but a profound gloom.

The sky below grew clearer as the Central European capital was approached.

So far they had been singularly lucky and had been challenged by no aeroplanes at all. The frontier scouts they must have passed in the night; probably these were mostly under the clouds; the world was wide and they had had luck in not coming close to any soaring sentinel. Their machine was painted a pale grey, that lay almost invisibly over the cloud levels below. But now the east was flushing with the near ascent of the sun, Berlin was but a score of miles ahead, and the luck of the Frenchmen held. By imperceptible degrees the clouds below dissolved. . . .

Away to the north-eastward, in a cloudless pool of gathering light and with all its nocturnal illuminations still blazing, was Berlin. The left finger of the steersman verified roads and open spaces below upon the mica-covered square of map that was fastened by his wheel. There in a series of lake-like expansions was the Havel away to the right; over by those forests must be Spandau; there the river split about the Potsdam island; and right ahead was Charlottenburg cleft by a great thoroughfare that fell like an indicating beam of light straight to the imperial headquarters. There, plain enough, was the Thiergarten; beyond rose the imperial palace, and to the right those tall buildings, those clustering, beflagged, bemasted roofs, must be the offices in which the Central European staff was housed. It was all coldly clear and colourless in the dawn.

He looked up suddenly as a humming sound grew out of nothing and became swiftly louder. Nearly overhead a German aeroplane was circling down from an immense height to challenge him. He made a gesture with his left arm to the gloomy man behind and then gripped his little wheel with both hands, crouched over it, and twisted his neck to look upward. He was attentive, tightly strung, but quite contemptuous of their ability to hurt him. No German alive, he was assured, could outfly him, or indeed any one of the best Frenchmen. He imagined they might strike at him as a hawk strikes, but they were men coming down out of the bitter cold up there, in a hungry, spiritless, morning mood; they came slanting down like a sword

swung by a lazy man, and not so rapidly but that he was able to slip away from under them and get between them and Berlin. They began challenging him in German with a megaphone when they were still perhaps a mile away. The words came to him, rolled up into a mere blob of hoarse sound. Then, gathering alarm from his grim silence, they gave chase and swept down, a hundred yards above him perhaps, and a couple of hundred behind. They were beginning to understand what he was. He ceased to watch them and concentrated himself on the city ahead, and for a time the two aeroplanes raced. . . .

A bullet came tearing through the air by him, as though someone was tearing paper. A second followed. Something tapped the machine.

It was time to act. The broad avenues, the park, the palaces below rushed widening out nearer and nearer to them. 'Ready!' said the steersman.

The gaunt face hardened to grimness, and with both hands the bomb-thrower lifted the big atomic bomb from the box and steadied it against the side. It was a black sphere two feet in diameter. Between its handles was a little celluloid stud, and to this he bent his head until his lips touched it. Then he had to bite in order to let the air in upon the inducive. Sure of its accessibility, he craned his neck over the side of the aeroplane and judged his pace and distance. Then very quickly he bent forward, bit the stud, and hoisted the bomb over the side.

'Round,' he whispered inaudibly.

The bomb flashed blinding scarlet in mid-air, and fell, a descending column of blaze eddying spirally in the midst of a whirlwind. Both the aeroplanes were tossed like shuttlecocks, hurled high and sideways and the steersman, with gleaming eyes and set teeth, fought in great banking curves for a balance. The gaunt man clung tight with hand and knees; his nostrils dilated, his teeth biting his lips. He was firmly strapped. . . .

When he could look down again it was like looking down upon the crater of a small volcano. In the open garden before the Imperial castle a shuddering star of evil splendour spurted and poured up smoke and flame towards them like an accusation. They were too high to distinguish people clearly, or mark the bomb's effect upon the building until suddenly the facade tottered and crumbled before the flare as sugar dissolves in water. The man stared for a moment, showed all his long teeth, and then staggered into the cramped standing position his straps permitted, hoisted out and bit another bomb, and sent it down after its fellow.

The explosion came this time more directly underneath the aeroplane and shot it upward edgeways. The bomb box tipped to the point of disgorgement, and the bomb-thrower was pitched forward upon the third bomb with his face close to its celluloid stud. He clutched its handles, and with a sudden gust of determination that the thing should not escape him, bit its stud. Before he could hurl it over, the monoplane was slipping sideways. Everything

was falling sideways. Instinctively he gave himself up to gripping, his body holding the bomb in its place.

Then that bomb had exploded also, and steersman, thrower, and aeroplane were just flying rags and splinters of metal and drops of moisture in the air, and a third column of fire rushed eddying down upon the doomed buildings below. . . .

SECTION 4

Never before in the history of warfare had there been a continuing explosive; indeed, up to the middle of the twentieth century the only explosives known were combustibles whose explosiveness was due entirely to their instantaneousness; and these atomic bombs which science burst upon the world that night were strange even to the men who used them. Those used by the Allies were lumps of pure Carolinum, painted on the outside with unoxidized cydonator inducive enclosed hermetically in a case of membranium. A little celluloid stud between the handles by which the bomb was lifted was arranged so as to be easily torn off and admit air to the inducive, which at once became active and set up radio-activity in the outer layer of the Carolinum sphere. This liberated fresh inducive, and so in a few minutes the whole bomb was a blazing continual explosion. The Central European bombs were the same, except that they were larger and had a more complicated arrangement for animating the inducive.

Always before in the development of warfare the shells and rockets fired had been but momentarily explosive, they had gone off in an instant once for all, and if there was nothing living or valuable within reach of the concussion and the flying fragments then they were spent and over. But Carolinum, which belonged to the beta group of Hyslop's so-called 'suspended degenerator' elements, once its degenerative process had been induced, continued a furious radiation of energy and nothing could arrest it. Of all Hyslop's artificial elements, Carolinum was the most heavily stored with energy and the most dangerous to make and handle. To this day it remains the most potent degenerator known. What the earlier twentieth-century chemists called its half period was seventeen days; that is to say, it poured out half of the huge store of energy in its great molecules in the space of seventeen days, the next seventeen days' emission was a half of that first period's outpouring, and so on. As with all radio-active substances this Carolinum, though every seventeen days its power is halved, though constantly it diminishes towards the imperceptible, is never entirely exhausted, and to this day the battle-fields and bomb fields of that frantic time in human history are sprinkled with radiant matter, and so centres of inconvenient rays.

What happened when the celluloid stud was opened was that the inducive oxidized and became active. Then the surface of the Carolinum began

to degenerate. This degeneration passed only slowly into the substance of the bomb. A moment or so after its explosion began it was still mainly an inert sphere exploding superficially, a big, inanimate nucleus wrapped in flame and thunder. Those that were thrown from aeroplanes fell in this state, they reached the ground still mainly solid, and, melting soil and rock in their progress, bored into the earth. There, as more and more of the Carolinum became active, the bomb spread itself out into a monstrous cavern of fiery energy at the base of what became very speedily a miniature active volcano. The Carolinum, unable to disperse, freely drove into and mixed up with a boiling confusion of molten soil and superheated steam, and so remained spinning furiously and maintaining an eruption that lasted for years or months or weeks according to the size of the bomb employed and the chances of its dispersal. Once launched, the bomb was absolutely unapproachable and uncontrollable until its forces were nearly exhausted, and from the crater that burst open above it, puffs of heavy incandescent vapour and fragments of viciously punitive rock and mud, saturated with Carolinum, and each a centre of scorching and blistering energy, were flung high and far.

Such was the crowning triumph of military science, the ultimate explosive that was to give the 'decisive touch' to war. . . .

SECTION 5

A recent historical writer has described the world of that time as one that 'believed in established words and was invincibly blind to the obvious in things'. Certainly it seems now that nothing could have been more obvious to the people of the earlier twentieth century than the rapidity with which war was becoming impossible. And as certainly they did not see it. They did not see it until the atomic bombs burst in their fumbling hands. Yet the broad facts must have glared upon any intelligent mind. All through the nineteenth and twentieth centuries the amount of energy that men were able to command was continually increasing. Applied to warfare that meant that the power to inflict a blow, the power to destroy, was continually increasing. There was no increase whatever in the ability to escape. Every sort of passive defence, armour, fortifications, and so forth, was being outmastered by this tremendous increase on the destructive side. Destruction was becoming so facile that any little body of malcontents could use it; it was revolutionizing the problems of police and internal rule. Before the last war began it was a matter of common knowledge that a man could carry about in a handbag an amount of latent energy sufficient to wreck half a city. These facts were before the minds of everybody; the children in the streets knew them. And yet the world still, as the Americans used to phrase it, 'fooled around' with the paraphernalia and pretensions of war.

It is only by realizing this profound, this fantastic divorce between the scientific and intellectual movement on the one hand, and the world of the lawyer-politician on the other, that the men of a later time can hope to understand this preposterous state of affairs. Social organization was still in the barbaric stage. There were already great numbers of actively intelligent men and much private and commercial civilization, but the community, as a whole, was aimless, untrained and unorganized to the pitch of imbecility. Collective civilization, the 'Modern State', was still in the womb of the future. . . .

SECTION 6

But let us return to Frederick Barnet's *Wander Jahre* and its account of the experiences of a common man during the war time. While these terrific disclosures of scientific possibility were happening in Paris and Berlin, Barnet and his company were industriously entrenching themselves in Belgian Luxembourg.

He tells of the mobilization and of his summer day's journey through the north of France and the Ardennes in a few vivid phrases. The country was browned by a warm summer, the trees a little touched with autumnal colour, and the wheat already golden. When they stopped for an hour at Hirson, men and women with tricolour badges upon the platform distributed cakes and glasses of beer to the thirsty soldiers, and there was much cheerfulness. 'Such good, cool beer it was,' he wrote. 'I had had nothing to eat nor drink since Epsom.'

A number of monoplanes, 'like giant swallows', he notes, were scouting in the pink evening sky.

Barnet's battalion was sent through the Sedan country to a place called Virton, and thence to a point in the woods on the line to Jemelle. Here they detrained, bivouacked uneasily by the railway – trains and stores were passing along it all night – and next morning he marched eastward through a cold, overcast dawn, and a morning, first cloudy and then blazing, over a large spacious countryside interspersed by forest towards Arlon.

There the infantry were set to work upon a line of masked entrenchments and hidden rifle pits between St Hubert and Virton that were designed to check and delay any advance from the east upon the fortified line of the Meuse. They had their orders, and for two days they worked without either a sight of the enemy or any suspicion of the disaster that had abruptly decapitated the armies of Europe, and turned the west of Paris and the centre of Berlin into blazing miniatures of the destruction of Pompeii.

And the news, when it did come, came attenuated. 'We heard there had been mischief with aeroplanes and bombs in Paris,' Barnet relates; 'but it didn't seem to follow that "They" weren't still somewhere elaborating their

plans and issuing orders. When the enemy began to emerge from the woods in front of us, we cheered and blazed away, and didn't trouble much more about anything but the battle in hand. If now and then one cocked up an eye into the sky to see what was happening there, the rip of a bullet soon brought one down to the horizontal again. . . .

That battle went on for three days all over a great stretch of country between Louvain on the north and Longwy to the south. It was essentially a rifle and infantry struggle. The aeroplanes do not seem to have taken any decisive share in the actual fighting for some days, though no doubt they effected the strategy from the first by preventing surprise movements. They were aeroplanes with atomic engines, but they were not provided with atomic bombs, which were manifestly unsuitable for field use, nor indeed had they any very effective kind of bomb. And though they manoeuvred against each other, and there was rifle shooting at them and between them, there was little actual aerial fighting. Either the airmen were indisposed to fight or the commanders on both sides preferred to reserve these machines for scouting. . . .

After a day or so of digging and scheming, Barnet found himself in the forefront of a battle. He had made his section of rifle pits chiefly along a line of deep dry ditch that gave a means of inter-communication, he had had the earth scattered over the adjacent field, and he had masked his preparations with tussocks of corn and poppy. The hostile advance came blindly and unsuspiciously across the fields below and would have been very cruelly handled indeed, if someone away to the right had not opened fire too soon.

'It was a queer thrill when these fellows came into sight,' he confesses; 'and not a bit like manoeuvres. They halted for a time on the edge of the wood and then came forward in an open line. They kept walking nearer to us and not looking at us, but away to the right of us. Even when they began to be hit, and their officers' whistles woke them up, they didn't seem to see us. One or two halted to fire, and then they all went back towards the wood again. They went slowly at first, looking round at us, then the shelter of the wood seemed to draw them, and they trotted. I fired rather mechanically and missed, then I fired again, and then I became earnest to hit something, made sure of my sighting, and aimed very carefully at a blue back that was dodging about in the corn. At first I couldn't satisfy myself and didn't shoot, his movements were so spasmodic and uncertain; then I think he came to a ditch or some such obstacle and halted for a moment. "Got you," I whispered, and pulled the trigger.

'I had the strangest sensations about that man. In the first instance, when I felt that I had hit him I was irradiated with joy and pride. . . .

'I sent him spinning. He jumped and threw up his arms. . . .

'Then I saw the corn tops waving and had glimpses of him flapping about. Suddenly I felt sick. I hadn't killed him. . . .

'In some way he was disabled and smashed up and yet able to struggle about. I began to think. . . .

'For nearly two hours that Prussian was agonizing in the corn. Either he was calling out or someone was shouting to him. . . .

'Then he jumped up – he seemed to try to get up upon his feet with one last effort; and then he fell like a sack and lay quite still and never moved again.

'He had been unendurable, and I believe someone had shot him dead. I had been wanting to do so for some time. . . .'

The enemy began sniping the rifle pits from shelters they made for themselves in the woods below. A man was hit in the pit next to Barnet, and began cursing and crying out in a violent rage. Barnet crawled along the ditch to him and found him in great pain, covered with blood, frantic with indignation, and with the half of his right hand smashed to a pulp. 'Look at this,' he kept repeating, hugging it and then extending it. 'Damned foolery! Damned foolery! My right hand, sir! My right hand!'

For some time Barnet could do nothing with him. The man was consumed by his tortured realization of the evil silliness of war, the realization which had come upon him in a flash with the bullet that had destroyed his skill and use as an artificer for ever. He was looking at the vestiges with a horror that made him impenetrable to any other idea. At last the poor wretch let Barnet tie up his bleeding stump and help him along the ditch that conducted him deviously out of range. . . .

When Barnet returned his men were already calling out for water, and all day long the line of pits suffered greatly from thirst. For food they had chocolate and bread.

'At first,' he says, 'I was extraordinarily excited by my baptism of fire. Then as the heat of the day came on I experienced an enormous tedium and discomfort. The flies became extremely troublesome, and my little grave of a rifle pit was invaded by ants. I could not get up or move about, for someone in the trees had got a mark on me. I kept thinking of the dead Prussian down among the corn, and of the bitter outcries of my own man. Damned foolery! It *was* damned foolery. But who was to blame? How had we got to this? . . .

'Early in the afternoon an aeroplane tried to dislodge us with dynamite bombs, but she was hit by bullets once or twice, and suddenly dived down over beyond the trees.

'"From Holland to the Alps this day," I thought, "there must be crouching and lying between half and a million of men, trying to inflict irreparable damage upon one another. The thing is idiotic to the pitch of impossibility. It is a dream. Presently I shall wake up." . . .

'Then the phrase changed itself in my mind. "Presently mankind will wake up."

'I lay speculating just how many thousands of men there were among these hundreds of thousands, whose spirits were in rebellion against all these ancient traditions of flag and empire. Weren't we, perhaps, already in the throes of the last crisis, in that darkest moment of a nightmare's horror before the sleeper will endure no more of it – and wakes?

'I don't know how my speculations ended. I think they were not so much ended as distracted by the distant thudding of the guns that were opening fire at long range upon Namur.'

SECTION 7

But as yet Barnet had seen no more than the mildest beginnings of modern warfare. So far he had taken part only in a little shooting. The bayonet attack by which the advanced line was broken was made at a place called Croix Rouge, more than twenty miles away, and that night under cover of the darkness the rifle pits were abandoned and he got his company away without further loss.

His regiment fell back unpressed behind the fortified lines between Namur and Sedan, entrained at a station called Mettet, and was sent northward by Antwerp and Rotterdam to Haarlem. Hence they marched into North Holland. It was only after the march into Holland that he began to realize the monstrous and catastrophic nature of the struggle in which he was playing his undistinguished part.

He describes very pleasantly the journey through the hills and open land of Brabant, the repeated crossing of arms of the Rhine, and the change from the undulating scenery of Belgium to the flat, rich meadows, the sunlit dyke roads, and the countless windmills of the Dutch levels. In those days there was unbroken land from Alkmaar and Leiden to the Dollart. Three great provinces, South Holland, North Holland and Zuiderzeeland, reclaimed at various times between the early tenth century and 1945 and all many feet below the level of the waves outside the dykes, spread out their lush polders to the northern sun and sustained a dense industrious population. An intricate web of laws and custom and tradition ensured a perpetual vigilance and a perpetual defence against the beleaguering sea. For more than two hundred and fifty miles from Walcheren to Friesland stretched a line of embankments and pumping stations that was the admiration of the world.

If some curious god had chosen to watch the course of events in those northern provinces while that flanking march of the British was in progress, he would have found a convenient and appropriate seat for his observation upon one of the great cumulus clouds that were drifting

slowly across the blue sky during all these eventful days before the great catastrophe. For that was the quality of the weather, hot and clear, with something of a breeze, and underfoot dry and a little inclined to be dusty. This watching god would have looked down upon broad stretches of sunlit green, sunlit save for the creeping patches of shadow cast by the clouds, upon sky-reflecting meres, fringed and divided up by masses of willow and large areas of silvery weeds, upon white roads lying bare to the sun and upon a tracery of blue canals. The pastures were alive with cattle, the roads had a busy traffic, of beasts and bicycles and gaily coloured peasants' automobiles, the hues of the innumerable motor barges in the canal vied with the eventfulness of the roadways; and everywhere in solitary steadings, amidst ricks and barns, in groups by the wayside, in straggling villages, each with its fine old church, or in compact towns laced with canals and abounding in bridges and clipped trees, were human habitations.

The people of this countryside were not belligerents. The interests and sympathies alike of Holland had been so divided that to the end she remained undecided and passive in the struggle of the world powers. And everywhere along the roads taken by the marching armies clustered groups and crowds of impartially observant spectators, women and children in peculiar white caps and old-fashioned sabots, and elderly, clean-shaven men quietly thoughtful over their long pipes. They had no fear of their invaders; the days when 'soldiering' meant bands of licentious looters had long since passed away. . . .

That watcher among the clouds would have seen a great distribution of khaki-uniformed men and khaki-painted material over the whole of the sunken area of Holland. He would have marked the long trains, packed with men or piled with great guns and war material, creeping slowly, alert for train-wreckers, along the north-going lines; he would have seen the Scheldt and Rhine choked with shipping, and pouring out still more men and still more material; he would have noticed halts and provisionings and detrainments, and the long, bustling caterpillars of cavalry and infantry, the maggot-like wagons, the huge beetles of great guns, crawling under the poplars along the dykes and roads northward, along ways lined by the neutral, unmolested, ambiguously observant Dutch. All the barges and shipping upon the canals had been requisitioned for transport. In that clear, bright, warm weather, it would all have looked from above like some extravagant festival of animated toys.

As the sun sank westward the spectacle must have become a little indistinct because of a golden haze; everything must have become warmer and more glowing, and because of the lengthening of the shadows more manifestly in relief. The shadows of the tall churches grew longer and longer, until they touched the horizon and mingled in the universal

shadow; and then, slow, and soft, and wrapping the world in fold after fold of deepening blue, came the night – the night at first obscurely simple, and then with faint points here and there, and then jewelled in darkling splendour with a hundred thousand lights. Out of that mingling of darkness and ambiguous glares the noise of an unceasing activity would have arisen, the louder and plainer now because there was no longer any distraction of sight.

It may be that watcher drifting in the pellucid gulf beneath the stars watched all through the night; it may be that he dozed. But if he gave way to so natural a proclivity, assuredly on the fourth night of the great flank march he was aroused, for that was the night of the battle in the air that decided the fate of Holland. The aeroplanes were fighting at last, and suddenly about him, above and below, with cries and uproar rushing out of the four quarters of heaven, striking, plunging, oversetting, soaring to the zenith and dropping to the ground, they came to assail or defend the myriads below.

Secretly the Central European power had gathered his flying machines together, and now he threw them as a giant might fling a handful of ten thousand knives over the low country. And amidst that swarming flight were five that drove headlong for the sea walls of Holland, carrying atomic bombs. From north and west and south, the allied aeroplanes rose in response and swept down upon this sudden attack. So it was that war in the air began. Men rode upon the whirlwind that night and slew and fell like archangels. The sky rained heroes upon the astonished earth. Surely the last fights of mankind were the best. What was the heavy pounding of your Homeric swordsmen, what was the creaking charge of chariots, beside this swift rush, this crash, this giddy triumph, this headlong swoop to death?

And then athwart this whirling rush of aerial duels that swooped and locked and dropped in the void between the lamp-lights and the stars, came a great wind and a crash louder than thunder, and first one and then a score of lengthening fiery serpents plunged hungrily down upon the Dutchmen's dykes and struck between land and sea and flared up again in enormous columns of glare and crimsoned smoke and steam.

And out of the darkness leapt the little land, with its spires and trees, aghast with terror, still and distinct, and the sea, tumbled with anger, red-foaming like a sea of blood. . . .

Over the populous country below went a strange multitudinous crying and a flurry of alarm bells. . . .

The surviving aeroplanes turned about and fled out of the sky, like things that suddenly know themselves to be wicked. . . .

Through a dozen thunderously flaming gaps that no water might quench, the waves came roaring in upon the land. . . .

SECTION 8

'We had cursed our luck,' says Barnet, 'that we could not get to our quarters at Alkmaar that night. There, we were told, were provisions, tobacco, and everything for which we craved. But the main canal from Zaandam and Amsterdam was hopelessly jammed with craft, and we were glad of a chance opening that enabled us to get out of the main column and lie up in a kind of little harbour very much neglected and weedgrown before a deserted house. We broke into this and found some herrings in a barrel, a heap of cheeses, and stone bottles of gin in the cellar; and with this I cheered my starving men. We made fires and toasted the cheese and grilled our herrings. None of us had slept for nearly forty hours, and I determined to stay in this refuge until dawn and then if the traffic was still choked leave the barge and march the rest of the way into Alkmaar.

'This place we had got into was perhaps a hundred yards from the canal and underneath a little brick bridge we could see the flotilla still, and hear the voices of the soldiers. Presently five or six other barges came through and lay up in the mere near by us, and with two of these, full of men of the Antrim regiment, I shared my find of provisions. In return we got tobacco. A large expanse of water spread to the westward of us and beyond were a cluster of roofs and one or two church towers. The barge was rather cramped for so many men, and I let several squads, thirty or forty perhaps altogether, bivouac on the bank. I did not let them go into the house on account of the furniture, and I left a note of indebtedness for the food we had taken. We were particularly glad of our tobacco and fires, because of the numerous mosquitoes that rose about us.

'The gate of the house from which we had provisioned ourselves was adorned with the legend, Vreugde bij Vrede, "Joy with Peace," and it bore every mark of the busy retirement of a comfort-loving proprietor. I went along his garden, which was gay and delightful with big bushes of rose and sweet brier, to a quaint little summerhouse, and there I sat and watched the men in groups cooking and squatting along the bank. The sun was setting in a nearly cloudless sky.

'For the last two weeks I had been a wholly occupied man, intent only upon obeying the orders that came down to me. All through this time I had been working to the very limit of my mental and physical faculties, and my only moments of rest had been devoted to snatches of sleep. Now came this rare, unexpected interlude, and I could look detachedly upon what I was doing and feel something of its infinite wonderfulness. I was irradiated with affection for the men of my company and with admiration at their cheerful acquiescence in the subordination and needs of our positions. I watched their proceedings and heard their pleasant voices. How willing those men were! How ready to accept leadership and forget themselves in collective ends! I thought how manfully they had gone through all the strains and toil

of the last two weeks, how they had toughened and shaken down to comrade-ship together, and how much sweetness there is after all in our foolish human blood. For they were just one casual sample of the species – their patience and readiness lay, as the energy of the atom had lain, still waiting to be properly utilized. Again it came to me with overpowering force that the supreme need of our race is leading, that the supreme task is to discover leading, to forget oneself in realizing the collective purpose of the race. Once more I saw life plain. . . .'

Very characteristic is that of the 'rather too corpulent' young officer, who was afterwards to set it all down in the *Wander Jahre*. Very characteristic, too, it is of the change in men's hearts that was even then preparing a new phase of human history.

He goes on to write of the escape from individuality in science and service, and of his discovery of this 'salvation.' All that was then, no doubt, very moving and original; now it seems only the most obvious common-place of human life.

The glow of the sunset faded, the twilight deepened into night. The fires burnt the brighter, and some Irishmen away across the mere started singing. But Barnet's men were too weary for that sort of thing, and soon the bank and the barge were heaped with sleeping forms.

'I alone seemed unable to sleep. I suppose I was over-weary, and after a little feverish slumber by the tiller of the barge I sat up, awake and uneasy. . . .

'That night Holland seemed all sky. There was just a little black lower rim to things, a steeple, perhaps, or a line of poplars, and then the great hemisphere swept over us. As at first the sky was empty. Yet my uneasiness referred itself in some vague way to the sky.

'And now I was melancholy. I found something strangely sorrowful and submissive in the sleepers all about me, those men who had marched so far, who had left all the established texture of their lives behind them to come upon this mad campaign, this campaign that signified nothing and consumed everything, this mere fever of fighting. I saw how little and feeble is the life of man, a thing of chances, preposterously unable to find the will to realize even the most timid of its dreams. And I wondered if always it would be so, if man was a doomed animal who would never to the last days of his time take hold of fate and change it to his will. Always, it may be, he will remain kindly but jealous, desirous but discursive, able and unwisely impul-sive, until Saturn who begot him shall devour him in his turn. . . .

'I was roused from these thoughts by the sudden realization of the pres-ence of a squadron of aeroplanes far away to the north-east and very high. They looked like little black dashes against the midnight blue. I remember that I looked up at them at first rather idly – as one might notice a flight of birds. Then I perceived that they were only the extreme wing of a great

fleet that was advancing in a long line very swiftly from the direction of the frontier and my attention tightened.

'Directly I saw that fleet I was astonished not to have seen it before.

'I stood up softly, undesirous of disturbing my companions, but with my heart beating now rather more rapidly with surprise and excitement. I strained my ears for any sound of guns along our front. Almost instinctively I turned about for protection to the south and west, and peered; and then I saw coming as fast and much nearer to me, as if they had sprung out of the darkness, three banks of aeroplanes; a group of squadrons very high, a main body at a height perhaps of one or two thousand feet, and a doubtful number flying low and very indistinct. The middle ones were so thick they kept putting out groups of stars. And I realized that after all there was to be fighting in the air.

'There was something extraordinarily strange in this swift, noiseless convergence of nearly invisible combatants above the sleeping hosts. Everyone about me was still unconscious; there was no sign as yet of any agitation among the shipping on the main canal, whose whole course, dotted with unsuspicious lights and fringed with fires, must have been clearly perceptible from above. Then a long way off towards Alkmaar I heard bugles, and after that shots, and then a wild clamour of bells. I determined to let my men sleep on for as long as they could. . . .

'The battle was joined with the swiftness of dreaming. I do not think it can have been five minutes from the moment when I first became aware of the Central European air fleet to the contact of the two forces. I saw it quite plainly in silhouette against the luminous blue of the northern sky. The allied aeroplanes – they were mostly French – came pouring down like a fierce shower upon the middle of the Central European fleet. They looked exactly like a coarser sort of rain. There was a crackling sound – the first sound I heard – it reminded one of the Aurora Borealis, and I supposed it was an interchange of rifle shots. There were flashes like summer lightning; and then all the sky became a whirling confusion of battle that was still largely noiseless. Some of the Central European aero- planes were certainly charged and overset; others seemed to collapse and fall and then flare out with so bright a light that it took the edge off one's vision and made the rest of the battle disappear as though it had been snatched back out of sight.

'And then, while I still peered and tried to shade these flames from my eyes with my hand, and while the men about me were beginning to stir, the atomic bombs were thrown at the dykes. They made a mighty thunder in the air, and fell like Lucifer in the picture, leaving a flaring trail in the sky. The night, which had been pellucid and detailed and eventful, seemed to vanish, to be replaced abruptly by a black background to these tremendous pillars of fire. . . .

'Hard upon the sound of them came a roaring wind, and the sky was filled with flickering lightnings and rushing clouds. . . .

'There was something discontinuous in this impact. At one moment I was a lonely watcher in a sleeping world; the next saw everyone about me afoot, the whole world awake and amazed. . . .

'And then the wind had struck me a buffet, taken my helmet and swept aside the summerhouse of Vreugde bij Vrede, as a scythe sweeps away grass. I saw the bombs fall, and then watched a great crimson flare leap responsive to each impact, and mountainous masses of red-lit steam and flying fragments clamber up towards the zenith. Against the glare I saw the countryside for miles standing black and clear, churches, trees, chimneys. And suddenly I understood. The Central Europeans had burst the dykes. Those flares meant the bursting of the dykes, and in a little while the sea-water would be upon us. . . .'

He goes on to tell with a certain prolixity of the steps he took – and all things considered they were very intelligent steps – to meet this amazing crisis. He got his men aboard and hailed the adjacent barges; he got the man who acted as barge engineer at his post and the engines working, he cast loose from his moorings. Then he bethought himself of food, and contrived to land five men, get in a few dozen cheeses, and ship his men again before the inundation reached them.

He is reasonably proud of this piece of coolness. His idea was to take the wave head-on and with his engines full speed ahead. And all the while he was thanking Heaven he was not in the jam of traffic in the main canal. He rather, I think, overestimated the probable rush of waters; he dreaded being swept away, he explains, and smashed against houses and trees.

He does not give any estimate of the time it took between the bursting of the dykes and the arrival of the waters, but it was probably an interval of about twenty minutes or half an hour. He was working now in darkness – save for the light of his lantern – and in a great wind. He hung out head and stern lights. . . .

Whirling torrents of steam were pouring up from the advancing waters, which had rushed, it must be remembered, through nearly incandescent gaps in the sea defences, and this vast uprush of vapour soon veiled the flaring centres of explosion altogether.

'The waters came at last, an advancing cascade. It was like a broad roller sweeping across the country. They came with a deep, roaring sound. I had expected a Niagara, but the total fall of the front could not have been much more than twelve feet. Our barge hesitated for a moment, took a dose over her bows, and then lifted. I signalled for full speed ahead and brought her head upstream, and held on like grim death to keep her there.

'There was a wind about as strong as the flood, and I found we were pounding against every conceivable buoyant object that had been between

us and the sea. The only light in the world now came from our lamps, the steam became impenetrable at a score of yards from the boat, and the roar of the wind and water cut us off from all remoter sounds. The black, shining waters swirled by, coming into the light of our lamps out of an ebony blackness and vanishing again into impenetrable black. And on the waters came shapes, came things that flashed upon us for a moment, now a half-submerged boat, now a cow, now a huge fragment of a house's timberings, now a muddle of packing-cases and scaffolding. The things clapped into sight like something shown by the opening of a shutter, and then bumped shatteringly against us or rushed by us. Once I saw very clearly a man's white face. . . .

'All the while a group of labouring, half-submerged trees remained ahead of us, drawing very slowly nearer. I steered a course to avoid them. They seemed to gesticulate a frantic despair against the black steam clouds behind. Once a great branch detached itself and tore shuddering by me. We did, on the whole, make headway. The last I saw of Vreugde bij Vrede before the night swallowed it was almost dead astern of us. . . .'

SECTION 9

Morning found Barnet still afloat. The bows of his barge had been badly strained, and his men were pumping or baling in relays. He had got about a dozen half-drowned people aboard whose boat had capsized near him, and he had three other boats in tow. He was afloat, and somewhere between Amsterdam and Alkmaar, but he could not tell where. It was a day that was still half night. Grey waters stretched in every direction under a dark grey sky, and out of the waves rose the upper parts of houses, in many cases ruined, the tops of trees, windmills, in fact the upper third of all the familiar Dutch scenery; and on it there drifted a dimly seen flotilla of barges, small boats, many overturned, furniture, rafts, timbering, and miscellaneous objects.

The drowned were under water that morning. Only here and there did a dead cow or a stiff figure still clinging stoutly to a box or chair or such-like buoy hint at the hidden massacre. It was not till the Thursday that the dead came to the surface in any quantity. The view was bounded on every side by a grey mist that closed overhead in a grey canopy. The air cleared in the afternoon, and then, far away to the west under great banks of steam and dust, the flaming red eruption of the atomic bombs came visible across the waste of water.

They showed flat and sullen through the mist, like London sunsets. 'They sat upon the sea,' says Barnet, 'like frayed-out waterlilies of flame.'

Barnet seems to have spent the morning in rescue work along the track of the canal, in helping people who were adrift, in picking up derelict boats, and in taking people out of imperilled houses. He found other military barges similarly employed, and it was only as the day wore on and the immediate

appeals for aid were satisfied that he thought of food and drink for his men, and what course he had better pursue. They had a little cheese, but no water. 'Orders', that mysterious direction, had at last altogether disappeared. He perceived he had now to act upon his own responsibility.

'One's sense was of a destruction so far-reaching and of a world so altered that it seemed foolish to go in any direction and expect to find things as they had been before the war began. I sat on the quarter-deck with Mylius my engineer and Kemp and two others of the non-commissioned officers, and we consulted upon our line of action. We were foodless and aimless. We agreed that our fighting value was extremely small, and that our first duty was to get ourselves in touch with food and instructions again. Whatever plan of campaign had directed our movements was manifestly smashed to bits. Mylius was of opinion that we could take a line westward and get back to England across the North Sea. He calculated that with such a motor barge as ours it would be possible to reach the Yorkshire coast within four-and-twenty hours. But this idea I overruled because of the shortness of our provisions, and more particularly because of our urgent need of water.

'Every boat we drew near now hailed us for water, and their demands did much to exasperate our thirst. I decided that if we went away to the south we should reach hilly country, or at least country that was not submerged, and then we should be able to land, find some stream, drink, and get supplies and news. Many of the barges adrift in the haze about us were filled with British soldiers and had floated up from the Nord See Canal, but none of them were any better informed than ourselves of the course of events. "Orders" had, in fact, vanished out of the sky.

'"Orders" made a temporary reappearance late that evening in the form of a megaphone hail from a British torpedo boat, announcing a truce, and giving the welcome information that food and water were being hurried down the Rhine and were to be found on the barge flotilla lying over the old Rhine above Leiden.' . . .

We will not follow Barnet, however, in the description of his strange overland voyage among trees and houses and churches by Zaandam and between Haarlem and Amsterdam, to Leiden. It was a voyage in a red-lit mist, in a world of steamy silhouette, full of strange voices and perplexity, and with every other sensation dominated by a feverish thirst. 'We sat,' he says, 'in a little huddled group, saying very little, and the men forward were mere knots of silent endurance. Our only continuing sound was the persistent mewing of a cat one of the men had rescued from a floating hayrick near Zaandam. We kept a southward course by a watch-chain compass Mylius had produced. . . .

'I do not think any of us felt we belonged to a defeated army, nor had we any strong sense of the war as the dominating fact about us. Our mental setting had far more of the effect of a huge natural catastrophe. The atomic

bombs had dwarfed the international issues to complete insignificance. When our minds wandered from the preoccupations of our immediate needs, we speculated upon the possibility of stopping the use of these frightful explosives before the world was utterly destroyed. For to us it seemed quite plain that these bombs and the still greater power of destruction of which they were the precursors might quite easily shatter every relationship and institution of mankind.

"'What will they be doing," asked Mylius, "what will they be doing? It's plain we've got to put an end to war. It's plain things have to be run some way. *This* – all this – is impossible."

'I made no immediate answer. Something – I cannot think what – had brought back to me the figure of that man I had seen wounded on the very first day of actual fighting. I saw again his angry, tearful eyes, and that poor, dripping, bloody mess that had been a skilful human hand five minutes before, thrust out in indignant protest. "Damned foolery," he had stormed and sobbed, "damned foolery. My right hand, sir! My *right* hand. . . ."

'My faith had for a time gone altogether out of me. "I think we are too – too silly," I said to Mylius, "ever to stop war. If we'd had the sense to do it, we should have done it before this. I think this—" I pointed to the gaunt black outline of a smashed windmill that stuck up, ridiculous and ugly, above the blood-lit waters – "this is the end."'

SECTION 10

But now our history must part company with Frederick Barnet and his barge-load of hungry and starving men.

For a time in western Europe at least it was indeed as if civilization had come to a final collapse. These crowning buds upon the tradition that Napoleon planted and Bismarck watered, opened and flared 'like waterlilies of flame' over nations destroyed, over churches smashed or submerged, towns ruined, fields lost to mankind for ever, and a million weltering bodies. Was this lesson enough for mankind, or would the flames of war still burn amidst the ruins?

Neither Barnet nor his companions, it is clear, had any assurance in their answers to that question. Already once in the history of mankind, in America, before its discovery by the whites, an organized civilization had given way to a mere cult of warfare, specialized and cruel, and it seemed for a time to many a thoughtful man as if the whole world was but to repeat on a larger scale this ascendancy of the warrior, this triumph of the destructive instincts of the race.

The subsequent chapters of Barnet's narrative do but supply body to this tragic possibility. He gives a series of vignettes of civilization, shattered, it seemed, almost irreparably. He found the Belgian hills swarming with refugees

and desolated by cholera; the vestiges of the contending armies keeping order under a truce, without actual battles, but with the cautious hostility of habit, and a great absence of plan everywhere.

Overhead aeroplanes went on mysterious errands, and there were rumours of cannibalism and hysterical fanaticisms in the valleys of the Semoy and the forest region of the eastern Ardennes. There was the report of an attack upon Russia by the Chinese and Japanese, and of some huge revolutionary outbreak in America. The weather was stormier than men had ever known it in those regions, with much thunder and lightning and wild cloud-bursts of rain. . . .

CHAPTER III

The Ending of War

SECTION 1

On the mountainside above the town of Brissago and commanding two long stretches of Lake Maggiore, looking eastward to Bellinzona, and southward to Luino, there is a shelf of grass meadows which is very beautiful in springtime with a great multitude of wild flowers. More particularly is this so in early June, when the slender asphodel Saint Bruno's lily, with its spike of white blossom, is in flower. To the westward of this delightful shelf there is a deep and densely wooded trench, a great gulf of blue some mile or so in width out of which arise great precipices very high and wild. Above the asphodel fields the mountains climb in rocky slopes to solitudes of stone and sunlight that curve round and join that wall of cliffs in one common skyline. This desolate and austere background contrasts very vividly with the glowing serenity of the great lake below, with the spacious view of fertile hills and roads and villages and islands to south and east, and with the hotly golden rice flats of the Val Maggia to the north. And because it was a remote and insignificant place, far away out of the crowding tragedies of that year of disaster, away from burning cities and starving multitudes, bracing and tranquillizing and hidden, it was here that there gathered the conference of rulers that was to arrest, if possible, before it was too late, the debacle of civilization. Here, brought together by the indefatigable energy of that impassioned humanitarian, Leblanc, the French ambassador at Washington, the chief Powers of the world were to meet in a last desperate conference to 'save humanity.'

Leblanc was one of those ingenuous men whose lot would have been insignificant in any period of security, but who have been caught up to an immortal role in history by the sudden simplification of human affairs through some tragical crisis, to the measure of their simplicity. Such a man was Abraham Lincoln, and such was Garibaldi. And Leblanc, with his transparent childish innocence, his entire self-forgetfulness, came into this confusion of distrust and intricate disaster with an invincible appeal for the manifest sanities of the situation. His voice, when he spoke, was 'full of remonstrance.' He was a little bald, spectacled man, inspired by that intellectual idealism which has been one of the peculiar gifts of France to humanity. He was possessed of one clear persuasion, that war must end, and that the only way to end war was to have but one government for mankind. He brushed aside all other considerations. At the very outbreak of the war, so soon as the two capitals of the belligerents had been wrecked,

he went to the president in the White House with this proposal. He made it as if it was a matter of course. He was fortunate to be in Washington and in touch with that gigantic childishness which was the characteristic of the American imagination. For the Americans also were among the simple peoples by whom the world was saved. He won over the American president and the American government to his general ideas; at any rate they supported him sufficiently to give him a standing with the more sceptical European governments, and with this backing he set to work – it seemed the most fantastic of enterprises – to bring together all the rulers of the world and unify them. He wrote innumerable letters, he sent messages, he went on desperate journeys, he enlisted whatever support he could find; no one was too humble for an ally or too obstinate for his advances; through the terrible autumn of the last wars this persistent little visionary in spectacles must have seemed rather like a hopeful canary twittering during a thunderstorm. And no accumulation of disasters daunted his conviction that they could be ended.

For the whole world was flaring then into a monstrous phase of destruction. Power after Power about the armed globe sought to anticipate attack by aggression. They went to war in a delirium of panic, in order to use their bombs first. China and Japan had assailed Russia and destroyed Moscow, the United States had attacked Japan, India was in anarchistic revolt with Delhi a pit of fire spouting death and flame; the redoubtable King of the Balkans was mobilizing. It must have seemed plain at last to everyone in those days that the world was slipping headlong to anarchy. By the spring of 1959 from nearly two hundred centres, and every week added to their number, roared the unquenchable crimson conflagrations of the atomic bombs, the flimsy fabric of the world's credit had vanished, industry was completely disorganized and every city, every thickly populated area was starving or trembled on the verge of starvation. Most of the capital cities of the world were burning; millions of people had already perished, and over great areas government was at an end. Humanity has been compared by one contemporary writer to a sleeper who handles matches in his sleep and wakes to find himself in flames.

For many months it was an open question whether there was to be found throughout all the race the will and intelligence to face these new conditions and make even an attempt to arrest the downfall of the social order. For a time the war spirit defeated every effort to rally the forces of preservation and construction. Leblanc seemed to be protesting against earthquakes, and as likely to find a spirit of reason in the crater of Etna. Even though the shattered official governments now clamoured for peace, bands of irreconcilables and invincible patriots, usurpers, adventurers, and political desperadoes, were everywhere in possession of the simple apparatus for the disengagement of atomic energy and the initiation of new centres

of destruction. The stuff exercised an irresistible fascination upon a certain type of mind. Why should anyone give in while he can still destroy his enemies? Surrender? While there is still a chance of blowing them to dust? The power of destruction which had once been the ultimate privilege of government was now the only power left in the world – and it was everywhere. There were few thoughtful men during that phase of blazing waste who did not pass through such moods of despair as Barnet describes, and declare with him: 'This is the end. . . .'

And all the while Leblanc was going to and fro with glittering glasses and an inexhaustible persuasiveness, urging the manifest reasonableness of his view upon ears that ceased presently to be inattentive. Never at any time did he betray a doubt that all this chaotic conflict would end. No nurse during a nursery uproar was ever so certain of the inevitable ultimate peace. From being treated as an amiable dreamer he came by insensible degrees to be regarded as an extravagant possibility. Then he began to seem even practicable. The people who listened to him in 1958 with a smiling impatience, were eager before 1959 was four months old to know just exactly what he thought might be done. He answered with the patience of a philosopher and the lucidity of a Frenchman. He began to receive responses of a more and more hopeful type. He came across the Atlantic to Italy, and there he gathered in the promises for this congress. He chose those high meadows above Brissago for the reasons we have stated. 'We must get away,' he said, 'from old associations.' He set to work requisitioning material for his conference with an assurance that was justified by the replies. With a slight incredulity the conference which was to begin a new order in the world, gathered itself together. Leblanc summoned it without arrogance, he controlled it by virtue of an infinite humility. Men appeared upon those upland slopes with the apparatus for wireless telegraphy; others followed with tents and provisions; a little cable was flung down to a convenient point upon the Locarno road below. Leblanc arrived, sedulously directing every detail that would affect the tone of the assembly. He might have been a courier in advance rather than the originator of the gathering. And then there arrived, some by the cable car, most by aeroplane, a few in other fashions, the men who had been called together to confer upon the state of the world. It was to be a conference without a name. Nine monarchs, the presidents of four republics, a number of ministers and ambassadors, powerful journalists, and such-like prominent and influential men, took part in it. There were even scientific men; and that world-famous old man, Holsten, came with the others to contribute his amateur statecraft to the desperate problem of the age. Only Leblanc would have dared so to summon figure heads and powers and intelligence, or have had the courage to hope for their agreement. . . .

SECTION 2

And one at least of those who were called to this conference of govern-
ments came to it on foot. This was King Egbert, the young king of the
most venerable kingdom in Europe. He was a rebel, and had always been
of deliberate choice a rebel against the magnificence of his position. He
affected long pedestrian tours and a disposition to sleep in the open air.
He came now over the Pass of Sta Maria Maggiore and by boat up the
lake to Brissago; thence he walked up the mountain, a pleasant path set
with oaks and sweet chestnut. For provision on the walk, for he did not
want to hurry, he carried with him a pocketful of bread and cheese. A
certain small retinue that was necessary to his comfort and dignity upon
occasions of state he sent on by the cable car, and with him walked his
private secretary, Firmin, a man who had thrown up the Professorship of
World Politics in the London School of Sociology, Economics, and Political
Science, to take up these duties. Firmin was a man of strong rather than
rapid thought, he had anticipated great influence in this new position, and
after some years he was still only beginning to apprehend how largely his
function was to listen. Originally he had been something of a thinker upon
international politics, an authority upon tariffs and strategy, and a valued
contributor to various of the higher organs of public opinion, but the
atomic bombs had taken him by surprise, and he had still to recover
completely from his pre-atomic opinions and the silencing effect of those
sustained explosives.

The king's freedom from the trammels of etiquette was very complete.
In theory – and he abounded in theory – his manners were purely democratic.
It was by sheer habit and inadvertency that he permitted Firmin, who had
discovered a rucksack in a small shop in the town below, to carry both
bottles of beer. The king had never, as a matter of fact, carried anything for
himself in his life, and he had never noted that he did not do so.

'We will have nobody with us,' he said, 'at all. We will be perfectly simple.'

So Firmin carried the beer.

As they walked up – it was the king made the pace rather than Firmin
– they talked of the conference before them, and Firmin, with a certain
want of assurance that would have surprised him in himself in the days of
his Professorship, sought to define the policy of his companion. 'In its broader
form, sir,' said Firmin; 'I admit a certain plausibility in this project of Leblanc's,
but I feel that although it may be advisable to set up some sort of general
control for International affairs – a sort of Hague Court with extended
powers – that is no reason whatever for losing sight of the principles of
national and imperial autonomy.'

'Firmin,' said the king, 'I am going to set my brother kings a good example.'

Firmin intimated a curiosity that veiled a dread.

'By chucking all that nonsense,' said the king.

He quickened his pace as Firmin, who was already a little out of breath, betrayed a disposition to reply.

'I am going to chuck all that nonsense,' said the king, as Firmin prepared to speak. 'I am going to fling my royalty and empire on the table – and declare at once I don't mean to haggle. It's haggling – about rights – has been the devil in human affairs, for – always. I am going to stop this nonsense.'

Firmin halted abruptly. 'But, sir!' he cried.

The king stopped six yards ahead of him and looked back at his adviser's perspiring visage.

'Do you really think, Firmin, that I am here as – as an infernal politician to put my crown and my flag and my claims and so forth in the way of peace? That little Frenchman is right. You know he is right as well as I do. Those things are over. We – we kings and rulers and representatives have been at the very heart of the mischief. Of course we imply separation, and of course separation means the threat of war, and of course the threat of war means the accumulation of more and more atomic bombs. The old game's up. But, I say, we mustn't stand here, you know. The world waits. Don't you think the old game's up, Firmin?'

Firmin adjusted a strap, passed a hand over his wet forehead, and followed earnestly. 'I admit, sir,' he said to a receding back, 'that there has to be some sort of hegemony, some sort of Amphictyonic council—'

'There's got to be one simple government for all the world,' said the king over his shoulder.

'But as for a reckless, unqualified abandonment, sir—'

'BANG!' cried the king.

Firmin made no answer to this interruption. But a faint shadow of annoyance passed across his heated features.

'Yesterday,' said the king, by way of explanation, 'the Japanese very nearly got San Francisco.'

'I hadn't heard, sir.'

'The Americans ran the Japanese aeroplane down into the sea and there the bomb got busted.'

'Under the sea, sir?'

'Yes. Submarine volcano. The steam is in sight of the Californian coast. It was as near as that. And with things like this happening, you want me to go up this hill and haggle. Consider the effect of that upon my imperial cousin – and all the others!'

'*He* will haggle, sir.'

'Not a bit of it,' said the king.

'But, sir.'

'Leblanc won't let him.'

Firmin halted abruptly and gave a vicious pull at the offending strap. 'Sir,

he will listen to his advisers,' he said, in a tone that in some subtle way seemed to implicate his master with the trouble of the knapsack.

The king considered him.

'We will go just a little higher,' he said. 'I want to find this unoccupied village they spoke of, and then we will drink that beer. It can't be far. We will drink the beer and throw away the bottles. And then, Firmin, I shall ask you to look at things in a more generous light. . . . Because, you know, you must. . . .'

He turned about and for some time the only sound they made was the noise of their boots upon the loose stones of the way and the irregular breathing of Firmin.

At length, as it seemed to Firmin, or quite soon, as it seemed to the king, the gradient of the path diminished, the way widened out, and they found themselves in a very beautiful place indeed. It was one of those upland clusters of sheds and houses that are still to be found in the mountains of North Italy, buildings that were used only in the high summer, and which it was the custom to leave locked up and deserted through all the winter and spring, and up to the middle of June. The buildings were of a soft-toned grey stone, buried in rich green grass, shadowed by chestnut trees and lit by an extraordinary blaze of yellow broom. Never had the king seen broom so glorious; he shouted at the light of it, for it seemed to give out more sunlight even than it received; he sat down impulsively on a lichenous stone, tugged out his bread and cheese, and bade Firmin thrust the beer into the shaded weeds to cool.

'The things people miss, Firmin,' he said, 'who go up into the air in ships!'

Firmin looked around him with an ungenial eye. 'You see it at its best, sir,' he said, 'before the peasants come here again and make it filthy.'

'It would be beautiful anyhow,' said the king.

'Superficially, sir,' said Firmin. 'But it stands for a social order that is fast vanishing away. Indeed, judging by the grass between the stones and in the huts, I am inclined to doubt if it is in use even now.'

'I suppose,' said the king, 'they would come up immediately the hay on this flower meadow is cut. It would be those slow, creamy-coloured beasts, I expect, one sees on the roads below, and swarthy girls with red handker-chiefs over their black hair. . . . It is wonderful to think how long that beautiful old life lasted. In the Roman times and long ages before ever the rumour of the Romans had come into these parts, men drove their cattle up into these places as the summer came on. . . . How haunted is this place! There have been quarrels here, hopes, children have played here and lived to be old crones and old gaffers, and died, and so it has gone on for thou-sands of lives. Lovers, innumerable lovers, have caressed amidst this golden broom. . . .'

He meditated over a busy mouthful of bread and cheese.

'We ought to have brought a tankard for that beer,' he said.

Firmin produced a folding aluminium cup, and the king was pleased to drink.

'I wish, sir,' said Firmin suddenly, 'I could induce you at least to delay your decision—'

'It's no good talking, Firmin,' said the king. 'My mind's as clear as daylight.'

'Sire,' protested Firmin, with his voice full of bread and cheese and genuine emotion, 'have you no respect for your kingship?'

The king paused before he answered with unwonted gravity. 'It's just because I have, Firmin, that I won't be a puppet in this game of international politics.' He regarded his companion for a moment and then remarked: 'Kingship! – what do YOU know of kingship, Firmin?

'Yes,' cried the king to his astonished counsellor. 'For the first time in my life I am going to be a king. I am going to lead, and lead by my own authority. For a dozen generations my family has been a set of dummies in the hands of their advisers. Advisers! Now I am going to be a real king – and I am going to – to abolish, dispose of, finish, the crown to which I have been a slave. But what a world of paralysing shams this roaring stuff has ended! The rigid old world is in the melting-pot again, and I, who seemed to be no more than the stuffing inside a regal robe, I am a king among kings. I have to play my part at the head of things and put an end to blood and fire and idiot disorder.'

'But, sir,' protested Firmin.

'This man Leblanc is right. The whole world has got to be a Republic, one and indivisible. You know that, and my duty is to make that easy. A king should lead his people; you want me to stick on their backs like some Old Man of the Sea. Today must be a sacrament of kings. Our trust for mankind is done with and ended. We must part our robes among them, we must part our kingship among them, and say to them all, now the king in everyone must rule the world. . . . Have you no sense of the magnificence of this occasion? You want me, Firmin, you want me to go up there and haggle like a damned little solicitor for some price, some compensation, some qualification. . . .'

Firmin shrugged his shoulders and assumed an expression of despair. Meanwhile, he conveyed, one must eat.

For a time neither spoke, and the king ate and turned over in his mind the phrases of the speech he intended to make to the conference. By virtue of the antiquity of his crown he was to preside, and he intended to make his presidency memorable. Reassured of his eloquence, he considered the despondent and sulky Firmin for a space.

'Firmin,' he said, 'you have idealized kingship.'

'It has been my dream, sir,' said Firmin sorrowfully, 'to serve.'

'At the levers, Firmin,' said the king.

'You are pleased to be unjust,' said Firmin, deeply hurt.

'I am pleased to be getting out of it,' said the king.

'Oh, Firmin,' he went on, 'have you no thought for me? Will you never realize that I am not only flesh and blood but an imagination – with its rights. I am a king in revolt against that fetter they put upon my head. I am a king awake. My reverend grandparents never in all their august lives had a waking moment. They loved the job that you, you advisers, gave them; they never had a doubt of it. It was like giving a doll to a woman who ought to have a child. They delighted in processions and opening things and being read addresses to, and visiting triplets and nonagenarians and all that sort of thing. Incredibly. They used to keep albums of cuttings from all the illustrated papers showing them at it, and if the press-cutting parcels grew thin they were worried. It was all that ever worried them. But there is something atavistic in me; I hark back to unconstitutional monarchs. They christened me too retrogressively, I think. I wanted to get things done. I was bored. I might have fallen into vice, most intelligent and energetic princes do, but the palace precautions were unusually thorough. I was brought up in the purest court the world has ever seen . . . alertly pure. . . . So I read books, Firmin, and went about asking questions. The thing was bound to happen to one of us sooner or later. Perhaps, too, very likely I'm not vicious. I don't think I am.'

He reflected. 'No,' he said.

Firmin cleared his throat. 'I don't think you are, sir,' he said. 'You prefer—'

He stopped short. He had been going to say 'talking'. He substituted 'ideas'.

'That world of royalty!' the king went on. 'In a little while no one will understand it any more. It will become a riddle. . . .

'Among other things, it was a world of perpetual best clothes. Everything was in its best clothes for us, and usually wearing bunting. With a cinema watching to see we took it properly. If you are a king, Firmin, and you go and look at a regiment, it instantly stops whatever it is doing, changes into full uniform and presents arms. When my august parents went in a train the coal in the tender used to be whitened. It did, Firmin, and if coal had been white instead of black I have no doubt the authorities would have blackened it. That was the spirit of our treatment. People were always walking about with their faces to us. One never saw anything in profile. One got an impression of a world that was insanely focused on ourselves. And when I began to poke my little questions into the Lord Chancellor and the archbishop and all the rest of them, about what I should see if people turned round, the general effect I produced was that I wasn't by any means displaying the Royal Tact they had expected of me. . . .'

He meditated for a time.

'And yet, you know, there is something in the kingship, Firmin. It stiffened

up my august little grandfather. It gave my grandmother a kind of awkward dignity even when she was cross – and she was very often cross. They both had a profound sense of responsibility. My poor father's health was wretched during his brief career; nobody outside the circle knows just how he screwed himself up to things. "My people expect it," he used to say of this tiresome duty or that. Most of the things they made him do were silly – it was part of a bad tradition, but there was nothing silly in the way he set about them. . . . The spirit of kingship is a fine thing, Firmin; I feel it in my bones; I do not know what I might not be if I were not a king. I could die for my people, Firmin, and you couldn't. No, don't say you could die for me, because I know better. Don't think I forget my kingship, Firmin, don't imagine that. I am a king, a kingly king, by right divine. The fact that I am also a chattering young man makes not the slightest difference to that. But the proper text-book for kings, Firmin, is none of the court memoirs and *Welt-Politik* books you would have me read; it is old Fraser's *Golden Bough*. Have you read that, Firmin?'

Firmin had. 'Those were the authentic kings. In the end they were cut up and a bit given to everybody. They sprinkled the nations – with Kingship.'

Firmin turned himself round and faced his royal master.

'What do you intend to do, sir?' he asked. 'If you will not listen to me, what do you propose to do this afternoon?'

The king flicked crumbs from his coat.

'Manifestly war has to stop for ever, Firmin. Manifestly this can only be done by putting all the world under one government. Our crowns and flags are in the way. Manifestly they must go.'

'Yes, sir,' interrupted Firmin, 'but *what* government? I don't see what government you get by a universal abdication!'

'Well,' said the king, with his hands about his knees, 'We shall be the government.'

'The conference?' exclaimed Firmin.

'Who else?' asked the king simply.

'It's perfectly simple,' he added to Firmin's tremendous silence.

'But,' cried Firmin, 'you must have sanctions! Will there be no form of election, for example?'

'Why should there be?' asked the king, with intelligent curiosity.

'The consent of the governed.'

'Firmin, we are just going to lay down our differences and take over government. Without any election at all. Without any sanction. The governed will show their consent by silence. If any effective opposition arises we shall ask it to come in and help. The true sanction of kingship is the grip upon the sceptre. We aren't going to worry people to vote for us. I'm certain the mass of men does not want to be bothered with such things. . . . We'll contrive a way for anyone interested to join in. That's quite enough in the

way of democracy. Perhaps later – when things don't matter. . . . We shall
govern all right, Firmin. Government only becomes difficult when the lawyers
get hold of it, and since these troubles began the lawyers are shy. Indeed,
come to think of it, I wonder where all the lawyers are. . . . Where are they?
A lot, of course, were bagged, some of the worst ones, when they blew up
my legislature. You never knew the late Lord Chancellor. . . .

'Necessities bury rights. And create them. Lawyers live on dead rights
disinterred. . . . We've done with that way of living. We won't have more
law than a code can cover and beyond that government will be free. . . .

'Before the sun sets today, Firmin, trust me, we shall have made our
abdications, all of us, and declared the World Republic, supreme and indi-
visible. I wonder what my august grandmother would have made of it! All
my rights! . . . And then we shall go on governing. What else is there to
do? All over the world we shall declare that there is no longer mine or thine,
but ours. China, the United States, two-thirds of Europe, will certainly fall
in and obey. They will have to do so. What else can they do? Their official
rulers are here with us. They won't be able to get together any sort of idea
of not obeying us. . . . Then we shall declare that every sort of property is
held in trust for the Republic. . . .'

'But, sir!' cried Firmin, suddenly enlightened. 'Has this been arranged
already?'

'My dear Firmin, do you think we have come here, all of us, to talk at
large? The talking has been done for half a century. Talking and writing. We
are here to set the new thing, the simple, obvious, necessary thing, going.'

He stood up.

Firmin, forgetting the habits of a score of years, remained seated.

'Well,' he said at last. 'And I have known nothing!'

The king smiled very cheerfully. He liked these talks with Firmin.

SECTION 3

That conference upon the Brissago meadows was one of the most hetero-
geneous collections of prominent people that has ever met together.
Principalities and powers, stripped and shattered until all their pride and
mystery were gone, met in a marvellous new humility. Here were kings and
emperors whose capitals were lakes of flaming destruction, statesmen whose
countries had become chaos, scared politicians and financial potentates.
Here were leaders of thought and learned investigators dragged reluctantly
to the control of affairs. Altogether there were ninety-three of them, Leblanc's
conception of the head men of the world. They had all come to the reali-
zation of the simple truths that the indefatigable Leblanc had hammered
into them; and, drawing his resources from the King of Italy, he had provi-
sioned his conference with a generous simplicity quite in accordance with

the rest of his character, and so at last was able to make his astonishing and entirely rational appeal. He had appointed King Egbert the president, he believed in this young man so firmly that he completely dominated him, and he spoke himself as a secretary might speak from the president's left hand, and evidently did not realize himself that he was telling them all exactly what they had to do. He imagined he was merely recapitulating the obvious features of the situation for their convenience. He was dressed in ill-fitting white silk clothes, and he consulted a dingy little packet of notes as he spoke. They put him out. He explained that he had never spoken from notes before, but that this occasion was exceptional.

And then King Egbert spoke as he was expected to speak, and Leblanc's spectacles moistened at that flow of generous sentiment, most amiably and lightly expressed. 'We haven't to stand on ceremony,' said the king, 'we have to govern the world. We have always pretended to govern the world and here is our opportunity.'

'Of course,' whispered Leblanc, nodding his head rapidly, 'of course.'

'The world has been smashed up, and we have to put it on its wheels again,' said King Egbert. 'And it is the simple common sense of this crisis for all to help and none to seek advantage. Is that our tone or not?'

The gathering was too old and seasoned and miscellaneous for any great displays of enthusiasm, but that was its tone, and with an astonishment that somehow became exhilarating it began to resign, repudiate, and declare its intentions. Firmin, taking notes behind his master, heard everything that had been foretold among the yellow broom, come true. With a queer feeling that he was dreaming, he assisted at the proclamation of the World State, and saw the message taken out to the wireless operators to be throbbed all round the habitable globe. 'And next,' said King Egbert, with a cheerful excitement in his voice, 'we have to get every atom of Carolinum and all the plant for making it, into our control. . . .'

Firman was not alone in his incredulity. Not a man there who was not a very amiable, reasonable, benevolent creature at bottom; some had been born to power and some had happened upon it, some had struggled to get it, not clearly knowing what it was and what it implied, but none was irreconcilably set upon its retention at the price of cosmic disaster. Their minds had been prepared by circumstances and sedulously cultivated by Leblanc; and now they took the broad obvious road along which King Egbert was leading them, with a mingled conviction of strangeness and necessity. Things went very smoothly; the King of Italy explained the arrangements that had been made for the protection of the camp from any fantastic attack; a couple of thousand of aeroplanes, each carrying a sharpshooter, guarded them, and there was an excellent system of relays, and at night all the sky would be searched by scores of lights, and the admirable Leblanc gave luminous reasons for their camping just where they were and going on with their administrative duties

forthwith. He knew of this place, because he had happened upon it when holiday-making with Madame Leblanc twenty years and more ago. 'There is very simple fare at present,' he explained, 'on account of the disturbed state of the countries about us. But we have excellent fresh milk, good red wine, beef, bread, salad, and lemons. . . . In a few days I hope to place things in the hands of a more efficient caterer. . . .'

The members of the new world government dined at three long tables on trestles, and down the middle of these tables Leblanc, in spite of the barrenness of his menu, had contrived to have a great multitude of beautiful roses. There was similar accommodation for the secretaries and attendants at a lower level down the mountain. The assembly dined as it had debated, in the open air, and over the dark crags to the west the glowing June sunset shone upon the banquet. There was no precedency now among the ninety-three, and King Egbert found himself between a pleasant little Japanese stranger in spectacles and his cousin of Central Europe, and opposite a great Bengali leader and the President of the United States of America. Beyond the Japanese was Holsten, the old chemist, and Leblanc was a little way down the other side.

The king was still cheerfully talkative and abounded in ideas. He fell presently into an amiable controversy with the American, who seemed to feel a lack of impressiveness in the occasion.

It was ever the Transatlantic tendency, due, no doubt, to the necessity of handling public questions in a bulky and striking manner, to over-emphasize and over-accentuate, and the president was touched by his national failing. He suggested now that there should be a new era, starting from that day as the first day of the first year.

The king demurred.

'From this day forth, sir, man enters upon his heritage,' said the American.

'Man,' said the king, 'is always entering upon his heritage. You Americans have a peculiar weakness for anniversaries – if you will forgive me saying so. Yes – I accuse you of a lust for dramatic effect. Everything is happening always, but you want to say this or this is the real instant in time and subordinate all the others to it.'

The American said something about an epoch-making day.

'But surely,' said the king, 'you don't want us to condemn all humanity to a worldwide annual Fourth of July for ever and ever more. On account of this harmless necessary day of declarations. No conceivable day could ever deserve that. Ah! You do not know, as I do, the devastations of the memorable. My poor grandparents were – *rubricated*. The worst of these huge celebrations is that they break up the dignified succession of one's contemporary emotions. They interrupt. They set back. Suddenly out come the flags and fireworks, and the old enthusiasms are furbished up – and it's sheer destruction of the proper thing that ought to be going on. Sufficient

unto the day is the celebration thereof. Let the dead past bury its dead. You see, in regard to the calendar, I am for democracy and you are for aristocracy. All things I hold, are august, and have a right to be lived through on their merits. No day should be sacrificed on the grave of departed events. What do you think of it, Wilhelm?'

'For the noble, yes, all days should be noble.'

'Exactly my position,' said the king, and felt pleased at what he had been saying.

And then, since the American pressed his idea, the king contrived to shift the talk from the question of celebrating the epoch they were making to the question of the probabilities that lay ahead. Here everyone became diffident. They could see the world unified and at peace, but what detail was to follow from that unification they seemed indisposed to discuss. This diffidence struck the king as remarkable. He plunged upon the possibilities of science. All the huge expenditure that had hitherto gone into unproductive naval and military preparations, must now, he declared, place research upon a new footing. 'Where one man worked we will have a thousand.' He appealed to Holsten. 'We have only begun to peep into these possibilities,' he said. 'You at any rate have sounded the vaults of the treasure house.'

'They are unfathomable,' smiled Holsten.

'Man,' said the American, with a manifest resolve to justify and reinstate himself after the flickering contradictions of the king, 'Man, I say, is only beginning to enter upon his heritage.'

'Tell us some of the things you believe we shall presently learn, give us an idea of the things we may presently do,' said the king to Holsten.

Holsten opened out the vistas. . . .

'Science,' the king cried presently, 'is the new king of the world.'

'*Our* view,' said the president, 'is that sovereignty resides with the people.'

'No!' said the king. 'The sovereign is a being more subtle than that. And less arithmetical. Neither my family nor your emancipated people. It is something that floats about us, and above us, and through us. It is that common impersonal will and sense of necessity of which Science is the best understood and most typical aspect. It is the mind of the race. It is that which has brought us here, which has bowed us all to its demands. . . .'

He paused and glanced down the table at Leblanc, and then re-opened at his former antagonist.

'There is a disposition,' said the king, 'to regard this gathering as if it were actually doing what it appears to be doing, as if we ninety-odd men of our own free will and wisdom were unifying the world. There is a temptation to consider ourselves exceptionally fine fellows, and masterful men, and all the rest of it. We are not. I doubt if we should average out as anything abler than any other casually selected body of ninety-odd men. We are no creators,

we are consequences, we are salvagers – or salvagees. The thing today is not ourselves but the wind of conviction that has blown us hither. . . .'

The American had to confess he could hardly agree with the king's estimate of their average.

'Holsten, perhaps, and one or two others, might lift us a little,' the king conceded. 'But the rest of us?'

His eyes flitted once more towards Leblanc.

'Look at Leblanc,' he said. 'He's just a simple soul. There are hundreds and thousands like him. I admit, a certain dexterity, a certain lucidity, but there is not a country town in France where there is not a Leblanc or so to be found about two o'clock in its principal cafe. It's just that he isn't complicated or Super-Mannish, or any of those things that has made all he has done possible. But in happier times, don't you think, Wilhelm, he would have remained just what his father was, a successful epicier, very clean, very accurate, very honest. And on holidays he would have gone out with Madame Leblanc and her knitting in a punt with a jar of something gentle and have sat under a large reasonable green-lined umbrella and fished very neatly and successfully for gudgeon. . . .'

The president and the Japanese prince in spectacles protested together.

'If I do him an injustice,' said the king, 'it is only because I want to elucidate my argument. I want to make it clear how small are men and days, and how great is man in comparison. . . .'

SECTION 4

So it was King Egbert talked at Brissago after they had proclaimed the unity of the world. Every evening after that the assembly dined together and talked at their ease and grew accustomed to each other and sharpened each other's ideas, and every day they worked together, and really for a time believed that they were inventing a new government for the world. They discussed a constitution. But there were matters needing attention too urgently to wait for any constitution. They attended to these incidentally. The constitution it was that waited. It was presently found convenient to keep the constitution waiting indefinitely as King Egbert had foreseen, and meanwhile, with an increasing self-confidence, that council went on governing . . .

On this first evening of all the council's gatherings, after King Egbert had talked for a long time and drunk and praised very abundantly the simple red wine of the country that Leblanc had procured for them, he fathered about him a group of congenial spirits and fell into a discourse upon simplicity, praising it above all things and declaring that the ultimate aim of art, religion, philosophy, and science alike was to simplify. He instanced himself as a devotee to simplicity. And Leblanc he instanced as a crowning instance of the splendour of this quality. Upon that they all agreed.

When at last the company about the tables broke up, the king found himself brimming over with a peculiar affection and admiration for Leblanc, he made his way to him and drew him aside and broached what he declared was a small matter. There was, he said, a certain order in his gift that, unlike all other orders and decorations in the world, had never been corrupted. It was reserved for elderly men of supreme distinction, the acuteness of whose gifts was already touched to mellowness, and it had included the greatest names of every age so far as the advisers of his family had been able to ascertain them. At present, the king admitted, these matters of stars and badges were rather obscured by more urgent affairs, for his own part he had never set any value upon them at all, but a time might come when they would be at least interesting, and in short he wished to confer the Order of Merit upon Leblanc. His sole motive in doing so, he added, was his strong desire to signalize his personal esteem. He laid his hand upon the Frenchman's shoulder as he said these things, with an almost brotherly affection. Leblanc received this proposal with a modest confusion that greatly enhanced the king's opinion of his admirable simplicity. He pointed out that eager as he was to snatch at the proffered distinction, it might at the present stage appear invidious, and he therefore suggested that the conferring of it should be postponed until it could be made the crown and conclusion of his services. The king was unable to shake this resolution, and the two men parted with expressions of mutual esteem.

The king then summoned Firmin in order to make a short note of a number of things that he had said during the day. But after about twenty minutes' work the sweet sleepiness of the mountain air overcame him, and he dismissed Firmin and went to bed and fell asleep at once, and slept with extreme satisfaction. He had had an active, agreeable day.

SECTION 5

The establishment of the new order that was thus so humanly begun, was, if one measures it by the standard of any preceding age, a rapid progress. The fighting spirit of the world was exhausted. Only here or there did fierceness linger. For long decades the combative side in human affairs had been monstrously exaggerated by the accidents of political separation. This now became luminously plain. An enormous proportion of the force that sustained armaments had been nothing more aggressive than the fear of war and warlike neighbours. It is doubtful if any large section of the men actually enlisted for fighting ever at any time really hungered and thirsted for bloodshed and danger. That kind of appetite was probably never very strong in the species after the savage stage was past. The army was a profession, in which killing had become a disagreeable possibility rather than an eventful certainty. If one reads the old newspapers and periodicals of that time, which

did so much to keep militarism alive, one finds very little about glory and adventure and a constant harping on the disagreeableness of invasion and subjugation. In one word, militarism was funk. The belligerent resolution of the armed Europe of the twentieth century was the resolution of a fiercely frightened sheep to plunge. And now that its weapons were exploding in its hands, Europe was only too eager to drop them, and abandon this fancied refuge of violence.

For a time the whole world had been shocked into frankness; nearly all the clever people who had hitherto sustained the ancient belligerent separations had now been brought to realize the need for simplicity of attitude and openness of mind; and in this atmosphere of moral renascence, there was little attempt to get negotiable advantages out of resistance to the new order. Human beings are foolish enough no doubt, but few have stopped to haggle on a fire-escape. The council had its way with them. The band of 'patriots' who seized the laboratories and arsenal just outside Osaka and tried to rouse Japan to revolt against inclusion in the Republic of Mankind found they had miscalculated the national pride and met the swift vengeance of their own countrymen. That fight in the arsenal was a vivid incident in this closing chapter of the history of war. To the last the 'patriots' were undecided whether, in the event of a defeat, they would explode their supply of atomic bombs or not. They were fighting with swords outside the iridium doors, and the moderates of their number were at bay and on the verge of destruction, only ten, indeed, remained unwounded, when the republicans burst in to the rescue. . . .

SECTION 6

One single monarch held out against the general acquiescence in the new rule, and that was that strange survival of mediaevalism, the 'Slavic Fox', the King of the Balkans. He debated and delayed his submissions. He showed an extraordinary combination of cunning and temerity in his evasion of the repeated summonses from Brissago. He affected ill-health and a great preoccupation with his new official mistress, for his semi-barbaric court was arranged on the best romantic models. His tactics were ably seconded by Doctor Pestovitch, his chief minister. Failing to establish his claims to complete independence, King Ferdinand Charles annoyed the conference by a proposal to be treated as a protected state. Finally he professed an unconvincing submission, and put a mass of obstacles in the way of the transfer of his national officials to the new government. In these things he was enthusiastically supported by his subjects, still for the most part an illiterate peasantry, passionately if confusedly patriotic, and so far with no practical knowledge of the effect of atomic bombs. More particularly he retained control of all the Balkan aeroplanes.

For once the extreme naiveté of Leblanc seems to have been mitigated by duplicity. He went on with the general pacification of the world as if the Balkan submission was made in absolute good faith, and he announced the disbandment of the force of aeroplanes that hitherto guarded the council at Brissago upon the approaching fifteenth of July. But instead he doubled the number upon duty on that eventful day, and made various arrangements for their disposition. He consulted certain experts, and when he took King Egbert into his confidence there was something in his neat and explicit foresight that brought back to that ex-monarch's mind his half-forgotten fantasy of Leblanc as a fisherman under a green umbrella.

About five o'clock in the morning of the seventeenth of July one of the outer sentinels of the Brissago fleet, which was soaring unobtrusively over the lower end of the lake of Garda, sighted and hailed a strange aeroplane that was flying westward, and, failing to get a satisfactory reply, set its wireless apparatus talking and gave chase. A swarm of consorts appeared very promptly over the westward mountains, and before the unknown aeroplane had sighted Como, it had a dozen eager attendants closing in upon it. Its driver seems to have hesitated, dropped down among the mountains, and then turned southward in flight, only to find an intercepting biplane sweeping across his bows. He then went round into the eye of the rising sun, and passed within a hundred yards of his original pursuer.

The sharpshooter therein opened fire at once, and showed an intelligent grasp of the situation by disabling the passenger first. The man at the wheel must have heard his companion cry out behind him, but he was too intent on getting away to waste even a glance behind. Twice after that he must have heard shots. He let his engine go, he crouched down, and for twenty minutes he must have steered in the continual expectation of a bullet. It never came, and when at last he glanced round, three great planes were close upon him, and his companion, thrice hit, lay dead across his bombs. His followers manifestly did not mean either to upset or shoot him, but inexorably they drove him down, down. At last he was curving and flying a hundred yards or less over the level fields of rice and maize. Ahead of him and dark against the morning sunrise was a village with a very tall and slender campanile and a line of cable bearing metal standards that he could not clear. He stopped his engine abruptly and dropped flat. He may have hoped to get at the bombs when he came down, but his pitiless pursuers drove right over him and shot him as he fell.

Three other aeroplanes curved down and came to rest amidst grass close by the smashed machine. Their passengers descended, and ran, holding their light rifles in their hands towards the debris and the two dead men. The coffin-shaped box that had occupied the centre of the machine had broken, and three black objects, each with two handles like the ears of a pitcher, lay peacefully amidst the litter.

These objects were so tremendously important in the eyes of their captors that they disregarded the two dead men who lay bloody and broken amidst the wreckage as they might have disregarded dead frogs by a country pathway.

'By God,' cried the first. 'Here they are!'

'And unbroken!' said the second.

'I've never seen the things before,' said the first.

'Bigger than I thought,' said the second.

The third comer arrived. He stared for a moment at the bombs and then turned his eyes to the dead man with a crushed chest who lay in a muddy place among the green stems under the centre of the machine.

'One can take no risks,' he said, with a faint suggestion of apology.

The other two now also turned to the victims. 'We must signal,' said the first man. A shadow passed between them and the sun, and they looked up to see the aeroplane that had fired the last shot. 'Shall we signal?' came a megaphone hail.

'Three bombs,' they answered together.

'Where do they come from?' asked the megaphone.

The three sharpshooters looked at each other and then moved towards the dead men. One of them had an idea. 'Signal that first,' he said, 'while we look.' They were joined by their aviators for the search, and all six men began a hunt that was necessarily brutal in its haste, for some indication of identity. They examined the men's pockets, their bloodstained clothes, the machine, the framework. They turned the bodies over and flung them aside. There was not a tattoo mark. . . . Everything was elaborately free of any indication of its origin.

'We can't find out!' they called at last.

'Not a sign?'

'Not a sign.'

'I'm coming down,' said the man overhead . . .

SECTION 7

The Slavic Fox stood upon a metal balcony in his picturesque Art Nouveau palace that gave upon the precipice that overhung his bright little capital, and beside him stood Pestovitch, grizzled and cunning, and now full of an ill-suppressed excitement. Behind them the window opened into a large room, richly decorated in aluminium and crimson enamel, across which the king, as he glanced ever and again over his shoulder with a gesture of enquiry, could see through the two open doors of a little azure walled antechamber the wireless operator in the turret working at his incessant transcription. Two pompously uniformed messengers waited listlessly in this apartment. The room was furnished with a stately dignity, and had in the middle of it a big green baize-covered table with the massive white metal

inkpots and antiquated sandboxes natural to a new but romantic monarchy. It was the king's council chamber and about it now, in attitudes of suspended intrigue, stood the half-dozen ministers who constituted his cabinet. They had been summoned for twelve o'clock, but still at half-past twelve the king loitered on the balcony and seemed to be waiting for some news that did not come.

The king and his minister had talked at first in whispers; they had fallen silent, for they found little now to express except a vague anxiety. Away there on the mountainside were the white metal roofs of the long farm buildings beneath which the bomb factory and the bombs were hidden. (The chemist who had made all these for the king had died suddenly after the declaration of Brissago.) Nobody knew of that store of mischief now but the king and his adviser and three heavily faithful attendants; the aviators who waited now in the midday blaze with their bomb-carrying machines and their passenger bomb-throwers in the exercising grounds of the motorcyclist barracks below were still in ignorance of the position of the ammunition they were presently to take up. It was time they started if the scheme was to work as Pestovitch had planned it. It was a magnificent plan. It aimed at no less than the Empire of the World. The government of idealists and professors away there at Brissago was to be blown to fragments, and then east, west, north, and south those aeroplanes would go swarming over a world that had disarmed itself, to proclaim Ferdinand Charles, the new Caesar, the Master, Lord of the Earth. It was a magnificent plan. But the tension of this waiting for news of the success of the first blow was – considerable.

The Slavic Fox was of a pallid fairness, he had a remarkably long nose, a thick, short moustache, and small blue eyes that were a little too near together to be pleasant. It was his habit to worry his moustache with short, nervous tugs whenever his restless mind troubled him, and now this motion was becoming so incessant that it irked Pestovitch beyond the limits of endurance.

'I will go,' said the minister, 'and see what the trouble is with the wireless. They give us nothing, good or bad.'

Left to himself, the king could worry his moustache without stint; he leant his elbows forward on the balcony and gave both of his long white hands to the work, so that he looked like a pale dog gnawing a bone. Suppose they caught his men, what should he do? Suppose they caught his men?

The clocks in the light gold-capped belfries of the town below presently intimated the half-hour after midday.

Of course, he and Pestovitch had thought it out. Even if they had caught those men, they were pledged to secrecy. . . . Probably they would be killed in the catching. . . . One could deny anyhow, deny and deny.

And then he became aware of half a dozen little shining specks very high in the blue. . . . Pestovitch came out to him presently. 'The government messages, sire, have all dropped into cipher,' he said. 'I have set a man—'

'*Look!*' interrupted the king, and pointed upward with a long, lean finger.

Pestovitch followed that indication and then glanced for one questioning moment at the white face before him.

'We have to face it out, sire,' he said.

For some moments they watched the steep spirals of the descending messengers, and then they began a hasty consultation. . . .

They decided that to be holding a council upon the details of an ultimate surrender to Brissago was as innocent-looking a thing as the king could well be doing, and so, when at last the ex-king Egbert, whom the council had sent as its envoy, arrived upon the scene, he discovered the king almost theatrically posed at the head of his councillors in the midst of his court. The door upon the wireless operators was shut.

The ex-king from Brissago came like a draught through the curtains and attendants that gave a wide margin to King Ferdinand's state, and the familiar confidence of his manner belied a certain hardness in his eye. Firmin trotted behind him, and no one else was with him. And as Ferdinand Charles rose to greet him, there came into the heart of the Balkan king again that same chilly feeling that he had felt upon the balcony – and it passed at the care-less gestures of his guest. For surely anyone might outwit this foolish talker who, for a mere idea and at the command of a little French rationalist in spectacles, had thrown away the most ancient crown in all the world.

One must deny, deny. . . .

And then slowly and quite tiresomely he realized that there was nothing to deny. His visitor, with an amiable ease, went on talking about everything in debate between himself and Brissago except—

Could it be that they had been delayed? Could it be that they had had to drop for repairs and were still uncaptured? Could it be that even now while this fool babbled, they were over there among the mountains heaving their deadly charge over the side of the aeroplane?

Strange hopes began to lift the tail of the Slavic Fox again.

What was the man saying? One must talk to him anyhow until one knew. At any moment the little brass door behind him might open with the news of Brissago blown to atoms. Then it would be a delightful relief to the present tension to arrest this chatterer forthwith. He might be killed perhaps. What?

The king was repeating his observation. 'They have a ridiculous fancy that your confidence is based on the possession of atomic bombs.'

King Ferdinand Charles pulled himself together. He protested.

'Oh, quite so,' said the ex-king, 'quite so.'

'What grounds?' The ex-king permitted himself a gesture and the ghost

of a chuckle – why the devil should he chuckle? 'Practically none,' he said. 'But of course with these things one has to be so careful.'

And then again for an instant something – like the faintest shadow of derision – gleamed out of the envoy's eyes and recalled that chilly feeling to King Ferdinand's spine.

Some kindred depression had come to Pestovitch, who had been watching the drawn intensity of Firmin's face. He came to the help of his master, who, he feared, might protest too much.

'A search!' cried the king. 'An embargo on our aeroplanes.'

'Only a temporary expedient,' said the ex-king Egbert, 'while the search is going on.'

The king appealed to his council.

'The people will never permit it, sire,' said a bustling little man in a gorgeous uniform.

'You'll have to make 'em,' said the ex-king, genially addressing all the councillors.

King Ferdinand glanced at the closed brass door through which no news would come.

'When would you want to have this search?'

The ex-king was radiant. 'We couldn't possibly do it until the day after tomorrow,' he said.

'Just the capital?'

'Where else?' asked the ex-king, still more cheerfully.

'For my own part,' said the ex-king confidentially, 'I think the whole business ridiculous. Who would be such a fool as to hide atomic bombs? Nobody. Certain hanging if he's caught – certain, and almost certain blowing up if he isn't. But nowadays I have to take orders like the rest of the world. And here I am.'

The king thought he had never met such detestable geniality. He glanced at Pestovitch, who nodded almost imperceptibly. It was well, anyhow, to have a fool to deal with. They might have sent a diplomatist. 'Of course,' said the king, 'I recognize the overpowering force – and a kind of logic – in these orders from Brissago.'

'I knew you would,' said the ex-king, with an air of relief, 'and so let us arrange—'

They arranged with a certain informality. No Balkan aeroplane was to adventure into the air until the search was concluded, and meanwhile the fleets of the world government would soar and circle in the sky. The towns were to be placarded with offers of reward to anyone who would help in the discovery of atomic bombs. . . .

'You will sign that,' said the ex-king.

'Why?'

'To show that we aren't in any way hostile to you.'

Pestovitch nodded 'yes' to his master.

'And then, you see,' said the ex-king in that easy way of his, 'we'll have a lot of men here, borrow help from your police, and run through all your things. And then everything will be over. Meanwhile, if I may be your guest. . . .' When presently Pestovitch was alone with the king again, he found him in a state of jangling emotions. His spirit was tossing like a wind-whipped sea. One moment he was exalted and full of contempt for 'that ass' and his search; the next he was down in a pit of dread. 'They will find them, Pestovitch, and then he'll hang us.'

'Hang us?'

The king put his long nose into his councillor's face. 'That grinning brute *wants* to hang us,' he said. 'And hang us he will, if we give him a shadow of a chance.'

'But all their Modern State Civilization!'

'Do you think there's any pity in that crew of Godless, Vivisecting Prigs?' cried this last king of romance. 'Do you think, Pestovitch, they understand anything of a high ambition or a splendid dream? Do you think that our gallant and sublime adventure has any appeal to them? Here am I, the last and greatest and most romantic of the Caesars, and do you think they will miss the chance of hanging me like a dog if they can, killing me like a rat in a hole? And that renegade! He who was once an anointed king! . . .

'I hate that sort of eye that laughs and keeps hard,' said the king.

'I won't sit still here and be caught like a fascinated rabbit,' said the king in conclusion. 'We must shift those bombs.'

'Risk it,' said Pestovitch. 'Leave them alone.'

'No,' said the king. 'Shift them near the frontier. Then while they watch us here – they will always watch us here now – we can buy an aeroplane abroad, and pick them up. . . .'

The king was in a feverish, irritable mood all that evening, but he made his plans nevertheless with infinite cunning. They must get the bombs away; there must be a couple of atomic hay lorries, the bombs could be hidden under the hay. . . . Pestovitch went and came, instructing trusty servants, planning and replanning . . . The king and the ex-king talked very pleasantly of a number of subjects. All the while at the back of King Ferdinand Charles's mind fretted the mystery of his vanished aeroplane. There came no news of its capture, and no news of its success. At any moment all that power at the back of his visitor might crumble away and vanish. . . .

It was past midnight, when the king, in a cloak and slouch hat that might equally have served a small farmer, or any respectable middle-class man, slipped out from an inconspicuous service gate on the eastward side of his palace into the thickly wooded gardens that sloped in a series of terraces down to the town. Pestovitch and his guard-valet Peter, both wrapped about in a similar disguise, came out among the laurels that bordered the pathway

and joined him. It was a clear, warm night, but the stars seemed unusually little and remote because of the aeroplanes, each trailing a searchlight, that drove hither and thither across the blue. One great beam seemed to rest on the king for a moment as he came out of the palace; then instantly and reassuringly it had swept away. But while they were still in the palace gardens another found them and looked at them.

'They see us,' cried the king.

'They make nothing of us,' said Pestovitch.

The king glanced up and met a calm, round eye of light, that seemed to wink at him and vanish, leaving him blinded. . . .

The three men went on their way. Near the little gate in the garden railings that Pestovitch had caused to be unlocked, the king paused under the shadow of an flex and looked back at the place. It was very high and narrow, a twentieth-century rendering of mediaevalism, mediaevalism in steel and bronze and sham stone and opaque glass. Against the sky it splashed a confusion of pinnacles. High up in the eastward wing were the windows of the apartments of the ex-king Egbert. One of them was brightly lit now, and against the light a little black figure stood very still and looked out upon the night.

The king snarled.

'He little knows how we slip through his fingers,' said Pestovitch.

And as he spoke they saw the ex-king stretch out his arms slowly, like one who yawns, knuckle his eyes and turn inward – no doubt to his bed.

Down through the ancient winding back streets of his capital hurried the king, and at an appointed corner a shabby atomic-automobile waited for the three. It was a hackney carriage of the lowest grade, with dinted metal panels and deflated cushions. The driver was one of the ordinary drivers of the capital, but beside him sat the young secretary of Pestovitch, who knew the way to the farm where the bombs were hidden.

The automobile made its way through the narrow streets of the old town, which were still lit and uneasy – for the fleet of airships overhead had kept the cafes open and people abroad – over the great new bridge, and so by straggling outskirts to the country. And all through his capital the king who hoped to outdo Caesar, sat back and was very still, and no one spoke. And as they got out into the dark country they became aware of the searchlights wandering over the countryside like the uneasy ghosts of giants. The king sat forward and looked at these flitting whitenesses, and every now and then peered up to see the flying ships overhead.

'I don't like them,' said the king.

Presently one of these patches of moonlight came to rest about them and seemed to be following their automobile. The king drew back.

'The things are confoundedly noiseless,' said the king. 'It's like being stalked by lean white cats.'

He peered again. 'That fellow is watching us,' he said.

And then suddenly he gave way to panic. 'Pestovitch,' he said, clutching his minister's arm, 'they are watching us. I'm not going through with this. They are watching us. I'm going back.'

Pestovitch remonstrated. 'Tell him to go back,' said the king, and tried to open the window. For a few moments there was a grim struggle in the automobile; a gripping of wrists and a blow. 'I can't go through with it,' repeated the king, 'I can't go through with it.'

'But they'll hang us,' said Pestovitch.

'Not if we were to give up now. Not if we were to surrender the bombs. It is you who brought me into this. . . .'

At last Pestovitch compromised. There was an inn perhaps half a mile from the farm. They could alight there and the king could get brandy, and rest his nerves for a time. And if he still thought fit to go back he could go back.

'See,' said Pestovitch, 'the light has gone again.'

The king peered up. 'I believe he's following us without a light,' said the king.

In the little old dirty inn the king hung doubtful for a time, and was for going back and throwing himself on the mercy of the council. 'If there is a council,' said Pestovitch. 'By this time your bombs may have settled it.'

'But if so, these infernal aeroplanes would go.'

'They may not know yet.'

'But, Pestovitch, why couldn't you do all this without me?'

Pestovitch made no answer for a moment. 'I was for leaving the bombs in their place,' he said at last, and went to the window. About their conveyance shone a circle of bright light. Pestovitch had a brilliant idea. 'I will send my secretary out to make a kind of dispute with the driver. Something that will make them watch up above there. Meanwhile you and I and Peter will go out by the back way and up by the hedges to the farm. . . .'

It was worthy of his subtle reputation and it answered passing well.

In ten minutes they were tumbling over the wall of the farm-yard, wet, muddy, and breathless, but unobserved. But as they ran towards the barns the king gave vent to something between a groan and a curse, and all about them shone the light – and passed.

But had it passed at once or lingered for just a second?

'They didn't see us,' said Peter.

'I don't think they saw us,' said the king, and stared as the light went swooping up the mountainside, hung for a second about a hayrick, and then came pouring back.

'In the barn!' cried the king.

He bruised his shin against something, and then all three men were inside the huge steel-girdered barn in which stood the two motor hay lorries that

were to take the bombs away. Kurt and Abel, the two brothers of Peter, had brought the lorries thither in daylight. They had the upper half of the loads of hay thrown off, ready to cover the bombs, so soon as the king should show the hiding-place. 'There's a sort of pit here,' said the king. 'Don't light another lantern. This key of mine releases a ring. . . .'

For a time scarcely a word was spoken in the darkness of the barn. There was the sound of a slab being lifted and then of feet descending a ladder into a pit. Then whispering and then heavy breathing as Kurt came struggling up with the first of the hidden bombs.

'We shall do it yet,' said the king. And then he gasped. 'Curse that light. Why in the name of Heaven didn't we shut the barn door?' For the great door stood wide open and all the empty, lifeless yard outside and the door and six feet of the floor of the barn were in the blue glare of an enquiring searchlight.

'Shut the door, Peter,' said Pestovitch.

'No,' cried the king, too late, as Peter went forward into the light. 'Don't show yourself!' cried the king. Kurt made a step forward and plucked his brother back. For a time all five men stood still. It seemed that light would never go and then abruptly it was turned off, leaving them blinded. 'Now,' said the king uneasily, 'now shut the door.'

'Not completely,' cried Pestovitch. 'Leave a chink for us to go out by. . . .'

It was hot work shifting those bombs, and the king worked for a time like a common man. Kurt and Abel carried the great things up and Peter brought them to the carts, and the king and Pestovitch helped him to place them among the hay. They made as little noise as they could. . . .

'Ssh!' cried the king. 'What's that?'

But Kurt and Abel did not hear, and came blundering up the ladder with the last of the load.

'Ssh!' Peter ran forward to them with a whispered remonstrance. Now they were still.

The barn door opened a little wider, and against the dim blue light outside they saw the black shape of a man.

'Anyone here?' he asked, speaking with an Italian accent.

The king broke into a cold perspiration. Then Pestovitch answered: 'Only a poor farmer loading hay,' he said, and picked up a huge hay fork and went forward softly.

'You load your hay at a very bad time and in a very bad light,' said the man at the door, peering in. 'Have you no electric light here?'

Then suddenly he turned on an electric torch, and as he did so Pestovitch sprang forward. 'Get out of my barn!' he cried, and drove the fork full at the intruder's chest. He had a vague idea that so he might stab the man to silence. But the man shouted loudly as the prongs pierced him and drove him backward, and instantly there was a sound of feet running across the yard.

'Bombs,' cried the man upon the ground, struggling with the prongs in his hand, and as Pestovitch staggered forward into view with the force of his own thrust, he was shot through the body by one of the two newcomers.

The man on the ground was badly hurt but plucky. 'Bombs,' he repeated, and struggled up into a kneeling position and held his electric torch full upon the face of the king. 'Shoot them,' he cried, coughing and spitting blood, so that the halo of light round the king's head danced about.

For a moment in that shivering circle of light the two men saw the king kneeling up in the cart and Peter on the barn floor beside him. The old fox looked at them sideways – snared, a white-faced evil thing. And then, as with a faltering suicidal heroism, he leant forward over the bomb before him, they fired together and shot him through the head.

The upper part of his face seemed to vanish.

'Shoot them,' cried the man who had been stabbed. 'Shoot them all!'

And then his light went out, and he rolled over with a groan at the feet of his comrades.

But each carried a light of his own, and in another moment everything in the barn was visible again. They shot Peter even as he held up his hands in sign of surrender.

Kurt and Abel at the head of the ladder hesitated for a moment, and then plunged backward into the pit. 'If we don't kill them,' said one of the sharpshooters, 'they'll blow us to rags. They've gone down that hatchway. Come! . . .

'Here they are. Hands up! I say. Hold your light while I shoot. . . .'

SECTION 8

It was still quite dark when his valet and Firmin came together and told the ex-king Egbert that the business was settled.

He started up into a sitting position on the side of his bed.

'Did he go out?' asked the ex-king.

'He is dead,' said Firmin. 'He was shot.'

The ex-king reflected. 'That's about the best thing that could have happened,' he said. 'Where are the bombs? In that farmhouse on the opposite hillside! Why! The place is in sight! Let us go. I'll dress. Is there anyone in the place, Firmin, to get us a cup of coffee?'

Through the hungry twilight of the dawn the ex-king's automobile carried him to the farmhouse where the last rebel king was lying among his bombs. The rim of the sky flashed, the east grew bright, and the sun was just rising over the hills when King Egbert reached the farmyard. There he found the hay lorries drawn out from the barn with the dreadful bombs still packed upon them. A couple of score of aviators held the yard, and outside a few peasants stood in a little group and stared, ignorant as yet of what had

happened. Against the stone wall of the farmyard five bodies were lying neatly side by side, and Pestovitch had an expression of surprise on his face and the king was chiefly identifiable by his long white hands and his blonde moustache. The wounded aeronaut had been carried down to the inn. And after the ex-king had given directions in what manner the bombs were to be taken to the new special laboratories above Zurich, where they could be unpacked in an atmosphere of chlorine, he turned to these five still shapes.

Their five pairs of feet stuck out with a curious stiff unanimity. . . .

'What else was there to do?' he said in answer to some internal protest.

'I wonder, Firmin, if there are any more of them?'

'Bombs, sir?' asked Firmin.

'No, such kings. . . .

'The pitiful folly of it!' said the ex-king, following his thoughts. 'Firmin, as an ex-professor of International Politics, I think it falls to you to bury them. There? . . . No, don't put them near the well. People will have to drink from that well. Bury them over there, some way off in the field.'

CHAPTER IV

The New Phase

SECTION 1

The task that lay before the Assembly of Brissago, viewed as we may view it now from the clarifying standpoint of things accomplished, was in its broad issues a simple one. Essentially it was to place social organization upon the new footing that the swift, accelerated advance of human knowledge had rendered necessary. The council was gathered together with the haste of a salvage expedition, and it was confronted with wreckage; but the wreckage was irreparable wreckage, and the only possibilities of the case were either the relapse of mankind to the agricultural barbarism from which it had emerged so painfully or the acceptance of achieved science as the basis of a new social order. The old tendencies of human nature, suspicion, jealousy, particularism, and belligerency, were incompatible with the monstrous destructive power of the new appliances the inhuman logic of science had produced. The equilibrium could be restored only by civilization destroying itself down to a level at which modern apparatus could no longer be produced, or by human nature adapting itself in its institutions to the new conditions. It was for the latter alternative that the assembly existed.

Sooner or later this choice would have confronted mankind. The sudden development of atomic science did but precipitate and render rapid and dramatic a clash between the new and the customary that had been gathering since ever the first flint was chipped or the first fire built together. From the day when man contrived himself a tool and suffered another male to draw near him, he ceased to be altogether a thing of instinct and untroubled convictions. From that day forth a widening breach can be traced between his egotistical passions and the social need. Slowly he adapted himself to the life of the homestead, and his passionate impulses widened out to the demands of the clan and the tribe. But widen though his impulses might, the latent hunter and wanderer and wonderer in his imagination outstripped their development. He was never quite subdued to the soil nor quite tamed to the home. Everywhere it needed teaching and the priest to keep him within the bounds of the plough-life and the beast-tending. Slowly a vast system of traditional imperatives superposed itself upon his instincts, imperatives that were admirably fitted to make him that cultivator, that cattle-mincer, who was for twice ten thousand years the normal man.

And, unpremeditated, undesired, out of the accumulations of his tilling came civilization. Civilization was the agricultural surplus. It appeared as trade and tracks and roads, it pushed boats out upon the rivers and presently

invaded the seas, and within its primitive courts, within temples grown rich and leisurely and amidst the gathering medley of the seaport towns rose speculation and philosophy and science, and the beginning of the new order that has at last established itself as human life. Slowly at first, as we traced it, and then with an accumulating velocity, the new powers were fabricated. Man as a whole did not seek them nor desire them; they were thrust into his hand. For a time men took up and used these new things and the new powers inadvertently as they came to him, recking nothing of the consequences. For endless generations change led him very gently. But when he had been led far enough, change quickened the pace. It was with a series of shocks that he realized at last that he was living the old life less and less and a new life more and more.

Already before the release of atomic energy the tensions between the old way of living and the new were intense. They were far intenser than they had been even at the collapse of the Roman imperial system. On the one hand was the ancient life of the family and the small community and the petty industry, on the other was a new life on a larger scale, with remoter horizons and a strange sense of purpose. Already it was growing clear that men must live on one side or the other. One could not have little trades-people and syndicated businesses in the same market, sleeping carters and motor trolleys on the same road, bows and arrows and aeroplane sharp-shooters in the same army, or illiterate peasant industries and power-driven factories in the same world. And still less was it possible that one could have the ideas and ambitions and greed and jealousy of peasants equipped with the vast appliances of the new age. If there had been no atomic bombs to bring together most of the directing intelligence of the world to that hasty conference at Brissago, there would still have been, extended over great areas and a considerable space of time perhaps, a less formal conference of responsible and understanding people upon the perplexities of this world-wide opposition. If the work of Holsten had been spread over centuries and imparted to the world by imperceptible degrees, it would nevertheless have made it necessary for men to take counsel upon and set a plan for the future. Indeed already there had been accumulating for a hundred years before the crisis a literature of foresight; there was a whole mass of 'Modern State' scheming available for the conference to go upon. These bombs did but accentuate and dramatize an already developing problem.

SECTION 2

This assembly was no leap of exceptional minds and super-intelligences into the control of affairs. It was teachable, its members trailed ideas with them to the gathering, but these were the consequences of the 'moral shock' the bombs had given humanity, and there is no reason for supposing its individual

personalities were greatly above the average. It would be possible to cite a thousand instances of error and inefficiency in its proceedings due to the forgetfulness, irritability, or fatigue of its members. It experimented considerably and blundered often. Excepting Holsten, whose gift was highly specialized, it is questionable whether there was a single man of the first order of human quality in the gathering. But it had a modest fear of itself, and a consequent directness that gave it a general distinction. There was, of course, a noble simplicity about Leblanc, but even of him it may be asked whether he was not rather good and honest-minded than in the fuller sense great.

The ex-king had wisdom and a certain romantic dash, he was a man among thousands, even if he was not a man among millions, but his memoirs, and indeed his decision to write memoirs, give the quality of himself and his associates. The book makes admirable but astonishing reading. Therein he takes the great work the council was doing for granted as a little child takes God. It is as if he had no sense of it at all. He tells amusing trivialities about his cousin Wilhelm and his secretary Firmin, he pokes fun at the American president, who was, indeed, rather a little accident of the political machine than a representative American, and he gives a long description of how he was lost for three days in the mountains in the company of the only Japanese member, a loss that seems to have caused no serious interruption of the work of the council. . . .

The Brissago conference has been written about time after time, as though it were a gathering of the very flower of humanity. Perched up there by the freak or wisdom of Leblanc, it had a certain Olympian quality, and the natural tendency of the human mind to elaborate such a resemblance would have us give its members the likenesses of gods. It would be equally reasonable to compare it to one of those enforced meetings upon the mountain-tops that must have occurred in the opening phases of the Deluge. The strength of the council lay not in itself but in the circumstances that had quickened its intelligence, dispelled its vanities, and emancipated it from traditional ambitions and antagonisms. It was stripped of the accumulation of centuries, a naked government with all that freedom of action that nakedness affords. And its problems were set before it with a plainness that was out of all comparison with the complicated and perplexing intimations of the former time.

SECTION 3

The world on which the council looked did indeed present a task quite sufficiently immense and altogether too urgent for any wanton indulgence in internal dissension. It may be interesting to sketch in a few phrases the condition of mankind at the close of the period of warring states, in the year of crisis that followed the release of atomic power. It was a world

extraordinarily limited when one measures it by later standards, and it was now in a state of the direst confusion and distress.

It must be remembered that at this time men had still to spread into enormous areas of the land surface of the globe. There were vast mountain wildernesses, forest wildernesses, sandy deserts, and frozen lands. Men still clung closely to water and arable soil in temperate or sub-tropical climates, they lived abundantly only in river valleys, and all their great cities had grown upon large navigable rivers or close to ports upon the sea. Over great areas even of this suitable land flies and mosquitoes, armed with infection, had so far defeated human invasion, and under their protection the virgin forests remained untouched. Indeed, the whole world even in its most crowded districts was filthy with flies and swarming with needless insect life to an extent which is now almost incredible. A population map of the world in 1950 would have followed seashore and river course so closely in its darker shading as to give an impression that homo sapiens was an amphibious animal. His roads and railways lay also along the lower contours, only here and there to pierce some mountain barrier or reach some holiday resort did they clamber above 3,000 feet. And across the ocean his traffic passed in definite lines; there were hundreds of thousands of square miles of ocean no ship ever traversed except by mischance.

Into the mysteries of the solid globe under his feet he had not yet pierced for five miles, and it was still not forty years since, with a tragic pertinacity, he had clambered to the poles of the earth. The limitless mineral wealth of the Arctic and Antarctic circles was still buried beneath vast accumulations of immemorial ice, and the secret riches of the inner zones of the crust were untapped and indeed unsuspected. The higher mountain regions were known only to a sprinkling of guide-led climbers and the frequenters of a few gaunt hotels, and the vast rainless belts of land that lay across the continental masses, from Gobi to Sahara and along the backbone of America, with their perfect air, their daily baths of blazing sunshine, their nights of cool serenity and glowing stars, and their reservoirs of deep-lying water, were as yet only desolations of fear and death to the common imagination.

And now under the shock of the atomic bombs, the great masses of population which had gathered into the enormous dingy town centres of that period were dispossessed and scattered disastrously over the surrounding rural areas. It was as if some brutal force, grown impatient at last at man's blindness, had with the deliberate intention of a rearrangement of population upon more wholesome lines, shaken the world. The great industrial regions and the large cities that had escaped the bombs were, because of their complete economic collapse, in almost as tragic plight as those that blazed, and the countryside was disordered by a multitude of wandering and lawless strangers. In some parts of the world famine raged, and in many regions there was plague. . . . The plains of north India, which had become more

and more dependent for the general welfare on the railways and that great system of irrigation canals which the malignant section of the patriots had destroyed, were in a state of peculiar distress, whole villages lay dead together, no man heeding, and the very tigers and panthers that preyed upon the emaciated survivors crawled back infected into the jungle to perish. Large areas of China were a prey to brigand bands. . . .

It is a remarkable thing that no complete contemporary account of the explosion of the atomic bombs survives. There are, of course, innumerable allusions and partial records, and it is from these that subsequent ages must piece together the image of these devastations.

The phenomena, it must be remembered, changed greatly from day to day, and even from hour to hour, as the exploding bomb shifted its position, threw off fragments or came into contact with water or a fresh texture of soil. Barnet, who came within forty miles of Paris early in October, is concerned chiefly with his account of the social confusion of the countryside and the problems of his command, but he speaks of heaped cloud masses of steam. 'All along the sky to the south-west' and of a red glare beneath these at night. Parts of Paris were still burning, and numbers of people were camped in the fields even at this distance watching over treasured heaps of salvaged loot. He speaks too of the distant rumbling of the explosion – 'like trains going over iron bridges'.

Other descriptions agree with this; they all speak of the 'continuous reverberations', or of the 'thudding and hammering', or some such phrase; and they all testify to a huge pall of steam, from which rain would fall suddenly in torrents and amidst which lightning played. Drawing nearer to Paris an observer would have found the salvage camps increasing in number and blocking up the villages, and large numbers of people, often starving and ailing, camping under improvised tents because there was no place for them to go. The sky became more and more densely overcast until at last it blotted out the light of day and left nothing but a dull red glare 'extraordinarily depressing to the spirit'. In this dull glare, great numbers of people were still living, clinging to their houses and in many cases subsisting in a state of partial famine upon the produce in their gardens and the stores in the shops of the provision dealers.

Coming in still closer, the investigator would have reached the police cordon, which was trying to check the desperate enterprise of those who would return to their homes or rescue their more valuable possessions within the 'zone of imminent danger'.

That zone was rather arbitrarily defined. If our spectator could have got permission to enter it, he would have entered also a zone of uproar, a zone of perpetual thunderings, lit by a strange purplish-red light, and quivering and swaying with the incessant explosion of the radio-active substance. Whole blocks of buildings were alight and burning fiercely, the

trembling, ragged flames looking pale and ghastly and attenuated in comparison with the full-bodied crimson glare beyond. The shells of other edifices already burnt rose, pierced by rows of window sockets against the red-lit mist.

Every step further would have been as dangerous as a descent within the crater of an active volcano. These spinning, boiling bomb centres would shift or break unexpectedly into new regions, great fragments of earth or drain or masonry suddenly caught by a jet of disruptive force might come flying by the explorer's head, or the ground yawn a fiery grave beneath his feet. Few who adventured into these areas of destruction and survived attempted any repetition of their experiences. There are stories of puffs of luminous, radio-active vapour drifting sometimes scores of miles from the bomb centre and killing and scorching all they overtook. And the first conflagrations from the Paris centre spread westward halfway to the sea.

Moreover, the air in this infernal inner circle of red-lit ruins had a peculiar dryness and a blistering quality, so that it set up a soreness of the skin and lungs that was very difficult to heal. . . .

Such was the last state of Paris, and such on a larger scale was the condition of affairs in Chicago, and the same fate had overtaken Berlin, Moscow, Tokyo, the eastern half of London, Toulon, Kiel and two hundred and eighteen other centres of population or armament. Each was a flaming centre of radiant destruction that only time could quench, that indeed in many instances time has still to quench. To this day, though indeed with a constantly diminishing uproar and vigour, these explosions continue. In the map of nearly every country of the world three or four or more red circles, a score of miles in diameter, mark the position of the dying atomic bombs and the death areas that men have been forced to abandon around them. Within these areas perished museums, cathedrals, palaces, libraries, galleries of masterpieces, and a vast accumulation of human achievement, whose charred remains lie buried, a legacy of curious material that only future generations may hope to examine. . . .

SECTION 4

The state of mind of the dispossessed urban population which swarmed and perished so abundantly over the countryside during the dark days of the autumnal months that followed the Last War, was one of blank despair. Barnet gives sketch after sketch of groups of these people, camped among the vineyards of Champagne, as he saw them during his period of service with the army of pacification.

There was, for example, that 'man-milliner' who came out from a field beside the road that rises up eastward out of Epernay, and asked how things were going in Paris. He was, says Barnet, a round-faced man, dressed very

neatly in black – so neatly that it was amazing to discover he was living close at hand in a tent made of carpets – and he had 'an urbane but insistent manner,' a carefully trimmed moustache and beard, expressive eyebrows, and hair very neatly brushed.

'No one goes into Paris,' said Barnet.

'But, Monsieur, that is very unenterprising,' the man by the wayside submitted.

'The danger is too great. The radiations eat into people's skins.'

The eyebrows protested. 'But is nothing to be done?'

'Nothing can be done.'

'But, Monsieur, it is extraordinarily inconvenient, this living in exile and waiting. My wife and my little boy suffer extremely. There is a lack of amenity. And the season advances. I say nothing of the expense and difficulty in obtaining provisions. . . . When does Monsieur think that something will be done to render Paris – possible?'

Barnet considered his interlocutor.

'I'm told,' said Barnet, 'that Paris is not likely to be possible again for several generations.'

'Oh! But this is preposterous! Consider, Monsieur! What are people like ourselves to do in the meanwhile? I am a costumier. All my connections and interests, above all my style, demand Paris. . . .'

Barnet considered the sky, from which a light rain was beginning to fall, the wide fields about them from which the harvest had been taken, the trimmed poplars by the wayside.

'Naturally,' he agreed, 'you want to go to Paris. But Paris is over.'

'Over!'

'Finished.'

'But then, Monsieur – what is to become – of *me*?'

Barnet turned his face westward, whither the white road led.

'Where else, for example, may I hope to find – opportunity?'

Barnet made no reply.

'Perhaps on the Riviera. Or at some such place as Homburg. Or some plague perhaps.'

'All that,' said Barnet, accepting for the first time facts that had lain evident in his mind for weeks; 'all that must be over, too.'

There was a pause. Then the voice beside him broke out. 'But, Monsieur, it is impossible! It leaves – nothing.'

'No. Not very much.'

'One cannot suddenly begin to grow potatoes!'

'It would be good if Monsieur could bring himself—'

'To the life of a peasant! And my wife – you do not know the distinguished delicacy of my wife, a refined helplessness, a peculiar dependent charm. Like some slender tropical creeper – with great white flowers. . . . But all this is

foolish talk. It is impossible that Paris, which has survived so many misfor-
tunes, should not presently revive.'

'I do not think it will ever revive. Paris is finished. London, too, I am
told – Berlin. All the great capitals were stricken. . . .'

'But—! Monsieur must permit me to differ.'

'It is so.'

'It is impossible. Civilizations do not end in this manner. Mankind will
insist.'

'On Paris?'

'On Paris.'

'Monsieur, you might as well hope to go down the Maelstrom and resume
business there.'

'I am content, Monsieur, with my own faith.'

'The winter comes on. Would not Monsieur be wiser to seek a house?'

'Further from Paris? No, Monsieur. But it is not possible, Monsieur, what
you say, and you are under a tremendous mistake. . . . Indeed you are in
error. . . . I asked merely for information. . . .'

'When last I saw him,' said Barnet, 'he was standing under the signpost
at the crest of the hill, gazing wistfully, yet it seemed to me a little doubtfully,
now, towards Paris, and altogether heedless of a drizzling rain that was wetting
him through and through. . . .'

SECTION 5

This effect of chill dismay, of a doom as yet imperfectly apprehended
deepens as Barnet's record passes on to tell of the approach of winter. It
was too much for the great mass of those unwilling and incompetent
nomads to realize that an age had ended, that the old help and guidance
existed no longer, that times would not mend again, however patiently
they held out. They were still in many cases looking to Paris when the
first snowflakes of that pitiless January came swirling about them. The
story grows grimmer. . . .

If it is less monstrously tragic after Barnet's return to England, it is, if
anything, harder. England was a spectacle of fear-embittered householders,
hiding food, crushing out robbery, driving the starving wanderers from
every faltering place upon the roads lest they should die inconveniently
and reproachfully on the doorsteps of those who had failed to urge them
onward. . . .

The remnants of the British troops left France finally in March, after
urgent representations from the provisional government at Orleans that they
could be supported no longer. They seem to have been a fairly well-behaved,
but highly parasitic force throughout, though Barnet is clearly of opinion
that they did much to suppress sporadic brigandage and maintain social

order. He came home to a famine-stricken country, and his picture of the England of that spring is one of miserable patience and desperate expedients. The country was suffering much more than France, because of the cessation of the overseas supplies on which it had hitherto relied. His troops were given bread, dried fish, and boiled nettles at Dover, and marched inland to Ashford and paid off. On the way thither they saw four men hanging from the telegraph posts by the roadside, who had been hung for stealing swedes. The labour refuges of Kent, he discovered, were feeding their crowds of casual wanderers on bread into which clay and sawdust had been mixed. In Surrey there was a shortage of even such fare as that. He himself struck across country to Winchester, fearing to approach the bomb-poisoned district round London, and at Winchester he had the luck to be taken on as one of the wireless assistants at the central station and given regular rations. The station stood in a commanding position on the chalk hill that overlooks the town from the east. . . .

Thence he must have assisted in the transmission of the endless cipher messages that preceded the gathering at Brissago, and there it was that the Brissago proclamation of the end of the war and the establishment of a world government came under his hands.

He was feeling ill and apathetic that day, and he did not realize what it was he was transcribing. He did it mechanically, as a part of his tedious duty.

Afterwards there came a rush of messages arising out of the declaration that strained him very much, and in the evening when he was relieved, he ate his scanty supper and then went out upon the little balcony before the station, to smoke and rest his brains after this sudden and as yet inexplicable press of duty. It was a very beautiful, still evening. He fell talking to a fellow operator, and for the first time, he declares, 'I began to understand what it was all about. I began to see just what enormous issues had been under my hands for the past four hours. But I became incredulous after my first stimulation. "This is some sort of Bunkum," I said very sagely.

'My colleague was more hopeful. "It means an end to bomb-throwing and destruction," he said. "It means that presently corn will come from America."

'"Who is going to send corn when there is no more value in money?" I asked.

'Suddenly we were startled by a clashing from the town below. The cathedral bells, which had been silent ever since I had come into the district, were beginning, with a sort of rheumatic difficulty, to ring. Presently they warmed a little to the work, and we realized what was going on. They were ringing a peal. We listened with an unbelieving astonishment and looking into each other's yellow faces.

'"They mean it," said my colleague.

'"But what can they do now?" I asked. "Everything is broken down. . . ."'

And on that sentence, with an unexpected artistry, Barnet abruptly ends his story.

SECTION 6

From the first the new government handled affairs with a certain greatness of spirit. Indeed, it was inevitable that they should act greatly. From the first they had to see the round globe as one problem; it was impossible any longer to deal with it piece by piece. They had to secure it universally from any fresh outbreak of atomic destruction, and they had to ensure a permanent and universal pacification. On this capacity to grasp and wield the whole round globe their existence depended. There was no scope for any further performance.

So soon as the seizure of the existing supplies of atomic ammunition and the apparatus for synthesizing Carolinum was assured, the disbanding or social utilization of the various masses of troops still under arms had to be arranged, the salvation of the year's harvests, and the feeding, housing, and employment of the drifting millions of homeless people. In Canada, in South America, and Asiatic Russia there were vast accumulations of provision that was immovable only because of the breakdown of the mone-tary and credit systems. These had to be brought into the famine districts very speedily if entire depopulation was to be avoided, and their transpor-tation and the revival of communications generally absorbed a certain proportion of the soldiery and more able unemployed. The task of housing assumed gigantic dimensions, and from building camps the housing committee of the council speedily passed to constructions of a more perma-nent type. They found far less friction than might have been expected in turning the loose population on their hands to these things. People were extraordinarily tamed by that year of suffering and death; they were disil-lusioned of their traditions, bereft of once obstinate prejudices; they felt foreign in a strange world, and ready to follow any confident leadership. The orders of the new government came with the best of all credentials, rations. The people everywhere were as easy to control, one of the old labour experts who had survived until the new time witnesses, 'as gangs of emigrant workers in a new land'. And now it was that the social possi-bilities of the atomic energy began to appear. The new machinery that had come into existence before the last wars increased and multiplied, and the council found itself not only with millions of hands at its disposal but with power and apparatus that made its first conceptions of the work it had to do seem pitifully timid. The camps that were planned in iron and deal were built in stone and brass; the roads that were to have been mere iron tracks became spacious ways that insisted upon architecture; the cultiva-tions of foodstuffs that were to have supplied emergency rations, were presently, with synthesizers, fertilizers, actinic light, and scientific direction, in excess of every human need.

The government had begun with the idea of temporarily reconstituting the social and economic system that had prevailed before the first coming

of the atomic engine, because it was to this system that the ideas and habits
of the great mass of the world's dispossessed population was adapted.
Subsequent rearrangement it had hoped to leave to its successors – whoever
they might be. But this, it became more and more manifest, was absolutely
impossible. As well might the council have proposed a revival of slavery.
The capitalist system had already been smashed beyond repair by the onset
of limitless gold and energy; it fell to pieces at the first endeavour to stand
it up again. Already before the war half of the industrial class had been out
of work, the attempt to put them back into wages employment on the old
lines was futile from the outset – the absolute shattering of the currency
system alone would have been sufficient to prevent that, and it was neces-
sary therefore to take over the housing, feeding, and clothing of this
worldwide multitude without exacting any return in labour whatever. In a
little while the mere absence of occupation for so great a multitude of people
everywhere became an evident social danger, and the government was obliged
to resort to such devices as simple decorative work in wood and stone, the
manufacture of hand-woven textiles, fruit-growing, flower-growing, and land-
scape gardening on a grand scale to keep the less adaptable out of mischief,
and of paying wages to the younger adults for attendance at schools that
would equip them to use the new atomic machinery. . . . So quite insensibly
the council drifted into a complete reorganization of urban and industrial
life, and indeed of the entire social system.

Ideas that are unhampered by political intrigue or financial considerations
have a sweeping way with them, and before a year was out the records of
the council show clearly that it was rising to its enormous opportunity, and
partly through its own direct control and partly through a series of specific
committees, it was planning a new common social order for the entire
population of the earth. 'There can be no real social stability or any general
human happiness while large areas of the world and large classes of people
are in a phase of civilization different from the prevailing mass. It is impos-
sible now to have great blocks of population misunderstanding the generally
accepted social purpose or at an economic disadvantage to the rest.' So the
council expressed its conception of the problem it had to solve. The peasant,
the field-worker, and all barbaric cultivators were at an 'economic disad-
vantage' to the more mobile and educated classes, and the logic of the
situation compelled the council to take up systematically the supersession
of this stratum by a more efficient organization of production. It developed
a scheme for the progressive establishment throughout the world of the
'modern system' in agriculture, a system that should give the full advantages
of a civilized life to every agricultural worker, and this replacement has
been going on right up to the present day. The central idea of the modern
system is the substitution of cultivating guilds for the individual cultivator,
and for cottage and village life altogether. These guilds are associations of

men and women who take over areas of arable or pasture land, and make themselves responsible for a certain average produce. They are bodies small enough as a rule to be run on a strictly democratic basis, and large enough to supply all the labour, except for a certain assistance from townspeople during the harvest, needed upon the land farmed. They have watchers' bungalows or chalets on the ground cultivated, but the ease and the cost-lessness of modern locomotion enables them to maintain a group of residences in the nearest town with a common dining-room and club house, and usually also a guild house in the national or provincial capital. Already this system has abolished a distinctively 'rustic' population throughout vast areas of the old world, where it has prevailed immemorially. That shy, unstimulated life of the lonely hovel, the narrow scandals and petty spites and persecutions of the small village, that hoarding, half inanimate existence away from books, thought, or social participation and in constant contact with cattle, pigs, poultry, and their excrement, is passing away out of human experience. In a little while it will be gone altogether. In the nineteenth century it had already ceased to be a necessary human state, and only the absence of any collective intelligence and an imagined need for tough and unintelligent soldiers and for a prolific class at a low level, prevented its systematic replacement at that time. . . .

And while this settlement of the country was in progress, the urban camps of the first phase of the council's activities were rapidly developing, partly through the inherent forces of the situation and partly through the council's direction, into a modern type of town. . . .

SECTION 7

It is characteristic of the manner in which large enterprises forced themselves upon the Brissago council, that it was not until the end of the first year of their administration and then only with extreme reluctance that they would take up the manifest need for a lingua franca for the world. They seem to have given little attention to the various theoretical universal languages which were proposed to them. They wished to give as little trouble to hasty and simple people as possible, and the worldwide distribution of English gave them a bias for it from the beginning. The extreme simplicity of its grammar was also in its favour.

It was not without some sacrifices that the English-speaking peoples were permitted the satisfaction of hearing their speech used universally. The language was shorn of a number of grammatical peculiarities, the distinctive forms for the subjunctive mood for example and most of its irregular plurals were abolished; its spelling was systematized and adapted to the vowel sounds in use upon the continent of Europe, and a process of incorporating foreign nouns and verbs commenced that speedily reached enormous proportions.

Within ten years from the establishment of the World Republic the New English Dictionary had swelled to include a vocabulary of 250,000 words, and a man of 1900 would have found considerable difficulty in reading an ordinary newspaper. On the other hand, the men of the new time could still appreciate the older English literature. . . . Certain minor acts of uniformity accompanied this larger one. The idea of a common understanding and a general simplification of intercourse once it was accepted led very naturally to the universal establishment of the metric system of weights and measures, and to the disappearance of the various makeshift calendars that had hitherto confused chronology. The year was divided into thirteen months of four weeks each, and New Year's Day and Leap Year's Day were made holidays, and did not count at all in the ordinary week. So the weeks and the months were brought into correspondence. And moreover, as the king put it to Firmin, it was decided to 'nail down Easter.' . . . In these matters, as in so many matters, the new civilization came as a simplification of ancient complications; the history of the calendar throughout the world is a history of inadequate adjustments, of attempts to fix seed-time and midwinter that go back into the very beginning of human society; and this final rectification had a symbolic value quite beyond its practical convenience. But the council would have no rash nor harsh innovations, no strange names for the months, and no alteration in the numbering of the years.

The world had already been put upon one universal monetary basis. For some months after the accession of the council, the world's affairs had been carried on without any sound currency at all. Over great regions money was still in use, but with the most extravagant variations in price and the most disconcerting fluctuations of public confidence. The ancient rarity of gold upon which the entire system rested was gone. Gold was now a waste product in the release of atomic energy, and it was plain that no metal could be the basis of the monetary system again. Henceforth all coins must be token coins. Yet the whole world was accustomed to metallic money, and a vast proportion of existing human relationships had grown up upon a cash basis, and were almost inconceivable without that convenient liquidating factor. It seemed absolutely necessary to the life of the social organization to have some sort of currency, and the council had therefore to discover some real value upon which to rest it. Various such apparently stable values as land and hours of work were considered. Ultimately the government, which was now in possession of most of the supplies of energy-releasing material, fixed a certain number of units of energy as the value of a gold sovereign, declared a sovereign to be worth exactly twenty marks, twenty-five francs, five dollars, and so forth, with the other current units of the world, and undertook, under various qualifications and conditions, to deliver energy upon demand as payment for every sovereign presented. On the whole, this worked satisfactorily. They saved the face of the pound sterling. Coin was rehabilitated,

and after a phase of price fluctuations, began to settle down to definite
equivalents and uses again, with names and everyday values familiar to the
common run of people. . . .

SECTION 8

As the Brissago council came to realize that what it had supposed to be
temporary camps of refugees were rapidly developing into great towns of a
new type, and that it was remoulding the world in spite of itself, it decided
to place this work of redistributing the non-agricultural population in the
hands of a compactor and better qualified special committee. That
committee is now, far more than the council of any other of its delegated
committees, the active government of the world. Developed from an almost
invisible germ of 'town-planning' that came obscurely into existence in
Europe or America (the question is still in dispute) somewhere in the closing
decades of the nineteenth century, its work, the continual active planning
and replanning of the world as a place of human habitation, is now so to
speak the collective material activity of the race. The spontaneous, disorderly
spreadings and recessions of populations, as aimless and mechanical as the
trickling of spilt water, which was the substance of history for endless years,
giving rise here to congestions, here to chronic devastating wars, and
everywhere to a discomfort and disorderliness that was at its best only
picturesque, is at an end. Men spread now, with the whole power of the
race to aid them, into every available region of the earth. Their cities are
no longer tethered to running water and the proximity of cultivation, their
plans are no longer affected by strategic considerations or thoughts of social
insecurity. The aeroplane and the nearly costless mobile car have abolished
trade routes; a common language and a universal law have abolished a
thousand restraining inconveniences, and so an astonishing dispersal of
habitations has begun. One may live anywhere. And so it is that our cities
now are true social gatherings, each with a character of its own and distinc-
tive interests of its own, and most of them with a common occupation.
They lie out in the former deserts, these long wasted sun-baths of the race,
they tower amidst eternal snows, they hide in remote islands, and bask on
broad lagoons. For a time the whole tendency of mankind was to desert
the river valleys in which the race had been cradled for half a million years,
but now that the War against Flies has been waged so successfully that this
pestilential branch of life is nearly extinct, they are returning thither with
a renewed appetite for gardens laced by watercourses, for pleasant living
amidst islands and houseboats and bridges, and for nocturnal lanterns
reflected by the sea.

Man who is ceasing to be an agricultural animal becomes more and more
a builder, a traveller and a maker. How much he ceases to be a cultivator

of the soil the returns of the Redistribution Committee showed. Every year the work of our scientific laboratories increases the productivity and simplifies the labour of those who work upon the soil, and the food now of the whole world is produced by less than one per cent of its population, a percentage which still tends to decrease. Far fewer people are needed upon the land than training and proclivity dispose towards it, and as a consequence of this excess of human attention, the garden side of life, the creation of groves and lawns and vast regions of beautiful flowers, has expanded enormously and continues to expand. For, as agricultural method intensifies and the quota is raised, one farm association after another, availing itself of the 1975 regulations, elects to produce a public garden and pleasaunce in the place of its former fields, and the area of freedom and beauty is increased. And the chemists' triumphs of synthesis, which could now give us an entirely artificial food, remain largely in abeyance because it is so much more pleasant and interesting to eat natural produce and to grow such things upon the soil. Each year adds to the variety of our fruits and the delightfulness of our flowers.

SECTION 9

The early years of the World Republic witnessed a certain recrudescence of political adventure. There was, it is rather curious to note, no revival of separatism after the face of King Ferdinand Charles had vanished from the sight of men, but in a number of countries, as the first urgent physical needs were met, there appeared a variety of personalities having this in common, that they sought to revive political trouble and clamber by its aid to positions of importance and satisfaction. In no case did they speak in the name of kings, and it is clear that monarchy must have been far gone in obsolescence before the twentieth century began, but they made appeals to the large survivals of nationalist and racial feeling that were everywhere to be found, they alleged with considerable justice that the council was overriding racial and national customs and disregarding religious rules. The great plain of India was particularly prolific in such agitators. The revival of newspapers, which had largely ceased during the terrible year because of the dislocation of the coinage, gave a vehicle and a method of organization to these complaints. At first the council disregarded this developing opposition, and then it recognized it with an entirely devastating frankness.

Never, of course, had there been so provisional a government. It was of an extravagant illegality. It was, indeed, hardly more than a club, a club of about a hundred persons. At the outset there were ninety-three, and these were increased afterwards by the issue of invitations which more than balanced its deaths, to as many at one time as one hundred and nineteen. Always its constitution has been miscellaneous. At no time were these

invitations issued with an admission that they recognized a right. The old institution or monarchy had come out unexpectedly well in the light of the new regime. Nine of the original members of the first government were crowned heads who had resigned their separate sovereignty, and at no time afterwards did the number of its royal members sink below six. In their case there was perhaps a kind of attenuated claim to rule, but except for them and the still more infinitesimal pretensions of one or two ex-presidents of republics, no member of the council had even the shade of a right to his participation in its power. It was natural, therefore, that its opponents should find a common ground in a clamour for representative government, and build high hopes upon a return, to parliamentary institutions.

The council decided to give them everything they wanted, but in a form that suited ill with their aspirations. It became at one stroke a representative body. It became, indeed, magnificently representative. It became so representative that the politicians were drowned in a deluge of votes. Every adult of either sex from pole to pole was given a vote, and the world was divided into ten constituencies, which voted on the same day by means of a simple modification of the world post. Membership of the government, it was decided, must be for life, save in the exceptional case of a recall; but the elections, which were held quinquennially, were arranged to add fifty members on each occasion. The method of proportional representation with one transferable vote was adopted, and the voter might also write upon his voting paper in a specially marked space, the name of any of his representatives that he wished to recall. A ruler was recallable by as many votes as the quota by which he had been elected, and the original members by as many votes in any constituency as the returning quotas in the first election.

Upon these conditions the council submitted itself very cheerfully to the suffrages of the world. None of its members were recalled, and its fifty new associates, which included twenty-seven which it had seen fit to recommend, were of an altogether too miscellaneous quality to disturb the broad trend of its policy. Its freedom from rules or formalities prevented any obstructive proceedings, and when one of the two newly arrived Home Rule members for India sought for information how to bring in a bill, they learnt simply that bills were not brought in. They asked for the speaker, and were privileged to hear much ripe wisdom from the ex-king Egbert, who was now consciously among the seniors of the gathering. Thereafter they were baffled men. . . .

But already by that time the work of the council was drawing to an end. It was concerned not so much for the continuation of its construction as for the preservation of its accomplished work from the dramatic instincts of the politician.

The life of the race becomes indeed more and more independent of the formal government. The council, in its opening phase, was heroic in spirit; a dragon-slaying body, it slashed out of existence a vast, knotted tangle of

obsolete ideas and clumsy and jealous proprietorships; it secured by a noble system of institutional precautions, freedom of enquiry, freedom of criticism, free communications, a common basis of education and understanding, and freedom from economic oppression. With that its creative task was accomplished. It became more and more an established security and less and less an active intervention. There is nothing in our time to correspond with the continual petty making and entangling of laws in an atmosphere of contention that is perhaps the most perplexing aspect of constitutional history in the nineteenth century. In that age they seem to have been perpetually making laws when we should alter regulations. The work of change which we delegate to these scientific committees of specific general direction which have the special knowledge needed, and which are themselves dominated by the broad intellectual process of the community, was in those days inextricably mixed up with legislation. They fought over the details; we should as soon think of fighting over the arrangement of the parts of a machine. We know nowadays that such things go on best within laws, as life goes on between earth and sky. And so it is that government gathers now for a day or so in each year under the sunshine of Brissago when Saint Bruno's lilies are in flower, and does little more than bless the work of its committees. And even these committees are less originative and more expressive of the general thought than they were at first. It becomes difficult to mark out the particular directive personalities of the world. Continually we are less personal. Every good thought contributes now, and every able brain falls within that informal and dispersed kingship which gathers together into one purpose the energies of the race.

SECTION 10

It is doubtful if we shall ever see again a phase of human existence in which 'politics', that is to say a partisan interference with the ruling sanities of the world, will be the dominant interest among serious men. We seem to have entered upon an entirely new phase in history in which contention as distinguished from rivalry, has almost abruptly ceased to be the usual occupation, and has become at most a subdued and hidden and discredited thing. Contentious professions cease to be an honourable employment for men. The peace between nations is also a peace between individuals. We live in a world that comes of age. Man the warrior, man the lawyer, and all the bickering aspects of life, pass into obscurity; the grave dreamers, man the curious learner and man the creative artist, come forward to replace these barbaric aspects of existence by a less ignoble adventure.

There is no natural life of man. He is, and always has been, a sheath of varied and even incompatible possibilities, a palimpsest of inherited dispositions. It was the habit of many writers in the early twentieth century to

speak of competition and the narrow, private life of trade and saving and suspicious isolation as though such things were in some exceptional way proper to the human constitution, and as though openness of mind and a preference for achievement over possession were abnormal and rather unsubstantial qualities. How wrong that was, the history of the decades immediately following the establishment of the world republic witnesses. Once the world was released from the hardening insecurities of a needless struggle for life that was collectively planless and individually absorbing, it became apparent that there was in the vast mass of people a long, smothered passion to make things. The world broke out into making, and at first mainly into aesthetic making. This phase of history, which has been not inaptly termed the 'Efflorescence', is still, to a large extent, with us. The majority of our population consists of artists, and the bulk of activity in the world lies no longer with necessities but with their elaboration, decoration and refinement. There has been an evident change in the quality of this making during recent years. It becomes more purposeful than it was, losing something of its first elegance and prettiness and gaining in intensity; but that is a change rather of hue than of nature. That comes with a deepening philosophy and a sounder education. For the first joyous exercises of fancy we perceive now the deliberation of a more constructive imagination. There is a natural order in these things, and art comes before science as the satisfaction of more elemental needs must come before art, and as play and pleasure come in a human life before the development of a settled purpose. Efflorescence. . .

For thousands of years this gathering impulse to creative work must have struggled in man against the limitations imposed upon him by his social ineptitude. It was a long smouldering fire that flamed out at last in all these things. The evidence of a pathetic, perpetually thwarted urgency to make something, is one of the most touching aspects of the relics and records of our immediate ancestors. There exists still in the death area about the London bombs, a region of deserted small homes that furnish the most illuminating comment on the old state of affairs. These homes are entirely horrible, uniform, square, squat, hideously proportioned, uncomfortable, dingy, and in some respects quite filthy, only people in complete despair of anything better could have lived in them, but to each is attached a ridiculous little rectangle of land called 'the garden,' containing usually a prop for drying clothes and a loathsome box of offal, the dustbin, full of egg-shells, cinders and such-like refuse. Now that one may go about this region in comparitive security – for the London radiations have dwindled to inconsiderable proportions – it is possible to trace in nearly every one of these gardens some effort to make. Here it is a poor little plank summerhouse, here it is a 'fountain' of bricks and oyster shells, here a 'rockery', here a 'workshop'. And in the houses everywhere there are pitiful little decorations, clumsy models, feeble drawings. These efforts are almost incredibly inept, like the drawings of blindfolded

men, they are only one shade less harrowing to a sympathetic observer than the scratchings one finds upon the walls of the old prisons, but there they are, witnessing to the poor buried instincts that struggled up towards the light. That god of joyous expression our poor fathers ignorantly sought, our freedom has declared to us. . . .

In the old days the common ambition of every simple soul was to possess a little property, a patch of land, a house uncontrolled by others, an 'independence' as the English used to put it. And what made this desire for freedom and prosperity so strong, was very evidently the dream of self-expression, of doing something with it, of playing with it, of making a personal delightfulness, a distinctiveness. Property was never more than a means to an end, nor avarice more than a perversion. Men owned in order to do freely. Now that everyone has his own apartments and his own privacy secure, this disposition to own has found its release in a new direction. Men study and save and strive that they may leave behind them a series of panels in some public arcade, a row of carven figures along a terrace, a grove, a pavilion. Or they give themselves to the penetration of some still opaque riddle in phenomena as once men gave themselves to the accumulation of riches. The work that was once the whole substance of social existence – for most men spent all their lives in earning a living – is now no more than was the burden upon one of those old climbers who carried knapsacks of provisions on their backs in order that they might ascend mountains. It matters little to the easy charities of our emancipated time that most people who have made their labour contribution produce neither new beauty nor new wisdom, but are simply busy about those pleasant activities and enjoyments that reassure them that they are alive. They help, it may be, by reception and reverberation, and they hinder nothing. . . .

SECTION 11

Now all this phase of gigantic change in the contours and appearances of human life which is going on about us, a change as rapid and as wonderful as the swift ripening of adolescence to manhood after the barbaric boyish years, is correlated with moral and mental changes at least as unprecedented. It is not as if old things were going out of life and new things coming in, it is rather that the altered circumstances of men are making an appeal to elements in his nature that have hitherto been suppressed, and checking tendencies that have hitherto been over-stimulated and over-developed. He has not so much grown and altered his essential being as turned new aspects to the light. Such turnings round into a new attitude the world has seen on a less extensive scale before. The Highlanders of the seventeenth century, for example, were cruel and bloodthirsty robbers, in the nineteenth their descendants were conspicuously trusty and honourable men. There was not

a people in Western Europe in the early twentieth century that seemed capable of hideous massacres, and none that had not been guilty of them within the previous two centuries. The free, frank, kindly, gentle life of the prosperous classes in any European country before the years of the last wars was in a different world of thought and feeling from that of the dingy, suspicious, secretive, and uncharitable existence of the respectable poor, or the constant personal violence, the squalor and naive passions of the lowest stratum. Yet there were no real differences of blood and inherent quality between these worlds; their differences were all in circumstances, suggestion, and habits of mind. And turning to more individual instances the constantly observed difference between one portion of a life and another consequent upon a religious conversion, were a standing example of the versatile possibilities of human nature.

The catastrophe of the atomic bombs which shook men out of cities and businesses and economic relations shook them also out of their old established habits of thought, and out of the lightly held beliefs and prejudices that came down to them from the past. To borrow a word from the old-fashioned chemists, men were made nascent; they were released from old ties; for good or evil they were ready for new associations. The council carried them forward for good; perhaps if his bombs had reached their destination King Ferdinand Charles might have carried them back to an endless chain of evils. But his task would have been a harder one than the council's. The moral shock of the atomic bombs had been a profound one, and for a while the cunning side of the human animal was overpowered by its sincere realization of the vital necessity for reconstruction. The litigious and trading spirits cowered together, scared at their own consequences; men thought twice before they sought mean advantages in the face of the unusual eagerness to realize new aspirations, and when at last the weeds revived again and 'claims' began to sprout, they sprouted upon the stony soil of law courts reformed, of laws that pointed to the future instead of the past, and under the blazing sunshine of a transforming world. A new literature, a new interpretation of history were springing into existence, a new teaching was already in the schools, a new faith in the young. The worthy man who forestalled the building of a research city for the English upon the Sussex downs by buying up a series of estates, was dispossessed and laughed out of court when he made his demand for some preposterous compensation; the owner of the discredited Dass patents makes his last appearance upon the scroll of history as the insolvent proprietor of a paper called The Cry for Justice, in which he duns the world for a hundred million pounds. That was the ingenuous Dass's idea of justice, that he ought to be paid about five million pounds annually because he had annexed the selvage of one of Holsten's discoveries. Dass came at last to believe quite firmly in his right, and he died a victim of conspiracy mania in a private hospital at Nice. Both of these men would

probably have ended their days enormously wealthy, and of course ennobled in the England of the opening twentieth century, and it is just this novelty of their fates that marks the quality of the new age.

The new government early discovered the need of a universal education to fit men to the great conceptions of its universal rule. It made no wrangling attacks on the local, racial, and sectarian forms of religious profession that at that time divided the earth into a patchwork of hatreds and distrusts; it left these organizations to make their peace with God in their own time; but it proclaimed as if it were a mere secular truth that sacrifice was expected from all, that respect had to be shown to all; it revived schools or set them up afresh all around the world, and everywhere these schools taught the history of war and the consequences and moral of the Last War; everywhere it was taught not as a sentiment but as a matter of fact that the salvation of the world from waste and contention was the common duty and occupation of all men and women. These things which are now the elementary commonplaces of human intercourse seemed to the councillors of Brissago, when first they dared to proclaim them, marvellously daring discoveries, not untouched by doubt, that flushed the cheek and fired the eye.

The council placed all this educational reconstruction in the hands of a committee of men and women, which did its work during the next few decades with remarkable breadth and effectiveness. This educational committee was, and is, the correlative upon the mental and spiritual side of the redistribution committee. And prominent upon it, and indeed for a time quite dominating it, was a Russian named Karenin, who was singular in being a congenital cripple. His body was bent so that he walked with difficulty, suffered much pain as he grew older, and had at last to undergo two operations. The second killed him. Already malformation, which was to be seen in every crowd during the middle ages so that the crippled beggar was, as it were, an essential feature of the human spectacle, was becoming a strange thing in the world. It had a curious effect upon Karenin's colleagues; their feeling towards him was mingled with pity and a sense of inhumanity that it needed usage rather than reason to overcome. He had a strong face, with little bright brown eyes rather deeply sunken and a large resolute thin-lipped mouth. His skin was very yellow and wrinkled, and his hair iron grey. He was at all times an impatient and sometimes an angry man, but this was forgiven him because of the hot wire of suffering that was manifestly thrust through his being. At the end of his life his personal prestige was very great. To him far more than to any contemporary is it due that self-abnegation, self-identification with the world spirit, was made the basis of universal education. That general memorandum to the teachers which is the key-note of the modern educational system, was probably entirely his work.

'Whosoever would save his soul shall lose it,' he wrote. 'That is the device upon the seal of this document, and the starting point of all we have to do.

It is a mistake to regard it as anything but a plain statement of fact. It is the basis for your work. You have to teach self-forgetfulness, and everything else that you have to teach is contributory and subordinate to that end. Education is the release of man from self. You have to widen the horizons of your children, encourage and intensify their curiosity and their creative impulses, and cultivate and enlarge their sympathies. That is what you are for. Under your guidance and the suggestions you will bring to bear on them, they have to shed the old Adam of instinctive suspicions, hostilities, and passions, and to find themselves again in the great being of the universe. The little circles of their egotisms have to be opened out until they become arcs in the sweep of the racial purpose. And this that you teach to others you must learn also sedulously yourselves. Philosophy, discovery, art, every sort of skill, every sort of service, love: these are the means of salvation from that narrow loneliness of desire, that brooding preoccupation with self and egotistical relationships, which is hell for the individual, treason to the race, and exile from God. . . .'

SECTION 12

As things round themselves off and accomplish themselves, one begins for the first time to see them clearly. From the perspectives of a new age one can look back upon the great and widening stream of literature with a complete understanding. Things link up that seemed disconnected, and things that were once condemned as harsh and aimless are seen to be but factors in the statement of a gigantic problem. An enormous bulk of the sincerer writing of the eighteenth, nineteenth, and twentieth centuries falls together now into an unanticipated unanimity; one sees it as a huge tissue of variations upon one theme, the conflict of human egotism and personal passion and narrow imaginations on the one hand, against the growing sense of wider necessities and a possible, more spacious life.

That conflict is in evidence in so early a work as Voltaire's *Candide*, for example, in which the desire for justice as well as happiness beats against human contrariety and takes refuge at last in a forced and inconclusive contentment with little things. *Candide* was but one of the pioneers of a literature of uneasy complaint that was presently an innumerable multitude of books. The novels more particularly of the nineteenth century, if one excludes the mere story-tellers from our consideration, witness to this uneasy realization of changes that call for effort and of the lack of that effort. In a thousand aspects, now tragically, now comically, now with a funny affectation of divine detachment, a countless host of witnesses tell their story of lives fretting between dreams and limitations. Now one laughs, now one weeps, now one reads with a blank astonishment at this huge and almost unpremeditated record of how the growing human spirit, now warily, now eagerly,

now furiously, and always, as it seems, unsuccessfully, tried to adapt itself to the maddening misfit of its patched and ancient garments. And always in these books as one draws nearer to the heart of the matter there comes a disconcerting evasion. It was the fantastic convention of the time that a writer should not touch upon religion. To do so was to rouse the jealous fury of the great multitude of professional religious teachers. It was permitted to state the discord, but it was forbidden to glance at any possible reconciliation. Religion was the privilege of the pulpit. . . .

It was not only from the novels that religion was omitted. It was ignored by the newspapers; it was pedantically disregarded in the discussion of business questions, it played a trivial and apologetic part in public affairs. And this was done not out of contempt but respect. The hold of the old religious organizations upon men's respect was still enormous, so enormous that there seemed to be a quality of irreverence in applying religion to the developments of every day. This strange suspension of religion lasted over into the beginnings of the new age. It was the clear vision of Marcus Karenin much more than any other contemporary influence which brought it back into the texture of human life. He saw religion without hallucinations, without superstitious reverence, as a common thing as necessary as food and air, as land and energy to the life of man and the well-being of the Republic. He saw that indeed it had already percolated away from the temples and hierarchies and symbols in which men had sought to imprison it, that it was already at work anonymously and obscurely in the universal acceptance of the greater state. He gave it clearer expression, rephrased it to the lights and perspectives of the new dawn. . . .

But if we return to our novels for our evidence of the spirit of the times it becomes evident as one reads them in their chronological order, so far as that is now ascertainable, that as one comes to the latter nineteenth and the earlier twentieth century the writers are much more acutely aware of secular change than their predecessors were. The earlier novelists tried to show 'life as it is', the latter showed life as it changes. More and more of their characters are engaged in adaptation to change or suffering from the effects of world changes. And as we come up to the time of the Last Wars, this newer conception of the everyday life as a reaction to an accelerated development is continually more manifest. Barnet's book, which has served us so well, is frankly a picture of the world coming about like a ship that sails into the wind. Our later novelists give a vast gallery of individual conflicts in which old habits and customs, limited ideas, ungenerous temperaments, and innate obsessions are pitted against this great opening out of life that has happened to us. They tell us of the feelings of old people who have been wrenched away from familiar surroundings, and how they have had to make peace with uncomfortable comforts and conveniences that are still strange to them. They give us the discord between the opening egotisms

of youths and the ill-defined limitations of a changing social life. They tell of the universal struggle of jealousy to capture and cripple our souls, of romantic failures and tragical misconceptions of the trend of the world, of the spirit of adventure, and the urgency of curiosity, and how these serve the universal drift. And all their stories lead in the end either to happiness missed or happiness won, to disaster or salvation. The clearer their vision and the subtler their art, the more certainly do these novels tell of the possibility of salvation for all the world. For any road in life leads to religion for those upon it who will follow it far enough. . . .

It would have seemed a strange thing to the men of the former time that it should be an open question as it is today whether the world is wholly Christian or not Christian at all. But assuredly we have the spirit, and as surely have we left many temporary forms behind. Christianity was the first expression of world religion, the first complete repudiation of tribalism and war and disputation. That it fell presently into the ways of more ancient rituals cannot alter that. The common sense of mankind has toiled through two thousand years of chastening experience to find at last how sound a meaning attaches to the familiar phrases of the Christian faith. The scientific thinker as he widens out to the moral problems of the collective life, comes inevitably upon the words of Christ, and as inevitably does the Christian, as his thought grows clearer, arrive at the world republic. As for the claims of the sects, as for the use of a name and successions, we live in a time that has shaken itself free from such claims and consistencies.

CHAPTER V

The Last Days of Marcus Karenin

SECTION 1

The second operation upon Marcus Karenin was performed at the new station for surgical work at Paran, high in the Himalayas above the Sutlej Gorge, where it comes down out of Tibet.

It is a place of such wildness and beauty as no other scenery in the world affords. The granite terrace which runs round the four sides of the low block of laboratories looks out in every direction upon mountains. Far below in the hidden depths of a shadowy blue cleft, the river pours down in its tumultuous passage to the swarming plains of India. No sound of its roaring haste comes up to those serenities. Beyond that blue gulf, in which whole forests of giant deodars seem no more than small patches of moss, rise vast precipices of many-coloured rock, fretted above, lined by snowfalls, and jagged into pinnacles. These are the northward wall of a towering wilderness of ice and snow which clambers southward higher and wilder and vaster to the culminating summits of our globe, to Dhaulagiri and Everest. Here are cliffs of which no other land can show the like, and deep chasms in which Mont Blanc might be plunged and hidden. Here are icefields as big as inland seas on which the tumbled boulders lie so thickly that strange little flowers can bloom among them under the untempered sunshine. To the northward, and blocking out any vision of the uplands of Tibet, rises that citadel of porcelain, that gothic pile, the Lio Porgyul, walls, towers and peaks, a clear twelve thousand feet of veined and splintered rock above the river. And beyond it and eastward and westward rise peaks behind peaks, against the dark blue Himalayan sky. Far away below to the south the clouds of the Indian rains pile up abruptly and are stayed by an invisible hand.

Hither it was that with a dreamlike swiftness Karenin flew high over the irrigations of Rajputana and the towers and cupolas of the ultimate Delhi; and the little group of buildings, albeit the southward wall dropped nearly five hundred feet, seemed to him as he soared down to it like a toy lost among these mountain wildernesses. No road came up to this place; it was reached only by flight.

His pilot descended to the great courtyard, and Karenin assisted by his secretary clambered down through the wing fabric and made his way to the officials who came out to receive him.

In this place, beyond infections and noise and any distractions, surgery had made for itself a house of research and a healing fastness. The building

itself would have seemed very wonderful to eyes accustomed to the flimsy architecture of an age when power was precious. It was made of granite, already a little roughened on the outside by frost, but polished within and of a tremendous solidity. And in a honeycomb of subtly lit apartments, were the spotless research benches, the operating tables, the instruments of brass, and fine glass and platinum and gold. Men and women came from all parts of the world for study or experimental research. They wore a common uniform of white and ate at long tables together, but the patients lived in an upper part of the buildings, and were cared for by nurses and skilled attendants. . . .

The first man to greet Karenin was Ciana, the scientific director of the institution. Beside him was Rachel Borken, the chief organizer. 'You are tired?' she asked, and old Karenin shook his head.

'Cramped,' he said. 'I have wanted to visit such a place as this.'

He spoke as if he had no other business with them.

There was a little pause.

'How many scientific people have you got here now?' he asked.

'Just three hundred and ninety-two,' said Rachel Borken.

'And the patients and attendants and so on?'

'Two thousand and thirty.'

'I shall be a patient,' said Karenin. 'I shall have to be a patient. But I should like to see things first. Presently I will be a patient.'

'You will come to my rooms?' suggested Ciana.

'And then I must talk to this doctor of yours,' said Karenin. 'But I would like to see a bit of this place and talk to some of your people before it comes to that.'

He winced and moved forward.

'I have left most of my work in order,' he said.

'You have been working hard up to now?' asked Rachel Borken.

'Yes. And now I have nothing more to do – and it seems strange . . . And it's a bother, this illness and having to come down to oneself. This doorway and the row of windows is well done; the grey granite and just the line of gold, and then those mountains beyond through that arch. It's very well done. . . .'

SECTION 2

Karenin lay on the bed with a soft white rug about him, and Fowler, who was to be his surgeon, sat on the edge of the bed and talked to him. An assistant was seated quietly in the shadow behind the bed. The examination had been made, and Karenin knew what was before him. He was tired but serene.

'So I shall die,' he said, 'unless you operate?'

Fowler assented. 'And then,' said Karenin, smiling, 'probably I shall die.'

'Not certainly.'

'Even if I do not die; shall I be able to work?'

'There is just a chance. . . .'

'So firstly I shall probably die, and if I do not, then perhaps I shall be a useless invalid?'

'I think if you live, you may be able to go on – as you do now.'

'Well, then, I suppose I must take the risk of it. Yet couldn't you, Fowler, couldn't you drug me and patch me instead of all this – vivisection? A few days of drugged and active life – and then the end?'

Fowler thought. 'We are not sure enough yet to do things like that,' he said.

'But a day is coming when you will be certain.'

Fowler nodded.

'You make me feel as though I was the last of deformity. Deformity is uncertainty – inaccuracy. My body works doubtfully, it is not even sure that it will die or live. I suppose the time is not far off when such bodies as mine will no longer be born into the world.'

'You see,' said Fowler, after a little pause, 'it is necessary that spirits such as yours should be born into the world.'

'I suppose,' said Karenin, 'that my spirit has had its use. But if you think that is because my body is as it is I think you are mistaken. There is no peculiar virtue in defect. I have always chafed against – all this. If I could have moved more freely and lived a larger life in health I could have done more. But some day perhaps you will be able to put a body that is wrong altogether right again. Your science is only beginning. It's a subtler thing than physics and chemistry, and it takes longer to produce its miracles. And meanwhile a few more of us must die in patience.'

'Fine work is being done and much of it,' said Fowler. 'I can say as much because I have nothing to do with it. I can understand a lesson, appreciate the discoveries of abler men and use my hands, but those others, Pigou, Masterton, Lie and the others, they are clearing the ground fast for the knowledge to come. Have you had time to follow their work?'

Karenin shook his head. 'But I can imagine the scope of it,' he said.

'We have so many men working now,' said Fowler. 'I suppose at present there must be at least a thousand thinking hard, observing, experimenting, for one who did so in nineteen hundred.'

'Not counting those who keep the records?'

'Not counting those. Of course, the present indexing of research is in itself a very big work, and it is only now that we are getting it properly done. But already we are feeling the benefit of that. Since it ceased to be a paid employment and became a devotion we have had only those people who obeyed the call of an aptitude at work upon these things. Here – I

must show you it today, because it will interest you – we have our copy of the encyclopaedic index – every week sheets are taken out and replaced by fresh sheets with new results that are brought to us by the aeroplanes of the Research Department. It is an index of knowledge that grows continually, an index that becomes continually truer. There was never anything like it before.'

'When I came into the education committee,' said Karenin, 'that index of human knowledge seemed an impossible thing. Research had produced a chaotic mountain of results, in a hundred languages and a thousand different types of publication. . . .' He smiled at his memories. 'How we groaned at the job!'

'Already the ordering of that chaos is nearly done. You shall see.'

'I have been so busy with my own work – Yes, I shall be glad to see.'

The patient regarded the surgeon for a time with interested eyes.

'You work here always?' he asked abruptly.

'No,' said Fowler.

'But mostly you work here?'

'I have worked about seven years out of the past ten. At times I go away – down there. One has to. At least I have to. There is a sort of greyness comes over all this, one feels hungry for life, real, personal passionate life, love-making, eating and drinking for the fun of the thing, jostling crowds, having adventures, laughter – above all laughter—'

'Yes,' said Karenin understandingly.

'And then one day, suddenly one thinks of these high mountains again. . . .'

'That is how I would have lived, if it had not been for my – defects,' said Karenin. 'Nobody knows but those who have borne it the exasperation of abnormality. It will be good when you have nobody alive whose body cannot live the wholesome everyday life, whose spirit cannot come up into these high places as it wills.'

'We shall manage that soon,' said Fowler.

'For endless generations man has struggled upward against the indignities of his body – and the indignities of his soul. Pains, incapacities, vile fears, black moods, despairs. How well I've known them. They've taken more time than all your holidays. It is true, is it not, that every man is something of a cripple and something of a beast? I've dipped a little deeper than most; that's all. It's only now when he has fully learnt the truth of that, that he can take hold of himself to be neither beast nor cripple. Now that he overcomes his servitude to his body, he can for the first time think of living the full life of his body. . . . Before another generation dies you'll have the thing in hand. You'll do as you please with the old Adam and all the vestiges from the brutes and reptiles that lurk in his body and spirit. Isn't that so?'

'You put it boldly,' said Fowler.

Karenin laughed cheerfully at his caution. . . . 'When,' asked Karenin suddenly, 'when will you operate?'

'The day after tomorrow,' said Fowler. 'For a day I want you to drink and eat as I shall prescribe. And you may think and talk as you please.'

'I should like to see this place.'

'You shall go through it this afternoon. I will have two men carry you in a litter. And tomorrow you shall lie out upon the terrace. Our mountains here are the most beautiful in the world. . . .'

SECTION 3

The next morning Karenin got up early and watched the sun rise over the mountains, and breakfasted lightly, and then young Gardener, his secretary, came to consult him upon the spending of his day. Would he care to see people? Or was this gnawing pain within him too much to permit him to do that?

'I'd like to talk,' said Karenin. 'There must be all sorts of lively-minded people here. Let them come and gossip with me. It will distract me – and I can't tell you how interesting it makes everything that is going on to have seen the dawn of one's own last day.'

'Your last day!'

'Fowler will kill me.'

'But he thinks not.'

'Fowler will kill me. If he does not he will not leave very much of me. So that this is my last day anyhow, the days afterwards if they come at all to me, will be refuse. I know. . . .'

Gardener was about to speak when Karenin went on again.

'I hope he kills me, Gardener. Don't be – old-fashioned. The thing I am most afraid of is that last rag of life. I may just go on – a scarred salvage of suffering stuff. And then – all the things I have hidden and kept down or discounted or set right afterwards will get the better of me. I shall be peevish. I may lose my grip upon my own egotism. It's never been a very firm grip. No, no, Gardener, don't say that! You know better, you've had glimpses of it. Suppose I came through on the other side of this affair, belittled, vain, and spiteful, using the prestige I have got among men by my good work in the past just to serve some small invalid purpose. . . .'

He was silent for a time, watching the mists among the distant precipices change to clouds of light, and drift and dissolve before the searching rays of the sunrise.

'Yes,' he said at last, 'I am afraid of these anaesthetics and these fag ends of life. It's life we are all afraid of. Death! – nobody minds just death. Fowler is clever – but some day surgery will know its duty better and not be so anxious just to save something . . . provided only that it quivers. I've tried

to hold my end up properly and do my work. After Fowler has done with
me I am certain I shall be unfit for work – and what else is there for me? . . .
I know I shall not be fit for work. . . .

'I do not see why life should be judged by its last trailing thread of
vitality. . . . I know it for the splendid thing it is – I who have been a
diseased creature from the beginning. I know it well enough not to confuse
it with its husks. Remember that, Gardener, if presently my heart fails me
and I despair, and if I go through a little phase of pain and ingratitude
and dark forgetfulness before the end. . . . Don't believe what I may say
at the last. . . . If the fabric is good enough the selvage doesn't matter. It
can't matter. So long as you are alive you are just the moment, perhaps,
but when you are dead then you are all your life from the first moment
to the last. . . .'

SECTION 4

Presently, in accordance with his wish, people came to talk to him, and he
could forget himself again. Rachel Borken sat for a long time with him and
talked chiefly of women in the world, and with her was a girl named Edith
Haydon who was already very well known as a cytologist. And several of
the younger men who were working in the place and a patient named Kahn,
a poet, and Edwards, a designer of plays and shows, spent some time with
him. The talk wandered from point to point and came back upon itself,
and became now earnest and now trivial as the chance suggestions deter-
mined. But soon afterwards Gardener wrote down notes of things he
remembered, and it is possible to put together again the outlook of Karenin
upon the world and how he thought and felt about many of the principal
things in life.

'Our age,' he said, 'has been so far an age of scene-shifting. We have
been preparing a stage, clearing away the setting of a drama that was played
out and growing tiresome. . . . If I could but sit out the first few scenes of
the new spectacle. . . .

'How encumbered the world had become! It was ailing as I am ailing
with a growth of unmeaning things. It was entangled, feverish, confused. It
was in sore need of release, and I suppose that nothing less than the violence
of those bombs could have released it and made it a healthy world again. I
suppose they were necessary. Just as everything turns to evil in a fevered
body so everything seemed turning to evil in those last years of the old time.
Everywhere there were obsolete organizations seizing upon all the new fine
things that science was giving to the world, nationalities, all sorts of political
bodies, the churches and sects, proprietorship, seizing upon those treat powers
and limitless possibilities and turning them to evil uses. And they would not
suffer open speech, they would not permit of education, they would let no

one be educated to the needs of the new time. . . . You who are younger cannot imagine the mixture of desperate hope and protesting despair in which we who could believe in the possibilities of science lived in those years before atomic energy came. . . .

'It was not only that the mass of people would not attend, would not understand, but that those who did understand lacked the power of real belief. They said the things, they saw the things, and the things meant nothing to them. . . .

'I have been reading some old papers lately. It is wonderful how our fathers bore themselves towards science. They hated it. They feared it. They permitted a few scientific men to exist and work – a pitiful handful. . . . "Don't find out anything about us," they said to them; "don't inflict vision upon us, spare our little ways of life from the fearful shaft of understanding. But do tricks for us, little limited tricks. Give us cheap lighting. And cure us of certain disagreeable things, cure us of cancer, cure us of consumption, cure our colds and relieve us after repletion. . . ." We have changed all that, Gardener. Science is no longer our servant. We know it for something greater than our little individual selves. It is the awakening mind of the race, and in a little while – in a little while – I wish indeed I could watch for that little while, now that the curtain has risen. . . .

'While I lie here they are clearing up what is left of the bombs in London,' he said. 'Then they are going to repair the ruins and make it all as like as possible to its former condition before the bombs fell. Perhaps they will dig out the old house in St John's Wood to which my father went after his expulsion from Russia. . . . That London of my memories seems to me like a place in another world. For you younger people it must seem like a place that could never have existed.'

'Is there much left standing?' asked Edith Haydon.

'Square miles that are scarcely shaken in the south and north-west, they say; and most of the bridges and large areas of dock. Westminster, which held most of the government offices, suffered badly from the small bomb that destroyed the Parliament, there are very few traces of the old thoroughfare of Whitehall or the Government region thereabout, but there are plentiful drawings to scale of its buildings, and the great hole in the east of London scarcely matters. That was a poor district and very like the north and the south. . . . It will be possible to reconstruct most of it. . . . It is wanted. Already it becomes difficult to recall the old time – even for us who saw it.'

'It seems very distant to me,' said the girl.

'It was an unwholesome world,' reflected Karenin. 'I seem to remember everybody about my childhood as if they were ill. They were ill. They were sick with confusion. Everybody was anxious about money and everybody was doing uncongenial things. They ate a queer mixture of foods,

either too much or too little, and at odd hours. One sees how ill they
were by their advertisements. All this new region of London they are
opening up now is plastered with advertisements of pills. Everybody must
have been taking pills. In one of the hotel rooms in the Strand they have
found the luggage of a lady covered up by falling rubble and unburnt,
and she was equipped with nine different sorts of pill and tablet. The
pill-carrying age followed the weapon-carrying age. They are equally
strange to us. People's skins must have been in a vile state. Very few
people were properly washed; they carried the filth of months on their
clothes. All the clothes they wore were old clothes; our way of pulping
our clothes again after a week or so of wear would have seemed fantastic
to them. Their clothing hardly bears thinking about. And the congestion
of them! Everybody was jostling against everybody in those awful towns.
In an uproar. People were run over and crushed by the hundred; every
year in London the cars and omnibuses alone killed or disabled twenty
thousand people, in Paris it was worse; people used to fall dead for want
of air in the crowded ways. The irritation of London, internal and external,
must have been maddening. It was a maddened world. It is like thinking
of a sick child. One has the same effect of feverish urgencies and acute
irrational disappointments.

'All history,' he said, 'is a record of a childhood. . . .

'And yet not exactly a childhood. There is something clean and keen
about even a sick child – and something touching. But so much of the old
times makes one angry. So much they did seems grossly stupid, obstinately,
outrageously stupid, which is the very opposite to being fresh and young.

'I was reading only the other day about Bismarck, that hero of
nineteenth-century politics, that sequel to Napoleon, that god of blood
and iron. And he was just a beery, obstinate, dull man. Indeed, that is
what he was, the commonest, coarsest man, who ever became great. I
looked at his portraits, a heavy, almost froggish face, with projecting eyes
and a thick moustache to hide a poor mouth. He aimed at nothing but
Germany, Germany emphasized, indurated, enlarged; Germany and his
class in Germany; beyond that he had no ideas, he was inaccessible to
ideas; his mind never rose for a recorded instant above a bumpkin's elab-
orate cunning. And he was the most influential man in the world, in the
whole world, no man ever left so deep a mark on it, because everywhere
there were gross men to resonate to the heavy notes he emitted. He
trampled on ten thousand lovely things, and a kind of malice in these
louts made it pleasant to them to see him trample. No – he was no child;
the dull, national aggressiveness he stood for, no childishness. Childhood
is promise. He was survival.

'All Europe offered its children to him, it sacrificed education, art, happi-
ness and all its hopes of future welfare to follow the clatter of his sabre. The

monstrous worship of that old fool's "blood and iron" passed all round the earth. Until the atomic bombs burnt our way to freedom again. . . .'

'One thinks of him now as one thinks of the megatherium,' said one of the young men.

'From first to last mankind made three million big guns and a hundred thousand complicated great ships for no other purpose but war.'

'Were there no sane men in those days,' asked the young man, 'to stand against that idolatry?'

'In a state of despair,' said Edith Haydon.

'He is so far off – and there are men alive still who were alive when Bismarck died!' . . . said the young man. . . .

SECTION 5

'And yet it may be I am unjust to Bismarck,' said Karenin, following his own thoughts. 'You see, men belong to their own age; we stand upon a common stock of thought and we fancy we stand upon the ground. I met a pleasant man the other day, a Maori, whose great-grandfather was a cannibal. It chanced he had a daguerreotype of the old sinner, and the two were marvellously alike. One felt that a little juggling with time and either might have been the other. People are cruel and stupid in a stupid age who might be gentle and splendid in a gracious one. The world also has its moods. Think of the mental food of Bismarck's childhood; the humiliations of Napoleon's victories, the crowded, crowning victory of the Battle of the Nations. . . . Everybody in those days, wise or foolish, believed that the division of the world under a multitude of governments was inevitable, and that it was going on for thousands of years more. It *was* inevitable until it was impossible. Anyone who had denied that inevitability publicly would have been counted – oh, a *silly* fellow! Old Bismarck was only just a little – forcible, on the lines of the accepted ideas. That is all. He thought that since there had to be national governments he would make one that was strong at home and invincible abroad. Because he had fed with a kind of rough appetite upon what we can see now were very stupid ideas, that does not make him a stupid man. We've had advantages; we've had unity and collectivism blasted into our brains. Where should we be now but for the grace of science? I should have been an embittered, spiteful, downtrodden member of the Russian intelligentsia, a conspirator, a prisoner or an assassin. You, my dear, would have been breaking dingy windows as a suffragette.'

'*Never*,' said Edith stoutly. . . .

For a time the talk broke into humorous personalities, and the young people gibed at each other across the smiling old administrator, and then presently one of the young scientific men gave things a new turn. He spoke like one who was full to the brim.

'You know, sir, I've a fancy – it is hard to prove such things – that civilization was very near disaster when the atomic bombs came banging into it, that if there had been no Holsten and no induced radio-activity, the world would have – smashed – much as it did. Only instead of its being a smash that opened a way to better things, it might have been a smash without a recovery. It is part of my business to understand economics, and from that point of view the century before Holsten was just a hundred years' crescendo of waste. Only the extreme individualism of that period, only its utter want of any collective understanding or purpose can explain that waste. Mankind used up material – insanely. They had got through three-quarters of all the coal in the planet, they had used up most of the oil, they had swept away their forests, and they were running short of tin and copper. Their wheat areas were getting weary and populous, and many of the big towns had so lowered the water level of their available hills that they suffered a drought every summer. The whole system was rushing towards bankruptcy. And they were spending every year vaster and vaster amounts of power and energy upon military preparations, and continually expanding the debt of industry to capital. The system was already staggering when Holsten began his researches. So far as the world in general went there was no sense of danger and no desire for enquiry. They had no belief that science could save them, nor any idea that there was a need to be saved. They could not, they would not, see the gulf beneath their feet. It was pure good luck for mankind at large that any research at all was in progress. And as I say, sir, if that line of escape hadn't opened, before now there might have been a crash, revolution, panic, social disintegration, famine, and – it is conceivable – complete disorder. . . . The rails might have rusted on the disused railways by now, the telephone poles have rotted and fallen, the big liners dropped into sheet-iron in the ports; the burnt, deserted cities become the ruinous hiding-places of gangs of robbers. We might have been brigands in a shattered and attenuated world. Ah, you may smile, but that had happened before in human history. The world is still studded with the ruins of broken-down civilizations. Barbaric bands made their fastness upon the Acropolis, and the tomb of Hadrian became a fortress that warred across the ruins of Rome against the Colosseum. . . . Had all that possibility of reaction ended so certainly in 1940? Is it all so very far away even now?'

'It seems far enough away now,' said Edith Haydon.

'But forty years ago?'

'No,' said Karenin with his eyes upon the mountains, 'I think you under-rate the available intelligence in those early decades of the twentieth century. Officially, I know, politically, that intelligence didn't tell – but it was there. And I question your hypothesis. I doubt if that discovery could have been delayed. There is a kind of inevitable logic now in the progress of research.

For a hundred years and more thought and science have been going their own way regardless of the common events of life. You see – they have got loose. If there had been no Holsten there would have been some similar man. If atomic energy had not come in one year it would have come in another. In decadent Rome the march of science had scarcely begun. . . . Nineveh, Babylon, Athens, Syracuse, Alexandria, these were the first rough experiments in association that made a security, a breathing-space, in which enquiry was born. Man had to experiment before he found out the way to begin. But already two hundred years ago he had fairly begun. . . . The politics and dignities and wars of the nineteenth and twentieth centuries were only the last phoenix blaze of the former civilization flaring up about the beginnings of the new. Which we serve. . . . Man lives in the dawn for ever,' said Karenin. 'Life is beginning and nothing else but beginning. It begins everlastingly. Each step seems vaster than the last, and does but gather us together for the rest. This Modern State of ours, which would have been a Utopian marvel a hundred years ago, is already the common-place of life. But as I sit here and dream of the possibilities in the mind of man that now gather to a head beneath the shelter of its peace, these great mountains here seem but little things. . . .'

SECTION 6

About eleven Karenin had his midday meal, and afterwards he slept among his artificial furs and pillows for two hours. Then he awoke and some tea was brought to him, and he attended to a small difficulty in connection with the Moravian schools in the Labrador country and in Greenland that Gardener knew would interest him. He remained alone for a little while after that, and then the two women came to him again. Afterwards Edwards and Kahn joined the group, and the talk fell upon love and the place of women in the renascent world. The cloudbanks of India lay under a quivering haze, and the blaze of the sun fell full upon the eastward precipices. Ever and again as they talked, some vast splinter of rock would crack and come away from these, or a wild rush of snow and ice and stone, pour down in thunder, hang like a wet thread into the gulfs below, and cease. . . .

SECTION 7

For a time Karenin said very little, and Kahn, the popular poet, talked of passionate love. He said that passionate, personal love had been the abiding desire of humanity since ever humanity had begun, and now only was it becoming a possible experience. It had been a dream that generation after generation had pursued, that always men had lost on the verge of attainment. To most of those who had sought it obstinately it had brought tragedy. Now,

lifted above sordid distresses, men and women might hope for realized and
triumphant love. This age was the Dawn of Love. . . .

Karenin remained downcast and thoughtful while Kahn said these things.
Against that continued silence Kahn's voice presently seemed to beat and
fail. He had begun by addressing Karenin, but presently he was including
Edith Haydon and Rachel Borken in his appeal. Rachel listened silently;
Edith watched Karenin and very deliberately avoided Kahn's eyes.

'I know,' said Karenin at last, 'that many people are saying this sort of
thing. I know that there is a vast release of love-making in the world. This
great wave of decoration and elaboration that has gone about the world,
this Efflorescence, has of course laid hold of that. I know that when you
say that the world is set free, you interpret that to mean that the world
is set free for love-making. Down there – under the clouds – the lovers
foregather. I know your songs, Kahn, your half-mystical songs, in which
you represent this old hard world dissolving into a luminous haze of love
– sexual love. . . . I don't think you are right or true in that. You are a
young, imaginative man, and you see life – ardently – with the eyes of
youth. But the power that has brought man into these high places under
this blue-veiled blackness of the sky and which beckons us on towards the
immense and awful future of our race, is riper and deeper and greater than
any such emotions. . . .

'All through my life – it has been a necessary part of my work – I have
had to think of this release of sexual love and the riddles that perfect freedom
and almost limitless power will put to the soul of our race. I can see now,
all over the world, a beautiful ecstasy of waste; "Let us sing and rejoice and
be lovely and wonderful." . . . The orgy is only beginning, Kahn. . . . It was
inevitable – but it is not the end of mankind. . . .

'Think what we are. It is but a yesterday in the endlessness of time that
life was a dreaming thing, dreaming so deeply that it forgot itself as it dreamt,
its lives, its individual instincts, its moments, were born and wondered and
played and desired and hungered and grew weary and died. Incalculable
successions of vision, visions of sunlit jungle, river wilderness, wild forest,
eager desire, beating hearts, soaring wings and creeping terror flamed hotly
and then were as though they had never been. Life was an uneasiness across
which lights played and vanished. And then we came, man came, and opened
eyes that were a question and hands that were a demand and began a mind
and memory that dies not when men die, but lives and increases for ever,
an over-mind, a dominating will, a question and an aspiration that reaches
to the stars. . . . Hunger and fear and this that you make so much of, this
sex, are but the elementals of life out of which we have arisen. All these
elementals, I grant you, have to be provided for, dealt with, satisfied, but all
these things have to be left behind.'

'But Love,' said Kahn.

'I speak of sexual love and the love of intimate persons. And that is what you mean, Kahn.'

Karenin shook his head. 'You cannot stay at the roots and climb the tree,' he said. . . .

'No,' he said after a pause, 'this sexual excitement, this love story, is just a part of growing up and we grow out of it. So far literature and art and sentiment and all our emotional forms have been almost altogether adolescent, plays and stories, delights and hopes, they have all turned on that marvellous discovery of the love interest, but life lengthens out now and the mind of adult humanity detaches itself. Poets who used to die at thirty live now to eighty-five. You, too, Kahn! There are endless years yet for you – and all full of learning. . . . We carry an excessive burden of sex and sexual tradition still, and we have to free ourselves from it. We do free ourselves from it. We have learnt in a thousand different ways to hold back death, and this sex, which in the old barbaric days was just sufficient to balance our dying, is now like a hammer that has lost its anvil, it plunges through human life. You poets, you young people want to turn it to delight. Turn it to delight. That may be one way out. In a little while, if you have any brains worth thinking about, you will be satisfied, and then you will come up here to the greater things. The old religions and their new offsets want still, I see, to suppress all these things. Let them suppress. If they can suppress. In their own people. Either road will bring you here at last to the eternal search for knowledge and the great adventure of power.'

'But incidentally,' said Rachel Borken; 'incidentally you have half of humanity, you have womankind, very much specialized for – for this love and reproduction that is so much less needed than it was.'

'Both sexes are specialized for love and reproduction,' said Karenin.

'But the women carry the heavier burden.'

'Not in their imaginations,' said Edwards.

'And surely,' said Kahn, 'when you speak of love as a phase – isn't it a necessary phase? Quite apart from reproduction the love of the sexes is necessary. Isn't it love, sexual love, which has released the imagination? Without that stir, without that impulse to go out from ourselves, to be reckless of ourselves and wonderful, would our lives be anything more than the contentment of the stalled ox?'

'The key that opens the door,' said Karenin, 'is not the goal of the journey.'

'But women!' cried Rachel. 'Here we are! What is our future – as women? Is it only that we have unlocked the doors of the imagination for you men? Let us speak of this question now. It is a thing constantly in my thoughts, Karenin. What do you think of us? You who must have thought so much of these perplexities.'

Karenin seemed to weigh his words. He spoke very deliberately. 'I do not care a rap about your future – as women. I do not care a rap about the

future of men – as males. I want to destroy these peculiar futures. I care for your future as intelligences, as parts of and contribution to the universal mind of the race. Humanity is not only naturally over-specialized in these matters, but all its institutions, its customs, everything, exaggerate, intensify this difference. I want to unspecialize women. No new idea. Plato wanted exactly that. I do not want to go on as we go now, emphasizing this natural difference; I do not deny it, but I want to reduce it and overcome it.'

'And – we remain women,' said Rachel Borken.

'Need you remain thinking of yourselves as women?'

'It is forced upon us,' said Edith Haydon.

'I do not think a woman becomes less of a woman because she dresses and works like a man,' said Edwards. 'You women here, I mean you scientific women, wear white clothing like the men, twist up your hair in the simplest fashion, go about your work as though there was only one sex in the world. You are just as much women, even if you are not so feminine, as the fine ladies down below there in the plains who dress for excitement and display, whose only thoughts are of lovers, who exaggerate every difference. . . . Indeed we love you more.'

'But we go about our work,' said Edith Haydon.

'So does it matter?' asked Rachel.

'If you go about your work and if the men go about their work then for Heaven's sake be as much woman as you wish,' said Karenin. 'When I ask you to unspecialize, I am thinking not of the abolition of sex, but the abolition of the irksome, restricting, obstructive obsession with sex. It may be true that sex made society, that the first society was the sex-cemented family, the first state a confederacy of blood relations, the first laws sexual taboos. Until a few years ago morality meant proper sexual behaviour. Up to within a few years of us the chief interest and motive of an ordinary man was to keep and rule a woman and her children and the chief concern of a woman was to get a man to do that. That was the drama, that was life. And the jealousy of these demands was the master motive in the world. You said, Kahn, a little while ago that sexual love was the key that let one out from the solitude of self, but I tell you that so far it has only done so in order to lock us all up again in a solitude of two. . . . All that may have been necessary but it is necessary no longer. All that has changed and changes still very swiftly. Your future, Rachel, *as women*, is a diminishing future.'

'Karenin,' asked Rachel, 'do you mean that women are to become men?'

'Men and women have to become human beings.'

'You would abolish women? But, Karenin, listen! There is more than sex in this. Apart from sex we are different from you. We take up life differently. Forget we are – females, Karenin, and still we are a different sort of human being with a different use. In some things we are amazingly secondary. Here am I in this place because of my trick of management, and Edith is here

because of her patient, subtle hands. That does not alter the fact that nearly the whole body of science is man made; that does not alter the fact that men do so predominatingly make history that you could nearly write a complete history of the world without mentioning a woman's name. And on the other hand we have a gift of devotion, of inspiration, a distinctive power for truly loving beautiful things, a care for life and a peculiar keen close eye for behaviour. You know men are blind beside us in these last matters. You know they are restless – and fitful. We have a steadfastness. We may never draw the broad outlines nor discover the new paths, but in the future isn't there a confirming and sustaining and supplying role for us? As important, perhaps, as yours? Equally important. We hold the world up, Karenin, though you may have raised it.'

'You know very well, Rachel, that I believe as you believe. I am not thinking of the abolition of woman. But I do want to abolish – the heroine, the sexual heroine. I want to abolish the woman whose support is jealousy and whose gift possession. I want to abolish the woman who can be won as a prize or locked up as a delicious treasure. And away down there the heroine flares like a divinity.'

'In America,' said Edwards, 'men are fighting duels over the praises of women and holding tournaments before Queens of Beauty.'

'I saw a beautiful girl in Lahore,' said Kahn, 'she sat under a golden canopy like a goddess, and three fine men, armed and dressed like the ancient paintings, sat on steps below her to show their devotion. And they wanted only her permission to fight for her.'

'That is the men's doing,' said Edith Haydon.

'I *said*,' cried Edwards, 'that man's imagination was more specialized for sex than the whole being of woman. What woman would do a thing like that? Women do but submit to it or take advantage of it.'

'There is no evil between men and women that is not a common evil,' said Karenin. 'It is you poets, Kahn, with your love songs which turn the sweet fellowship of comrades into this woman-centred excitement. But there is something in women, in many women, which responds to these provocations; they succumb to a peculiarly self-cultivating egotism. They become the subjects of their own artistry. They develop and elaborate themselves as scarcely any man would ever do. They *look* for golden canopies. And even when they seem to react against that, they may do it still. I have been reading in the old papers of the movements to emancipate women that were going on before the discovery of atomic force. These things which began with a desire to escape from the limitations and servitude of sex ended in an inflamed assertion of sex, and women more heroines than ever. Helen of Holloway was at last as big a nuisance in her way as Helen of Troy, and so long as you think of yourselves as women' – he held out a finger at Rachel and smiled gently – 'instead of thinking of yourselves as intelligent beings,

you will be in danger of – Helenism. To think of yourselves as women is to think of yourselves in relation to men. You can't escape that consequence. You have to learn to think of yourselves – for our sakes and your own sakes – in relation to the sun and stars. You have to cease to be our adventure, Rachel, and come with us upon our adventures. . . .' He waved his hand towards the dark sky above the mountain crests.

SECTION 8

'These questions are the next questions to which research will bring us answers,' said Karenin. 'While we sit here and talk idly and inexactly of what is needed and what may be, there are hundreds of keen-witted men and women who are working these things out, dispassionately and certainly, for the love of knowledge. The next sciences to yield great harvests now will be psychology and neural physiology. These perplexities of the situation between man and woman and the trouble with the obstinacy of egotism, these are temporary troubles, the issue of our own times. Suddenly all these differences that seem so fixed will dissolve, all these incompatibles will run together, and we shall go on to mould our bodies and our bodily feelings and personal reactions as boldly as we begin now to carve mountains and set the seas in their places and change the currents of the wind.'

'It is the next wave,' said Fowler, who had come out upon the terrace and seated himself silently behind Karenin's chair.

'Of course, in the old days,' said Edwards, 'men were tied to their city or their country, tied to the homes they owned or the work they did. . . .'

'I do not see,' said Karenin, 'that there is any final limit to man's power of self-modification.'

'There is none,' said Fowler, walking forward and sitting down upon the parapet in front of Karenin so that he could see his face. 'There is no absolute limit to either knowledge or power. . . . I hope you do not tire yourself talking.'

'I am interested,' said Karenin. 'I suppose in a little while men will cease to be tired. I suppose in a little time you will give us something that will hurry away the fatigue products and restore our jaded tissues almost at once. This old machine may be made to run without slacking or cessation.'

'That is possible, Karenin. But there is much to learn.'

'And all the hours we give to digestion and half living; don't you think there will be some way of saving these?'

Fowler nodded assent.

'And then sleep again. When man with his blazing lights made an end to night in his towns and houses – it is only a hundred years or so ago that that was done – then it followed he would presently resent his eight

hours of uselessness. Shan't we presently take a tablet or lie in some field of force that will enable us to do with an hour or so of slumber and rise refreshed again?'

'Frobisher and Ameer Ali have done work in that direction.'

'And then the inconveniences of age and those diseases of the system that come with years; steadily you drive them back and you lengthen and lengthen the years that stretch between the passionate tumults of youth and the contractions of senility. Man who used to weaken and die as his teeth decayed now looks forward to a continually lengthening, continually fuller term of years. And all those parts of him that once gathered evil against him, the vestigial structures and odd, treacherous corners of his body, you know better and better how to deal with. You carve his body about and leave it re-modelled and unscarred. The psychologists are learning how to mould minds, to reduce and remove bad complexes of thought and motive, to relieve pressures and broaden ideas. So that we are becoming more and more capable of transmitting what we have learnt and preserving it for the race. The race, the racial wisdom, science, gather power continually to subdue the individual man to its own end. Is that not so?'

Fowler said that it was, and for a time he was telling Karenin of new work that was in progress in India and Russia. 'And how is it with heredity?' asked Karenin.

Fowler told them of the mass of enquiry accumulated and arranged by the genius of Tchen, who was beginning to define clearly the laws of inher-itance and how the sex of children and the complexions and many of the parental qualities could be determined.

'He can actually *do*—?'

'It is still, so to speak, a mere laboratory triumph,' said Fowler, 'but tomorrow it will be practicable.'

'You see,' cried Karenin, turning a laughing face to Rachel and Edith, 'while we have been theorizing about men and women, here is science getting the power for us to end that old dispute for ever. If woman is too much for us, we'll reduce her to a minority, and if we do not like any type of men and women, we'll have no more of it. These old bodies, these old animal limita-tions, all this earthly inheritance of gross inevitabilities falls from the spirit of man like the shrivelled cocoon from an imago. And for my own part, when I hear of these things I feel like that – like a wet, crawling new moth that still fears to spread its wings. Because where do these things take us?'

'Beyond humanity,' said Kahn.

'No,' said Karenin. 'We can still keep our feet upon the earth that made us. But the air no longer imprisons us, this round planet is no longer chained to us like the ball of a galley slave. . . .

'In a little while men who will know how to bear the strange gravitations, the altered pressures, the attenuated, unfamiliar gases and all the fearful

strangenesses of space will be venturing out from this earth. This ball will
be no longer enough for us; our spirit will reach out. . . . Cannot you see
how that little argosy will go glittering up into the sky, twinkling and glit-
tering smaller and smaller until the blue swallows it up. They may succeed
out there; they may perish, but other men will follow them. . . .

'It is as if a great window opened,' said Karenin.

SECTION 9

As the evening drew on Karenin and those who were about him went up
upon the roof of the buildings, so that they might the better watch the
sunset and the flushing of the mountains and the coming of the afterglow.
They were joined by two of the surgeons from the laboratories below, and
presently by a nurse who brought Karenin refreshment in a thin glass cup.
It was a cloudless, windless evening under the deep blue sky, and far away
to the north glittered two biplanes on the way to the observatories on
Everest, two hundred miles distant over the precipices to the east. The
little group of people watched them pass over the mountains and vanish
into the blue, and then for a time they talked of the work that the obser-
vatory was doing. From that they passed to the whole process of research
about the world, and so Karenin's thoughts returned again to the mind
of the world and the great future that was opening upon man's imagina-
tion. He asked the surgeons many questions upon the detailed possibilities
of their science, and he was keenly interested and excited by the things
they told him. And as they talked the sun touched the mountains, and
became very swiftly a blazing and indented hemisphere of liquid flame
and sank.

Karenin looked blinking at the last quivering rim of incandescence, and
shaded his eyes and became silent.

Presently he gave a little start.

'What?' asked Rachel Borken.

'I had forgotten,' he said.

'What had you forgotten?'

'I had forgotten about the operation tomorrow. I have been so interested
as Man today that I have nearly forgotten Marcus Karenin. Marcus Karenin
must go under your knife tomorrow, Fowler, and very probably Marcus
Karenin will die.' He raised his slightly shrivelled hand. 'It does not matter,
Fowler. It scarcely matters even to me. For indeed is it Karenin who has
been sitting here and talking; is it not rather a common mind, Fowler, that
has played about between us? You and I and all of us have added thought
to thought, but the thread is neither you nor me. What is true we all have;
when the individual has altogether brought himself to the test and winnowing
of expression, then the individual is done. I feel as though I had already

been emptied out of that little vessel, that Marcus Karenin, which in my youth held me so tightly and completely. Your beauty, dear Edith, and your broad brow, dear Rachel, and you, Fowler, with your firm and skilful hands, are now almost as much to me as this hand that beats the arm of my chair. And as little to me. And the spirit that desires to know, the spirit that resolves to do, that spirit that lives and has talked in us today, lived in Athens, lived in Florence, lives on, I know, for ever. . . .

'And you, old Sun, with your sword of flame searing these poor eyes of Marcus for the last time of all, beware of me! You think I die – and indeed I am only taking off one more coat to get at you. I have threatened you for ten thousand years, and soon I warn you I shall be coming. When I am altogether stripped and my disguises thrown away. Very soon now, old Sun, I shall launch myself at you, and I shall reach you and I shall put my foot on your spotted face and tug you about by your fiery locks. One step I shall take to the moon, and then I shall leap at you. I've talked to you before, old Sun, I've talked to you a million times, and now I am beginning to remember. Yes – long ago, long ago, before I had stripped off a few thousand generations, dust now and forgotten, I was a hairy savage and I pointed my hand at you and – clearly I remember it! – I saw you in a net. Have you forgotten that, old Sun? . . .

'Old Sun, I gather myself together out of the pools of the individual that have held me dispersed so long. I gather my billion thoughts into science and my million wills into a common purpose. Well may you slink down behind the mountains from me, well may you cower. . . .'

SECTION 10

Karenin desired that he might dream alone for a little while before he returned to the cell in which he was to sleep. He was given relief for a pain that began to trouble him and wrapped warmly about with furs, for a great coldness was creeping over all things, and so they left him, and he sat for a long time watching the afterglow give place to the darkness of night.

It seemed to those who had to watch over him unobtrusively lest he should be in want of any attention, that he mused very deeply.

The white and purple peaks against the golden sky sank down into cold, blue remoteness, glowed out again and faded again, and the burning cressets of the Indian stars, that even the moonrise cannot altogether quench, began their vigil. The moon rose behind the towering screen of dark precipices to the east, and long before it emerged above these, its slanting beams had filled the deep gorges below with luminous mist and turned the towers and pinnacles of Lio Porgyul to a magic dreamcastle of radiance and wonder. . . .

Came a great uprush of ghostly light above the black rim of rocks, and
then like a bubble that is blown and detaches itself the moon floated off
clear into the unfathomable dark sky. . . .

And then Karenin stood up. He walked a few paces along the terrace
and remained for a time gazing up at that great silver disc, that silvery shield
that must needs be man's first conquest in outer space. . . .

Presently he turned about and stood with his hands folded behind him,
looking at the northward stars. . . .

At length he went to his own cell. He lay down there and slept peacefully
till the morning. And early in the morning they came to him and the anaes-
thetic was given him and the operation performed.

It was altogether successful, but Karenin was weak and he had to lie very
still; and about seven days later a blood clot detached itself from the healing
scar and travelled to his heart, and he died in an instant in the night.